THE UNABRIDGED MARK TWAIN
Volume II

Samuel Langhorne Clemens (1835–1910), c. 1872

THE UNABRIDGED

MARK TWAIN

VOLUME II

Edited by Lawrence Teacher

Running Press
Philadelphia, Pennsylvania

Canadian representatives: John Wiley & Sons Canada, Ltd.
22 Worcester Road, Rexdale, Ontario M9W 1L1

International representatives: Kaiman & Polon, Inc.
2175 Lemoine Avenue, Fort Lee, New Jersey 07024

9 8 7 6
Digit on the right indicates the number of this printing

Library of Congress Cataloging in Publication Data

Clemens, Samuel Langhorne, 1835–1910
Twain unabridged, vol. 2
I. Title
PZ3.C59Tw   1979   PS1302   813'.4   79–9576
ISBN 0–89471–086–9 paperback
ISBN 0–89471–087–7 library binding

Cover illustration by Charles Santore
Cover design by James Wizard Wilson
Cover calligraphy by Peter Ruge
Interior illustration by Suzanne Clee
Design by Peter John Dorman & Stuart Teacher
Research assistance by Richard Scholl

This book was typeset from first editions of Mark Twain's works. The publisher wishes to thank Lyman W. Riley, Assistant Director of Libraries for Special Collections, Van Pelt Library, University of Pennsylvania, for his help in procuring these first editions.

Typography: English Times, with Garamond, by Comp•Art, Inc.,
Philadelphia, Pennsylvania; composition direction by J. Richard Conklin
Printed and bound by Port City Press, Baltimore, Maryland

This book may be ordered directly from the publisher.
Please include 75 cents postage.
Try your bookstore first.

RUNNING PRESS
125 South Twenty-Second Street
Philadelphia, Pennsylvania 19103

EDITOR'S NOTE

This volume represents a completed journey through the best of Mark Twain's fiction. If you already own *The Unabridged Mark Twain,* this book completes your library and is the last of Twain that this house will publish.

Because so many typesetters, writers, editors, and publishers altered Twain's words, I have attempted to go back and set stories and novels exclusively from his first editions. These were the only works that came close to being approved by him. Each novel and short story is preceded by a little note containing an occasional anecdote and a brief chronology of its publication.

My pleasure in working on *The Unabridged Mark Twain 2* was greatly enhanced by the contributions of my editorial associate, Alida Becker. This book has been an especially rewarding experience for me and there is a certain sadness that I feel in running out of first-rate Twain.

LAWRENCE TEACHER
PHILADELPHIA, PA.

CONTENTS

Mark Twain's Burlesque Autobiography and First Romance *was a small volume brought out in 1871 by Sheldon and Company, publishers of* Galaxy, *a magazine to which Twain was a regular contributor. Although Twain was not happy with the book (several years later he bought the plates and had them destroyed), he did include both the autobiography and the romance in later collections of his work. "A Burlesque Biography" appeared in* The $30,000 Bequest and Other Stories, *published by Harper & Brothers in 1906.*

A Burlesque Biography

Two or three persons having at different times intimated that if I would write an autobiography they would read it when they got leisure, I yield at last to this frenzied public demand and herewith tender my history.

Ours is a noble old house, and stretches a long way back into antiquity. The earliest ancestor the Twains have any record of was a friend of the family by the name of Higgins. This was in the eleventh century, when our people were living in Aberdeen, county of Cork, England. Why it is that our long line has ever since borne the maternal name (except when one of them now and then took a playful refuge in an alias to avert foolishness), instead of Higgins, is a mystery which none of us has ever felt much desire to stir. It is a kind of vague, pretty romance, and we leave it alone. All the old families do that way.

Arthour Twain was a man of considerable note—a solicitor on the highway in William Rufus's time. At about the age of thirty he went to one of those fine old English places of resort called Newgate, to see about something, and never returned again. While there he died suddenly.

Augustus Twain seems to have made something of a stir about the year 1160. He was as full of fun as he could be, and used to take his old sabre and sharpen it up, and get in a convenient place on a dark night, and stick it through people as they went by, to see them jump. He was a born humorist. But he got to' going too far with it; and the first time he was found stripping one of these parties, the authorities removed one end of him, and put it up on a nice high place on Temple

Bar, where it could contemplate the people and have a good time. He never liked any situation so much or stuck to it so long.

Then for the next two hundred years the family tree shows a succession of soldiers—noble, high-spirited fellows, who always went into battle singing, right behind the army, and always went out a-whooping, right ahead of it.

This is a scathing rebuke to old dead Froissart's poor witticism that our family tree never had but one limb to it, and that that one stuck out at right angles, and bore fruit winter and summer.

Early in the fifteenth century we have Beau Twain, called "the Scholar." He wrote a beautiful, beautiful hand. And he could imitate anybody's hand so closely that it was enough to make a person laugh his head off to see it. He had infinite sport with his talent. But by-and-by he took a contract to break stone for a road, and the roughness of the work spoiled his hand. Still, he enjoyed life all the time he was in the stone business, which, with inconsiderable intervals, was some forty-two years. In fact, he died in harness. During all those long years he gave such satisfaction that he never was through with one contract a week till the government gave him another. He was a perfect pet. And he was always a favorite with his fellow-artists, and was a conspicuous member of their benevolent secret society, called the Chain Gang. He always wore his hair short, had a preference for striped clothes, and died lamented by the government. He was a sore loss to his country. For he was so regular.

Some years later we have the illustrious John Morgan Twain. He came over to this country with Columbus in 1492 as a passenger. He appears to have been of a crusty, uncomfortable disposition. He complained of the food all the way over, and was always threatening to go ashore unless there was a change. He wanted fresh shad. Hardly a day passed over his head that he did not go idling about the ship with his nose in the air, sneering about the commander, and saying he did not believe Columbus knew where he was going to or had ever been there before. The memorable cry of "Land ho!" thrilled every heart in the ship but his. He gazed a while through a piece of smoked glass at the pencilled line lying on the distant water, and then said: "Land be hanged,—it's a raft!"

When this questionable passenger came on board the ship, he brought nothing with him but an old newspaper containing a handkerchief marked "B.G.," one cotton sock marked "L.W.C.," one woollen one marked "D.F.," and a night-shirt marked "O.M.R." And yet during the voyage he worried more about his "trunk," and gave himself more airs about it, than all the rest of the passengers put together. If the ship was "down by the head," and would not steer, he would go and move his "trunk" farther aft, and then watch the effect. If the ship was "by the stern," he would suggest to Columbus to detail some men to "shift that baggage." In storms he had to be gagged, because his wailings about his "trunk" made it impossible for the men to hear the orders. The man does not appear to have been openly charged with any gravely unbecoming thing, but it is noted in the ship's log as a "curious circumstance" that albeit he brought his baggage on board the ship in a newspaper, he took it ashore in four trunks, a queensware crate, and a couple of champagne baskets. But when he came back insinuating, in an insolent, swaggering way, that some of his things were missing, and was going to search the other passengers' baggage, it was too much, and they threw him overboard. They watched long and wonderingly for him to come up, but not even a bubble rose on the quietly ebbing tide. But while every one was most absorbed in gazing over the side, and the interest was momentarily increasing, it was observed with consternation that the vessel was adrift and the anchor-cable hanging limp from the bow. Then in the ship's dimmed and ancient log we find this quaint note:

"In time it was discouvered yt ye troblesome passenger hadde gonne downe and got ye anchor, and toke ye same and solde it to ye dam sauvages from ye interior, saying yt he hadde founde it, ye sonne of a ghun!"

Yet this ancestor had good and noble instincts, and it is with pride that we call to mind the fact that he was the first white person who ever interested himself in the work of elevating and civilizing our Indians. He built a commodious jail and put up a gallows, and to his dying day he claimed with satisfaction that he had had a more restraining and elevating influence on the Indians than any other reformer that ever labored among them. At this point the chronicle becomes less frank and chatty, and closes abruptly by saying that the old voyager went to see his gallows perform on the first white man ever hanged in America, and while there received injuries which terminated in his death.

The great-grandson of the "Reformer" flourished in sixteen hundred and something, and was known in our annals as "the old Admiral," though in history he had other titles. He was long in command of fleets of swift vessels, well armed and manned, and did great service in hurrying up merchantmen. Vessels which he followed and kept his eagle eye on, always made good fair time across the ocean. But if a ship still loitered in spite of all he could do, his indignation would grow till he could contain himself no longer—and then he would take that ship home where he lived and keep it there carefully, expecting the owners to come for it, but they never did. And he would try to get the idleness and sloth out of the sailors of that ship by compelling them to take invigorating exercise and a bath. He called it "walking a plank." All the pupils liked it. At any rate they never found any fault with it after trying it. When the owners were late coming for their ships, the Admiral always burned them, so that the insurance money should not be lost. At last this fine old tar was cut down in the fulness of his years and honors. And to her dying day, his poor heart-broken widow believed that if he had been cut down fifteen minutes sooner he might have been resuscitated.

Charles Henry Twain lived during the latter part of the seventeenth century, and was a zealous and distinguished missionary. He converted sixteen thousand South Sea islanders, and taught them that a dog-tooth necklace and a pair of spectacles was not enough clothing to come to divine service in. His poor flock loved him very, very dearly; and when his funeral was over, they got up in a body (and came out of the restaurant) with tears in their eyes, and saying, one to another, that he was a good tender missionary, and they wished they had some more of him.

Pah-go-to-wah-wah-pukketekeewis (Mighty-Hunter-with-a-Hog-Eye-Twain) adorned the middle of the eighteenth century, and aided General Braddock with all his heart to resist the oppressor Washington. It was this ancestor who fired seventeen times at our Washington from behind a tree. So far the beautiful romantic narrative in the moral story-books is correct; but when that narrative goes on to say that at the seventeenth round the awe-stricken savage said solemnly that that man was being reserved by the Great Spirit for some mighty mission, and he dared not lift his sacrilegious rifle against him again, the narrative seriously impairs the integrity of history. What he did say was:

"It ain't no (hic) use. 'At man's so drunk he can't stan' still long enough for a man to hit him. I (hic) I can't 'ford to fool away any more am'nition on him."

That was why he stopped at the seventeenth round, and it was a good, plain, matter-of-fact reason, too, and one that easily commends itself to us by the eloquent, persuasive flavor of probability there is about it.

I always enjoyed the story-book narrative, but I felt a marring misgiving that every Indian at Braddock's Defeat who fired at a soldier a couple of times (two easily grows to seventeen in a century), and missed him, jumped to the conclusion that the Great Spirit was reserving that soldier for some grand mission; and so I somehow feared that the only reason why Washington's case is remembered and the others forgotten is, that in his the prophecy came true, and in that of the others it didn't. There are not books enough on earth to contain the record of the prophecies Indians and other unauthorized parties have made; but one may carry in his overcoat-pockets the record of all the prophecies that have been fulfilled.

I will remark here, in passing, that certain ancestors of mine are so thoroughly well-known in history by their aliases, that I have not felt it to be worth while to dwell upon them, or even mention them in the order of their birth. Among these may be mentioned Richard Brinsley Twain, alias Guy Fawkes; John Wentworth Twain, alias Jack Sheppard; Ananias Twain, alias Baron Munchausen; John George Twain, alias Captain Kydd; and then there are George Francis Train, Tom Pepper, Nebuchadnezzar, and Baalam's Ass—they all belong to our family, but to a branch of it somewhat distinctly removed from the honorable direct line—in fact, a collateral branch, whose members chiefly differ from the ancient stock in that, in order to acquire the notoriety we have always yearned and hungered for, they have got into a low way of going to jail instead of getting hanged.

It is not well, when writing an autobiography, to follow your ancestry down too close to your own time—it is safest to speak only vaguely of your great-grandfather, and then skip from there to yourself, which I now do.

I was born without teeth—and there Richard III had the advantage of me; but I was born without a humpback, likewise, and there I had the advantage of him. My parents were neither very poor nor conspicuously honest.

But now a thought occurs to me. My own history would really seem so tame contrasted with that of my ancestors, that it is simply wisdom to leave it unwritten until I am hanged. If some other biographies I have read had stopped with the ancestry until a like event occurred, it would have been a felicitous thing for the reading public. How does it strike you?

THE UNABRIDGED

MARK TWAIN

VOLUME II

The Tragedy of Pudd'nhead Wilson *first appeared in the* Century *magazine from December 1893 to June 1894. To promote the serialization, the* Century *printed up a pamphlet called* Pudd'nhead Wilson's Calendar, *composed of the maxims that open each chapter of the novel, and distributed it to subscribers, newstands, and bookshops. When the American Publishing Company brought out* The Tragedy of Pudd'nhead Wilson *in book form in November of 1894, it was paired with* The Comedy Those Extraordinary Twins, *which had at one time been incorporated into the novel.*

The Tragedy of
Pudd'nhead Wilson

A WHISPER TO THE READER

There is no character, howsoever good and fine, but it can be destroyed by ridicule, howsoever poor and witless. Observe the ass, for instance: his character is about perfect, he is the choicest spirit among all the humbler animals, yet see what ridicule has brought him to. Instead of feeling complimented when we are called an ass, we are left in doubt.—*Pudd'nhead Wilson's Calendar.*

A person who is ignorant of legal matters is always liable to make mistakes when he tries to photograph a court scene with his pen; and so I was not willing to let the law chapters in this book go to press without first subjecting them to rigid and exhausting revision and correction by a trained barrister—if that is what they are called. These chapters are right, now, in every detail, for they were rewritten under the immediate eye of William Hicks, who studied law part of a while in southwest Missouri thirty-five years ago and then came over here to Florence for his health and is still helping for exercise and board in Macaroni Vermicelli's horse-feed shed which is up the back alley as you turn around the corner out of the Piazza del Duomo just beyond the house where that stone that Dante used to sit on six hundred years ago is let into the wall when he let on to be watching them built Giotto's campanile and yet always got tired looking as soon as Beatrice passed along on her way to get a chunk of chestnut cake to defend herself with in case of a Ghibelline outbreak before she got to school, at the same old stand where they sell the same old cake to this day and it is just as light and good as it was then, too, and this is not flattery, far from it. He was a little rusty on his law, but he rubbed up for this book, and those two or three legal chapters are right and straight, now. He told me so himself.

Given under my hand this second day of January, 1893, at the Villa Viviani, village of Settignano, three miles back of Florence, on the hills—the same certainly affording the most charming view to be found on this planet, and with it the most dream-like and enchanting sunsets to be found in any planet or even in any solar system—and given, too, in the swell room of the house, with the busts of Cerretani senators and other grandees of this line looking approvingly down upon me as they used to look down upon Dante, and mutely asking me to adopt them into my family, which I do with pleasure, for my remotest ancestors are but spring chickens compared with these robed and stately antiques, and it will be a great and satisfying lift for me, that six hundred years will.

Mark Twain.

CHAPTER I

Tell the truth or trump—but get the trick.—Pudd'nhead Wilson's Calendar.

The scene of this chronicle is the town of Dawson's Landing, on the Missouri side of the Mississippi, half a day's journey, per steamboat, below St. Louis.

In 1830 it was a snug little collection of modest one-and two-story frame dwellings whose whitewashed exteriors were almost concealed from sight by climbing tangles of rose-vines, honey-suckles and morning-glories. Each of these pretty homes had a garden in front fenced with white palings and opulently stocked with hollyhocks, marigolds, touch-me-nots, prince's-feathers and other old-fashioned flowers; while on the window-sills of the houses stood wooden boxes containing moss-rose plants and terra-cotta pots in which grew a breed of geranium whose spread of intensely red blossoms accented the prevailing pink tint of the rose-clad house-front like an explosion of flame. When there was room on the ledge outside of the pots and boxes for a cat, the cat was there—in sunny weather—stretched at full length, asleep and blissful, with her furry belly to the sun and a paw curved over her nose. Then that house was complete, and its contentment and peace were made manifest to the world by this symbol, whose testimony is infallible. A home without a cat—and a well-fed, well-petted and properly revered cat—may be a perfect home, perhaps, but how can it prove title?

All along the streets, on both sides, at the outer edge of the brick sidewalks, stood locust-trees with trunks protected by wooden boxing, and these furnished shade for summer and a sweet fragrance in spring when the clusters of buds came forth. The main street, one block back from the river, and running parallel with it, was the sole business street. It was six blocks long, and in each block two or three brick stores three stories high towered above interjected bunches of little frame shops. Swinging signs creaked in the wind, the street's whole length. The candy-striped pole which indicates nobility proud and an-cient along the palace-bordered canals of Venice, indicated merely the humble barbershop along the main street of Dawson's Landing. On a chief corner stood a lofty unpainted pole wreathed from top to bottom with tin pots and pans and cups, the chief tinmonger's noisy notice to the world (when the wind blew) that his shop was on hand for business at that corner.

The hamlet's front was washed by the clear waters of the great river; its body stretched itself rearward up a gentle incline; its most rearward border fringed itself out and scattered its houses about the base-line of the hills; the hills rose high, inclosing the town in a half-moon curve, clothed with forests from foot to summit.

Steamboats passed up and down every hour or so. Those belonging to the little Cairo line and the little Memphis line always stopped; the big Orleans liners stopped for hails only, or to land passengers or freight; and this was the case also with the great flotilla of "transients." These latter came out of a dozen rivers—the Illinois, the Missouri, the Upper Mississippi, the Ohio, the Monongahela, the Tennessee, the Red River, the White River, and so on; and were bound every whither and stocked with every imaginable comfort or necessity which the Mississippi's communities could want, from the frosty Falls of St. Anthony down through nine climates to torrid New Orleans.

Dawson's Landing was a slaveholding town, with a rich slave-worked grain and pork country back of it. The town was sleepy and comfortable and contented. It was fifty years old, and was growing slowly—very slowly, in fact, but still it was growing.

The chief citizen was York Leicester Driscoll, about forty years old, judge of the county court. He was very proud of his old Virginian ancestry, and in his hospitalities and his rather formal and stately manners he kept up its traditions. He was fine and just and generous. To be a gentleman—a gentleman without stain or blemish—was his only religion, and to it he was always faithful. He was respected, esteemed and beloved by all the community. He was well off, and was gradually adding to his store. He and his wife were very nearly happy, but not quite, for they had no children. The longing for the treasure of a child had grown stronger and stronger as the years slipped away, but the blessing never came—and was never to come.

With this pair lived the Judge's widowed sister, Mrs. Rachel Pratt, and she also was childless—childless, and sorrowful for that reason, and not to be comforted. The women were good and commonplace people, and did their duty and had their reward in clear consciences and the community's approbation. They were Presbyterians, the Judge was a free-thinker.

Pembroke Howard, lawyer and bachelor, aged about forty, was another old Virginian grandee with proved descent from the First Families. He was a fine, brave, majestic creature, a gentleman according to the nicest requirements of the Virginia rule, a devoted Presbyterian, an authority on the "code," and a man always courteously ready to stand up before you in the field if any act or word of his had seemed doubtful or suspicious to you, and explain it with any weapon you might prefer from

21

brad-awls to artillery. He was very popular with the people, and was the Judge's dearest friend.

Then there was Colonel Cecil Burleigh Essex, another F. F. V. of formidable caliber—however, with him we have no concern.

Percy Northumberland Driscoll, brother to the Judge, and younger than he by five years, was a married man, and had had children around his hearthstone; but they were attacked in detail by measles, croup and scarlet fever, and this had given the doctor a chance with his effective antediluvian methods; so the cradles were empty. He was a prosperous man, with a good head for speculations, and his fortune was growing. On the 1st of February, 1830, two boy babes were born in his house: one to him, the other to one of his slave girls, Roxana by name. Roxana was twenty years old. She was up and around the same day, with her hands full, for she was tending both babies.

Mrs. Percy Driscoll died within the week. Roxy remained in charge of the children. She had her own way, for Mr. Driscoll soon absorbed himself in his speculations and left her to her own devices.

In that same month of February, Dawson's Landing gained a new citizen. This was Mr. David Wilson, a young fellow of Scotch parentage. He had wandered to this remote region from his birthplace in the interior of the State of New York, to seek his fortune. He was twenty-five years old, college-bred, and had finished a post-college course in an Eastern law school a couple of years before.

He was a homely, freckled, sandy-haired young fellow, with an intelligent blue eye that had frankness and comradeship in it and a covert twinkle of a pleasant sort. But for an unfortunate remark of his, he would no doubt have entered at once upon a successful career at Dawson's Landing. But he made his fatal remark the first day he spent in the village, and it "gaged" him. He had just made the acquaintance of a group of citizens when an invisible dog began to yelp and snarl and howl and make himself very comprehensively disagreeable, whereupon young Wilson said, much as one who is thinking aloud—

"I wish I owned half of that dog."

"Why?" somebody asked.

"Because I would kill my half."

The group searched his face with curiosity, with anxiety even, but found no light there, no expression that they could read. They fell away from him as from something uncanny, and went into privacy to dicuss him. One said:

" 'Pears to be a fool."

" 'Pears?" said another. "*Is,* I reckon you better say."

"Said he wished he owned *half* of the dog, the idiot," said a third. "What did he reckon would become of the other half if he killed his half? Do you reckon he thought it would live?"

"Why, he must have thought it, unless he *is* the downrightest fool in the world; because if he hadn't thought it, he would have wanted to own the whole dog, knowing that if he killed his half and the other half died, he would be responsible for that half just the same as if he had killed that half instead of his own. Don't it look that way to you, gents?"

"Yes, it does. If he owned one half of the general dog, it would be so; if he owned one end of the dog and another person owned the other end, it would be so, just the same; particularly in the first case, because if you kill one half of a general dog, there ain't any man that can tell whose half it was, but if he owned one end of the dog, maybe he could kill his end of it and——"

"No, he couldn't either; he couldn't and not be responsible if the other end died, which it would. In my opinion the man ain't in his right mind."

"In my opinion he hain't *got* any mind."

No. 3 said: "Well, he's a lummox, anyway."

"That's what he is," said No. 4, "he's a labrick—just a Simon-pure labrick, if ever there was one."

"Yes, sir, he's a dam fool, that's the way I put him up," said No. 5. "Anybody can think different that wants to, but those are my sentiments."

"I'm with you, gentlemen," said No. 6. "Perfect jackass— yes, and it ain't going too far to say he is a pudd'nhead. If he ain't a pudd'nhead, I ain't no judge, that's all."

Mr. Wilson stood elected. The incident was told all over the town, and gravely discussed by everybody. Within a week he had lost his first name; Pudd'nhead took its place. In time he came to be liked, and well liked too; but by that time the nickname had got well stuck on, and it stayed. That first day's verdict made him a fool, and he was not able to get it set aside, or even modified. The nickname soon ceased to carry any harsh or unfriendly feeling with it, but it held its place, and was to continue to hold its place for twenty long years.

CHAPTER II

Adam was but human—this explains it all. He did not want the apple for the apple's sake, he wanted it only because it was forbidden. The mistake was in not forbidding the serpent; then he would have eaten the serpent.—*Pudd'nhead Wilson's Calendar.*

Pudd'nhead Wilson had a trifle of money when he arrived, and he bought a small house on the extreme western verge of the town. Between it and Judge Driscoll's house there was only a grassy yard, with a paling fence dividing the properties in the middle. He hired a small office down in the town and hung out a tin sign with these words on it:

DAVID WILSON.

ATTORNEY AND COUNSELOR-AT-LAW.
SURVEYING, CONVEYANCING, ETC.

But his deadly remark had ruined his chance—at least in the law. No clients came. He took down his sign, after a while, and put it up on his own house with the law features knocked out of it. It offered his services now in the humble capacities of land-surveyor and expert accountant. Now and then he got a job of surveying to do, and now and then a merchant got him to straighten out his books. With Scotch patience and pluck he resolved to live down his reputation and work his way into the legal field yet. Poor fellow, he could not foresee that it was going to take him such a weary long time to do it.

He had a rich abundance of idle time, but it never hung heavy on his hands, for he interested himself in every new thing that was born into the universe of ideas, and studied it and experimented upon it at his house. One of his pet fads was palmistry. To another one he gave no name, neither would he explain to anybody what its purpose was, but merely said it was an amusement. In fact he had found that his fads added to his reputation as a pudd'nhead; therefore he was growing chary of being too communicative about them. The fad without a name was one which dealt with people's finger-marks. He carried in his coat pocket a shallow box with grooves in it, and in the grooves strips of glass five inches long and three inches wide. Along the lower edge of each strip was pasted a slip of white paper. He asked people to pass their hands through their hair (thus collecting upon them a thin coating of the natural oil) and then make a thumb-mark on a glass strip, following it with the mark of the ball of each finger in succession. Under this row of faint grease-prints he would write a record on the strip of white paper—thus:

JOHN SMITH, *right hand*—

and add the day of the month and the year, then take Smith's left hand on another glass strip, and add name and date and the words "left hand." The strips were now returned to the grooved box, and took their place among what Wilson called his "records."

He often studied his records, examining and poring over them with absorbing interest until far into the night; but what he found there—if he found anything—he revealed to no one. Sometimes he copied on paper the involved and delicate pattern left by the ball of a finger, and then vastly enlarged it with a pantograph so that he could examine its web of curving lines with ease and convenience.

One sweltering afternoon—it was the first day of July, 1830— he was at work over a set of tangled account-books in his workroom, which looked westward over a stretch of vacant lots, when a conversation outside disturbed him. It was carried on in yells, which showed that the people engaged in it were not close together:

"Say, Roxy, how does yo' baby come on?" This from the distant voice.

"Fust-rate; how does *you* come on, Jasper?" This yell was from close by.

"Oh, I's middlin'; hain't got noth'n' to complain of. I's gwine to come a-court'n' you bimeby, Roxy."

"*You* is, you black mud-cat! Yah—yah—yah! I got somep'n' better to do den 'sociat'n' wid niggers as black as you is. Is ole Miss Cooper's Nancy done give you de mitten?" Roxy followed this sally with another discharge of care-free laughter.

"You's jealous, Roxy, dat's what's de matter wid *you,* you hussy—yah—yah—yah! Dat's de time I got you!"

"Oh, yes, *you* got me, hain't you. 'Clah to goodness if dat conceit o' yo'n strikes in, Jasper, it gwine to kill you sho'. If you b'longed to me I'd sell you down de river 'fo' you git too fur gone. Fust time I runs acrost yo' marster, I's gwine to tell him so."

This idle and aimless jabber went on and on, both parties enjoying the friendly duel and each well satisfied with his own share of the wit exchanged—for wit they considered it.

Wilson stepped to the window to observe the combatants; he could not work while their chatter continued. Over in the vacant lots was Jasper, young, coal-black and of magnificent build, sitting on a wheelbarrow in the pelting sun—at work, supposably, whereas he was in fact only preparing for it by taking an hour's rest before beginning. In front of Wilson's porch stood Roxy, with a local hand-made baby-wagon, in which sat her two charges—one at each end and facing each other. From Roxy's manner of speech, a stranger would have expected her to be

25

black, but she was not. Only one sixteenth of her was black, and that sixteenth did not show. She was of majestic form and stature, her attitudes were imposing and statuesque, and her gestures and movements distinguished by a noble and stately grace. Her complexion was very fair, with the rosy glow of vigorous health in the cheeks, her face was full of character and expression, her eyes were brown and liquid, and she had a heavy suit of fine soft hair which was also brown, but the fact was not apparent because her head was bound about with a checkered handkerchief and the hair was concealed under it. Her face was shapely, intelligent and comely—even beautiful. She had an easy, independent carriage—when she was among her own caste—and a high and "sassy" way, withal; but of course she was meek and humble enough where white people were.

To all intents and purposes Roxy was as white as anybody, but the one sixteenth of her which was black outvoted the other fifteen parts and made her a negro. She was a slave, and salable as such. Her child was thirty-one parts white, and he, too, was a slave, and by a fiction of law and custom a negro. He had blue eyes and flaxen curls like his white comrade, but even the father of the white child was able to tell the children apart—little as he had commerce with them—by their clothes: for the white babe wore ruffled soft muslin and a coral necklace, while the other wore merely a coarse tow-linen shirt which barely reached to its knees, and no jewelry.

The white child's name was Thomas à Becket Driscoll, the other's name was Valet de Chambre: no surname—slaves hadn't the privilege. Roxana had heard that phrase somewhere, the fine sound of it had pleased her ear, and as she had supposed it was a name, she loaded it on to her darling. It soon got shortened to "Chambers," of course.

Wilson knew Roxy by sight, and when the duel of wit began to play out, he stepped outside to gather in a record or two. Jasper went to work energetically, at once, perceiving that his leisure was observed. Wilson inspected the children and asked—

"How old are they, Roxy?"

"Bofe de same age, sir—five months. Bawn de fust o' Feb'uary."

"They're handsome little chaps. One's just as handsome as the other, too."

A delighted smile exposed the girl's white teeth, and she said:

"Bless yo' soul, Misto Wilson, it's pow'ful nice o' you to say dat, 'ca'se one of 'em ain't on'y a nigger. Mighty prime little nigger, *I* al'ays says, but dat's ca'se it's mine, o' course."

"How do you tell them apart, Roxy, when they haven't any clothes on?"

Roxy laughed a laugh proportioned to her size, and said:

"Oh, *I* kin tell 'em 'part, Misto Wilson, but I bet Marse Percy couldn't, not to save his life."

Wilson chatted along for awhile, and presently got Roxy's finger-prints for his collection—right hand and left—on a couple of his glass strips; then labeled and dated them, and took the "records" of both children, and labeled and dated them also.

Two months later, on the 3d of September, he took this trio of finger-marks again. He liked to have a "series," two or three "takings" at intervals during the period of childhood, these to be followed by others at intervals of several years.

The next day—that is to say, on the 4th of September—something occurred which profoundly impressed Roxana. Mr. Driscoll missed another small sum of money—which is a way of saying that this was not a new thing, but had happened before. In truth it had happened three times before. Driscoll's patience was exhausted. He was a fairly humane man toward slaves and other animals; he was an exceedingly humane man toward the erring of his own race. Theft he could not abide, and plainly there was a thief in his house. Necessarily the thief must be one of his negroes. Sharp measures must be taken. He called his servants before him. There were three of these, besides Roxy: a man, a woman, and a boy twelve years old. They were not related. Mr. Driscoll said:

"You have all been warned before. It has done no good. This time I will teach you a lesson. I will sell the thief. Which of you is the guilty one?"

They all shuddered at the threat, for here they had a good home, and a new one was likely to be a change for the worse. The denial was general. None had stolen anything—not money, anyway—a little sugar, or cake, or honey, or something like that, that "Marse Percy wouldn't mind or miss," but not money—never a cent of money. They were eloquent in their protestations, but Mr. Driscoll was not moved by them. He answered each in turn with a stern "Name the thief!"

The truth was, all were guilty but Roxana; she suspected that the others were guilty, but she did not know them to be so. She was horrified to think how near she had come to being guilty herself; she had been saved in the nick of time by a revival in the colored Methodist Church, a fortnight before, at which time and place she "got religion." The very next day after that gracious experience, while her change of style was fresh upon her and she

27

was vain of her purified condition, her master left a couple of dollars lying unprotected on his desk, and she happened upon that temptation when she was polishing around with a dust-rag. She looked at the money awhile with a steadily rising resentment, then she burst out with—

"Dad blame dat revival, I wisht it had 'a' be'n put off till tomorrow!"

Then she covered the tempter with a book, and another member of the kitchen cabinet got it. She made this sacrifice as a matter of religious etiquette; as a thing necessary just now, but by no means to be wrested into a precedent; no, a week or two would limber up her piety, then she would be rational again, and the next two dollars that got left out in the cold would find a comforter—and she could name the comforter.

Was she bad? Was she worse than the general run of her race? No. They had an unfair show in the battle of life, and they held it no sin to take military advantage of the enemy—in a small way; in a small way, but not in a large one. They would smouch provisions from the pantry whenever they got a chance; or a brass thimble, or a cake of wax, or an emery-bag, or a paper of needles, or a silver spoon, or a dollar bill, or small articles of clothing, or any other property of light value; and so far were they from considering such reprisals sinful, that they would go to church and shout and pray the loudest and sincerest with their plunder in their pockets. A farm smoke-house had to be kept heavily padlocked, for even the colored deacon himself could not resist a ham when Providence showed him in a dream, or otherwise, where such a thing hung lonesome and longed for some one to love. But with a hundred hanging before him the deacon would not take two—that is, on the same night. On frosty nights the humane negro prowler would warm the end of a plank and put it up under the cold claws of chickens roosting in a tree; a drowsy hen would step on to the comfortable board, softly clucking her gratitude, and the prowler would dump her into his bag, and later into his stomach, perfectly sure that in taking this trifle from the man who daily robbed him of an inestimable treasure—his liberty—he was not committing any sin that God would remember against him in the Last Great Day.

"Name the thief!"

For the fourth time Mr. Driscoll had said it, and always in the same hard tone. And now he added these words of awful import:

"I give you one minute"—he took out his watch. "If at the end of that time you have not confessed, I will not only sell all four of you, *but*—I will sell you down the river!"

It was equivalent to condemning them to hell! No Missouri negro doubted this. Roxy reeled in her tracks and the color vanished out of her face; the others dropped to their knees as if they had been shot; tears gushed from their eyes, their supplicating hands went up, and three answers came in the one instant:

"I done it!"

"I done it!"

"I done it!—have mercy, marster—Lord have mercy on us po' niggers!"

"Very good," said the master, putting up his watch, "I will sell you *here* though you don't deserve it. You ought to be sold down the river."

The culprits flung themselves prone, in an ecstasy of gratitude, and kissed his feet, declaring that they would never forget his goodness and never cease to pray for him as long as they lived. They were sincere, for like a god he had stretched forth his mighty hand and closed the gates of hell against them. He knew, himself, that he had done a noble and gracious thing, and was privately well pleased with his magnanimity; and that night he set the incident down in his diary, so that his son might read it in after years, and be thereby moved to deeds of gentleness and humanity himself.

CHAPTER III

Whoever has lived long enough to find out what life is, knows how deep a debt of gratitude we owe to Adam, the first great benefactor of our race. He brought death into the world.—*Pudd'nhead Wilson's Calendar.*

Percy Driscoll slept well the night he saved his house-minions from going down the river, but no wink of sleep visited Roxy's eyes. A profound terror had taken possession of her. Her child could grow up and be sold down the river! The thought crazed her with horror. If she dozed and lost herself for a moment, the next moment she was on her feet flying to her child's cradle to see if it was still there. Then she would gather it to her heart and pour out her love upon it in a frenzy of kisses, moaning, crying, and saying "Dey sha'n't, oh, dey *sha'n't!*—yo' po' mammy will kill you fust!"

Once, when she was tucking it back in its cradle again, the other child nestled in its sleep and attracted her attention. She went and stood over it a long time communing with herself:

"What has my po' baby done, dat he couldn't have yo' luck? He hain't done noth'n'. God was good to you; why warn't he

29

good to him? Dey can't sell *you* down de river. I hates yo' pappy; he hain't got no heart—for niggers he hain't, anyways. I hates him, en I could kill him!'' She paused awhile, thinking; then she burst into wild sobbings again, and turned away, saying, "Oh, I got to kill my chile, dey ain't no yuther way,—killin' *him* wouldn't save de chile fum goin' down de river. Oh, I got to do it, yo' po' mammy's got to kill you to save you, honey"—she gathered her baby to her bosom, now, and began to smother it with caresses—"Mammy's got to kill you—how *kin* I do it! But yo' mammy ain't gwine to desert you—no, no; *dah,* don't cry—she gwine *wid* you, she gwine to kill herself too. Come along, honey, come along wid mammy; we gwine to jump in de river, den de troubles o' dis worl' is all over—dey don't sell po' niggers down the river over *yonder.''*

She started toward the door, crooning to the child and hushing it; midway she stopped, suddenly. She had caught sight of her new Sunday gown—a cheap curtain-calico thing, a conflagration of gaudy colors and fantastic figures. She surveyed it wistfully, longingly.

"Hain't ever wore it yet," she said, "en it's jist lovely.'' Then she nodded her head in response to a pleasant idea, and added, "No, I ain't gwine to be fished out, wid everybody lookin' at me, in dis mis'able ole linsey-woolsey.''

She put down the child and made the change. She looked in the glass and was astonished at her beauty. She resolved to make her death-toilet perfect. She took off her handkerchief-turban and dressed her glossy wealth of hair "like white folks"; she added some odds and ends of rather lurid ribbon and a spray of atrocious artificial flowers; finally she threw over her shoulders a fluffy thing called a "cloud" in that day, which was of a blazing red complexion. Then she was ready for the tomb.

She gathered up her baby once more; but when her eye fell upon its miserably short little gray tow-linen shirt and noted the contrast between its pauper shabbiness and her own volcanic irruption of infernal splendors, her mother-heart was touched, and she was ashamed.

"No, dolling, mammy ain't gwine to treat you so. De angels is gwine to 'mire you jist as much as dey does yo' mammy. Ain't gwine to have 'em putt'n' dey han's up 'fo' dey eyes en sayin' to David en Goliah en dem yuther prophets, 'Dat chile is dress' too indelicate fo' dis place.' ''

By this time she had stripped off the shirt. Now she clothed the naked little creature in one of Thomas à Becket's snowy long babygowns, with its bright blue bows and dainty flummery of ruffles.

"Dah—now you's fixed." She propped the child in a chair and stood off to inspect it. Straightway her eyes began to widen with astonishment and admiration, and she clapped her hands and cried out, "Why, it do beat all!—I *never* knowed you was so lovely. Marse Tommy ain't a bit puttier—not a single bit."

She stepped over and glanced at the other infant; she flung a glance back at her own; then one more at the heir of the house. Now a strange light dawned in her eyes, and in a moment she was lost in thought. She seemed in a trance; when she came out of it she muttered, "When I 'uz a-washin' 'em in de tub, yistiddy, his own pappy asked me which of 'em was his'n."

She began to move about like one in a dream. She undressed Thomas à Becket, stripping him of everything, and put the tow-linen shirt on him. She put his coral necklace on her own child's neck. Then she placed the children side by side, and after earnest inspection she muttered—

"Now who would b'lieve clo'es could do de like o' dat? Dog my cats if it ain't all *I* kin do to tell t' other fum which, let alone his pappy."

She put her cub in Tommy's elegant cradle and said—

"You's young Marse *Tom* fum dis out, en I got to practise and git used to 'memberin' to call you dat, honey, or I 's gwine to make a mistake some time en git us bofe into trouble. Dah—now you lay still en don't fret no mo', Marse Tom—oh, thank de good Lord in heaven, you's saved, you's saved!—dey ain't no man kin ever sell mammy's po' little honey down de river now!"

She put the heir of the house in her own child's unpainted pine cradle, and said, contemplating its slumbering form uneasily—

"I 's sorry for you, honey; I 's sorry, God knows I is,—but what *kin* I do, what *could* I do? Yo' pappy would sell him to somebody, some time, en den he'd go down de river, sho', en I couldn't, couldn't, *couldn't* stan' it."

She flung herself on her bed and began to think and toss, toss and think. By and by she sat suddenly upright, for a comforting thought had flown through her worried mind—

" 'T ain't no sin—*white* folks has done it! It ain't no sin, glory to goodness it ain't no sin! *Dey 's* done it—yes, en dey was de biggest quality in de whole bilin', too—*kings!*"

She began to muse; she was trying to gather out of her memory the dim particulars of some tale she had heard some time or other. At last she said—

"Now I 's got it; now I 'member. It was dat ole nigger preacher dat tole it, de time he come over here fum Illinois en preached in de nigger church. He said dey ain't nobody kin save his own self—can't do it by faith, can't do it by works, can't do

31

it no way at all. Free grace is de *on'y* way, en dat don't come fum nobody but jis' de Lord; en *he* kin give it to anybody he please, saint or sinner—*he* don't kyer. He do jis' as he's a mineter. He s'lect out anybody dat suit him, en put another one in his place, en make de fust one happy forever en leave t' other one to burn wid Satan. De preacher said it was jist like dey done in Englan' one time, long time ago. De queen she lef' her baby layin' aroun' one day, en went out callin'; en one o' de niggers roun' 'bout de place dat was 'mos' white, she come in en see de chile layin' aroun', en tuck en put her own chile's clo'es on de queen's chile, en put de queen's chile's clo'es on her own chile, en den lef' her own chile layin' aroun' en tuck en toted de queen's chile home to de nigger-quarter, en nobody ever foun' it out, en her chile was de king bimeby, en sole de queen's chile down de river one time when dey had to settle up·de estate. Dah, now—de preacher said it his own self, en it ain't no sin, 'ca'se white folks done it. *Dey* done it—yes, *dey* done it; en not on'y jis' common white folks nuther, but de biggest quality dey is in de whole bilin'. Oh, I 's *so* glad I 'member 'bout dat!''

She got up light-hearted and happy, and went to the cradles and spent what was left of the night "practising." She would give her own child a light pat and say humbly, "Lay still, Marse Tom," then give the real Tom a pat and say with severity, "Lay *still,* Chambers!—does you want me to take somep'n' *to* you?''

As she progressed with her practice, she was surprised to see how steadily and surely the awe which had kept her tongue reverent and her manner humble toward her young master was transferring itself to her speech and manner toward the usurper, and how similarly handy she was becoming in transferring her motherly curtness of speech and peremptoriness of manner to the unlucky heir of the ancient house of Driscoll.

She took occasional rests from practising, and absorbed herself in calculating her chances.

"Dey'll sell dese niggers to-day fo' stealin' de money, den dey'll buy some mo' dat don't know de chillen—so *dat's* all right. When I takes de chillen out to git de air, de minute I 's roun' de corner I 's gwine to gaum dey mouths all roun' wid jam, den dey can't *nobody* notice dey's changed. Yes, I gwine-ter do dat till I 's safe, if it's a year.

"Dey ain't but one man dat I 's afeard of, en dat's dat Pudd'nhead Wilson. Dey calls him a pudd'nhead, en says he's a fool. My lan', dat man ain't no mo' fool den I is! He's de smartes' man in dis town, less'n it's Jedge Driscoll or maybe Pem Howard. Blame dat man, he worries me wid dem ornery glasses o' hisn; *I* b'lieve he's a witch. But nemmine, I 's gwine to happen aroun' dah one o' dese days en let on dat I reckon he wants to print de chillen's fingers ag'in; en if *he* don't notice dey's changed, I bound dey ain't nobody gwine to notice it, en den I 's safe, sho'. But I reckon I 'll tote along a hoss-shoe to keep off de witch-work.''

The new negroes gave Roxy no trouble, of course. The master gave her none, for one of his speculations was in jeopardy, and his mind was so occupied that he hardly saw the children when he looked at them, and all Roxy had to do was to get them both into a gale of laughter when he came about; then their faces were mainly cavities exposing gums, and he was gone again before the spasm passed and the little creatures resumed a human aspect.

Within a few days the fate of the speculation became so dubious that Mr. Percy went away with his brother the Judge, to see what could be done with it. It was a land speculation as usual, and it had gotten complicated with a lawsuit. The men were gone seven weeks. Before they got back Roxy had paid her visit to Wilson, and was satisfied. Wilson took the finger-prints, labeled them with the names and with the date—October the first—put them carefully away and continued his chat with Roxy, who seemed very anxious that he should admire the great advance in flesh and beauty which the babies had made since he took their finger-prints a month before. He complimented their improvement to her contentment; and as they were without any disguise of jam or other stain, she trembled all the while and was miserably frightened lest at any moment he—

But he didn't. He discovered nothing; and she went home jubilant, and dropped all concern about the matter permanently out of her mind.

CHAPTER IV

Adam and Eve had many advantages, but the principal one was, that they escaped teething.—*Pudd'nhead Wilson's Calendar.*

There is this trouble about special providences—namely, there is so often a doubt as to which party was intended to be the beneficiary. In the case of the children, the bears and the prophet, the bears got more real satisfaction out of the episode than the prophet did, because they got the children.—*Pudd'nhead Wilson's Calendar.*

This history must henceforth accommodate itself to the change which Roxana has consummated, and call the real heir ''Chambers'' and the usurping little slave ''Thomas à

Becket"— shortening this latter name to "Tom," for daily use, as the people about him did.

"Tom" was a bad baby, from the very beginning of his usurpation. He would cry for nothing; he would burst into storms of devilish temper without notice, and let go scream after scream and squall after squall, then climax the thing with "holding his breath"— that frightful specialty of the teething nursling, in the throes of which the creature exhausts its lungs, then is convulsed with noiseless squirmings and twistings and kickings in the effort to get its breath, while the lips turn blue and the mouth stands wide and rigid, offering for inspection one wee tooth set in the lower rim of a hoop of red gums; and when the appalling stillness has endured until one is sure the lost breath will never return, a nurse comes flying, and dashes water in the child's face, and—presto! the lungs fill, and instantly discharge a shriek, or a yell, or a howl which bursts the listening ear and surprises the owner of it into saying words which would not go well with a halo if he had one. The baby Tom would claw anybody who came within reach of his nails, and pound anybody he could reach with his rattle. He would scream for water until he got it, and then throw cup and all on the floor and scream for more. He was indulged in all his caprices, howsoever troublesome and exasperating they might be; he was allowed to eat anything he wanted, particularly things that would give him the stomach-ache.

When he got to be old enough to begin to toddle about and say broken words and get an idea of what his hands were for, he was a more consummate pest than ever. Roxy got no rest while he was awake. He would call for anything and everything he saw, simply saying "Awnt it!" (want it), which was a command. When it was brought, he said in a frenzy, and motioning it away with his hands, "Don't awnt it! don't awnt it!" and the moment it was gone he set up frantic yells of "Awnt it! awnt it! awnt it!" and Roxy had to give wings to her heels to get that thing back to him again before he could get time to carry out his intention of going into convulsions about it.

What he preferred above all other things was the tongs. This was because his "father" had forbidden him to have them lest he break windows and furniture with them. The moment Roxy's back was turned he would toddle to the presence of the tongs and say "Like it!" and cock his eye to one side to see if Roxy was observing; then, "Awnt it!" and cock his eye again; then, "Hab it!" with another furtive glance; and finally, "Take it!"—and the prize was his. The next moment the heavy implement was raised aloft; the next, there was a crash and a squall, and the cat was off on three legs to meet an engagement; Roxy would arrive just as the lamp or a window went to irremediable smash.

Tom got all the petting, Chambers got none. Tom got all the delicacies, Chambers got mush and milk, and clabber without sugar. In consequence Tom was a sickly child and Chambers wasn't. Tom was "fractious," as Roxy called it, and overbearing; Chambers was meek and docile.

With all her splendid common sense and practical every-day ability, Roxy was a doting fool of a mother. She was this toward her child—and she was also more than this: by the fiction created by herself, he was become her master; the necessity of recognizing this relation outwardly and of perfecting herself in the forms required to express the recognition, had moved her to such diligence and faithfulness in practicing these forms that this exercise soon concreted itself into habit; it became automatic and unconscious; then a natural result followed: deceptions intended solely for others gradually grew practically into self-deceptions as well; the mock reverence became real reverence, the mock obsequiousness real obsequiousness, the mock homage real homage; the little counterfeit rift of separation between imitation-slave and imitation-master widened and widened, and became an abyss, and a very real one—and on one side of it stood Roxy, the dupe of her own deceptions, and on the other stood her child, no longer a usurper to her, but her accepted and recognized master. He was her darling, her master, and her deity all in one, and in her worship of him she forgot who she was and what he had been.

In babyhood Tom cuffed and banged and scratched Chambers unrebuked, and Chambers early learned that between meekly bearing it and resenting it, the advantage all lay with the former policy. The few times that his persecutions had moved him beyond control and made him fight back had cost him very dear at headquarters; not at the hands of Roxy, for if she ever went beyond scolding him sharply for "forgitt'n' who his young marster was," she at least never extended her punishment beyond a box on the ear. No, Percy Driscoll was the person. He told Chambers that under no provocation whatever was he privileged to lift his hand against his little master. Chambers overstepped the line three times, and got three such convincing canings from the man who was his father and did n't know it, that he took Tom's cruelties in all humility after that, and made no more experiments.

Outside of the house the two boys were together all through their boyhood. Chambers was strong beyond his years, and a good fighter; strong because he was coarsely fed and hard worked about the house, and a good fighter because Tom furnished him plenty of practice—on white boys whom he hated and was afraid of. Chambers was his constant body-guard, to and from school; he was present on the playground at recess to protect his charge. He fought himself into such a formidable reputation, by and by, that Tom could have changed clothes with him, and "ridden in peace," like Sir Kay in Launcelot's armor.

He was good at games of skill, too. Tom staked him with marbles to play "keeps" with, and then took all the winnings away from him. In the winter season Chambers was on hand, in Tom's worn-out clothes, with "holy" red mittens, and "holy" shoes, and pants "holy" at the knees and seat, to drag a sled up the hill for Tom, warmly clad, to ride down on; but he never got a ride himself. He built snow men and snow fortifications under Tom's directions. He was Tom's patient target when Tom wanted to do some snowballing, but the target couldn't fire back. Chambers carried Tom's skates to the river and strapped them on him, then trotted around after him on the ice, so as to be on hand when wanted; but he wasn't ever asked to try the skates himself.

In summer the pet pastime of the boys of Dawson's Landing was to steal apples, peaches, and melons from the farmers' fruit wagons,—mainly on account of the risk they ran of getting their heads laid open with the butt of the farmer's whip. Tom was a distinguished adept at these thefts—by proxy. Chambers did his stealing, and got the peach-stones, apple-cores, and melon-rinds for his share.

Tom always made Chambers go in swimming with him, and stay by him as a protection. When Tom had had enough, he would slip out and tie knots in Chambers' shirt, dip the knots in the water to make them hard to undo, then dress himself and sit by and laugh while the naked shiverer tugged at the stubborn knots with his teeth.

Tom did his humble comrade these various ill turns partly out of native viciousness, and partly because he hated him for his superiorities of physique and pluck, and for his manifold clevernesses. Tom couldn't dive, for it gave him splitting headaches. Chambers could dive without inconvenience, and was fond of doing it. He excited so much admiration, one day, among a crowd of white boys, by throwing back somersaults from the stern of a canoe, that it wearied Tom's spirit, and at last he shoved the canoe underneath Chambers while he was in the air— so he came down on the canoe-bottom; and while he lay unconscious, several of Tom's ancient adversaries saw that their long-desired opportunity was come, and they gave the false heir such a drubbing that with Chambers's best help he was hardly able to drag himself home afterward.

When the boys were fifteen and upward, Tom was "showing off" in the river one day, when he was taken with a cramp, and shouted for help. It was a common trick with the boys— particularly if a stranger was present—to pretend a cramp and howl for help; then when the stranger came tearing hand over hand to the rescue, the howler would go on struggling and howling till he was close at hand, then replace the howl with a sarcastic smile and swim blandly away, while the town boys assailed the dupe with a volley of jeers and laughter. Tom had never tried this joke as yet, but was supposed to be trying it now, so the boys held warily back; but Chambers believed his master was in earnest, therefore he swam out, and arrived in time, unfortunately, and saved his life.

This was the last feather. Tom had managed to endure everything else but to have to remain publicly and permanently under such an obligation as this to a nigger, and to this nigger of all niggers—this was too much. He heaped insults upon Chambers for "pretending to think he was in earnest in calling for help, and said that anybody but a block-headed nigger would have known he was funning and left him alone.

Tom's enemies were in strong force here, so they came out with their opinions quite freely. They laughed at him, and called him coward, liar, sneak, and other sorts of pet names, and told him they meant to call Chambers by a new name after this, and make it common in town—"Tom Driscoll's niggerpappy,"—to signify that he had had a second birth into this life, and that Chambers was the author of his new being. Tom grew frantic under these taunts, and shouted—

"Knock their heads off, Chambers! knock their heads off! What do you stand there with your hands in your pockets for?"

Chambers expostulated, and said, "But, Marse Tom, dey's too many of 'em—dey's—"

"Do you hear me?"

"Please, Marse Tom, don't make me! Dey's so many of 'em dat———"

Tom sprang at him and drove his pocketknife into him two or three times before the boys could snatch him away and give the wounded lad a chance to escape. He was considerably hurt, but not seriously. If the blade had been a little longer his career would have ended there.

Tom had long ago taught Roxy "her place." It had been many a day now since she had ventured a caress or a fondling epithet in his quarter. Such things, from a "nigger," were repulsive to him, and she had been warned to keep her distance and remember who she was. She saw her darling gradually cease from being her son, she saw *that* detail perish utterly; all that was left was master—master, pure and simple, and it was not a gentle mastership, either. She saw herself sink from the sublime height of motherhood to the somber depths of unmodified slavery. The abyss of separation between her and her boy was complete. She was merely his chattel, now, his convenience, his dog, his cringing and helpless slave, the humble and unresisting victim of his capricious temper and vicious nature.

Sometimes she could not go to sleep, even when worn out with fatigue, because her rage boiled so high over the day's experiences with her boy. She would mumble and mutter to herself—

"He struck me, en I warn't no way to blame—struck me in de face, right before folks. En he's al'ays callin' me nigger-wench, en hussy, en all dem mean names, when I's doin' de very bes' I kin. Oh, Lord, I done so much for him—I lift'd him away up to what he is—en dis is what I git for it."

Sometimes when some outrage of peculiar offensiveness stung her to her heart, she would plan schemes of vengeance and revel in the fancied spectacle of his exposure to the world as an imposter and a slave; but in the midst of these joys fear would strike her: she had made him too strong; she could prove nothing, and—heavens, she might get sold down the river for her pains! So her schemes always went for nothing, and she laid them aside in impotent rage against the fates, and against herself for playing the fool on that fatal September day in not providing herself with a witness for use in the day when such a thing might be needed for the appeasing of her vengeance-hungry heart.

And yet the moment Tom happened to be good to her, and kind,—and this occurred every now and then,—all her sore places were healed, and she was happy; happy and proud, for this was her son, her nigger son, lording it among the whites and securely avenging their crimes against her race.

There were two grand funerals in Dawson's Landing that fall—the fall of 1845. One was that of Colonel Cecil Burleigh Essex, the other that of Percy Driscoll.

On his death-bed Driscoll set Roxy free and delivered his idolized ostensible son solemnly into the keeping of his brother, the Judge and his wife. Those childless people were glad to get him. Childless people are not difficult to please.

Judge Driscoll had gone privately to his brother, a month before, and bought Chambers. He had heard that Tom had been trying to get his father to sell the boy down the river, and he wanted to prevent the scandal—for public sentiment did not approve of that way of treating family servants for light cause or for no cause.

Percy Driscoll had worn himself out in trying to save his great speculative landed estate, and had died without succeeding. He was hardly in his grave before the boom collapsed and left his hitherto envied young devil of an heir a pauper. But that was nothing; his uncle told him he should be his heir and have all his fortune when he died; so Tom was comforted.

Roxy had no home, now; so she resolved to go around and say good-by to her friends and then clear out and see the world—that is to say, she would go chambermaiding on a steamboat, the darling ambition of her race and sex.

Her last call was on the black giant, Jasper. She found him chopping Pudd'nhead Wilson's winter provision of wood.

Wilson was chatting with him when Roxy arrived. He asked her how she could bear to go off chambermaiding and leave her boys; and chaffingly offered to copy off a series of their fingerprints, reaching up to their twelfth year, for her to remember them by; but she sobered in a moment, wondering if he suspected anything; then she said she believed she did n't want them. Wilson said to himself, "The drop of black blood in her is superstitious; she thinks there's some devilry, some witch-business about my glass mystery somewhere; she used to come here with an old horseshoe in her hand; it could have been an accident, but I doubt it."

CHAPTER V

Training is everything. The peach was once a bitter almond; cauliflower is nothing but cabbage with a college education—*Pudd'nhead Wilson's Calendar.*

Remark of Dr. Baldwin's concerning upstarts: We don't care to eat toadstools that think they are truffles.—*Pudd'nhead Wilson's Calendar.*

Mrs. York Driscoll enjoyed two years of bliss with that prize, Tom—bliss that was troubled a little at times, it is true, but bliss nevertheless; then she died, and her husband and his childless sister, Mrs. Pratt, continued the bliss-business at the old stand. Tom was petted and indulged and spoiled to his entire content—or nearly that. This went on till he was nineteen, then he was sent to Yale. He went handsomely equipped with "conditions," but otherwise he was not an object of distinction there. He remained at Yale two years, and then threw up the struggle. He came home with his manners a good deal improved; he had lost his surliness and brusqueness, and was rather pleasantly soft and smooth, now; he was furtively, and sometimes openly, ironical of speech, and given to gently touching people on the raw, but he did it with a good-natured semiconscious air that carried it off safely, and kept him from getting into trouble. He was as indolent as ever and showed no very strenuous desire to hunt up an occupation. People argued from this that he preferred to be supported by his uncle until his uncle's shoes should become vacant. He brought back one or two new habits with him, one of which he rather openly practised—tippling—but concealed another, which was gambling. It would not do to gamble where his uncle could hear of it; he knew that quite well.

Tom's Eastern polish was not popular among the young people. They could have endured it, perhaps, if Tom had stopped there; but he wore gloves, and that they couldn't stand, and wouldn't; so he was mainly without society. He brought home with him a suit of clothes of such exquisite style and cut and fashion,—Eastern fashion, city fashion,—that it filled everybody with anguish and was regarded as a peculiarly wanton affront. He enjoyed the feeling which he was exciting, and paraded the town serene and happy all day; but the young fellows set a tailor to work that night, and when Tom started out on his parade next morning he found the old deformed negro bell-ringer straddling along in his wake tricked out in a flamboyant curtain-calico exaggeration of his finery, and imitating his fancy Eastern graces as well as he could.

Tom surrendered, and after that clothed himself in the local fashion. But the dull country town was tiresome to him, since his acquaintanceship with livelier regions, and it grew daily more and more so. He began to make little trips to St. Louis for refreshment. There he found companionship to suit him, and pleasures to his taste, along with more freedom, in some particulars, than he could have at home. So, during the next two years his visits to the city grew in frequency and his tarryings there grew steadily longer in duration.

He was getting into deep waters. He was taking chances, privately, which might get him into trouble some day—in fact, *did*.

Judge Driscoll had retired from the bench and from all business activities in 1850, and had now been comfortably idle three years. He was president of the Free-thinkers' Society, and Pudd'nhead Wilson was the other member. The society's weekly discussions were now the old lawyer's main interest in life.

Pudd'nhead was still toiling in obscurity at the bottom of the ladder, under the blight of that unlucky remark which he had let fall twenty-three years before about the dog.

Judge Driscoll was his friend, and claimed that he had a mind above the average, but that was regarded as one of the Judge's whims, and it failed to modify the public opinion. Or rather, that was one of the reasons why it failed, but there was another and better one. If the Judge had stopped with bare assertion, it would have had a good deal of effect; but he made the mistake of trying to prove his position. For some years Wilson had been privately at work on a whimsical almanac, for his amusement—a calendar, with a little dab of ostensible philosophy, usually in ironical form, appended to each date; and the Judge thought that these quips and fancies of Wilson's were neatly turned and cute; so he carried a handful of them around, one day, and read them to some of the chief citizens. But irony was not for those people; their mental vision was not focussed for it. They read those playful trifles in the solidest earnest, and decided without hesitancy that if there had ever been any doubt that Dave Wilson was a pudd'nhead—which there hadn't—this revelation removed that doubt for good and all. That is just the way in this world; an enemy can partly ruin a man, but it takes a good-natured injudicious friend to complete the thing and make it perfect. After this the Judge felt tenderer than ever toward Wilson, and surer than ever that his calendar had merit.

Judge Driscoll could be a free-thinker and still hold his place in society because he was the person of most consequence in the community, and therefore could venture to go his own way and follow out his own notions. The other member of his pet organization was allowed the like liberty because he was a cipher in the estimation of the public, and nobody attached any importance to what he thought or did. He was liked, he was welcome enough all around, but he simply didn't count for anything.

The widow Cooper—affectionately called "aunt Patsy" by everybody—lived in a snug and comely cottage with her daughter Rowena, who was nineteen, romantic, amiable, and very pretty, but otherwise of no consequence. Rowena had a couple of young brothers—also of no consequence.

The widow had a large spare room which she let to a lodger, with board, when she could find one, but this room had been empty for a year now, to her sorrow. Her income was only sufficient for the family support, and she needed the lodging-money for trifling luxuries. But now, at last, on a flaming June day, she found herself happy; her tedious wait was ended; her year-worn

advertisement had been answered; and not by a village applicant, oh, no!—this letter was from away off yonder in the dim
great world to the North: it was from St. Louis. She sat on her
porch gazing out with unseeing eyes upon the shining reaches of
the mighty Mississippi, her thoughts steeped in her good fortune. Indeed it was specially good fortune, for she was to have
two lodgers instead of one.

She had read the letter to the family, and Rowena had danced
away to see to the cleaning and airing of the room by the slave
woman Nancy, and the boys had rushed abroad in the town to
spread the great news, for it was matter of public interest, and
the public would wonder and not be pleased if not informed.
Presently Rowena returned, all ablush with joyous excitement,
and begged for a re-reading of the letter. It was framed thus:

Honored Madam: My brother and I have seen your advertisement,
by chance, and beg leave to take the room you offer. We are twenty-
four years of age and twins. We are Italians by birth, but have lived
long in the various countries of Europe, and several years in the United
States. Our names are Luigi and Angelo Capello. You desire but one
guest; but dear Madam, if you will allow us to pay for two, we will not
incommode you. We shall be down Thursday.

"Italians! How romantic! Just think, ma—there's never been
one in this town, and everybody will be dying to see them, and
they're all *ours!* Think of that!"

"Yes, I reckon they'll make a grand stir."

"Oh, indeed they will. The whole town will be on its head!
Think—they've been in Europe and everywhere! There's never
been a traveler in this town before. Ma, I shouldn't wonder if
they've seen kings!"

"Well, a body can't tell; but they'll make stir enough, without
that."

"Yes, that's of course. Luigi—Angelo. They're lovely names;
and so grand and foreign—not like Jones and Robinson and
such. Thursday they are coming, and this is only Tuesday; it's a
cruel long time to wait. Here comes Judge Driscoll in at the gate.
He's heard about it. I'll go and open the door."

The Judge was full of congratulations and curiosity. The letter
was read and discussed. Soon Justice Robinson arrived with
more congratulations, and there was a new reading and a new
discussion. This was the beginning. Neighbor after neighbor, of
both sexes, followed, and the procession drifted in and out all
day and evening and all Wednesday and Thursday. The letter
was read and re-read until it was nearly worn out; everybody
admired its courtly and gracious tone, and smooth and practised

style, everybody was sympathetic and excited, and the Coopers were steeped in happiness all the while.

The boats were very uncertain in low water, in these primitive times. This time the Thursday boat had not arrived at ten at night—so the people had waited at the landing all day for nothing; they were driven to their homes by a heavy storm without having had a view of the illustrious foreigners.

Eleven o'clock came; and the Cooper house was the only one in the town that still had lights burning. The rain and thunder were booming yet, and the anxious family were still waiting, still hoping. At last there was a knock at the door and the family jumped to open it. Two negro men entered, each carrying a trunk, and proceeded up-stairs toward the guest-room. Then entered the twins—the handsomest, the best dressed, the most distinguished-looking pair of young fellows the West had ever seen. One was a little fairer than the other, but otherwise they were exact duplicates.

CHAPTER VI

Let us endeavor so to live that when we come to die even the undertaker will be sorry.—*Pudd'nhead Wilson's Calendar.*

Habit is habit, and not to be flung out of the window by any man, but coaxed down-stairs a step at a time.—*Pudd'nhead Wilson's Calendar.*

At breakfast in the morning the twins' charm of manner and easy and polished bearing made speedy conquest of the family's good graces. All constraint and formality quickly disappeared, and the friendliest feeling succeeded. Aunt Patsy called them by their Christian names almost from the beginning. She was full of the keenest curiosity about them, and showed it; they responded by talking about themselves, which pleased her greatly. It presently appeared that in their early youth they had known poverty and hardship. As the talk wandered along the old lady watched for the right place to drop in a question or two concerning that matter, and when she found it she said to the blond twin who was now doing the biographies in his turn while the brunette one rested—

"If it ain't asking what I ought not to ask, Mr. Angelo, how did you come to be so friendless and in such trouble when you were little? Do you mind telling? But don't if you do."

"Oh, we don't mind it at all, madam; in our case it was merely misfortune, and nobody's fault. Our parents were well to do, there in Italy, and we were their only child. We were of the old Florentine nobility''—Rowena's heart gave a great bound, her nostrils expanded, and a fine light played in her eyes—''and when the war broke out my father was on the losing side and had to fly for his life. His estates were confiscated, his personal property seized, and there we were, in Germany, strangers, friendless, and in fact paupers. My brother and I were ten years old, and well educated for that age, very studious, very fond of our books, and well grounded in the German, French, Spanish, and English languages. Also, we were marvelous musical prodigies—if you will allow me to say it, it being only the truth.

"Our father survived his misfortunes only a month, our mother soon followed him, and we were alone in the world. Our parents could have made themselves comfortable by exhibiting us as a show, and they had many and large offers; but the thought revolted their pride, and they said they would starve and die first. But what they wouldn't consent to do we had to do without the formality of consent. We were seized for the debts occasioned by their illness and their funerals, and placed among the attractions of a cheap museum in Berlin to earn the liquidation money. It took us two years to get out of that slavery. We traveled all about Germany receiving no wages, and not even our keep. We had to be exhibited for nothing, and beg our bread.

"Well, madam, the rest is not of much consequence. When we escaped from that slavery at twelve years of age, we were in some respects men. Experience had taught us some valuable things; among others, how to take care of ourselves, how to avoid and defeat sharks and sharpers, and how to conduct our own business for our own profit and without other people's help. We traveled everywhere—years and years—picking up smatterings of strange tongues, familiarizing ourselves with strange sights and strange customs, accumulating an education of a wide and varied and curious sort. It was a pleasant life. We went to Venice—to London, Paris, Russia, India, China, Japan—''

At this point Nancy the slave woman thrust her head in at the door and exclaimed:

"Ole Missus, de house is plum' jam full o' people, en dey's jes a-spi'lin' to see de gen'lmen!'' She indicated the twins with a nod of her head, and tucked it back out of sight again.

It was a proud occasion for the widow, and she promised herself high satisfaction in showing off her fine foreign birds before her neighbors and friends—simple folk who had hardly ever seen a foreigner of any kind, and never one of any distinction or style. Yet her feeling was moderate indeed when contrasted with Rowena's. Rowena was in the clouds, she walked on air; this was to be the greatest day, the most romantic episode, in the colorless history of that dull country town. She was to be familiarly near the source of its glory and feel the full flood of it pour over her and about her; the other girls could only gaze and envy, not partake.

The widow was ready, Rowena was ready, so also were the foreigners.

The party moved along the hall, the twins in advance, and entered the open parlor door, whence issued a low hum of conversation. The twins took a position near the door the widow stood at Luigi's side, Rowena stood beside Angelo, and the march-past and the introductions began. The widow was all smiles and contentment. She received the procession and passed it on to Rowena.

"Good mornin', Sister Cooper"—hand-shake.

"Good morning, Brother Higgins—Count Luigi Capello, Mr. Higgins"—hand-shake, followed by a devouring stare and "I'm glad to see ye," on the part of Higgins, and a courteous inclination of the head and a pleasant "Most happy!" on the part of Count Luigi.

"Good mornin', Roweny"—hand-shake.

"Good morning, Mr. Higgins—present you to Count Angelo Capello." Hand-shake, admiring stare, "Glad to see ye,"—courteous nod, smily "Most happy!" and Higgins passes on.

None of these visitors was at ease, but, being honest people, they didn't pretend to be. None of them had ever seen a person bearing a title of nobility before, and none had been expecting to see one now, consequently the title came upon them as a kind of pile-driving surprise and caught them unprepared. A few tried to rise to the emergency, and got out an awkward "My Lord," or "Your lordship," or something of that sort, but the great majority were overwhelmed by the unaccustomed word and its dim and awful associations with gilded courts and stately ceremony and anointed kingship, so they only fumbled through the hand-shake and passed on, speechless. Now and then, as happens at all receptions everywhere, a more than ordinarily friendly soul blocked the procession and kept it waiting while he inquired how the brothers liked the village, and how long they were going to stay, and if their families were well, and dragged in the weather, and hoped it would get cooler soon, and all that sort of thing, so as to be able to say, when they got home, "I had quite a long talk with them"; but nobody did or said anything of a regrettable kind, and so the great affair went through to the end in a creditable and satisfactory fashion.

General conversation followed, and the twins drifted about from group to group, talking easily and fluently and winning approval, compelling admiration and achieving favor from all. The widow followed their conquering march with a proud eye, and every now and then Rowena said to herself with deep satisfaction, "And to think they are ours—all ours!"

There were no idle moments for mother or daughter. Eager inquiries concerning the twins were pouring into their enchanted ears all the time; each was the constant center of a group of breathless listeners; each recognized that she knew now for the first time the real meaning of that great word Glory, and perceived the stupendous value of it, and understood why men in all ages had been willing to throw away meaner happinesses, treasure, life itself, to get a taste of its sublime and supreme joy. Napoleon and all his kind stood accounted for—and justified.

When Rowena had at last done all her duty by the people in the parlor, she went up-stairs to satisfy the longings of an overflow-meeting there, for the parlor was not big enough to hold all the comers. Again she was besieged by eager questioners and again she swam in sunset seas of glory. When the forenoon was nearly gone, she recognized with a pang that this most splendid episode of her life was almost over, that nothing could prolong it, that nothing quite its equal could ever fall to her fortune again. But never mind, it was sufficient unto itself, the grand occasion had moved on an ascending scale from the start, and was a noble and memorable success. If the twins could but do some crowning act, now, to climax it, something unusual, something startling, something to concentrate upon themselves the company's loftiest admiration, something in the nature of an electric surprise—

Here a prodigious slam-banging broke out below, and everybody rushed down to see. It was the twins knocking out a classic four-handed piece on the piano, in great style. Rowena was satisfied—satisfied down to the bottom of her heart.

The young strangers were kept long at the piano. The villagers were astonished and enchanted with the magnificence of their performance, and could not bear to have them stop. All the music that they had ever heard before seemed spiritless prenticework and barren of grace or charm when compared with these intoxicating floods of melodious sound. They realized that for once in their lives they were hearing masters.

CHAPTER VII

One of the most striking differences between a cat and a lie is that a cat has only nine lives.—*Pudd'nhead Wilson's Calendar.*

The company broke up reluctantly, and drifted toward their several homes, chatting with vivacity, and all agreeing that it would be many a long day before Dawson's Landing would see the equal of this one again. The twins had accepted several invitations while the reception was in progress, and had also volunteered to play some duets at an amateur entertainment for the benefit of a local charity. Society was eager to receive them to its bosom. Judge Driscoll had the good fortune to secure them for an immediate drive, and to be the first to display them in public. They entered his buggy with him, and were paraded down the main street, everybody flocking to the windows and sidewalks to see.

The Judge showed the strangers the new graveyard, and the jail, and where the richest man lived, and the Freemasons' hall, and the Methodist church, and the Presbyterian church, and where the Baptist church was going to be when they got some money to build it with, and showed them the town hall and the slaughter-house, and got out the independent fire company in uniform and had them put out an imaginary fire; then he let them inspect the muskets of the militia company, and poured out an exhaustless stream of enthusiasm over all these splendors, and seemed very well satisfied with the responses he got, for the twins admired his admiration, and paid him back the best they could, though they could have done better if some fifteen or sixteen hundred thousand previous experiences of this sort in various countries had not already rubbed off a considerable part of the novelty of it.

The Judge laid himself out hospitably to make them have a good time, and if there was a defect anywhere it was not his fault. He told them a good many humorous anecdotes, and always forgot the nub, but they were always able to furnish it, for these yarns were of a pretty early vintage, and they had had many a rejuvenating pull at them before. And he told them all about his several dignities, and how he had held this and that and the other place of honor or profit, and had once been to the legislature, and was now president of the Society of Freethinkers. He said the society had been in existence four years, and already had two members, and was firmly established. He would call for the brothers in the evening if they would like to attend a meeting of it.

Accordingly he called for them, and on the way he told them all about Pudd'nhead Wilson, in order that they might get a favorable impression of him in advance and be prepared to like him. This scheme succeeded—the favorable impression was achieved. Later it was confirmed and solidified when Wilson proposed that out of courtesy to the strangers the usual topics be put aside and the hour be devoted to conversation upon ordinary subjects and the cultivation of friendly relations and good-fellowship,—a proposition which was put to vote and carried.

The hour passed quickly away in lively talk, and when it was ended the lonesome and neglected Wilson was richer by two friends than he had been when it began. He invited the twins to look in at his lodgings, presently, after disposing of an intervening engagement, and they accepted with pleasure.

Toward the middle of the evening they found themselves on the road to his house. Pudd'head was at home waiting for them and putting in his time puzzling over a thing which had come under his notice that morning. The matter was this: He happened to be up very early—at dawn, in fact; and he crossed the hall which divided his cottage through the center, and entered a room to something there. The window of the room had no curtains, for that side of the house had long been unoccupied, and through this window he caught sight of something which surprised and interested him. It was a young woman—a young woman where properly no young woman belonged; for she was in Judge Driscoll's house, and in the bedroom over the Judge's private study or sitting-room. This was young Tom Dricoll's bedroom. He and the Judge, the Judge's widowed sister Mrs. Pratt and three negro servants were the only people who belonged in the house. Who, then, might this young lady be? The two houses were separated by an ordinary yard, with a low fence running back through its middle from the street in front to the lane in the rear. The distance was not great, and Wilson was able to see the girl very well, the window-shades of the room she was in being up, and the window also. The girl had on a neat and trim summer dress, patterned in broad stripes of pink and white, and her bonnet was equipped with a pink veil. She was practising steps, gaits and attitudes, apparently; she was doing the thing gracefully, and was very much absorbed in her work. Who could she be, and how came she to be in young Tom Driscoll's room?

Wilson had quickly chosen a position from which he could watch the girl without running much risk of being seen by her, and he remained there hoping she would raise her veil and betray her face. But she disappointed him. After a matter of twenty minutes she disappeared, and although he stayed at his post half an hour longer, she came no more.

Toward noon he dropped in at the Judge's and talked with Mrs. Pratt about the great event of the day, and levee of the distinguished foreigners at Aunt Patsy Cooper's. He asked after her nephew Tom, and she said he was on his way home, and that she was expecting him to arrive a little before night; and added that she and the Judge were gratified to gather from his letters that he was conducting himself very nicely and creditably—at which Wilson winked to himself privately. Wilson did not ask if there was a newcomer in the house, but he asked questions that would have brought light-throwing answers as to that matter if Mrs. Pratt had had any light to throw; so he went away satisfied that he knew of things that were going on in her house of which she herself was not aware.

He was now waiting for the twins, and still puzzling over the problem of who that girl might be, and how she happened to be in that young fellow's room at daybreak in the morning.

CHAPTER VIII

The holy passion of Friendship is of so sweet and steady and loyal and enduring a nature that it will last through a whole lifetime, if not asked to lend money.—*Pudd'nhead Wilson's Calendar.*

Consider well the proportions of things. It is better to be a young June-bug than an old bird of paradise.—*Pudd'nhead Wilson's Calendar.*

It is necessary now, to hunt up Roxy.

At the time she was set free and went away chambermaiding, she was thirty-five. She got a berth as second chambermaid on a Cincinnati boat in the New Orleans trade, the *Grand Mogul*. A couple of trips made her wonted and easy-going at the work, and infatuated her with the stir and adventure and independence of steamboat life. Then she was promoted and became head chambermaid. She was a favorite with the officers, and exceedingly proud of their joking and friendly ways with her.

During eight years she served three parts of the year on that boat, and the winters on a Vicksburg packet. But now for two months she had had rheumatism in her arms, and was obliged to let the wash-tub alone. So she resigned. But she was well fixed —rich, as she would have described it; for she had lived a steady life, and had banked four dollars every month in New Orleans as a provision for her old age. She said in the start that she had "put shoes on one bar' footed nigger to tromple on her with," and that one mistake like that was enough; she would be independent of the human race thenceforth forevermore if hard work and economy could accomplish it. When the boat touched the levee at New Orleans she bade good-by to her comrades on the *Grand Mogul* and moved her kit ashore.

But she was back in an hour. The bank had gone to smash and carried her four hundred dollars with it. She was a pauper, and homeless. Also disabled bodily, at least for the present. The officers were full of sympathy for her in her trouble, and made up a little purse for her. She resolved to go to her birthplace; she had friends there among the negroes, and the unfortunate always help the unfortunate, she was well aware of that; those lowly comrades of her youth would not let her starve.

She took the little local packet at Cairo, and now she was on the home-stretch. Time had worn away her bitterness against her son, and she was able to think of him with serenity. She put the vile side of him out of her mind, and dwelt only on recollections of his occasional acts of kindness to her. She gilded and otherwise decorated these, and made them very pleasant to contemplate. She began to long to see him. She would go and fawn upon him, slave-like—for this would have to be her attitude, of course—and maybe she would find that time had modified him, and that he would be glad to see his long-forgotten old nurse and treat her gently. That would be lovely; that would make her forget her woes and her poverty.

Her poverty! That thought inspired her to add another castle to her dream: maybe he would give her a trifle now and then—maybe a dollar, once a month, say; any little thing like that would help, oh, ever so much.

By the time she reached Dawson's Landing she was her old self again; her blues were gone, she was in high feather. She would get along, surely; there were many kitchens where the servants would share their meals with her, and also steal sugar and apples and other dainties for her to carry home—or give her a chance to pilfer them herself, which would answer just as well. And there was the church. She was a more rabid and devoted Methodist than ever, and her piety was no sham, but was strong and sincere. Yes, with plenty of creature comforts and her old place in the amen-corner in her possession again, she would be perfectly happy and at peace thenceforward to the end.

She went to Judge Driscoll's kitchen first of all. She was received there in great form and with vast enthusiasm. Her wonderful travels, and the strange countries she had seen and the adventures she had had, made her a marvel, and a heroine of romance. The negroes hung enchanted upon the great story of her experiences, interrupting her all along with eager questions, with laughter, exclamations of delight and expressions of applause; and she was obliged to confess to herself that if there was anything better in this world than steamboating, it was the glory to be got by telling about it. The audience loaded her stomach with their dinners, and then stole the pantry bare to load up her basket.

Tom was in St. Louis. The servants said he had spent the best part of his time there during the previous two years. Roxy came every day, and had many talks about the family and its affairs. Once she asked why Tom was away so much. The ostensible "Chambers" said:

"De fac' is, ole marster kin git along better when young marster's away den he kin when he's in de town; yes, en he love him better, too; so he gives him fifty dollahs a month—"

"No, is dat so? Chambers, you's a-jokin', ain't you?"

"'Clah to goodness I ain't, mammy; Marse Tom tole me so his own self. But nemmine, 't ain't enough?"

"My lan', what de reason 't ain't enough?"

"Well, I's gwine to tell you, if you gimme a chanst, mammy. De reason it ain't enough is 'ca'se Marse Tom gambles."

Roxy threw up her hands in astonishment and Chambers went on—

"Ole marster found it out, 'ca'se he had to pay two hundred dollahs for Marse Tom's gamblin' debts, en dat's true, mammy, jes as dead certain as you's bawn."

"Two—hund'd—dollahs! Why, what is you talkin' 'bout? Two—hund'd—dollahs. Sakes alive, it's 'mos' enough to buy a tol'able good second-hand nigger wid. En you ain't lyin', honey?—you wouldn't lie to yo' ole mammy?"

"It's God's own truth, jes as I tell you—two hund'd dollahs—I wisht I may never stir outen my tracks if it ain't so. En, oh, my lan', ole Marse was jes a-hoppin'! he was b'ilin' mad, I tell you! He tuck 'n' dissenhurrit him."

He licked his chops with relish after that stately word. Roxy struggled with it a moment, then gave it up and said—

"Dissen*whiched* him?"

"Dissenhurrit him."

"What's dat? What do it mean?"

"Means he bu'sted de will."

"Bu's—ted de will! He wouldn't *ever* treat him so! Take it back, you mis'able imitation nigger dat I bore in sorrow en tribilation."

Roxy's pet castle—an occasional dollar from Tom's pocket—was tumbling to ruin before her eyes. She could not abide such a disaster as that; she couldn't endure the thought of it. Her remark amused Chambers:

"Yah-yah-yah! jes listen to dat! If I's imitation, what is you? Bofe of us is imitation *white* —dat's what we is—en pow'ful good imitation, too—yah-yah-yah!—we don't 'mount to noth'n as imitation *niggers;* en as for—"

"Shet up yo' foolin', 'fo' I knock you side de head, en tell me 'bout de will. Tell me't ain't bu'sted—do, honey, en I'll never forgit you."

"Well, *'tain't* —'ca'se dey's a new one made, en Marse Tom's all right ag'in. But what is you in sich a sweat 'bout it for, mammy? 'Tain't none o' your business I don't reckon."

"'Tain't none o' my business? Whose business is it den, I'd like to know? Wuz I his mother tell he was fifteen years old, or wus n't I?—you answer me dat. En you speck I could see him turned out po'en ornery on de worl' en never care noth 'n 'bout it? I reckon if you'd ever be'n a mother yo'self, Valet de Chambers, you wouldn't talk sich foolishness as dat."

"Well, den, ole Marse forgive him en fixed up de will ag'in—do dat satisfy you?"

Yes, she was satisfied now, and quite happy and sentimental over it. She kept coming daily, and at last she was told that Tom had come home. She began to tremble with emotion, and straightway sent to beg him to let his "po' ole nigger mammy have jes one sight of him en die for joy."

Tom was stretched at his lazy ease on a sofa when Chambers brought the petition. Time had not modified his ancient detestation of the humble drudge and protector of his boyhood; it was still bitter and uncompromising. He sat up and bent a severe gaze upon the fair face of the young fellow whose name he was unconsciously using and whose family rights he was enjoying. He maintained the gaze until the victim of it had become satisfactorily pallid with terror, then he said—

"What does the old rip want with me?"

The petition was meekly repeated.

"Who gave you permission to come and disturb me with the social attentions of niggers?"

Tom had risen. The other young man was trembling now, visibly. He saw what was coming, and bent his head sideways, and put up his left arm to shield it. Tom rained cuffs upon the head and its shield, saying no word: the victim received each blow with a beseeching "Please, Marse Tom!—oh, please,

Marse Tom!'' Seven blows—then Tom said, ''Face the door—march!'' He followed behind with one, two, three solid kicks. The last one helped the pure-white slave over the door-sill, and he limped away mopping his eyes with his old ragged sleeve. Tom shouted after him, ''Send her in!''

Then he flung himself panting on the sofa again, and rasped out the remark, ''He arrived just at the right moment; I was full to the brim with bitter thinkings, and nobody to take it out of. How refreshing it was! I feel better.''

Tom's mother entered now, closing the door behind her, and approached her son with all the wheedling and supplicating servilities that fear and interest can impart to the words and attitudes of the born slave. She stopped a yard from her boy and made two or three admiring exclamations over his manly stature and general handsomeness, and Tom put an arm under his head and hoisted a leg over the sofa-back in order to look properly indifferent.

''My lan', how you is growed, honey! 'Clah to goodness, I wouldn't a-knowed you, Marse Tom! 'deed I wouldn't! Look at me good; does you 'member old Roxy?—does you know yo' old nigger mammy, honey? Well now, I kin lay down en die in peace, 'ca'se I 'se seed—''

''Cut it short,—it, cut it short! What is it you want?''

''You heah dat? Jes de same old Marse Tom, al'ays so gay and funnin' wid de ole mammy. I 'uz jes as shore—''

''Cut it short, I tell you, and get along! What do you want.''

This was a bitter disappointment. Roxy had for so many days nourished and fondled and petted her notion that Tom would be glad to see his old nurse, and would make her proud and happy to the marrow with a cordial word or two, that it took two rebuffs to convince her that he was not funning, and that her beautiful dream was a fond and foolish vanity, a shabby and pitiful mistake. She was hurt to the heart, and so ashamed that for a moment she did not quite know what to do or how to act. Then her breast began to heave, the tears came, and in her forlornness she was moved to try that other dream of hers—an appeal to her boy's charity; and so, upon the impulse, and without reflection, she offered her supplication:

''Oh, Marse Tom, de po' ole mammy is in sich hard luck dese days; en she's kinder crippled in de arms en can't work, en if you could gimme a dollah—on'y jes one little dol—''

Tom was on his feet so suddenly that the supplicant was startled into a jump herself.

''A dollar!—give you a dollar! I've a notion to strangle you!

Is *that* your errand here? Clear out! and be quick about it!''

Roxy backed slowly toward the door. When she was half-way he stopped, and said mournfully:

"Marse Tom, I nussed you when you was a little baby, en I raised you all by myself tell you was 'most a young man; en now you is young en rich, en I is po' en gitt'n ole, en I come heah b'lievin' dat you would he'p de ole mammy 'long down de little road dat's lef' 'twix' her en de grave, en—"

Tom relished this tune less than any that had preceded it, for it began to wake up a sort of echo in his conscience; so he interrupted and said with decision, though without asperity, that he was not in a situation to help her, and wasn't going to do it.

"Ain't you ever gwine to he'p me, Marse Tom?"

"No! Now go away and don't bother me any more."

Roxy's head was down, in an attitude of humility. But now the fires of her old wrongs flamed up in her breast and began to burn fiercely. She raised her head slowly, till it was well up, and at the same time her great frame unconsciously assumed an erect and masterful attitude, with all the majesty and grace of her vanished youth in it. She raised her finger and punctuated with it:

"You has said de word. You has had yo' chance, en you has trompled it under yo' foot. When you git another one, you'll git down on yo' knees en *beg* for it!"

A cold chill went to Tom's heart, he didn't know why; for he did not reflect that such words, from such an incongruous source, and so solemnly delivered, could not easily fail of that effect. However, he did the natural thing: he replied with bluster and mockery:

"*You'll* give me a chance—*you!* Perhaps I'd better get down on my knees now! But in case I don't—just for argument's sake—what's going to happen, pray?"

"Dis is what is gwine to happen. I's gwine as straight to yo' uncle as I kin walk, en tell him every las' thing I knows 'bout you."

Tom's cheek blenched, and she saw it. Disturbing thoughts began to chase each other through his head. "How can she know? And yet she must have found out—she looks it. I've had the will back only three months, and am already deep in debt again, and moving heaven and earth to save myself from exposure and destruction, with a reasonably fair show of getting the thing covered up if I'm let alone, and now this fiend has gone and found me out somehow or other. I wonder how much she knows? Oh, oh, oh, it's enough to break a body's heart! But I've got to humor her—there's no other way."

Then he worked up a rather sickly sample of a gay laugh and a hollow chipperness of manner, and said:

"Well, well, Roxy dear, old friends like you and me mustn't quarrel. Here's your dollar—now tell me what you know."

He held out the wild-cat bill; she stood as she was, and made no movement. It was her turn to scorn persuasive foolery, now, and she did not waste it. She said, with a grim implacability in voice and manner which made Tom almost realize that even a former slave can remember for ten minutes insults and injuries returned for compliments and flatteries received, and can also enjoy taking revenge for them when the opportunity offers:

"What does I know? I'll tell you what I knows. I knows enough to bu'st dat will to flinders—en more, mind you, *more!*"

Tom was aghast.

"More? " he said. "What do you call more? Where's there any room for more?"

Roxy laughed a mocking laugh, and said scoffingly, with a toss of her head, and her hands on her hips—

"Yes!—oh, I reckon! *Co'se* you'd like to know—wid yo' po' little ole rag dollah. What you reckon I's gwine to tell *you* for?—you ain't got no money. I's gwine to tell yo' uncle—en I'll do it dis minute, too—he'll gimme *five* dollahs for de news, en mighty glad, too."

She swung herself around disdainfully, and started away. Tom was in a panic. He seized her skirts, and implored her to wait. She turned and said, loftiiy—

"Look-a-heah, what 'uz it I tole you?"

"You—you—I don't remember anything. What was it you told me?"

"I tole you dat de next time I give you a chance you'd git down on yo' knees en beg for it."

Tom was stupefied for a moment. He was panting with excitement. Then he said:

"Oh, Roxy, you wouldn't require your young master to do such a horrible thing. You can't mean it."

"I'll let you know mighty quick whether I means it or not! You call me names, en as good as spit on me when I comes here po' en ornery en 'umble, to praise you for bein' growed up so fine en handsome, en tell you how I used to nuss you en tend you en watch you when you 'uz sick en hadn't no mother but me in de whole worl', en beg you to give de po' ole nigger a dollah for to git her som'n' to eat, en you call me names—*names,* dad blame you! Yassir, I gives you jes one chance mo', and dat's *now,* en it las' on'y a half a second—you hear?"

Tom slumped to his knees and began to beg, saying—

"You see I 'm begging, and it's honest begging, too! Now tell me, Roxy, tell me."

The heir of two centuries of unatoned insult and outrage looked down on him and seemed to drink in deep draughts of satisfaction. Then she said—

"Fine nice young white gen'l'man kneelin' down to a nigger-wench! I's wanted to see dat jes once befo' I's called. Now, Gabr'el, blow de hawn, I's ready . . . Git up!"

Tom did it. He said, humbly—

"Now, Roxy, don't punish me any more. I deserved what I've got, but be good and let me off with that. Don't go to uncle. Tell me—I'll give you the five dollars."

"Yes, I bet you will; en you won't stop dah, nuther. But I ain't gwine to tell you heah—"

"Good gracious, no!"

"Is you 'feared o' de ha'nted house?"

"N-no."

"Well, den, you come to de ha'nted house 'bout ten or 'leven to-night, en climb up de ladder, 'ca'se de sta'r-steps is broke down, en you'll find me. I's a-roostin' in de ha'nted house 'ca'se I can't 'ford to roos' nowhers' else." She started toward the door, but stopped and said, "Gimme de dollah bill!" He gave it to her. She examined it and said, "H'm—like enough de bank 's bu'sted." She started again, but halted again. "Has you got any whisky?"

"Yes, a little."

"Fetch it!"

He ran to his room overhead and brought down a bottle which was two-thirds full. She tilted it up and took a drink. Her eyes sparkled with satisfaction, and she tucked the bottle under her shawl, saying, "It's prime. I'll take it along."

Tom humbly held the door for her, and she marched out as grim and erect as a grenadier.

CHAPTER IX

Why is it that we rejoice at a birth and grieve at a funeral? It is because we are not the person involved.—*Pudd'nhead Wilson's Calendar.*

It is easy to find fault, if one has that disposition. There was once a man who, not being able to find any other fault with his coal, complained that there were too many prehistoric toads in it.—*Pudd'nhead Wilson's Calendar.*

Tom flung himself on the sofa, and put his throbbing head in his hands, and rested his elbows on his knees. He rocked himself back and forth and moaned.

"I've knelt to a nigger wench!" he muttered. "I thought I had struck the deepest depths of degradation before, but oh, dear, it was nothing to this . . . . Well, there is one consolation, such as it is—I've struck bottom this time; there's nothing lower."

But that was a hasty conclusion.

At ten that night he climbed the ladder in the haunted house, pale, weak and wretched. Roxy was standing in the door of one of the rooms, waiting, for she had heard him.

This was a two-story log house which had acquired the reputation a few years before of being haunted, and that was the end of its usefulness. Nobody would live in it afterward, or go near it by night, and most people even gave it a wide berth in the daytime. As it had no competition, it was called *the* haunted house. It was getting crazy and ruinous, now, from long neglect. It stood three hundred yards beyond Pudd'nhead Wilson's house, with nothing between but vacancy. It was the last house in the town at that end.

Tom followed Roxy into the room. She had a pile of clean straw in the corner for a bed, some cheap but well-kept clothing was hanging on the wall, there was a tin lantern freckling the floor with little spots of light, and there were various soap-and-candle boxes scattered about, which served for chairs. The two sat down. Roxy said—

"Now den, I'll tell you straight off, en I'll begin to k'leck de money later on; I ain't in no hurry. What does you reckon I's gwine to tell you?"

"Well, you—you—oh, Roxy, don't make it too hard for me! Come right out and tell me you've found out somehow what a shape I'm in on account of dissipation and foolishness."

"Disposition en foolishness! *No* sir, dat ain't it. Dat jist ain't nothin' at all, 'longside o' what *I* knows."

Tom stared at her, and said—

"Why, Roxy, what do you mean?"

She rose, and gloomed above him like a Fate.

"I means dis—en it's de Lord's truth. You ain't no more kin to ole Marse Driscoll den I is!—*dat's* what I means!" and her eyes flamed with triumph.

"What!"

"Yassir, en *dat* ain't all! You's a *nigger!—bawn* a nigger en a *slave!* —en you's a nigger en a slave dis minute; en if I opens my mouf ole Marse Driscoll 'll sell you down de river befo' you is two days older den what you is now!"

57

"It's a thundering lie, you miserable old blatherskite!"

"It ain't no lie, nuther. It's jes de truth, en nothin' *but* de truth, so he'p me. Yassir—you's my *son*—"

"You devil!"

"En dat po' boy dat you's be'n a-kickin' en a-cuffin' to-day is Percy Driscoll's son en yo' *marster*—"

"You beast!"

"En *his* name's Tom Driscoll, en *yo'* name's Valet de Chambers, en you ain't *got* no fambly name, beca'se niggers don't *have* em!"

Tom sprang up and seized a billet of wood and raised it but his mother only laughed at him and said—

"Set down, you pup! Does you think you kin skyer me? It ain't in you, nor de likes of you. I reckon you'd shoot me in de back, maybe, if you got a chance, for dat's jist yo' style— *I* knows you, throo en throo—but I don't mind gitt'n killed, beca'se all dis is down in writin' en it's in safe hands, too, en de man dat's got it knows whah to look for de right man when I gits killed. Oh, bless yo' soul, if you puts yo' mother up for as big a fool as *you* is, you's pow'ful mistaken, I kin tell you! Now den, you set still en behave yo'self; en don't you git up ag'in till I tell you!"

Tom fretted and chafed awhile in a whirlwind of disorganizing sensations and emotions, and finally said, with something like settled conviction—

"The whole thing is moonshine; now then, go ahead and do your worst; I'm done with you."

Roxy made no answer. She took the lantern and started toward the door. Tom was in a cold panic in a moment.

"Come back, come back!" he wailed. "I didn't mean it, Roxy; I take it all back, and I'll never say it again! Please come back, Roxy!"

The woman stood a moment, then she said gravely:

"Dat's one thing you's got to stop, Valet de Chambers. You can't call me *Roxy,* same as if you was my equal. Chillen don't speak to dey mammies like dat. You'll call me ma or mammy, dat's what you'll call me—leastways when dey ain't nobody aroun'. *Say* it!"

It cost Tom a struggle, but he got it out.

"Dat's all right. Don't you ever forget it ag'in, if you knows what's good for you. Now den, you has said you wouldn't ever call it lies en moonshine ag'in. I'll tell you dis, for a warnin': if you ever does say it ag'in, it's de *las'* time you'll ever say it to me; I'll tramp as straight to de Judge as I kin walk, en tell him who you is, en *prove* it. Does you b'lieve me when I says dat?"

"Oh," groaned Tom, "I more than believe it; I *know* it."

Roxy knew her conquest was complete. She could have proved nothing to anybody, and her threat about the writings was a lie; but she knew the person she was dealing with, and had made both statements without any doubt as to the effect they would produce.

She went and sat down on her candle-box, and the pride and pomp of her victorious attitude made it a throne. She said—

"Now den, Chambers, we's gwine to talk business, en dey ain't gwine to be no mo' foolishness. In de fust place, you gits fifty dollahs a month; you's gwine to han' over half of it to yo' ma. Plank it out!"

But Tom had only six dollars in the world. He gave her that, and promised to start fair on next month's pension.

"Chambers, how much is you in debt?"

Tom shuddered, and said—

"Nearly three hundred dollars."

"How is you gwine to pay it?"

Tom groaned out—"Oh, I don't know; don't ask me such awful questions."

But she stuck to her point until she wearied a confession out of him: he had been prowling about in disguise, stealing small valuables from private houses; in fact, had made a good deal of a raid on his fellow-villagers a fortnight before, when he was supposed to be in St. Louis; but he doubted if he had sent away enough stuff to realize the required amount, and was afraid to make a further venture in the present excited state of the town. His mother approved of his conduct, and offered to help, but this frightened him. He tremblingly ventured to say that if she would retire from the town he should feel better and safer, and could hold his head higher—and was going on to make an argument, but she interrupted and surprised him pleasantly by saying she was ready; it didn't make any difference to her where she stayed, so that she got her share of the pension regularly. She said she would not go far, and would call at the haunted house once a month for her money. Then she said—

"I don't hate you so much now, but I've hated you a many a year—and anybody would. Didn't I change you off, en give you a good fambly en a good name, en made you a white gen'l'man en rich, wid store clothes on—en what did I git for it? You despised me all de time, en was al'ays sayin' mean hard things to me befo' folks, en wouldn't ever let me forgit I's a nigger—en—en—"

She fell to sobbing, and broke down. Tom said—"But you know I didn't know you were my mother; and besides—"

"Well, nemmine 'bout dat, now; let it go. I's gwine to fo'git it." Then she added fiercely, "En don't ever make me remember it ag'in, or you'll be sorry, *I* tell you."

When they were parting, Tom said, in the most persuasive way he could command—

"Ma, would you mind telling me who was my father?"

He had supposed he was asking an embarrassing question. He was mistaken. Roxy drew herself up with a proud toss of her head, and said—

"Does I mine tellin' you? No, dat I don't! You ain't got no 'casion to be shame' o' yo' father, *I* kin tell you. He wuz de highest quality in dis whole town—ole Virginny stock. Fust famblies, he wuz. Jes as good stock as de Driscolls en de Howards, de bes' day dey ever seed." She put on a little prouder air, if possible, and added impressively: "Does you 'member Cunnel Cecil Burleigh Essex, dat died de same year yo' young Marse Tom Driscoll's pappy died, en all de Masons en Odd Fellers en Churches turned out en give him de bigges' funeral dis town ever seed? Dat's de man."

Under the inspiration of her soaring complacency the departed graces of her earlier days returned to her, and her bearing took to itself a dignity and state that might have passed for queenly if her surroundings had been a little more in keeping with it.

"Dey ain't another nigger in dis town dat's as high-bawn as you is. Now den, go 'long! En jes you hold yo' head up as high as you want to—you has de right, en dat I kin swah."

CHAPTER X

All say, "How hard it is that we have to die"—a strange complaint to come from the mouths of people who have had to live.—*Pudd'nhead Wilson's Calendar.*

When angry, count four; when very angry, swear.—*Pudd'nhead Wilson's Calendar.*

Every now and then, after Tom went to bed, he had sudden wakings out of his sleep, and his first thought was, "Oh, joy, it was all a dream!" Then he laid himself heavily down again, with a groan and the muttered words, "A nigger! I am a nigger! Oh, I wish I was dead!"

He woke at dawn with one more repetition of this horror, and then he resolved to meddle no more with that treacherous sleep.

He began to think. Sufficiently bitter thinkings they were. They wandered along something after this fashion:

"Why were niggers *and* whites made? What crime did the uncreated first nigger commit that the curse of birth was decreed for him? And why is this awful difference made between white and black? . . . How hard the nigger's fate seems, this morning!—yet until last night such a thought never entered my head."

He sighed and groaned an hour or more away. Then "Chambers" came humbly in to say that breakfast was nearly ready. "Tom" blushed scarlet to see this aristocratic white youth cringe to him, a nigger, and call him "Young Marster." He said roughly—

"Get out of my sight!" and when the youth was gone, he muttered, "He has done me no harm, poor wretch, but he is an eyesore to me now, for he is Driscoll the young gentleman, and I am a—oh, I wish I was dead!"

A gigantic irruption, like that of Krakatoa a few years ago, with the accompanying earthquakes, tidal waves, and clouds of volcanic dust, changes the face of the surrounding landscape beyond recognition, bringing down the high lands, elevating the low, making fair lakes where deserts had been, and deserts where green prairies had smiled before. The tremendous catastrophe which had befallen Tom had changed his moral landscape in much the same way. Some of his low places he found lifted to ideals, some of his ideals had sunk to the valleys, and lay there with the sackcloth and ashes of pumice-stone and sulphur on their ruined heads.

For days he wandered in lonely places, thinking, thinking, thinking—trying to get his bearings. It was new work. If he met a friend, he found that the habit of a lifetime had in some mysterious way vanished—his arm hung limp, instead of involuntarily extending the hand for a shake. It was the "nigger" in him asserting its humility, and he blushed and was abashed. And the "nigger" in him was surprised when the white friend put out his hand for a shake with him. He found the "nigger" in him involuntarily giving the road, on the sidewalk, to the white rowdy and loafer. When Rowena, the dearest thing his heart knew, the idol of his secret worship, invited him in, the "nigger" in him made an embarrassed excuse and was afraid to enter and sit with the dread white folks on equal terms. The "nigger" in him went shrinking and skulking here and there and yonder, and fancying it saw suspicion and maybe detection in all faces, tones, and gestures. So strange and uncharacteristic was Tom's conduct that people noticed it, and turned to look after him when he

passed on; and when he glanced back—as he could not help doing, in spite of his best resistance—and caught that puzzled expression in a person's face, it gave him a sick feeling, and he
took himself out of view as quickly as he could. He presently
came to have a hunted sense and a hunted look, and then he fled
away to the hill-tops and the solitudes. He said to himself that
the curse of Ham was upon him.

He dreaded his meals; the "nigger" in him was ashamed to sit
at the white folks' table, and feared discovery all the time; and
once when Judge Driscoll said, "What's the matter with you?
You look as meek as a nigger," he felt as secret murderers are
said to feel when the accuser says, "Thou art the man!" Tom
said he was not well, and left the table.

His ostensible "aunt's" solicitudes and endearments were
become a terror to him, and he avoided them.

And all the time, hatred of his ostensible "uncle" was steadily
growing in his heart; for he said to himself, "He is white; and I
am his chattel, his property, his goods, and he can sell me, just
as he could his dog."

For as much as a week after this, Tom imagined that his character had undergone a pretty radical change. But that was because he did not know himself.

In several ways his opinions were totally changed, and would
never go back to what they were before, but the main structure
of his character was not changed, and could not be changed.
One or two very important features of it were altered, and in
time effects would result from this, if opportunity offered— effects of a quite serious nature, too. Under the influence of a
great mental and moral upheaval his character and habits had
taken on the appearance of complete change, but after a while
with the subsidence of the storm both began to settle toward
their former places. He dropped gradually back into his old
frivolous and easy-going ways and conditions of feeling and
manner of speech, and no familiar of his could have detected
anything in him that differentiated him from the weak and careless Tom of other days.

The theft-raid which he had made upon the village turned out
better than he had ventured to hope. It produced the sum necessary to pay his gaming-debts, and saved him from exposure to
his uncle and another smashing of the will. He and his mother
learned to like each other fairly well. She couldn't love him, as
yet, because there "warn't nothing *to* him," as she expressed it,
but her nature needed something or somebody to rule over, and
he was better than nothing. Her strong character and aggressive
and commanding ways compelled Tom's admiration in spite of

the fact that he got more illustrations of them than he needed for his comfort. However, as a rule her conversation was made up of racy tattle about the privacies of the chief families of the town (for she went harvesting among their kitchens every time she came to the village), and Tom enjoyed this. It was just in his line. She always collected her half of his pension punctually, and he was always at the haunted house to have a chat with her on these occasions. Every now and then she paid him a visit there on between-days also.

Occasionally he would run up to St. Louis for a few weeks, and at last temptation caught him again. He won a lot of money, but lost it, and with it a deal more besides, which he promised to raise as soon as possible.

For this purpose he projected a new raid on his town. He never meddled with any other town, for he was afraid to venture into houses whose ins and outs he did not know and the habits of whose households he was not acquainted with. He arrived at the haunted house in disguise on the Wednesday before the advent of the twins—after writing his aunt Pratt that he would not arrive until two days after—and lay in hiding there with his mother until toward daylight Friday morning, when he went to his uncle's house and entered by the back way with his own key, and slipped up to his room, where he could have the use of mirror and toilet articles. He had a suit of girl's clothes with him in a bundle as a disguise for his raid, and was wearing a suit of his mother's clothing, with black gloves and veil. By dawn he was tricked out for his raid, but he caught a glimpse of Pudd'nhead Wilson through the window over the way, and knew that Pudd'nhead had caught a glimpse of him. So he entertained Wilson with some airs and graces and attitudes for a while, then stepped out of sight and resumed the other disguise, and by and by went down and out the back way and started down town to reconnoiter the scene of his intended labors.

But he was ill at ease. He had changed back to Roxy's dress, with the stoop of age added to the disguise, so that Wilson would not bother himself about a humble old woman leaving a neighbor's house by the back way in the early morning, in case he was still spying. But supposing Wilson had seen him leave, and had thought it suspicious, and had also followed him? The thought made Tom cold. He gave up the raid for the day, and hurried back to the haunted house by the obscurest route he knew. His mother was gone; but she came back, by and by, with the news of the grand reception at Patsy Cooper's, and soon persuaded him that the opportunity was like a special providence, it was so inviting and perfect. So he went raiding, after all, and made a nice success of it while everybody was gone to Patsy Cooper's. Success gave him nerve and even actual intrepidity; insomuch, indeed, that after he had conveyed his harvest to his mother in a back alley, he went to the reception himself, and added several of the valuables of that house to his takings.

* After this long digression we have now arrived once more at the point where Pudd'nhead Wilson, while waiting for the arrival of the twins on that same Friday evening, sat puzzling over the strange apparition of that morning—a girl in young Tom Driscoll's bedroom; fretting, and guessing, and puzzling over it, and wondering who the shameless creature might be.

CHAPTER XI

There are three infallible ways of pleasing an author, and the three form a rising scale of compliment: 1, to tell him you have read one of his books; 2, to tell him you have read all of his books; 3, to ask him to let you read the manuscript of his forthcoming book. No. 1 admits you to his respect; No. 2 admits you to his admiration; No. 3 carries you clear into his heart.—*Pudd'nhead Wilson's Calendar.*

As to the Adjective: when in doubt, strike it out.—*Pudd'nhead Wilson's Calendar.*

The twins arrived presently, and talk began. It flowed along chattily and sociably, and under its influence the new friendship gathered ease and strength. Wilson got out his Calendar, by request, and read a passage or two from it, which the twins praised quite cordially. This pleased the author so much that he complied gladly when they asked him to lend them a batch of the work to read at home. In the course of their wide travels they had found out that there are three sure ways of pleasing an author; they were now working the best of the three.

There was an interruption, now. Young Tom Driscoll appeared, and joined the party. He pretended to be seeing the distinguished strangers for the first time when they rose to shake hands; but this was only a blind, as he had already had a glimpse of them, at the reception, while robbing the house. The twins made mental note that he was smooth-faced and rather handsome, and smooth and undulatory in his movements—graceful, in fact. Angelo thought he had a good eye; Luigi thought there was something veiled and sly about it. Angelo thought he had a pleasant free-and-easy way of talking; Luigi thought it was more so than was agreeable. Angelo thought he was a sufficiently nice

young man; Luigi reserved his decision. Tom's first contribution
to the conversation was a question which he had put to Wilson a
hundred times before. It was always cheerily and good-naturedly
put, and always inflicted a little pang, for it touched a secret
sore; but this time the pang was sharp, since strangers were present.

"Well, how does the law come on? Had a case yet?"

Wilson bit his lip, but answered, "No—not yet," with as
much indifference as he could assume. Judge Driscoll had
generously left the law feature out of the Wilson biography
which he had furnished to the twins. Young Tom laughed pleasantly, and said:

"Wilson's a lawyer, gentlemen, but he doesn't practise
now."

The sarcasm bit, but Wilson kept himself under control, and
said without passion:

"I don't practise, it is true. It is true that I have never had a
case, and have had to earn a poor living for twenty years an an
expert accountant in a town where I can't get hold of a set of
books to untangle as often as I should like. But it is also true that
I did fit myself well for the practice of the law. By the time I was
your age, Tom, I had chosen a profession, and was soon competent to enter upon it." Tom winced. "I never got a chance to try
my hand at it, and I may never get a chance; and yet if I ever do
get it I shall be found ready, for I have kept up my law-studies
all these years."

"That's it; that's good grit! I like to see it. I've a notion to
throw all my business your way. My business and your law-
practice ought to make a pretty gay team, Dave," and the young
fellow laughed again.

"If you will throw—" Wilson had thought of the girl in
Tom's bedroom, and was going to say, "If you will throw the
surreptitious and disreputable part of your business my way, it
may amount to something;" but thought better of it and said,
"However, this matter doesn't fit well in a general conversation."

"All right, we'll change the subject; I guess you were about to
give me another dig, anyway, so I'm willing to change. How's
the Awful Mystery flourishing these days? Wilson's got a
scheme for driving plain window-glass out of the market by
decorating it with greasy finger-marks, and getting rich by
selling it at famine prices to the crowned heads over in Europe to
outfit their palaces with. Fetch it out, Dave."

Wilson brought three of his glass strips, and said—

"I get the subject to pass the fingers of his right hand through his hair, so as to get a little coating of the natural oil on them, and then press the balls of them on the glass. A fine and delicate print of the lines in the skin results, and is permanent, if it doesn't come in contact with something able to rub it off. You begin, Tom."

"Why, I think you took my finger-marks once or twice before."

"Yes; but you were a little boy the last time, only about twelve years old."

"That's so. Of course I've changed entirely since then, and variety is what the crowned heads want, I guess."

He passed his fingers through his crop of short hair, and pressed them one at a time on the glass. Angelo made a print of his fingers on another glass, and Luigi followed with the third. Wilson marked the glasses with names and date, and put them away. Tom gave one of his little laughs, and said—

"I thought I wouldn't say anything, but if variety is what you are after, you have wasted a piece of glass. The hand-print of one twin is the same as the hand-print of the fellow-twin."

"Well, it's done now, and I like to have them both, anyway," said Wilson, returning to his place.

"But look here, Dave," said Tom, "you used to tell people's fortunes, too, when you took their finger-marks. Dave's just an all-round genius—a genius of the first water, gentlemen; a great scientist running to seed here in this village, a prophet with the kind of honor that prophets generally get at home—for here they don't give shucks for his scientifics, and they call his skull a notion-factory—hey, Dave, ain't it so? But never mind; he'll make his mark some day—finger-mark, you know, he-he! But really, you want to let him take a shy at your palms once; it's worth twice the price of admission or your money's returned at the door. Why, he'll read your wrinkles as easy as a book, and not only tell you fifty or sixty things that's going to happen to you, but fifty or sixty thousand that ain't. Come, Dave, show the gentlemen what an inspired Jack-at-all-science we've got in this town, and don't know it."

Wilson winced under this nagging and not very courteous chaff, and the twins suffered with him and for him. They rightly judged, now, that the best way to relieve him would be to take the thing in earnest and treat it with respect, ignoring Tom's rather overdone raillery; so Luigi said—

"We have seen something of palmistry in our wanderings, and know very well what astonishing things it can do. If it isn't a science, and one of the greatest of them, too, I don't know what its

66

other name ought to be. In the Orient—"

Tom looked surprised and incredulous. He said—

"That juggling a science? But really, you ain't serious, are you?"

"Yes, entirely so. Four years ago we had our hands read out to us as if our palms had been covered with print."

"Well, do you mean to say there was actually anything in it?" asked Tom, his incredulity beginning to weaken a little.

"There was this much in it," said Angelo: "what was told us of our characters was minutely exact—we could not have bettered it ourselves. Next, two or three memorable things that had happened to us were laid bare—things which no one present but ourselves could have known about."

"Why, it's rank sorcery!" exclaimed Tom, who was now becoming very much interested. "And how did they make out with what was going to happen to you in the future?"

"On the whole, quite fairly," said Luigi. "Two or three of the most striking things foretold have happened since; much the most striking one of all happened within that same year. Some of the minor prophecies have come true; some of the minor and some of the major ones have not been fulfilled yet, and of course may never be: still, I should be more surprised if they failed to arrive than if the didn't."

Tom was entirely sobered, and profoundly impressed. He said, apologetically—

"Dave, I wasn't meaning to belittle that science; I was only chaffing—chattering, I reckon I'd better say. I wish you would look at their palms. Come, won't you?"

"Why certainly, if you want me to; but you know I've had no chance to become an expert, and don't claim to be one. When a past event is somewhat prominently recorded in the palm I can generally detect that, but minor ones often escape me,—not always, of course, but often,—but I haven't much confidence in myself when it comes to reading the future. I am talking as if palmistry was a daily study with me, but that is not so. I haven't examined half a dozen hands in the last half dozen years; you see, the people got to joking about it, and I stopped to let the talk die down. I'll tell you what we'll do, Count Luigi: I'll make a try at your past, and if I have any success there—no, on the whole, I'll let the future alone; that's really the affair of an expert."

He took Luigi's hand. Tom said—

"Wait—don't look yet, Dave! Count Luigi, here's paper and pencil. Set down that thing that you said was the most striking one that was foretold to you, and happened less than a year afterward, and give it to me so I can see if Dave finds it in your hand."

Luigi wrote a line privately, and folded up the piece of paper, and handed it to Tom, saying—

"I'll tell you when to look at it, if he finds it."

Wilson began to study Luigi's palm, tracing life lines, heart lines, head lines, and so on, and noting carefully their relations with the cobweb of finer and more delicate marks and lines that enmeshed them on all sides; he felt the fleshy cushion at the base of the thumb, and noted its shape; he felt of the fleshy side of the hand between the wrist and the base of the little finger, and noted its shape also; he painstakingly examined the fingers, observing their form, proportions, and natural manner of disposing themselves when in repose. All this process was watched by the three spectators with absorbing interest, their heads bent together over Luigi's palm, and nobody disturbing the stillness with a word. Wilson now entered upon a close survey of the palm again, and his revelations began.

He mapped out Luigi's character and disposition, his tastes, aversions, proclivities, ambitions, and eccentricities in a way which sometimes made Luigi wince and the others laugh, but both twins declared that the chart was artistically drawn and was correct.

Next, Wilson took up Luigi's history. He proceeded cautiously and with hesitation, now, moving his finger slowly along the great lines of the palm, and now and then halting it at a "star" or some such landmark, and examining that neighborhood minutely. He proclaimed one or two past events, Luigi confirmed his correctness, and the search went on. Presently Wilson glanced up suddenly with a surprised expression—

"Here is record of an incident which you would perhaps not wish me to—"

"Bring it out," said Luigi, good-naturedly; "I promise you it sha'n't embarrass me."

But Wilson still hesitated, and did not seem quite to know what to do. Then he said—

"I think it is too delicate a matter to—to—I believe I would rather write it or whisper it to you, and let you decide for yourself whether you want it talked out or not."

"That will answer," said Luigi; "write it."

Wilson wrote something on a slip of paper and handed it to Luigi, who read it to himself and said to Tom—

"Unfold your slip and read it, Mr. Driscoll."

Tom read:

"It was prophesied that I would kill a man. It came true before the year was out."

Tom added, "Great Scott!"

Luigi handed Wilson's paper to Tom, and said—

"Now read this one."

Tom read:

"You have killed some one, but whether man, woman or child, I do not make out."

"Caesar's ghost!" commented Tom, with astonishment. "It beats anything that was ever heard of! Why, a man's own hand is his deadliest enemy! Just think of that—a man's own hand keeps a record of the deepest and fatalest secrets of his life, and is treacherously ready to expose him to any black-magic stranger that comes along. But what do you let a person look at your hand for, with that awful thing printed in it?"

"Oh," said Luigi, reposefully, "I don't mind it. I killed the man for good reasons, and I don't regret it."

"What were the reasons?"

"Well, he needed killing."

"I'll tell you why he did it, since he won't say himself," said Angelo, warmly. "He did it to save my life, that's what he did it for. So it was a noble act, and not a thing to be hid in the dark."

"So it was, so it was," said Wilson; "to do such a thing to save a brother's life is a great and fine action."

"Now come," said Luigi, "it is very pleasant to hear you say these things, but for unselfishness, or heroism, or magnanimity, the circumstances won't stand scrutiny. You overlook one detail; suppose I hadn't saved Angelo's life, what would have become of mine? If I had let the man kill him, wouldn't he have killed me, too? I saved my own life, you see."

"Yes; that is your way of talking," said Angelo, "but I know you—I don't believe you thought of yourself at all. I keep that weapon yet that Luigi killed the man with, and I'll show it to you sometime. That incident makes it interesting, and it had a history before it came into Luigi's hands which adds to its interest. It was given to Luigi by a great Indian prince, the Gaikowar of Baroda, and it had been in his family two or three centuries. It killed a good many disagreeable people who troubled that hearthstone at one time and another. It isn't much to look at, except that it isn't shaped like other knives, or dirks, or whatever it may be called—here, I'll draw it for you." He took a sheet of paper and made a rapid sketch. "There it is—a broad and murderous blade, with edges like a razor for sharpness. The devices engraved on it are the ciphers or names of its long line of possessors—I had Luigi's name added in Roman letters myself with our coat of arms, as you see. You notice what a curious handle the thing has. It is solid ivory, polished like a mirror, and is four or five inches long—round, and as thick as a large man's wrist, with the end squared off flat, for your thumb to rest on; for you grasp it, with your thumb resting on the blunt end—so— and lift it aloft and strike downward. The Gaikowar showed us how the thing was done when he gave it to Luigi, and before that night was ended Luigi had used the knife, and the Gaikowar was a man short by reason of it. The sheath is magnificently ornamented with gems of great value. You will find the sheath more worth looking at than the knife itself, of course.''

Tom said to himself—

"It's lucky I came here. I would have sold that knife for a song; I supposed the jewels were glass.''

"But go on; don't stop,'' said Wilson. "Our curiosity is up now, to hear about the homicide. Tell us about that.''

"Well, briefly, the knife was to blame for that, all around. A native servant slipped into our room in the palace in the night, to kill us and steal the knife on account of the fortune incrusted on its sheath, without a doubt. Luigi had it under his pillow; we were in bed together. There was a dim night-light burning. I was asleep, but Luigi was awake, and he thought he detected a vague form nearing the bed. He slipped the knife out of the sheath and was ready, and unembarrassed by hampering bed-clothes, for the weather was hot and we hadn't any. Suddenly that native rose at the bedside, and bent over me with his right hand lifted and a dirk in it aimed at my throat; but Luigi grabbed his wrist, pulled him downward, and drove his own knife into the man's neck. That is the whole story.''

Wilson and Tom drew deep breaths, and after some general chat about the tragedy, Pudd'nhead said, taking Tom's hand—

"Now, Tom, I've never had a look at your palms, as it happens; perhaps you've got some little questionable privacies that need—hel-lo!''

Tom had snatched away his hand, and was looking a good deal confused.

"Why, he's blushing!'' said Luigi.

Tom darted an ugly look at him, and said sharply—

"Well, if I am, it ain't because I'm a murderer!'' Luigi's dark face flushed, but before he could speak or move, Tom added with anxious haste: "Oh, I beg a thousand pardons. I didn't mean that; it was out before I thought, and I'm very, very sorry—you must forgive me!''

Wilson came to the rescue, and smoothed things down as well as he could; and in fact was entirely successful as far as the twins were concerned, for they felt sorrier for the affront put upon him by his guest's outburst of ill manners than for the insult offered to Luigi. But the success was not so pronounced with the offender. Tom tried to seem at his ease, and he went through the motions fairly well, but at bottom he felt resentful toward all the three witnesses of his exhibition; in fact, he felt so annoyed at them for having witnessed it and noticed it that he almost forgot to feel annoyed at himself for placing it before them. However, something presently happened which made him almost comfortable, and brought him nearly back to a state of charity and friendliness. This was a little spat between the twins; not much of a spat, but still a spat; and before they got far with it they were in a decided condition of irritation with each other. Tom was charmed; so pleased, indeed, that he cautiously did what he could to increase the irritation while pretending to be actuated by more respectable motives. By his help the fire got warmed up to the blazing-point, and he might have had the happiness of seeing the flames show up, in another moment, but for the interruption of a knock on the door—an interruption which fretted him as much as it gratified Wilson. Wilson opened the door.

The visitor was a good-natured, ignorant, energetic, middle-aged Irishman named John Buckstone, who was a great politician in a small way, and always took a large share in public matters of every sort. One of the town's chief excitements, just now, was over the matter of rum. There was a strong rum party and a strong anti-rum party. Buckstone was training with the rum party, and he had been sent to hunt up the twins and invite them to attend a mass-meeting of that faction. He delivered his errand, and said the clans were already gathering in the big hall over the market-house. Luigi accepted the invitation cordially, Angelo less cordially, since he disliked crowds, and did not drink the powerful intoxicants of America. In fact, he was even a teetotaler sometimes—when it was judicious to be one.

The twins left with Buckstone, and Tom Driscoll joined company with them uninvited.

In the distance one could see a long wavering line of torches drifting down the main street, and could hear the throbbing of the bass drum, the clash of cymbals, the squeaking of a fife or two, and the faint roar of remote hurrahs. The tail-end of this procession was climbing the market-house stairs when the twins arrived in its neighborhood; when they reached the hall it was full of people, torches, smoke, noise and enthusiasm. They were conducted to the platform by Buckstone—Tom Driscoll still following—and were delivered to the chairman in the midst of a prodigious explosion of welcome. When the noise had moderated a little, the chair proposed that "our illustrious guests be at once elected, by complimentary acclamation, to membership in our ever-glorious organization, the paradise of the free and the perdition of the slave."

This eloquent discharge opened the floodgates of enthusiasm again, and the election was carried with thundering unanimity. Then arose a storm of cries:

"Wet them down! Wet them down! Give them a drink!"

Glasses of whisky were handed to the twins. Luigi waved his aloft, then brought it to his lips; but Angelo set his down. There was another storm of cries:

"What's the matter with the other one?" "What is the blond one going back on us for?" "Explain! Explain!"

The chairman inquired, and then reported—

"We have made an unfortunate mistake, gentlemen. I find that the Count Angelo Cappello is opposed to our creed—is a teetotaler, in fact, and was not intending to apply for membership with us. He desires that we reconsider the vote by which he was elected. What is the pleasure of the house?"

There was a general burst of laughter, plentifully accented with whistlings and cat-calls, but the energetic use of the gavel presently restored something like order. Then a man spoke from the crowd, and said that while he was very sorry that the mistake had been made, it would not be possible to rectify it at the present meeting. According to the by-laws it must go over to the next regular meeting for action. He would not offer a motion, as none was required. He desired to apologize to the gentleman in the name of the house, and begged to assure him that as far as it might lie in the power of the Sons of Liberty, his temporary membership in the order would be made pleasant to him.

This speech was received with great applause, mixed with cries of—

"That's the talk!" "He's a good fellow, anyway, if he *is* a teetotaler!" "Drink his health!" "Give him a rouser, and no heeltaps!"

Glasses were handed around, and everybody on the platform drank Angelo's health, while the house bellowed forth in song:

> For he's a jolly good fel-low,
> For he's a jolly good fel-low,
> For he's a jolly good fe-el-low,—
> Which nobody can deny.

Tom Driscoll drank. It was his second glass, for he had drunk Angelo's the moment that Angelo had set it down. The two drinks made him very merry—almost idiotically so—and he

began to take a most lively and prominent part in the proceedings, particularly in the music and cat-calls and side-
remarks.

The chairman was still standing at the front, the twins at his
side. The extraordinarily close resemblance of the brothers to
each other suggested a witticism to Tom Driscoll, and just as the
chairman began a speech he skipped forward and said with an
air of tipsy confidence to the audience—

"Boys, I move that he keeps still and lets this human
philopena snip you out a speech."

The descriptive aptness of the phrase caught the house, and a
mighty burst of laughter followed.

Luigi's southern blood leaped to the boiling-point in a moment under the sharp humiliation of this insult delivered in the
presence of four hundred strangers. It was not in the young
man's nature to let the matter pass, or to delay the squaring of
the account. He took a couple of strides and halted behind the
unsuspecting joker. Then he drew back and delivered a kick of
such titanic vigor that it lifted Tom clear over the footlights and
landed him on the heads of the front row of the Sons of Liberty.

Even a sober person does not like to have a human being emptied on him when he is not doing any harm; a person who is not
sober cannot endure such an attention at all. The nest of Sons of
Liberty that Driscoll landed in had not a sober bird in it; in fact
there was probably not an entirely sober one in the auditorium.
Driscoll was promptly and indignantly flung on to the heads of
Sons in the next row, and these Sons passed him on toward the
rear, and then immediately began to pummel the front-row Sons
who had passed him to them. This course was strictly followed
by bench after bench as Driscoll traveled in his tumultuous and
airy flight toward the door; so he left behind him an ever length-
ening wake of raging and plunging and fighting and swearing
humanity. Down went group after group of torches, and
presently above the deafening clatter of the gavel, roar of angry
voices, and crash of succumbing benches, rose the paralyzing cry
of "FIRE!"

The fighting ceased instantly; the cursing ceased; for one
distinctly defined moment there was a dead hush, a motionless
calm, where the tempest had been; then with one impulse the
multitude awoke to life and energy again, and went surging and
struggling and swaying, this way and that, its outer edges
melting away through windows and doors and gradually lessen-
ing the pressure and relieving the mass.

The fire-boys were never on hand so suddenly before; for
there was no distance to go, this time, their quarters being in the

rear end of the market-house. There was an engine company and a hook-and-ladder company. Half of each was composed of rummies and the other half of anti-rummies, after the moral and political share-and-share-alike fashion of the frontier town of the period. Enough anti-rummies were loafing in quarters to man the engine and the ladders. In two minutes they had their red shirts and helmets on—they never stirred officially in unofficial costume—and as the mass meeting overhead smashed through the long row of windows and poured out upon the roof of the arcade, the deliverers were ready for them with a powerful stream of water which washed some of them off the roof and nearly drowned the rest. But water was preferable to fire, and still the stampede from the windows continued, and still the pitiless drenchings assailed it until the building was empty; then the fire-boys mounted to the hall and flooded it with water enough to annihilate forty times as much fire as there was there; for a village fire-company does not often get a chance to show off, and so when it does get a chance it makes the most of it. Such citizens of that village as were of a thoughtful and judicious temperament did not insure against fire; they insured against the fire-company.

CHAPTER XII

Courage is resistance to fear, mastery of fear—not absence of fear. Except a creature be part coward it is not a compliment to say it is brave; it is merely a loose misapplication of the word. Consider the flea!—incomparably the bravest of all the creatures of God, if ignorance of fear were courage. Whether you are asleep or awake he will attack you, caring nothing for the fact that in bulk and strength you are to him as are the massed armies of the earth to a sucking child; he lives both day and night and all days and nights in the very lap of peril and the immediate presence of death, and yet is no more afraid than is the man who walks the streets of a city that was threatened by an earthquake ten centuries before. When we speak of Clive, Nelson, and Putnam as men who "didn't know what fear was," we ought always to add the flea— and put him at the head of the procession.—*Pudd'nhead Wilson's Calendar.*

Judge Driscoll was in bed and asleep by ten o'clock on Friday night, and he was up and gone a-fishing before daylight in the morning with his friend Pembroke Howard. These two had been boys together in Virginia when that State still ranked as the chief and most imposing member of the Union, and they still coupled the proud and affectionate adjective "old" with her name when they spoke of her. In Missouri a recognized superiority attached to any person who hailed from Old Virginia; and this superiority was exalted to supremacy when a person of such nativity could also prove descent from the First Families of that great commonwealth. The Howards and Driscolls were of this aristocracy. In their eyes it was a nobility. It had its unwritten laws, and they were as clearly defined and as strict as any that could be found among the printed statutes of the land. The F.F.V. was born a gentleman; his highest duty in life was to watch over that great inheritance and keep it unsmirched. He must keep his honor spotless. Those laws were his chart; his course was marked out on it; if he swerved from it by so much as half a point of the compass it meant shipwreck to his honor; that is to say, degradation from his rank as a gentleman. These laws required certain things of him which his religion might forbid: then his religion must yield—the laws could not be relaxed to accommodate religions or anything else. Honor stood first; and the laws defined what it was and wherein it differed in certain details from honor as defined by church creeds and by the social laws and customs of some of the minor divisions of the globe that had got crowded out when the sacred boundaries of Virginia were staked out.

If Judge Driscoll was the recognized first citizen of Dawson's Landing, Pembroke Howard was easily its recognized second citizen. He was called "the great lawyer"—an earned title. He and Driscoll were of the same age—a year or two past sixty.

Although Driscoll was a free-thinker and Howard a strong and determined Presbyterian, their warm intimacy suffered no impairment in consequence. They were men whose opinions were their own property and not subject to revision and amendment, suggestion or criticism, by anybody, even their friends.

The day's fishing finished, they came floating down stream in their skiff, talking national politics and other high matters, and presently met a skiff coming up from town, with a man in it who said:

"I reckon you know one of the new twins gave your nephew a kicking last night, Judge?"

"Did *what?*"

"Gave him a kicking."

The old Judge's lips paled, and his eyes began to flame. He choked with anger for a moment, then he got out what he was trying to say—

"Well—well—go on! give me the details."

The man did it. At the finish the Judge was silent a minute, turning over in his mind the shameful picture of Tom's flight over the footlights; then he said, as if musing aloud—"H'm—I don't understand it. I was asleep at home. He didn't wake me. Thought he was competent to manage his affair without my help, I reckon." His face lit up with pride and pleasure at that thought, and he said with a cheery complacency, "I like that—it's the true old blood—hey, Pembroke?"

Howard smiled an iron smile, and nodded his head approvingly. Then the news-bringer spoke again—

"But Tom beat the twin on the trial."

The Judge looked at the man wonderingly, and said—

"The trial? What trial?"

"Why, Tom had him up before Judge Robinson for assault and battery."

The old man shrank suddenly together like one who has received a death-stroke. Howard sprang for him as he sank forward in a swoon, and took him in his arms, and bedded him on his back in the boat. He sprinkled water in his face, and said to the startled visitor—

"Go, now—don't let him come to and find you here. You see what an effect your heedless speech has had; you ought to have been more considerate than to blurt out such a cruel piece of slander as that."

"I'm right down sorry I did it now, Mr. Howard, and I wouldn't have done it if I had thought: but it ain't slander; it's perfectly true, just as I told him."

He rowed away. Presently the old Judge came out of his faint and looked up piteously into the sympathetic face that was bent over him.

"Say it ain't true, Pembroke; tell me it ain't true!" he said in a weak voice.

There was nothing weak in the deep organ-tones that responded—

"You know it's a lie as well as I do, old friend. He is of the best blood of the Old Dominion."

"God bless you for saying it!" said the old gentleman, fervently. "Ah, Pembroke, it was such a blow!"

Howard stayed by his friend, and saw him home, and entered the house with him. It was dark, and past supper-time, but the Judge was not thinking of supper; he was eager to hear the slander refuted from headquarters, and as eager to have Howard hear it, too. Tom was sent for, and he came immediately. He was bruised and lame, and was not a happy-looking object. His uncle made him sit down, and said—

"We have been hearing about your adventure, Tom, with a

handsome lie added to it for embellishment. Now pulverize that lie to dust! What measures have you taken? How does the thing stand?"

Tom answered guilelessly: "It don't stand at all; it's all over. I had him up in court and beat him. Pudd'nhead Wilson defended him—first case he ever had, and lost it. The judge fined the miserable hound five dollars for the assault."

Howard and the Judge sprang to their feet with the opening sentence—why, neither knew; then they stood gazing vacantly at each other. Howard stood a moment, then sat mournfully down without saying anything. The Judge's wrath began to kindle, and he burst out—

"You cur! You scum! You vermin! Do you mean to tell me that blood of my race has suffered a blow and crawled to a court of law about it? Answer me!"

Tom's head drooped, and he answered with an eloquent silence. His uncle stared at him with a mixed expression of amazement and shame and incredulity that was sorrowful to see. At last he said—

"Which of the twins was it?"

"Count Luigi."

"You have challenged him?"

"N—no," hesitated Tom, turning pale.

"You will challenge him to-night. Howard will carry it."

Tom began to turn sick, and to show it. He turned his hat round and round in his hand, his uncle glowering blacker and blacker upon him as the heavy seconds drifted by; then at last he began to stammer, and said piteously—

"Oh, please don't ask me to do it, uncle! He is a murderous devil—I never could—I—I'm afraid of him!"

Old Driscoll's mouth opened and closed three times before he could get it to perform its office; then he stormed out—

"A coward in my family! A Driscoll a coward! Oh, what have I done to deserve this infamy!" He tottered to his secretary in the corner repeating that lament again and again in heart-breaking tones, and got out of a drawer a paper, which he slowly tore to bits scattering the bits absently in his track as he walked up and down the room, still grieving and lamenting. At last he said—

"There it is, shreds and fragments once more—my will. Once more you have forced me to disinherit you, you base son of a most noble father! Leave my sight! Go—before I spit on you!"

The young man did not tarry. Then the Judge turned to Howard:

"You will be my second, old friend?"

"Of course."

"There is pen and paper. Draft the cartel, and lose no time."

"The Count shall have it in his hands in fifteen minutes," said Howard.

Tom was very heavy-hearted. His appetite was gone with his property and his self-respect. He went out the back way and wandered down the obscure lane grieving, and wondering if any course of future conduct, however discreet and carefully perfected and watched over, could win back his uncle's favor and persuade him to reconstruct once more that generous will which had just gone to ruin before his eyes. He finally concluded that it could. He said to himself that he had accomplished this sort of triumph once already, and that what had been done once could be done again. He would set about it. He would bend every energy to the task, and he would score that triumph once more, cost what it might to his convenience, limit as it might his frivolous and liberty-loving life.

"To begin," he said to himself, "I'll square up with the proceeds of my raid, and then gambling has got to be stopped—and stopped short off. It's the worst vice I've got—from my standpoint, anyway, because it's the one he can most easily find out, through the impatience of my creditors. He thought it expensive to have to pay two hundred dollars to them for me once. Expensive—*that!* Why, it cost me the whole of his fortune—but of course he never thought of that; some people can't think of any but their own side of a case. If he had known how deep I am in, now, the will would have gone to pot without waiting for a duel to help. Three hundred dollars! It's a pile! But he'll never hear of it, I'm thankful to say. The minute I've cleared it off, I'm safe; and I'll never touch a card again. Anyway, I won't while he lives, I make oath to that. I'm entering on my last reform—I know it—yes, and I'll win; but after that, if I ever slip again I'm gone."

CHAPTER XIII

When I reflect upon the number of disagreeable people who I know have gone to a better world, I am moved to lead a different life.—*Pudd'nhead Wilson's Calendar.*

October. This is one of the peculiarly dangerous months to speculate in stocks in. The others are July, January, September, April, November, May, March, June, December, August, and February. —*Pudd'nhead Wilson's Calendar.*

Thus mournfully communing with himself Tom moped along

the lane past Pudd'nhead Wilson's house, and still on and on between fences inclosing vacant country on each hand till he neared the haunted house, then he came moping back again, with many sighs and heavy with trouble. He sorely wanted cheerful company. Rowena! His heart gave a bound at the thought, but the next thought quieted it—the detested twins would be there.

He was on the inhabited side of Wilson's house, and now as he approached it he noticed that the sitting-room was lighted. This would do; others made him feel unwelcome sometimes, but Wilson never failed in courtesy toward him, and a kindly courtesy does at least save one's feelings, even if it is not professing to stand for a welcome. Wilson heard footsteps at his threshold, then the clearing of a throat.

"It's that fickle-tempered, dissipated young goose—poor devil, he finds friends pretty scarce to-day, likely, after the disgrace of carrying a personal-assault case into a law-court."

A dejected knock. "Come in!"

Tom entered, and drooped into a chair, without saying anything. Wilson said kindly—

"Why, my boy, you look desolate. Don't take it so hard. Try and forget you have been kicked."

"Oh, dear," said Tom, wretchedly, "it's not that, Pudd'nhead—it's not that. It's a thousand times worse than that—oh, yes, a million times worse."

"Why, Tom, what do you mean? Has Rowena—"

"Flung me? No, but the old man has."

Wilson said to himself, "Aha!" and thought of the mysterious girl in the bedroom. "The Driscolls have been making discoveries!" Then he said aloud, gravely:

"Tom, there are some kinds of dissipation which—"

"Oh, shucks, this hasn't got anything to do with dissipation. He wanted me to challenge that derned Italian savage, and I wouldn't do it."

"Yes, of course he would do that," said Wilson in a meditative matter-of-course way, "but the thing that puzzled me was, why he didn't look to that last night, for one thing, and why he let you carry such a matter into a court of law at all, either before the duel or after it. It's no place for it. It was not like him. I couldn't understand it. How did it happen?"

"It happened because he didn't know anything about it. He was asleep when I got home last night."

"And you didn't wake him? Tom, is that possible?"

Tom was not getting much comfort here. He fidgeted a moment, then said:

"I didn't choose to tell him—that's all. He was going a-fishing before the dawn, with Pembroke Howard, and if I got the twins into the common calaboose—and I thought sure I could—I never dreamed of their slipping out on a paltry fine for such an outrageous offense—well, once in the calaboose they would be disgraced, and uncle wouldn't want any duels with that sort of characters, and wouldn't allow any."

"Tom, I am ashamed of you! I don't see how you could treat your good old uncle so. I am a better friend of his than you are; for if I had known the circumstances I would have kept that case out of court until I got word to him and let him have a gentleman's chance."

"You would?" exclaimed Tom, with lively surprise. "And it your first case! And you know perfectly well there never would have *been* any case if he had got that chance, don't you? And you'd have finished your days a pauper nobody, instead of being an actually launched and recognized lawyer to-day. And you would really have done that, would you?"

"Certainly."

Tom looked at him a moment or two, then shook his head sorrowfully and said—

"I believe you·–upon my word I do. I don't know why I do, but I do. Pudd'nhead Wilson, I think you're the biggest fool I ever saw."

"Thank you."

"Don't mention it."

"Well, he has been requiring you to fight the Italian and you have refused. You degenerate remnant of an honorable line! I'm thoroughly ashamed of you, Tom!"

"Oh, that's nothing! I don't care for anything, now that the will's torn up again."

"Tom, tell me squarely—didn't he find any fault with you for anything but those two things—carrying the case into court and refusing to fight?"

He watched the young fellow's face narrowly, but it was entirely reposeful, and so also was the voice that answered:

"No, he didn't find any other fault with me. If he had had any to find, he would have begun yesterday, for he was just in the humor for it. He drove that jack-pair around town and showed them the sights, and when he came home he couldn't find his father's old silver watch that don't keep time and he thinks so much of, and couldn't remember what he did with it three or four days ago when he saw it last; and so when I arrived he was all in a sweat about it, and when I suggested that it probably wasn't lost but stolen, it put him in a regular passion and he said

I was a fool—which convinced me, without any trouble, that that was just what he was afraid *had* happened, himself, but did not want to believe it, because lost things stand a better chance of being found again than stolen ones.''

"Whe-ew!" whistled Wilson; "score another on the list."

"Another what?"

"Another theft!"

"Theft?"

"Yes, theft. That watch isn't lost, it's stolen. There's been another raid on the town—and just the same old mysterious sort of thing that has happened once before, as you remember."

"You don't mean it!"

"It's as sure as you are born! Have you missed anything yourself?"

"No. That is, I did miss a silver pencil-case that Aunt Mary Pratt gave me last birthday—"

"You'll find it stolen—that's what you'll find."

"No, I sha'n't; for when I suggested theft about the watch and got such a rap, I went and examined my room, and the pencil-case was missing, but it was only mislaid, and I found it again."

"You are sure you missed nothing else?"

"Well, nothing of consequence. I missed a small plain gold ring worth two or three dollars, but that will turn up. I'll look again."

"In my opinion you'll not find it. There's been a raid, I tell you, Come *in!*"

Mr. Justice Robinson entered, followed by Buckstone and the town-constable, Jim Blake. They sat down, and after some wandering and aimless weather-conversation Wilson said—

"By the way, we've just added another to the list of thefts, maybe two. Judge Driscoll's old silver watch is gone, and Tom here has missed a gold ring."

"Well, it is a bad business," said the Justice, "and gets worse the further it goes. The Hankses, the Dobsons, the Pilligrews, the Ortons, the Grangers, the Hales, the Fullers, and Holcombs, in fact everybody that lives around about Patsy Cooper's has been robbed of little things like trinkets and teaspoons and such-like small valuables that are easily carried off. It's perfectly plain that the thief took advantage of the reception at Patsy Cooper's when all the neighbors were in her house and all their niggers hanging around her fence for a look at the show, to raid the vacant houses undisturbed. Patsy is miserable about it; miserable on account of the neighbors, and particularly miserable on account of her foreigners, of course; so miserable on their account that she hasn't any room to worry about her own little losses."

"It's the same old raider," said Wilson. "I suppose there isn't any doubt about that."

"Constable Blake doesn't think so."

"No, you're wrong there." said Blake; "the other times it was a man; there was plenty of signs of that, as we know, in the profession, though we never got hands on him; but this time it's a woman."

Wilson thought of the mysterious girl straight off. She was always in his mind now. But she failed him again. Blake continued:

"She's a stoop-shouldered old woman with a covered basket on her arm, in a black veil, dressed in mourning. I saw her going aboard the ferry-boat yesterday. Lives in Illinois, I reckon; but I don't care where she lives, I'm going to get her—she can make herself sure of that."

"What makes you think she's the thief?"

"Well, there ain't any other, for one thing; and for another, some of the nigger draymen that happened to be driving along saw her coming out of or going into houses, and told me so—and it just happens that they was *robbed* houses, every time."

It was granted that this was plenty good enough circumstantial evidence. A pensive silence followed, which lasted some moments, then Wilson said—

"There's one good thing, anyway. She can't either pawn or sell Count Luigi's costly Indian dagger."

"My!" said Tom, "is *that* gone?"

"Yes."

"Well, that was a haul! But why can't she pawn it or sell it?"

"Because when the twins went home from the Sons of Liberty meeting last night, news of the raid was sifting in from everywhere, and Aunt Patsy was in distress to know if they had lost anything. They found that the dagger was gone, and they notified the police and pawnbrokers everywhere. It was a great haul, yes, but the old woman won't get anything out of it, because she'll get caught."

"Did they offer a reward?" asked Buckstone.

"Yes; five hundred dollars for the knife, and five hundred more for the thief."

"What a leather-headed idea!" exclaimed the constable. "The thief da'sn't go near them, nor send anybody. Whoever goes is going to get himself nabbed, for there ain't any pawnbroker that's going to lose the chance to—"

If anybody had noticed Tom's face at that time, the gray-green color of it might have provoked curiosity; but nobody did.

He said to himself: "I'm gone! I never can square up; the rest of the plunder won't pawn or sell for half of the bill. Oh, I know it—I'm gone, I'm gone—and this time it's for good. Oh, this is awful—I don't know what to do, nor which way to turn!"

"Softly, softly," said Wilson to Blake. "I planned their scheme for them at midnight last night, and it was all finished up ship-shape by two this morning. They'll get their dagger back, and then I'll explain to you how the thing was done."

There were strong signs of a general curiosity, and Buckstone said—

"Well, you have whetted us up pretty sharp, Wilson, and I'm free to say that if you don't mind telling us in confidence—"

"Oh, I'd as soon tell as not, Buckstone, but as long as the twins and I agreed to say nothing about it, we must let it stand so. But you can take my word for it you won't be kept waiting three days. Somebody will apply for that reward pretty promptly, and I'll show you the thief and the dagger both very soon afterward."

The constable was disappointed, and also perplexed. He said—

"It may all be—yes, and I hope it will, but I'm blamed if I can see my way through it. It's too many for yours truly."

The subject seemed about talked out. Nobody seemed to have anything further to offer. After a silence the justice of the peace informed Wilson that he and Buckstone and the constable had come as a committee, on the part of the Democratic party, to ask him to run for mayor—for the little town was about to become a city and the first charter election was approaching. It was the first attention which Wilson had ever received at the hands of any party; it was a sufficiently humble one, but it was a recognition of his début into the town's life and activities at last; it was a step upward, and he was deeply gratified. He accepted, and the committee departed, followed by young Tom.

CHAPTER XIV

The true Southern watermelon is a boon apart, and not to be mentioned with commoner things. It is chief of this world's luxuries, king by the grace of God over all the fruits of the earth. When one has tasted it, he knows what the angels eat. It was not a Southern watermelon that Eve took: we know it because she repented.—*Pudd'nhead Wilson's Calendar.*

About the time that Wilson was bowing the committee out, Pembroke Howard was entering the next house to report. He found the old Judge sitting grim and straight in his chair, waiting.

"Well, Howard—the news?"

"The best in the world."

"Accepts, does he?" and the light of battle gleamed joyously in the Judge's eye.

"Accepts? Why, he jumped at it."

"Did, did he? Now that's fine—that's very fine. I like that. When is it to be?"

"Now! Straight off! To-night! An admirable fellow— admirable!"

"Admirable? He's a darling! Why, it's an honor as well as a pleasure to stand up before such a man. Come—off with you! Go and arrange everything—and give him my heartiest compliments. A rare fellow, indeed; an admirable fellow, as you have said!"

Howard hurried away, saying—

"I'll have him in the vacant stretch between Wilson's and the haunted house within the hour, and I'll bring my own pistols."

Judge Driscoll began to walk the floor in a state of pleased excitement; but presently he stopped, and began to think—began to think of Tom. Twice he moved toward the secretary, and twice he turned away again; but finally he said—

"This may be my last night in the world—I must not take the chance. He is worthless and unworthy, but it is largely my fault. He was intrusted to me by my brother on his dying bed, and I have indulged him to his hurt, instead of training him up severely, and making a man of him. I have violated my trust, and I must not add the sin of desertion to that. I have forgiven him once already, and would subject him to a long and hard trial before forgiving him again, if I could live; but I must not run that risk. No, I must restore the will. But if I survive the duel, I will hide it away, and he will not know, and I will not tell him until he reforms, and I see that his reformation is going to be permanent."

He re-drew the will, and his ostensible nephew was heir to a fortune again. As he was finishing his task, Tom, wearied with another brooding tramp, entered the house and went tiptoeing past the sitting-room door. He glanced in, and hurried on, for the sight of his uncle had nothing but terrors for him to-night. But his uncle was writing! That was unusual at this late hour. What could he be writing? A chill of anxiety settled down upon Tom's heart. Did that writing concern him? He was afraid so. He reflected that when ill luck begins, it does not come in sprinkles, but in showers. He said he would get a glimpse of that document or know the reason why. He heard some one coming, and stepped out of sight and hearing. It was Pembroke Howard. What could be hatching.

Howard said, with great satisfaction:

"Everything's right and ready. He's gone to the battle-ground with his second and the surgeon—also with his brother. I've arranged it all with Wilson—Wilson's his second. We are to have three shots apiece."

"Good! How is the moon?"

"Bright as day, nearly. Perfect, for the distance—fifteen yards. No wind—not a breath; hot and still."

"All good; all first-rate. Here, Pembroke, read this, and witness it."

Pembroke read and witnessed the will, then gave the old man's hand a hearty shake and said:

"Now that's right, York—but I knew you would do it. You couldn't leave that poor chap to fight along without means or profession, with certain defeat before him, and I knew you wouldn't, for his father's sake if not for his own."

"For his dead father's sake I couldn't, I know; for poor Percy—but you know what Percy was to me. But mind—Tom is not to know of this unless I fall to-night."

"I understand. I'll keep the secret."

The Judge put the will away, and the two started for the battle-ground. In another minute the will was in Tom's hands. His misery vanished, his feelings underwent a tremendous revulsion. He put the will carefully back in its place, and spread his mouth and swung his hat once, twice, three times around his head, in imitation of three rousing huzzas, no sound issuing from his lips. He fell to communing with himself excitedly and joyously, but every now and then he let off another volley of dumb hurrahs.

He said to himself: "I've got the fortune again, but I'll not let on that I know about it. And this time I'm going to hang on to it. I take no more risks. I'll gamble no more, I'll drink no more, because—well, because I'll not go where there is any of that sort of thing going on, again. It's the sure way, and the only sure way; I might have thought of that sooner—well, yes, if I had wanted to. But now—dear me, I've had a scare this time, and I'll take no more chances. Not a single chance more. Land! I persuaded myself this evening that I could fetch him around without any great amount of effort, but I've been getting more and more heavy-hearted and doubtful straight along, ever since. If he tells me about this thing, all right; but if he doesn't, I sha'n't, let on. I—well, I'd like to tell Pudd'nhead Wilson, but—no, I'll think about that; perhaps I won't." He whirled off another dead huzza, and said, "I'm reformed, and this time I'll stay so, sure!"

He was about to close with a final grand silent demonstration, when he suddenly recollected that Wilson had put it out of his power to pawn or sell the Indian knife, and that he was once more in awful peril of exposure by his creditors for that reason. His joy collapsed utterly, and he turned away and moped toward the door moaning and lamenting over the bitterness of his luck. He dragged himself up-stairs, and brooded in his room a long time disconsolate and forlorn, with Luigi's Indian knife for a text. At last he sighed and said:

"When I supposed these stones were glass and this ivory bone, the thing hadn't any interest for me because it hadn't any value, and couldn't help me out of my trouble. But now—why, now it is full of interest; yes, and of a sort to break a body's heart. It's a bag of gold that has turned to dirt and ashes in my hands. It could save me, and save me so easily, and yet I've got to go to ruin. It's like drowning with a life-preserver in my reach. All the hard luck comes to me, and all the good luck goes to other people—Pudd'nhead Wilson, for instance; even his career has got a sort of a little start at last, and what has he done to deserve it, I should like to know? Yes, he has opened his own road, but he isn't content with that, but must block mine. It's a sordid, selfish world, and I wish I was out of it." He allowed the light of the candle to play upon the jewels of the sheath, but the flashings and sparklings had no charm for his eye; they were only just so many pangs to his heart. "I must not say anything to Roxy about this thing," he said, "she is too daring. She would be for digging these stones out and selling them, and then—why, she would be arrested and the stones traced, and then—" The thought made him quake, and he hid the knife away, trembling all over and glancing furtively about, like a criminal who fancies that the accuser is already at hand.

Should he try to sleep? Oh, no, sleep was not for him; his trouble was too haunting, too afflicting for that. He must have somebody to mourn with. He would carry his despair to Roxy.

He had heard several distant gunshots, but that sort of thing was not uncommon, and they had made no impression upon him. He went out at the back door, and turned westward. He passed Wilson's house and proceeded along the lane, and presently saw several figures approaching Wilson's place through the vacant lots. These were the duelists returning from the fight; he thought he recognized them, but as he had no desire for white people's company, he stooped down behind the fence until they were out of his way.

Roxy was feeling fine. She said:

"Whah was you, child? Warn't you in it?"

"In what?"

"In de duel."

"Duel? Has there been a duel?"

" 'Co'se dey has. De ole Jedge has be'n havin' a duel wid one o' dem twins."

"Great Scott!" Then he added to himself: "That's what made him re-make the will; he thought he might get killed, and it softened him toward me. And that's what he and Howard were so busy about. . . . Oh dear, if the twin had only killed him, I should be out of my—"

"What is you mumblin' bout, Chambers? Whah was you? Didn't you know dey was gwyne to be a duel?"

"No, I didn't. The old man tried to get me to fight one with Count Luigi, but he didn't succeed, so I reckon he concluded to patch up the family honor himself."

He laughed at the idea, and went rambling on with a detailed account of his talk with the Judge, and how shocked and ashamed the Judge was to find that he had a coward in his family. He glanced up at last, and got a shock himself. Roxana's bosom was heaving with suppressed passion, and she was glowering down upon him with measureless contempt written in her face.

"En you refuse' to fight a man dat kicked you, 'stid o' jumpin' at de chance! En you ain't got no mo' feelin' den to come en tell me, dat fetched sich a po' low-down ornery rabbit into de worl'! Pah! it make me sick! It's de nigger in you, dat's what it is. Thirty-one parts o' you is white, en on'y one part nigger, en dat po' little one part is yo' *soul*. Tain't wuth savin'; tain't wuth totin' out on a shovel en throwin' in de gutter. You has disgraced yo' birth. What would yo' pa think o' you? It's enough to make him turn in his grave."

The last three sentences stung Tom into a fury, and he said to himself that if his father were only alive and in reach of assassination his mother would soon find that he had a very clear notion of the size of his indebtedness to that man, and was willing to pay it up in full, and would do it too, even at risk of his life; but he kept his thought to himself; that was safest in his mother's present state.

"Whatever has come o' yo' Essex blood? Dat's what I can't understan'. En it ain't on'y jist Essex blood dat's in you, not by a long sight—'deed it ain't! My great-great-great-gran'father en yo' great-great-great-great-gran'father was Ole Cap'n John Smith, de highest blood dat Ole Virginny ever turned out, en *his* great-great-gran'mother or somers along back dah, was Pocahontas de Injun queen, en her husbun' was a nigger king outen Africa— en yit here you is, a slinkin' outen a duel en disgracin' our whole line like a ornery low-down hound! Yes, it's de nigger in you!''

She sat down on her candle-box and fell into a reverie. Tom did not disturb her; he sometimes lacked prudence, but it was not in circumstances of this kind. Roxana's storm went gradually down, but it died hard, and even when it seemed to be quite gone, it would now and then break out in a distant rumble, so to speak, in the form of muttered ejaculations. One of these was, "Ain't nigger enough in him to show in his finger-nails, en dat takes mighty little—yit dey's enough to paint his soul.''

Presently she muttered. "Yassir, enough to paint a whole thimbleful of 'em.'' At last her ramblings ceased altogether, and her countenance began to clear—a welcome sign to Tom, who had learned her moods, and knew she was on the threshold of good-humor, now. He noticed that from time to time she unconsciously carried her finger to the end of her nose. He looked close and said:

"Why, mammy, the end of your nose is skinned. How **did** that come?''

She sent out the sort of whole-hearted peal of laughter which God has vouchsafed in its perfection to none but the happy angels in heaven and the bruised and broken black slave on the earth, and said:

"Dad fetch dat duel, I be'n in it myself.''

"Gracious! did a bullet do that?''

"Yassir, you bet it did!''

"Well, I declare! Why, how did that happen?''

"Happened dis-away. I 'uz a-sett'n' here kinder dozin' in de dark, en *che-bang!* goes a gun, right out dah. I skips along out towards t'other end o' de house to see what's gwyne on, en stops by de ole winder on de side to wards Pudd'nhead Wilson's house dat ain't got no sash in it,—but dey ain't none of 'em got any sashes, fur as dat's concerned,—en I stood dah in de dark en look out, en dar in de moonlight, right down under me 'uz one o' de twins a-cussin'— not much, but jist a-cussin' soft—'uz de brown one dat 'uz cussin', ca'se he 'uz hit in de shoulder. En Doctor Claypool he 'uz a-workin' at him, en Pudd'nhead Wilson he 'uz a-he'pin', en ole Jedge Driscoll en Pem Howard 'uz a-standin' out yonder a little piece waitin' for 'em to git ready agin. En trecky dey squared off en give de word, en *bang-bang* went de pistols, en de twin he say, 'Ouch!'—hit him on de han' dis time,—en I hear dat same bullet go *spat!* ag'in' de logs under de winder; en de nex' time dey shoot, de twin say, 'Ouch!' ag'in, en I done it too, 'ca'se de bullet glance' on his cheed-bone en skip up here en glance on de side o' de winder en whiz' right acrost my face en tuck de hide off'n my nose—why, if I'd 'a' be'n jist a inch or a inch en a half furder 't would 'a' tuck de whole nose en disfiggered me. Here's de bullet; I hunted her up.''

"Did you stand there all the time?"

"Dat's a question to ask, ain't it! What else would I do? Does I git a chance to see a duel every day?"

"Why, you were right in range! Weren't you afraid?"

The woman gave a sniff of scorn.

" 'Fraid! De Smith-Pocahontases ain't 'fraid o' nothin', let alone bullets.''

"They've got pluck enough, I suppose; what they lack is judg-ment. *I* wouldn't have stood there.''

"Nobody's accusin' you!"

"Did anybody else get hurt?"

"Yes, we all got hit 'cep' de blon' twin en de doctor en de seconds. De Jedge didn't git hurt, but I hear Pudd'nhead say de bullet snip some o' his ha'r off.''

" 'George!'' said Tom to himself, "to come so near being out of my trouble, and miss it by an inch. Oh dear, dear, he will live to find me out and sell me to some nigger-trader yet—yes, and he would do it in a minute." Then he said aloud, in a grave tone—

"Mother, we are in an awful fix.''

Roxana caught her breath with a spasm, and said—

"Chile! What you hit a body so sudden for, like dat? What's be'n en gone en happen'?''

"Well, there's one thing I didn't tell you. When I wouldn't fight, he tore up the will again, and—

Roxana's face turned a dead white, and she said—

"Now you's *done!*—done forever! Dat's de end. Bofe un us is gwyne to starve to—''

"Wait and hear me through, can't you! I reckon that when he resolved to fight, himself, he thought he might get killed and not have a chance to forgive me any more in this life, so he made the will again, and I've seen it, and it's all right. But—''

"Oh, thank goodness, den we's safe ag'in!—safe! en so what did you want to come here en talk sich dreadful—''

"Hold *on,* I tell you, and let me finish. The swag I gathered won't half square me up, and the first thing we know, my creditors—well, you know what'll happen.''

Roxana dropped her chin, and told her son to leave her alone—she must think this matter out. Presently she said impressively:

"You got to go mighty keerful now, I tell you! En here's what you got to do. He didn't git killed, en if you gives him de least reason, he'll bust de will ag'in, en dat's de *las'* time, now you hear me! So—you's got to show him what you kin do in de nex' few days. You's got to be pison good, en let him see it; you got to do everything dat'll make him b'lieve in you, en you got to sweeten aroun' ole Aunt Pratt, too,—she's pow'ful strong wid de Jedge, en de bes' frien' you got. Nex', you'll go 'long away to Sent Louis, en dat'll *keep* him in yo' favor. Den you go en make a bargain wid dem people. You tell 'em he ain't gwyne to live long—en dat's de fac', too,—en tell 'em you'll pay 'em intrust, en big intrust, too,—ten per—what you call it?''

"Ten per cent, a month?"

"Dat's it. Den you take and sell yo' truck aroun', a little at a time, en pay de intrust. How long will it las'?''

"I think there's enough to pay the interest five or six months.''

"Den you's all right. If he don't die in six months, dat don't make no diff'rence—Providence'll provide. You's gwyne to be safe—if you behaves." She bent an austere eye on him and added, "En you *is* gwyne to behave—does you know dat?''

He laughed and said he was going to try, anyway. She did not unbend. She said gravely:

"Tryin' ain't de thing. You's gwyne to *do* it. You ain't gwyne to steal a pin—'ca'se it ain't safe no mo'; en you ain't gwyne into no bad comp'ny—not even once, you understand; en you ain't gwyne to drink a drop—nary single drop; en you ain't gwyne to gamble one single gamble—not one! Dis ain't what you's gwyne to *try* to do, it's what you's gwyne to *do*. En I'll tell you how I knows it. Dis is how. I's gwyne to foller along to Sent Louis my own self; en you's gwyne to come to me every day o' yo life, en I'll look you over; en if you fails in one single one o' dem things—jist *one*—I take my oath I'll come straight down to dis town en tell de Jedge you's a nigger en a slave—en *prove* it!'' She paused to let her words sink home. Then she added, "Chambers, does you b'lieve me when I says dat?''

Tom was sober enough now. There was no levity in his voice when he answered:

"Yes, mother, I know, now, that I am reformed—and permanently. Permanently—and beyond the reach of any human temptation.

"Den g' long home en begin!"

CHAPTER XV

Nothing so needs reforming as other people's habits.—*Pudd'nhead Wilson's Calendar.*

Behold, the fool saith, "Put not all thine eggs in the one basket"—which is but a manner of saying, "Scatter your money and your attention;" but the wise man saith, "Put all your eggs in the one basket and—WATCH THAT BASKET."—*Pudd'nhead Wilson's Calendar.*

What a time of it Dawson's Landing was having! All its life it had been asleep, but now it hardly got a chance for a nod, so swiftly did big events and crashing surprises come along in one another's wake: Friday morning, first glimpse of Real Nobility, also grand reception at Aunt Patsy Cooper's, also great robber-raid; Friday evening, dramatic kicking of the heir of the chief citizen in presence of four hundred people; Saturday morning, emergence as practising lawyer of the long-submerged Pudd'nhead Wilson; Saturday night, duel between chief citizen and titled stranger.

The people took more pride in the duel than in all the other events put together, perhaps. It was a glory to their town to have such a thing happen there. In their eyes the principals had reached the summit of human honor. Everybody paid homage to their names; their praises were in all mouths. Even the duelists' subordinates came in for a handsome share of the public approbation: wherefore Pudd'nhead Wilson was suddenly become a man of consequence. When asked to run for the mayoralty Saturday night he was risking defeat, but Sunday morning found him a made man and his success assured.

The twins were prodigiously great, now; the town took them to its bosom with enthusiasm. Day after day, and night after night, they went dining and visiting from house to house, making friends, enlarging and solidifying their popularity, and charming and surprising all with their musical prodigies, and now and then heightening the effects with samples of what they could do in other directions, out of their stock of rare and curious accomplishments. They were so pleased that they gave the regulation thirty days' notice, the required preparation for citizenship, and resolved to finish their days in this pleasant place. That was the climax. The delighted community rose as one man and applauded; and when the twins were asked to stand for seats in the forthcoming aldermanic board, and consented, the public contentment was rounded and complete.

Tom Driscoll was not happy over these things; they sunk deep, and hurt all the way down. He hated the one twin for kicking him, and the other one for being the kicker's brother.

Now and then the people wondered why nothing was heard of the raider, or of the stolen knife or the other plunder, but nobody was able to throw any light on that matter. Nearly a week had drifted by, and still the thing remained a vexed mystery.

On Saturday Constable Blake and Pudd'nhead Wilson met on the street, and Tom Driscoll joined them in time to open their conversation for them. He said to Blake—"You are not looking well, Blake; you seem to be annoyed about something. Has anything gone wrong in the detective business? I believe you fairly and justifiably claim to have a pretty good reputation in that line, isn't it so?"—which made Blake feel good, and look it; but Tom added, "for a country detective"—which made Blake feel the other way, and not only look it, but betray it in his voice—

"Yes, sir, I *have* got a reputation; and it's as good as anybody's in the profession, too, country or no country."

"Oh, I beg pardon; I didn't mean any offense. What I started out to ask was only about the old woman that raided the town—the stoop-shouldered old woman, you know, that you said you were going to catch; and I knew you would, too, because you have the reputation of never boasting, and—well, you—you've caught the old woman?"

"D——the old woman!"

"Why, sho! you don't mean to say you haven't caught her?"

"No; I haven't caught her. If anybody could have caught her, I could; but nobody couldn't, I don't care who he is."

"I am sorry, real sorry—for your sake; because, when it gets around that a detective has expressed himself so confidently, and then——"

"Don't you worry, that's all—don't you worry; and as for the town, the town needn't worry, either. She's my meat—make yourself easy about that. I'm on her track; I've got clues that——"

"That's good! Now if you could get an old veteran detective down from St. Louis to help you find what the clues mean, and where they lead to, and then——"

"I'm plenty veteran enough myself, and I don't need anybody's help. I'll have her inside of a we—inside of a month. That I'll swear to!"

Tom said carelessly—

"I suppose that will answer—yes, that will answer. But I reckon she is pretty old, and old people don't often outlive the cautious pace of the professional detective when he has got his clues together and is out on his still-hunt."

Blake's dull face flushed under this gibe, but before he could set his retort in order Tom had turned to Wilson, and was saying, with placid indifference of manner and voice—

"Who got the reward, Pudd'head?"

Wilson winced slightly, and saw that his own turn was come.

"What reward?"

"Why, the reward for the thief, and the other one for the knife."

Wilson answered—and rather uncomfortably, to judge by his hesitating fashion of delivering himself—

"Well, the—well, in fact, nobody has claimed it yet."

Tom seemed surprised.

"Why, is that so?"

Wilson showed a trifle of irritation when he replied—

"Yes, it's so. And what of it?"

"Oh, nothing. Only I thought you had struck out a new idea, and invented a scheme that was going to revolutionize the time-worn and ineffectual methods of the——" He stopped, and turned to Blake, who was happy now that another had taken his place on the gridiron: "Blake, didn't you understand him to intimate that it wouldn't be necessary for you to hunt the old woman down?"

"B'George, he said he'd have thief and swag both inside of three days—he did, by hokey! and that's just about a week ago. Why, I said at the time that no thief and no thief's pal was going to try to pawn or sell a thing where he knowed the pawnbroker could get both rewards by taking *him* into camp *with* the swag. It was the blessedest idea that ever *I* struck!"

"You'd change your mind," said Wilson, with irritated bluntness, "if you knew the entire scheme instead of only part of it."

"Well," said the constable, pensively, "I had the idea that it wouldn't work, and up to now I'm right anyway."

"Very well, then, let it stand at that, and give it a further show. It has worked at least as well as your own methods, you perceive."

The constable hadn't anything handy to hit him back with, so he discharged a discontented sniff, and said nothing.

After the night that Wilson had partly revealed his scheme at his house, Tom had tried for several days to guess out the secret of the rest of it, but had failed. Then it occurred to him to give Roxana's smarter head a chance at it. He made up a supposititious case, and laid it before her. She thought it over, and delivered her verdict upon it. Tom said to himself, "She's hit it, sure!" He thought he would test that verdict, now, and watch Wilson's face; so he said reflectively—

"Wilson, you're not a fool—a fact of recent discovery. Whatever your scheme was, it had sense in it, Blake's opinion to the contrary notwithstanding, I don't ask you to reveal it, but I will suppose a case—a case which will answer as a starting-point for the real thing I am going to come at, and that's all I want. You offered five hundred dollars for the knife, and five hundred for the thief. We will suppose, for argument's sake, that the first reward is *advertised* and the second offered by *private letter* to pawnbrokers and——"

Blake slapped his thigh, and cried out—

"By Jackson, he's got you, Pudd'nhead! Now why couldn't I or *any* fool have thought of that?"

Wilson said to himself, "Anybody with a reasonably good head would have thought of it. I am not surprised that Blake didn't detect it; I am only surprised that Tom did. There is more to him than I supposed." He said nothing aloud, and Tom went on:

"Very well. The thief would not suspect that there was a trap, and he would bring or send the knife, and say he bought it for a song, or found it in the road, or something like that, and try to collect the reward, and be arrested—wouldn't he?"

"Yes," said Wilson.

"I think so," said Tom. "There can't be any doubt of it. Have you ever seen that knife?"

"No."

"Has any friend of yours?"

"Not that I know of."

"Well, I begin to think I understand why your scheme failed."

"What do you mean, Tom? What are you driving at?" asked Wilson, with a dawning sense of discomfort.

"Why, that there *isn't* any such knife."

"Look here, Wilson," said Blake, "Tom Driscoll's right, for a thousand dollars—if I had it."

Wilson's blood warmed a little, and he wondered if he had been played upon by those strangers; it certainly had something of that look. But what could they gain by it? He threw out that suggestion. Tom replied:

"Gain? Oh, nothing that you would value, maybe. But they are strangers making their way in a new community. Is it nothing to them to appear as pets of an Oriental prince—at no expense? Is it nothing to them to be able to dazzle this poor little town with thousand-dollar rewards—at no expense? Wilson, there isn't any such knife, or your scheme would have fetched it to light. Or if there is any such knife, they've got it yet. I believe, myself, that they've seen such a knife, for Angelo pictured it out with his pencil too swiftly and handily for him to have been inventing it, and of course I can't swear that they've never had it; but this I'll go bail for—if they had it when they came to this town, they've got it yet."

Blake said—

"It looks mighty reasonable, the way Tom puts it; it most certainly does."

Tom responded, turning to leave—

"You find the old woman, Blake, and if she can't furnish the knife, go and search the twins!"

Tom sauntered away. Wilson felt a good deal depressed. He hardly knew what to think. He was loth to withdraw his faith from the twins, and was resolved not to do it on the present indecisive evidence; but—well, he would think, and then decide how to act.

"Blake, what do you think of this matter?"

"Well, Pudd'nhead, I'm bound to say I put it the way Tom does. They hadn't the knife; or if they had it, they've got it yet."

The men parted. Wilson said to himself:

"I believe they had it; if it had been stolen, the scheme would have restored it, that is certain. And so I believe they've got it yet."

Tom had no purpose in his mind when he encountered those two men. When he began his talk he hoped to be able to gall them a little and get a trifle of malicious entertainment out of it. But when he left, he left in great spirits, for he perceived that just by pure luck and no troublesome labor he had accomplished several delightful things: he had touched both men on a raw spot and seen them squirm; he had modified Wilson's sweetness for the twins with one small bitter taste that he wouldn't be able to get out of his mouth right away; and, best of all, he had taken the hated twins down a peg with the community; for Blake would gossip around freely, after the manner of detectives, and within a week the town would be laughing at them in its sleeve for offering a gaudy reward for a bauble which they either never possessed or hadn't lost. Tom was very well satisfied with himself.

Tom's behavior at home had been perfect during the entire week. His uncle and aunt had seen nothing like it before. They could find no fault with him anywhere.

Saturday evening he said to the Judge—

"I've had something preying on my mind, uncle, and as I am going away, and might never see you again, I can't bear it any longer. I made you believe I was afraid to fight that Italian adventurer. I had to get out of it on some pretext or other, and maybe I chose badly, being taken unawares, but no honorable person could consent to meet him in the field, knowing what I knew about him."

"Indeed? What was that?"

"Count Luigi is a confessed assassin."

"Incredible!"

"It is perfectly true. Wilson detected it in his hand, by palmistry, and charged him with it, and cornered him up so close that he had to confess; but both twins begged us on their knees to keep the secret, and swore they would lead straight lives here; and it was all so pitiful that we gave our word of honor never to expose them while they kept that promise. You would have done it yourself, uncle."

"You are right, my boy; I would. A man's secret is still his own property, and sacred, when it has been surprised out of him like that. You did well, and I am proud of you." Then he added mournfully, "But I wish I could have been saved the shame of meeting an assassin on the field of honor."

"It couldn't be helped, uncle. If I had known you were going to challenge him I should have felt obliged to sacrifice my pledged word in order to stop it, but Wilson couldn't be expected to do otherwise than keep silent."

"Oh no; Wilson did right, and is in no way to blame. Tom, Tom, you have lifted a heavy load from my heart; I was stung to the very soul when I seemed to have discovered that I had a coward in my family."

"You may imagine what it cost *me* to assume such a part, uncle."

"Oh, I know it, poor boy, I know it. And I can understand how much it has cost you to remain under that unjust stigma to this time. But it is all right now, and no harm is done. You have restored my comfort of mind, and with it your own; and both of us had suffered enough."

The old man sat awhile plunged in thought; then he looked up with a satisfied light in his eye, and said: "That this assassin should have put the affront upon me of letting me meet him on the field of honor as if he were a gentleman is a matter which I will presently settle—but not now. I will not shoot him until after election. I see a way to ruin them both before; I will attend to that first. Neither of them shall be elected, that I promise. You are sure that the fact that he is an assassin has not got abroad?"

"Perfectly certain of it, sir."

"It will be a good card. I will fling a hint at it from the stump on the polling-day. It will sweep the ground from under both of them."

"There's no doubt of it. It will finish them."

"That and outside work among the voters will, to a certainty. I want you to come down here by and by and work privately among the rag-tag and bobtail. You shall spend money among them; I will furnish it."

Another point scored against the detested twins! Really it was a great day for Tom. He was encouraged to chance a parting shot, now, at the same target, and did it.

"You know that wonderful Indian knife that the twins have been making such a to-do about? Well, there's no track or trace of it yet; so the town is beginning to sneer and gossip and laugh. Half the people believe they never had any such knife, the other half believe they had it and have got it still. I've heard twenty people talking like that today."

Yes, Tom's blemishless week had restored him to the favor of his aunt and uncle.

His mother was satisfied with him, too. Privately, she believed she was coming to love him, but she did not say so. She told him to go along to St. Louis, now, and she would get ready and follow. Then she smashed her whisky bottle and said—

"Dah now! I's a-gwyne to make you walk straight as a string, Chambers, en so I's bown' you ain't gwyne to git no bad example out o' yo' mammy. I tole you you couldn't go into no bad comp'ny. Well, you's gwyne into my comp'ny, en I's gwyne to fill de bill. Now, den, trot along, trot along!"

Tom went aboard one of the big transient boats that night with his heavy satchel of miscellaneous plunder, and slept the sleep of the unjust, which is serener and sounder than the other kind, as we know by the hanging-eve history of a million rascals. But when he got up in the morning, luck was against him again: A brother-thief had robbed him while he slept, and gone ashore at some intermediate landing.

CHAPTER XVI

If you pick up a starving dog and make him prosperous, he will not bite you. This is the principal difference between a dog and a man.
—*Pudd'nhead Wilson's Calendar.*

We know all about the habits of the ant, we know all about the habits of the bee, but we know nothing at all about the habits of the oyster. It seems almost certain that we have been choosing the wrong time for studying the oyster.—*Pudd'nhead Wilson's Calendar.*

When Roxana arrived, she found her son in such despair and misery that her heart was touched and her motherhood rose up strong in her. He was ruined past hope, now; his destruction would be immediate and sure, and he would be an outcast and friendless. That was reason enough for a mother to love a child; so she loved him, and told him so. It made him wince, secretly—for she was a "nigger." That he was one himself was far from reconciling him to that despised race.

Roxana poured out endearments upon him, to which he responded uncomfortably, but as well as he could. And she tried to comfort him, but that was not possible. These intimacies quickly became horrible to him, and within the hour he began to try to get up courage enough to tell her so, and require that they be discontinued or very considerably modified. But he was afraid of her; and besides, there came a lull, now, for she had begun to think. She was trying to invent a saving plan. Finally she started up, and said she had found a way out. Tom was almost suffocated by the joy of this sudden good news. Roxana said:

"Here is de plan, en she'll win, sure. I's a nigger, en nobody ain't gwyne to doubt it dat hears me talk. I's wuth six hund'd dollahs. Take en sell me, en pay off dese gamblers."

Tom was dazed. He was not sure he had heard aright. He was dumb for a moment; then he said:

"Do you mean that you would be sold into slavery to save me?"

"Ain't you my chile? En does you know anything dat a mother won't do for her chile? Dey ain't nothin a white mother won't do for her chile. Who made 'em so? De Lord done it. En who made de niggers? De Lord made 'em. In de inside, mothers is all de same. De good Lord he made 'em so. I's gwyne to be sole into slavery, en in a year you's gwyne to buy yo' ole mammy free ag'in. I'll show you how. Dat's de plan."

Tom's hopes began to rise, and his spirits along with them. He said—

"It's lovely of you, mammy—it's just—"

"Say it ag'in! En keep on sayin' it? It's all de pay a body kin want in dis worl', en it's mo'den enough. Laws bless you, honey, when I's slavin' aroun', en dey 'buses me, if I knows you's a-sayin' dat, 'way off yonder somers, it'll heal up all de sore places, en I kin stan' 'em."

"I *do* say it again, mammy, and I'll keep on saying it, too. But how am I going to sell you? You're free, you know."

"Much diff'rence dat make! White folks ain't partic'lar. De law kin sell me now if dey tell me to leave de State in six months en I don't go. You draw up a paper—bill o' sale—en put it 'way off yonder, down in de middle 'o Kaintuck somers, en sign some names to it, en say you'll sell me cheap 'ca'se you's hard up; you'll find you ain't gwyne to have no trouble. You take me up de country a piece, en sell me on a farm; dem people ain't gwyne to ask no questions if I's a bargain."

Tom forged a bill of sale and sold his mother to an Arkansas cotton-planter for a trifle over six hundred dollars. He did not want to commit this treachery, but luck threw the man in his way, and this saved him the necessity of going up country to hunt up a purchaser, with the added risk of having to answer a lot of questions, whereas this planter was so pleased with Roxy that he asked next to none at all. Besides, the planter insisted that Roxy wouldn't know where she was, at first, and that by the time she found out she would already have become contented. And Tom argued with himself that it was an immense advantage for Roxy to have a master who was so pleased with her, as this planter manifestly was. In almost no time his flowing reasonings carried him to the point of even half believing he was doing Roxy a splendid surreptitious service in selling her "down the river." And then he kept diligently saying to himself all the time: "It's for only a year. In a year I buy her free again; she'll keep that in mind, and it'll reconcile her." Yes; the little deception could do no harm, and everything would come out right and pleasant in the end, any way. By agreement, the conversation in Roxy's presence was all about the man's "upcountry" farm, and how pleasant a place it was, and how happy the slaves were there; so poor Roxy was entirely deceived; and easily, for she was not dreaming that her own son could be guilty of treason to a mother who, in voluntarily going into slavery—slavery of any kind, mild or severe, or of any duration, brief or long—was making a sacrifice for him compared with which death would have been a poor and commonplace one. She lavished tears and loving caresses upon him privately, and then went away with her owner—went away broken-hearted, and yet proud of what she was doing, and glad that it was in her power to do it.

Tom squared his accounts, and resolved to keep to the very letter of his reform, and never to put that will in jeopardy again. He had three hundred dollars left. According to his mother's plan, he was to put that safely away, and add her half of his pension to it monthly. In one year this fund would buy her free again.

For a whole week he was not able to sleep well, so much the villiany which he had played upon his trusting mother preyed upon his rag of a conscience; but after that he began to get comfortable again, and was presently able to sleep like any other miscreant.

The boat bore Roxy away from St. Louis at four in the afternoon, and she stood on the lower guard abaft the paddle-box and watched Tom through a blur of tears until he melted into the throng of people and disappeared; then she looked no more, but sat there on a coil of cable crying till far into the night. When she went to her foul steerage-bunk at last, between the clashing engines, it was not to sleep, but only to wait for the morning, and, waiting, grieve.

It had been imagined that she "would not know," and would think she was traveling up stream. She! Why, she had been steamboating for years. At dawn she got up and went listlessly and sat down on the cable-coil again. She passed many a snag whose "break" could have told her a thing to break her heart, for it showed a current moving in the same direction that the boat was going; but her thoughts were elsewhere, and she did not notice. But at last the roar of a bigger and nearer break than usual brought her out of her torpor, and she looked up, and her practised eye fell upon that tell-tale rush of water. For one moment her petrified gaze fixed itself there. Then her head dropped upon her breast, and she said—

"Oh, de good Lord God have mercy on po' sinful me—*I's sole down de river!*"

CHAPTER XVII

Even popularity can be overdone. In Rome, along at first, you are full of regrets that Michaelangelo died; but by and by you only regret that you didn't see him do it.—*Pudd'nhead Wilson's Calendar.*

July 4. Statistics show that we lose more fools on this day than in all the other days of the year put together. This proves, by the number left in stock, that one Fourth of July per year is now inadequate, the country has grown so.—*Pudd'nhead Wilson's Calendar.*

The summer weeks dragged by, and then the political campaign opened—opened in pretty warm fashion, and waxed hotter and hotter daily. The twins threw themselves into it with their whole heart, for their self-love was engaged. Their popularity, so general at first, had suffered afterward; mainly because they had been *too* popular, and so a natural reaction had followed. Besides, it had been diligently whispered around that it was curious—indeed, *very* curious—that that wonderful knife of theirs did not turn up—*if* it was so valuable, or *if* it had ever existed. And with the whisperings went chucklings and nudgings and winks, and such things have an effect. The twins considered that success in the election would reinstate them, and that defeat would work them irreparable damage. Therefore they worked hard, but not harder than Judge Driscoll and Tom worked against them in the closing days of the canvas. Tom's conduct had remained so letter-perfect during two whole months, now, that his uncle not only trusted him with money with which to persuade voters, but trusted him to go and get it himself out of the safe in the private sitting-room.

The closing speech of the campaign was made by Judge Driscoll, and he made it against both of the foreigners. It was disastrously effective. He poured out rivers of ridicule upon them, and forced the big mass-meeting to laugh and applaud. He scoffed at them as adventurers, mountebanks, side-show riff-raff, dime museum freaks; he assailed their showy titles with measureless derision; he said they were back-alley barbers disguised as nobilities, peanut pedlers masquerading as gentlemen, organ-grinders bereft of their brother monkey. At last he stopped and stood still. He waited until the place had become absolutely silent and expectant, then he delivered his deadliest shot; delivered it with ice-cold seriousness and deliberation, with a significant emphasis upon the closing words: he said he believed that the reward offered for the lost knife was humbug and buncombe, and that its owner would know where to find it whenever he should have occasion *to assassinate somebody*.

Then he stepped from the stand, leaving a startled and impressive hush behind him instead of the customary explosion of cheers and party cries.

The strange remark flew far and wide over the town and made an extraordinary sensation. Everybody was asking, "What could he mean by that?" And everybody went on asking that question, but in vain; for the Judge only said he knew what he was talking about, and stopped there; Tom said he hadn't any idea what his uncle meant, and Wilson, whenever he was asked what he thought it meant, parried the question by asking the questioner what *he* thought it meant.

Wilson was elected, the twins were defeated—crushed, in fact, and left forlorn and substantially friendless. Tom went back to St. Louis happy.

Dawson's Landing had a week of repose, now, and it needed it. But it was in an expectant state, for the air was full of rumors of a new duel. Judge Driscoll's election labors had prostated him, but it was said that as soon as he was well enough to entertain a challenge he would get one from Count Luigi.

The brother withdrew entirely from society, and nursed their humiliation in privacy. They avoided the people, and went out for exercise only late at night, when the streets were deserted.

CHAPTER XVIII

Gratitude and treachery are merely the two extremities of the same procession. You have seen all of it that is worth staying for when the band and the gaudy officials have gone by.—*Pudd'nhead Wilson's Calendar*.

Thanksgiving Day. Let all give humble, hearty, and sincere thanks, now, but the turkeys. In the island of Fiji they do not use turkeys; they use plumbers. It does not become you and me to sneer at Fiji.—*Pudd'nhead Wilson's Calendar*.

The Friday after the election was a rainy one in St. Louis. It rained all day long, and rained hard, apparently trying its best to wash that soot-blackened town white, but of course not succeeding. Toward midnight Tom Driscoll arrived at his lodgings from the theatre in the heavy downpour, and closed his umbrella and let himself in; but when he would have shut the door, he found that there was another person entering—doubtless another lodger; this person closed the door and tramped upstairs behind Tom. Tom found his door in the dark, and entered it and turned up the gas. When he faced about, lightly whistling, he saw the back of a man. The man was closing and locking his door for him. His whistle faded out and he felt uneasy. The man turned around, a wreck of shabby old clothes, sodden with rain and all a-drip, and showed a black face under an old slouch hat. Tom was frightened. He tried to order the man out, but the words refused to come, and the other man got the start. He said, in a low voice—

"Keep still—I's yo' mother!"

Tom sunk in a heap on a chair, and gasped out—

"It was mean of me, and base—I know it; but I meant it for the best, I did indeed—I can swear it."

Roxana stood awhile looking mutely down on him while he writhed in shame and went on incoherently babbling self- accusations mixed with pitiful attempts at explanation and palliation of his crime; then she seated herself and took off her hat, and her unkempt masses of long brown hair tumbled down about her shoulders.

"It ain't no fault o' yo'n dat dat ain't gray," she said sadly, noticing the hair.

"I know it, I know it! I'm a scoundrel. But I swear I meant it for the best. It was a mistake, of couse, but I thought it was for the best, I truly did."

Roxy began to cry softly, and presently words began to find their way out between her sobs. They were uttered lamentingly, rather than angrily—

"Sell a pusson down de river—*down de river!*—for de bes'! I wouldn't treat a dog so! I is all broke down en wore out, now, en so I reckon it ain't in me to storm aroun' no mo', like I used to when I 'uz trompled on en 'bused. I don't know—but maybe it's so. Leastways, I's suffered so much dat mournin' seem to come mo' handy to me now den stormin'."

These words should have touched Tom Driscoll, but if they did, that effect was obliterated by a stronger one—one which removed the heavy weight of fear which lay upon him, and gave his crushed spirit a most grateful rebound, and filled all his small soul with a deep sense of relief. But he kept prudently still, and ventured no comment. There was a voiceless interval of some duration, now, in which no sounds were heard but the beating of the rain upon the panes, the sighing and complaining of the winds, and now and then a muffled sob from Roxana. The sobs became more and more infrequent, and at last ceased. The refugee began to talk again:

"Shet down dat light a little. More. More yit. A pusson dat is hunted don't like de light. Dah—dat'll do. I kin see whah you is, en dat's enough. I's gwine to tell you de tale, en cut it jes as short as I kin, en den I'll tell you what you's got to do. Dat man dat bought me ain't a bad man; he's good enough, as planters goes; en if he could 'a' had his way I'd 'a' be'n a house servant in his fambly en be'n comfortable: but his wife she was a Yank, en not right down good lookin', en she riz up agin me straight off; so den dey sent me out to de quarter 'mongst de common fiel' han's. Dat woman warn't satisfied even wid dat, but she worked up de overseer ag'in' me, she 'uz dat jealous en hateful; so de overseer he had me out befo' day in de mawnin's en worked me de whole long day as long as dey'uz any light to see by; en many's de lashin's I got 'ca'se I couldn't come up to de work o' de stronges'. Dat overseer wuz a Yank, too, outen New Englan', en anybody down South kin tell you what dat mean. *Dey* knows how to work a nigger to death, en day knows how to whale 'em, too—whale 'em till dey backs is welted like a washboard. 'Long at fust my marster say de good word for me to de overseer, but dat 'uz bad for me; for de mistis she fine it out, en arter dat I jist ketched it at every turn—dey warn't no mercy for me no mo'."

Tom's heart was fired—with fury 'against the planter's wife; and he said to himself, "But for that meddlesome fool, everything would have gone all right." He added a deep and bitter curse against her.

The expression of this sentiment was fiercely written in his face, and stood thus revealed to Roxana by a white glare of lightning which turned the somber dusk of the room into dazzling day at that moment. She was pleased—pleased and grateful; for did not that expression show that her child was capable of grieving for his mother's wrongs and of feeling resentment toward her persecutors?—a thing which she had been doubting. But her flash of happiness was only a flash, and went out again and left her spirit dark; for she said to herself, "He sole me down de river—he can't feel for a body long: dis'll pass en go." Then she took up her tale again.

" 'Bout ten days ago I 'uz sayin' to myself dat I couldn't las' many mo' weeks I 'uz so wore out wid de awful work en de lashin's, en so downhearted en misable. En I didn't care no mo', nuther—life warn't wuth noth'n' to me, if I got to go on like dat. Well, when a body is in a frame o' mine like dat, what do a body care what a body do? Dey was a little sickly nigger wench 'bout ten year ole dat 'uz good to me, en hadn't no mammy, po' thing, en I loved her en she loved me; en she come out whah I 'uz workin 'en she had a roasted tater, en tried to slip it to me,— robbin' herself, you see, 'ca'se she knowed de overseer didn't gimme enough to eat,—en he ketched her at it, en give her a lick acrost de back wid his stick, which 'uz as thick as a broom- handle, en she drop' screamin' on de groun', en squirmin' en wallerin' aroun' in de dust like a spider dat's got crippled. I couldn't stan' it. All de hell-fire dat 'uz ever in my heart flame' up, en I snatch de stick outen his han' en laid him flat. He laid dah moanin' en cussin', en all out of his head, you know, en de niggers 'uz plumb sk'yerd to death. Dey gathered roun' him to hep' him, en I jumped on his hoss en took out for de river as tight as I could go. I knowed what dey would do wid me. Soon as he got well he would start in en work me to death if marster let him; en if dey didn't do dat, they'd sell me furder down de river, en dat's de same thing. So I 'lowed to drown myself en git out o' my troubles. It 'uz gitt'n' towards dark. I 'uz at de river in two minutes. Den I see a canoe, en I says dey ain't no use to drown myself tell I got to; so I ties de hoss in de edge o' de timber en shove out down de river, keepin' in under de shelter o' de bluff bank en prayin' for de dark to shet down quick. I had a pow'ful good start, 'ca'se de big house 'uz three mile back f'om de river en on'y de work-mules to ride dah on, en on'y niggers to ide 'em, en *day* warn't gwine to hurry—dey'd gimme all de chance dey could. Befo' a body could go to de house en back it would be long pas' dark, en dey couldn't track de hoss en fine out which way I went tell mawnin', en de niggers would tell 'em all de lies dey could 'bout it.

"Well, de dark come, en I went on a-spinnin' down de river. I paddled mo'n two hours, den I warn't worried no mo', so I quit paddlin, en floated down de current, considerin' what I 'uz gwine to do if I didn't have to drown myself. I made up some plans, en floated along, turnin' 'em over in my mine. Well, when it 'uz a little pas' midnight, as I reckoned, en I had come fifteen or twenty mile, I see de lights o' a steamboat layin' at de bank, whah dey warn't no town en no woodyard, en putty soon I ketched de shape o' de chimbly-tops ag'in' de stars, en de good gracious me, I 'most jumped out o' my skin for joy! It 'uz de *Gran' Mogul*—I 'uz chambermaid on her for eight seasons in de Cincinnati en Orleans trade. I slid 'long pas'—don't see nobody stirrin' nowhah—hear 'em a-hammerin' away in de engine-room, den I knowed what de matter was—some o' de machin-ery's broke. I got asho' below de boat and turn' de canoe loose, den I goes 'long up, en dey 'uz jes one plank out, en I step' 'board de boat. It 'uz pow'ful hot, deckhan's en roustabouts 'uz sprawled aroun' asleep on de fo'cas'l', de second mate, Jim Bangs, he sot dah on de bitts wid his head down, asleep—'ca'se dat's de way de second mate stan' de cap'n's watch!—en de ole watchman, Billy Hatch, he 'uz a-noddin' on de companion-way;—en I knowed 'em all; 'en, lan', but dey did look good! I says to myself, I wished old marster'd come along *now* en try to take me—bless yo' heart, I's 'mong frien's, I is. So I tromped right along 'mongst 'em, en went up on de b'iler deck en 'way back aft to de ladies' cabin guard, en sot down dah in de same cheer dat I'd sot in 'mos' a hund'd million times, I reckon; en it 'uz jist home ag'in, I tell you!

"In 'bout an hour I heard de ready-bell jingle, en den de racket begin. Putty soon I hear de gong strike. 'Set her back on de outside,' I says to myself—'I reckon I knows dat music!' I hear de gong ag'in. 'Come ahead on de inside,' I says. Gong ag'in. 'Stop de outside.' Gong ag'in. 'Come ahead on de outside—now we's pinted for Sent Louis, en I's outer de woods en ain't got to drown myself at all.' I knowed de *Mogul* 'uz in de Sent Louis trade now, you see. It 'uz jes fair daylight when we passed our plantation, en I seed a gang o' niggers en white folks huntin' up en down de sho', en troublin' deyselves a good deal 'bout me; but I warn't troublin' myself none 'bout dem.

"Bout dat time Sally Jackson, dat used to be my second chambermaid en 'uz head chambermaid now, she come out on de guard, en 'uz pow'ful glad to see me, en so 'uz all de officers; en I tole 'em I'd got kidnapped en sole down de river, en dey made me up twenty dollahs en give it to me, en Sally she rigged me out wid good clo'es, en when I got here I went straight to whah you used to wuz, en den I come to dis house, en dey say you's away but 'spected back every day; so I didn't dast to go down de river to Dawson's, 'ca'se I might miss you.

"Well, las' Monday I 'uz pass'n' by one o' dem places in Fourth street whah deh sticks up runaway-nigger bills, en he'ps to ketch 'em, en I seed my marster! I 'mos' flopped down on de groun', I felt so gone. He had his back to me, en 'uz talkin' to de man en givin' him some bills—nigger-bills, I reckon, en I'se de nigger. He's offerin' a reward—dat's it. Ain't I right, don't you reckon?"

Tom had been gradually sinking into a state of ghastly terror, and he said to himself, now: "I'm lost, no matter what turn things take! This man has said to me that he thinks there was something suspicious about that sale. He said he had a letter from a passenger on the *Grand Mogul* saying that Roxy came here on that boat and that everybody on board knew all about the case; so he says that hercoming here instead of flying to a free State looks bad for me, and that if I don't find her for him, and that pretty soon, he will make trouble for me. I never believed that story; I couldn't believe she would be so dead to all motherly instincts as to come here, knowing the risk she would run of getting me into irremediable trouble. And after all, here she is! And I stupidly swore I would help him find her, thinking it was a perfectly safe thing to promise. If I venture to deliver her up, she—she—but how can I help myself? I've got to do that or pay the money, and where's the money to come from? I—I— well, I should think that if he would swear to treat her kindly hereafter—and she says, herself, that he is a good man—and if he would swear to never allow her to be overworked, or ill fed, or—"

A flash of lightning exposed Tom's pallid face, drawn and

rigid with these worrying thoughts. Roxana spoke up sharply now, and there was apprehension in her voice—

"Turn up dat light! I want to see yo' face better. Dah now—lemme look at you. Chambers, you's as white as yo' shirt! Has you seen dat man? Has he be'n to see you?"

"Ye-s."

"When?"

"Monday noon."

"Monday noon! Was he on my track?"

"He—well, he thought he was. That is, he hoped he was. This is the bill you saw." He took it out of his pocket.

"Read it to me!"

She was panting with excitement, and there was a dusky glow in her eyes that Tom could not translate with certainty, but there seemed to be something threatening about it. The handbill had the usual rude woodcut of a turbaned negro woman running, with the customary bundle on a stick over her shoulder, and the heading in bold type, "$100 REWARD." Tom read the bill aloud—at least the part that described Roxana and named the master and his St. Louis address and the address of the Fourth-street agency; but he left out the item that applicants for the reward might also apply to Mr. Thomas Driscoll.

"Gimme de bill!"

Tom had folded it and was putting it in his pocket. He felt a chilly streak creeping down his back, but said as carelessly as he could—

"The bill? Why, it isn't any use to you, you can't read it. What do you want with it?"

"Gimme de bill!" Tom gave it to her, but with a reluctance which he could not entirely disguise. "Did you read it *all* to me?"

"Certainly I did."

"Hole up yo' han' en swah to it."

Tom did it. Roxana put the bill carefully away in her pocket, with her eyes fixed upon Tom's face all the while; then she said—

"Yo's lyin'!"

"What would I want to lie about it for?"

"I don't know—but you is. Dat's my opinion, anyways. But nemmine 'bout dat. When I seed dat man I 'uz dat sk'yerd dat I could sca'cely wobble home. Den I give a nigger man a dollar for dese clo'es, en I ain't be'n in a house sence, night ner day, till now. I blacked my face en laid hid in de cellar of a ole house dat's burnt down, daytimes, en robbed de sugar hogsheads en grain sacks on de wharf, nights, to git somethin' to eat, en never dast to try to buy noth'n', en I's 'mos' starved. En I never dast to come near dis place till dis rainy night, when dey ain't no people roun' sca'cely. But to-night I be'n a-stannin' in de dark alley ever sence night come, waitin' for you to go by. En here I is.''

She fell to thinking. Presently she said—

"You seed dat man at noon, las' Monday?"

"Yes."

"I seed him de middle o' dat arternoon. He hunted you up, didn't he?"

"Yes."

"Did he give you de bill dat time?"

"No, he hadn't got it printed yet."

Roxana darted a suspicious glance at him.

"Did you he'p him fix up de bill?"

Tom cursed himself for making that stupid blunder, and tried to rectify it by saying he remembered, now, that it *was* at noon Monday that the man gave him the bill. Roxana said—

"You's lyin' ag'in, sho." Then she straightened up and raised her finger:

"Now den! I's gwine to ask you a question, en I wants to know how you's gwine to git aroun' it. You knowed he 'uz arter me; en if you run off, 'stid o' stayin' here to he'p him, he'd know dey 'uz somethin' wrong 'bout dis business, en den he would inquire 'bout you, en dat would take him to yo' uncle, en yo' uncle would read de bill en see dat you be'n sellin' a free nigger down de river, en you know *him,* I reckon! He'd t'ar up de will en kick you outen de house. Now, den, you answer me dis question: hain't you tole dat man dat I would be sho' to come here, en den you would fix it so he could set a trap en ketch me?"

Tom recognized that neither lies nor arguments could help him any longer—he was in a vise, with the screw turned on, and out of it there was no budging. His face began to take on an ugly look, and presently he said, with a snarl—

"Well, what could I do? You see, yourself, that I was in his grip and couldn't get out."

Roxy scorched him with a scornful gaze awhile, then she said—

"What could you do? You could be Judas to yo' own mother to save yo' wuthless hide! Would anybody b'lieve it? No—a dog couldn't! You is de low-downest orneriest hound dat was ever pup'd into dis worl'—en I's 'sponsible for it!''—and she spat on him.

He made no effort to resent this. Roxy reflected a moment, then she said—

"Now I'll tell you what you's gwine to do. You's gwine to give dat man de money dat you's got laid up, en make him wait till you kin go to de Jedge en git de res' en buy me free agin."

"Thunder! what are you thinking of? Go and ask him for three hundred dollars and odd? What would I tell him I want with it, pray?"

Roxy's answer was delivered in a serene and level voice—

"You'll tell him you's sole me to pay yo' gamblin' debts en dat you lied to me en was a villain, en dat I 'quires you to git dat money en buy me back ag'in."

"Why, you've gone stark mad! He would tear the will to shreds in a minute—don't you know that?"

"Yes, I does."

"Then you don't believe I'm idiot enough to go to him, do you?"

"I don't b'lieve nothin' 'bout it—I *knows* you's a-goin'. I knows it 'ca'se you knows dat if you don't raise dat money I'll go to him myself, en den he'll sell *you* down de river, en you kin see how you like it!"

Tom rose, trembling and excited, and there was an evil light in his eye. He strode to the door and said he must get out of this suffocating place for a moment and clear his brain in the fresh air so that he could determine what to do. The door wouldn't open. Roxy smiled grimly, and said—

"I's got de key, honey—set down. You needn't cle'r up yo' brain none to fine out what you gwine to do—*I* knows what you's gwine to do." Tom sat down and began to pass his hands through his hair with a helpless and desperate air. Roxy said, "Is dat man in dis house?"

Tom glanced up with a surprised expression, and asked—

"What gave you such an idea?"

"You done it. Gwine out to cle'r yo' brain! In de fust place you ain't got none to cle'r, en in de second place yo' ornery eye tole on you. You's de low-downest hound dat ever—but I done tole you dat befo'. Now den, dis is Friday. You kin fix it up wid dat man, en tell him you's gwine away to git de res' o' de money, en dat you'll be back wid it nex' Tuesday, or maybe Wednesday. You understan'?"

Tom answered sullenly—

"Yes."

"En when you gits de new bill o' sale dat sells me to my own self, take en send it in de mail to Mr. Pudd'nhead Wilson, en write on de back dat he's to keep it tell I come. You understan'?"

"Yes."

"Dat's all den. Take yo' umbreller, en put on yo' hat."

"Why?"

"Beca'se you's gwine to see me home to de wharf. You see dis knife? I's toted it aroun' sence de day I seed dat man en bought dese clo'es en it. If he ketch me, I's gwine to kill myself wid it. Now start along, en go sof', en lead de way; en if you gives a sign in dis house, or if anybody comes up to you in de street, I's gwine to jam it right into you. Chambers, does you b'lieve me when I says dat?"

"It's no use to bother me with that question. I know your word's good."

"Yes, it's diff'rent from yo'n! Shet de light out en move along—here's de key."

They were not followed. Tom trembled every time a late straggler brushed by them on the street, and half expected to feel the cold steel in his back. Roxy was right at his heels and always in reach. After tramping a mile they reached a wide vacancy on the deserted wharves, and in this dark and rainy desert they parted.

As Tom trudged home his mind was full of dreary thoughts and wild plans; but at last he said to himself, wearily—

"There is but the one way out. I must follow her plan. But with a variation—I will not ask for the money and ruin myself; I will *rob* the old skinflint."

CHAPTER XIX

Few things are harder to put up with than the annoyance of a good example.—*Pudd'nhead Wilson's Calendar.*

It were not best that we should all think alike; it is difference of opinion that makes horse-races.—*Pudd'nhead Wilson's Calendar.*

Dawson's Landing was comfortably finishing its season of dull repose and waiting patiently for the duel. Count Luigi was waiting, too; but not patiently, rumor said. Sunday came, and Luigi insisted on having his challenge conveyed. Wilson carried it. Judge Driscoll declined to fight with an assassin—"that is," he added significantly, "in the field of honor."

Elsewhere, of course, he would be ready. Wilson tried to convince him that if he had been present himself when Angelo told about the homicide committed by Luigi, he would not have considered the act discreditable to Luigi; but the obstinate old man was not to be moved.

Wilson went back to his principal and reported the failure of his mission. Luigi was incensed, and asked how it could be that the old gentleman, who was by no means dull-witted, held his trifling nephew's evidence and inferences to be of more value than Wilson's. But Wilson laughed, and said—

"That is quite simple; that is easily explicable. I am not his doll—his baby—his infatuation: his nephew is. The Judge and his late wife never had any children. The Judge and his wife were past middle age when this treasure fell into their lap. One must make allowances for a parental instinct that has been starving for twenty-five or thirty years. It is famished, it is crazed with hunger by that time, and will be entirely satisfied with anything that comes handy; its taste is atrophied, it can't tell mud-cat from shad. A devil born to a young couple is measurably recognizable by them as a devil before long, but a devil adopted by an old couple is an angel to them, and remains so, through thick and thin. Tom is this old man's angel; he is infatuated with him. Tom can persuade him into things which other people can't—not all things; I don't mean that, but a good many— particularly one class of things: the things that create or abolish personal partialities or prejudices in the old man's mind. The old man liked both of you. Tom conceived a hatred for you. That was enough; it turned the old man around at once. The oldest and strongest friendship must go to the ground when one of these late-adopted darlings throws a brick at it."

"It's a curious philosophy," said Luigi.

"It ain't a philosophy at all—it's a fact. And there is something pathetic and beautiful about it, too. I think there is nothing more pathetic than to see one of these poor old childless couples taking a menagerie of yelping little worthless dogs to their hearts; and then adding some cursing and squawking parrots and a jackass-voiced macaw; and next a couple of hundred screeching songbirds, and presently some fetid guinea-pigs and rabbits, and a howling colony of cats. It is all a groping and ignorant effort to construct out of base metal and brass filings, so to speak, something to take the place of that golden treasure denied them by Nature, a child. But this is a digression. The unwritten law of this region requires you to kill Judge Driscoll on sight, and he and the community will expect that attention at your hands—though of course your own death by his bullet will answer every purpose. Look out for him! Are you heeled—that is, fixed?"

"Yes; he shall have his opportunity. If he attacks me I will respond."

As Wilson was leaving, he said—

"The Judge is still a little used up by his campaign work, and will not get out for a day or so; but when he does get out, you want to be on the alert."

About eleven at night the twins went out for exercise, and started on a long stroll in the veiled moonlight.

Tom Driscoll had landed at Hackett's Store, two miles below Dawson's, just about half an hour earlier, the only passenger for that lonely spot, and had walked up the shore road and entered Judge Driscoll's house without having encountered any one either on the road or under the roof.

He pulled down his window-blinds and lighted his candle. He laid off his coat and hat and began his preparations. He unlocked his trunk and got his suit of girl's clothes out from under the male attire in it, and laid it by. Then he blacked his face with burnt cork and put the cork in his pocket. His plan was, to slip down to his uncle's private sitting-room below, pass into the bedroom, steal the safe-key from the old gentleman's clothes, and then go back and rob the safe. He took up his candle to start. His courage and confidence were high, up to this point, but both began to waver a little, now. Suppose he should make a noise, by some accident, and get caught—say, in the act of opening the safe? Perhaps it would be well to go armed. He took the Indian knife from its hiding-place, and felt a pleasant return of his wandering courage. He slipped stealthily down the narrow stair, his hair rising and his pulses halting at the slightest creak. When he was half-way down, he was disturbed to perceive that the landing below was touched by a faint glow of light. What could that mean? Was his uncle still up? No, that was not likely; he must have left his night-taper there when he went to bed. Tom crept on down, pausing at every step to listen. He found the door standing open, and glanced in. What he saw pleased him beyond measure. His uncle was asleep on the sofa; on a small table at the head of the sofa a lamp was burning low, and by it stood the old man's small tin cash-box, closed. Near the box was a pile of bank-notes and a piece of paper covered with figures in pencil. The safe-door was not open. Evidently the sleeper had wearied himself with work upon his finances, and was taking a rest.

Tom set his candle on the stairs, and began to make his way toward the pile of notes, stooping low as he went. When he was passing his uncle, the old man stirred in his sleep, and Tom stopped instantly—stopped, and softly drew the knife from its sheath, with his heart thumping, and his eyes fastened upon his benefactor's face. After a moment or two he ventured forward again—one step—reached for his prize and seized it, dropping the knife-sheath. Then he felt the old man's strong grip upon him, and a wild cry of "Help! help!" rang in his ear. Without hesitation he drove the knife home—and was free. Some of the notes escaped from his left hand and fell in the blood on the floor. He dropped the knife and snatched them up and started to fly; transferred them to his left hand, and seized the knife again, in his fright and confusion, but remembered himself and flung it from him, as being a dangerous witness to carry away with him.

He jumped for the stair-foot, and closed the door behind him; and as he snatched his candle and fled upward, the stillness of the night was broken by the sound of urgent footsteps approaching the house. In another moment he was in his room and the twins were standing aghast over the body of the murdered man!

Tom put on his coat, buttoned his hat under it, threw on his suit of girl's clothes, dropped the veil, blew out his light, locked the room door by which he had just entered, taking the key, passed through his other door into the back hall, locked that door and kept the key, then worked his way along in the dark and descended the back stairs. He was not expecting to meet anybody, for all interest was centered in the other part of the house, now; his calculation proved correct. By the time he was passing through the backyard, Mrs. Pratt, her servants, and a dozen half-dressed neighbors had joined the twins and the dead, and accessions were still arriving at the front door.

As Tom, quaking as with a palsy, passed out at the gate, three women came flying from the house on the opposite side of the lane. They rushed by him and in at the gate, asking him what the trouble was there, but not waiting for an answer. Tom said to himself, "Those old maids waited to dress—they did the same thing the night Stevens's house burned down next door." In a few minutes he was in the haunted house. He lighted a candle and took off his girl-clothes. There was blood on him all down his left side, and his right hand was red with the stains of the blood-soaked notes which he had crushed in it; but otherwise he was free from this sort of evidence. He cleansed his hand on the straw, and cleaned most of the smut from his face. Then he burned his male and female attire to ashes, scattered the ashes, and put on a disguise proper for a tramp. He blew out his light, went below, and was soon loafing down the river road with the intent to borrow and use one of Roxy's devices. He found a canoe and paddled off down-stream, setting the canoe adrift as dawn approached, and making his way by land to the next village, where he kept out of sight till a transient steamer came along, and then took deck passage for St. Louis. He was ill at

113

ease until Dawson's Landing was behind him; then he said to himself, "All the detectives on earth couldn't trace me now; there's not a vestige of a clue left in the world; that homicide will take its place with the permanent mysteries, and people won't get done trying to guess out the secret of it for fifty years."

In St. Louis, next morning, he read this brief telegram in the papers—dated at Dawson's Landing:

Judge Driscoll, an old and respected citizen, was assassinated here about midnight by a profligate Italian nobleman or barber on account of a quarrel growing out of the recent election. The assassin will probably be lynched.

"One of the twins!" soliloquized Tom; "how lucky! It is the knife that has done him this grace. We never know when fortune is trying to favor us. I actually cursed Pudd'nhead Wilson in my heart for putting it out of my power to sell that knife. I take it back, now."

Tom was now rich and independent. He arranged with the planter, and mailed to Wilson the new bill of sale which sold Roxana to herself; then he telegraphed his Aunt Pratt:

Have seen the awful news in the papers and am almost prostrated with grief. Shall start by packet to-day. Try to bear up till I come.

When Wilson reached the house of mourning and had gathered such details as Mrs. Pratt and the rest of the crowd could tell him, he took command as mayor, and gave orders that nothing should be touched, but everything left as it was until Justice Robinson should arrive and take the proper measures as coroner. He cleared everybody out of the room but the twins and himself. The sheriff soon arrived and took the twins away to jail. Wilson told them to keep heart, and promised to do his best in their defense when the case should come to trial. Justice Robinson came presently, and with him Constable Blake. They examined the room thoroughly. They found the knife and the sheath. Wilson noticed that there were finger-prints on the knife-handle. That pleased him, for the twins had required the earliest comers to make a scrutiny of their hands and clothes, and neither these people nor Wilson himself had found any blood-stains upon them. Could there be a possibility that the twins had spoken the truth when they said they found the man dead when they ran into the house in answer to the cry for help? He thought of that mysterious girl at once. But this was not the sort of work for a girl to be engaged in. No matter; Tom Driscoll's room must be examined.

After the coroner's jury had viewed the body and its surroundings, Wilson suggested a search up-stairs, and he went along. The jury forced an entrance to Tom's room, but found nothing, of course.

The coroner's jury found that the homicide was committed by Luigi, and that Angelo was accessory to it.

The town was bitter against the unfortunates, and for the first few days after the murder they were in constant danger of being lynched. The grand jury presently indicted Luigi for murder in the first degree, and Angelo as accessory before the fact. The twins were transferred from the city jail to the county prison to await trial.

Wilson examined the finger-marks on the knife-handle and said to himself, "Neither of the twins made those marks." Then manifestly there was another person concerned, either in his own interest or as hired assassin.

But who could it be? That, he must try to find out. The safe was not open, the cash-box was closed, and had three thousand dollars in it. Then robbery was not the motive, and revenge was. Where had the murdered man an enemy except Luigi? There was but that one person in the world with a deep grudge against him.

The mysterious girl! The girl was a great trial to Wilson. If the motive had been robbery, the girl might answer; but there wasn't any girl that would want to take this old man's life for revenge. He had no quarrels with girls; he was a gentleman.

Wilson had perfect tracings of the finger-marks of the knife-handle; and among his glass-records he had a great array of the finger-prints of women and girls, collected during the last fifteen or eighteen years, but he scanned them in vain, they successfully withstood every test; among them were no duplicates of the prints on the knife.

The presence of the knife on the stage of the murder was a worrying circumstance for Wilson. A week previously he had as good as admitted to himself that he believed Luigi had possessed such a knife, and that he still possessed it notwithstanding his pretense that it had been stolen. And now here was the knife, and with it the twins. Half the town had said the twins were humbugging when they claimed that they had lost their knife, and now these people were joyful, and said, "I told you so!"

If their finger-prints had been on the handle—but it was useless to bother any further about that; the finger-prints on the handle were *not* theirs—that he knew perfectly.

Wilson refused to suspect Tom; for first, Tom couldn't murder anybody—he hadn't character enough; secondly, if he could murder a person he wouldn't select his doting benefactor and nearest relative; thirdly, self-interest was in the way; for while the uncle lived, Tom was sure of a free support and a chance to get the destroyed will revived again, but with the uncle gone, that chance was gone, too. It was true the will had really been revived, as was now discovered, but Tom could not have been aware of it, or he would have spoken of it, in his native talky, unsecretive way. Finally, Tom was in St. Louis when the murder was done, and got the news out of the morning journals, as was shown by his telegram to his aunt. These speculations were unemphasized sensations rather than articulated thoughts, for Wilson would have laughed at the idea of seriously connecting Tom with the murder.

Wilson regarded the case of the twins as desperate—in fact, about hopeless. For he argued that if a confederate was not found, an enlightened Missouri jury would hang them, sure; if a confederate was found, that would not improve the matter, but simply furnish one more person for the sheriff to hang. Nothing could save the twins but the discovery of a person who did the murder on his sole personal account—an undertaking which had all the aspect of the impossible. Still, the person who made the finger-prints must be sought. The twins might have no case *with* him, but they certainly would have none without him.

So Wilson mooned around, thinking, thinking, guessing, guessing, day and night, and arriving nowhere. Whenever he ran across a girl or a woman he was not acquainted with, he got her finger-prints, on one pretext or another; and they always cost him a sigh when he got home, for they never tallied with the finger-marks on the knife-handle.

As to the mysterious girl, Tom swore he knew no such girl, and did not remember ever seeing a girl wearing a dress like the one described by Wilson. He admitted that he did not always lock his room, and that sometimes the servants forgot to lock the house doors; still, in his opinion the girl must have made but few visits or she would have been discovered. When Wilson tried to connect her with the stealing-raid, and thought she might have been the old woman's confederate, if not the very thief herself disguised as an old woman, Tom seemed struck, and also much interested, and said he would keep a sharp eye out for this person or persons, although he was afraid that she or they would be too smart to venture again into a town where everybody would now be on the watch for a good while to come.

Everybody was pitying Tom, he looked so quiet and sorrowful, and seemed to feel his great loss so deeply. He was playing a part, but it was not all a part. The picture of his alleged uncle, as he had last seen him, was before him in the dark pretty frequently, when he was awake, and called again in his dreams, when he was asleep. He wouldn't go into the room where the tragedy had happened. This charmed the doting Mrs. Pratt, who realized now, "as she had never done before," she said, what a sensitive and delicate nature her darling had, and how he adored his poor uncle.

CHAPTER XX

Even the clearest and most perfect circumstantial evidence is likely to be at fault, after all, and therefore ought to be received with great caution. Take the case of any pencil, sharpened by any woman: if you have witnesses, you will find she did it with a knife; but if you take simply the aspect of the pencil, you will say she did it with her teeth.—*Pudd'nhead Wilson's Calendar.*

The weeks dragged along, no friend visiting the jailed twins but their counsel and Aunt Patsy Cooper, and the day of trial came at last—the heaviest day in Wilson's life; for with all his tireless diligence he had discovered no sign or trace of the missing confederate. "Confederate" was the term he had long ago privately accepted for that person—not as being unquestionably the right term, but as being at least possibly the right one, though he was never able to understand why the twins did not vanish and escape, as the confederate had done, instead of remaining by the murdered man and getting caught there.

The court-house was crowded, of course, and would remain so to the finish, for not only in the town itself, but in the country for miles around, the trial was the one topic of conversation among the people. Mrs. Pratt, in deep mourning, and Tom with a weed on his hat, had seats near Pembroke Howard, the public prosecutor, and back of them sat a great array of friends of the family. The twins had but one friend present to keep their counsel in countenance, their poor old sorrowing landlady. She sat near Wilson, and looked her friendliest. In the "nigger corner" sat Chambers; also Roxy, with good clothes on, and her bill of sale in her pocket. It was her most precious possession, and she never parted with it, day or night. Tom had allowed her thirty-five dollars a month ever since he came into his property, and had said that he and she ought to be grateful to the twins for making them rich; but had roused such a temper in her by this speech that he did not repeat the argument afterward. She said the old Judge had treated her child a thousand times better than he deserved, and had never done her an unkindness in his life; so she hated these outlandish devils for killing him, and shouldn't ever sleep satisfied till she saw them hanged for it. She was here to watch the trial, now, and was going to lift up just one "hooraw" over it if the County Judge put her in jail a year for it. She gave her turbaned head a toss and said, "When dat ver-dic' comes, I's gwine to lif' dat *roof,* now, I *tell* you."

Pembroke Howard briefly sketched the State's case. He said he would show by a chain of circumstantial evidence without break or fault in it anywhere, that the principal prisoner at the bar committed the murder; that the motive was partly revenge, and partly a desire to take his own life out of jeopardy, and that his brother, by his presence, was a consenting accessory to the crime; a crime which was the basest known to the calendar of human misdeeds—assassination; that it was conceived by the blackest of hearts and consummated by the cowardliest of hands; a crime which had broken a loving sister's heart, blighted the happiness of a young nephew who was as dear as a son, brought inconsolable grief to many friends, and sorrow and loss to the whole community. The utmost penalty of the outraged law would be exacted, and upon the accused, now present at the bar, that penalty would unquestionably be executed. He would reserve further remark until his closing speech.

He was strongly moved, and so also was the whole house; Mrs. Pratt and several other women were weeping when he sat down, and many an eye that was full of hate was riveted upon the unhappy prisoners.

Witness after witness was called by the State, and questioned at length; but the cross-questioning was brief. Wilson knew they could furnish nothing valuable for his side. People were sorry for Pudd'nhead; his budding career would get hurt by this trial.

Several witnesses swore they heard Judge Driscoll say in his public speech that the twins would be able to find their lost knife again when they needed it to assassinate somebody with. This was not news, but now it was seen to have been sorrowfully pro-phetic, and a profound sensation quivered through the hushed court-room when those dismal words were repeated.

The public prosecutor rose and said that it was within his knowledge, through a conversation held with Judge Driscoll on the last day of his life, that counsel for the defense had brought him a challenge from the person charged at this bar with murder; that he had refused to fight with a confessed assassin—"that is, on the field of honor," but had added significantly, that he would be ready for him elsewhere. Presumably the per-son here charged with murder was warned that he must kill or be killed the first time he should meet Judge Driscoll. If counsel for the defense chose to let the statement stand so, he would not call him to the witness stand. Mr. Wilson said he would offer no denial. [Murmurs in the house—"It is getting worse and worse for Wilson's case."]

Mrs. Pratt testified that she heard no outcry, and did not know what woke her up, unless it was the sound of rapid footsteps approaching the front door. She jumped up and ran out in the hall just as she was, and heard the footsteps flying up the front steps and then following behind her as she ran to the sitting-room. There she found the accused standing over her murdered brother. [Here she broke down and sobbed. Sensation in the court.] Resuming, she said the persons entering behind her were Mr. Rogers and Mr. Buckstone.

Cross-examined by Wilson, she said the twins proclaimed their innocence; declared that they had been taking a walk, and had hurried to the house in response to a cry for help which was so loud and strong that they had heard it at a considerable distance; that they begged her and the gentlemen just mentioned to examine their hands and clothes—which was done, and no blood stains found.

Confirmatory evidence followed from Rogers and Buckstone.

The finding of the knife was verified, the advertisement minutely describing it and offering a reward for it was put in evidence, and its exact correspondence with that description proved. Then followed a few minor details, and the case for the State was closed.

Wilson said that he had three witnesses, the Misses Clarkson, who would testify that they met a veiled young woman leaving Judge Driscoll's premises by the back gate a few minutes after the cries for help were heard, and that their evidence, taken with certain circumstantial evidence which he would call the court's attention to, would in his opinion convince the court that there was still one person concerned in this crime who had not yet been found, and also that a stay of proceedings ought to be granted, in justice to his clients, until that person should be discovered. As it was late, he would ask leave to defer the examination of his three witnesses until the next morning.

The crowd poured out of the place and went flocking away in excited groups and couples, talking the events of the session over with vivacity and consuming interest, and everybody seemed to have had a satisfactory and enjoyable day except the accused, their counsel, and their old-lady friend. There was no cheer among these, and no substantial hope.

In parting with the twins Aunt Patsy did attempt a good-night with a gay pretense of hope and cheer in it, but broke down without finishing.

Absolutely secure as Tom considered himself to be, the opening solemnities of the trial had nevertheless oppressed him with a vague uneasiness, his being a nature sensitive to even the smallest alarms; but from the moment that the poverty and weakness of Wilson's case lay exposed to the court, he was comfortable once more, even jubilant. He left the court-room sarcastically sorry for Wilson. "The Clarksons met an unknown woman in the back lane," he said to himself—*"that* is his case! I'll give him a century to find her in—a couple of them if he likes. A woman who doesn't exist any longer, and the clothes that gave her her sex burnt up and the ashes thrown away—oh, certainly, he'll find *her* easy enough!" This reflection set him to admiring, for the hundredth time, the shrewd ingenuities by which he had insured himself against detection—more, against even suspicion.

"Nearly always in cases like this there is some little detail or other overlooked, some wee little track or trace left behind, and detection follows; but here there's not even the faintest suggestion of a trace left. No more than a bird leaves when it flies through the air—yes, through the night, you may say. The man that can track a bird through the air in the dark and find that bird is the man to track me out and find the Judge's assassin— no other need apply. And that is the job that has been laid out for poor Pudd'nhead Wilson, of all people in the world! Lord, it will be pathetically funny to see him grubbing and groping after that woman that don't exist, and the right person sitting under his very nose all the time!" The more he thought the situation over, the more the humor of it struck him. Finally he said, "I'll never let him hear the last of that woman. Every time I catch him in company, to his dying day, I'll ask him in the guileless affectionate way that used to gavel him so when I inquired how his unborn law-business was coming along, 'Got on her track yet— hey, Pudd'nhead?' " He wanted to laugh, but that would not have answered; there were people about, and he was mourning for his uncle. He made up his mind that it would be good entertainment to look in on Wilson that night and watch him worry over his barren law-case and goad him with an exasperating word or two of sympathy and commiseration now and then.

Wilson wanted no supper, he had no appetite. He got out all the finger-prints of girls and women in his collection of records and pored gloomily over them an hour or more, trying to convince himself that that troublesome girl's marks were there somewhere and had been overlooked. But it was not so. He drew back his chair, clasped his hands over his head, and gave himself up to dull and arid musings.

Tom Driscoll dropped in, an hour after dark, and said with a pleasant laugh as he took a seat—

"Hello, we've gone back to the amusements of our days of neglect and obscurity for consolation, have we?" and he took up one of the glass strips and held it against the light to inspect it. "Come, cheer up, old man; there's no use in losing your grip and going back to this child's-play merely because this big sunspot is drifting across your shiny new disk. It'll pass, and you'll be all right again,"—and he laid the glass down. "Did you think you could win always?"

"Oh, no," said Wilson, with a sigh, "I didn't expect that, but I can't believe Luigi killed your uncle, and I feel very sorry for him. It makes me blue. And you would feel as I do, Tom, if you were not prejudiced against those young fellows."

"I don't know about that," and Tom's countenance darkened, for his memory reverted to his kicking; "I owe them no good will, considering the brunette one's treatment of me that night. Prejudice or no prejudice, Pudd'nhead, I don't like them, and when they get their deserts you're not going to find me sitting on the mourner's bench."

He took up another strip of glass, and exclaimed—

"Why, here's old Roxy's label! Are you going to ornament the royal palaces with nigger paw-marks, too? By the date here, I was seven months old when this was done, and she was nursing me and her little nigger cub. There's a line straight across her thumb-print. How comes that?" and Tom held out the piece of glass to Wilson.

"That is common," said the bored man, wearily. "Scar of a cut or a scratch, usually"—and he took the strip of glass indifferently, and raised it toward the lamp.

All the blood sunk suddenly out of his face; his hand quaked, and he gazed at the polished surface before him with the glassy stare of a corpse.

"Great Heavens, what's the matter with you, Wilson? Are you going to faint?"

Tom sprang for a glass of water and offered it, but Wilson shrank shuddering from him and said—

"No, no!—take it away!" His breast was rising and falling, and he moved his head about in a dull and wandering way, like a person who has been stunned. Presently he said, "I shall feel better when I get to bed; I have been overwrought to-day; yes, and over worked for many days."

"Then I'll leave you and let you to get to your rest. Goodnight, old man." But as Tom went out he couldn't deny himself a small parting gibe: "Don't take it so hard; a body can't win every time; you'll hang somebody yet."

Wilson muttered to himself, "It is no lie to say I am sorry I have to begin with you, miserable dog though you are!"

He braced himself up with a glass of cold whisky, and went to work again. He did not compare the new finger-marks unintentionally left by Tom a few minutes before on Roxy's glass with the tracings of the marks left on the knife-handle, there being no need of that (for his trained eye), but busied himself with another matter, muttering from time to time, "Idiot that I was!—Nothing but a *girl* would do me—a man in girl's clothes never occurred to me." First, he hunted out the plate containing the finger-prints made by Tom when he was twelve years old, and laid it by itself; then he brought forth the marks made by Tom's baby fingers when he was a suckling of seven months, and placed these two plates with the one containing this subject's newly (and unconsciously) made record.

"Now the series is complete," he said with satisfaction, and sat down to inspect these things and enjoy them.

But his enjoyment was brief. He stared a considerable time at the three strips, and seemed stupefied with astonishment. At last he put them down and said, "I can't make it out at all—hang it, the baby's don't tally with the others!"

He walked the floor for half an hour puzzling over his enigma, then he hunted out two other glass plates.

He sat down and puzzled over these things a good while, but kept muttering, "It's no use; I can't understand it. They don't tally right, and yet I'll swear the names and dates are right, and so of course they *ought* to tally. I never labeled one of these things carelessly in my life. There is a most extraordinary mystery here."

He was tired out, now, and his brains were beginning to clog. He said he would sleep himself fresh, and then see what he could do with this riddle. He slept through a troubled and unrestful hour, then unconsciousness began to shred away, and presently he rose drowsily to a sitting posture. "Now what was that dream?" he said, trying to recall it; "what was that dream?—it seemed to unravel that puz—"

He landed in the middle of the floor at a bound, without finishing the sentence, and ran and turned up his light and seized his "records." He took a single swift glance at them and cried out—

"It's so! Heavens, what a revelation! And for twenty-three years no man has ever suspected it!"

CHAPTER XXI

He is useless on top of the ground; he ought to be under it, inspiring the cabbages.—Pudd'nhead Wilson's Calendar.

April 1. This is the day upon which we are reminded of what we are on the other three hundred and sixty-four.—*Pudd'nhead Wilson's Calendar.*

Wilson put on enough clothes for business purposes and went to work under a high pressure of steam. He was awake all over. All sense of weariness had been swept away by the invigorating refreshment of the great and hopeful discovery which he had made. He made fine and accurate reproductions of a number of his "records," and then enlarged them on a scale of ten to one with his pantograph. He did these pantograph enlargements on sheets of white cardboard, and made each individual line of the bewildering maze of whorls or curves or loops which constituted the "pattern," of a "record" stand out bold and black by rein-forcing it with ink. To the untrained eye the collection of delicate originals made by the human finger on the glass plates looked about alike; but when enlarged ten times they resembled the markings of a block of wood that has been sawed across the grain, and the dullest eye could detect at a glance, and at a distance of many feet, that no two of the patterns were alike. When Wilson had at last finished his tedious and difficult work, he arranged its results according to a plan in which a progressive order and sequence was a principal feature; then he added to the batch several pantograph enlargements which he had made from time to time in bygone years.

The night was spent and the day well advanced, now. By the time he had snatched a trifle of breakfast it was nine o'clock, and the court was ready to begin its sitting. He was in his place twelve minutes later with his "records."

Tom Driscoll caught a slight glimpse of the records, and nudged his nearest friend and said, with a wink, "Pudd'nhead's got a rare eye to business—thinks that as long as he can't win his case it's at least a noble good chance to advertise his palace-window decorations without any expense." Wilson was informed that his witnesses had been delayed, but would arrive presently; but he rose and said he should probably not have occasion to make use of their testimony. [An amused murmur ran through the room—"It's a clean backdown! he gives up without hitting a lick!"] Wilson continued—"I have other testimony—and bet-ter. [This compelled interest, and evoked murmurs of surprise that had a detectible ingredient of disappointment in them.] If I

123

seem to be springing this evidence upon the court, I offer as my justification for this, that I did not discover its existence until late last night, and have been engaged in examining and classifying it ever since, until half an hour ago. I shall offer it presently; but first I wish to say a few preliminary words.

"May it please the Court, the claim given the front place, the claim most persistently urged, the claim most strenuously and I may even say aggressively and defiantly insisted upon by the prosecution, is this—that the person whose hand left the blood-stained finger-prints upon the handle of the Indian knife is the person who committed the murder." Wilson paused, during several moments, to give impressiveness to what he was about to say, and then added tranquilly, *"We grant that claim."*

It was an electrical surprise. No one was prepared for such an admission. A buzz of astonishment rose on all sides, and people were heard to intimate that the overworked lawyer had lost his mind. Even the veteran judge, accustomed as he was to legal ambushes and masked batteries in criminal procedure, was not sure that his ears were not deceiving him, and asked counsel what it was he had said. Howard's impassive face betrayed no sign, but his attitude and bearing lost something of their careless confidence for a moment. Wilson resumed:

"We not only grant that claim, but we welcome it and strongly endorse it. Leaving that matter for the present, we will now proceed to consider other points in the case which we propose to establish by evidence, and shall include that one in the chain in its proper place."

He had made up his mind to try a few hardy guesses, in mapping out his theory of the origin and motive of the murder—guesses designed to fill up gaps in it—guesses which could help if they hit, and would probably do no harm if they didn't.

"To my mind, certain circumstances of the case before the court seem to suggest a motive for the homicide quite different from the one insisted on by the State. It is my conviction that the motive was not revenge, but robbery. It has been urged that the presence of the accused brothers in that fatal room, just after notification that one of them must take the life of Judge Driscoll or lose his own the moment the parties should meet, clearly signifies that the natural instinct of self-preservation moved my clients to go there secretly and save Count Luigi by destroying his adversary.

"Then why did they stay there, after the deed was done? Mrs. Pratt had time, although she did not hear the cry for help, but woke up some moments later, to run to that room—and there she found these men standing and making no effort to escape. If they were guilty, they ought to have been running out of the house at the same time that she was running to that room. If they had had such a strong instinct toward self-preservation as to move them to kill that unarmed man, what had become of it now, when it should have been more alert than ever? Would any of us have remained there? Let us not slander our intelligence to that degree.

"Much stress has been laid upon the fact that the accused offered a very large reward for the knife with which this murder was done; that no thief came forward to claim that extraordinary reward; that the latter fact was good circumstantial evidence that the claim that the knife had been stolen was a vanity and a fraud; that these details taken in connection with the memorable and apparently prophetic speech of the deceased concerning that knife, and the final discovery of that very knife in the fatal room where no living person was found present with the slaughtered man but the owner of the knife and his brother, form an indestructible chain of evidence which fixes the crime upon those unfortunate strangers.

"But I shall presently ask to be sworn, and shall testify that there was a large reward offered for the *thief,* also; that it was offered secretly and not advertised; that this fact was indiscreetly mentioned—or at least tacitly admitted—in what was supposed to be safe circumstances, but may *not* have been. The thief may have been present himself. [Tom Driscoll had been looking at the speaker, but dropped his eyes at this point.] In that case he would retain the knife in his possession, not daring to offer it for sale, or for pledge in a pawn-show. [There was a nodding of heads among the audience by way of admission that this was not a bad stroke.] I shall prove to the satisfaction of the jury that there *was* a person in Judge Driscoll's room several minutes before the accused entered it. [This produced a strong sensation; the last drowsy-head in the court-room roused up, now, and made preparation to listen.] If it shall seem necessary, I will prove by the Misses Clarkson that they met a veiled person— ostensibly a woman—coming out of the back gate a few minutes after the cry for help was heard. This person was not a woman, but a man dressed in woman's clothes." Another sensation. Wilson had his eye on Tom when he hazarded this guess, to see what effect it would produce. He was satisfied with the result, and said to himself, "It was a success—he's hit!"

"The object of that person in that house was robbery, not murder. It is true that the safe was not open, but there was an ordinary tin cash-box on the table, with three thousand dollars in it. It is easily supposable that the thief was concealed in the house; that he knew of this box, and of its owner's habit of counting its contents and arranging his accounts at night—if he had that habit, which I do not assert, of course;—that he tried to take the box while its owner slept, but made a noise and was seized, and had to use the knife to save himself from capture; and that he fled without his booty because he heard help coming.

"I have now done with my theory, and will proceed to the evidences by which I propose to try to prove its soundness." Wilson took up several of his strips of glass. When the audience recognized these familiar mementoes of Pudd'nhead's old-time childish "puttering" and folly, the tense and funereal interest vanished out of their faces, and the house burst into volleys of relieving and refreshing laughter, and Tom chirked up and joined in the fun himself; but Wilson was apparently not disturbed. He arranged his records on the table before him, and said—

"I beg the indulgence of the court while I make a few remarks in explanation of some evidence which I am about to introduce, and which I shall presently ask to be allowed to verify under oath on the witness stand. Every human being carries with him from his cradle to his grave certain physical marks which do not change their character, and by which he can always be identified—and that without shade of doubt or question. These marks are his signature, his physiological autograph, so to speak, and this autograph can not be counterfeited, nor can he disguise it or hide it away, nor can it become illegible by the wear and mutations of time. This signature is not his face—age can change that beyond recognition; it is not his hair, for that can fall out; it is not his height, for duplicates of that exist; it is not his form, for duplicates of that exist also, whereas this signature is each man's very own—there is no duplicate of it among the swarming populations of the globe! [The audience was interested once more.]

"This autograph consists of the delicate lines or corrugations with which Nature marks the insides of the hands and the soles of the feet. If you will look at the balls of your fingers,—you that have very sharp eyesight,—you will observe that these dainty curving lines lie close together, like those that indicate the borders of oceans in maps, and that they form various clearly defined patterns, such as arches, circles, long curves, whorls, etc., and that these patterns differ on the different fingers. [Every man in the room had his hand up to the light, now, and his head canted to one side, and was minutely scrutinizing the balls of his fingers; there were whispered ejaculations of "Why, it's so—I never noticed that before!"] The patterns on the right hand are not the same as those on the left. [Ejaculations of "Why, that's so, too!"] Taken finger for finger, your patterns differ from your neighbor's. [Comparisons were made all over the house—even the judge and jury were absorbed in this curious work.] The patterns of a twin's right hand are not the same as those on his left. One twin's patterns are never the same as his fellow-twin's patterns—the jury will find that the patterns upon the finger-balls of the accused follow this rule. [An examination of the twins' hands was begun at once.] You have often heard of twins who were so exactly alike that when dressed alike their own parents could not tell them apart. Yet there was never a twin born into this world that did not carry from birth to death a sure identifier in this mysterious and marvelous natal autograph. That once known to you, his fellow-twin could never personate him and deceive you."

Wilson stopped and stood silent. Inattention dies a quick and sure death when a speaker does that. The stillness gives warning that something is coming. All palms and finger-balls went down, now, all slouching forms straightened, all heads came up, all eyes were fastened upon Wilson's face. He waited yet one, two, three moments, to let his pause complete and perfect its spell upon the house; then, when through the profound hush he could hear the ticking of the clock on the wall, he put out his hand and took the Indian knife by the blade and held it aloft where all could see the sinister spots upon its ivory handle; then he said, in a level and passionless voice—

"Upon this haft stands the assassin's natal autograph, written in the blood of that helpless and unoffending old man who loved you and whom you all loved. There is but one man in the whole earth whose hand can duplicate that crimson sign,"—he paused and raised his eyes to the pendulum swinging back and forth,—"and please God we will produce that man in this room before the clock strikes noon!"

Stunned, distraught, unconscious of its own movement, the house half rose, as if expecting to see the murderer appear at the door, and a breeze of muttered ejaculations swept the place. "Order in the court!—sit down!" This from the sheriff. He was obeyed, and quiet reigned again. Wilson stole a glance at Tom, and said to himself, "He is flying signals of distress, now; even people who despise him are pitying him; they think this is a hard ordeal for a young fellow who has lost his benefactor by so cruel a stroke—and they are right." He resumed his speech:

"For more than twenty years I have amused my compulsory leisure with collecting these curious physical signatures in this town. At my house I have hundreds upon hundreds of them. Each and every one is labelled with name and date; not labelled the next day or even the next hour, but in the very minute that the impression was taken. When I go upon the witness stand I will repeat under oath the things which I am now saying. I have the finger-prints of the court, the sheriff, and every member of the jury. There is hardly a person in this room, white or black, whose natal signature I cannot produce, and not one of them can so disguise himself that I cannot pick him out from a multitude of his fellow-creatures and unerringly identify him by his hands. And if he and I should live to be a hundred I could still do it. [The interest of the audience was steadily deepening, now.]

"I have studied some of these signatures so much that I know them as well as the bank cashier knows the autograph of his oldest customer. While I turn my back now, I beg that several persons will be so good as to pass their fingers through their hair, and then press them upon one of the panes of the window near the jury, and that among them the accused may set *their* finger-marks. Also, I beg that these experimenters, or others, will set their finger-marks upon another pane, and add again the marks of the accused, but not placing them in the same order or relation to the other signatures as before—for, by one chance in a million, a person might happen upon the right marks by pure guess-work *once,* therefore I wish to be tested twice."

He turned his back, and the two panes were quickly covered with delicately-lined oval spots, but visible only to such persons as could get a dark background for them—the foliage of a tree, outside, for instance. Then, upon call, Wilson went to the window, made his examination and said—

"This is Count Luigi's right hand; this one, three signatures below, is his left. Here is Count Angelo's right; down here is his left. Now for the other pane: here and here are his brother's." He faced about. "Am I right?"

A deafening explosion of applause was the answer. The Bench said—

"This certainly approaches the miraculous!"

Wilson turned to the window again and remarked, pointing with his finger—

"This is the signature of Mr. Justice Robinson. [Applause.] This, of Constable Blake. [Applause.] This, of John Mason, juryman. [Applause.] This, of the sheriff. [Applause.] I cannot name the others, but I have them all at home, named and dated, and could identify them all by my finger-print records."

He moved to his place through a storm of applause—which the sheriff stopped, and also made the people sit down, for they were all standing and struggling to see, of course. Court, jury, sheriff, and everybody had been too absorbed in observing Wilson's performance to attend to the audience earlier.

"Now, then," said Wilson, "I have here the natal autographs of two children—thrown up to ten times the natural size by the pantograph, so that any one who can see at all can tell the markings apart at a glance. We will call the children A and B. Here are A's finger-marks, taken at the age of five months. Here they are again, taken at seven months. [Tom started.] They are alike, you see. Here are B's at five months, and also at seven months. They, too, exactly copy each other, but the patterns are quite different from A's, you observe. I shall refer to these again presently, but we will turn them face down, now.

"Here, thrown up ten sizes, are the natal autographs of the two persons who are here before you accused of murdering Judge Driscoll. I made these pantograph copies last night, and will so swear when I go upon the witness stand. I ask the jury to compare them with the finger-marks of the accused upon the window panes, and tell the court if they are the same."

He passed a powerful magnifying-glass to the foreman.

One juryman after another took the cardboard and the glass and made the comparison. Then the foreman said to the judge—

"Your honor, we are all agreed that they are identical."

Wilson said to the foreman—

"Please turn that cardboard face down, and take this one, and compare it searchingly, by the magnifier, with the fatal signature upon the knife-handle, and report your finding to the court."

Again the jury made minute examinations, and again reported—

"We find them to be exactly identical, your honor."

Wilson turned toward the counsel for the prosecution, and there was a clearly recognizable note of warning in his voice when he said—

"May it please the court, the State has claimed, strenuously and persistently, that the blood-stained finger-prints upon that knife-handle were left there by the assassin of Judge Driscoll. You have heard us grant that claim, and welcome it." He turned to the jury: "Compare the finger-prints of the accused with the finger-prints left by the assassin—and report."

The comparison began. As it proceeded, all movement and all sound ceased, and the deep silence of an absorbed and waiting suspense settled upon the house; and when at last the words came—

"They do not even resemble," a thunder-crash of applause followed and the house sprang to its feet, but was quickly repressed by official force and brought to order again. Tom was altering his position every few minutes, now, but none of his changes brought repose nor any small trifle of comfort. When the house's attention was become fixed once more, Wilson said gravely, indicating the twins with a gesture—

"These men are innocent—I have no further concern with them. [Another outbreak of applause began, but was promptly checked.] We will now proceed to find the guilty. [Tom's eyes were starting from their sockets—yes, it was a cruel day for the bereaved youth, everybody thought.] We will return to the infant autographs of *A* and *B*. I will ask the jury to take these large pantograph facsimiles of *A's* marked five months and seven months. Do they tally?"

The foreman responded—

"Perfectly."

"Now examine this pantograph, taken at eight months, and also marked *A*. Does it tally with the other two?"

The surprised response was—

"No—they differ widely!"

"You are quite right. Now take these two pantographs of *B's* autograph, marked five months and seven months. Do they tally with each other?"

"Yes—perfectly."

"Take this third pantograph marked *B,* eight months. Does it tally with *B's* other two?"

"By no means!"

"Do you know how to account for those strange discrepancies? I will tell you. For a purpose unknown to us, but probably a selfish one, somebody changed those children in the cradle."

This produced a vast sensation, naturally; Roxana was astonished at this admirable guess, but not disturbed by it. To guess the exchange was one thing, to guess who did it quite another. Pudd'nhead Wilson could do wonderful things, no doubt, but he couldn't do impossible ones. Safe? She was perfectly safe. She smiled privately.

"Between the ages of seven months and eight months those children were changed in the cradle"—he made one of his effect-collecting pauses, and added—"and the person who did it is in this house!"

Roxy's pulses stood still! The house was thrilled as with an electric shock, and the people half rose as if to seek a glimpse of the person who had made that exchange. Tom was growing limp; the life seemed oozing out of him. Wilson resumed:

"*A* was put into *B's* cradle in the nursery; *B* was transferred to the kitchen and became a negro and a slave, [Sensation— confusion of angry ejaculations]—but within a quarter of an hour he will stand before you white and free! [Burst of applause, checked by the officers.] From seven months onward until now, *A* has still been a usurper, and in my finger-record he bears *B's* name. Here is his pantograph at the age of twelve. Compare it with the assassin's signature upon the knife-handle. Do they tally?"

The foreman answered—

"To the minutest detail!"

Wilson said, solemnly—

"The murderer of your friend and mine—York Driscoll of the generous hand and the kindly spirit—sits in among you. Valet de Chambre, negro and slave,—falsely called Thomas à Becket Driscoll,—make upon the window the finger-prints that will hang you!"

Tom turned his ashen face imploringly toward the speaker, made some impotent movements with his white lips, then slid limp and lifeless to the floor.

Wilson broke the awed silence with the words—

"There is no need. He has confessed."

Roxy flung herself upon her knees, covered her face with her hands, and out through her sobs the words struggled—

"De Lord have mercy on me, po' misable sinner dat I is!"

The clock struck twelve.

The court rose; the new prisoner, handcuffed, was removed.

CONCLUSION

It is often the case that the man who can't tell a lie thinks he is the best judge of one.—*Pudd'nhead Wilson's Calendar.*

October 12, the Discovery. It was wonderful to find America, but it would have been more wonderful to miss it.—*Pudd'nhead Wilson's Calendar.*

The town sat up all night to discuss the amazing events of the day and swap guesses as to when Tom's trial would begin. Troop after troop of citizens came to serenade Wilson, and require a speech, and shout themselves hoarse over every sentence that fell from his lips—for all his sentences were golden, now, all were marvelous. His long fight against hard luck and prejudice was ended; he was a made man for good.

And as each of these roaring gangs of enthusiasts marched away, some remorseful member of it was quite sure to raise his voice and say—

"And this is the man the likes of us have called a pudd'nhead for more than twenty years. He has resigned from that position, friends."

"Yes, but it isn't vacant—we're elected."

The twins were heroes of romance, now, and with rehabilitated reputations. But they were weary of Western adventure, and straightway retired to Europe.

Roxy's heart was broken. The young fellow upon whom she had inflicted twenty-three years of slavery continued the false heir's pension of thirty-five dollars a month to her, but her hurts were too deep for money to heal; the spirit in her eye was quenched, her martial bearing departed with it, and the voice of her laughter ceased in the land. In her church and its affairs she found her only solace.

The real heir suddenly found himself rich and free, but in a most embarrassing situation. He could neither read nor write, and his speech was the basest dialect of the negro quarter. His gait, his attitudes, his gestures, his bearing, his laugh—all were vulgar and uncouth; his manners were the manners of a slave. Money and fine clothes could not mend these defects or cover them up; they only made them the more glaring and the more pathetic. The poor fellow could not endure the terrors of the white man's parlor, and felt at home and at peace nowhere but in the kitchen. The family pew was a misery to him, yet he could nevermore enter into the solacing refuge of the "nigger gallery"—that was closed to him for good and all. But we cannot follow his curious fate further—that it would be a long story.

The false heir made a full confession and was sentenced to imprisonment for life. But now a complication came up. The Percy Driscoll estate was in such a crippled shape when its owner died that it could pay only sixty per cent of its great indebtedness, and was settled at that rate. But the creditors came forward, now, and complained that inasmuch as through an error for which *they* were in no way to blame the false heir was not inventoried at that time with the rest of the property, great wrong and loss had thereby been inflicted upon them. They rightly claimed that "Tom" was lawfully their property and had been so for eight years; that they had already lost sufficiently in being deprived of his services during that long period, and ought not to be required to add anything to that loss; that if he had been delivered up to them in the first place, they would have sold him and he could not have murdered Judge Driscoll; therefore it was not he that had really committed the murder, the guilt lay with the erroneous inventory. Everybody saw that there was reason in this. Everybody granted that if "Tom" were white and free it would be unquestionably right to punish him—it would be no loss to anybody; but to shut up a valuable slave for life—that was quite another matter.

As soon as the Governor understood the case, he pardoned Tom at once, and the creditors sold him down the river.

The Comedy Those Extraordinary Twins *was a story that, as Twain says, "got tangled together" with* Pudd'nhead Wilson *as his work on the novel progressed. "I pulled one of the stories out by the roots, and left the other one—a kind of literary Caesarean operation." The comedy that he had originally excised was thus given the subtitle "The Suppressed Farce" when it was published in one volume with* The Tragedy of Pudd'nhead Wilson *by the American Publishing Company in 1894.*

The Comedy
Those Extraordinary Twins

A man who is not born with the novel-writing gift has a troublesome time of it when he tries to build a novel. I know this from experience. He has no clear idea of his story; in fact he has no story. He merely has some people in his mind, and an incident or two, also a locality. He knows these people, he knows the selected locality, and he trusts that he can plunge those people into those incidents with interesting results. So he goes to work. To write a novel? No—that is a thought which comes later; in the beginning he is only proposing to tell a little tale; a very little tale; a six-page tale. But as it is a tale which he is not acquainted with, and can only find out what it is by listening as it goes along telling itself, it is more apt to go on and on and on till it spreads itself into a book. I know about this, because it has happened to me so many times.

And I have noticed another thing: that as the short tale grows into the long tale, the original intention (or motif) is apt to get abolished and find itself superseded by a quite different one. It was so in the case of a magazine sketch which I once started to write—a funny and fantastic sketch about a prince and a pauper; it presently assumed a grave cast of its own accord, and in that new shape spread itself out into a book. Much the same thing happened with "Pudd'nhead Wilson." I had a sufficiently hard time with that tale, because it changed itself from a farce to a tragedy while I was going along with it,—a most embarrassing circumstance. But what was a great deal worse was, that it was not one story, but two stories tangled together; and they obstructed and interrupted each other at every turn and created no end of confusion and annoyance. I could not offer the book for publication, for I was afraid it would unseat the reader's reason, I did not know what was the matter with it, for I had not noticed, as yet, that it was two stories in one. It took me months to make that discovery. I carried the manuscript back and forth across the Atlantic two or three times, and read it and studied over it on shipboard; and at last I saw where the difficulty lay. I had no further trouble. I pulled one of the stories out by the roots, and left the other one—a kind of literary Cæsarean operation.

Would the reader care to know something about the story which I pulled out? He has been told many a time how the born-and-trained novelist works; won't he let me round and complete his knowledge by telling him how the jack-leg does it?

Originally the story was called "Those Extraordinary Twins." I meant to make it very short. I had seen a picture of a youthful

135

Italian "freak"—or "freaks"—which was—or which were—on exhibition in our cities—a combination consisting of two heads and four arms joined to a single body and a single pair of legs—and I thought I would write an extravagantly fantastic little story with this freak of nature for hero—or heroes—a silly young Miss for heroine, and two old ladies and two boys for the minor parts. I lavishly elaborated these people and their doings, of course. But the tale kept spreading along, and other people got to intruding themselves and taking up more and more room with their talk and their affairs. Among them came a stranger named Pudd'nhead Wilson, and a woman named Roxana; and presently the doings of these two pushed up into prominence a young fellow named Tom Driscoll, whose proper place was away in the obscure background. Before the book was half finished those three were taking things almost entirely into their own hands and working the whole tale as a private venture of their own—a tale which they had nothing at all to do with, by rights.

When the book was finished and I came to look around to see what had become of the team I had originally started out with—Aunt Patsy Cooper, Aunt Betsy Hale, the two boys, and Rowena the light-weight heroine—they were nowhere to be seen; they had disappeared from the story some time or other. I hunted about and found them—found them stranded, idle, forgotten, and permanently useless. It was very awkward. It was awkward all around, but more particularly in the case of Rowena, because there was a lovematch on, between her and one of the twins that constituted the freak, and I had worked it up to a blistering heat and thrown in a quite dramatic love-quarrel, wherein Rowena scathingly denounced her betrothed for getting drunk, and scoffed at his explanation of how it had happened, and wouldn't listen to it, and had driven him from her in the usual "forever" way; and now here she sat crying and broken-hearted; for she had found that he had spoken only the truth; that it was not he, but the other half of the freak that had drunk the liquor that made him drunk; that her half was a prohibitionist and had never drunk a drop in his life, and although tight as a brick three days in the week, was wholly innocent of blame; and indeed, when sober, was constantly doing all he could to reform his brother, the other half, who never got any satisfaction out of drinking, anyway, because liquor never affected him. Yes, here she was, stranded with that deep injustice of hers torturing her poor torn heart.

I didn't know what to do with her. I was as sorry for her as anybody could be, but the campaign was over, the book was finished, she was side-tracked, and there was no possible way of crowding her in, anywhere. I could not leave her there, of course; it would not do. After spreading her out so, and making such a to-do over her affairs, it would be absolutely necessary to account to the reader for her. I thought and thought and studied and studied; but I arrived at nothing. I finally saw plainly that there was really no way but one—I must simply give her the grand bounce. It grieved me to do it, for after associating with her so much I had come to kind of like her after a fashion, notwithstanding she was such an ass and said such stupid, irritating things and was so nauseatingly sentimental. Still it had to be done. So at the top of Chapter XVII. I put a "Calendar" remark concerning July the Fourth, and began the chapter with this statistic:

"Rowena went out in the back yard after supper to see the fireworks and fell down the well and got drowned."

It seemed abrupt, but I thought maybe the reader wouldn't notice it, because I changed the subject right away to something else. Anyway it loosened up Rowena from where she was stuck and got her out of the way, and that was the main thing. It seemed a prompt good way of weeding out people that had got stalled, and a plenty good enough way for those others; so I hunted up the two boys and said "they went out back one night to stone the cat and fell down the well and got drowned." Next I searched around and found old Aunt Patsy Cooper and Aunt Betsy Hale where they were aground, and said "they went out back one night to visit the sick and fell down the well and got drowned." I was going to drown some of the others, but I gave up the idea, partly because I believed that if I kept that up it would arouse attention, and perhaps sympathy with those people, and partly because it was not a large well and would not hold any more anyway.

Still the story was unsatisfactory. Here was a set of new characters who are become inordinately prominent and who persisted in remaining so to the end; and back yonder was an older set who made a large noise and a great to-do for a little while and then suddenly played out utterly and fell down the well. There was a radical defect somewhere, and I must search it out and cure it.

The defect turned out to be the one already spoken of—two stories in one, a farce and a tragedy. So I pulled out the farce and left the tragedy. This left the original team in, but only as mere names, not as characters. Their prominence was wholly gone; they were not even worth drowning; so I removed that detail. Also I took those twins apart and made two separate men of them. They had no occasion to have foreign names now, but it was too much trouble to remove them all through, so I left them christened as they were and made no explanation.

The Suppressed Farce

CHAPTER I

The conglomerate twins were brought on the stage in Chapter I of the original extravaganza. Aunt Patsy Cooper has received their letter applying for board and lodging, and Rowena, her daughter, insane with joy, is begging for a hearing of it:

"Well, set down then, and be quiet a minute and don't fly around so; it fairly makes me tired to see you. It starts off so: 'HONORED MADAM—' "

"I like that, ma, don't you? It shows they're high-bred."

"Yes, I noticed that when I first read it. 'My brother and I have seen your advertisement, by chance, in a copy of your local journal——' "

"It's so beautiful and smooth, ma—don't you think so?"

"Yes, seems so to me—'and beg leave to take the room you offer. We are twenty-four years of age, and twins——' "

"Twins! How sweet! I do hope they are handsome, and I just know they are! Don't you hope they are, ma?"

"Land, I ain't particular. 'We are Italians by birth——' "

"It's so romantic! Just think—there's never been one in this town, and everybody will want to see them, and they're all *ours!* Think of that!"

"—'but have lived in the various countries of Europe, and several years in the United States.' "

"Oh, just think what wonders they've seen, ma! Won't it be good to hear them talk?"

"I reckon so; yes, I reckon so. 'Our names are Luigi and Angelo Capello——' "

"Beautiful, perfectly beautiful! Not like Jones and Robinson and those horrible names."

" 'You desire but one guest, but dear madam, if you will allow us to pay for two we will not discommode you. We will sleep together in the same bed. We have always been used to this, and prefer it.' And then he goes on to say they will be down Thursday."

"And this is Tuesday—I don't know how I'm ever going to wait, ma! The time does drag along so, and I'm so dying to see them! Which of them do you reckon is the tallest, ma?"

"How do you s'pose I can tell, child? Mostly they are the same size—twins are."

"Well then, which do you reckon is the best looking?"

"Goodness knows—I don't."

"I think Angelo is; it's the prettiest name, anyway. Don't you think it's a sweet name, ma?"

"Yes, it's well enough. I'd like both of them better if I knew the way to pronounce them—the Eyetalian way, I mean. The Missouri way and the Eyetalian way is different I judge."

"Maybe—yes. It's Luigi that writes the letter. What do you reckon is the reason Angelo didn't write it?"

"Why, how can I tell? What's the difference who writes it, so long as it's done?"

"Oh, I hope it wasn't because he is sick! You don't think he is sick, do you, ma?"

"Sick your granny; what's to make him sick?"

"Oh, there's never any telling. These foreigners with that kind of names are so delicate, and of course that kind of names are not suited to our climate—you wouldn't expect it."

[And so-on and so-on, no end. The time drags along; Thursday comes; the boat arrives in a pouring storm toward midnight.]

At last there was a knock at the door and the anxious family jumped to open it. Two negro men entered, each carrying a trunk, and proceeded up-stairs toward the guest-room. Then followed a stupefying apparition—a double-headed human creature with four arms, one body, and a single pair of legs!

It—or they, as you please—bowed with elaborate foreign formality, but the Coopers could not respond immediately; they were paralyzed. At this moment there came from the rear of the group a fervent ejaculation—"My lan'!"—followed by a crash of crockery, and the slave-wench Nancy stood petrified and staring, with a tray of wrecked tea-things at her feet. The incident broke the spell, and brought the family to consciousness. The beautiful heads of the new-comer bowed again, and one of them said with easy grace and dignity:

"I crave the honor, madam and miss, to introduce to you my brother, Count Luigi Capello," (the other head bowed) "and myself—Count Angelo; and at the same time offer sincere apologies for the lateness of our coming, which was unavoidable," and both heads bowed again.

The poor old lady was in a whirl of amazement and confusion, but she managed to stammer out:

"I'm sure I'm glad to make your acquaintance, sir—I mean, gentlemen. As for the delay, it is nothing, don't mention it. This is my daughter Rowena, sir—gentlemen. Please step into the parlor and sit down and have a bite and sup; you are dreadful wet and must be uncomfortable—both of you, I mean."

But to the old lady's relief they courteously excused themselves, saying it would be wrong to keep the family out of their beds longer; then each bowed in turn and uttered a friendly good-night, and the singular figure moved away in the wake of Rowena's small brothers, who bore candles, and disappeared up the stairs.

The widow tottered into the parlor and sank into the chair with a gasp, and Rowena followed, tongue-tied and dazed. The two sat silent in the throbbing summer heat unconscious of the million-voiced music of the mosquitoes, unconscious of the roaring gale, the lashing and thrashing of the rain along the windows and the roof, the white glare of the lightning, the tumultuous booming and bellowing of the thunder; conscious of nothing but that prodigy, that uncanny apparition that had come and gone so suddenly—that weird strange thing that was so soft-spoken and so gentle of manner and yet had shaken them up like an earthquake with the shock of its gruesome aspect. At last a cold little shudder quivered along down the widow's meager frame and she said in a weak voice:

"Ugh, it was awful—just the mere look of that phillipene!"

Rowena did not answer. Her faculties were still caked, she had not yet found her voice. Presently the widow said, a little resentfully:

"Always been *used* to sleeping together—in fact, *prefer* it. And I was thinking it was to accommodate me. I thought it was very good of them, whereas a person situated as that young man is——"

"Ma, you oughtn't to begin by getting up a prejudice against him. I'm sure he is good-hearted and means well. Both of his faces show it."

"I'm not so certain about that. The one on the left—I mean the one on *it's* left—hasn't near as good a face, in my opinion, as its brother."

"That's Luigi."

"Yes, Luigi; anyway it's the dark-skinned one; the one that was west of his brother when they stood in the door. Up to all kinds of mischief and disobedience when he was a boy, I'll be bound. I lay his mother had trouble to lay her hand on him when she wanted him. But the one on the right is as good as gold, I can see that."

"That's Angelo."

"Yes, Angelo, I reckon, though I can't tell t' other from which by their names, yet awhile. But it's the right-hand one—the blonde one. He has such kind blue eyes, and curly copper hair and fresh complexion——"

"And such a noble face!—oh, it *is* a noble face, ma, just royal, you may say! And beautiful—deary me, how beautiful! But both are that; the dark one's as beautiful as a picture. There's no such wonderful faces and handsome heads in this town——none that even begin. And such hands—especially Angelo's—so shapely and——"

"Stuff, how could you tell which they belonged to?—they had gloves on."

"Why, didn't I see them take off their hats?"

"That don't signify. They might have taken off each other's hats. Nobody could tell. There was just a wormy squirming of arms in the air—seemed to be a couple of dozen of them, all writhing at once, and it just made me dizzy to see them go."

"Why, ma, I hadn't any difficulty. There's two arms on each shoulder——"

"There, now. One arm on each shoulder belongs to each of the creatures, don't it? For a person to have two arms on one shoulder wouldn't do him any good, would it? Of course not. Each has an arm on each shoulder. Now then, you tell me which of them belongs to which, if you can. *They* don't know themselves—they just work whichever arm comes handy. Of course they do; especially if they are in a hurry and can't stop to think which belongs to which."

The mother seemed to have the rights of the argument, so the daughter abandoned the struggle. Presently the widow rose with a yawn and said:

"Poor thing. I hope it won't catch cold; it was powerful wet, just drenched, you may say. I hope it has left its boots outside, so they can be dried." Then she gave a little start, and looked perplexed. "Now I remember I heard one of them ask Joe to call him at half after seven—I think it was the one on the left—no, it was the one to the east of the other one—but I didn't hear the other one say anything. I wonder if he wants to be called too. Do you reckon it's too late to ask?"

"Why, ma, it's not necessary. Calling one is calling both. If one gets up, the other's *got* to."

"Sho, of course; I never thought of that. Well, come along, maybe we can get some sleep, but I don't know, I'm so shook up with what we've been through."

The stranger had made an impression on the boys, too. They

had a word of talk as they were getting to bed. Henry, the gentle, the humane, said:

"I feel ever so sorry for it, don't you, Joe?"

But Joe was a boy of this world, active, enterprising, and had a theatrical side to him:

"Sorry? Why, how you talk! It can't stir a step without attracting attention. It 's just grand!"

Henry said, reproachfully:

"Instead of pitying it, Joe, you talk as if——"

"Talk as if *what?* I know one thing mighty certain: if you can fix me so I can eat for two and only have to stub toes for one, I ain't going to fool away no such chance just for sentiment."

The twins were wet and tired, and they proceeded to undress without any preliminary remarks. The abundance of sleeves made the partnership-coat hard to get off, for it was like skinning a tarantula; but it came at last, after much tugging and perspiring. The mutual vest followed. Then the brothers stood up before the glass, and each took off his own cravat and collar. The collars were of the standing kind, and came high up under the ears, like the sides of a wheelbarrow, as required by the fashion of the day. The cravats were as broad as a bank bill, with fringed ends which stood far out to right and left like wings of a dragon-fly, and this also was strictly in accordance with the fashion of the time. Each cravat, as to color, was in perfect taste, so far as its owner's complexion was concerned—a delicate pink, in the case of the blonde brother, a violent scarlet in the case of the brunette—but as a combination they broke all the laws of taste known to civilization. Nothing more fiendish and irreconcilable than those shrieking and blaspheming colors could have been contrived. The wet boots gave no end of trouble—to Luigi. When they were off at last, Angelo said, with bitterness:

"I wish you wouldn't wear such tight boots, they hurt my feet."

Luigi answered with indifference:

"My friend, when I am in command of our body, I choose my apparel according to my own convenience, as I have remarked more than several times already. When you are in command, I beg you will do as you please."

Angelo was hurt, and the tears came into his eyes. There was gentle reproach in his voice, but not anger, when he replied:

"Luigi, I often consult your wishes, but you never consult mine. When I am in command I treat you as a guest; I try to make you feel at home; when you are in command you treat me as an intruder, you make me feel unwelcome. It embarrasses me cruelly in company, for I can see that people notice it and comment on it.''

"Oh, damn the people,'' responded the brother languidly, and with the air of one who is tired of the subject.

A slight shudder shook the frame of Angelo, but he said nothing and the conversation ceased. Each buttoned his own share of the night-shirt in silence; then Luigi, with Paine's "Age of Reason" in his hand, sat down in one chair and put his feet in another and lit his pipe, while Angelo took his "Whole Duty of Man," and both began to read. Angelo presently began to cough; his coughing increased and became mixed with gaspings for breath, and he was finally obliged to make an appeal to his brother's humanity:

"Luigi, if you would only smoke a little milder tobacco, I am sure I could learn not to mind it in time, but this is so strong, and the pipe is so rank that——"

"Angelo, I wouldn't be such a baby. I have learned to smoke in a week, and the trouble is already over with me; if you would try, you could learn too, and then you would stop spoiling my comfort with your everlasting complaints."

"Ah, brother, that is a strong word—everlasting—and isn't quite fair. I only complain when I suffocate; you know I don't complain when we are in the open air."

"Well, anyway, you could learn to smoke yourself."

"But my *principles,* Luigi, you forget my principles. You would not have me do a thing which I regard as a sin?"

"Oh, bosh!"

The conversation ceased again, for Angelo was sick and discouraged and strangling; but after some time he closed his book and asked Luigi to sing "From Greenland's Icy Mountains" with him, but he would not, and when he tried to sing by himself Luigi did his best to drown his plaintive tenor with a rude and rollicking song delivered in a thundering bass.

After the singing there was silence, and neither brother was happy. Before blowing the light out Luigi swallowed half a tumbler of whiskey, and Angelo, whose sensitive organization could not endure intoxicants of any kind, took a pill to keep it from giving him the headache.

CHAPTER II

The family sat in the breakfast-room waiting for the twins to come down. The widow was quiet, the daughter was all alive with happy excitement. She said:

"Ah, they're a boon, ma, just a boon! don't you think so?"

"Laws, I hope so, I don't know."

"Why, ma, yes you do. They're so fine and handsome, and high-bred and polite, so every way superior to our gawks here in this village; why, they'll make life different from what it was—so humdrum and commonplace, you know—oh, you may be sure they're full of accomplishments, and knowledge of the world, and all that, that will be an immense advantage to society here. Don't you think so, ma?"

"Mercy on me, how should I know, and I've hardly set eyes on them yet." After a pause she added, "They made considerable noise after they went up."

"Noise? Why, ma, they were singing! And it was beautiful, too."

"Oh, it was well enough, but too mixed-up, seemed to me."

"Now, ma, honor bright, did you ever hear 'Greenland's Icy Mountains' sung sweeter—now did you?"

"If it had been sung by itself, it would have been uncommon sweet, I don't deny it; but what they wanted to mix it up with 'Old Bob Ridley' for, I can't make out. Why, they don't go together at all. They are not of the same nature. 'Bob Ridley' is a common rackety slam-bang secular song, one of the rippingest and rantingest and noisiest there is. I am no judge of music, and I don't claim it, but in my opinion nobody can make those two songs go together right."

"Why, ma, I thought——"

"It don't make any difference what you thought, it can't be done. They tried it, and to my mind it was a failure. I never heard such a crazy uproar; seemed to me, sometimes, the roof would come off; and as for the cats—well, I've lived a many a year, and seen cats aggravated in more ways than one, but I've never seen cats take on the way they took on last night."

"Well, I don't think that that goes for anything, ma, because it is the nature of cats that any sound that is unusual——"

"Unusual! You may well call it so. Now if they are going to sing duets every night, I do hope they will both sing the same tune at the same time, for in my opinion a duet that is made up of two different tunes is a mistake; especially when the tunes ain't any kin to one another, that way."

"But, ma, I think it must be a foreign custom; and it must be right too, and the best way, because they have had every opportunity to know what is right, and it don't stand to reason that with their education they would do anything but what the highest musical authorities have sanctioned. You can't help but admit that, ma."

The argument was formidably strong; the old lady could not find any way around it; so, after thinking it over a while she gave in with a sigh of discontent, and admitted that the daughter's position was probably correct. Being vanquished, she had no mind to continue the topic at that disadvantage, and was about to seek a change when a change came of itself. A footstep was heard on the stairs, and she said:

"There—he's coming!"

"*They,* ma—you ought to say *they*—it's nearer right."

The new lodger, rather shoutingly dressed but looking superbly handsome, stepped with courtly carriage into the trim little breakfast-room and put out all his cordial arms at once, like one of those pocket-knives with a multiplicity of blades, and shook hands with the whole family simultaneously. He was so easy and pleasant and hearty that all embarrassment presently thawed away and disappeared, and a cheery feeling of friendliness and comradeship took its place. He—or preferably they—were asked to occupy the seat of honor at the foot of the table. They consented with thanks, and carved the beefsteak with one set of their hands while they distributed it at the same time with the other set.

"Will you have coffee, gentlemen, or tea?"

"Coffee for Luigi, if you please, madam, tea for me."

"Cream and sugar?"

"For me, yes, madam; Luigi takes his coffee black. Our natures differ a good deal from each other, and our tastes also."

The first time the negro girl Nancy appeared in the door and saw the two heads turned in opposite directions and both talking at once, then saw the commingling arms feed potatoes into one mouth and coffee into the other at the same time, she had to pause and pull herself out of a faintness that came over her; but after that she held her grip and was able to wait on the table with fair courage.

Conversation fell naturally into the customary grooves. It was a little jerky, at first, because none of the family could get smoothly through a sentence without a wobble in it here and a break there, caused by some new surprise in the way of attitude or gesture on the part of the twins. The weather suffered the most. The weather was all finished up and disposed of, as a subject, before the simple Missourians had gotten sufficiently wonted to the spectacle of one body feeding two heads to feel composed and reconciled in the presence of so bizarre a miracle. And even after everybody's mind became tranquilized there was still one slight distraction left: the hand that picked up a biscuit carried it to the wrong head, as often as any other way, and the wrong mouth devoured it. This was a puzzling thing, and marred the talk a little. It bothered the widow to such a degree that she presently dropped out of the conversation without knowing it, and fell to watching and guessing and talking to herself:

"Now that hand is going to take that coffee to—no, it's gone to the other mouth; I can't understand it; and now, here is the dark complected hand with a potato on its fork, I'll see what goes with it—there, the light complected head's got it, as sure as I live!" Finally Rowena said:

"Ma, what is the matter with you? Are you dreaming about something?"

The old lady came to herself and blushed; then she explained with the first random thing that came into her mind: "I saw Mr. Angelo take up Mr. Luigi's coffee, and I thought maybe he—sha'n't I give *you* a cup, Mr. Angelo?"

"Oh no, madam, I am very much obliged, but I never drink coffee, much as I would like to. You did see me take up Luigi's cup, it is true, but if you noticed, I didn't carry it to my mouth, but to his."

"Y—es, I thought you did. Did you mean to?"

"How?"

The widow was a little embarrassed again. She said:

"I don't know but what I'm foolish, and you mustn't mind; but you see, he got the coffee I was expecting to see you drink, and you got a potato that I thought he was going to get. So I thought it might be a mistake all around, and everybody getting what wasn't intended for him."

Both twins laughed and Luigi said:

"Dear madam, there wasn't any mistake. We are always helping each other that way. It is a great economy for us both; it saves time and labor. We have a system of signs which nobody can notice or understand but ourselves. If I am using both my hands and want some coffee, I make the sign and Angelo furnishes it to me; and you saw that when he needed a potato I delivered it."

"How convenient!"

"Yes, and often of the extremest value. Take the Mississippi boats, for instance. They are always over-crowded. There is table-room for only half of the passengers, therefore they have to set a second table for the second half. The stewards rush both parties, they give them no time to eat a satisfying meal, both divisions leave the table hungry. It isn't so with us. Angelo books himself for the one table, I book myself for the other. Neither of us eats anything at the other's table, but just simply works—works. Thus, you see there are four hands to feed Angelo, and the same four to feed me. Each of us eats two meals.''

The old lady was dazed with admiration, and kept saying, "It is *per*fectly wonderful, perfectly wonderful!" and the boy Joe licked his chops enviously, but said nothing—at least aloud.

"Yes," continued Luigi, "our construction may have its disadvantages—in fact, *has*—but it also has its compensations, of one sort and another. Take travel, for instance. Travel is enormously expensive, in all countries; we have been obliged to do a vast deal of it—come, Angelo, don't put any more sugar in your tea, I'm just over one indigestion and don't want another right away—been obliged to do a great deal of it, as I was saying. Well, we always travel as one person, since we occupy but one seat; so we save half the fare."

"How romantic!" interjected Rowena, with effusion.

"Yes, my dear young lady, and how practical too, and economical. In Europe, beds in the hotels are not charged with the board, but separately—another saving, for we stood to our rights and paid for the one bed only. The landlords often insisted that as both of us occupied the bed we ought——"

"No, they didn't," said Angelo. "They did it only twice, and in both cases it was a double bed—a rare thing in Europe—and the double bed gave them some excuse. Be fair to the landlords; twice doesn't constitute 'often.' "

"Well, that depends—that depends. I knew a man who fell down a well twice. He said he didn't mind the first time, but he thought the second time was once too often. Have I misused that word, Mrs. Cooper?"

"To tell the truth, I was afraid you had, but it seems to look, now, like you hadn't." She stopped, and was evidently struggling with the difficult problem a moment, then she added in the tone of one who is convinced without being converted, "It seems so, but I can't somehow tell why."

Rowena thought Luigi's retort was wonderfully quick and bright, and she remarked to herself with satisfaction that there wasn't any young native of Dawson's Landing that could have risen to the occasion like that. Luigi detected the applause in her face, and expressed his pleasure and his thanks with his eyes; and so eloquently withal, that the girl was proud and pleased, and hung out the delicate sign of it on her cheeks.

Luigi went on, with animation:

"Both of us get a bath for one ticket, theater seat for one ticket, pew-rent is on the same basis, but at peep-shows we pay double."

147

"We have much to be thankful for," said Angelo, impressively, with a reverent light in his eye and a reminiscent tone in his voice, "we have been greatly blessed. As a rule, what one of us has lacked, the other, by the bounty of Providence, has been able to supply. My brother is hardy, I am not; he is very masculine, assertive, aggressive; I am much less so. I am subject to illness, he is never ill. I cannot abide medicines, and cannot take them, but he has no prejudice against them, and——"

"Why, goodness gracious," interrupted the widow, "when you are sick, does he take the medicine for you?"

"Always, madam."

"Why, I never heard such a thing in my life! I think it's beautiful of you."

"Oh, madam, it's nothing, don't mention it, it's really nothing at all."

"But I say it's beautiful, and I stick to it!" cried the widow, with a speaking moisture in her eye. "A well brother to take the medicine for his poor sick brother—I wish I had such a son," and she glanced reproachfully at her boys. "I declare I'll never rest till I've shook you by the hand," and she scrambled out of her chair in a fever of generous enthusiasm, and made for the twins, blind with her tears, and began to shake. The boy Joe corrected her:

"You're shaking the wrong one, ma."

This flurried her, but she made a swift change and went on shaking.

"Got the wrong one again ma," said the boy.

"Oh, shut up, can't you!" said the widow, embarrassed and irritated. "Give me *all* your hands, I want to shake them all; for I know you are both just as good as you can be."

It was a victorious thought, a master-stroke of diplomacy, though, that never occurred to her and she cared nothing for diplomacy. She shook the four hands in turn cordially, and went back to her place in a state of high and fine exaltation that made her look young and handsome.

"Indeed I owe everything to Luigi," said Angelo, affectionately. "But for him I could not have survived our boyhood days, when we were friendless and poor—ah, so poor! We lived from hand to mouth—lived on the coarse fare of unwilling charity, and for weeks and weeks together not a morsel of food passed my lips, for its character revolted me and I could not eat it. But for Luigi I should have died. He ate for us both."

"How noble!" sighed Rowena.

"Do you hear that?" said the widow, severely, to her boys.

"Let it be an example to you—I mean you, Joe."

Joe gave his head a barely perceptible disparaging toss and said: "Et for both. It ain't anything—I'd a done it."

"Hush, if you haven't got any better manners than that. You don't see the point at all. It wasn't good food."

"I don't care—it was food, and I'd 'a et it if it was rotten."

"Shame! Such language! Can't you understand? They were starving—actually starving—and he ate for both, and——"

"Shucks! you gimme a chance and I'll—"

"There, now—close your head! and don't you open it again till you're asked."

[Angelo goes on and tells how his parents the Count and Countess had to fly from Florence for political reasons, and died poor in Berlin bereft of their great property by confiscation; and how he and Luigi had to travel with a freak-show during two years and suffer semi-starvation.]

* "That hateful black-bread! but I seldom ate anything during that time; that was poor Luigi's affair——"

"I'll never *Mister* him again!" cried the widow, with strong emotion, "he's Luigi to me, from this out!"

"Thank you a thousand times, madam, a thousand times! though in truth I don't deserve it."

"Ah, Luigi is always the fortunate one when honors are showering," said Angelo, plaintively, "now what have I done, Mrs. Cooper, that you leave me out? Come, you must strain a point in my favor."

"Call you Angelo? Why, certainly I will; what are you thinking of! In the case of twins, why——"

"But, ma, you're breaking up the story—do let him go on."

"You keep still, Rowena Cooper, and he can go on all the better, I reckon. One interruption don't hurt, it's two that makes the trouble."

"But you've added one, now, and that is three."

"Rowena! I will not allow you to talk back at me when you have got nothing rational to say."

CHAPTER III

[After breakfast the whole village crowded in, and there was a grand reception in honor of the twins; and at the close of it the gifted "freak" captured everybody's admiration by sitting down at the piano and knocking out a classic four-handed piece in great style. Then the Judge took it—or them—driving in his buggy and showed off his village.]

All along the streets the people crowded the windows and stared at the amazing twins. Troops of young boys flocked after the buggy, excited and yelling. At first the dogs showed no interest. They thought they merely saw three men in a buggy—a matter of no consequence; but when they found out the facts of the case, they altered their opinion pretty radically, and joined the boys, expressing their minds as they came. Other dogs got interested; indeed all the dogs. It was a spirited sight to see them coming leaping fences, tearing around corners, swarming out of every by-street and alley. The noise they made was something beyond belief—or praise. They did not seem to be moved by malice but only by prejudice, the common human prejudice against lack of conformity. If the twins turned their heads, the broke and fled in every direction, but stopped at a safe distance and faced about; and then formed and came on again as soon as the strangers showed them their back. Negroes and farmers' wives took to the woods when the buggy came upon them suddenly, and altogether the drive was pleasant and animated, and a refreshment all around.

[It was a long and lively drive. Angelo was a Methodist; Luigi was a Freethinker. The Judge was very proud of his Freethinker Society, which was flourishing along in a most prosperous way and already had two members— himself and the obscure and neglected Pudd'nhead Wilson. It was to meet that evening, and he invited Luigi to join; a thing which Luigi was glad to do, partly because it would please himself, and partly because it would gravel Angelo.]

They had now arrived at the widow's gate, and the excursion ended. The twins politely expressed their obligations for the pleasant outing which had been afforded them; to which the Judge bowed his thanks, and then said he would now go and arrange for the Freethinkers' meeting, and would call for Count Luigi in the evening.

"For you also, dear sir," he added hastily, turning to Angelo and bowing. "In addressing myself particularly to your brother, I was not meaning to leave you out. It was an unintentional rudeness, I assure you, and due wholly to accident—accident and preoccupation. I beg you to forgive me."

His quick eye had seen the sensitive blood mount into Angelo's face, betraying the wound that had been inflicted. The sting of the slight had gone deep, but the apology was so prompt, and so evidently sincere, that the hurt was almost immediately healed, and a forgiving smile testified to the kindly Judge that all was well again.

Concealed behind Angelo's modest and unassuming exterior, and unsuspected by any but his intimates, was a lofty pride, a pride of almost abnormal proportions indeed, and this rendered him ever the prey of slights; and although they were almost always imaginary ones, they hurt none the less on that account. By ill fortune Judge Driscoll had happened to touch his sorest point, *i. e.,* his conviction that his brother's presence was welcomer everywhere than his own; that he was often invited, out of mere courtesy, where only his brother was wanted, and that in a majority of cases he would not be included in an invitation if he could be left out without offence. A sensitive nature like this is necessarily subject to moods; moods which traverse the whole gamut of feeling; moods which know all the climes of emotion, from the sunny heights of joy to the black abyss of despair. At times, in his seasons of deepest depression, Angelo almost wished that he and his brother might become segregated from each other and be separate individuals, like other men. But of course as soon as his mind cleared and these diseased imaginings passed away, he shuddered at the repulsive thought, and earnestly prayed that it might visit him no more. To be separate, and as other men are! How awkward it would seem; how unendurable. What would he do with is hands, his arms? How would his legs feel? How odd, and strange, and grotesque every action, attitude, movement, gesture would be. To sleep by himself, eat by himself, walk by himself—how lonely, how unspeakably lonely! No, no, any fate but that. In every way and from every point, the idea was revolting.

This was of course natural; to have felt otherwise would have been unnatural. He had known no life but a combined one; he had been familiar with it from his birth; he was not able to conceive of any other as being agreeable, or even bearable. To him, in the privacy of his secret thoughts, all other men were monsters, deformities; and during three-fourths of his life their aspect had filled him with what promised to be an unconquerable aversion. But at eighteen his eye began to take note of female beauty; and little by little, undefined longings grew up in his heart, under whose softening influences the old stubborn aversion gradually diminished, and finally disappeared. Men were still monstrosities to him, still deformities, and in his sober moments he had no desire to be like them, but their strange and unsocial and uncanny construction was no longer offensive to him.

151

This had been a hard day for him, physically and mentally. He had been called in the morning before he had quite slept off the effects of the liquor which Luigi had drunk; and so, for the first half hour had had the seedy feeling, and languor, the brooding depression, the cobwebby mouth and druggy taste that come of dissipation and are so ill a preparation for bodily or intellectual activities; the long violent strain of the reception had followed; and this had been followed, in turn, by the dreary sight-seeing, the Judge's wearying explanations and laudations of the sights, and the stupefying clamor of the dogs. As a congrous conclusion, a fitting end, his feelings had been hurt, a slight had been put upon him. He would have been glad to forego dinner and betake himself to rest and sleep, but he held his peace and said no word, for he knew his brother, Luigi, was fresh, unweary, full of life, spirit, energy; he would have scoffed at the idea of wasting valuable time on a bed or a sofa, and would have refused permission.

CHAPTER IV

Rowena was dining out, Joe and Harry were belated at play, there were but three chairs and four persons that noon at the home dinner-table—the twins, the widow, and her chum, Aunt Betsy Hale. The widow soon perceived that Angelo's spirits were as low as Luigi's were high, and also that he had a jaded look. Her motherly solicitude was aroused, and she tried to get him interested in the talk and win him to a happier frame of mind, but the cloud of sadness remained on his countenance. Luigi lent his help, too. He used a form and a phrase which he was always accustomed to employ in these circumstances. He gave his brother an affectionate slap on the shoulder and said, encouragingly:

"Cheer up, the worst is yet to come!"

But this did no good. It never did. If anything it made the matter worse, as a rule, because it irritated Angelo. This made it a favorite with Luigi. By and by the widow said:

"Angelo, you are tired, you've overdone yourself; you go right to bed, after dinner, and get a good nap and a rest, then you'll be all right."

"Indeed I would give anything if I could do that, madam."

"And what's to hender, I'd like to know? Land, the room's yours to do what you please with! The idea that you can't do what you like with your own!"

"But you see, there's one prime essential—an essential of the very first importance—which isn't my own."

"What is that?"

"My body."

The old ladies looked puzzled, and Aunt Betsy Hale said:

"Why bless your heart, how is that?"

"It's my brother's."

"Your brother's! I don't quite understand. I supposed it belonged to both of you."

"So it does. But not to both at the same time."

"That is mighty curious; I don't see how it can be. I shouldn't think it could be managed that way."

"Oh, it's a good enough arrangement, and goes very well; in fact it wouldn't do to have it otherwise. I find that the teetotalers and the anti-teetotalers hire the use of the same hall for their meetings. Both parties don't use it at the same time, do they?"

"You bet they don't!" said both old ladies in a breath.

"And moreover," said Aunt Betsy, "the Freethinkers and the Baptist Bible-class use the same room over the Market-house, but you can take my word for it they don't mush up together and use it at the same time."

"Very well," said Angelo, "you understand it now. And it stands to reason that the arrangement couldn't be improved. I'll prove it to you. If our legs tried to obey two wills, how could we ever get anywhere? I would start one way, Luigi would start another, at the same moment—the result would be a standstill, wouldn't it?"

"As sure as you are born! Now ain't that wonderful! A body would never have thought of it."

"We should always be arguing and fussing and disputing over the merest trifles. We should lose worlds of time, for we couldn't go down-stairs or up, couldn't go to bed, couldn't rise, couldn't wash, couldn't dress, couldn't stand up, couldn't sit down, couldn't even cross our legs, without calling a meeting first and explaining the case and passing resolutions, and getting consent. It wouldn't ever do—now would it?"

"Do? Why, it would wear a person out in a week! Did you ever hear anything like it, Patsy Cooper?"

"Oh, you 'll find there's more than one thing about them that ain't commonplace," said the widow, with the complacent air of a person with a property-right in a novelty that is under admiring scrutiny.

"Well now, how ever do you manage it? I don't mind saying I'm suffering to know."

"He who made us," said Angelo reverently, "and with us this difficulty, also provided a way out of it. By a mysterious law of our being, each of us has utter and indisputable command of our body a week at a time, turn and turn about."

"Well, I never! Now ain't that beautiful!"

"Yes, it is beautiful and infinitely wise and just. The week ends every Saturday at midnight to the minute, to the second, to the last shade of a fraction of a second, infallibly, unerringly, and in that instant the one brother's power over the body vanishes and the other brother takes possession, asleep or awake."

"How marvelous are His ways, and past finding out!"

Luigi said: "So exactly to the instant does the change come, that during our stay in many of the great cities of the world, the public clocks were regulated by it; and as hundreds of thousands of private clocks and watches were set and corrected in accordance with the public clocks, we really furnished the standard time for the entire city."

"Don't tell me that He don't do miracles any more! Blowing down the walls of Jericho with rams' horns wa'n't as difficult, in my opinion."

"And that is not all," said Angelo. "A thing that is even more marvelous, perhaps, is the fact that the change takes note of longitude and fits itself to the meridian we are on. Luigi is in command this week. Now, if on Saturday night at a moment before midnight we could fly in an instant to a point fifteen degrees west of here, he would hold possession of the power another hour, for the change observes *local* time and no other."

Betsy Hale was deeply impressed, and said with solemnity:

"Patsy Cooper, for *de*tail it lays over the Passage of the Red Sea."

"Now, I shouldn't go as far as that," said Aunt Patsy, "but if you've a mind to say Sodom and Gomorrah, I am with you, Betsy Hale."

"I am agreeable, then, though I do think I was right, and I believe Parson Maltby would say the same. Well now, there's another thing. Suppose one of you wants to borrow the legs a minute from the one that's got them, could he let him?"

"Yes, but we hardly ever do that. There were disagreeable results, several times, and so we very seldom ask or grant the privilege, nowdays, and we never even think of such a thing unless the case is extremely urgent. Besides, a week's possession at a time seems so little that we can't bear to spare a minute of it. People who have the use of their legs all the time never think of what a blessing it is, of course. It never occurs to them; it's just their natural ordinary condition, and so it does not excite them at all. But when I wake up, on Sunday morning, and it's my week and I feel the power all through me, oh, such a wave of exultation and thanksgiving goes surging over me, and I want to shout 'I can walk! I can walk!' Madam, do you ever, at your uprising want to shout 'I can walk! I can walk'?''

"No, you poor unfortunate cretur', but I'll never get out of my bed again without *doing* it! Laws, to think I've had this unspeakable blessing all my long life and never had the grace to thank the good Lord that gave it to me!"

Tears stood in the eyes of both the old ladies and the widow said, softly:

"Betsy Hale, we have learned something, you and me."

The conversation now drifted wide, but by and by floated back once more to that admired detail, the rigid and beautiful impartiality with which the possession of power had been distributed between the twins. Aunt Betsy saw in it a far finer justice than human law exhibits in related cases. She said:

"In my opinion it ain't right now, and never has been right, the way a twin born a quarter of a minute sooner than the other one gets all the land and grandeurs and nobilities in the old countries and his brother has to go bare and be a nobody. Which of you was born first?"

Angelo's head was resting against Luigi's; weariness had overcome him, and for the past five minutes he had been peacefully sleeping. The old ladies had dropped their voices to a lulling drone, to help him steal the rest his brother wouldn't take him up-stairs to get. Luigi listened a moment to Angelo's regular breathing, then said in a voice barely audible:

"We were both born at the same time, but I am six months older than he is."

"For the land's sake!"

" 'Sh! don't wake him up; he wouldn't like my telling this. It has always been kept secret till now."

"But how in the world can it be? If you were both born at the same time, how can one of you be older than the other?"

"It is very simple, and I assure you it is true. I was born with a full crop of hair, he was as bald as an egg for six months. I could walk six months before he could make a step. I finished teething six months ahead of him. I began to take solids six months before he left the breast. I began to talk six months before he could say a word. Last, and absolutely unassailable proof, *the sutures in my skull closed six months ahead of his*. Always just that six months difference to a day. Was that accident? Nobody is going to claim that, I'm sure. It was ordained—it was law—it had its meaning, and we know what that meaning was. Now what does this overwhelming body of evidence establish? It establishes just one thing, and that thing it establishes beyond any peradventure whatever. Friends, we would not have it known for the world, and I must beg you to keep it strictly to yourselves, but the truth is, *we are no more twins than you are*.''

The two old ladies were stunned, paralyzed—petrified, one may almost say—and could only sit and gaze vacantly at each other for some moments; then Aunt Betsy Hale said impressively:

"There's no getting around proof like that. I do believe it's the most amazing thing I ever heard of.'' She sat silent a moment or two and breathing hard with excitement, then she looked up and surveyed the strangers steadfastly a little while, and added: "Well, it does beat me, but I would have took you for twins anywhere.''

"So would I, so would I,'' said Aunt Patsy with the emphasis of a certainty that is not impaired by any shade of doubt.

"*Any*body would—anybody in the world, I don't care who he is,'' said Aunt Betsy with decision.

"You won't tell,'' said Luigi, appealingly.

"Oh, dear no!'' answered both ladies promptly, "you can trust us, don't you be afraid.''

"That is good of you, and kind. Never let on; treat us always as if we were twins.''

"You can depend on us,'' said Aunt Betsy, "but it won't be easy, because now that I know you ain't, you don't *seem* so.''

Luigi muttered to himself with satisfaction: "That swindle has gone through without change of cars.''

It was not very kind of him to load the poor things up with a secret like that, which would always be flying to their tongues' ends every time they heard any one speak of the strangers as twins, and would become harder and harder to hang on to with every recurrence of the temptation to tell it, while the torture of retaining it would increase with every new strain that was applied; but he never thought of that, and probably would not have worried much about it if he had.

A visitor was announced—some one to see the twins. They withdrew to the parlor, and the two old ladies began to discuss with interest the strange things which they had been listening to. When they had finished the matter to their satisfaction, and Aunt Betsy rose to go, she stopped to ask a question:

"How does things come on between Roweny and Tom Driscoll?''

"Well, about the same. He writes tolerable often, and she answers tolerable seldom.''

"Where is he?''

"In St. Louis, I believe, though he's such a gad-about that a body can't be very certain of him, I reckon."

"Don't Roweny know?"

"Oh, yes, like enough. I haven't asked her lately."

"Do you know how him and the Judge are getting along now?"

"First-rate, I believe. Mrs. Pratt says so; and being right in the house, and sister to the one and aunt to t'other, of course she ought to know. She says the Judge is real fond of him when he's away, but frets when he's around and is vexed with his ways, and not sorry to have him go again. He has been gone three weeks this time—a pleasant thing for both of them, I reckon."

"Tom's ruther harum-scarum, but there ain't anything bad in him, I guess."

"Oh no, he's just young, that's all. Still, twenty-three is old, in one way. A young man ought to be earning his living by that time. If Tom were doing that, or was even trying to do it, the Judge would be a heap better satisfied with him. Tom's always going to begin, but somehow he can't seem to find just the opening he likes."

"Well now, it's partly the Judge's own fault. Promising the boy his property wasn't the way to set him earning a fortune of his own. But what do you think—is Roweny beginning to lean any towards him, or ain't she?"

Aunt Patsy had a secret in her bosom; she wanted to keep it there, but nature was too strong for her. She drew Aunt Betsy aside, and said in her most confidential and mysterious manner:

"Don't you breathe a syllable to a soul—I'm going to tell you something. In my opinion Tom Driscoll's chances were considerable better yesterday than they are today."

"Patsy Cooper, what *do* you mean?"

"It's so, as sure as you're born. I wish you could 'a' been at breakfast and seen for yourself."

"You don't mean it!"

"Well, if I'm any judge, there's a leaning—there's a leaning, sure."

"My land! Which one of 'em is it?"

"I can't say for certain, but I think it's the youngest one—Anjy."

Then there were handshakings, and congratulations, and hopes, and so on, and the old ladies parted, perfectly happy—the one in knowing something which the rest of the town didn't, and the other in having been the sole person able to furnish that knowledge.

The visitor who had called to see the twins was the Rev. Mr. Hotchkiss, pastor of the Baptist church. At the reception Angelo had told him he had lately experienced a change in his religious views, and was now desirous of becoming a Baptist, and would immediately join Mr. Hotchkiss's church. There was no time to say more, and the brief talk ended at that point. The minister was much gratified, and had dropped in for a moment, now, to invite the twins to attend his Bible-class at eight that evening. Angelo accepted, and was expecting Luigi to decline, but he did not, because he knew that the Bible-class and the Freethinkers met in the same room, and he wanted to treat his brother to the embarrassment of being caught in freethinking company.

CHAPTER V

[A long and vigorous quarrel follows, between the twins. And there is plenty to quarrel about, for Angelo was always seeking truth, and this obliged him to change and improve his religion with frequency, which wearied Luigi, and annoyed him too; for he had to be present at each new enlistment—which placed him in the false position of seeming to indorse and approve his brother's fickleness; moreover, he had to go to Angelo's prohibition meetings, and he hated them. On the other hand, when it was *his* week to command the legs he gave Angelo just cause of complaint, for he took him to circuses and horse-races and fandangoes, exposing him to all sorts of censure and criticism; and he drank, too; and whatever he drank went to Angelo's head instead of his own and made him act disgracefully. When the evening was come, the two attended the Freethinkers' meeting, where Angelo was sad and silent; then came the Bible-class and looked upon him coldly, finding him in such company. Then they went to Wilson's house, and Chapter XI of "Pudd'nhead Wilson" follows, which tells of the girl seen in Tom Driscoll's room; and closes with the kicking of Tom by Luigi at the anti-temperance mass meeting of the Sons of Liberty; with the addition of some account of Roxy's adventures as a chambermaid on a Mississippi boat. Her exchange of the children had been flippantly and farcically described in an earlier chapter.]

Next morning all the town was a-buzz with great news; Pudd'nhead Wilson had a law-case! The public astonishment was so great and the public curiosity so intense, that when the justice of the peace opened his court, the place was packed with people, and even the windows were full. Everybody was flushed and perspiring, the summer heat was almost unendurable.

Tom Driscoll had brought a charge of assault and battery against the twins. Robert Allen was retained by Driscoll, David Wilson by the defense. Tom, his native cheerfulness unannihilated by his back-breaking and bone-bruising passage across the massed heads of the Sons of Liberty the previous night, laughed his little customary laugh, and said to Wilson:

"I've kept my promise, you see: I'm throwing my business your way. Sooner than I was expecting, too."

"It's very good of you—particularly if you mean to keep it up."

"Well, I can't tell about that, yet. But we'll see. If I find you deserve it I'll take you under my protection and make your fame and fortune for you."

"I'll try to deserve it, Tom."

A jury was sworn in; then Mr. Allen said:

"We will detain your honor but a moment with this case. It is not one where any doubt of the fact of the assault can enter in. These gentlemen—the accused—kicked my client at the Market Hall last night; they kicked him with violence; with extraordinary violence; with even unprecedented violence, I may say; insomuch that he was lifted entirely off his feet and discharged into the midst of the audience. We can prove this by four hundred witnesses—we shall call but three. Mr. Harkness will take the stand."

Mr. Harkness being sworn, testified that he was chairman upon the occasion mentioned; that he was close at hand and saw the defendants in this action kick the plaintiff into the air and saw him descend among the audience.

"Take the witness," said Allen.

"Mr. Harkness," said Wilson, "you say you saw these gentlemen, my clients kick the plaintiff. Are you sure—and please remember that you are on oath—are you perfectly sure that you saw *both* of them kick him, or only one? Now be careful."

A bewildered look began to spread itself over the witness's face. He hesitated, stammered, but got out nothing. His eyes wandered to the twins and fixed themselves there with a vacant gaze.

"Please answer, Mr. Harkness, you are keeping the court waiting. It is a very simple question."

Counsel for the prosecution broke in with impatience:

"Your honor, the question is an irrelevant triviality. Necessarily they both kicked him, for they have but the one pair of legs, and both are responsible for them."

Wilson said, sarcastically:

"Will your honor permit this new witness to be sworn? He seems to possess knowledge which can be of the utmost value just at this moment—knowledge which would at once dispose of what every one must see is a very difficult question in this case. Brother Allen, will take the stand?"

"Go on with your case!" said Allen petulantly. The audience laughed, and got a warning from the court.

"Now, Mr. Harkness," said Wilson, insinuatingly, "we shall have to insist upon an answer to that question."

"I—er—well, of course I do not absolutely *know*, but in my opinion—"

"Never mind your opinion, sir—answer the question."

"I—why, I *can't* answer it."

"That will do, Mr. Harkness. Stand down."

The audience tittered, and the discomfited witness retired in a state of great embarrassment.

Mr. Wakeman took the stand and swore that he saw the twins kick the plaintiff off the platform. The defence took the witness.

"Mr. Wakeman, you have sworn that you saw these gentlemen kick the plaintiff. Do I understand you to swear that you saw them *both* do it?"

"Yes, sir,"—with decision.

"How do you know that both did it?"

"Because I *saw* them do it."

The audience laughed, and got another warning from the court.

"But by what means do you know that both, and not one, did it?"

"Well, in the first place, the insult was given to both of them equally, for they were called a pair of scissors. Of course they would both want to resent it, and so—"

"Wait! You are theorizing now. Stick to facts—counsel will attend to the arguments. Go on."

"Well, they both went over there—*that* I saw."

"Very good. Go on."

"And they both kicked him—I swear to it."

"Mr. Wakeman, was Count Luigi, here, willing to join the Sons of Liberty last night?"

"Yes, sir, he was. He did join, too, and drank a glass or two of whisky, like a man."

"Was his brother willing to join?"

"No, sir, he wasn't. He is a teetotaler, and was elected through a mistake."

"Was he given a glass of whisky?"

"Yes, sir, but of course that was another mistake, and not intentional. He wouldn't drink it. He set it down." A slight pause, then he added, casually and quite simply: "The plaintiff reached for it and hogged it."

There was a fine outburst of laughter, but as the justice was caught out himself, his reprimand was not very vigorous.

Mr. Allen jumped up and exclaimed: "I protest against these foolish irrelevancies. What have they to do with the case?"

Wilson said: "Calm yourself, brother, it was only an experiment. Now, Mr. Wakeman, if one of these gentlemen chooses to join an association and the other doesn't; and if one of them enjoys whisky and the other doesn't, but sets it aside and leaves it unprotected" (titter from the audience), "it seems to show that they have independent minds and tastes and preferences, and that one of them is able to approve of a thing at the very moment that the other is heartily disapproving of it. Doesn't it seem so to you?"

"Certainly it does. It's perfectly plain."

"Now then, it might be—I only say it might be—that one of these brothers wanted to kick the plaintiff last night, and that the other didn't want that humiliating punishment inflicted upon him in that public way and before all those people. Isn't that possible?

"Of course it is. It's more than possible. I don't believe the blonde one would kick anybody. It was the other one that——"

"Silence!" shouted the plaintiff's counsel, and went on with an angry sentence which was lost in the wave of laughter that swept the house.

"That will do, Mr. Wakemen," said Wilson, "you may stand down."

The third witness was called. He had seen the twins kick the plaintiff. Mr. Wilson took the witness.

"Mr. Rogers, you say you saw these accused gentlemen kick the plaintiff?"

"Yes, sir."

"Both of them?"

"Yes, sir."

"Which of them kicked him first?"

"Why—they—they both kicked him at the same time."

"Are you perfectly sure of that?"

"Yes, sir."

"What makes you sure of it?"

"Why, I stood right behind them, and *saw* them do it."

"How many kicks were delivered?"

"Only one."

"If two men kick, the result should be two kicks, shouldn't it?"

"Why—why—yes, as a rule."

"Then what do you think went with the other kick?"

"I—well—the fact is, I wasn't thinking of two being necessary, this time."

161

"What do you think now?"

"Well, I—I'm sure I don't quite know what to think, but I reckon that one of them did half of the kick and the other one did the other half."

Somebody in the crowd sung out: "It's the first sane thing that any of them has said."

The audience applauded. The judge said: "Silence! or I will clear the court."

Mr. Allen looked pleased, but Wilson did not seem disturbed. He said:

"Mr. Rogers, you have favored us with what you think and what you reckon, but as thinking and reckoning are not evidence, I will now give you a chance to come out with something positive, one way or the other, and shall require you to produce it. I will ask the accused to stand up and repeat the phenomenal kick of last night." The twins stood up. "Now, Mr. Rogers, please stand behind them."

A Voice: "No, stand in front!" (Laughter. Silenced by the court.) Another Voice: "No, give Tommy another highst!" (Laughter. Sharply rebuked by the court.)

"Now then, Mr. Rogers, two kicks shall be delivered, one after the other, and I give you my word that at least one of the two shall be delivered by one of the twins alone, without the slightest assistance from his brother. Watch sharply, for you have got to render a decision without any if's and and's in it." Rogers bent himself behind the twins with his palms just above his knees, in the modern attitude of the catcher at a base-ball match, and riveted his eyes on the pair of legs in front of him. "Are you ready, Mr. Rogers?"

"Ready, sir."

"Kick!"

The kick was launched.

"Have you got that one classified, Mr. Rogers?"

"Let me study a minute, sir."

"Take as much time as you please. Let me know when you are ready."

For as much as a minute Rogers pondered, with all eyes and a breathless interest fastened upon him. Then he gave the word: "Ready, sir."

"Kick!"

The kick that followed was an exact duplicate of the first one.

"Now then, Mr. Rogers, one of those kicks was an individual kick, not a mutual one. You will now state positively which was the mutual one."

The witness said, with a crestfallen look:

"I've got to give up. There ain't any man in the world that could tell t'other from which, sir."

"Do you still assert that last night's kick was a mutual kick?"

"Indeed I don't, sir."

"That will do, Mr. Rogers. If my brother Allen desires to address the court, your honor, very well; but as far as I am concerned I am ready to let the case be at once delivered into the hands of this intelligent jury without comment."

Mr. Justice Robinson had been in office only two months, and in that short time had not had many cases to try, of course. He had no knowledge of laws and courts except what he had picked up since he came into office. He was a sore trouble to the lawyers, for his rulings were pretty eccentric sometimes, and he stood by them with Roman simplicity and fortitude; but the people were well satisfied with him, for they saw that his intentions were always right, that he was entirely impartial, and that he usually made up in good sense what he lacked in technique, so to speak. He now perceived that there was likely to be a miscarriage of justice here, and he rose to the occasion.

"Wait a moment, gentlemen," he said, "it is plain that an assault has been committed—it is plain to anybody; but the way things are going, the guilty will certainly escape conviction. I cannot allow this. Now—"

"But, your honor!" said Wilson, interrupting him, earnestly but respectfully, "you are deciding the case yourself, whereas the jury—"

"Never mind the jury, Mr. Wilson; the jury will have a chance when there is a reasonable doubt for them to take hold of—which there isn't, so far. There is no doubt whatever that an assault has been committed. The attempt to show that both of the accused committed it has failed. Are they both to escape justice on that account? Not in this court, if I can prevent it. It appears to have been a mistake to bring the charge against them as a corporation; each should have been charged in his capacity as an individual, and—"

"But your honor!" said Wilson, "in fairness to my clients I must insist that inasmuch as the prosecution did not separate the—"

"No wrong will be done your clients, sir—they will be protected; also the public and the offended laws. Mr. Allen, you will amend your pleadings, and put one of the accused on trial at a time."

Wilson broke in: "But your honor! this is wholly unprecedented! To imperil an accused person by arbitrarily altering and widening the charge against him in order to compass his conviction when the charge as originally brought promises to fail to convict, is a thing unheard of before.''

''Unheard of *where?*''

''In the courts of this or any other State.''

The judge said with dignity: ''I am not acquainted with the customs of other courts, and am not concerned to know what they are. I am responsible for this court, and I cannot conscientiously allow my judgment to be warped and my judicial liberty hampered by trying to conform to the caprices of other courts, be they—,''

''But, your honor, the oldest and highest courts in Europe—''

''This court is not run on the European plan, Mr. Wilson; it is not run on any plan but its own. It has a plan of its own; and that plan is, to find justice for both State and accused, no matter what happens to be practice and custom in Europe or anywhere else.'' (Great applause.) ''Silence! It has not been the custom of this court to imitate other courts; it has not been the custom of this court to take shelter behind the decisions of other courts, and we will not begin now. We will do the best we can by the light that God has given us, and while this court continues to have His approval, it will remain indifferent to what other organizations may think of it.'' (Applause.) ''Gentlemen, I *must* have order!—quiet yourselves! Mr. Allen, you will now proceed against the prisoners one at a time. Go on with the case.''

Allen was not at his ease. However, after whispering a moment with his client and with one or two other people, he rose and said:

''Your honor, I find it to be reported and believed that the accused are able to act independently in many ways, but that this independence does not extend to their legs, authority over their legs being vested exclusively in the one brother during a specific term of days, and then passing to the other brother for a like term, and so on, by regular alternation. I could call witnesses who would prove that the accused had revealed to them the existence of this extraordinary fact, and had also made known which of them was in possession of the legs yesterday—and this would of course indicate where the guilt of the assault belongs— but as this would be mere hearsay evidence, these revelations not having been made under oath—''

''Never mind about that, Mr. Allen. It may not all be hearsay. We shall see. It may at least help to put us on the right track. Call the witnesses.''

''Then I will call Mr. John Buckstone, who is now present, and I beg that Mrs. Patsy Cooper may be sent for. Take the stand, Mr. Buckstone.''

Buckstone took the oath, and then testified that on the previous evening the Count Angelo Cappello had protested against going to the hall, and had called all present to witness that he was going by compulsion and would not go if he could help himself. Also, that the Count Luigi had replied sharply that he would *go*, just the same, and that he, Count Luigi, would see to that, himself. Also, that upon Count Angelo's complaining about being kept on his legs so long, Count Luigi retorted with apparent surprise, '*Your* legs!—I like your impudence!' ''

"*Now* we are getting at the kernel of the thing," observed the judge, with grave and earnest satisfaction. "It looks as if the Count Luigi was in possession of the battery at the time of the assault."

Nothing further was elicited from Mr. Buckstone on direct examination. Mr. Wilson took the witness.

"Mr. Buckstone, about what time was it that that conversation took place?"

"Toward nine yesterday evening, sir."

"Did you then proceed directly to the hall?"

"Yes, sir."

"How long did it take you to go there?"

"Well, we walked; and as it was from the extreme edge of town, and there was no hurry, I judge it took us about twenty minutes, maybe a trifle more."

"About what hour was the kick delivered?"

"At thirteen minutes and a half to ten."

"Admirable! You are a pattern witness, Mr. Buckstone. How did you happen to look at your watch at that particular moment?"

"I always do it when I see an assault. It's likely I shall be called as a witness, and it's a good point to have."

"It would be well if others were as thoughtful. Was anything said, between the conversation at my house and the assault, upon the detail which we are now examining into?"

"No, sir."

"If power over the mutual legs was in the possession of one brother at nine, and passed into the possession of the other one during the next thirty or forty minutes, do you think you could have detected the change?"

"By no means!"

"That is all, Mr. Buckstone."

Mrs. Patsy Cooper was called. The crowd made way for her, and she came smiling and bowing through the narrow human lane, with Betsy Hale, as escort and support, smiling and bowing in her wake, the audience breaking into welcoming cheers as the old favorites filed along. The judge did not check this kindly demonstration of homage and affection, but let it run its course unrebuked.

The old ladies stopped and shook hands with the twins with effusion, then gave the judge a friendly nod, and bustled into the seats provided for them. They immediately began to deliver a volley of eager questions at the friends around them: "What is this thing for?" "What is that thing for?" "Who is that young man that's writing at the desk? Why, I declare, it's Jack Bunce! I thought he was sick." "Which is the jury? Why, is *that* the jury? Billy Price and Job Turner, and Jack Lounsbury, and—well, I never!" "Now who would ever a'thought—"

But they were gently called to order at this point, and asked not to talk in court. Their tongues fell silent, but the radiant interest in their faces remained, and their gratitude for the blessing of a new sensation and a novel experience still beamed undimmed from their eyes. Aunt Patsy stood up and took the oath, and Mr. Allen explained the point in issue, and asked her to go on, now, in her own way, and throw as much light upon it as she could. She toyed with her reticule a moment or two, as if considering where to begin, then she said:

"Well, the way of it is this. They are Luigi's legs a week at a time, and then they are Angelo's, and he can do whatever he wants to with them."

"You are making a mistake, Aunt Patsy Cooper," said the judge. "You shouldn't state that as a *fact,* because you don't know it to *be* a fact."

"What's the reason I don't?" said Aunt Patsy, bridling a little.

"What is the reason that you do know it?"

"The best in the world—because they told me."

"That isn't a reason."

"Well, for the land's sake! Betsy Hale, do you hear that?"

"*Hear* it? I should think so," said Aunt Betsy, rising and facing the court. "Why, Judge, I was there and heard it myself. Luigi says to Angelo—no, it was Angelo said it to—"

"Come, come, Mrs. Hale, pray sit down, and—"

"Certainly, it's all right, I'm going to sit down presently, but not until I've—"

"But you *must* sit down!"

"*Must!* Well, upon my word if things ain't getting to a pretty pass when—"

The house broke into laughter, but was promptly brought to order, and meantime Mr. Allen persuaded the old lady to take her seat. Aunt Patsy continued:

"Yes, they told me that, and I know it's true. They're Luigi's legs this week, but—"

"Ah, *they* told you that, did they?" said the justice, with interest.

"Well no, I don't know that *they* told me, but that's neither here nor there. I know, without that, that at dinner yesterday, Angelo was as tired as a dog, and yet Luigi wouldn't lend him the legs to go up-stairs and take a nap with."

"Did he ask for them?"

"Let me see—it seems to me somehow, that—that—Aunt Betsy, do you remember whether he—"

"Never mind about what Aunt Betsy remembers—she is not a witness; we only want to know what you remember, yourself," said the judge.

"Well, it does seem to me that you are most cantankerously particular about a little thing, Sim Robinson. Why, when I can't remember a thing myself, I always—"

"Ah, *please* go on!"

"Now how *can* she when you keep fussing at her all the time?" said Aunt Betsy. "Why, with a person pecking at *me* that way, I should get that fuzzled and fuddled that—"

She was on her feet again, but Allen coaxed her into her seat once more, while the court squelched the mirth of the house. Then the judge said:

"Madam, do you know—do you absolutely *know,* independently of anything these gentlemen have told you—that the power over their legs passes from the one to the other regularly every week?"

"Regularly? Bless your heart, regularly ain't any name for the exactness of it! All the big cities in Europe used to set the clocks by it." (Laughter, *suppressed by the court.*)

"How do you *know?* That is the question. Please answer it plainly and squarely."

"Don't you talk to me like that, Sim Robinson—I won't have it. How do I know, indeed! How do *you* know what you know? Because somebody told you. You didn't invent it out of your own head, did you? Why, these twins are the truthfulest people in the world; and I don't think it becomes you to sit up there and throw slurs at them when they haven't been doing anything to you. And they are orphans besides—both of them. All—"

But Aunt Betsy was up again, now, and both old ladies were talking at once and with all their might; but as the house was weltering in a storm of laughter, and the judge was hammering his desk with an iron paper-weight, one could only see them talk, not hear them. At last, when quiet was restored, the court said:

167

"Let the ladies retire."

"But, your honor, I have the right, in the interest of my clients, to cross-exam—"

"You'll not need to exercise it, Mr. Wilson—the evidence is thrown out."

"Thrown out!" said Aunt Patsy, ruffled; "and what's it thrown out for, I'd like to know."

"And so would I, Patsy Cooper. It seems to me that if we can save these poor persecuted strangers, it is our bounden duty to stand up here and talk for them till—"

"There, there, there, *do* sit down!"

It cost some trouble and a good deal of coaxing, but they were got into their seats at last. The trial was soon ended, now. The twins themselves became witnesses in their own defense. They established the fact, upon oath, that the leg-power passed from one to the other every Saturday night at twelve o'clock, sharp. But on cross-examination their counsel would not allow them to tell whose week of power the current week was. The judge insisted upon their answering, and proposed to compel them; but even the prosecution took fright and came to the rescue then, and helped stay the sturdy jurist's revolutionary hand. So the case had to go to the jury with that important point hanging in the air. They were out an hour, and brought in this verdict:

"We the jury do find: 1, that an assault was committed, as charged; 2, that it was committed by one of the persons accused, he having been seen to do it by several credible witnesses: 3, but that his identity is so merged in his brother's that we have not been able to tell which was him. We cannot convict both, for only one is guilty. We cannot acquit both, for only one is innocent. Our verdict is that justice has been defeated by dispensation of God, and ask to be discharged from further duty."

This was read aloud in court and brought out a burst of hearty applause. The old ladies made a spring at the twins, to shake and congratulate, but were gently disengaged by Mr. Wilson and softly crowded back into their places.

The Judge rose in his little tribune, laid aside his silver-bowed spectacles, roached his gray hair up with his fingers, and said, with dignity and solemnity, and even with a certain pathos:

"In all my experience on the bench, I have not seen Justice bow her head in shame in this court until this day. You little realize what far-reaching harm has just been wrought here under the fickle forms of law. Imitation is the bane of courts—I thank God that this one is free from the contamination of that vice—and in no long time you will see the fatal work of this hour seized upon by profligate so-called guardians of justice in all the wide circumstance of this plane and perpetuated in their pernicious decisions. I wash my hands of this iniquity. I would have compelled these culprits to expose their guilt, but support failed me where I had most right to expect aid and encouragement. And I was confronted by a law made in the interest of crime, which protects the criminal from testifying against himself. Yet I had precedents of my own whereby I had set aside that law on two different occasions and thus succeeded in convicting criminals to whose crimes there were no witnesses but themselves. What have you accomplished this day? Do you realize it? You have set adrift, unadmonished, in this community, two men endowed with an awful and mysterious gift, a hidden and grisly power for evil—a power by which each in his turn may commit crime after crime of the most heinous character, and no man be able to tell which is the guilty or which the innocent party in any case of them all. Look to your homes—look to your property—look to your lives—for you have need!

"Prisoners at the bar, stand up. Through suppression of evidence, a jury of your—our—countrymen have been obliged to deliver a verdict concerning your case which stinks to heaven with the rankness of its injustice. By its terms you, the guilty one, go free with the innocent. Depart in peace, and come no more! The costs devolve upon the outraged plaintiff—another iniquity. The Court stands dissolved."

Almost everybody crowded forward to overwhelm the twins and their counsel with congratulations; but presently the two old aunties dug the duplicates out and bore them away in triumph through the hurrahing crowd, while lots of new friends carried Pudd'nhead Wilson off tavern-wards to feast him and "wet down" his great and victorious entry into the legal arena. To Wilson, so long familiar with neglect and depreciation, this strange new incense of popularity and admiration was as a fragrance blown from the fields of paradise. A happy man was Wilson.

CHAPTER VI

[A deputation came in the evening and conferred upon Wilson the welcome honor of a nomination for mayor; for the village has just been converted into a city by charter. Tom skulks out of challenging the twins. Judge Driscoll thereupon challenges Angelo, (accused by Tom of doing the kicking;) he declines, but Luigi accepts in his place against Angelo's timid protest.]

It was late Saturday night—nearing eleven.

169

The Judge and his second found the rest of the war party at the further end of the vacant ground, near the haunted house. Pudd'nhead Wilson advanced to meet them, and said anxiously—

"I must say a word in behalf of my principal's proxy, Count Luigi, to whom you have kindly granted the privilege of fighting my principal's battle for him. It is growing late and Count Luigi is in great trouble lest midnight shall strike before the finish."

"It is another testimony," said Howard, approvingly. "That young man is fine all through. He wishes to save his brother the sorrow of fighting on the Sabbath, and he is right; it is the right and manly feeling and does him credit. We will make all possible haste."

Wilson said—

"There is also another reason—a consideration, in fact, which deeply concerns Count Luigi himself. These twins have command of their mutual legs turn about. Count Luigi is in command, now; but at midnight, possession will pass to my principal, Count Angelo, and—well, you can foresee what will happen. He will march straight off the field, and carry Luigi with him."

"Why! sure enough!" cried the Judge, "we have heard something about that extraordinary law of their being, already— nothing very definite, it is true, as regards dates and durations of the power, but I see it is definite enough as regards to-night. Of course we must give Luigi every chance. Omit all the ceremonial possible, gentlemen, and place us in position."

The seconds at once tossed up a coin; Howard won the choice. He placed the Judge sixty feet from the haunted house and facing it; Wilson placed the twins within fifteen feet of the house and facing the Judge—necessarily. The pistol-case was opened and the long slim tubes taken out; when the moonlight glinted from them a shiver went through Angelo. The doctor was a fool, but a thoroughly well-meaning one, with a kind heart and a sincere disposition to oblige, but along with it an absence of tact which often hurt its effectiveness. He brought his box of lint and bandages, and asked Angelo to feel and see how soft and comfortable they were. Angelo's head fell over against Luigi's in a faint, and precious time was lost in bringing him to; which provoked Luigi into expressing his mind to the doctor with a good deal of vigor and frankness. After Angelo came to he was still so weak that Luigi was obliged to drink a stiff horn of brandy to brace him up.

The seconds now stepped at once to their posts, half way between the combatants, one of them on each side of the line of fire. Wilson was to count, very deliberately, "One—two—three—fire!—stop!" and the duelists could bang away at any time they chose during that recitation, but not after the last word. Angelo grew very nervous when he saw Wilson's hand rising slowly into the air as a sign to make ready, and he leaned his head against Luigi's and said—

"O, please take me away from here, I can't stay, I know I can't!"

"What in the world are you doing? Straighten up! What's the matter with you?—*you're* in no danger—nobody's going to shoot at you. Straighten up, I tell you!"

Angelo obeyed, just in time to hear—

"One—!"

"Bang!" Just one report, and a little tuft of white hair floated slowly to the Judge's feet in the moonlight. The Judge did not swerve; he still stood erect and motionless, like a statue, with his pistol-arm hanging straight down at his side. He was reserving his fire.

"Two—!"

"Three—!"

"Fire—!"

Up came the pistol-arm instantly—Angelo dodged with the report. He said "Ouch!" and fainted again.

The doctor examined and bandaged the wound. It was of no consequence, he said—bullet through fleshy part of arm—no bones broken—the gentleman was still able to fight—let the duel proceed.

Next time Angelo jumped just as Luigi fired, which disordered his aim and caused him to cut a chip out of Howard's ear. The Judge took his time again, and when he fired Angelo jumped and got a knuckle skinned. The doctor inspected and dressed the wounds. Angelo now spoke out and said he was content with the satisfaction he had got, and if the Judge—but Luigi shut him roughly up, and asked him not to make an ass of himself; adding—

"And I want you to stop dodging. You take a great deal too prominent a part in this thing for a person who has got nothing to do with it. You should remember that you are here only by courtesy, and are without official recognition; officially you are not here at all; officially you do not even exist. To all intents and purposes you are absent from this place, and you ought for your own modesty's sake to reflect that it cannot become a person who is not present here to be taking this sort of public and indecent prominence in a matter in which he is not in the slightest degree concerned. Now, don't dodge again; the bullets are not for you, they are for me; if I want them dodged I will attend to it myself. I never saw a person act so."

Angelo saw the reasonableness of what his brother had said, and he did try to reform, but it was of no use; both pistols went off at the same instant, and he jumped once more; he got a sharp scrape along his cheek from the Judge's bullet, and so deflected Luigi's aim that his ball went wide and chipped a flake of skin from Pudd'nhead Wilson's chin. The doctor attended to the wounded.

By the terms, the duel was over. But Luigi was entirely out of patience, and begged for one more exchange of shots, insisting that he had had no fair chance, on account of his brother's in-delicate behavior. Howard was opposed to granting so unusual a privilege, but the Judge took Luigi's part, and added that indeed he himself might fairly be considered entitled to another trial, because although the proxy on the other side was in no way to blame for his (the Judge's) humiliatingly resultless work, the gentleman with whom he was fighting this duel was to blame for it, since if he had played no advantages and had held his head still, his proxy would have been disposed of early. He added—

"Count Luigi's request for another exchange is another proof that he is a brave and chivalrous gentleman, and I beg that the courtesy he asks may be accorded him."

"I thank you most sincerely for this generosity, Judge Driscoll," said Luigi, with a polite bow, and moving to his place. Then he added—to Angelo, "Now hold your grip, hold your *grip*, I tell you, and I'll land him, sure!"

The men stood erect, their pitsol-arms at their sides, the two seconds stood at their official posts, the doctor stood five paces in Wilson's rear with his instruments and bandages in his hands. The deep stillness, the peaceful moonlight, the motionless figures, made an impressive picture and the impending fatal possibilities augmented this impressiveness to solemnity. Wilson's hand began to rise—slowly—slowly—higher—still higher—in another moment—

"*Boom!*"—the first stroke of midnight swung up out of the distance: Angelo was off like a deer!

"Oh, you unspeakable traitor!" wailed his brother, as they went soaring over the fence.

The others stood astonished and gazing; and so stood, watching that strange spectacle until distance dissolved it and swept it from their view. Then they rubbed their eyes like people waking out of a dream.

"Well, I've never seen anything like that before!" said the

Judge. "Wilson, I am going to confess, now, that I wasn't quite able to believe in that leg-business, and had a suspicion that it was a put-up convenience between those twins; and when Count Angelo fainted I thought I saw the whole scheme—thought it was pretext No. 1, and would be followed by others till twelve o'clock should arrive and Luigi would get off with all the credit of seeming to want to fight and yet not have to fight, after all. But I was mistaken. His pluck proved it. He's a brave fellow and did want to fight."

"There isn't any doubt about that," said Howard, and added in a grieved tone, "but what an unworthy sort of Christian that Angelo is—I hope and believe there are not many like him. It is not right to engage in a duel on the Sabbath—I could not approve of that myself; but to finish one that has been begun—that is a duty, let the day be what it may."

They strolled along, still wondering, still talking.

"It is a curious circumstance," remarked the surgeon, halting Wilson a moment to paste some more court plaster on his chin, which had gone to leaking blood again, "that in this duel neither of the parties who handled the pistols lost blood, while nearly all the persons present in the mere capacity of guests got hit. I have not heard of such a thing before. Don't you think it unusual?"

"Yes," said the Judge, "it has struck me as peculiar. Peculiar and unfortunate. I was annoyed at it, all the time. In the case of Angelo it made no great difference, because he was in a measure concerned, though not officially; but it troubled me to see the seconds compromised, and yet I knew no way to mend the matter."

"There was no way to mend it," said Howard, whose ear was being readjusted now by the doctor; "the code fixes our place, and it would not have been lawful to change it. If we could have stood at your side, or behind you, or in front of you, it—but it would not have been legitimate and the other parties would have had a just right to complain of our trying to protect ourselves from danger; infractions of the code are certainly not permissible in any case whatever."

Wilson offered no remarks. It seemed to him that there was very little place here for so much solemnity, but he judged that if a duel where nobody was in danger or got crippled but the seconds and the outsiders had nothing ridiculous about for these gentlemen, his pointing out that feature would probably not help them to see it.

He invited them in to take a nightcap, and Howard and the Judge accepted, but the doctor said he would have to go and see how Angelo's principal wound was getting on.

[It was now Sunday, and in the afternoon Angelo was to be received into the Baptist communion by immersion—a doubtful prospect, the doctor feared.]

CHAPTER VII

When the doctor arrived at Aunt Patsy Cooper's house, he found the lights going and everybody up and dressed and in a great state of solicitude and excitement. The twins were stretched on a sofa in the sitting-room, Aunt Patsy was fussing at Angelo's arm, Nancy was flying around under her commands, the two young boys were trying to keep out of the way and always getting in it, in order to see and wonder, Rowena stood apart, helpless with apprehension and emotion, and Luigi was growling in unappeasable fury over Angelo's shameful flight.

As has been reported before, the doctor was a fool—a kind-hearted and well-meaning one, but with no tact; and as he was by long odds the most learned physician in the town, and was quite well aware of it, and could talk his learning with ease and precision, and liked to show off when he had an audience, he was sometimes tempted into revealing more of a case than was good for the patient.

He examined Angelo's wound, and was really minded to say nothing for once; but Aunt Patsy was so anxious and so pressing that he allowed his caution to be overcome, and proceeded to empty himself as follows, with scientific relish—

"Without going too much into detail, madam—for you would probably not understand it anyway—I concede that great care is going to be necessary here; otherwise exudation of the aesophagus is nearly sure to ensue, and this will be followed by ossification and extradition of the maxillaris superioris, which must decompose the granular surfaces of the great infusorial ganglionic system, thus obstructing the action of the posterior varioloid arteries and precipitating compound strangulated sorosis of the valvular tissues, and ending unavoidably in the dispersion and combustion of the marsupial fluxes and the consequent embrocation of the bicuspid populo redax referendum rotulorum."

A miserable silence followed. Aunt Patsy's heart sank, the pallor of despair invaded her face, she was not able to speak; poor Rowena wrung her hands in privacy and silence, and said to herself in the bitterness of her young grief, "There is no hope—it is plain there is no hope;" the good-hearted negro wench, Nancy, paled to chocolate, then to orange, then to amber, and thought to herself with yearning sympathy and sorrow, "Po' thing, he ain' gwyne to las' throo de half o' dat;" small Henry choked up, and turned his head away to hide his rising tears, and his brother Joe said to himself, with a sense of loss, "The baptizing's busted, that's sure." Luigi was the only person who had any heart to speak. He said, a little bit sharply, to the doctor—

"Well, well, there's nothing to be gained by wasting precious time: give him a barrel of pills—I'll take them for him."

"You?" asked the doctor.

"Yes. Did you suppose he was going to take them himself?"

"Why, of course."

"Well, it's a mistake. He never took a dose of medicine in his life. He can't."

"Well, upon my word, it's the most extraordinary thing I ever heard of!"

"Oh," said Aunt Patsy, as pleased as a mother whose child is being admired and wondered at, "you'll find that there's more about them that's wonderful than their just being made in the image of God like the rest of His creatures, now you can depend on that, *I* tell you," and she wagged her complacent head like one who could reveal marvelous things if she chose.

The boy Joe began—

"Why, ma, they *ain't* made in the im——"

"You shut up, and wait till you're asked, Joe. I'll let you know when I want help. Are you looking for something, Doctor?"

The doctor asked for a few sheets of paper and a pen, and said he would write a prescription; which he did. It was one of Galen's; in fact, it was Galen's favorite, and had been slaying people for sixteen thousand years. Galen used it for everything, applied it to everything, said it would remove everything, from warts all the way through to lungs—and it generally did. Galen was still the only medical authority recognized in Missouri; his practice was the only practice known to the Missouri doctors, and his prescriptions were the only ammunition they carried when they went out for game. By and by Dr. Claypool laid down his pen and read the result of his labors aloud, carefully and deliberately, for this battery must be constructed on the premises by the family, and mistakes could occur; for he wrote a doctor's hand—the hand which from the beginning of time has been so disastrous to the apothecary and so profitable to the undertaker:

"Take of afarabocca, henbane, corpobalsamum, each two drams and a half; of cloves, opium, myrrh, cyperus, each two

175

drams; of opobalsamum, Indian leaf, cinnamon, zedoary, ginger, coftus, coral, cassia, euphorbium, gum tragacanth, frankincense, styrax calamita, celtic, nard, spignel, hartwort, mustard, saxifrage, dill, anise, each one dram; of xylaloes, rheum ponticum, alipta moschata, castor, spikenard, galangals, opoponax, anacardium, mastich, brimstone, peony, eringo, pulp of dates, red and white hermodactyls, roses, thyme, acorns, pennyroyal, gentian, the bark of the root of mandrake, germander, valerian, bishop's weed, bay-berries, long and white pepper, xylobalsamum, carnabadium, macedonian, parsley-seeds, lovage, the seeds of rue, and sinon, of each a dram and a half; of pure gold, pure silver, pearls not perforated, the blatta byzantina, the bone of the stag's heart, of each the quantity of fourteen grains of wheat; of sapphire, emerald and jasper stones, each one dram; of hazel-nut, two drams; of pellitory of Spain, shavings of ivory, calamus odoratus, each the quantity of twenty-nine grains of wheat; of honey or sugar a sufficient quantity. Boil down and skim off.''

"There," he said, "that will fix the patient; give his brother a dipperful every three-quarters of an hour——"

—"while he survives," muttered Luigi—

—"and see that the room is kept wholesomely hot, and the doors and windows closed tight. Keep Count Angelo nicely covered up with six or seven blankets, and when he is thirsty—which will be frequently—moisten a rag in the vapor of the tea-kettle and let his brother suck it. When he is hungry—which will also be frequently—he must not be humored oftener than every seven or eight hours; then toast part of a cracker until it begins to brown, and give it to his brother."

"That is all very well, as far as Angelo is concerned," said Luigi, "but what am I to eat?"

"I do not see that there is anything the matter with you," the doctor answered, "you may of course eat what you please."

"And also drink what I please, I suppose?"

"Oh, certainly—at present. When the violent and continuous perspiring has reduced your strength, I shall have to reduce your diet, of course, and also bleed you, but there is no occasion for that yet awhile." He turned to Aunt Patsy and said: "He must be put to bed, and sat up with, and tended with the greatest care, and not allowed to stir for several days and nights."

"For one, I'm sacredly thankful for that," said Luigi, "it postpones the funeral—I'm not to be drowned to-day, any-how."

Angelo said quietly to the doctor:

"I will cheerfully submit to all your requirements, sir, up to two o'clock this afternoon, and will resume them after three, but cannot be confined to the house during that intermediate hour."

"Why, may I ask?"

"Because I have entered the Baptist communion, and by appointment am to be baptized in the river at that hour."

"Oh, insanity!—it cannot be allowed!"

Angelo answered with placid firmness—

"Nothing shall prevent it, if I am alive."

"Why, consider, my dear sir, in your condition it might prove fatal."

A tender and ecstatic smile beamed from Angelo's eyes, and he broke forth in a tone of joyous fervency—

"Ah, how blessed it would be to die for such a cause—it would be martyrdom!"

"But your brother—consider your brother; you would be risking his life, too."

"He risked mine an hour ago," responded Angelo, gloomily; "did he consider me?" A thought swept through his mind that made him shudder. "If I had not run, I might have been killed in a duel on the Sabbath day, and my soul would have been lost—lost."

"Oh, don't fret, it wasn't in any danger," said Luigi, irritably; "they wouldn't waste it for a little thing like that; there's a glass case all ready for it in the heavenly museum, and a pin to stick it up with."

Aunt Patsy was shocked, and said—

"Looy, Looy!—don't talk so, dear!"

Rowena's soft heart was pierced by Luigi's unfeeling words, and she murmured to herself, "Oh, if I but had the dear privilege of protecting and defending him with my weak voice!—but alas, this sweet boon is denied me by the cruel conventions of social intercourse."

"Get their bed ready," said Aunt Patsy to Nancy, "and shut up the windows and doors, and light their candles, and see that you drive all the mosquitoes out of their bar, and make up a good fire in their stove, and carry up some bags of hot ashes to lay to his feet——"

—"and a shovel of fire for his head, and a mustard plaster for his neck, and some gum shoes for his ears," Luigi interrupted, with temper; and added, to himself, "Damnation, I'm going to be roasted alive, I just know it!"

"Why, Looy! Do be quiet; I never saw such a fractious thing. A body would think you didn't care for your brother."

177

"I don't—to *that* extent, Aunt Patsy. I was glad the drowning was postponed a minute ago, but I'm not, now. No, that is all gone by: I want to be drowned."

"You'll bring a judgment on yourself just as sure as you live, if you go on like that. Why, I never heard the beat of it. Now, there,—there! you've said enough. Not another word out of you,—I won't have it!"

"But, Aunt Patsy——"

"Luigi! Didn't you hear what I told you?"

"But, Aunt Patsy, I—why, I'm not going to set my heart and lungs afloat in that pail of sewage which this criminal here has been prescri——"

"Yes, you are, too. You are going to be good, and do everything I tell you, like a dear," and she tapped his cheek affectionately with her finger. "Rowena, take the prescription and go in the kitchen and hunt up the things and lay them out for me. I'll sit up with my patient the rest of the night, Doctor; I can't trust Nancy, she couldn't make Luigi take the medicine. Of course you'll drop in again during the day. Have you got any more directions?"

"No, I believe not, Aunt Patsy. If I don't get in earlier, I'll be along by early candlelight, anyway. Meantime, don't allow him to get out of his bed."

Angelo said, with calm determination—

"I shall be baptized at two o'clock. Nothing but death shall prevent me."

The doctor said nothing aloud, but to himself he said:

"Why, this chap's got a manly side, after all! Physically he's a coward, but morally he's a lion. I'll go and tell the others about this; it will raise him a good deal in their estimation—and the public will follow their lead, of course."

Privately, Aunt Patsy applauded too, and was proud of Angelo's courage in the moral field as she was of Luigi's in the field of honor.

The boy Henry was troubled, but the boy Joe said, inaudibly, and gratefully, "We're all hunky, after all; and no postponement on account of the weather."

CHAPTER VIII

By nine o'clock the town was humming with the news of the midnight duel, and there were but two opinions about it: one, that Luigi's pluck in the field was most praiseworthy and Angelo's flight most scandalous; the other, that Angelo's courage in flying the field for conscience' sake was as fine and creditable as was Luigi's in holding the field in the face of the bullets. The one opinion was held by half of the town, the other one was maintained by the other half. The division was clean and exact, and it made two parties, an Angelo party and a Luigi party. The twins had suddenly become popular idols along with Pudd'nhead Wilson, and haloed with a glory as intense as his. The children talked the duel all the way to Sunday-school, their elders talked it all the way to church, the choir discussed it behind their red curtain, it usurped the place of pious thought in the "nigger gallery."

By noon the doctor had added the news, and spread it, that Count Angelo, in spite of his wound and all warnings and supplications, was resolute in his determination to be baptised at the hour appointed. This swept the town like wildfire, and mightily reinforced the enthusiasm of the Angelo faction, who said, "If any doubted that it was moral courage that took him from the field, what have they to say now!"

Still the excitement grew. All the morning it was traveling countrywards, toward all points of the compass; so, whereas before only the farmers and their wives were intending to come and witness the remarkable baptism, a general holiday was now proclaimed and the children and negroes admitted to the privileges of the occasion. All the farms for ten miles around were vacated, all the converging roads emptied long processions of wagons, horses and yeomanry into the town. The pack and cram of people vastly exceeded any that had ever been seen in that sleepy region before. The only thing that had ever even approached it, was the time long gone by, but never forgotten, nor even referred to without wonder and pride, when two circuses and a Fourth of July fell together. But the glory of that occasion was extinguished, now, for good. It was but a freshet to this deluge.

The great invasion massed itself on the river bank and waited hungrily for the immense event. Waited, and wondered if it would really happen, or if the twin who was not a "professor" would stand out and prevent it.

But they were not to be disappointed. Angelo was as good as his word. He came attended by an escort of honor composed of several hundred of the best citizens, all of the Angelo party; and when the immersion was finished they escorted him back home; and would even have carried him on their shoulders, but that people might think they were carrying Luigi.

Far into the night the citizens continued to discuss and wonder over the strangely-mated pair of incidents that had distinguished and exalted the past twenty-four hours above any other twenty-four in the history of their town for picturesqueness and splendid interest; and long before the lights were out and burghers asleep it had been decided on all hands that in capturing these twins Dawson's Landing had drawn a prize in the great lottery of municipal fortune.

At midnight Angelo was sleeping peacefully. His immersion had not harmed him, it had merely made him wholesomely drowsy, and he had been dead asleep many hours now. It had made Luigi drowsy, too, but he had got only brief naps, on account of his having to take the medicine every three-quarters of an hour—and Aunt Betsy Hale was there to see that he did it. When he complained and resisted, she was quietly firm with him, and said in a low voice:

"No—no, that won't do; you mustn't talk, and you mustn't retch and gag that way, either—you'll wake up your poor brother."

'Well, what of it, Aunt Betsy, he——"

" 'Sh-h! Don't make a noise, dear. You mustn't forget that your poor brother is sick and——"

"Sick, is he? Well, I wish I——"

"Sh-h-h! Will you be quiet, Luigi! Here, now, take the rest of it— don't keep me holding the dipper all night. I declare if you haven't left a good fourth of it in the bottom! Come—that's a good boy."

"Aunt Betsy, don't make me! I feel like I've swallowed a cemetery; I do, indeed. Do let me rest a little—just a little; I can't take any more of the devilish stuff now."

"Luigi! Using such language here, and him just baptised! Do you want the roof to fall on you?"

"I wish to goodness it would!"

"Why, you dreadful thing! I've a good notion to—let that blanket alone; do you want your brother to catch his death?"

"Aunt Betsy, I've *got* to have it off, I'm being roasted alive; nobody could stand it—you couldn't, yourself."

"Now, then, you're sneezing again—I just expected it."

"Because I've caught a cold in my head. I always do, when I go in the water with my clothes on. And it takes me weeks to get over it, too. I think it was a shame to serve me so."

"Luigi, you are unreasonable; you know very well they couldn't baptise him dry. I should think you would be willing to undergo a little inconvenience for your brother's sake."

"Inconvenience! Now how you talk, Aunt Betsy. I came as near as anything to getting drowned—you saw that, yourself; and do you call this inconvenience?—the room shut up as tight as a drum, and so hot the mosquitoes are trying to get out; and a cold in the head, and dying for sleep and no chance to get any on account of this infamous medicine that that assassin prescri——"

"There, you're sneezing again. I'm going down and mix some more of this truck for you, dear."

CHAPTER IX

During Monday, Tuesday and Wednesday the twins grew steadily worse; but then the doctor was summoned south to attend his mother's funeral and they got well in forty-eight hours. They appeared on the street on Friday, and were welcomed with enthusiasm by the new-born parties, the Luigi and Angelo factions. The Luigi faction carried its strength into the Democratic party, the Angelo faction entered into a combination with the Whigs. The Democrats nominated Luigi for alderman under the new city government, and the Whigs put up Angelo against him. The democrats nominated Pudd'nhead Wilson for mayor, and he was left alone in this glory, for the Whigs had no man who was willing to enter the lists against such a formidable opponent. No politician had scored such a compliment as this before in the history of the Mississippi Valley.

The political campaign in Dawson's Landing opened in a pretty warm fashion, and waxed hotter every week. Luigi's whole heart was in it, and even Angelo developed a surprising amount of interest—which was natural, because he was not merely representing Whigism, a matter of no consequence to him, but he was representing something immensely finer and greater—to wit, Reform. In him was centred the hopes of the whole reform element of the town; he was the chosen and admired champion of every clique that had a pet reform of any sort or kind at heart. He was president of the great Teetotaller's Union, its chiefest prophet and mouthpiece.

But as the canvass went on, troubles began to spring up all around—troubles for the twins, and through them for all the parties and segments and fractions of parties. Whenever Luigi had possession of the legs, he carried Angelo to balls, rum shops, Sons of Liberty parades, horse races, campaign riots, and everywhere else that could damage him with his party and the church; and when it was Angelo's week he carried Luigi diligently to all manner of moral and religious gatherings, doing his best to regain the ground he had lost before. As a result of these double performances, there was a storm blowing all the time, an ever rising storm, too—a storm of frantic criticism of the twins, and rage over their extravagant, incomprehensible conduct.

Luigi had the final chance. The legs were his for the closing week of the canvas. He led his brother a fearful dance.

But he saved his best card for the very eve of the election. There was to be a grand turn-out of the Teetotaller's Union that day, and Angelo was to march at the head of the procession and deliver a great oration afterward. Luigi drank a couple of glasses of whiskey—which steadied his nerves and clarified his mind, but made Angelo drunk. Everybody who saw the march, saw that the Champion of the Teetotallers was half seas over, and noted also that his brother, who made no hypocritical pretensions to extra temperance virtues, was dignified and sober. This eloquent fact could not be unfruitful at the end of a hot political canvass. At the mass meeting Angelo tried to make his great temperance oration but was so discommoded by hiccoughs and thickness of tongue that he had to give it up; then drowsiness overtook him and his head drooped against Luigi's and he went to sleep. Luigi apologized for him, and was going on to improve his opportunity with an appeal for a moderation of what he called "the prevailing teetotal madness," but persons in the audience began to howl and throw things at him, and then the meeting rose in wrath and chased him home.

This episode was a crusher for Angelo in another way. It destroyed his chances with Rowena. Those chances had been growing, right along, for two months. Rowena had partly confessed that she loved him, but wanted time to consider. Now the tender dream was ended, and she told him so, the moment he was sober enough to understand. She said she would never marry a man who drank.

"But I don't drink," he pleaded.

"That is nothing to the point," she said, coldly, "you get drunk, and that is worse."

[There was a long and sufficiently idiotic discussion here, which ended as reported in a previous note.]

CHAPTER X

Dawson's Landing had a week of repose, after the election, and it needed it, for the frantic and variegated nightmare which had tormented it all through the preceding week had left it limp, haggard and exhausted at the end. It got the week of repose because Angelo had the legs, and was in too subdued a condition to want to go out and mingle with an irritated community that had come to distrust and detest him because there was such a lack of harmony between his morals, which were confessedly excellent, and his methods of illustrating them, which were distinctly damnable.

The new city officers were sworn in on the following Monday—at least all but Luigi. There was a complication in his case. His election was conceded, but he could not sit in the board of aldermen without his brother, and his brother could not sit there because he was not a member. There seemed to be no way out of the difficulty but to carry the matter into the courts, so this was resolved upon. The case was set for the Monday fortnight. In due course the time arrived. In, the meantime the city government had been at a stand-still, because without Luigi there was a tie in the board of aldermen, whereas with him the liquor interest—the richest in the political field—would have one majority. But the court decided that Angelo could not sit in the board with him, either in public or executive sessions, and at the same time forbade the board to deny admission to Luigi, a fairly and legally chosen alderman. The case was carried up and up from court to court, yet still the same old original decision was confirmed every time. As a result, the city government not only stood still, with its hands tied, but everything it was created to protect and care for went a steady gait toward rack and ruin. There was no way to levy a tax, so the minor officials had to resign or starve; therefore they resigned. There being no city money, the enormous legal expenses on both sides had to be defrayed by private subscription. But at last the people came to their senses, and said—

"Pudd'nhead was right, at the start—we ought to have hired the official half of that human phillipene to resign; but it's too late, now; some of us haven't got anything left to hire him with."

"Yes, we have," said another citizen, "we've got this"—and he produced a halter.

Many shouted, "That's the ticket." But others said, "No—Count Angelo is innocent; we mustn't hang him."

"Who said anything about hanging him? We are only going to hang the other one."

"Then that is all right—there is no objection to that."

So they hanged Luigi. And so ends the history of "Those Extraordinary Twins."

FINAL REMARKS

As you see, it was an extravagant sort of a tale, and had no purpose but to exhibit that monstrous "freak" in all sorts of grotesque lights. But when Roxy wandered into the tale she had to be furnished with something to do; so she changed the children in the cradle: this necessitated the invention of a reason for it; this in turn resulted in making the children prominent personages—nothing could prevent it, of course. Their career began to take a tragic aspect, and some one had to be brought in to help work the machinery; so Pudd'nhead Wilson was introduced and taken on trial. By this time the whole show was being run by the new people and in their interest, and the original show was become side-tracked and forgotten; the twin-monster and the heroine and the lads and the old ladies had dwindled to inconsequentialities and were merely in the way. Their story was one story, the new people's story was another story, and there was no connection between them, no interdependence, no kinship. It is not practicable or rational to try to tell two stories at the same time; so I dug out the farce and left the tragedy.

The reader already knew how the expert works; he knows now how the other kind do it.

MARK TWAIN.

"The Awful German Language" was an appendix to an *illustrated volume of European travel sketches called* A Tramp Abroad *that was brought out by the American Publishing Company in 1880 in an attempt to repeat the success of* The Innocents Abroad. *Although* A Tramp Abroad *accomplished this commercial aim, it was, unlike its predecessor, a very uneven performance.*

The Awful German Language

A little learning makes the whole world kin.—Proverbs xxxii, 7.

I went often to look at the collection of curiosities in Heidelberg Castle, and one day I surprised the keeper of it with my German. I spoke entirely in that language. He was greatly interested; and after I had talked awhile he said my German was very rare, possibly a "unique;" and wanted to add it to his museum.

If he had known what it had cost me to acquire my art, he would also have known that it would break any collector to buy it. Harris and I had been hard at work on our German during several weeks at that time, and although we had made good progress, it had been accomplished under great difficulty and annoyance, for three of our teachers had died in the meantime. A person who has not studied German can form no idea of what a perplexing language it is.

Surely there is not another language that is so slip-shod and systemless, and so slippery and elusive to the grasp. One is washed about in it, hither and hither, in the most helpless way; and when at last he thinks he has captured a rule which offers firm ground to take a rest on amid the general rage and turmoil of the ten parts of speech, he turns over the page and reads, "Let the pupil make careful note of the following *exceptions.*" He runs his eye down and finds that there are more exceptions to the rule than instances of it. So overboard he goes again, to hunt for another Ararat and find another quicksand. Such has been, and continues to be, my experience. Every time I think I have got one of these four confusing "cases" where I am master of it, a seemingly insignificant preposition intrudes itself into my sentence, clothed with an awful and unsuspected power, and crumbles the ground from under me. For instance, my book inquires after a certain bird—(it is always inquiring after things which are of no sort of consequence to anybody): "Where is the bird?" Now the answer to this question,—according to the book,—is that the bird is waiting in the blacksmith shop on account of the rain. Of course no bird would do that, but then you must stick to the book. Very well, I begin to cipher out the German for that answer. I begin at the wrong end, necessarily, for that is the German idea. I say to myself, "*Regen*, (rain,) is masculine—or maybe it is feminine—or possibly neuter—it is too much trouble to look, now. Therefore, it is either *der* (the) Regen, or *die* (the) Regen, or *das* (the) Regen, according to which gender it may turn out to be when I look. In the interest of science, I will cipher it out on the hypothesis that it is masculine. Very well—then *the* rain is *der* Regen, if it is simply in the quiescent state of being *mentioned*, without enlargement or discussion—Nominative case; but if this rain is lying around, in a kind of a general way on the ground, it is then definitely located, it is *doing something*—that is, *resting*, (which is one of the German grammar's ideas of doing something,) and this throws the rain into the Dative case, and makes it *dem* Regen. However, this rain is not resting, but is doing something *actively*,—it is falling,—to interfere with the bird, likely,—and this indicates *movement*, which has the effect of sliding it into the Accusative case and changing *dem* Regen into *den* Regen." Having completed the grammatical horoscope of this matter, I answer up confidently and state in German that the bird is staying in the blacksmith shop "wegen (on account of) *den* Regen." Then the teacher lets me softly down with the remark that whenever the word "wegen" drops into a sentence, it *always* throws that subject into the *Genitive* case, regardless of consequences—and that therefore this bird staid in the blacksmith shop "wegen *des* Regens."

N.B. I was informed, later, by a higher authority, that there was an "exception" which permits one to say "wegen *den* Regen" in certain peculiar and complex circumstances, but that this exception is not extended to anything *but* rain.

There are ten parts of speech, and they are all troublesome. An average sentence, in a German newspaper, is a sublime and impressive curiosity; it occupies a quarter of a column; it contains all the ten parts of speech—not in regular order, but mixed;

it is built mainly of compound words constructed by the writer on the spot, and not to be found in any dictionary—six or seven words compacted into one, without joint or seam—that is, without hyphens; it treats of fourteen or fifteen different subjects, each enclosed in a parenthesis of its own, with here and there extra parentheses which re-enclose three or four of the minor parentheses, making pens within pens; finally, all the parentheses and re-parentheses are massed together between a couple of king-parentheses, one of which is placed in the first line of the majestic sentence and the other in the middle of the last line of it—*after which comes the* VERB, and you find out for the first time what the man has been talking about; and after the verb—merely by way of ornament, as far as I can make out,—the writer shovels in *"haben sind gewesen gehabt haben geworden sein,"* or words to that effect, and the monument is finished. I suppose that this closing hurrah is in the nature of the flourish to a man's signature—not necessary, but pretty. German books are easy enough to read when you hold them before the looking-glass or stand on your head,—so as to reverse the construction,—but I think that to learn to read and understand a German newspaper is a thing which must always remain an impossibility to a foreigner.

Yet even the German books are not entirely free from attacks of the Parenthesis distemper—though they are usually so mild as to cover only a few lines, and therefore when you at last get down to the verb it carries some meaning to your mind because you are able to remember a good deal of what has gone before.

Now here is a sentence from a popular and excellent German novel,—with a slight parenthesis in it. I will make a perfectly literal translation, and throw in the parenthesis-marks and some hyphens for the assistance of the reader,—though in the original there are no parenthesis-marks or hyphens, and the reader is left to flounder through to the remote verb the best way he can:

"But when he, upon the street, the (in-satin-and-silk-covered-now-very-unconstrainedly-after-the-newest-fashion-dressed) government counseller's wife *met"* etc., etc.*

That is from "The Old Mamselle's Secret," by Mrs. Marlitt. And that sentence is constructed upon the most approved German model. You observe how far that verb is from the reader's base of operations; well, in a German newspaper they put their verb away over on the next page; and I have heard that sometimes after stringing along on exciting preliminaries and paren-

---

* Wenn er aber auf der Strasse der in Sammt und Seide gehüllten jetz sehr ungenirt nach der neusten mode gekleideten Regierungsrathin begegnet."

theses for a column or two, they get in a hurry and have to go to press without getting to the verb at all. Of course, then, the reader is left in a very exhausted and ignorant state.

We have the Parenthesis disease in our literature, too; and one may see cases of it every day in our books and newspapers: but with us it is the mark and sign of an unpractised writer or a cloudy intellect, whereas with the Germans it is doubtless the mark and sign of a practised pen and of the presence of that sort of luminous intellectual fog which stands for clearness among these people. For surely it is *not* clearness,—it necessarily can't be clearness. Even a jury would have penetration enough to discover that. A writer's ideas must be a good deal confused, a good deal out of line and sequence, when he starts out to say that a man met a counsellor's wife in the street, and then right in the midst of this so simple undertaking halts these approaching people and makes them stand still until he jots down an inventory of the woman's dress. That is manifestly absurd. It reminds a person of those dentists who secure your instant and breathless interest in a tooth by taking a grip on it with the forceps, and then stand there and drawl through a tedious anecdote before they give the dreaded jerk. Parentheses in literature and dentistry are in bad taste.

The Germans have another kind of parenthesis, which they make by splitting a verb in two and putting half of it at the beginning of an exciting chapter and the *other half* at the end of it. Can any one conceive of anything more confusing than that? These things are called "separable verbs." The German grammar is blistered all over with separable verbs; and the wider the two portions of one of them are spread apart, the better the author of the crime is pleased with his performance. A favorite one is *reiste ab*,—which means, *departed*. Here is an example which I culled from a novel and reduced to English:

"The trunks being now ready, he DE-after kissing his mother and sisters, and once more pressing to his bosom his adored Gretchen, who, dressed in simple white muslin, with a single tube-rose in the ample folds of her rich brown hair, had tottered feebly down the stairs, still pale from the terror and excitement of the past evening, but longing to lay her poor aching head yet once again upon the breast of him whom she loved more dearly than life itself, PARTED."

However, it is not well to dwell too much on the separable verbs. One is sure to lose his temper early; and if he sticks to the subject, and will not be warned, it will at last either soften his brain or petrify it. Personal pronouns and adjectives are a fruitful nuisance in this language, and should have been left out. For instance, the same sound, *sie*, means *you*, and it means *she*, and it means *her*, and it means *it*, and it means *they*, and it means *them*. Think of the ragged poverty of a language which has to make one word do the work of six,—and a poor little weak thing of only three letters at that. But mainly, think of the exasperation of never knowing which of these meanings the speaker is trying to convey. This explains why, whenever a person says *sie* to me, I generally try to kill him, if a stranger.

Now observe the Adjective. Here was a case where simplicity would have been an advantage; therefore, for no other reason, the inventor of this language complicated it all he could. When we wish to speak of our "good friend or friends," in our enlightened tongue, we stick to the one form and have no trouble or hard feeling about it; but with the German tongue it is different. When a German gets his hands on an adjective, he declines it, and keeps on declining it until the common sense is all declined out of it. It is as bad as Latin. He says, for instance:

SINGULAR.

Nominative—Mein gut*er* Freund, my good friend.
Genitive—Mein*es* gut*en* Freund*es*, of my good friend.
Dative—Mein*em* gut*en* Freund, to my good friend.
Accusative—Mein*en* gut*en* Freund, my good friend.

PLURAL.

N.—Mein*e* gut*en* Freund*e*, my good friends.
G.—Mein*er* gut*en* Freund*e*, of my good friends.
D.—Mein*en* gut*en* Freund*en*, to my good friends.
A.—Mein*e* gut*en* Freund*e*, my good friends.

Now let the candidate for the asylum try to memorize those variations, and see how soon he will be elected. One might better go without friends in Germany than take all this trouble about them. I have shown what a bother it is to decline a good (male) friend; well, this is only a third of the work, for there is a variety of new distortions of the adjective to be learned when the object is feminine, and still another when the object is neuter. Now there are more adjectives in this language than there are black cats in Switzerland, and they must all be as elaborately declined as the examples above suggested. Difficult?—troublesome?—these words cannot describe it. I heard a Californian student in Heidelberg, say, in one of his calmest moods, that he would rather decline two drinks than one German adjective.

The inventor of the language seems to have taken pleasure in complicating it in every way he could think of. For instance, if one is casually referring to a house, *Haus*, or a horse, *Pferd*, or a dog, *Hund*, he spells these words as I have indicated; but if he is referring to them in the Dative case, he sticks on a foolish and unnecessary *e* and spells them Hause, Pferde, Hunde. So, as an added *e* often signifies the plural, as the *s* does with us, the new student is likely to go on for a month making twins out of a Dative dog before he discovers his mistake; and on the other hand, many a new student who could ill afford loss, has bought and paid for two dogs and only got one of them, because he ignorantly bought that dog in the Dative singular when he really supposed he was talking plural,—which left the law on the seller's side, of course, by the strict rules of grammar, and therefore a suit for recovery could not lie.

In German, all the Nouns begin with a capital letter. Now that is a good idea; and a good idea, in this language, is necessarily conspicuous from its lonesomeness. I consider this capitalizing of nouns a good idea, because by reason of it you are almost always able to tell a noun the minute you see it. You fall into error occasionally, because you mistake the name of a person for the name of a thing, and waste a good deal of time trying to dig a meaning out of it. German names almost always do mean something, and this helps to deceive the student. I translated a passage one day, which said that "the infuriated tigress broke loose and utterly ate up the unfortunate fir-forest," (*Tannenwald*.) When I was girding up my loins to doubt this, I found out that Tannenwald, in this instance, was a man's name.

Every noun has a gender, and there is no sense or system in the distribution; so the gender of each must be learned separately and by heart. There is no other way. To do this, one has to have a memory like a memorandum book. In German, a young lady has no sex, while a turnip has. Think what overwrought reverence that shows for the turnip, and what callous disrespect for the girl. See how it looks in print—I translate this from a conversation in one of the best of the German Sunday-school books:

"*Gretchen.*   Wilhelm, where is the turnip?

"*Wilhelm.*   She has gone to the kitchen.

"*Gretchen.* Where is the accomplished and beautiful English maiden?

"*Wilhelm.* It has gone to the opera."

To continue with the German genders: a tree is male, its buds are female, its leaves are neuter; horses are sexless, dogs are male, cats are female,—Tom-cats included, of course; a person's mouth, neck, bosom, elbows, fingers, nails, feet, and body, are of the male sex, and his head is male or neuter according to the word selected to signify it, and *not* according to the sex of the individual who wears it,—for in Germany all the women wear either male heads or sexless ones; a person's nose, lips, shoulders, breast, hands, hips, and toes are of the female sex; and his hair, ears, eyes, chin, legs, knees, heart, and conscience, haven't any sex at all. The inventor of the language probably got what he knew about a conscience from hearsay.

Now, by the above dissection, the reader will see that in Germany a man may *think* he is a man, but when he comes to look into the matter closely, he is bound to have his doubts; he finds that in sober truth he is a most ridiculous mixture; and if he ends by trying to comfort himself with the thought that he can at least depend on a third of this mess as being manly and masculine, the humiliating second thought will quickly remind him that in this respect he is no better off than any woman or cow in the land.

In the German it is true that by some oversight of the inventor of the language, a Woman is a female; but a Wife, (*Weib*,) is not,—which is unfortunate. A Wife, here, has no sex; she is neuter; so, according to the grammar, a fish is *he*, his scales are *she*, but a fishwife is neither. To describe a wife as sexless, may be called under-description; that is bad enough, but over-description is surely worse. A German speaks of an Englishman as the *Engländer*; to change the sex, he adds *inn*, and that stands for Englishwoman,—*Engländerinn*. That seems descriptive enough, but still it is not exact enough for a German; so he precedes the word with that article which indicates that the creature to follow is feminine, and writes it down thus: "*die* Englander*inn*,"—which means "the *she-Englishwoman*." I consider that that person is over-described.

Well, after the student has learned the sex of a great number of nouns, he is still in a difficulty, because he finds it impossible to persuade his tongue to refer to things as "*he*" and "*she*," and "*him*" and "*her*," which it has been always accustomed to refer to as "*it*." When he even frames a German sentence in his mind, with the hims and hers in the right places, and then works up his courage to the utterance-point, it is no use,—the moment he begins to speak his tongue flies the track and all those labored males and females come out as *"its."* And even when he is reading German to himself, he always calls those things *"it;"* whereas he ought to read in this way:

TALE OF THE FISHWIFE AND ITS SAD FATE.*

It is a bleak Day. Hear the Rain, how he pours, and the Hail, how he rattles; and see the Snow, how he drifts along, and oh the Mud, how deep he is! Ah the poor Fishwife, it is stuck fast in the Mire; it has dropped its Basket of Fishes; and its Hands have been cut by the Scales as it seized some of the falling Creatures; and one Scale has even got into its Eye, and it cannot get her out. It opens its Mouth to cry for Help; but if any Sound comes out of him, alas he is drowned by the raging of the Storm. And now a Tomcat has got one of the Fishes and she will surely escape with him. No, she bites off a Fin, she holds her in her Mouth,— will she swallow her? No, the Fishwife's brave Mother-Dog deserts his Puppies and rescues the Fin,—which he eats, himself, as his Reward. O, horror, the Lightning has struck the Fishbasket, he sets him on Fire; see the Flame, how she licks the doomed Utensil with her red and angry Tongue; now she attacks the helpless Fishwife's Foot,—she burns him up, all but the big Toe, and even *she* is partly consumed; and still she spreads, still she waves her fiery Tongues; she attacks the Fishwife's Leg and destroys *it*; she attacks its Hand and destroys *her*; she attacks its poor worn Garment and destroys *her* also; she attacks its Body and consumes *him*; she wreathes herself about its Heart and *it* is consumed; next about its Breast, and in a Moment *she* is a Cinder; now she reaches its Neck,—*he* goes; now its Chin,—*it* goes; now its Nose,—*she* goes. In another Moment, except Help come, the Fishwife will be no more. Time presses,—is there none to succor and save? Yes! Joy, joy, with flying Feet the she-Englishwoman comes! But alas, the generous she-Female is too late: where now is the fated Fishwife? It has ceased from its Sufferings, it has gone to a better Land; all that is left of it for its loved Ones to lament over, is this poor smouldering Ash-heap. Ah, woful, woful Ash-heap! Let us take him up tenderly, reverently, upon the lowly Shovel, and bear him to his long Rest, with the Prayer that when he rises again it will be in a Realm where he will have one good square responsible Sex, and have it all to himself, instead of having a mangy lot of assorted Sexes scattered all over him in Spots.

*I capitalize the nouns, in the German (and ancient English) fashion.

There, now, the reader can see for himself that this pronoun-business is a very awkward thing for the unaccustomed tongue.

I suppose that in all languages the similarities of look and sound between words which have no similarity in meaning are a fruitful source of perplexity to the foreigner. It is so in our tongue, and it is notably the case in the German. Now there is that troublesome word *vermählt:* to me it has so close a resemblance,—either real or fancied,—to three or four other words, that I never know whether it means despised, painted, suspected, or married; until I look in the dictionary, and then I find it means the latter. There are lots of such words, and they are a great torment. To increase the difficulty there are words which *seem* to resemble each other, and yet do not; but they make just as much trouble as if they did. For instance, there is the word *vermiethen*, (to let, to lease, to hire); and the word *verheirathen*, (another way of saying to *marry*.) I heard of an Englishman who knocked at a man's door in Heidelberg and proposed, in the best German he could command, to "verheirathen" that house. Then there are some words which mean one thing when you emphasize the first syllable, but mean something very different if you throw the emphasis on the last syllable. For instance, there is a word which means a run-away, or the act of glancing through a book, according to the placing of the emphasis; and another word which signifies to *associate* with a man, or to *avoid* him, according to where you put the emphasis,—and you can generally depend on putting it in the wrong place and getting into trouble.

There are some exceedingly useful words in this language. *Schlag*, for example; and *Zug*. There are three-quarters of a column of Schlags in the dictionary, and a column and a half of Zugs. The world Schlag means Blow, Stroke, Dash, Hit, Shock, Clap, Slap, Time, Bar, Coin, Stamp, Kind, Sort, Manner, Way, Apoplexy, Wood-Cutting, Enclosure, Field, Forest-Clearing. This is its simple and *exact* meaning,—that is to say, its restricted, its fettered meaning; but there are ways by which you can set it free, so that it can soar away, as on the wings of the morning, and never be at rest. You can hang any word you please to its tail, and make it mean anything you want to. You can begin with *Schlag-ader*, which means artery, and you can hang on the whole dictionary, word by word, clear through the alphabet to *Schlag-wasser*, which means bilge-water,—and including *Schlag-mutter*, which means mother-in-law.

Just the same with *Zug*. Strictly speaking, Zug means Pull, Tug, Draught, Procession, March, Progress, Flight, Direction, Expedition, Train, Caravan, Passage, Stroke, Touch, Line,

Flourish, Trait of Character, Feature, Lineament, Chess-move, Organstop, Team, Whiff, Bias, Drawer, Propensity, Inhalation, Disposition: but that thing which it does *not* mean,—when all its legitimate pendants have been hung on, has not been discovered yet.

One cannot over-estimate the usefulness of Schlag and Zug. Armed just with these two, and the word *Also*, what cannot the foreigner on German soil accomplish? The German word *Also* is the equivalent of the English phrase "You know," and does not mean anything at all,—in *talk*, though it sometimes does in print. Every time a German opens his mouth an *Also* falls out; and every time he shuts it he bites one in two that was trying to *get* out.

Now, the foreigner, equipped with these three noble words, is master of the situation. Let him talk right along, fearlessly; let him pour his indifferent German forth, and when he lacks for a word, let him heave a *Schlag* into the vacuum; all the chances are, that it fits it like a plug; but if it doesn't, let him promptly heave a *Zug* after it; the two together can hardly fail to bung the hole; but if, by a miracle, they *should* fail, let him simply say *Also*! and this will give him a moment's chance to think of the needful word. In Germany, when you load your conversational gun it is always best to throw in a *Schlag* or two and a *Zug* or two; because it doesn't make any difference how much the rest of the charge may scatter, you are bound to bag something with *them*. Then you blandly say *Also*, and load up again. Nothing gives such an air of grace and elegance and unconstraint to a German or an English conversation as to scatter it full of "Also's" or "You-knows."

In my note-book I find this entry:

July 1.-In the hospital, yesterday, a word of thirteen syllables was successfully removed from a patient,—a North-German from near Hamburg; but as most unfortunately the surgeons had opened him in the wrong place, under the impression that he contained a panorama, he died. The sad event has cast a gloom over the whole community.

That paragraph furnished a text for a few remarks about one of the most curious and notable features of my subject,—the length of German words. Some German words are so long that they have a perspective. Observe these examples:

Freudschaftsbezeigungen.

Dilletantenaufdringlichkeiten.

Stadtverordnetenversammlungen.

These things are not words, they are alphabetical processions. And they are not rare; one can open a German newspaper any time and see them marching majestically across the page,—and if he has any imagination he can see the banners and hear the music, too. They impart a martial thrill to the meekest subject. I take a great interest in these curiosities. Whenever I come across a good one, I stuff it and put it in my museum. In this way I have made quite a valuable collection. When I get duplicates, I exchange with other collectors, and thus increase the variety of my stock. Here are some specimens which I lately bought at an auction sale of the effects of a bankrupt bric-a-brac hunter:

GENERALSTAATSVERORDNETENVERSAMMLUGEN.

ALTERTHUMSWISSENSCHAFTEN.

KINDERBEWAHRUNGSANSTALTEN.

UNABHAENGIGKEITSERKLAERUNGEN.

WIEDERHERSTELLUNGSBESTREBUNGEN.

WAFFENSTILLSTANDSUNTERHANDLUNGEN.

Of course when one of these grand mountain ranges goes stretching across the printed page, it adorns and ennobles that literary landscape,—but at the same time it is a great distress to the new student, for it blocks up his way; he cannot crawl under it, or climb over it or tunnel through it. So he resorts to the dictionary for help; but there is no help there. The dictionary must draw the line somewhere,—so it leaves this sort of words out. And it is right, because these long things are hardly legitimate words, but are rather combinations of words, and the inventor of them ought to have been killed. They are compound words, with the hyphens left out. The various words used in building them are in the dictionary, but in a very scattered condition; so you can hunt the materials out, one by one, and get at the meaning at last, but it is a tedious and harrassing business. I have tried this process upon some of the above examples. 'Freundschaftsbezeigungen" seems to be "Friendship demonstrations," which is only a foolish and clumsy way of saying "demonstrations of friendship." "Unabhaengigkeitserklaerungen" seems to be "Independencedeclarations," which is no improvement upon "Declarations of Independence," as far as I can see. "Generalstaatsverordnetenversammlungen" seems to be "Generalstatesrepresentativesmeetings," as nearly as I can get at it,—a mere rhythmical, gushy euphuism for "meetings of the legislature," I judge. We used to have a good deal of this sort of crime in our literature, but it has gone out, now. We used to speak of a thing as a "never-to-be-forgotten" circumstance, instead of cramping it into the simple and sufficient word "memorable" and then going calmly about our business as if nothing had happened. In those days we were not content to embalm the thing and bury it decently, we wanted to build a monument over it.

But in our newspapers the compounding-disease lingers a little to the present day, but with the hyphens left out, in the German fashion. This is the shape it takes: instead of saying "Mr. Simmons, clerk of the country and district courts, was in town yesterday," the new form puts it thus: "Clerk of the County and District Court Simmons was in town yesterday." This saves neither time nor ink, and has an awkward sound besides. One often sees a remark like this in our papers: "*Mrs.*Assistant District Attorney Johnson returned to her city residence yesterday for the season." That is a case of really unjustifiable compounding; because it not only saves no time or trouble, but confers a title on Mrs. Johnson which she has no right to. But these little instances are trifles indeed, contrasted with the ponderous and dismal German system of piling jumbled compounds together. I wish to submit the following local item, from a Mannheim journal, by way of illustration:

"In the daybeforeyesterdayshortlyaftereleveno'clock Night, the inthistownstandingtavern called "The Wagoner" was downburnt. When the fire to the onthedownburninghouseresting Stork's Nest reached, flew the parent Storks away. But when the byteraging, firesurrounded Nest *itself* caught Fire, straightway plunged the quickreturning Mother-Stork into the Flames and died, her Wings over young ones outspread."

Even the cumbersome German construction is not able to take the pathos out of that picture,—indeed it somehow seems to strengthen it. This item is dated away back yonder months ago. I could have used it sooner, but I was waiting to hear from the Father-Stork. I am still waiting.

"*Also!*" If I have not shown that the German is a difficult language, I have at least intended to do it. I have heard of an American student who was asked how he was getting along with his German, and who answered promptly: "I am not getting along at all. I have worked at it hard for three level months, and all I have got to show for it is one solitary German phrase,—'*Zwei glas,*' " (two glasses of beer.) He paused a moment, reflectively, then added with feeling, "But I've got that *solid!*"

And if I have not also shown that German is a harassing and infuriating study, my execution has been at fault, and not my intent. I heard lately of a worn and sorely tried American student who used to fly to a certain German word for relief when he could bear up under his aggravations no longer,—the only word in the whole language whose sound was sweet and precious to his ear and healing to his lacerated spirit. This was the word *Damit*.

It was only the *sound* that helped him, not the meaning*; and so, at last, when he learned that the emphasis was not on the first syllable, his only stay and support was gone, and he faded away and died.

I think that a description of any loud, stirring, tumultuous episode must be tamer in German than in English. Our descriptive words of this character have such a deep, strong, resonant sound, while their German equivalents do seem so thin and mild and energyless. Boom, burst, crash, roar, storm, bellow, blow, thunder, explosion; howl, cry, shout, yell, groan; battle, hell. These are magnificent words; they have a force and magnitude of sound befitting the things which they describe. But their German equivalents would be ever so nice to sing the children to sleep with, or else my awe-inspiring ears were made for display and not for superior usefulness in analyzing sounds. Would any man want to die in a battle which was called by so tame a term as a *Schlacht?* Or would not a consumptive feel too much bundled up, who was about to go out, in a shirt collar and a seal ring, into a storm which the bird-song word *Gewitter* was employed to describe? And observe the strongest of the several German equivalents for explosion,—*Ausbruch.* Our word Toothbrush is more powerful than that. It seems to me that the Germans could do worse than import it into their language to describe particularly tremendous explosions with. The German word for hell,—Hölle,—sounds more like *helly* than anything else; therefore, how necessarily chipper, frivolous and unimpressive it is. If a man were told in German to go there, could he really rise to the dignity of feeling insulted?

Having now pointed out, in detail, the several vices of this language, I now come to the brief and pleasant task of pointing out its virtues. The capitalizing of the nouns, I have already mentioned. But far before this virtue stands another,—that of spelling a word according to the sound of it. After one short lesson in the alphabet, the student can tell how any German word is pronounced, without having to ask; whereas in our language if a student should inquire of us "What does B,O,W, spell?" we should be obliged to reply, "Nobody can tell what it spells, when you set it off by itself,—you can only tell by referring to the context and finding out what it signifies,—whether it is a thing to shoot arrows with, or a nod of one's head, or the forward end of a boat."

There are some German words which are singularly and

---

*It merely means, in its general sense, *"herewith."*

powerfully effective. For instance, those which describe lowly, peaceful and affectionate home life; those which deal with love, in any and all forms, from mere kindly feeling and honest good will toward the passing stranger, clear up to courtship; those which deal with out door Nature, in its softest and loveliest aspects,—with meadows, and forests, and birds and flowers, the fragrance and sunshine of summer, and the moonlight of peaceful winter nights; in a word, those which deal with any and all forms of rest, repose, and peace; those also which deal with the creatures and marvels of fairyland; and lastly and chiefly, in those words which express pathos, is the language surpassingly rich and effective. There are German songs which can make a stranger to the language cry. That shows that the *sound* of the words is correct,—it interprets the meanings with truth and with exactness; and so the ear is informed, and through the ear, the heart.

The Germans do not seem to be afraid to repeat a word when it is the right one. They repeat it several times, if they choose. That is wise. But in English when we have used a word a couple of times in a paragraph, we imagine we are growing tautological, and so we are weak enough to exchange it for some other word which only approximates exactness, to escape what we wrongly fancy is a greater blemish. Repetition may be bad, but surely inexactness is worse.

———

There are people in the world who will take a great deal of trouble to point out the faults in a religion or a language, and then go blandly about their business without suggesting any remedy. I am not that kind of a person. I have shown that the German language needs reforming. Very well, I am ready to reform it. At least I am ready to make the proper suggestions. Such a course as this might be immodest in another; but I have devoted upwards of nine full weeks, first and last, to a careful and critical study of this tongue, and thus have acquired a confidence in my ability to reform it which no mere superficial culture could have conferred upon me.

In the first place, I would leave out the Dative Case. It confuses the plurals; and besides, nobody ever knows when he is in the Dative Case, except he discover it by accident,—and then he does not know when or where it was that he got into it, or how long he has been in it, or how he is ever going to get out of it again. The Dative Case is but an ornamental folly,—it is better to discard it.

In the next place, I would move the Verb further up to the

front. You may load up with ever so good a Verb, but I notice that you never really bring down a subject with it at the present German range,—you only cripple it. So I insist that this important part of speech should be brought forward to a position where it may be easily seen with the naked eye.

Thirdly, I would import some strong words from the English tongue,—to swear with, and also to use in describing all sorts of vigorous things in a vigorous way.*

Fourthly, I would reorganize the sexes, and distribute them according to the will of the Creator. This as a tribute of respect, if nothing else.

Fifthly, I would do away with those great long compounded words; or require the speaker to deliver them in sections, with intermissions for refreshments. To wholly do away with them would be best, for ideas are more easily received and digested when they come one at a time than when they come in bulk. Intellectual food is like any other; it is pleasanter and more beneficial to take it with a spoon than with a shovel.

Sixthly, I would require a speaker to stop when he is done, and not hang a string of those useless "haben sind gewesen gehabt haben geworden seins" to the end of his oration. This sort of gew-gaws undignify a speech, instead of adding a grace. They are therefore an offense, and should be discarded.

Seventhly, I would discard the Parenthesis. Also the re-Parenthesis, the re-re-parenthesis, and the re-re-re-re-re-re-parentheses, and likewise the final wide-reaching all-enclosing King-parenthesis. I would require every individual, be he high or low, to unfold a plain straightforward tale, or else coil it and sit on it and hold his peace. Infractions of this law should be punishable with death.

And eighthly and lastly, I would retain *Zug* and *Schlag,* with their pendants, and discard the rest of the vocabulary. This would simplify the language.

I have now named what I regard as the most necessary and important changes. These are perhaps all I could be expected to name for nothing; but there are other suggestions which I can

---

*"*Verdammt,*" and its variations and enlargements, are word which have plenty of meaning, but the *sounds* are so mild and ineffectual that German ladies can use them without sin. German ladies who could not be induced to commit a sin by any persuasion or compulsion, promptly rip out one of these harmless little words when they tear their dresses or don't like the soup. It sounds about as wicked as our "My gracious." German ladies are constantly saying, "Ach! Gott!" "Mein Gott!" "Gott in Himmel!" "Herr Gott!" "Der Herr Jesus!" etc. They think our ladies have the same custom, perhaps, for I once heard a gentle and lovely old German lady say to a sweet young American girl, "The two languages are so alike—how pleasant that is; we say 'Ach! Gott!' you say '*Goddam.*' "

and will make in case my proposed application shall result in my being formally employed by the government in the work of re-forming the language.

My philological studies have satisfied me that a gifted person ought to learn English (barring spelling and pronouncing), in 30 hours, French in 30 days, and German in 30 years. It seems manifest, then, that the latter tongue ought to be trimmed down and repaired. If it is to remain as it is, it ought to be gently and reverently set aside among the dead languages, for only the dead have time to learn it.

A FOURTH OF JULY ORATION IN THE GERMAN TONGUE, DELIVERED AT A BANQUET OF THE ANGLO-AMERICAN CLUB OF STUDENTS BY THE AUTHOR OF THIS BOOK.

GENTLEMEN: Since I arrived, a month ago, in this old wonderland, this vast garden of Germany, my English tongue has so often proved a useless piece of baggage to me, and so troublesome to carry around, in a country where they haven't the checking system for luggage, that I finally set to work, last week, and learned the German language. Also! Es freüt mich dass dies so ist, denn es muss, in ein hauptsächlich degree, höflich sein, dass man aüf ein occasion like this, sein Rede in die Sprache des Landes worin he boards, aüssprechen soll. Dafür habe ich, aus reinische Verlegenheit,—no Vergangenheit,—no, I mean Höflichkeit,—aüs reinische Höflichkeit habe ich resolved to tackle this business in the German language, üm Gottes willen! Also! Sie müssen so freündlich sein, ünd verzeih mich die interlarding von ein oder zwei Englischer Worte, hie ünd da, denn ich finde dass die deutches is not a very copious language, and so when you've really got anything to say, you've got to draw on a language that can stand the strain.

Wenn aber man kann nicht meinem Rede verstehen, so werde ich ihm spater dasselbe übersetz, wenn er solche Dienst verlangen wollen haben werden sollen sein hätte. (I don't know what wollen haben werden sollen sein hätte means, but I notice they always put it at the end of a German sentence—merely for general literary gorgeousness, I suppose.)

This is a great and justly honored day,—a day which is worthy of the veneration in which it is held by the true patriots of all climes and nationalities,—a day which offers a fruitful theme for thought and speech; ünd meinem Freünde,—no, meinen Freüden,—meines Freündes,—well, take your choice, they're all the same price; I don't know which one is right,—also! ich habe gehabt haben worden gewesen sein, as Goethe says, in his

Paradise Lost,—ich,—ich,—that is to say,—ich,—but let us change cars.

Also! Die Anblich so viele Grossbrittanischer ünd Amerikanischer hier zusammengetroffen in Bruderliche concord, ist zwar a welcome and inspiriting spectacle. And what has moved you to it? Can the terse German tongue rise to the expression of this impulse? Is it Freündschaftsbezeigüngenstadtverordnetenversammlungenfamilieneigenthümlichkeiten? Nein, o nein! This is a crisp and noble word, but it fails to pierce the marrow of the impulse which has gathered this friendly meeting and produced diese Anblick,—eine Anblick welche ist güt zu sehen,—güt für die Aügen in a foreign land and a far country,—eine Anblick solche als in die gewönliche Heidelberger phrase nennt man ein "schönes Aussicht!" Ja, freilich natürlich wahrscheinlich ebensowohl! Also! Die Aussich aüf dem Königstuhl mehr grösserer ist, aber geistlische sprechend nicht so schön, lob' Gott! Because sie sind hier zusammengetroffen, in Bruderlichem concord, ein grossen Tag zu feiern, whose high benefits were not for one land and one locality only, but have conferred a measure of good upon all lands that know liberty to day, and love it. Hündert Jahre vorüber, waren die Engländer ünd die Amerikaner Feinde; aber heüte sind sie herzlichen Freünde, Gott sei Dank! May this good fellowship endure; may these banners here blended in amity, so remain; may they never any more wave over opposing hosts, or be stained with blood which was kindred, is kindred, and always will be kindred, until a line drawn upon a map shall be able to say, *"This* bars the ancestral blood from flowing in the veins of the descendant!"

Chapters IV through XVII of Life on the Mississippi *were originally written as a series for the prestigious Boston literary magazine, the* Atlantic, *which was edited by Twain's friend, William Dean Howells. This material was titled "Old Times on the Mississippi" when it appeared in the magazine from January to June of 1875, and also for its publication in book form by Belford Brothers of Toronto in 1876 and in London the following year. To fill out the narrative to a suitable length for the subscription format of his American publishers, Twain returned to the river in 1882 and set down an account of that later trip. The expanded narrative was retitled* Life on the Mississippi *when it was published by James R. Osgood and Company in 1883.*

Life on the Mississippi

THE "BODY OF THE NATION"

But *the basin of the Mississippi is the* BODY OF THE NATION. All the other parts are but members, important in themselves, yet more important in their relations to this. Exclusive of the Lake basin and of 300,000 square miles in Texas and New Mexico, which, in many aspects form a part of it, this basin contains about 1,250,000 square miles. In extent it is the second great valley of the world, being exceeded only by that of the Amazon. The valley of the frozen Obi approaches it in extent; that of the La Plata comes next in space, and probably in habitable capacity, having about 8/9 of its area; then comes that of the Yenisei, with about 7/9; the Lena, Amoor, Hoang-ho, Yang-tse-kiang, and Nile, 5/9; the Ganges, less than 1/2; the Indus, less than 1/3; the Euphrates, 1/5; the Rhine, 1/15. It exceeds in extent the whole of Europe, exclusive of Russia, Norway, and Sweden. *It would contain Austria four times, Germany or Spain five times, France six times, the British Islands or Italy ten times.* Conceptions formed from the river-basins of Western Europe are rudely shocked when we consider the extent of the valley of the Mississippi; nor are those formed from the sterile basins of the great rivers of Siberia, the lofty plateaus of Central Asia, or the mighty sweep of the swampy Amazon more adequate. Latitude, elevation, and rainfall all combine to render every part of the Mississippi Valley capable of supporting a dense population. *As* a dwelling-place for civilized man it is by far the first upon our globe.—EDITOR'S TABLE, *Harper's Magazine, February,* 1863.

CHAPTER I

THE RIVER AND ITS HISTORY

The Mississippi is well worth reading about. It is not a commonplace river, but on the contrary is in all ways remarkable. Considering the Missouri its main branch, it is the longest river in the world—four thousand three hundred miles. It seems safe to say that it is also the crookedest river in the world, since in one part of its journey it uses up one thousand three hundred miles to cover the same ground that the crow would fly over in six hundred and seventy-five. It discharges three times as much water as the St. Lawrence, twenty-five times as much as the Rhine, and three hundred and thirty-eight times as much as the Thames. No other river has so vast a drainage-basin: it draws its water supply from twenty-eight States and Territories; from Delaware, on the Atlantic seaboard, and from all the country between that and Idaho on the Pacific slope—a spread of forty-five degrees of longitude. The Mississippi receives and carries to the Gulf water from fifty-four subordinate rivers that are navigable by steamboats, and from some hundreds that are navigable by flats and keels. The area of its drainage-basin is as great as the combined areas of England, Wales, Scotland, Ireland, France, Spain, Portugal, Germany, Austria, Italy, and Turkey; and almost all this wide region is fertile; the Mississippi valley, proper, is exceptionally so.

It is a remarkable river in this: that instead of widening toward its mouth, it grows narrower; grows narrower and deeper. From the junction of the Ohio to a point half way down to the sea, the width averages a mile in high water: thence to the sea the width steadily diminishes, until, at the "Passes," above the mouth, it is but little over half a mile. At the junction of the Ohio the Mississippi's depth is eighty-seven feet; the depth increases gradually, reaching one hundred and twenty-nine just above the mouth.

The difference in rise and fall is also remarkable—not in the upper, but in the lower river. The rise is tolerably uniform down to Natchez (three hundred and sixty miles above the mouth)—about fifty feet. But at Bayou La Fourche the river rises only twenty-four feet; at New Orleans only fifteen, and just above the mouth only two and one half.

An article in the New Orleans "Times-Democrat," based upon reports of able engineers, states that the river annually empties four hundred and six million tons of mud into the Gulf of Mexico—which brings to mind Captain Marryat's rude name for the Mississippi—"the Great Sewer." This mud, solidified, would make a mass a mile square and two hundred and forty-one feet high.

The mud deposit gradually extends the land—but only gradually; it has extended it not quite a third of a mile in the two hundred years which have elapsed since the river took its place in history. The belief of the scientific people is, that the mouth used to be at Baton Rouge, where the hills cease, and that the two hundred miles of land between there and the Gulf was built by the river. This gives us the age of that piece of country, without any trouble at all—one hundred and twenty thousand years. Yet it is much the youthfulest batch of country that lies around there anywhere.

The Mississippi is remarkable in still another way—its disposition to make prodigious jumps by cutting through narrow necks of land, and thus straightening and shortening itself. More than once it has shortened itself thirty miles at a single jump! These cut-offs have had curious effects: they have thrown several river towns out into the rural districts, and built up sand bars and forests in front of them. The town of Delta used to be three miles below Vicksburg: a recent cut-off has radically changed the position, and Delta is now *two miles above* Vicksburg.

Both of these river towns have been retired to the country by that cut-off. A cut-off plays havoc with boundary lines and jurisdictions: for instance, a man is living in the State of Mississippi to-day, a cut-off occurs to-night, and to-morrow the man finds himself and his land over on the other side of the river, within the boundaries and subject to the laws of the State of Louisiana! Such a thing, happening in the upper river in the old times, could have transferred a slave from Missouri to Illinois and made a free man of him.

The Mississippi does not alter its locality by cut-offs alone: it is always changing its habitat *bodily*—is always moving bodily *sidewise*. At Hard Times, La., the river is two miles west of the region it used to occupy. As a result, the original *site* of that settlement is not now in Louisiana at all, but on the other side of the river, in the State of Mississippi. *Nearly the whole of that one thousand three hundred miles of old Mississippi River which La Salle floated down in his canoes, two hundred years ago, is good solid dry ground now.* The river lies to the right of it, in places, and to the left of it in other places.

Although the Mississippi's mud builds land but slowly, down at the mouth, where the Gulf's billows interfere with its work, it builds fast enough in better protected regions higher up: for instance, Prophet's Island contained one thousand five hundred acres of land thirty years ago; since then the river has added seven hundred acres to it.

But enough of these examples of the mighty stream's eccentricities for the present—I will give a few more of them further along in the book.

Let us drop the Mississippi's physical history, and say a word about its historical history—so to speak. We can glance briefly at its slumbrous first epoch in a couple of short chapters; at its second and wider-awake epoch in a couple more; at its flushest and widest-awake epoch in a good many succeeding chapters; and then talk about its comparatively tranquil present epoch in what shall be left of the book.

The world and the books are so accustomed to use, and overuse, the word "new" in connection with our country, that we early get and permanently retain the impression that there is nothing old about it. We do of course know that there are several comparatively old dates in American history, but the mere figures convey to our minds no just idea, no distinct realization, of the stretch of time which they represent. To say that De Soto, the first white man who ever saw the Mississippi River, saw it in 1542, is a remark which states a fact without interpreting it: it is something like giving the dimensions of a sunset by astronomical measurements, and cataloguing the colors by their scientific names;—as a result, you get the bald fact of the sunset, but you don't see the sunset. It would have been better to paint a picture of it.

The date 1542, standing by itself, means little or nothing to us; but when one groups a few neighboring historical dates and facts around it, he adds perspective and color, and then realizes that this is one of the American dates which is quite respectable for age.

For instance, when the Mississippi was first seen by a white man, less than a quarter of a century had elapsed since Francis I.'s defeat at Pavia; the death of Raphael; the death of Bayard, *sans peur et sans reproche;* the driving out of the Knights-Hospitallers from Rhodes by the Turks; and the placarding of the Ninety-Five Propositions,—the act which began the Reformation. When De Soto took his glimpse of the river, Ignatius Loyola was an obscure name; the order of the Jesuits was not yet a year old; Michael Angelo's paint was not yet dry on the Last Judgment in the Sistine Chapel; Mary Queen of Scots was not yet born, but would be before the year closed. Catherine de Medici was a child; Elizabeth of England was not yet in her teens; Calvin, Benvenuto Cellini, and the Emperor Charles V. were at the top of their fame, and each was manufacturing history after his own peculiar fashion; Margaret of Navarre was writing the "Heptameron" and some religious books,—the first survives, the others are forgotten, wit and indelicacy being sometimes better literature-preservers than holiness; lax court morals and the absurd chivalry business were in full feather, and the joust and the tournament were the frequent pastime of titled fine gentlemen who could fight better than they could spell, while religion was the passion of their ladies, and the classifying their offspring into children of full rank and children by brevet their pastime. In fact, all around, religion was in a peculiarly blooming condition: the Council of Trent was being called; the Spanish Inquisition was roasting, and racking, and burning, with a free hand; elsewhere on the continent the nations were being persuaded to holy living by the sword and fire; in England, Henry VIII. had suppressed the monasteries, burnt Fisher and another bishop or two, and was getting his English reformation and his harem effectively started. When De Soto stood on the banks of the Mississippi, it was still two years before Luther's death; eleven years before the burning of Servetus; thirty years before the St. Bartholomew slaughter; Rabelais was not yet published; "Don Quixote" was not yet written; Shakespeare was not yet born; a hundred long years must still elapse before Englishmen would hear the name of Oliver Cromwell.

Unquestionably the discovery of the Mississippi is a datable fact which considerably mellows and modifies the shiny newness of our country, and gives her a most respectable outside-aspect of rustiness and antiquity.

De Soto merely glimpsed the river, then died and was buried in it by his priests and soldiers. One would expect the priests and the soldiers to multiply the river's dimensions by ten—the Spanish custom of the day—and thus move other adventurers to go at once and explore it. On the contrary, their narratives when they reached home, did not excite that amount of curiosity. The Mississippi was left unvisited by whites during a term of years which seems incredible in our energetic days. One may "sense" the interval to his mind, after a fashion, by dividing it up in this way: After De Soto glimpsed the river, a fraction short of a quarter of a century elapsed, and then Shakespeare was born; lived a trifle more than half a century, then died; and when he had been in his grave considerably more than half a century, the *second* white man saw the Mississippi. In our day we don't allow a hundred and thirty years to elapse between glimpses of a marvel. If somebody should discover a creek in the county next to the one that the North Pole is in, Europe and America would start fifteen costly expeditions thither: one to explore the creek, and the other fourteen to hunt for each other.

For more than a hundred and fifty years there had been white settlements on our Atlantic coasts. These people were in intimate communication with the Indians: in the south the Spaniards were robbing, slaughtering, enslaving and converting them; higher up, the English were trading beads and blankets to them for a consideration, and throwing in civilization and whiskey, "for lagniappe;"* and in Canada the French were schooling them in a rudimentary way, missionarying among them, and drawing whole populations of them at a time to Quebec, and later to Montreal, to buy furs of them. Necessarily, then, these various clusters of whites must have heard of the great river of the far west; and indeed, they did hear of it vaguely,—so vaguely and indefinitely, that its course, proportions, and locality were hardly even guessable. The mere mysteriousness of the matter ought to have fired curiosity and compelled exploration; but this did not occur. Apparently nobody happened to want such a river, nobody needed it, nobody was curious about it; so, for a century and a half the Mississippi remained out of the market and undisturbed. When De Soto found it, he was not hunting for a river, and had no present occasion for one; consequently he did not value it or even take any particular notice of it.

But at last La Salle the Frenchman conceived the idea of seeking out that river and exploring it. It always happens that when a man seizes upon a neglected and important idea, people inflamed with the same notion crop up all around. It happened so in this instance.

Naturally the question suggests itself, Why did these people want the river now when nobody had wanted it in the five preceding generations? Apparently it was because at this late day they thought they had discovered a way to make it useful; for it had come to be believed that the Mississippi emptied into the Gulf of California, and therefore afforded a short cut from Canada to China. Previously the supposition had been that it emptied into the Atlantic, or Sea of Virginia.

*See page 414.

CHAPTER II

THE RIVER AND ITS EXPLORERS

La Salle himself sued for certain high privileges, and they were graciously accorded him by Louis XIV. of inflated memory. Chief among them was the privilege to explore, far and wide, and build forts, and stake out continents, and hand the same over to the king, and pay the expenses himself; receiving, in return, some little advantages of one sort or another; among them the monopoly of buffalo hides. He spent several years and about all of his money, in making perilous and painful trips between Montreal and a fort which he had built on the Illinois, before he at last succeeded in getting his expedition in such a shape that he could strike for the Mississippi.

And meantime other parties had had better fortune. In 1673 Joliet the merchant, and Marquette the priest, crossed the country and reached the banks of the Mississippi. They went by way of the Great Lakes; and from Green Bay, in canoes, by way of Fox River and the Wisconsin. Marquette had solemnly contracted, on the feast of the Immaculate Conception, that if the Virgin would permit him to discover the great river, he would name it Conception, in her honor. He kept his word. In that day, all explorers travelled with an outfit of priests. De Soto had twenty-four with him. La Salle had several, also. The expeditions were often out of meat, and scant of clothes, but they always had the furniture and other requisites for the mass; they were always prepared, as one of the quaint chroniclers of the time phrased it, to "explain hell to the salvages."

On the 17th of June, 1673, the canoes of Joliet and Marquette and their five subordinates reached the junction of the Wisconsin with the Mississippi. Mr. Parkman says: "Before them a wide and rapid current coursed athwart their way, by the foot of lofty heights wrapped thick in forests." He continues: "Turning southward, they paddled down the stream, through a solitude unrelieved by the faintest trace of man."

A big cat-fish collided with Marquette's canoe, and startled him; and reasonably enough, for he had been warned by the Indians that he was on a foolhardy journey, even a fatal one, for the river contained a demon "whose roar could be heard at a great distance, and who would engulf them in the abyss where he dwelt." I have seen a Mississippi cat-fish that was more than six feet long, and weighed two hundred and fifty pounds; and if Marquette's fish was the fellow to that one, he had a fair right to think the river's roaring demon was come.

211

"At length the buffalo began to appear, grazing in herds on the great prairies which then bordered the river; and Marquette describes the fierce and stupid look of the old bulls as they stared at the intruders through the tangled mane which nearly blinded them."

The voyagers moved cautiously: "Landed at night and made a fire to cook their evening meal; then extinguished it, embarked again, paddled some way farther, and anchored in the stream, keeping a man on the watch till morning."

They did this day after day and night after night; and at the end of two weeks they had not seen a human being. The river was an awful solitude, then. And it is now, over most of its stretch.

But at the close of the fortnight they one day came upon the footprints of men in the mud of the western bank—a Robinson Crusoe experience which carries an electric shiver with it yet, when one stumbles on it in print. They had been warned that the river Indians were as ferocious and pitiless as the river demon, and destroyed all comers without waiting for provocation; but no matter, Joliet and Marquette struck into the country to hunt up the proprietors of the tracks. They found them, by and by, and were hospitably received and well treated—if to be received by an Indian chief who has taken off his last rag in order to appear at his level best is to be received hospitably; and if to be treated abundantly to fish, porridge, and other game, including dog, and have these things forked into one's mouth by the ungloved fingers of Indians is to be well treated. In the morning the chief and six hundred of his tribesmen escorted the Frenchmen to the river and bade them a friendly farewell.

On the rocks above the present city of Alton they found some rude and fantastic Indian paintings, which they describe. A short distance below "a torrent of yellow mud rushed furiously athwart the calm blue current of the Mississippi, boiling and surging and sweeping in its course logs, branches, and uprooted trees." This was the mouth of the Missouri, "that savage river," which "descending from its mad career through a vast unknown of barbarism, poured its turbid floods into the bosom of its gentle sister."

By and by they passed the mouth of the Ohio; they passed canebrakes; they fought mosquitoes; they floated along, day after day, through the deep silence and loneliness of the river, drowsing in the scant shade of makeshift awnings, and broiling with the heat; they encountered and exchanged civilities with another party of Indians; and at last they reached the mouth of the Arkansas (about a month out from their starting-point), where a tribe of war-whooping savages swarmed out to meet and murder them; but they appealed to the Virgin for help; so in place of a fight there was a feast, and plenty of pleasant palaver and fol-de-rol.

They had proved to their satisfaction, that the Mississippi did not empty into the Gulf of California, or into the Atlantic. They believed it emptied into the Gulf of Mexico. They turned back, now, and carried their great news to Canada.

But belief is not proof. It was reserved for La Salle to furnish the proof. He was provokingly delayed, by one misfortune after another, but at last got his expedition under way at the end of the year 1681. In the dead of winter he and Henri de Tonty, son of Lorenzo Tonty, who invented the tontine, his lieutenant, started down the Illinois, with a following of eighteen Indians brought from New England, and twenty-three Frenchmen. They moved in procession down the surface of the frozen river, on foot, and dragging their canoes after them on sledges.

At Peoria Lake they struck open water, and paddled thence to the Mississippi and turned their prows southward. They ploughed through the fields of floating ice, past the mouth of the Missouri; past the mouth of the Ohio, by and by; "and, gliding by the wastes of bordering swamp, landed on the 24th of February near the Third Chickasaw Bluffs," where they halted and built Fort Prudhomme.

"Again," says Mr. Parkman, "they embarked; and with every stage of their adventurous progress, the mystery of this vast new world was more and more unveiled. More and more they entered the realms of spring. The hazy sunlight, the warm and drowsy air, the tender foliage, the opening flowers, betokened the reviving life of nature."

Day by day they floated down the great bends, in the shadow of the dense forests, and in time arrived at the mouth of the Arkansas. First, they were greeted by the natives of this locality as Marquette had before been greeted by them—with the booming of the war drum and the flourish of arms. The Virgin composed the difficulty in Marquette's case; the pipe of peace did the same office for La Salle. The white man and the red man struck hands and entertained each other during three days. Then, to the admiration of the savages, La Salle set up a cross with the arms of France on it, and took possession of the whole country for the king—the cool fashion of the time—while the priest piously consecrated the robbery with a hymn. The priest explained the mysteries of the faith "by signs," for the saving of the savages; thus compensating them with possible possessions in Heaven for the certain ones on earth which they had just been

213

robbed of. And also, by signs, La Salle drew from these simple children of the forest acknowledgments of fealty to Louis the Putrid, over the water. Nobody smiled at these colossal ironies.

These performances took place on the site of the future town of Napoleon, Arkansas, and there the first confiscation-cross was raised on the banks of the great river. Marquette's and Joliet's voyage of discovery ended at the same spot—the site of the future town of Napoleon. When De Soto took his fleeting glimpse of the river, away back in the dim early days, he took it from that same spot—the site of the future town of Napoleon, Arkansas. Therefore, three out of the four memorable events connected with the discovery and exploration of the mighty river occurred, by accident, in one and the same place. It is a most curious distinction, when one comes to look at it and think about it. France stole that vast country on that spot, the future Napoleon; and by and by Napoleon himself was to give the country back again!—make restitution, not to the owners, but to their white American heirs.

The voyagers journeyed on, touching here and there; "passed the sites, since become historic, of Vicksburg and Grand Gulf;" and visited an imposing Indian monarch in the Teche country, whose capital city was a substantial one of sun-baked bricks mixed with straw—better houses than many that exist there now. The chief's house contained an audience room forty feet square; and there he received Tonty in State, surrounded by sixty old men clothed in white cloaks. There was a temple in the town, with a mud wall about it ornamented with skulls of enemies sacrificed to the sun.

The voyagers visited the Natchez Indians, near the site of the present city of that name, where they found a "religious and political despotism, a privileged class descended from the sun, a temple and a sacred fire." It must have been like getting home again; it was home with an advantage, in fact, for it lacked Louis XIV.

A few more days swept swiftly by, and La Salle stood in the shadow of his confiscating cross, at the meeting of the waters from Delaware, and from Itaska, and from the mountain ranges close upon the Pacific, with the waters of the Gulf of Mexico, his task finished, his prodigy achieved. Mr. Parkman, in closing his fascinating narrative, thus sums up:

"On that day, the realm of France received on parchment a stupendous accession. The fertile plains of Texas; the vast basin of the

Mississippi, from its frozen northern springs to the sultry borders of the Gulf; from the woody ridges of the Alleghanies to the bare peaks of the Rocky Mountains—a region of savannas and forests, sun-cracked deserts and grassy prairies, watered by a thousand rivers, ranged by a thousand warlike tribes, passed beneath the sceptre of the Sultan of Versailles; and all by virture of a feeble human voice, inaudible at half a mile.''

CHAPTER III

FRESCOES FROM THE PAST

Apparently the river was ready for business, now. But no, the distribution of a population along its banks was as calm and deliberate and time-devouring a process as the discovery and exploration had been.

Seventy years elapsed, after the exploration, before the river's borders had a white population worth considering; and nearly fifty more before the river had a commerce. Between La Salle's opening of the river and the time when it may be said to have become the vehicle of anything like a regular and active commerce, seven sovereigns had occupied the throne of England, America had become an independent nation, Louis XIV. and Louis XV. had rotted and died, the French monarchy had gone down in the red tempest of the revolution, and Napoleon was a name that was beginning to be talked about. Truly, there were snails in those days.

The river's earliest commerce was in great barges—keel-boats, broadhorns. They floated and sailed from the upper rivers to New Orleans, changed cargoes there, and were tediously warped and poled back by hand. A voyage down and back sometimes occupied nine months. In time this commerce increased until it gave employment to hordes of rough and hardy men; rude, uneducated, brave, suffering terrific hardships with sailor-like stoicism; heavy drinkers, coarse frolickers in moral sties like the Natchez-under-the-hill of that day, heavy fighters, reckless fellows, every one, elephantinely jolly, foul-witted, profane; prodigal of their money, bankrupt at the end of the trip, fond of barbaric finery, prodigious braggarts; yet, in the main, honest, trustworthy, faithful to promises and duty, and often picturesquely magnanimous.

By and by the steamboat intruded. Then, for fifteen or twenty years, these men continued to run their keelboats down-stream, and the steamers did all of the up-stream business, the keelboat-men selling their boats in New Orleans, and returning home as deck passengers in the steamers.

But after a while the steamboats so increased in number and in speed that they were able to absorb the entire commerce; and then keelboating died a permanent death. The keelboatman be-came a deck hand, or a mate, or a pilot on the steamer; and when steamer-berths were not open to him, he took a berth on a Pittsburgh coal-flat, or on a pine-raft constructed in the forests up toward the sources of the Mississippi.

In the heyday of the steamboating prosperity, the river from end to end was flaked with coal-fleets and timber rafts, all managed by hand, and employing hosts of the rough characters whom I have been trying to describe. I remember the annual processions of mighty rafts that used to glide by Hannibal when I was a boy,—an acre or so of white, sweet-smelling boards in each raft, a crew of two dozen men or more, three or four wigwams scattered about the raft's vast level space for storm-quarters,—and I remember the rude ways and the tremendous talk of their big crews, the ex-keelboatmen and their admiringly patterning successors; for we used to swim out a quarter or third of a mile and get on these rafts and have a ride.

By way of illustrating keelboat talk and manners, and that now-departed and hardly-remembered raft-life, I will throw in, in this place, a chapter from a book which I have been working at, by fits and starts, during the past five or six years, and may possibly finish in the course of five or six more. The book is a story which details some passages in the life of an ignorant village boy, Huck Finn, son of the town drunkard of my time out west, there. He has run away from his persecuting father, and from a persecuting good widow who wishes to make a nice, truth-telling, respectable boy of him; and with him a slave of the widow's has also escaped. They have found a fragment of a lumber raft (it is high water and dead summer time), and are floating down the river by night, and hiding in the willows by day,—bound for Cairo,—whence the negro will seek freedom in the heart of the free States. But in a fog, they pass Cairo without knowing it. By and by they begin to suspect the truth, and Huck Finn is persuaded to end the dismal suspense by swimming down to a huge raft which they have seen in the distance ahead of them, creeping aboard under cover of the darkness, and gather-ing the needed information by eavesdropping:—

But you know a young person can't wait very well when he is impa-tient to find a thing out. We talked it over, and by and by Jim said it was such a black night, now, that it wouldn't be no risk to swim down to the big raft and crawl aboard and listen,—they would talk about Cairo, because they would be calculating to go ashore there for a spree, maybe, or anyway they would send boats ashore to buy whiskey or fresh meat or something. Jim had a wonderful level head, for a nigger: he could most always start a good plan when you wanted one.

I stood up and shook my rags off and jumped into the river, and struck out for the raft's light. By and by, when I got down nearly to her, I eased up and went slow and cautious. But everything was all right—nobody at the sweeps. So I swum down along the raft till I was most abreast the camp fire in the middle, then I crawled aboard and inched along and got in amongst some bundles of shingles on the weather side of the fire. There was thirteen men there—they was the watch on deck of course. And a mighty rough-looking lot, too. They had a jug, and tin cups, and they kept the jug moving. One man was singing— roaring, you may say; and it wasn't a nice song—for a parlor anyway. He roared through his nose, and strung out the last word of every line very long. When he was done they all fetched a kind of Injun war-whoop, and then another was sung. It begun:—

> "There was a woman in our towdn,
> In our towdn did dwed'l (dwell,)
> She loved her husband dear-i-lee,
> But another man twyste as wed'l.
>
> Singing too, riloo, riloo, riloo,
> Ri-too, riloo, rilay- - -e,
> She loved her husband dear-i-lee,
> But another man twyste as wed'l.''

And so on—fourteen verses. It was kind of poor, and when he was going to start on the next verse one of them said it was the tune the old cow died on; and another one said, "Oh, give us a rest." And another one told him to take a walk. They made fun of him till he got mad and jumped up and begun to cuss the crowd, and said he could lam any thief in the lot.

They was all about to make a break for him, but the biggest man there jumped up and says:

"Set whar you are, gentlemen. Leave him to me; he's my meat."

Then he jumped up in the air three times and cracked his heels together every time. He flung off a buckskin coat that was all hung with fringes, and says, "You lay thar tell the chawin-up's done;" and flung his hat down, which was all over ribbons, and says, "You lay thar tell his sufferins is over."

Then he jumped up in the air and cracked his heels together again and shouted out:—

"Whoo-oop! I'm the old original iron-jawed, brass-mounted, copper-bellied corpse-maker from the wilds of Arkansaw!—Look at me! I'm the man they call Sudden Death and General Desolation! Sired by a hurricane, dam'd by an earthquake, half-brother to the cholera, nearly related to the small-pox on the mother's side! Look at me! I take nineteen alligators and a bar'l of whiskey for breakfast when I'm in robust health, and a bushel of rattlesnakes and a dead body when I'm ailing! I split the everlasting rocks with my glance, and I squouch the thunder when I speak! Whoo-oop! Stand back and give me room according to my strength! Blood's my natural drink, and the wails of the dying is music to my ear! Cast your eye on me, genltemen!—and lay low and hold your breath, for I'm bout to turn myself loose!"

All the time he was getting this off, he was shaking his head and looking fierce, and kind of swelling around in a little circle, tucking up his wrist-bands, and now and then straightening up and beating his breast with his fist, saying, "Look at me, gentlemen!" When he got through, he jumped up and cracked his heels together three times, and let off a roaring "whoo-oop! I'm the bloodiest son of a wildcat that lives!"

Then the man that had started the row tilted his old slouch hat down over his right eye; then he bent stooping forward, with his back sagged and his south end sticking out far, and his fists a-shoving out and drawing in in front of him, and so went around in a little circle about three times, swelling himself up and breathing hard. Then he straightened, and jumped up and cracked his heels together three times before he lit again (that made them cheer), and he begun to shout like this:—

"Whoo-oop! bow your neck and spread, for the kingdom of sorrow's a-coming! Hold me down to the earth, for I feel my powers a-working! whoo-oop! I'm a child of sin, *don't* let me get a start! Smoked glass, here, for all! Don't attempt to look at me with the naked eye, gentlemen! When I'm playful I use the meridians of longitude and parallels of latitude for a seine, and drag the Atlantic Ocean for whales! I scratch my head with the lightning and purr myself to sleep with the thunder! When I'm cold, I bile the Gulf of Mexico and bathe in it; when I'm hot I fan myself with an equinoctial storm; when I'm thirsty I reach up and suck a cloud dry like a sponge; when I range the earth hungry, famine follows in my tracks! Woo-oop! Bow your neck and spread! I put my hand on the sun's face and make it night in the earth; I bite a piece out of the moon and hurry the seasons; I shake myself and crumble the mountains! Contemplate me through leather—*don't* use the naked eye! I'm the man with a petrified heart and biler-iron bowels! The massacre of isolated communities is the pastime of my idle moments, the destruction of nationalities the serious business of my life! The boundless vastness of the great American desert is my enclosed property, and I bury my dead on my own premises!" He jumped up and cracked his heels together three times before he lit (they cheered him again), and as he come down he shouted out: "Whoo-oop! bow your neck and spread, for the pet child of calamity's a-coming!"

Then the other one went to swelling around and blowing again—the first one—the one they called Bob; next, the Child of Calamity chipped in again, bigger than ever; then they both got at it at the same time, swelling round and round each other and punching their fists most into each other's faces, and whooping and jawing like Injuns; then Bob called the Child names, and the Child called him names back again: next, Bob called him a heap rougher names and the Child come back at him with the very worst kind of language; next, Bob knocked the Child's hat off, and the Child picked it up and kicked Bob's ribbony hat about six foot; Bob went and got it and said never mind, this warn't going to be the last of this thing, because he was a man that never forgot and never forgive, and so the Child better look out, for there was a time a-coming, just as sure as he was a living man, that he would have to answer to him with the best blood in his body. The Child said no man was willinger than he was for that time to come, and he would give Bob fair warning, *now,* never to cross his path again, for he could never rest till he had waded in his blood, for such was his nature, though he was sparing him now on account of his family, if he had one.

Both of them was edging away in different directions, growling and shaking their heads and going on about what they was going to do; but a little black-whiskered chap skipped up and says:—

"Come back here, you couple of chicken-livered cowards, and I'll thrash the two of ye!"

And he done it, too. He snatched them, he jerked them this way and that, he booted them around, he knocked them sprawling faster than they could get up. Why, it warn't two minutes till they begged like dogs—and how the other lot did yell and laugh and clap their hands all the way through, and shout "Sail in, Corpse-Maker!" "Hi! at him again, Child of Calamity!" "Bully for you, little Davy!" Well, it was a perfect pow-wow for a while. Bob and the Child had red noses and black eyes when they got through. Little Davy made them own up that they was sneaks and cowards and not fit to eat with a dog or drink with a nigger; then Bob and the Child shook hands with each other, very solemn, and said they had always respected each other and was willing to let bygones be bygones. So then they washed their faces in the river; and just then there was a loud order to stand by for a crossing, and some of them went forward to man the sweeps there, and the rest went aft to handle the after-sweeps.

I laid still and waited for fifteen minutes, and had a smoke out of a pipe that one of them left in reach; then the crossing was finished, and they stumped back and had a drink around and went to talking and singing again. Next they got out an old fiddle, and one played, and another patted juba, and the rest turned themselves loose on a regular old-fashioned keel-boat break-down. Then couldn't keep that up very long without gettting winded, so by and by they settled around the jug again.

They sung "jolly, jolly raftsman's the life for me," with a rousing chorus, and then they got to talking about differences betwixt hogs, and their different kind of habits; and next about women and their different ways; and next about the best ways to put out houses that was afire; and next about what ought to be done with the Injuns; and next about what a king had to do, and how much he got; and next about how to make cats fight; and next about what to do when a man has fits; and next about differences betwixt clearwater rivers and muddy-water ones. The man they called Ed said the muddy Mississippi water was wholesomer to drink than the clear water of the Ohio; he said if you let a pint of this yaller Mississippi water settle, you would have about a half to three quarters of an inch of mud in the bottom, according to the stage of the river, and then it warn't no better than Ohio water—what you wanted to do was to keep it stirred up—and when the river was low, keep mud on hand to put in and thicken the water up the way it ought to be.

The Child of Calamity said that was so; he said there was nutritiousness in the mud, and a man that drunk Mississippi water could grow corn in his stomach if he wanted to. He says:—

"You look at the graveyards; that tells the tale. Trees won't grow worth shucks in a Cincinnati graveyard, but in a Sent Louis graveyard they grow upwards of eight hundred foot high. It's all on account of the water the people drunk before they laid up. A Cincinnati corpse don't richen a soil any."

And they talked about how Ohio water didn't like to mix with Mississippi water. Ed said if you take the Mississippi on a rise when the Ohio is low, you'll find a wide band of clear water all the way down the east side of the Mississippi for a hundred mile or more, and the minute you get out a quarter of a mile from shore and pass the line, it is all thick and yaller the rest of the way across. Then they talked about how to keep tobacco from getting mouldy, and from that they went into ghosts and told about a lot that other folks had seen; but Ed says:—

" 'Why don't you tell something that you've seen yourselves? Now let me have a say. Five years ago I was on a raft as big as this, and right along here it was a bright moonshiny night, and I was on watch and boss of the stabboard oar forrard, and one of my pards was a man named Dick Allbright, and he come along to where I was sitting, forrard—gaping and stretching, he was—and stooped down on the edge of the raft and washed his face in the river, and come and set down by me and got out his pipe, and had just got it filled, when he looks up and says,—

" 'Why looky-here,' he says, 'ain't that Buck Miller's place, over yander in the bend?''

" 'Yes,' says I, 'it is—why?' He laid his pipe down and leant his head on his hand, and says,—

" 'I thought we'd be furder down.' I says,—

" 'I thought it too, when I went off watch'—we was standing six hours on and six off—'but the boys told me,' I says, 'that the raft didn't seem to hardly move, for the last hour,'—says I, 'though she's a slipping along all right, now,' says I. He give a kind of a groan, and says,—

" 'I've seed a raft act so before, along here,' he says, ''pears to me the current has most quit above the head of this bend durin' the last two years,' he says.

"Well, he raised up two or three times, and looked away off and around on the water. That started me at it, too. A body is always doing what he sees somebody else doing, though there mayn't be no sense in it. Pretty soon I see a black something floating on the water away off to stabboard and quartering behind us. I see he was looking at it, too. I says,—

" 'What's that?' He says, sort of pettish,—

" 'Tain't nothing but an old empty bar'l.'

" 'An empty bar'l!' says I, 'why,' says I, 'a spy-glass is a fool to *your* eyes. How can you tell it's an empty bar'l?' He says,—

" 'I don't know; I reckon it ain't a bar'l, but I thought it might be,' says he.

" 'Yes,' I says, 'so it might be, and it might be anything else, too; a body can't tell nothing about it, such a distance as that,' I says.

"We hadn't nothing else to do, so we kept on watching it. By and by I says,—

" 'Why looky-here, Dick Allbright, that thing's a-gaining on us, I believe.'

"He never said nothing. The thing gained and gained, and I judged it must be a dog that was about tired out. Well, we swung down into the crossing, and the thing floated across the bright streak of the moonshine, and, by George, it *was* a bar'l. Says I,—

" 'Dick Allbright, what made you think that thing was a bar'l, when it was a half a mile off,' says I. Says he,—

" 'I don't know.' Says I,—

" 'You tell me, Dick Allbright.' He says,—

" 'Well, I knowed it was a bar'l; I've seen it before; lots has seen it; they says it's a hanted bar'l.'

"I called the rest of the watch, and they come and stood there, and I told them what Dick said. It floated right along abreast, now, and didn't gain any more. It was about twenty foot off. Some was for having it aboard, but the rest didn't want to. Dick Allbright said rafts that had fooled with it had got bad luck by it. The captain of the watch said he didn't believe in it. He said he reckoned the bar'l gained on us because it was in a little better current than what we was. He said it would leave by and by.

"So then we went to talking about other things, and we had a song, and then a breakdown; and after that the captain of the watch called for another song; but it was clouding up, now, and the bar'l stuck right thar in the same place, and the song didn't seem to have much warm-up to it, somehow, and so they didn't finish it, and there wasn't any cheers, but it sort of dropped flat, and nobody said anything for a minute. Then everybody tried to talk at once, and one chap got off a joke, but it warn't no use, they didn't laugh, and even the chap that made the joke didn't laugh at it, which ain't usual. We all just settled down glum, and watched the bar'l, and was oneasy and oncomfortable. Well, sir, it shut down black and still, and then the wind begin to moan around, and next the lightning begin to play and the thunder to grumble. And pretty soon there was a regular storm, and in the middle of it a man that was running aft stumbled and fell and sprained his ankle so that he had to lay up. This made the boys shake their heads. And every time the lightning come, there was that bar'l with the blue lights winking around it. We was always on the look-out for it. But by and by, towards dawn, she was gone. When the day come we couldn't see her anywhere, and we warn't sorry, neither.

"But next night about half-past nine, when there was songs and high jinks going on, here she comes again, and took her old roost on the stabboard side. There warn't no more high jinks. Everybody got solemn; nobody talked; you couldn't get anybody to do anything but set around moody and look at the bar'l. It begun to cloud up again. When the watch changed, the off watch stayed up, 'stead of turning in. The storm ripped and roared around all night, and in the middle of it another man tripped and sprained his ankle, and had to knock off. The bar'l left towards day, and nobody see it go.

"Everybody was sober and down in the mouth all day. I don't mean the kind of sober that comes of leaving liquor alone,—not that. They was quiet, but they all drunk more than usual,—not together,—but each man sidled off and took it private, by himself.

"After dark the off watch didn't turn in; 'nobody sung, nobody talked; the boys didn't scatter around, neither; they sort of huddled together, forrard; and for two hours they set there, perfectly still, looking steady in the one direction, and heaving a sigh once in a while. And then, here comes the bar'l again. She took up her old place. She staid there all night; nobody turned in. The storm come on again, after midnight. It got awful dark; the rain poured down; hail, too; the thunder boomed and roared and bellowed; the wind blowed a hurricane; and the lightning spread over everything in big sheets of glare, and showed the whole raft as plain as day; and the river lashed up white as milk as far as you could see for miles, and there was that bar'l jiggering along, same as ever. The captain ordered the watch to man the after sweeps for a crossing, and nobody would go,—no more sprained ankles for them, they said. They wouldn't even *walk* aft. Well then, just then the sky split wide open, with a crash, and the lightning killed two men of the after watch, and crippled two more. Crippled them how, says you? Why, *sprained their ankles!*

"The bar'l left in the dark betwixt lightnings, towards dawn. Well, not a body eat a bite at breakfast that morning. After that the men loafed around, in twos and threes, and talked low together. But none of them herded with Dick Allbright. They all give him the cold shake. If he come around where any of the men was, they split up and sidled away. They wouldn't man the sweeps with him. The captain had all the skiffs hauled up on the raft, alongside of his wigwam, and wouldn't let the dead men be took ashore to be planted; he didn't believe a man that got ashore would come back; and he was right.

"After night come, you could see pretty plain that there was going to be trouble if that bar'l come again; there was such a muttering going on. A good many wanted to kill Dick Allbright, because he'd seen the bar'l on other trips, and that had an ugly look. Some wanted to put him ashore. Some said, let's all go ashore in a pile, if the bar'l comes again.

"This kind of whispers was still going on, the men being bunched together forrard watching for the bar'l, when, lo and behold you, here she comes again. Down she comes, slow and steady, and settles into her old tracks. You could a heard a pin drop. Then up comes the captain, and says:—

" 'Boys, don't be a pack of children and fools; I don't want this bar'l to be dogging us all the way to Orleans, and *you* don't; well, then, how's the best way to stop it? Burn it up,—that's the way. I'm going to fetch it aboard,' he says. And before anybody could say a word, in he went.

"He swum to it, and as he come pushing it to the raft, the men spread to one side. But the old man got it aboard and busted in the head, and there was a baby in it! Yes sir, a stark naked baby. It was Dick Allbright's baby; he owned up and said so.

" 'Yes,' he says, a-leaning over it, 'yes, it is my own lamented darling, my poor lost Charles William Allbright deceased,' says he,— for he could curl his tongue around the bulliest words in the language when he was a mind to, and lay them before you withoug a jint started, anywheres. Yes, he said he used to live up at the head of this bend, and one night he choked his child, which was crying, not intending to kill it,—which was prob'ly a lie,—and then he was scared, and buried it in a bar'l, before his wife got home, and off he went, and struck the northern trail and went to rafting; and this was the third year that the bar'l had chased him. He said the bad luck always begun light, and lasted till four men was killed, and then the bar'l didn't come any more after that. He said if the men would stand it one more night,—and was a-going on like that,—but the men had got enough. They started to get out a boat to take him ashore and lynch him, but he grabbed the little child all of a sudden and jumped overboard with it hugged up to his breast and shedding tears, and we never see him again in this life, poor old suffering soul, nor Charles William neither."

"*Who* was shedding tears?" says Bob; "was it Allbright or the baby?"

"Why, Allbright, of course; didn't I tell you the baby was dead? Been dead three years—how could it cry?"

"Well, never mind how it could cry—how could it *keep* all that time?" says Davy. "You answer me that."

"I don't know how it done it," says Ed. "It done it though—that's all I know about it."

"Say—what did they do with the bar'l?" says the Child of Calamity.

"Why, they hove it overboard, and it sunk like a chunk of lead."

"Edward, did the child look like it was choked?" says one.

"Did it have its hair parted?" says another.

"What was the brand on that bar'l, Eddy?" says a fellow they called Bill.

"Have you got the papers for them statistics, Edmund?" says Jimmy.

"Say, Edwin, was you one of the men that was killed by the lightning?" says Davy.

"Him? O, ho, he was both of 'em," says Bob. Then they all haw-hawed.

"Say, Edward, don't you reckon you'd better take a pill? You look bad— don't you feel pale?" says the Child of Calamity.

"O, come, now, Eddy," says Jimmy, "show up; you must a kept part of that bar'l to prove the thing by. Show us the bunghole—do—and we'll all believe you."

"Say, boys," says Bill, "less divide it up. Thar's thirteen of us. I can swaller a thirteenth of the yard, if you can worry down the rest."

Ed got up mad and said they could all go to some place which he ripped out pretty savage, and then walked off aft cussing to himself, and they yelling and jeering at him, and roaring and laughing so you could hear them a mile.

"Boys, we'll split a watermelon on that," says the Child of Calamity; and he come rummaging around in the dark amongst the shingle bundles where I was, and put his hand on me. I was warm and soft and naked; so he says "Ouch!" and jumped back.

"Fetch a lantern or a chunk of fire here, boys—there's a snake here as big as a cow!"

So they run there with a lantern and crowded up and looked in on me.

"Come out of that, you beggar!" says one.

"Who are you?" says another.

"What are you after here? Speak up prompt, or overboard you go."

"Snake him out, boys. Snatch him out by the heels."

I began to beg, and crept out amongst them trembling. They looked me over, wondering, and the Child of Calamity says:—

"A cussed thief! Lend a hand and less heave him overboard!"

"No," says Big Bob, "less get out the paint-pot and paint him a sky blue all over from head to heel, and *then* heave him over!"

"Good! that's it. Go for the paint, Jimmy."

When the paint come, and Bob took the brush and was just going to begin, the others laughing and rubbing their hands, I begun to cry, and that sort of worked on Davy, and he says:—

"'Vast there! He's nothing but a cub. I'll paint the man that tetches him!"

So I looked around on them, and some of them grumbled and growled, and Bob put down the paint, and the others didn't take it up.

"Come here to the fire, and less see what you're up to here," says Davy. "Now set down there and give an account of yourself. How long have you been aboard here?"

"Not over a quarter of a minute, sir," says I.

"How did you get dry so quick?"

"I don't know, sir. I'm always that way, mostly."

"Oh, you are, are you? What's your name?"

I warn't going to tell my name. I didn't know what to say, so I just says:

"Charles William Allbright, sir."

Then they roared—the whole crowd; and I was mighty glad I said

224

that, because maybe laughing would get them in a better humor.

When they got done laughing, Davy says:—

"It won't hardly do, Charles William. You couldn't have growed this much in five year, and you was a baby when you come out of the bar'l, you know, and dead at that. Come, now, tell a straight story, and nobody'll hurt you, if you ain't up to anything wrong. What *is* your name?"

"Aleck Hopkins, sir. Aleck James Hopkins."

"Well, Aleck, where did you come from, here?"

"From a trading scow. She lays up the bend yonder. I was born on her. Pap has traded up and down here all his life; and he told me to swim off here, because when you went by he said he would like to get some of you to speak to a Mr. Jonas Turner, in Cairo, and tell him—"

"Oh, come!"

"Yes, sir, it's as true as the world; Pap he says—"

"Oh, your grandmother!"

They all laughed, and I tried again to talk, but they broke in on me and stopped me.

"Now, looky-here," says Davy; "you're scared, and so you talk wild. Honest, now, do you live in a scow, or is it a lie?"

"Yes, sir, in a trading scow. She lays up at the head of the bend. But I warn't born in her. It's our first trip."

"Now you're talking! What did you come aboard here, for? To steal?"

"No, sir, I didn't.—It was only to get a ride on the raft. All boys does that."

"Well, I know that. But what did you hide for?"

"Sometimes they drive the boys off."

"So they do. They might steal. Looky-here; if we let you off this time, will you keep out of these kind of scrapes hereafter?"

"'Deed I will, boss. You try me."

"All right, then. You ain't but little ways from shore. Overboard with you, and don't you make a fool of yourself another time this way.—Blast it, boy, some raftsmen would rawhide you till you were black and blue!"

I didn't wait to kiss good-bye, but went overboard and broke for shore. When Jim come along by and by, the big raft was away out of sight around the point. I swum out and got aboard, and was mighty glad to see home again.

The boy did not get the information he was after, but his adventure has furnished the glimpse of the departed raftsman and keelboatman which I desire to offer in this place.

I now come to a phase of the Mississippi River life of the flush times of steamboating, which seems to me to warrant full examination—the marvellous science of piloting, as displayed there. I believe there has been nothing like it elsewhere in the world.

CHAPTER IV

THE BOYS' AMBITION

When I was a boy, there was but one permanent ambition among my comrades in our village* on the west bank of the Mississippi River. That was, to be a steamboatman. We had transient ambitions of other sorts, but they were only transient. When a circus came and went, it left us all burning to become clowns; the first negro minstrel show that came to our section left us all suffering to try that kind of life; now and then we had a hope that if we lived and were good, God would permit us to be pirates. These ambitions faded out, each in its turn; but the ambition to be a steamboatman always remained.

Once a day a cheap, gaudy packet arrived upward from St. Louis, and another downward from Keokuk. Before these events, the day was glorious with expectancy; after them, the day was a dead and empty thing. Not only the boys, but the whole village, felt this. After all these years I can picture that old time to myself now, just as it was then: the white town drowsing in the sunshine of a summer's morning; the streets empty, or pretty nearly so; one or two clerks sitting in front of the Water Street stores, with their splint-bottomed chairs tilted back against the wall, chins on breasts, hats slouched over their faces, asleep—with shingle-shavings enough around to show what broke them down; a sow and a litter of pigs loafing along the sidewalk, doing a good business in watermelon rinds and seeds; two or three lonely little freight piles scattered about the "levee;" a pile of "skids" on the slope of the stone-paved wharf, and the fragrant town drunkard asleep in the shadow of them; two or three wood flats at the head of the wharf, but nobody to listen to the peaceful lapping of the wavelets against them; the great Mississippi, the majestic, the magnificent Mississippi, rolling its mile-wide tide along, shining in the sun; the dense forest away on the other side; the "point" above the town, and the "point" below, bounding the river-glimpse and turning it into a sort of sea, and withal a very still and brilliant and lonely one. Presently a film of dark smoke appears above one of those remote "points;" instantly a negro drayman, famous for his quick eye and prodigious voice, lifts up the cry, "S-t-e-a-m-boat a-comin'!" and the scene changes! The town drunkard stirs, the clerks wake up, a furious clatter of drays follows, every house and store pours out a human contribution,

*Hannibal, Missouri.

and all in a twinkling the dead town is alive and moving. Drays, carts, men, boys, all go hurrying from many quarters to a common centre, the wharf. Assembled there, the people fasten their eyes upon the coming boat as upon a wonder they are seeing for the first time. And the boat *is* rather a handsome sight, too. She is long and sharp and trim and pretty; she has two tall, fancy-topped chimneys, with a gilded device of some kind swung between them; a fanciful pilot-house, all glass and "gingerbread," perched on top of the "texas" deck behind them; the paddle-boxes are gorgeous with a picture or with gilded rays above the boat's name; the boiler deck, the hurricane deck, and the texas deck are fenced and ornamented with clean white railings; there is a flag gallantly flying from the jack-staff; the furnace doors are open and the fires glaring bravely; the upper decks are black with passengers, the captain stands by the big bell, calm, imposing, the envy of all; great volumes of the blackest smoke are rolling and tumbling out of the chimneys—a husbanded grandeur created with a bit of pitch pine just before arriving at a town; the crew are grouped on the forecastle; the broad stage is run far out over the port bow, and an envied deck-hand stands picturesquely on the end of it with a coil of rope in his hand; the pent steam is screaming through the gauge-cocks; the captain lifts his hand, a bell rings, the wheels stop; then they turn back, churning the water to foam, and the steamer is at rest. Then such a scramble as there is to get aboard, and to get ashore, and to take in freight and to discharge freight, all at one and the same time; and such a yelling and cursing as the mates facilitate it all with! Ten minutes later the steamer is under way again, with no flag on the jack-staff and no black smoke issuing from the chimneys. After ten more minutes the town is dead again, and the town drunkard asleep by the skids once more.

My father was a justice of the peace, and I supposed he possessed the power of life and death over all men and could hang anybody that offended him. This was distinction enough for me as a general thing; but the desire to be a steamboatman kept intruding, nevertheless. I first wanted to be a cabin-boy, so that I could come out with a white apron on and shake a table-cloth over the side, where all my old comrades could see me; later I thought I would rather be the deck-hand who stood on the end of the stage-plank with the coil of rope in his hand, because he was particularly conspicuous. But these were only day-dreams,—they were too heavenly to be contemplated as real possibilities. By and by one of our boys went away. He was not heard of for a long time. At last he turned up as apprentice engineer or "striker" on a steamboat. This thing shook the bottom out of all my Sunday-school teachings. That boy had been notoriously worldly, and I just the reverse; yet he was exalted to this eminence, and I left in obscurity and misery. There was nothing generous about this fellow in his greatness. He would always manage to have a rusty bolt to scrub while his boat tarried at our town, and he would sit on the inside guard and scrub it, where we could all see him and envy him and loathe him. And whenever his boat was laid up he would come home and swell around the town in his blackest and greasiest clothes, so that nobody could help remembering that he was a steamboatman; and he used all sorts of steamboat technicalities in his talk, as if he were so used to them that he forgot common people could not understand them. He would speak of the "labboard" side of a horse in an easy, natural way that would make one wish he was dead. And he was always talking about "St. Looy" like an old citizen; he would refer casually to occasions when he "was coming down Fourth Street," or when he was "passing by the Planter's House," or when there was a fire and he took a turn on the brakes of "the old Big Missouri;" and then he would go on and lie about how many towns the size of ours were burned down there that day. Two or three of the boys had long been persons of consideration among us because they had been to St. Louis once and had a vague general knowledge of its wonders, but the day of their glory was over now. They lapsed into a humble silence, and learned to disappear when the ruthless "cub"-engineer approached. This fellow had money, too, and hair oil. Also an ignorant silver watch and a showy brass watch chain. He wore a leather belt and used no suspenders. If ever a youth was cordially admired and hated by his comrades, this one was. No girl could withstand his charms. He "cut out" every boy in the village. When his boat blew up at last, it diffused a tranquil contentment among us such as we had not known for months. But when he came home the next week, alive, renowned, and appeared in church all battered up and bandaged, a shining hero, stared at and wondered over by everybody, it seemed to us that the partiality of Providence for an undeserving reptile had reached a point where it was open to criticism.

This creature's career could produce but one result, and it speedily followed. Boy after boy managed to get on the river. The minister's son became an engineer. The doctor's and the post-master's sons became "mud clerks;" the wholesale liquor dealer's son became a bar-keeper on a boat; four sons of the chief merchant, and two sons of the county judge, became pilots. Pilot was the grandest position of all. The pilot, even in those days of trivial wages, had a princely salary—from a hundred and fifty to two hundred and fifty dollars a month, and no board to pay. Two months of his wages would pay a preacher's salary for a year. Now some of us were left disconsolate. We could not get on the river—at least our parents would not let us.

So by and by I ran away. I said I never would come home again till I was a pilot and could come in glory. But somehow I could not manage it. I went meekly aboard a few of the boats that lay packed together like sardines at the long St. Louis wharf, and very humbly inquired for the pilots, but got only a cold shoulder and short words from mates and clerks. I had to make the best of this sort of treatment for the time being, but I had comforting day-dreams of a future when I should be a great and honored pilot, with plenty of money, and could kill some of these mates and clerks and pay for them.

CHAPTER V

I WANT TO BE A CUB-PILOT

Months afterward the hope within me struggled to a reluctant death, and I found myself without an ambition. But I was ashamed to go home. I was in Cincinnati, and I set work to map out a new career. I had been reading about the recent exploration of the river Amazon by an expedition sent out by our government. It was said that the expedition, owing to difficulties, had not thoroughly explored a part of the country lying about the head-waters, some four thousand miles from the mouth of the river. It was only about fifteen hundred miles from Cincinnati to New Orleans, where I could doubtless get a ship. I had thirty dollars left; I would go and complete the exploration of the Amazon. This was all the thought I gave to the subject. I never was great in matters of detail. I packed my valise, and took passage on an ancient tub called the "Paul Jones," for New Orleans. For the sum of sixteen dollars I had the scarred and tarnished splendors of "her" main saloon principally to myself, for she was not a creature to attract the eye of wiser travellers.

When we presently got under way and went poking down the broad Ohio, I became a new being, and the subject of my own admiration. I was a traveller! A word never had tasted so good in my mouth before. I had an exultant sense of being bound for mysterious lands and distant climes which I never have felt in so uplifting a degree since. I was in such a glorified condition that

229

all ignoble feelings departed out of me, and I was able to look down and pity the untravelled with a compassion that had hardly a trace of contempt in it. Still, when we stopped at villages and wood-yards, I could not help lolling carelessly upon the railings of the boiler deck to enjoy the envy of the country boys on the bank. If they did not seem to discover me, I presently sneezed to attract their attention, or moved to a position where they could not help seeing me. And as soon as I knew they saw me I gaped and stretched, and gave other signs of being mightily bored with travelling.

I kept my hat off all the time, and stayed where the wind and the sun could strike me, because I wanted to get the bronzed and weather-beaten look of an old traveller. Before the second day was half gone, I experienced a joy which filled me with the purest gratitude; for I saw that the skin had begun to blister and peel off my face and neck. I wished that the boys and girls at home could see me now.

We reached Louisville in time—at least the neighborhood of it. We stuck hard and fast on the rocks in the middle of the river, and lay there four days. I was now beginning to feel a strong sense of being a part of the boat's family, a sort of infant son to the captain and younger brother to officers. There is no estimating the pride I took in this grandeur, or the affection that began to swell and grow in me for those people. I could not know how the lordly steamboatman scorns that sort of presumption in a mere landsman. I particularly longed to acquire the least trifle of notice from the big stormy mate, and I was on the alert for an opportunity to do him a service to that end. It came at last. The riotous powwow of setting a spar was going on down on the forecastle, and I went down there and stood around in the way—or mostly skipping out of it—till the mate suddenly roared a general order for somebody to bring him a capstan bar. I sprang to his side and said: "Tell me where it is—I'll fetch it!"

If a rag-picker had offered to do a diplomatic service for the Emperor of Russia, the monarch could not have been more astounded than the mate was. He even stopped swearing. He stood and stared down at me. It took him ten seconds to scrape his disjointed remains together again. Then he said impressively: "Well, if this don't beat hell!" and turned to his work with the air of a man who had been confronted with a problem too abstruse for solution.

I crept away, and courted solitude for the rest of the day. I did not go to dinner; I stayed away from supper until everybody else had finished. I did not feel so much like a member of the boat's family now as before. However, my spirits returned, in instalments, as we pursued our way down the river. I was sorry I hated the mate so, because it was not in (young) human nature not to admire him. He was huge and muscular, his face was bearded and whiskered all over; he had a red woman and a blue woman tattooed on his right arm,—one on each side of a blue anchor with a red rope to it; and in the matter of profanity he was sublime. When he was getting out cargo at a landing, I was always where I could see and hear. He felt all the majesty of his great position, and made the world feel it, too. When he gave even the simplest order, he discharged it like a blast of lightning, and sent a long, reverberating peal of profanity thundering after it. I could not held contrasting the way in which the average landsman would give an order, with the mate's way of doing it. If the landsman should wish the gang-plank moved a foot farther forward, he would probably say: "James, or William, one of you push that plank forward, please;" but put the mate in his place, and he would roar out: "Here, now, start that gang-plank for'ard! Lively, now! *What*'re you about! *Snatch* it! There! there! Aft again! aft again! Don't you hear me? Dash it to dash! are you going to *sleep* over it! *'Vast* heaving. 'Vast heaving, I tell you! Going to heave it clear astern? WHERE're you going with that barrel! *for'ard* with it 'fore I make you swallow it, you dash-dash-dash-*dashed* split between a tired mudturtle and crippled hearse-horse!"

I wished I could talk like that.

When the soreness of my adventure with the mate had somewhat worn off, I began timidly to make up to the humblest official connected with the boat—the night watchman. He snubbed my advances at first, but I presently ventured to offer him a new chalk pipe, and that softened him. So he allowed me to sit with him by the big bell on the hurricane deck, and in time he melted in conversation. He could not well have helped it, I hung with such homage on his words and so plainly showed that I felt honored by his notice. He told me the names of dim capes and shadowy islands as we glided by them in the solemnity of the night, under the winking stars, and by and by got to talking about himself. He seemed over-sentimental for a man whose salary was six dollars a week—or rather he might have seemed so to an older person that I. But I drank in his words hungrily, and with a faith that might have moved mountains if it had been applied judiciously. What was it to me that he was soiled and seedy and fragrant with gin? What was it to me that his grammar was bad, his construction worse, and his profanity so void of art that it was an element of weakness rather than strength in his conversation? He was a wronged man, a man who had seen trouble, and that was enough for me. As he mellowed into his plaintive history his tears dripped upon the lantern in his lap, and I cried, too, from sympathy. He said he was the son of an English nobleman—either an earl or an alderman, he could not remember which, but believed was both; his father, the nobleman, loved him, but his mother hated him from the cradle; and so while he was still a little boy he was sent to "one of them old, ancient colleges"—he couldn't remember which; and by and by his father died and his mother seized the property and "shook" him, as he phrased it. After his mother shook him, members of the nobility with whom he was acquainted used their influence to get him the position of "lob-lolly-boy in a ship;" and from that point my watchman threw off all trammels of date and locality and branched out into a narrative that bristled all along with incredible adventures; a narrative that was so reeking with bloodshed and so crammed with hair-breadth escapes and the most engaging and unconscious personal villanies, that I sat speechless, enjoying, shuddering, wondering, worshipping.

It was a sore blight to find out afterwards that he was a low, vulgar, ignorant, sentimental, half-witted humbug, an untravelled native of the wilds of Illinois, who had absorbed wildcat literature and appropriated its marvels, until in time he had woven odds and ends of the mess into this yarn, and then gone on telling it to fledglings like me, until he had come to believe it himself.

CHAPTER VI

A CUB-PILOT'S EXPERIENCE

What with lying on the rocks four days at Louisville, and some other delays, the poor old "Paul Jones" fooled away about two weeks in making the voyage from Cincinnati to New Orleans. This gave me a chance to get acquainted with one of the pilots, and he taught me how to steer the boat, and thus made the fascination of river life more potent than ever for me.

It also gave me a chance to get acquainted with a youth who had taken deck passage—more's the pity; for he easily borrowed six dollars of me on a promise to return to the boat and pay it back to me the day after we should arrive. But he probably died or forgot, for he never came. It was doubtless the former, since he had said his parents were wealthy, and he only travelled deck passage because it was cooler.*

*"Deck" passage—*i.e.*, steerage passage.

I soon discovered two things. One was that a vessel would not be likely to sail for the mouth of the Amazon under ten or twelve years; and the other was that the nine or ten dollars still left in my pocket would not suffice for so imposing an exploration as I had planned, even if I could afford to wait for a ship. Therefore it followed that I must contrive a new career. The "Paul Jones" was now bound for St. Louis. I planned a siege against my pilot, and at the end of three hard days he surrendered. He agreed to teach me the Mississippi River from New Orleans to St. Louis for five hundred dollars, payable out of the first wages I should receive after graduating. I entered upon the small enterprise of "learning" twelve or thirteen hundred miles of the great Mississippi River with the easy confidence of my time of life. If I had really known what I was about to require of my faculties, I should not have had the courage to begin. I supposed that all a pilot had to do was to keep his boat in the river, and I did not consider that that could be much of a trick, since it was so wide.

The boat backed out from New Orleans at four in the afternoon, and it was "our watch" until eight. Mr. Bixby, my chief, "straightened her up," plowed her along past the sterns of the other boats that lay at the Levee, and then said, "Here, take her; shave those steamships as close as you'd peel an apple." I took the wheel, and my heart-beat fluttered up into the hundreds; for it seemed to me that we were about to scrape the side off every ship in the line, we were so close. I held my breath and began to claw the boat away from the danger; and I had my own opinion of the pilot who had known no better than to get us into such peril, but I was too wise to express it. In half a minute I had a wide margin of safety intervening between the "Paul Jones" and the ships; and within ten seconds more I was set aside in disgrace, and Mr. Bixby was going into danger again and flaying me alive with abuse of my cowardice. I was stung, but I was obliged to admire the easy confidence with which my chief loafed from side to side of his wheel, and trimmed the ships so closely that disaster seemed ceaselessly imminent. When he had cooled a little he told me that the easy water was close ashore and the current outside, and therefore we must hug the bank, up-stream, to get the benefit of the former, and stay well out, down-stream, to take advantage of the latter. In my own mind I resolved to be a down-stream pilot and leave the up-streaming to people dead to prudence.

Now and then Mr. Bixby called my attention to certain things. Said he, "This is Six-Mile Point." I assented. It was pleasant enough information, but I could not see the bearing of it. I was not conscious that it was a matter of any interest to me. Another time he said, "This is Nine-Mile Point." Later he said, "This is Twelve-Mile Point." They were all about level with the water's Twelve-Mile Point." They were all about level with the water's edge; they all looked about alike to me; they were monotonously unpicturesque. I hoped Mr. Bixby would change the subject. But no; he would crowd up around a point, hugging the shore with affection, and then say: "The slack water ends here, abreast this bunch of China-trees; now we cross over." So he crossed over. He gave me the wheel once or twice, but I had no luck. I either came near shipping off the edge of a sugar plantation, or I yawed too far from shore, and so dropped back into disgrace again and got abused.

The watch was ended at last, and we took supper and went to bed. At midnight the glare of a lantern shone in my eyes, and the night watchman said:—

"Come! turn out!"

And then he left. I could not understand this extraordinary procedure; so I presently gave up trying to, and dozed off to sleep. Pretty soon the watchman was back again, and this time he was gruff. I was annoyed. I said:—

"What do you want to come bothering around here in the middle of the night for? Now as like as not I'll not get to sleep again to-night."

The watchman said:—

"Well, if this an't good, I'm blest."

The "off-watch" was just turning in, and I heard some brutal laughter from them, and such remarks as "Hello, watchman! an't the new cub turned out yet? He's delicate, likely. Give him some sugar in a rag and send for the chambermaid to sing rock-a-by-baby to him."

About this time Mr. Bixby appeared on the scene. Something like a minute later I was climbing the pilot-house steps with some of my clothes on and the rest in my arms. Mr. Bixby was close behind, commenting. Here was something fresh—this thing of getting up in the middle of the night to go to work. It was a detail in piloting that had never occurred to me at all. I knew that boats ran all night, but somehow I had never happened to reflect that somebody had to get up out of a warm bed to run them. I began to fear that piloting was not quite so romantic as I had imagined it was; there was something very real and work-like about this new phase of it.

It was a rather dingy night, although a fair number of stars were out. The big mate was at the wheel, and he had the old tub pointed at a star and was holding her straight up the middle of the river. The shores on either hand were not much more than half a mile apart, but they seemed wonderfully far away and ever so vague and indistinct. The mate said:—

"We've got to land at Jones's plantation, sir."

The vengeful spirit in me exulted. I said to myself, I wish you joy of your job, Mr. Bixby; you'll have a good time finding Mr. Jones's plantation such a night as this; and I hope you never *will* find it as long as you live.

Mr. Bixby said to the mate:—

"Upper end of the plantation, or the lower?"

"Upper."

"I can't do it. The stumps there are out of water at this stage. It's no great distance to the lower, and you'll have to get along with that."

"All right, sir. If Jones don't like it he'll have to lump it, I reckon."

And then the mate left. My exultation began to cool and my wonder to come up. Here was a man who not only proposed to find this plantation on such a night, but to find either end of it you preferred. I dreadfully wanted to ask a question, but I was carrying about as many short answers as my cargo-room would admit of, so I held my peace. All I desired to ask Mr. Bixby was the simple question whether he was ass enough to really imagine he was going to find that plantation on a night when all plantations were exactly alike and all the same color. But I held in. I used to have fine inspirations of prudence in those days.

Mr. Bixby made for the shore and soon was scraping it, just the same as if it had been daylight. And not only that, but singing—

"Father in heaven, the day is declining," etc.

It seemed to me that I had put my life in the keeping of a peculiarly reckless outcast. Presently he turned on me and said:—

"What's the name of the first point above New Orleans?"

I was gratified to be able to answer promptly, and I did. I said I didn't know.

"Don't *know*?"

This manner jolted me. I was down at the foot again, in a moment. But I had to say just what I had said before.

"Well, you're a smart one," said Mr. Bixby. "What's the name of the *next* point?"

Once more I didn't know.

"Well, this beats anything. Tell me the name of *any* point or place I told you."

I studied a while and decided that I couldn't.

"Look here! What do you start out from, above Twelve-Mile Point, to cross over?"

"I—I—don't know."

"You—you—don't know?" mimicking my drawling manner of speech. What *do* you know?"

"I—I—nothing, for certain."

"By the great Caesar's ghost, I believe you! You're the stupidest dunderhead I ever saw or ever heard of, so help me Moses! The idea of *you* being a pilot—*you!* Why, you don't know enough to pilot a cow down a lane."

Oh, but his wrath was up! He was a nervous man, and he shuffled from one side of his wheel to the other as if the floor was hot. He would boil a while to himself, and then overflow and scald me again.

"Look here! What do you suppose I told you the names of those points for?"

I tremblingly considered a moment, and then the devil of temptation provoked me to say:—

"Well—to—to—be entertaining, I thought."

This was a red rag to the bull. He raged and stormed so (he was crossing the river at the time) that I judge it made him blind, because he ran over the steering-oar of a trading-scow. Of course the traders sent up a volley of red-hot profanity. Never was a man so grateful as Mr. Bixby was: because he was brim full, and here were subjects who would *talk back*. He threw open a window, thrust his head out, and such an irruption followed as I never had heard before. The fainter and farther away the scowmen's curses drifted, the higher Mr. Bixby lifted his voice and the weightier his adjectives grew. When he closed the window he was empty. You could have drawn a seine through his system and not caught curses enough to disturb your mother with. Presently he said to me in the gentlest way:—

"My boy, you must get a little memorandum-book, and every time I tell you a thing, put it down right away. There's only one way to be a pilot, and that is to get this entire river by heart. You have to know it just like A B C."

That was a dismal revelation to me; for my memory was never loaded with anything but blank cartridges. However, I did not feel discouraged long. I judged that it was best to make some allowances, for doubtless Mr. Bixby was "stretching." Presently he pulled a rope and struck a few strokes on the big bell. The stars were all gone now, and the night was as black as ink. I could hear the wheels churn along the bank, but I was not entirely certain that I could see the shore. The voice of the invisible watchman called up from the hurricane deck:—

"What's this, sir?"

"Jones's plantation."

I said to myself, I wish I might venture to offer a small bet that it isn't. But I did not chirp. I only waited to see. Mr. Bixby handled the engine bells, and in due time the boat's nose came to the land, a torch glowed from the forecastle, a man skipped ashore, a darky's voice on the bank said, "Gimme de k'yarpet-bag, Mars' Jones," and the next moment we were standing up the river again, all serene. I reflected deeply a while, and then said,—but not aloud,—Well, the finding of that plantation was the luckiest accident that ever happened; but it couldn't happen again in a hundred years. And I fully believed it *was* an accident, too.

By the time we had gone seven or eight hundred miles up the river, I had learned to be a tolerably plucky upstream steersman, in daylight, and before we reached St. Louis I had made a trifle of progress in night-work, but only a trifle. I had a note-book that fairly bristled with the names of towns, "points," bars, islands, bends, reaches, etc.; but the information was to be found only in the note-book—none of it was in my head. It made my heart ache to think I had only got half of the river set down; for as our watch was four hours off and four hours on, day and night, there was a long four-hour gap in my book for every time I had slept since the voyage began.

My chief was presently hired to go on a big New Orleans boat, and I packed my satchel and went with him. She was a grand affair. When I stood in her pilot-house I was so far above the water that I seemed perched on a mountain; and her decks stretched so far away, fore and aft, below me, that I wondered how I could ever have considered the little "Paul Jones" a large craft. There were other differences, too. The "Paul Jones's" pilot-house was a cheap, dingy, battered rattle-trap, cramped for room: but here was a sumptuous glass temple; room enough to have a dance in; showy red and gold window-curtains; an imposing sofa; leather cushions and a back to the high bench where visiting pilots sit, to spin yarns and "look at the river;" bright, fanciful "cuspadores" instead of a broad wooden box filled with sawdust; nice new oilcloth on the floor; a hospitable big stove for winter; a wheel as high as my head, costly with inlaid work; a wire tiller-rope; bright brass knobs for the bells; and a tidy, white-aproned, black "texas-tender," to bring up tarts and ices and coffee during mid-watch, day and night. Now this was "something like;" and so I began to take heart once more to believe that piloting was a romantic sort of occupation after all. The moment we were under way I began to prowl about the great steamer and fill myself with joy. She was as clean and as dainty as a drawing-room; when I looked down her long, gilded saloon, it was like gazing through a splendid tunnel; she had an oil-picture, by some gifted signpainter, on every state-room door; she glittered with no end of prism-fringed chandeliers; the clerk's office was elegant, the bar was marvellous, and the bar-keeper had been barbered and upholstered at incredible cost. The boiler deck (*i.e.*, the second story of the boat, so to speak), was as spacious as a church, it seemed to me; so with the forecastle; and there was no pitiful handful of deck-hands, firemen, and roust-abouts down there, but a whole battalion of men. The fires were fiercely glaring from a long row of furnaces, and over them were eight huge boilers! This was unutterable pomp. The mighty engines—but enough of this. I had never felt so fine before. And when I found that the regiment of natty servants respectfully "sir'd" me, my satisfaction was complete.

CHAPTER VII

A DARING DEED

When I returned to the pilot-house St. Louis was gone and I was lost. Here was a piece of river which was all down in my book, but I could make neither head nor tail of it: you understand, it was turned around. I had seen it when coming up-stream, but I had never faced about to see how it looked when it was behind me. My heart broke again, for it was plain that I had got to learn this troublesome river *both ways*.

The pilot-house was full of pilots, going down to "look at the river." What is called the "upper river" (the two hundred miles between St. Louis and Cairo, where the Ohio comes in) was low; and the Mississippi changes its channel so constantly that the pilots used to always find it necessary to run down to Cairo to take a fresh look, when their boats were to lie in port a week; that is, when the water was at a low stage. A deal of this "look-ing at the river" was done by poor fellows who seldom had a berth, and whose only hope of getting one lay in their being always freshly posted and therefore ready to drop into the shoes of some reputable pilot, for a single trip, on account of such pilot's sudden illness, or some other necessity. And a good many of them constantly ran up and down inspecting the river, not because they ever really hoped to get a berth, but because (they being guests of the boat) it was cheaper to "look at the river" than stay ashore and pay board. In time these fellows grew dainty in their tastes, and only infested boats that had an established reputation for setting good tables. All visiting pilots were useful, for they were always ready and willing, winter or summer, night or day, to go out in the yawl and help buoy the channel or assist the boat's pilots in any way they could. They were likewise welcome because all pilots are tireless talkers, when gathered together, and as they talk only about the river they are always understood and are always interesting. Your true pilot cares nothing about anything on earth but the river, and his pride in his occupation surpasses the pride of kings.

We had a fine company of these river-inspectors along, this trip. There were eight or ten; and there was abundance of room for them in our great pilot-house. Two or three of them wore polished silk hats, elaborate shirt-fronts, diamond breastpins, kid gloves, and patent-leather boots.They were choice in their English, and bore themselves with a dignity proper to men of solid means and prodigious reputation as pilots. The others were more or less loosely clad, and wore upon their heads tall felt cones that were suggestive of the days of the Commonwealth.

I was a cipher in this august company, and felt subdued, not to say torpid. I was not even of sufficient consequence to assist at the wheel when it was necessary to put the tiller hard down in a hurry; the guest that stood nearest did that when occasion required—and this was pretty much all the time, because of the crookedness of the channel and the scant water. I stood in a corner; and the talk I listened to took the hope all out of me. One visitor said to another:—

"Jim, how did you run Plum Point, coming up?"

"It was in the night, there, and I ran it the way one of the boys on the 'Diana' told me; started out about fifty yards above the wood pile on the false point, and held on the cabin under Plum Point till I raised the reef—quarter less twain—then straightened up for the middle bar till I got well abreast the old one-limbed cotton-wood in the bend, then got my stern on the cotton-wood and head on the low place above the point, and came through a-booming—nine and a half."

"Pretty square crossing, an't it?"

"Yes, but the upper bar's working down fast."

Another pilot spoke up and said:—

"I had better water than that, and ran it lower down; started out from the false point—mark twain—raised the second reef abreast the big snag in the bend, and had quarter less twain."

One of the gorgeous ones remarked:—

"I don't want to find fault with your leadsmen, but that's a good deal of water for Plum Point, it seems to me."

There was an approving nod all around as this quiet snub dropped on the boaster and "settled" him. And so they went on talk-talk-talking. Meantime, the thing that was running in my mind was, "Now if my ears hear aright, I have not only to get the names of all the towns and islands and bends, and so on, by heart, but I must even get up a warm personal acquaintanceship with every old snag and one-limbed cotton-wood and obscure wood pile that ornaments the banks of this river for twelve hundred miles; and more than that, I must actually know where these things are in the dark, unless these guests are gifted with eyes that can pierce through two miles of solid blackness; I wish the piloting business was in Jericho and I had never thought of it."

At dusk Mr. Bixby tapped the big bell three times (the signal to land), and the captain emerged from his drawing-room in the forward end of the texas, and looked up inquiringly. Mr. Bixby said:—

"We will lay up here all night, captain."

"Very well, sir."

That was all. The boat came to shore and was tied up for the night. It seemed to me a fine thing that the pilot could do as he pleased, without asking so grand a captain's permission. I took my supper and went immediately to bed, discouraged by my day's observations and experiences. My late voyage's note-booking was but a confusion of meaningless names. It had tangled me all up in a knot every time I had looked at it in the daytime. I now hoped for respite in sleep; but no, it revelled all through my head till sunrise again, a frantic and tireless nightmare.

Next morning I felt pretty rusty and low-spirited. We went booming along, talking a good many chances, for we were anxious to "get out of the river" (as getting out to Cairo was called) before night should overtake us. But Mr. Bixby's partner, the other pilot, presently grounded the boat, and we lost so much time getting her off that it was plain the darkness would overtake us a good long way above the mouth. This was a great misfortune, especially to certain of our visiting pilots, whose boats would have to wait for their return, no matter how long that might be. It sobered the pilot-house talk a good deal. Coming up-stream, pilots did not mind low water or any kind of darkness; nothing stopped them but fog. But down-stream work was different; a boat was too nearly helpless, with a stiff current pushing behind her; so it was not customary to run down-stream at night in low water.

There seemed to be one small hope, however: if we could get

through the intricate and dangerous Hat Island crossing before night, we could venture the rest, for we would have plainer sailing and better water. But it would be insanity to attempt Hat Island at night. So there was a deal of looking at watches all the rest of the day, and a constant ciphering upon the speed we were making; Hat Island was the eternal subject; sometimes hope was high and sometimes we were delayed in a bad crossing, and down it went again. For hours all hands lay under the burden of this suppressed excitement; it was even communicated to me, and I got to feeling so solicitous about Hat Island, and under such an awful pressure of responsibility, that I wished I might have five minutes on shore to draw a good, full, relieving breath, and start over again. We were standing no regular watches. Each of our pilots ran such portions of the river as he had run when coming up-stream, because of his greater familiarity with it; but both remained in the pilot-house constantly.

An hour before sunset, Mr. Bixby took the wheel and Mr. W—— stepped aside. For the next thirty minutes every man held his watch in his hand and was restless, silent, and uneasy. At last somebody said, with a doomful sigh,—

"Well yonder's Hat Island—and we can't make it."

All the watches closed with a snap, everybody sighed and muttered something about its being "too bad, too bad—ah, if we could *only* have got here half an hour sooner!" and the place was thick with the atmosphere of disappointment. Some started to go out, but loitered, hearing no bell-tap to land. The sun dipped behind the horizon, the boat went on. Inquiring looks passed from one guest to another; and one who had his hand on the door-knob and had turned it, waited, then presently took away his hand and let the knob turn back again. We bore steadily down the bend. More looks were exchanged, and nods of surprised admiration—but no words. Insensibly the men drew together behind Mr. Bixby, as the sky darkened and one or two dim stars came out. The dead silence and sense of waiting became oppressive. Mr. Bixby pulled the cord, and two deep, mellow notes from the big bell floated off on the night. Then a pause, and one more note was struck. The watchman's voice followed, from the hurricane deck:—

"Labboard lead, there! Stabboard lead!"

The cries of the leadsmen began to rise out of the distance, and were gruffly repeated by the word-passers on the hurricane deck.

"M-a-r-k three! .... M-a-r-k three! .... Quarter-less-three! .... Half twain! .... Quarter twain! .... M-a-r-k twain! .... Quarter-less"—

Mr. Bixby pulled two bell-ropes, and was answered by faint jinglings far below in the engine room, and our speed slackened. The steam began to whistle through the gaugecocks. The cries of the leadsmen went on—and it is a weird sound, always, in the night. Every pilot in the lot was watching now, with fixed eyes, and talking under his breath. Nobody was calm and easy but Mr. Bixby. He would put his wheel down and stand on a spoke, and as the steamer swung into her (to me) utterly invisible marks—for we seemed to be in the midst of a wide and gloomy sea—he would meet and fasten her there. Out of the murmur of half-audible talk, one caught a coherent sentence now and then—such as:

"There; she's over the first reef all right!"

After a pause, another subdued voice:—

"Her stern's coming down just *exactly* right, by *George!*"

"Now she's in the marks; over she goes!"

Somebody else muttered:—

Oh, it was done beautiful—*beautiful!*"

Now the engines were stopped altogether, and we drifted with the current. Not that I could see the boat drift, for I could not, the stars being all gone by this time. This drifting was the dismalest work; it held one's heart still. Presently I discovered a blacker gloom than that which surrounded us. It was the head of the island. We were closing right down upon it. We entered its deeper shadow, and so imminent seemed the peril that I was likely to suffocate; and I had the strongest impulse to do *something,* anything, to save the vessel. But still Mr. Bixby stood by his wheel, silent, intent as a cat, and all the pilots stood shoulder to shoulder at his back.

"She'll not make it!" somebody whispered.

The water grew shoaler and shoaler, by the leadsman's cries, till it was down to—

"Eight-and-a-half! . . . . E-i-g-h-t feet! . . . . E-i-g-h-t feet! . . . . Seven-and"—

Mr. Bixby said warningly through his speaking tube to the engineer:—

"Stand by, now!"

"Aye-aye, sir!"

"Seven-and-a-half! Seven feet! *Six*-and"—

We touched bottom! Instantly Mr. Bixby set a lot of bells ringing, shouted through the tube, *"Now,* let her have it—every ounce you've got!" then to his partner, "Put her hard down! snatch her! snatch her!" The boat rasped and ground her way through the sand, hung upon the apex of disaster a single tremendous instant, and then over she went! And such a shout as went up at Mr. Bixby's back never loosened the roof of a pilot-house before!

There was no more trouble after that. Mr. Bixby was a hero that night; and it was some little time, too, before his exploit ceased to be talked about by river men.

Fully to realize the marvellous precision required in laying the great steamer in her marks in that murky waste of water, one should know that not only must she pick her intricate way through snags and blind reefs, and then shave the head of the island so closely as to brush the overhanging foliage with her stern, but at one place she must pass almost within arm's reach of a sunken and invisible wreck that would snatch the hull timbers from under her if she should strike it, and destroy a quarter of a million dollars' worth of steamboat and cargo in five minutes, and maybe a hundred and fifty human lives into the bargain.

The last remark I heard that night was a compliment to Mr. Bixby, uttered in soliloquy and with unction by one of our guests. He said:—

"By the Shadow of Death, but he's a lightning pilot!"

CHAPTER VIII

PERPLEXING LESSONS

At the end of what seemed a tedious while, I had managed to pack my head full of islands, towns, bars, "points," and bends; and a curiously inanimate mass of lumber it was, too. However, inasmuch as I could shut my eyes and reel off a good long string of these names without leaving out more than ten miles of river in every fifty, I began to feel that I could take a boat down to New Orleans if I could make her skip those little gaps. But of course my complacency could hardly get start enough to lift my nose a trifle into the air, before Mr. Bixby would think of something to fetch it down again. One day he turned on me suddenly with this settler:—

"What is the shape of Walnut Bend?"

He might as well have asked me my grandmother's opinion of protoplasm. I reflected respectfully, and then said I didn't know it had any particular shape. My gunpowdery chief went off with a bang, of course, and then went on loading and firing until he was out of adjectives.

I had learned long ago that he only carried just so many rounds of ammunition, and was sure to subside into a very placable and even remorseful old smooth-bore as soon as they were all gone. That word "old" is merely affectionate; he was not more than thirty-four. I waited. By and by he said,—

"My boy, you've got to know the *shape* of the river perfectly. It is all there is left to steer by on a very dark night. Everything else is blotted out and gone. But mind you, it hasn't the same shape in the night that it has in the day-time."

"How on earth am I ever going to learn it, then?"

"How do you follow a hall at home in the dark? Because you know the shape of it. You can't see it."

"Do you mean to say that I've got to know all the million trifling variations of shape in the banks of this interminable river as well as I know the shape of the front hall at home?"

"On my honor, you've got to know them *better* than any man ever did know the shapes of the halls in his own house."

"I wish I was dead!"

"Now I don't want to discourage you, but"—

"Well, pile it on me: I might as well have it now as another time."

"You see, this has got to be learned; there isn't any getting around it. A clear starlight night throws such heavy shadows that if you didn't know the shape of a shore perfectly you would claw away from every bunch of timber, because you would take the black shadow of it for a solid cape; and you see you would be getting scared to death every fifteen minutes by the watch. You would be fifty yards from shore all the time when you ought to be within fifty feet of it. You can't see a snag in one of those shadows, but you know exactly where it is, and the shape of the river tells you when you are coming to it. Then there's your pitch-dark night; the river is a very different shape on a pitch-dark night from what it is on a starlight night. All shores seem to be straight lines, then, and mighty dim ones, too; and you'd *run* them for straight lines only you know better. You boldly drive your boat right into what seems to be a solid, straight wall (you knowing very well that in reality there is a curve there), and that wall falls back and makes way for you. Then there's your gray mist. You take a night when there's one of these grisly, drizzly, gray mists, and then there isn't *any* particular shape to a shore. A gray mist would tangle the head of the oldest man that ever lived. Well, then, different kinds of *moonlight* change the shape of the river in different ways. You see"—

"Oh, don't say any more, please! Have I got to learn the shape of the river according to all these fivdifferent ways? If I tried to carry all that cargo in my head it would make me stoop-shouldered."

"*No!* you only learn *the* shape of the river; and you learn it with such absolute certainty that you can always steer by the shape that's *in your head,* and never mind the one that's before your eyes."

"Very well, I'll try it; but after I have learned it can I depend on it? Will it keep the same form and not go fooling around?"

Before Mr. Bixby could answer, Mr. W—— came in to take the watch, and he said,—

"Bixby, you'll have to look out for President's Island and all that country clear away up above the Old Hen and Chickens. The banks are caving and the shape of the shores changing like everything. Why, you wouldn't know the point above 40. You can go up inside the old sycamore snag, now."*

So that question was answered. Here were leagues of shore changing shape. My spirits were down in the mud again. Two things seemed pretty apparent to me. One was, that in order to be a pilot a man had got to learn more than any one man ought to be allowed to know; and the other was, that he must learn it all over again in a different way every twenty-four hours. That night we had the watch until twelve. Now it was an ancient river custom for the two pilots to chat a bit when the watch changed. While the relieving pilot put on his gloves and lit his cigar, his partner, the retiring pilot, would say something like this:—

"I judge the upper bar is making down a little at Hale's Point; had quarter twain with the lower lead and mark twain** with the other."

"Yes, I thought it was making down a little, last trip. Meet any boats?"

"Met one abreast the head of 21, but she was away over hugging the bar, and I couldn't make her out entirely. I took her for the 'Sunny South'—hadn't any skylights forward of the chimneys."

And so on. And as the relieving pilot took the wheel his partner† would mention that we were in such-and-such a bend, and say we were abreast of such-and-such a man's wood-yard or plantation. This was courtesy; I supposed it was *necessity.* But Mr. W—— came on watch full twelve minutes late on this particular night,—a tremendous breach of etiquette; in fact, it is the unpardonable sin among pilots. So Mr. Bixby gave him no greeting whatever, but simply surrendered the wheel and

---

* It may not be necessary, but still it can do no harm to explain that "inside" means between the snag and the shore.—M.T.

** Two fathoms. Quarter twain is 2¼ fathoms, 13½ feet. Mark three is three fathoms.

† "Partner" is technical for "the other pilot."

marched out of the pilot-house without a word. I was appalled; it was a villanous night for blackness, we were in a particularly wide and blind part of the river, where there was no shape or substance to anything, and it seemed incredible that Mr. Bixby should have left that poor fellow to kill the boat trying to find out where he was. But I resolved that I would stand by him any way. He should find that he was not wholly friendless. So I stood around, and waited to be asked where we were. But Mr. W—— plunged on serenely through the solid firmament of black cats that stood for an atmosphere, and never opened his mouth. Here is a proud devil, thought I; here is a limb of Satan that would rather send us all to destruction than put himself under obligations to me, because I am not yet one of the salt of the earth and privileged to snub captains and lord it over everything dead and alive in a steamboat. I presently climbed up on the bench; I did not think it was safe to go to sleep while this lunatic was on watch.

However, I must have gone to sleep in the course of time, because the next thing I was aware of was the fact that day was breaking, Mr. W—— gone, and Mr. Bixby at the wheel again. So it was four o'clock and all well—but me; I felt like a skinful of dry bones and all of them trying to ache at once.

Mr. Bixby asked me what I had stayed up there for. I confessed that it was to do Mr. W—— a benevolence,—tell him where he was. It took five minutes for the entire preposterousness of the thing to filter into Mr. Bixby's system, and then I judge it filled him nearly up to the chin; because he paid me a compliment—and not much of a one either. He said,—

"Well, taking you by-and-large, you do seem to be more different kinds of an ass than any creature I ever saw before. What did you suppose he wanted to know for?"

I said I thought it might be a convenience to him.

"Convenience! D-nation! Didn't I tell you that a man's got to know the river in the night the same as he'd know his own front hall?"

"Well, I can follow the front hall in the dark if I know it *is* the front hall; but suppose you set me down in the middle of it in the dark and not tell me which hall it is; how am *I* to know?"

"Well, you've *got* to, on the river!"

"All right. Then I'm glad I never said anything to Mr. W——"

"I should say so. Why, he'd have slammed you through the window and utterly ruined a hundred dollars' worth of window-sash and stuff."

I was glad this damage had been saved, for it would have made me unpopular with the owners. They always hated anybody who had the name of being careless, and injuring things.

I went to work now to learn the shape of the river; and of all the eluding and ungraspable objects that ever I tried to get mind or hands on, that was the chief. I would fasten my eyes upon a sharp, wooded point that projected far into the river some miles ahead of me, and go to laboriously photographing its shape upon my brain; and just as I was beginning to succeed to my satisfaction, we would draw up toward it and the exasperating thing would begin to melt away and fold back into the bank! If there had been a conspicuous dead tree standing upon the very point of the cape, I would find that tree inconspicuously merged into the general forest, and occupying the middle of a straight shore, when I got abreast of it! No prominent hill would stick to its shape long enough for me to make up my mind what its form really was, but it was as dissolving and changeful as if it had been a mountain of butter in the hottest corner of the tropics. Nothing ever had the same shape when I was coming down-stream that it had borne when I went up. I mentioned these little difficulties to Mr. Bixby. He said,—

"That's the very main virtue of the thing. If the shapes didn't change every three seconds they wouldn't be of any use. Take this place where we are now, for instance. As long as that hill over yonder is only one hill, I can boom right along the way I'm going; but the moment it splits at the top and forms a V, I know I've got to scratch to starboard in a hurry, or I'll bang this boat's brains out against a rock; and then the moment one of the prongs of the V swings behind the other, I've got to waltz to lar-board again, or I'll have a misunderstanding with a snag that would snatch the keelson out of this steamboat as neatly as if it were a sliver in your hand. If that hill didn't change its shape on bad nights there would be an awful steamboat grave-yard around here inside of a year."

It was plain that I had got to learn the shape of the river in all the different ways that could be thought of,—upside down, wrong end first, inside out, for-and-aft, and "thortships,"—and then know what to do on gray nights when it hadn't any shape at all. So I set about it. In the course of time I began to get the best of this knotty lesson, and my self-complacency moved to the front once more. Mr. Bixby was all fixed, and ready to start it to the rear again. He opened on me after this fashion:—

"How much water did we have in the middle crossing at Hole-in-the-Wall, trip before last?"

I considered this an outrage. I said:—

"Every trip, down and up, the leadsmen are singing through that tangled place for three quarters of an hour on a stretch. How do you reckon I can remember such a mess as that?"

"My boy, you've got to remember it. You've got to remember the exact spot and the exact marks the boat lay in when we had the shoalest water, in every one of the five hundred shoal places between St. Louis and New Orleans; and you mustn't get the shoal soundings and marks of one trip mixed up with the shoal soundings and marks of another, either, for they're not often twice alike. You must keep them separate."

When I came to myself again, I said,—

"When I get so that I can do that, I'll be able to raise the dead, and then I won't have to pilot a steamboat to make a living. I want to retire from this business. I want a slush-bucket and a brush; I'm only fit for a roustabout. I haven't got brains enough to be a pilot; and if I had I wouldn't have strength enough to carry them around, unless I went on crutches."

"Now drop that! When I say I'll learn* a man the river, I mean it. And you can depend on it, I'll learn him or kill him."

CHAPTER IX

CONTINUED PERPLEXITIES

There was no use in arguing with a person like this. I promptly put such a strain on my memory that by and by even the shoal water and the countless crossing-marks began to stay with me. But the result was just the same. I never could more than get one knotty thing learned before another presented itself. Now I had often seen pilots gazing at the water and pretending to read it as if it were a book; but it was a book that told me nothing. A time came at last, however, when Mr. Bixby seemed to think me far enough advanced to bear a lesson on water-reading. So he began:—

"Do you see that long slanting line on the face of the water? Now, that's a reef. Moreover, it's a bluff reef. There is a solid sand-bar under it that is nearly as straight up and down as the side of a house. There is plenty of water close up to it, but mighty little on top of it. If you were to hit it you would knock the boat's brains out. Do you see where the line fringes out at the upper end and begins to fade away?"

"Yes, sir."

*"Teach" is not in the river vocabulary.

"Well, that is a low place; that is the head of the reef. You can climb over there, and not hurt anything. Cross over, now, and follow along close under the reef—easy water there—not much current."

I followed the reef along till I approached the fringed end. Then Mr. Bixby said,—

"Now get ready. Wait till I give the word. She won't want to mount the reef; a boat hates shoal water. Stand by—wait—*wait*—keep her well in hand. *Now* cramp her down! Snatch her! snatch her!"

He seized the other side of the wheel and helped to spin it around until it was hard down, and then we held it so. The boat resisted, and refused to answer for a while, and next she came surging to starboard, mounted the reef, and sent a long, angry ridge of water foaming away from her bows.

"Now watch her; watch her like a cat, or she'll get away from you. When she fights strong and the tiller slips a little, in a jerky, greasy sort of way, let up on her a trifle; it is the way she tells you at night that the water is too shoal; but keep edging her up, little by little, toward the point. You are well up on the bar, now; there is a bar under every point, because the water that comes down around it forms an eddy and allows the sediment to sink. Do you see those fine lines on the face of the water that branch out like the ribs of a fan? Well, those are little reefs; you want to just miss the ends of them, but run them pretty close. Now look out—look out! Don't you crowd that slick, greasy-looking place; there ain't nine feet there; she won't stand it. She begins to smell it; look sharp, I tell you! Oh blazes, there you go! Stop the starboard wheel! Quick! Ship up to back! Set her back!"

The engine bells jingled and the engines answered promptly, shooting white columns of steam far aloft out of the 'scape pipes, but it was too late. The boat had "smelt" the bar in good earnest; the foamy ridges that radiated from her bows suddenly disappeared, a great dead swell came rolling forward and swept ahead of her, she careened far over to larboard, and went tearing away toward the other shore as if she were about scared to death. We were a good mile from where we ought to have been, when we finally got the upper hand of her again.

During the afternoon watch the next day, Mr. Bixby asked me if I knew how to run the next few miles. I said:—

"Go inside the first snag above the point, outside the next one, start out from the lower end of Higgins's wood-yard, make a square crossing and"—

"That's all right. I'll be back before you close up on the next point."

But he wasn't. He was still below when I rounded it and entered upon a piece of river which I had some misgivings about. I did not know that he was hiding behind a chimney to see how I would perform. I went gayly along, getting prouder and prouder, for he had never left the boat in my sole charge such a length of time before. I even got to "setting" her and letting the wheel go, entirely, while I vaingloriously turned my back and inspected the stern marks and hummed a tune, a sort of easy indifference which I had prodigiously admired in Bixby and other great pilots. Once I inspected rather long, and when I faced to the front again my heart flew into my mouth so suddenly that if I hadn't clapped my teeth together I should have lost it. One of those frightful bluff reefs was stretching its deadly length right across our bows! My head was gone in a moment; I did not know which end I stood on; I gasped and could not get my breath; I spun the wheel down with such rapidity that it wove itself together like a spider's web; the boat answered and turned square away from the reef, but the reef followed her! I fled, and still it followed still it kept—right across my bows! I never looked to see where I was going, I only fled. The awful crash was imminent—why didn't that villain come! If I committed the crime of ringing a bell, I might get thrown overboard. But better that than kill the boat. So in blind desperation I started such a rattling "shivaree" down below as never had astounded an engineer in this world before, I fancy. Amidst the frenzy of the bells the engines began to back and fill in a furious way, and my reason forsook its throne—we were about to crash into the woods on the other side of the river. Just then Mr. Bixby stepped calmly into view on the hurricane deck. My soul went out to him in gratitude. My distress vanished; I would have felt safe on the brink of Niagara, with Mr. Bixby on the hurricane deck. He blandly and sweetly took his tooth-pick out of his mouth between his fingers, as if it were a cigar,—we were just in the act of climbing an overhanging big tree, and the passengers were scudding astern like rats,—and lifted up these commands to me ever so gently:—

"Stop the starboard. Stop the larboard. Set her back on both."

The boat hesitated, halted, pressed her nose among the boughs a critical instant, then reluctantly began to back away.

"Stop the larboard. Come ahead on it. Stop the starboard. Come ahead on it. Point her for the bar."

I sailed away as serenely as a summer's morning. Mr. Bixby came in and said, with mock simplicity,—

"When you have a hail, my boy, you ought to tap the big bell three times before you land, so that the engineers can get ready."

I blushed under the sarcasm, and said I hadn't had any hail.

"Ah! Then it was for wood, I suppose. The officer of the watch will tell you when he wants to wood up."

I went on consuming, and said I wasn't after wood.

"Indeed? Why, what could you want over here in the bend, then? Did you ever know of a boat following a bend up-stream at this stage of the river?"

"No, sir,—and *I* wasn't trying to follow it. I was getting away from a bluff reef."

"No, it wasn't a bluff reef; there isn't one within three miles of where you were."

"But I saw it. It was as bluff as that one yonder."

"Just about. Run over it!"

"Do you give it as an order?"

"Yes. Run over it."

"If I don't, I wish I may die."

"All right; I am taking the responsibility."

I was just as anxious to kill the boat, now, as I had been to save her before. I impressed my orders upon my memory, to be used at the inquest, and made a straight break for the reef. As it disappeared under our bows I held my breath; but we slid over it like oil.

"Now don't you see the difference? It wasn't anything but a *wind* reef. The wind does that."

"So I see. But it is exactly like a bluff reef. How am I ever going to tell them apart?"

"I can't tell you. It is an instinct. By and by you will just naturally *know* one from the other, but you never will be able to explain why or how you know them apart."

It turned out to be true. The face of the water, in time, became a wonderful book—a book that was a dead language to the uneducated passenger, but which told its mind to me without reserve, delivering its most cherished secrets as clearly as if it uttered them with a voice. And it was not a book to be read once and thrown aside, for it had a new story to tell every day. Throughout the long twelve hundred miles there was never a page that was void of interest, never one that you could leave unread without loss, never one that you would want to skip, thinking you could find higher enjoyment in some other thing. There never was so wonderful a book written by man; never one whose interest was so absorbing, so unflagging, so sparklingly renewed with every re-perusal. The passenger who could not read it was charmed with a peculiar sort of faint dimple on its

251

surface (on the rare occasions when he did not overlook it altogether); but to the pilot that was an *italicized* passage; indeed, it was more than that, it was a legend of the largest capitals, with a string of shouting exclamation points at the end of it; for it meant that a wreck or a rock was buried there that could tear the life out of the strongest vessel that ever floated. It is the faintest and simplest expression the water ever makes, and the most hideous to a pilot's eye. In truth, the passenger who could not read this book saw nothing but all manner of pretty pictures in it, painted by the sun and shaded by the clouds, whereas to the trained eye these were not pictures at all, but the grimmest and most dead-earnest of reading-matter.

Now when I had mastered the language of this water and had come to know every trifling feature that bordered the great river as familiarly as I knew the letters of the alphabet, I had made a valuable acquisition. But I had lost something, too. I had lost something which could never be restored to me while I lived. All the grace, the beauty, the poetry had gone out of the majestic river! I still keep in mind a certain wonderful sunset which I witnessed when steamboating was new to me. A broad expanse of the river was turned to blood; in the middle distance the red hue brightened into gold, through which a solitary log came floating, black and conspicuous; in one place a long, slanting mark lay sparkling upon the water; in another the surface was broken by boiling, tumbling rings, that were as many-tinted as an opal; where the ruddy flush was faintest, was a smooth spot that was covered with graceful circles and radiating lines, ever so delicately traced; the shore on our left was densely wooded, and the sombre shadow that fell from this forest was broken in one place by a long, ruffled trail that shone like silver; and high above the forest wall a clean-stemmed dead tree waved a single leafy bough that glowed like a flame in the unobstructed splendor that was flowing from the sun. There were graceful curves, reflected images, woody heights, soft distances; and over the whole scene, far and near, the dissolving lights drifted steadily, enriching it, every passing moment, with new marvels of coloring.

I stood like one bewitched. I drank it in, in a speechless rapture. The world was new to me, and I had never seen anything like this at home. But as I have said, a day came when I began to cease from noting the glories and the charms which the moon and the sun and the twilight wrought upon the river's face; another day came when I ceased altogether to note them. Then, if that sunset scene had been repeated, I should have looked upon it without rapture, and should have commented upon it, inwardly, after this fashion: This sun means that we are going to have wind to-morrow; that floating log means that the river is rising, small thanks to it; that slanting mark on the water refers to a bluff reef which is going to kill somebody's steamboat one of these nights, if it keeps on stretching out like that; those tumbling "boils" show a dissolving bar and a changing channel there; the lines and circles in the slick water over yonder are a warning that that troublesome place is shoaling up dangerously; that silver streak in the shadow of the forest is the "break" from a new snag, and he has located himself in the very best place he could have found to fish for steamboats; that tall dead tree, with a single living branch, is not going to last long, and then how is a body ever going to get through this blind place at night without the friendly old landmark?

No, the romance and the beauty were all gone from the river. All the value any feature of it had for me now was the amount of usefulness it could furnish toward compassing the safe piloting of a steamboat. Since those days, I have pitied doctors from my heart. What does the lovely flush in a beauty's cheek mean to a doctor but a "break" that ripples above some deadly disease? Are not all her visible charms sown thick with what are to him the signs and symbols of hidden decay? Does he ever see her beauty at all, or doesn't he simply view her professionally, and comment upon her unwholesome condition all to himself? And doesn't he sometimes wonder whether he has gained most or lost most by learning his trade?

CHAPTER X

COMPLETING MY EDUCATION

Whosoever has done me the courtesy to read my chapters which have preceded this may possibly wonder that I deal so minutely with piloting as a science. It was the prime purpose of those chapters; and I am not quite done yet. I wish to show, in the most patient and painstaking way, what a wonderful science it is. Ship channels are buoyed and lighted, and therefore it is a comparatively easy undertaking to learn to run them; clearwater rivers, with gravel bottoms, change their channels very gradually, and therefore one needs to learn them but once; but piloting becomes another matter when you apply it to vast streams like the Mississippi and the Missouri, whose alluvial banks cave and change constantly, whose snags are always hunting up new quarters, whose sandbars are never at rest, whose channels are forever dodging and shirking, and whose obstructions must be confronted in all nights and all weathers without the aid of a single light-house or a single buoy; for there is neither light nor buoy to be found anywhere in all this three or four thousand miles of villanous river.* I feel justified in enlarging upon this great science for the reason that I feel sure no one has ever yet written a paragraph about it who had piloted a steamboat himself, and so had a practical knowledge of the subject. If the theme were hackneyed, I should be obliged to deal gently with the reader; but since it is wholly new, I have felt at liberty to take up a considerable degree of room with it.

When I had learned the name and position of every visible feature of the river; when I had so mastered its shape that I could shut my eyes and trace it from St. Louis to New Orleans; when I had learned to read the face of the water as one would cull the news from the morning paper; and finally, when I had trained my dull memory to treasure up an endless array of soundings and crossing-marks, and keep fast hold of them, I judged that my education was complete: so I got to tilting my cap to the side of my head, and wearing a toothpick in my mouth at the wheel. Mr. Bixby had his eye on these airs. One day he said,—

"What is the height of that bank yonder, at Burgess's?"

"How can I tell, sir? It is three quarters of a mile away."

"Very poor eye—very poor. Take the glass."

I took the glass, and presently said,—

"I can't tell. I suppose that that bank is about a foot and a half high."

"Foot and a half! That's a six-foot bank. How high was the bank along here last trip?"

"I don't know; I never noticed."

"You didn't? Well, you must always do it hereafter."

"Why?"

"Because you'll have to know a good many things that it tells you. For one thing, it tells you the stage of the river—tells you whether there's more water or less in the river along here than there was last trip."

"The leads tell me that." I rather thought I had the advantage of him there.

"Yes, but suppose the leads lie? The bank would tell you so, and then you'd stir those leadsmen up a bit. There was a ten-foot

---

* True at the time referred to; not true now (1882).

bank here last trip, and there is only a six-foot bank now. What does that signify?"

"That the river is four feet higher than it was last trip."

"Very good. Is the river rising or falling?"

"Rising."

"No it ain't."

"I guess I am right, sir. Yonder is some driftwood floating down the stream."

"A rise *starts* the drift-wood, but then it keeps on floating a while after the river is done rising. Now the bank will tell you about this. Wait till you come to a place where it shelves a little. Now here; do you see this narrow belt of fine sediment? That was deposited while the water was higher. You see the drift-wood begins to strand, too. The bank helps in other ways. Do you see that stump on the false point?"

"Ay, ay, sir."

"Well, the water is just up to the roots of it. You must make a note of that."

"Why?"

"Because that means that there's seven feet in the chute of 103."

"But 103 is a long way up the river yet."

"That's where the benefit of the bank comes in. There is water enough in 103 *now,* yet there may not be by the time we get there; but the bank will keep us posted all along. You don't run close chutes on a falling river, upstream, and there are precious few of them that you are allowed to run at all downstream. There's a law of the United States against it. The river may be rising by the time we get to 103, and in that case we'll run it. We are drawing—how much?"

"Six feet aft,—six and a half forward."

"Well, you do seem to know something."

"But what I particularly want to know is, if I have got to keep up an everlasting measuring of the banks of this river, twelve hundred miles, month in and month out?"

"Of course!"

My emotions were too deep for words for a while. Presently I said,—

"And how about these chutes? Are there many of them?"

"I should say so. I fancy we shan't run any of the river this trip as you've ever seen it run before—so to speak. If the river begins to rise again, we'll go up behind bars that you've always seen standing out of the river, high and dry like the roof of a house; we'll cut across low places that you've never noticed at

255

all, right through the middle of bars that cover three hundred acres of river; we'll creep through cracks where you've always thought was solid land; we'll dart through the woods and leave twenty-five miles of river off to one side; we'll see the hind-side of every island between New Orleans and Cairo."

"Then I've got to go to work and learn just as much more river as I already know."

"Just about twice as much more, as near as you can come at it."

"Well, one lives to find out. I think I was a fool when I went into this business."

"Yes, that is true. And you are yet. But you'll not be when you've learned it."

"Ah, I never can learn it."

"I will see that you *do.*"

By and by I ventured again:—

"Have I got to learn all this thing just as I know the rest of the river—shapes and all—and so I can run it at night?"

"Yes. And you've got to have good fair marks from one end of the river to the other, that will help the bank tell you when there is water enough in each of these countless places,—like that stump, you know. When the river first begins to rise, you can run half a dozen of the deepest of them; when it rises a foot more you can run another dozen; the next foot will add a couple of dozen, and so on: so you see you have to know your banks and marks to a dead moral certainty, and never get them mixed; for when you start through one of those cracks, there's no backing out again, as there is in the big river; you've got to go through, or stay there six months if you get caught on a falling river. There are about fifty of these cracks which you can't run at all except when the river is brim full and over the banks."

"This new lesson is a cheerful prospect."

"Cheerful enough. And mind what I've just told you; when you start into one of those places you've got to go through. They are too narrow to turn around in, too crooked to back out of, and the shoal water is always *up at the head;* never elsewhere. And the head of them is always likely to be filling up, little by little, so that the marks you reckon their depth by, this season, may not answer for next."

"Learn a new set, then, every year?"

"Exactly. Cramp her up to the bar! What are you standing up through the middle of the river for?"

The next few months showed me strange things. On the same day that we held the conversation above narrated, we met a great rise coming down the river. The whole vast face of the stream was black with drifting dead logs, broken boughs, and great trees that had caved in and been washed away. It required the nicest steering to pick one's way through this rushing raft, even in the day-time, when crossing from point to point; and at night the difficulty was mightily increased; every now and then a huge log, lying deep in the water, would suddenly appear right under our bows, coming head-on; no use to try to avoid it then; we could only stop the engines, and one wheel would walk over that log from one end to the other, keeping up a thundering racket and careening the boat in a way that was very uncomfortable to passengers. Now and then we would hit one of these sunken logs a rattling bang, dead in the centre, with a full head of steam, and it would stun the boat as if she had hit a continent. Sometimes this log would lodge, and stay right across our nose, and back the Mississippi up before it; we would have to do a little crawfishing, then, to get away from the obstruction. We often hit *white* logs, in the dark, for we could not see them till we were right on them; but a black log is a pretty distinct object at night. A white snag is an ugly customer when the daylight is gone.

Of course, on the great rise, down came a swarm of prodigious timber-rafts from the head waters of the Mississippi, coal barges from Pittsburgh, little trading scows from everywhere, and broad-horns from "Posey County," Indiana, freighted with "fruit and furniture"—the usual term for describing it, though in plain English the freight thus aggrandized was hoop-poles and pumpkins. Pilots bore a mortal hatred to these craft; and it was returned with usury. The law required all such helpless traders to keep a light burning, but it was a law that was often broken. All of a sudden, on a murky night, a light would hop up, right under our bows, almost, and an agonized voice, with the backwoods "whang" to it, would wail out:—

"Whar'n the——you goin'to! Cain't you see nothin', you dash—dashed aig-suckin', sheep-stealin', one-eyed son of a stuffed monkey!"

Then for an instant, as we whistled by, the red glare from our furnaces would reveal the scow and the form of the gesticulating orator as if under a lightning-flash, and in that instant our firemen and deck-hands would send and receive a tempest of missiles and profanity, one of our wheels would walk off with the crashing fragments of a steering-oar, and down the dead blackness would shut again. And that flatboatman would be sure to go into New Orleans and sue our boat, swearing stoutly that he had a light burning all the time, when in truth his gang had the lantern down below to sing and lie and drink and gamble by, and no watch on deck. Once, at night, in one of those forest-bordered crevices (behind an island) which steamboatmen intensely describe with the phrase "as dark as the inside of a cow," we should have eaten up a Posey County family, fruit, furniture, and all, but that they happened to be fiddling down below and we just caught the sound of the music in time to sheer off, doing no serious damage, unfortunately, but coming so near it that we had good hopes for a moment. These people brought up their lantern, then, of course; and as we backed and filled to get away, the precious family stood in the light of it—both sexes and various ages —and cursed us till everything turned blue. Once a coalboatman sent a bullet through our pilot-house, when we borrowed a steering-oar of him in a very narrow place.

CHAPTER XI

THE RIVER RISES

During this big rise these small-fry craft were an intolerable nuisance. We were running chute after chute,—a new world to me,—and if there was a particularly cramped place in a chute, we would be pretty sure to meet a broad-horn there; and if he failed to be there, we would find him in a still worse locality, namely, the head of the chute, on the shoal water. And then there would be no end of profane cordialities exchanged.

Sometimes, in the big river, when we would be feeling our way cautiously along through a fog, the deep hush would suddenly be broken by yells and a clamor of tin pans, and all in an instant a log raft would appear vaguely through the webby veil, close upon us; and then we did not wait to swap knives, but snatched our engine bells out by the roots and piled on all the steam we had, to scramble out of the way! One doesn't hit a rock or a solid log raft with a steamboat when he can get excused.

You will hardly believe it, but many steamboat clerks always carried a large assortment of religious tracts with them in those old departed steamboating days. Indeed they did. Twenty times a day we would be cramping up around a bar, while a string of these small-fry rascals were drifting down into the head of the bend away above and beyond us a couple of miles. Now a skiff would dart away from one of them, and come fighting its laborious way across the desert of water. It would "ease all," in the shadow of our forecastle, and the panting oarsmen would shout, "Gimme a pa-a-per!" as the skiff drifted swiftly astern.

The clerk would throw over a file of New Orleans journals. If these were picked up *without comment,* you might notice that now a dozen other skiffs had been drifting down upon us without saying anything. You understand, they had been waiting to see how No. 1 was going to fare. No. 1 making no comment, all the rest would bend to their oars and come on, now; and as fast as they came the clerk would heave over neat bundles of religious tracts, tied to shingles. The amount of hard swearing which twelve packages of religious literature will command when impartially divided up among twelve raftsmen's crews, who have pulled a heavy skiff two miles on a hot day to get them, is simply incredible.

As I have said, the big rise brought a new world under my vision. By the time the river was over its banks we had forsaken our old paths and were hourly climbing over bars that had stood ten feet out of water before; we were shaving stumpy shores, like that at the foot of Madrid Bend, which I had always seen avoided before; we were clattering through chutes like that of 82, where the opening at the foot was an unbroken wall of timber till our nose was almost at the very spot. Some of these chutes were utter solitudes. The dense, untouched forest overhung both banks of the crooked little crack, and one could believe that human creatures had never intruded there before. The swinging grape-vines, the grassy nooks and vistas glimpsed as we swept by, the flowering creepers waving their red blossoms from the tops of dead trunks, and all the spendthrift richness of the forest foliage, were wasted and thrown away there. The chutes were lovely places to steer in; they were deep, except at the head; the current was gentle; under the "points" the water was absolutely dead, and the invisible banks so bluff that where the tender willow thickets projected you could bury your boat's broadside in them as you tore along, and then you seemed fairly to fly.

Behind other islands we found wretched little farms, and wretcheder little log-cabins; there were crazy rail fences sticking a foot or two above the water, with one or two jeans-clad, chills-racked, yellow-faced male miserables roosting on the top-rail, elbows on knees, jaws in hands, grinding tobacco and discharging the result at floating chips through crevices left by lost teeth; while the rest of the family and the few farm-animals were huddled together in an empty wood-flat riding at her moorings close at hand. In this flatboat the family would have to cook and eat and sleep for a lesser or greater number of days (or possibly weeks), until the river should fall two or three feet and let them get back to their log-cabin and their chills again—chills being a merciful provision of an all-wise Providence to enable them to take exercise without exertion. And this sort of watery camping out was a thing which these people were rather liable to be treated to a couple of times a year: by the December rise out of the Ohio, and the June rise out of the Mississippi. And yet these were kindly dispensations, for they at least enabled the poor things to rise from the dead now and then, and look upon life when a steamboat went by. They appreciated the blessing, too, for they spread their mouths and eyes wide open and made the most of these occasions. Now what *could* these banished creatures find to do to keep from dying of the blues during the low-water season!

Once, in one of these lovely island chutes, we found our course completely bridged by a great fallen tree. This will serve to show how narrow some of the chutes were. The passengers had an hour's recreation in a virgin wilderness, while the boat-hands chopped the bridge away; for there was no such thing as turning back, you comprehend.

From Cairo to Baton Rouge, when the river is over its banks, you have no particular trouble in the night, for the thousand-mile wall of dense forest that guards the two banks all the way is only gapped with a farm or wood-yard opening at intervals, and so you can't "get out of the river" much easier than you could get out of a fenced lane; but from Baton Rouge to New Orleans it is a different matter. The river is more than a mile wide, and very deep—as much as two hundred feet, in places. Both banks, for a good deal over a hundred miles, are shorn of their timber and bordered by continuous sugar plantations, with only here and there a scattering sapling or row of ornamental China-trees. The timber is shorn off clear to the rear of the plantations, from two to four miles. When the first frost threatens to come, the planters snatch off their crops in a hurry. When they have finished grinding the cane, they form the refuse of the stalks (which they call *bagasse*) into great piles and set fire to them, though in other sugar countries the bagasse is used for fuel in the furnaces of the sugar mills. Now the piles of damp bagasse burn slowly, and smoke like Satan's own kitchen.

An embankment ten or fifteen feet high guards both banks of the Mississippi all the way down that lower end of the river, and this embankment is set back from the edge of the shore from ten to perhaps a hundred feet, according to circumstances; say thirty or forty feet, as a general thing. Fill that whole region with an impenetrable gloom of smoke from a hundred miles of burning bagasse piles, when the river is over the banks, and turn a steamboat loose along there at midnight and see how she will feel. And see how you will feel, too! You find yourself away out in the midst of a vague dim sea that is shoreless, that fades out and loses itself in the murky distances; for you cannot discern the thin rib of embankment, and you are always imagining you see a straggling tree when you don't. The plantations themselves are transformed by the smoke, and look like a part of the sea. All through your watch you are tortured with the exquisite misery of uncertainty. You hope you are keeping in the river, but you do not know. All that you are sure about is that you are likely to be within six feet of the bank *and* destruction, when you think you are a good half-mile from shore. And you are sure, also, that if you chance suddenly to fetch up against the embankment and topple your chimneys overboard, you will have the small comfort of knowing that it is about what you were expecting to do. One of the great Vicksburg packets darted out into a sugar plantation one night, at such a time, and had to stay there a week. But there was no novelty about it; it had often been done before.

I thought I had finished this chapter, but I wish to add a curious thing, while it is in my mind. It is only relevant in that it is connected with piloting. There used to be an excellent pilot on the river, a Mr. X., who was a somnambulist. It was said that if his mind was troubled about a bad piece of river, he was pretty sure to get up and walk in his sleep and do strange things. He was once fellow-pilot for a trip or two with George Ealer, on a great New Orleans passenger packet. During a considerable part of the first trip George was uneasy, but got over it by and by, as X. seemed content to stay in his bed when asleep. Late one night the boat was approaching Helena, Arkansas; the water was low, and the crossing above the town in a very blind and tangled condition. X. had seen the crossing since Ealer had, and as the night was particularly drizzly, sullen, and dark, Ealer was considering whether he had not better have X. called to assist in running the place, when the door opened and X. walked in. Now on very dark nights, light is a deadly enemy to piloting; you are aware that if you stand in a lighted room, on such a night, you cannot see things in the street to any purpose; but if you put out the lights and stand in the gloom you can make out objects in the street pretty well. So, on very dark nights, pilots do not smoke; they allow no fire in the pilot-house stove if there is a crack which can allow the least ray to escape; they order the furnaces to be curtained with huge tarpaulins and the sky-lights to be closely blinded. Then no light whatever issues from the boat. The undefinable shape that now entered the pilot-house had Mr. X.'s voice. This said,—

"Let me take her, George; I've seen this place since you have, and it is so crooked that I reckon I can run it myself easier than I could tell you how to do it."

"It is kind of you, and I swear *I* am willing. I haven't got another drop of perspiration left in me. I have been spinning around and around the wheel like a squirrel. It is so dark I can't tell which way she is swinging till she is coming around like a whirligig."

So Ealer took a seat on the bench, panting and breathless. The black phantom assumed the wheel without saying anything, steadied the waltzing steamer with a turn or two, and then stood at ease, coaxing her a little to this side and then to that, as gently and as sweetly as if the time had been noonday. When Ealer observed this marvel of steering, he wished he had not confessed! He stared, and wondered, and finally said,—

"Well, I thought I knew how to steer a steamboat, but that was another mistake of mine."

X. said nothing, but went serenely on with his work. He rang for the leads; he rang to slow down the steam; he worked the boat carefully and neatly into invisible marks, then stood at the centre of the wheel and peered blandly out into the blackness, fore and aft, to verify his position; as the leads shoaled more and more, he stopped the engines entirely, and the dead silence and suspense of "drifting" followed; when the shoalest water was struck, he cracked on the steam, carried her handsomely over, and then began to work her warily into the next system of shoal marks; the same patient, heedful use of leads and engines followed, the boat slipped through without touching bottom, and entered upon the third and last intricacy of the crossing; imperceptibly she moved through the gloom, crept by inches into her marks, drifted tediously tili the shoalest water was cried, and then, under a tremendous head of steam, went swinging over the reef and away into deep water and safety!

Ealer let his long-pent breath pour out in a great, relieving sigh, and said:—

"That's the sweetest piece of piloting that was ever done on the Mississippi River! I wouldn't believed it could be done, if I hadn't seen it."

There was no reply, and he added:—

"Just hold her five minutes longer, partner, and let me run down and get a cup of coffee."

A minute later Ealer was biting into a pie, down in the "texas," and comforting himself with coffee. Just then the night watchman happened in, and was about to happen out again, when he noticed Ealer and exclaimed,—

"Who is at the wheel, sir?"

"X."

"Dart for the pilot-house, quicker than lightning!"

The next moment both men were flying up the pilot-house companion-way, three steps at a jump! Nobody there! The great steamer was whistling down the middle of the river at her own sweet will! The watchman shot out of the place again; Ealer seized the wheel, set an engine back with power, and held his breath while the boat reluctantly swung away from a "towhead" which she was about to knock into the middle of the Gulf of Mexico!

By and by the watchman came back and said,—

"Didn't that lunatic tell you he was asleep, when he first came up here?"

"No."

"Well, he was. I found him walking along on top of the railings, just as unconcerned as another man would walk a pavement; and I put him to bed; now just this minute there he was again, away astern, going through that sort of tightrope deviltry the same as before."

"Well, I think I'll stay by, next time he has one of those fits. But I hope he'll have them often. You just ought to have seen him take this boat through Helena crossing. *I* never saw anything so gaudy before. And if he can do such gold-leaf, kid-glove, diamond-breastpin piloting when he is sound asleep, what *couldn't* he do if he was dead!"

CHAPTER XII

SOUNDING

When the river is very low, and one's steamboat is "drawing all the water" there is in the channel,—or a few inches more, as was often the case in the old times,—one must be painfully circumspect in his piloting. We used to have to "sound" a number of particularly bad places almost every trip when the river was at a very low stage. Sounding is done in this way. The boat ties up at the shore, just above the shoal crossing; the pilot not on watch takes his "cub" or steersman and a picked crew of men (sometimes an officer also), and goes out in the yawl—provided the boat has not that rare and sumptuous luxury, a regularly-devised "sounding-boat"—and proceeds to hunt for the best water, the pilot on duty watching his movements through a spy-glass, meantime, and in some instances assisting by signals of the boat's whistle, signifying "try higher up" or "try lower down;" for the surface of the water, like an oil-painting, is more expressive and intelligible when inspected from a little distance than very close at hand. The whistle signals are seldom necessary, however; never, perhaps, except when the wind confuses the significant ripples upon the water's surface. When the yawl has reached the shoal place, the speed is slackened, the pilot begins to sound the depth with a pole ten or twelve feet long, and the steersman at the tiller obeys the order to "hold her up to starboard;" or "let her fall off to larboard;"* or "steady—steady as you go."

When the measurements indicate that the yawl is approaching the shoalest part of the reef, the command is given to "ease all!" Then the men stop rowing and the yawl drifts with the current. The next order is, "Stand by with the buoy!" The moment the shallowest point is reached, the pilot delivers the order, "Let go the buoy!" and over she goes. If the pilot is not satisfied, he sounds the place again; if he finds better water higher up or lower down, he removes the buoy to that place. Being finally satisfied, he gives the order, and all the men stand their oars straight up in the air, in line; a blast from the boat's whistle indicates that the signal has been seen; then the men "give way" on their oars and lay the yawl alongside the buoy; the steamer comes creeping carefully down, is pointed straight at the buoy, husbands her power for the coming struggle, and presently, at the critical moment, turns on all her steam and goes grinding and wallowing over the buoy and the sand, and gains the deep water beyond. Or maybe she doesn't; maybe she "strikes and swings." Then she has to while away several hours (or days) sparring herself off.

Sometimes a buoy is not laid at all, but the yawl goes ahead, hunting the best water, and the steamer follows along in its wake. Often there is a deal of fun and excitement about sounding, especially if it is a glorious summer day, or a blustering night. But in winter the cold and the peril take most of the fun out of it.

A buoy is nothing but a board four or five feet long, with one end turned up; it is a reversed school-house bench, with one of the supports left and the other removed. It is anchored on the shoalest part of the reef by a rope with a heavy stone made fast to the end of it. But for the resistance of the turned-up end of the reversed bench, the current would pull the buoy under water. At

---

* The term "larboard" is never used at sea, now, to signify the left hand; but was always used on the river in my time.

night, a paper lantern with a candle in it is fastened on top of the buoy, and this can be seen a mile or more, a little glimmering spark in the waste of blackness.

Nothing delights a cub so much as an opportunity to go out sounding. There is such an air of adventure about it; often there is danger; it is so gaudy and man-of-war-like to sit up in the stern-sheets and steer a swift yawl; there is something fine about the exultant spring of the boat when an experienced old sailor crew throw their souls into the oars; it is lovely to see the white foam stream away from the bows; there is music in the rush of the water; it is deliciously exhilarating, in summer, to go speeding over the breezy expanses of the river when the world of wavelets is dancing in the sun. It is such grandeur, too, to the cub, to get a chance to give an order; for often the pilot will simply say, "Let her go about!" and leave the rest to the cub, who instantly cries, in his sternest tone of command, "Ease starboard! Strong on the larboard! Starboard give way! With a will, men!" The cub enjoys sounding for the further reason that the eyes of the passengers are watching all the yawl's movements with absorbing interest if the time be daylight; and if it be night he knows that those same wondering eyes are fastened upon the yawl's lantern as it glides out into the gloom and dims away in the remote distance.

One trip a pretty girl of sixteen spent her time in our pilot-house with her uncle and aunt, every day and all day long. I fell in love with her. So did Mr. Thornburg's cub, Tom G——. Tom and I had been bosom friends until this time; but now a coolness began to arise. I told the girl a good many of my river adventures, and made myself out a good deal of a hero; Tom tried to make himself appear to be a hero, too, and succeeded to some extent, but then he always had a way of embroidering. However, virtue is its own reward, so I was a barely perceptible trifle ahead in the contest. About this time something happened which promised handsomely for me: the pilots decided to sound the crossing at the head of 21. This would occur about nine or ten o'clock at night, when the passengers would be still up; it would be Mr. Thornburg's watch, therefore my chief would have to do the sounding. We had a perfect love of a sounding-boat—long, trim, graceful, and as fleet as a greyhound; her thwarts were cushioned; she carried twelve oarsmen; one of the mates was always sent in her to transmit orders to her crew, for ours was a steamer where no end of "style" was put on.

We tied up at the shore above 21, and got ready. It was a foul night, and the river was so wide, there, that a landsman's uneducated eyes could discern no opposite shore through such a gloom. The passengers were alert and interested; everything was satisfactory. As I hurried through the engine-room, picturesquely gotten up in storm toggery, I met Tom, and could not forbear delivering myself of a mean speech:—

"Ain't you glad *you* don't have to go out sounding?"

Tom was passing on, but he quickly turned, and said,—

"Now just for that, you can go and get the sounding-pole yourself. I was going after it, but I'd see you in Halifax, now, before I'd do it."

"Who wants you to get it? *I* don't. It's in the sounding-boat."

"It ain't, either. It's been new-painted; and it's been up on the ladies cabin guards two days, drying."

I flew back, and shortly arrived among the crowd of watching and wondering ladies just in time to hear the command:

"Give way, men!"

I looked over, and there was the gallant sounding-boat booming away, the unprincipled Tom presiding at the tiller, and my chief sitting by him with the sounding-pole which I had been sent on a fool's errand to fetch. Then that young girl said to me,—

"Oh, how awful to have to go out in that little boat on such a night! Do you think there is any danger?"

I would rather have been stabbed. I went off, full of venom, to help in the pilot-house. By and by the boat's lantern disappeared, and after an interval a wee spark glimmered upon the face of the water a mile away. Mr. Thornburg blew the whistle, in acknowledgment, backed the steamer out, and made for it. We flew along for a while, then slackened steam and went cautiously gliding toward the spark. Presently Mr. Thornburg exclaimed,—

"Hello, the buoy-lantern's out!"

He stopped the engines. A moment or two later he said,—

"Why, there it is again!"

So he came ahead on the engines once more, and rang for the leads. Gradually the water shoaled up, and then began to deepen again! Mr. Thornburg muttered:—

"Well, I don't understand this. I believe that buoy has drifted off the reef. Seems to be a little too far to the left. No matter, it is safest to run over it, anyhow."

So, in that solid world of darkness we went creeping down on the light. Just as our bows were in the act of plowing over it, Mr. Thornburg seized the bell-ropes, rang a startling peal, and exclaimed,—

"My soul, it's the sounding-boat!"

A sudden chorus of wild alarms burst out far below—a

pause—and then a sound of grinding and crashing followed. Mr. Thornburg exclaimed,—

"There! the paddle-wheel has ground the sounding-boat to lucifer matches! Run! See who is killed!"

I was on the main deck in the twinkling of an eye. My chief and the third mate and nearly all the men were safe. They had discovered their danger when it was too late to pull out of the way; then, when the great guards overshadowed them a moment later, they were prepared and knew what to do; at my chief's order they sprang at the right instant, seized the guard, and were hauled aboard. The next moment the sounding-yawl swept aft to the wheel and was struck and splintered to atoms. Two of the men and the cub Tom, were missing—a fact which spread like wildfire over the boat. The passengers came flocking to the forward gangway, ladies and all, anxious-eyed, white-faced, and talked in awed voices of the dreadful thing. And often and again I heard them say, "Poor fellows! poor boy, poor boy!"

By this time the boat's yawl was manned and away, to search for the missing. Now a faint call was heard, off to the left. The yawl had disappeared in the other direction. Half the people rushed to one side to encourage the swimmer with their shouts; the other half rushed the other way to shriek to the yawl to turn about. By the callings, the swimmer was approaching, but some said the sound showed failing strength. The crowd massed themselves against the boiler-deck railings, leaning over and staring into the gloom; and every faint and fainter cry wrung from them such words as "Ah, poor fellow, poor fellow! is there *no* way to save him?"

But still the cries held out, and drew nearer, and presently the voice said pluckily,—

"I can make it! Stand by with a rope!"

What a rousing cheer they gave him! The chief mate took his stand in the glare of a torch-basket, a coil of rope in his hand, and his men grouped about him. The next moment the swimmer's face appeared in the circle of light, and in another one the owner of it was hauled aboard, limp and drenched, while cheer on cheer went up. It was that devil Tom.

The yawl crew searched everywhere, but found no sign of the two men. They probably failed to catch the guard, tumbled back, and were struck by the wheel and killed. Tom had never jumped for the guard at all, but had plunged head-first into the river and dived under the wheel. It was nothing; I could have done it easy enough, and I said so; but everybody went on just the same, making a wonderful to-do over that ass, as if he had done something great. That girl couldn't seem to have enough of that pitiful "hero" the rest of the trip; but little I cared; I loathed her, any way.

The way we came to mistake the sounding-boat's lantern for the buoy-light was this. My chief said that after laying the buoy he fell away and watched it till it seemed to be secure; then he took up a position a hundred yards below it and a little to one side of the steamer's course, headed the sounding-boat up-stream, and waited. Having to wait some time, he and the officer got to talking; he looked up when he judged that the steamer was about on the reef; saw that the buoy was gone, but supposed that the steamer had already run over it; he went on with his talk; he noticed that the steamer was getting very close down on him, but that was the correct thing; it was her business to shave him closely, for convenience in taking him aboard; he was expecting her to sheer off, until the last moment; then if flashed upon him that she was trying to run him down, mistaking his lantern for the buoy-light; so he sang out, "Stand by to spring for the guard, men!" and the next instant the jump was made.

CHAPTER XIII

A PILOT'S NEEDS

But I am wandering from what I was intending to do, that is, make plainer than perhaps appears in the previous chapters, some of the peculiar requirements of the science of piloting. First of all, there is one faculty which a pilot must incessantly cultivate until he has brought it to absolute perfection. Nothing short of perfection will do. That faculty is memory. He cannot stop with merely thinking a thing is so and so; he must *know* it; for this eminently one of the "exact" sciences. With what scorn a pilot was looked upon, in the old times, if he ever ventured to deal in that feeble phrase "I think," instead of the vigorous one "I know!" One cannot easily realize what a tremendous thing it is to know every trivial detail of twelve hundred miles of river and know it with absolute exactness. If you will take the longest street in New York, and travel up and down it, conning its features patiently until you know every house and window and door and lamp-post and big and little sign by heart, and know them so accurately that you can instantly name the one you are abreast of when you are set down at random in that street in the middle of an inky black night, you will then have a tolerable notion of the amount and the exactness of a pilot's knowledge who carries the Mississippi River in his head. And then if you will go on until you know every street crossing, the character, size, and position of the crossing-stones, and the varying depth of mud in each of those numberless places, you will have some idea of what the pilot must know in order to keep a Mississippi steamer out of trouble. Next, if you will take half of the signs in that long street, and *change their places* once a month, and still manage to know their new positions accurately on dark nights, and keep up with these repeated changes without making any mistakes, you will understand what is required of a pilot's peerless memory by the fickle Mississippi.

I think a pilot's memory is about the most wonderful thing in the world. To know the Old and New Testaments by heart, and be able to recite them glibly, forward or backward, or begin at random anywhere in the book and recite both ways and never trip or make a mistake, is no extravagant mass of knowledge, and no marvellous facility, compared to a pilot's massed knowledge of the Mississippi and his marvellous facility in the handling of it. I make this comparison deliberately, and believe I am not expanding the truth when I do it. Many will think my figure too strong, but pilots will not.

And how easily and comfortably the pilot's memory does its work; how placidly effortless is its way; how *unconsciously* it lays up its vast stores, hour by hour, day by day, and never loses or mislays a single valuable package of them all! Take an instance. Let a leadsman cry, "Half twain! half twain! half twain! half twain! half twain!" until it becomes as monotonous as the ticking of a clock; let conversation be going on all the time, and the pilot be doing his share of the talking, and no longer consciously listening to the leadsman; and in the midst of this endless string of half twains let a single "quarter twain!" be interjected, without emphasis, and then the half twain cry go on again, just as before: two or three weeks later that pilot can describe with precision the boat's position in the river when that quarter twain was uttered, and give you such a lot of headmarks, stern marks, and side marks to guide you, that you ought to be able to take the boat there and put her in that same spot again yourself! The cry of "quarter twain" did not really take his mind from his talk, but his trained faculties instantly photographed the bearings, noted the change of depth, and laid up the important details for future reference without requiring any assistance from *him* in the matter. If you were walking and talking with a friend, and another friend at your side kept up a monotonous repetition of the vowel sound A, for a couple of blocks, and then in the midst interjected an R, thus, A, A, A, A, A, R, A, A, A, etc., and gave the R no emphasis, you would not be able to state, two or three weeks afterward, that the R had been put in, nor be able to tell what objects you were passing at the moment it was done. But you could if your memory had been patiently and laboriously trained to do that sort of thing mechanically.

Give a man a tolerably fair memory to start with, and piloting will develop it into a very colossus of capability. But *only in the matters it is daily drilled in.* A time would come when the man's faculties could not help noticing landmarks and soundings, and his memory could not help holding on to them with the grip of a vice; but if you asked that same man at noon what he had had for breakfast, it would be ten chances to one that he could not tell you. Astonishing things can be done with the human memory if you will devote it faithfully to one particular line of business.

At the time that wages soared so high on the Missouri River, my chief, Mr. Bixby, went up there and learned more than a thousand miles of that stream with an ease and rapidity that were astonishing. When he had seen each division *once* in the daytime and *once* at night, his education was so nearly complete that he took out a "daylight" license; a few trips later he took out a full license, and went to piloting day and night,—and he ranked A 1, too.

Mr. Bixby placed me as steersman for a while under a pilot whose feats of memory were a constant marvel to me. However, his memory was born in him, I think, not built. For instance, somebody would mention a name. Instantly Mr. Brown would break in:—

"Oh, I knew *him.* Sallow-faced, red-headed fellow, with a little scar on the side of his throat, like a splinter under the flesh. He was only in the Southern trade six months. That was thirteen years ago. I made a trip with him. There was five feet in the upper river then; the 'Henry Blake' grounded at the foot of Tower Island drawing four and a half; the 'George Elliott' unshipped her rudder on the wreck of the 'Sunflower' "—

"Why, the 'Sunflower' didn't sink until"—

"*I* know when she sunk; it was three years before that, on the 2d of December; Asa Hardy was captain of her, and his brother John was first clerk; and it was his first trip in her, too; Tom Jones told me these things a week afterward in New Orleans; he was first mate of the 'Sunflower.' Captain Hardy stuck a nail in his foot the 6th of July of the next year, and died of the lockjaw on the 15th. His brother John died two years after,—3d of

March,—erysipelas. I never saw either of the Hardys,—they were Alleghany River men,—but people who knew them told me all these things. And they said Captain Hardy wore yarn socks winter and summer just the same, and his first wife's name was Jane Shook,—she was from New England,—and his second one died in a lunatic asylum. It was in the blood. She was from Lexington, Kentucky. Name was Horton before she was married.''

And so on, by the hour, the man's tongue would go. He could *not* forget any thing. It was simply impossible. The most trivial details remained as distinct and luminous in his head, after they had lain there for years, as the most memorable events. His was not simply a pilot's memory; its grasp was universal. If he were talking about a trifling letter he had received seven years before, he was pretty sure to deliver you the entire screed from memory. And then without observing that he was departing from the true line of his talk, he was more than likely to hurl in a long-drawn parenthetical biography of the writer of that letter; and you were lucky indeed if he did not take up that writer's relatives, one by one, and give you their biographies, too.

Such a memory as that is a great misfortune. To it, all occurrences are of the same size. Its possessor cannot distinguish an interesting circumstance from an uninteresting one. As a talker, he is bound to clog his narrative with tiresome details and make himself an insufferable bore. Moreover, he cannot stick to his subject. He picks up every little grain of memory he discerns in his way, and so is led aside. Mr. Brown would start out with the honest intention of telling you a vastly funny anecdote about a dog. He would be "so full of laugh" that he could hardly begin; then his memory would start with the dog's breed and personal appearance; drift into a history of his owner; of his owner's family, with descriptions of weddings and burials that had occurred in it, together with recitals of congratulatory verses and obituary poetry provoked by the same; then this memory would recollect that one of these events occurred during the celebrated "hard winter" of such and such a year, and a minute description of that winter would follow, along with the names of people who were frozen to death, and statistics showing the high figures which pork and hay went up to. Pork and hay would suggest corn and fodder; corn and fodder would suggest cows and horses; cows and horses would suggest the circus and certain celebrated bare-back riders; the transition from the circus to the menagerie was easy and natural; from the elephant to equatorial Africa was but a step; then of course the heathen savages would suggest religion; and at the end of three or four hours' tedious jaw, the watch would change, and Brown would go out of the pilot-house muttering extracts from sermons he had heard years before about the efficacy of prayer as a means of grace. And the original first mention would be all you had learned about that dog, after all this waiting and hungering.

A pilot must have a memory; but there are two higher qualities which he must also have. He must have good and quick judgment and decision, and a cool, calm courage that no peril can shake. Give a man the merest trifle of pluck to start with, and by the time he has become a pilot he cannot be unmanned by any danger a steamboat can get into; but one cannot quite say the same for judgment. Judgment is a matter of brains, and a man must *start* with a good stock of that article or he will never succeed as a pilot.

The growth of courage in the pilot-house is steady all the time, but it does not reach a high and satisfactory condition until some time after the young pilot has been "standing his own watch," alone and under the staggering weight of all the responsibilities connected with the position. When an apprentice has become pretty thoroughly acquainted with the river, he goes clattering along so fearlessly with his steamboat, night or day, that he presently begins to imagine that it is *his* courage that animates him; but the first time the pilot steps out and leaves him to his own devices he finds out it was the other man's. He discovers that the article has been left out of his own cargo altogether. The whole river is bristling with exigencies in a moment; he is not prepared for them; he does not know how to meet them; all his knowledge forsakes him; and within fifteen minutes he is as white as a sheet and scared almost to death. Therefore pilots wisely train these cubs by various strategic tricks to look danger in the face a little more calmly. A favorite way of theirs is to play a friendly swindle upon the candidate.

Mr. Bixby served me in this fashion once, and for years afterward I used to blush even in my sleep when I thought of it. I had become a good steersman; so good, indeed, that I had all the work to do on our watch, night and day; Mr. Bixby seldom made a suggestion to me; all he ever did was to take the wheel on particularly bad nights or in particularly bad crossings, land the boat when she needed to be landed, play gentleman of leisure nine tenths of the watch, and collect the wages. The lower river was about bank-full, and if anybody had questioned my ability to run any crossing between Cairo and New Orleans without help or instruction, I should have felt irreparably hurt. The idea of being afraid of any crossing in the lot, in the *day-time*, was a thing too preposterous for contemplation. Well, one matchless summer's day I was bowling down the bend above island 66, brimful of self-conceit and carrying my nose as high as a giraffe's, when Mr. Bixby said,—

"I am going below a while. I suppose you know the next crossing?"

This was almost an affront. It was about the plainest and simplest crossing in the whole river. One couldn't come to any harm, whether he ran it right or not; and as for depth, there never had been any bottom there. I knew all this, perfectly well.

"Know how to *run* it? Why, I can run it with my eyes shut."

"How much water is there in it?"

"Well, that is an odd question. I couldn't get bottom there with a church steeple."

"You think so, do you?"

The very tone of the question shook my confidence. That was what Mr. Bixby was expecting. He left, without saying anything more. I began to imagine all sorts of things. Mr. Bixby, unknown to me, of course, sent somebody down to the forecastle with some mysterious instructions to the leadsmen, another messenger was sent to whisper among the officers, and then Mr. Bixby went into hiding behind a smoke-stack where he could observe results. Presently the captain stepped out on the hurricane deck; next the chief mate appeared; then a clerk. Every moment or two a straggler was added to my audience; and before I got to the head of the island I had fifteen or twenty people assembled down there under my nose. I began to wonder what the trouble was. As I started across, the captain glanced aloft at me and said, with a sham uneasiness in his voice,—

"Where is Mr. Bixby?"

"Gone below, sir."

But that did the business for me. My imagination began to construct dangers out of nothing, and they multiplied faster than I could keep the run of them. All at once I imagined I saw shoal water ahead! The wave of coward agony that surged through me then came near dislocating every joint in me. All my confidence in that crossing vanished. I seized the bell-rope; dropped it, ashamed; seized it again; dropped it once more; clutched it tremblingly once again, and pulled it so feebly that I could hardly hear the stroke myself. Captain and mate sang out instantly, and both together,—

"Starboard lead there! and quick about it!"

This was another shock. I began to climb the wheel like a squirrel; but I would hardly get the boat started to port before I would see new dangers on that side, and away I would spin to the other; only to find perils accumulating to starboard, and be crazy to get to port again. Then came the leadsman's sepulchral cry:—

"D-e-e-p four!"

Deep four in a bottomless crossing! The terror of it took my breath away.

"M-a-r-k three! . . . M-a-r-k three . . . Quarter less three! . . . Half twain!"

This was frightful! I seized the bell-ropes and stopped the engines.

"Quarter twain! Quarter twain! *Mark* twain!"

I was helpless. I did not know what in the world to do. I was quaking from head to foot, and I could have hung my hat on my eyes, they stuck out so far.

"Quarter *less* twain! Nine and a *half!*"

We were *drawing* nine! My hands were in a nerveless flutter. I could not ring a bell intelligibly with them. I flew to the speaking-tube and shouted to the engineer,—

"Oh, Ben, if you love me, *back* her! Quick, Ben! Oh, back the immortal *soul* out of her!"

I heard the door close gently. I looked around, and there stood Mr. Bixby, smiling a bland, sweet smile. Then the audience on the hurricane deck sent up a thundergust of humiliating laughter. I saw it all, now, and I felt meaner than the meanest man in human history. I laid in the lead, set the boat in her marks, came ahead on the engines, and said:—

"It was a fine trick to play on an orphan, *wasn't* it? I suppose I'll never hear the last of how I was ass enough to heave the lead at the head of 66."

"Well, no, you won't, maybe. In fact I hope you won't; for I want you to learn something by that experience. Didn't you *know* there was no bottom in that crossing?"

"Yes, sir, I did."

"Very well, then. You shouldn't have allowed me or anybody else to shake your confidence in that knowledge. Try to remember that. And another thing: when you get into a dangerous place, don't turn coward. That isn't going to help matters any."

It was a good enough lesson, but pretty hardly learned. Yet about the hardest part of it was that for months I so often had to hear a phrase which I had conceived a particular distaste for. It was, "Oh, Ben, if you love me, back her!"

CHAPTER XIV

RANK AND DIGNITY OF PILOTING

In my preceding chapters I have tried, by going into the minutiae of the science of piloting, to carry the reader step by step to a comprehension of what the science consists of; and at the same time I have tried to show him that it is a very curious and wonderful science, too, and very worthy of his attention. If I have seemed to love my subject, it is no surprising thing, for I loved the profession far better than any I have followed since, and I took a measureless pride in it. The reason is plain: a pilot, in those days was the only unfettered and entirely independent human being that lived in the earth. Kings are but the hampered servants of parliament and people; parliaments sit in chains forged by their constituency; the editor of a newspaper cannot be independent, but must work with one hand tied behind him by party and patrons, and be content to utter only half or two thirds of his mind; no clergyman is a free man and may speak the whole truth, regardless of his parish's opinions; writers of all kinds are manacled servants of the public. We write frankly and fearlessly, but then we "modify" before we print. In truth, every man and woman and child has a master, and worries and frets in servitude; but in the day I write of, the Mississippi pilot had *none*. The captain could stand upon the hurricane deck, in the pomp of a very brief authority, and give him five or six orders while the vessel backed into the stream, and then that skipper's reign was over. The moment that the boat was under way in the river, she was under the sole and unquestioned control of the pilot. He could do with her exactly as he pleased, run her when and whither he chose, and tie her up to the bank whenever his judgment said that that course was best. His movements were entirely free; he consulted no one, he received commands from nobody, he promptly resented even the merest suggestions. Indeed, the law of the United States forbade him to listen to commands or suggestions, rightly considering that the pilot necessarily knew better how to handle the boat than anybody could tell him. So here was the novelty of a king without a keeper, an absolute monarch who was absolute in sober truth and not by a fiction of words. I have seen a boy of eighteen taking a great steamer serenely into what seemed almost certain destruction, and the aged captain standing mutely by, filled with apprehension but powerless to interfere. His interference, in that particular instance, might have been an excellent thing, but to permit it would have been to establish a

275

most pernicious precedent. It will easily be guessed, considering the pilot's boundless authority, that he was a great personage in the old steamboating days. He was treated with marked courtesy by the captain and with marked deference by all the officers and servants; and this deferential spirit was quickly communicated to the passengers, too. I think pilots were about the only people I ever knew who failed to show, in some degree, embarrassment in the presence of travelling foreign princes. But then, people in one's own grade of life are not usually embarrassing objects.

By long habit, pilots came to put all their wishes in the form of commands. It "gravels" me, to this day, to put my will in the weak shape of a request, instead of launching it in the crisp language of an order.

In those old days, to load a steamboat at St. Louis, take her to New Orleans and back, and discharge cargo, consumed about twenty-five days, on an average. Seven or eight of these days the boat spent at the wharves of St. Louis and New Orleans, and every soul on board was hard at work, except the two pilots; *they* did nothing but play gentleman up town, and receive the same wages for it as if they had been on duty. The moment the boat touched the wharf at either city, they were ashore; and they were not likely to be seen again till the last bell was ringing and everything in readiness for another voyage.

When a captain got hold of a pilot of particularly high reputation, he took pains to keep him. When wages were four hundred dollars a month on the Upper Mississippi, I have known a captain to keep such a pilot in idleness, under full pay, three months at a time, while the river was frozen up. And one must remember that in those cheap times four hundred dollars was a salary of almost inconceivable splendor. Few men on shore got such pay as that, and when they did they were mightily looked up to. When pilots from either end of the river wandered into our small Missouri village, they were sought by the best and the fairest, and treated with exalted respect. Lying in port under wages was a thing which many pilots greatly enjoyed and appreciated; especially if they belonged in the Missouri River in the heyday of that trade (Kansas times), and got nine hundred dollars a trip, which was equivalent to about eighteen hundred dollars a month. Here is a conversation of that day. A chap out of the Illinois River, with a little stern-wheel tub, accosts a couple of ornate and gilded Missouri River pilots:—

"Gentlemen, I've got a pretty good trip for the up-country, and shall want you about a month. How much will it be?"

"Eighteen hundred dollars apiece."

"Heavens and earth! You take my boat, let me have your wages, and I'll divide!"

I will remark, in passing, that Mississippi steamboatmen were important in landsmen's eyes (and in their own, too, in a degree) according to the dignity of the boat they were on. For instance, it was a proud thing to be of the crew of such stately craft as the "Aleck Scott" or the "Grand Turk." Negro firemen, deck hands, and barbers belonging to those boats were distinguished personages in their grade of life, and they were well aware of that fact, too. A stalwart darkey once gave offence at a negro ball in New Orleans by putting on a good many airs. Finally one of the managers bustled up to him and said,—

"Who *is* you, any way? Who *is* you? dat's what *I* wants to know!"

The offender was not disconcerted in the least, but swelled himself up and threw that into his voice which showed that he knew he was not putting on all those airs on a stinted capital.

"Who *is* I? Who *is* I? I let you know mighty quick who I is! I want you niggers to understan' dat I fires de middle do'* on de 'Aleck Scott!'"

That was sufficient.

The barber of the "Grand Turk" was a spruce young negro, who aired his importance with balmy complacency, and was greatly courted by the circle in which he moved. The young colored population of New Orleans were much given to flirting, at twilight, on the banquettes of the back streets. Somebody saw and heard something like the following, one evening, in one of those localities. A middle-aged negro woman projected her head through a broken pane and shouted (very willing that the neighbors should hear and envy), "You Mary Ann, come in de house dis minute! Stannin' out dah foolin' 'long wid dat low trash, an' heah's de barber off'n de 'Gran' Turk' wants to converse wid you!"

My reference, a moment ago, to the face that a pilot's peculiar official position placed him out of the reach of criticism or command, brings Stephen W—— naturally to my mind. He was a gifted pilot, a good fellow, a tireless talker, and had both wit and humor in him. He had a most irreverent independence, too, and was deliciously easy-going and comfortable in the presence of age, official dignity, and even the most august wealth. He always had work, he never saved a penny, he was a most persuasive borrower, he was in debt to every pilot on the river, and

* Door.

277

to the majority of the captains. He could throw a sort of splendor around a bit of harum-scarum, devil-may-care piloting, that made it almost fascinating—but not to everybody. He made a trip with good old Captain Y——once, and was "relieved" from duty when the boat got to New Orleans. Somebody expressed surprise at the discharge. Captain Y——shuddered at the mere mention of Stephen. Then his poor, thin old voice piped out something like this:—

"Why, bless me! I wouldn't have such a wild creature on my boat for the world—not for the whole world! He swears, he sings, he whistles, he yells—I never saw such an Injun to yell. All times of the night—it never made any difference to him. He would just yell that way, not for anything in particular, but merely on account of a kind of devilish comfort he got out of it. I never could get into a sound sleep but he would fetch me out of bed, all in a cold sweat, with one of those dreadful war-whoops. A queer being,—very queer being; no respect for anything or anybody. Sometimes he called me 'Johnny.' And he kept a fiddle, and a cat. He played execrably. This seemed to distress the cat, and so the cat would howl. Nobody could sleep where that man—and his family—was. And reckless? There never was anything like it. Now you may believe it or not, but as sure as I am sitting here, he brought my boat a-tilting down through those awful snags at Chicot under a rattling head of steam, and the wind a-blowing like the very nation, at that! My officers will tell you so. They saw it. And, sir, while he was a-tearing right down through those snags, and I a-shaking in my shoes and praying, I wish I may never speak again if he didn't pucker up his mouth and go to *whistling!* Yes, sir; whistling 'Buffalo gals, can't you come out to-night, can't you come out to-night, can't you come out to-night;' and doing it as calmly as if we were attending a funeral and weren't related to the corpse. And when I remonstrated with him about it, he smiled down on me as if I was his child, and told me to run in the house and try to be good, and not be meddling with my superiors!"*

Once a pretty mean captain caught Stephen in New Orleans out of work and as usual out of money. He laid steady siege to Stephen, who was in a very "close place," and finally persuaded him to hire with him at one hundred and twenty-five dollars per month, just half wages, the captain agreeing not to divulge the secret and so bring down the contempt of all the guild upon the

---

* Considering a captain's ostentatious but hollow chieftainship, and a pilot's real authority, there was something impudently apt and happy about that way of phrasing it.

poor fellow. But the boat was not more than a day out of New Orleans before Stephen discovered that the captain was boasting of his exploit, and that all the officers had been told. Stephen winced, but said nothing. About the middle of the afternoon the captain stepped out on the hurricane deck, cast his eye around, and looked a good deal surprised. He glanced inquiringly aloft at Stephen, but Stephen was whistling placidly, and attending to business. The captain stood around a while in evident discomfort, and once or twice seemed about to make a suggestion; but the etiquette of the river taught him to avoid that sort of rashness, and so he managed to hold his peace. He chafed and puzzled a few minutes longer, then retired to his apartments. But soon he was out again, and apparently more perplexed than ever. Presently he ventured to remark, with deference,—

"Pretty good stage of the river now, ain't it, sir?"

"Well, I should say so! Bank-full *is* a pretty liberal stage."

"Seems to be a good deal of current here."

"Good deal don't describe it! It's worse than a millrace."

"Isn't it easier in toward shore than it is out here in the middle?"

"Yes, I reckon it is; but a body can't be too careful with a steamboat. It's pretty safe out here; can't strike any bottom here, you can depend on that."

The captain departed, looking rueful enough. At this rate, he would probably die of old age before his boat got to St. Louis. Next day he appeared on deck and again found Stephen faithfully standing up the middle of the river, fighting the whole vast force of the Mississippi, and whistling the same placid tune. This thing was becoming serious. In by the shore was a slower boat clipping along in the easy water and gaining steadily; she began to make for an island chute; Stephen stuck to middle of the river. Speech was *wrung* from the captain. He said,—

"Mr. W——, don't that chute cut off a good deal of distance?"

"I think it does, but I don't know."

"Don't know! Well, isn't there water enough in it now to go through?"

"I expect there is, but I am not certain."

"Upon my word this is odd! Why, those pilots on that boat yonder are going to try it. Do you mean to say that you don't know as much as they do?"

"*They!* Why, *they* are two-hundred-and-fifty-dollar pilots! But don't you be uneasy; I know as much as any man can afford to know for a hundred and twenty-five!"

The captain surrendered.

Five minutes later Stephen was bowling through the chute and showing the rival boat a two-hundred-and-fifty-dollar pair of heels.

CHAPTER XV

THE PILOTS' MONOPOLY

One day, on board the "Aleck Scott," my chief, Mr. Bixby, was crawling carefully through a close place at Cat Island, both leads going, and everybody holding his breath. The captain, a nervous, apprehensive man, kept still as long as he could, but finally broke down and shouted from the hurricane deck,—

"For gracious' sake, give her steam, Mr. Bixby! give her steam! She'll never raise the reef on this headway!"

For all the effect that was produced upon Mr. Bixby, one would have supposed that no remark had been made. But five minutes later, when the danger was past and the leads laid in, he burst instantly into a consuming fury, and gave the captain the most admirable cursing I ever listened to. No bloodshed ensued; but that was because the captain's cause was weak; for ordinarily he was not a man to take correction quietly.

Having now set forth in detail the nature of the science of piloting, and likewise described the rank which the pilot held among the fraternity of steamboatmen, this seems a fitting place to say a few words about an organization which the pilots once formed for the protection of their guild. It was curious and noteworthy in this, that it was perhaps the compactest, the completest, and the strongest commercial organization ever formed among men.

For a long time wages had been two hundred and fifty dollars a month; but curiously enough, as steamboats multiplied and business increased, the wages began to fall little by little. It was easy to discover the reason of this. Too many pilots were being "made." It was nice to have a "cub," a steersman, to do all the hard work for a couple of years, gratis, while his master sat on a high bench and smoked; all pilots and captains had sons or nephews who wanted to be pilots. By and by it came to pass that nearly every pilot on the river had a steersman. When a steersman had made an amount of progress that was satisfactory to any two pilots in the trade, they could get a pilot's license for him by signing an application directed to the United States Inspector. Nothing further was needed; usually no questions were asked, no proofs of capacity required.

Very well, this growing swarm of new pilots presently began to undermine the wages, in order to get berths. Too late— apparently—the knights of the tiller perceived their mistake. Plainly, something had to be done, and quickly; but what was to be the needful thing? A close organization. Nothing else would answer. To compass this seemed an impossibility; so it was talked, and talked, and then dropped. It was too likely to ruin whoever ventured to move in the matter. But at last about a dozen of the boldest—and some of them the best—pilots on the river launched themselves into the enterprise and took all the chances. They got a special charter from the legislature, with large powers, under the name of the Pilots' Benevolent Association; elected their officers, completed their organization, contributed capital, put "association" wages up to two hundred and fifty dollars at once—and then retired to their homes, for they were promptly discharged from employment. But there were two or three unnoticed trifles in their by-laws which had the seeds of propagation in them. For instance, all idle members of the association, in good standing, were entitled to a pension of twenty-five dollars per month. This began to bring in one straggler after another from the ranks of the new-fledged pilots, in the dull (summer) season. Better have twenty-five dollars than starve; the initiation fee was only twelve dollars, and no dues required from the unemployed.

Also, the widows of deceased members in good standing could draw twenty-five dollars per month, and a certain sum for each of their children. Also, the said deceased would be buried at the association's expense. These things resurrected all the superannuated and forgotten pilots in the Mississippi Valley. They came from farms, they came from interior villages, they came from everywhere. They came on crutches, on drays, in ambulances,— any way, so they got there. They paid in their twelve dollars, and straightway began to draw out twenty-five dollars a month and calculate their burial bills.

By and by, all the useless, helpless pilots, and a dozen first-class ones, were in the association, and nine tenths of the best pilots out of it and laughing at it. It was the laughing-stock of the whole river. Everybody joked about the by-law requiring members to pay ten per cent of their wages, every month, into the treasury for the support of the association, whereas all the members were outcast and tabooed, and no one would employ them. Everybody was derisively grateful to the association for taking all the worthless pilots out of the way and leaving the whole field to the excellent and the deserving; and everybody was not only jocularly grateful for that, but for a result which naturally followed, namely, the gradual advance of wages as the busy season approached. Wages had gone up from the low figure of one hundred dollars a month to one hundred and twenty-five, and in some cases to one hundred and fifty; and it was great fun to enlarge upon the fact that this charming thing had been accomplished by a body of men not one of whom received a particle of benefit from it. Some of the jokers used to call at the association rooms and have a good time chaffing the members and offering them the charity of taking them as steersmen for a trip, so that they could see what the forgotten river looked like. However, the association was content; or at least it gave no sign to the contrary. Now and then it captured a pilot who was "out of luck," and added him to its list; and these later additions were very valuable, for they were good pilots; the incompetent ones had all been absorbed before. As business freshened, wages climbed gradually up to two hundred and fifty dollars—the association figure—and became firmly fixed there; and still without benefiting a member of that body, for no member was hired. The hilarity at the association's expense burst all bounds, now. There was no end to the fun which that poor martyr had to put up with.

However, it is a long lane that has no turning. Winter approached, business doubled and trebled, and an avalanche of Missouri, Illinois, and Upper Mississippi River boats came pouring down to take a chance in the New Orleans trade. All of a sudden, pilots were in great demand, and were correspondingly scarce. The time for revenge was come. It was a bitter pill to have to accept association pilots at last, yet captains and owners agreed that there was no other way. But none of these outcasts offered! So there was a still bitterer pill to be swallowed: they must be sought out and asked for their services. Captain—— was the first man who found it necessary to take the dose, and he had been the loudest derider of the organization. He hunted up one of the best of the association pilots and said,—

"Well, you boys have rather got the best of us for a little while, so I'll give in with as good a grace as I can. I've come to hire you; get your trunk aboard right away. I want to leave at twelve o'clock."

"I don't know about that. Who is your other pilot?"

"I've got I. S——. Why?"

"I can't go with him. He don't belong to the association."

"What!"

"It's so."

"Do you mean to tell me that you won't turn a wheel with one of the very best and oldest pilots on the river because he don't belong to your association?"

"Yes, I do."

"Well, if this isn't putting on airs! I supposed I was doing you a benevolence; but I begin to think that I am the party that wants a favor done. Are you acting under a law of the concern?"

"Yes."

"Show it to me."

So they stepped into the association rooms, and the secretary soon satisfied the captain, who said,—

"Well, what am I to do? I have hired Mr. S—— for the entire season."

"I will provide for you," said the secretary. "I will detail a pilot to go with you, and he shall be on board at twelve o'clock."

"But if I discharge S——, he will come on me for the whole season's wages."

"Of course that is a matter between you and Mr. S——, captain. We cannot meddle in your private affairs."

The captain stormed, but to no purpose. In the end he had to discharge S——, pay him about a thousand dollars, and take an association pilot in his place. The laugh was beginning to turn the other way, now. Every day, thenceforward, a new victim fell; every day some outraged captain discharged a non-association pet, with tears and profanity, and installed a hated association man in his berth. In a very little while, idle non-associationists began to be pretty plenty, brisk as business was, and much as their services were desired. The laugh was shifting to the other side of their mouths most palpably. These victims, together with the captains and owners, presently ceased to laugh altogether, and began to rage about the revenge they would take when the passing business "spurt" was over.

Soon all the laughers that were left were the owner and crews of boats that had two non-association pilots. But their triumph was not very long-lived. For this reason: It was a rigid rule of the association that its members should never, under any circumstances whatever, give information about the channel to any "outsider." By this time about half the boats had none but association pilots, and the other half had none but outsiders. At the first glance one would suppose that when it came to forbidding information about the river these two parties could play equally at that game; but this was not so. At every good-sized town from one end of the river to the other, there was a "wharf-boat" to land at, instead of a wharf or a pier. Freight was stored in it for transportation; waiting passengers slept in its cabins. Upon each of these wharf-boats the association's officers placed a strong box, fastened with a peculiar lock which was used in no other service but one—the United States mail service. It was the letter-bag lock, a sacred governmental thing. By dint of much beseeching the government had been persuaded to allow the association to use this lock. Every association man carried a key which would open these boxes. That key, or rather a peculiar way of holding it in the hand when its owner was asked for river information by a stranger,—for the success of the St. Louis and New Orleans association had now bred tolerably thriving branches in a dozen neighboring steamboat trades,—was the association man's sign and diploma of membership; and if the stranger did not respond by producing a similar key and holding it in a certain manner duly prescribed, his question was politely ignored. From the association's secretary each member received a package of more or less gorgeous blanks, printed like a bill-head, on handsome paper, properly ruled in columns; a bill-head worded something like this:—

STEAMER GREAT REPUBLIC.
JOHN SMITH, MASTER.
Pilots, John Jones and Thomas Brown.

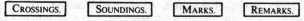

These blanks were filled up, day by day, as the voyage progressed, and deposited in the several wharf-boat boxes. For instance, as soon as the first crossing, out from St. Louis, was completed, the times would be entered upon the blank, under the appropriate headings, thus:—

"St. Louis. Nine and a half (feet). Stern on courthouse, head on dead cottonwood above wood-yard, until you raise the first reef, then pull up square." Then under head of Remarks: "Go just outside the wrecks; this is important. New snag just where you straighten down; go above it."

The pilot who deposited that blank in the Cairo box (after adding to it the details of every crossing all the way down from St. Louis) took out and read half a dozen fresh reports (from upward-bound steamers) concerning the river between Cairo and Memphis, posted himself thoroughly, returned them to the box, and went back aboard his boat again so armed against accident that he could not possibly get his boat into trouble without bringing the most ingenious carelessness to his aid.

Imagine the benefits of so admirable a system in a piece of river twelve or thirteen hundred miles long, whose channel was shifting every day! The pilot who had formerly been obliged to put up with seeing a shoal place once or possibly twice a month, had a hundred sharp eyes to watch it for him, now, and bushels of intelligent brains to tell him how to run it. His information about it was seldom twenty-four hours old. If the reports in the last box chanced to leave any misgivings on his mind concerning a treacherous crossing, he had his remedy; he blew his steam-whistle in a peculiar way as soon as he saw a boat approaching; the signal was answered in a peculiar way if that boat's pilots were association men; and then the two steamers ranged alongside and all uncertainties were swept away by fresh information furnished to the inquirer by word of mouth and in minute detail.

The first thing a pilot did when he reached New Orleans or St. Louis was to take his final and elaborate report to the association parlors and hang it up there,—*after* which he was free to visit his family. In these parlors a crowd was always gathered together, discussing changes in the channel, and the moment there was a fresh arrival, everybody stopped talking till this witness had told the newest news and settled the latest uncertainty. Other craftsmen can "sink the shop," sometimes, and interest themselves in other matters. Not so with a pilot; he must devote himself wholly to his profession and talk of nothing else; for it would be small gain to be perfect one day and imperfect the next. He has no time or words to waste if he would keep "posted."

But the outsiders had a hard time of it. No particular place to meet and exchange information, no wharf-boat reports, none but chance and unsatisfactory ways of getting news. The consequence was that a man sometimes had to run five hundred miles of river on information that was a week or ten days old. At a fair stage of the river that might have answered; but when the dead low water came it was destructive.

Now came another perfectly logical result. The outsiders began to ground steamboats, sink them, and get into all sorts of trouble, whereas accidents seemed to keep entirely away from the association men. Wherefore even the owners and captains of boats furnished exclusively with outsiders, and previously considered to be wholly independent of the association and free to comfort themselves with brag and laughter, began to feel pretty uncomfortable. Still, they made a show of keeping up the brag, until one black day when every captain of the lot was formally ordered to immediately discharge his outsiders and take association pilots in their stead. And who was it that had the dashing presumption to do that? Alas, it came from a power behind the throne that was greater than the throne itself. It was the underwriters!

It was no time to "swap knives." Every outsider had to take his trunk ashore at once. Of course it was supposed that there was collusion between the association and the underwriters, but this was not so. The latter had come to comprehend the excellence of the "report" system of the association and the safety it secured, and so they had made their decision among themselves and upon plain business principles.

There was weeping and wailing and gnashing of teeth in the camp of the outsiders now. But no matter, there was but one course for them to pursue, and they pursued it. They came forward in couples and groups, and proffered their twelve dollars and asked for membership. They were surprised to learn that several new by-laws had been long ago added. For instance, the initiation fee had been raised to fifty dollars; that sum must be tendered, and also ten per cent of the wages which the applicant had received each and every month since the founding of the association. In many cases this amounted to three or four hundred dollars. Still, the association would not entertain the application until the money was present. Even then a single adverse vote killed the application. Every member had to vote yes or no in person and before witnesses; so it took weeks to decide a candidacy, because many pilots were so long absent on voyages. However, the repentant sinners scraped their savings together, and one by one, by our tedious voting process, they were added to the fold. A time came, at last, when only about ten remained outside. They said they would starve before they would apply. They remained idle a long while, because of course nobody could venture to employ them.

By and by the association published the fact that upon a certain date the wages would be raised to five hundred dollars per month. All the branch associations had grown strong, now, and the Red River one had advanced wages to seven hundred dollars a month. Reluctantly the ten outsiders yielded, in view of these things, and made application. There was *another* new by-law, by this time, which required them to pay dues not only on all the wages they had received since the association was born, but also on what they would have received if they had continued at work up to the time of their application, instead of going off to pout in idleness. It turned out to be a difficult matter to elect them, but it was accomplished at last. The most virulent sinner of this batch had stayed out and allowed "dues" to accumulate against him so long that he had to send in six hundred and twenty-five dollars with his application.

The association had a good bank account now, and was very strong. There was no longer an outsider. A by-law was added forbidding the reception of any more cubs or apprentices for five years; after which time a limited number would be taken, not by individuals, but by the association, upon these terms: the applicant must not be less than eighteen years old, and of respectable family and good character; he must pass an examination as to education, pay a thousand dollars in advance for the privilege of becoming an apprentice, and must remain under the commands of the association until a great part of the membership (more than half, I think) should be willing to sign his application for a pilot's license.

All previously-articled apprentices were now taken away from their masters and adopted by the association. The president and secretary detailed them for service on one boat or another, as they chose, and changed them from boat to boat according to certain rules. If a pilot could show that he was in infirm health and needed assistance, one of the cubs would be ordered to go with him.

The widow and orphan list grew, but so did the association's financial resources. The association attended its own funerals in state, and paid for them. When occasion demanded, it sent members down the river upon searches for the bodies of brethren lost by steamboat accidents; a search of this kind sometimes cost a thousand dollars.

The association procured a charter and went into the insurance business, also. It not only insured the lives of its members, but took risks on steamboats.

The organization seemed indestructible. It was the tightest monopoly in the world. By the United States law, no man could become a pilot unless two duly licensed pilots signed his application; and now there was nobody outside of the association competent to sign. Consequently the making of pilots was at an end. Every year some would die and others become incapacitated by age and infirmity; there would be no new ones to take their places. In time, the association could put wages up to any figure it chose; and as long as it should be wise enough not to carry the thing too far and provoke the national government into amending the licensing system, steamboat owners would have to submit, since there would be no help for it.

The owners and captains were the only obstruction that lay between the association and absolute power; and at last this one was removed. Incredible as it may seem, the owners and captains deliberately did it themselves. When the pilots' association announced, months beforehand, that on the first day of September, 1861, wages would be advanced to five hundred dollars per month, the owners and captains instantly put freights up a few cents, and explained to the farmers along the river the necessity of it, by calling their attention to the burdensome rate of wages about to be established. It was a rather slender argument, but the farmers did not seem to detect it. It looked reasonable to them that to add five cents freight on a bushel of corn was justifiable under the circumstances, overlooking the fact that this advance on a cargo of forty thousand sacks was a good deal more than necessary to cover the new wages.

So, straightway the captains and owners got up an association of their own, and proposed to put captains' wages up to five hundred dollars, too, and move for another advance in freights. It was a novel idea, but of course an effect which had been produced once could be produced again. The new association decreed (for this was before all the outsiders had been taken into the pilots' association) that if any captain employed a non-association pilot, he should be forced to discharge him, and also pay a fine of five hundred dollars. Several of these heavy fines were paid before the captains' organization grew strong enough to exercise full authority over its membership; but that all ceased, presently. The captains tried to get the pilots to decree that no member of their corporation should serve under a non-association captain; but this proposition was declined. The pilots saw that they would be backed up by the captains and the underwriters anyhow, and so they wisely refrained from entering into entangling alliances.

As I have remarked, the pilots' association was now the compactest monopoly in the world, perhaps, and seemed simply indestructible. And yet the days of its glory were numbered. First, the new railroad stretching up through Mississippi, Tennessee, and Kentucky, to Northern railway centres, began to divert the passenger travel from the steamers; next the war came and almost entirely annihilated the steamboating industry during several years, leaving most of the pilots idle, and the cost of living advancing all the time; then the treasurer of the St. Louis association put his hand into the till and walked off with every dollar of the ample fund; and finally, the railroads intruding everywhere, there was little for steamers to do, when the war was over, but carry freights; so straightway some genius from the Atlantic coast introduced the plan of towing a dozen steamer cargoes down to New Orleans at the tail of a vulgar little tug-boat; and behold, in the twinkling of an eye, as it were, the association and the noble science of piloting were things of the dead and pathetic past!

CHAPTER XVI

RACING DAYS

It was always the custom for the boats to leave New Orleans between four and five o'clock in the afternoon. From three o'clock onward they would be burning rosin and pitch pine (the sign of preparation), and so one had the picturesque spectacle of a rank, some two or three miles long, of tall, ascending columns of coal-black smoke; a colonnade which supported a sable roof of the same smoke blended together and spreading abroad over the city. Every outward-bound boat had its flag flying at the jack-staff, and sometimes a duplicate on the verge staff astern. Two or three miles of mates were commanding and swearing with more than usual emphasis; countless processions of freight barrels and boxes were spinning athwart the levee and flying aboard the stage-planks; belated passengers were dodging and skipping among these frantic things, hoping to reach the fore-castle companion way alive, but having their doubts about it; women with reticules and bandboxes were trying to keep up with husbands freighted with carpet-sacks and crying babies, and making a failure of it by losing their heads in the whirl and roar and general distraction; drays and baggage-vans were clattering hither and thither in a wild hurry, every now and then getting blocked and jammed together, and then during ten seconds one could not see them for the profanity, except vaguely and dimly; every windlass connected with every fore-hatch, from one end of that long array of steamboats to the other, was keeping up a deafening whiz and whir, lowering freight into the hold, and the half-naked crews of perspiring negroes that worked them were roaring such songs as "De Las' Sack! De Las' Sack!"—inspired to unimaginable exaltation by the chaos of turmoil and racket that was driving everybody else mad. By this time the hurricane and boiler decks of the steamers would be packed and black with passengers. The "last bells" would begin to clang, all down the line, and then the powwow seemed to double; in a moment or two the final warning came,—a simultaneous din of Chinese gongs, with the cry, "All dat ain't goin', please to git asho'!"—and behold, the powwow quadrupled! People came swarming ashore, overturning excited stragglers that were trying to swarm aboard. One more moment later a long array of stage-planks was being hauled in, each with its customary latest passenger clinging to the end of it with teeth, nails, and everything else, and the customary latest procrastinator making a wild spring shoreward over his head.

Now a number of the boats slide backward into the stream, leaving wide gaps in the serried rank of steamers. Citizens crowd the decks of boats that are not to go, in order to see the sight. Steamer after steamer straightens herself up, gathers all her strength, and presently comes swinging by, under a tremendous head of steam, with flag flying, black smoke rolling, and her entire crew of firemen and deck-hands (usually swarthy negroes) massed together on the forecastle, the best "voice" in the lot towering from the mist (being mounted on the capstan), waving his hat or a flag, and all roaring a mighty chorus, while the parting cannons boom and the multitudinous spectators swing their hats and huzza! Steamer after steamer falls into line, and the stately procession goes winging its flight up the river.

In the old times, whenever two fast boats started out on a race, with a big crowd of people looking on, it was inspiring to hear the crews sing, especially if the time were night-fall, and the forecastle lit up with the red glare of the torch-baskets. Racing was royal fun. The public always had an idea that racing was dangerous; whereas the opposite was the case—that is, after the laws were passed which restricted each boat to just so many pounds of steam to the square inch. No engineer was ever sleepy or careless when his heart was in a race. He was constantly on the alert, trying gauge-cocks and watching things. The dangerous place was on slow, plodding boats, where the engineers drowsed around and allowed chips to get into the "doctor" and shut off the water supply from the boilers.

In the "flush times" of steam-boating, a race between two notoriously fleet steamers was an event of vast importance. The date was set for it several weeks in advance, and from that time foreward, the whole Mississippi Valley was in a state of consuming excitement. Politics and the weather were dropped, and people talked only of the coming race. As the time approached, the two steamers "stripped" and got ready. Every incumbrance that added weight, or exposed a resisting surface to wind or water, was removed, if the boat could possibly do without it. The "spars," and sometimes even their supporting derricks, were sent ashore, and no means left to set the boat afloat in case she got aground. When the "Eclipse" and the "A.L. Shotwell" ran their great race many years ago, it was said that pains were taken to scrape the gilding off the fanciful device which hung between the "Eclipse's" chimneys, and that for that one trip the captain left off his kid gloves and had his head shaved. But I always doubted these things.

If the boat was known to make her best speed when drawing five and a half feet forward and five feet aft, she was carefully loaded to that exact figure—she wouldn't enter a dose of homoeopathic pills on her manifest after that. Hardly any passengers were taken, because they not only add weight but they never will "trim boat." They always run to the side when there is anything to see, whereas a conscientious and experienced steamboatman would stick to the centre of the boat and part his hair in the middle with a spirit level.

No way-freights and no way-passengers were allowed, for the racers would stop only at the largest towns, and then it would be only "touch and go." Coal flats and wood flats were contracted for beforehand, and these were kept ready to hitch on to the flying streamers at a moment's warning. Double crews were carried, so that all work could be quickly done.

The chosen date being come, and all things in readiness, the two great steamers back into the stream, and lie there jockeying a moment, and apparently watching each other's slightest movement, like sentient creatures; flags drooping, the pent steam shrieking through safety-valves, the black smoke rolling and tumbling from the chimneys and darkening all the air. People, people everywhere; the shores, the house-tops, the steamboats, the ships, are packed with them, and you know that the borders of the broad Mississippi are going to be fringed with humanity thence northward twelve hundred miles, to welcome these racers.

Presently tall columns of steam burst from the 'scapepipes of both steamers, two guns boom a good-by, two red-shirted heroes mounted on capstans wave their small flags above the massed crews on the forecastles, two plaintive solos linger on the air a few waiting seconds, two mighty choruses burst forth—and here they come! Brass bands bray Hail Columbia, huzza after huzza thunders from the shores, and the stately creatures go whistling by like the wind.

Those boats will never halt a moment between New Orleans and St. Louis, except for a second or two at large towns, or to hitch thirty-cord wood-boats alongside. You should be on board when they take a couple of those wood-boats in tow and turn a swarm of men into each; by the time you have wiped your glasses and put them on, you will be wondering what has become of that wood.

Two nicely matched steamers will stay in sight of each other

day after day. They might even stay side by side, but for the fact
that pilots are not all alike, and the smartest pilots will win the
race. If one of the boats has a "lightning" pilot, whose "partner" is a trifle his inferior, you can tell which one is on watch by
noting whether that boat has gained ground or lost some during
each four-hour stretch. The shrewdest pilot can delay a boat if
he has not a fine genius for steering. Steering is a very high art.
One must not keep a rudder dragging across a boat's stern if he
wants to get up the river fast.

There is a great difference in boats, of course. For a long time
I was on a boat that was so slow we used to forget what year it
was we left port in. But of course this was at rare intervals.
Ferry-boats used to lose valuable trips because their passengers
grew old and died, waiting for us to get by. This was at still rarer
intervals. I had the documents for these occurrences, but
through carelessness they have been mislaid. This boat, the
"John J. Roe," was so slow that when she finally sunk in
Madrid Bend, it was five years before the owners heard of it.
That was always a confusing fact to me, but it is according to the
record, any way. She was dismally slow; still, we often had
pretty exciting times racing with islands, and rafts, and such
things. One trip, however, we did rather well. We went to
St. Louis in sixteen days. But even at this rattling gait I think we
changed watches three times in Fort Adams reach, which is five
miles long. A "reach" is a piece of straight river, and of course
the current drives through such a place in a pretty lively way.
That trip we went to Grand Gulf, from New Orleans, in four
days (three hundred and forty miles); the "Eclipse" and
"Shotwell" did it in one. We were nine days out, in the chute of
63 (seven hundred miles); the "Eclipse" and "Shotwell" went
there in two days. Something over a generation ago, a boat
called the "J. M. White" went from New Orleans to Cairo in
three days, six hours, and forty-four minutes. In 1853 the
"Eclipse" made the same trip in three days, three hours, and
twenty minutes.* In 1870 the "R. E. Lee" did it in three days
and *one* hour. This last is called the fastest trip on record. I will
try to show that it was not. For this reason: the distance between
New Orleans and Cairo, when the "J. M. White" ran it, was
about eleven hundred and six miles; consequently her average
speed was a trifle over fourteen miles per hour. In the
"Eclipse's" day the distance between the two ports had become
reduced to one thousand and eighty miles; consequently her
average speed was a shade under fourteen and three eighths

---

* Time disputed. Some authorities add 1 hour and 16 minutes to this.

miles per hour. In the "R. E. Lee's" time the distance had diminished to about one thousand and thirty miles; consequently her average was about fourteen and one eighth miles per hour. Therefore the "Eclipse's" was consequently the fastest time that has ever been made.

THE RECORD OF SOME FAMOUS TRIPS.

[From Commodore Rollingpin's Almanac.]

FAST TIME ON THE WESTERN WATERS.

FROM NEW ORLEANS TO NATCHEZ — 268 MILES.

				D.	H.	M.						H.	M.
1814.	Orleans made the run in			6	6	40	1844.	Sultana . . made the run in			19	45
1814.	Comet	,,	,,	5	10		1851.	Magnolia	,,	,,		19	50
1815.	Enterprise	,,	,,	4	11	20	1853.	A. L. Shotwell	,,	,,		19	49
1817.	Washington	,,	,,	4			1853.	Southern Belle	,,	,,		20	3
1817.	Shelby	,,	,,	3	20		1853.	Princess (No. 4)	,,	,,		20	26
1819.	Paragon	,,	,,	3	8		1853.	Eclipse	,,	,,		19	47
1828.	Tecumseh	,,	,,	3	1	20	1855.	Princess (New)	,,	,,		18	53
1834.	Tuscarora	,,	,,	1	21		1855.	Natchez (New)	,,	,,		17	30
1838.	Natchez	,,	,,	1	17		1856.	Princess (New)	,,	,,		17	30
1840.	Ed. Shippen	,,	,,	1	8		1870.	Natchez		,,		17	17
1842.	Belle of the West	,,	,,	1	18		1870.	R. E. Lee		,,		17	11

FROM NEW ORLEANS TO CAIRO — 1,024 MILES.

				D.	H.	M						D.	H.	M.
1844.	J. M. White made the run in			3	6	44	1869.	Dexter . . . made the run in				3	6	20
1852.	Reindeer	,,	,,	3	12	45	1870.	Natchez	,,	,,		3	4	34
1853.	Eclipse	,,	,,	3	4	4	1870.	R. E. Lee	,,	,,		3	1	
1853.	A. L. Shotwell	,,	,,	3	3	40								

FROM NEW ORLEANS TO LOUISVILLE — 1,440 MILES.

				D.	H.	M.						D.	H.	M.
1815.	Enterprise made the run in			25	2	40	1840.	Ed. Shippen made the run in				5	14	
1817.	Washington	,,	,,	25			1842.	Belle of the West	,,	,,		6	14	
1817.	Shelby	,,	,,	20	4	20	1843.	Duke of Orleans	,,	,,		5	23	
1819.	Paragon	,,	,,	18	10		1844.	Sultana	,,	,,		5	12	
1828.	Tecumseh	,,	,,	8	4		1849.	Bostona	,,	,,		5	8	
1834.	Tuscarora	,,	,,	7	16		1851.	Belle Key	,,	,,		4	23	
1837.	Gen. Brown	,,	,,	6	22		1852.	Reindeer	,,	,,		4	20	45
1837.	Randolph	,,	,,	6	22		1852.	Eclipse	,,	,,		4	19	
1837.	Empress	,,	,,	6	17		1853.	A. L. Shotwell	,,	,,		4	10	20
1837.	Sultana	,,	,,	6	15		1853.	Eclipse	,,	,,		4	9	30

FROM NEW ORLEANS TO DONALDSVILLE — 78 MILES.

				H.	M.						H.	M.
1852.	A. L. Shotwell made the run in			5	42	1860.	Atlantic . . . made the run in				5	11
1852.	Eclipse	,,	,,	5	42	1860.	Gen. Quitman	,,	,,		5	6
1854.	Sultana	,,	,,	5	12	1865.	Ruth	,,	,,		4	43
1856.	Princess	,,	,,	4	51	1870.	R. E. Lee	,,	,,		4	59

FROM NEW ORLEANS TO ST. LOUIS — 1,218 MILES.

				D.	H.	M.						D.	H.	M.
1844.	J. M. White made the run in			3	23	9	1870.	Natchez . . made the run in				3	21	58
1849.	Missouri	,,	,,	4	19		1870.	R. E. Lee	,,	,,		3	18	14
1869.	Dexter	,,	,,	4	9									

FROM LOUISVILLE TO CINCINNATI — 141 MILES.

				D.	H.	M.						D.	H.	M.
1819.	Gen. Pike made the run in			1	16		1843.	Congress . . made the run in				12	20	
1819.	Paragon	,,	,,	1	14	20	1846.	Ben Franklin (No. 6)		,,		11	45	
1822.	Wheeling Packet	,,	,,	1	10		1852.	Alleghaney	,,	,,		10	38	
1837.	Moselle	,,	,,		12		1852.	Pittsburgh	,,	,,		10	23	
1843.	Duke of Orleans	,,	,,		12		1853.	Telegraph No. 3	,,	,,		9	52	

FROM LOUISVILLE TO ST. LOUIS   750 MILES.

			D.	H.	M.					D.	H.	M.
1843.	Congress	.. made the run in	2	1		1854.	Northerner	made the run in	1	22	30
1854.	Pike	,, ,,	1	23		1855.	Southerner	,, ,,	1	19	

FROM CINCINNATI TO PITTSBURG — 490 MILES.

			D.	H.				D.	H.
1850.	Telegraph No. 2 made the run in	1	17	1852.	Pittsburgh . . . made the run in	1	15
1851.	Buckeye State	,, ,,	1	16				

FROM ST. LOUIS TO ALTON — 30 MILES.

			H.	M.				H.	M.
1853.	Altona . . . . . made the run in	1	35	1876.	War Eagle . . . made the run in	1	37
1876.	Golden Eagle	,, ,,	1	37			

MISCELLANEOUS RUNS.

In June, 1859, the St. Louis and Keokuk Packet, City of Louisiana, made the run from St. Louis to Keokuk (214 miles) in 16 hours and 20 minutes, the best time on record.

In 1868 the steamer Hawkeye State, of the Northern Line Packet Company, made the run from St. Louis to St. Paul (800 miles) in 2 days and 20 hours. Never was beaten.

In 1853 the steamer Polar Star made the run from St. Louis to St. Joseph, on the Missouri River in 64 hours. In July, 1856, the steamer Jas. H. Lucas, Andy Wineland, Master, made the same run in 60 hours and 57 minutes. The distance between the ports is 600 miles, and when the difficulties of navigating the turbulent Missouri are taken into consideration, the performance of the Lucas deserves especial mention.

THE RUN OF THE ROBERT E. LEE.

The time made by the R. E. Lee from New Orleans to St. Louis in 1870, in her famous race with the Natchez, is the best on record, and, inasmuch as the race created a national interest, we give below her time table from port to port.

Left New Orleans, Thursday, June 30th, 1870, at 4 o'clock and 55 minutes, p. m. ; reached

	D.	H.	M.		D.	H.	M.
Carrollton			27½	Vicksburg	1		38
Harry Hills	1	00½		Milliken's Bend	1	2	37
Red Church	1	39		Bailey's	1	3	48
Bonnet Carre	2	38		Lake Providence	1	5	47
College Point	3	50½		Greenville	1	10	55
Donaldsonville	4	59		Napoleon	1	16	22
Plaquemine	7	05½		White River	1	16	56
Baton Rouge	8	25		Australia	1	19	
Bayou Sara	10	26		Helena	1	23	25
Red River	12	56		Half Mile Below St. Francis . .	2		
Stamps	13	56		Memphis	2	6	9
Bryaro	15	51½		Foot of Island 37	2	9	
Hinderson's	16	29		Foot of Island 26	2	13	30
Natchez	17	11		Tow-head, Island 14 . . .	2	17	23
Cole's Creek	19	21		New Madrid	2	19	50
Waterproof	18	53		Dry Bar No. 10	2	20	37
Rodney	20	45		Foot of Island 8	2	21	25
St. Joseph	21	02		Upper Tow-head — Lucas Bend .	3		
Grand Gulf	22	06		Cairo	3	1	
Hard Times	22	18		St. Louis	3	18	14
Half Mile Below Warrenton . .	1						

The Lee landed at St. Louis at 11.25 A. M., on July 4th, 1870 — six hours and thirty-six minutes ahead of the Natchez. The officers of the Natchez claimed seven hours and one minute stoppage on account of fog and repairing machinery. The R. E. Lee was commanded by Captain John W. Cannon, and the Natchez was in charge of that veteran Southern boatman, Captain Thomas P. Leathers.

CHAPTER XVII

CUT-OFFS AND STEPHEN

These dry details are of importance in one particular. They give me an opportunity of introducing one of the Mississippi's oddest peculiarities,—that of shortening its length from time to time. If you will throw a long, pliant apple-paring over your shoulder, it till pretty fairly shape itself into an average section of the Mississippi River; that is, the nine or ten hundred miles stretching from Cairo, Illinois, southward to New Orleans, the same being wonderfully crooked, with a brief straight bit here and there at wide intervals. The two-hundred-mile stretch from Cairo northward to St. Louis is by no means so crooked, that being a rocky country which the river cannot cut much.

The water cuts the alluvial banks of the "lower" river into deep horseshoe curves; so deep, indeed, that in some places if you were to get ashore at one extremity of the horseshoe and walk across the neck, half or three quarters of a mile, you could sit down and rest a couple of hours while your steamer was coming around the long elbow, at a speed of ten miles an hour, to take you aboard again. When the river is rising fast, some scoundrel whose plantation is back in the country, and therefore of inferior value, has only to watch his chance, cut a little gutter across the narrow neck of land some dark night, and turn the water into it, and in a wonderfully short time a miracle has happened: to wit, the whole Mississippi has taken possession of that little ditch, and placed the countryman's plantation on its bank (quadrupling its value), and that other party's formerly valuable plantation finds itself away out yonder on a big island; the old water-course around it will soon shoal up, boats cannot approach within ten miles of it, and down goes its value to a fourth of its former worth. Watches are kept on those narrow necks, at needful times, and if a man happens to be caught cutting a ditch across them, the chances are all against his ever having another opportunity to cut a ditch.

Pray observe some of the effects of this ditching business. Once there was a neck opposite Port Hudson, Louisiana, which was only half a mile across, in its narrowest place. You could walk across there in fifteen minutes; but if you made the journey around the cape on a raft, you travelled thirty-five miles to accomplish the same thing. In 1722 the river darted through that neck, deserted its old bed, and thus shortened itself thirty-five miles. In the same way it shortened itself twenty-five miles at Black Hawk Point in 1699. Below Red River Landing, Raccourci cut-off was made (forty or fifty years ago, I think). This shortened the river twenty-eight miles. In our day, if you travel by river from the southernmost of these three cut-offs to the northernmost, you go only seventy miles. To do the same thing a hundred and seventy-six years ago, one had to go a hundred and fifty-eight miles!—a shortening of eighty-eight miles in that trifling distance. At some forgotten time in the past, cut-offs were made above Vidalia, Louisiana; at island 92; at island 84; and at Hale's Point. These shortened the river, in the aggregate, seventy-seven miles.

Since my own day on the Mississippi, cut-offs have been made at Hurricane Island; at island 100; at Napoleon, Arkansas; at Walnut Bend; and at Council Bend. These shortened the river, in the aggregate, sixty-seven miles. In my own time a cut-off was made at American Bend, which shortened the river ten miles or more.

Therefore, the Mississippi between Cairo and New Orleans was twelve hundred and fifteen miles long one hundred and seventy-six years ago. It was eleven hundred and eighty after the cut-off of 1722. It was one thousand and forty after the American Bend cut-off. It has lost sixty-seven miles since. Consequently its length is only nine hundred and seventy-three miles at present.

Now, if I wanted to be one of those ponderous scientific people, and "let on" to prove what had occurred in the remote past by what had occurred in a given time in the recent past, or what will occur in the far future by what has occurred in late years, what an opportunity is here! Geology never had such a chance, nor such exact data to argue from! Nor "development of species," either! Glacial epochs are great things, but they are vague—vague. Please observe:—

In the space of one hundred and seventy-six years the Lower Mississippi has shortened itself two hundred and forty-two miles. That is an average of a trifle over one mile and a third per year. Therefore, any calm person, who is not blind or idiotic, can see that in the Old Oölitic Silurian Period, just a million years ago next November, the Lower Mississippi River was upwards of one million three hundred thousand miles long, and stuck out over the Gulf of Mexico like a fishing-rod. And by the same token any person can see that seven hundred and forty-two years from now the Lower Mississippi will be only a mile and three quarters long, and Cairo and New Orleans will have joined their streets together, and be plodding comfortably along under a single mayor and a mutual board of aldermen. There is something fascinating about science. One gets such wholesale returns of conjecture out of such a trifling investment of fact.

When the water begins to flow through one of those ditches I have been speaking of, it is time for the people thereabouts to move. The water cleaves the banks away like a knife. By the time the ditch has become twelve or fifteen feet wide, the calamity is as good as accomplished, for no power on earth can stop it now. When the width has reached a hundred yards, the banks begin to peel off in slices half an acre wide. The current flowing around the bend travelled formerly only five miles an hour; now it is tremendously increased by the shortening of the distance. I was on board the first boat that tried to go through the cut-off at American Bend, but we did not get through. It was toward midnight, and a wild night it was—thunder, lightning, and torrents of rain. It was estimated that the current in the cut-off was making about fifteen or twenty miles an hour; twelve or thirteen was the best our boat could do, even in tolerably slack water, therefore perhaps we were foolish to try the cut-off. However, Mr. Brown was ambitious, and he kept on trying. The eddy running up the bank, under the "point," was about as swift as the current out in the middle; so we would go flying up the shore like a lightning express train, get on a big head of steam, and "stand by for a surge" when we struck the current that was whirling by the point. But all our preparations were useless. The instant the current hit us it spun us around like a top, the water deluged the forecastle, and the boat careened so far over that one could hardly keep his feet. The next instant we were away down the river, clawing with might and main to keep out of the woods. We tried the experiment four times. I stood on the forecastle companion way to see. It was astonishing to observe how suddenly the boat would spin around and turn tail the moment she emerged from the eddy and the current struck her nose. The sounding concussion and the quivering would have been about the same if she had come full speed against a sand-bank. Under the lightning flashes one could see the plantation cabins and the goodly acres tumble into the river; and the crash they made was not a bad effort at thunder. Once, when we spun around, we only missed a house about twenty feet, that had a light burning in the window; and in the same instant that house went overboard. Nobody could stay on our forecastle; the water swept across it in a torrent every time we plunged athwart the current. At the end of our fourth effort we brought up in the woods two miles below the cut-off; all the country there was overflowed, of course. A day or two later the cut-off was three quarters of a mile wide, and boats passed up through it without much difficulty, and so saved ten miles.

The old Raccourci cut-off reduced the river's length twenty-eight miles. There used to be a tradition connected with it. It was said that a boat came along there in the night and went around the enormous elbow the usual way, the pilots not knowing that the cut-off had been made. It was a grisly, hideous night, and all shapes were vague and distorted. The old bend had already begun to fill up, and the boat got to running away from mysterious reefs, and occasionally hitting one. The perplexed pilots fell to swearing, and finally uttered the entirely unnecessary wish that they might never get out of that place. As always happens in such cases, that particular prayer was answered, and the others neglected. So to this day that phantom steamer is still butting around in that deserted river, trying to find her way out. More than one grave watchman has sworn to me that on drizzly, dismal nights, he has glanced fearfully down that forgotten river as he passed the head of the island, and seen the faint glow of the spectre steamer's lights drifting through the distant gloom, and heard the muffled cough of her 'scapepipes and the plaintive cry of her leads-men.

In the absence of further statistics, I beg to close this chapter with one more reminiscence of "Stephen."

Most of the captains and pilots held Stephen's note for borrowed sums, ranging from two hundred and fifty dollars upward. Stephen never paid one of these notes, but he was very prompt and very zealous about renewing them every twelve month.

Of course there came a time, at last, when Stephen could no longer borrow of his ancient creditors; so he was obliged to lie in wait for new men who did not know him. Such a victim was good-hearted, simple-natured young Yates (I use a fictitious name, but the real name began, as this one does, with a Y). Young Yates graduated as a pilot, got a berth, and when the month ended and he stepped up to the clerk's office and received his two hundred and fifty dollars in crisp new bills, Stephen was there! His silvery tongue began to wag, and in a very little while Yate's two hundred and fifty dollars had changed hands. The fact was soon known at pilot headquarters, and the amusement and satisfaction of the old creditors were large and generous. But innocent Yates never suspected that Stephen's promise to pay promptly at the end of the week was a worthless one. Yates called for his money at the stipulated time; Stephen sweetened him up and put him off a week. He called then, according to agreement, and came away sugar-coated again, but suffering under another postponement. So the thing went on. Yates haunted Stephen week after week, to no purpose, and at last gave it up. And then straightway Stephen began to haunt Yates! Wherever Yates appeared, there was the inevitable Stephen. And not only there, but beaming with affection and gushing with apologies for not being able to pay. By and by, whenever poor Yates saw him coming, he would turn and fly, and drag his company with him, if he had company; but it was of no use; his debtor would run him down and corner him. Panting and red-faced,

Stephen would come, with outstretched hands and eager eyes, invade the conversation, shake both of Yates's arms loose in their sockets, and begin:—

"My, what a race I've had! I saw you didn't see me, and so I clapped on all steam for fear I'd miss you entirely. And here you are! there, just stand so, and let me look at you! Just the same old noble countenance." [To Yates's friend:] "Just look at him! *Look* at him! Ain't it just *good* to look at him! *Ain't* it now? Ain't he just a picture! *Some* call him a picture; *I* call him a panorama! That's what he is—an entire panorama. And now I'm reminded! How I do wish I could have seen you an hour earlier! For twenty-four hours I've been saving up that two hundred and fifty dollars for you; been looking for you everywhere. I waited at the Planter's from six yesterday evening till two o'clock this morning, without rest or food; my wife says, 'Where have you been all night?' I said, 'This debt lies heavy on my mind.' She says, 'In all my days I never saw a man take a debt to heart the way you do.' I said, 'It's my nature; how can *I* change it?' She says, 'Well, do go to bed and get some rest.' I said, 'Not till that poor, noble young man has got his money.' So I set up all night, and this morning out I shot, and the first man I struck told me you had shipped on the 'Grand Turk' and gone to New Orleans. Well sir, I had to lean up against a building and cry. So help me goodness, I couldn't help it. The man that owned the place come out cleaning up with a rag, and said he didn't like to have people cry against his building, and then it seemed to me that the whole world had turned against me, and it wasn't any use to live any more; and coming along an hour ago, suffering no man knows what agony, I met Jim Wilson and paid him the two hundred and fifty dollars on account; and to think that here you are, now, and I haven't got a cent! But as sure as I am standing here on this ground on this particular brick,—there, I've scratched a mark on the brick to remember it by,—I'll borrow that money and pay it over to you at twelve o'clock sharp, to-morrow! Now, stand so; let me look at you just once more."

And so on. Yates's life became a burden to him. He could not escape his debtor and his debtor's awful sufferings on account of not being able to pay. He dreaded to show himself in the street, lest he should find Stephen lying in wait for him at the corner.

Bogart's billiard saloon was a great resort for pilots in those days. They met there about as much to exchange river news as to play. One morning Yates was there; Stephen was there, too, but kept out of sight. But by and by, when about all the pilots had arrived who were in town, Stephen suddenly appeared in the midst, and rushed for Yates as for a long-lost brother.

"*Oh,* I am so glad to see you! Oh my soul, the sight of you is such a comfort to my eyes! Gentlemen, I owe all of you money; among you I owe probably forty thousand dollars. I want to pay it; I intend to pay it—every last cent of it. You all know, without my telling you, what sorrow it has cost me to remain so long under such deep obligations to such patient and generous friends; but the sharpest pang I suffer—by far the sharpest—is from the debt I owe to this noble young man here; and I have come to this place this morning especially to make the announcement that I have at last found a method whereby I can pay off all my debts! And most especially I wanted *him* to be here when I announced it. Yes, my faithful friend,—my benefactor, I've found the method! I've found the method to pay off *all* my debts, and you'll get your money!" Hope dawned in Yates's eye; then Stephen, beaming benignantly, and placing his hand upon Yates's head, added, "I am going to pay them off in alphabetical order!"

Then he turned and disappeared. The full significance of Stephen's "method" did not dawn upon the perplexed and musing crowd for some two minutes; and then Yates murmured with a sigh:—

"Well, the Y's stand a gaudy chance. He won't get any further than the C's in *this* world, and I reckon that after a good deal of eternity has wasted away in the next one, I'll still be referred to up there as 'that poor, ragged pilot that came here from St. Louis in the early days!' "

CHAPTER XVIII

I TAKE A FEW EXTRA LESSONS

During the two or two and a half years of my apprenticeship, I served under many pilots, and had experience of many kinds of steamboatmen and many varieties of steamboats; for it was not always convenient for Mr. Bixby to have me with him, and in such cases he sent me with somebody else. I am to this day profiting somewhat by that experience; for in that brief, sharp schooling, I got personally and familiarly acquainted with about all the different types of human nature that are to be found in fiction, biography, or history. The fact is daily borne in upon me, that the average shore-employment requires as much as for-

ty years to equip a man with this sort of education. When I say I
am still profiting by this thing, I do not mean that it has constituted me a judge of men—no, it has not done that; for judges
of men are born, not made. My profit is various in kind and
degree; but the feature of it which I value most is the zest which
that early experience has given to my later reading. When I find
a well- drawn character in fiction or biography, I generally take
a warm personal interest in him, for the reason that I have
known him before—met him on the river.

The figure that comes before me oftenest, out of the shadows
of that vanished time, is that of Brown, of the steamer
"Pennsylvania"—the man referred to in a former chapter,
whose memory was so good and tiresome. He was a middle-
aged, long, slim, bony, smooth-shaven, horse-faced, ignorant,
stingy, malicious, snarling, fault-hunting, mote-magnifying
tyrant. I early got the habit of coming on watch with dread at my
heart. No matter how good a time I might have been having with
the off-watch below, and no matter how high my spirits might
be when I started aloft, my soul became lead in my body the moment I approached the pilot-house.

I still remember the first time I ever entered the presence of
that man. The boat had backed out from St. Louis and was
"straightening down;" I ascended to the pilot-house in high
feather, and very proud to be semi-officially a member of the executive family of so fast and famous a boat. Brown was at the
wheel. I paused in the middle of the room, all fixed to make my
bow, but Brown did not look around. I thought he took a furtive
glance at me out of the corner of his eye, but as not even this
notice was repeated, I judged I had been mistaken. By this time
he was picking his way among some dangerous "breaks"
abreast the wood-yards; therefore it would not be proper to interrupt him; so I stepped softly to the high bench and took a
seat.

There was silence for ten minutes; then my new boss turned
and inspected me deliberately and painstakingly from head to
heel for about—as it seemed to me—a quarter of an hour. After
which he removed his countenance and I saw it no more for
some seconds; then it came around once more, and this question
greeted me:—

"Are you Horace Bigsby's cub?"

"Yes, sir."

After this there was a pause and another inspection. Then:

"What's your name?"

I told him. He repeated it after me. It was probably the only thing he ever forgot; for although I was with him many months he never addressed himself to me in any other way than "Here!" and then his command followed.

"Where was you born?"

"In Florida, Missouri."

A pause. Then:—

"Dern sight better staid there!"

By means of a dozen or so of pretty direct questions, he pumped my family history out of me.

The leads were going now, in the first crossing. This interrupted the inquest. When the leads had been laid in, he resumed:—

"How long you been on the river?"

I told him. After a pause:—

"Where'd you get them shoes?"

I gave him the information.

"Hold up your foot!"

I did so. He stepped back, examined the shoe minutely and contemptuously, scratching his head thoughtfully, tilting his high sugar-loaf hat well forward to facilitate the operation, then ejaculated, "Well, I'll be dod derned!" and returned to his wheel.

What occasion there was to be dod derned about it is a thing which is still as much of a mystery to me now as it was then. It must have been all of fifteen minutes—fifteen minutes of dull, homesick silence—before that long horse-face swung round upon me again—and then, what a change! It was as red as fire, and every muscle in it was working. Now came this shriek:

"Here!—You going to set there all day?"

I lit in the middle of the floor, shot there by the electric suddenness of the surprise. As soon as I could get my voice I said, apologetically:—"I have had no orders, sir." "You've had no *orders!* My, what a fine bird we are! We must have *orders!* Our father was a *gentleman*—owned slaves—and *we've* been to *school.* Yes, *we* are a gentleman, *too,* and got to have *orders!* ORDERS, is it? ORDERS is what you want! Dod dern my skin, *I'll* learn you to swell yourself up and blow around *here* about your dod-derned *orders!* G' way from the wheel!" (I had approached it without knowing it.)

I moved back a step or two, and stood as in a dream, all my senses stupefied by this frantic assault.

"What you standing there for? Take that ice-pitcher down to the texas-tender—come, move along, and don't you be all day about it!"

The moment I got back to the pilot-house, Brown said:—

"Here! What was you doing down there all this time?"

"I couldn't find the texas-tender; I had to go all the way to the pantry."

"Derned likely story! Fill up the stove."

I proceeded to do so. He watched me like a cat. Presently he shouted:—

"Put down that shovel! Derndest numskull I ever saw—ain't even got sense enough to load up a stove."

All through the watch this sort of thing went on. Yes, and the subsequent watches were much like it, during a stretch of months. As I have said, I soon got the habit of coming on duty with dread. The moment I was in the presence, even in the darkest night, I could feel those yellow eyes upon me, and knew their owner was watching for a pretext to spit out some venom on me. Preliminarily he would say:—

"Here! Take the wheel."

Two minutes later:—

"*Where* in the nation you going to? Pull her down! pull her down!"

After another moment:—

"Say! You going to hold her all day? Let her go—meet her! meet her!"

Then he would jump from the bench, snatch the wheel from me, and meet her himself, pouring out wrath upon me all the time.

George Ritchie was the other pilot's cub. He was having good times now; for his boss, George Ealer, was as kind-hearted as Brown wasn't. Ritchie had steered for Brown the season before; consequently he knew exactly how to entertain himself and plague me, all by the one operation. Whenever I took the wheel for a moment on Ealer's watch, Ritchie would sit back on the bench and play Brown, with continual ejaculations of "Snatch her! snatch her! Derndest mud-cat I ever saw!" "Here! Where you going *now?* Going to run over that snag?" "Pull her *down!* Don't you hear me? Pull her *down!*" "There she goes! *Just* as I expected! I *told* you not to cramp that reef. G'way from the wheel!"

So I always had a rough time of it, no matter whose watch it was; and sometimes it seemed to me that Ritchie's good-natured badgering was pretty nearly as aggravating as Brown's dead-earnest nagging.

I often wanted to kill Brown, but this would not answer. A cub had to take everything his boss gave, in the way of vigorous comment and criticism; and we all believed that there was a United States law making it a penitentiary offence to strike or threaten a pilot who was on duty. However, I could *imagine* myself killing Brown; there was no law against that; and that was the thing I used always to do the moment I was abed. Instead of going over my river in my mind as was my duty, I threw business aside for pleasure, and killed Brown. I killed Brown every night for months; not in old, stale, commonplace ways, but in new and picturesque ones,—ways that were sometimes surprising for freshness of design and ghastliness of situation and environment.

Brown was *always* watching for a pretext to find fault; and if he could find no plausible pretext, he would invent one. He would scold you for shaving a shore, and for not shaving it; for hugging a bar, and for not hugging it; for "pulling down" when not invited, and for *not* pulling down when not invited; for firing up without orders, and for waiting *for* orders. In a word, it was his invariable rule to find fault with *everything* you did; and another invariable rule of his was to throw all his remarks (to you) into the form of an insult.

One day we were approaching New Madrid, bound down and heavily laden. Brown was at one side of the wheel, steering; I was at the other, standing by to "pull down" or "shove up." He cast a furtive glance at me every now and then. I had long ago learned what that meant; viz., he was trying to invent a trap for me. I wondered what shape it was going to take. By and by he stepped back from the wheel and said in his usual snarly way:—

"Here!—See if you've got gumption enough to round her to."

This was simply *bound* to be a success; nothing could prevent it; for he had never allowed me to round the boat to before; consequently, no matter how I might do the thing, he could find free fault with it. He stood back there with his greedy eye on me, and the result was what might have been foreseen: I lost my head in a quarter of a minute, and didn't know what I was about; I started too early to bring the boat around, but detected a green gleam of joy in Brown's eye, and corrected my mistake; I started around once more while too high up, but corrected myself again in time; I made other false moves, and still managed to save myself; but at last I grew so confused and anxious that I tumbled into the very worst blunder of all—I got too far *down* before beginning to fetch the boat around. Brown's chance was come.

His face turned red with passion; he made one bound, hurled me across the house with a sweep of his arm, spun the wheel down, and began to pour out a stream of vituperation upon me which lasted till he was out of breath. In the course of this speech he called me all the different kinds of hard names he could think of, and once or twice I thought he was even going to

304

swear—but he had never done that, and he didn't this time. "Dod dern" was the nearest he ventured to the luxury of swearing, for he had been brought up with a wholesome respect for future fire and brimstone.

That was an uncomfortable hour; for there was a big audience on the hurricane deck. When I went to bed that night, I killed Brown in seventeen different ways—all of them new.

CHAPTER XIX

BROWN AND I EXCHANGE COMPLIMENTS

Two trips later, I got into serious trouble. Brown was steering; I was "pulling down." My younger brother appeared on the hurricane deck, and shouted to Brown to stop at some landing or other a mile or so below. Brown gave no intimation that he had heard anything. But that was his way: he never condescended to take notice of an under clerk. The wind was blowing; Brown was deaf (although he always pretended he wasn't), and I very much doubted if he had heard the order. If I had had two heads, I would have spoken; but as I had only one, it seemed judicious to take care of it; so I kept still.

Presently, sure enough, we went sailing by that plantation. Captain Klinefelter appeared on the deck, and said:—

"Let her come around, sir, let her come around. Didn't Henry tell you to land here?"

"*No,* sir!"

"I sent him up to do it."

"He *did* come up; and that's all the good it done, the dodderned fool. He never said anything."

"Didn't *you* hear him?" asked the captain of me.

Of course I didn't want to be mixed up in this business, but there was no way to avoid it; so I said:—

"Yes, sir."

I knew what Brown's next remark would be, before he uttered it; it was:—

"Shut your mouth! you never heard anything of the kind."

I closed my mouth according to instructions. An hour later, Henry entered the pilot-house, unaware of what had been going on. He was a thoroughly inoffensive boy, and I was sorry to see him come, for I knew Brown would have no pity on him. Brown began, straightway:—

"Here! why didn't you tell me we'd got to land at that plantation?"

"I did tell you, Mr. Brown."

"It's a lie!"

I said:—

"You lie, yourself. He did tell you."

Brown glared at me in unaffected surprise; and for as much as a moment he was entirely speechless; then he shouted to me:—

"I'll attend to your case in a half a minute!" then to Henry, "And you leave the pilot-house; out with you!"

It was pilot law, and must be obeyed. The boy started out, and even had his foot on the upper step outside the door, when Brown, with a sudden access of fury, picked up a ten-pound lump of coal and sprang after him; but I was between, with a heavy stool, and I hit Brown a good honest blow which stretched him out.

I had committed a crime of crimes,—I had lifted my hand against a pilot on duty! I supposed I was booked for the penitentiary sure, and couldn't be booked any surer if I went on and squared my long account with this person while I had the chance; consequently I stuck to him and pounded him with my fists a considerable time,—I do not know how long, the pleasure of it probably made it seem longer than it really was;—but in the end he struggled free and jumped up and sprang to the wheel: a very natural solicitude, for, all this time, here was this steamboat tearing down the river at the rate of fifteen miles an hour and nobody at the helm! However, Eagle Bend was two miles wide at this bank-full stage, and correspondingly long and deep; and the boat was steering herself straight down the middle and taking no chances. Still, that was only luck—a body *might* have found her charging into the woods.

Perceiving, at a glance, that the "Pennsylvania" was in no danger, Brown gathered up the spy-glass, war-club fashion, and ordered me out of the pilot-house with more than Comanche bluster. But I was not afraid of him now; so, instead of going, I tarried, and criticised his grammer; I reformed his ferocious speeches for him, and put them into good English, calling his attention to the advantage of pure English over the bastard dialect of the Pennsylvanian collieries whence he was extracted. He could have done his part to admiration in a cross-fire of mere vituperation, of course; but he was not equipped for this species of controversy; so he presently laid aside his glass and took the wheel, muttering and shaking his head; and I retired to the bench. The racket had brought everybody to the hurricane deck, and I trembled when I saw the old captain looking up from the midst of the crowd. I said to myself, "Now I *am* done for!"— For although, as a rule, he was so fatherly and indulgent toward the boat's family, and so patient of minor shortcomings, he could be stern enough when the fault was worth it.

I tried to imagine what he *would* do to a cub pilot who had been guilty of such a crime as mine, committed on a boat guard-deep with costly freight and alive with passengers. Our watch was nearly ended. I thought I would go and hide somewhere till I got a chance to slide ashore. So I slipped out of the pilot-house, and down the steps, and around to the texas door,—and was in the act of gliding within, when the captain confronted me! I dropped my head, and he stood over me in silence a moment or two, then said impressively,—

"Follow me."

I dropped into his wake; he led the way to his parlor in the forward end of the texas. We were alone, now. He closed the after door; then moved slowly to the forward one and closed that. He sat down; I stood before him. He looked at me some little time, then said,—

"So you have been fighting Mr. Brown?"

I answered meekly:—

"Yes, sir."

"Do you know that that is a very serious matter?"

"Yes, sir."

"Are you aware that this boat was ploughing down the river fully five minutes with no one at the wheel?"

"Yes, sir."

"Did you strike him first?"

"Yes, sir."

"What with?"

"A stool, sir."

"Hard?"

"Middling, sir."

"Did it knock him down?"

"He—he fell, sir."

"Did you follow it up? Did you do anything further?"

"Yes, sir."

"What did you do?"

"Pounded him, sir."

"Pounded him?"

"Yes, sir."

"Did you pound him much?—that is, severely?"

"One might call it that, sir, maybe."

"I'm deuced glad of it! Hark ye, never mention that I said that. You have been guilty of a great crime; and don't you ever be guilty of it again, on this boat. *But*—lay for him ashore! Give him a good sound thrashing, do you hear? I'll pay the expenses.

Now go—and mind you, not a word of this to anybody. Clear out with you!—you've been guilty of a great crime, you whelp!''

I slid out, happy with the sense of a close shave and a mighty deliverance; and I heard him laughing to himself and slapping his fat thighs after I had closed his door.

When Brown came off watch he went straight to the captain, who was talking with some passengers on the boiler deck, and demanded that I be put ashore in New Orleans—and added:—

"I'll never turn a wheel on this boat again while that cub stays."

The captain said:—

"But he needn't come round when you are on watch, Mr. Brown."

"I won't even stay on the same boat with him. *One* of us has got to go ashore."

"Very well," said the captain, "let it be yourself;" and resumed his talk with the passengers.

During the brief remainder of the trip, I knew how an emancipated slave feels; for I was an emancipated slave myself. While we lay at landings, I listened to George Ealer's flute; or to his readings from his two bibles, that is to say, Goldsmith and Shakespeare; or I played chess with him—and would have beaten him sometimes, only he always took back his last move and ran the game out differently.

CHAPTER XX

A CATASTROPHE

We lay three days in New Orleans, but the captain did not succeed in finding another pilot; so he proposed that I should stand a daylight watch, and leave the night watches to George Ealer. But I was afraid; I had never stood a watch of any sort by myself, and I believed I should be sure to get into trouble in the head of some chute, or ground the boat in a near cut through some bar or other. Brown remained in his place; but he would not travel with me. So the captain gave me an order on the captain of the "A.T. Lacey," for a passage to St. Louis, and said he would find a new pilot there and my steersman's berth could then be resumed. The "Lacey" was to leave a couple of days after the "Pennsylvania."

The night before the "Pennsylvania" left, Henry and I sat chatting on a freight pile on the levee till midnight. The subject of the chat, mainly, was one which I think we had not exploited before—steamboat disasters. One was then on its way to us, little as we suspected it; the water which was to make the steam which should cause it, was washing past some point fifteen hundred miles up the river while we talked;—but it would arrive at the right time and the right place. We doubted if persons not clothed with authority were of much use in cases of disaster and attendant panic; still, they might be of *some* use; so we decided that if a disaster ever fell within our experience we would at least stick to the boat, and give such minor service as chance might throw in the way. Henry remembered this, afterward, when the disaster came, and acted accordingly.

The "Lacey" started up the river two days behind the "Pennsylvania." We touched at Greenville, Mississippi, a couple of days out, and somebody shouted:—

"The 'Pennsylvania' is blown up at Ship Island, and a hundred and fifty lives lost!"

At Napoleon, Arkansas, the same evening, we got an extra, issued by a Memphis paper, which gave some particulars. It mentioned my brother, and said he was not hurt.

Further up the river we got a later extra. My brother was again mentioned; but this time as being hurt beyond help. We did not get full details of the catastrophe until we reached Memphis. This is the sorrowful story:—

It was six o'clock on a hot summer morning. The "Pennsylvania" was creeping along, north of Ship Island, about sixty miles below Memphis on a half-head of steam, towing a wood-flat which was fast being emptied. George Ealer was in the pilot-house—alone, I think; the second engineer and a striker had the watch in the engine room; the second mate had the watch on deck; George Black, Mr. Wood, and my brother, clerks, were asleep, as were also Brown and the head engineer, the carpenter, the chief mate, and one striker; Capt. Klinefelter was in the barber's chair, and the barber was preparing to shave him. There were a good many cabin passengers aboard, and three or four hundred deck passengers—so it was said at this time—and not very many of them were astir. The wood being nearly all out of the flat now, Ealer rang to "come ahead" full steam, and the next moment four of the eight boilers exploded with a thunderous crash, and the whole forward third of the boat was hoisted toward the sky! The main part of the mass, with the chimneys, dropped upon the boat again, a mountain of riddled and chaotic rubbish—and then, after a little, fire broke out.

Many people were flung to considerable distances, and fell in the river; among these were Mr. Wood and my brother, and the carpenter. The carpenter was still stretched upon his mattress when he struck the water seventy-five feet from the boat. Brown, the pilot, and George Black, chief clerk, were never seen or heard of after the explosion. The barber's chair, with Captain Klinefelter in it and unhurt, was left with its back overhanging vacancy—everything forward of it, floor and all, had disappeared; and the stupefied barber, who was also unhurt, stood with one toe projecting over space, still stirring his lather unconsciously, and saying not a word.

When George Ealer saw the chimneys plunging aloft in front of him, he knew what the matter was; so he muffled his face in the lapels of his coat, and pressed both hands there tightly to keep this protection in its place so that no steam could get to his nose or mouth. He had ample time to attend to these details while he was going up and returning. He presently landed on top of the unexploded boilers, forty feet below the former pilothouse, accompanied by his wheel and a rain of other stuff, and enveloped in a cloud of scalding steam. All of the many who breathed that steam, died; none escaped. But Ealer breathed none of it. He made his way to the free air as quickly as he could; and when the steam cleared away he returned and climbed up on the boilers again, and patiently hunted out each and every one of his chessmen and the several joints of his flute.

By this time the fire was beginning to threaten. Shrieks and groans filled the air. A great many persons had been scalded, a great many crippled; the explosion had driven an iron crowbar through one man's body—I think they said he was a priest. He did not die at once, and his sufferings were very dreadful. A young French naval cadet, of fifteen, son of a French admiral, was fearfully scalded, but bore his tortures manfully. Both mates were badly scalded, but they stood to their posts, nevertheless. They drew the wood-boat aft, and they and the captain fought back the frantic herd of frightened immigrants till the wounded could be brought there and placed in safety first.

When Mr. Wood and Henry fell into the water, they struck out for shore, which was only a few hundred yards away; but Henry presently said he believed he was not hurt, (what an unaccountable error!) and therefore would swim back to the boat and help save the wounded. So they parted, and Henry returned.

By this time the fire was making fierce headway, and several persons who were imprisoned under the ruins were begging piteously for help. All efforts to conquer the fire proved fruitless; so the buckets were presently thrown aside and the officers fell-to with axes and tried to cut the prisoners out. A striker was one of the captives; he said he was not injured, but could not free himself; and when he saw that the fire was likely to drive away the workers, he begged that some one would shoot him, and thus save him from the more dreadful death. The fire did drive the axe-men away, and they had to listen, helpless, to this poor fellow's supplications till the flames ended his miseries.

The fire drove all into the wood-flat that could be accommodated there; it was cut adrift, then, and it and the burning steamer floated down the river toward Ship Island. They moored the flat at the head of the island, and there, unsheltered from the blazing sun, the half-naked occupants had to remain, without food or stimulants, or help for their hurts, during the rest of the day. A steamer came along, finally, and carried the unfortunates to Memphis, and there the most lavish assistance was at once forthcoming. By this time Henry was insensible. The physicians examined his injuries and saw that they were fatal, and naturally turned their main attention to patients who could be saved.

Forty of the wounded were placed upon pallets on the floor of a great public hall, and among these was Henry. There the ladies of Memphis came every day, with flowers, fruits, and dainties and delicacies of all kinds, and there they remained and nursed the wounded. All the physicians stood watches there, and all the medical students; and the rest of the town furnished money, or whatever else was wanted. And Memphis knew how to do all these things well; for many a disaster like the "Pennsylvania's" had happened near her doors, and she was experienced, above all other cities on the river, in the gracious office of the Good Samaritan.

The sight I saw when I entered that large hall was new and strange to me. Two long rows of prostrate forms—more than forty, in all—and every face and head a shapeless wad of loose raw cotton. It was a grewsome spectacle. I watched there six days and nights, and a very melancholy experience it was. There was one daily incident which was peculiarly depressing: this was the removal of the doomed to a chamber apart. It was done in order that the *morale* of the other patients might not be injuriously affected by seeing one of their number in the death-agony. The fated one was always carried out with as little stir as possible, and the stretcher was always hidden from sight by a wall of assistants; but no matter: everybody knew what that cluster of bent forms, with its muffled step and its slow movement meant; and all eyes watched it wistfully, and a shudder went abreast of it like a wave.

I saw many poor fellows removed to the "death-room," and saw them no more afterward. But I saw our chief mate carried thither more than once. His hurts were frightful, especially his scalds. He was clothed in linseed oil and raw cotton to his waist, and resembled nothing human. He was often out of his mind; and then his pains would make him rave and shout and sometimes shriek. Then, after a period of dumb exhaustion, his disordered imagination would suddenly transform the great apartment into a forecastle, and the hurrying throng of nurses into the crew; and he would come to a sitting posture and shout, "Hump yourselves, *hump* yourselves, you petrifactions, snail-bellies, pall-bearers! going to be all *day* getting that hatful of freight out?" and supplement this explosion with a firmament-obliterating irruption of profanity which nothing could stay or stop till his crater was empty. And now and then while these frenzies possessed him, he would tear off handfuls of the cotton and expose his cooked flesh to view. It was horrible. It was bad for the others, of course—this noise and these exhibitions; so the doctors tried to give him morphine to quiet him. But, in his mind or out of it, he would not take it. He said his wife had been killed by that treacherous drug, and he would die before he would take it. He suspected that the doctors were concealing it in his ordinary medicines and in his water—so he ceased from putting either to his lips. Once, when he had been without water during two sweltering days, he took the dipper in his hand, and the sight of the limpid fluid, and the misery of his thirst, tempted him almost beyond his strength; but he mastered himself and threw it away, and after that he allowed no more to be brought near him. Three times I saw him carried to the death-room, insensible and supposed to be dying; but each time he revived, cursed his attendants, and demanded to be taken back. He lived to be mate of a steamboat again.

But he was the only one who went to the death-room and returned alive. Dr. Peyton, a principal physician, and rich in all the attributes that go to constitute high and flawless character, did all that educated judgment and trained skill could do for Henry; but, as the newspapers had said in the beginning, his hurts were past help. On the evening of the sixth day his wandering mind busied itself with matters far away, and his nerveless fingers "picked at this coverlet." His hour had struck; we bore him to the death-room, poor boy.

CHAPTER XXI

A SECTION IN MY BIOGRAPHY

In due course I got my license. I was a pilot now, full fledged. I dropped into casual employments; no misfortunes resulting, intermittent work gave place to steady and protracted engagements. Time drifted smoothly and prosperously on, and I supposed—and hoped—that I was going to follow the river the rest of my days, and die at the wheel when my mission was ended. But by and by the war came, commerce was suspended, my occupation was gone.

I had to seek another livelihood. So I became a silver miner in Nevada; next, a newspaper reporter; next, a gold miner, in California; next, a reporter in San Francisco; next, a special correspondent in the Sandwich Islands; next, a roving correspondent in Europe and the East; next, an instructional torch-bearer on the lecture platform; and, finally, I became a scribbler of books, and an immovable fixture among the other rocks of New England.

In so few words have I disposed of the twenty-one slow-drifting years that have come and gone since I last looked from the windows of a pilot-house.

Let us resume, now.

CHAPTER XXII

I RETURN TO MY MUTTONS

After twenty-one years' absence, I felt a very strong desire to see the river again, and the steamboats, and such of the boys as might be left; so I resolved to go out there. I enlisted a poet for company, and a stenographer to "take him down," and started westward about the middle of April.

As I proposed to make notes, with a view to printing, I took some thought as to methods of procedure. I reflected that if I were recognized, on the river, I should not be as free to go and come, talk, inquire, and spy around, as I should be if unknown; I remembered that it was the custom of steamboatmen in the old times to load up the confiding stranger with the most picturesque and admirable lies, and put the sophisticated friend off with dull and ineffectual facts: so I concluded, that, from a business point of view, it would be an advantage to disguise our party with fictitious names. The idea was certainly good, but it bred infinite bother; for although Smith, Jones, and Johnson are easy names to remember when there is no occasion to remember them, it is next to impossible to recollect them when they are wanted. How do criminals manage to keep a brand-new *alias* in mind? This is a great mystery. I was innocent; and yet was seldom able to lay my hand on my new name when it was needed; and it seemed to me that if I had had a crime on my con-science to further confuse me, I could never have kept the name by me at all.

We left per Pennsylvania Railroad, at 8 A.M. April 18.

"*Evening*. Speaking of dress. Grace and picturesqueness drop gradually out of it as one travels away from New York."

I find that among my notes. It makes no difference which direc-tion you take, the fact remains the same. Whether you move north, south, east, or west, no matter: you can get up in the morning and guess how far you have come, by noting what degree of grace and picturesqueness is by that time lacking in the costumes of the new passengers;—I do not mean of the women alone, but of both sexes. It may be that *carriage* is at the bottom of this thing; and I think it is; for there are plenty of ladies and gentlemen in the provincial cities whose garments are all made by the best tailors and dressmakers of New York; yet this has no perceptible effect upon the grand fact: the educated eye never mistakes those people for New-Yorkers. No, there is a godless grace, and snap, and style about a born and bred New-Yorker which mere clothing cannot effect.

"*April* 19. This morning, struck into the region of full goatees—sometimes accompanied by a moustache, but only occasionally."

It was odd to come upon this thick crop of an obsolete and un-comely fashion; it was like running suddenly across a forgotten acquaintance whom you had supposed dead for a generation. The goatee extends over a wide extent of country; and is ac-companied by an iron-clad belief in Adam and the biblical history of creation, which has not suffered from the assaults of the scientists.

"*Afternoon*. At the railway stations the loafers carry *both* hands in their breeches pockets; it was observable, heretofore, that one hand was sometimes out of doors,—here, never. This is an important fact in geography."

If the loafers determined the character of a country, it would be still more important, of course.

"Heretofore, all along, the station-loafer has been often observed to scratch one shin with the other foot; here, these remains of activity are wanting. This has an ominous look."

By and by, we entered the tobacco-chewing region. Fifty years ago, the tobacco-chewing region covered the Union. It is greatly restricted now.

Next, boots began to appear. Not in strong force, however. Later—away down the Mississippi—they became the rule. They disappeared from other sections of the Union with the mud; no doubt they will disappear from the river villages, also, when proper pavements come in.

We reached St. Louis at ten o'clock at night. At the counter of the hotel I tendered a hurriedly-invented fictitious name, with a miserable attempt at careless ease. The clerk paused, and inspected me in the compassionate way in which one inspects a respectable person who is found in doubtful circumstances; then he said,—

"It's all right; I know what sort of a room you want. Used to clerk at the St. James, in New York."

An unpromising beginning for a fraudulent career. We started to the supper room, and met two other men whom I had known elsewhere. How odd and unfair it is: wicked impostors go around lecturing under my *nom de guerre*, and nobody suspects them; but when an honest man attempts an imposture, he is exposed at once.

One thing seemed plain: we must start down the river the next day, if people who could not be deceived were going to crop up at this rate: an unpalatable disappointment, for we had hoped to have a week in St. Louis. The Southern was a good hotel, and we could have had a comfortable time there. It is large, and well conducted, and its decorations do not make one cry, as do those of the vast Palmer House, in Chicago. True, the billiard-tables were of the Old Silurian Period, and the cues and balls of the Post-Pliocene; but there was refreshment in this, not discomfort; for there is rest and healing in the contemplation of antiquities.

The most notable absence observable in the billiard room, was the absence of the river man. If he was there he had taken in his sign, he was in disguise. I saw there none of the swell airs and graces, and ostentatious displays of money, and pompous squanderings of it, which used to distinguish the steamboat crowd from the dry-land crowd in the bygone days, in the thronged billiard-rooms of St. Louis. In those times, the principal saloons were always populous with river men; given fifty players present, thirty or thirty-five were likely to be from the river. But I suspected that the ranks were thin now, and the steamboatmen no longer an aristocracy. Why, in my time they used to call the "barkeep" Bill, or Joe, or Tom, and slap him on the shoulder; I watched for that. But none of these people did it. Manifestly a glory that once was had dissolved and vanished away in these twenty-one years.

When I went up to my room, I found there the young man called Rogers, crying. Rogers was not his name; neither was Jones, Brown, Dexter, Ferguson, Bascom, nor Thompson; but he answered to either of these that a body found handy in an emergency; or to any other name, in fact, if he perceived that you meant him. He said:—

"What is a person to do here when he wants a drink of water?—drink this slush?"

"Can't you drink it?"

"I could if I had some other water to wash it with."

Here was a thing which had not changed; a score of years had not affected this water's mulatto complexion in the least; a score of centuries would succeed no better, perhaps. It comes out of the turbulent, bank-caving Missouri, and every tumblerful of it holds nearly an acre of land in solution. I got this fact from the bishop of the diocese. If you will let your glass stand half an hour, you can separate the land from the water as easy as Genesis; and then you will find them both good: the one good to eat, the other good to drink. The land is very nourishing, the water is thoroughly wholesome. The one appeases hunger; the other, thirst. But the natives do not take them separately, but together, as nature mixed them. When they find an inch of mud in the bottom of a glass, they stir it up, and then take the draught as they would gruel. It is difficult for a stranger to get used to this batter, but once used to it he will prefer it to water. This is really the case. It is good for steamboating, and good to drink; but it is worthless for all other purposes, except baptizing.

Next morning, we drove around town in the rain. The city seemed but little changed. It *was* greatly changed, but it did not seem so; because in St. Louis, as in London and Pittsburgh, you can't persuade a new thing to look new; the coal smoke turns it into an antiquity the moment you take your hand off it. The place had just about doubled its size, since I was a resident of it, and was now become a city of 400,000 inhabitants; still, in the solid business parts, it looked about as it had looked formerly. Yet I am sure there is not as much smoke in St. Louis now as there used to be. The smoke used to bank itself in a dense billowy black canopy over the town, and hide the sky from view. This shelter is very much thinner now; still, there is a sufficiency of smoke there, I think. I heard no complaint.

However, on the outskirts changes were apparent enough; notably in dwelling-house architecture. The fine new homes are noble and beautiful and modern. They stand by themselves, too, with green lawns around them; whereas the dwellings of a former day are packed together in blocks, and are all of one pattern, with windows all alike, set in an arched frame-work of twisted stone; a sort of house which was handsome enough when it was rarer.

There was another change—the Forest Park. This was new to

me. It is beautiful and very extensive, and has the excellent merit of having been made mainly by nature. There are other parks, and fine ones, notably Tower Grove and the Botanical Gardens; for St. Louis interested herself in such improvements at an earlier day than did the most of our cities.

The first time I ever saw St. Louis, I could have bought it for six million dollars, and it was the mistake of my life that I did not do it. It was bitter now to look abroad over this domed and steepled metropolis, this solid expanse of bricks and mortar stretching away on every hand into dim, measure-defying distances, and remember that I had allowed that opportunity to go by. Why I should have allowed it to go by seems, of course, foolish and inexplicable to-day, at a first glance; yet there were reasons at the time to justify this course.

A Scotchman, Hon. Charles Augustus Murray, writing some forty-five or fifty years ago, said: "The streets are narrow, ill paved and ill lighted." Those streets are narrow still, of course; many of them are ill paved yet; but the reproach of ill lighting cannot be repeated, now. The "Catholic New Church" was the only notable building then, and Mr. Murray was confidently called upon to admire it, with its "species of Grecian portico, surmounted by a kind of steeple, much too diminutive in its proportions, and surmounted by sundry ornaments" which the unimaginative Scotchman found himself "quite unable to describe;" and therefore was grateful when a German tourist helped him out with the exclamation: "By—, they look exactly like bed-posts!" St. Louis is well equipped with stately and noble public buildings now, and the little church, which the people used to be so proud of, lost its importance a long time ago. Still, this would not surprise Mr. Murray, if he could come back; for he prophesied the coming greatness of St. Louis with strong confidence.

The further we drove in our inspection-tour, the more sensibly I realized how the city had grown since I had seen it last; changes in detail became steadily more apparent and frequent than at first, too: changes uniformly evidencing progress, energy, prosperity.

But the change of changes was on the "levee." This time, a departure from the rule. Half a dozen sound-asleep steamboats where I used to see a solid mile of wide-awake ones! This was melancholy, this was woful. The absence of the pervading and jocund steamboatman from the billiard-saloon was explained. He was absent because he is no more. His occupation is gone, his power has passed away, he is absorbed into the common herd, he grinds at the mill, a shorn Samson and inconspicuous. Half a dozen lifeless steamboats, a mile of empty wharves, a negro fatigued with whiskey stretched asleep, in a wide and soundless vacancy, where the serried hosts of commerce used to contend!* Here was desolation, indeed.

> "The old, old sea, as one in tears,
> Comes murmuring, with foamy lips,
> And knocking at the vacant pipers,
> Calls for his long-lost multitude of shops."

The towboat and the railroad had done their work, and done it well and completely. The mighty bridge, stretching along over our heads, had done its share in the slaughter and spoliation. Remains of former steamboatmen told me, with wan satisfaction, that the bridge doesn't pay. Still, it can be no sufficient compensation to a corpse, to know that the dynamite that laid him out was not of as good quality as it had been supposed to be.

The pavements along the river front were bad; the sidewalks were rather out of repair; there was a rich abundance of mud. All this was familiar and satisfying; but the ancient armies of drays, and struggling throngs of men, and mountains of freight, were gone; and Sabbath reigned in their stead. The immemorial mile of cheap foul doggeries remained, but business was dull with them; the multitudes of poison-swilling Irishmen had departed, and in their places were a few scattering handfuls of ragged negroes, some drinking, some drunk, some nodding, others asleep. St. Louis is a great and prosperous and advancing city; but the river-edge of it seems dead past resurrection.

Mississippi steamboating was born about 1812; at the end of thirty years, it had grown to mighty proportions; and in less than thirty more, it was dead! A strangely short life for so majestic a creature. Of course it is not absolutely dead; neither is a crippled octogenarian who could once jump twenty-two feet on level ground; but as contrasted with what it was in its prime vigor, Mississippi steamboating may be called dead.

It killed the old-fashioned keel-boating, by reducing the freight-trip to New Orleans to less than a week. The railroads have killed the steamboat passenger traffic by doing in two or three days what the steamboats consumed a week in doing; and the towing-fleets have killed the through-freight traffic by dragging six or seven steamer-loads of stuff down the river at a time, at an expense so trivial that steamboat competition was out of the question.

---

* Capt. Marryat, writing forty-five years ago, says: "St. Louis has 20,000 inhabitants. The *river abreast of the town is crowded with steamboats, lying in two or three tiers.*"

Freight and passenger way-traffic remains to the steamers. This is in the hands—along the two thousand miles of river between St. Paul and New Orleans—of two or three close corporations well fortified with capital; and by able and thoroughly business-like management and system, these make a sufficiency of money out of what is left of the once prodigious steamboating industry. I suppose that St. Louis and New Orleans have not suffered materially by the change, but alas for the wood-yard man!

He used to fringe the river all the way; his close-ranked merchandise stretched from the one city to the other, along the banks, and he sold uncountable cords of it every year for cash on the nail; but all the scattering boats that are left burn coal now, and the seldomest spectacle on the Mississippi to-day is a wood-pile. Where now is the once wood-yard man?

CHAPTER XXIII

TRAVELLING INCOGNITO

My idea was, to tarry a while in every town between St. Louis and New Orleans. To do this, it would be necessary to go from place to place by the short packet lines. It was an easy plan to make, and would have been an easy one to follow, twenty years ago—but not now. There are wide intervals between boats, these days.

I wanted to begin with the interesting old French settlements of St. Genevieve and Kaskaskia, sixty miles below St. Louis. There was only one boat advertised for that section—a Grand Tower packet. Still, one boat was enough; so we went down to look at her. She was a venerable rack-heap, and a fraud to boot; for she was playing herself for personal property, whereas the good honest dirt was so thickly caked all over her that she was righteously taxable as real estate. There are places in New England where her hurricane deck would be worth a hundred and fifty dollars an acre. The soil on her forecastle was quite good—the new crop of wheat was already springing from the cracks in protected places. The companionway was of a dry sandy character, and would have been well suited for grapes, with a southern exposure and a little subsoiling. The soil of the boiler deck was thin and rocky, but good enough for grazing purposes. A colored boy was on watch here—nobody else visible. We gathered from him that this calm craft would go, as advertised, "if she got her trip;" if she didn't get it, she would wait for it.

"Has she got any of her trip?"

319

"Bless you, no, boss. She ain't unloadened, yit. She only come in dis mawnin'."

He was uncertain as to when she might get her trip, but thought it might be to-morrow or maybe next day. This would not answer at all; so we had to give up the novelty of sailing down the river on a farm. We had one more arrow in our quiver: a Vicksburg packet, the "Gold Dust," was to leave at 5 P.M. We took passage in her for Memphis, and gave up the idea of stopping off here and there, as being impracticable. She was neat, clean, and comfortable. We camped on the boiler deck, and bought some cheap literature to kill time with. The vender was a venerable Irishman with a benevolent face and a tongue that worked easily in the socket, and from him we learned that he had lived in St. Louis thirty-four years and had never been across the river during that period. Then he wandered into a very flowing lecture, filled with classic names and allusions, which was quite wonderful for fluency until the fact became rather apparent that this was not the first time, nor perhaps the fiftieth, that the speech had been delivered. He was a good deal of a character, and much better company than the sappy literature he was selling. A random remark, connecting Irishmen and beer, brought this nugget of information out of him:—

"They don't drink it, sir. They *can't* drink it, sir. Give an Irishman lager for a month, and he's a dead man. An Irishman is lined with copper, and the beer corrodes it. But whiskey polishes the copper and is the saving of him, sir."

At eight o'clock, promptly, we backed out and—crossed the river. As we crept toward the shore, in the thick darkness, a blinding glory of white electric light burst suddenly from our forecastle, and lit up the water and the warehouses as with a noon-day glare. Another big change, this,—no more flickering, smoky, pitch-dripping, ineffectual torch-baskets, now: their day is past. Next, instead of calling out a score of hands to man the stage, a couple of men and a hatful of steam lowered it from the derrick where it was suspended, launched it, deposited it in just the right spot, and the whole thing was over and done-with before a mate in the olden time could have got his profanity-mill adjusted to begin the preparatory services. Why this new and simple method of handling the stages was not thought of when the first steamboat was built, is a mystery which helps one to realize what a dull-witted slug the average human being is.

We finally got away at two in the morning, and when I turned out at six, we were rounding to at a rocky point where there was an old stone warehouse—at any rate, the ruins of it; two or three decayed dwelling-houses were near by, in the shelter of the leafy hills; but there were no evidences of human or other animal life to be seen. I wondered if I had forgotten the river; for I had no recollection whatever of this place; the shape of the river, too, was unfamiliar; there was nothing in sight, anywhere, that I could remember ever having seen before. I was surprised, disappointed, and annoyed.

We put ashore a well-dressed lady and gentleman, and two well-dressed, lady-like young girls, together with sundry Russia-leather bags. A strange place for such folk! No carriage was waiting. The party moved off as if they had not expected any, and struck down a winding country road afoot.

But the mystery was explained when we got under way again; for these people were evidently bound for a large town which lay shut in behind a tow-head (*i.e.*, new island) a couple of miles below this landing. I couldn't remember that town; I couldn't place it, couldn't call its name. So I lost part of my temper. I suspected that it might be St. Genevieve—and so it proved to be. Observe what this eccentric river had been about: it had built up this huge useless tow-head directly in front of this town, cut off its river communications, fenced it away completely, and made a ''country'' town of it. It is a fine old place, too, and deserved a better fate. It was settled by the French, and is a relic of a time when one could travel from the mouths of the Mississippi to Quebec and be on French territory and under French rule all the way.

Presently I ascended to the hurricane deck and cast a longing glance toward the pilot-house.

CHAPTER XXIV

MY INCOGNITO IS EXPLODED

After a close study of the face of the pilot on watch, I was satisfied that I had never seen him before; so I went up there. The pilot inspected me; I re-inspected the pilot. These customary preliminaries over, I sat down on the high bench, and he faced about and went on with his work. Every detail of the pilot-house was familiar to me, with one exception,—a large-mouthed tube under the breast-board. I puzzled over that thing a considerable time; then gave up and asked what it was for.

"To hear the engine-bells through."

It was another good contrivance which ought to have been invented half a century sooner. So I was thinking, when the pilot asked,—

"Do you know what this rope is for?"

I managed to get around this question, without committing myself.

"Is this the first time you were ever in a pilot-house?"

I crept under that one.

"Where are you from?"

"New England."

"First time you have ever been West?"

I climbed over this one.

"If you take an interest in such things, I can tell you what all these things are for."

I said I should like it.

"This," putting his hand on a backing-bell rope, "is to sound the fire-alarm; this," putting his hand on a go-a-head bell, "is to call the texas-tender; this one," indicating the whistle-lever, "is to call the captain"—and so he went on, touching one object after another, and reeling off his tranquil spool of lies.

I had never felt so like a passenger before. I thanked him, with emotion, for each new fact, and wrote it down in my note-book. The pilot warmed to his opportunity, and proceeded to load me up in the good old-fashioned way. At times I was afraid he was going to rupture his invention; but it always stood the strain, and he pulled through all right. He drifted, by easy stages, into revealments of the river's marvellous eccentricities of one sort and another, and backed them up with some pretty gigantic illustrations. For instance,—

"Do you see that little bowlder sticking out of the water yonder? well, when I first came on the river, that was a solid ridge of rock, over sixty feet high and two miles long. All washed away but that." [This with a sigh.]

I had a mighty impulse to destroy him, but it seemed to me that killing, in any ordinary way, would be too good for him.

Once, when an odd-looking craft, with a vast coal-scuttle slanting aloft on the end of a beam, was steaming by in the distance, he indifferently drew attention to it, as one might to an object grown wearisome through familiarity, and observed that it was an "alligator boat."

"An alligator boat? What's it for?"

"To dredge out alligators with."

"Are they so thick as to be troublesome?"

"Well, not now, because the government keeps them down. But they used to be. Not everywhere; but in favorite places, here and there, where the river is wide and shoal—like Plum Point, and Stack Island, and so on—places they call alligator beds."

"Did they actually impede navigation?"

"Years ago, yes, in very low water; there was hardly a trip, then, that we didn't get aground on alligators."

It seemed to me that I should certainly have to get out my tomahawk. However, I restrained myself and said,—

"It must have been dreadful."

"Yes, it was one of the main difficulties about piloting. It was so hard to tell anything about the water; the damned things shift around so—never lie still five minutes at a time. You can tell a wind-reef, straight off, by the look of it; you can tell a break; you can tell a sand-reef—that's all easy; but an alligator reef doesn't show up, worth anything. Nine times in ten you can't tell where the water is; and when you *do* see where it is, like as not it ain't there when *you* get there, the devils have swapped around so, meantime. Of course there were some few pilots that could judge of alligator water nearly as well as they could of any other kind, but they had to have natural talent for it; it wasn't a thing a body could *learn*, you had to be born with it. Let me see: there was Ben Thornburg, and Beck Jolly, and Squire Bell, and Horace Bixby, and Major Downing, and John Stevenson, and Billy Gordon, and Jim Brady, and George Ealer, and Billy Youngblood— all A 1 alligator pilots. *They* could tell alligator water as far as another Christian could tell whiskey. Read it?—Ah, *couldn't* they, though! I only wish I had as many dollars as they could read alligator water a mile and a half off. Yes, and it paid them to do it, too. A good alligator pilot could always get fifteen hundred dollars a month. Nights, other people had to lay up for alligators, but those fellows never laid up for alligators; they never laid up for anything but fog. They could *smell* the best alligator water—so it was said; I don't know whether it was so or not, and I think a body's got his hands full enough if he sticks to just what he knows himself, without going around backing up other people's say-so's, though there's a plenty that ain't backward about doing it, as long as they can roust out something wonderful to tell. Which is not the style of Robert Styles, by as much as three fathom—maybe quarter-*less*."

[My! Was this Rob Styles?—This moustached and stately figure?—A slim enough cub, in my time. How he has improved in comeliness in five and twenty years—and in the noble art of inflating his facts.] After these musings, I said aloud,—

"I should think that dredging out the alligators wouldn't have done much good, because they could come back again right away."

"If you had had as much experience of alligators as I have, you wouldn't talk like that. You dredge an alligator once and he's *convinced*. It's the last you hear of *him*. He wouldn't come back for pie. If there's one thing that an alligator is more down on than another, it's being dredged. Besides, they were not simply shoved out of the way; the most of the scoopful were scooped aboard; they emptied them into the hold; and when they had got a trip, they took them to Orleans to the Government works."

"What for?"

"Why, to make soldier-shoes out of their hides. All the Government shoes are made of alligator hide. It makes the best shoes in the world. They last five years, and they won't absorb water. The alligator fishery is a Government monopoly. All the alligators are Government property—just like the live-oaks. You cut down a live-oak, and Government fines you fifty dollars; you kill an alligator, and up you go for misprision of treason—lucky duck if they don't hang you, too. And they will, if you're a Democrat. The buzzard is the sacred bird of the South, and you can't touch him; the alligator is the sacred bird of the Government, and you've got to let him alone."

"Do you ever get aground on the alligators now?"

"Oh, no! it hasn't happened for years."

"Well, then, why do they still keep the alligator boats in service?"

"Just for police duty—nothing more. They merely go up and down now and then. The present generation of alligators know them as easy as a burglar knows a roundsman; when they see one coming, they break camp and go for the woods."

After rounding-out and finishing-up and polishing-off the alligator business, he dropped easily and comfortably into the historical vein, and told of some tremendous feats of half a dozen old-time steamboats of his acquaintance, dwelling at special length upon a certain extraordinary performance of his chief favorite among this distinguished fleet—and then adding:—

"That boat was the 'Cyclone,'—last trip she ever made—she sunk, that very trip—captain was Tom Ballou, the most immortal liar that ever I struck. He couldn't ever seem to tell the truth, in *any* kind of weather. Why, he would make you fairly shudder. He *was* the most scandalous liar! I left him, finally; I couldn't stand it. The proverb says, 'like master, like man;' and if you stay with that kind of a man, you'll come under suspicion by and by, just as sure as you live. He paid first-class wages; but said I, What's wages when your reputation's in danger? So I let the wages go, and froze to my reputation. And I've never regretted it. Reputation's worth everything, ain't it? That's the way I look at it. He had more selfish organs than any seven men in the world—all packed in the stern-sheets of his skull, of course, where they belonged. They weighed down the back of his head so that it made his nose tilt up in the air. People thought it was vanity, but it wasn't, it was malice. If you only saw his foot, you'd take him to be nineteen feet high, but he wasn't; it was because his foot was out of drawing. He was intended to be nineteen feet high, no doubt, if his foot was made first, but he didn't get there; he was only five feet ten. That's what he was, and what's what he is. You take the lies out of him, and he'll shrink to the size of your hat; you take the malice out of him, and he'll disappear. That 'Cyclone' was a rattler to go, and the sweetest thing to steer that ever walked the waters. Set her amidships, in a big river, and just let her go; it was all you had to do. She would hold herself on a star all night, if you let her alone. You couldn't ever feel her rudder. It wasn't any more labor to steer her than it is to count the Republican vote in a South Carolina election. One morning, just at daybreak, the last trip she ever made, they took her rudder aboard to mend it; I didn't know anything about it; I backed her out from the wood-yard and went a- weaving down the river all serene. When I had gone about twenty-three miles, and made four horribly crooked crossings—"

"Without any rudder?"

"Yes—old Capt. Tom appeared on the roof and began to find fault with me for running such a dark night—"

"Such a *dark night*?—Why, you said—"

"Never mind what I said,—'twas as dark as Egypt *now*, though pretty soon the moon began to rise, and—"

"You mean the *sun*—because you started out just at break of—look here! Was this *before* you quitted the captain on account of his lying, or—"

"It was before—oh, a long time before. And as I was saying, he—"

"But was this the trip she sunk, or was—"

"Oh, no!—months afterward. And so the old man, he—"

"Then she made *two* last trips, because you said—"

He stepped back from the wheel, swabbing away his perspiration, and said—

"Here!" (calling me by name), "*you* take her and lie a while—you're handier at it than I am. Trying to play yourself for a stranger and an innocent!—why, I knew you before you had spoken seven words; and I made up my mind to find out what was your little game. It was to *draw me out*. Well, I let you, didn't I? Now take the wheel and finish the watch; and next time play fair, and you won't have to work your passage."

Thus ended the fictitious-name business. And not six hours

out from St. Louis! but I had gained a privilege, anyway, for I had been itching to get my hands on the wheel, from the beginning. I seemed to have forgotten the river, but I hadn't forgotten how to steer a steamboat, nor how to enjoy it, either.

CHAPTER XXV

FROM CAIRO TO HICKMAN

The scenery, from St. Louis to Cairo—two hundred miles—is varied and beautiful. The hills were clothed in the fresh foliage of spring now, and were a gracious and worthy setting for the broad river flowing between. Our trip began auspiciously, with a perfect day, as to breeze and sunshine, and our boat threw the miles out behind her with satisfactory despatch.

We found a railway intruding at Chester, Illinois; Chester has also a penitentiary now, and is otherwise marching on. At Grand Tower, too, there was a railway; and another at Cape Girardeau. The former town gets its name from a huge, squat pillar of rock, which stands up out of the water on the Missouri side of the river—a piece of nature's fanciful handiwork—and is one of the most picturesque features of the scenery of that region. For nearer or remoter neighbors, the Tower has the Devil's Bake Oven—so called, perhaps, because it does not powerfully resemble anybody else's bake oven; and the Devil's Tea Table—this latter a great smooth-surfaced mass of rock, with diminishing wine-glass stem, perched some fifty or sixty feet above the river, beside a beflowered and garlanded precipice, and sufficiently like a tea-table to answer for anybody, Devil or Christian. Away down the river we have the Devil's Elbow and the Devil's Race-course, and lots of other property of his which I cannot now call to mind.

The Town of Grand Tower was evidently a busier place than it had been in old times, but it seemed to need some repairs here and there, and a new coat of whitewash all over. Still, it was pleasant to me to see the old coat once more. "Uncle" Mumford, our second officer, said the place had been suffering from high water and consequently was not looking its best now. But he said it was not strange that it didn't waste whitewash on itself, for more lime was made there, and of a better quality, than anywhere in the West; and added,—"On a dairy farm you never can get any milk for your coffee, nor any sugar for it on a sugar plantation; and it is against sense to go to a lime town to hunt for whitewash." In my own experience I knew the first two items to be true; and also that people who sell candy don't care for candy; therefore there was plausibility in Uncle Mumford's final observation that "people who make lime run more to religion than whitewash." Uncle Mumford said, further, that Grand Tower was a great coaling centre and a prospering place.

Cape Girardeau is situated on a hillside, and makes a handsome appearance. There is a great Jesuit school for boys at the foot of the town by the river. Uncle Mumford said it had as high a reputation for thoroughness as any similar institution in Missouri. There was another college higher up on an airy summit,—a bright new edifice, picturesquely and peculiarly towered and pinnacled—a sort of gigantic casters, with the cruets all complete. Uncle Mumford said that Cape Girardeau was the Athens of Missouri, and contained several colleges besides those already mentioned; and all of them on a religious basis of one kind or another. He directed my attention to what he called the "strong and pervasive religious look of the town," but I could not see that it looked more religious than the other hill towns with the same slope and built of the same kind of bricks. Partialities often make people see more than really exists.

Uncle Mumford has been thirty years a mate on the river. He is a man of practical sense and a level head; has observed; has had much experience of one sort and another; has opinions; has, also, just a perceptible dash of poetry in his composition, an easy gift of speech, a thick growl in his voice, and an oath or two where he can get at them when the exigencies of his office require a spiritual lift. He is a mate of the blessed old-time kind; and goes gravely damning around, when there is work to the fore, in a way to mellow the ex-steamboatman's heart with sweet soft longings for the vanished days that shall come no more. "*Git* up, there,—— —you! Going to be all day? Why d'n't you *say* you was petrified in your hind legs, before you shipped!"

He is a steady man with his crew; kind and just, but firm; so they like him, and stay with him. He is still in the slouchy garb of the old generation of mates; but next trip the Anchor Line will have him in uniform—a natty blue naval uniform, with brass buttons, along with all the officers of the line—and then he will be a totally different style of scenery from what he is now.

Uniforms on the Mississippi! It beats all the other changes put together, for surprise. Still, there is another surprise—that it was not made fifty years ago. It is so manifestly sensible, that it might have been thought of earlier, one would suppose. During fifty years, out there, the innocent passenger in need of help and information, has been mistaking the mate for the cook, and the captain for the barber—and being roughly entertained for it, too. But his troubles are ended now. And the greatly improved aspect of the boat's staff is another advantage achieved by the dress-reform period.

Steered down the bend below Cape Girardeau. They used to call it "Steersman's Bend;" plain sailing and plenty of water in it, always; about the only place in the Upper River, that a new cub was allowed to take a boat through, in low water.

Thebes, at the head of the Grand Chain, and Commerce at the foot of it, were towns easily rememberable, as they had not undergone conspicuous alteration. Nor the Chain, either—in the nature of things; for it is a chain of sunken rocks admirably arranged to capture and kill steamboats on bad nights. A good many steamboat corpses lie buried there, out of sight; among the rest my first friend the "Paul Jones;" she knocked her bottom out, and went down like a pot, so the historian told me—Uncle Mumford. He said she had a gray mare aboard, and a preacher. To me, this sufficiently accounted for the disaster; as it did, of course to Mumford, who added,—"But there are many ignorant people who would scoff at such a matter, and call it superstition. But you will always notice that they are people who have never travelled with a gray mare and a preacher. I went down the river once in such company. We grounded at Bloody Island; we grounded at Hanging Dog; we grounded just below this same Commerce; we jolted Beaver Dam Rock; we hit one of the worst breaks in the 'Graveyard' behind Goose Island; we had a roustabout killed in a fight; we burnt a boiler; broke a shaft; collapsed a flue; and went into Cairo with nine feet of water in the hold— may have been more, may have been less. I remember it as if it were yesterday. The men lost their heads with terror. They painted the mare blue, in sight of town, and threw the preacher overboard, or we should not have arrived at all. The preacher was fished out and saved. He acknowledged, himself, that he had been to blame. I remember it all, as if it were yesterday."

That this combination—of preacher and gray mare—should breed calamity, seems strange, and at first glance unbelievable; but the fact is fortified by so much unassailable proof that to doubt is to dishonor reason. I myself remember a cast where a captain was warned by numerous friends against taking a gray mare and a preacher with him, but persisted in his purpose in spite of all that could be said; and the same day,—it may have been the next, and some say it was, though I think it was the same day,—he got drunk and fell down the hatchway and was borne to his home a corpse. This is literally true.

No vestige of Hat Island is left now; every shred of it is

washed away. I do not even remember what part of the river it used to be in, except that it was between St. Louis and Cairo somewhere. It was a bad region—all around and about Hat Island, in early days. A farmer who lived on the Illinois shore there, said that twenty-nine steamboats had left their bones strung along within sight from his house. Between St. Louis and Cairo the steamboat wrecks average one to the mile;—two hundred wrecks, altogether.

I could recognize big changes from Commerce down. Beaver Dam Rock was out in the middle of the river now, and throwing a prodigious "break;" it used to be close to the shore, and boats went down outside of it. A big island that used to be away out in mid-river, has retired to the Missouri shore, and boats do not go near it any more. The island called Jacket Pattern is whittled down to a wedge now, and is booked for early destruction. Goose Island is all gone but a little dab the size of a steamboat. The perilous "Graveyard," among whose numberless wrecks we used to pick our way so slowly and gingerly, is far away from the channel now, and a terror to nobody. One of the islands formerly called the Two Sisters is gone entirely; the other, which used to lie close to the Illinois shore, is now on the Missouri side, a mile away; it is joined solidly to the shore, and it takes a sharp eye to see where the seam is—but it is Illinois ground yet, and the people who live on it have to ferry themselves over and work the Illinois roads and pay Illinois taxes: singular state of things!

Near the mouth of the river several islands were missing—washed away. Cairo was still there—easily visible across the long, flat point upon whose further verge it stands; but we had to steam a long way around to get to it. Night fell as we were going out of the "Upper River" and meeting the floods of the Ohio. We dashed along without anxiety; for the hidden rock which used to lie right in the way has moved up stream a long distance out of the channel; or rather, about one county has gone into the river from the Missouri point, and the Cairo point has "made down" and added to its long tongue of territory correspondingly. The Mississippi is a just and equitable river; it never tumbles one man's farm overboard without building a new farm just like it for that man's neighbor. This keeps down hard feelings.

Going into Cairo, we came near killing a steamboat which paid no attention to our whistle and then tried to cross our bows. By doing some strong backing, we saved him; which was a great loss, for he would have made good literature.

Cairo is a brisk town now; and is substantially built, and has a city look about it which is in noticeable contrast to its former estate, as per Mr. Dickens's portrait of it. However, it was already building with bricks when I had seen it last—which was when Colonel (now General) Grant was drilling his first command there. Uncle Mumford says the libraries and Sunday-schools have done a good work in Cairo, as well as the brick masons. Cairo has a heavy railroad and river trade, and her situation at the junction of the two great rivers is so advantageous that she cannot well help prospering.

When I turned out, in the morning, we had passed Columbus, Kentucky, and were approaching Hickman, a pretty town, perched on a handsome hill. Hickman is in a rich tobacco region, and formerly enjoyed a great and lucrative trade in that staple, collecting it there in her warehouses from a large area of country and shipping it by boat; but Uncle Mumford says she built a railway to facilitate this commerce a little more, and he thinks it facilitated in the wrong way—took the bulk of the trade out of her hands by "collaring it along the line without gathering it at her doors."

CHAPTER XXVI

UNDER FIRE

Talk began to run upon the war now, for we were getting down into the upper edge of the former battle-stretch by this time. Columbus was just behind us, so there was a good deal said about the famous battle of Belmont. Several of the boat's officers had seen active service in the Mississippi war-fleet. I gathered that they found themselves sadly out of their element in that kind of business at first, but afterward got accustomed to it, reconciled to it, and more or less at home in it. One of our pilots had his first war experience in the Belmont fight, as a pilot on a boat in the Confederate service. I had often had a curiosity to know how a green hand might feel, in his maiden battle, perched all solitary and alone on high in a pilot house, a target for Tom, Dick and Harry, and nobody at his elbow to shame him from showing the white feather when matters grew hot and perilous around him; so, to me his story was valuable—it filled a gap for me which all histories had left till that time empty.

THE PILOT'S FIRST BATTLE

He said:—

It was the 7th of November. The fight began at seven in the morning. I was on the "R. H. W. Hill." Took over a load of troops from Columbus. Came back, and took over a battery of artillery. My partner said he was going to see the fight; wanted me to go along. I said, no, I wasn't anxious, I would look at it from the pilot-house. He said I was a coward, and left.

That fight was an awful sight. General Cheatham made his men strip their coats off and throw them in a pile, and said, "Now follow me to hell or victory!" I heard him say that from the pilot-house; and then he galloped in, at the head of his troops. Old General Pillow, with his white hair, mounted on a white horse, sailed in, too, leading his troops as lively as a boy. By and by the Federals chased the rebels back, and here they came! tearing along, everybody for himself and Devil take the hindmost! and down under the bank they scrambled, and took shelter. I was sitting with my legs hanging out of the pilot-house window. All at once I noticed a whizzing sound passing my ear. Judged it was a bullet. I didn't stop to think about anything, I just tilted over backwards and landed on the floor, and stayed there. The balls came booming around. Three cannon-balls went through the chimney; one ball took off the corner of the pilot-house; shells were screaming and bursting all around. Mighty warm times—I wished I hadn't come. I lay there on the pilot-house floor, while the shots came faster and faster. I crept in behind the big stove, in the middle of the pilot-house. Presently a minie-ball came through the stove, and just grazed my head, and cut my hat. I judged it was time to go away from there. The captain was on the roof with a red-headed major from Memphis—a fine-looking man. I heard him say he wanted to leave here, but "that pilot is killed." I crept over to the starboard side to pull the bell to set her back; raised up and took a look, and I saw about fifteen shot holes through the window panes; had come so lively I hadn't noticed them. I glanced out on the water, and the spattering shot were like a hail-storm. I thought best to get out of that place. I went down the pilot-house guy, head first—not feet first but head first—slid down—before I struck the deck, the captain said we must leave there. So I climbed up the guy and got on the floor again. About that time, they collared my partner and were bringing him up to the pilot-house between two soldiers. Somebody had said I was killed. He put his head in and saw me on the floor reaching for the backing bells. He said, "Oh, hell, he ain't shot," and jerked away from the men who had him by the collar, and ran below. We were there until three o'clock in the afternoon, and then got away all right.

The next time I saw my partner, I said, "Now, come out, be honest, and tell me the truth. Where did you go when you went to see that battle?'' He says, ''I went down in the hold.''

All through that fight I was scared nearly to death. I hardly knew anything, I was so frightened; but you see, nobody knew that but me. Next day General Polk sent for me, and praised me for my bravery and gallant conduct. I never said anything, I let it go at that. I judged it wasn't so, but it was not for me to contradict a general officer.

Pretty soon after that I was sick, and used up, and had to go off to the Hot Springs. When there, I got a good many letters from commanders saying they wanted me to come back. I declined, because I wasn't well enough or strong enough; but I kept still, and kept the reputation I had made.

A plain story, straightforwardly told; but Mumford told me that that pilot had ''gilded that scare of his, in spots;'' that his subsequent career in the war was proof of it.

We struck down through the chute of Island No. 8, and I went below and fell into conversation with a passenger, a handsome man, with easy carriage and an intelligent face. We were approaching Island No. 10, a place so celebrated during the war. This gentleman's home was on the main shore in its neighborhood. I had some talk with him about the war times; but presently the discourse fell upon ''feuds,'' for in no part of the South has the vendetta flourished more briskly, or held out longer between warring families, than in this particular region. This gentleman said:—

''There's been more than one feud around here, in old times, but I reckon the worst one was between the Darnells and the Watsons. Nobody don't know what the first quarrel was about, it's so long ago; the Darnells and the Watsons, if there's any of them living, which I don't think there is. Some says it was about a horse or a cow—anyway, it was a little matter; the money in it wasn't of no consequence—none in the world—both families was rich. The thing could have been fixed up, easy enough; but no, that wouldn't do. Rough words had been passed; and so, nothing but blood could fix it up after that. That horse or cow, whichever it was, cost sixty years of killing and crippling! Every year or so somebody was shot, on one side or the other; and as fast as one generation was laid out, their sons took up the feud and kept it a-going. And it's just as I say; they went on shooting each other, year in and year out—making a kind of a religion of it, you see—till they'd done forgot, long ago, what it was all about. Wherever a Darnell caught a Watson, or a Watson caught a Darnell, one of 'em was going to get hurt—only question was, which of them got the drop on the other. They'd shoot one another down, right in the presence of the family. They didn't *hunt* for each other, but when they happened to meet, they pulled and begun. Men would shoot boys, boys would shoot men. A man shot a boy twelve years old—happened on him in the woods, and didn't give him no chance. If he *had* 'a' given him a chance, the boy'd 'a' shot *him*. Both families belonged to the same church (everybody around here is religious); through all this fifty or sixty years' fuss, both tribes was there every Sunday, to worship. The lived each side of the line, and the church was at a landing called Compromise. Half the church and half the aisle was in Kentucky, the other half in Tennessee. Sundays you'd see the families drive up, all in their Sunday clothes, men, women, and children, and file up the aisle, and set down, quiet and orderly, one lot on the Tennessee side of the church and the other on the Kentucky side; and the men and boys would lean their guns up against the wall, handy, and then all hands would join in with the prayer and praise; though they say the man next the aisle didn't kneel down, along with the rest of the family; kind of stood guard. I don't know; never was at that church in my life; but I remember that that's what used to be said.

"Twenty or twenty-five years ago, one of the feud families caught a young man of nineteen out and killed him. Don't remember whether it was the Darnells and Watsons, or one of the other feuds; but anyway, this young man rode up—steamboat laying there at the time—and the first thing he saw was a whole gang of the enemy. He jumped down behind a wood-pile, but they rode around and begun on him, he firing back, and they galloping and cavorting and yelling and banging away with all their might. Think he wounded a couple of them; but they closed in on him and chased him into the river; and as he swum along down stream, they followed along the bank and kept on shooting at him; and when he struck shore he was dead. Windy Marshall told me about it. He saw it. He was captain of the boat.

"Years ago, the Darnells was so thinned out that the old man and his two sons concluded they'd leave the country. They started to take steamboat just above No. 10; but the Watsons got wind of it; and they arrived just as the two young Darnells was walking up the companion-way with their wives on their arms. The fight begun then, and they never got no further—both of them killed. After that, old Darnell got into trouble with the man that run the ferry, and the ferry-man got the worst of it—and died. But his friends shot old Darnell through and through—filled him full of bullets, and ended him."

The country gentleman who told me these things had been reared in ease and comfort, was a man of good parts, and was college bred. His loose grammar was the fruit of careless habit, not ignorance. This habit among educated men in the West is not universal, but it is prevalent—prevalent in the towns, certainly, if not in the cities; and to a degree which one cannot help noticing, and marvelling at. I heard a Westerner who would be accounted a highly educated man in any country, say "never mind, it *don't make no difference,* anyway." A life-long resident who was present heard it, but it made no impression upon her. She was able to recall the fact afterward, when reminded of it; but she confessed that the words had not grated upon her ear at the time—a confession which suggests that if educated people can hear such blasphemous grammar, from such a source, and be unconscious of the deed, the crime must be tolerably common—so common that the general ear has become dulled by familiarity with it, and is no longer alert, no longer sensitive to such affronts.

No one in the world speaks blemishless grammar; no one has ever written it—*no* one, either in the world or out of it (taking the Scriptures for evidence on the latter point); therefore it would not be fair to exact grammatical perfection from the peoples of the Valley; but they and all other peoples may justly be required to refrain from *knowingly* and *purposely* debauching their grammar.

I found the river greatly changed at Island No. 10. The island which I remembered was some three miles long and a quarter of a mile wide, heavily timbered, and lay near the Kentucky shore—within two hundred yards of it, I should say. Now, however, one had to hunt for it with a spy-glass. Nothing was left of it but an insignificant little tuft, and this was no longer near the Kentucky shore; it was clear over against the opposite shore, a mile away. In war times the island had been an important place, for it commanded the situation; and, being heavily fortified, there was no getting by it. It lay between the upper and lower divisions of the Union forces, and kept them separate, until a junction was finally effected across the Missouri neck of land; but the island being itself joined to that neck now, the wide river is without obstruction.

In this region the river passes from Kentucky into Tennessee, back into Missouri, then back into Kentucky, and thence into Tennessee again. So a mile or two of Missouri sticks over into Tennessee.

The town of New Madrid was looking very unwell; but otherwise unchanged from its former condition and aspect. Its blocks of frame-houses were still grouped in the same old flat plain, and environed by the same old forests. It was as tranquil as formerly, and apparently had neither grown nor diminished in size. It was said that the recent high water had invaded it and damaged its looks. This was surprising news; for in low water the river bank is very high there (fifty feet), and in my day an overflow had always been considered an impossibility. This present flood of 1882 will doubtless be celebrated in the river's history for several generations before a deluge of like magnitude shall be seen. It put all the unprotected low lands under water, from Cairo to the mouth; it broke down the levees in a great many places, on both sides of the river; and in some regions south when the flood was at its highest, the Mississippi was *seventy miles* wide! a number of lives were lost, and the destruction of property was fearful. The crops were destroyed, houses washed away, and shelterless men and cattle forced to take refuge on scattering elevations here and there in field and forest, and wait in peril and suffering until the boats put in commission by the national and local governments and by newspaper enterprise could come and rescue them. The properties of multitudes of people were under water for months, and the poorer ones must have starved by the hundred if succor had not been promptly afforded.* The water had been falling during a considerable time now, yet as a rule we found the banks still under water.

CHAPTER XXVII

SOME IMPORTED ARTICLES

We met two steamboats at New Madrid. Two steamboats in sight at once! an infrequent spectacle now in the lonesome Mississippi. The loneliness of this solemn, stupendous flood is impressive—and depressing. League after league, and still league after league, it pours its chocolate tide along, between its solid forest walls, its almost untenanted shores, with seldom a sail or a moving object of any kind to disturb the surface and break the monotony of the blank, watery solitude; and so the day goes, the night comes, and again the day—and still the same, night after night and day after day,—majestic, unchanging sameness of serenity, repose, tranquillity, lethargy, vacancy,—symbol of eternity, realization of the heaven pictured

* For a detailed and interesting description of the great flood, written on board of the New Orleans "Times-Democrat's" relief-boat, see Appendix A.

by priest and prophet, and longed for by the good and thoughtless!

Immediately after the war of 1812, tourists began to come to America, from England; scattering ones at first, then a sort of procession of them—a procession which kept up its plodding, patient march through the land during many, many years. Each tourist took notes, and went home and published a book—a book which was usually calm, truthful, reasonable, kind; but which seemed just the reverse to our tender-footed progenitors. A glance at these tourist-books shows us that in certain of its aspects the Mississippi has undergone no change since those strangers visited it, but remains to-day about as it was then. The emotions produced in those foreign breasts by these aspects were not all formed on one pattern, of course; they *had* to be various, along at first, because the earlier tourists were obliged to originate their emotions, whereas in older countries one can always borrow emotions from one's predecessors. And, mind you, emotions are among the toughest things in the world to manufacture out of whole cloth; it is easier to manufacture seven facts than one emotion. Captain Basil Hall, R. N., writing fifty-five years ago, says:—

"Here I caught the first glimpse of the object I had so long wished to behold, and felt myself amply repaid at that moment for all the trouble I had experienced in coming so far; and stood looking at the river flowing past till it was too dark to distinguish anything. But it was not till I had visited the same spot a dozen times, that I came to a right comprehension of the grandeur of the scene."

Following are Mrs. Trollope's emotions. She is writing a few months later in the same year, 1827, and is coming in at the mouth of the Mississippi:—

"The first indication of our approach to land was the appearance of this mighty river pouring forth its muddy mass of waters, and mingling with the deep blue of the Mexican Gulf. I never beheld a scene so utterly desolate as this entrance of the Mississippi. Had Dante seen it, he might have drawn images of another Bolgia from its horrors. Only one object rears itself above the eddying waters; this is the mast of a vessel long since wrecked in attempting to cross the bar, and it still stands, a dismal witness of the destruction that has been, and a boding prophet of that which is to come."

Emotions of Hon. Charles Augustus Murray (near St. Louis), seven years later:—

336

"It is only when you ascend the mighty current for fifty or a hundred miles, and use the eye of imagination as well as that of nature, that you begin to understand all his might and majesty. You see him fertilizing a boundless valley, bearing along in his course the trophies of his thousand victories over the shattered forest—here carrying away large masses of soil with all their growth, and there forming islands, destined at some future period to be the residence of man; and while indulging in this prospect, it is then time for reflection to suggest that the current before you has flowed through two or three thousand miles, and has yet to travel one thousand three hundred more before reaching its ocean destination."

Receive, now, the emotions of Captain Marryat, R. N. author of the sea tales, writing in 1837, three years after Mr. Murray:—

"Never, perhaps, in the records of nations, was there an instance of a century of such unvarying and unmitigated crime as is to be collected from the history of the turbulent and blood-stained Mississippi. The stream itself appears as if appropriate for the deeds which have been committed. It is not like most rivers, beautiful to the sight, bestowing fertility in its course; not one that the eye loves to dwell upon as it sweeps along, nor can you wander upon its bank, or trust yourself without danger to its stream. It is a furious, rapid, desolating torrent, loaded with alluvial soil; and few of those who are received into its waters ever rise again,* or can support themselves long upon its surface without assistance from some friendly log. It contains the coarsest and most uneatable of fish, such as the cat-fish and such genus, and as you descend, its banks are occuped with the fetid alligator, while the panther basks as its edge in the cane-brakes, almost impervious to man. Pouring its impetuous waters through wild tracks covered with trees of little value except for firewood, it sweeps down whole forests in its course, which disappear in tumultuous confusion, whirled away by the stream now loaded with the masses of soil which nourished their roots, often blocking up and changing for a time the channel of the river, which, as if in anger at its being opposed, inundates and devastates the whole country round; and as soon as it forces its way through its former channel, plants in every direction the uprooted monarchs of the forest (upon whose branches the bird will never again perch, or the raccoon, the opossum, or the squirrel climb) as traps to the adventurous navigators of its waters by steam, who, borne down upon these concealed dangers which pierce through the planks, very often have not time to steer for and gain the shore before they sink to the bottom. There are no pleasing associations connected with the great common sewer of the Western America, which pours out its mud into the Mexican Gulf, polluting the clear blue sea for many miles beyond its mouth. It is a river of desolation; and instead of reminding you, like other beautiful rivers, of an angel which has descended for the benefit of

* There was a foolish superstition of some little prevalence in that day, that the Mississippi would neither buoy up a swimmer, nor permit a drowned person's body to rise to the surface.

man, you imagine it a devil, whose energies have been only overcome by the wonderful power of steam."

It is pretty crude literature for a man accustomed to handling a pen; still, as a panorama of the emotions sent weltering through this noted visitor's breast by the aspect and traditions of the "great common sewer," it has a value. A value, though marred in the matter of statistics by inaccuracies; for the catfish is a plenty good enough fish for anybody, and there are no panthers that are "impervious to man."

Later still comes Alexander Mackay, of the Middle Temple, Barrister at Law, with a better digestion, and no catfish dinner aboard, and feels as follows:—

"The Mississippi! It was with indescribable emotions that I first felt myself afloat upon its waters. How often in my school-boy dreams, and in my waking visions afterwards, had my imagination pictured to itself the lordly stream, rolling with tumultuous current through the boundless region to which it has given its name, and gathering into itself, in its course to the ocean, the tributary waters of almost every latitude in the temperate zone! Here it was then in its reality, and I, at length, steaming against its tide. I looked upon it with that reverence with which every one must regard a great feature of external nature."

So much for the emotions. The tourists, one and all, remark upon the deep, brooding loneliness and desolation of the vast river. Captain Basil Hall, who saw it at floodstage, says:—

"Sometimes we passed along distances of twenty or thirty miles without seeing a single habitation. An artist, in search of hints for a painting of the deluge, would here have found them in abundance."

The first shall be last, etc. Just two hundred years ago, the old original first and gallantest of all the foreign tourists, pioneer, head of the procession, ended his weary and tedious discovery-voyage down the solemn stretches of the great river—La Salle, whose name will last as long as the river itself shall last. We quote from Mr. Parkman:—

"And now they neared their journey's end. On the sixth of April, the river divided itself into three broad channels. La Salle followed that of the west, and D'Autray that of the east; while Tonty took the middle passage. As he drifted down the turbid current, between the low and marshy shores, the brackish water changed to brine, and the breeze grew fresh with the salt breath of the sea. Then the broad bosom of the great Gulf opened on his sight, tossing its restless billows, limitless, voiceless, lonely as when born of chaos, without a sail, without a sign of life."

338

Then, on a spot of solid ground, La Salle reared a column "bearing the arms of France; the Frenchmen were mustered under arms; and while the New England Indians and their squaws looked on in wondering silence, they chanted the *Te Deum,* the *Exaudiat,* and the *Domine salvum fac regem."*

Then, whilst the musketry volleyed and rejoicing shouts burst forth, the victorious discoverer planted the column, and made proclamation in a loud voice, taking formal possession of the river and the vast countries watered by it, in the name of the King. The column bore this inscription:—

LOUIS LE GRAND, ROY DE FRANCE ET DE NAVARRE, REGNE;
LE NEUVIEME AVRIL, 1682.

New Orleans intended to fittingly celebrate, this present year, the bicentennial anniversary of this illustrious event; but when the time came, all her energies and surplus money were required in other directions, for the flood was upon the land then, making havoc and devastation everywhere.

CHAPTER XXVIII

UNCLE MUMFORD UNLOADS

All day we swung along down the river, and had the stream almost wholly to ourselves. Formerly, at such a stage of the water, we should have passed acres of lumber rafts, and dozens of big coal barges; also occasional little trading-scows, peddling along from farm to farm, with the pedler's family on board; possibly, a random scow, bearing a humble Hamlet and Co. on an itinerant dramatic trip. But these were all absent. Far along in the day, we saw one steamboat; just one, and no more. She was lying at rest in the shade, within the wooded mouth of the Obion River. The spy-glass revealed the fact that she was named for me—or *he* was named for me, whichever you prefer. As this was the first time I had ever encountered this species of honor, it seems excusable to mention it, and at the same time call the attention of the authorities to the tardiness of my recognition of it.

Noted a big change in the river, at Island 21. It was a very large island, and used to lie out toward mid-stream; but it is joined fast to the main shore now, and has retired from business as an island.

As we approached famous and formidable Plum Point, darkness fell, but that was nothing to shudder about—in these modern times. For now the national government has turned the Mississippi into a sort of two-thousand-mile torch-light procession. In the head of every crossing, and in the foot of every crossing, the government has set up a clear-burning lamp. You are never entirely in the dark, now; there is always a beacon in sight, either before you, or behind you, or abreast. One might almost say that lamps have been squandered there. Dozens of crossings are lighted which were not shoal when they were created, and have never been shoal since; crossings so plain, too, and also so straight, that a steamboat can take herself through them without any help, after she has been through once. Lamps in such places are of course not wasted; it is much more convenient and comfortable for a pilot to hold on them than on a spread of formless blackness that won't stay still; and money is saved to the boat, at the same time, for she can of course make more miles with her rudder amidships than she can with it squared across her stern and holding her back.

But this thing has knocked the romance out of piloting, to a large extent. It and some other things together, have knocked all the romance out of it. For instance, the peril from snags is not now what it once was. The government's snag-boats go patrolling up and down, in these matter-of-fact days, pulling the river's teeth; they have rooted out all the old clusters which made many localities so formidable; and they allow no new ones to collect. Formerly, if your boat got away from you, on a black night, and broke for the woods, it was an anxious time with you; so was it also, when you were groping your way through solidified darkness in a narrow chute; but all that is changed now,— you flash out your electric light, transform night into day in the twinkling of an eye, and your perils and anxieties are at an end. Horace Bixby and George Ritchie have charted the crossings and laid out the courses by compass; they have invented a lamp to go with the chart, and have patented the whole. With these helps, one may run in the fog now, with considerable security, and with a confidence unknown in the old days.

With these abundant beacons, the banishment of snags, plenty of daylight in a box and ready to be turned on whenever needed, and a chart and compass to fight the fog with, piloting, at a good stage of water, is now nearly as safe and simple as driving stage, and is hardly more than three times as romantic.

And now in these new days, these days of infinite change, the Anchor Line have raised the captain above the pilot by giving him the bigger wages of the two. This was going far, but they have not stopped there. They have decreed that the pilot shall remain at his post, and stand his watch clear through, whether the boat be under way or tied up to the shore. We, that were once the aristocrats of the river, can't go to bed now, as we used to do, and sleep while a hundred tons of freight are lugged aboard; no, we must sit in the pilot-house; and keep awake, too. Verily we are being treated like a parcel of mates and engineers. The Government has taken away the romance of our calling; the Company has taken away its state and dignity.

Plum Point looked as it had always looked by night, with the exception that now there were beacons to mark the crossings, and also a lot of other lights on the Point and along its shore; these latter glinting from the fleet of the United States River Commission, and from a village which the officials have built on the land for offices and for the employés of the service. The military engineers of the Commission have taken upon their shoulders the job of making the Mississippi over again,—a job transcended in size by only the original job of creating it. They are building wing-dams here and there, to deflect the current; and dikes to confine it in narrower bounds; and other dikes to make it stay there; and for unnumbered miles along the Mississippi, they are felling the timber-front for fifty yards back, with the purpose of shaving the bank down to low-water mark with the slant of a house-roof, and ballasting it with stones; and in many places they have protected the wasting shores with rows of piles. One who knows the Mississippi will promptly aver—not aloud, but to himself—that ten thousand River Commissions, with the mines of the world at their back, cannot tame that lawless stream, cannot curb it or confine it, cannot say to it, Go here, or Go there, and make it obey; cannot save a shore which it has sentenced; cannot bar its path with an obstruction which it will not tear down, dance over, and laugh at. But a discreet man will not put these things into spoken words; for the West Point engineers have not their superiors anywhere; they know all that can be known of their abstruse science; and so, since they conceive that they can fetter and handcuff that river and boss him, it is but wisdom for the unscientific man to keep still, lie low, and wait till they do it. Captain Eads, with his jetties, has done a work at the mouth of the Mississippi which seemed clearly impossible; so we do not feel full confidence now to prophesy against like impossibilities. Otherwise one would pipe out and say the Commission might as well bully the comets in their courses and undertake to make them behave, as try to bully the Mississippi into right and reasonable conduct.

I consulted Uncle Mumford concerning this and cognate matters; and I give here the result, stenographically reported, and therefore to be relied on as being full and correct; except that I have here and there left out remarks which were addressed to the men, such as *"where* in the blazes are you going with that barrel now?" and which seemed to me to break the flow of the written statement, without compensating by adding to its information or its clearness. Not that I have ventured to strike out all such interjections; I have removed only those which were obviously irrelevant; wherever one occurred which I felt any question about, I have judged it safest to let it remain.

UNCLE MUMFORD'S IMPRESSIONS

Uncle Mumford said:—

"As long as I have been mate of a steamboat,—thirty years—I have watched this river and studied it. Maybe I could have learnt more about it at West Point, but if I believe it I wish I may be WHAT *are you sucking your fingers there for?—Collar that kag of nails!* Four years at West Point, and plenty of books and schooling, will learn a man a good deal, I reckon, but it won't learn him the river. You turn one of those little European rivers over to this Commission, with its hard bottom and clear water, and it would just be a holiday job for them to wall it, and pile it, and dike it, and tame it down, and boss it around, and make it go wherever they wanted it to, and stay where they put it, and do just as they said, every time. But this ain't that kind of a river. They have started in here with big confidence, and the best intentions in the world; but they are going to get left. What does Ecclesiastes vii. 13 say? Says enough to knock *their* little game galley-west, don't it? Now you look at their methods once. There at Devil's Island, in the Upper River, they wanted the water to go one way, the water wanted to go another. So they put up a stone wall. But what does the river care for a stone wall? When it got ready, it just bulged through it. Maybe they can build another that will stay; that is, up there—but not down here they can't. Down here in the Lower River, they drive some pegs to turn the water away from the shore and stop it from slicing off the bank; very well, don't it go straight over and cut somebody else's bank? Certainly. Are they going to peg *all* the banks? Why, they could buy ground and build a new Mississippi cheaper. They are pegging Bulletin Tow-head now. It won't do any good. If the river has got a mortgage on that island, it will foreclose, sure, pegs or no pegs. Away down yonder, they have driven two rows of piles straight through the middle of a dry bar half a mile long, which is forty foot out of the water when the river is low. What do you reckon that is for? If I know, I wish I may land in—HUMP *yourself, you son of an undertaker!—out with that coal-oil, now, lively,* LIVELY! And just look at what they are trying to do down there at Milliken's Bend. There's been a cut-off in that section, and Vicksburg is left out in the cold. It's a country town now. The river strikes in below it; and a boat can't go up to the town except in high water. Well, they are going to build wing-dams in the bend opposite the foot of 103, and throw the water over and cut off the foot of the island and plow down into an old ditch where the river used to be in ancient times; and they think they can persuade the water around that way, and get it to strike in above Vicksburg, as it used to do, and fetch the town back into the world again. That is, they are going to take this whole Mississippi, and twist it around and make it run several miles *up stream*. Well, you've got to admire men that deal in ideas of that size and can tote them around without crutches; but you haven't got to believe they can *do* such miracles, have you? And yet you ain't absolutely obliged to believe they can't. I reckon the safe way, where a man can afford it, is to *copper* the operation, and at the same time buy enough property in Vicksburg to square you up in case they win. Government is doing a deal for the Mississippi, now—spending loads of money on her. When there used to be four thousand steamboats and ten thousand acres of coal-barges, and rafts and trading scows, there wasn't a lantern from St. Paul to New Orleans, and the snags were thicker than bristles on a hog's back; and now when there's three dozen steamboats and nary barge or raft, Government has snatched out all the snags on the river as she'd be in heaven. And I reckon that by the time there ain't any boats left at all, the Commission will have the old thing all reorganized, and dredged out, and fenced in, and tidied up, to a degree that will make navigation just simply perfect, and absolutely safe and profitable; and all the days will be Sundays, and all the mates will be Sunday-school suWHAT-*in-the-nation-you-fooling-around-there-for, you sons of unrighteousness, heirs of perdition! Going to be a* YEAR *getting that hogshead ashore?"*

During our trip to New Orleans and back, we had many conversations with river men, planters, journalists, and officers of the River Commission — with conflicting and confusing results. To wit:—

1. Some believed in the Commission's scheme to arbitrarily and permanently confine (and thus deepen) the channel, preserve threatened shores, etc.

2. Some believed that the Commission's money ought to be spent only on building and repairing the great system of levees.

3. Some believed that the higher you build your levee, the higher the river's bottom will rise; and that consequently the levee system is a mistake.

4. Some believed in the scheme to relieve the river, in flood-time, by turning its surplus waters off into Lake Borgne, etc.

5. Some believed in the scheme of northern lake-reservoirs to replenish the Mississippi in low-water seasons.

Wherever you find a man down there who believes in one of these theories you may turn to the next man and frame your talk upon the hypothesis that he does *not* believe in that theory; and after you have had experience, you do not take this course doubtfully, or hesitatingly, but with the confidence of a dying murderer—converted one, I mean. For you will have come to know, with a deep and restful certainty, that you are not going to meet two people sick of the same theory, one right after the other. No, there will always be one or two with the other diseases along between. And as you proceed, you will find out one or two other things. You will find out that there is no distemper of the lot but is contagious; and you cannot go where it is without catching it. You may vaccinate yourself with deterrent facts as much as you please—it will do no good; it will seem to "take," but it doesn't; the moment you rub against any one of those theorists, make up your mind that it is time to hang out your yellow flag.

Yes, you are his sure victim: yet his work is not all to your hurt—only part of it; for he is like your family physician, who comes and cures the mumps, and leaves the scarlet-fever behind. If your man is a Lake-Borgne-relief theorist, for instance, he will exhale a cloud of deadly facts and statistics which will lay you out with that disease, sure; but at the same time he will cure you of any other of the five theories that may have previously got into your system.

I have had all the five; and had them "bad;" but ask me not, in mournful numbers, which one racked me hardest, or which one numbered the biggest sick list, for I do not know. In truth, no one can answer the latter question. Mississippi Improvement is a mighty topic, down yonder. Every man on the river banks, south of Cairo, talks about it every day, during such moments as he is able to spare from talking about the war; and each of the several chief theories has its host of zealous partisans; but, as I have said, it is not possible to determine which cause numbers the most recruits.

All were agreed upon one point, however: if Congress would make a sufficient appropriation, a colossal benefit would result. Very well; since then the appropriation has been made—possibly a sufficient one, certainly not too large a one. Let us hope that the prophecy will be amply fulfilled.

One thing will be easily granted by the reader; that an opinion from Mr. Edward Atkinson, upon any vast national commercial matter, comes as near ranking as authority, as can the opinion of any individual in the Union. What he has to say about Mississippi River Improvement will be found in the Appendix.*

Sometimes, half a dozen figures will reveal, as with a lightning-flash, the importance of a subject which ten thousand labored words, with the same purpose in view, had left at last but dim and uncertain. Here is a case of the sort—paragraph from the "Cincinnati Commercial:"—

"The towboat 'Jos. B. Williams' is on her way to New Orleans with a tow of thirty-two barges, containing six hundred thousand bushels (seventy-six pounds to the bushel) of coal exclusive of her own fuel, being the largest tow ever taken to New Orleans or anywhere else in the world. Her freight bill, at 3 cents a bushel, amounts to $18,000. It would take eighteen hundred cars, of three hundred and thirty-three bushels to the car, to transport this amount of coal. At $10 per ton, or $100 per car, which would be a fair price for the distance by rail, the freight bill would amount to $180,000, or $162,000 more by rail than by river. The tow will be taken from Pittsburg to New Orleans in fourteen or fifteen days. It would take one hundred trains of eighteen cars to the train to transport this one tow of six hundred thousand bushels of coal, and even if it made the usual speed of fast freight lines, it would take one whole summer to put it through by rail."

When a river in good condition can enable one to save $162,00 and a whole summer's time, on a single cargo, the wisdom of taking measures to keep the river in good condition is made plain to even the uncommercial mind.

CHAPTER XXIX

A FEW SPECIMEN BRICKS

We passed through the Plum Point region, turned Craighead's Point, and glided unchallenged by what was once the formidable Fort Pillow, memorable because of the massacre perpetrated there during the war. Massacres are sprinkled with some frequency through the histories of several Christian nations, but this is almost the only one that can be found in American history; perhaps it is the only one which rises to a size

* See Appendix B.

correspondent to that huge and sombre title. We have the "Boston Massacre," where two or three people were killed; but we must bunch Anglo-Saxon history together to find the fellow to the Fort Pillow tragedy; and doubtless even then we must travel back to the days and the performances of Coeur de Lion, that fine "hero," before we accomplish it.

More of the river's freaks. In times past, the channel used to strike above Island 37, by Brandywine Bar, and down towards Island 39. Afterward, changed its course and went from Brandywine down through Vogelman's chute in the Devil's Elbow, to Island 39—part of this course reversing the old order; the river running *up* four or five miles, instead of down, and cutting off, throughout, some fifteen miles of distance. This in 1876. All that region is now called Centennial Island.

There is a tradition that Island 37 was one of the principal abiding places of the once celebrated "Murel's Gang." This was a colossal combination of robbers, horse-thieves, negro-stealers, and counterfeiters, engaged in business along the river some fifty or sixty years ago. While our journey across the country towards St. Louis was in progress we had had no end of Jesse James and his stirring history; for he had just been assassinated by an agent of the Governor of Missouri, and was in consequence occupying a good deal of space in the newspapers. Cheap histories of him were for sale by train boys. According to these, he was the most marvellous creature of his kind that had ever existed. It was a mistake. Murel was his equal in boldness; in pluck; in rapacity; in cruelty, brutality, heartlessness, treachery, and in general and comprehensive vileness and shamelessness; and very much his superior in some larger aspects. James was a retail rascal; Murel, wholesale. James's modest genius dreamed of no loftier flight than the planning of raids upon cars, coaches, and country banks; Murel projected negro insurrections and the capture of New Orleans; and furthermore, on occasion, this Murel could go into a pulpit and edify the congregation. What are James and his half-dozen vulgar rascals compared with this stately old-time criminal, with his sermons, his meditated insurrections and city-captures, and his majestic following of ten hundred men, sworn to do his evil will! Here is a paragraph or two concerning this big operator, from a now-forgotten book which was published half a century ago.—

He appears to have been a most dexterous as well as consummate villain. When he travelled, his usual disguise was that of an itinerant preacher; and it is said that his discourses were very "soul-moving"—

interesting the hearers so much that they forgot to look after their horses, which were carried away by his confederates while he was preaching. But the stealing of horses in one State, and selling them in another, was but a small portion of their business; the most lucrative was the enticing slaves to run away from their masters, that they might sell them in another quarter. This was arranged as follows; they would tell a negro that if he would run away from his master, and allow them to sell him, he should receive a portion of the money paid for him, and that upon his return to them a second time they would send him to a free State, where he would be safe. The poor wretches complied with this request, hoping to obtain money and freedom; they would be sold to another master, and run away again to their employers; sometimes they would be sold in this manner three or four times, until they had realized three or four thousand dollars by them; but as, after this, there was fear of detection, the usual custom was to get rid of the only witness that could be produced against them, which was the negro himself, by murdering him, and throwing his body into the Mississippi. Even if it was established that they had stolen a negro, before he was murdered, they were always prepared to evade punishment; for they concealed the negro who had run away, until he was advertised, and a reward offered to any man who would catch him. An advertisement of this kind warrants the person to take the property, if found. And then the negro becomes a property in trust, when, therefore, they sold the negro, it only became a breach of trust, not stealing; and for a breach of trust, the owner of the property can only have redress by a civil action, which was useless, as the damages were never paid. It may be inquired, how it was that Murel escaped Lynch law under such circumstances? This will be easily understood when it is stated that he had *more than a thousand sworn confederates,* all ready at a moment's notice to support any of the gang who might be in trouble. The names of all the principal confederates of Murel were obtained from himself, in a manner which I shall presently explain. The gang was composed of two classes: the Heads or Council, as they were called, who planned and concerted, but seldom acted; they amounted to about four hundred. The other class were the active agents, and were termed strikers, and amounted to about six hundred and fifty. These were the tools in the hands of the others; they ran all the risk, and received but a small portion of the money; they were in the power of the leaders of the gang, who would sacrifice them at any time by handing them over to justice, or sinking their bodies in the Mississippi. The general rendezvous of this gang of miscreants was on the Arkansas side of the river, where they concealed their negroes in the morasses and cane-brakes.

The depredations of this extensive combination were severely felt; but so well were their plans arranged, that although Murel, who was always active, was everywhere suspected, there was no proof to be obtained. It so happened, however, that a young man of the name of Stewart, who was looking after two slaves which Murel had decoyed away, fell in with him and obtained his confidence, took the oath, and was admitted into the gang as one of the General Council. By this means all was discovered; for Stewart turned traitor, although he had taken the oath, and having obtained every information, exposed the whole concern, the names of all the parties, and finally succeeded in bringing home sufficient evidence against Murel, to procure his conviction and sentence to the Penitentiary (Murel was sentenced to fourteen years' imprisonment); so many people who were supposed to be honest, and bore a respectable name in the different States, were found to be among the list of the Grand Council as published by Stewart, that every attempt was made to throw discredit upon his assertions—his character was vilified, and more than one attempt was made to assassinate him. He was obliged to quit the Southern States in consequence. It is, however, now well ascertained to have been all true; and although some blame Mr. Stewart for having violated his oath, they no longer attempt to deny that his revelations were correct. I will quote one or two portions of Murel's confessions to Mr. Stewart, made to him when they were journeying together. I ought to have observed, that the ultimate intentions of Murel and his associates were, by his own account, on a very extended scale; having no less an object in view than *raising the blacks against the whites, taking possession of, and plundering New Orleans, and making themselves possessors of the territory.* The following are a few extracts:—

"I collected all my friends about New Orleans at one of our friends' houses in that place, and we sat in council three days before we got all our plans to our notion; we then determined to undertake the rebellion at every hazard, and make as many friends as we could for that purpose. Every man's business being assigned him, I started to Natchez on foot, having sold my horse in New Orleans,—with the intention of stealing another after I started. I walked four days, and no opportunity offered for me to get a horse. The fifth day, about twelve, I had become tired, and stopped at a creek to get some water and rest a little. While I was sitting on a log, looking down the road the way that I had come, a man came in sight riding on a good-looking horse. The very moment I saw him, I was determined to have his horse, if he was in the garb of a traveller. He rode up, and I saw from his equipage that he was a traveller. I arose and drew an elegant rifle pistol on him and ordered him to dismount. He did so, and I took his horse by the bridle and pointed down the creek, and ordered him to walk before me. He went a few hundred yards and stopped. I hitched his horse, and then made him undress himself, all to his shirt and drawers, and ordered him to turn his back to me. He said, 'If you are determined to kill me, let me have time to pray before I die.' I told him I had no time to hear him pray. He turned around and dropped on his knees, and I shot him through the back of the head. I ripped open his belly and took out his entrails, and sunk him in the creek. I then searched his pockets, and found four hundred dollars and thirty seven cents, and a number of papers that I did not take time to examine. I sunk the pocket-book and papers and his hat, in the creek. His boots were bran-new, and fitted me genteelly; and I put them on and sunk my old shoes in the creek, to atone for them. I rolled up his clothes and put them into his portmanteau, as they were bran-new cloth of the best quality. I mounted as fine a horse as ever I straddled, and directed my course for Natchez in much better style than I had been for the last five days.

"Myself and a fellow by the name of Crenshaw gathered four good horses and started for Georgia. We got in company with a young South Carolinian just before we got to Cumberland Mountain, and Crenshaw soon knew all about his business. He had been to Tennessee to buy a drove of hogs, but when he got there pork was dearer than he calculated, and he declined purchasing. We concluded he was a prize. Crenshaw winked at me; I understood his idea. Crenshaw had travelled the road before, but I never had; we had travelled several miles on the mountain, when he passed near a great precipice; just before we passed it Crenshaw asked me for my whip, which had a pound of lead in the butt; I handed it to him, and he rode up by the side of the South Carolinian, and gave him a blow on the side of the head and tumbled him from his horse; we lit from our horses and fingered his pockets; we got twelve hundred and sixty-two dollars. Crenshaw said he knew a place to hide him, and he gathered him under his arms, and I by his feet, and conveyed him to a deep crevice in the brow of the precipice, and tumbled him into it, and he went out of sight; we then tumbled in his saddle, and took his horse with us, which was worth two hundred dollars.

"We were detained a few days, and during that time our friend went to a little village in the neighborhood and saw the negro advertised (a negro in our possession), and a description of the two men of whom he had been purchased, and giving his suspicions of the men. It was rather squally times, but any port in a storm: we took the negro that night on the bank of a creek which runs by the farm of our friend, and Crenshaw shot him through the head. We took out his entrails and sunk him in the creek.

"He had sold the other negro the third time on Arkansaw River for upwards of five hundred dollars; and then stole him and delivered him into the hand of his friend, who conducted him to a swamp, and veiled the tragic scene, and got the last gleanings and sacred pledge of secrecy; as a game of that kind will not do unless it ends in a mystery to all but the fraternity. He sold the negro, first and last, for nearly two thousand dollars, and then put him forever out of the reach of all pursuers; and they can never graze him unless they can find the negro; and that they cannot do, for his carcass has fed many a tortoise and catfish before this time, and the frogs have sung this many a long day to the silent repose of his skeleton."

We were approaching Memphis, in front of which city, and witnessed by its people, was fought the most famous of the river battles of the Civil War. Two men whom I had served under, in my river days, took part in that fight: Mr. Bixby, head pilot of the Union fleet, and Montgomery, Commodore of the Confederate fleet. Both saw a great deal of active service during the war, and achieved high reputations for pluck and capacity.

As we neared Memphis, we began to cast about for an excuse

to stay with the "Gold Dust" to the end of her course—Vicksburg. We were so pleasantly situated, that we did not wish to make a change. I had an errand of considerable importance to do at Napoleon, Arkansas, but perhaps I could manage it without quitting the "Gold Dust." I said as much; so we decided to stick to present quarters.

The boat was to tarry at Memphis till ten the next morning. It is a beautiful city, nobly situated on a commanding bluff overlooking the river. The streets are straight and spacious, though not paved in a way to incite distempered admiration. No, the admiration must be reserved for the town's sewerage system, which is called perfect; a recent reform, however, for it was just the other way, up to a few years ago—a reform resulting from the lesson taught by a desolating visitation of the yellow-fever. In those awful days the people were swept off by hundreds, by thousands; and so great was the reduction caused by flight and by death together, that the population was diminished three-fourths, and so remained for a time. Business stood nearly still, and the streets bore an empty Sunday aspect.

Here is a picture of Memphis, at that disastrous time, drawn by a German tourist who seems to have been an eyewitness of the scenes which he describes. It is from Chapter VII., of his book, just published, in Leipzig, "Mississippi-Fahrten, von Ernest von Hesse-Wartegg."—

"In August the yellow-fever had reached its extremest height. Daily, hundreds fell a sacrifice to the terrible epidemic. The city was become a mighty graveyard, two-thirds of the population had deserted the place, and only the poor, the aged and the sick, remained behind, a sure prey for the insidious enemy. The houses were closed: little lamps burned in front of many—a sign that here death had entered. Often, several lay dead in a single house; from the windows hung black crape. The stores were shut up, for their owners were gone away or dead.

"Fearful evil! In the briefest space it struck down and swept away even the most vigorous victim. A slight indisposition, then an hour of fever, then the hideous delirium, then—the Yellow Death! On the street corners, and in the squares, lay sick men, suddenly overtaken by the disease; and even corpses, distorted and rigid. Food failed. Meat spoiled in a few hours in the fetid and pestiferous air, and turned black.

"Fearful clamors issue from many houses; then after a season they cease, and all is still: noble, self-sacrificing men come with the coffin, nail it up, and carry it away, to the graveyard. In the night stillness reigns. Only the physicians and the hearses hurry through the streets; and out of the distance, at intervals, comes the muffled thunder of the railway train, which with the speed of the wind, and as if hunted by furies, flies by the pest-ridden city without halting."

But there is life enough there now. The population exceeds forty thousand and is augmenting, and trade is in a flourishing condition. We drove about the city; visited the park and the sociable horde of squirrels there; saw the fine residences, rose-clad and in other ways enticing to the eye; and got a good breakfast at the hotel.

A thriving place is the Good Samaritan City of the Mississippi: has a great wholesale jobbing trade; foundries, machine shops; and manufactories of wagons, carriages, and cotton-seed oil; and is shortly to have cotton mills and elevators.

Her cotton receipts reached five hundred thousand bales last year—an increase of sixty thousand over the year before. Out from her healthy commercial heart issue five trunk lines of railway; and a sixth is being added.

This is a very different Memphis from the one which the vanished and unremembered procession of foreign tourists used to put into their books long time ago. In the days of the now forgotten but once renowned and vigorously hated Mrs. Trollope, Memphis seems to have consisted mainly of one long street of log-houses, with some outlying cabins sprinkled around rearward toward the woods; and now and then a pig, and no end of mud. That was fifty-five years ago. She stopped at the hotel. Plainly it was not the one which gave us our breakfast. She says:—

"The table was laid for fifty persons, and was nearly full. They ate in perfect silence, and with such astonishing rapidity that their dinner was over literally before ours was begun; the only sounds heard were those produced by the knives and forks, with the unceasing chorus of coughing, *etc.*"

"Coughing, *etc.*" The "etc." stands for an unpleasant word there, a word which she does not always charitably cover up, but sometimes prints. You will find it in the following description of a steamboat dinner which she ate in company with a lot of aristocratic planters; wealthy, well-born, ignorant swells they were, tinselled with the usual harmless military and judicial titles of that old day of cheap shams and windy pretence:—

"The total want of all the usual courtesies of the table; the voracious rapidity with which the viands were seized and devoured; the strange uncouth phrases and pronunciation; the loathsome spitting from the contamination of which it was absolutely impossible to protect our dresses; the frightful manner of feeding with their knives, till the whole blade seemed to enter into the mouth; and the still more frightful manner of cleaning the teeth afterward with a pocket knife, soon forced us to feel that we were not surrounded by the generals, colonels, and majors of the old world; and that the dinner hour was to be anything rather than an hour of enjoyment.''

CHAPTER XXX

SKETCHES BY THE WAY

It was a big river, below Memphis; banks brimming full, everywhere, and very frequently more than full, the waters pouring out over the land, flooding the woods and fields for miles into the interior; and in places, to a depth of fifteen feet; signs, all about, of men's hard work gone to ruin, and all to be done over again, with straitened means and a weakened courage. A melancholy picture, and a continuous one;—hundreds of miles of it. Sometimes the beacon lights stood in water three feet deep, in the edge of dense forests which extended for miles without farm, wood-yard, clearing, or break of any kind; which meant that the keeper of the light must come in a skiff a great distance to discharge his trust,—and often in desperate weather. Yet I was told that the work is faithfully performed, in all weathers; and not always by men, sometimes by women, if the man is sick or absent. The Government furnishes oil, and pays ten or fifteen dollars a month for the lighting and tending. A Government boat distributes oil and pays wages once a month.

The Ship Island region was as woodsy and tenantless as ever. The island has ceased to be an island; has joined itself compactly to the main shore, and wagons travel, now, where the steamboats used to navigate. No signs left of the wreck of the ''Pennsylvania.'' Some farmer will turn up her bones with his plow one day, no doubt, and be surprised.

We were getting down now into the migrating negro region. These poor people could never travel when they were slaves; so they make up for the privation now. They stay on a plantation till the desire to travel seizes them; then they pack up, hail a steamboat, and clear out. Not for any particular place; no, nearly any place will answer; they only want to be moving. The amount of money on hand will answer the rest of the conundrum of them. If it will take them fifty miles, very well; let it be fifty. If not, a shorter flight will do.

During a couple of days, we frequently answered these hails. Sometimes there was a group of high-water-stained, tumbledown cabins, populous with colored folk, and no whites visible;

with grassless patches of dry ground here and there; a few felled trees, with skeleton cattle, mules, and horses, eating the leaves and gnawing the bark—no other food for them in the flood-wasted land. Sometimes there was a single lonely landing- cabin; near it the colored family that had hailed us; little and big, old and young, roosting on the scant pile of household goods; these consisting of a rusty gun, sone bedticks, chests, tinware, stools, a crippled looking-glass, a venerable arm-chair, and six or eight base-born and spiritless yellow curs, attached to the family by strings. They must have their dogs; can't go without their dogs. Yet the dogs are never willing; they always object; so, one after another, in ridiculous procession, they are dragged aboard; all four feet braced and sliding along the stage, head likely to be pulled off; but the tugger marching determinedly forward, bending to his work, with the rope over his shoulder for better purchase. Sometimes a child is forgotten and left on the bank; but never a dog.

The usual river-gossip going on in the pilot-house. Island No. 63—an island with a lovely "chute," or passage, behind it in the former times. They said Jesse Jamieson, in the "Skylark," had a visiting pilot with him one trip—a poor old broken-down, super-annuated fellow—left him at the wheel, at the foot of 63, to run off the watch. The ancient mariner went up through the chute, and down the river outside; and up the chute and down the river again; and yet again and again; and handed the boat over to the relieving pilot, at the end of three hours of honest endeavor, at the same old foot of the island where he had originally taken the wheel! A darkey on shore who had observed the boat go by, about thirteen times, said, " 'clar to gracious, I wouldn't be s'prised if dey's a whole line o' dem Sk'ylarks!"

Anecdote illustrative of influence of reputation in the changing of opinion. The "Eclipse" was renowned for her swiftness. One day she passed along; an old darkey on shore, absorbed in his own matters, did not notice what steamer it was. Presently some one asked:—

"Any boat gone up?"

"Yes, sah."

"Was she going fast?"

"Oh, so-so—loafin' along."

"Now, do you know what boat that was?"

"No, sah."

"Why, uncle, that was the 'Eclipse.' "

"No! Is dat so? Well, I bet it was—cause she jes' went by here a-*sparklin'!*"

Piece of history illustrative of the violent style of some of the people down along here. During the early weeks of high water, A's fence rails washed down on B's ground, and B's rails washed up in the eddy and landed on A's ground. A said, "Let the thing remain so; I will use your rails, and you use mine." But B objected—wouldn't have it so. One day, A came down on B's ground to get his rails. B said, "I'll kill you!" and proceeded for him with his revolver. A said, "I'm not armed." So B, who wished to do only what was right, threw down his revolver; then pulled a knife, and cut A's throat all around, but gave his principal attention to the front, and so failed to sever the jugular. Struggling around, A managed to get his hands on the discarded revolver, and shot B dead with it—and recovered from his own injuries.

Further gossip;—after which, everybody went below to get afternoon coffee, and left me at the wheel, alone. Something presently reminded me of our last hour in St. Louis, part of which I spent on this boat's hurricane deck, aft. I was joined there by a stranger, who dropped into conversation with me—a brisk young fellow, who said he was born in a town in the interior of Wisconsin, and had never seen a steamboat until a week before. Also said that on the way down from La Crosse he had inspected and examined his boat so diligently and with such passionate interest that he had mastered the whole thing from stem to rudder-blade. Asked me where I was from. I answered, New England. "Oh, a Yank!" said he; and went chatting straight along, without waiting for assent or denial. He immediately proposed to take me all over the boat and tell me the names of her different parts, and teach me their uses. Before I could enter protest or excuse, he was already rattling glibly away at his benevolent work; and when I perceived that he was misnaming the things, and inhospitably amusing himself at the expense of an innocent stranger from a far country, I held my peace, and let him have his way. He gave me a world of misinformation; and the further he went, the wider his imagination expanded, and the more he enjoyed his cruel work of deceit. Sometimes, after palming off a particularly fantastic and outrageous lie upon me, he was so "full of laugh" that he had to step aside for a minute, upon one pretext or another, to keep me from suspecting. I staid faithfully by him until his comedy was finished. Then he remarked that he had undertaken to "learn" me all about a steamboat, and had done it; but that if he had overlooked anything, just ask him and he would supply the lack. "Anything about this boat that you don't know the name of or the purpose of, you come to me and I'll tell you." I said I would, and took my departure; disappeared, and approached him from another quarter, whence he could not see me. There he sat, all alone, doubling himself up and writhing this way and that, in the throes of unappeasable laughter. He must have made himself sick; for he was not publicly visible afterward for several days. Meantime, the episode dropped out of my mind.

The thing that reminded me of it now, when I was alone at the wheel, was the spectacle of this young fellow standing in the pilot-house door, with the knob in his hand, silently and severely inspecting me. I don't know when I have seen anybody look so injured as he did. He did not say anything—simply stood there and looked; reproachfully looked and pondered. Finally he shut the door, and started away; halted on the texas a minute; came slowly back and stood in the door again, with that grieved look in his face; gazed upon me a while in meek rebuke, then said:—

"You let me learn you all about a steamboat, *didn't* you?"

"Yes,"I confessed.

"Yes, you did—*didn't* you?"

"Yes."

"*You* are the feller that—that—"

Language failed. Pause—impotent struggle for further words—then he gave it up, choked out a deep, strong oath, and departed for good. Afterward I saw him several times below during the trip; but he was cold—would not look at me. Idiot, if he had not been in such a sweat to play his witless practical joke upon me, in the beginning, I would have persuaded his thoughts into some other direction, and saved him from committing that wanton and silly impoliteness.

I had myself called with the four o'clock watch, mornings, for one cannot see too many summer sunrises on the Mississippi. They are enchanting. First, there is the eloquence of silence; for a deep hush broods everywhere. Next, there is the haunting sense of loneliness, isolation, remoteness from the worry and bustle of the world. The dawn creeps in stealthily; the solid walls of black forest soften to gray, and vast stretches of the river open up and reveal themselves; the water is glass-smooth, gives off spectral little wreaths of white mist, there is not the faintest breath of wind, nor stir of leaf; the tranquillity is profound and infinitely satisfying. Then a bird pipes up, another follows, and soon the pipings develop into a jubilant riot of music. You see none of the birds; you simply move through an atmosphere of song which seems to sing itself. When the light has become a little stronger, you have one of the fairest and softest pictures imaginable. You have the intense green of the massed and crowded foliage near by; you see it paling shade by shade in front of you; upon the next projecting cape, a mile off or more, the tint has lightened to the tender young green of spring; the cape beyond that one has almost lost color, and the furthest one, miles away under the horizon, sleeps upon the water a mere dim vapor, and hardly separable from the sky above it and about it. And all this stretch of river is a mirror, and you have the shadowy reflections of the leafage and the curving shores and the receding capes pictured in it. Well, that is all beautiful; soft and rich and beautiful; and when the sun gets well up, and distributes a pink flush here and a powder of gold yonder and a purple haze where it will yield the best effect, you grant that you have seen something that is worth remembering.

We had the Kentucky Bend country in the early morning—scene of a strange and tragic accident in the old times. Captain Poe had a small stern-wheel boat, for years the home of himself and his wife. One night the boat struck a snag in the head of Kentucky Bend, and sank with astonishing suddenness; water already well above the cabin floor when the captain got aft. So he cut into his wife's stateroom from above with an axe; she was asleep in the upper berth, the roof a flimsier one than was supposed; the first blow crashed down through the rotten boards and clove her skull.

This bend is all filled up now—result of a cut-off; and the same agent has taken the great and once much-frequented Walnut Bend, and set it away back in a solitude far from the accustomed track of passing steamers.

Helena we visited, and also a town I had not heard of before, it being of recent birth—Arkansas City. It was born of a railway; the Little Rock, Mississippi River and Texas Railroad touches the river there. We asked a passenger who belonged there what sort of a place it was. "Well," said he, after considering, and with the air of one who wishes to take time and be accurate, "It's a hell of a place." A description which was photographic for exactness. There were several rows and clusters of shabby frame-houses, and a supply of mud sufficient to insure the town against a famine in that article for a hundred years; for the overflow had but lately subsided. There were stagnant ponds in the streets, here and there, and a dozen rude scows were scattered about, lying aground wherever they happened to have been when the waters drained off and people could do their visiting and shopping on foot once more. Still, it is a thriving place, with a rich country behind it, an elevator in front of it, and also a fine big mill for the manufacture of cotton-seed oil. I had never seen this kind of a mill before.

Cotton-seed was comparatively valueless in my time; but it is worth $12 or $13 a ton now, and none of it is thrown away. The oil made from it is colorless, tasteless, and almost if not entirely odorless. It is claimed that it can, by proper manipulation, be made to resemble and perform the office of any and all oils, and be produced at a cheaper rate than the cheapest of the originals. Sagacious people shipped it to Italy, doctored it, labelled it, and brought it back as olive oil. This trade grew to be so formidable that Italy was obliged to put a prohibitory impost upon it to keep it from working serious injury to her oil industry.

Helena occupies one of the prettiest situations on the Mississippi. Her perch is the last, the southernmost group of hills which one sees on that side of the river. In its normal condition it is a pretty town; but the flood (or possibly the seepage) had lately been ravaging it; whole streets of houses had been invaded by the muddy water, and the outsides of the buildings were still belted with a broad stain extending upwards from the foundations. Stranded and discarded scows lay all about; plank sidewalks on stilts four feet high were still standing; the board sidewalks on the ground level were loose and ruinous,—a couple of men trotting along them could make a blind man think a cavalry charge was coming; everywhere the mud was black and deep, and in many places malarious pools of stagnant water were standing. A Mississippi inundation is the next most wasting and desolating infliction to a fire.

We had an enjoyable time here, on this sunny Sunday: two full hours' liberty ashore while the boat discharged freight. In the back streets but few white people were visible, but there were plenty of colored folk—mainly women and girls; and almost without exception upholstered in bright new clothes of swell and elaborate style and cut—a glaring and hilarious contrast to the mournful mud and the pensive puddles.

Helena is the second town in Arkansas, in point of population—which is placed at five thousand. The country about it is exceptionally productive. Helena has a good cotton trade; handles from forty to sixty thousand bales annually; she has a large lumber and grain commerce; has a foundry, oil mills, machine shops and wagon factories—in brief has $1,000,000 invested in manufacturing industries. She has two railways, and is the commercial centre of a broad and prosperous region. Her gross receipts of money, annually, from all sources, are placed by the New Orleans "Times-Democrat" at $4,000,000.

CHAPTER XXXI

A THUMB-PRINT AND WHAT CAME OF IT

We were approaching Napoleon, Arkansas. So I began to think about my errand there. Time, noonday; and bright and sunny. This was bad—not best, anyway; for mine was not (preferably) a noonday kind of errand. The more I thought, the more that fact pushed itself upon me—now in one form, now in another. Finally, it took the form of a distinct question: is it good common sense to do the errand in daytime, when, by a little sacrifice of comfort and inclination, you can have night for it, and no inquisitive eyes around? This settled it. Plain question and plain answer make the shortest road out of most perplexities.

I got my friends into my stateroom, and said I was sorry to create annoyance and disappointment, but that upon reflection it really seemed best that we put our luggage ashore and stop over at Napoleon. Their disapproval was prompt and loud; their language mutinous. Their main argument was one which has always been the first to come to the surface, in such cases, since the beginning of time: "But you decided and *agreed* to stick to this boat, etc.;" as if, having determined to do an unwise thing, one is thereby bound to go ahead and make *two* unwise things of it, by carrying out that determination.

I tried various mollifying tactics upon them, with reasonably good success: under which encouragement, I increased my efforts; and, to show them that *I* had not created this annoying errand, and was in no way to blame for it, I presently drifted into its history—substantially as follows:

Toward the end of last year, I spent a few months in Munich, Bavaria. In November I was living in Fräulein Dahlweiner's *pension, 1a,* Karlstrasse; but my working quarters were a mile from there, in the house of a widow who supported herself by taking lodgers. She and her two young children used to drop in every morning and talk German to me—by request. One day, during a ramble about the city, I visited one of the two establishments where the Government keeps and watches corpses until the doctors decide that they are permanently dead, and not in a trance state. It was a grisly place, that spacious room. There were thirty-six corpses of adults in sight, stretched on their backs on slightly slanted boards, in three long rows—all of them with wax-white, rigid faces, and all of them wrapped in white shrouds. Along the sides of the room were deep alcoves, like bay windows; and in each of these lay several marble-visaged babes, utterly hidden and buried under banks of fresh flowers, all but their faces and crossed hands. Around a finger of each of these fifty still forms, both great and small, was a ring; and from the ring a wire led to the ceiling, and thence to a bell in a watch-room yonder, where, day and night, a watchman sits always alert and ready to spring to the aid of any of that pallid company who, waking out of death, shall make a movement—for any even the slightest movement will twitch the wire and ring that fearful bell. I imagined myself a death-sentinel drowsing there alone, far in the dragging watches of some wailing, gusty night, and having in a twinkling all my body stricken to quivering jelly by the sudden clamor of that awful summons! So I inquired about this thing; asked what resulted usually? if the watchman died, and the restored corpse came and did what it could to make his last moments easy? But I was rebuked for trying to feed an idle and frivolous curiosity in so solemn and so mournful a place; and went my way with a humbled crest.

Next morning I was telling the widow my adventure, when she exclaimed—

"Come with me! I have a lodger who shall tell you all you want to know. He has been a night watchman there."

He was a living man, but he did not look it. He was abed, and had his head propped high on pillows; his face was wasted and colorless, his deep-sunken eyes were shut; his hand, lying on his breast, was talon-like, it was so bony and long-fingered. The widow began her introduction of me. The man's eyes opened slowly, and glittered wickedly out from the twilight of their caverns; he frowned a black frown; he lifted his lean hand and waved us peremptorily away. But the widow kept straight on, till she had got out the fact that I was a stranger and an American. The man's face changed at once; brightened, became even eager—and the next moment he and I were alone together.

I opened up in cast-iron German; he responded in quite flexible English; thereafter we gave the German language a permanent rest.

This consumptive and I became good friends. I visited him every day, and we talked about everything. At least, about everything but wives and children. Let anybody's wife or anybody's child be mentioned, and three things always followed: the most gracious and loving and tender light glimmered in the man's eyes for a moment; faded out the next, and in its place came that deadly look which had flamed there the first time I ever saw his lids unclose; thirdly, he ceased from speech, there and then for that day; lay silent, abstracted, and absorbed; apparently heard nothing that I said; took no notice of my good-byes, and plainly did not know, by either sight or hearing, when I left the room.

When I had been this Karl Ritter's daily and sole intimate during two months, he one day said, abruptly,—

"I will tell you my story."

A DYING MAN'S CONFESSION

Then he went on as follows:—

I have never given up, until now. But now I have given up. I am going to die. I made up my mind last night that it must be, and very soon, too. You say you are going to revisit your river, by and by, when you find opportunity. Very well; that, together with a certain strange experience which fell to my lot last night, determines me to tell you my history—for you will see Napoleon, Arkansas; and for my sake you will stop there, and do a certain thing for me—a thing which you will willingly undertake after you shall have heard my narrative.

Let us shorten the story wherever we can, for it will need it, being long. You already know how I came to go to America, and how I came to settle in that lonely region in the South. But you do not know that I had a wife. My wife was young, beautiful, loving, and oh, so divinely good and blameless and gentle! And our little girl was her mother in miniature. It was the happiest of happy households.

One night—it was toward the close of the war—I woke up out of a sodden lethargy, and found myself bound and gagged, and the air tainted with chloroform! I saw two men in the room, and one was saying to the other, in a hoarse whisper, "I *told* her I would, if she made a noise, and as for the child—"

The other man interrupted in a low, half-crying voice—

"You said we'd only gag them and rob them, not hurt them; or I wouldn't have come."

"Shut up your whining; *had* to change the plan when they waked up; you done all *you* could to protect them, now let that satisfy you; come, help rummage."

Both men were masked, and wore coarse, ragged "nigger" clothes; they had a bull's-eye lantern, and by its light I noticed that the gentler robber had no thumb on his right hand. They rummaged around my poor cabin for a moment; the head bandit then said, in his stage whisper,—

"It's a waste of time—*he* shall tell where it's hid. Undo his gag, and revive him up."

The other said—

"All right—provided no clubbing."

"No clubbing it is, then—provided he keeps still."

They approached me; just then there was a sound outside; a sound of voices and trampling hoofs; the robbers held their breath and listened; the sounds came slowly nearer and nearer; then came a shout—

"*Hello*, the house! Show a light, we want water."

"The captain's voice, by G—!" said the stage-whispering ruffian, and both robbers fled by the way of the back door, shutting off their bull's-eye as they ran.

The strangers shouted several times more, then rode by—there seemed to be a dozen of the horses—and I heard nothing more.

I struggled, but could not free myself from my bonds. I tried to speak, but the gag was effective; I could not make a sound. I listened for my wife's voice and my child's—listened long and intently, but no sound came from the other end of the room where their bed was. This silence became more and more awful, more and more ominous, every moment. Could you have endured an hour of it, do you think? Pity me, then, who had to endure three. Three hours?—it was three ages! Whenever the clock struck, it seemed as if years had gone by since I had heard it last. All this time I was struggling in my bonds; and at last, about dawn, I got myself free, and rose up and stretched my stiff limbs. I was able to distinguish details pretty well. The floor was littered with things thrown there by the robbers during their search for my savings. The first object that caught my particular attention was a document of mine which I had seen the rougher of the two ruffians glance at and then cast away. It had blood on it! I staggered to the other end of the room. Oh, poor unoffending, helpless ones, there they lay, their troubles ended, mine begun!

Did I appeal to the law—I? Does it quench the pauper's thirst if the King drink for him? Oh, no, no, no—I wanted no impertinent interference of the law. Laws and the gallows could not pay the debt that was owing to me! Let the laws leave the matter in my hands, and have no fears: I would find the debtor and collect the debt. How accomplish this, do you say? How accomplish it, and feel so sure about it, when I had neither seen the robbers' faces, nor heard their natural voices, nor had any idea who they might be? Nevertheless, I *was* sure—quite sure, quite confident. I had a clue—a clue which you would not have valued—a clue which would not have greatly helped even a detective, since he would lack the secret of how to apply it. I shall come to that, presently—you shall see. Let us go on, now, taking things in their due order. There was one circumstance which gave me a slant in a definite direction to begin with: Those two robbers were manifestly soldiers in tramp disguise; and not new to military service, but old in it—regulars, perhaps; they did not acquire their soldierly attitude, gestures, carriage, in a day, nor a month, nor yet in a year. So I thought, but said nothing. And one of them had said, "the captain's voice, by G—!"—the one whose life I would have. Two miles away, several regiments were in camp, and two companies of U.S. cavalry. When I learned that Captain Blakely, of Company C had passed our way, that night, with an escort, I said nothing, but in that company I resolved to seek my man. In conversation I studiously and persistently described the robbers as tramps, camp followers; and among this class the people made useless search, none suspecting the soldiers but me.

Working patiently, by night, in my desolated home, I made a disguise for myself out of various odds and ends of clothing; in the nearest village I bought a pair of blue goggles. By and by, when the military camp broke up, and Company C was ordered a hundred miles north, to Napoleon, I secreted my small hoard of money in my belt, and took my departure in the night. When Company C arrived in Napoleon, I was already there. Yes, I was there, with a new trade—fortune-teller. Not to seem partial, I made friends and told fortunes among all the companies garrisoned there; but I gave Company C the great bulk of my attentions. I made myself limitlessly obliging to these particular men; they could ask me no favor, put upon me no risk, which I would decline. I became the willing butt of their jokes; this perfected my popularity; I became a favorite.

I early found a private who lacked a thumb—what joy it was to me! And when I found that he alone, of all the company, had lost a thumb, my last misgiving vanished; I was *sure* I was on the right track. This man's name was Kruger, a German. There were nine Germans in the company. I watched, to see who might be his intimates; but he seemed to have no especial intimates. But *I* was his intimate; and I took care to make the intimacy grow. Sometimes I so hungered for my revenge that I could hardly restrain myself from going on my knees and begging him to point out the man who had murdered my wife and child; but I managed to bridle my tongue. I bided my time, and went on telling fortunes, as opportunity offered.

My apparatus was simple: a little red paint and a bit of white paper. I painted the ball of the client's thumb, took a print of it on the paper, studied it that night, and revealed his fortune to him next day. What was my idea in this nonsense? It was this: When I was a youth, I knew an old Frenchman who had been a prison-keeper for thirty years, and he told me that there was one thing about a person which never changed, from the cradle to the grave—the lines in the ball of the thumb; and he said that these lines were never exactly alike in the thumbs of any two human beings. In these days, we photograph the new criminal, and hang his picture in the Rogues' Gallery for future reference; but that Frenchman, in his day, used to take a print of the ball of a new prisoner's thumb and put that away for future reference. He always said that pictures were no good—future disguises could make them useless; "The thumb's the only sure thing," said he; "you can't disguise that." And he used to prove his theory, too, on my friends and acquaintances; it always succeeded.

I went on telling fortunes. Every night I shut myself in, all alone, and studied the day's thumb-prints with a magnifying-glass. Imagine the devouring eagerness with which I pored over those mazy red spirals, with that document by my side which bore the right-hand thumb-and-finger-marks of that unknown murderer, printed with the dearest blood—to me—that was ever shed on this earth! And many and many a time I had to repeat the same old disappointed remark, "will they *never* correspond!"

But my reward came at last. It was the print of the thumb of the forty-third man of Company C whom I had experimented on—private Franz Adler. An hour before, I did not know the murderer's name, or voice, or figure, or face, or nationality; but now I knew all these things! I believed I might feel sure; the Frenchman's repeated demonstrations being so good a warranty. Still, there was a way to *make* sure. I had an impression of Kruger's left thumb. In the morning I took him aside when he was off duty; and when we were out of sight and hearing of witnesses, I said, impressively:—

"A part of your fortune is so grave, that I thought it would be better for you if I did not tell it in public. You and another man, whose fortune I was studing last night,—private Adler,— have been murdering a woman and a child! You are being dogged: within five days both of you will be assassinated."

He dropped on his knees, frightened out of his wits; and for five minutes he kept pouring out the same set of words, like a demented person, and in the same half-crying way which was one of my memories of that murderous night in my cabin:—

"I didn't do it; upon my soul I didn't do it; and I tried to keep *him* from doing it; I did, as God is my witness. He did it alone."

This was all I wanted. And I tried to get rid of the fool; but no, he clung to me, imploring me to save him from the assassin. He said,—

"I have money—ten thousand dollars—hid away, the fruit of

loot and thievery; save me—tell me what to do, and you shall have it, every penny. Two thirds of it is my cousin Adler's; but you can take it all. We hid it when we first came here. But I hid it in a new place yesterday, and have not told him—shall not tell him. I was going to desert, and get away with it all. It is gold, and too heavy to carry when one is running and dodging; but a woman who has been gone over the river two days to prepare my way for me is going to follow me with it; and if I got no chance to describe the hiding-place to her I was going to slip my silver watch into her hand, or send it to her, and she would understand. There's a piece of paper in the back of the case, which tells it all. Here, take the watch—tell me what to do!''

He was trying to press his watch upon me, and was exposing the paper and explaining it to me, when Adler appeared on the scene, about a dozen yards away. I said to poor Kruger:—

"Put up your watch, I don't want it. You shan't come to any harm. Go, now; I must tell Adler his fortune. Presently I will tell you how to escape the assassin; meantime shall have to examine your thumb-mark again. Say nothing to Adler about this thing—say nothing to anybody."

He went away filled with fright and gratitude, poor devil. I told Adler a long fortune,—purposely so long that I could not finish it; promised to come to him on guard, that night, and tell him the really important part of it—the tragical part of it, I said,—so must be out of reach of eavesdroppers. They always kept a picket-watch outside the town,—mere discipline and ceremony,—no occasion for it, no enemy around.

Toward midnight I set out, equipped with the counter-sign, and picked my way toward the lonely region where Adler was to keep his watch. It was so dark that I stumbled right on a dim figure almost before I could get out a protecting word. The sentinel hailed and I answered, both at the same moment. I added, "It's only me—the fortune-teller." Then I slipped to the poor devil's side, and without a word I drove my dirk into his heart! *Ja wohl*, laughed I, it *was* the tragedy part of his fortune, indeed! As he fell from his horse, he clutched at me, and my blue goggles remained in his hand; and away plunged the beast dragging him, with his foor in the stirrup.

I fled through the woods, and made good my escape, leaving the accusing goggles behind me in that dead man's hand.

This was fifteen or sixteen years ago. Since then I have wandered aimlessly about the earth, sometimes at work, sometimes idle; sometimes with money, sometimes with none; but always tired of life, and wishing it was done, for my mission here was finished, with the act of that night; and the only pleasure, solace, satisfaction I had, in all those tedious years, was in the daily reflection, "I have killed him!"

Four years ago, my health began to fail. I had wandered into Munich, in my purposeless way. Being out of money, I sought work, and got it; did my duty faithfully about a year, and was then given the berth of night watchman yonder in that dead-house which you visited lately. The place suited my mood. I liked it. I liked being with the dead—liked being alone with them. I used to wander among those rigid corpses, and peer into their austere faces, by the hour. The later the time, the more impressive it was; I preferred the late time. Sometimes I turned the lights low: this gave perspective, you see; and the imagination could play; always, the dim receding ranks of the dead inspired one with weird and fascinating fancies. Two years ago—I had been there a year then—I was sitting all alone in the watch-room, one gusty winter's night, chilled, numb, comfortless; drowsing gradually into unconsciousness; the sobbing of the wind and the slamming of distant shutters falling fainter and fainter upon my dulling ear each moment, when sharp and suddenly that dead-bell rang out a blood-curdling alarum over my head! The shock of it nearly paralyzed me; for it was the first time I had ever heard it.

I gathered myself together and flew to the corpse-room. About midway down the outside rank, a shrouded figure was sitting upright, wagging its head slowly from one side to the other—a grisly spectacle! Its side was toward me. I hurried to it and peered into its face. Heavens, it was Adler!

Can you divine what my first thought was? Put into words, it was this: "It seems, then, you escaped me once: there will be a different result this time!"

Evidently this creature was suffering unimaginable terrors. Think what it must have been to wake up in the midst of that voiceless hush, and look over that grim congregation of the dead! What gratitude shone in his skinny white face when he saw a living form before him! And how the fervency of this mute gratitude was augmented when his eyes fell upon the life-giving cordials which I carried in my hands! Then imagine the horror which came into this pinched face when I put the cordials behind me, and said mockingly,—

"Speak up, Franz Adler—call upon these dead. Doubtless they will listen and have pity; but here there is none else that will."

He tried to speak, but that part of the shroud which bound his jaws, held firm and would not let him. He tried to lift imploring hands, but they were crossed upon his breast and tied. I said—

"Shout, Franz Adler; make the sleepers in the distant streets hear you and bring help. Shout—and lose no time, for there is little to lose. What, you cannot? That is a pity; but it is no matter—it does not always bring help. When you and your cousin murdered a helpless woman and child in a cabin in Arkansas—my wife, it was, and my child!—they shrieked for help, you remember; but it did no good; you remember that it did no good, is it not so? Your teeth chatter—then why cannot you shout? Loosen the bandages with your hands—then you can. Ah, I see—your hands are tied, they cannot aid you. How strangely things repeat themselves, after long years; for *my* hands were tied, that night, you remember? Yes, tied much as yours are now—how odd that is. I could not pull free. It did not occur to you to untie me; it does not occur to me to untie you. Sh—! there's a late footstep. It is coming this way. Hark, how near it is! One can count the footfalls—one—two—three. There—it is just outside. Now is the time! Shout, man, shout!— it is the one sole chance between you and eternity! Ah, you see you have delayed too long—it is gone by. There—it is dying out. It is gone! Think of it—reflect upon it—you have heard a human footstep for the last time. How curious it must be, to listen to so common a sound as that, and know that one will never hear the fellow to it again."

Oh, my friend, the agony in that shrouded face was ecstasy to see! I thought of a new torture, and applied it—assisting myself with a trifle of lying invention:—

"That poor Kruger tried to save my wife and child, and I did him a grateful good turn for it when the time came. I persuaded him to rob you; and I and a woman helped him to desert, and got him away in safety."

A look as of surprise and triumph shone out dimly through the anguish in my victim's face. I was disturbed, disquieted. I said—

"What, then,—didn't he escape?"

A negative shake of the head.

"No? What happened, then?"

The satisfaction in the shrouded face was still plainer. The man tried to mumble out some words—could not succeed; tried to express something with his obstructed hands—failed; paused a moment, then feebly tilted his head, in a meaning way, toward the corpse that lay nearest him.

"Dead?" I asked. "Failed to escape?—caught in the act and shot?"

Negative shake of the head.

"How, then?"

Again the man tried to do something with his hands. I watched closely, but could not guess the intent. I bent over and watched still more intently. He had twisted a thumb around and was weakly punching at his breast with it.

"Ah—stabbed, do you mean?"

Affirmative nod, accompanied by a spectral smile of such peculiar devilishness, that it struck an awakening light through my dull brain, and I cried—

"Did *I* stab him, mistaking him for you?—for that stroke was meant for none but you."

The affirmative nod of the re-dying rascal was as joyous as his failing strength was able to put into its expression.

"O, miserable, miserable me, to slaughter the pitying soul that stood a friend to my darlings when they were helpless, and would have saved them if he could! miserable, oh, miserable, miserable me!"

I fancied I heard the muffled gurgle of a mocking laugh. I took my face out of my hands, and saw my enemy sinking back upon his inclined board.

He was a satisfactory long time dying. He had a wonderful vitality, an astonishing constitution. Yes, he was a pleasant long time at it. I got a chair and a newspaper, and sat down by him and read. Occasionally I took a sip of brandy. This was necessary, on account of the cold. But I did it partly because I saw, that along at first, whenever I reached for the bottle, he thought I was going to give him some. I read aloud: mainly imaginary accounts of people snatched from the grave's threshold and restored to life and vigor by a few spoonsful of liquor and a warm bath. Yes, he had a long, hard death of it—three hours and six minutes, from the time he rang his bell.

It is believed that in all these eighteen years that have elapsed since the institution of the corpse-watch, no shrouded occupant of the Bavarian dead-houses has ever rung its bell. Well, it is a harmless belief. Let it stand at that.

The chill of that death-room had penetrated my bones. It revived and fastened upon me the disease which had been afflicting me, but which, up to that night, had been steadily disappearing. That man murdered my wife and my child; and in three days hence he will have added me to his list. No matter—God! how delicious the memory of it!—I caught him escaping from his grave, and thrust him back into it!

After that night, I was confined to my bed for a week; but as soon as I could get about, I went to the dead-house books and got the number of the house which Adler had died in. A wretched lodging house, it was. It was my idea that he would naturally have gotten hold of Kruger's effects, being his cousin; and I wanted to get Kruger's watch, if I could. But while I was sick, Adler's things had been sold and scattered, all except a few old letter, and some odds and ends of no value. However, through those letters, I traced out a son of Kruger's, the only relative he left. He is a man of thirty, now, a shoemaker by trade, and living at No. 14 Königstrasse, Mannheim—widower, with several small children. Without explaining to him why, I have furnished two thirds of his support, ever since.

Now, as to that watch—see how strangely things happen! I traced it around and about Germany for more than a year, at considerable cost in money and vexation; and at last I got it. Got it, and was unspeakably glad; opened it, and found nothing in it! Why, I might have known that that bit of paper was not going to stay there all this time. Of course I gave up that ten thousand dollars then; gave it up, and dropped it out of my mind: and most sorrowfully, for I had wanted it for Kruger's son.

Last night, when I consented at last that I must die, I began to make ready. I proceeded to burn all useless papers; and sure enough, from a batch of Adler's, not previously examined with thoroughness, out dropped that long-desired scrap! I recognized it in a moment. Here it is—I will translate it:

"Brick livery stable, stone foundation, middle of town, corner of Orleans and Market. Corner toward Court-house. Third stone, fourth row. Stick notice there, saying how many are to come."

There—take it, and preserve it. Kruger explained that that stone was removable; and that it was in the north wall of the foundation, fourth row from the top, and third stone from the west. The money is secreted behind it. He said the closing sentence was a blind, to mislead in case the paper should fall into wrong hands. It probably performed that office for Adler.

Now I want to beg that when you make your intended journey down the river, you will hunt out that hidden money, and send it to Adam Kruger, care of the Mannheim address which I have mentioned. It will make a rich man of him, and I shall sleep the sounder in my grave for knowing that I have done what I could for the son of the man who tried to save my wife and child— albeit my hand ignorantly struck him down, whereas the impulse of my heart would have been to shield and serve him.

CHAPTER XXXII

THE DISPOSAL OF A BONANZA

"Such was Ritter's narrative," said I to my two friends.

There was a profound and impressive silence, which lasted a considerable time; then both men broke into a fusillade of excited and admiring ejaculations over the strange incidents of the tale; and this, along with a rattling fire of questions, was kept up until all hands were about out of breath. Then my friends began to cool down, and draw off, under shelter of occasional volleys, into silence and abysmal reverie. For ten minutes now, there was stillness. Then Rogers said dreamily:—

"Ten thousand dollars." Adding, after a considerable pause,—

"Ten thousand. It is a heap of money."

Presently the poet inquired,—

"Are you going to send it to him right away?"

"Yes," I said. "It is a queer question."

No reply. After a little, Rogers asked, hesitatingly:

"*All* of it?— That is— I mean—"

"*Certainly,* all of it."

I was going to say more, but stopped,—was stopped by a train of thought which started up in me. Thompson spoke, but my mind was absent and I did not catch what he said. But I heard Rogers answer,—

"Yes, it seems so to me. It ought to be quite sufficient; for I don't see that *he* has done anything."

Presently the poet said,—

"When you come to look at it, it is *more* than sufficient. Just look at it—five thousand dollars! Why, he couldn't spend it in a lifetime! And it would injure him, too; perhaps ruin him—you want to look at that. In a little while he would throw his last away, shut up his shop, maybe take to drinking, maltreat his motherless children, drift into other evil courses, go steadily from bad to worse—"

"Yes, that's it," interrupted Rogers, fervently, "I've seen it a hundred times—yes, more than a hundred. You put money into the hands of a man like that, if you want to destroy him, that's all; just put money into his hands, it's all you've got to do; and if it don't pull him down, and take all the usefulness out of him, and all the self-respect and everything, then I don't know human nature—ain't that so, Thompson? And even if we were to give him a *third* of it; why, in less than six months—"

"Less than six *weeks,* you'd better say!" said I, warming up and breaking in. "Unless he had that three thousand dollars in safe hands where he couldn't touch it, he would no more last you six weeks than—"

"Or *course* he wouldn't," said Thompson; "I've edited books for that kind of people; and the moment they get their hands on the royalty—maybe it's three thousand, maybe it's two thousand—"

"What business has that shoemaker with two thousand dollars, I should like to know?" broke in Rogers, earnestly. "A man perhaps perfectly contented now, there in Mannheim, surrounded by his own class, eating his bread with the appetite which laborious industry alone can give, enjoying his humble life, honest, upright, pure in heart; and *blest!*—yes, I say blest! blest above all the myriads that go in silk attire and walk the empty artificial round of social folly—but just you put *that* temptation before him once! just you lay fifteen hundred dollars before a man like that, and say—"

"Fifteen hundred devils!" cried I, *"five* hundred would rot his principles, paralyze his industry, drag him to the rumshop, thence to the gutter, thence to the almshouse, thence to—"

"Why put upon ourselves this crime, gentlemen?" interrupted the poet earnestly and appealingly. "He is happy where he is, and *as* he is. Every sentiment of honor, every sentiment of charity, every sentiment of high and sacred benevolence warns us, beseeches us, commands us to leave him undisturbed. That is real friendship, that is true friendship. We could follow other courses that would be more showy; but none that would be so truly kind and wise, depend upon it."

After some further talk, it became evident that each of us, down in his heart, felt some misgivings over this settlement of the matter. It was manifest that we all felt that we ought to send the poor shoemaker *something*. There was long and thoughtful discussion of this point; and we finally decided to send him a chromo.

Well, now that everything seemed to be arranged satisfactorily to everybody concerned, a new trouble broke out: it transpired that these two men were expecting to share equally in the money with me. That was not my idea. I said that if they got half of it between them they might consider themselves lucky. Rogers said:—

"Who would have had *any* if it hadn't been for me? I flung out the first hint—but for that it would all have gone to the shoemaker."

Thompson said that he was thinking of the thing himself at the very moment that Rogers had originally spoken.

I retorted that the idea would have occurred to me plenty soon enough, and without anybody's help. I was slow about thinking, maybe, but I was sure.

This matter warmed up into a quarrel; then into a fight; and each man got pretty badly battered. As soon as I had got myself mended up after a fashion, I ascended to the hurricane deck in a pretty sour humor. I found Captain McCord there, and said, as pleasantly as my humor would permit:—

"I have come to say good-bye, captain. I wish to go ashore at Napoleon."

"Go ashore where?"

"Napoleon."

The captain laughed; but seeing that I was not in a jovial mood, stopped that and said,—

"But are you serious?"

"Serious? I certainly am."

"The captain glanced up at the pilot-house and said,—

"He wants to get off at Napoleon!"

"Napoleon?"

"That's what he says."

"Great Caesar's ghost!"

Uncle Mumford approached along the deck. The captain said,—

"Uncle, here's a friend of yours wants to get off at Napoleon!"

"Well, by—!"

I said,—

"Come, what is all this about? Can't a man go ashore at Napoleon if he wants to?"

"Why, hang it, don't you know? There *isn't* any Napoleon any more. Hasn't been for years and years. The Arkansas River burst through it, tore it all to rags, and emptied it into the Mississippi!"

"Carried the *whole* town away?—banks, churches, jails, newspaper-offices, court-house, theatre, fire department, livery stable,—*everything?*"

"Everything. Just a fifteen-minute job, or such a matter. Didn't leave hide nor hair, shred nor shingle of it, except the fag-end of a shanty and one brick chimney. This boat is paddling along right now, where the dead-centre of that town used to be; yonder is the brick chimney,—all that's left of Napoleon. These dense woods on the right used to be a mile back of the town.

371

Take a look behind you—up-stream—now you begin to recognize this country, don't you?"

"Yes, I do recognize it now. It is the most wonderful thing I ever heard of; by a long shot the most wonderful—and unexpected."

Mr. Thompson and Mr. Rogers had arrived, meantime, with satchels and umbrellas, and had silently listened to the captain's news. Thompson put a half-dollar in my hand and said softly:—

"For my share of the chromo."

Rogers followed suit.

Yes, it was an astonishing thing to see the Mississippi rolling between unpeopled shores and straight over the spot where I used to see a good big self-complacent town twenty years ago. Town that was county-seat of a great and important county; town with a big United States marine hospital; town of innumerable fights—an inquest every day; town where I had used to know the prettiest girl, and the most accomplished in the whole Mississippi Valley; town where we were handed the first printed news of the "Pennsylvania's" mournful disaster a quarter of a century ago; a town no more—swallowed up, vanished, gone to feed the fishes; nothing left but a fragment of a shanty and a crumbling brick chimney!

CHAPTER XXXIII

REFRESHMENTS AND ETHICS

In regard to Island 74, which is situated not far from the former Napoleon, a freak of the river here has sorely perplexed the laws of men and made them a vanity and a jest. When the State of Arkansas was chartered, she controlled "to the centre of the river"—a most unstable line. The State of Mississippi claimed "to the channel"—another shifty and unstable line. No. 74 belonged to Arkansas. By and by a cut-off threw this big island out of Arkansas, and yet not *within* Mississippi. "Middle of the river" on one side of it, "channel" on the other. That is as I understand the problem. Whether I have got the details right or wrong, this *fact* remains: that here is this big and exceedingly valuable island of four thousand acres, thrust out in the cold, and belonging to neither the one State nor the other; paying taxes to neither, owing allegiance to neither. One man owns the whole island, and of right is "the man without a country."

Island 92 belongs to Arkansas. The river moved it over and joined it to Mississippi. A chap established a whiskey shop there, without a Mississippi license, and enriched himself upon Mississippi custom under Arkansas protection (where no license was in those days required).

We glided steadily down the river in the usual privacy—steamboat or other moving thing seldom seen. Scenery as always: stretch upon stretch of almost unbroken forest, on both sides of the river; soundless solitude. Here and there a cabin or two, standing in small openings on the gray and grassless banks—cabins which had formerly stood a quarter or half-mile farther to the front, and gradually been pulled farther and farther back as the shores caved in. As at Pilcher's Point, for instance, where the cabins had been moved back three hundred yards in three months, so we were told; but the caving banks had already caught up with them, and they were being conveyed rearward once more.

Napoleon had but small opinion of Greenville, Mississippi, in the old times; but behold, Napoleon is gone to the catfishes, and here is Greenville full of life and activity, and making a considerable flourish in the Valley; having three thousand inhabitants, it is said, and doing a gross trade of $2,500,000 annually. A growing town.

There was much talk on the boat about the Calhoun Land Company, an enterprise which is expected to work wholesome results. Colonel Calhoun, a grandson of the statesman, went to Boston and formed a syndicate which purchased a large tract of land on the river, in Chicot County, Arkansas,—some ten thousand acres—for cotton-growing. The purpose is to work on a cash basis: buy at first hands, and handle their own product; supply their negro laborers with provisions and necessaries at a trifling profit, say 8 or 10 per cent; furnish them comfortable quarters, etc., and encourage them to save money and remain on the place. If this proves a financial success, as seems quite certain, they propose to establish a banking-house in Greenville, and lend money at an unburdensome rate of interest—6 per cent is spoken of.

The trouble heretofore has been—I am quoting remarks of planters and steamboatmen—that the planters, although owning the land, were without cash capital; had to hypothecate both land and crop to carry on the business. Consequently, the commission dealer who furnishes the money takes some risk and demands big interest—usually 10 per cent, and 2½ per cent for negotiating the loan. The planter has also to buy his supplies through the same dealer, paying commissions and profits. Then when he ships his crop, the dealer adds his commissions, insurance, etc. So, taking it by and large, and first and last, the dealer's share of that crop is about 25 per cent.*

A cotton-planter's estimate of the average margin of profit on planting, in his section: One man and mule will raise ten acres of cotton, giving ten bales cotton, worth, say, $500; cost of producing, say $350; net profit, $150, or $15 per acre. There is also a profit now from the cotton-seed, which formerly had little value—none where much transportation was necessary. In sixteen hundred pounds crude cotton, four hundred are lint, worth, say, ten cents a pound; and twelve hundred pounds of seed, worth $12 or $13 per ton. Maybe in future even the *stems* will not be thrown away. Mr. Edward Atkinson says that for each bale of cotton there are fifteen hundred pounds of stems, and that these are very rich in phosphate of lime and potash; that when ground and mixed with ensilage or cotton-seed meal (which is too rich for use as fodder in large quantities), the stem mixture makes a superior food, rich in all the elements needed for the production of milk, meat, and bone. Heretofore the stems have been considered a nuisance.

Complaint is made that the planter remains grouty toward the former slave, since the war; will have nothing but a chill business relation with him, no sentiment permitted to intrude; will not keep a "store" himself, and supply the negro's wants and thus protect the negro's pocket and make him able and willing to stay on the place and an advantage to him to do it, but lets that privilege to some thrifty Israelite, who encourages the thoughtless negro and wife to buy all sorts of things which they could do without,—buy on credit, at big prices, month after month, credit based on the negro's share of the growing crop; and at the end of the season, the negro's share belongs to the Israelite, the negro is in debt besides, is discouraged, dissatisfied, restless, and both he and the planter are injured; for he will take steamboat and migrate, and the planter must get a stranger in his place who does not know him, does not care for him, will flatten the Israelite a season, and follow his predecessor per steamboat.

It is hoped that the Calhoun Company will show, by its humane and protective treatment of its laborers, that its method is the most profitable for both planter and negro; and it is believed that a general adoption of that method will then follow.

---

*"But what can the state do where the people are under subjection to rates of interest ranging from 18 to 30 per cent, and are also under the necessity of purchasing their crops in advance even of planting, at these rates, for the privilege of purchasing all their supplies at 100 per cent profit?"—*Edward Atkinson.*

And where so many are saying their say, shall not the barkeeper testify? He is thoughtful, observant, never drinks; endeavors to earn his salary, and *would* earn it if there were custom enough. He says the people along here in Mississippi and Louisiana will send up the river to buy vegetables rather than raise them, and they will come aboard at the landings and buy fruits of the barkeeper. Thinks they "don't know anything but cotton;" believes they don't know how to raise vegetables and fruit—"at least the most of them." Says "a nigger will go to H for a watermelon" ("H" is all I find in the stenographer's report—means Halifax probably, though that seems a good way to go for a watermelon). Barkeeper buys watermelons for five cents up the river, brings them down and sells them for fifty. "Why does he mix such elaborate and picturesque drinks for the nigger hands on the boat?" Because they won't have any other. "They want a *big* drink; don't make any difference what you make it of, they want the worth of their money. You give a nigger a plain gill of half-a-dollar brandy for five cents—will he touch it? No. Ain't size enough to it. But you put up a pint of all kinds of worthless rubbish, and heave in some red stuff to make it beautiful—red's the main thing—and he wouldn't put down that glass to go to a circus." All the bars on this Anchor Line are rented and owned by one firm. They furnish the liquors from their own establishment, and hire the barkeepers "on salary." Good liquors? Yes, on some of the boats, where there are the kind of passengers that want it and can pay for it. On the other boats? No. Nobody but the deck hands and firemen to drink it. "Brandy? Yes, I've got brandy, plenty of it; but you don't want any of it unless you've made your will." It isn't as it used to be in the old times. Then everybody travelled by steamboat, everybody drank, and everybody treated everybody else. "Now most everybody goes by railroad, and the rest don't drink." In the old times, the barkeeper owned the bar himself, "and was gay and smarty and talky and all jewelled up, and was the toniest aristocrat on the boat; used to make $2,000 on a trip. A father who left his son a steamboat bar, left him a fortune. Now he leaves him board and lodging; yes, and washing, if a shirt a trip will do. Yes, indeedy, times are changed. Why, do you know, on the principal line of boats on the Upper Mississippi, they don't have any bar at all! Sounds like poetry, but it's the petrified truth."

CHAPTER XXXIV

TOUGH YARNS

Stack Island. I remembered Stack Island; also Lake Providence, Louisiana—which is the first distinctly Southern-looking town you come to, downward-bound; lies level and low, shade-trees hung with venerable gray beards of Spanish moss; "restful, pensive, Sunday aspect about the place," commends Uncle Mumford, with feeling—also with truth.

A Mr. H. furnished some minor details of fact concerning this region which I would have hesitated to believe if I had not known him to be a steamboat mate. He was a passenger of ours, a resident of Arkansas City, and bound to Vicksburg to join his boat, a little Sunflower packet. He was an austere man, and had the reputation of being singularly unworldly, for a river man. Among other things, he said that Arkansas had been injured and kept back by generations of exaggerations concerning the mosquitoes there. One may smile, said he, and turn the matter off as being a small thing; but when you come to look at the effects produced, in the way of discouragement of immigration, and diminished values of property, it was quite the opposite of a small thing, or thing in any wise to be coughed down or sneered at. These mosquitoes had been persistently represented as being formidable and lawless; whereas "the truth is, they are feeble, insignificant in size, diffident to a fault, sensitive"—and so on, and so on; you would have supposed he was talking about his family. But if he was soft on the Arkansas mosquitoes, he was hard enough on the mosquitoes of Lake Providence to make up for it—"those Lake Providence colossi," as he finely called them. He said that two of them could whip a dog, and that four of them could hold a man down; and except help come, they would kill him—"butcher him," as he expressed it. Referred in a sort of casual way—and yet significant way—to "the fact that the life policy in its simplest form is unknown in Lake Providence—they take out a mosquito policy besides." He told many remarkable things about those lawless insects. Among others, said he had seen them try to *vote*. Noticing that this statement seemed to be a good deal of a strain on us, he modified it a little: said he might have been mistaken, as to that particular, but knew he had seen them around the polls "canvassing."

There was another passenger—friend of H.'s—who backed up the harsh evidence against those mosquitoes, and detailed some stirring adventures which he had had with them. The stories were pretty sizable, merely pretty sizable; yet Mr. H. was continually interrupting with a cold, inexorable "Wait—knock off twenty-five per cent of that; now go on;" or, "Wait—you are getting that too strong; cut it down, cut it down—you get a leetle too much costumery on to your statements: always dress a fact in tights, never in an ulster;" or, "Pardon, once more: if you are going to load anything more on to that statement, you want to get a couple of lighters and tow the rest, because it's drawing all the water there is in the river already; stick to facts— just stick to the cold facts; what these gentlemen want for a book is the frozen truth—ain't that so, gentlemen?" He explained privately that it was necessary to watch this man all the time, and keep him within bounds; it would not do to neglect this precaution, as he, Mr. H., "knew to his sorrow." Said he, "I will not deceive you; he told me such a monstrous lie once, that it swelled my left ear up, and spread it so that I was actually not able to see out around it; it remained so for months, and people came miles to see me fan myself with it."

CHAPTER XXXV

VICKSBURG DURING THE TROUBLE

We used to plough past the lofty hill-city, Vicksburg, downstream; but we cannot do that now. A cutoff has made a country town of it, like Osceola, St. Genevieve, and several others. There is currentless water—also a big island—in front of Vicksburg now. You come down the river the other side of the island, then turn and come up to the town; that is, in high water: in low water you can't come up, but must land some distance below it.

Signs and scars still remain, as reminders of Vicksburg's tremendous war-experiences; earthworks, trees crippled by the cannon balls, cave-refuges in the clay precipices, etc. The caves did good service during the six weeks' bombardment of the city—May 18 to July 4, 1863. They were used by the noncombatants—mainly by the women and children; not to live in constantly, but to fly to for safety on occasion. They were mere holes, tunnels, driven into the perpendicular clay bank, then branched Y shape, within the hill. Life in Vicksburg, during the six weeks was perhaps—but wait; here are some materials out of which to reproduce it:—

Population, twenty-seven thousand soldiers and three thousand non-combatants; the city utterly cut off from the world— walled solidly in, the frontage by gunboats, the rear by soldiers and batteries; hence, no buying and selling with the outside; no passing to and fro; no God-speeding a parting guest, no welcoming a coming one; no printed acres of world-wide news to be read at breakfast, mornings—a tedious dull absence of such matter, instead; hence, also, no running to see steamboats smoking into view in the distance up or down, and ploughing toward the town—for none came, the river lay vacant and undisturbed; no rush and turmoil around the railway station, no struggling over bewildered swarms of passengers by noisy mobs of hackmen—all quiet there; flour two hundred dollars a barrel, sugar thirty, corn ten dollars a bushel, bacon five dollars a pound, rum a hundred dollars a gallon; other things in proportion: consequently, no roar and racket of drays and carriages tearing along the streets; nothing for them to do, among that handful of non-combatants of exhausted means; at three o'clock in the morning, silence; silence so dead that the measured tramp of a sentinel can be heard a seemingly impossible distance; out of hearing of this lonely sound, perhaps the stillness is absolute: all in a moment come ground-shaking thunder-crashes of artillery, the sky is cobwebbed with the cris-crossing red lines streaming from soaring bomb-shells, and a rain of iron fragments descends upon the city; descends upon the empty streets: streets which are not empty a moment later, but mottled with dim figures of frantic women and children skurrying from home and bed toward the cave dungeons—encouraged by the humorous grim soldiery, who shout "Rats, to your holes!" and laugh.

The cannon-thunder rages, shells scream and crash overhead, the iron rain pours down, one hour, two hours, three, possibly six, then stops; silence follows, but the streets are still empty; the silence continues; by and by a head projects from a cave here and there and yonder, and reconnoitres, cautiously; the silence still continuing, bodies follow heads, and jaded, half-smothered creatures group themselves about, stretch their cramped limbs, draw in deep draughts of the grateful fresh air, gossip with the neighbors from the next cave; maybe straggle off home presently, or take a lounge through the town, if the stillness continues; and will skurry to the holes again, by and by, when the war-tempest breaks forth once more.

There being but three thousand of these cave-dwellers— merely the population of a village—would they not come to know each other, after a week or two, and familiarly; insomuch that the fortunate or unfortunate experiences of one would be of interest to all?

Those are the materials furnished by history. From them

might not almost anybody reproduce for himself the life of that time in Vicksburg? Could you, who did not experience it, come nearer to reproducing it to the imagination of another non- participant than could a Vicksburger who *did* experience it? It seems impossible; and yet there are reasons why it might not really be. When one makes his first voyage in a ship, it is an experience which multitudinously bristles with striking novelties; novelties which are in such sharp contrast with all this person's former experiences that they take a seemingly deathless grip upon his imagination and memory. By tongue or pen he can make a landsman live that strange and stirring voyage over with him; make him see it all and feel it all. But if he wait? If he make ten voyages in succession—what then? Why, the thing has lost color, snap, surprise; and has become commonplace. The man would have nothing to tell that would quicken a landsman's pulse.

Years ago, I talked with a couple of the Vicksburg noncombatants—a man and his wife. Left to tell their story in their own way, those people told it without fire, almost without interest.

A week of their wonderful life there would have made their tongues eloquent forever perhaps; but they had six weeks of it, and that wore the novelty all out; they got used to being bombshelled out of home and into the ground; the matter became commonplace. After that, the possibility of their ever being startlingly interested in their talks about it was gone. What the man said was to this effect:—

"It got to be Sunday all the time. Seven Sundays in the week—to us, anyway. We hadn't anything to do, and time hung heavy. Seven Sundays, and all of them broken up at one time or another, in the day or in the night, by a few hours of the awful storm of fire and thunder and iron. At first we used to shin for the holes a good deal faster than we did afterwards. The first time, I forgot the children, and Maria fetched them both along. When she was all safe in the cave she fainted. Two or three weeks afterwards, when she was running for the holes, one morning, through a shell-shower, a big shell burst near her and covered her all over with dirt, and a piece of the iron carried away her game-bag of false hair from the back of her head. Well, she stopped to get that game-bag before she shoved along again! Was getting used to things already, you see. We all got so that we could tell a good deal about shells; and after that we didn't always go under shelter if it was a light shower. Us men would loaf around and talk; and a man would say, 'There she goes!' and name the kind of shell it was from the sound of it, and go on talking—if there wasn't any danger from it. If a shell was bursting close over us, we stopped talking and stood still;—uncomfortable, yes, but it wasn't safe to move. When it let go, we went on talking again, if nobody hurt—maybe saying, 'That was a ripper!' or some such commonplace comment before we resumed; or, maybe, we would see a shell poising itself away high in the air overhead. In that case, every fellow just whipped out a sudden, 'See you again, gents!' and shoved. Often and often I saw gangs of ladies promenading the streets, looking as cheerful as you please, and keeping an eye canted up watching the shells; and I've seen them stop still when they were uncertain about what a shell was going to do, and wait and make certain; and after that they s'antered along again, or lit out for shelter, according to the verdict. Streets in some towns have a litter of pieces of paper, and odds and ends of one sort or another lying around. Ours hadn't; they had *iron* litter. Sometimes a man would gather up all the iron fragments and unbursted shells in his neighborhood, and pile them into a kind of monument in his front yard—a ton of it, sometimes. No glass left; glass couldn't stand such a bombardment; it was all shivered out. Windows of the houses vacant—looked like eye-holes in a skull. *Whole* panes were as scarce as news.

"We had church Sundays. Not many there, along at first; but by and by pretty good turnouts. I've seen service stop a minute, and everybody sit quiet—no voice heard, pretty funeral-like then—and all the more so on account of the awful boom and crash going on outside and overhead; and pretty soon, when a body could be heard, service would go on again. Organs and church-music mixed up with a bombardment is a powerful queer combination—along at first. Coming out of church, one morning, we had an accident—the only one that happened around me on a Sunday. I was just having a hearty hand-shake with a friend I hadn't seen for a while, and saying, 'Drop into our cave to-night, after bombardment; we've got hold of a pint of prime wh—.' Whiskey, I was going to say, you know, but a shell interrupted. A chunk of it cut the man's arm off, and left it dangling in my hand. And do you know the thing that is going to stick the longest in my memory, and outlast everything else, little and big, I reckon, is the mean thought I had then? It was 'the whiskey *is saved.*' And yet, don't you know, it was kind of excusable; because it was as scarce as diamonds, and we had only just that little; never had another taste during the siege.

"Sometimes the caves were desperately crowded, and always hot and close. Sometimes a cave had twenty or twenty-five people packed into it; no turning-room for anybody; air so foul, sometimes, you couldn't have made a candle burn in it. A child was born in one of those caves one night. Think of that; why, it was like having it born in a trunk.

"Twice we had sixteen people in our cave; and a number of times we had a dozen. Pretty suffocating in there. We always had eight; eight belonged there. Hunger and misery and sickness and fright and sorrow, and I don't know what all, got so loaded into them that none of them were ever rightly their old selves after the siege. They all died but three of us within a couple of years. One night a shell burst in front of the hole and caved it in and stopped it up. It was lively times, for a while, digging out. Some of us came near smothering. After that we made two openings—ought to have thought of it at first.

"Mule meat? No, we only got down to that the last day or two. Of course it was good; anything is good when you are starving."

This man had kept a diary during—six weeks? No, only the first six days. The first day, eight close pages; the second, five; the third, one—loosely written; the fourth, three or four lines; a line or two the fifth and sixth days; seventh day, diary abandoned; life in terrific Vicksburg having now become commonplace and matter of course.

The war history of Vicksburg has more about it to interest the general reader than that of any other of the river-towns. It is full of variety, full of incident, full of the picturesque. Vicksburg held out longer than any other important river-town, and saw warfare in all its phases, both land and water—the siege, the mine, the assault, the repulse, the bombardment, sickness, captivity, famine.

The most beautiful of all the national cemeteries is here. Over the great gateway is this inscription:—

"HERE REST IN PEACE 16,600 WHO DIED FOR THEIR COUNTRY IN THE YEARS 1861 TO 1865."

The grounds are nobly situated; being very high and commanding a wide prospect of land and river. They are tastefully laid out in broad terraces, with winding roads and paths; and there is profuse adornment in the way of semi-tropical shrubs and flowers; and in one part is a piece of native wild-wood, left just as it grew, and, therefore, perfect in its charm. Everything about this cemetery suggests the hand of the national Government. The Government's work is always conspicuous for excellence, solidity, thoroughness, neatness. The Government does its work well in the first place, and then takes care of it.

By winding-roads—which were often cut to so great a depth between perpendicular walls that they were mere roofless tunnels—we drove out a mile or two and visited the monument which stands upon the scene of the surrender of Vicksburg to General Grant by General Pemberton. Its metal will preserve it from the hackings and chippings which so defaced its predecessor, which was of marble; but the brick foundations are crumbling, and it will tumble down by and by. It overlooks a picturesque region of wooded hills and ravines; and is not unpicturesque itself, being well smothered in flowering weeds. The battered remnant of the marble monument has been removed to the National Cemetery.

On the road, a quarter of a mile townward, an aged colored

man showed us, with pride, an unexploded bomb-shell which has lain in his yard since the day it fell there during the siege.

"I was a-stannin' heah, an' de dog was a-stannin' heah; de dog he went for de shell, gwine to pick a fuss wid it; but I didn't; I says, 'Jes' make youseff at home heah; lay still whah you is, or bust up de place, jes' as you's a mind to, but *I's* got business out in de woods, *I* has!'"

Vicksburg is a town of substantial business streets and pleasant residences; it commands the commerce of the Yazoo and Sunflower Rivers; is pushing railways in several directions, through rich agricultural regions, and has a promising future of prosperity and importance.

Apparently, nearly all the river towns, big and little, have made up their minds that they must look mainly to railroads for wealth and upbuilding, henceforth. They are acting upon this idea. The signs are, that the next twenty years will bring about some noteworthy changes in the Valley, in the direction of increased population and wealth, and in the intellectual advancement and the liberalizing of opinion which go naturally with these. And yet, if one may judge by the past, the river towns will manage to find and use a chance, here and there, to cripple and retard their progress. They kept themselves back in the days of steamboating supremacy, by a system of wharfage-dues so stupidly graded as to prohibit what may be called small *retail* traffic in freights and passengers. Boats were charged such heavy wharfage that they could not afford to land for one or two passengers or a light lot of freight. Instead of encouraging the bringing of trade to their doors, the towns diligently and effectively discouraged it. They could have had many boats and low rates; but their policy rendered few boats and high rates compulsory. It was a policy which extended—and extends—from New Orleans to St. Paul.

We had a strong desire to make a trip up the Yazoo and the Sunflower—an interesting region at any time, but additionally interesting at this time, because up there the great inundation was still to be seen in force,—but we were nearly sure to have to wait a day or more for a New Orleans boat on our return; so we were obliged to give up the project.

Here is a story which I picked up on board the boat that night. I insert it in this place merely because it is a good story, not because it belongs here—for it doesn't. It was told by a passenger—a college professor—and was called to the surface in the course of a general conversation which began with talk about horses, drifted into talk about astronomy, then into talk about the lynching of the gamblers in Vicksburg half a century ago, then into talk about dreams and superstitions; and ended, after midnight, in a dispute over free trade and protection.

CHAPTER XXXVI

THE PROFESSOR'S YARN

It was in the early days. I was not a college professor then. I was a humble-minded young land-surveyor, with the world before me—to survey, in case anybody wanted it done. I had a contract to survey a route for a great mining-ditch in California, and I was on my way thither, by sea—a three or four weeks' voyage. There were a good many passengers, but I had very little to say to them; reading and dreaming were my passions, and I avoided conversation in order to indulge these appetites. There were three professional gamblers on board—rough, repulsive fellows. I never had any talk with them, yet I could not help seeing them with some frequency, for they gambled in an upper-deck state-room every day and night, and in my promenades I often had glimpses of them through their door, which stood a little ajar to let out the surplus tobacco smoke and profanity. They were an evil and hateful presence, but I had to put up with it, of course.

There was one other passenger who fell under my eye a good deal, for he seemed determined to be friendly with me, and I could not have gotten rid of him without running some chance of hurting his feelings, and I was far from wishing to do that. Besides, there was something engaging in his countrified simplicity and his beaming good-nature. The first time I saw this Mr. John Backus, I guessed, from his clothes and his looks, that he was a grazier or farmer from the back woods of some western State—doubtless Ohio—and afterward when he dropped into his personal history and I discovered that he *was* a cattle-raiser from interior Ohio, I was so pleased with my own penetration that I warmed toward him for verifying my instinct.

He got to dropping alongside me every day, after breakfast, to help me make my promenade; and so, in the course of time, his easy-working jaw had told me everything about his business, his prospects, his family, his relatives, his politics—in fact everything that concerned a Backus, living or dead. And meantime I think he had managed to get out of me everything I knew about my trade, my tribe, my purposes, my prospects, and myself. He was a gentle and persuasive genius, and this thing showed it; for I was not given to talking about my matters. I said something about triangulation, once; the stately word pleased his ear; he inquired what it meant; I explained; after that he quietly and inoffensively ignored my name, and always called me Triangle.

What an enthusiast he was in cattle! At the bare name of a bull or a cow, his eye would light and his eloquent tongue would turn itself loose. As long as I would walk and listen, he would walk and talk; he knew all breeds, he loved all breeds, he caressed them all with his affectionate tongue. I tramped along in voiceless misery whilst the cattle question was up; when I could endure it no longer, I used to deftly insert a scientific topic into the conversation; then my eye fired and his faded; my tongue fluttered, his stopped; life was a joy to me, and a sadness to him.

One day he said, a little hesitatingly, and with somewhat of diffidence:—

"Triangle, would you mind coming down to my state-room a minute, and have a little talk on a certain matter?"

I went with him at once. Arrived there, he put his head out, glanced up and down the saloon warily, then closed the door and locked it. We sat down on the sofa, and he said:—

"I'm a-going to make a little proposition to you, and if it strikes you favorable, it'll be a middling good thing for both of us. You ain't a-going out to Californy for fun, nuther am I—it's *business,* ain't that so? Well, you can do me a good turn, and so can I you, if we see fit. I've raked and scraped and saved, a considerable many years, and I've got it all here." He unlocked an old hair trunk, tumbled a chaos of shabby clothes aside, and drew a short stout bag into view for a moment, then buried it again and relocked the trunk. Dropping his voice to a cautious low tone, he continued, "She's all there—a round ten thousand dollars in yellow-boys; now this is my little idea: What I don't know about raising cattle, ain't worth knowing. There's mints of money in it, in Californy. Well, I know, and you know, that all along a line that's being surveyed, there's little dabs of land that they call 'gores,' that fall to the surveyor free gratis for nothing. All you've got to do, on your side, is to survey in such a way that the 'gores' will fall on good fat land, then you turn 'em over to me, I stock 'em with cattle, *in* rolls the cash, I plank out your share of the dollars regular, right along, and—"

I was sorry to wither his blooming enthusiasm, but it could not be helped. I interrupted, and said severely,—"I am not that kind of a surveyor. Let us change the subject, Mr. Backus."

It was pitiful to see his confusion and hear his awkward and shamefaced apologies. I was as much distressed as he was—especially as he seemed so far from having suspected that there was anything improper in his proposition. So I hastened to console him and lead him on to forget his mishap in a conversational orgy about cattle and butchery. We were lying at Acapulco; and, as we went on deck, it happened luckily that the crew were just beginning to hoist some beeves aboard in slings. Backus's melancholy vanished instantly, and with it the memory of his late mistake.

"Now only look at that!" cried he; "My goodness, Triangle, what *would* they say to it in *Ohio?* Wouldn't their eyes bug out, to see 'em handled like that?—wouldn't they, though?"

All the passengers were on deck to look—even the gamblers—and Backus knew them all, and had afflicted them all with his pet topic. As I moved away, I saw one of the gamblers approach and accost him; then another of them; then the third. I halted; waited; watched; the conversation continued between the four men; it grew earnest; Backus drew gradually away; the gamblers followed, and kept at his elbow. I was uncomfortable. However, as they passed me presently, I heard Backus say, with a tone of persecuted annoyance:—

"But it ain't any use, gentlemen; I tell you again, as I've told you a half a dozen times before, I warn't raised to it, and I ain't a-going to resk it."

I felt relieved. "His level head will be his sufficient protection," I said to myself.

During the fortnight's run from Acapulco to San Francisco I several times saw the gamblers talking earnestly with Backus, and once I threw out a gentle warning to him. He chuckled comfortably and said,—

"Oh, yes! they tag around after me considerable—want me to play a little, just for amusement, they say—but laws-a-me, if my folks have told me once to look out for that sort of live-stock, they've told me a thousand times, I reckon."

By and by, in due course, we were approaching San Francisco. It was an ugly black night, with a strong wind blowing, but there was not much sea. I was on deck, alone. Toward ten I started below. A figure issued from the gamblers' den, and disappeared in the darkness. I experienced a shock, for I was sure it was Backus. I flew down the companion-way, looked about for him, could not find him, then returned to the deck just in time to catch a glimpse of him as he re-entered that confounded nest of rascality. Had he yielded at last? I feared it. What had he gone below for?—His bag of coin? Possibly. I drew near the door, full of bodings. It was a-crack, and I glanced in and saw a sight that made me bitterly wish I had given my attention to saving my poor cattle-friend, instead of reading and dreaming my foolish time away. He was gambling. Worse still, he was being plied with champagne, and was already showing some effect from it. He praised the "cider," as he called it, and said now that he had got a taste of it he almost believed he would drink it if it was spirits, it was so good and so ahead of anything he had ever run across before. Surreptitious smiles, at this, passed from one rascal to another, and they filled all the glasses, and whilst Backus honestly drained his to the bottom they pretended to do the same, but threw the wine over their shoulders.

I could not bear the scene, so I wandered forward and tried to interest myself in the sea and the voices of the wind. But no, my uneasy spirit kept dragging me back at quarter-hour intervals; and always I saw Backus drinking his wine—fairly and squarely, and the others throwing theirs away. It was the painfulest night I ever spent.

The only hope I had was that we might reach our anchorage with speed—that would break up the game. I helped the ship along all I could with my prayers. At last we went booming through the Golden Gate, and my pulses leaped for joy. I hurried back to that door and glanced in. Alas, there was small room for hope—Backus's eyes were heavy and bloodshot, his sweaty face was crimson, his speech maudlin and thick, his body sawed drunkenly about with the weaving motion of the ship. He drained another glass to the dregs, whilst the cards were being dealt.

He took his hand, glanced at it, and his dull eyes lit up for a moment. The gamblers observed it, and showed their gratification by hardly perceptible signs.

"How many cards?"

"None!" said Backus.

One villain—named Hank Wiley—discarded one card, the others three each. The betting began. Heretofore the bets had been trifling—a dollar or two; but Backus started off with an eagle now, Wiley hesitated a moment, then "saw it" and "went ten dollars better." The other two threw up their hands.

Backus went twenty better. Wiley said,—

"I see that, and go you a *hundred* better!" then smiled and reached for the money.

"Let it alone," said Backus, with drunken gravity.

"What! you mean to say you're going to cover it?"

"Cover it? Well I reckon I am—and lay another hundred on top of it, too."

He reached down inside his overcoat and produced the required sum.

"Oh, that's your little game, is it? I see your raise, and raise it five hundred!" said Wiley.

"Five hundred *better!*" said the foolish bull-driver, and pulled out the amount and showered it on the pile. The three conspirators hardly tried to conceal their exultation.

All diplomacy and pretence were dropped now, and the sharp exclamations came thick and fast, and the yellow pyramid grew higher and higher. At last ten thousand dollars lay in view. Wiley cast a bag of coin on the table, and said with mocking gentleness,—

"Five thousand dollars better, my friend from the rural districts—what do you say *now?*"

"I *call* you!" said Backus, heaving his golden shot-bag on the pile. "What have you got?"

"Four kings, you d—d fool!" and Wiley threw down his cards and surrounded the stakes with his arms.

"Four *aces,* you ass!" thundered Backus, covering his man with a cocked revolver. "*I'm a professional gambler myself, and I've been laying for you duffers all this voyage!*"

Down went the anchor, rumbledy-dum-dum! and the long trip was ended.

Well—well, it is a sad world. On of the three gamblers was Backus's "pal." It was he that dealt the fateful hands. According to an understanding with the two victims, he was to have given Backus four queens, but alas, he didn't.

A week later, I stumbled upon Backus—arrayed in the height of fashion—in Montgomery Street. He said, cheerily, as we were parting,—

"Ah, by-the-way, you needn't mind about those gores. I don't really know anything about cattle, except what I was able to pick up in a week's apprenticeship over in Jersey just before we sailed. My cattle-culture and cattle-enthusiasm have served their turn—I shan't need them any more."

———

Next day we reluctantly parted from the "Gold Dust" and her officers, hoping to see that boat and all those officers again, some day. A thing which the fates were to render tragically impossible!

CHAPTER XXXVII

THE END OF THE "GOLD DUST"

For, three months later, August 8, while I was writing one of these foregoing chapters, the New York papers brought this telegram:—

A TERRIBLE DISASTER

SEVENTEEN PERSONS KILLED BY AN EXPLOSION OF THE STEAMER "GOLD DUST"

"NASHVILLE, Aug. 7.—A despatch from Hickman, Ky., says:—

"The steamer 'Gold Dust' exploded her boilers at three o'clock today, just after leaving Hickman. Forty-seven persons were scalded and seventeen are missing. The boat was landed in the eddy just above the town, and through the exertions of the citizens the cabin passengers, officers, and part of the crew and deck passengers were taken ashore and removed to the hotels and residences. Twenty-four of the injured were lying in Holcomb's dry-goods store at one time, where they received every attention before being removed to more comfortable places."

A list of the names followed, whereby it appeared that of the seventeen dead, one was the barkeeper; and among the forty-seven wounded, were the captain, chief mate, second mate, and second and third clerks; also Mr. Lem S. Gray, pilot, and several members of the crew.

In answer to a private telegram, we learned that none of these was severely hurt, except Mr. Gray. Letters received afterward confirmed this news, and said that Mr. Gray was improving and would get well. Later letters spoke less hopefully of his case; and finally came one announcing his death. A good man, a most companionable and manly man, and worthy of a kindlier fate.

CHAPTER XXXVIII

THE HOUSE BEAUTIFUL

We took passage in a Cincinnati boat for New Orleans; or on a Cincinnati boat—either is correct; the former is the eastern form of putting it, the latter the western.

Mr. Dickens declined to agree that the Mississippi steamboats

were "magnificent," or that they were "floating palaces,"—
terms which had always been applied to them; terms which did
not over-express the admiration with which the people viewed
them.

Mr. Dickens's position was unassailable, possibly; the people's position was certainly unassailable. If Mr. Dickens was
comparing these boats with the crown jewels; or with the Taj, or
with the Matterhorn; or with some other priceless or wonderful
thing which he had seen, they were not magnificent—he was
right. The people compared them with what *they* had seen; and,
thus measured, thus judged, the boats were magnificent—the
term was the correct one, it was not at all too strong. The people
were as right as was Mr. Dickens. The steamboats were finer
than anything on shore. Compared with superior dwelling-
houses and first class hotels in the Valley, they were indubitably
magnificent, they were "palaces." To a few people living in New
Orleans and St. Louis, they were not magnificent, perhaps; not
palaces; but to the great majority of those populations, and to
the entire populations spread over both banks between Baton
Rouge and St. Louis, they were palaces; they tallied with the
citizen's dream of what magnificence was, and satisfied it.

Every town and village along that vast stretch of double river-
frontage had a best dwelling, finest dwelling, mansion,—the
home of its wealthiest and most conspicuous citizen. It is easy to
describe it: large grassy yard, with paling fence painted white—
in fair repair; brick walk from gate to door; big, square, two-
story "frame" house, painted white and porticoed like a Grecian temple—with this difference, that the imposing fluted columns and Corinthian capitals were a pathetic sham, being made
of white pine, and painted; iron knocker; brass door knob—
discolored, for lack of polishing. Within, an uncarpeted hall, of
planed boards; opening out of it, a parlor, fifteen feet by
fifteen—in some instances five or ten feet larger; ingrain carpet;
mahogany centre-table; lamp on it, with green-paper shade—
standing on a gridiron, so to speak, made of high-colored yarns,
by the young ladies of the house, and called a lampmat; several
books, piled and disposed, with cast-iron exactness, according
to an inherited and unchangeable plan; among them, Tupper,
much pencilled; also, "Friendship's Offering," and "Affection's Wreath," with their sappy inanities illustrated in die-away
mezzotints; also, Ossian; "Alonzo and Melissa;" maybe "Ivanhoe;" also "Album," full of original "poetry" of the Thou-
hast-wounded-the-spirit-that-loved-thee breed; two or three
goody-goody works—"Shepherd of Salisbury Plain," etc.; current number of the chaste and innocuous Godey's "Lady's

Book," with painted fashion-plate of wax-figure women with mouths all alike—lips and eyelids the same size—each five-foot woman with a two-inch wedge sticking from under her dress and letting-on to be half of her foot. Polished air-tight stove (new and deadly invention), with pipe passing through a board which closes up the discarded good old fireplace. On each end of the wooden mantel, over the fireplace, a large basket of peaches and other fruits, natural size, all done in plaster, rudely, or in wax, and painted to resemble the originals—which they don't. Over middle of mantel, engraving—Washington Crossing the Delaware; on the wall by the door, copy of it done in thunder-and-lightning crewels by one of the young ladies—work of art which would have made Washington hesitate about crossing, if he could have foreseen what advantage was going to be taken of it. Piano—kettle in disguise—with music, bound and unbound, piled on it, and on a stand near by: Battle of Prague; Bird Waltz; Arkansas Traveller; Rosin the Bow; Marseilles Hymn; On a Lone Barren Isle (St. Helena); The Last Link is Broken; She wore a Wreath of Roses the Night when last we met; Go, forget me, Why should Sorrow o'er that Brow a Shadow fling; Hours there were to Memory Dearer; Long, Long Ago; Days of Absence; A Life on the Ocean Wave, a Home on the Rolling Deep; Bird at Sea; and spread open on the rack, where the plaintive singer has left it, *Ro*-holl on, silver *moo*-hoon, guide the *trav*-el-lerr his *way,* etc. Tilted pensively against the piano, a guitar—guitar capable of playing the Spanish Fandango by itself, if you give it a start. Frantic work of art on the wall—pious motto, done on the premises, sometimes in colored yarns, sometimes in faded grasses: progenitor of the "God Bless Our Home" of modern commerce. Framed in black mouldings on the wall, other works of art, conceived and committed on the premises, by the young ladies; being grim black-and-white crayons; landscapes, mostly: lake, solitary sail-boat, petrified clouds, pre-geological trees on shore, anthracite precipice; name of criminal conspicuous in the corner. Lithograph, Napoleon Crossing the Alps. Lithograph, The Grave at St. Helena. Steel-plates, Trumbull's Battle of Bunker Hill, and the Sally from Gibraltar. Copper-plates, Moses Smiting the Rock, and Return of the Prodigal Son. In big gilt frame, slander of the family in oil: papa holding a book ("Constitution of the United States"); guitar leaning against mamma, blue ribbons fluttering from its neck; the young ladies, as children, in slippers and scalloped pantelettes, one embracing toy horse, the other beguiling kitten with ball of yarn, and both simpering up at mamma, who simpers back. These persons all fresh, raw, and red— apparently skinned. Opposite, in gilt frame, grandpa and grandma, at thirty and twenty-two, stiff, old-fashioned, high-collared, puff-sleeved, glaring pallidly out from a background of solid Egyptian night. Under a glass French clock dome, large bouquet of stiff flowers done in corpsy white wax. Pyramidal what-not in the corner, the shelves occupied chiefly with bric-a-brac of the period, disposed with an eye to best effect: shell, with the Lord's Prayer carved on it; another shell—of the long-oval sort, narrow, straight orifice, three inches long, running from end to end—portrait of Washington carved on it; not well done; the shell had Washington's mouth, originally—artist should have built to that. These two are memorials of the long-ago bridal trip to New Orleans and the French Market. Other bric-a-brac: Californian "specimens"—quartz, with gold wart adhering; old Guinea-gold locket, with circlet of ancestral hair in it; Indian arrow-heads, of flint; pair of bead moccasins, from uncle who crossed the Plains; three "alum" baskets of various colors— being skeleton-frame of wire, clothed-on with cubes of crystallized alum in the rock-candy style—works of art which were achieved by the young ladies; their doubles and duplicates to be found upon all what-nots in the land; convention of desiccated bugs and butterflies pinned to a card; painted toy-dog, seated upon bellows-attachment—drop its under jaw and squeaks when pressed upon; sugar-candy rabbit—limbs and features merged together, not strongly defined; pewter presidential-campaign medal; miniature card-board wood-sawyer, to be attached to the stovepipe and operated by the heat; small Napoleon, done in wax; spread-open daguerreotypes of dim children, parents, cousins, aunts, and friends, in all attitudes but customary ones; no templed portico at back, and manufactured landscape stretching away in the distance—that came in later, with the photograph; all these vague figures lavishly chained and ringed—metal indicated and secured from doubt by stripes and splashes of vivid gold bronze; all of them too much combed, too much fixed up; and all of them uncomfortable in inflexible Sunday-clothes of a pattern which the spectator cannot realize could ever have been in fashion; husband and wife generally grouped together—husband sitting, wife standing, with hand on his shoulder—and both preserving, all these fading years, some traceable effect of the daguerreotypist's brisk "Now smile, if you please!" Bracketed over what-not—place of special sacredness— an outrage in water-color, done by the young niece that came on a visit long ago, and died. Pity, too; for she might have repented of this in time. Horse-hair chairs, horse-hair sofa which keeps sliding from under you. Window shades, of oil stuff, with milk-maids and ruined castles stencilled on them in fierce colors. Lambrequins dependent from gaudy boxings of beaten tin, gilded. Bedrooms with rag carpets; bedsteads of the "corded" sort, with a sag in the middle, the cords needing tightening; snuffy feather-bed—not aired often enough; cane-seat chairs, splint-bottomed rocker; looking-glass on wall, school-slate size, veneered frame; inherited bureau; wash-bowl and pitcher, possibly—but not certainly; brass candlestick, tallow candle, snuffers. Nothing else in the room. Not a bath-room in the house; and no visitor likely to come along who has ever seen one.

That was the residence of the principal citizen, all the way from the suburbs of New Orleans to the edge of St. Louis. When he stepped aboard a big fine steamboat, he entered a new and marvellous world: chimney-tops cut to counterfeit a spraying crown of plumes—and maybe painted red; pilot-house, hur-ricane deck, boiler-deck guards, all garnished with white wooden filagree work of fanciful patterns; gilt acorns topping the derricks; gilt deer-horns over the big bell; gaudy symbolical picture on the paddle-box, possibly; big roomy boiler-deck, painted blue, and furnished with Windsor arm-chairs; inside, a far receding snow-white "cabin;" porcelain knob and oil-pic-ture on every state-room door; curving patterns of filagree-work touched up with gilding, stretching overhead all down the converging vista; big chandeliers every little way, each an April shower of glittering glass-drops; lovely rainbow-light falling everywhere from the colored glazing of the skylights; the whole a long-drawn, resplendent tunnel, a bewildering and soul-satis-fying spectacle! in the ladies' cabin a pink and white Wilton carpet, as soft as mush, and glorified with a ravishing pattern of gigantic flowers. Then the Bridal Chamber—the animal that in-vented that idea was still alive and unhanged, at that day—Bridal Chamber whose pretentious flummery was necessarily overawing to the now tottering intellect of that hosannahing citizen. Every state-room had its couple of cosy clean bunks, and perhaps a looking-glass and a snug closet; and sometimes there was even a washbowl and pitcher, and part of a towel which could be told from mosquito netting by an expert—though gen-erally these things were absent, and the shirt-sleeved passengers cleansed themselves at a long row of stationary bowls in the barber shop, where were also public towels, public combs, and public soap.

Take the steamboat which I have just described, and you have her in her highest and finest, and most pleasing, and com-fortable, and satisfactory estate. Now cake her over with a layer of ancient and obdurate dirt, and you have the Cincinnati steamer awhile ago referred to. Not all over—only inside; for she was ably officered in all departments except the steward's.

But wash that boat and repaint her, and she would be about the counterpart of the most complimented boat of the old flush times: for the steamboat architecture of the West has undergone no change; neither has steamboat furniture and ornamentation undergone any.

CHAPTER XXXIX

MANUFACTURES AND MISCREANTS

Where the river, in the Vicksburg region, used to be corkscrewed, it is now comparatively straight—made so by cut-off; a former distance of seventy miles is reduced to thirty-five. It is a change which threw Vicksburg's neighbor, Delta, Louisiana, out into the country and ended its career as a river town. Its whole river-frontage is now occupied by a vast sand-bar, thickly covered with young trees—a growth which will magnify itself into a dense forest, by and by, and completely hide the exiled town.

In due time we passed Grand Gulf and Rodney, of war fame, and reached Natchez, the last of the beautiful hill-cities—for Baton Rouge, yet to come, is not on a hill, but only on high ground. Famous Natchez-under-the-hill has not changed notably in twenty years; in outward aspect—judging by the descriptions of the ancient procession of foreign tourists—it has not changed in sixty; for it is still small, straggling, and shabby. It had a desperate reputation, morally, in the old keel-boating and early steamboating times—plenty of drinking, carousing, fisticuffing, and killing there, among the riff-raff of the river, in those days. But Natchez-on-top-of-the-hill is attractive; has always been attractive. Even Mrs. Trollope (1827) had to confess its charms:

"At one or two points the wearisome level line is relieved by *bluffs,* as they call the short intervals of high ground. The town of Natchez is beautifully situated on one of those high spots. The contrast that its bright green hill forms with the dismal line of black forest that stretches on every side, the abundant growth of the paw-paw, palmetto and orange, the copious variety of sweet-scented flowers that flourish there, all make it appear like an oasis in the desert. Natchez is the furthest point to the north at which oranges ripen in the open air, or endure the winter without shelter. With the exception of this sweet spot, I thought all the little towns and villages we passed wretched-looking in the extreme.''

Natchez, like her near and far river neighbors, has railways now, and is adding to them—pushing them hither and thither into all rich outlying regions that are naturally tributary to her. And like Vicksburg and New Orleans, she has her ice-factory; she makes thirty tons of ice a day. In Vicksburg and Natchez, in my time, ice was jewelry; none but the rich could wear it. But anybody and everybody can have it now. I visited one of the ice-factories in New Orleans, to see what the polar regions might look like when lugged into the edge of the tropics. But there was nothing striking in the aspect of the place. It was merely a spacious house, with some innocent steam machinery in one end of it and some big porcelain pipes running here and there. No, not porcelain—they merely seemed to be; they were iron, but the ammonia which was being breathed through them had coated them to the thickness of your hand with solid milk-white ice. It ought to have melted; for one did not require winter clothing in that atmosphere: but it did not melt; the inside of the pipe was too cold.

Sunk into the floor were numberless tin boxes, a foot square and two feet long, and open at the top end. These were full of clear water; and around each box, salt and other proper stuff was packed; also, the ammonia gases were applied to the water in some way which will always remain a secret to me, because I was not able to understand the process. While the water in the boxes gradually froze, men gave it a stir or two with a stick occasionally—to liberate the air-bubbles, I think. Other men were continually lifting out boxes whose contents had become hard frozen. They gave the box a single dip into a vat of boiling water, to melt the block of ice free from its tin coffin, then they shot the block out upon a platform car, and it was ready for market. These big blocks were hard, solid, and crystal-clear. In certain of them, big bouquets of fresh and brilliant tropical flowers had been frozen-in; in others, beautiful silken-clad French dolls, and other pretty objects. These blocks were to be set on end in a platter, in the centre of dinner-tables, to cool the tropical air; and also to be ornamental, for the flowers and things imprisoned in them could be seen as through plate glass. I was told that this factory could retail its ice, by wagon, throughout New Orleans, in the humblest dwelling house quantities, at six or seven dollars a ton, and make a sufficient profit. This being the case, there is business for ice factories in the

North; for we get ice on no such terms there, if one takes less than three hundred and fifty pounds at a delivery.

The Rosalie Yarn Mill, of Natchez, has a capacity of 6,000 spindles and 160 looms, and employs 100 hands. The Natchez Cotton Mills Company began operations four years ago in a two-story building of 50 × 190 feet, with 4,000 spindles and 128 looms; capital $105,000, all subscribed in the town. Two years later, the same stockholders increased their capital to $225,000; added a third story to the mill, increased its length to 317 feet; added machinery to increase the capacity to 10,300 spindles and 304 looms. The company now employ 250 operatives, many of whom are citizens of Natchez. "The mill works 5,000 bales of cotton annually and manufactures the best standard quality of brown shirtings and sheetings and drills, turning out 5,000,000 yards of these goods per year."* A close corporation—stock held at $5,000 per share, but none in the market.

The changes in the Mississippi River are great and strange, yet were to be expected; but I was not expecting to live to see Natchez and these other river towns become manufacturing strongholds and railway centres.

Speaking of manufactures reminds me of a talk upon that topic which I heard—which I overheard—on board the Cincinnati boat. I awoke out of a fretted sleep, with a dull confusion of voices in my ears. I listened—two men were talking; subject, apparently, the great inundation. I looked out through the open transom. The two men were eating a late breakfast; sitting opposite each other; nobody else around. They closed up the inundation with a few words—having used it, evidently, as a mere ice-breaker and acquaintanceship-breeder—then they dropped into business. It soon transpired that they were drummers—one belonging in Cincinnati, the other in New Orleans. Brisk men, energetic of movement and speech; the dollar their god, how to get it their religion.

"Now as to this article," said Cincinnati, slashing into the ostensible butter and holding forward a slab of it on his knifeblade, "It's from our house; look at it—smell of it—taste it. Put any test on it you want to. Take your own time—no hurry—make it thorough. There now—what do you say? butter, ain't it? Not by a thundering sight—it's oleomargarine! Yes, sir, that's what it is—oleomargarine. You can't tell it from butter; by George, an *expert* can't. It's from our house. We supply most of the boats in the West; there's hardly a pound of butter on one

*"New Orleans Times-Democrat," Aug. 26, 1882.

of them. We are crawling right along—*jumping* right along is the word. We are going to have that entire trade. Yes, and the hotel trade, too. You are going to see the day, pretty soon, when you can't find an ounce of butter to bless yourself with, in any hotel in the Mississippi and Ohio Valleys, outside of the biggest cities. Why, we are turning out oleomargarine *now* by the thousands of tons. And we can sell it so dirt-cheap that the whole country has *got* to take it—can't get around it you see. Butter don't stand any show—there ain't any chance for competition. Butter's had its *day*—and from this out, butter goes to the wall. There's more money in oleomargarine than—why, you can't imagine the business we do. I've stopped in every town, from Cincinnati to Natchez; and I've sent home big orders from every one of them."

And so-forth and so-on, for ten minutes longer, in the same fervid strain. Then New Orleans piped up and said:—

"Yes, it's a first-rate imitation, that's a certainty; but it ain't the only one around that's first-rate. For instance, they make olive-oil out of cotton-seed oil, now-a-days, so that you can't tell them apart."

"Yes, that's so," responded Cincinnati, "and it was a tip-top business for a while. They sent it over and brought it back from France and Italy, with the United States custom-house mark on it to indorse it for genuine, and there was no end of cash in it; but France and Italy broke up the game—of course they naturally would. Cracked on such a rattling impost that cotton-seed olive-oil couldn't stand the raise; had to hang up and quit."

"Oh, it *did,* did it?" You wait here a minute."

Goes to his state-room, brings back a couple of long bottles, and takes out the corks—says:—

"There now, smell them, taste them, examine the bottles, inspect the labels. One of 'm's from Europe, the other's never been out of this country. One's European olive-oil, the other's American cotton-seed olive-oil. Tell 'm apart? 'Course you can't. Nobody can. People that want to, can go to the expense and trouble of shipping their oils to Europe and back—it's their privilege; but our firm knows a trick worth six of that. We turn out the whole thing—clean from the word go—in our factory in New Orleans: labels, bottles, oil, everything. Well, no, not labels: been buying *them* abroad—get them dirt-cheap there. You see, there's just one little wee speck, essence, or whatever it is, in a gallon of cotton-seed oil, that gives it a smell, or a flavor, or something—get that out, and you're all right—perfectly easy then to turn the oil into any kind of oil you want to, and there ain't anybody that can detect the true from the false. Well, we know how to get that one little particle out—and we're the only firm that does. And we turn out an olive-oil that is just simply perfect—undetectable! We are doing a ripping trade, too—as I could easily show you by my order-book for this trip. Maybe you'll butter everybody's bread pretty soon, but we'll cotton-seed his salad for him from the Gulf to Canada, and that's a dead-certain thing.''

Cincinnati glowed and flashed with admiration. The two scoundrels exchanged business-cards, and rose. As they left the table, Cincinnati said,—

"But you have to have custom-house marks, don't you? How do you manage that?"

I did not catch the answer.

We passed Port Hudson, scene of two of the most terrific episodes of the war—the night-battle there between Farragut's fleet and the Confederate land batteries, April 14th, 1863; and the memorable land battle, two months later, which lasted eight hours—eight hours of exceptionally fierce and stubborn fighting—and ended, finally, in the repulse of the Union forces with great slaughter.

CHAPTER XL

CASTLES AND CULTURE

Baton Rouge was clothed in flowers, like a bride—no, much more so; like a greenhouse. For we were in the absolute South now—no modifications, no compromises, no half-way measures. The magnolia-trees in the Capitol grounds were lovely and fragrant, with their dense rich foliage and huge snow-ball blossoms. The scent of the flower is very sweet, but you want distance on it, because it is so powerful. They are not good bedroom blossoms—they might suffocate one in his sleep. We were certainly in the South at last; for here the sugar region begins, and the plantations—vast green levels, with sugar-mill and negro quarters clustered together in the middle distance—were in view. And there was a tropical sun overhead and a tropical swelter in the air.

And at this point, also, begins the pilot's paradise: a wide river hence to New Orleans, abundance of water from shore to shore, and no bars, snags, sawyers, or wrecks in his road.

Sir Walter Scott is probably responsible for the Capitol building; for it is not conceivable that this little sham castle would ever have been built if he had not run the people mad, a couple of generations ago, with his mediaeval romances. The South has not yet recovered from the debilitating influence of his books. Admiration of his fantastic heroes and their grotesque "chivalry" doings and romantic juvenilities still survives here, in an atmosphere in which is already perceptible the wholesome and practical nineteenth-century smell of cotton-factories and locomotives; and traces of its inflated language and other windy humbuggeries survive along with it. It is pathetic enough, that a whitewashed castle with turrets and things—materials all ungenuine within and without, pretending to be what they are not—should ever have been built in this otherwise honorable place; but it is much more pathetic to see this architectural falsehood undergoing restoration and perpetuation in our day, when it would have been so easy to let dynamite finish what a charitable fire began, and then devote this restoration-money to the buildingof something genuine.

Baton Rouge has no patent on imitation castles, however, and no monopoly of them. Here is a picture from the advertisement of the "Female Institute" of Columbia, Tennessee. The following remark is from the same advertisement:—

"The Institute building has long been famed as a model of striking and beautiful architecture. Visitors are charmed with its resemblance to the old castles of song and story, with its towers, turreted walls, and ivy-mantled porches."

Keeping school in a castle is a romantic thing; as romantic as keeping hotel in a castel.

By itself the imitation castle is doubtless harmless, and well enough; but as a symbol and breeder and sustainer of maudlin Middle-Age romanticism here in the midst of the plainest and sturdiest and infinitely greatest and worthiest of all the centuries the world has seen, it is necessarily a hurtful thing and a mistake.

Here is an extract from the prospectus of a Kentucky "Female College." Female college sounds well enough; but since the phrasing it in that unjustifiable way was done purely in the interest of brevity, it seems to me that she-college would have been still better—because shorter, and means the same thing: that is, if either phrase means anything at all:—

"The president is southern by birth, by rearing, by education, and by sentiment; the teachers are all southern in sentiment, and with the exception of those born in Europe were born and raised in the south. Believing the southern to be the highest type of civilization this continent has seen,* the young ladies are trained according to the southern ideas of delicacy, refinement, womanhood, religion, and propriety; hence we offer a first-class female college for the south and solicit southern patronage.''

---

*Illustrations of it thoughtlessly omitted by the advertiser:

KNOXVILLE, Tenn., October 19.—This morning a few minutes after ten o'clock, General Joseph A. Mabry, Thomas O'Connor, and Joseph A. Mabry, Jr., were killed in a shooting affray. The difficulty began yesterday afternoon by General Mabry attacking Major O'Connor and threatening to kill him. This was at the fair grounds, and O'Connor told Mabry that it was not the place to settle their difficulties. Mabry then told O'Connor he should not live. It seems that Mabry was armed and O'Connor was not. The cause of the difficulty was an old feud about the transfer of some property from Mabry to O'Connor. Later in the afternoon Mabry sent word to O'Connor that he would kill him on sight. This morning Major O'Connor was standing in the door of the Mechanics' National Bank, of which he was president. General Mabry and another gentleman walked down Gay Street on the opposite side from the bank. O'Connor stepped into the bank, got a shot gun, took deliberate aim at General Mabry and fired. Mabry fell dead, being shot in the left side. As he fell O'Connor fired again, the shot taking effect in Mabry's thigh. O'Connor then reached into the bank and got another shot gun. About this time Joseph A. Mabry, Jr., son of General Mabry, came rushing down the street, unseen by O'Connor until within forty feet, when the young man fired a pistol, the shot taking effect in O'Connor's right breast, passing through the body near the heart. The instant Mabry shot, O'Connor turned and fired, the load taking effect in young Mabry's right breast and side. Mabry fell pierced with twenty buckshot, and almost instantly O'Connor fell dead without a struggle. Mabry tried to rise, but fell back dead. The whole tragedy occurred within two minutes, and neither of the three spoke after he was shot. General Mabry had about thirty buckshot in his body. A bystander was painfully wounded in the thigh with a buckshot, and another was wounded in the arm. Four other men had their clothing pierced by buckshot. The affair caused great excitement, and Gay Street was thronged with thousands of people. General Mabry and his son Joe were acquitted only a few days ago of the murder of Moses Lusby and Don Lusby, father and son, whom they killed a few weeks ago. Will Mabry was killed by Don Lusby last Christmas. Major Thomas O'Connor was President of the Mechanics' National Bank here, and was the wealthiest man in the State.—*Associated Press Telegram.*

One day last month, Professor Sharpe, of the Somerville, Tenn., Female College, "a quiet and gentlemanly man," was told that his brother-in-law, a Captain Burton, had threatened to kill him. Burton, it seems, had already killed one man and driven his knife into another. The Professor armed himself with a double-barrelled shot gun, started out in search of his brother-in-law, found him playing billiards in a saloon, and blew his brains out. The "Memphis Avalanche" reports that the Professor's course met with pretty general approval in the community; knowing that the law was powerless, in the actual condition of public sentiment, to protect him, he protected himself.

About the same time, two young men in North Carolina quarrelled about a girl, and "hostile messages" were exchanged. Friends tried to reconcile them, but had their labor for their pains. On the 24th the young men met in the public highway. One of them had a heavy club in his hand, the other an axe. The man with the club fought desperately for his life, but it was a hopeless fight from the first. A well-directed blow sent his club whirling out of his grasp, and the next moment he was a dead man.

About the same time, two"highly connected" young Virginians, clerks in a hardware store at Charlottesville, while "skylarking," came to blows. Peter Dick threw pepper in Charles Road's eyes; Roads demanded an apology; Dick refused to give it, and it was agreed that a duel was inevitable, but a difficulty arose; the parties had no pistols, and it was too late at night to procure them. One of them suggested that butcher-knives would answer the purpose, and the other accepted the suggestion; the result was that Roads fell to the floor with a gash in his abdomen that may or may not prove fatal. If Dick has been arrested, the news has not reached us. He "expressed deep regret," and we are told by a Staunton correspondent of the "Philadelphia Press" that "every effort has been made to hush the matter up."—*Extracts from the Public Journals.*

What, warder, ho! the man that can blow so complacent a blast as that, probably blows it from a castle.

From Baton Rouge to New Orleans, the great sugar plantations border both sides of the river all the way, and stretch their league-wide levels back to the dim forest-walls of bearded cypress in the rear. Shores lonely no longer. Plenty of dwellings all the way, on both banks—standing so close together, for long distances, that the broad river lying between the two rows, becomes a sort of spacious street. A most home-like and happy-looking region. And now and then you see a pillared and porticoed great manor-house, embowered in trees. Here is testimony of one or two of the procession of foreign tourists that filed along here half a century ago. Mrs. Trollope says:—

"The unbroken flatness of the banks of the Mississippi continued unvaried for many miles above New Orleans; but the graceful and luxuriant palmetto, the dark and noble ilex, and the bright orange, were everywhere to be seen, and it was many days before we were weary of looking at them."

Captain Basil Hall:—

"The district of country which lies adjacent to the Mississippi, in the lower parts of Louisiana, is everywhere thickly peopled by sugar planters, whose showy houses, gay piazzas, trig gardens, and numerous slave-villages, all clean and neat, gave an exceedingly thriving air to the river scenery."

All the procession paint the attractive picture in the same way. The descriptions of fifty years ago do not need to have a word changed in order to exactly describe the same region as it appears to-day—except as to the "trigness" of the houses. The whitewash is gone from the negro cabins now; and many, possibly most, of the big mansions, once so shining white, have worn out their paint and have a decayed, neglected look. It is the blight of the war. Twenty-one years ago everything was trim and trig and bright along the "coast," just as it had been in 1827, as described by those tourists.

Unfortunate tourists! People humbugged them with stupid and silly lies, and then laughed at them for believing and printing the same. They told Mrs. Trollope that the alligators—or crocodiles, as she calls them—were terrible creatures; and backed up the statement with a blood-curdling account of how one of these slandered reptiles crept into a squatter cabin one night, and ate up a woman and five children. The woman, by herself, would have satisfied any ordinarily-impossible alligator; but no, these liars must make him gorge the five children besides. One would not imagine that jokers of this robust breed would be sensitive—but they were. It is difficult, at this day, to understand, and impossible to justify, the reception which the book of the grave, honest, intelligent, gentle, manly, charitable, well-meaning Capt. Basil Hall got. Mrs. Trollope's account of it may perhaps entertain the reader; therefore I have put it in the Appendix.*

CHAPTER XLI

THE METROPOLIS OF THE SOUTH

The approaches to New Orleans were familiar; general aspects were unchanged. When one goes flying through London along a railway propped in the air on tall arches, he may inspect miles of upper bedrooms through the open windows, but the lower half of the houses is under his level and out of sight. Similarly, in high-river stage, in the New Orleans region, the water is up to the top of the enclosing levee-rim, the flat country behind it lies low—representing the bottom of a dish—and as the boat swims along, high on the flood, one looks down upon the houses and into the upper windows. There is nothing but that frail breast-work of earth between the people and destruction.

The old brick salt-warehouses clustered at the upper end of the city looked as they had always looked; warehouses which had had a kind of Aladdin's lamp experience, however, since I had seen them; for when the war broke out the proprietor went to bed one night leaving them packed with thousands of sacks of vulgar salt, worth a couple of dollars a sack, and got up in the morning and found his mountain of salt turned into a mountain of gold, so to speak, so suddenly and to so dizzy a height had the war news sent up the price of the article.

The vast reach of plank wharves remained unchanged, and there were as many ships as ever: but the long array of steam-boats had vanished; not altogether, of course, but not much of it was left.

The city itself had not changed—to the eye. It had greatly increased in spread and population, but the look of the town was not altered. The dust, waste-paper-littered, was still deep in the streets; the deep, trough-like gutters alongside the curb-stones

* See Appendix C.

401

were still half full of reposeful water with a dusty surface; the sidewalks were still—in the sugar and bacon region—incumbered by casks and barrels and hogsheads; the great blocks of austerely plain commercial houses were as dusty-looking as ever.

Canal Street was finer, and more attractive and stirring than formerly, with its drifting crowds of people, its several processions of hurrying street-cars, and—toward evening—its broad second-story verandas crowded with gentlemen and ladies clothed according to the latest mode.

Not that there is any "architecture" in Canal Street: to speak in broad, general terms, there is no architecture in New Orleans, except in the cemeteries. It seems a strange thing to say of a wealthy, far-seeing, and energetic city of a quarter of a million inhabitants, but it is true. There is a huge granite U.S. Customhouse—costly enough, genuine enough, but as a decoration it is inferior to a gasometer. It looks like a state prison. But it was built before the war. Architecture in America may be said to have been born since the war. New Orleans, I believe, has had the good luck—and in a sense the bad luck—to have had no great fire in late years. It must be so. If the opposite had been the case, I think one would be able to tell the "burnt district" by the radical improvement in its architecture over the old forms. One can do this in Boston and Chicago. The "burnt district" of Boston was commonplace before the fire; but now there is no commercial district in any city in the world that can surpass it—or perhaps even rival it—in beauty, elegance, and tastefulness.

However, New Orleans has begun—just this moment, as one may say. When completed, the new Cotton Exchange will be a stately and beautiful building; massive, substantial, full of architectural graces; no shams or false pretenses or uglinesses about it anywhere. To the city, it will be worth many times its cost, for it will breed its species. What has been lacking hitherto, was a model to build toward; something to educate eye and taste; a *suggester,* so to speak.

The city is well outfitted with progressive men—thinking, sagacious, long-headed men. The contrast between the spirit of the city and the city's architecture is like the contrast between waking and sleep. Apparently there is a "boom" in everything but that one dead feature. The water in the gutters used to be stagnant and slimy, and a potent disease-breeder; but the gutters are flushed now, two or three times a day, by powerful machinery; in many of the gutters the water never stands still, but has a steady current. Other sanitary improvements have been made; and with such effect that New Orleans claims to be (during the long intervals between the occasional yellow-fever assaults) one of the healthiest cities in the Union. There's plenty of ice now for everybody, manufactured in the town. It is a driving place commercially, and has a great river, ocean, and railway business. At the date of our visit, it was the best lighted city in the Union, electrically speaking. The New Orleans electric lights were more numerous than those of New York, and very much better. One had this modified noonday not only in Canal and some neighboring chief streets, but all along a stretch of five miles of river frontage. There are good clubs in the city now— several of them but recently organized—and inviting modern-style pleasure resorts at West End and Spanish Fort. The telephone is everywhere. One of the most notable advances is in journalism. The newspapers, as I remember them, were not a striking feature. Now they are. Money is spent upon them with a free hand. They get the news, let it cost what it may. The editorial work is not hackgrinding, but literature. As an example of New Orleans journalistic achievement, it may be mentioned that the "Times-Democrat" of August 26, 1882, contained a report of the year's business of the towns of the Mississippi Valley, from New Orleans all the way to St. Paul—two thousand miles. That issue of the paper consisted of *forty* pages; seven columns to the page; two hundred and eighty columns in all; fifteen hundred words to the column; an aggregate of four hundred and twenty thousand words. That is to say, not much short of three times as many words as there are in this book. One may with sorrow contrast this with the architecture of New Orleans.

I have been speaking of public architecture only. The domestic article in New Orleans is reproachless, notwithstanding it remains as it always was. All the dwellings are of wood—in the American part of the town, I mean—and all have a comfortable look. Those in the wealthy quarter are spacious; painted snow-white usually, and generally have wide verandas, or double-verandas, supported by ornamental columns. These mansions stand in the centre of large grounds, and rise, garlanded with roses, out of the midst of swelling masses of shining green foliage and many-colored blossoms. No houses could well be in better harmony with their surroundings, or more pleasing to the eye, or more home-like and comfortable-looking.

One even becomes reconciled to the cistern presently; this is a mighty cask, painted green, and sometimes a couple of stories high, which is propped against the house-corner on stilts. There is a mansion-and-brewery suggestion about the combination which seems very incongruous at first. But the people cannot have wells, and so they take rain-water. Neither can they conveniently have cellars, or graves;* the town being built upon "made" ground; so they do without both, and few of the living complain, and none of the others.

CHAPTER XLII

HYGIENE AND SENTIMENT

They bury their dead in vaults, above the ground.

These vaults have a resemblance to houses—sometimes to temples; are built of marble, generally; are architecturally graceful and shapely; they face the walks and driveways of the cemetery; and when one moves through the midst of a thousand or so of them and sees their white roofs and gables stretching into the distance on every hand, the phrase "city of the dead" has all at once a meaning to him. Many of the cemeteries are beautiful, and are kept in perfect order. When one goes from the levee or the business streets near it, to a cemetery, he observes to himself that if those people down there would live as neatly while they are alive as they do after they are dead, they would find many advantages in it; and besides, their quarter would be the wonder and admiration of the business world. Fresh flowers, in vases of water, are to be seen at the portals of many of the vaults; placed there by the pious hands of bereaved parents and children, husbands and wives, and renewed daily. A milder form of sorrow finds its inexpensive and lasting remembrancer in the coarse and ugly but indestructible "immortelle"—which is a wreath or cross or some such emblem, made of rosettes of black linen, with sometimes a yellow rosette at the conjunction of the cross's bars,—kind of sorrowful breastpin, so to say. The immortelle requires no attention: you just hang it up, and there you are; just leave it alone, it will take care of your grief for you, and keep it in mind better than you can; stands weather first-rate, and lasts like boiler-iron.

On sunny days, pretty little chameleons—gracefullest of legged reptiles—creep along the marble fronts of the vaults, and catch flies. Their changes of color—as to variety—are not up to the creature's reputation. They change color when a person comes along and hangs up an immortelle; but that is nothing: any right-feeling reptile would do that.

I will gradually drop this subject of graveyards. I have been

---

*The Israelites are buried in graves—by permission, I take it, not requirement; but none else, except the destitute, who are buried at public expense. The graves are but three or four feet deep.

trying all I could to get down to the sentimental part of it, but I cannot accomplish it. I think there is no genuinely sentimental part to it. It is all grotesque, ghastly, horrible. Graveyards may have been justifiable in the bygone ages, when nobody knew that for every dead body put into the ground, to glut the earth and the plant-roots and the air with disease-germs, five or fifty, or maybe a hundred, persons must die before their proper time; but they are hardly justifiable now, when even the children know that a dead saint enters upon a century-long career of assassination the moment the earth closes over his corpse. It is a grim sort of a thought. The relics of St. Anne, up in Canada, have now, after nineteen hundred years, gone to curing the sick by the dozen. But it is merest matter-of-course that these same relics, within a generation after St. Anne's death and burial, *made* several thousand people sick. Therefore these miracle-performances are simply compensation, nothing more. St. Anne is somewhat slow pay, for a Saint, it is true; but better a debt paid after nineteen hundred years, and outlawed by the statute of limitations, than not paid at all; and most of the knights of the halo do not pay at all. Where you find one that pays—like St. Anne—you find a hundred and fifty that take the benefit of the statute. And none of them pay any more than the principal of what they owe—they pay none of the interest either simple or compound. A Saint can never *quite* return the principal, however; for his dead body *kills* people, whereas his relics *heal* only—they never restore the dead to life. That part of the account is always left unsettled.

"Dr. F. Julius Le Moyne, after fifty years of medical practice, wrote: 'The inhumation of human bodies, dead from infectious diseases, results in constantly loading the atmosphere, and polluting the waters, with not only the germs that rise from simply putrefaction, but also with the *specific* germs of the diseases from which death resulted.'

"The gases (from buried corpses) will rise to the surface through eight or ten feet of gravel, just as coal-gas will do, and there is practically no limit to their power of escape.

"During the epidemic in New Orleans in 1853, Dr. E.H. Barton reported that in the Fourth District the mortality was four hundred and fifty-two per thousand—more than double that of any other. In this district were three large cemeteries, in which during the previous year more than three thousand bodies had been buried. In other districts the proximity of cemeteries seemed to aggravate the disease.

"In 1828 Professor Bianchi demonstrated how the fearful reappearance of the plague at Modena was caused by excavations in ground where, *three hundred years previously* the victims of the pestilence had been buried. Mr. Cooper, in explaining the causes of some epidemics, remarks that the opening of the plague burial-grounds at Eyam resulted in an immediate outbreak of disease."—*North American Review, No. 3, Vol.* 135.

In an address before the Chicago Medical Society, in advocacy of cremation, Dr. Charles W. Purdy made some striking comparisons to show what a burden is laid upon society by the burial of the dead:—

"One and one-fourth times more money is expended annually in funerals in the United States than the Government expends for public-school purposes. Funerals cost this country in 1880 enough money to pay the liabilities of all the commercial failures in the United States during the same year, and give each bankrupt a capital of $8,630 with which to resume business. Funerals cost annually more money than the value of the combined gold and silver yield of the United States in the year 1880! These figures do not include the sums invested in burial-grounds and expended in tombs and monuments, nor the loss from depreciation of property in the vicinity of cemeteries."

For the rich, cremation would answer as well as burial; for the ceremonies connected with it could be made as costly and ostentatious as a Hindoo *suttee;* while for the poor, cremation would be better than burial, because so cheap*—so cheap until the poor got to imitating the rich, which they would do by and by. The adoption of cremation would relieve us of a muck of threadbare burial-witticisms; but, on the other hand, it would resurrect a lot of mildewed old cremation-jokes that have had a rest for two thousand years.

I have a colored acquaintance who earns his living by odd jobs and heavy manual labor. He never earns above four hundred dollars in a year, and as he has a wife and several young children, the closest scrimping is necessary to get him through to the end of the twelve months debtless. To such a man a funeral is a colossal financial disaster. While I was writing one of the preceding chapters, this man lost a little child. He walked the town over with a friend, trying to find a coffin that was within his means. He bought the very cheapest one he could find, plain wood, stained. It cost him *twenty-six dollars.* It would have cost less than four, probably, if it had been built to put something useful into. He and his family will feel that outlay a good many months.

*Four or five dollars is the minimum cost.

CHAPTER XLIII

THE ART OF INHUMATION

About the same time, I encountered a man in the street, whom I had not seen for six or seven years; and something like this talk followed. I said,—

"But you used to look sad and oldish; you don't now. Where did you get all this youth and bubbling cheerfulness? Give me the address."

He chuckled blithely, took off his shining tile, pointed to a notched pink circlet of paper pasted into its crown, with something lettered on it, and went on chuckling while I read, "J. B—, UNDERTAKER." Then he clapped his hat on, gave it an irreverent tilt to leeward, and cried out,—

"That's what's the matter! It used to be rough times with me when you knew me—insurance-agency business, you know; mighty irregular. Big fire, all right—brisk trade for ten days while people scared; after that, dull policy-business till next fire. Town like this don't have fires often enough—a fellow strikes so many dull weeks in a row that he gets discouraged. But you bet you, *this* is the business! People don't wait for examples to *die*. No, sir, they drop off right along—there ain't any dull spots in the undertaker line. I just started in with two or three little old coffins and a hired hearse, and *now* look at the thing! I've worked up a business here that would satisfy any man, don't care who he is. Five years ago, lodged in an attic; live in a swell house now, with a mansard roof, and all the modern inconveniences."

"Does a coffin pay so well? Is there much profit on a coffin?"

"*Go*-way! How you talk!" Then, with a confidential wink, a dropping of the voice, and an impressive laying of his hand on my arm; "Look here; there's one thing in this world which isn't ever cheap. That's a coffin. There's one thing in this world which a person don't ever try to jew you down on. That's a coffin. There's one thing in this world which a person don't say,— 'I'll look around a little, and if I find I can't do better I'll come back and take it.' That's a coffin. There's one thing in this world which a person won't take in pine if he can go walnut; and won't take in walnut if he can go mahogany; and won't take in mahogany if he can go an iron casket with silver door-plate and bronze handles. That's a coffin. And there's one thing in this world which you don't have to worry around after a person to get him to pay for. And *that's* a coffin. Undertaking?—why it's the dead-surest business in Christendom, and the nobbiest.

"Why, just look at it. A rich man won't have anything but your very best; and you can just pile it on, too—pile it on and sock it to him—he won't ever holler. And you take in a poor man, and if you work him right he'll bust himself on a single layout. Or especially a woman. F'r instance: Mrs. O'Flaherty comes in—widow—wiping her eyes and kind of moaning. Unhandkerchiefs one eye, bats it around tearfully over the stock; says,—

" 'And fhat might ye ask for that wan?'

" 'Thirty-nine dollars, madam,' says I.

" 'It's a foine big price, sure, but Pat shall be buried like a gintleman, as he was, if I have to work me fingers off for it. I'll have that wan, sor.'

" 'Yes, madam,' says I, 'and it is a very good one, too; not costly, to be sure, but in this life we must cut our garment to our clothes, as the saying is.' And as she starts out, I heave in, kind of casually, 'This one with the white satin lining is a beauty, but I am afraid—well, sixty-five dollars *is* a rather—rather—but no matter, I felt obliged to say to Mrs. O'Shaughnessy,—'

" 'D'ye mane to soy that Bridget O'Shaughnessy bought the mate to that joo-ul box to ship that dhrunken divil to Purgatory in?'

" 'Yes, madam.'

" 'Then Pat shall go to heaven in the twin to it, if it takes the last rap the O'Flaherties can raise; and moind you, stick on some extras, too, and I'll give ye another dollar.'

"And as I lay-in with the livery stables, of course I don't forget to mention that Mrs. O'Shaughnessy hired fifty-four dollars' worth of hacks and flung as much style into Dennis's funeral as if he had been a duke or an assassin. And of course she sails in and goes the O'Shaughnessy about four hacks and an omnibus better. That *used* to be, but that's all played now; that is, in this particular town. The Irish got to piling up hacks so, on their funerals, that a funeral left them ragged and hungry for two years afterward; so the priest pitched in and broke it all up. He don't allow them to have but two hacks now, and sometimes only one."

"Well," said I, "if you are so light-hearted and jolly in ordinary times, what *must* you be in an epidemic?"

He shook his head.

"No, you're off, there. We don't like to see an epidemic. An epidemic don't pay. Well, of course I don't mean that, exactly; but it don't pay in proportion to the regular thing. Don't it occur to you, why?"

"No."

"Think."

"I can't imagine. What is it?"

"It's just two things."

"Well, what *are* they?"

"One's Embamming."

"And what's the other?"

"Ice."

"How is that?"

"Well, in ordinary times, a person dies, and we lay him up in ice; one day, two days, maybe three, to wait for friends to come. Takes a lot of it—melts fast. We charge jewelry rates for that ice, and war-prices for attendance. Well, don't you know, when there's an epidemic, they rush 'em to the cemetery the minute the breath's out. No market for ice in an epidemic. Same with Embamming. You take a family that's able to embam, and you've got a soft thing. You can mention sixteen different ways to do it—though there *ain't* only one or two ways, when you come down to the bottom facts of it—and they'll take the highest-priced way, every time. It's human nature—human nature in grief. It don't reason, you see. 'Time being, it don't care a dam. All it wants is physical immortality for deceased, and they're willing to pay for it. All you've got to do is to just be ca'm and stack it up—they'll stand the racket. Why, man, you can take a defunct that you couldn't *give* away; and get your em-bamming traps around you and go to work; and in a couple of hours he is worth a cool six hundred—that's what *he's* worth. There ain't anything equal to it but trading rats for di'monds in time of famine. Well, don't you see, when there's an epidemic, people don't wait to embam. No, indeed they don't; and it hurts the business like hellth, as we say—hurts it like hell-th, *health*, see?— Our little joke in the trade. Well, I must be going. Give me a call whenever you need any—I mean, when you're going by, sometime."

In his joyful high spirits, he did the exaggerating himself, if any has been done. I have not enlarged on him.

With the above brief references to inhumation, let us leave the subject. As for me, I hope to be cremated. I made that remark to my pastor once, who said, with what he seemed to think was an impressive manner,—

"I wouldn't worry about that, if I had your chances."

Much he knew about it—the family all so opposed to it.

CHAPTER XLIV

CITY SIGHTS

The old French part of New Orleans—anciently the Spanish part—bears no resemblance to the American end of the city: the American end which lies beyond the intervening brick business-centre. The houses are massed in blocks; are austerely plain and dignified; uniform of pattern, with here and there a departure from it with pleasant effect; all are plastered on the outside, and nearly all have long, iron-railed verandas running along the several stories. Their chief beauty is the deep, warm, varicolored stain with which time and the weather have enriched the plaster. It harmonizes with all the surroundings, and has as natural a look of belonging there as has the flush upon sunset clouds. This charming decoration cannot be successfully imitated; neither is it to be found elsewhere in America.

The iron railings are a specialty, also. The pattern is often exceedingly light and dainty, and airy and graceful—with a large cipher or monogram in the centre, a delicate cobweb of baffling, intricate forms, wrought in steel. The ancient railings are hand-made, and are now comparatively rare and proportionately valuable. They are become bric-a-brac.

The party had the privilege of idling through this ancient quarter of New Orleans with the South's finest literary genius, the author of "the Grandissimes." In him the South has found a masterly delineator of its interior life and its history. In truth, I find by experience, that the untrained eye and vacant mind can inspect it and learn of it and judge of it more clearly and profitably in his books than by personal contact with it.

With Mr. Cable along to see for you, and describe and explain and illuminate, a jog through that old quarter is a vivid pleasure. And you have a vivid *sense* as of unseen or dimly seen things—vivid, and yet fitful and darkling; you glimpse salient features, but lose the fine shades or catch them imperfectly through the vision of the imagination: a case, as it were, of ignorant near-sighted stranger traversing the rim of wide vague horizons of Alps with an inspired and enlightened long-sighted native.

We visited the old St. Louis Hotel, now occupied by municipal offices. There is nothing strikingly remarkable about it; but one can say of it as of the Academy of Music in New York, that if a broom or a shovel has ever been used in it there is no circumstantial evidence to back up the fact. It is curious that cabbages and hay and things do not grow in the Academy of Music; but no doubt it is on account of the interruption of the light by the benches, and the impossibility of hoeing the crop except in the aisles. The fact that the ushers grow their buttonhole-bouquets on the premises shows what might be done if they had the right kind of an agricultural head to the establishment.

We visited also the venerable Cathedral, and the pretty square in front of it; the one dim with religious light, the other brilliant with the wordly sort, and lovely with orange trees and blossomy shrubs; then we drove in the hot sun through the wilderness of houses and out on to the wide dead level beyond, where the villas are, and the water wheels to drain the town, and the commons populous with cows and children; passing by an old cemetery where we were told lie the ashes of an early pirate; but we took him on trust, and did not visit him. He was a pirate with a tremendous and sanguinary history; and as long as he preserved unspotted, in retirement, the dignity of his name and the grandeur of his ancient calling, homage and reverence were his from high and low; but when at last he descended into politics and became a paltry alderman, the public "shook" him, and turned aside and wept. When he died, they set up a monument over him; and little by little he has come into respect again; but it is respect for the pirate, not the alderman, To-day the loyal and generous remember only what he was, and charitably forget what he became.

Thence, we drove a few miles across a swamp, along a raised shell road, with a canal on one hand and a dense wood on the other; and here and there, in the distance, a ragged and angular-limbed and moss-bearded cypress, top standing out, clear cut against the sky, and as quaint of form as the apple-trees in Japanese pictures—such was our course and the surroundings of it. There was an occasional alligator swimming comfortably along in the canal, and an occasional picturesque colored person on the bank, flinging his statue-rigid reflection upon the still water and watching for a bite.

And by and by we reached the West End, a collection of hotels of the usual light summer-resort pattern, with broad verandas all around, and the waves of the wide and blue Lake Pontchartrain lapping the thresholds. We had dinner on a ground-veranda over the water—the chief dish the renowned fish called the pompano, delicious as the less criminal forms of sin.

Thousands of people come by rail and carriage to West End and to Spanish Fort every evening, and dine, listen to the bands, take strolls in the open air under the electric lights, go sailing on the lake, and entertain themselves in various and sundry other ways.

We had opportunities on other days and in other places to test the pompano. Notably, at an editorial dinner at one of the clubs in the city. He was in his last possible perfection there, and justified his fame. In his suite was a tall pyramid of scarlet crayfish—large ones; as large as one's thumb; delicate, palatable, appetizing. Also devilled whitebait; also shrimps of choice quality; and a platter of small soft-shell crabs of a most superior breed. The other dishes were what one might get at Delmonico's, or Buckingham Palace; those I have spoken of can be had in similar perfection in New Orleans only, I suppose.

In the West and South they have a new institution,—the Broom Brigade. It is composed of young ladies who dress in a uniform costume, and go through the infantry drill, with broom in place of musket. It is a very pretty sight, on private view. When they perform on the stage of a theatre, in the blaze of colored fires, it must be a fine and fascinating spectacle. I saw them go through their complex manual with grace, spirit, and admirable precision. I saw them do everything which a human being can possibly do with a broom, except sweep. I did not see them sweep. But I know they could learn. What they have already learned proves that. And if they ever should learn, and should go on the war-path down Tchoupitoulas or some of those other streets around there, those thoroughfares would bear a greatly improved aspect in a very few minutes. But the girls themselves wouldn't; so nothing would be really gained, after all.

The drill was in the Washington Artillery building. In this building we saw many interesting relics of the war. Also a fine oil-painting representing Stonewall Jackson's last interview with General Lee. Both men are on horseback. Jackson has just ridden up, and is accosting Lee. The picture is very valuable, on account of the portraits, which are authentic. But, like many another historical picture, it means nothing without its label. And one label will fit it as well as another:—

First Interview between Lee and Jackson.
Last Interview between Lee and Jackson.
Jackson Introducing Himself to Lee.
Jackson Accepting Lee's Invitation to Dinner.
Jackson Declining Lee's Invitation to Dinner—with Thanks.
Jackson Apologizing for a Heavy Defeat.
Jackson Reporting a Great Victory.
Jackson Asking Lee for a Match.

It tells *one* story, and a sufficient one; for it says quite plainly and satisfactorily, "Here are Lee and Jackson together." The artist would have made it tell that this is Lee and Jackson's last interview if he could have done it. But he couldn't, for there wasn't any way to do it. A good legible label is usually worth, for information, a ton of significant attitude and expression in a historical picture. In Rome, people with fine sympathetic natures stand up and weep in front of the celebrated "Beatrice Cenci the Day before her Execution." It shows what a label can do. If they did not know the picture, they would inspect it unmoved, and say, "Young girl with hay fever; young girl with her head in a bag."

I found the half-forgotten Southern intonations and elisions as pleasing to my ear as they had formerly been. A Southerner talks music. At least it is music to me, but then I was born in the South. The educated Southerner has no use for an *r*, except at the beginning of a word. He says "honah," and "dinnah," and "Gove'nuh," and "befo' the waw," and so on. The words may lack charm to the eye, in print, but they have it to the ear. When did the *r* disappear from Southern speech, and how did it come to disappear? The custom of dropping it was not borrowed from the North, nor inherited from England. Many Southerners—most Southerners—put a *y* into occasional words that begin with the *k* sound. For instance, they say Mr. K'yahtah (Carter) and speak of playing k'yahds or of riding in the k'yahs. And they have the pleasant custom—long ago fallen into decay in the North—of frequently employing the respectful "Sir." Instead of the curt Yes, and the abrupt No, they say "Yes, Suh"; "No, Suh."

But there are some infelicities. Such as "like" for "as," and the addition of an "at" where it isn't needed. I heard an educated gentleman say, "Like the flag-officer did." His cook or his butler would have said, "Like the flag-officer done." You hear gentlemen say, "Where have you been at?" And here is the aggravated form—heard a ragged street Arab say it to a comrade: "I was a-ask'n' Tom whah you was a-sett'n' at." The very elect carelessly say "will" when they mean "shall"; and many of them say, "I didn't go to do it," meaning "I didn't mean to do it." The Northern word "guess"—imported from England, where it used to be common, and now regarded by satirical Englishmen as a Yankee original—is but little used among Southerners. They say "reckon." They haven't any "doesn't" in their language; they say "don't" instead. The unpolished often use "went" for "gone." It is nearly as bad as the Northern "hadn't ought." This reminds me that a remark of a very peculiar nature was made here in my neighborhood (in the North) a few days ago: "He hadn't ought to have went." How is that? Isn't that a good deal of a triumph? One knows the orders combined in this half-breed's architecture without inquiring:

THE UNABRIDGED MARK TWAIN II

one parent Northern, the other Southern. To-day I heard a school-mistress ask, "Where is John gone?" This form is so common—so nearly universal, in fact—that if she had used "whither" instead of "where," I think it would have sounded like an affectation.

We picked up one excellent word—a word worth traveling to New Orleans to get; a nice limber, expressive, handy word— "Lagniappe." They pronounce it lanny-*yap*. It is Spanish—so they said. We discovered it at the head of a column of odds and ends in the Picayune, the first day; heard twenty people use it the second; inquired what it meant the third; adopted it and got facility in swinging it the fourth. It has a restricted meaning, but I think the people spread it out a little when they choose. It is the equivalent of the thirteenth roll in a "baker's dozen." It is something thrown in, gratis, for good measure. The custom originated in the Spanish quarter of the city. When a child or a servant buys something in a shop—or even the mayor or the governor, for aught I know—he finishes the operation by saying,—

"Give me something for lagniappe."

The shopman always responds; gives the child a bit of liquorice-root, gives the servant a cheap cigar or a spool of thread, gives the governor—I don't know what he gives the governor; support, likely.

When you are invited to drink,—and this does occur now and then in New Orleans,—and you say, "What, again?—no, I've had enough;" the other party says, "But just this one time more,—this is for lagniappe." When the beau perceives that he is stacking his compliments a trifle too high, and sees by the young lady's countenance that the edifice would have been better with the top compliment left off, he puts his "I beg pardon,—no harm intended," into the briefer form of "Oh, that's for lagniappe." If the waiter in the restaurant stumbles and spills a gill of coffee down the back of your neck, he says, "For lagniappe, sah," and gets you another cup without extra charge.

CHAPTER XLV

SOUTHERN SPORTS

In the North one hears the war mentioned, in social conversation, once a month; sometimes as often as once a week; but as a distinct subject for talk, it has long ago been relieved of duty. There are sufficient reasons for this. Given a dinner company of six gentlemen to-day, it can easily happen that four of them—and possibly five—were not in the field at all. So the chances are four to two, or five to one, that the war will at no time during the evening become the topic of conversation; and the chances are still greater that if it become the topic it will remain so but a little while. If you add six ladies to the company, you have added six people who saw so little of the dread realities of the war that they ran out of talk concerning them years ago, and now would soon weary of the war topic if you brought it up.

The case is very different in the South. There, every man you meet was in the war; and every lady you meet saw the war. The war is the great chief topic of conversation. The interest in it is vivid and constant; the interest in other topics is fleeting. Mention of the war will wake up a dull company and set their tongues going, when nearly any other topic would fail. In the South, the war is what A.D. is elsewhere: they date from it. All day long you hear things "placed" as having happened since the waw; or du'in' the waw; or befo' the waw; or right aftah the waw; or 'bout two yeahs or five yeahs or ten yeahs befo' the waw or aftah the waw. It shows how intimately every individual was visited, in his own person, by that tremendous episode. It gives the inexperienced stranger a better idea of what a vast and comprehensive calamity invasion is than he can ever get by reading books at the fireside.

At a club one evening, a gentleman turned to me and said, in an aside:—

"You notice, of course, that we are nearly always talking about the war. It isn't because we haven't anything else to talk about, but because nothing else has so strong an interest for us. And there is another reason: In the war, each of us, in his own person, seems to have sampled all the different varieties of human experience; as a consequence, you can't mention an outside matter of any sort but it will certainly remind some listener of something that happened during the war,—and out he comes with it. Of course that brings the talk back to the war. You may try all you want to, to keep other subjects before the house, and we may all join in and help, but there can be but one result: the most random topic would load every man up with war reminiscences, and *shut* him up, too; and talk would be likely to stop presently, because you can't talk pale inconsequentialities when you've got a crimson fact or fancy in your head that you are burning to fetch out."

The poet was sitting some little distance away; and presently he began to speak—about the moon.

The gentleman who had been talking to me remarked in an

"aside:" "There, the moon is far enough from the seat of war, but you will see that it will suggest something to somebody about the war; in ten minutes from now the moon, as a topic, will be shelved."

The poet was saying he had noticed something which was a surprise to him; had had the impression that down here, toward the equator, the moonlight was much stronger and brighter than up North; had had the impression that when he visited New Orleans, many years ago, the moon—

Interruption from the other end of the room:—

"Let me explain that. Reminds me of an anecdote. Everything is changed since the war, for better or for worse; but you'll find people down here born grumblers, who see no change except the change for the worse. There was an old negro woman of this sort. A young New-Yorker said in her presence, 'What a wonderful moon you have down here!' She sighed and said, 'Ah, bless yo' heart, honey, you ought to seen dat moon befo' de waw!'"

The new topic was dead already. But the poet resurrected it, and gave it a new start.

A brief dispute followed, as to whether the difference between Northern and Southern moonlight really existed or was only imagined. Moonlight talk drifted easily into talk about artificial methods of dispelling darkness. Then somebody remembered that when Farragut advanced upon Port Hudson on a dark night—and did not wish to assist the aim of the Confederate gunners—he carried no battle-lanterns, but painted the decks of his ships white, and thus created a dim but valuable light, which enabled his own men to grope their way around with considerable facility. At this point the war got the floor again—the ten minutes not quite up yet.

I was not sorry, for war talk by men who have been in a war is always interesting; whereas moon talk by a poet who has not been in the moon is likely to be dull.

We went to a cockpit in New Orleans on a Saturday afternoon. I had never seen a cock-fight before. There were men and boys there of all ages and all colors, and of many languages and nationalities. But I noticed one quite conspicuous and surprising absence: the traditional brutal faces. There were no brutal faces. With no cock-fighting going on, you could have played the gathering on a stranger for a prayer-meeting; and after it began, for a revival,— provided you blindfolded your stranger,—for the shouting was something prodigious.

A negro and a white man were in the ring; everybody else outside. The cocks were brought in in sacks; and when time was called, they were taken out by the two bottle-holders, stroked, caressed, poked toward each other, and finally liberated. The big black cock plunged instantly at the little gray one and struck him on the head with his spur. The gray responded with spirit. Then the Babel of many-tongued shoutings broke out, and ceased not thenceforth. When the cocks had been fighting some little time, I was expecting them momently to drop dead, for both were blind, red with blood, and so exhausted that they frequently fell down. Yet they would not give up, neither would they die. The negro and the white man would pick them up every few seconds, wipe them off, blow cold water on them in a fine spray, and take their heads in their mouths and hold them there a moment—to warm back the perishing life perhaps; I do not know. Then, being set down again, the dying creatures would totter gropingly about, with dragging wings, find each other, strike a guess-work blow or two, and fall exhausted once more.

I did not see the end of the battle. I forced myself to endure it as long as I could, but it was too pitiful a sight; so I made frank confession to that effect, and we retired. We heard afterward that the black cock died in the ring, and fighting to the last.

Evidently there is abundant fascination about this "sport" for such as have had a degree of familiarity with it. I never saw people enjoy anything more than this gathering enjoyed this fight. The case was the same with old gray-heads and with boys of ten. They lost themselves in frenzies of delight. The "cocking-main" is an inhuman sort of entertainment, there is no question about that; still, it seems a much more respectable and far less cruel sport than fox-hunting—for the cocks like it; they experience, as well as confer enjoyment; which is not the fox's case.

We assisted—in the French sense—at a mule race, one day. I believe I enjoyed this contest more than any other mule there. I enjoyed it more than I remember having enjoyed any other animal race I ever saw. The grand stand was well filled with the beauty and the chivalry of New Orleans. That phrase is not original with me. It is the Southern reporter's. He has used it for two generations. He uses it twenty times a day, or twenty thousand times a day; or a million times a day—according to the exigencies. He is obliged to use it a million times a day, if he have occasion to speak of respectable men and women that often; for he has no other phrase for such service except that single one. He never tires of it; it always has a fine sound to him. There is a kind of swell mediaeval bulliness and tinsel about it that pleases his gaudy barbaric soul. If he had been in Palestine in the early times, we should have had no references to "much people" out of him. No, he would have said "the beauty and the chivalry of

Galilee'' assembled to hear the Sermon on the Mount. It is likely that the men and women of the South are sick enough of that phrase by this time, and would like a change, but there is no immediate prospect of their getting it.

The New Orleans editor has a strong, compact, direct, unflowery style; wastes no words, and does not gush. Not so with his average correspondent. In the Appendix I have quoted a good letter, penned by a trained hand; but the average correspondent hurls a style which differs from that. For instance:—

The "Times-Democrat" sent a relief-steamer up one of the bayous, last April. This steamer landed at a village, up there somewhere, and the Captain invited some of the ladies of the village to make a short trip with him. They accepted and came aboard, and the steamboat shoved out up the creek. That was all there was "to it." And that is all that the editor of the "Times-Democrat" would have got out of it. There was nothing in the thing but statistics, and he would have got nothing else out of it. He would probably have even tabulated them, partly to secure perfect clearness of statement, and partly to save space. But his special correspondent knows other methods of handling statistics. He just throws off all restraint and wallows in them:—

"On Saturday, early in the morning, the beauty of the place graced our cabin, and proud of her fair freight the gallant little boat glided up the bayou."

Twenty-two words to say the ladies came aboard and the boat shoved out up the creek, is a clean waste of ten good words, and is also destructive of compactness of statement.

The trouble with the Southern reporter is—Women. They unsettle him; they throw him off his balance. He is plain, and sensible, and satisfactory, until a woman heaves in sight. Then he goes all to pieces; his mind totters, he becomes flowery and idiotic. From reading the above extract, you would imagine that this student of Sir Walter Scott is an apprentice, and knows next to nothing about handling a pen. On the contrary, he furnishes plenty of proofs, in his long letter, that he knows well enough how to handle it when the women are not around to give him the artificial-flower complaint. For instance:—

"At 4 o'clock ominous clouds began to gather in the southeast, and presently from the Gulf there came a blow which increased in severity every moment. It was not safe to leave the landing then, and there was a delay. The oaks shook off long tresses of their mossy beards to the tugging of the wind, and the bayou in its ambition put on miniature waves in mocking of much larger bodies of water. A lull permitted a start, and homewards we steamed, an inky sky overhead and a heavy wind blowing. As darkness crept on, there were few on board who did not wish themselves nearer home.''

There is nothing the matter with that. It is good description, compactly put. Yet there was great temptation, there, to drop into lurid writing.

But let us return to the mule. Since I left him, I have rummaged around and found a full report of the race. In it I find confirmation of the theory which I broached just now—namely, that the trouble with the Southern reporter is Women: Women, supplemented by Walter Scott and his knights and beauty and chivalry, and so on. This is an excellent report, as long as the women stay out of it. But when they intrude, we have this frantic result:—

"It will be probably a long time before the ladies' stand presents such a sea of foam-like loveliness as it did yesterday. The New Orleans women are always charming, but never so much so as at this time of the year, when in their dainty spring costumes they bring with them a breath of balmy freshness and an odor of sanctity unspeakable. The stand was so crowded with them that, walking at their feet and seeing no possibility of approach, many a man appreciated as he never did before the Peri's feeling at the Gates of Paradise, and wondered what was the priceless boon that would admit him to their sacred presence. Sparkling on their white-robed breasts or shoulders were the colors of their favorite knights, and were it not for the fact that the doughty heroes appeared on unromantic mules, it would have been easy to imagine one of King Arthur's gala-days.''

There were thirteen mules in the first heat; all sorts of mules, they were; all sorts of complexions, gaits, dispositions, aspects. Some were handsome creatures, some were not; some were sleek, some hadn't had their fur brushed lately; some were innocently gay and frisky; some were full of malice and all unrighteousness; guessing from looks, some of them thought the matter on hand was war, some thought it was a lark, the rest took it for a religious occasion. And each mule acted according to his convictions. The result was an absence of harmony well compensated by a conspicuous presence of variety—variety of picturesque and entertaining sort.

All the riders were young gentlemen in fashionable society. If the reader has been wondering why it is that the ladies of New Orleans attend so humble an orgy as a mule-race, the thing is explained now. It is a fashion-freak; all connected with it are people of fashion.

419

It is great fun, and cordially liked. The mule-race is one of the marked occasions of the year. It has brought some pretty fast mules to the front. One of these had to be ruled out, because he was so fast that he turned the thing into a one-mule contest, and robbed it of one of its best features—variety. But every now and then somebody disguises him with a new name and a new complexion, and rings him in again.

The riders dress in full jockey costumes of bright-colored silks, satins, and velvets.

The thirteen mules got away in a body, after a couple of false starts, and scampered off with prodigious spirit. As each mule and each rider had a distinct opinion of his own at to how the race ought to be run, and which side of the track was best in certain circumstances, and how often the track ought to be crossed, and when a collision ought to be accomplished, and when it ought to be avoided, these twenty-six conflicting opinions created a most fantastic and picturesque confusion, and the resulting spectacle was killingly comical.

Mile heat; time, 2:22. Eight of the thirteen mules distanced. I had a bet on a mule which would have won if the procession had been reversed. The second heat was good fun; and so was the "consolation race for beaten mules," which followed later; but the first heat was the best in that respect.

I think that much the most enjoyable of all races is a steamboat race; but, next to that, I prefer the gay and joyous mule-rush. Two red-hot steamboats raging along, neck-and-neck, straining every nerve—that is to say, every rivet in the boilers—quaking and shaking and groaning from stem to stern, spouting white steam from the pipes, pouring black smoke from the chimneys, raining down sparks, parting the river into long breaks of hissing foam—this is sport that makes a body's very liver curl with enjoyment. A horse-race is pretty tame and colorless in comparison. Still, a horse-race might be well enough, in its way, perhaps, if it were not for the tiresome false starts. But then, nobody is ever killed. At least, nobody was ever killed when I was at a horse-race. They have been crippled, it it true; but this is little to the purpose.

CHAPTER XLVI

ENCHANTMENTS AND ENCHANTERS

The largest annual event in New Orleans is a something which we arrived too late to sample—the Mardi-Gras festivities. I saw the procession of the Mystic Crew of Comus there, twenty-four years ago—with knights and nobles and so on, clothed in silken and golden Paris-made gorgeousnesses, planned and bought for that single night's use; and in their train all manner of giants, dwarfs, monstrosities, and other diverting grotesquerie—a startling and wonderful sort of show, as it filed solemnly and silently down the street in the light of its smoking and flickering torches; but it is said that in these latter days the spectacle is mightily augmented, as to cost, splendor, and variety. There is a chief personage—"Rex;" and if I remember rightly, neither this king nor any of his great following of subordinates is known to any outsider. All these people are gentlemen of position and consequence; and it is a proud thing to belong to the organization; so the mystery in which they hide their personality is merely for romance's sake, and not on account of the police.

Mardi-Gras is of course a relic of the French and Spanish occupation; but I judge that the religious feature has been pretty well knocked out of it now. Sir Walter has got the advantage of the gentlemen of the cowl and rosary, and he will stay. His mediaeval business, supplemented by the monsters and the oddities, and the pleasant creatures from fairy-land, is finer to look at than the poor fantastic inventions and performances of the revelling rabble of the priest's day, and serves quite as well, perhaps, to emphasize the day and admonish men that the graceline between the worldly season and the holy one is reached.

This Mardi-Gras pageant was the exclusive possession of New Orleans until recently. But now it has spread to Memphis and St. Louis and Baltimore. It has probably reached its limit. It is a thing which could hardly exist in the practical North; would certainly last but a very brief time; as brief a time as it would last in London. For the soul of it is the romantic, not the funny and the grotesque. Take away the romantic mysteries, the kings and knights and big-sounding titles, and Mardi-Gras would die, down there in the South. The very feature that keeps it alive in the South— girly-girly romance—would kill it in the North or in London. Puck and Punch, and the press universal, would fall upon it and make merciless fun of it, and its first exhibition would be also its last.

Against the crimes of the French Revolution and of Bonaparte may be set two compensating benefactions: the Revolution broke the chains of the *ancien régime* and of the Church, and made of a nation of abject slaves a nation of freemen; and Bonaparte instituted the setting of merit above birth, and also so completely stripped the divinity from royalty, that whereas crowned heads in Europe were gods before, they are only men, since, and can never be gods again, but only figure-heads, and answerable for their acts like common clay. Such benefactions as these compensate the temporary harm which Bonaparte and the Revolution did, and leave the world in debt to them for these great and permanent services to liberty, humanity, and progress.

Then comes Sir Walter Scott with his enchantments, and by his single might checks this wave of progress, and even turns it back; sets the world in love with dreams and phantoms; with decayed and swinish forms of religion; with decayed and degraded systems of government; with the sillinesses and emptinesses, sham grandeurs, sham gauds, and sham chivalries of a brainless and worthless long-vanished society. He did measureless harm; more real and lasting harm, perhaps, than any other individual that ever wrote. Most of the world has now outlived good part of these harms, though by no means all of them; but in our South they flourish pretty forcefully still. Not so forcefully as half a generation ago, perhaps, but still forcefully. There, the genuine and wholesome civilization of the nineteenth century is curiously confused and commingled with the Walter Scott Middle-Age sham civilization and so you have practical, common-sense, progressive ideas, and progressive works, mixed up with the duel, the inflated speech, and the jejune romanticism of an absurd past that is dead, and out of charity ought to be buried. But for the Sir Walter disease, the character of the Southerner—or Southron, according to Sir Walter's starchier way of phrasing it—would be wholly modern, in place of modern and mediaeval mixed, and the South would be fully a generation further advanced than it is. It was Sir Walter that made every gentleman in the South a Major or a Colonel, or a General or a Judge, before the war; and it was he, also, that made these gentlemen value these bogus decorations. For it was he that created rank and caste down there, and also reverence for rank and caste, and pride and pleasure in them. Enough is laid on slavery, without fathering upon it these creations and contributions of Sir Walter.

Sir Walter had so large a hand in making Southern character, as it existed before the war, that he is in great measure responsible for the war. It seems a little harsh toward a dead man to say that we never should have had any war but for Sir Walter; and yet something of a plausible argument might, perhaps, be made in support of that wild proposition. The Southerner of the American revolution owned slaves; so did the Southerner of the Civil War: but the former resembles the latter as an Englishman resembles a Frenchman. The change of character can be traced rather more easily to Sir Walter's influence than to that of any other thing or person.

One may observe, by one or two signs, how deeply that influence penetrated, and how strongly it holds. If one take up a Northern or Southern literary periodical of forty or fifty years ago, he will find it filled with wordy, windy, flowery "eloquence," romanticism, sentimentality—all imitated from Sir Walter, and sufficiently badly done, too—innocent travesties of his style and methods, in fact. This sort of literature being the fashion in both sections of the country, there was opportunity for the fairest competition; and as a consequence, the South was able to show as many well-known literary names, proportioned to population, as the North could.

But a change has come, and there is no opportunity now for a fair competition between North and South. For the North has thrown out that old inflated style, whereas the Southern writer still clings to it—clings to it and has a restricted market for his wares, as a consequence. There is as much literary talent in the South, now, as ever there was, of course; but its work can gain but slight currency under present conditions; the authors write for the past, not the present; they use obsolete forms, and a dead language. But when a Southerner of genius writes modern English, his book goes upon crutches no longer, but upon wings; and they carry it swiftly all about America and England, and through the great English reprint publishing houses of Germany—as witness the experience of Mr. Cable and Uncle Remus, two of the very few Southern authors who do not write in the southern style. Instead of three or four widely-known literary names, the South ought to have a dozen or two—and will have them when Sir Walter's time is out.

A curious exemplification of the power of a single book for good or harm is shown in the effects wrought by Don Quixote and those wrought by Ivanhoe. The first swept the world's admiration for the mediaeval chivalry-silliness out of existence; and the other restored it. As far as our South is concerned, the good work done by Cervantes is pretty nearly a dead letter, so effectually has Scott's pernicious work undermined it.

CHAPTER XLVII

UNCLE REMUS AND MR. CABLE

Mr. Joel Chandler Harris ("Uncle Remus") was to arrive from Atlanta at seven o'clock Sunday morning; so we got up and received him. We were able to detect him among the crowd of arrivals at the hotel-counter by his correspondence with a description of him which had been furnished us from a trust-worthy source. He was said to be undersized, red-haired, and somewhat freckled. He was the only man in the party whose out-side tallied with this bill of particulars. He was said to be very shy. He is a shy man. Of this there is no doubt. It may not show on the surface, but the shyness is there. After days of intimacy one wonders to see that it is still in about as strong force as ever. There is a fine and beautiful nature hidden behind it, as all know who have read the Uncle Remus book; and a fine genius, too, as all know by the same sign. I seem to be talking quite freely about this neighbor; but in talking to the public I am but talking to his personal friends, and these things are permissible among friends.

He deeply disappointed a number of children who had flocked eagerly to Mr. Cable's house to get a glimpse of the illustrious sage and oracle of the nation's nurseries. They said:—

"Why, he's white!"

They were grieved about it. So, to console them, the book was brought, that they might hear Uncle Remus's Tar-Baby story from the lips of Uncle Remus himself—or what, in their out-raged eyes, was left of him. But it turned out that he had never read aloud to people, and was too shy to venture the attempt now. Mr. Cable and I read from books of ours, to show him what an easy trick it was; but his immortal shyness was proof against even this sagacious strategy, so we had to read about Brer Rabbit ourselves.

Mr. Harris ought to be able to read the negro dialect better than anybody else, for in the matter of writing it he is the only master the country has produced. Mr. Cable is the only master in the writing of French dialects that the country has produced; and he reads them in perfection. It was a great treat to hear him read about Jean-ah Poquelin, and about Innerarity and his famous "pigshoo" representing "Louisihanna *Rif*-fusing to Hanter the Union," along with passages of nicely-shaded Ger-man dialect from a novel which was still in manuscript.

It came out in conversation, that in two different instances Mr. Cable got into grotesque trouble by using, in his books, next-to-impossible French names which nevertheless happened to be borne by living and sensitive citizens of New-Orleans. His names were either inventions or were borrowed from the ancient and obsolete past, I do not now remember which; but at any rate living bearers of them turned up, and were a good deal hurt at having attention directed to themselves and their affairs in so excessively public a manner.

Mr. Warner and I had an experience of the same sort when we wrote the book called "The Gilded Age." There is a character in it called "Sellers." I do not remember what his first name was, in the beginning; but anyway, Mr. Warner did not like it, and wanted it improved. He asked me if I was able to imagine a person named "Eschol Sellers." Of course I said I could not, without stimulants. He said that away out West, once, he had met, and contemplated, and actually shaken hands with a man bearing that impossible name—"Eschol Sellers." He added,—

"It was twenty years ago; his name has probably carried him off before this; and if it hasn't, he will never see the book anyhow. We will confiscate his name. The name you are using is common, and therefore dangerous; there are probably a thousand Sellerses bearing it, and the whole horde will come after us; but Eschol Sellers is a safe name—it is a rock."

So we borrowed that name; and when the book had been out about a week, one of the stateliest and handsomest and most aristocratic looking white men that ever lived, called around, with the most formidable libel suit in his pocket that ever—well, in brief, we got his permission to suppress an edition of ten million* copies of the book and change that name to "Mulberry Sellers" in future editions.

CHAPTER XLVIII

SUGAR AND POSTAGE

One day, on the street, I encountered the man whom, of all men, I most wished to see—Horace Bixby; formerly pilot under me—or rather, over me—now captain of the great steamer "City of Baton Rouge," the latest and swiftest addition to the Anchor Line. The same slender figure, the same tight curls, the same springy step, the same alertness, the same decision of eye and answering decision of hand, the same erect military bearing; not an inch gained or lost in girth, not an ounce gained or lost in weight, not a hair turned. It is a curious thing, to leave a man thirty-five years old, and come back at the end of twenty-one years and find him still only thirty-five. I have not had an experience of this kind before, I believe. There were some crow's-

* Figures taken from memory, and probably incorrect. Think it was more.

feet, but they counted for next to nothing, since they were inconspicuous.

His boat was just in. I had been waiting several days for her, purposing to return to St. Louis in her. The captain and I joined a party of ladies and gentlemen, guests of Major Wood, and went down the river fifty-four miles, in a swift tug, to ex-Governor Warmouth's sugar plantation. Strung along below the city, were a number of decayed, ram-shackly, superannuated old steamboats, not one of which I had ever seen before. They had all been built, and worn out, and thrown aside, since I was here last. This gives one a realizing sense of the frailness of a Mississippi boat and the briefness of its life.

Six miles below town a fat and battered brick chimney, sticking above the magnolias and live-oaks, was pointed out as the monument erected by an appreciative nation to celebrate the battle of New Orleans—Jackson's victory over the British, January 8, 1815. The war had ended, the two nations were at peace, but the news had not yet reached New Orleans. If we had had the cable telegraph in those days, this blood would not have been spilt, those lives would not have been wasted; and better still, Jackson would probably never have been president. We have gotten over the harms done us by the war of 1812, but not over some of those done us by Jackson's presidency.

The Warmouth plantation covers a vast deal of ground, and the hospitality of the Warmouth mansion is graduated to the same large scale. We saw steam-plows at work, here, for the first time. The traction engine travels about on its own wheels, till it reaches the required spot; then it stands still and by means of a wire rope pulls the huge plow toward itself two or three hundred yards across the field, between the rows of cane. The thing cuts down into the black mould a foot and a half deep. The plow looks like a fore-and-aft brace of a Hudson river steamer, inverted. When the negro steersman sits on one end of it, that end tilts down near the ground, while the other sticks up high in air. This great see-saw goes rolling and pitching like a ship at sea, and it is not every circus rider that could stay on it.

The plantation contains two thousand six hundred acres; six hundred and fifty are in cane; and there is a fruitful orange grove of five thousand trees. The cane is cultivated after a modern and intricate scientific fashion, too elaborate and complex for me to attempt to describe; but it lost $40,000 last year. I forget the other details. However, this year's crop will reach ten or twelve hundred tons of sugar, consequently last year's loss will not matter. These troublesome and expensive scientific methods achieve a yield of a ton and a half, and from that to two tons, to the acre; which is three or four times what the yield of an acre was in my time.

The drainage-ditches were everywhere alive with little crabs—"fiddlers." One saw them scampering sidewise in every direction whenever they heard a disturbing noise. Expensive pests, these crabs; for they bore into the levees, and ruin them.

The great sugar-house was a wilderness of tubs and tanks and vats and filters, pumps, pipes, and machinery. The process of making sugar is exceedingly interesting. First, you heave your cane into the centrifugals and grind out the juice; then run it through the evaporating pan to extract the fibre; then through the bone-filter to remove the alcohol; then through the clarifying tanks to discharge the molasses; then through the granulating pipes to condense it; then through the vacuum pan to extract the vacuum. It is now ready for market. I have jotted these particulars down from memory. The thing looks simple and easy. Do not deceive yourself. To make sugar is really one of the most difficult things in the world. And to make it right, is next to impossible. If you will examine your own supply every now and then for a term of years, and tabulate the result, you will find that not two men in twenty can make sugar without getting sand into it.

We could have gone down to the mouth of the river and visited Captain Eads' great work, the "jetties," where the river has been compressed between walls, and thus deepened to twenty-six feet; but it was voted useless to go, since at this stage of the water everything would be covered up and invisible.

We could have visited that ancient and singular burg, "Pilot-town," which stands on stilts in the water—so they say; where nearly all communication is by skiff and canoe, even to the attending of weddings and funerals; and where the littlest boys and girls are as handy with the oar as unamphibious children are with the velocipede.

We could have done a number of other things; but on account of limited time, we went back home. The sail up the breezy and sparkling river was a charming experience, and would have been satisfyingly sentimental and romantic but for the interruptions of the tug's pet parrot, whose tireless comments upon the scenery and the guests were always this-worldly, and often profane. He had also a superabundance of the discordant, ear-splitting, metallic laugh common to his breed,—a machine-made laugh, a Frankenstein laugh, with the soul left out of it. He applied it to every sentimental remark, and to every pathetic song. He cackled it out with hideous energy after "Home again, home again, from a foreign shore," and said he "wouldn't give a damn for a tug-load of such rot.'' Romance and sentiment cannot long survive this sort of discouragement; so the singing and talking presently ceased; which so delighted the parrot that he cursed himself hoarse for joy.

Then the male members of the party moved to the forecastle, to smoke and gossip. There were several old steamboatmen along, and I learned from them a great deal of what had been happening to my former river friends during my long absence. I learned that a pilot whom I used to steer for is become a spiritualist, and for more than fifteen years has been receiving a letter every week from a deceased relative, through a New York spiritualistic medium named Manchester—postage graduated by distance: from the local post-office in Paradise to New York, five dollars; from New York to St. Louis, three cents. I remember Mr. Manchester very well. I called on him once, ten years ago, with a couple of friends, one of whom wished to inquire after a deceased uncle. This uncle had lost his life in a peculiarly violent and unusual way, half a dozen years before: a cyclone blew him some three miles and knocked a tree down with him which was four feet through at the butt and sixty-five feet high. He did not survive this triumph. At the *séance* just referred to, my friend questioned his late uncle, through Mr. Manchester, and the late uncle wrote down his replies, using Mr. Manchester's hand and pencil for that purpose. The following is a fair example of the questions asked, and also of the sloppy twaddle in the way of answers, furnished by Manchester under the pretence that it came from the spectre. If this man is not the paltriest fraud that lives, I owe him an apology:—

Question. Where are you?

Answer. In the spirit world.

Q. Are you happy?

A. Very happy. Perfectly happy.

Q. How do you amuse yourself?

A. Conversation with friends, and other spirits.

Q. What else?

A. Nothing else. Nothing else is necessary.

Q. What do you talk about?

A. About how happy we are; and about friends left behind in the earth, and how to influence them for their good.

Q. When your friends in the earth all get to the spirit land, what shall you have to talk about then?— nothing but about how happy you all are?

No reply. It is explained that spirits will not answer frivolous questions.

Q. How is it that spirits that are content to spend an eternity in frivolous employments, and accept it as happiness, are so fastidious about frivolous questions upon the subject?

No reply.

Q. Would you like to come back?

A. No.

Q. Would you say that under oath?

A. Yes.

Q. What do you eat there?

A. We do not eat.

Q. What do you drink?

A. We do not drink.

Q. What do you smoke?

A. We do not smoke.

Q. What do you read?

A. We do not read.

Q. Do all the good people go to your place?

A. Yes.

Q. You know my present way of life. Can you suggest any additions to it, in the way of crime, that will reasonably insure my going to some other place?

A. No reply.

Q. When did you die?

A. I did not die, I passed away.

Q. Very well, then, when did you pass away? How long have you been in the spirit land?

A. We have no measurements of time here.

Q. Though you may be indifferent and uncertain as to dates and times in your present condition and environment, this has nothing to do with your former condition. You had dates then. One of these is what I ask for. You departed on a certain day in a certain year. Is not this true?

A. Yes.

Q. Then name the day of the month.

(Much fumbling with pencil, on the part of the medium, accompanied by violent spasmodic jerkings of his head and body, for some little time. Finally, explanation to the effect that spirits often forget dates, such things being without importance to them.)

Q. Then this one has actually forgotten the date of its translation to the spirit land?

This was granted to be the case.

Q. This is very curious. Well, then, what year was it?

(More fumbling, jerking, idiotic spasms, on the part of the medium. Finally, explanation to the effect that the spirit has forgotten the year.)

Q. This is indeed stupendous. Let me put one more question, one last question, to you, before we part to meet no more;—for even if I fail to avoid your asylum, a meeting there will go for nothing *as* a meeting, since by that time you will easily have forgotten me and my name: did you die a natural death, or were you cut off by a catastrophe?

A. (After long hesitation and many throes and spasms.) *Natural death.*

This ended the interview. My friend told the medium that when his relative was in this poor world, he was endowed with an extraordinary intellect and an absolutely defectless memory, and it seemed a great pity that he had not been allowed to keep some shred of these for his amusement in the realms of everlasting contentment, and for the amazement and admiration of the rest of the population there.

This man had plenty of clients—has plenty yet. He receives letters from spirits located in every part of the spirit world, and delivers them all over this country through the United States mail. These letter are filled with advice—advice from "spirits" who don't know as much as a tadpole—and this advice is religiously followed by the receivers. One of these clients was a man whom the spirits (if one may thus plurally describe the ingenious Manchester) were teaching how to contrive an improved railway car-wheel. It is coarse employment for a spirit, but it is higher and wholesomer activity than talking forever about "how happy we are."

CHAPTER XLIX

EPISODES IN PILOT LIFE

In the course of the tug-boat gossip, it came out that out of every five of my former friends who had quitted the river, four had chosen farming as an occupation. Of course this was not because they were peculiarly gifted, agriculturally, and thus more likely to succeed as farmers than in other industries: the reason for their choice must be traced to some other source. Doubtless they chose farming because that life is private and secluded from irruptions of undesirable strangers,—like the pilot-house hermitage. And doubtless they also chose it because on a thousand nights of black storm and danger they had noted the twinkling lights of solitary farm-houses, as the boat swung by, and pictured to themselves the serenity and security and cosiness of such refuges at such times, and so had by and by come to dream of that retired and peaceful life as the one desirable thing to long for, anticipate, earn, and at last enjoy.

But I did not learn that any of these pilot-farmers had astonished anybody with their successes. Their farms do not support them: they support their farms. The pilot-farmer disappears from the river annually, about the breaking of spring, and is seen no more till next frost. Then he appears again, in damaged homespun, combs the hay-seed out of his hair, and takes a pilot-house berth for the winter. In this way he pays the debts which his farming has achieved during the agricultural season. So his river bondage is but half broken; he is still the river's slave the hardest half of the year.

One of these men bought a farm, but did not retire to it. He knew a trick worth two of that. He did not propose to pauperize his farm by applying his personal ignorance to working it. No, he put the farm into the hands of an agricultural expert to be worked on shares—out of every three loads of corn the expert to have two and the pilot the third. But at the end of the season the pilot received no corn. The expert explained that *his* share was not reached. The farm produced only two loads.

Some of the pilots whom I had known had had adventures;— the outcome fortunate, sometimes, but not in all cases. Captain Montgomery, whom I had steered for when he was a pilot, commanded the Confederate fleet in the great battle before Memphis; when his vessel went down, he swam ashore, fought his way through a squad of soldiers, and made a gallant and narrow escape. He was always a cool man; nothing could disturb his serenity. Once when he was captain of the "Cresent City," I was bringing the boat into port at New Orleans, and momently expecting orders from the hurricane deck, but received none. I had stopped the wheels, and there my authority and responsibility ceased. It was evening—dim twilight—the captain's hat was perched upon the big bell, and I supposed the intellectual end of the captain was in it, but such was not the case. The captain was very strict; therefore I knew better than to touch a bell without orders. My duty was to hold the boat steadily on her calamitous course, and leave the consequences to take care of themselves— which I did. So we went plowing past the sterns of steamboats and getting closer and closer—the crash was bound to come very soon—and still that hat never budged; for alas, the captain was napping in the texas. . . . Things were becoming exceedingly nervous and uncomfortable. It seemed to me that the captain was not going to appear in time to see the entertainment. But he did. Just as we were walking into the stern of a steamboat, he stepped out on deck, and said, with heavenly serenity, "Set her back on both''—which I did; but a trifle late, however, for the next moment we went smashing through that other boat's flimsy outer works with a most prodigious racket. The captain never said a word to me about the matter afterwards, except to remark that I had done right, and that he hoped I would not hesitate to act in the same way again in like circumstances.

One of the pilots whom I had known when I was on the river had died a very honorable death. His boat caught fire, and he remained at the wheel until he got her safe to land. Then he went out over the breast-board with his clothing in flames, and was the last person to get ashore. He died from his injuries in the course of two or three hours, and his was the only life lost.

The history of Mississippi piloting affords six or seven instances of this sort of martyrdom, and half a hundred instances of escapes from a like fate which came within a second or two of being fatally too late; *but there is no instance of a pilot deserting his post to save his life while by remaining and sacrificing it he might secure other lives from destruction.* It is well worth while to set down this noble fact, and well worth while to put it in italics, too.

The ''cub'' pilot is early admonished to despise all perils connected with a pilot's calling, and to prefer any sort of death to the deep dishonor of deserting his post while there is any possibility of his being useful in it. And so effectively are these admonitions inculcated, that even young and but half-tried pilots can be depended upon to stick to the wheel, and die there when occasion requires. In a Memphis graveyard is buried a young fellow who perished at the wheel a great many years ago, in White River, to save the lives of other men. He said to the captain that if the fire would give him time to reach a sand bar, some distance away, all could be saved, but that to land against the bluff bank of the river would be to insure the loss of many lives. He reached the bar and grounded the boat in shallow water; but by that time the flames had closed around him, and in escaping through them he was fatally burned. He had been urged to fly sooner, but had replied as became a pilot to reply:—

''I will not go. If I go, nobody will be saved; if I stay, no one will be lost but me. I will stay.''

There were two hundred persons on board, and no life was lost but the pilot's. There used to be a monument to this young fellow, in that Memphis graveyard. While we tarried in Memphis on our down trip, I started out to look for it, but our time was so brief that I was obliged to turn back before my object was accomplished.

The tug-boat gossip informed me that Dick Kennet was

dead—blown up, near Memphis, and killed; that several others whom I had known had fallen in the war—one or two of them shot down at the wheel; that another and very particular friend, whom I had steered many trips for, had stepped out of his house in New Orleans, one night years ago, to collect some money in a remote part of the city, and had never been seen again,—was murdered and thrown into the river, it was thought; that Ben Thornburgh was dead long ago; also his wild "cub" whom I used to quarrel with, all through every daylight watch. A heedless, reckless creature he was, and always in hot water, always in mischief. An Arkansas passenger brought an enormous bear aboard, one day, and chained him to a life-boat on the hurricane deck. Thornburgh's "cub" could not rest till he had gone there and unchained the bear, to "see what he would do." He was promptly gratified. The bear chased him around and around the deck, for miles and miles, with two hundred eager faces grinning through the railings for audience, and finally snatched off the lad's coat-tail and went into the texas to chew it. The off-watch turned out with alacrity; and left the bear in sole possession. He presently grew lonesome, and started out for recreation. He ranged the whole boat—visited every part of it, with an advance guard of fleeing people in front of him and a voiceless vacancy behind him; and when his owner captured him at last, those two were the only visible beings anywhere; everybody else was in hiding, and the boat was a solitude.

I was told that one of my pilot friends fell dead at the wheel, from heart disease, in 1869. The captain was on the roof at the time. He saw the boat breaking for the shore; shouted, and got no answer; ran up, and found the pilot lying dead on the floor.

Mr. Bixby had been blown up, in Madrid bend; was not injured, but the other pilot was lost.

George Ritchie had been blown up near Memphis—blown into the river from the wheel, and disabled. The water was very cold; he clung to a cotton bale—mainly with his teeth—and floated until nearly exhausted, when he was rescued by some deck hands who were on a piece of the wreck. They tore open the bale and packed him in the cotton, and warmed the life back into him, and got him safe to Memphis. He is one of Bixby's pilots on the "Baton Rouge" now.

Into the life of a steamboat clerk, now dead, had dropped a bit of romance,—somewhat grotesque romance, but romance nevertheless. When I knew him he was a shiftless young spendthrift, boisterous, good-hearted, full of careless generosities, and pretty conspicuously promising to fool his possibilities away early, and come to nothing. In a Western city lived a rich and childless old foreigner and his wife; and in their family was a comely young girl—sort of friend, sort of servant. The young clerk of whom I have been speaking,—whose name was not George Johnson, but who shall be called George Johnson for the purposes of this narrative,—got acquainted with this young girl, and they sinned; and the old foreigner found them out, and rebuked them. Being ashamed, they lied, and said they were married; that they had been privately married. Then the old foreigner's hurt was healed, and he forgave and blessed them. After that, they were able to continue their sin without concealment. By and by the foreigner's wife died; and presently he followed after her. Friends of the family assembled to mourn; and among the mourners sat the two young sinners. The will was opened and solemnly read. It bequeathed every penny of that old man's great wealth to *Mrs. George Johnson!*

And there was no such person. The young sinners fled forth then, and did a very foolish thing: married themselves before an obscure Justice of the Peace, and got him to antedate the thing. That did no sort of good. The distant relatives flocked in and exposed the fraudful date with extreme suddenness and surprising ease, and carried off the fortune, leaving the Johnsons very legitimately, and legally, and irrevocably chained together in honorable marriage, but with not so much as a penny to bless themselves withal. Such are the actual facts; and not all novels have for a base so telling a situation.

CHAPTER L

THE "ORIGINAL JACOBS"

We had some talk about Captain Isaiah Sellers, now many years dead. He was a fine man, a high-minded man, and greatly respected both ashore and on the river. He was very tall, well built, and handsome; and in his old age—as I remember him— his hair was as black as an Indian's, and his eye and hand were as strong and steady and his nerve and judgment as firm and clear as anybody's, young or old, among the fraternity of pilots. He was the patriarch of the craft; he had been a keelboat pilot before the day of steamboats; and a steamboat pilot before any other steamboat pilot, still surviving at the time I speak of, had ever turned a wheel. Consequently his brethren held him in the sort of awe in which illustrious survivors of a bygone age are always held by their associates. He knew how he was regarded, and perhaps this fact added some trifle of stiffening to his natural dignity, which had been sufficiently stiff in its original state.

He left a diary behind him; but apparently it did not date back to his first steamboat trip, which was said to be 1811, the year the first steamboat disturbed the waters of the Mississippi. At the time of his death a correspondent of the "St. Louis Republican" culled the following items from the diary:—

"In February, 1825, he shipped on board the steamer 'Rambler,' at Florence, Ala., and made during that year three trips to New Orleans and back,—this on the 'Gen. Carrol,' between Nashville and New Orleans. It was during his stay on this boat that Captain Sellers introduced the tap of the bell as a signal to heave the lead, previous to which time it was the custom for the pilot to speak to the men below when soundings were wanted. The proximity of the forecastle to the pilot-house, no doubt, rendered this an easy matter; but how different on one of our palaces of the present day.

"In 1827 we find him on board the 'President,' a boat of two hundred and eighty-five tons burden, and plying between Smithland and New Orleans. Thence he joined the 'Jubilee' in 1828, and on this boat he did his first piloting in the St. Louis trade; his first watch extending from Herculaneum to St. Genevieve. On May 26, 1836, he completed and left Pittsburg in charge of the steamer 'Prairie,' a boat of four hundred tons, and the first steamer with a *state-room cabin* ever seen at St. Louis. In 1857 he introduced the signal for meeting boats, and which has, with some slight change, been the universal custom of this day; in fact, is rendered obligatory by act of Congress.

"As general items of river history, we quote the following marginal notes from his general log:—

"In March, 1825, Gen. Lafayette left New Orleans for St. Louis on the low-pressure steamer 'Natchez.'

"In January, 1828, twenty-one steamers left the New Orleans wharf to celebrate the occasion of Gen. Jackson's visit to that city.

"In 1830 the 'North American' made the run from New Orleans to Memphis in six days—best time on record to that date. It has since been made in two days and ten hours.

"In 1831 the Red River cut-off formed.

"In 1832 steamer 'Hudson' made the run from White River to Helena, a distance of seventy-five miles, in twelve hours. This was the source of much talk and speculation among parties directly interested.

"In 1839 Great Horseshoe cut-off formed.

"Up to the present time, a term of thirty-five years, we ascertain, by reference to the diary, he has made four hundred and sixty round trips to New Orleans, which gives a distance of one million one hundred and four thousand miles, or an average of eighty-six miles a day."

Whenever Captain Sellers approached a body of gossiping pilots, a chill fell there, and talking ceased. For this reason: whenever six pilots were gathered together, there would always be one or two newly fledged ones in the lot, and the elder ones would be always "showing off" before these poor fellows; making them sorrowfully feel how callow they were, how recent their nobility, and how humble their degree, by talking largely and vaporously of old-time experiences on the river; always making it a point to date everything back as far as they could, so as to make the new men feel their newness to the sharpest degree possible, and envy the old stagers in the like degree. And how these complacent baldheads *would* swell, and brag, and lie, and date back—ten, fifteen, twenty years,—and how they did enjoy the effect produced upon the marvelling and envying youngsters!

And perhaps just at this happy stage of the proceedings, the stately figure of Captain Isaiah Sellers, that real and only genuine Son of Antiquity, would drift solemnly into the midst. Imagine the size of the silence that would result on the instant. And imagine the feelings of those bald-heads, and the exultation of their recent audience when the ancient captain would begin to drop casual and indifferent remarks of a reminiscent nature,— about islands that had disappeared, and cut-offs that had been made, a generation before the oldest bald-head in the company had ever set his foot in a pilot-house!

Many and many a time did this ancient mariner appear on the scene in the above fashion, and spread disaster and humiliation around him. If one might believe the pilots, he always dated his islands back to the misty dawn of river history; and he never used the same island twice; and never did he employ an island that still existed, or give one a name which anybody present was old enough to have heard of before. If you might believe the pilots, he was always conscientiously particular about little details; never spoke of "the State of Mississippi," for instance,—no, he would say, "When the State of Mississippi was where Arkansas now is;" and would never speak of Louisiana or Missouri in a general way, and leave an incorrect impression on your mind,—no, he would say, "When Louisiana was up the river farther," or "When Missouri was on the Illinois side."

The old gentleman was not of literary turn or capacity, but he used to jot down brief paragraphs of plain practical information about the river, and sign them "Mark Twain," and give them to the "New Orleans Picayune." They related to the stage and condition of the river, and were accurate and valuable; and thus far, they contained no poison. But in speaking of the stage of the river today, at a given point, the captain was pretty apt to drop in a little remark about this being the first time he had seen the water so high or so low at that particular point for forty-nine years; and now and then he would mention Island so and so, and follow it, in parentheses, with some such observation as "disappeared in 1807, if I remember rightly." In these antique interjections lay poison and bitterness for the other old pilots, and they used to chaff the "Mark Twain" paragraphs with unsparing mockery.

It so chanced that one of these paragraphs* became the text for my first newspaper article. I burlesqued it broadly, very broadly, stringing my fantastics out to the extent of eight hundred or a thousand words. I was a "cub" at the time. I showed my performance to some pilots, and they eagerly rushed it into print in the "New Orleans True Delta." It was a great pity; for it did nobody any worthy service, and it sent a pang deep into a good man's heart. There was no malice in my rubbish; but it laughed at the captain. It laughed at a man to whom such a thing was new and strange and dreadful. I did not know then, though I do now, that there is no suffering comparable with that which a private person feels when he is for the first time pilloried in print.

Captain Sellers did me the honor to profoundly detest me from that day forth. When I say he did me the honor, I am not using empty words. It was a very real honor to be in the thoughts of so great a man as Captain Sellers, and I had wit enough to appreciate it and be proud of it. It was distinction to be loved by such a man; but it was a much greater distinction to be hated by him, because he loved scores of people; but he didn't sit up nights to hate anybody but me.

He never printed another paragraph while he lived, and he never again signed "Mark Twain" to anything. At the time that the telegraph brought the news of his death, I was on the Pacific coast. I was a fresh new journalist, and needed a *nom de guerre;* so I confiscated the ancient mariner's discarded one, and have done my best to make it remain what it was in his hands—a sign and symbol and warrant that whatever is found in its company may be gambled on as being the petrified truth; how I have succeeded, it would not be modest in me to say.

---

* The original MS. of it, in the captain's own hand, has been sent to me from New Orleans. It reads as follows:—

"VICKSBURG, May 4, 1959.

"My opinion for the benefit of the citizens of New Orleans: The water is higher this far up than it has been since 1815. My opinion is that the water will be 4 feet deep in Canal street before the first of next June. Mrs. Turner's plantation at the head of Big Black Island is all under water, and it has not been since 1815.

"I. SELLERS."

The captain had an honorable pride in his profession and an abiding love for it. He ordered his monument before he died, and kept it near him until he did die. It stands over his grave now, in Bellefontaine cemetery, St. Louis. It is his image, in marble, standing on duty at the pilot wheel; and worthy to stand and confront criticism, for it represents a man who in life would have staid there till he burned to a cinder, if duty required it.

The finest thing we saw on our whole Mississippi trip, we saw as we approached New Orleans in the steam-tug. This was the curving frontage of the crescent city lit up with the white glare of five miles of electric lights. It was a wonderful sight, and very beautiful.

CHAPTER LI

REMINISCENCES

We left for St. Louis in the "City of Baton Rouge," on a delightfully hot day, but with the main purpose of my visit but lamely accomplished. I had hoped to hunt up and talk with a hundred steamboatmen, but got so pleasantly involved in the social life of the town that I got nothing more than mere five-minute talks with a couple of dozen of the craft.

I was on the bench of the pilot-house when we backed out and "straightened up" for the start—the boat pausing for a "good ready," in the old-fashioned way, and the black smoke piling out of the chimneys equally in the old-fashioned way. Then we began to gather momentum, and presently were fairly under way and booming along. It was all as natural and familiar—and so were the shoreward sights—as if there had been no break in my river life. There was a "cub," and I judged that he would take the wheel now; and he did. Captain Bixby stepped into the pilot-house. Presently the cub closed up on the rank of steamships. He made me nervous, for he allowed too much water to show between our boat and the ships. I knew quite well what was going to happen, because I could date back in my own life and inspect the record. The captain looked on, during a silent half-minute, then took the wheel himself, and crowded the boat in, till she went scraping along within a hand-breadth of the ships. It was exactly the favor which he had done me, about a quarter of a century before, in that same spot, the first time I ever steamed out of the port of New Orleans. It was a very great and sincere pleasure to me to see the thing repeated—with somebody else as victim.

We made Natchez (three hundred miles) in twenty-two hours and a half,—much the swiftest passage I have ever made over that piece of water.

The next morning I came on·with the four o'clock watch, and saw Ritchie successfully run half a dozen crossings in a fog, using for his guidance the marked chart devised and patented by Bixby and himself. This sufficiently evidenced the great value of the chart.

By and by, when the fog began to clear off, I noticed that the reflection of a tree in the smooth water of an overflowed bank, six hundred yards away, was stronger and blacker than the ghostly tree itself. The faint spectral trees, dimly glimpsed through the shredding fog, were very pretty things to see.

We had a heavy thunder-storm at Natchez, another at Vicksburg, and still another about fifty miles below Memphis. They had an old-fashioned energy which had long been unfamiliar to me. This third storm was accompanied by a raging wind. We tied up to the bank when we saw the tempest coming, and everybody left the pilot-house but me. The wind bent the young trees down, exposing the pale underside of the leaves; and gust after gust followed, in quick succession, thrashing the branches violently up and down, and to this side and that, and creating swift waves of alternating green and white according to the side of the leaf that was exposed, and these waves raced after each other as do their kind over a wind-tossed field of oats. No color that was visible anywhere was quite natural,—all tints were charged with a leaden tinge from the solid cloud-bank overhead. The river was leaden; all distances the same; and even the far-reaching ranks of combing white-caps were dully shaded by the dark, rich atmosphere through which their swarming legions marched. The thunder-peals were constant and deafening; explosion followed explosion with but inconsequential intervals between, and the reports grew steadily sharper and higher-keyed, and more trying to the ear; the lightning was as diligent as the thunder, and produced effects which enchanted the eye and sent electric ecstasies of mixed delight and apprehension shivering along every nerve in the body in unintermittent procession. The rain poured down in amazing volume; the ear-splitting thunder-peals broke nearer and nearer; the wind increased in fury and began to wrench off boughs and tree-tops and send them sailing away through space; the pilot-house fell to rocking and straining and cracking and surging, and I went down in the hold to see what time it was.

People boast a good deal about Alpine thunder-storms; but the storms which I have had the luck to see in the Alps were not the equals of some which I have seen in the Mississippi Valley. I may not have seen the Alps do their best, of course, and if they can beat the Mississippi, I don't wish to.

On this up trip I saw a little towhead (infant island) half a mile long, which had been formed during the past nineteen years. Since there was so much time to spare that nineteen years of it could be devoted to the construction of a mere towhead, where was the use, originally, in rushing this whole globe through in six days? It is likely that if more time had been taken, in the first place, the world would have been made right, and this ceaseless improving and repairing would not be necessary now. But if you hurry a world or a house, you are nearly sure to find out by and by, that you have left out a towhead, or a broom-closet, or some other little convenience, here and there, which has got to be supplied, no matter how much expense and vexation it may cost.

We had a succession of black nights, going up the river, and it was observable that whenever we landed, and suddenly inundated the trees with the intense sunburst of the electric light, a certain curious effect was always produced: hundreds of birds flocked instantly out from the masses of shining green foliage, and went careering hither and thither through the white rays, and often a song-bird tuned up and fell to singing. We judged that they mistook this superb artificial day for the genuine article.

We had a delightful trip in that thoroughly well-ordered steamer, and regretted that it was accomplished so speedily. By means of diligence and activity, we managed to hunt out nearly all the old friends. One was missing, however; he went to his reward, whatever it was, two years ago. But I found out all about him. His case helped me to realize how lasting can be the effect of a very trifling occurrence. When he was an apprentice-blacksmith in our village, and I a schoolboy, a couple of young Englishmen came to the town and sojourned a while; and one day they got themselves up in cheap royal finery and did the Richard III. sword-fight with maniac energy and prodigious powwow, in the presence of the village boys. This blacksmith cub was there, and the histrionic poison entered his bones. This vast, lumbering, ignorant, dull-witted lout was stage-struck, and irrecoverably. He disappeared, and presently turned up in St. Louis. I ran across him there, by and by. He was standing musing on a street corner, with his right hand on his hip, the thumb of his left supporting his chin, face bowed and frowning, slouch hat pulled down over his forehead—imagining himself to be Othello or some such character, and imagining that the passing crowd marked his tragic bearing and were awestruck.

I joined him, and tried to get him down out of the clouds, but did not succeed. However, he casually informed me, presently, that he was a member of the Walnut Street theatre company,— and he tried to say it with indifference, but the indifference was thin, and a mighty exultation showed through it. He said he was cast for a part in Julius Caesar, for that night, and if I should come I would see him. *If* I should come! I said I wouldn't miss it if I were dead.

I went away stupefied with astonishment, and saying to myself, "How strange it is! *we* always thought this fellow a fool; yet the moment he comes to a great city, where intelligence and appreciation abound, the talent concealed in this shabby napkin is at once discovered, and promptly welcomed and honored."

But I came away from the theatre that night disappointed and offended; for I had had no glimpse of my hero, and his name was not in the bills. I met him on the street the next morning, and before I could speak, he asked:—

"Did you see me?"

"No, you weren't there."

He looked surprised and disappointed. He said:—

"Yes, I was. Indeed I was. I was a Roman soldier."

"Which one?"

"Why, didn't you see them Roman soldiers that stood back there in a rank, and sometimes marched in procession around the stage?"

"Do you mean the Roman army?—those six sandalled roustabouts in nightshirts, with tin shields and helmets, that marched around treading on each other's heels, in charge of a spider-legged consumptive dressed like themselves?"

"That's it! that's it! I was one of them Roman soldiers. I was the next to the last one. A half a year ago I used to always be the last one; but I've been promoted."

Well, they told me that the poor fellow remained a Roman soldier to the last—a matter of thirty-four years. Sometimes they cast him for a "speaking part," but not an elaborate one. He could be trusted to go and say, "My lord, the carriage waits," but if they ventured to add a sentence or two to this, his memory felt the strain and he was likely to miss fire. Yet, poor devil, he had been patiently studying the part of Hamlet for more than thirty years, and he lived and died in the belief that some day he would be invited to play it!

And this is what came of that fleeting visit of those young Englishmen to our village such ages and ages ago! What noble horseshoes this man might have made, but for those Englishmen; and what an inadequate Roman soldier he *did* make!

A day or two after we reached St. Louis, I was walking along Fourth Street when a grizzly-headed man gave a sort of start as he passed me, then stopped, came back, inspected me narrowly, with a clouding brow, and finally said with deep asperity:—

"Look here, *have you got that drink yet?*"

A maniac, I judged, at first. But all in a flash I recognized him. I made an effort to blush that strained every muscle in me, and answered as sweetly and winningly as ever I knew how:—

"Been a little slow, but am just this minute closing in on the place where they keep it. Come in and help."

He softened, and said make it a bottle of champagne and he was agreeable. He said he had seen my name in the papers, and had put all his affairs aside and turned out, resolved to find me or die; and make me answer that question satisfactorily, or kill me; though the most of his late asperity had been rather counterfeit than otherwise.

This meeting brought back to me the St. Louis riots of about thirty years ago. I spent a week there, at that time, in a boarding-house, and had this young fellow for a neighbor across the hall. We saw some of the fightings and killings; and by and by we went one night to an armory where two hundred young men had met, upon call, to be armed and go forth against the rioters, under command of a military man. We drilled till about ten o'clock at night; then news came that the mob were in great force in the lower end of the town, and were sweeping everything before them. Our column moved at once. It was a very hot night, and my musket was very heavy. We marched and marched; and the nearer we approached the seat of war, the hotter I grew and the thirstier I got. I was behind my friend; so, finally, I asked him to hold my musket while I dropped out and got a drink. Then I branched off and went home. I was not feeling any solicitude about *him* of course, because I knew he was so well armed, now, that he could take care of himself without any trouble. If I had had any doubts about that, I would have borrowed another musket for him. I left the city pretty early the next morning, and if this grizzled man had not happened to encounter my name in the papers the other day in St. Louis, and felt moved to seek me out, I should have carried to my grave a heart-torturing uncertainty as to whether he ever got out of the riots all right or not. I ought to have inquired, thirty years ago; I know that. And I would have inquired, if I had had the muskets; but, in the circumstances, he seemed better fixed to conduct the investigations than I was.

One Monday, near the time of our visit to St. Louis, the "Globe-Democrat" came out with a couple of pages of Sunday statistics, whereby it appeared that 119,448 St. Louis people attended the morning and evening church services the day before, and 23,102 children attended Sunday-school. Thus 142,550 persons, out of the city's total of 400,000 population, respected the day religious-wise. I found these statistics, in a condensed form, in a telegram of the Associated Press, and preserved them. They made it apparent that St. Louis was in a higher state of grace than she could have claimed to be in my time. But now that I canvass the figures narrowly, I suspect that the telegraph mutilated them. It cannot be that there are more than 150,000 Catholics in the town; the other 250,000 must be classified as Protestants. Out of these 250,000, according to this questionable telegram, only 26,362 attended church and Sunday-school, while out of the 150,000 Catholics, 116,188 went to church and Sunday-school.

CHAPTER LII

A BURNING BRAND

All at once the thought came into my mind, "I have not sought out Mr. Brown."

Upon that text I desire to depart from the direct line of my subject, and make a little excursion. I wish to reveal a secret which I have carried with me nine years, and which has become burdensome.

Upon a certain occasion, nine years ago, I had said, with strong feeling, "If ever I see St. Louis again, I will seek out Mr. Brown, the great grain merchant, and ask of him the privilege of shaking him by the hand."

The occasion and the circumstances were as follows. A friend of mine, a clergyman, came one evening and said:—

"I have a most remarkable letter here, which I want to read to you, if I can do it without breaking down. I must preface it with some explanations, however. The letter is written by an ex-thief and ex-vagabond of the lowest origin and basest rearing, a man all stained with crime and steeped in ignorance; but, thank God, with a mine of pure gold hidden away in him, as you shall see. His letter is written to a burglar named Williams, who is serving a nine-year term in a certain State prison, for burglary. Williams was a particularly daring burglar, and plied that trade during a number of years; but he was caught at last and jailed, to await trial in a town where he had broken into a house at night, pistol in hand, and forced the owner to hand over to him $8,000 in government bonds. Williams was not a common sort of person, by any means; he was a graduate of Harvard College, and came of good New England stock. His father was a clergyman. While lying in jail, his health began to fail, and he was threatened with consumption. This fact, together with the opportunity for reflection afforded by solitary confinement, had its effect—its natural effect. He fell into serious thought: his early training asserted itself with power, and wrought with strong influence upon his mind and heart. He put his old life behind him, and became an earnest Christian. Some ladies in the town heard of this, visited him, and by their encouraging words supported him in his good resolutions and strengthened him to continue in his new life. The trial ended in his conviction and sentence to the State prison for the term of nine years, as I have before said. In the prison he became acquainted with the poor wretch referred to in the beginning of my talk, Jack Hunt, the writer of the letter which I am going to read. You will see that the acquaintanceship bore fruit for Hunt. When Hunt's time was out, he wandered to St. Louis; and from that place he wrote his letter to Williams. The letter got no further than the office of the prison warden, of course; prisoners are not often allowed to receive letters from outside. The prison authorities read this letter, but did not destroy it. They had not the heart to do it. They read it to several persons, and eventually it fell into the hands of those ladies of whom I spoke a while ago. The other day I came across an old friend of mine—a clergyman—who had seen this letter, and was full of it. The mere remembrance of it so moved him that he could not talk of it without his voice breaking. He promised to get a copy of it for me; and here it is,—an exact copy, with all the imperfections of the original preserved. It has many slang expressions in it—thieves' *argot*—but their meaning has been interlined, in parentheses, by the prison authorities:"—

St. Louis, June 9th, 1872.

Mr. W——friend Charlie if i may call you so: i no you are surprised to get a letter from me, but i hope you won't be mad at my writing to you. i want to tell you my thanks for the way you talked to me when i was in prison—it has led me to try and be a better man; i guess you thought i did not cair for what you said, & at the first go off I didn't, but i noed you was a man who had don big work with good men & want no sucker, nor want gasing & all the boys knod it.

I used to think at nite what you said, & for it i nocked off swearing 5 months before my time was up, for i saw it want no good, nohow—the day my time was up you told me if i would shake the cross, *(quit stealing)* & live on the square for 3 months, it would be the best job i ever done in my life. The state agent give me a ticket to here, & on the car i thought more of what you said to me, but didn't make up my mind. When we got to Chicago on the cars from there to here, I pulled off an old woman's leather; *(robbed her of her pocketbook)* i hadn't no more than got it off when i wished i hadn't done it, for awhile before that i made up my mind to be a square bloke, for 3 months on your word, but forgot it when i saw the leather was a grip *(easy to get)*—but i kept clos to her & when she got out of the cars at a way place i said, marm have you lost anything? & she tumbled *(discovered)* her leather was off *(gone)*—is this it says i, giving it to her—well if you aint honest, says she, but i hadnt got cheak enough to stand that sort of talk, so i left her in a hurry. When i got here i had $1 and 25 cents left & i didn't get no work for 3 days as i aint strong enough for roust about on a steam bote *(for a deck hand)*—The afternoon of the 3rd day I spent my last 10 cts for 2 moons *(large, round sea-biscuit)* & cheese & i felt pretty rough & was thinking i would have to go on the dipe *(picking pockets)* again, when i thought of what you once said about a fellows calling on the Lord when he was in hard luck, & i thought i would try it once anyhow, but when i tryed it i got stuck on the start & all i could get off wos, Lord give a poor fellow a chance to square it for 3 months for Christ's sake, amen; & i kept a thinking, of it over and over as i went along—about an hour after that i was in 4th St. & this is what happened & is the cause of my being where i am now & about which i will tell you before i get done writing. As i was walking along i herd a big noise & saw a horse running away with a carriage with 2 children in it, & I grabed up a peace of box cover from the side walk & run in the middle of the street, & when the horse came up i smashed him over the head as hard as i could drive— the bord split to peces & the horse checked up a little & i grabbed the reigns & pulled his head down until he stopped—the gentleman what owned him came running up & soon as he saw the children were all rite, he shook hands with me & gave me a $50 green back, & my asking the Lord to help me come into my head, & i was so thunderstruck i couldn't drop the reigns nor say nothing—he saw something was up, & coming back to me said, my boy are you hurt? & the thought come into my head just then to ask him for work; & i asked him to take back the bill and give me a job—says he, jump in here & lets talk about it, but keep the money—he asked me if i could take care of horses & i said yes, for i used to hang round livery stables & often would help clean & drive horses, he told me he wanted a man for that work, & would give me $16. a month & bord me. You bet i took that chance at once. that nite in my little room over the stable i sat a long time thinking over my past life & of what had just happened & i just got down on my nees & thanked the Lord for the job & to help me to square it, & to bless you for putting me up to it, & the next morning i done it again & got me some new togs *(clothes)* & a bible for i *made up my mind* after what the Lord had done for me i would read the bible every nite and morning, & ask him to keep an eye on me. When I had been there about a week Mr. Brown (that's his name) came in my room one nite & saw me reading the bible—he asked me if i was a Christian & i told him no—he asked me how it was i read the bible instead of papers & books—Well Charlie i thought i had

better give him a square deal in the start, so i told him all about my
being in prison & about you, & how i had almost done give up looking
for work & how the Lord got me the job when i asked him; & the only
way i had to pay him back was to read the bible & square it, & i asked
him to give me a chance for 3 months—he talked to me like a father for
a long time, & told me i could stay & then i felt better than ever i had
done in my life, for i had given Mr. Brown a fair start with me & now i
didn't fear no one giving me a back cap *(exposing his past life)* & running me off the job—the next morning he called me into the library &
gave me another square talk, & advised me to study some every day, &
he would help me one or 2 hours every nite, & he gave me a Arithmetic,
a spelling book, a Geography & a writing book, & he hers me every
nite—he lets me come into the house to prayers every morning, & got
me put in a bible class in the Sunday School which i likes very much for
it helps me to understand my bible better.

Now, Charlie the 3 months on the square are up 2 months ago, & as
you said, it is the best job i ever did in my life, & i commenced another
of the same sort right away, only it is to God helping me to last a
lifetime Charlie—i wrote this letter to tell you I do think God has
forgiven my sins & herd your prayers, for you told me you should pray
for me—i no i love to read his word & tell him all my troubles & he
helps me i know for i have plenty of chances to steal but i don't feel to
as i once did & now i take more pleasure in going to church than to the
theatre & that wasnt so once—our minister and others often talk with
me & a month ago they wanted me to join the church, but I said no, not
now, i may be mistaken in my feelings, i will wait awhile, but now i feel
that God has called me & on the first Sunday in July i will join the
church—dear friend i wish i could write to you as i feel, but i cant do it
yet—you no i learned to read and write while in prisons & i aint got well
enough along to write as i would talk; i no i aint spelled all the words
rite in this & lots of other mistakes but you will excuse it i no, for you
no i was brought up in a poor house until i run away, & that i never new
who my father and mother was & i dont no my rite name, & i hope you
wont be mad at me, but i have as much rite to one name as another & i
have taken your name, for you wont use it when you get out i no, & you
are the man i think most of in the world; so i hope you wont be mad—I
am doing well, i put $10 a month in bank with $25 of the $50—if you
ever want any or all of it let me know, & it is yours. i wish you would let
me send you some now. I send you with this a receipt for a year of Lit-
tles Living Age, i didn't know what you would like & i told Mr. Brown
& he said he thought you would like it—i wish i was nere you so i could
send you chuck *(refreshments)* on holidays; it would spoil this weather
from here, but i will send you a box next thanksgiving any way—next
week Mr. Brown takes me into his store as lite porter & will advance me
as soon as i know a little more—he keeps a big granary store,
wholesale—i forgot to tell you of my mission school, sunday school
class—the school is in the sunday afternoon, i went out two sunday
afternoons, and picked up seven kids *(little boys)* & got them to come
in. two of them new as much as i did & i had them put in a class where

they could learn something. i dont no much myself, but as these kids cant read i get on nicely with them. i make sure of them by going after them every Sunday ½ hour before school time, i also got 4 girls to come. tell Mack and Harry about me, if they will come out here when their time is up i will get them jobs at once. i hope you will excuse this long letter & all mistakes, i wish i could see you for i cant write as i would talk—i hope the warm weather is doing your lungs good—i was afraid when you was bleeding you would die—give my respects to all the boys and tell them how i am doing—i am doing well and every one here treats me as kind as they can—Mr Brown is going to write to you sometime—i hope some day you will write to me, this letter is from your very true friend

C—— W——
who you know as Jack Hunt.

I send you Mr Brown's card. Send my letter to him.

Here was true eloquence; irresistible eloquence; and without a single grace or ornament to help it out. I have seldom been so deeply stirred by any piece of writing. The reader of it halted, all the way through, on a lame and broken voice; yet he had tried to fortify his feelings by several private readings of the letter before venturing into company with it. He was practising upon me to see if there was any hope of his being able to read the document to his prayer-meeting with anything like a decent command over his feelings. The result was not promising. However, he determined to risk it; and did. He got through tolerably well; but his audience broke down early, and stayed in that condition to the end.

The fame of the letter spread through the town. A brother minister came and borrowed the manuscript, put it bodily into a sermon, preached the sermon to twelve hundred people on a Sunday morning, and the letter drowned them in their own tears. Then my friend put it into a sermon and went before his Sunday morning congregation with it. It scored another triumph. The house wept as one individual.

My friend went on summer vacation up into the fishing regions of our northern British neighbors, and carried this sermon with him, since he might possibly chance to need a sermon. He was asked to preach, one day. The little church was full. Among the people present were the late Dr. J. G. Holland, the late Mr. Seymour of the "New York Times," Mr. Page, the philanthropist and temperance advocate, and, I think, Senator Frye, of Maine. The marvellous letter did its wonted work; all the people were moved, all the people wept; the tears flowed in a steady stream down Dr. Holland's cheeks, and nearly the same can be said with regard to all who were there. Mr. Page was so full of enthusiasm over the letter that he said he would not rest until he made pilgrimage to that prison, and had speech with the man who had been able to inspire a fellow-unfortunate to write so priceless a tract.

Ah, that unlucky Page!—and another man. If they had only been in Jericho, that letter would have rung through the world and stirred all the hearts of all the nations for a thousand years to come, and nobody might ever have found out that it was the confoundedest, brazenest, ingeniousest piece of fraud and humbuggery that was ever concocted to fool poor confiding mortals with!

The letter was a pure swindle, and that is the truth. And take it by and large, it was without a compeer among swindles. It was perfect, it was rounded, symmetrical, complete, colossal!

The reader learns it at this point; but we didn't learn it till some miles and weeks beyond this stage of the affair. My friend came back from the woods, and he and other clergymen and lay missionaries began once more to inundate audiences with their tears and the tears of said audiences; I begged hard for permission to print the letter in a magazine and tell the watery story of its triumphs; numbers of people got copies of the letter, with permission to circulate them in writing, but not in print; copies were sent to the Sandwich Islands and other far regions.

Charles Dudley Warner was at church, one day, when the worn letter was read and wept over. At the church door, afterward, he dropped a peculiarly cold iceberg down the clergyman's back with the question,—

"Do you know that letter to be genuine?"

It was the first suspicion that had ever been voiced; but it had that sickening effect which first-uttered suspicions against one's idol always have. Some talk followed:—

"Why—what should make you suspect that it isn't genuine?"

"Nothing that I know of, except that it is too neat, and compact, and fluent, and nicely put together for an ignorant person, an unpractised hand. I think it was done by an educated man."

The literary artist had detected the literary machinery. If you will look at the letter now, you will detect it yourself—it is observable in every line.

Straightway the clergyman went off, with this seed of suspicion sprouting in him, and wrote to a minister residing in that town where Williams had been jailed and converted; asked for light; and also asked if a person in the literary line (meaning me) might be allowed to print the letter and tell its history. He presently received this answer:—

Rev.——.

My Dear Friend,—In regard to that "convict's letter" there can be
no doubt as to its genuineness. "Williams," to whom it was written, lay
in our jail and professed to have been converted, and Rev. Mr. ——,
the chaplain, had great faith in the genuineness of the change—as much
as one can have in any such case.

The letter was sent to one of our ladies, who is a Sunday-school
teacher,—sent either by Williams himself, or the chaplain of the State's
prison, probably. She has been greatly annoyed in having so much
publicity, lest it might seem a breach of confidence, or be an injury to
Williams. In regard to its publication, I can give no permission; though
if the names and places were omitted, and especially if sent out of the
country, I think you might take the responsibility and do it.

It is a wonderful letter, which no Christian genius, much less one un-
sanctified, could ever have written. As showing the work of grace in a
human heart, and in a very degraded and wicked one, it proves its own
origin and reproves our weak faith in its power to cope with any form
of wickedness.

"Mr. Brown" of St. Louis, some one said, was a Hartford man. Do
all whom you send from Hartford serve their Master as well?

P.S. Williams is still in the State's prison, serving out a long
sentence—of nine years, I think. He has been sick and threatened with
consumption, but I have not inquired after him lately. This lady that I
speak of corresponds with him, I presume, and will be quite sure to
look after him.

This letter arrived a few days after it was written—and up went
Mr. Williams's stock again. Mr. Warner's low-down suspicion
was laid in the cold, cold grave, where it apparently belonged. It
was a suspicion based upon mere internal evidence, anyway; and
when you come to internal evidence, it's a big field and a game
that two can play at: as witness this other internal evidence, discovered by the writer of the note above quoted, that "it is a
wonderful letter—which no Christian genius, much less one un-
sanctified, could ever have written."

I had permission now to print—provided I suppressed names
and places and sent my narrative out of the country. So I chose
an Australian magazine for vehicle, as being far enough out of
the country, and set myself to work on my article. And the
ministers set the pumps going again, with the letter to work the
handles.

But meantime Brother Page had been agitating. He had not
visited the penitentiary, but he had sent a copy of the illustrious
letter to the chaplain of that institution, and accompanied it
with—apparently—inquiries. He got an answer, dated four days
later than that other Brother's reassuring epistle; and before my

article was complete, it wandered into my hands. The original is before me, now, and I here append it. It is pretty well loaded with internal evidence of the most solid description:—

July 11, 1873.

DEAR BRO. Page,—Herewith please fine the letter kindly leased me. I am afraid its genuineness cannot be established. It purports to be addressed to some prisoner here. No such letter ever came to a prisoner here. All letters received are carefully read by officers of the prison before they go into the hands of the convicts, and any such letter could not be forgotten. Again, Charles Williams is not a Christian man, but a dissolute, cunning prodigal, whose father is a minister of the gospel. His name is an assumed one. I am glad to have made your acquaintance. I am preparing a lecture upon life seen through prison bars, and should like to deliver the same in your vicinity.

And so ended that little drama. My poor article went into the fire; for whereas the materials for it were now more abundant and infinitely richer than they had previously been, there were parties all around me, who, although longing for the publication before, were a unit for suppression at this stage and complexion of the game. They said,—"Wait—the wound is too fresh, yet." All the copies of the famous letter except mine, disappeared suddenly; and from that time onward, the aforetime same old drought set in in the churches. As a rule, the town was on a spacious grin for a while, but there were places in it where the grin did not appear, and where it was dangerous to refer to the ex-convict's letter.

A word of explanation. "Jack Hunt," the professed writer of the letter, was an imaginary person. The burglar Williams—Harvard graduate, son of a minister—wrote the letter himself, *to* himself: got it smuggled out of the prison; got it conveyed to persons who had supported and encouraged him in his conversion—where he knew two things would happen: the genuineness of the letter would not be doubted or inquired into; and the nub of it would be noticed, and would have valuable effect—the effect, indeed, of starting a movement to get Mr. Williams pardoned out of prison.

That "nub" is so ingeniously, so casually, flung in, and immediately left there in the tail of the letter, undwelt upon, that an indifferent reader would never suspect that it was the heart and core of the epistle, if he even took note of it at all. This is the "nub":—

i hope the warm weather is doing your lungs good—*i was afraid when you was bleeding you would die*—give my respects," etc.

That is all there is of it—simply touch and go—no dwelling upon it. Nevertheless it was intended for an eye that would be swift to see it; and it was meant to move a kind heart to try to effect the liberation of a poor reformed and purified fellow lying in the fell grip of consumption.

When I for the first time heard that letter read, nine years ago, I felt that it was the most remarkable one I had ever encountered. And it so warmed me toward Mr. Brown of St. Louis that I said that if ever I visited that city again, I would seek out that excellent man and kiss the hem of his garment if it was a new one. Well, I visited St. Louis, but I did not hunt for Mr. Brown; for, alas! the investigations of long ago had proved that the benevolent Brown, like "Jack Hunt," was not a real person, but a sheer invention of that gifted rascal, Williams—burglar, Harvard graduate, son of a clergyman.

CHAPTER LIII

MY BOYHOOD HOME

We took passage in one of the fast boats of the St. Louis and St. Paul Packet Company, and started up the river.

When I, as a boy, first saw the mouth of the Missouri River, it was twenty-two or twenty-three miles above St. Louis, according to the estimate of pilots; the wear and tear of the banks has moved it down eight miles since then; and the pilots say that within five years the river will cut through and move the mouth down five miles more, which will bring it within ten miles of St. Louis.

About nightfall we passed the large and flourishing town of Alton, Illinois; and before daylight next morning the town of Louisiana, Missouri, a sleepy village in my day, but a brisk railway centre now; however, all the towns out there are railway centres now. I could not clearly recognize the place. This seemed odd to me, for when I retired from the rebel army in '61 I retired upon Louisiana in good order; at least in good enough order for a person who had not yet learned how to retreat according to the rules of war, and had to trust to native genius. It seemed to me that for a first attempt at a retreat it was not badly done. I had done no advancing in all that campaign that was at all equal to it.

There was a railway bridge across the river here well sprinkled with glowing lights, and a very beautiful sight it was.

At seven in the morning we reached Hannibal, Missouri, where my boyhood was spent. I had had a glimpse of it fifteen years ago, and another glimpse six years earlier, but both were so brief that they hardly counted. The only notion of the town that remained in my mind was the memory of it as I had known it when I first quitted it twenty-nine years ago. That picture of it was still as clear and vivid to me as a photograph. I stepped ashore with the feeling of one who returns out of a dead-and-gone generation. I had a sort of realizing sense of what the Bastille prisoners must have felt when they used to come out and look upon Paris after years of captivity, and note how curiously the familiar and the strange were mixed together before them. I saw the new houses—saw them plainly enough—but they did not affect the older picture in my mind, for through their solid bricks and mortar I saw the vanished houses, which had formerly stood there, with perfect distinctness.

It was Sunday morning, and everybody was abed yet. So I passed through the vacant streets, still seeing the town as it was, and not as it is, and recognizing and metaphorically shaking hands with a hundred familiar objects which no longer exist; and finally climbed Holiday's Hill to get a comprehensive view. The whole town lay spread out below me then, and I could mark and fix every locality, every detail. Naturally, I was a good deal moved. I said, "Many of the people I once knew in this tranquil refuge of my childhood are now in heaven; some, I trust, are in the other place."

The things about me and before me made me feel like a boy again—convinced me that I was a boy again, and that I had simply been dreaming an unusually long dream; but my reflections spoiled all that; for they forced me to say, "I see fifty old houses down yonder, into each of which I could enter and find either a man or a woman who was a baby or unborn when I noticed those houses last, or a grandmother who was a plump young bride at that time."

From this vantage ground the extensive view up and down the river, and wide over the wooded expanses of Illinois, is very beautiful,—one of the most beautiful on the Mississippi, I think, which is a hazardous remark to make, for the eight hundred miles of river between St. Louis and St. Paul afford an unbroken succession of lovely pictures. It may be that my affection for the one in question biases my judgment in its favor; I cannot say as to that. No matter, it was satisfyingly beautiful to me, and it had this advantage over all the other friends whom I was about to greet again: it had suffered no change; it was as young and fresh and comely and gracious as ever it had been; whereas, the faces of the others would be old, and scarred with the campaigns of life, and marked with their griefs and defeats, and would give me no upliftings of spirit.

An old gentleman, out on an early morning walk, came along, and we discussed the weather, and then drifted into other matters. I could not remember his face. He said he had been living here twenty-eight years. So he had come after my time, and I had never seen him before. I asked him various questions; first about a mate of mine in Sunday school—what became of him?

"He graduated with honor in an Eastern college, wandered off into the world somewhere, succeeded at nothing, passed out of knowledge and memory years ago, and is supposed to have gone to the dogs."

"He was bright, and promised well when he was a boy."

"Yes, but the thing that happened is what became of it all."

I asked after another lad, altogether the brightest in our village school when I was a boy.

"He, too, was graduated with honors, from an Eastern college; but life whipped him in every battle, straight along, and died in one of the Territories, years ago, a defeated man."

I asked after another of the bright boys.

"He is a success, always has been, always will be, I think."

I inquired after a young fellow who came to the town to study for one of the professions when I was a boy.

"He went at something else before he got through—went from medicine to law, or from law to medicine—then to some other new thing; went away for a year, came back with a young wife; fell to drinking, then to gambling behind the door; finally took his wife and two young children to her father's, and went off to Mexico; went from bad to worse, and finally died there, without a cent to buy a shroud, and without a friend to attend the funeral."

"Pity, for he was the best-natured, and most cheery and hopeful young fellow that ever was."

I named another boy.

"Oh, he is all right. Lives here yet; has a wife and children, and is prospering."

Same verdict concerning other boys.

I named three school-girls.

"The first two live here, are married and have children; the other is long ago dead—never married."

I named, with emotion, one of my early sweethearts.

"She is all right. Been married three times; buried two husbands, divorced from the third, and I hear she is getting ready to marry an old fellow out in Colorado somewhere. She's got children scattered around here and there, most everywheres."

The answer to several other inquiries was brief and simple,—

"Killed in the war."

I named another boy.

"Well, now, his case *is* curious! There wasn't a human being in this town but knew that that boy was a perfect chucklehead; perfect dummy; just a stupid ass, as you may say. Everybody knew it, and everybody said it. Well, if that very boy isn't the first lawyer in the State of Missouri to-day, I'm a Democrat!"

"Is that so?"

"It's actually so. I'm telling you the truth."

"How do you account for it?"

"Account for it? There ain't any accounting for it, except that if you send a damned fool to St. Louis, and you don't tell them he's a damned fool *they'll* never find it out. There's one thing sure—if I had a damned fool I should know what to do with him: ship him to St. Louis—it's the noblest market in the world for that kind of property. Well, when you come to look at it all around, and chew at it and think it over, *don't* it just bang anything you ever heard of?"

"Well, yes, it does seem to. But don't you think maybe it was the Hannibal people who were mistaken about the boy, and not the St. Louis people?"

"Oh, nonsense! The people here have known him from the very cradle—they knew him a hundred times better than the St. Louis idiots *could* have known him. No, if you have got any damned fools that you want to realize on, take my advice—send them to St. Louis."

I mentioned a great number of people whom I had formerly known. Some were dead, some were gone away, some had prospered, some had come to naught; but as regarded a dozen or so of the lot, the answer was comforting:

"Prosperous—live here yet—town littered with their children."

I asked about Miss ——.

"Died in the insane asylum three or four years ago—never was out of it from the time she went in; and was always suffering, too; never got a shred of her mind back."

If he spoke the truth, here was a heavy tragedy, indeed. Thirty-six years in a madhouse, that some young fools might have some fun! I was a small boy, at the time; and I saw those giddy young ladies come tiptoeing into the room where Miss —— sat reading at midnight by a lamp. The girl at the head of the file wore a shroud and a doughface; she crept behind the victim, touched her on the shoulder, and she looked up and screamed, and then fell into convulsions. She did not recover from the fright, but went mad. In these days it seems incredible that people believed in ghosts so short a time ago. But they did.

After asking after such other folk as I could call to mind, I finally inquired about *myself:*

"Oh, he succeeded well enough—another case of damned fool. If they'd sent him to St. Louis, he'd have succeeded sooner."

It was with much satisfaction that I recognized the wisdom of having told this candid gentleman, in the beginning, that my name was Smith.

CHAPTER LIV

PAST AND PRESENT

Being left to myself, up there, I went on picking out old houses on the distant town, and calling back their former inmates out of the mouldy past. Among them I presently recognized the house of the father of Lem Hackett (fictitious name). It carried me back more than a generation in a moment, and landed me in the midst of a time when the happenings of life were not the natural and logical results of great general laws, but of special orders, and were freighted with very precise and distinct purposes—partly punitive in intent, partly admonitory; and usually local in application.

When I was a small boy, Lem Hackett was drowned—on a Sunday. He fell out of an empty flat-boat, where he was playing. Being loaded with sin, he went to the bottom like an anvil. He was the only boy in the village who slept that night. We others all lay awake, repenting. We had not needed the information, delivered from the pulpit that evening, that Lem's was a case of special judgment—we knew that, already. There was a ferocious thunder-storm, that night, and it raged continuously until near dawn. The winds blew, the windows rattled, the rain swept along the roof in pelting sheets, and at the briefest of intervals the inky blackness of the night vanished, the houses over the way glared out white and blinding for a quivering instant, then the solid darkness shut down again and a splitting peal of thunder followed which seemed to rend everything in the neighborhood to shreds and splinters. I sat up in bed quaking and shuddering, waiting for the destruction of the world, and expecting it. To me there was nothing strange or incongruous in heaven's making such an uproar about Lem Hackett. Apparently it was the right and proper thing to do. Not a doubt entered my mind that all the angels were grouped together, discussing this boy's case and

455

observing the awful bombardment of our beggarly little village with satisfaction and approval. There was one thing which disturbed me in the most serious way; that was the thought that this centering of the celestial interest on our village could not fail to attract the attention of the observers to people among us who might otherwise have escaped notice for years. I felt that I was not only one of those people, but the very one most likely to be discovered. That discovery could have but one result: I should be in the fire with Lem before the chill of the river had been fairly warmed out of him. I knew that this would be only just and fair. I was increasing the chances against myself all the time, by feeling a secret bitterness against Lem for having attracted this fatal attention to me, but I could not help it—this sinful thought persisted in infesting my breast in spite of me. Every time the lightning glared I caught my breath, and judged I was gone. In my terror and misery, I meanly began to suggest other boys, and mention acts of theirs which were wickeder than mine, and peculiarly needed punishment—and I tried to pretend to myself that I was simply doing this in a casual way, and without intent to divert the heavenly attention to them for the purpose of getting rid of it myself. With deep sagacity I put these mentions into the form of sorrowing recollections and left-handed sham-supplications that the sins of those boys might be allowed to pass unnoticed—"Possibly they may repent." "It is true that Jim Smith broke a window and lied about it—but maybe he did not mean any harm. And although Tom Holmes says more bad words than any other boy in the village, he probably intends to repent—though he has never said he would. And whilst it is a fact that John Jones did fish a little on Sunday, once, he didn't really catch anything but only just one small useless mud-cat; and maybe that wouldn't have been so awful if he had thrown it back—as he says he did, but he didn't. Pity but they would repent of these dreadful things—and maybe they will yet."

But while I was shamefully trying to draw attention to these poor chaps—who were doubtless directing the celestial attention to me at the same moment, though I never once suspected that—I had heedlessly left my candle burning. It was not a time to neglect even trifling precautions. There was no occasion to add anything to the facilities for attracting notice to me—so I put the light out.

It was a long night to me, and perhaps the most distressful one I ever spent. I endured agonies of remorse for sins which I knew I had committed, and for others which I was not certain about, yet was sure that they had been set down against me in a book by an angel who was wiser than I and did not trust such important matters to memory. It struck me, by and by, that I had been making a most foolish and calamitous mistake, in one respect: doubtless I had not only made my own destruction sure by directing attention to those other boys, but had already accomplished theirs!—Doubtless the lightning had stretched them all dead in their beds by this time! The anguish and the fright which this thought gave me made my previous sufferings seem trifling by comparison.

Things had become truly serious. I resolved to turn over a new leaf instantly; I also resolved to connect myself with the church the next day, if I survived to see its sun appear. I resolved to cease from sin in all its forms, and to lead a high and blameless life forever after. I would be punctual at church and Sunday-school; visit the sick; carry baskets of victuals to the poor (simply to fulfil the regulation conditions, although I knew we had none among us so poor but they would smash the basket over my head for my pains); I would instruct other boys in right ways, and take the resulting trouncings meekly; I would subsist entirely on tracts; I would invade the rum shop and warn the drunkard—and finally, if I escaped the fate of those who early become too good to live, I would go for a missionary.

The storm subsided toward daybreak, and I dozed gradually to sleep with a sense of obligation to Lem Hackett for going to eternal suffering in that abrupt way, and thus preventing a far more freadful disaster—my own loss.

But when I rose refreshed, by and by, and found that those other boys were still alive, I had a dim sense that perhaps the whole thing was a false alarm; that the entire turmoil had been on Lem's account and nobody's else. The world looked so bright and safe that there did not seem to be any real occasion to turn over a new leaf. I was a little subdued, during that day, and perhaps the next; after that, my purpose of reforming slowly dropped out of my mind, and I had a peaceful, comfortable time again, until the next storm.

That storm came about three weeks later; and it was the most unaccountable one, to me, that I had ever experienced; for on the afternoon of the day, "Dutchy" was drowned. Dutchy belonged to our Sunday-school. He was a German lad who did not know enough to come in out of the rain; but he was exasperatingly good, and had a prodigious memory. One Sunday he made himself the envy of all the youth and the talk of all the admiring village, by reciting three thousand verses of Scripture without missing a word; then he went off the very next day and got drowned.

Circumstances gave to his death a peculiar impressiveness. We were all bathing in a muddy creek which had a deep hole in it, and in this hole the coopers had sunk a pile of green hickory hoop poles to soak, some twelve feet under water. We were diving and "seeing who could stay under longest." We managed to remain down by holding on to the hoop poles. Dutchy made such a poor success of it that he was hailed with laughter and derision every time his head appeared above water. At last he seemed hurt with the taunts, and begged us to stand still on the bank and be fair with him and give him an honest count—"be friendly and kind just this once, and not miscount for the sake of having the fun of laughing at him." Treacherous winks were exchanged, and all said "All right, Dutchy—go ahead, we'll play fair."

Dutchy plunged in, but the boys, instead of beginning to count, followed the lead of one of their number and scampered to a range of blackberry bushes close by and hid behind it. They imagined Dutchy's humiliation, when he should rise after a superhuman effort and find the place silent and vacant, nobody there to applaud. They were "so full of laugh" with the idea, that they were continually exploding into muffled cackles. Time swept on, and presently one who was peeping through the briers, said, with surprise:—

"Why, he hasn't come up, yet!"

The laughing stopped.

"Boys, it's a splended dive," said one.

"Never mind that," said another, "the joke on him is all the better for it."

There was a remark or two more, and then a pause. Talking ceased, and all began to peer through the vines. Before long, the boys' faces began to look uneasy, then anxious, then terrified. Still there was no movement of the placid water. Hearts began to beat fast, and faces to turn pale. We all glided out, silently, and stood on the bank, our horrified eyes wandering back and forth from each other's countenances to the water.

"Somebody must go down and see!"

Yes, that was plain; but nobody wanted that grisly task.

"Draw straws!"

So we did—with hands which shook so, that we hardly knew what we were about. The lot fell to me, and I went down. The water was so muddy I could not see anything, but I felt around among the hoop poles, and presently grasped a limp wrist which gave me no response—and if it had I should not have known it, I let it go with such a frightened suddenness.

The boy had been caught among the hoop poles and entangled there, helplessly. I fled to the surface and told the awful news.

Some of us knew that if the boy were dragged out at once he might possibly be resuscitated, but we never thought of that. We did not think of anything; we did not know what to do, so we did nothing—except that the smaller lads cried, piteously, and we all struggled frantically into our clothes, putting on anybody's that came handy, and getting them wrong-side-out and upside-down, as a rule. Then we scurried away and gave the alarm, but none of us went back to see the end of the tragedy. We had a more important thing to attend to: we all flew home, and lost not a moment on getting ready to lead a better life.

The night presently closed down. Then came on that tremendous and utterly unaccountable storm. I was perfectly dazed; I could not understand it. It seemed to me that there must be some mistake. The elements were turned loose, and they rattled and banged and blazed away in the most blind and frantic manner. All heart and hope went out of me, and the dismal thought kept floating through my brain, "If a boy who knows three thousand verses by heart is not satisfactory, what chance is there for anybody else?"

Of course I never questioned for a moment that the storm was on Dutchy's account, or that he or any other inconsequential animal was worthy of such a majestic demonstration from on high; the lesson of it was the only thing that troubled me; for it convinced me that if Dutchy, with all his perfections, was not a delight, it would be vain for me to turn over a new leaf, for I must infallibly fall hopelessly short of that boy, no matter how hard I might try. Nevertheless I did turn it over—a highly educated fear compelled me to do that—but succeeding days of cheerfulness and sunshine came bothering around, and within a month I had so drifted backward that again I was as lost and comfortable as ever.

Breakfast time approached while I mused these musings and called these ancient happenings back to mind; so I got me back into the present and went down the hill.

On my way through town to the hotel, I saw the house which was my home when I was a boy. At present rates, the people who now occupy it are of no more value than I am; but in my time they would have been worth not less than five hundred dollars apiece. They are colored folk.

After breakfast, I went out alone again, intending to hunt up some of the Sunday-schools and see how this generation of pupils might compare with their progenitors who had sat with me in those places and had probably taken me as a model— though I do not remember as to that now. By the public square there had been in my day a shabby little brick church called the

"Old Ship of Zion," which I had attended as a Sunday-school scholar; and I found the locality easily enough, but not the old church; it was gone, and a trig and rather hilarious new edifice was in its place. The pupils were better dressed and better looking than were those of my time; consequently they did not resemble their ancestors; and consequently there was nothing familiar to me in their faces. Still, I contemplated them with a deep interest and a yearning wistfulness, and if I had been a girl I would have cried; for they were offspring, and represented, and occupied the places, of boys and girls some of whom I had loved to love, and some of whom I had loved to hate, but all of whom were dear to me for the one reason or the other, so many years gone by—and, Lord, where be they now!

I was mightily stirred, and would have been grateful to be allowed to remain unmolested and look my fill; but a bald-summited superintendent who had been a tow-headed Sunday-school mate of mine on that spot in the early ages, recognized me, and I talked a flutter of wild nonsense to those children to hide the thoughts which were in me, and which could not have been spoken without a betrayal of feeling that would have been recognized as out of character with me.

Making speeches without preparation is no gift of mine; and I was resolved to shirk any new opportunity, but in the next and larger Sunday-school I found myself in the rear of the assemblage; so I was very willing to go on the platform a moment for the sake of getting a good look at the scholars. On the spur of the moment I could not recall any of the old idiotic talks which visitors used to insult me with when I was a pupil there; and I was sorry for this, since it would have given me time and excuse to dawdle there and take a long and satisfying look at what I feel at liberty to say was an array of fresh young comeliness not matchable in another Sunday-school of the same size. As I talked merely to get a chance to inspect; and as I strung out the random rubbish solely to prolong the inspection, I judged it but decent to confess these low motives, and I did so.

If the Model Boy was in either of these Sunday-schools, I did not see him. The Model Boy of my time—we never had but the one—was perfect: perfect in manners, perfect in dress, perfect in conduct, perfect in filial piety, perfect in exterior godliness; but at bottom he was a prig; and as for the contents of his skull, they could have changed place with the contents of a pie and nobody would have been the worse off for it but the pie. This fellow's reproachlessness was a standing reproach to every lad in the village. He was the admiration of all the mothers, and the detestation of all their sons. I was told what became of him, but as it was a disappointment to me, I will not enter into details. He succeeded in life.

CHAPTER LV

A VENDETTA AND OTHER THINGS

During my three days' stay in the town, I woke up every morning with the impression that I was a boy—for in my dreams the faces were all young again, and looked as they had looked in the old times—but I went to bed a hundred years old, every night—for meantime I had been seeing those faces as they are now.

Of course I suffered some surprises, along at first, before I had become adjusted to the changed state of things. I met young ladies who did not seem to have changed at all; but they turned out to be the daughters of the young ladies I had in mind—sometimes their grand-daughters. When you are told that a stranger of fifty is a grandmother, there is nothing surprising about it; but if, on the contrary, she is a person whom you knew as a little girl, it seems impossible. You to say yourself, "How can a little girl be a grandmother?" It takes some little time to accept and realize the fact that while you have been growing old, your friends have not been standing still, in that matter.

I noticed that the greatest changes observable were with the women, not the men. I saw men whom thirty years had changed but slightly; but their wives had grown old. These were good women; it is very wearing to be good.

There was a saddler whom I wished to see; but he was gone. Dead, these many years, they said. Once or twice a day, the saddler used to go tearing down the street, putting on his coat as he went; and then everybody knew a steamboat was coming. Everybody knew, also, that John Stavely was not expecting anybody by the boat—or any freight, either; and Stavely must have known that everybody knew this, still it made no difference to him; he liked to seem to himself to be expecting a hundred thousand tons of saddles by this boat, and so he went on all his life, enjoying being faithfully on hand to receive and receipt for those saddles, in case by any miracle they should come. A malicious Quincy paper used always to refer to this town, in derision as "Stavely's Landing." Stavely was one of my earliest admirations; I envied him his rush of imaginary business, and the display he was able to make of it, before strangers, as he went flying down the street struggling with his fluttering coat.

But there was a carpenter who was my chiefest hero. He was a mighty liar, but I did not know that; I believed everything he said. He was a romantic, sentimental, melodramatic fraud, and his bearing impressed me with awe. I vividly remember the first time he took me into his confidence. He was planing a board, and every now and then he would pause and heave a deep sigh; and occasionally mutter broken sentences—confused and not intelligible—but out of their midst an ejaculation sometimes escaped which made me shiver and did me good: one was, "O God, it is his blood!" I sat on the tool-chest and humbly and shudderingly admired him; for I judged he was full of crime. At last he said in a low voice:—

"My little friend, can you keep a secret?"

I eagerly said I could.

"A dark and dreadful one?"

I satisfied him on that point.

"Then I will tell you some passages in my history; for oh, I *must* relieve my burdened soul, or I shall die!"

He cautioned me once more to be "as silent as the grave;" then he told me he was a "red-handed murderer." He put down his plane, held his hands out before him, contemplated them sadly, and said:—

"Look—with these hands I have taken the lives of thirty human beings!"

The effect which this had upon me was an inspiration to him, and he turned himself loose upon his subject with interest and energy. He left generalizing, and went into details,—began with his first murder; described it, told what measures he had taken to avert suspicion; then passed to his second homicide, his third, his fourth, and so on. He had always done his murders with a bowie-knife, and he made all my hairs rise by suddenly snatching it out and showing it to me.

At the end of this first *séance* I went home with six of his fearful secrets among my freightage, and found them a great help to my dreams, which had been sluggish for a while back. I sought him again and again, on my Saturday holidays; in fact I spent the summer with him—all of it which was valuable to me. His fascinations never diminished, for he threw something fresh and stirring, in the way of horror, into each successive murder. He always gave names, dates, places—everything. This by and by enabled me to note two things: that he had killed his victims in every quarter of the globe, and that these victims were always named Lynch. The destruction of the Lynches went serenely on, Saturday after Saturday, until the original thirty had multiplied to sixty,—and more to be heard from yet; then my curiosity got the better of my timidity, and I asked how it happened that these justly punished persons all bore the same name.

My hero said he had never divulged that dark secret to any living being; but felt that he could trust me, and therefore he would lay bare before me the story of his sad and blighted life. He had loved one "too fair for earth," and she had reciprocated "with all the sweet affection of her pure and noble nature." But he had a rival, a "base hireling" named Archibald Lynch, who said the girl should be his, or he would "dye his hands in her heart's best blood." The carpenter, "innocent and happy in love's young dream," gave no weight to the threat, but led his "golden-haired darling to the altar," and there, the two were made one; there also, just as the minister's hands were stretched in blessing over their heads, the fell deed was done—with a knife—and the bride fell a corpse at her husband's feet. And what did the husband do? He plucked forth that knife, and kneeling by the body of his lost one, swore to "consecrate his life to the extermination of all the human scum that bear the hated name of Lynch."

That was it. He had been hunting down the Lynches and slaughtering them, from that day to this—twenty years. He had always used that same consecrated knife; with it he had murdered his long array of Lynches, and with it he had left.upon the forehead of each victim a peculiar mark—a cross, deeply incised. Said he:—

"The cross of the Mysterious Avenger is known in Europe, in America, in China, in Siam, in the Tropics, in the Polar Seas, in the deserts of Asia, in all the earth. Wherever in the uttermost parts of the globe, a Lynch has penetrated, there has the Mysterious Cross been seen, and those who have seen it have shuddered and said, 'it is his mark, he has been here.' You have heard of the Mysterious Avenger—look upon him, for before you stands no less a person! But beware—breathe not a word to any soul. Be silent, and wait. Some morning this town will flock aghast to view a gory corpse; on its brow will be seen the awful sign, and men will tremble and whisper, 'he has been here,—it is the Mysterious Avenger's mark!' You will come here, but I shall have vanished; you will see me no more."

This ass has been reading the "Jibbenainosay," no doubt, and had had his poor romantic head turned by it; but as I had not yet seen the book then, I took his inventions for truth, and did not suspect that he was a plagiarist.

However, we had a Lynch living in the town; and the more I reflected upon his impending doom, the more I could not sleep.

It seemed my plain duty to save him, and a still plainer and more important duty to get some sleep for myself, so at last I ventured to go to Mr. Lynch and tell him what was about to happen to him—under strict secrecy. I advised him to "fly," and certainly expected him to do it. But he laughed at me; and he did not stop there; he led me down to the carpenter's shop, gave the carpenter a jeering and scornful lecture upon his silly pretensions, slapped his face, made him get down on his knees and beg—then went off and left me to contemplate the cheap and pitiful ruin of what, in my eyes, had so lately been a majestic and incomparable hero. The carpenter blustered, flourished his knife, and doomed this Lynch in his usual volcanic style, the size of his fateful words undiminished; but it was all wasted upon me; he was a hero to me no longer but only a poor, foolish, exposed humbug. I was ashamed of him, and ashamed of myself; I took no further interest in him, and never went to his shop any more. He was a heavy loss to me, for he was the greatest hero I had ever known. The fellow must have had some talent; for some of his imaginary murders were so vividly and dramatically described that I remember all their details yet.

The people of Hannibal are not more changed than is the town. It is no longer a village; it is a city, with a mayor, and a council, and water-works, and probably a debt. It has fifteen thousand people, is a thriving and energetic place, and is paved like the rest of the west and south—where a well-paved street and a good sidewalk are things so seldom seen, that one doubts them when he does see them. The customary half-dozen railways centre in Hannibal now, and there is a new depot which cost a hundred thousand dollars. In my time the town had no specialty, and no commercial grandeur; the daily packet usually landed a passenger and bought a catfish, and took away another passenger and a hatful of freight; but now a huge commerce in lumber has grown up and a large miscellaneous commerce is one of the results. A deal of money changes hands there now.

Bear Creek—so called, perhaps, because it was always so particularly bare of bears—is hidden out of sight now, under islands and continents of piled lumber, and nobody but an expert can find it. I used to get drowned in it every summer regularly, and be drained out, and inflated and set going again by some chance enemy; but not enough of it is unoccupied now to drown a person in. It was a famous breeder of chills and fever in its day. I remember one summer when everybody in town had this disease at once. Many chimneys were shaken down, and all the houses were so racked that the town had to be rebuilt. The chasm or gorge between Lover's Leap and the hill west of it is supposed by scientists to have been caused by glacial action. This is a mistake.

There is an interesting cave a mile or two below Hannibal, among the bluffs. I would have liked to revisit it, but had not time. In my time the person who then owned it turned it into a mausoleum for his daughter, aged fourteen. The body of this poor child was put into a copper cylinder filled with alcohol, and this was suspended in one of the dismal avenues of the cave. The top of the cylinder was removable; and it was said to be a common thing for the baser order of tourists to drag the dead face into view and examine it and comment upon it.

CHAPTER LVI

A QUESTION OF LAW

The slaughter-house is gone from the mouth of Bear Creek and so is the small jail (or "calaboose") which once stood in its neighborhood. A citizen asked, "Do you remember when Jimmy Finn, the town drunkard, was burned to death in the calaboose?"

Observe, now, how history becomes defiled, through lapse of time and the help of the bad memories of men. Jimmy Finn was not burned in the calaboose, but died a natural death in a tan vat, of a combination of delirium tremens and spontaneous combustion. When I say natural death, I mean it was a natural death for Jimmy Finn to die. The calaboose victim was not a citizen; he was a poor stranger, a harmless whiskey-sodden tramp. I knew more about his case than anybody else; I knew too much of it, in that bygone day, to relish speaking of it. That tramp was wandering about the streets one chilly evening, with a pipe in his mouth, and begging for a match; he got neither matches nor courtesy; on the contrary, a troop of bad little boys followed him around and amused themselves with nagging and annoying him. I assisted; but at last, some appeal which the wayfarer made for forbearance, accompanying it with a pathetic reference to his forlorn and friendless condition, touched such sense of shame and remnant of right feeling as were left in me, and I went away and got him some matches, and then hied me home and to bed, heavily weighted as to conscience, and unbuoyant in spirit. An hour or two afterward, the man was arrested and locked up in the calaboose by the marshal—large name for a constable, but that was his title. At two in the morning, the church bells rang for fire, and everybody turned out, of course—I with the rest. The tramp had used his matches disastrously: he had set his straw bed on fire, and the oaken sheathing of the room had caught. When I reached the ground, two hundred men, women, and children stood massed together, transfixed with horror, and staring at the grated windows of the jail. Behind the iron bars, and tugging frantically at them, and screaming for help, stood the tramp; he seemed like a black object set against a sun, so white and intense was the light at his back. That marshal could not be found, and he had the only key. A battering-ram was quickly improvised, and the thunder of its blows upon the door had so encouraging a sound that the spectators broke into wild cheering, and believed the merciful battle won. But it was not so. The timbers were too strong; they did not yield. It was said that the man's death-grip still held fast to the bars after he was dead; and that in this position the fires wrapped him about and consumed him. As to this, I do not know. What was seen after I recognized the face that was pleading through the bars was seen by others, not by me.

I saw that face, so situated, every night for a long time afterward; and I believed myself as guilty of the man's death as if I had given him the matches purposely that he might burn himself up with them. I had not a doubt that I should be hanged if my connection with this tragedy were found out. The happenings and the impressions of that time are burnt into my memory, and the study of them entertains me as much now as they themselves distressed me then. If anybody spoke of that grisly matter, I was all ears in a moment, and alert to hear what might be said, for I was always dreading and expecting to find out that I was suspected; and so fine and so delicate was the perception of my guilty conscience, that it often detected suspicion in the most purposeless remarks, and in looks, gestures, glances of the eye which had no significance, but which sent me shivering away in a panic of fright, just the same. And how sick it made me when somebody dropped, howsoever carelessly and barren of intent, the remark that "murder will out!" For a boy of ten years, I was carrying a pretty weighty cargo.

All this time I was blessedly forgetting one thing—the fact that I was an inveterate talker in my sleep. But one night I awoke and found my bed-mate—my younger brother—sitting up in bed and contemplating me by the light of the moon. I said:—

"What is the matter?"

"You talk so much I can't sleep."

I came to a sitting posture in an instant, with my kidneys in my throat and my hair on end.

"What did I say? Quick—out with it—what did I say?"

"Nothing much."

"It's a lie—you know everything."

"Everything about what?"

"You know well enough. About *that*."

"About *what*?—I don't know what you are talking about. I think you are sick or crazy or something. But anyway, you're awake, and I'll get to sleep while I've got a chance."

He fell asleep and I lay there in a cold sweat, turning this new terror over in the whirling chaos which did duty as my mind. The burden of my thought was, How much did I divulge? How much does he know?—what a distress is this uncertainty! But by and by I evolved an idea—I would wake my brother and probe him with a supposititious case. I shook him up, and said—

"Suppose a man should come to you drunk—"

"This is foolish—I never get drunk."

"I don't mean you, idiot—I mean the man. Suppose a *man* should come to you drunk, and borrow a knife, or a tomahawk, or a pistol, and you forgot to tell him it was loaded, and—"

"How could you load a tomahawk?"

"I don't mean the tomahawk, and I didn't *say* the tomahawk; I said the pistol. Now don't you keep breaking in that way, because this is serious. There's been a man killed."

"What! In this town?"

"Yes, in this town."

"Well, go on—I won't say a single word."

"Well, then, suppose you forgot to tell him to be careful with it, because it was loaded, and he went off and shot himself with that pistol,—fooling with it, you know, and probably doing it by accident, being drunk. Well, would it be murder?"

"No—suicide."

"No, No. I don't mean *his* act, I mean yours: would you be a murderer for letting him have that pistol?"

After deep thought came this answer,—

"Well, I should think I was guilty of something—maybe murder—yes, probably murder, but I don't quite know."

This made me very uncomfortable. However, it was not a decisive verdict. I should have to set out the real case—there seemed to be no other way. But I would do it cautiously, and keep a watch out for suspicious effects. I said:—

"I was supposing a case, but I am coming to the real one now. Do you know how the man came to be burned up in the calaboose?"

"No."

"Haven't you the least idea?"

"Not the least."

"Wish you may die in your tracks if you have?"

"Yes, wish I may die in my tracks."

"Well, the way of it was this. The man wanted some matches to light his pipe. A boy got him some. The man set fire to the calaboose with those very matches, and burnt himself up."

"Is that so?"

"Yes, it is. Now, is that boy a murderer, do you think?"

"Let me see. The man was drunk?"

"Yes, he was drunk."

"Very drunk?"

"Yes."

"And the boy knew it?"

"Yes, he knew it."

There was a long pause. Then came this heavy verdict:—

"If the man was drunk, and the boy knew it, the boy murdered that man. This is certain."

Faint, sickening sensations crept along all the fibres of my body, and I seemed to know how a person feels who hears his death sentence pronounced from the bench. I waited to hear what my brother would say next. I believed I knew what it would be, and I was right. He said,—

"I know the boy."

I had nothing to say; so I said nothing. I simply shuddered. Then he added,—

"Yes, before you got half through telling about the thing, I knew perfectly well who the boy was; it was Ben Coontz!"

I came out of my collapse as one who rises from the dead. I said, with admiration:—

"Why, how in the world did you ever guess it?"

"You told it in your sleep."

I said to myself, "How splendid that is! This is a habit which must be cultivated."

My brother rattled innocently on:—

"When you were talking in your sleep, you kept mumbling something about 'matches,' which I couldn't make anything out of; but just now, when you began to tell me about the man and the calaboose and the matches, I remembered that in your sleep you mentioned Ben Coontz two or three times; so I put this and that together, you see, and right away I knew it was Ben that burnt that man up."

I praised his sagacity effusively. Presently he asked,—

"Are you going to give him up to the law?"

"No," I said; "I believe that this will be a lesson to him. I shall keep an eye on him, of course, for that is but right; but if he stops where he is and reforms, it shall never be said that I betrayed him."

"How good you are!"

"Well, I try to be. It is all a person can do in a world like this."

And now, my burden being shifted to other shoulders, my terrors soon faded away.

The day before we left Hannibal, a curious thing fell under my notice,—the surprising spread which longitudinal time undergoes there. I learned it from one of the most unostentatious of men,—the colored coachman of a friend of mine, who lives three miles from town. He was to call for me at the Park Hotel at 7.30 P.M., and drive me out. But he missed it considerably,—did not arrive till ten. He excused himself by saying:—

"De time is mos' an hour en a half slower in de country en what it is in de town; you'll be in plenty time, boss. Sometimes we shoves out early for church, Sunday, en fetches up dah right plum in de middle er de sermon. Diffunce in de time. A body can't make no calculations 'bout it."

I had lost two hours and a half; but I had learned a fact worth four.

CHAPTER LVII

AN ARCHANGEL

From St. Louis northward there are all the enlivening signs of the presence of active, energetic, intelligent, prosperous, practical nineteenth-century populations. The people don't dream, they work. The happy result is manifest all around in the substantial outside aspect of things, and the suggestions of wholesome life and comfort that everywhere appear.

Quincy is a notable example,—a brisk, handsome, well-ordered city; and now, as formerly, interested in art, letters, and other high things.

But Marion City is an exception. Marion City has gone backwards in a most unaccountable way. This metropolis promised so well that the projectors tacked "city" to its name in the very beginning, with full confidence; but it was bad prophecy. When I first saw Marion City, thirty-five years ago, it contained one street, and nearly or quite six houses. It contains but one house now, and this one, in a state of ruin, is getting ready to follow the former five into the river.

Doubtless Marion City was too near to Quincy. It had another disadvantage: it was situated in a flat mud bottom, below high-water mark, whereas Quincy stands high up on the slope of a hill.

In the beginning Quincy had the aspect and ways of a model New England town: and these she has yet: broad, clean streets, trim, neat dwellings and lawns, fine mansions, stately blocks of commercial buildings. And there are ample fair-grounds, a well kept park, and many attractive drives; library, reading-rooms, a couple of colleges, some handsome and costly churches, and a grand court-house, with grounds which occupy a square. The population of the city is thirty thousand. There are some large factories here, and manufacturing, of many sorts, is done on a great scale.

La Grange and Canton are growing towns, but I missed Alexandria; was told it was under water, but would come up to blow in the summer.

Keokuk was easily recognizable. I lived there in 1857,—an extraordinary year there in real-estate matters. The "boom" was something wonderful. Everybody bought, everybody sold,— except widows and preachers; they always hold on; and when the tide ebbs, they get left. Anything in the semblance of a town lot, no matter how situated, was salable, and at a figure which would still have been high if the ground had been sodded with greenbacks.

The town has a population of fifteen thousand now, and is progressing with a healthy growth. It was night, and we could not see details, for which we were sorry, for Keokuk has the reputation of being a beautiful city. It was a pleasant one to live in long ago, and doubtless has advanced, not retrograded, in that respect.

A mighty work which was in progress there in my day is finished now. This is the canal over the Rapids. It is eight miles long, three hundred feet wide, and is in no place less than six feet deep. Its masonry is of the majestic kind which the War Department usually deals in, and will endure like a Roman aqueduct. The work cost four or five millions.

After an hour or two spent with former friends, we started up the river again. Keokuk, a long time ago, was an occasional loafing-place of that erratic genius, Henry Clay Dean. I believe I never saw him but once; but he was much talked of when I lived there. This is what was said of him:—

He began life poor and without education. But he educated himself—on the curb-stones of Keokuk. He would sit down on a curb-stone with his book, careless or unconscious of the clatter of commerce and the tramp of the passing crowds, and bury himself in his studies by the hour, never changing his position except to draw in his knees now and then to let a dray pass unobstructed; and when his book was finished, its contents, however abstruse, had been burnt into his memory, and were his permanent possession. In this way he acquired a vast hoard of all sorts of learning, and had it pigeonholed in his head where he could put his intellectual hand on it whenever it was wanted.

His clothes differed in no respect from a "wharf-rat's", except that they were raggeder, more ill-assorted and inharmonious (and therefore more extravagantly picturesque), and several layers dirtier. Nobody could infer the master-mind in the top of that edifice from the edifice itself.

He was an orator,—by nature in the first place, and later by the training of experience and practice. When he was out on a canvass, his name was a loadstone which drew the farmers to his stump from fifty miles around. His theme was always politics. He used no notes, for a volcano does not need notes. In 1862, a son of Keokuk's late distinguished citizen, Mr. Claggett, gave me this incident concerning Dean:

The war feeling was running high in Keokuk (in '61), and a great mass meeting was to be held on a certain day in the new Althenaeum. A distinguished stranger was to address the house. After the building had been packed to its utmost capacity with sweltering folk of both sexes, the stage still remained vacant,— the distinguished stranger had failed to connect. The crowd grew impatient, and by and by indignant and rebellious. About this time a distressed manager discovered Dean on a curb-stone, explained the dilemma to him, took his book away from him, rushed him into the building the back way, and told him to make for the stage and save his country.

Presently a sudden silence fell upon the grumbling audience, and everybody's eyes sought a single point,—the wide, empty, carpetless stage. A figure appeared there whose aspect was familiar to hardly a dozen persons present. It was the scarecrow Dean,—in foxy shoes, down at the heels; socks of odd colors, also "down;" damaged trousers, relics of antiquity, and a world too short, exposing some inches of naked ankle; an unbuttoned vest, also too short, and exposing a zone of soiled and wrinkled linen between it and the waistband; shirt bosom open; long black handkerchief, wound round and round the neck like a bandage; bob-tailed blue coat, reaching down to the small of the back, with sleeves which left four inches of forearm unprotected; small, stiff-brimmed soldier-cap hung on a corner of the bump of—whichever bump it was. This figure moved gravely out upon the stage and, with sedate and measured step, down to the front, where it paused, and dreamily inspected the house, saying no word. The silence of surprise held its own for a moment, then was broken by a just audible ripple of merriment which swept the sea of faces like the wash of a wave. The figure remained as before, thoughtfully inspecting. Another wave started,—laughter, this time. It was followed by another, then a third,—this last one boisterous.

And now the stranger stepped back one pace, took off his soldier-cap, tossed it into the wing, and began to speak, with deliberation, nobody listening, everybody laughing and whispering. The speaker talked on unembarrassed, and presently delivered a shot which went home, and silence and attention resulted. He followed it quick and fast, with other telling things; warmed to his work and began to pour his words out, instead of dripping them; grew hotter and hotter, and fell to discharging lightnings and thunder,—and now the house began to break into applause, to which the speaker gave no heed, but went hammering straight on; unwound his black bandage and cast it away, still thundering; presently discarded the bob-tailed coat and flung it aside, firing up higher and higher all the time; finally flung the vest after the coat; and then for an untimed period stood there, like another Vesuvius, spouting smoke and flame, lava and ashes, raining pumice-stone and cinders, shaking the moral earth with intellectual crash upon crash, explosion upon explosion, while the mad multitude stood upon their feet in a solid body, answering back with a ceaseless hurricane of cheers, through a thrashing snow-storm of waving handkerchiefs.

"When Dean came," said Claggett, "the people thought he was an escaped lunatic; but when he went, they thought he was an escaped archangel."

Burlington, home of the sparkling Burdette, is another hill city; and also a beautiful one; unquestionably so; a fine and flourishing city, with a population of twenty-five thousand, and belted with busy factories of nearly every imaginable description. It was a very sober city, too—for the moment—for a most sobering bill was pending; a bill to forbid the manufacture, exportation, importation, purchase, sale, borrowing, lending, stealing, drinking, smelling, or possession, by conquest, inheritance, intent, accident, or otherwise, in the State of Iowa, of each and every deleterious beverage known to the human race, except water. This measure was approved by all the rational people in the State; but not by the bench of Judges.

Burlington has the progressive modern city's full equipment of devices for right and intelligent government; including a paid fire department, a thing which the great city of New Orleans is without, but still employs that relic of antiquity, the independent system.

In Burlington, as in all these Upper-River towns, one breathes a go-ahead atmosphere which tastes good in the nostrils. An opera-house has lately been built there which is in strong contrast with the shabby dens which usually do duty as theatres in cities of Burlington's size.

We had not time to go ashore in Muscatine, but had a daylight view of it from the boat. I lived there awhile, many years ago, but the place, now, had a rather unfamiliar look; so I suppose it has clear outgrown the town which I used to know. In fact, I know it has; for I remember it as a small place—which it isn't now. But I remember it best for a lunatic who caught me out in the fields, one Sunday, and extracted a butcher-knife from his boot and proposed to carve me up with it, unless I acknowledged him to be the only son of the Devil. I tried to compromise on an acknowledgment that he was the only member of the family I had met; but that did not satisfy him; he wouldn't have any half-measures; I must say he was the sole and only son of the Devil—and he whetted his knife on his boot. It did not seem worth while to make trouble about a little thing like that; so I swung round to his view of the matter and saved my skin whole. Shorty afterward, he went to visit his father; and as he has not turned up since, I trust he is there yet.

And I remember Muscatine—still more pleasantly—for its summer sunsets. I have never seen any, on either side of the ocean, that equalled them. They used the broad smooth river as a canvas, and painted on it every imaginable dream of color, from the mottled daintinesses and delicacies of the opal, all the way up, through cumulative intensities, to blinding purple and crimson conflagrations which were enchanting to the eye, but sharply tried it at the same time. All the Upper Mississippi region has these extraordinary sunsets as a familiar spectacle. It is the true Sunset Land: I am sure no other country can show so good a right to the name. The sunrises are also said to be exceedingly fine. I do not know.

CHAPTER LVIII

ON THE UPPER RIVER

The big towns drop in, thick and fast, now: and between stretch processions of thrifty farms, not desolate solitude. Hour by hour, the boat plows deeper and deeper into the great and populous Northwest; and with each successive section of it which is revealed, one's surprise and respect gather emphasis and increase. Such a people, and such achievements as theirs, compel homage. This is an independent race who think for themselves, and who are competent to do it, because they are educated and enlightened; they read, they keep abreast of the best and newest thought, they fortify every weak place in their land with a school, a college, a library, and a newspaper; and they live under law. Solicitude for the future of a race like this is not in order.

This region is new; so new that it may be said to be still in its babyhood. By what it has accomplished while still teething, one may forecast what marvels it will do in the strength of its maturity. It is so new that the foreign tourist has not heard of it yet; and has not visited it. For sixty years, the foreign tourist has steamed up and down the river between St. Louis and New Orleans, and then gone home and written his book, believing he had seen all of the river that was worth seeing or that had anything to see. In not six of all these books is there mention of these Upper-River towns—for the reason that the five or six tourists who penetrated this region did it before these towns were projected. The latest tourist of them all (1878) made the same old regulation trip—he had not heard that there was anything north of St. Louis.

Yet there was. There was this amazing region, bristling with great towns, projected day before yesterday, so to speak, and built next morning. A score of them number from fifteen hundred to five thousand people. Then we have Muscatine, ten thousand; Winona, ten thousand; Moline, ten thousand; Rock Island, twelve thousand; La Crosse, twelve thousand; Burlington, twenty-five thousand; Dubuque, twenty-five thousand; Davenport, thirty thousand; St. Paul, fifty-eight thousand; Minneapolis, sixty thousand and upward.

The foreign tourist has never heard of these; there is no note of them in his books. They have sprung up in the night, while he slept. So new is this region, that I, who am comparatively young, am yet older than it is. When I was born, St. Paul had a population of three persons, Minneapolis had just a third as many. The then population of Minneapolis died two years ago; and when he died he had seen himself undergo an increase, in forty years, of fifty-nine thousand nine hundred and ninety-nine persons. He had a frog's fertility.

I must explain that the figures set down above, as the population of St. Paul and Minneapolis, are several months old. These towns are far larger now. In fact, I have just seen a newspaper estimate which gives the former seventy-one thousand, and the latter seventy-eight thousand. This book will not reach the public for six or seven months yet; none of the figures will be worth much then.

We had a glimpse of Davenport, which is another beautiful city, crowning a hill—a phrase which applies to all these towns; for they are all comely, all well built, clean, orderly, pleasant to the eye, and cheering to the spirit; and they are all situated upon hills. Therefore we will give that phrase a rest. The Indians have a tradition that Marquette and Joliet camped where Davenport now stands, in 1673. The next white man who camped there, did it about a hundred and seventy years later—in 1834. Davenport has gathered its thirty thousand people within the past thirty years. She sends more children to her schools now, than her whole population numbered twenty-three years ago. She has the usual Upper-River quota of factories, newspapers, and institutions of learning; she has telephones, local telegraphs, an electric alarm, and an admirable paid fire department, consisting of six hook and ladder companies, four steam fire engines, and thirty churches. Davenport is the official residence of two bishops— Episcopal and Catholic.

Opposite Davenport is the flourishing town of Rock Island, which lies at the foot of the Upper Rapids. A great railroad bridge connects the two towns—one of the thirteen which fret the Mississippi and the pilots, between St. Louis and St. Paul.

The charming island of Rock Island, three miles long and half a mile wide, belongs to the United States, and the Government has turned it into a wonderful park, enhancing its natural attractions by art, and threading its fine forests with many miles of drives. Near the centre of the island one catches glimpses, through the trees, of ten vast stone four-story buildings, each of which covers an acre of ground. These are the Government workshops; for the Rock Island establishment is a national armory and arsenal.

We move up the river—always through enchanting scenery, there being no other kind on the Upper Mississippi—and pass Moline, a centre of vast manufacturing industries; and Clinton and Lyons, great lumber centres; and presently reach Dubuque, which is situated in a rich mineral region. The lead mines are very productive, and of wide extent. Dubuque has a great number of manufacturing establishments; among them a plough factory which has for customers all Christendom in general. At least so I was told by an agent of the concern who was on the boat. He said:—

"You show me any country under the sun where they really know *how* to plough, and if I don't show you our mark on the plough they use, I'll eat that plough; and I won't ask for any Woostershyre sauce to flavor it up with, either."

All this part of the river is rich in Indian history and traditions. Black Hawk's was once a puissant name hereabouts; as was Keokuk's, further down. A few miles below Dubuque is the Tete de Mort—Death's-head rock, or bluff—to the top of which the French drove a band of Indians, in early times, and cooped them up there, with death for a certainty, and only the manner of it matter of choice—to starve, or jump off and kill themselves. Black Hawk adopted the ways of the white people, toward the end of his life; and when he died he was buried, near Des Moines, in Christian fashion, modified by Indian custom; that is to say, clothed in a Christian military uniform, and with a Christian cane in his hand, but deposited in the grave in a sitting posture. Formerly, a horse had always been buried with a chief. The substitution of the cane shows that Black Hawk's haughty nature was really humbled, and he expected to walk when he got over.

We noticed that above Dubuque the water of the Mississippi was olive-green—rich and beautiful and semi-transparent, with the sun on it. Of course the water was nowhere as clear or of as fine a complexion as it is in some other seasons of the year; for now it was at flood stage, and therefore dimmed and blurred by the mud manufactured from caving banks.

The majestic bluffs that overlook the river, along through this region, charm one with the grace and variety of their forms, and the soft beauty of their adornment. The steep verdant slope, whose base is at the water's edge, is topped by a lofty rampart of broken, turreted rocks, which are exquisitely rich and mellow in color—mainly dark browns and dull greens, but splashed with other tints. And then you have the shining river, winding here and there and yonder, its sweep interrupted at intervals by clusters of wooded islands threaded by silver channels; and you have glimpses of distant villages, asleep upon capes; and of stealthy rafts slipping along in the shade of the forest walls; and of white steamers vanishing around remote points. And it is all as tranquil and reposeful as dreamland, and has nothing this-worldly about it—nothing to hang a fret or a worry upon.

Until the unholy train comes tearing along—which it presently does, ripping the sacred solitude to rags and tatters with its devil's warwhoop and the roar and thunder of its rushing wheels—and straightway you are back in this world, and with one of its frets ready to hand for your entertainment: for you remember that this is the very road whose stock always goes down after you buy it, and always goes up again as soon as you sell it. It makes me shudder to this day, to remember that I once came near not getting rid of my stock at all. It must be an awful thing to have a railroad left on your hands.

The locomotive is in sight from the deck of the steamboat almost the whole way from St. Louis to St. Paul—eight hundred miles. These railroads have made havoc with the steamboat commerce. The clerk of our boat was a steamboat clerk before these roads were built. In that day the influx of population was so great, and the freight business so heavy, that the boats were not able to keep up with the demands made upon their carrying capacity; consequently the captains were very independent and airy—pretty "biggity", as Uncle Remus would say. The clerk nut-shelled the contrast between the former time and the present, thus:—

"Boat used to land—captain on hurricane roof—mighty stiff and straight—iron ramrod for a spine—kid gloves, plug tile, hair parted behind—man on shore takes off hat and says:—

" 'Got twenty-eight tons of wheat, cap'n—be great favor if you can take them.'

"Captain says:—

" ' 'll take two of them'—and don't even condescend to look at him.

"But now-a-days the captain takes off his old slouch, and smiles all the way around to the back of his ears, and gets off a bow which he hasn't got any ramrod to interfere with, and says:—

" 'Glad to see you, Smith, glad to see you—you're looking well—haven't seen you looking so well for years—what you got for us?'

" 'Nuth'n', says Smith; and keeps his hat on, and just turns his back and goes to talking with somebody else.

"Oh, yes, eight years ago, the captain was on top; but it's Smith's turn now. Eight years ago a boat used to go up the river with every stateroom full, and people piled five and six deep on the cabin floor; and a solid deck-load of immigrants and harvesters down below, into the bargain. To get a first-class stateroom, you'd got to prove sixteen quarterings of nobility and four hundred years of descent, or be personally acquainted with the nigger that blacked the captain's boots. But it's all changed now; plenty staterooms above, no harvesters below—there's a patent self-binder now, and they don't have harvesters any more; they've gone where the woodbine twineth—and they didn't go by steamboat, either; went by the train."

Up in this region we met massed acres of lumber rafts coming down—but not floating leisurely along, in the old-fashioned way, manned with joyous and reckless crews of fiddling, song-singing, whiskey-drinking, breakdown-dancing rapscallions; no, the whole thing was shoved swiftly along by a powerful stern-wheeler, modern fashion, and the small crews were quiet, order-ly men, of a sedate business aspect, with not a suggestion of romance about them anywhere.

Along here, somewhere, on a black night, we ran some ex-ceedingly narrow and intricate island-chutes by aid of the elec-tric light. Behind was solid blackness—a crackless bank of it; ahead, a narrow elbow of water, curving between dense walls of foliage that almost touched our bows on both sides; and here every individual leaf, and every individual ripple stood out in its natural color, and flooded with a glare as of noonday inten-sified. The effect was strange, and fine, and very striking.

We passed Prairie du Chien, another of Father Marquette's camping-places; and after some hours of progress through varied and beautiful scenery, reached La Crosse. Here is a town of twelve or thirteen thousand population, with electric lighted streets, and with blocks of buildings which are stately enough, and also architecturally fine enough, to command respect in any city. It is a choice town, and we made satisfactory use of the hour allowed us, in roaming it over, though the weather was rainier than necessary.

CHAPTER LIX

LEGENDS AND SCENERY

We added several passengers to our list, at La Crosse; among others an old gentleman who had come to this northwestern region with the early settlers, and was familiar with every part of it. Pardonably proud of it, too. He said:—

"You'll find scenery between here and St. Paul that can give the Hudson points. You'll have the Queen's Bluff—seven hun-dred feet high, and just as imposing a spectacle as you can find anywheres; and Trempeleau Island, which isn't like any other island in America, I believe, for it is a gigantic mountain, with precipitous sides, and is full of Indian traditions, and used to be full of rattlesnakes; if you catch the sun just right there, you will have a picture that will stay with you. And above Winona you'll have lovely prairies; and then come the Thousand Islands, too beautiful for anything; green? why you never saw foliage so green, nor packed so thick; it's like a thousand plush cushions afloat on a looking-glass—when the water's still; and then the monstrous bluffs on both sides of the river—ragged, rugged, dark-complected—just the frame that's wanted; you always want a strong frame, you know, to throw up the nice points of a delicate picture and make them stand out.''

The old gentleman also told us a touching Indian legend or two—but not very powerful ones.

After this excursion into history, he came back to the scenery, and described it, detail by detail, from the Thousand Islands to St. Paul; naming its names with such facility, tripping along his theme with such nimble and confident ease, slamming in a three-ton word, here and there, with such a complacent air of 't isn't-anything,-I-can-do-it-any-time-I-want-to, and letting off fine surprises of lurid eloquence at such judicious intervals, that I presently began to suspect—

But no matter what I began to suspect. Hear him:—

"Ten miles above Winona we come to Fountain City, nestling sweetly at the feet of cliffs that lift their awful fronts, Jovelike, toward the blue depths of heaven, bathing them in virgin atmospheres that have known no other contact save that of angels' wings.

"And next we glide through silver waters, amid lovely and stupendous aspects of nature that attune our hearts to adoring admiration, about twelve miles, and strike Mount Vernon, six hundred feet high, with romantic ruins of a once first-class hotel perched far among the cloud shadows that mottle its dizzy heights—sole remnant of once-flourishing Mount Vernon, town of early days, now desolate and utterly deserted.

"And so we move on. Past Chimney Rock we fly—noble shaft of six hundred feet; then just before landing at Minnieska our attention is attracted by a most striking promontory rising over five hundred feet—the ideal mountain pyramid. Its conic shape—thickly-wooded surface girding its sides, and its apex like that of a cone, cause the spectator to wonder at nature's workings. From its dizzy heights superb views of the forests, streams, bluffs, hills and dales below and beyond for miles are brought within its focus. What grander river scenery can be conceived, as we gaze upon this enchanting landscape, from the uppermost point of these bluffs upon the valleys below? The primeval wildness and awful loneliness of these sublime creations of nature and nature's God, excite feelings of unbounded admiration, and the recollection of which can never be effaced from the memory, as we view them in any direction.

"Next we have the Lion's Head and the Lioness's Head, carved by nature's hand, to adorn and dominate the beauteous stream; and then anon the river widens, and a most charming and magnificent view of the valley before us suddenly bursts upon our vision; rugged hills, clad with verdant forests from summit to base, level prairie lands, holding in their lap the beautiful Wabasha, City of the Healing Waters, puissant foe of Bright's disease, and that grandest conception of nature's works, incomparable Lake Pepin—these constitute a picture whereon the tourist's eye may gaze uncounted hours, with rapture unappeased and unappeasable.

"And so we glide along; in due time encountering those majestic domes, the mighty Sugar Loaf, and the sublime Maiden's Rock—which latter, romantic superstition has invested with a voice; and oft-times as the birch canoe glides near, at twilight, the dusky paddler fancies he hears the soft sweet music of the long-departed Winona, darling of Indian song and story.

"Then Frontenac looms upon our vision, delightful resort of jaded summer tourists; then progressive Red Wing; and Diamond Bluff, impressive and preponderous in its lone sublimity; then Prescott and the St. Croix; and anon we see bursting upon us the domes and steeples of St. Paul, giant young chief of the North, marching with seven-league stride in the van of progress, banner-bearer of the highest and newest civilization, carving his beneficent way with the tomahawk of commercial enterprise, sounding the warwhoop of Christian culture, tearing off the reeking scalp of sloth and superstition to plant there the steamplow and the school-house—ever in his front stretch arid lawlessness, ignorance, crime, despair; ever in his wake bloom the jail, the gallows, and the pulpit; and ever—"

"Have you ever travelled with a panorama?"

"I have formerly served in that capacity."

My suspicion was confirmed.

"Do you still travel with it?"

"No, she is laid up till the fall season opens. I am helping now to work up the materials for a Tourist's Guide which the St. Louis and St. Paul Packet Company are going to issue this summer for the benefit of travellers who go by that line."

"When you were talking of Maiden's Rock, you spoke of the long-departed Winona, darling of Indian song and story. Is she the maiden of the rock?—and are the two connected by legend?"

"Yes, and a very tragic and painful one. Perhaps the most celebrated, as well as the most pathetic, of all the legends of the Mississippi."

We asked him to tell it. He dropped out of his conversational vein and back into his lecture-gait without an effort, and rolled on as follows:—

"A little distance above Lake City is a famous point known as Maiden's Rock, which is not only a picturesque spot, but is full of romantic interest from the event which gave it its name. Not many years ago this locality was a favorite resort for the Sioux Indians on account of the fine fishing and hunting to be had there, and large numbers of them were always to be found in this locality. Among the families which used to resort here, was one belonging to the tribe of Wabasha. We-no-na (first-born) was the name of a maiden who had plighted her troth to a lover belonging to the same band. But her stern parents had promised her hand to another, a famous warrior, and insisted on her wedding him. The day was fixed by her parents, to her great grief. She appeared to accede to the proposal and accompany them to the rock, for the purpose of gathering flowers for the feast. On reaching the rock, We-no-na ran to its summit and standing on its edge upbraided her parents who were below, for their cruelty, and then singing a death-dirge, threw herself from the precipice and dashed them in pieces on the rock below."

"Dashed who in pieces—her parents?"

"Yes."

"Well, it certainly was a tragic business, as you say. And moreover, there is a startling kind of dramatic surprise about it which I was not looking for. It is a distinct improvement upon the threadbare form of Indian legend. There are fifty Lover's Leaps along the Mississippi from whose summit disappointed Indian girls have jumped, but this is the only jump in the lot that turned out in the right and satisfactory way. What became of Winona?"

"She was a good deal jarred up and jolted: but she got herself together and disappeared before the coroner reached the fatal spot; and 't is said she sought and married her true love, and wandered with him to some distant clime, where she lived happy ever after, her gentle spirit mellowed and chastened by the romantic incident which had so early deprived her of the sweet guidance of a mother's love and a father's protecting arm, and thrown her, all unfriended, upon the cold charity of a censorious world."

I was glad to hear the lecturer's description of the scenery, for it assisted my appreciation of what I saw of it, and enabled me to imagine such of it as we lost by the intrusion of night.

As the lecturer remarked, this whole region is blanketed with Indian tales and traditions. But I reminded him that people

481

usually merely mentioned this fact—doing it in a way to make a body's mouth water—and judiciously stopped there. Why? Because the impression left, was that these tales were full of incident and imagination—a pleasant impression which would be promptly dissipated if the tales were told. I showed him a lot of this sort of literature which I had been collecting, and he confessed that it was poor stuff, exceedingly sorry rubbish; and I ventured to add that the legends which he had himself told us were of this character, with the single exception of the admirable story of Winona. He granted these facts, but said that if I would hunt up Mr. Schoolcraft's book, published near fifty years ago, and now doubtless out of print, I would find some Indian inventions in it that were very far from being barren on incident and imagination; that the tales in Hiawatha were of this sort, and they came from Schoolcraft's book; and that there were others in the same book which Mr. Longfellow could have turned into verse with good effect. For instance, there was the legend of "The Undying Head." He could not tell it, for many of the details had grown dim in his memory; but he would recommend me to find it and enlarge my respect for the Indian imagination. He said that this tale, and most of the others in the book, were current among the Indians along this part of the Mississippi when he first came here; and that the contributors to Schoolcraft's book had got them directly from Indian lips, and had written them down with strict exactness, and without embellishments of their own.

I have found the book. The lecturer was right. There are several legends in it which confirm what he said. I will offer two of them—"The Undying Head," and "Peboan and Seegwun, an Allegory of the Seasons." The latter is used in Hiawatha; but it is worth reading in the original form, if only that one may see how effective a genuine poem can be without the helps and graces of poetic measure and rhythm:—

PEBOAN AND SEEGWUN

An old man was sitting alone in his lodge, by the side of a frozen stream. It was the close of winter, and his fire was almost out. He appeared very old and very desolate. His locks were white with age, and he trembled in every joint. Day after day passed in solitude, and he heard nothing but the sound of the tempest, sweeping before it the new-fallen snow.

One day, as his fire was just dying, a handsome young man approached and entered his dwelling. His cheeks were red with the blood of youth, his eyes sparkled with animation, and a smile played upon his lips. He walked with a light and quick step. His forehead was bound with a wreath of sweet grass, in place of a warrior's frontlet, and he carried a bunch of flowers in his hand.

"Ah, my son," said the old man, "I am happy to see you. Come in. Come and tell me of your adventures, and what strange lands you have been to see. Let us pass the night together. I will tell you of my prowess and exploits, and what I can perform. You shall do the same, and we will amuse ourselves."

He then drew from his sack a curiously wrought antique pipe, and having filled it with tobacco, rendered mild by a mixture of certain leaves, handed it to his guest. When this ceremony was concluded they began to speak.

"I blow my breath," said the old man, "and the stream stands still. The water becomes stiff and hard as clear stone."

"I breathe," said the young man, "and flowers spring up over the plain."

"I shake my locks," retorted the old man, "and snow covers the land. The leaves fall from the trees at my command, and my breath blows them away. The birds get up from the water, and fly to a distant land. The animals hide themselves from my breath, and the very ground becomes as hard as flint."

"I shake my ringlets," rejoined the young man, "and warm showers of soft rain fall upon the earth. The plants lift up their heads out of the earth, like the eyes of children glistening with delight. My voice recalls the birds. The warmth of my breath unlocks the streams. Music fills the groves wherever I walk, and all nature rejoices."

At length the sun began to rise. A gentle warmth came over the place. The tongue of the old man became silent. The robin and bluebird began to sing on the top of the lodge. The stream began to murmur by the door, and the fragrance of growing herbs and flowers came softly on the vernal breeze.

Daylight fully revealed to the young man the character of his entertainer. When he looked upon him, he had the icy visage of *Peboan*.* Streams began to flow from his eyes. As the sun increased, he grew less and less in stature, and anon had melted completely away. Nothing remained on the place of his lodge-fire but the *miskodeed*†, a small white flower, with a pink border, which is one of the earliest species of northern plants.

"The Undying Head" is a rather long tale, but it makes up in weird conceits, fairy-tale prodigies, variety of incident, and energy of movement, for what it lacks in brevity‡.

---

* Winter.　　　　　　† The *trailing arbutus*.　　　　　　‡ See Appendix D.

CHAPTER LX

SPECULATIONS AND CONCLUSIONS

We reached St. Paul, at the head of navigation of the Mississippi, and there our voyage of two thousand miles from New Orleans ended. It is about a ten-day trip by steamer. It can probably be done quicker by rail. I judge so because I know that one may go by rail from St. Louis to Hannibal—a distance of at least a hundred and twenty miles—in seven hours. This is better than walking; unless one is in a hurry.

The season being far advanced when we were in New Orleans, the roses and magnolia blossoms were falling; but here in St. Paul it was the snow. In New Orleans we had caught an occasional withering breath from over a crater, apparently; here in St. Paul we caught a frequent benumbing one from over a glacier, apparently.

I am not trying to astonish by these statistics. No, it is only natural that there should be a sharp difference between climates which lie upon parallels of latitude which are one or two thousand miles apart. I take this position, and I will hold it and maintain it in spite of the newspapers. The newspaper thinks it isn't a natural thing; and once a year, in February, it remarks, with ill-concealed exclamation points, that while we, away up here are fighting snow and ice, folds are having new strawberries and peas down South; callas are blooming out of doors, and the people are complaining of the warm weather. The newspaper never gets done being surprised about it. It is caught regularly every February. There must be a reason for this; and this reason must be change of hands at the editorial desk. You cannot surprise an individual more than twice with the same marvel—not even with the February miracles of the Southern climate; but if you keep putting new hands at the editorial desk every year or two, and forget to vaccinate them against the annual climatic surprise, that same old thing is going to occur right along. Each year one new hand will have the disease, and be safe from its recurrence; but this does not save the newspaper. No, the newspaper is in as bad case as ever; it will forever have its new hand; and so, it will break out with the strawberry surprise every February as long as it lives. The new hand is curable; the newspaper itself is incurable. An act of Congress—no, Congress could not prohibit the strawberry surprise without questionably stretching its powers. An amendment to the Constitution might fix the thing, and that is probably the best and quickest way to get at it. Under authority of such an amendment, Congress could then pass an act inflicting imprisonment for life for the first offence, and some sort of lingering death for subsequent ones; and this, no doubt, would presently give us a rest. At the same time, the amendment and the resulting act and penalties might easily be made to cover various cognate abuses, such as the Annual-Veteran-who-has-Voted-for-Every-President-from-Washington-down,-and-Walked-to-the-Polls-Yesterday-with-as-Bright-an-Eye-and-as-Firm-a-Step-as-Ever, and ten or eleven other weary yearly marvels of that sort, and of the Oldest-Freemason, and Oldest-Printer, and Oldest-Baptist-Preacher, and Oldest-Alumnus sort, and Three-Children-Born-at-a-Birth sort, and so on, and so on. And then England would take it up and pass a law prohibiting the further use of Sidney Smith's jokes, and appointing a commissioner to construct some new ones. Then life would be a sweet dream of rest and peace, and the nations would cease to long for heaven.

But I wander from my theme. St. Paul is a wonderful town. It is put together in solid blocks of honest brick and stone, and has the air of intending to stay. Its post-office was established thirty-six years ago; and by and by, when the postmaster received a letter, he carried it to Washington, horseback, to inquire what was to be done with it. Such is the legend. Two frame houses were built that year, and several persons were added to the population. A recent number of the leading St. Paul paper, the "Pioneer Press," gives some statistics which furnish a vivid contrast to that old state of things, to wit: Population, autumn of the present year (1882), 71,000; number of letters handled, first half of the year, 1,209,387; number of houses built during three-quarters of the year, 989; their cost, $3,186,000. The increase of letters over the corresponding six months of last year was fifty per cent. Last year the new buildings added to the city cost above $4,500,000. St. Paul's strength lies in her commerce—I mean his commerce. He is a manufacturing city, of course—all the cities of that region are—but he is peculiarly strong in the matter of commerce. Last year his jobbing trade amounted to upwards of $52,000,000.

He has a custom-house, and is building a costly capitol to replace the one recently burned—for he is the capital of the State. He has churches without end; and not the cheap poor kind, but the kind that the rich Protestant puts up, the kind that the poor Irish "hired-girl" delights to erect. What a passion for building majestic churches the Irish hired-girl has. It is a fine thing for our architecture; but too often we enjoy her stately fanes without giving her a grateful thought. In fact, instead of reflecting that "every brick and every stone in this beautiful edifice represents an ache or a pain, and a handful of sweat, and hours of heavy fatigue, contributed by the back and forehead and bones of poverty," it is our habit to forget these things entirely, and merely glorify the mighty temple itself, without vouchsafing one praiseful thought to its humble builder, whose rich heart and withered purse it symbolizes.

This is a land of libraries and schools. St. Paul has three public libraries, and they contain, in the aggregate, some forty thousand books. He has one hundred and sixteen school-houses, and pays out more than seventy thousand dollars a year in teachers' salaries.

There is an unusually fine railway station; so large is it, in fact, that it seemed somewhat overdone, in the matter of size, at first; but at the end of a few months it was perceived that the mistake was distinctly the other way. The error is to be corrected.

The town stands on high ground; it is about seven hundred feet above the sea level. It is so high that a wide view of river and lowland is offered from its streets.

It is a very wonderful town indeed, and is not finished yet. All the streets are obstructed with building material, and this is being compacted into houses as fast as possible, to make room for more—for other people are anxious to build, as soon as they can get the use of the streets to pile up their bricks and stuff in.

How solemn and beautiful is the thought, that the earliest pioneer of civilization, the van-leader of civilization, is never the steamboat, never the railroad, never the newspaper, never the Sabbath-school, never the missionary—but always whiskey! Such is the case. Look history over; you will see. The missionary comes after the whiskey—I mean he arrives after the whiskey has arrived; next comes the poor immigrant, with axe and hoe and rifle; next, the trader; next, the miscellaneous rush; next, the gambler, the desperado, the highwayman, and all their kindred in sin of both sexes; and next, the smart chap who has bought up an old grant that covers all the land; this brings the lawyer tribe; the vigilance committee brings the undertaker. All these interests bring the newspaper; the newspaper starts up politics and a railroad; all hands turn to and build a church and a jail,—and behold, civilization is established forever in the land. But whiskey, you see, was the van-leader in this beneficent work. It always is. It was like a foreigner—and excusable in a foreigner—to be ignorant of this great truth, and wander off into astronomy to borrow a symbol. But if he had been conversant with the facts, he would have said,—

Westward the Jug of Empire takes its way.

This great van-leader arrived upon the ground which St. Paul now occupies, in June, 1837. Yes, at that date, Pierre Parrant, a Canadian, built the first cabin, uncorked his jug, and began to sell whiskey to the Indians. The result is before us.

All that I have said of the newness, briskness, swift progress, wealth, intelligence, fine and substantial architecture, and general slash and go, and energy of St. Paul, will apply to his near neighbor, Minneapolis—with the addition that the latter is the bigger of the two cities.

These extraordinary towns were ten miles apart, a few months ago, but were growing so fast that they may possibly be joined now, and getting along under a single mayor. At any rate, within five years from now there will be at least such a substantial ligament of buildings stretching between them and uniting them that a stranger will not be able to tell where the one Siamese twin leaves off and the other begins. Combined, they will then number a population of two hundred and fifty thousand, if they continue to grow as they are now growing. Thus, this centre of population at the head of Mississippi navigation, will then begin a rivalry as to numbers, with that centre of population at the foot of it—New Orleans.

Minneapolis is situated at the falls of St. Anthony, which stretch across the river, fifteen hundred feet, and have a fall of eighty-two feet—a waterpower which, by art, has been made of inestimable value, business-wise, though somewhat to the damage of the Falls as a spectacle, or as a background against which to get your photograph taken.

Thirty flouring mills turn out two million barrels of the very choicest of flour every year; twenty sawmills produce two hundred million feet of lumber annually; then there are woollen mills, cotton mills, paper and oil mills; and sash, nail, furniture, barrel, and other factories, without number, so to speak. The great flouring-mills here and at St. Paul use the "new process" and mash the wheat by rolling, instead of grinding it.

Sixteen railroads meet in Minneapolis, and sixty-five passenger trains arrive and depart daily.

In this place, as in St. Paul, journalism thrives. Here there are three great dailies, ten weeklies, and three monthlies.

There is a university, with four hundred students—and, better still, its good efforts are not confined to enlightening the one sex. There are sixteen public schools, with buildings which cost $500,000; there are six thousand pupils and one hundred and twenty-eight teachers. There are also seventy churches existing, and a lot more projected. The banks aggregate a capital of $3,000,000, and the wholesale jobbing trade of the town amounts to $50,000,000 a year.

Near St. Paul and Minneapolis are several points of interest— Fort Snelling, a fortress occupying a river-bluff a hundred feet high; the falls of Minnehaha; White-bear Lake, and so forth. The beautiful falls of Minnehaha are sufficiently celebrated— they do not need a lift from me, in that direction. The White-bear Lake is less known. It is a lovely sheet of water, and is being utilized as a summer resort by the wealth and fashion of the State. It has its club-house, and its hotel, with the modern improvements and conveniences; its fine summer residences; and plenty of fishing, hunting, and pleasant drives. There are a dozen minor summer resorts around about St. Paul and Minneapolis, but the White-bear Lake is *the* resort. Connected with White-bear Lake is a most idiotic Indian legend. I would resist the temptation to print it here, if I could, but the task is beyond my strength. The guide-book names the preserver of the legend, and compliments his "facile pen." Without further comment or delay then, let us turn the said facile pen loose upon the reader:—

A LEGEND OF WHITE-BEAR LAKE

Every spring, for perhaps a century, or as long as there has been a nation of red men, an island in the middle of White-bear Lake has been visited by a band of Indians for the purpose of making maple sugar.

Tradition says that many springs ago, while upon this island, a young warrior loved and wooed the daughter of his chief, and it is said, also, the maiden loved the warrior. He had again and again been refused her hand by her parents, the old chief alleging that he was no brave, and his old consort called him a woman!

The sun had again set upon the "sugar-bush," and the bright moon rose high in the bright blue heavens, when the young warrior took down his flute and went out alone, once more to sing the story of his love, the mild breeze gently moved the two gay feathers in his head-dress, and as he mounted on the trunk of a leaning tree, the damp snow fell from his feet heavily. As he raised his flute to his lips, his blanket slipped from his well-formed shoulders, and lay partly on the snow beneath. He began his weird, wild love-song, but soon felt that he was cold, and as he reached back for his blanket, some unseen hand laid it gently on his shoulders; it was the hand of his love, his guardian angel. She took her place beside him, and for the present they were happy; for the Indian has a heart to love, and in this pride he is as noble as in his own freedom, which makes him the child of the forest. As the legend runs, a large white-bear, thinking, perhaps, that polar snows and dismal winter weather extended everywhere, took up his journey southward. He at length approached the northern shore of the lake which now bears his name, walked down the bank and made his way noiselessly through the deep heavy snow toward the island. It was the same spring ensuing that the lovers met. They had left their first retreat, and were now seated among the branches of a large elm which hung far over the lake. (The same tree is still standing, and excites universal curiosity and interest.) For fear of being detected, they talked almost in a whisper, and now, that they might get back to camp in good time and thereby avoid suspicion, they were just rising to return, when the maiden uttered a shriek which was heard at the camp, and bounding toward the young brave, she caught his blanket, but missed the direction of her foot and fell, bearing the blanket with her into the great arms of the ferocious monster. Instantly every man, woman, and child of the band were upon the bank, but all unarmed. Cries and wailings went up from every mouth. What was to be done? In the meantime this white and savage beast held the breathless maiden in his huge grasp, and fondled with his precious prey as if he were used to scenes like this. One deafening yell from the lover warrior is heard above the cries of hundreds of his tribe, and dashing away to his wigwam he grasps his faithful knife, returns almost at a single bound to the scene of fear and fright, rushes out along the leaning tree to the spot where his treasure fell, and springing with the fury of a mad panther, pounced upon his prey. The animal turned, and with one stroke of his huge paw brought the lovers heart to heart, but the next moment the warrior, with one plunge of the blade of his knife, opened the crimson sluices of death, and the dying bear relaxed his hold.

That night there was no more sleep for the band or the lovers, and as the young and the old danced about the carcass of the dead monster, the gallant warrior was presented with another plume, and ere another moon had set he had a living treasure added to his heart. Their children for many years played upon the skin of the white-bear—from which the lake derives its name—and the maiden and the brave remembered long the fearful scene and rescue that made them one, for Kis-se-me-pa and Ka-go-ka could never forget their fearful encounter with the huge monster that came so near sending them to the happy hunting-ground.

It is a perplexing business. First, she fell down out of the tree—she and the blanket; and the bear caught her and fondled her—her and the blanket; then she fell up into the tree again—leaving the blanket; meantime the lover goes war-whooping home and comes back "heeled," climbs the tree, jumps down on the bear, the girl jumps down after him—apparently, for she was up the tree—resumes her place in the bear's arms along with the blanket, the lover rams his knife into the bear, and saves—whom, the blanket? No—nothing of the sort. You get yourself all worked up and excited about that blanket, and then all of a sudden, just when a happy climax seems imminent, you are let down flat—nothing saved but the girl. Whereas, one is not interested in the girl; she is not the prominent feature of the legend. Nevertheless, there you are left, and there you must remain; for if you live a thousand years you will never know who got the blanket. A dead man could get up a better legend than this one. I don't mean a fresh dead man either; I mean a man that's been dead weeks and weeks.

We struck the home-trail now, and in a few hours were in that astonishing Chicago—a city where they are always rubbing the lamp, and fetching up the genii, and contriving and achieving new impossibilities. It is hopeless for the occasional visitor to try to keep up with Chicago—she out-grows his prophecies faster than he can make them. She is always a novelty; for she is never the Chicago you saw when you passed through the last time. The Pennsylvania road rushed us to New York without missing schedule time ten minutes anywhere on the route; and there ended one of the most enjoyable five-thousand-mile journeys I have ever had the good fortune to make.

APPENDIX

A

[From the New-Orleans Times-Democrat, of March 29, 1882.]

VOYAGE OF THE TIMES-DEMOCRAT'S RELIEF BOAT THROUGH THE INUNDATED REGIONS

It was nine o'clock Thursday morning when the "Susie" left the Mississippi and entered Old River, or what is now called the mouth of the Red. Ascending on the left, a flood was pouring in through and over the levees on the Chandler plantation, the most northern point in Pointe Coupée parish. The water completely covered the place, although the levees had given way but a short time before. The stock had been gathered in a large flat-boat, where, without food, as we passed, the animals were huddled together, waiting for a boat to tow them off. On the right-hand side of the river is Turnbull's Island, and on it is a large plantation which formerly was pronounced one of the most fertile in the State. The water has hitherto allowed it to go scot-free in usual floods, but now broad sheets of water told only where fields were. The top of the protecting levee could be seen here and there, but nearly all of it was submerged.

The trees have put on a greener foliage since the water has poured in, and the woods look bright and fresh, but this pleasant aspect to the eye is neutralized by the interminable waste of water. We pass mile after mile, and it is nothing but trees standing up to their branches in water. A water-turkey now and again rises and flies ahead into the long avenue of silence. A pirogue sometimes flits from the bushes and crosses the Red River on its way out to the Mississippi, but the sad-faced paddlers never turn their heads to look at our boat. The puffing of the boat is music in this gloom, which affects one most curiously. It is not the gloom of deep forests or dark caverns, but a peculiar kind of solemn silence and impressive awe that holds one perforce to its recognition. We passed two negro families on a raft tied up in the willows this morning. They were evidently of the well-to-do class, as they had a supply of meal and three or four hogs with them. Their rafts were about twenty feet square, and in front of an improvised shelter earth had been placed, on which they built their fire.

The current running down the Atchafalaya was very swift, the Mississippi showing predilection in that direction, which needs only to be seen to enforce the opinion of that river's desperate endeavors to find a short way to the Gulf. Small boats, skiffs, pirogues, etc., are in great demand, and many have been stolen by piratical negroes, who take them where they will bring the greatest price. From what was told me by Mr. C.P. Ferguson, a planter near Red River Landing, whose place has just gone under, there is much suffering in the rear of that place. The negroes had given up all thoughts of a crevasse there, as the upper levee had stood so long, and when it did come they were at its mercy. On Thursday a number were taken out of trees and off of cabin roofs and brought in, many yet remaining.

One does not appreciate the sight of earth until he has travelled through a flood. At sea one does not expect or look for it, but here, with fluttering leaves, shadowy forest aisles, house-tops barely visible, it is expected. In fact a grave-yard, if the mounds were above water, would be appreciated. The river here is known only because there is an opening in the trees, and that is all. It is in width, from Fort Adams on the left bank of the Mississippi to the bank of Rapides Parish, a distance of about sixty miles. A large portion of this was under cultivation, particularly along the Mississippi and back of the Red. When Red River proper was entered, a strong current was running directly across it, pursuing the same direction as that of the Mississippi.

After a run of some hours, Black River was reached. Hardly was it entered before signs of suffering became visible. All the willows along the banks were stripped of their leaves. One man, whom your correspondent spoke to, said that he had had one hundred and fifty head of cattle and one hundred head of hogs. At the first appearance of water he had started to drive them to the high lands of Avoyelles, thirty-five miles off, but he lost fifty head of the beef cattle and sixty hogs. Black River is quite picturesque, even if its shores are under water. A dense growth of ash, oak, gum, and hickory make the shores almost impenetrable, and where one can get a view down some avenue in the trees, only the dim outlines of distant trucks can be barely distinguished in the gloom.

A few miles up this river, the depth of water on the banks was fully eight feet, and on all sides could be seen, still holding against the strong current, the tops of cabins. Here and there one overturned was surrounded by drift-wood, forming the nucleus of possibly some future island.

In order to save coal, as it was impossible to get that fuel at any point to be touched during the expedition, a lookout was kept for a wood-pile. On rounding a point a pirogue, skilfully paddled by a youth, shot out, and in its bow was a girl of fifteen, of fair face, beautiful black eyes, and demure manners. The boy asked for a paper, which was thrown to him, and the couple pushed their tiny craft out into the swell of the boat.

Presently a little girl, not certainly over twelve years, paddled out in the smallest little canoe and handled it with all the deftness of an old voyageur. The little one looked more like an Indian than a white child, and laughed when asked if she were afraid. She had been raised in a pirogue and could go anywhere. She was bound out to pick willow leaves for the stock, and she pointed to a house near by with water three inches deep on the floors. At its back door was moored a raft about thirty feet square, with a sort of fence built upon it, and inside of this some sixteen cows and twenty hogs were standing. The family did not complain, except on account of losing their stock, and promptly brought a supply of wood in a flat.

From this point to the Mississippi River, fifteen miles, there is not a spot of earth above water, and to the westward for thirty-five miles there is nothing but the river's flood. Black River had risen during Thursday, the 23d, 1 3/4 inches, and was going up at night still. As we progress up the river habitations become more frequent, but are yet still miles apart. Nearly all of them are deserted, and the out-houses floated off. To add to the gloom, almost every living thing seems to have departed, and not a whistle of a bird nor the bark of the squirrel can be heard in this solitude. Sometimes a morose gar will throw his tail aloft and disappear in the river, but beyond this everything is quiet—the quiet of dissolution. Down the river floats now a neatly whitewashed hen-house, then a cluster of neatly split fence-rails, or a door and a bloated carcass, solemnly guarded by a pair of buzzards, the only bird to be seen, which feast on the carcass as it bears them along. A picture-frame in which there was a cheap lithograph of a soldier on horseback, as it floated on told of some hearth invaded by the water and despoiled of this ornament.

At dark, as it was not prudent to run, a place alongside the woods was hunted and to a tall gum-tree the boat was made fast for the night.

A pretty quarter of the moon threw a pleasant light over forest and river, making a picture that would be a delightful piece of landscape study, could an artist only hold it down to his canvas. The motion of the engines had ceased, the puffing of the escaping steam was stilled, and the enveloping silence closed upon us, and such silence it was! Usually in a forest at night one can hear the piping of frogs, the hum of insects, or the dropping of limbs; but here nature was dumb. The dark recesses, those aisles into this cathedral, gave forth no sound, and even the ripplings of the current die away.

At daylight Friday morning all hands were up, and up the Black we started. The morning was a beautiful one, and the river, which is remarkably straight, put on its loveliest garb. The blossoms of the haw perfumed the air deliciously, and a few birds whistled blithely along the banks. The trees were larger, and the forest seemed of older growth than below. More fields were passed than nearer the mouth, but the same scene presented itself—smokehouses drifting out in the pastures, negro quarters anchored in confusion against some oak, and the modest residence just showing its eaves above water. The sun came up in a glory of carmine, and the trees were brilliant in their varied shades of green. Not a foot of soil is to be seen anywhere, and the water is apparently growing deeper and deeper, for it reaches up to the branches of the largest trees. All along, the bordering willows have been denuded of leaves, showing how long the people have been at work gathering this fodder for their animals. An old man in a pirogue was asked how the willow leaves agreed with his cattle. He stopped in his work, and with an ominous shake of his head replied: "Well, sir, it's enough to keep warmth in their bodies and that's all we expect, but it's hard on the hogs, particularly the small ones. They is dropping off powerful fast. But what can you do? It's all we've got."

At thirty miles above the mouth of Black River the water extends from Natchez on the Mississippi across to the pine hills of Louisiana, a distance of seventy-three miles, and there is hardly a spot that is not ten feet under it. The tendency of the current up the Black is toward the west. In fact, so much is this the case, the waters of Red River have been driven down from toward the Calcasieu country, and the waters of the Black enter the Red some fifteen miles above the mouth of the former, a thing never before seen by even the oldest steamboatmen. The water now in sight of us is entirely from the Mississippi.

Up to Trinity, or rather Troy, which is but a short distance below, the people have nearly all moved out, those remaining having enough for their present personal needs. Their cattle, though, are suffering and dying off quite fast, as the confinement on rafts and the food they get breeds disease.

After a short stop we started, and soon came to a section where there were many open fields and cabins thickly scattered about. Here were seen more pictures of distress. On the inside of the houses the inmates had built on boxes a scaffold on which they placed the furniture. The bed-posts were sawed off on top, as the ceiling was not more than four feet from the improvised floor. The buildings looked very insecure, and threaten every moment to float off. Near the houses were cattle standing breast high in the water, perfectly impassive. They did not move in their places, but stood patiently waiting for help to come. The sight was a distressing one, and the poor creatures will be sure to die unless speedily rescued. Cattle differ from horses in this peculiar quality. A horse, after finding no relief comes, will swim off in search of food, whereas a beef will stand in its tracks until with exhaustion it drops in the water and drowns.

At half-past twelve o'clock a hail was given from a flat-boat inside the line of the bank. Rounding to we ran alongside, and General York stepped aboard. He was just then engaged in getting off stock, and welcomed the "Times-Democrat Boat" heartily, as he said there was much need for her. He said that the distress was not exaggerated in the least. People were in a condition it was difficult even for one to imagine. The water was so high there was great danger of their houses being swept away. It had already risen so high that it was approaching the eaves, and when it reaches this point there is always imminent risk of their being swept away. If this occurs, there will be great loss of life. The General spoke of the gallant work of many of the people in their attempts to save their stock, but thought that fully twenty-five per cent had perished. Already twenty-five hundred people had received rations from Troy, on Black River, and he had towed out a great many cattle, but a very great quantity remained and were in dire need. The water was now eighteen inches higher than in 1874, and there was no land between Vidalia and the hills of Catahoula.

At two o'clock the "Susie" reached Troy, sixty-five miles above the mouth of Black River. Here on the left comes in Little River; just beyond that the Ouachita, and on the right the Tensas. These three rivers form the Black River. Troy, or a portion of it, is situated on and around three large Indian mounds, circular in shape, which rise above the present water about twelve feet. They are about one hundred and fifty feet in diameter and are about two hundred yards apart. The houses are all built between these mounds, and hence are all flooded to a depth of eighteen inches on their floors.

These elevations, built by the aborigines hundreds of years ago, are the only points of refuge for miles. When we arrived we found them crowded with stock, all of which was thin and hardly able to stand up. They were mixed together, sheep, hogs, horses, mules, and cattle. One of these mounds has been used for many years as the grave-yard, and to-day we saw attenuated cows lying against the marble tomb-stones, chewing their cud in contentment, after a meal of corn furnished by General York. Here, as below, the remarkable skill of the women and girls in the management of the smaller pirogues was noticed. Children were paddling about in these most ticklish crafts with all the nonchalance of adepts.

General York has put into operation a perfect system in regard to furnishing relief. He makes a personal inspection of the place where it is asked, sees what is necessary to be done, and then, having two boats chartered, with flats, sends them promptly to the place, when the cattle are loaded and towed to the pine hills and uplands of Catahoula. He has made Troy his headquarters, and to this point boats come for their supply of feed for cattle. On the opposite side of Little River, which branches to the left out of Black, and between it and the Ouachita, is situated the town of Trinity, which is hourly threatened with destruction. It is much lower than Troy, and the water is eight and nine feet deep in the houses. A strong current sweeps through it, and it is remarkable that all of its houses have not gone before. The residents of both Troy and Trinity have been cared for, yet some of their stock have to be furnished with food.

As soon as the "Susie" reached Troy, she was turned over to General York and placed at his disposition to carry out the work of relief more rapidly. Nearly all her supplies were landed on one of the mounds to lighten her, and she was headed down stream to relieve those below. At Tom Hooper's place, a few miles from Troy, a large flat, with about fifty head of stock on board, was taken in tow. The animals were fed, and soon regained some strength. To-day we go on Little River, where the suffering is greatest.

DOWN BLACK RIVER

SATURDAY EVENING, MARCH 25

We started down Black River quite early, under the direction of General York, to bring out what stock could be reached. Going down river a flat in tow was left in a central locality, and from there men poled her back in the rear of plantations, picking up the animals wherever found. In the loft of a gin-house there were seventeen head found, and after a gangway was built they were led down into the flat without difficulty. Taking a skiff with the General, your reporter was pulled up to a little house of two rooms, in which the water was standing two feet on the floors. In one of the large rooms were huddled the horses and cows of the place, while in the other the Widow Taylor and her son were seated on a scaffold raised on the floor. One or two dugouts were drifting about in the room ready to be put in service at any time. When the flat was brought up, the side of the house was cut away as the only means of getting the animals out, and the cattle were driven on board the boat. General York, in this as in every case, inquired if the family desired to leave, informing them that Major Burke, of "The Times-Democrat," has sent the "Susie" up for that purpose. Mrs. Taylor said she thanked Major Burke, but she would try and hold out. The remarkable tenacity of the people here to their homes is beyond all comprehension. Just below, at a point sixteen miles from Troy, information was received that the house of Mr. Tom Ellis was in danger, and his family were all in it. We steamed there immediately, and a sad picture was presented. Looking out of the half of the window left above water was Mrs. Ellis, who is in feeble health, whilst at the door were her seven children, the oldest not fourteen years. One side of the house was given up to the work animals, some twelve head, besides hogs. In the next room the family lived, the water coming within two inches of the bed-rail. The stove was below water, and the cooking was done on a fire on top of it. The house threatened to give way at any moment: one end of it was sinking, and, in fact, the building looked a mere shell. As the boat rounded to, Mr. Ellis came out in a dug-out, and General York told him that he had come to his relief; that "The Times- Democrat" boat was at his service, and would remove his family at once to the hills, and on Monday a flat would take out his stock, as, until that time, they would be busy. Notwithstanding the deplorable situation himself and family were in, Mr. Ellis did not want to leave. He said he thought he would wait until Monday, and take the risk of his house falling. The children around the door looked perfectly contented, seeming to care little for the danger they were in. These are but two instances of the many. After weeks of privation and suffering, people still cling to their houses and leave only when there is not room between the water and the ceiling to build a scaffold on which to stand. It seemed to be incomprehensible, yet the love for the old place was stronger than that for safety.

After leaving the Ellis place, the next spot touched at was the Oswald place. Here the flat was towed alongside the gin-house where there were fifteen head standing in water; and yet, as they stood on scaffolds, their heads were above the top of the entrance. It was found impossible to get them out without cutting away a portion of the front; and so axes were brought into requisition and a gap made. After much labor the horses and mules were securely placed on the flat.

At each place we stop there are always three, four, or more dugouts arriving, bringing information of stock in other places in need. Notwithstanding the fact that a great many had driven a part of their stock to the hills some time ago, there yet remains a large quantity, which General York, who is working with indomitable energy, will get landed in the pine hills by Tuesday.

All along Black River the "Susie" has been visited by scores of planters, whose tales are the repetition of those already heard of suffering and loss. An old planter, who has lived on the river since 1844, said there never was such a rise, and he was satisfied more than one quarter of the stock has been lost. Luckily the people cared first for their work stock, and when they could find it horses and mules were housed in a place of safety. The rise which still continues, and was two inches last night, compels them to get them out to the hills; hence it is that the work of General York is of such a great value. From daylight to late at night he is going this way and that, cheering by his kindly words and directing with calm judgment what is to be done. One unpleasant story, of a certain merchant in New Orleans, is told all along the river. It appears for some years past the planters have been dealing with this individual, and many of them had balances in his hands. When the overflow came they wrote for coffee, for meal, and, in fact, for such little necessities as were required. No response to these letters came, and others were written, and yet these old customers, with plantations under water, were refused even what was necessary to sustain life. It is needless to say he is not popular now on Black River.

The hills spoken of as the place of refuge for the people and stock on Black River are in Catahoula parish, twenty-four miles from Black River.

After filling the flat with cattle we took on board the family of T.S. Hooper, seven in number, who could not longer remain in their dwelling, and we are now taking them up Little River to the hills.

THE FLOOD STILL RISING

TROY, MARCH 27, 1882, NOON.

The flood here is rising about three and a half inches every twenty-four hours, and rains have set in which will increase this. General York feels now that our efforts ought to be directed towards saving life, as the increase of the water has jeopardized many houses. We intend to go up the Tensas in a few minutes, and then we will return and go down Black River to take off families. There is a lack of steam transportation here to meet the emergency. The General has three boats chartered, with flats in tow, but the demand for these to tow out stock is greater than they can meet with promptness. All are working night and day, and the "Susie" hardly stops for more than an hour anywhere. The rise has placed Trinity in a dangerous plight, and momentarily it is expected that some of the houses will float off. Troy is a little higher, yet all are in the water. Reports have come in that a woman and child have been washed away below here, and two cabins floated off. Their occupants are the same who refused to come off day before yesterday. One would not believe the utter passiveness of the people.

As yet no news has been received of the steamer "Delia," which is supposed to be the one sunk in yesterday's storm on Lake Catahoula. She is due here now, but has not arrived. Even the mail here is most uncertain, and this I send by skiff to Natchez to get it to you. It is impossible to get accurate data as to past crops, etc., as those who know much about the matter have gone, and those who remain are not well versed in the production of this section.

General York desires me to say that the amount of rations formerly sent should be duplicated and sent at once. It is impossible to make any estimate, for the people are fleeing to the hills, so rapid is the rise. The residents here are in a state of commotion that can only be appreciated when seen, and complete demoralization has set in.

If rations are drawn for any particular section hereabouts, they would not be certain to be distributed, so everything should be sent to Troy as a centre, and the General will have it properly disposed of. He has sent for one hundred tents, and, if all go to the hills who are in motion now, two hundred will be required.

B

The condition of this rich valley of the Lower Mississippi, immediately after and since the war, constituted one of the disastrous effects of war most to be deplored. Fictitious property in slaves was not only righteously destroyed, but very much of the work which had depended upon the slave labor was also destroyed or greatly impaired, especially the levee system.

It might have been expected by those who have not investigated the subject, that such important improvements as the construction and maintenance of the levees would have been assumed at once by the several States. But what can the State do where the people are under subjection to rates of interest ranging from 18 to 30 per cent, and are also under the necessity of pledging their crops in advance even of planting, at these rates, for the privilege of purchasing all of their supplies at 100 per cent profit?

It has needed but little attention to make it perfectly obvious that the control of the Mississippi River, if undertaken at all, must be undertaken by the national government, and cannot be compassed by States. The river must be treated as a unit; its control cannot be compassed under a divided or separate system of administration.

Neither are the States especially interested competent to combine among themselves for the necessary operations. The work must begin far up the river; at least as far as Cairo, if not beyond; and must be conducted upon a consistent general plan throughout the course of the river.

It does not need technical or scientific knowledge to comprehend the elements of the case if one will give a little time and attention to the subject, and when a Mississippi River commission has been constituted, as the existing commission is, of thoroughly able men of different walks in life, may it not be suggested that their verdict in the case should be accepted as conclusive, so far as any *a priori* theory of construction or control can be considered conclusive?

It should be remembered that upon this board are General Gilmore, General Comstock, and General Suter, of the United States Engineers; Professor Henry Mitchell (the most competent authority on the question of hydrography), of the United States Coast Survey; B. B. Harrod, the State Engineer of Louisiana; Jas. B. Eads, whose success with the jetties at New Orleans is a warrant of his competency, and Judge Taylor, of Indiana.

It would be presumption on the part of any single man, however skilled, to contest the judgment of such a board as this.

The method of improvement proposed by the commission is at once in accord with the results of engineering experience and with observations of nature where meeting our wants. As in nature the growth of trees and their proneness where undermined to fall across the slope and support the bank secures at some points a fair depth of channel and some degree of permanence, so in the project of the engineer the use of timber and brush and the encouragement of forest growth are the main features. It is proposed to reduce the width where excessive by brushwood dykes, at first low, but raised higher and higher as the mud of the river settles under their shelter, and finally slope them back at the angle upon which willows will grow freely. In this work there are many details connected with the forms of these shelter dykes, their arrangements so as to present a series of settling basins, etc., a description of which would only complicate the conception. Through the larger part of the river works of contraction will not be required, but nearly all the banks on the concave side of the bends must be held against the wear of the stream, and much of the opposite banks defended at critical points. The works having in view this conservative object may be generally designated works of revetment; and these also will be largely of brushwood, woven in continuous carpets, or twined into wire-netting. This veneering process has been successfully employed on the Missouri River; and in some cases they have so covered themselves with sediments, and have become so overgrown with willows, that they may be regarded as permanent. In securing these mats rubble-stone is to be used in small quantities, and in some instances the dressed slope between high and low river will have to be more or less paved with stone.

Any one who has been on the Rhine will have observed operations not unlike those to which we have just referred; and, indeed, most of the rivers of Europe flowing among their own alluvia have required similar treatment in the interest of navigation and agriculture.

The levee is the crowning work of bank revetment, although not necessarily in immediate connection. It may be set back a short distance from the revetted bank; but it is, in effect, the requisite parapet. The flood river and the low river cannot be brought into register, and compelled to unite in the excavation of a single permanent channel, without a complete control of all the stages; and even the abnormal rise must be provided against, because this would endanger the levee, and once in force behind the works of revetment would tear them also away.

Under the general principle that the local slope of a river is the result and measure of the resistance of its bed, it is evident that a narrow and deep stream should have less slope, because it has less frictional surface in proportion to capacity; *i.e.,* less perimeter in proportion to area of cross section. The ultimate effect of levees and revetments confining the floods and bringing all the stages of the river into register is to deepen the channel and let down the slope. The first effect of the levees is to raise the surface; but this, by inducing greater velocity of flow, inevitably causes an enlargement of section, and if this enlargement is prevented from being made at the expense of the banks, the bottom must give way and the form of the waterway be so improved as to admit this flow with less rise. The actual experience with levees upon the Mississippi River, with no attempt to hold the banks, has been favorable, and no one can doubt, upon the evidence furnished in the reports of the commission, that if the earliest levees had been accompanied by revetment of banks, and made complete, we should have to-day a river navigable at low water and an adjacent country safe from inundation.

Of course it would be illogical to conclude that the constrained river can ever lower its flood slope so as to make levees unnecessary, but it is believed that, by this lateral constraint, the river as a conduit may be so improved in form that even those rare floods which result from the coincident rising of many tributaries will find vent without destroying levees of ordinary height. That the actual capacity of a channel through alluvium depends upon its service during floods has been often shown, but this capacity does not include anomalous, but recurrent, floods.

It is hardly worth while to consider the projects for relieving the Mississippi River floods by creating new outlets, since these sensational propositions have commended themselves only to unthinking minds, and have no support among engineers. Were the river bed cast-iron, a resort to openings for surplus waters might be a necessity; but as the bottom is yielding, and the best form of outlet is a single deep channel, as realizing the least ratio of perimeter to area of cross section, there could not well be a more unphilosophical method of treatment than the multiplication of avenues of escape.

In the foregoing statement the attempt has been made to condense in as limited a space as the importance of the subject would permit, the general elements of the problem, and the general features of the proposed method of improvement which has been adopted by the Mississippi River Commission.

The writer cannot help feeling that it is somewhat presumptuous on his part to attempt to present the facts relating to an enterprise which calls for the highest scientific skill; but it is a matter which interests every citizen of the United States, and is one of the methods of reconstruction which ought to be approved. It is a war claim which implies no private gain, and no compensation except for one of the cases of destruction incident to war, which may well be repaired by the people of the whole country.

EDWARD ATKINSON.

BOSTON, April 14, 1882.

C

RECEPTION OF CAPTAIN BASIL HALL'S BOOK IN THE UNITED STATES

Having now arrived nearly at the end of our travels, I am induced, ere I conclude, again to mention what I consider as one of the most remarkable traits in the national character of the Americans; namely, their exquisite sensitiveness and soreness respecting everything said or written concerning them. Of this, perhaps, the most remarkable example I can give is the effect produced on nearly every class of readers by the appearance of Captain Basil Hall's "Travels in North America." In fact, it was a sort of moral earthquake, and the vibration it occasioned through the nerves of the republic, from one corner of the Union to the other, was by no means over when I left the country in July, 1831, a couple of years after the shock.

I was in Cincinnati when these volumes came out, but it was not till July, 1830, that I procured a copy of them. One bookseller to whom I applied told me that he had had a few copies before he understood the nature of the work, but that, after becoming acquainted with it, nothing should induce him to sell another. Other persons of his profession must, however, have been less scrupulous; for the book was read in city, town, village, and hamlet, steamboat, and stage-coach, and a sort of war-whoop was sent forth perfectly unprecedented in my recollection upon any occasion whatever.

An ardent desire for approbation, and a delicate sensitiveness under censure, have always, I believe, been considered as amiable traits of character; but the condition into which the appearance of Captain Hall's work threw the republic shows plainly that these feelings, if carried to excess, produce a weakness which amounts to imbecility.

It was perfectly astonishing to hear men who, on other subjects, were of some judgment utter their opinions upon this. I never heard of any instance in which the common-sense generally found in national criticism was so overthrown by passion. I do not speak of the want of justice, and of fair and liberal interpretation: these, perhaps, were hardly to be expected. Other nations have been called thin-skinned, but the citizens of the Union have, apparently, no skins at all; they wince if a breeze blows over them, unless it be tempered with adulation. It was not, therefore, very surprising that the acute and forcible observations of a traveller they knew would be listened to should be received testily. The extraordinary features of the business were, first, the excess of the rage into which they lashed themselves; and, secondly, the puerility of the inventions by which they attempted to account for the severity with which they fancied they had been treated.

Not content with declaring that the volumes contained no word of truth from beginning to end (which is an assertion I heard made very nearly as often as they were mentioned), the whole country set to work to discover the causes why Captain Hall had visited the United States, and why he had published his book.

I have heard it said with as much precision and gravity as if the statement had been conveyed by an official report, that Captain Hall had been sent out by the British government expressly for the purpose of checking the growing admiration of England for the government of the United States,—that it was by a commission from the treasury he had come, and that it was only in obedience to orders that he had found anything to object to.

I do not give this as the gossip of a coterie; I am persuaded that it is the belief of a very considerable portion of the country. So deep is the conviction of this singular people that they cannot be seen without being admired, that they will not admit the possibility that any one should honestly and sincerely find aught to disapprove in them or their country.

The American Reviews are, many of them, I believe, well known in England; I need not, therefore, quote them here, but I sometimes wondered that they, none of them, ever thought of translating Obadiah's curse into classic American; if they had done so, on placing (he, Basil Hall,) between brackets, instead of (he, Obadiah,) it would have saved them a world of trouble.

I can hardly describe the curiosity with which I sat down at length to peruse these tremendous volumes; still less can I do justice to my surprise at their contents. To say that I found not one exaggerated statement throughout the work is by no means saying enough. It is impossible for any one who knows the country not to see that Captain Hall earnestly sought out things to admire and commend. When he praises, it is with evident pleasure; and when he finds fault, it is with evident reluctance and restraint, excepting where motives purely patriotic urge him to state roundly what it is for the benefit of his country should be known.

In fact, Captain Hall saw the country to the greatest possible advantage. Furnished, of course, with letters of introduction to the most distinguished individuals, and with the still more influential recommendation of his own reputation, he was received in full drawing-room style and state from one end of the Union to the other. He saw the country in full dress, and had little or no opportunity of judging of it unhouselled, unanointed, unannealed, with all its imperfections on its head, as I and my family too often had.

Captain Hall had certainly excellent opportunities of making himself acquainted with the form of the government and the laws; and of receiving, moreover, the best oral commentary upon them, in conversation with the most distinguished citizens. Of these opportunities he made excellent use; nothing important met his eye which did not receive that sort of analytical attention which an experienced and philosophical traveller alone can give. This has made his volumes highly interesting and valuable; but I am deeply persuaded, that were a man of equal penetration to visit the United States with no other means of becoming acquainted with the national character than the ordinary working-day intercourse of life, he would conceive an infinitely lower idea of the moral atmosphere of the country than Captain Hall appears to have done; and the internal conviction on my mind is strong, that if Captain Hall had not placed a firm restraint on himself, he must have given expression to far deeper indignation than any he has uttered against many points in the American character, with which he shows from other circumstances that he was well acquainted. His rule appears to have been to state just so much of the truth as would leave on the mind of his readers a correct impression, at the least cost of pain to the sensitive folks he was writing about. He states his own opinions and feelings, and leaves it to be inferred that he has good grounds for adopting them; but he spares the Americans the bitterness which a detail of the circumstances would have produced.

If any one chooses to say that some wicked antipathy to twelve millions of strangers is the origin of my opinion, I must bear it; and were the question of mere idle speculation, I certainly would not court the abuse I must meet for stating it. But it is not so.

. . . .

The candor which he expresses, and evidently feels, they mistake for irony, or totally distrust; his unwillingness to give pain to persons from whom he has received kindness, they scornfully reject as affectation, and although they must know right well, in their own secret hearts, how infinitely more they lay at his mercy than he has chosen to betray; they pretend, even to themselves, that he has exaggerated the bad points of their character and institutions; whereas, the truth is, that he has let them off with a degree of tenderness which may be quite suitable for him to exercise, however little merited; while, at the same time, he has most industriously magnified their merits, whenever he could possibly find anything favorable.

D

THE UNDYING HEAD

In a remote part of the North lived a man and his sister, who had never seen a human being. Seldom, if ever, had the man any cause to go from home; for, as his wants demanded food, he had only to go a little distance from the lodge, and there, in some particular spot, place his arrows, with their barbs in the ground. Telling his sister where they had been placed, every morning she would go in search, and never fail of finding each stuck through the heart of a deer. She had then only to drag them into the lodge and prepare their food. Thus she lived till she attained womanhood, when one day her brother, whose name was Iamo, said to her: "Sister, the time is at hand when you will be ill. Listen to my advice. If you do not, it will probably be the cause of my death. Take the implements with which we kindle our fires. Go some distance from our lodge and build a separate fire. When you are in want of food, I will tell you where to find it. You must cook for youself, and I will for myself. When you are ill, do not attempt to come near the lodge, or bring any of the utensils you use. Be sure always to fasten to your belt the implements you need, for you do not know when the time will come. As for myself, I must do the best I can." His sister promised to obey him in all he had said.

Shortly after, her brother had cause to go from home. She was alone in her lodge, combing her hair. She had just untied the belt to which the implements were fastened, when suddenly the event, to which her brother had alluded, occurred. She ran out of the lodge, but in her haste forgot the belt. Afraid to return, she stood for some time thinking. Finally, she decided to enter the lodge and get it. For, thought she, my brother is not at home, and I will stay but a moment to catch hold of it. She went back. Running in suddenly, she caught hold of it, and was coming out when her brother came in sight. He knew what was the matter. "Oh," he said, "did I not tell you to take care? But now you have killed me." She was going on her way, but her brother said to her, "What can you do there now? The accident has happened. Go in, and stay where you have always stayed. And what will become of you? You have killed me."

He then laid aside his hunting-dress and accoutrements, and soon after both his feet began to turn black, so that he could not move. Still he directed his sister where to place the arrows, that she might always have food. The inflammation continued to increase, and had now reached his first rib; and he said: "Sister, my end is near. You must do as I tell you. You see my medicine-sack, and my war-club tied to it. It contains all my medicines, and my war-plumes, and my paints of all colors. As soon as the inflammation reaches my breast, you will take my war-club. It has a sharp point, and you will cut off my head. When it is free from my body, take it, place its neck in the sack, which you must open at one end. Then hang it up in its former place. Do not forget my bow and arrows. One of the last you will take to procure food. The remainder, tie in my sack, and then hang it up, so that I can look towards the door. Now and then I will speak to you, but not often." His sister again promised to obey.

In a little time his breast was affected. "Now," said he, "take the club and strike off my head." She was afraid, but he told her to muster courage. *"Strike,"* said he, and a smile was on his face. Mustering all her courage, she gave the blow and cut off the head. "Now," said the head, "place me where I told you." And fearfully she obeyed it in all its commands. Retaining its animation, it looked around the lodge as usual, and it would command its sister to go in such places as it thought would procure for her the flesh of different animals she needed. One day the head said: "The time is not distant when I shall be freed from this situation, and I shall have to undergo many sore evils. So the superior manito decrees, and I must bear all patiently." In this situation we must leave the head.

In a certain part of the country was a village inhabited by a numerous and warlike band of Indians. In this village was a family of ten young men—brothers. It was in the spring of the year that the youngest of these blackened his face and fasted. His dreams were propitious. Having ended his fast, he went secretly for his brothers at night, so that none in the village could overhear or find out the direction they intended to go. Though their drum was heard, yet that was a common occurrence. Having ended the usual formalities, he told how favorable his dreams were, and that he had called them together to know if they would accompany him in a war excursion. They all answered they would. The third brother from the eldest, noted for his oddities, coming up with his war-club when his brother had ceased speaking, jumped up. "Yes," said he, "I will go, and this will be the way I will treat those I am going to fight;" and he struck the post in the centre of the lodge, and gave a yell. The others spoke to him, saying: "Slow, slow, Mudjikewis, when you are in other people's lodges." So he sat down. Then, in turn, they took the drum, and sang their songs, and closed with a feast. The youngest told them not to whisper their intention to their wives, but secretly to prepare for their journey. They all promised obedience, and Mudjikewis was the first to say so.

The time for their departure drew near. Word was given to assemble on a certain night, when they would depart immediately. Mudjikewis was loud in his demands for his moccasins. Several times his wife asked him the reason. "Besides," said she, "you have a good pair on." "Quick, quick," said he, "since you must know, we are going on a war excursion; so be quick." He thus revealed the secret. That night they met and started. The snow was on the ground, and they travelled all night, lest others should follow them. When it was daylight, the leader took snow and made a ball of it, then tossing it into the air, he said: "It was in this way I saw snow fall in a dream, so that I could not be tracked." And he told them to keep close to each other for fear of losing themselves, as the snow began to fall in very large flakes. Near as they walked, it was with difficulty they could see each other. The snow continued falling all that day and the following night, so it was impossible to track them.

They had now walked for several days, and Mudjikewis was always in the rear. One day, running suddenly forward, he gave the *saw-saw-quan*,* and struck a tree with his war-club, and it broke into pieces as if struck with lightning. "Brothers," said he, "this will be the way I will serve those we are going to fight." The leader answered, "Slow, slow, Mudjikewis, the one I lead you to is not to be thought of so lightly." Again he fell back and thought to himself: "What! what! who can this be he is leading us to?" He felt fearful and was silent. Day after day they travelled on, till they came to an extensive plain, on the borders of which human bones were bleaching in the sun. The leader spoke: "They are the bones of those who have gone before us. None has ever yet returned to tell the sad tale of their fate." Again Mudjikewis became restless, and, running forward, gave the accustomed yell. Advancing to a large rock which stood above the ground, he struck it, and it fell to pieces. "See, brothers," said he, "thus will I treat those whom we are going to fight." "Still, still," once more said the leader; "he to whom I am leading you is not to be compared to the rock."

Mudjikewis fell back thoughtful, saying to himself: "I wonder who this can be that he is going to attack;" and he was afraid. Still they continued to see the remains of former warriors, who had been to the place where they were now going, some of whom had retreated as far back as the place where they first saw the bones, beyond which no one had ever escaped. At last they came to a piece of rising ground, from which they plainly distinguished, sleeping on a distant mountain, a mammoth bear.

The distance between them was very great, but the size of the animal caused him to be plainly seen. "There," said the leader, "it is he to whom I am leading you; here our troubles will commence, for he is a mishemokwa and a manito. It is he who has that we prize so dearly (*i.e.* wampum), to obtain which, the warriors whose bones we saw, sacrificed their lives. You must not be fearful; be manly. We shall find him asleep." Then the leader went forward and touched the belt around the animal's neck. "This," said he, "is what we must get. It contains the wampum." Then they requested the eldest to try and slip the belt over the bear's head, who appeared to be fast asleep, as he was not in the least disturbed by the attempt to obtain the belt. All their efforts were in vain, till it came to the one next the youngest. He tried, and the belt moved nearly over the monster's head, but he could get it no farther. Then the youngest one, and the leader, made his attempt, and succeed-

* War-whoop.

ed. Placing it on the back of the oldest, he said, "Now we must run," and off they started. When one became fatigued with its weight, another would relieve him. Thus they ran till they had passed the bones of all former warriors, and were some distance beyond, when, looking back, they saw the monster slowly rising. He stood some time before he missed his wampum. Soon they heard his tremendous howl, like distant thunder, slowly filling all the sky; and then they heard him speak and say, "Who can it be that has dared to steal my wampum? earth is not so large but that I can find them;" and he descended from the hill in pursuit. As if convulsed, the earth shook with every jump he made. Very soon he approached the party. They, however, kept the belt, exchanging it from one to another, and encouraging each other; but he gained on them fast. "Brothers," said the leader, "has never any one of you, when fasting, dreamed of some friendly spirit who would aid you as a guardian?" A dead silence followed. "Well," said he, "fasting, I dreamed of being in danger of instant death, when I saw a small lodge, with smoke curling from its top. An old man lived in it, and I dreamed he helped me; and may it be verified soon," he said, running forward and giving the peculiar yell, and a howl as if the sounds came from the depths of his stomach, and what is called *checaudum*. Getting upon a piece of rising ground, behold! a lodge, with smoke curling from its top, appeared. This gave them all new strength, and they ran forward and entered it. The leader spoke to the old man who sat in the lodge, saying, "Nemesho, help us; we claim your protection, for the great bear will kill us." "Sit down and eat, my grandchildren," said the old man. "Who is a great manito?" said he. "There is none but me; but let me look," and he opened the door of the lodge, when, lo! at a little distance he saw the enraged animal coming on, with slow but powerful leaps. He closed the door. "Yes," said he, "he is indeed a great manito: my grandchildren, you will be the cause of my losing my life; you asked my protection, and I granted it; so now, come what may, I will protect you. When the bear arrives at the door, you must run out of the other door of the lodge." Then putting his hand to the side of the lodge where he sat, he brought out a bag which he opened. Taking out two small black dogs, he placed them before him. "These are the ones I use when I fight," said he; and he commenced patting with both hands the sides of one of them, and he began to swell out, so that he soon filled the lodge by his bulk; and he had great strong teeth. When he attained his full size he growled, and from that moment, as from instinct, he jumped out at the door and met the bear, who in another leap would have reached the lodge. A terrible combat ensued. The skies rang with the howls of the fierce monsters. The remaining dog soon took the field. The brothers, at the onset, took the advice of the old man, and escaped through the opposite side of the lodge. They had not proceeded far before they heard the dying cry of one of the dogs, and soon after of the other. "Well," said the leader, "the old man will share their fate: so run; he will soon be after us." They started with fresh vigor, for they had received food from the old man: but very soon the bear came in sight, and again was fast gaining upon them. Again the leader asked the brothers if they could do nothing for their safety. All were silent. The leader, running forward, did as before. "I dreamed," he cried, "that, being in great trouble, an old man helped me who was a manito; we shall soon see his lodge." Taking courage, they still went on. After going a short distance they saw the lodge of the old manito. They entered immediately and claimed his protection, telling him a manito was after them. The old man, setting meat before them, said: "Eat! who is a manito? there is no manito but me; there is none whom I fear;" and the earth trembled as the monster advanced. The old man opened the door and saw him coming. He shut it slowly, and said: "Yes, my grandchildren, you have brought trouble upon me." Procuring his medicine-sack, he took out his small war-clubs of black stone, and told the young men to run through the other side of the lodge. As he handled the clubs, they became very large, and the old man stepped out just as the bear reached the door. Then striking him with one of the clubs, it broke in pieces; the bear stumbled. Renewing the attempt with the other war-club, that also was broken, but the bear fell senseless. Each blow the old man gave him sounded like a clap of thunder, and the howls of the bear ran along till they filled the heavens.

The young men had now run some distance, when they looked back. They could see that the bear was recovering from the blows. First he moved his paws, and soon they saw him rise on his feet. The old man shared the fate of the first, for they now heard his cries as he was torn in pieces. Again the monster was in pursuit, and fast overtaking them. Not yet discouraged, the young men kept on their way; but the bear was now so close, that the leader once more applied to his brothers, but they could do nothing. "Well," said he, "my dreams will soon be exhausted; after this I have but one more." He advanced, invoking his guardian spirit to aid him. "Once," said he, "I dreamed that, being sorely pressed, I came to a large lake, on the shore of which was a canoe, partly out of water, having ten paddles all in readiness. Do not fear," he cried, "we shall soon get it." And so it was, even as he had said. Coming to the lake, they saw the canoe with ten paddles, and immediately they embarked. Scarcely had they reached the centre of the lake, when they saw the bear arrive at its borders. Lifting himself on his hind legs, he looked all around. Then he waded into the water; then losing his footing he turned back, and commenced making the circuit of the lake. Meantime the party remained stationary in the centre to watch his movements. He travelled all around, till at last he came to the place from whence he started. Then he commenced drinking up the water, and they saw the current fast setting in towards his open mouth. The leader encouraged them to paddle hard for the opposite shore. When only a short distance from land, the current had increased so much, that they were drawn back by it, and all their efforts to reach it were in vain.

Then the leader again spoke, telling them to meet their fates manfully. "Now is the time, Mudjikewis," said he, "to show your prowess. Take courage and sit at the bow of the canoe; and when it approaches his mouth, try what effect your club will have on his head." He obeyed, and stood ready to give the blow; while the leader, who steered, directed the canoe for the open mouth of the monster.

Rapidly advancing, they were just about to enter his mouth, when Mudjikewis struck him a tremendous blow on the head, and gave the *saw-saw-quan*. The bear's limbs doubled under him, and he fell, stunned by the blow. But before Mudjikewis could renew it, the monster disgorged all the water he had drank, with a force which sent the canoe with great velocity to the opposite shore. Instantly leaving the canoe, again they fled, and on they went till they were completely exhausted. The earth again shook, and soon they saw the monster hard after them. Their spirits drooped, and they felt discouraged. The leader exerted himself, by actions and words, to cheer them up; and once more he asked them if they thought of nothing, or could do nothing for their rescue; and, as before, all were silent. "Then," he said, "this is the last time I can apply to my guardian spirit. Now, if we do not succeed, our fates are decided." He ran forward, invoking his spirit with great earnestness, and gave the yell. "We shall soon arrive," said he to his brothers, "at the place where my last guardian spirit dwells. In him I place great confidence. Do not, do not be afraid, or your limbs will be fear-bound. We shall soon reach his lodge. Run, run," he cried.

Returning now to Iamo, he had passed all the time in the same condition we had left him, the head directing his sister, in order to procure food, where to place the magic arrows, and speaking at long intervals. One day the sister saw the eyes of the head brighten, as if with pleasure. At last it spoke. "Oh, sister," it said, "in what a pitiful situation you have been the cause of placing me! Soon, very soon, a party of young men will arrive and apply to me for aid; but alas! How can I give what I would have done with so much pleasure? Nevertheless, take two arrows, and place them where you have been in the habit of placing the others, and have meat prepared and cooked before they arrive. When you hear them coming and calling on my name, go out and say, 'Alas! it is long ago that an accident befell him. I was the cause of it.' If they still come near, ask them in, and set meat before them. And now you must follow my directions strictly. When the bear is near, go out and meet him. You will take my medicine-sack, bows and arrows, and my head. You must then untie the sack, and spread out before you my paints of all colors, my war-eagle feathers, my tufts of dried hair, and whatever else it contains. As the bear approaches, you will take all these articles, one by one, and say to him, 'This is my deceased brother's paint,' and so on with all the other articles, throwing each of them as far as you can. The virtues contained in them will cause him to totter; and, to complete his destruction, you will take my head, and that too you will cast as far off as you can, crying aloud, 'See, this is my deceased brother's head.' He will then fall senseless. By this time the young men will have eaten, and you will call them to your assistance. You must then cut the carcass into pieces, yes, into small pieces, and scatter them to the four winds; for, unless you do this, he will again revive." She promised that all should be done as he said. She had only time to prepare the meat, when the voice of the leader was heard calling upon Iamo for aid. The woman went out and said as her brother had directed. But the war party being closely pursued, came up to the lodge. She invited them in, and placed the meat before them. While they were eating, they heard the bear approaching. Untying the medicine-sack and taking the head, she had all in readiness for his approach. When he came up she did as she had been told; and, before she had expended the paints and feathers, the bear began to totter, but, still advancing, came close to the woman. Saying as she was commanded, she then took the head, and cast it as far from her as she could. As it rolled along the ground, the blood, excited by the feelings of the head in this terrible scene, gushed from the nose and mouth. The bear, tottering, soon fell with a tremendous noise. Then she cried for help, and the young men came rushing out, having partially regained their strength and spirits.

Mudjikewis, stepping up, gave a yell and struck him a blow upon the head. This he repeated, till it seemed like a mass of brains, while the others, as quick as possible, cut him into very small pieces, which they then scattered in every direction. While thus employed, happening to look around where they had thrown the meat, wonderful to behold, they saw starting up and running off in every direction small black bears, such as are seen at the present day. The country was soon overspread with these black animals. And it was from this monster that the present race of bears derived their origin.

Having thus overcome their pursuer, they returned to the lodge. In the mean time, the woman, gathering the implements she had used, and the head, placed them again in the sack. But the head did not speak again, probably from its great exertion to overcome the monster.

Having spent so much time and traversed so vast a country in their flight, the young men gave up the idea of ever returning to their own country, and game being plenty, they determined to remain where they now were. One day they moved off some distance from the lodge for the purpose of hunting, having left the wampum with the woman. They were very successful, and amused themselves, as all young men do when alone, by talking and jesting with each other. One of them spoke and said, "We have all this sport to ourselves; let us go and ask our sister if she will not let us bring the head to this place, as it is still alive. It may be pleased to hear us talk, and be in our company. In the mean time take food to our sister." They went and requested the head. She told them to take it, and they took it to their hunting-grounds, and tried to amuse it, but only at times did they see its eyes beam with pleasure. One day, while busy in their encampment, they were unexpectedly attacked by unknown Indians. The skirmish was long contested and bloody; many of their foes were slain, but still they were thirty to one. The young men fought desperately till they were all killed. The attacking party then retreated to a height of ground, to muster their men, and to count the number of missing and slain. One of their young men had stayed away, and, in endeavoring to overtake them, came to the place where the head was hung up. Seeing that alone retain animation, he eyed it for some time with fear and surprise. However, he took it down and opened the sack, and was much pleased to see the beautiful feathers, one of which he placed on his head.

Starting off, it waved gracefully over him till he reached his party, when he threw down the head and sack, and told them how he had found it, and that the sack was full of paints and feathers. They all looked at the head and made sport of it. Numbers of the young men took the paint and painted themselves, and one of the party took the head by the hair and said:—

"Look, you ugly thing, and see your paints on the faces of warriors."

But the feathers were so beautiful, that numbers of them also placed them on their heads. Then again they used all kinds of indignity to the head, for which they were in turn repaid by the death of those who had used the feathers. Then the chief commanded them to throw away all except the head. "We will see," said he, "when we get home, what we can do with it. We will try to make it shut its eyes."

When they reached their homes they took it to the council-lodge, and hung it up before the fire, fastening it with raw hide soaked, which would shrink and become tightened by the action of fire. "We will then see," they said, "if we cannot make it shut its eyes."

Meantime, for several days, the sister had been waiting for the young men to bring back the head; till, at last, getting impatient, she went in search of it. The young men she found lying within short distances of each other, dead, and covered with wounds. Various other bodies lay scattered in different directions around them. She searched for the head and sack, but they were nowhere to be found. She raised her voice and wept, and blackened her face. Then she walked in different directions, till she came to the place from whence the head had been taken. Then she found the magic bow and arrows, where the young men, ignorant of their qualities, had left them. She thought to herself that she would find her brother's head, and came to a piece of rising ground, and there saw some of his paints and feathers. These she carefully put up, and hung upon the branch of a tree till her return.

At dusk she arrived at the first lodge of a very extensive village. Here she used a charm, common among Indians when they wish to meet with a kind reception. On applying to the old man and woman of the lodge, she was kindly received. She made known her errand. The old man promised to aid her, and told her the head was hung up before the council-fire, and that the chiefs of the village, with their young men, kept watch over it continually. The former are considered as manitoes. She said she only wished to see it, and would be satisfied if she could only get to the door of the lodge. She knew she had not sufficient power to take it by force. "Come with me," said the Indian, "I will take you there." They went, and they took their seats near the door. The council-lodge was filled with warriors, amusing themselves with games, and constantly keeping up a fire to smoke the head, as they said, to make dry meat. They saw the head move, and not knowing what to make of it, one spoke and said: "Ha! ha! It is beginning to feel the effects of the smoke." The sister looked up from the door, and her eyes met those of her brother, and tears rolled down the cheeks of the head. "Well," said the chief, "I thought we would make you do something at last. Look! look at it—shedding tears," said he to those around him; and they all laughed and passed their jokes upon it. The chief, looking around, and observing the woman, after some time said to the man who came with her: "Who have you got there? I have never seen that woman before in our village." "Yes," replied the man, "you have seen her; she is a relation of mine, and seldom goes out. She stays at my lodge, and asked me to allow her to come with me to this place." In the centre of the lodge sat one of those young men who are always forward, and fond of boasting and displaying themselves before others. "Why", said he, "I have seen her often, and it is to this lodge I go almost every night to court her." All the others laughed and continued their games. The young man did not know he was telling a lie to the woman's advantage, who by that means escaped.

She returned to the man's lodge, and immediately set out for her own country. Coming to the spot where the bodes of her adopted brothers lay, she placed them together, their feet toward the east. Then taking an axe which she had, she cast it up into the air, crying out, "Brothers, get up from under it, or it will fall on you." This she repeated three times, and the third time the brothers all arose and stood on their feet.

Mudjikewis commenced rubbing his eyes and stretching himself. "Why," said he, "I have overslept myself." "No, indeed," said one of the others, "do you not know we were all killed, and that it is our sister who has brought us to life?" The young men took the bodies of their enemies and burned them. Soon after, the woman went to procure wives for them, in a distant country, they knew not where; but she returned with ten young women, which she gave to the ten young men, beginning with the eldest. Mudjikewis stepped to and fro, uneasy lest he should not get the one he liked. But he was not disappointed, for she fell to his lot. And they were well matched, for she was a female magician. They then all moved into a very large lodge, and their sister told them that the women must now take turns in going to her brother's head every night, trying to untie it. They all said they would do so with pleasure. The eldest made the first attempt, and with a rushing noise she fled through the air.

Toward daylight she returned. She had been unsuccessful, as she succeeded in untying only one of the knots. All took their turns regularly, and each one succeeded in untying only one knot each time. But when the youngest went, she commenced the work as soon as she reached the lodge; although it had always been occupied, still the Indians never could see any one. For ten nights now, the smoke had not ascended, but filled the lodge and drove them out. This last night they were all driven out, and the young woman carried off the head.

The young people and the sister heard the young woman coming high through the air, and they heard her saying: "Prepare the body of our brother." And as soon as they heard it, they went to a small lodge where the black body of Iamo lay. His sister commenced cutting the neck part, from which the neck had been severed. She cut so deep as to cause it to bleed; and the others who were present, by rubbing the body and applying medicines, expelled the blackness. In the mean time the one who brought it, by cutting the neck of the head, caused that also to bleed.

As soon as she arrived, they placed that close to the body, and, by aid of medicines and various other means, succeeded in restoring Iamo to all his former beauty and manliness. All rejoiced in the happy termination of their troubles, and they had spent some time joyfully together, when Iamo said: "Now I will divide the wampum;" and getting the belt which contained it, he commenced with the eldest, giving it in equal portions. But the youngest got the most splendid and beautiful, as the bottom of the belt held the richest and rarest.

They were told that, since they had all once died, and were restored to life, they were no longer mortal, but spirits, and they were assigned different stations in the invisible world. Only Mudjukewis's place was, however, named. He was to direct the west wind, hence generally called Kebeyun, there to remain forever. They were commanded, as they had it in their power, to do good to the inhabitants of the earth, and, forgetting their sufferings in procuring the wampum, to give all things with a liberal hand. And they were also commanded that it should also be held by them sacred; those grains or shells of the pale hue to be emblematic of peace, while those of the darker hue would lead to evil and war.

The spirits then, amid songs and shouts, took their flight to their respective abodes on high; while Iamo, with his sister Iamoqua, descended into the depths below.

"A Medieval Romance" was first called *"Awful, Terrible Medieval Romance"* when it appeared as a feature in the Buffalo Express *on January 1, 1870. The story acquired its shortened title when it was published in 1871 in a slim volume along with* Mark Twain's Burlesque Autobiography. *Twain included "A Medieval Romance" in* Mark Twain's Sketches New and Old, *which appeared in 1875.*

A Medieval Romance

CHAPTER I

THE SECRET REVEALED

It was night. Stillness reigned in the grand old feudal castle of Klugenstein. The year 1222 was drawing to a close. Far away up in the tallest of the castle's towers a single light glimmered. A secret council was being held there. The stern old lord of Klugenstein sat in a chair of state meditating. Presently he said, with a tender accent—"My daughter!"

A young man of noble presence, clad from head to heel in knightly mail, answered—"Speak, father!"

"My daughter, the time is come for the revealing of the mystery that hath puzzled all your young life. Know, then, that it had its birth in the matter which I shall now unfold. My brother Ulrich is the great Duke of Brandenburgh. Our father, on his deathbed, decreed that if no son were born to Ulrich the succession should pass to my house, provided a *son* were born to me. And further, in case no son were born to either, but only daughters, then the succession should pass to Ulrich's daughter if she proved stainless; if she did not, my daughter should succeed if she retained a blameless name. And so I and my old wife here prayed fervently for the good boon of a son, but the prayer was vain. You were born to us. I was in despair. I saw the mighty prize slipping from my grasp—the splendid dream vanishing away! And I had been so hopeful! Five years had Ulrich lived in wedlock, and yet his wife had borne no heir of either sex.

" 'But hold,' I said, 'all is not lost.' A saving scheme had shot athwart my brain. You were born at midnight. Only the leech, the nurse, and six waiting-women knew your sex. I hanged them every one before an hour sped. Next morning all the barony went mad with rejoicing over the proclamation that a *son* was born to Klugenstein—an heir to mighty Brandenburgh! And well the secret has been kept. Your mother's own sister nursed your infancy, and from that time forward we feared nothing.

"When you were ten years old a daughter was born to Ulrich. We grieved, but hoped for good results from measles, or physicians, or other natural enemies of infancy, but were always disappointed. She lived, she throve—Heaven's malison upon her! But it is nothing. We are safe. For, ha! ha! have we not a son? And is not our son the future Duke? Our well-beloved Conrad, is it not so?—for woman of eight-and-twenty years as you are, my child, none other name than that hath ever fallen to *you!*

"Now it hath come to pass that age hath laid its hand upon my brother, and he waxes feeble. The cares of state do tax him sore, therefore he wills that you shall come to him and be already Duke in act, though not yet in name. Your servitors are ready—you journey forth to-night.

"Now listen well. Remember every word I say. There is a law as old as Germany, that if any woman sit for a single instant in the great ducal chair before she hath been absolutely crowned in presence of the people—SHE SHALL DIE! So heed my words. Pretend humility. Pronounce your judgments from the Premier's chair, which stands at the *foot* of the throne. Do this until you are crowned and safe. It is not likely that your sex will ever be discovered, but still it is the part of wisdom to make all things as safe as may be in this treacherous earthly life."

"O my father! is it for this my life hath been a lie? Was it that I might cheat my unoffending cousin of her rights? Spare me, father, spare your child!"

"What, hussy! Is this my reward for the august fortune my brain has wrought for thee? By the bones of my father, this puling sentiment of thine but ill accords with my humor. Betake thee to the Duke instantly, and beware how thou meddlest with my purpose!"

Let this suffice of the conversation. It is enough for us to know that the prayers, the entreaties, and the tears of the gentle-natured girl availed nothing. Neither they nor anything could move the stout old lord of Klugenstein. And so, at last, with a heavy heart, the daughter saw the castle gates close behind her, and found herself riding away in the darkness surrounded by a knightly array of armed vassals and a brave following of servants.

The old baron sat silent for many minutes after his daughter's departure, and then he turned to his sad wife, and said—

"Dame, our matters seem speeding fairly. It is full three months since I sent the shrewd and handsome Count Detzin on his devilish mission to my brother's daughter Constance. If he fail we are not wholly safe, but if he do succeed no power can bar our girl from being Duchess, e'en though ill fortune should decree she never should be Duke!"

"My heart is full of bodings; yet all may still be well."

"Tush, woman! Leave the owls to croak. To bed with ye, and dream of Brandenburgh and grandeur!"

CHAPTER II

FESTIVITY AND TEARS

Six days after the occurrences related in the above chapter, the brilliant capital of the Duchy of Brandenburgh was resplendent with military pageantry, and noisy with the rejoicings of loyal multitudes, for Conrad, the young heir to the crown, was come. The old Duke's heart was full of happiness, for Conrad's handsome person and graceful bearing had won his love at once. The great halls of the palace were thronged with nobles, who welcomed Conrad bravely; and so bright and happy did all things seem, that he felt his fears and sorrows passing away, and giving place to a comforting contentment.

But in a remote apartment of the palace a scene of a different nature was transpiring. By a window stood the Duke's only child, the Lady Constance. Her eyes were red and swollen, and full of tears. She was alone. Presently she fell to weeping anew, and said aloud—

"The villain Detzin is gone—has fled the dukedom! I could not believe it at first, but, alas! it is too true. And I loved him so. I dared to love him though I knew the Duke my father would never let me wed him. I loved him—but now I hate him! With all my soul I hate him! Oh, what is to become of me? I am lost, lost, lost! I shall go mad!"

CHAPTER III

THE PLOT THICKENS

A few months drifted by. All men published the praises of the young Conrad's government, and extolled the wisdom of his judgments, the mercifulness of his sentences, and the modesty with which he bore himself in his great office. The old Duke soon gave everything into his hands, and sat apart and listened with proud satisfaction while his heir delivered the decrees of the crown from the seat of the Premier. It seemed plain that one so loved and praised and honored of all men as Conrad was could not be otherwise than happy. But, strangely enough, he was not. For he saw with dismay that the Princess Constance had begun to love him! The love of the rest of the world was happy fortune for him, but this was freighted with danger! And he saw, moreover, that the delighted Duke had discovered his daughter's passion likewise, and was already dreaming of a marriage. Every day somewhat of the deep sadness that had been in the princess's face faded away; every day hope and animation beamed brighter from her eye; and by and by even vagrant smiles visited the face that had been so troubled.

Conrad was appalled. He bitterly cursed himself for having yielded to the instinct that had made him seek the companionship of one of his own sex when he was new and a stranger in the palace—when he was sorrowful and yearned for a sympathy such as only women can give or feel. He now began to avoid his cousin. But this only made matters worse, for naturally enough, the more he avoided her the more she cast herself in his way. He marvelled at this at first, and next it startled him. The girl haunted him; she hunted him; she happened upon him at all times and in all places, in the night as well as in the day. She seemed singularly anxious. There was surely a mystery somewhere.

This could not go on for ever. All the world was talking about it. The Duke was beginning to look perplexed. Poor Conrad was becoming a very ghost through dread and dire distress. One day as he was emerging from a private ante-room attached to the picture gallery Constance confronted him, and seizing both his hands in hers, exclaimed—

"Oh, why do you avoid me? What have I done—what have I said, to lose your kind opinion of me—for surely I had it once? Conrad, do not despise me, but pity a tortured heart? I cannot, cannot hold the words unspoken longer, lest they kill me—I LOVE

YOU, CONRAD! There, despise me if you must, but they *would* be uttered!''

Conrad was speechless. Constance hesitated a moment, and then, misinterpreting his silence, a wild gladness flamed in her eyes, and she flung her arms about his neck and said—

"You relent! you relent! You *can* love me—you *will* love me! Oh, say you will, my own, my worshipped Conrad!''

Conrad groaned aloud. A sickly pallor overspread his countenance, and he trembled like an aspen. Presently, in desperation, he thrust the poor girl from him, and cried—

"You know not what you ask! It is for ever and ever impossible!'' And then he fled like a criminal, and left the princess stupefied with amazement. A minute afterward she was crying and sobbing there, and Conrad was crying and sobbing in his chamber. Both were in despair. Both saw ruin staring them in the face.

By and by Constance rose slowly to her feet and moved away, saying—

"To think that he was despising my love at the very moment that I thought it was melting his cruel heart! I hate him! He spurned me—did this man—he spurned me from him like a dog!''

CHAPTER IV

THE AWFUL REVELATION

Time passed on. A settled sadness rested once more upon the countenance of the good Duke's daughter. She and Conrad were seen together no more now. The Duke grieved at this. But as the weeks wore away Conrad's color came back to his cheeks, and his old-time vivacity to his eye, and he administered the government with a clear and steadily ripening wisdom.

Presently a strange whisper began to be heard about the palace. It grew louder; it spread farther. The gossips of the city got hold of it. It swept the dukedom. And this is what the whisper said—

"The Lady Constance hath given birth to a child!''

When the lord of Klugenstein heard it he swung his plumed helmet thrice around his head and shouted—

"Long live Duke Conrad!—for lo, his crown is sure from this day forward! Detzin has done his errand well, and the good scoundrel shall be rewarded!''

And he spread the tidings far and wide, and for eight-and-forty hours no soul in all the barony but did dance and sing, carouse and illuminate, to celebrate the great event, and all at proud and happy old Klugenstein's expense.

CHAPTER V

THE FRIGHTFUL CATASTROPHE

The trial was at hand. All the great lords and barons of Brandenburgh were assembled in the Hall of Justice in the ducal palace. No space was left unoccupied where there was room for a spectator to stand or sit. Conrad, clad in purple and ermine, sat in the Premier's chair, and on either side sat the great judges of the realm. The old Duke had sternly commanded that the trial of his daughter should proceed without favor, and then had taken to his bed broken-hearted. His days were numbered. Poor Conrad had begged, as for his very life, that he might be spared the misery of sitting in judgment upon his cousin's crime, but it did not avail.

The saddest heart in all that great assemblage was in Conrad's breast.

The gladdest was in his father's, for, unknown to his daughter "Conrad," the old Baron Klugenstein was come, and was among the crowd of nobles triumphant in the swelling fortunes of his house.

After the heralds had made due proclamation and the other preliminaries had followed, the venerable Lord Chief-Justice said—"Prisoner, stand forth!"

The unhappy princess rose, and stood unveiled before the vast multitude. The Lord Chief-Justice continued—

"Most noble lady, before the great judges of this realm it hath been charged and proven that out of holy wedlock your Grace hath given birth unto a child, and by our ancient law the penalty is death excepting in one sole contingency, whereof his Grace the acting Duke, our good Lord Conrad, will advertise you in his solemn sentence now; wherefore give heed."

Conrad stretched forth his reluctant sceptre, and in the self-same moment the womanly heart beneath his robe yearned pityingly toward the doomed prisoner, and the tears came into his eyes. He opened his lips to speak, but the Lord Chief-Justice said quickly—

"Not there, your Grace, not there! It is not lawful to pronounce judgment upon any of the ducal line SAVE FROM THE DUCAL THRONE!"

A shudder went to the heart of poor Conrad, and a tremor shook the iron frame of his old father likewise. CONRAD HAD NOT BEEN CROWNED—dared he profane the throne? He hesitated and turned pale with fear. But it must be done. Wondering eyes were already upon him. They would be suspicious eyes if he hesitated longer. He ascended the throne. Presently he stretched forth the sceptre again, and said—

"Prisoner, in the name of our sovereign Lord Ulrich, Duke of Brandenburgh, I proceed to the solemn duty that hath devolved upon me. Give heed to my words. By the ancient law of the land, except you produce the partner of your guilt and deliver him up to the executioner you must surely die. Embrace this opportunity—save yourself while yet you may. Name the father of your child!"

A solemn hush fell upon the great court—a silence so profound that men could hear their own hearts beat. Then the princess slowly turned, with eyes gleaming with hate, and pointing her finger straight at Conrad, said—

"Thou art the man!"

An appalling conviction of his helpless, hopeless peril struck a chill to Conrad's heart like the chill of death itself. What power on earth could save him! To disprove the charge he must reveal that he was a woman, and for an uncrowned woman to sit in the ducal chair was death! At one and the same moment he and his grim old father swooned and fell to the ground.

* * * * * * * * *

The remainder of this thrilling and eventful story will not be found in this or any other publication, either now or at any future time.

The truth is, I have got my hero (or heroine) into such a particularly close place that I do not see how I am ever going to get him (or her) out of it again, and therefore I will wash my hands of the whole business, and leave that person to get the best way that offers—or else stay there. I thought it was going to be easy enough to straighten out that little difficulty, but it looks different now.

For the first publication of "Extracts from Adam's Diary" in the Niagara Book, *a souvenir publication sold at the Buffalo World's Fair in 1893, Twain obligingly added several references to Niagara Falls. This material was cut when the story was published in the London edition of* Tom Sawyer, Detective *in 1897, and later in the New York edition of* The $30,000 Bequest *in 1906, but it was retained in the version that appeared as a separate volume in New York in 1904. This edition was reprinted in 1931 along with a companion piece, "Eve's Diary," as* The Private Lives of Adam and Eve.

Extracts from Adam's Diary

Translated from the original Ms.

[NOTE. — *I translated a portion of this diary some years ago, and a friend of mine printed a few copies in an incomplete form, but the public never got them. Since then I have deciphered some more of Adam's hieroglyphics, and think he has now become sufficiently important as a public character to justify this publication.—M.T.]*

Monday

This new creature with the long hair is a good deal in the way. It is always hanging around and following me about. I don't like this; I am not used to company. I wish it would stay with the other animals. . . . Cloudy to-day, wind in the east; think we shall have rain. . . . *We?* Where did I get that word? . . . I remember now—the new creature uses it.

Tuesday

Been examining the great waterfall. It is the finest thing on the estate, I think. The new creature calls it Niagara Falls—why, I am sure I do not know. Says it *looks* like Niagara Falls. That is not a reason; it is mere waywardness and imbecility. I get no chance to name anything myself. The new creature names everything that comes along, before I can get in a protest. And always that same pretext is offered—it *looks* like the thing. There is the dodo, for instance. Says the moment one looks at it one sees at a glance that it "looks like a dodo." It will have to keep that name, no doubt. It wearies me to fret about it, and it does no good, anyway. Dodo! It looks no more like a dodo than I do.

523

Wednesday

Built me a shelter against the rain, but could not have it to myself in peace. The new creature intruded. When I tried to put it out it shed water out of the holes it looks with, and wiped it away with the back of its paws, and made a noise such as some of the other animals make when they are in distress. I wish it would not talk; it is always talking. That sounds like a cheap fling at the poor creature, a slur; but I do not mean it so. I have never heard the human voice before, and any new and strange sound intruding itself here upon the solemn hush of these dreaming solitudes offends my ear and seems a false note. And this new sound is so close to me; it is right at my shoulder, right at my ear, first on one side and then on the other, and I am used only to sounds that are more or less distant from me.

Friday

The naming goes recklessly on, in spite of anything I can do. I had a very good name for the estate, and it was musical and pretty—GARDEN-OF-EDEN. Privately, I continue to call it that, but not any longer publicly. The new creature says it is all woods and rocks and scenery, and therefore has no resemblance to a garden. Says it *looks* like a park, and does not look like anything *but* a park. Consequently, without consulting me, it has been new-named—NIAGARA FALLS PARK. This is sufficiently high-handed, it seems to me. And already there is a sign up:

> **KEEP OFF**
> **THE GRASS**

My life is not as happy as it was.

Saturday

The new creature eats too much fruit. We are going to run short, most likely. "We" again—that is *its* word; mine too, now, from hearing it so much. Good deal of fog this morning. I do not go out in the fog myself. The new creature does. It goes out in all weathers, and stumps right in with its muddy feet. And talks. It used to be so pleasant and quiet here.

Sunday

Pulled through. This day is getting to be more and more trying. It was selected and set apart last November as a day of rest. I already had six of them per week, before. This morning found the new creature trying to clod apples out of that forbidden tree.

Monday

The new creature says its name is Eve. That is all right, I have no objections. Says it is to call it by when I want it to come. I said it was superfluous, then. The word evidently raised me in its respect; and indeed it is a large, good word, and will bear repetition. It says it is not an It, it is a She. This is probably doubtful; yet it is all one to me; what she is were nothing to me if she would but go by herself and not talk.

Tuesday

She has littered the whole estate with execrable names and offensive signs:

☞ THIS WAY TO THE WHIRLPOOL.

☞ THIS WAY TO GOAT ISLAND.

☞ CAVE OF THE WINDS THIS WAY.

She says this park would make a tidy summer resort, if there was any custom for it. Summer resort—another invention of hers—just words, without any meaning. What is a summer resort? But it is best not to ask her, she has such a rage for explaining.

Friday

She has taken to beseeching me to stop going over the Falls. What harm does it do? Says it makes her shudder. I wonder why. I have always done it—always liked the plunge, and the excitement, and the coolness. I supposed it was what the Falls were for. They have no other use that I can see, and they must have been made for something. She says they were only made for scenery—like the rhinoceros and the mastodon.

I went over the Falls in a barrel—not satisfactory to her. Went over in a tub—still not satisfactory. Swam the Whirlpool and the Rapids in a fig-leaf suit. It got much damaged. Hence, tedious complaints about my extravagance. I am too much hampered here. What I need is change of scene.

Saturday

I escaped last Tuesday night, and travelled two days, and built me another shelter, in a secluded place, and obliterated my tracks as well as I could, but she hunted me out by means of a beast which she has tamed and calls a wolf, and came making

525

that pitiful noise again, and shedding that water out of the places she looks with. I was obliged to return with her, but will presently emigrate again, when occasion offers. She engages herself in many foolish things: among others, trying to study out why the animals called lions and tigers live on grass and flowers, when, as she says, the sort of teeth they wear would indicate that they were intended to eat each other. This is foolish, because to do that would be to kill each other, and that would introduce what, as I understand it, is called "death"; and death, as I have been told, has not yet entered the Park. Which is a pity. on some accounts.

Sunday
Pulled through.

Monday
I believe I see what the week is for: it is to give time to rest up from the weariness of Sunday. It seems a good idea. . . . She has been climbing that tree again. Clodded her out of it. She said nobody was looking. Seems to consider that a sufficient justification for chancing any dangerous thing. Told her that. The word justification moved her admiration—and envy too, I thought. It is a good word.

Tuesday
She told me she was made out of a rib taken from my body. This is at least doubtful, if not more than that. I have not missed any rib. . . . She is in much trouble about the buzzard; says grass does not agree with it; is afraid she can't raise it; thinks it was intended to live on decayed flesh. The buzzard must get along the best it can with what is provided. We cannot overturn the whole scheme to accommodate the buzzard.

Saturday
She fell in the pond yesterday, when she was looking at herself in it, which she is always doing. She nearly strangled, and said it was most uncomfortable. This made her sorry for the creatures which live in there, which she calls fish, for she continues to fasten names on to things that don't need them and don't come when they are called by them, which is a matter of no consequence to her, as she is such a numskull anyway; so she got a lot of them out and brought them in last night and put them in my bed to keep warm, but I have noticed them now and then all day, and I don't see that they are any happier there than they were before, only quieter. When night comes I shall throw them out-

doors. I will not sleep with them again, for I find them clammy and unpleasant to lie among when a person hasn't anything on.

Sunday
Pulled through.

Tuesday
She has taken up with a snake now. The other animals are glad, for she was always experimenting with them and bothering them; and I am glad, because the snake talks, and this enables me to get a rest.

Friday
She says the snake advises her to try the fruit of that tree, and says the result will be a great and fine and noble education. I told her there would be another result, too—it would introduce death into the world. That was a mistake—it had been better to keep the remark to myself; it only gave her an idea—she could save the sick buzzard, and furnish fresh meat to the despondent lions and tigers. I advised her to keep away from the tree. She said she wouldn't. I foresee trouble. Will emigrate.

Wednesday
I have had a variegated time. I escaped that night, and rode a horse all night as fast as he could go, hoping to get clear out of the Park and hide in some other country before the trouble should begin; but it was not to be. About an hour after sunup, as I was riding through a flowery plain where thousands of animals were grazing, slumbering, or playing with each other, according to their wont, all of a sudden they broke into a tempest of frightful noises, and in one moment the plain was in a frantic commotion and every beast was destroying its neighbor. I knew what it meant—Eve had eaten that fruit, and death was come into the world. . . . The tigers ate my horse, paying no attention when I ordered them to desist, and they would even have eaten me if I had stayed—which I didn't, but went away in much haste. . . . I found this place, outside the Park, and was fairly comfortable for a few days, but she has found me out. Found me out, and has named the place Tonawanda—says it *looks* like that. In fact, I was not sorry she came, for there are but meagre pickings here, and she brought some of those apples. I was obliged to eat them, I was so hungry. It was against my principles, but I find that principles have no real force except when one is well fed. . . . She came curtained in boughs and bunches of leaves, and when I asked her what she meant by such

nonsense, and snatched them away and threw them down, she tittered and blushed. I had never seen a person titter and blush before, and to me it seemed unbecoming and idiotic. She said I would soon know how it was myself. This was correct. Hungry as I was, I laid down the apple half eaten—certainly the best one I ever saw, considering the lateness of the season—and arrayed myself in the discarded boughs and branches, and then spoke to her with some severity and ordered her to go and get some more and not make such a spectacle of herself. She did it, and after this we crept down to where the wild-beast battle had been, and collected some skins, and I made her patch together a couple of suits proper for public occasions. They are uncomfortable, it is true, but stylish, and that is the main point about clothes. . . . I find she is a good deal of a companion. I see I should be lonesome and depressed without her, now that I have lost my property. Another thing, she says it is ordered that we work for our living hereafter. She will be useful. I will superintend.

Ten Days Later

She accuses *me* of being the cause of our disaster! She says, with apparent sincerity and truth, that the Serpent assured her that the forbidden fruit was not apples, it was chestnuts. I said I was innocent, then, for I had not eaten any chestnuts. She said the Serpent informed her that "chestnut" was a figurative term meaning an aged and mouldy joke. I turned pale at that, for I have made many jokes to pass the weary time, and some of them could have been of that sort, though I had honestly supposed that they were new when I made them. She asked me if I had made one just at the time of the catastrophe. I was obliged to admit that I had made one to myself, though not aloud. It was this. I was thinking about the Falls, and I said to myself, "How wonderful it is to see that vast body of water tumble down there!" Then in an instant a bright thought flashed into my head, and I let it fly, saying, "It would be a deal more wonderful to see it tumble *up* there!"—and I was just about to kill myself with laughing at it when all nature broke loose in war and death, and I had to flee for my life. "There," she said, with triumph, "that is just it; the Serpent mentioned that very jest, and called it the First Chestnut, and said it was coeval with the creation." Alas, I am indeed to blame. Would that I were not witty; oh, would that I had never had that radiant thought!

Next Year

We have named it Cain. She caught it while I was up country trapping on the North Shore of the Erie; caught it in the timber a couple of miles from our dug-out—or it might have been four, she isn't certain which. It resembles us in some ways, and may be a relation. That is what she thinks, but this is an error, in my judgment. The difference in size warrants the conclusion that it is a different and new kind of animal—a fish, perhaps, though when I put it in the water to see, it sank, and she plunged in and snatched it out before there was opportunity for the experiment to determine the matter. I still think it is a fish, but she is indifferent about what it is, and will not let me have it to try. I do not understand this. The coming of the creature seems to have changed her whole nature and made her unreasonable about experiments. She thinks more of it than she does of any of the other animals, but is not able to explain why. Her mind is disordered—everything shows it. Sometimes she carries the fish in her arms half the night when it complains and wants to get to the water. At such times the water comes out of the places in her face that she looks out of, and she pats the fish on the back and makes soft sounds with her mouth to soothe it, and betrays sorrow and solicitude in a hundred ways. I have never seen her do like this with any other fish, and it troubles me greatly. She used to carry the young tigers around so, and play with them, before we lost our property; but it was only play; she never took on about them like this when their dinner disagreed with them.

Sunday

She doesn't work Sundays, but lies around all tired out, and likes to have the fish wallow over her; and she makes fool noises to amuse it, and pretends to chew its paws, and that makes it laugh. I have not seen a fish before that could laugh. This makes me doubt. . . . I have come to like Sunday myself. Superintending all the week tires a body so. There ought to be more Sundays. In the old days they were tough, but now they come handy.

Wednesday

It isn't a fish. I cannot quite make out what it is. It makes curious, devilish noises when not satisfied, and says "goo-goo" when it is. It is not one of us, for it doesn't walk; it is not a bird, for it doesn't fly; it is not a frog, for it doesn't hop; it is not a snake, for it doesn't crawl; I feel sure it is not a fish, though I cannot get a chance to find out whether it can swim or not. It merely lies around, and mostly on its back, with its feet up. I have not seen any other animal do that before. I said I believed it was an enigma, but she only admired the word without understanding it. In my judgment it is either an enigma or some kind of a bug. If it dies, I will take it apart and see what its arrangements are. I never had a thing perplex me so.

Three Months Later

The perplexity augments instead of diminishing. I sleep but little. It has ceased from lying around, and goes about on its four legs now. Yet it differs from the other four-legged animals in that its front legs are unusually short, consequently this causes the main part of its person to stick up uncomfortably high in the air, and this is not attractive. It is built much as we are, but its method of travelling shows that it is not of our breed. The short front legs and long hind ones indicate that it is of the kangaroo family, but it is a marked variation of the species, since the true kangaroo hops, whereas this one never does. Still, it is a curious and interesting variety, and has not been catalogued before. As I discovered it, I have felt justified in securing the credit of the discovery by attaching my name to it, and hence have called it *Kangaroorum Adamiensis*. . . . It must have been a young one when it came, for it has grown exceedingly since. It must be five times as big, now, as it was then, and when discontented is able to make from twenty-two to thirty-eight times the noise it made at first. Coercion does not modify this, but has the contrary effect. For this reason I discontinued the system. She reconciles it by persuasion, and by giving it things which she had previously told it she wouldn't give it. As already observed, I was not at home when it first came, and she told me she found it in the woods. It seems odd that it should be the only one, yet it must be so, for I have worn myself out these many weeks trying to find another one to add to my collection, and for this one to play with; for surely then it would be quieter, and we could tame it more easily. But I find none, nor any vestige of any; and strangest of all, no tracks. It has to live on the ground, it cannot help itself; therefore, how does it get about without leaving a track? I have set a dozen traps, but they do no good. I catch all small animals except that one; animals that merely go into the trap out of curiosity, I think, to see what the milk is there for. They never drink it.

Three Months Later

The kangaroo still continues to grow, which is very strange and perplexing. I never knew one to be so long getting its growth. It has fur on its head now; not like kangaroo fur, but exactly like our hair, except that it is much finer and softer, and instead of being black is red. I am like to lose my mind over the capricious and harassing developments of this unclassifiable zoological freak. If I could catch another one—but that is hopeless; it is a new variety, and the only sample; this is plain. But I caught a true kangaroo and brought it in, thinking that this one, being lonesome, would rather have that for company than have no kin at all, or any animal it could feel a nearness to or get sympathy from in its forlorn condition here among strangers who do not know its ways or habits, or what to do to make it feel that it is among friends; but it was a mistake—it went into such fits at the sight of the kangaroo that I was convinced it had never seen one before. I pity the poor noisy little animal, but there is nothing I can do to make it happy. If I could tame it—but that is out of the question; the more I try, the worse I seem to make it. It grieves me to the heart to see it in its little storms of sorrow and passion. I wanted to let it go, but she wouldn't hear of it. That seemed cruel and not like her; and yet she may be right. It might be lonelier than ever; for since I cannot find another one, how could *it?*

Five Months Later

It is not a kangaroo. No, for it supports itself by holding to her finger, and thus goes a few steps on its hind legs, and then falls down. It is probably some kind of a bear; and yet it has no tail—as yet—and no fur, except on its head. It still keeps on growing—that is a curious circumstance, for bears get their growth earlier than this. Bears are dangerous—since our catastrophe—and I shall not be satisfied to have this one prowling about the place much longer without a muzzle on. I have offered to get her a kangaroo if she would let this one go, but it did no good—she is determined to run us into all sorts of foolish risks, I think. She was not like this before she lost her mind.

A Fortnight Later

I examined its mouth. There is no danger yet; it has only one tooth. It has no tail yet. It makes more noise now than it ever did before—and mainly at night. I have moved out. But I shall go over, mornings, to breakfast, and to see if it has more teeth. If it gets a mouthful of teeth, it will be time for it to go, tail or no tail, for a bear does not need a tail in order to be dangerous.

Four Months Later

I have been off hunting and fishing a month, up in the region that she calls Buffalo; I don't know why, unless it is because there are not any buffaloes there. Meantime the bear has learned to paddle around all by itself on its hind legs, and says "poppa" and "momma." It is certainly a new species. This resemblance to words may be purely accidental, of course, and may have no purpose or meaning; but even in that case it is still extraordinary, and is a thing which no other bear can do. This imitation of speech, taken together with general absence of fur and entire absence of tail, sufficiently indicates that this is a new kind of bear. The further study of it will be exceedingly interesting. Meantime I will go off on a far expedition among the forests of the North and make an exhaustive search. There must certainly be another one somewhere, and this one will be less dangerous when it has company of its own species. I will go straightway; but I will muzzle this one first.

Three Months Later

It has been a weary, weary hunt, yet I have had no success. In the mean time, without stirring from the home estate, she has caught another one! I never saw such luck. I might have hunted these woods a hundred years, I never should have run across that thing.

Next Day

I have been comparing the new one with the old one, and it is perfectly plain that they are the same breed. I was going to stuff one of them for my collection, but she is prejudiced against it for some reason or other; so I have relinquished the idea, though I think it is a mistake. It would be an irreparable loss to science if they should get away. The old one is tamer than it was, and can laugh and talk like the parrot, having learned this, no doubt, from being with the parrot so much, and having the imitative faculty in a highly developed degree. I shall be astonished if it turns out to be a new kind of parrot; and yet I ought not to be astonished, for it has already been everything else it could think of, since those first days when it was a fish. The new one is as ugly now as the old one was at first; has the same sulphur-and-raw-meat complexion and the same singular head without any fur on it. She calls it Abel.

Ten Years Later

They are boys; we found it out long ago. It was their coming in that small, immature shape that puzzled us; we were not used to it. There are some girls now. Abel is a good boy, but if Cain had stayed a bear it would have improved him. After all these years, I see that I was mistaken about Eve in the beginning; it is better to live outside the Garden with her than inside it without her. At first I thought she talked too much; but now I should be

sorry to have that voice fall silent and pass out of my life.
Blessed be the chestnut that brought us near together and taught
me to know the goodness of her heart and the sweetness of her
spirit!

"Eve's Diary" was written in 1905; its epitaph becomes especially poignant when one remembers that Twain's wife, Livy, had died the previous June. The story made its first appearance in the December 1905 issue of Harper's *magazine, and in March of the following year it was included in* Their Husband's Wives. *Several months later, in June 1906, the story was issued in a separate volume. In 1931, it was collected with "Extracts from Adam's Diary" in* The Private Lives of Adam and Eve.

Eve's Diary

Translated from the Original

Saturday

I am almost a whole day old, now. I arrived yesterday. That is
as it seems to me. And it must be so, for if there was a day-
before-yesterday I was not there when it happened, or I should
remember it. It could be, of course, that it did happen, and that
I was not noticing. Very well; I will be very watchful, now, and
if any day-before-yesterdays happen I will make a note of it. It
will be best to start right and not let the record get confused, for
some instinct tells me that these details are going to be important
to the historian some day. For I feel like an experiment, I feel exactly like an experiment; it would be impossible for a person to
feel more like an experiment than I do, and so I am coming to
feel convinced that that is what I *am*—an experiment; just an experiment, and nothing more.

Then if I am an experiment, am I the whole of it? No, I think
not; I think the rest of it is part of it. I am the main part of it, but
I think the rest of it has its share in the matter. Is my position
assured, or do I have to watch it and take care of it? The latter,
perhaps. Some instinct tells me that eternal vigilance is the price
of supremacy. [That is a good phrase, I think, for one so
young.]

Everything looks better to-day than it did yesterday. In the
rush of finishing up yesterday, the mountains were left in a ragged condition, and some of the plains were so cluttered with rubbish and remnants that the aspects were quite distressing. Noble
and beautiful works of art should not be subjected to haste; and

535

this majestic new world is indeed a most noble and beautiful work. And certainly marvellously near to being perfect, notwithstanding the shortness of the time. There are too many stars in some places and not enough in others, but that can be remedied presently, no doubt. The moon got loose last night, and slid down and fell out of the scheme—a very great loss; it breaks my heart to think of it. There isn't another thing among the ornaments and decorations that is comparable to it for beauty and finish. It should have been fastened better. If we can only get it back again—

But of course there is no telling where it went to. And besides, whoever gets it will hide it; I know it because I would do it myself. I believe I can be honest in all other matters, but I already begin to realize that the core and centre of my nature is love of the beautiful, a passion for the beautiful, and that it would not be safe to trust me with a moon that belonged to another person and that person didn't know I had it. I could give up a moon that I found in the daytime, because I should be afraid some one was looking; but if I found it in the dark, I am sure I should find some kind of an excuse for not saying anything about it. For I do love moons, they are so pretty and so romantic. I wish we had five or six; I would never go to bed; I should never get tired lying on the moss-bank and looking up at them.

Stars are good, too. I wish I could get some to put in my hair. But I suppose I never can. You would be surprised to find how far off they are, for they do not look it. When they first showed, last night, I tried to knock some down with a pole, but it didn't reach, which astonished me; then I tried clods till I was all tired out, but I never got one. It was because I am left-handed and cannot throw good. Even when I aimed at the one I wasn't after I couldn't hit the other one, though I did make some close shots, for I saw the black blot of the clod sail right into the midst of the golden clusters forty or fifty times, just barely missing them, and if I could have held out a little longer maybe I could have got one.

So I cried a little, which was natural, I suppose, for one of my age, and after I was rested I got a basket and started for a place on the extreme rim of the circle, where the stars were close to the ground and I could get them with my hands, which would be better, anyway, because I could gather them tenderly then, and not break them. But it was farther than I thought, and at last I had to give it up; I was so tired I couldn't drag my feet another step; and besides, they were sore and hurt me very much.

I couldn't get back home; it was too far, and turning cold; but

I found some tigers, and nestled in among them and was most adorably comfortable, and their breath was sweet and pleasant, because they live on strawberries. I had never seen a tiger before, but I knew them in a minute by the stripes. If I could have one of those skins, it would make a lovely gown.

To-day I am getting better ideas about distances. I was so eager to get hold of every pretty thing that I giddily grabbed for it, sometimes when it was too far off, and sometimes when it was but six inches away but seemed a foot—alas, with thorns between! I learned a lesson; also I made an axiom, all out of my own head—my very first one: *The scratched Experiment shuns the thorn*. I think it is a very good one for one so young.

I followed the other Experiment around, yesterday afternoon, at a distance, to see what it might be for, if I could. But I was not able to make out. I think it is a man. I had never seen a man, but it looked like one, and I feel sure that that is what it is. I realize that I feel more curiosity about it than about any of the other reptiles. If it is a reptile, and I suppose it is; for it has frowsy hair and blue eyes, and looks like a reptile. It has no hips; it tapers like a carrot; when it stands, it spreads itself apart like a derrick; so I think it is a reptile, though it may be architecture.

I was afraid of it at first, and started to run every time it turned around, for I thought it was going to chase me; but by-and-by I found it was only trying to get away, so after that I was not timid any more, but tracked it along, several hours, about twenty yards behind, which made it nervous and unhappy. At last it was a good deal worried, and climbed a tree. I waited a good while, then gave it up and went home.

To-day the same thing over. I've got it up the tree again.

Sunday

It is up there yet. Resting, apparently. But that is a subterfuge: Sunday isn't the day of rest; Saturday is appointed for that. It looks to me like a creature that is more interested in resting than in anything else. It would tire me to rest so much. It tires me just to sit around and watch the tree. I do wonder what it is for; I never see it do anything.

They returned the moon last night, and I was *so* happy! I think it is very honest of them. It slid down and fell off again, but I was not distressed; there is no need to worry when one has that kind of neighbors; they will fetch it back. I wish I could do something to show my appreciation. I would like to send them some stars, for we have more than we can use. I mean I, not we, for I can see that the reptile cares nothing for such things.

It has low tastes, and is n r   v er ! went there yesterday evening in the gloaming it had crept down and was trying to catch the little speckled fishes that play in the pool, and I had to clod it to make it go up the tree again and let them alone. I wonder if *that* is what it is for? Hasn't it any heart? Hasn't it any compassion for those little creatures? Can it be that it was designed and manufactured for such ungentle work? It has the look of it. One of the clods took it back of the ear, and it used language. It gave me a thrill, for it was the first time I had ever heard speech, except my own. I did not understand the words, but they seemed expressive.

When I found it could talk, I felt a new interest in it, for I love to talk; I talk all day, and in my sleep, too, and I am very interesting, but if I had another to talk to I could be twice as interesting, and would never stop, if desired.

If this reptile is a man, it isn't an *it,* is it? That wouldn't be grammatical, would it? I think it would be *he.* I think so. In that case one would parse it thus: nominative, *he*; dative, *him*; possessive, *his'n*. Well, I will consider it a man and call it he until it turns out to be something else. This will be handier than having so many uncertainties.

Next week Sunday

All the week I tagged around after him and tried to get acquainted. I had to do the talking, because he was shy, but I don't mind it. He seemed pleased to have me around, and I used the sociable "we" a good deal, because it seemed to flatter him to be included.

Wednesday

We are getting along very well indeed, now, and getting better and better acquainted. He does not try to avoid me any more, which is a good sign, and shows that he likes to have me with him. That pleases me, and I study to be useful to him in every way I can, so as to increase his regard. During the last day or two I have taken all the work of naming things off his hands, and this has been a great relief to him, for he has no gift in that line, and is evidently very grateful. He can't think of a rational name to save him, but I do not let him see that I am aware of his defect. Whenever a new creature comes along, I name it before he has time to expose himself by an awkward silence. In this way I have saved him many embarrassments. I have no defect like his. The minute I set eyes on an animal I know what it is. I don't have to reflect a moment; the right name comes out instantly, just as if it were an inspiration, as no doubt it is, for I am sure it wasn't in me half a minute before. I seem to know just by the shape of the creature and the way it acts what animal it is.

When the dodo came along he thought it was a wildcat—I saw it in his eye. But I saved him. And I was careful not to do it in a way that could hurt his pride. I just spoke up in a quite natural way of pleased surprise, and not as if I was dreaming of conveying information, and said, "Well, I do declare if there isn't the dodo!" I explained—without seeming to be explaining—how I knew it for a dodo, and although I thought maybe he was a little piqued that I knew the creature when he didn't, it was quite evident that he admired me. That was very agreeable, and I thought of it more than once with gratification before I slept. How little a thing can make us happy when we feel that we have earned it.

Thursday

My first sorrow. Yesterday he avoided me and seemed to wish I would not talk to him. I could not believe it, and thought there was some mistake, for I loved to be with him, and loved to hear him talk, and so how could it be that he could feel unkind towards me when I had not done anything? But at last it seemed true, so I went away and sat lonely in the place where I first saw him the morning that we were made and I did not know what he was and was indifferent about him; but now it was a mournful place, and every little thing spoke of him, and my heart was very sore. I did not know why very clearly, for it was a new feeling; I had not experienced it before, and it was all a mystery, and I could not make it out.

But when night came I could not bear the lonesomeness, and went to the new shelter which he has built, to ask him what I had done that was wrong and how I could mend it and get back his kindness again; but he put me out in the rain, and it was my first sorrow.

Sunday

It is pleasant again, now, and I am happy; but those were heavy days; I do not think of them when I can help it.

I tried to get him some of those apples, but I cannot learn to throw straight. I failed, but I think the good intention pleased him. They are forbidden, and he says I shall come to harm; but so I come to harm through pleasing him, why shall I care for that harm?

Monday

This morning I told him my name, hoping it would interest

him. But he did not care for it. It is strange. If he should tell me his name, I would care. I think it would be pleasanter in my ears than any other sound.

He talks very little. Perhaps it is because he is not bright, and is sensitive about it and wishes to conceal it. It is such a pity that he should feel so, for brightness is nothing; it is in the heart that the values lie. I wish I could make him understand that a loving good heart is riches, and riches enough, and that without it intellect is poverty.

Although he talks so little he has quite a considerable vocabulary. This morning he used a surprisingly good word. He evidently recognized, himself, that it was a good one, for he worked it in twice afterwards, casually. It was not good casual art, still it showed that he possesses a certain quality of perception. Without a doubt that seed can be made to grow, if cultivated.

Where did he get that word? I do not think I have ever used it.

No, he took no interest in my name. I tried to hide my disappointment, but I suppose I did not succeed. I went away and sat on the moss-bank with my feet in the water. It is where I go when I hunger for companionship, some one to look at, some one to talk to. It is not enough—that lovely white body painted there in the pool—but it is something, and something is better than utter loneliness. It talks when I talk; it is sad when I am sad; it comforts me with its sympathy; it says, "Do not be downhearted, you poor friendless girl; I will be your friend." It *is* a good friend to me, and my only one; it is my sister.

That first time that she forsook me! ah, I shall never forget that—never, never. My heart was lead in my body! I said, "She was all I had, and now she is gone!" In my despair I said, "Break, my heart; I cannot bear my life any more!" and hid my face in my hands, and there was no solace for me. And when I took them away, after a little, there she was again, white and shining and beautiful, and I sprang into her arms!

That was perfect happiness; I had known happiness before, but it was not like this, which was ecstasy. I never doubted her afterwards. Sometimes she stayed away—maybe an hour, maybe almost the whole day, but I waited and did not doubt; I said, "She is busy, or she is gone a journey, but she will come." And it was so: she always did. At night she would not come if it was dark, for she was a timid little thing; but if there was a moon she would come. I am not afraid of the dark, but she is younger than I am; she was born after I was. Many and many are the visits I have paid her; she is my comfort and my refuge when my life is hard—and it is mainly that.

Tuesday

All the morning I was at work improving the estate; and I purposely kept away from him in the hope that he would get lonely and come. But he did not.

At noon I stopped for the day and took my recreation by flitting all about with the bees and butterflies and revelling in the flowers, those beautiful creatures that catch the smile of God out of the sky and preserve it! I gathered them, and made them into wreaths and garlands and clothed myself in them while I ate my luncheon—apples, of course; then I sat in the shade and wished and waited. But he did not come.

But no matter. Nothing would have come of it, for he does not care for flowers. He calls them rubbish, and cannot tell one from another, and thinks it is superior to feel like that. He does not care for me, he does not care for flowers, he does not care for the painted sky at eventide—is there anything he does care for, except building shacks to coop himself up in from the good clean rain, and thumping the melons, and sampling the grapes, and fingering the fruit on the trees, to see how those properties are coming along?

I laid a dry stick on the ground and tried to bore a hole in it with another one, in order to carry out a scheme that I had, and soon I got an awful fright. A thin, transparent, bluish film rose out of the hole, and I dropped everything and ran! I thought it was a spirit, and I *was* so frightened! But I looked back, and it was not coming; so I leaned against a rock and rested and panted, and let my limbs go on trembling until they got steady again; then I crept warily back, alert, watching, and ready to fly if there was occasion; and when I was come near, I parted the branches of a rose-bush and peeped through—wishing the man was about, I was looking so cunning and pretty—but the sprite was gone. I went there, and there was a pinch of delicate pink dust in the hole. I put my finger in, to feel it, and said *ouch!* and took it out again. It was a cruel pain. I put my finger in my mouth; and by standing first on one foot and then the other, and grunting, I presently eased my misery; then I was full of interest, and began to examine.

I was curious to know what the pink dust was. Suddenly the name of it occurred to me, though I had never heard of it before. It was *fire!* I was as certain of it as a person could be of anything in the world. So without hesitation I named it that—fire.

I had created something that didn't exist before; I had added a new thing to the world's uncountable properties; I realized this, and was proud of my achievement, and was going to run and find him and tell him about it, thinking to raise myself in his esteem—but I reflected, and did not do it. No—he would not care for it. He would ask what it was good for, and what could I answer? For it was not *good* for something, but only beautiful, merely beautiful—

So I sighed, and did not go. For it wasn't good for anything; it could not build a shack, it could not improve melons, it could not hurry a fruit crop; it was useless, it was a foolishness and a vanity; he would despise it and say cutting words. But to me it was not despicable; I said, "Oh, you fire, I love you, you dainty pink creature, for you are *beautiful*—and that is enough!" and was going to gather it to my breast. But refrained. Then I made another maxim out of my own head, though it was so nearly like the first one that I was afraid it was only a plagiarism: *"The burnt Experiment shuns the fire."*

I wrought again; and when I had made a good deal of fire-dust I emptied it into a handful of dry brown grass, intending to carry it home and keep it always and play with it; but the wind struck it and it sprayed up and spat out at me fiercely, and I dropped it and ran. When I looked back the blue spirit was towering up and stretching and rolling away like a cloud, and instantly I thought of the name of it—*smoke!*—though, upon my word, I had never heard of smoke before.

Soon, brilliant yellow-and-red flares shot up through the smoke, and I named them in an instant—*flames!*—and I was right, too, though these were the very first flames that had ever been in the world. They climbed the trees, they flashed splendidly in and out of the vast and increasing volume of tumbling smoke, and I had to clap my hands and laugh and dance in my rapture, it was so new and strange and so wonderful and so beautiful!

He came running, and stopped and gazed, and said not a word for many minutes. Then he asked what it was. Ah, it was too bad that he should ask such a direct question. I had to answer it, of course, and I did. I said it was fire. If it annoyed him that I should know and he must ask, that was not my fault; I had no desire to annoy him. After a pause he asked:

"How did it come?"

Another direct question, and it also had to have a direct answer.

"I made it."

The fire was travelling farther and farther off. He went to the edge of the burned place and stood looking down, and said:

"What are these?"

"Fire-coals."

He picked up one to examine it, but changed his mind and put it down again. Then he went away. *Nothing* interests him.

But I was interested. There were ashes, gray and soft and delicate and pretty—I knew what they were at once. And the embers; I knew the embers, too. I found my apples, and raked. them out, and was glad; for I am very young and my appetite is active. But I was disappointed; they were all burst open and spoiled. Spoiled apparently; but it was not so; they were better than raw ones. Fire is beautiful; some day it will be useful, I think.

Friday

I saw him again, for a moment, last Monday at nightfall, but only for a moment. I was hoping he would praise me for trying to improve the estate, for I had meant well and had worked hard. But he was not pleased, and turned away and left me. He was also displeased on another account: I tried once more to persuade him to stop going over the Falls. That was because the fire had revealed to me a new passion—quite new, and distinctly different from love, grief, and those others which I had already discovered—*fear*. And it is horrible!—I wish I had never discovered it; it gives me dark moments, it spoils my happiness, it makes me shiver and tremble and shudder. But I could not persuade him, for he has not discovered fear yet, and so he could not understand me.

Extract from Adam's Diary

Perhaps I ought to remember that she is very young, a mere girl, and make allowances. She is all interest, eagerness, vivacity, the world is to her a charm, a wonder, a mystery, a joy; she can't speak for delight when she finds a new flower, she must pet it and caress it and smell it and talk to it, and pour out endearing names upon it. And she is color-mad: brown rocks, yellow sand, gray moss, green foliage, blue sky; the pearl of the dawn, the purple shadows on the mountains, the golden islands floating in crimson seas at sunset, the pallid moon sailing through the shredded cloud-rack, the star-jewels glittering in the wastes of space—none of them is of any practical value, so far as I can see, but because they have color and majesty, that is enough for her, and she loses her mind over them. If she could quiet down and keep still a couple of minutes at a time, it would be a reposeful spectacle. In that case I think I could enjoy looking at her; indeed I am sure I could, for I am coming to realize that she is a quite remarkably comely creature—lithe, slender, trim, rounded, shapely, nimble, graceful; and once when she was standing marble-white and sun-drenched on a bowlder, with her young head tilted back and her hand shading her eyes, watching the flight of a bird in the sky, I recognized that she was beautiful.

Monday noon.—If there is anything on the planet that she is not interested in it is not in my list. There are animals that I am indifferent to, but it is not so with her. She has no discrimination, she takes to all of them, she thinks they are all treasures, every new one is welcome.

When the mighty brontosaurus came striding into camp, she regarded it as an acquisition, I considered it a calamity; that is a good sample of the lack of harmony that prevails in our views of things. She wanted to domesticate it, I wanted to make it a present of the homestead and move out. She believed it could be tamed by kind treatment and would be a good pet; I said a pet twenty-one feet high and eighty-four feet long would be no proper thing to have about the place, because, even with the best intentions and without meaning any harm, it could sit down on the house and mash it, for any one could see by the look of its eye that it was absent-minded.

Still, her heart was set upon having that monster, and she couldn't give it up. She thought we could start a dairy with it, and wanted me to help her milk it; but I wouldn't; it was too risky. The sex wasn't right, and we hadn't any ladder anyway. Then she wanted to ride it, and look at the scenery. Thirty or forty feet of its tail was lying on the ground, like a fallen tree, and she thought she could climb it, but she was mistaken; when she got to the steep place it was too slick and down she came, and would have hurt herself but for me.

Was she satisfied now? No. Nothing ever satisfies her but demonstration; untested theories are not in her line, and she won't have them. It is the right spirit, I concede it; it attracts me; I feel the influence of it; if I were with her more I think I should take it up myself. Well, she had one theory remaining about this colossus: she thought that if we could tame him and make him friendly we could stand him in the river and use him for a bridge. It turned out that he was already plenty tame enough—at least as far as she was concerned—so she tried her theory, but it failed; every time she got him properly placed in the river and went ashore to cross over on him, he came out and followed her around like a pet mountain. Like the other animals. They all do that.

Tuesday—Wednesday—Thursday—and to-day: all without

seeing him. It is a long time to be alone; still, it is better to be alone than unwelcome.

I *had* to have company—I was made for it, I think—so I made friends with the animals. They are just charming, and they have the kindest disposition and the politest ways; they never look sour, they never let you feel that you are intruding, they smile at you and wag their tail, if they've got one, and they are always ready for a romp or an excursion or anything you want to propose. I think they are perfect gentlemen. All these days we have had such good times, and it hasn't been lonesome for me, ever. Lonesome! No, I should say not. Why, there's always a swarm of them around—sometimes as much as four or five acres—you can't count them; and when you stand on a rock in the midst and look out over the furry expanse, it is so mottled and splashed and gay with color and frisking sheen and sun-flash, and so rippled with stripes, that you might think it was a lake, only you know it isn't; and there's storms of sociable birds, and hurricanes of whirring wings; and when the sun strikes all that feathery commotion, you have a blazing up of all the colors you can think of, enough to put your eyes out.

We have made long excursions, and I have seen a great deal of the world—almost all of it, I think; and so I am the first traveller, and the only one. When we are on the march, it is an imposing sight—there's nothing like it anywhere. For comfort I ride a tiger or a leopard, because it is soft and has a round back that fits me, and because they are such pretty animals; but for long distance or for scenery I ride the elephant. He hoists me up with his trunk, but I can get off myself; when we are ready to camp, he sits and I slide down the back way.

The birds and animals are all friendly to each other, and there are no disputes about anything. They all talk, and they all talk to me, but it must be a foreign language, for I cannot make out a word they say; yet they often understand me when I talk back, particularly the dog and the elephant. It makes me ashamed. It shows that they are brighter than I am, and are therefore my superiors. It annoys me, for I want to be the principal Experiment myself—and I intend to be, too.

I have learned a number of things, and am educated, now, but I wasn't at first. I was ignorant at first. At first it used to vex me because, with all my watching, I was never smart enough to be around when the water was running up-hill; but now I do not mind it. I have experimented and experimented until now I know it never does run up-hill, except in the dark. I know it does in the dark, because the pool never goes dry; which it would, of course, if the water didn't come back in the night. It is best to prove things by actual experiment; then you *know;* whereas if you depend on guessing and supposing and conjecturing, you will never get educated.

Friday

Some things you *can't* find out; but you will never know you can't by guessing and supposing: no, you have to be patient and go on experimenting until you find out that you can't find out. And it is delightful to have it that way, it makes the world so interesting. If there wasn't anything to find out, it would be dull. Even trying to find out and not finding out is just as interesting as trying to find out and finding out, and I don't know but more so. The secret of the water was a treasure until I *got* it; then the excitement all went away, and I recognized a sense of loss.

By experiment I know that wood swims, and dry leaves, and feathers, and plenty of other things; therefore by all that cumulative evidence you know that a rock will swim; but you have to put up with simply knowing it, for there isn't any way to prove it—up to now. But I shall find a way—then *that* excitement will go. Such things make me sad; because by-and-by when I have found out everything there won't be any more excitements, and I do love excitements so! The other night I couldn't sleep for thinking about it.

At first I couldn't make out what I was made for, but now I think it was to search out the secrets of this wonderful world and be happy and thank the Giver of it all for devising it. I think there are many things to learn yet—I hope so; and by economizing and not hurrying too fast I think they will last weeks and weeks. I hope so. When you cast up a feather it sails away on the air and goes out of sight; then you throw up a clod and it doesn't. It comes down, every time. I have tried it and tried it, and it is always so. I wonder why it is? Of course it *doesn't* come down, but why should it *seem* to? I suppose it is an optical illusion. I mean, one of them is. I don't know which one. It may be the feather, it may be the clod; I can't prove which it is, I can only demonstrate that one or the other is a fake, and let a person take his choice.

By watching, I know that the stars are not going to last. I have seen some of the best ones melt and run down the sky. Since one can melt, they can all melt; since they can all melt, they can all melt the same night. That sorrow will come—I know it. I mean to sit up every night and look at them as long as I can keep awake; and I will impress those sparkling fields on my memory, so that by-and-by when they are taken away I can by my fancy restore those lovely myriads to the black sky and make them sparkle again, and double them by the blur of my tears.

After the Fall

When I look back, the Garden is a dream to me. It was beautiful, surpassingly beautiful, enchantingly beautiful; and now it is lost, and I shall not see it any more.

The Garden is lost, but I have found *him,* and am content. He loves me as well as he can; I love him with all the strength of my passionate nature, and this, I think, is proper to my youth and sex. If I ask myself why I love him, I find I do not know, and do not really much care to know; so I suppose that this kind of love is not a product of reasoning and statistics, like one's love for other reptiles and animals. I think that this must be so. I love certain birds because of their song; but I do not love Adam on account of his singing—no, it is not that; the more he sings the more I do not get reconciled to it. Yet I ask him to sing, because I wish to learn to like everything he is interested in. I am sure I can learn, because at first I could not stand it, but now I can. It sours the milk, but it doesn't matter; I can get used to that kind of milk.

It is not on account of his brightness that I love him—no, it is not that. He is not to blame for his brightness, such as it is, for he did not make it himself; he is as God made him, and that is sufficient. There was a wise purpose in it; *that* I know. In time it will develop, though I think it will not be sudden; and, besides, there is no hurry; he is well enough just as he is.

It is not on account of his gracious and considerate ways and his delicacy that I love him. No, he has lacks in these regards, but he is well enough just so, and is improving.

It is not on account of his industry that I love him—no, it is not that. I think he has it in him, and I do not know why he conceals it from me. It is my only pain. Otherwise he is frank and open with me, now. I am sure he keeps nothing from me but this. It grieves me that he should have a secret from me, and sometimes it spoils my sleep, thinking of it, but I will put it out of my mind; it shall not trouble my happiness, which is otherwise full to overflowing.

It is not on account of his education that I love him—no, it is not that. He is self-educated, and does really know a multitude of things, but they are not so.

It is not on account of his chivalry that I love him—no, it is not that. He told on me, but I do not blame him; it is a peculiarity of sex, I think, and he did not make his sex. Of course I would

547

not have told on him, I would have perished first; but that is a peculiarity of sex, too, and I do not take credit for it, for I did not make my sex.

Then why is it that I love him? *Merely because he is masculine,* I think.

At bottom he is good, and I love him for that, but I could love him without it. If he should beat me and abuse me, I should go on loving him. I know it. It is a matter of sex, I think.

He is strong and handsome, and I love him for that, and I admire him and am proud of him, but I could love him without those qualities. If he were plain, I should love him; if he were a wreck, I should love him; and I would work for him, and slave over him, and pray for him, and watch by his bedside until I died.

Yes, I think I love him merely because he is *mine* and is *masculine.* There is no other reason, I suppose. And so I think it is as I first said: that this kind of love is not a product of reasonings and statistics. It just *comes*—none knows whence—and cannot explain itself. And doesn't need to.

It is what I think. But I am only a girl, and the first that has examined this matter, and it may turn out that in my ignorance and inexperience I have not got it right.

Forty Years Later

It is my prayer, it is my longing, that we may pass from this life together—a longing which shall never perish from the earth, but shall have place in the heart of every wife that loves, until the end of time; and it shall be called by my name.

But if one of us must go first, it is my prayer that it shall be I; for he is strong, I am weak, I am not so necessary to him as he is to me—life without him would not be life; how could I endure it? This prayer is also immortal, and will not cease from being offered up while my race continues. I am the first wife; and in the last wife I shall be repeated.

At Eve's Grave

ADAM: Wheresoever she was, *there* was Eden.

The Innocents Abroad, *a book of travel sketches published in 1869, was an immediate success and established Twain's reputation as a writer. Eager to capitalize on this popularity, the American Publishing Company urged him to bring out a volume based on his experiences in the West. Twain obliged with* Roughing It, *a lively description of his adventures in Nevada, California, and the Sandwich Islands. The book appeared in 1872.*

Roughing It

CHAPTER I

My brother had just been appointed Secretary of Nevada Territory—an office of such majesty that it concentrated in itself the duties and dignities of Treasurer, Comptroller, Secretary of State, and Acting Governor in the Governor's absence. A salary of eighteen hundred dollars a year and the title of "Mr. Secretary," gave to the great position an air of wild and imposing grandeur. I was young and ignorant, and I envied my brother. I coveted his distinction and his financial splendor, but particularly and especially the long, strange journey he was going to make, and the curious new world he was going to explore. He was going to travel! I never had been away from home, and that word "travel" had a seductive charm for me. Pretty soon he would be hundreds and hundreds of miles away on the great plains and deserts, and among the mountains of the Far West, and would see buffaloes and Indians, and prairie dogs, and antelopes, and have all kinds of adventures, and may be get hanged or scalped, and have ever such a fine time, and write home and tell us all about it, and be a hero. And he would see the gold mines and the silver mines, and maybe go about of an afternoon when his work was done, and pick up two or three pailfuls of shining slugs, and nuggets of gold and silver on the hillside. And by and by he would become very rich, and return home by sea, and be able to talk as calmly about San Francisco and the ocean, and "the isthmus" as if it was nothing of any consequence to have seen those marvels face to face. What I suffered in contemplating his happiness, pen cannot describe. And so, when he offered me, in cold blood, the sublime position of private secretary under him, it appeared to me that the heavens and the earth passed away, and the firmament was rolled together as a scroll! I had nothing more to desire. My contentment was complete. At the end of an hour or two I was ready for the journey. Not much packing up was necessary, because we were going in the overland stage from the Missouri frontier to Nevada, and passengers were only allowed a small quantity of baggage apiece. There was no Pacific railroad in those fine times of ten or twelve years ago—not a single rail of it.

I only proposed to stay in Nevada three months—I had no thought of staying longer than that. I meant to see all I could that was new and strange, and then hurry home to business. I little thought that I would not see the end of that three-month pleasure excursion for six or seven uncommonly long years!

I dreamed all night about Indians, deserts, and silver bars, and in due time, next day, we took shipping at the St. Louis wharf on board a steamboat bound up the Missouri River.

We were six days going from St. Louis to "St. Jo."—a trip that was so dull, and sleepy, and eventless that it has left no more impression on my memory than if its duration had been six minutes instead of that many days. No record is left in my mind, now, concerning it, but a confused jumble of savage-looking snags, which we deliberately walked over with one wheel or the other; and of reefs which we butted and butted, and then retired from and climbed over in some softer place; and of sand-bars which we roosted on occasionally, and rested, and then got out our crutches and sparred over. In fact, the boat might almost as well have gone to St. Jo. by land, for she was walking most of the time, anyhow—climbing over reefs and clambering over snags patiently and laboriously all day long. The captain said she was a "bully" boat, and all she wanted was more "shear" and a bigger wheel. I thought she wanted a pair of stilts, but I had the deep sagacity not to say so.

CHAPTER II

The first thing we did on that glad evening that landed us at St. Joseph was to hunt up the stage-office, and pay a hundred and fifty dollars apiece for tickets per overland coach to Carson City, Nevada.

The next morning, bright and early, we took a hasty breakfast, and hurried to the starting-place. Then an inconvenience presented itself which we had not properly appreciated before, namely, that one cannot make a heavy traveling trunk stand for twenty-five pounds of baggage—because it weighs a good deal more. But that was all we could take—twenty-five pounds each. So we had to snatch our trunks open, and make a selection in a good deal of a hurry. We put our lawful twenty-five pounds apiece all in one valise, and shipped the trunks back to St. Louis again. It was a sad parting, for now we had no swallow-tail coats and white kid gloves to wear at Pawnee receptions in the Rocky Mountains, and no stovepipe hats nor patent-leather boots, nor anything else necessary to make life calm and peaceful. We were reduced to a war-footing. Each of us put on a rough, heavy suit of clothing, woolen army shirt and "stogy" boots included; and into the valise we crowded a few white shirts, some under-clothing and such things. My brother, the Secretary, took along about four pounds of United States statutes and six pounds of Unabridged Dictionary; for we did not know—poor innocents—that such things could be bought in San Francisco on one day and received in Carson City the next. I was armed to the teeth with a pitiful little Smith & Wesson's seven-shooter, which carried a ball like a homoeopathic pill, and it took the whole seven to make a dose for an adult. But I thought it was grand. It appeared to me to be a dangerous weapon. It only had one fault—you could not hit anything with it. One of our "conductors" practiced awhile on a cow with it, and as long as she stood still and behaved herself she was safe; but as soon as she went to moving about, and he got to shooting at other things, she came to grief. The Secretary had a small-sized Colt's revolver strapped around him for protection against the Indians, and to guard against accidents he carried it uncapped. Mr. George Bemis was dismally formidable. George Bemis was our fellow-traveler. We had never seen him before. He wore in his belt an old original "Allen" revolver, such as irreverent people called a "pepper-box." Simply drawing the trigger back, cocked and fired the pistol. As the trigger came back, the hammer would begin to rise and the barrel to turn over, and presently down would drop the hammer, and away would speed the ball. To aim along the turning barrel and hit the thing aimed at was a feat which was probably never done with an "Allen" in the world. But George's was a reliable weapon, nevertheless, because, as one of the stage-drivers afterward said, "If she didn't get what she went after, she would fetch something else." And so she did. She went after a deuce of spades nailed against a tree, once, and fetched a mule standing about thirty yards to the left of it. Bemis did not want the mule; but the owner came out with a double-barreled shotgun and persuaded him to buy it, anyhow. It was a cheerful weapon—the "Allen." Sometimes all its six barrels would go off at once, and then there was no safe place in all the region round about, but behind it.

We took two or three blankets for protection against frosty weather in the mountains. In the matter of luxuries we were modest—we took none along but some pipes and five pounds of smoking tobacco. We had two large canteens to carry water in, between stations on the Plains, and we also took with us a little shot-bag of silver coin for daily expenses in the way of breakfasts and dinners.

By eight o'clock everything was ready, and we were on the other side of the river. We jumped into the stage, the driver cracked his whip, and we bowled away and left "the States" behind us. It was a superb summer morning, and all the landscape was brilliant with sunshine. There was a freshness and breeziness, too, and an exhilarating sense of emancipation from all sorts of cares and responsibilities, that almost made us feel that the years we had spent in the close, hot city, toiling and slaving, had been wasted and thrown away. We were spinning along through Kansas, and in the course of an hour and a half we were fairly abroad on the great Plains. Just here the land was rolling—a grand sweep of regular elevations and depressions as far as the eye could reach—like the stately heave and swell of the ocean's bosom after a storm. And everywhere were cornfields, accenting with squares of deeper green, this limitless expanse of grassy land. But presently this sea upon dry ground was to lose its "rolling" character and stretch away for seven hundred miles as level as a floor!

Our coach was a great swinging and swaying stage, of the most sumptuous description—an imposing cradle on wheels. It was drawn by six handsome horses, and by the side of the driver sat the "conductor," the legitimate captain of the craft; for it was his business to take charge and care of the mails, baggage, express matter, and passengers. We three were the only passengers, this trip. We sat on the back seat, inside. About all the rest of the coach was full of mail bags—for we had three days' delayed mails with us. Almost touching our knees, a perpendicular wall of mail matter rose up to the roof. There was a great pile of it strapped on top of the stage, and both the fore and hind boots were full. We had twenty-seven hundred pounds of it aboard, the driver said—"a little for Brigham, and Carson, and 'Frisco, but the heft of it for the Injuns, which is powerful troublesome 'thout they get plenty of truck to read." But as he just then got up a fearful convulsion of his countenance which was suggestive of a wink being swallowed by an earthquake, we guessed that his remark was intended to be facetious, and to mean that we would unload the most of our mail matter somewhere on the Plains and leave it to the Indians, or whosoever wanted it.

We changed horses every ten miles, all day long, and fairly flew over the hard, level road. We jumped out and stretched our legs every time the coach stopped, and so the night found us still vivacious and unfatigued.

After supper a woman got in, who lived about fifty miles further on, and we three had to take turns at sitting outside with the driver and conductor. Apparently she was not a talkative woman. She would sit there in the gathering twilight and fasten her steadfast eyes on a mosquito rooting into her arm, and slowly she would raise her other hand till she had got his range, and then she would launch a slap at him that would have jolted a cow; and after that she would sit and contemplate the corpse with tranquil satisfaction—for she never missed her mosquito; she was a dead shot at short range. She never removed a carcass, but left them there for bait. I sat by this grim Sphynx and watched her kill thirty or forty mosquitoes—watched her, and waited for her to say something, but she never did. So I finally opened the conversation myself. I said:

"The mosquitoes are pretty bad, about here, madam."

"You bet!"

"What did I understand you to say, madam?"

"You BET!"

Then she cheered up, and faced around and said:

"Danged if I didn't begin to think you fellers was deef and dumb. I did, b'gosh. Here I've sot, and sot, and sot, a-bust'n muskeeters and wonderin' what was ailin' ye. Fust I thot you was deef and dumb, then I thot you was sick or crazy, or suthin', and then by and by I begin to reckon you was a passel of sickly fools that couldn't think of nothing to say. Wher'd ye come from?"

The Sphynx was a Sphynx no more! The fountains of her great deep were broken up, and she rained the nine parts of speech forty days and forty nights, metaphorically speaking, and buried us under a desolating deluge of trivial gossip that left not a crag or pinnacle of rejoinder projecting above the tossing waste of dislocated grammar and decomposed pronunciation!

How we suffered, suffered, suffered! She went on, hour after hour, till I was sorry I ever opened the mosquito question and gave her a start. She never did stop again until she got to her journey's end toward daylight; and then she stirred us up as she was leaving the stage (for we were nodding, by that time), and said:

"Now you git out at Cottonwood, you fellers, and lay over a couple o' days, and I'll be along some time to-night, and if I can do ye any good by edgin' in a word now and then, I'm right thar. Folks 'll tell you 't I've always ben kind o' offish and partic'lar for a gal that's raised in the woods, and I *am*, with the rag-tag and bob-tail, and a gal *has* to be, if she wants to *be* anything, but when people comes along which is my equals, I reckon I'm a pretty sociable heifer after all."

We resolved not to "lay by at Cottonwood."

CHAPTER III

About an hour and a half before daylight we were bowling along smoothly over the road—so smoothly that our cradle only rocked in a gentle, lulling way, that was gradually soothing us to sleep, and dulling our consciousness—when something gave away under us! We were dimly aware of it, but indifferent to it. The coach stopped. We heard the driver and conductor talking together outside, and rummaging for a lantern, and swearing because they could not find it—but we had no interest in whatever had happened, and it only added to our comfort to think of those people out there at work in the murky night, and we snug in our nest with the curtains drawn. But presently, by the sounds, there seemed to be an examination going on, and then the driver's voice said:

"By George, the thoroughbrace is broke!"

This started me broad awake—as an undefined sense of calamity is always apt to do. I said to myself: "Now, a thoroughbrace is probably part of a horse; and doubtless a vital part, too, from the dismay in the driver's voice. Leg, maybe— and yet how could he break his leg waltzing along such a road as this? No, it can't be his leg. That is impossible, unless he was reaching for the driver. Now, what can be the thoroughbrace of a horse, I wonder? Well, whatever comes, I shall not air my ignorance in this crowd, anyway."

Just then the conductor's face appeared at a lifted curtain, and his lantern glared in on us and our wall of mail matter. He said:

"Gents, you'll have to turn out a spell. Thoroughbrace is broke."

We climbed out into a chill drizzle, and felt ever so homeless and dreary. When I found that the thing they called a "thoroughbrace" was the massive combination of belts and springs which the coach rocks itself in, I said to the driver:

"I never saw a thoroughbrace used up like that, before, that I can remember. How did it happen?"

"Why, it happened by trying to make one coach carry three days' mail—that's how it happened," said he. "And right here is the very direction which is wrote on all the newspaper-bags which was to be put out for the Injuns for to keep 'em quiet. It's most uncommon lucky, becuz it's so nation dark I should 'a' gone by unbeknowns if that air thoroughbrace hadn't broke."

I knew that he was in labor with another of those winks of his, though I could not see his face, because he was bent down at work; and wishing him a safe delivery, I turned to and helped the rest get out the mail-sacks. It made a great pyramid by the roadside when it was all out. When they had mended the thoroughbrace we filled the two boots again, but put no mail on top, and only half as much inside as there was before. The conductor bent all the seat-backs down, and then filled the coach just half full of mail-bags from end to end. We objected loudly to this, for it left us no seats. But the conductor was wiser than we, and said a bed was better than seats, and moreover, this plan would protect his thoroughbraces. We never wanted any seats after that. The lazy bed was infinitely preferable. I had many an exciting day, subsequently, lying on it reading the statutes and the dictionary, and wondering how the characters would turn out.

The conductor said he would send back a guard from the next station to take charge of the abandoned mail-bags, and we drove on.

It was now just dawn; and as we stretched our cramped legs full length on the mail sacks, and gazed out through the windows across the wide wastes of greensward clad in cool, powdery mist, to where there was an expectant look in the eastern horizon, our perfect enjoyment took the form of a tranquil and contented ecstasy. The stage whirled along at a spanking gait, the breeze flapping curtains and suspended coats in a most exhilarating way; the cradle swayed and swung luxuriously, the pattering of the horses' hoofs, the cracking of the driver's whip, and his "Hi-yi! g'lang!" were music; the spinning ground and the waltzing trees appeared to give us a mute hurrah as we went by, and then slack up and look after us with interest, or envy, or something; and as we lay and smoked the pipe of peace and compared all this luxury with the years of tiresome city life that had gone before it, we felt that there was only one complete and satisfying happiness in the world, and we had found it.

After breakfast, at some station whose name I have forgotten, we three climbed up on the seat behind the driver, and let the conductor have our bed for a nap. And by and by, when the sun made me drowsy, I lay down on my face on top of the coach, grasping the slender iron railing, and slept for an hour or more. That will give one an appreciable idea of those matchless roads. Instinct will make a sleeping man grip a fast hold of the railing when the stage jolts, but when it only swings and sways, no grip is necessary. Overland drivers and conductors used to sit in their places and sleep thirty or forty minutes at a time, on good roads, while spinning along at the rate of eight or ten miles an hour. I saw them do it, often. There was no danger about it; a sleeping man *will* seize the irons in time when the coach jolts. These men were hard worked, and it was not possible for them to stay awake all the time.

By and by we passed through Marysville, and over the Big Blue and Little Sandy; thence about a mile, and entered Nebraska. About a mile further on, we came to the Big Sandy—one hundred and eighty miles from St. Joseph.

As the sun was going down, we saw the first specimen of an animal known familiarly over two thousand miles of mountain and desert—from Kansas clear to the Pacific Ocean—as the "jackass rabbit." He is well named. He is just like any other rabbit, except that he is from one third to twice as large, has longer legs in proportion to his size, and has the most preposterous ears that ever were mounted on any creature *but* a jackass. When he is sitting quiet, thinking about his sins, or is absent-minded or unapprehensive of danger, his majestic ears project above him conspicuously; but the breaking of a twig will scare him nearly to death, and then he tilts his ears back gently and starts for home. All you can see, then, for the next minute, is his long gray form stretched out straight and "streaking it" through the low sage-brush, head erect, eyes right, and ears just canted a little to the rear, but showing you where the animal is, all the time, the same as if he carried a jib. Now and then he makes a marvelous spring with his long legs, high over the stunted sage-brush, and scores a leap that would make a horse envious. Presently he comes down to a long, graceful "lope," and shortly he mysteriously disappears. He has crouched behind a sage-bush, and will sit there and listen and tremble until you get within six feet of him, when he will get under way again. But one must shoot at this creature once, if he wishes to see him throw his heart into his heels, and do the best he knows how. He is frightened clear through, now, and he lays his long ears down on his back, straightens himself out like a yard-stick every spring he makes, and scatters miles behind him with an easy indifference that is enchanting.

Our party made this specimen "hump himself," as the conductor said. The secretary started him with a shot from the Colt; I commenced spitting at him with my weapon; and all in the same instant the old "Allen's" whole broadside let go with a rattling crash, and it is not putting it too strong to say that the rabbit was frantic! He dropped his ears, set up his tail, and left for San Francisco at a speed which can only be described as a flash and a vanish! Long after he was out of sight we could hear him whiz.

I do not remember where we first came across "sage-brush," but as I have been speaking of it I may as well describe it. This is easily done, for if the reader can imagine a gnarled and venerable live oak-tree reduced to a little shrub two feet high, with its rough bark, its foliage, its twisted boughs, all complete, he can picture the "sage-brush" exactly. Often, on lazy afternoons in the mountains, I have lain on the ground with my face under a sage-bush, and entertained myself with fancying that the gnats among its foliage were liliputian birds, and that the ants marching and countermarching about its base were liliputian flocks and herds, and myself some vast loafer from Brobdignag waiting to catch a little citizen and eat him.

It is an imposing monarch of the forest in exquisite miniature, is the "sage-brush." Its foliage is a grayish green, and gives that tint to desert and mountain. It smells like our domestic sage, and "sage-tea" made from it tastes like the sage-tea which all boys are so well acquainted with. The sage-brush is a singularly hardy plant, and grows right in the midst of deep sand, and among barren rocks, where nothing else in the vegetable world would try to grow, except "bunch-grass."* The sage-bushes grow from three to six or seven feet apart, all over the mountains and deserts of the Far West, clear to the borders of California. There is not a tree of any kind in the deserts, for hundreds of miles— there is no vegetation at all in a regular desert, except the sage-brush and its cousin the "greasewood," which is so much like the sage-brush that the difference amounts to little. Camp-fires and hot suppers in the deserts would be impossible but for the friendly sage-brush. Its trunk is as large as a boy's wrist (and

---

* "Bunch-grass" grows on the bleak mountain-sides of Nevada and neighboring territories, and offers excellent feed for stock, even in the dead of winter, wherever the snow is blown aside and exposes it; notwithstanding its unpromising home, bunch-grass is a better and more nutritious diet for cattle and horses than almost any other hay or grass that is known—so stock men say.

from that up to a man's arm), and its crooked branches are half as large as its trunk—all good, sound, hard wood, very like oak.

When a party camps, the first thing to be done is to cut sage-brush; and in a few minutes there is an opulent pile of it ready for use. A hole a foot wide, two feet deep, and two feet long, is dug, and sage-brush chopped up and burned in it till it is full to the brim with glowing coals. Then the cooking begins, and there is no smoke, and consequently no swearing. Such a fire will keep all night, with very little replenishing; and it makes a very sociable camp-fire, and one around which the most impossible reminiscences sound plausible, instructive, and profoundly entertaining.

Sage-brush is very fair fuel, but as a vegetable it is a distinguished failure. Nothing can abide the taste of it but the jackass and his illegitimate child the mule. But their testimony to its nutritiousness is worth nothing, for they will eat pine knots, or anthracite coal, or brass filings, or lead pipe, or old bottles, or anything that comes handy, and then go off looking as grateful as if they had had oysters for dinner. Mules and donkeys and camels have appetites that anything will relieve temporarily, but nothing satisfy. In Syria, once, at the head-waters of the Jordan, a camel took charge of my overcoat while the tents were being pitched, and examined it with a critical eye, all over, with as much interest as if he had an idea of getting one made like it; and then, after he was done figuring on it as an arti-cle of apparel, he began to contemplate it as an article of diet. He put his foot on it, and lifted one of the sleeves out with his teeth, and chewed and chewed at it, gradually taking it in, and all the while opening and closing his eyes in a kind of religious ecstasy, as if he had never tasted anything as good as an overcoat before, in his life. Then he smacked his lips once or twice, and reached after the other sleeve. Next he tried the velvet collar, and smiled a smile of such contentment that it was plain to see that he regarded that as the daintiest thing about an overcoat. The tails went next, along with some percussion caps and cough can-dy, and some fig-paste from Constantinople. And then my newspaper correspondence dropped out, and he took a chance in that—manuscript letters written for the home papers. But he was treading on dangerous ground, now. He began to come across solid wisdom in those documents that was rather weighty on his stomach; and occasionally he would take a joke that would shake him up till it loosened his teeth; it was getting to be perilous times with him, but he held his grip with good courage and hopefully, till at last he began to stumble on statements that not even a camel could swallow with impunity. He began to gag and gasp, and his eyes to stand out, and his forelegs to spread, and in about a quarter of a minute he fell over as stiff as a carpenter's work-bench, and died a death of indescribable agony. I went and pulled the manuscript out of his mouth, and found that the sensitive creature had choked to death on one of the mildest and gentlest statements of fact that I ever laid before a trusting public.

I was about to say, when diverted from my subject, that occasionally one finds sage-bushes five or six feet high, and with a spread of branch and foliage in proportion, but two or two and a half feet is the usual height.

CHAPTER IV

As the sun went down and the evening chill came on, we made preparation for bed. We stirred up the hard leather letter-sacks, and the knotty canvas bags of printed matter (knotty and uneven because of projecting ends and corners of magazines, boxes and books). We stirred them up and redisposed them in such a way as to make our bed as level as possible. And we *did* improve it, too, though after all our work it had an upheaved and billowy look about it, like a little piece of a stormy sea. Next we hunted up our boots from odd nooks among the mail-bags where they had settled, and put them on. Then we got down our coats, vests, pantaloons and heavy woolen shirts, from the arm-loops where they had been swinging all day, and clothed ourselves in them—for, there being no ladies either at the stations or in the coach, and the weather being hot, we had looked to our comfort by stripping to our underclothing, at nine o'clock in the morning. All things being now ready, we stowed the uneasy Dictionary where it would lie as quiet as possible, and placed the water canteens and pistols where we could find them in the dark. Then we smoked a final pipe, and swapped a final yarn; after which, we put the pipes, tobacco and bag of coin in snug holes and caves among the mail-bags, and then fastened down the coach curtains all around, and made the place as "dark as the inside of a cow," as the conductor phrased it in his picturesque way. It was certainly as dark as any place could be—nothing was even dimly visible in it. And finally, we rolled ourselves up like silk-worms, each person in his own blanket, and sank peacefully to sleep.

Whenever the stage stopped to change horses, we would wake up, and try to recollect where we were—and succeed—and in a minute or two the stage would be off again, and we likewise. We began to get into country, now, threaded here and there with little streams. These had high, steep banks on each side, and every time we flew down one bank and scrambled up the other, our party inside got mixed somewhat. First we would all be down in a pile at the forward end of the stage, nearly in a sitting posture, and in a second we would shoot to the other end, and stand on our heads. And we would sprawl and kick, too, and ward off ends and corners of mail-bags that came lumbering over us and about us; and as the dust rose from the tumult, we would all sneeze in chorus, and the majority of us would grumble, and probably say some hasty thing, like: "Take your elbow out of my ribs!—can't you quit crowding?"

Every time we avalanched from one end of the stage to the other, the Unabridged Dictionary would come too; and every time it came it damaged somebody. One trip it "barked" the Secretary's elbow; the next trip it hurt me in the stomach, and the third it tilted Bemis's nose up till he could look down his nostrils—he said. The pistols and coin soon settled to the bottom, but the pipes, pipe-stems, tobacco and canteens clattered and floundered after the Dictionary every time it made an assault on us, and aided and abetted the book by spilling tobacco in our eyes, and water down our backs.

Still, all things considered, it was a very comfortable night. It wore gradually away, and when at last a cold gray light was visible through the puckers and chinks in the curtains, we yawned and stretched with satisfaction, shed our cocoons, and felt that we had slept as much as was necessary. By and by, as the sun rose up and warmed the world, we pulled off our clothes and got ready for breakfast. We were just pleasantly in time, for five minutes afterward the driver sent the weird music of his bugle winding over the grassy solitudes, and presently we detected a low hut or two in the distance. Then the rattling of the coach, the clatter of our six horses' hoofs, and the driver's crisp commands, awoke to a louder and stronger emphasis, and we went sweeping down on the station at our smartest speed. It was fascinating—that old overland stage-coaching.

We jumped out in undress uniform. The driver tossed his gathered reins out on the ground, gaped and stretched complacently, drew off his heavy buckskin gloves with great deliberation and insufferable dignity—taking not the slightest notice of a dozen solicitous inquiries after his health, and humbly facetious and flattering accostings, and obsequious tenders of service, from five or six hairy and half-civilized station-keepers and hostlers who were nimbly unhitching our steeds and bringing the fresh team out of the stables—for in the eyes of the stage-driver of that day, station-keepers and hostlers were a sort of good enough low creatures, useful in their place, and helping to make up a world, but not the kind of beings which a person of distinction could afford to concern himself with; while, on the contrary, in the eyes of the station-keeper and the hostler, the stage-driver was a hero—a great and shining dignitary, the world's favorite son, the envy of the people, the observed of the nations. When they spoke to him they received his insolent silence meekly, and as being the natural and proper conduct of so great a man; when he opened his lips they all hung on his words with admiration (he never honored a particular individual with a remark, but addressed it with a broad generality to the horses, the stables, the surrounding country *and* the human underlings); when he discharged a facetious insulting personality at a hostler, that hostler was happy for the day; when he uttered his one jest—old as the hills, coarse, profane, witless, and inflicted on the same audience, in the same language, every time his coach drove up there—the varlets roared, and slapped their thighs, and swore it was the best thing they'd ever heard in all their lives. And how they would fly around when he wanted a basin of water, a gourd of the same, or a light for his pipe!—but they would instantly insult a passenger if he so far forgot himself as to crave a favor at their hands. They could do that sort of insolence as well as the driver they copied it from—for, let it be borne in mind, the overland driver had but little less contempt for his passengers than he had for his hostlers.

The hostlers and station-keepers treated the really powerful *conductor* of the coach merely with the best of what was their idea of civility, but the *driver* was the only being they bowed down to and worshipped. How admiringly they would gaze up at him in his high seat as he gloved himself with lingering deliberation, while some happy hostler held the bunch of reins aloft, and waited patiently for him to take it! And how they would bombard him with glorifying ejaculations as he cracked his long whip and went careering away.

The station buildings were long, low huts, made of sun-dried, mud-colored bricks, laid up without mortar (*adobes*, the Spaniards call these bricks, and Americans shorten it to *'dobies*). The roofs, which had no slant to them worth speaking of, were thatched and then sodded or covered with a thick layer of earth, and from this sprung a pretty rank growth of weeds and grass. It was the first time we had ever seen a man's front yard on top of his house. The buildings consisted of barns, stable-room for twelve or fifteen horses, and a hut for an eating-room for passengers. This latter had bunks in it for the station-keeper and a hostler or two. You could rest your elbow on its eaves, and you had to bend in order to get in at the door. In place of a window there was a square hole about large enough for a man to crawl through, but this had no glass in it. There was no flooring, but the ground was packed hard. There was no stove, but the fire-place served all needful purposes. There were no shelves, no cupboards, no closets. In a corner stood an open sack of flour, and nestling against its base were a couple of black and venerable tin coffee-pots, a tin tea-pot, a little bag of salt, and a side of bacon.

By the door of the station-keeper's den, outside, was a tin wash-basin, on the ground. Near it was a pail of water and a piece of yellow bar soap, and from the eaves hung a hoary blue woolen shirt, significantly—but this latter was the station-keeper's private towel, and only two persons in all the party might venture to use it—the stage-driver and the conductor. The latter would not, from a sense of decency; the former would not, because he did not choose to encourage the advances of a station-keeper. We had towels—in the valise; they might as well have been in Sodom and Gomorrah. We (and the conductor) used our handkerchiefs, and the driver his pantaloons and sleeves. By the door, inside, was fastened a small old-fashioned looking-glass frame, with two little fragments of the original mirror lodged down in one corner of it. This arrangement afforded a pleasant double-barreled portrait of you when you looked into it, with one half of your head set up a couple of inches above the other half. From the glass frame hung the half of a comb by a string—but if I had to describe that patriarch or die, I believe I would order some sample coffins. It had come down from Esau and Samson, and had been accumulating hair ever since—along with certain impurities. In one corner of the room stood three or four rifles and muskets, together with horns and pouches of ammunition. The station-men wore pantaloons of coarse, country-woven stuff, and into the seat and the inside of the legs were sewed ample additions of buckskin, to do duty in place of leggings, when the man rode horseback—so the pants were half dull blue and half yellow, and unspeakably picturesque. The pants were stuffed into the tops of high boots, the heels whereof were armed with great Spanish spurs, whose little iron clogs and chains jingled with every step. The man wore a huge beard and mustachios, an old slouch hat, a blue woolen shirt, no suspenders, no vest, no coat—in a leathern sheath in his belt, a great long "navy" revolver (slung on right side, hammer to the front), and projecting from his boot a horn-handled bowie-knife. The furniture of the hut was neither gorgeous nor much in the way. The rocking-chairs and sofas were not present, and never had been, but they were represented by two three- legged stools, a pine-board bench four feet long, and two empty candle-boxes. The table was a greasy board on stilts, and the table-cloth and napkins had not come—and they were not looking for them, either. A battered tin platter, a knife and fork, and a tin pint cup, were at each man's place, and the driver had a queensware saucer that had seen better days. Of course this duke sat at the head of the table. There was one isolated piece of table furniture that bore about it a touching air of grandeur in misfortune. This was the caster. It was German silver, and crippled and rusty, but it was so preposterously out of place there that it was suggestive of a tattered exiled king among barbarians, and the majesty of its native position compelled respect even in its degradation. There was only one cruet left, and that was a stopperless, fly-specked, broken-necked thing, with two inches of vinegar in it, and a dozen preserved flies with their heels up and looking sorry they had invested there.

The station-keeper upended a disk of last week's bread, of the shape and size of an old-time cheese, and carved some slabs from it which were as good as Nicholson pavement, and tenderer.

He sliced off a piece of bacon for each man, but only the experienced old hands made out to eat it, for it was condemned army bacon which the United States would not feed to its soldiers in the forts, and the stage company had bought it cheap for the sustenance of their passengers and employes. We may have found this condemned army bacon further out on the plains than the section I am locating it in, but we *found* it—there is no gainsaying that.

Then he poured for us a beverage which he called *"Slumgullion,"* and it is hard to think he was not inspired when he named it. It really pretented to be tea, but there was too much dish-rag, and sand, and old bacon-rind in it to deceive the intelligent traveler. He had no sugar and no milk—not even a spoon to stir the ingredients with.

We could not eat the bread or the meat, nor drink the "slumgullion." And when I looked at that melancholy vinegar-cruet, I thought of the anecdote (a very, very old one, even at that day) of the traveler who sat down to a table which had nothing on it but a mackerel and a pot of mustard. He asked the landlord if this was all. The landlord said:

"All! Why, thunder and lightning, I should think there was mackerel enough there for six."

"But I don't like mackerel."

"Oh—then help yourself to the mustard."

In other days I had considered a good, a very good, anecdote, but there was a dismal plausibility about it, here, that took all the humor out of it.

Our breakfast was before us, but our teeth were idle.

I tasted and smelt, and said I would take coffee, I believed. The station-boss stopped dead still, and glared at me speechless. At last, when he came to, he turned away and said, as one who communes with himself upon a matter too vast to grasp:

"*Coffee!* Well, if that don't go clean ahead of me, I'm d——d!"

We could not eat, and there was no conversation among the hostlers and herdsmen—we all sat at the same board. At least there was no conversation further than a single hurried request, now and then, from one employe to another. It was always in the same form, and always gruffly friendly. Its western freshness and novelty startled me, at first, and interested me; but it presently grew monotonous, and lost its charm. It was:

"Pass the bread, you son of a skunk!" No, I forget—skunk was not the word; it seems to me it was still stronger than that; I know it was, in fact, but it is gone from my memory, apparently. However, it is no matter—probably it was too strong for print, anyway. It is the landmark in my memory which tells me where I first encountered the vigorous new vernacular of the occidental plains and mountains.

We gave up the breakfast, and paid our dollar apiece and went back to our mail-bag bed in the coach, and found comfort in our pipes. Right here we suffered the first diminution of our princely state. We left our six fine horses and took six mules in their place. But they were wild Mexican fellows, and a man had to stand at the head of each of them and hold him fast while the driver gloved and got himself ready. And when at last he grasped the reins and gave the word, the men sprung suddenly away from the mules' heads and the coach shot from the station as if it had issued from a cannon. How the frantic animals did scamper! It was a fierce and furious gallop—and the gait never altered for a moment till we reeled off ten or twelve miles and swept up to the next collection of little station-huts and stables.

So we flew along all day. At 2 P.M. the belt of timber that fringes the North Platte and marks its windings through the vast level floor of the Plains came in sight. At 4 P.M. we crossed a branch of the river, and at 5 P.M. we crossed the Platte itself, and landed at Fort Kearney, *fifty-six hours out from St. Joe*—THREE HUNDRED MILES!

Now that was stage-coaching on the great overland, ten or twelve years ago, when perhaps not more than ten men in America, all told, expected to live to see a railroad follow that route to the Pacific. But the railroad is there, now, and it pictures a thousand odd comparisons and contrasts in my mind to read the following sketch, in the New York *Times,* of a recent trip over almost the very ground I have been describing. I can scarcely comprehend the new state of things:

ACROSS THE CONTINENT

"At 4.20 P.M., Sunday, we rolled out of the station at Omaha, and started westward on our long jaunt. A couple of hours out, dinner was announced—an "event" to those of us who had yet to experience what it is to eat in one of Pullman's hotels on wheels; so, stepping into the car next forward of our sleeping palace, we found ourselves in the dining-car. It was a revelation to us, that first dinner on Sunday. And though we continued to dine for four days, and had as many breakfasts and suppers, our whole party never ceased to admire the perfection of the arrangements, and the marvelous results achieved. Upon tables covered with snowy linen, and garnished with services of solid silver, Ethiop waiters, flitting about in spotless white, placed as by magic a repast at which Delmonico himself could have had no occasion to blush; and, indeed, in some respects it would be hard for that distinguished *chef* to match our *menu*; for, in addition to all that ordinarily makes up a first-chop dinner, had we not our antelope steak (the gormand who has not experienced this—bah! what does he know of the feast of fat things?) our delicious mountain-brook trout, and choice fruits and berries, and (sauce piquant and unpurchasable!) our sweet-scented, appetite-compelling air of the prairies? You may depend upon it, we all did justice to the good things, and as we washed them down with bumpers of sparkling Krug, whilst we sped along at the rate of thirty miles an hour, agreed it was the *fastest* living we had ever experienced. (We beat that, however, two days afterward when we made *twenty-seven miles in twenty-seven minutes*, while our Champagne glasses filled to the brim spilled not a drop!) After dinner we repaired to our drawing-room car, and, as it was Sabbath eve, intoned some of the grand old hymns—"Praise God from whom," etc.; "Shining Shore," "Coronation," etc.—the voices of the men singers and of the women singers blending sweetly in the evening air, while our train, with its great glaring Polyphemus eye, lighting up long vistas of prairie, rushed into the night and the Wild. Then to bed in luxurious couches, where we slept the sleep of the just and only awoke the next morning (Monday) at eight o'clock, to find ourselves at the crossing of the North Platte, three hundred miles from Omaha—*fifteen hours and forty minutes out.*"

CHAPTER V

Another night of alternate tranquillity and turmoil. But morning came, by and by. It was another glad awakening to fresh breezes, vast expanses of level greensward, bright sunlight, an impressive solitude utterly without visible human beings or human habitations, and an atmosphere of such amazing magnifying properties that trees that seemed close at hand were more than three miles away. We resumed undress uniform, climbed atop of the flying coach, dangled our legs over the side, shouted occasionally at our frantic mules, merely to see them lay their ears back and scamper faster, tied our hats on to keep our hair from blowing away, and leveled an outlook over the world-wide carpet about us for things new and strange to gaze at. Even at this day it thrills me through and through to think of the life, the gladness and the wild sense of freedom that used to make the blood dance in my veins on those fine overland mornings!

Along about an hour after breakfast we saw the first prairie-dog villages, the first antelope, and the first wolf. If I remember rightly, this latter was the regular *cayote* (pronounced ky-o-te) of the farther deserts. And if it *was*, he was not a pretty creature or respectable either, for I got well acquainted with his race afterward, and can speak with confidence. The cayote is a long, slim, sick and sorry-looking skeleton, with a gray wolf-skin stretched over it, a tolerably bushy tail that forever sags down with a despairing expression of forsakenness and misery, a furtive and evil eye, and a long, sharp face, with slightly lifted lip and exposed teeth. He has a general slinking expression all over. The cayote is a living, breathing allegory of Want. He is *always* hungry. He is always poor, out of luck and friendless. The meanest creatures despise him, and even the fleas would desert him for a velocipede. He is so spiritless and cowardly that even while his exposed teeth are pretending a threat, the rest of his face is apologizing for it. And he is *so* homely!—so scrawny, and ribby, and coarse-haired, and pitiful. When he sees you he lifts his lip and lets a flash of his teeth out, and then turns a little out of the course he was pursuing, depresses his head a bit, and strikes a long, soft-footed trot through the sage-brush, glancing over his shoulder at you, from time to time, till he is about out of easy pistol range, and then he stops and takes a deliberate survey of you; he will trot fifty yards and stop again—another fifty and stop again; and finally the gray of his gliding body blends with the gray of the sage-brush, and he disappears. All this is when you make no demonstration against him; but if you do, he develops a livelier interest in his journey, and instantly electrifies his heels and puts such a deal of real estate between himself and your weapon, that by the time you have raised the hammer you see that you need a minie rifle, and by the time you have got him in line you need a rifled cannon, and by the time you have "drawn a bead" on him you see well enough that nothing but an unusually long-winded streak of lightning could reach him where he is now. But if you start a swift-footed dog after him, you will enjoy it ever so much—especially if it is a dog that has a good opinion of himself, and has been brought up to think he knows something about speed. The cayote will go swinging gently off on that deceitful trot of his, and every little while he will smile a fraudful smile over his shoulder that will fill that dog entirely full of encouragement and worldly ambition, and make him lay his head still lower to the ground, and stretch his neck further to the front, and pant more fiercely, and stick his tail out straighter behind, and move his furious legs with a yet wilder frenzy, and leave a broader and broader, and higher and denser cloud of desert sand smoking behind, and marking his long wake across the level plain! And all this time the dog is only a short twenty feet behind the cayote, and to save the soul of him he cannot understand why it is that he cannot get perceptibly closer; and he begins to get aggravated, and it makes him madder and madder to see how gently the cayote glides along and never pants or sweats or ceases to smile; and he grows still more and more incensed to see how shamefully he has been taken in by an entire stranger, and what an ignoble swindle that long, calm, soft-footed trot is; and next he notices that he is getting fagged, and that the cayote actually has to slacken speed a little to keep from running away from him—and *then* that town-dog is mad in earnest and he begins to strain and weep and swear, and paw the sand higher than ever, and reach for the cayote with concentrated and desperate energy. This "spurt" finds him six feet behind the gliding enemy, and two miles from his friends. And then, in the instant that a wild new hope is lighting up his face, the cayote turns and smiles blandly upon him once more, and with a something about it which seems to say: "Well, I shall have to tear myself away from you, bub—business is business, and it will not do for me to be fooling along this way all day"— and forthwith there is a rushing sound, and the sudden splitting of a long crack through the atmosphere, and behold that dog is solitary and alone in the midst of a vast solitude!

It makes his head swim. He stops, and looks all around; climbs the nearest sand-mound, and gazes into the distance; shakes his head reflectively, and then, without a word, he turns and jogs along back to his train, and takes up a humble position under the hindmost wagon, and feels unspeakably mean, and looks ashamed, and hangs his tail at half-mast for a week. And for as much as a year after that, whenever there is a great hue and cry after a cayote, that dog will merely glance in that direction without emotion, and apparently observe to himself, "I believe I do not wish any of the pie."

The cayote lives chiefly in the most desolate and forbidding deserts, along with the lizard, the jackass-rabbit and the raven, and gets an uncertain and precarious living, and earns it. He seems to subsist almost wholly on the carcases of oxen, mules and horses that have dropped out of emigrant trains and died, and upon windfalls of carrion, and occasional legacies of offal bequeathed to him by white men who have been opulent enough to have something better to butcher than condemned army bacon. He will eat anything in the world that his first cousins, the desert-frequenting tribes of Indians will, and they will eat anything they can bite. It is a curious fact that these latter are the only creatures known to history who will eat nitro-glycerine and ask for more if they survive.

The cayote of the deserts beyond the Rocky Mountains has a peculiarly hard time of it, owing to the fact that his relations, the Indians, are just as apt to be the first to detect a seductive scent on the desert breeze, and follow the fragrance to the late ox it emanated from, as he is himself; and when this occurs he has to content himself with sitting off at a little distance watching those people strip off and dig out everything edible, and walk off with it. Then he and the waiting ravens explore the skeleton and polish the bones. It is considered that the cayote, and the obscene bird, and the Indian of the desert, testify their blood kinship with each other in that they live together in the waste places of the earth on terms of perfect confidence and friendship, while hating all other creatures and yearning to assist at their funerals. He does not mind going a hundred miles to breakfast, and a hundred and fifty to dinner, because he is sure to have three or four days between meals, and he can just as well be traveling and looking at the scenery as lying around doing nothing and adding to the burdens of his parents.

We soon learned to recognize the sharp, vicious bark of the cayote as it came across the murky plain at night to disturb our dreams among the mail-sacks; and remembering his forlorn aspect and his hard fortune, made shift to wish him the blessed novelty of a long day's good luck and a limitless larder the morrow.

CHAPTER VI

Our new conductor (just shipped) had been without sleep for twenty hours. Such a thing was very frequent. From St. Joseph, Missouri, to Sacramento, California, by stage-coach, was nearly nineteen hundred miles, and the trip was often made in fifteen days (the cars do it in four and a half, now), but the time specified in the mail contracts, and required by the schedule, was eighteen or nineteen days, if I remember rightly. This was to make fair allowance for winter storms and snows, and other unavoidable causes of detention. The stage company had everything under strict discipline and good system. Over each two hundred and fifty miles of road they placed an agent or superintendent, and invested him with great authority. His beat or jurisdiction of two hundred and fifty miles was called a "division." He purchased horses, mules harness, and food for men and beasts, and distributed these things among his stage stations, from time to time, according to his judgment of what each station needed. He erected station buildings and dug wells. He attended to the paying of the station-keepers, hostlers, drivers and blacksmiths, and discharged them whenever he chose. He was a very, very great man in his "division"—a kind of Grand Mogul, a Sultan of the Indies, in whose presence common men were modest of speech and manner, and in the glare of whose greatness even the dazzling stage-driver dwindled to a penny dip. There were about eight of these kings, all told, on the overland route.

Next in rank and importance to the division-agent came the "conductor." His beat was the same length as the agent's—two hundred and fifty miles. He sat with the driver, and (when necessary) rode that fearful distance, night and day, without other rest or sleep than what he could get perched thus on top of the flying vehicle. Think of it! He had absolute charge of the mails, express matter, passengers, and stage-coach, until he delivered them to the next conductor, and got his receipt for them. Consequently he had to be a man of intelligence, decision and considerable executive ability. He was usually a quiet, pleasant man, who attended closely to his duties, and was a good deal of a gentleman. It was not absolutely necessary that the division-agent should be a gentleman, and occasionally he wasn't. But he was always a general in administrative ability, and a bulldog in courage and determination—otherwise the chieftainship over the lawless underlings of the overland service would never in any instance have been to him anything but an equivalent for a month of insolence and distress and a bullet and a coffin at the

571

end of it. There were about sixteen or eighteen conductors on the overland, for there was a daily stage each way, and a conductor on every stage.

Next in *real* and official rank and importance, *after* the conductor, came my delight, the driver—next in real but not *apparent* importance—for we have seen that in the eyes of the common herd the driver was to the conductor as an admiral is to the captain of the flag-ship. The driver's beat was pretty long, and his sleeping-time at the stations pretty short, sometimes; and so, but for the grandeur of his position his would have been a sorry life, as well as a hard and a wearing one. We took a new driver every day or every night (for they drove backward and forward over the same piece of road all the time), and therefore we never got as well acquainted with them as we did with the conductors; and besides, they would have been above being familiar with such rubbish as passengers, anyhow, as a general thing. Still, we were always eager to get a sight of each and every new driver as soon as the watch changed, for each and every day we were either anxious to get rid of an unpleasant one, or loath to part with a driver we had learned to like and had come to be sociable and friendly with. And so the first question we asked the conductor whenever we got to where we were to exchange drivers, was always, "Which is him?" The grammar was faulty, maybe, but we could not know, then, that it would go into a book some day. As long as everything went smoothly, the overland driver was well enough situated, but if a fellow driver got sick suddenly it made trouble, for the coach *must* go on, and so the potentate who was about to climb down and take a luxurious rest after his long night's siege in the midst of wind and rain and darkness, had to stay where he was and do the sick man's work. Once, in the Rocky Mountains, when I found a driver sound asleep on the box, and the mules going at the usual break-neck pace, the conductor said never mind him, there was no danger, and he was doing double duty—had driven seventy-five miles on one coach, and was now going back over it on this without rest or sleep. A hundred and fifty miles of holding back of six vindictive mules and keeping them from climbing the trees! It sounds incredible, but I remember the statement well enough.

The station-keepers, hostlers, etc., were low, rough characters, as already described; and from western Nebraska to Nevada a considerable sprinkling of them might be fairly set down as outlaws—fugitives from justice, criminals whose best security was a section of country which was without law and without even the pretence of it. When the "division-agent" issued an order to one of these parties he did it with the full understanding that he might have to enforce it with a navy six-shooter, and so he always went "fixed" to make things go along smoothly. Now and then a division-agent was really obliged to shoot a hostler through the head to teach him some simple matter that he could have taught him with a club if his circumstances and surroundings had been different. But they were snappy, able men, those division-agents, and when they tried to teach a subordinate anything, that subordinate generally "got it through his head."

A great portion of this vast machinery—these hundreds of men and coaches, and thousands of mules and horses—was in the hands of Mr. Ben Holliday. All the western half of the business was in his hands. This reminds me of an incident of Palestine travel which is pertinent here, and so I will transfer it just in the language in which I find it set down in my Holy Land note-book:

No doubt everybody has heard of Ben Holliday—a man of prodigious energy, who used to send mails and passengers flying across the continent in his overland stage-coaches like a very whirlwind—two thousand long miles in fifteen days and a half, by the watch! But this fragment of history is not about Ben Holliday, but about a young New York boy by the name of Jack, who traveled with our small party of pilgrims in the Holy Land (and who had traveled to California in Mr. Holliday's overland coaches three years before, and had by no means forgotten it or lost his gushing admiration of Mr. H.) Aged nineteen. Jack was a good boy—a good-hearted and always well-meaning boy, who had been reared in the city of New York, and although he was bright and knew a great many useful things, his Scriptural education had been a good deal neglected—to such a degree, indeed, that all Holy Land history was fresh and new to him, and all Bible names mysteries that had never disturbed his virgin ear. Also in our party was an elderly pilgrim who was the reverse of Jack, in that he was learned in the Scriptures and an enthusiast concerning them. He was our encyclopedia, and we were never tired of listening to his speeches, nor he of making them. He never passed a celebrated locality, from Bashan to Bethlehem, without illuminating it with an oration. One day, when camped near the ruins of Jericho, he burst forth with something like this:

"Jack, do you see that range of mountains over yonder that bounds the Jordan valley? The mountains of Moab, Jack! Think of it, my boy—the actual mountains of Moab—renowned in Scripture history! We are actually standing face to face with those illustrious crags and peaks—and for all we know"]dropping his voice impressively], "*our eyes may be resting at this very moment upon the spot* WHERE LIES THE MYSTERIOUS GRAVE OF MOSES! Think of it, Jack!"

"Moses *who?*" (falling inflection).

"Moses *who!* Jack, you ought to be ashamed of yourself— you ought to be ashamed of such criminal ignorance. Why, Moses, the great guide, soldier, poet, lawgiver of ancient Israel! Jack, from this spot where we stand, to Egypt, stretches a fearful desert three hundred miles in extent—and across that desert that wonderful man brought the children of Israel!—guiding them with unfailing sagacity for forty years over the sandy desolation and among the obstructing rocks and hills, and landed them at last, safe and sound, with insight of this very spot; and where we now stand they entered the Promised Land with anthems of rejoicing! It was a wonderful, wonderful thing to do, Jack! Think of it!"

"*Forty years? Only three hundred miles?* Humph! Ben Holliday would have fetched them through in thirty-six hours!"

The boy meant no harm. He did not know that he had said anything that was wrong or irreverent. And so no one scolded him or felt offended with him—and nobody *could* but some ungenerous spirit incapable of excusing the heedless blunders of a boy.

At noon on the fifth day out, we arrived at the "Crossing of the South Platte," *alias* "Julesburg," *alias* "Overland City," four hundred and seventy miles from St. Joseph—the strangest, quaintest, funniest frontier town that our untraveled eyes had ever stared at and been astonished with.

CHAPTER VII

It did seem strange enough to see a town again after what appeared to us such a long acquaintance with deep, still, almost lifeless and houseless solitude! We tumbled out into the busy street feeling like meteoric people crumbled off the corner of some other world, and wakened up suddenly in this. For an hour we took as much interest in Overland City as if we had never seen a town before. The reason we had an hour to spare was because we had to change out stage (for a less sumptuous affair, called a "mud-wagon") and transfer our freight of mails.

Presently we got under way again. We came to the shallow, yellow, muddy South Platte, with its low banks and its scattering flat sand-bars and pigmy islands—a melancholy stream straggling through the centre of the enormous flat plain, and only saved from being impossible to find with the naked eye by its sentinel rank of scattering trees standing on either bank. The Platte was "up," they said—which made me wish I could see it when it was down, if it could look any sicker and sorrier. They said it was a dangerous stream to cross, now, because its quicksands were liable to swallow up horses, coach and passengers if an attempt was made to ford it. But the mails had to go, and we made the attempt. Once or twice in midstream the wheels sunk into the yielding sands so threateningly that we half believed we had dreaded and avoided the sea all our lives to be shipwrecked in a "mud-wagon" in the middle of a desert at last. But we dragged through and sped away toward the setting sun.

Next morning, just before dawn, when about five hundred and fifty miles from St. Joseph, our mud-wagon broke down. We were to be delayed five or six hours, and therefore we took horses, by invitation, and joined a party who were just starting on a buffalo hunt. It was noble sport galloping over the plain in the dewy freshness of the morning, but our part of the hunt ended in disaster and disgrace, for a wounded buffalo bull chased the passenger Bemis nearly two miles, and then he forsook his horse and took to a lone tree. He was very sullen about the matter for some twenty-four hours, but at last he began to soften little by little, and finally he said:

"Well, it was not funny, and there was no sense in those gawks making themselves so facetious over it. I tell you I was angry in earnest for awhile. I should have shot that long gangly lubber they called Hank, if I could have done it without crippling six or seven other people—but of course I couldn't, the old 'Allen's' so confounded comprehensive. I wish those loafers had been up in the tree; they wouldn't have wanted to laugh so. If I had had a horse worth a cent—but no, the minute he saw that buffalo bull wheel on him and give a bellow, he raised straight up in the air and stood on his heels. The saddle began to slip, and I took him round the neck and laid close to him, and began to pray. Then he came down and stood up on the other end awhile, and the bull actually stopped pawing sand and bellowing to contemplate the inhuman spectacle. Then the bull made a pass at him and uttered a bellow that sounded perfectly frightful, it was so close to me, and that seemed to literally prostrate my horse's reason, and make a raving distracted maniac of him, and I wish I may die if he didn't stand on his head for a quarter of a minute and shed tears. He was absolutely out of his mind—he was, as sure as truth itself, and he really didn't know what he was doing. Then the bull came charging at us, and my horse dropped down on all fours and took a fresh start—and then for the next ten minutes he would actually throw one handspring after another so fast that the bull began to get unsettled, too, and didn't know where to start in—and so he stood there sneezing, and shovelling dust over his back, and bellowing every now and them, and thinking he had got a fifteen-hundred dollar circus horse for breakfast, certain. Well, I was first out on his neck—the horse's, not the bull's—and then underneath, and next on his rump, and sometimes head up, and sometimes heels—but I tell you it seemed solemn and awful to be ripping and tearing and carrying on so in the presence of death, as you might say. Pretty soon the bull made a snatch for us and brought away some of my horse's tail (I suppose, but do not know, being pretty busy at the time), but *something* made him hungry for solitude and suggested to him to get up and hunt for it. And then you ought to have seen that spider-legged old skeleton go! and you ought to have seen the bull cut out after him, too—head down, tongue out, tail up, bellowing like everything, and actually mowing down the weeds, and tearing up the earth, and boosting up the sand like a whirlwind! By George, it was a hot race! I and the saddle were back on the rump, and I had the bridle in my teeth and holding on to the pommel with both hands. First we left the dogs behind; then we passed a jackass rabbit; then we overtook a cayote, and were gaining on an antelope when the rotten girth let go and threw me about thirty yards off to the left, and as the saddle went down over the horse's rump he gave it a lift with his heels that sent it more than four hundred yards up in the air, I wish I may die in a minute if he didn't. I fell at the foot of the only solitary tree there was in nine counties adjacent (as any creature could see with the naked eye), and the next second I had hold of the bark with four sets of nails and my teeth, and the next second after that I was astraddle of the main limb and blaspheming my luck in a way that made my breath smell of brimstone. I *had* the bull, now, if he did not think of *one* thing. But that one thing I dreaded. I dreaded it very seriously. There was a possibility that the bull might not think of it, but there were greater chances that he would. I made up my mind what I would do in case he did. It was a little over forty feet to the ground from where I sat. I cautiously unwound the lariat from the pommel of my saddle—"

"Your *saddle?* Did you take your saddle up in the tree with you?"

"Take it up in the tree with me? Why, how you talk. Of course I didn't. No man could do that. It *fell* in the tree when it came down."

"Oh—exactly."

"Certainly. I unwound the lariat, and fastened one end of it to the limb. It was the very best green raw-hide, and capable of sustaining tons. I made a slip-noose in the other end, and then hung it down to see the length. It reached down twenty-two feet—half way to the ground. I then loaded every barrel of the Allen with a double charge. I felt satisfied. I said to myself, if he never thinks of that one thing that I dread, all right—but if he does, all right anyhow—I am fixed for him. But don't you know that the very thing a man dreads is the thing that always happens? Indeed it is so. I watched the bull, now, with anxiety—anxiety which no one can conceive of who has not been in such a situation and felt that at any moment death might come. Presently a thought came into the bull's eye. I knew it! said I—if my nerve fails now, I am lost. Sure enough, it was just as I had dreaded, he started in to climb the tree—''

"What, the bull?"

"Of course—who else?"

"But a bull can't climb a tree."

"He can't, can't he? Since you know so much about it, did you ever see a bull try?"

"No! I never dreamt of such a thing."

"Well, then, what is the use of your talking that way, then? Because you never saw a thing done, is that any reason why it can't be done?"

"Well, all right—go on. What did you do?"

"The bull started up, and got along well for about ten feet, then slipped and slid back. I breathed easier. He tried it again—got up a little higher—slipped again. But he came at it once more, and this time he was careful. He got gradually higher and higher, and my spirits went down more and more. Up he came—an inch at a time—with his eyes hot, and his tongue hanging out. Higher and higher—hitched his foot over the stump of a limb, and looked up, as much as to say, 'You are my meat, friend.' Up again—higher and higher, and getting more excited the closer he got. He was within ten feet of me! I took a long breath,—and then said I, 'It is now or never.' I had the coil of the lariat all ready; I paid it out slowly, till it hung right over his head; all of a sudden I let go of the slack, and the slipnoose fell fairly round his neck! Quicker than lightning I out with the Allen and let him have it in the face. It was an awful roar, and must have scared the bull out of his senses. When the smoke cleared away, there he was, dangling in the air, twenty foot from the ground, and going out of one convulsion into another faster than you could count! I didn't stop to count, anyhow—I shinned down the tree and shot for home.''

"Bemis, is all that true, just as you have stated it?"

"I wish I may rot in my tracks and die the death of a dog if it isn't."

"Well, we can't refuse to believe it, and we don't. But if there were some proofs—"

"Proofs! Did I bring back my lariat?"

"No."

"Did I bring back my horse?"

"No."

"Did you ever see the bull again?"

"No."

"Well, then, what more do you want? I never saw anybody as particular as you are about a little thing like that."

I made up my mind that if this man was not a liar he only missed it by the skin of his teeth. This episode reminds me of an incident of my brief sojourn in Siam, years afterward. The European citizens of a town in the neighborhood of Bangkok had a prodigy among them by the name of Eckert, an Englishman—a person famous for the number, ingenuity and imposing magnitude of his lies. They were always repeating his most celebrated falsehoods, and always trying to "draw him out" before strangers; but they seldom succeeded. Twice he was invited to the house where I was visiting, but nothing could seduce him into a specimen lie. One day a planter named Bascom, an influential man, and a proud and sometimes irascible one, invited me to ride over with him and call on Eckert. As we jogged along, said he:

"Now, do you know where the fault lies? It lies in putting Eckert on his guard. The minute the boys go to pumping at Eckert he knows perfectly well what they are after, and of course he shuts up his shell. Anybody might know he would. But when we get there, we must play him finer than that. Let him shape the conversation to suit himself—let him drop it or change it whenever he wants to. Let him see that nobody is trying to draw him out. Just let him have his own way. He will soon forget himself and begin to grind out lies like a mill. Don't get impatient—just keep quiet, and let me play him. I will make him lie. It does seem to me that the boys must be blind to overlook such an obvious and simple trick as that."

Eckert received us heartily—a pleasant-spoken, gentleman-nered creature. We sat in the veranda an hour, sipping English ale, and talking about the king, and the sacred white elephant, the Sleeping Idol, and all manner of things; and I noticed that my comrade never led the conversation himself or shaped it, but simply followed Eckert's lead, and betrayed no solicitude and no anxiety about anything. The effect was shortly perceptible. Eckert began to grow communicative; he grew more and more at his ease, and more and more talkative and sociable. Another hour passed in the same way, and then all of a sudden Eckert said:

"Oh, by the way! I came near forgetting. I have got a thing here to astonish you. Such a thing as neither you nor any other man ever heard of—I've got a cat that will eat cocoanut! Common green cocoanut—and not only eat the meat, but drink the milk. It is so—I'll swear to it.''

A quick glance from Bascom—a glance that I understood—then:

"Why, bless my soul, I never heard of such a thing. Man, it is impossible.''

"I knew you would say it. I'll fetch the cat.''

He went in the house. Bascom said:

"There—what did I tell you? Now, that is the way to handle Eckert. You see, I have petted him along patiently, and put his suspicions to sleep. I am glad we came. You tell the boys about it when you go back. Cat eat a cocoanut—oh, my! Now, that is just his way, exactly—he will tell the absurdest lie, and trust to luck to get out of it again. Cat eat a cocoanut—the innocent fool!''

Eckert approached with his cat, sure enough.

Bascom smiled. Said he:

"I'll hold the cat—you bring a cocoanut.''

Eckert split one open, and chopped up some pieces. Bascom smuggled a wink to me, and proffered a slice of the fruit to puss. She snatched it, swallowed it ravenously, and asked for more!

We rode our two miles in silence, and wide apart. At least I was silent, though Bascom cuffed his horse and cursed him a good deal, notwithstanding the horse was behaving well enough. When I branched off homeward, Bascom said:

"Keep the horse till morning. And—you need not speak of this—foolishness to the boys.''

CHAPTER VIII

In a little while all interest was taken up in stretching our necks and watching for the "pony-rider"—the fleet messenger who sped across the continent from St. Joe to Sacramento, carrying letters nineteen hundred miles in eight days! Think of that for perishable horse and human flesh and blood to do! The pony-rider was usually a little bit of a man, brimful of spirit and endurance. No matter what time of the day or night his watch came on, and no matter whether it was winter or summer, raining, snowing, hailing, or sleeting, or whether his "beat" was a level straight road or a crazy trail over mountain crags and precipices, or whether it led through peaceful regions or regions that swarmed with hostile Indians, he must be always ready to leap into the saddle and be off like the wind! There was no idling-time for a pony-rider on duty. He rode fifty miles without stopping, by daylight, moonlight, starlight, or through the blackness of darkness—just as it happened. He rode a splendid horse that was born for a racer and fed and lodged like a gentleman; kept him at his utmost speed for ten miles, and then, as he came crashing up to the station where stood two men holding fast a fresh, impatient steed, the transfer of rider and mail-bag was made in the twinkling of an eye, and away flew the eager pair and were out of sight before the spectator could get hardly the ghost of a look. Both rider and horse went "flying light." The rider's dress was thin, and fitted close; he wore a "roundabout," and a skull-cap, and tucked his pantaloons into his boot-tops like a race-rider. He carried no arms—he carried nothing that was not absolutely necessary, for even the postage on his literary freight was worth *five dollars a letter*. He got but little frivolous correspondence to carry—his bag had business letters in it, mostly. His horse was stripped of all unnecessary weight, too. He wore a little wafer of a racing-saddle, and no visible blanket. He wore light shoes, or none at all. The little flat mail-pockets strapped under the rider's thighs would each hold about the bulk of a child's primer. They held many and many an important business chapter and newspaper letter, but these were written on paper as airy and thin as gold-leaf, nearly, and thus bulk and weight were economized. The stage-coach traveled about a hundred to a hundred and twenty-five miles a day (twenty-four hours), the pony-rider about two hundred and fifty. There were about eighty pony-riders in the saddle all the time, night and day, stretching in a long, scattering procession from Missouri to California, forty flying eastward, and forty toward the west, and among them making four hundred gallant horses earn a stirring livelihood and see a deal of scenery every single day in the year.

We had had a consuming desire, from the beginning, to see a pony-rider, but somehow or other all that passed us and all that met us managed to streak by in the night, and so we heard only a whiz and a hail, and the swift phantom of the desert was gone before we could get our heads out of the windows. But now we were expecting one along every moment, and would see him in broad daylight. Presently the driver exclaims:

"HERE HE COMES!"

Every neck is stretched further, and every eye strained wider. Away across the endless dead level of the prairie a black speck appears against the sky, and it is plain that it moves. Well, I should think so! In a second or two it becomes a horse and rider, rising and falling, rising and falling—sweeping toward us nearer and nearer—growing more and more distinct, more and more sharply defined—nearer and still nearer, and the flutter of the hoofs comes faintly to the ear—another instant a whoop and a hurrah from our upper deck, a wave of the rider's hand, but no reply, and man and horse burst past our excited faces, and go winging away like a belated fragment of a storm!

So sudden is it all, and so like a flash of unreal fancy, that but for the flake of white foam left quivering and perishing on a mail-sack after the vision had flashed by and disappeared, we might have doubted whether we had seen any actual horse and man at all, maybe.

We rattled through Scott's Bluffs Pass, by and by. It was along here somewhere that we first came across genuine and unmistakable alkali water in the road, and we cordially hailed it as a first-class curiosity, and a thing to be mentioned with eclat in letters to the ignorant at home. This water gave the road a soapy appearance, and in many places the ground looked as if it had been whitewashed. I think the strange alkali water excited us as much as any wonder we had come upon yet, and I know we felt very complacent and conceited, and better satisfied with life after we had added it to our list of things which *we* had seen and some other people had not. In a small way we were the same sort of simpletons as those who climb unnecessarily the perilous peaks of Mont Blanc and the Matterhorn, and derive no pleasure from it except the reflection that it isn't a common experience. But once in a while one of those parties trips and comes darting down the long mountain-crags in a sitting posture, making the crusted snow smoke behind him, flitting from bench to bench, and from terrace to terrace, jarring the earth where he strikes, and still glancing and flitting on again, sticking an iceberg into himself every now and then, and tearing his clothes, snatching at things to save himself, taking hold of trees and fetching them along with him, roots and all, starting little rocks now and then, then big boulders, then acres of ice and snow and patches of forest, gathering and still gathering as he goes, adding and still adding to his massed and sweeping grandeur as he nears a three thousand-foot precipice, till at last he waves his hat magnificently and rides into eternity on the back of a raging and tossing avalanche!

This is all very fine, but let us not be carried away by excitement, but ask calmly, how does this person feel about it in his cooler moments next day, with six or seven thousand feet of snow and stuff on top of him?

We crossed the sand hills near the scene of the Indian mail robbery and massacre of 1856, wherein the driver and conductor perished, and also all the passengers but one, it was supposed; but this must have been a mistake, for at different times afterward on the Pacific coast I was personally acquainted with a hundred and thirty-three or four people who were wounded during that massacre, and barely escaped with their lives. There was no doubt of the truth of it—I had it from their own lips. One of these parties told me that he kept coming across arrow-heads in his system for nearly seven years after the massacre; and another of them told me that he was stuck so literally full of arrows that after the Indians were gone and he could raise up and examine himself, he could not restrain his tears, for his clothes were completely ruined.

The most trustworthy tradition avers, however, that only one man, a person named Babbitt, survived the massacre, and he was desperately wounded. He dragged himself on his hands and knee (for one leg was broken) to a station several miles away. He did it during portions of two nights, lying concealed one day and part of another, and for more than forty hours suffering unimaginable anguish from hunger, thirst and bodily pain. The Indians robbed the coach of everything it contained, including quite an amount of treasure.

CHAPTER IX

We passed Fort Laramie in the night, and on the seventh morning out we found ourselves in the Black Hills, with Laramie Peak at our elbow (apparently) looming vast and solitary—a deep, dark, rich indigo blue in hue, so portentously did the old colossus frown under his beetling brows of storm-cloud. He was thirty or forty miles away, in reality, but he only seemed removed a little beyond the low ridge at our right. We breakfasted at Horse-Shoe Station, six hundred and seventy-six miles out from St. Joseph. We had now reached a hostile Indian country, and during the afternoon we passed Laparelle Station, and enjoyed great discomfort all the time we were in the neighborhood, being aware that many of the trees we dashed by at arm's length concealed a lurking Indian or two. During the preceding night an ambushed savage had sent a bullet through the pony-rider's jacket, but he had ridden on, just the same, because pony-riders were not allowed to stop and inquire into such things except when killed. As long as they had life enough left in them they had to stick to the horse and ride, even if the Indians had been waiting for them a week, and were entirely out of patience.

About two hours and a half before we arrived at Laparelle Station, the keeper in charge of it had fired four times at an Indian, but he said with an injured air that the Indian had "skipped around so's to spile everything—and ammunition's blamed skurse, too." The most natural inference conveyed by his manner of speaking was, that in "skipping around," the Indian had taken an unfair advantage. The coach we were in had a neat hold through its front—a reminiscence of its last trip through this region. The bullet that made it wounded the driver slightly, but he did not mind it much. He said the place to keep a man "huffy" was down on the Southern Overland, among the Apaches, before the company moved the stageline up on the northern route. He said the Apaches used to annoy him all the time down there, and that he came as near as anything to starving to death in the midst of abundance, because they kept him so leaky with bullet holes that he "couldn't hold his vittles." This person's statement were not generally believed.

We shut the blinds down very tightly that first night in the hostile Indian country, and lay on our arms. We slept on them some, but most of the time we only lay on them. We did not talk much, but kept quiet and listened. It was an inky-black night, and occasionally rainy. We were among woods and rocks, hills and gorges—so shut in, in fact, that when we peeped through a chink in a curtain, we could discern nothing. The driver and conductor on top were still, too, or only spoke at long intervals, in low tones, as is the way of men in the midst of invisible dangers. We listened to rain-drops pattering on the roof; and the grinding of the wheels through the muddy gravel; and the low wailing of the wind; and all the time we had that absurd sense upon us, inseparable from travel at night in a close-curtained vehicle, the sense of remaining perfectly still in one place, notwithstanding the jolting and swaying of the vehicle, the trampling of the horses, and the grinding of the wheels. We listened a long time, with intent faculties and bated breath; every time one of us would relax, and draw a long sigh of relief and start to say something, a comrade would be sure to utter a sudden "Hark!" and instantly the experimenter was rigid and listening again. So the tiresome minutes and decades of minutes dragged away, until at last our tense forms filmed over with a dulled consciousness, and we slept, if one might call such a condition by so strong a name—for it was a sleep set with a hair-trigger. It was a sleep seething and teeming with a weird and distressful confusion of shreds and fag-ends of dreams—a sleep that was a chaos. Presently, dreams and sleep and the sullen hush of the night were startled by a ringing report, and cloven by *such* a long, wild, agonizing shriek! Then we heard—ten steps from the stage—

"Help! help! help!" [It was our driver's voice.]

"Kill him! Kill him like a dog!"

"I'm being murdered! Will no man lend me a pistol?"

"Look out! head him off! head him off!"

[Two pistol shots; a confusion of voices and the trampling of many feet, as if a crowd were closing and surging together around some object; several heavy, dull blows, as with a club; a voice that said appealingly, "Don't, gentlemen, please don't—I'm a dead man!" Then a fainter groan, and another blow, and away sped the stage into the darkness, and left the grisly mystery behind us.]

What a startle it was! Eight seconds would amply cover the time it occupied—maybe even five would do it. We only had time to plunge at a curtain and unbuckle and unbutton part of it in an awkward and hindering flurry, when our whip cracked sharply overhead, and we went rumbling and thundering away, down a mountain "grade."

We fed on that mystery the rest of the night—what was left of it, for it was waning fast. It had to remain a present mystery, for all we could get from the conductor in answer to our hails was something that sounded, through the clatter of the wheels, like "Tell you in the morning!"

So we lit our pipes and opened the corner of a curtain for a chimney, and lay there in the dark, listening to each other's story of how he first felt and how many thousand Indians he first thought had hurled themselves upon us, and what his remembrance of the subsequent sounds was, and the order of their occurrence. And we theorized, too, but there was never a theory that would account for our driver's voice being out there, nor yet account for his Indian murderers talking such good English, if they *were* Indians.

So we chatted and smoked the rest of the night comfortably away, our boding anxiety being somehow marvelously dissipated by the real presence of something to be anxious *about*.

We never did get much satisfaction about that dark occurrence. All that we could make out of the odds and ends of the information we gathered in the morning, was that the disturbance occurred at a station; that we changed drivers there, and that the driver that got off there had been talking roughly about some of the outlaws that infested the region ("for there wasn't a man around there but had a price on his head and didn't dare show himself in the settlements," the conductor said); he had talked roughly about these characters, and ought to have "drove up there with his pistol cocked and ready on the seat alongside of him, and begun business himself, because any softy would know they would be laying for him."

That was all we could gather, and we could see that neither the conductor nor the new driver were much concerned about the matter. They plainly had little respect for a man who would deliver offensive opinions of people and then be so simple as to come into their presence unprepared to "back his judgment," as they pleasantly phrased the killing of any fellow-being who did not like said opinions. And likewise they plainly had a contempt for the man's poor discretion in venturing to rouse the wrath of such utterly reckless wild beasts as those outlaws—and the conductor added:

"I tell you it's as much as Slade himself wants to do!"

This remark created an entire revolution in my curiosity. I cared nothing now about the Indians, and even lost interest in the murdered driver. There was such magic in that name, SLADE! Day or night, now, I stood always ready to drop any subject in hand, to listen to something new about Slade and his ghastly exploits. Even before we got to Overland City, we had begun to hear about Slade and his "division" (for he was a "division-agent") on the Overland; and from the hour we had left Overland City we had heard drivers and conductors talk about only three things—"Californy," the Nevada silver mines, and this desperado Slade. And a deal the most of the talk was about Slade. We had gradually come to have a realizing sense of the fact that Slade was a man whose heart and hands and soul were steeped in the blood of offenders against his dignity; a man who awfully avenged all injuries, affronts, insults or slights, of whatever kind—on the spot if he could, years afterward if lack of earlier opportunity compelled it; a man whose hate tortured him day and night till vengeance appeased it—and not an ordinary vengeance either, but his enemy's absolute death— nothing less; a man whose face would light up with a terrible joy when he surprised a foe and had him at a disadvantage. A high and efficient servant of the Overland, an outlaw among outlaws and yet their relentless scourge, Slade was at once the most bloody, the most dangerous and the most valuable citizen that inhabited the savage fastnesses of the mountains.

CHAPTER X

Really and truly, two thirds of the talk of drivers and conductors had been about this man Slade, ever since the day before we reached Julesburg. In order that the eastern reader may have a clear conception of what a Rocky Mountain desperado is, in his highest state of development, I will reduce all this mass of overland gossip to one straightforward narrative, and present it in the following shape:

Slade was born in Illinois, of good parentage. At about twenty-six years of age he killed a man in a quarrel and fled the country. At St. Joseph, Missouri, he joined one of the early California-bound emigrant trains, and was given the post of train-master. One day on the plains he had an angry dispute with one of his wagon-drivers, and both drew their revolvers. But the driver was the quicker artist, and had his weapon cocked first. So Slade said it was a pity to waste life on so small a matter, and proposed that the pistols be thrown on the ground and the quarrel settled by a fist-fight. The unsuspecting driver agreed, and threw down his pistol—whereupon Slade laughed at his simplicity, and shot him dead!

He made his escape, and lived a wild life for awhile, dividing his time between fighting Indians and avoiding an Illinois sheriff, who had been sent to arrest him for his first murder. It is said that in one Indian battle he killed three savages with his own hand, and afterward cut their ears off and sent them, with his compliments, to the chief of the tribe.

Slade soon gained a name for fearless resolution, and this was sufficient merit to procure for him the important post of overland division-agent at Julesburg, in place of Mr. Jules, removed. For some time previously, the company's horses had been frequently stolen, and the coaches delayed, by gangs of outlaws, who were wont to laugh at the idea of any man's having the temerity to resent such outrages. Slade resented them promptly. The outlaws soon found that the new agent was a man who did not fear anything that breathed the breath of life. He made short work of all offenders. The result was that delays ceased, the company's property was let alone, and no matter what happened or who suffered, Slade's coaches went through, every time! True, in order to bring about this wholesome change, Slade had to kill several men—some say three, others say four, and others six—but the world was the richer for their loss. The first prominent difficulty he had was with the ex-agent Jules, who bore the reputation of being a reckless and desperate man himself. Jules hated Slade for supplanting him, and a good fair occasion for a

586

fight was all he was waiting for. By and by Slade dared to employ a man whom Jules had once discharged. Next, Slade seized a team of stage-horses which he accused Jules of having driven off and hidden somewhere for his own use. War was declared, and for a day or two the two men walked warily about the streets, seeking each other, Jules armed with a double-barreled shot gun, and Slade with his history-creating revolver. Finally, as Slade stepped into a store, Jules poured the contents of his gun into him from behind the door. Slade was pluck, and Jules got several bad pistol wounds in return. Then both men fell, and were carried to their respective lodgings, both swearing that better aim should do deadlier work next time. Both were bedridden a long time, but Jules got on his feet first, and gathering his possessions together, packed them on a couple of mules, and fled to the Rocky Mountains to gather strength in safety against the day of reckoning. For many months he was not seen or heard of, and was gradually dropped out of the remembrance of all save Slade himself. But Slade was not the man to forget him. On the contrary, common report said that Slade kept a reward standing for his capture, dead or alive!

After awhile, seeing that Slade's energetic administration had restored peace and order to one of the worst divisions of the road, the overland stage company transferred him to the Rocky Ridge division in the Rocky Mountains, to see if he could perform a like miracle there. It was the very paradise of outlaws and desperadoes. There was absolutely no semblance of law there. Violence was the rule. Force was the only recognized authority. The commonest misunderstandings were settled on the spot with the revolver or the knife. Murders were done in open day, and with sparkling frequency, and nobody thought of inquiring into them. It was considered that the parties who did the killing had their private reasons for it; for other people to meddle would have been looked upon as indelicate. After a murder, all that Rocky Mountain etiquette required of a spectator was, that he should help the gentleman bury his game—otherwise his churlishness would surely be remembered against him the first time he killed a man himself and needed a neighborly turn in interring him.

Slade took up his residence sweetly and peacefully in the midst of this hive of horse-thieves and assassins, and the very first time one of them aired his insolent swaggerings in his presence he shot him dead! He began a raid on the outlaws, and in a singularly short space of time he had completely stopped their depredations on the stage stock, recovered a large number of stolen horses, killed several of the worst desperadoes of the district, and gained such a dread ascendancy over the rest that they respected him, admired him, feared him, obeyed him! He wrought the same marvelous change in the ways of the community that had marked his administration at Overland City. He captured two men who had stolen overland stock, and with his own hands he hanged them. He was supreme judge in his district, and he was jury and executioner likewise—and not only in the case of offences against his employers, but against passing emigrants as well. On one occasion some emigrants had their stock lost or stolen, and told Slade, who chanced to visit their camp. With a single companion he rode to a ranch, the owners of which he suspected, and opening the door, commenced firing, killing three, and wounding the fourth.

From a bloodthirstily interesting little Montana book* I take this paragraph:

While on the road, Slade held absolute sway. He would ride down to a station, get into a quarrel, turn the house out of windows, and maltreat the occupants most cruelly. The unfortunates had no means of redress, and were compelled to recuperate as best they could. On one of these occasions, it is said he killed the father of the fine little half-breed boy Jemmy, whom he adopted, and who lived with his widow after his execution. Stories of Slade's hanging men, and of innumerable assaults, shootings, stabbings and beatings, in which he was a principal actor, form part of the legends of the stage line. As for minor quarrels and shootings, it is absolutely certain that a minute history of Slade's life would be one long record of such practices.

Slade was a matchless marksman with a navy revolver. The legends say that one morning at Rocky Ridge, when he was feeling comfortable, he saw a man approaching who had offended him some days before—observe the fine memory he had for matters like that—and, "Gentleman," said Slade, drawing, "it is a good twenty-yard shot—I'll clip the third button on his coat!" Which he did. The bystanders all admired it. And they all attended the funeral, too.

On one occasion a man who kept a little whisky-shelf at the station did something which angered Slade—and went and made his will. A day or two afterward Slade came in and called for some brandy. The man reached under the counter (ostensibly to get a bottle—possibly to get something else), but Slade smiled upon him that peculiarly bland and satisfied smile of his which the neighbors had long ago learned to recognize as a death-warrant in disguise, and told him to "none of that!—pass out

*"The Vigilantes of Montana," by Prof. Thos. J. Dimsdale.

the high-priced article." So the poor bar-keeper had to turn his back and get the high-priced brandy from the shelf; and when he faced around again he was looking into the muzzle of Slade's pistol. "And the next instant," added my informant, impressively, "he was one of the deadest men that ever lived."

The stage-drivers and conductors told us that sometimes Slade would leave a hated enemy wholly unmolested, unnoticed and unmentioned, for weeks together—had done it once or twice at any rate. And some said they believed he did it in order to lull the victims into unwatchfulness, so that he could get the advantage of them, and others said they believed he saved up an enemy that way, just as a schoolboy saves up a cake, and made the pleasure go as far as it would by gloating over the anticipation. One of these cases was that of a Frenchman who had offended Slade. To the surprise of everybody Slade did not kill him on the spot, but let him alone for a considerable time. Finally, however, he went to the Frenchman's house very late one night, knocked, and when his enemy opened the door, shot him dead—pushed the corpse inside the door with his foot, set the house on fire and burned up the dead man, his widow and three children! I heard this story from several different people, and they evidently believed what they were saying. It may be true, and it may not. "Give a dog a bad name," etc.

Slade was captured, once, by a party of men who intended to lynch him. They disarmed him, and shut him up in a strong loghouse, and placed a guard over him. He prevailed on his captors to send for his wife, so that he might have a last interview with her. She was a brave, loving, spirited woman. She jumped on a horse and rode for life and death. When she arrived they let her in without searching her, and before the door could be closed she whipped out a couple of revolvers, and she and her lord marched forth defying the party. And then, under a brisk fire, they mounted double and galloped away unharmed!

In the fulness of time Slade's myrmidons captured his ancient enemy Jules, whom they found in a well-chosen hiding-place in the remote fastnesses of the mountains, gaining a precarious livelihood with his rifle. They brought him to Rocky Ridge, bound hand and foot, and deposited him in the middle of the cattle-yard with his back against a post. It is said that the pleasure that lit Slade's face when he heard of it was something fearful to contemplate. He examined his enemy to see that he was securely tied, and then went to bed, content to wait till morning before enjoying the luxury of killing him. Jules spent the night in the cattle-yard, and it is a region where warm nights are never known. In the morning Slade practised on him with his revolver, nipping the flesh here and there, and occasionally clipping off a finger, while Jules begged him to kill him outright and put him out of his misery. Finally Slade reloaded, and walking up close to his victim, made some characteristic remarks and then dispatched him. The body lay there half a day, nobody venturing to touch it without orders, and then Slade detailed a party and assisted at the burial himself. But he first cut off the dead man's ears and put them in his vest pocket, where he carried them for some time with great satisfaction. That is the story as I have frequently heard it told and seen it in print in California newspapers. It is doubtless correct in all essential particulars.

In due time we rattled up to a stage-station, and sat down to breakfast with a half-savage, half-civilized company of armed and bearded mountaineers, ranchmen and station employees. The most gentlemanly-appearing, quiet and affable officer we had yet found along the road in the Overland Company's service was the person who sat at the head of the table, at my elbow. Never youth stared and shivered as I did when I heard them call him SLADE!

Here was romance, and I sitting face to face with it!—looking upon it—touching it—hobnobbing with it, as it were! Here, right by my side, was the actual ogre who, in fights and brawls and various ways, *had taken the lives of twenty-six human beings,* or all men lied about him! I suppose I was the proudest stripling that ever traveled to see strange lands and wonderful people.

He was so friendly and so gentle-spoken that I warmed to him in spite of his awful history. It was hardly possible to realize that this pleasant person was the pitiless scourge of the outlaws, the raw-head-and-bloody-bones the nursing mothers of the mountains terrified their children with. And to this day I can remember nothing remarkable about Slade except that his face was rather broad across the cheek bones, and that the cheek bones were low and the lips peculiarly thin and straight. But that was enough to leave something of an effect upon me, for since then I seldom see a face possessing those characteristics without fancying that the owner of it is a dangerous man.

The coffee ran out. At least it was reduced to one tin-cupful, and Slade was about to take it when he saw that my cup was empty. He politely offered to fill it, but although I wanted it, I politely declined. I was afraid he had not killed anybody that morning, and might be needing diversion. But still with firm politeness he insisted on filling my cup, and said I had traveled all night and better deserved it than he—and while he talked he placidly poured the fluid, to the last drop. I thanked him and drank it, but it gave me no comfort, for I could not feel sure that he would not be sorry, presently, that he had given it away, and proceed to kill me to distract his thoughts from the loss. But nothing of the kind occurred. We left him with only twenty-six dead people to account for, and I felt a tranquil satisfaction in the thought that in so judiciously taking care of No. 1 at that breakfast-table I had pleasantly escaped being No. 27. Slade came out to the coach and saw us off, first ordering certain rearrangements of the mail-bags for our comfort, and then we took leave of him, satisfied that we should hear of him again, some day, and wondering in what connection.

CHAPTER XI

And sure enough, two or three years afterward, we did hear of him again. News came to the Pacific coast that the Vigilance Committee in Montana (whither Slade had removed from Rocky Ridge) had hanged him. I find an account of the affair in the thrilling little book I quoted a paragraph from in the last chapter—"The Vigilantes of Montana; being a Reliable Account of the Capture, Trial and Execution of Henry Plummer's Notorious Road Agent Band: By Prof. Thos. J. Dimsdale, Virginia City, M.T." Mr. Dimsdale's chapter is well worth reading, as a specimen of how the people of the frontier deal with criminals when the courts of law prove inefficient. Mr. Dimsdale makes two remarks about Slade, both of which are accurately descriptive, and one of which is exceedingly picturesque: "Those who saw him in his natural state only, would pronounce him to be a kind husband, a most hospitable host and a courteous gentleman; on the contrary, those who met him when maddened with liquor and surrounded by a gang of armed roughs, would pronounce him a fiend incarnate." And this: "From Fort Kearney, west, he was feared *a great deal more than the Almighty.*" For compactness, simplicity and vigor of expression, I will "back" that sentence against anything in literature. Mr. Dimsdale's narrative is as follows. In all places where italics occur, they are mine:

After the execution of the five men on the 14th of January, the Vigilantes considered that their work was nearly ended. They had freed the country of highwaymen and murderers to a great extent, and they determined that in the absence of the regular civil authority they would establish a People's Court where all offenders should be tried by judge and jury. This was the nearest approach to social order that the circumstances permitted, and, though strict legal authority was wanting, yet the people were firmly determined to maintain its efficiency, and to enforce its decrees. It may here be mentioned that the overt act which was the last round on the fatal ladder leading to the scaffold on which Slade perished, *was the tearing in pieces and stamping upon a writ of this court, followed by his arrest of the Judge, Alex. Davis, by authority of a presented Derringer, and with his own hands.*

J.A. Slade was himself, we have been informed, a Vigilante; he openly boasted of it, and said he knew all that they knew. He was never accused, or even suspected, of either murder or robbery, committed in this Territory (the latter crime was never laid to his charge, in any place); but that he had killed several men in other localities was notorious, and his bad reputation in this respect was a most powerful argument in determining his fate, when he was finally arrested for the offence above mentioned. On returning from Milk River he became more and more addicted to drinking, until at last it was a common feat for him and his friends to "take the town." He and a couple of his dependents might often be seen on one horse, galloping through the streets, shouting and yelling, firing revolvers, etc. On many occasions he would ride his horse into stores, break up bars, toss the scales out of doors and use most insulting language to parties present. Just previous to the day of his arrest, he had given a fearful beating to one of his followers; but such was his influence over them that the man wept bitterly at the gallows, and begged for his life with all his power. *It had become quite common, when Slade was on a spree, for the shopkeepers and citizens to close the stores and put out all the lights;* being fearful of some outrage at his hands. For his wanton destruction of goods and furniture, he was always ready to pay, when sober, if he had money; but there were not a few who regarded payment as small satisfaction for the outrage, and these men were his personal enemies.

From time to time Slade received warnings from men that he well knew would not deceive him, of the certain end of his conduct. There was not a moment, for weeks previous to his arrest, in which the public did not expect to hear of some bloody outrage. The dread of his very name, and the presence of the armed band of hangers-on who followed him alone prevented a resistance which must certainly have ended in the instant murder or mutilation of the opposing party.

Slade was frequently arrested by order of the court whose organization we have described, and had treated it with respect by paying one or two fines and promising to pay the rest when he had money; but in the transaction that occurred at this crisis, he forgot even this caution, and goaded by passion and the hatred of restraint, he sprang into the embrace of death.

Slade had been drunk and "cutting up" all night. He and his companions had made the town a perfect hell. In the morning, J.M. Fox, the sheriff, met him, arrested him, took him into court and commenced reading a warrant that he had for his arrest, by way of arraignment. He became uncontrollably furious, and *seizing the writ, he tore it up, threw it on the ground and stamped upon it.* The clicking of the locks of his companions' revolvers was instantly heard, and a crisis was expected. The sheriff did not attempt his retention; but being at least as prudent as he was valiant, he succumbed, leaving Slade the *master of the situation and the conqueror and ruler of the courts, law and lawmakers.* This was a declaration of war, and was so accepted. The Vigilance Committee now felt that the question of social order and the preponderance of the law-abiding citizens had then and there to be decided. They knew the character of Slade, and they were well aware that they must submit to his rule without murmur, or else that he must be dealt with in such fashion as would prevent his being able to wreak his vengeance on the committee, who could never have hoped to live in the Territory secure from outrage or death, and who could never leave it without encountering his friends, whom his victory would have emboldened and stimulated to a pitch that would have rendered them reckless of consequences. The day previous he had ridden into Dorris's store, and on being requested to leave, he drew his revolver and threatened to kill the gentleman who spoke to him. Another saloon he had led his horse into, and buying a bottle of wine, he tried to make the animal drink it. This was not considered an uncommon performance, as he had often entered saloons and commenced firing at the lamps, causing a wild stampede.

A leading member of the committee met Slade, and informed him in the quiet, earnest manner of one who feels the importance of what he is saying: "Slade, get your horse at once, and go home, or there will be——to pay." Slade started and took a long look, with his dark and piercing eyes, at the gentleman. "What do you mean?" said he. "You have no right to ask me what I mean," was the quiet reply, "get your horse at once, and remember what I tell you." After a short pause he promised to do so, and actually got into the saddle; but, being still intoxicated, he began calling aloud to one after another of his friends, and at last seemed to have forgotten the warning he had received and became again uproarious, shouting the name of a well-known courtezan in company with those of two men whom he considered heads of the committee, as a sort of challenge; perhaps, however, as a simple act of bravado. It seems probable that the intimation of personal danger he had received had not been forgotten entirely; though fatally for him, he took a foolish way of showing his remembrance of it. He sought out Alexander Davis, the Judge of the Court, and drawing a cocked Derringer, he presented it at his head, and told him that he should hold him as a hostage for his own safety. As the judge stood perfectly quiet, and offered no resistance to his captor, no further outrage followed on this score. Previous to this, on account of the critical state of affairs, the committee had met, and at last resolved to arrest him. His execution had not been agreed upon, and, at that time, would have been negatived, most assuredly. A messenger rode down to Nevada to inform the leading men of what was on hand, as it was desirable to show that there was a feeling of unanimity on the subject, all along the gulch.

The miners turned out almost *en masse,* leaving their work and forming in solid column, about six hundred strong, armed to the teeth, they marched up to Virginia. The leader of the body well knew the temper of his men on the subject. He spurred on ahead of them, and hastily calling a meeting of the executive, he told them plainly that the miners meant "business," and that, if they came up, the would not stand in the street to be shot down by Slade's friends: but that they would take him and hang him. The meeting was small, as the Virginia men were loath to act at all. This momentous announcement of the feeling of the Lower Town was made to a cluster of men, who were deliberating behind a wagon, at the rear of a store on Main street.

The committee were most unwilling to proceed to extremities. All the duty they had ever performed seemed as nothing to the task before them; but they had to decide, and that quickly. It was finally agreed that if the whole body of the miners were of the opinion that he should be hanged, that the committee left it in their hands to deal with him. Off, at hot speed, rode the leader of the Nevada men to join his command.

Slade had found out what was intended, and the news sobered him instantly. He went into P.S. Pfouts' store, where Davis was, and apologized for his conduct, saying that he would take it all back.

The head of the column now wheeled into Wallace street and marched up at quick time. Halting in front of the store, the executive officer of the committee stepped forward and arrested Slade, who was at once informed of his doom, and inquiry was made as to whether he had any business to settle. Several parties spoke to him on the subject; but to all such inquiries he turned a deaf ear, being entirely absorbed in the terrifying reflections on his own awful position. He never ceased his entreaties for life, and to see his dear wife. The unfortunate lady referred to, between whom and Slade there existed a warm affection, was at this time living at their ranch on the Madison. She was possessed of considerable personal attractions; tall, well-formed, of graceful carriage, pleasing manners, and was, withal, an accomplished horsewoman.

A messenger from Slade rode at full speed to inform her of her husband's arrest. In an instant she was in the saddle, and with all the energy that love and despair could lend to an ardent temperament and a strong physique, she urged her fleet charger over the twelve miles of rough and rocky ground that intervened between her and the object of her passionate devotion.

Meanwhile a party of volunteers had made the necessary preparations for the execution, in the valley traversed by the branch. Beneath the site of Pfouts and Russell's stone building there was a corral, the gate-posts of which were strong and high. Across the top was laid a beam, to which the rope was fastened, and a dry-goods box served for the platform. To this place Slade was marched, surrounded by a guard, composing the best armed and most numerous force that has ever appeared in Montana Territory.

The doomed man had so exhausted himself by tears, prayers and lamentations, that he had scarcely strength left to stand under the fatal beam. He repeatedly exclaimed, "My God! my God! must I die? Oh, my dear wife!"

On the return of the fatigue party, they encountered some friends of Slade, staunch and reliable citizens and members of the committee, but who were personally attached to the condemned. On hearing of his sentence, one of them, a stout-hearted man, pulled out his handkerchief and walked away, weeping like a child. Slade still begged to see his wife, most piteously, and it seemed hard to deny his request; but the bloody consequences that were sure to follow the inevitable attempt at a rescue, that her presence and entreaties would have certainly incited, forbade the granting of his request. Several gentlemen were sent for to see him, in his last moments, one of whom (Judge Davis) made a short address to the people; but in such low tones as to be inaudible, save to a few in his immediate vicinity. One of his friends, after exhausting his powers of entreaty, threw off his coat and declared that the prisoner could not be hanged until he himself was killed. A hundred guns were instantly leveled at him; whereupon he turned and fled; but, being brought back, he was compelled to resume his coat, and to give a promise of future peaceable demeanor.

Scarcely a leading man in Virginia could be found, though numbers of the citizens joined the ranks of the guard when the arrest was made. All lamented the stern necessity which dictated the execution.

Everything being ready, the command was given, "Men, do your duty," and the box being instantly slipped from beneath his feet, he died almost instantaneously.

The body was cut down and carried to the Virginia Hotel, where, in a darkened room, it was scarcely laid out, when the unfortunate and bereaved companion of the deceased arrived, at headlong speed, to find that all was over, and that she was a widow. Her grief and heart-piercing cries were terrible evidences of the depth of her attachment for her lost husband, and a considerable period elapsed before she could regain the command of her excited feelings.

There is something about the desperado-nature that is wholly unaccountable—at least it looks unaccountable. It is this. The true desperado is gifted with splendid courage, and yet he will take the most infamous advantage of his enemy; armed and free, he will stand up before a host and fight until he is shot all to pieces, and yet when he is under the gallows and helpless he will cry and plead like a child. Words are cheap, and it is easy to call Slade a coward (all executed men who do not "die game" are promptly called cowards by unreflecting people), and when we read of Slade that he "had so exhausted himself by tears, prayers and lamentations, that he had scarcely strength left to stand under the fatal beam," the disgraceful word suggests itself in a moment—yet in frequently defying and inviting the vengeance of banded Rocky Mountain cut-throats by shooting down their comrades and leaders, and never offering to hide or fly, Slade showed that he was a man of peerless bravery. No coward would dare that. Many a notorious coward, many a chicken-livered poltroon, coarse, brutal, degraded, has made his dying speech without a quaver in his voice and been swung into eternity with what looked liked the calmest fortitude, and so we are justified in believing, from the low intellect of such a creature, that it was not *moral* courage that enabled him to do it. Then, if moral courage is not the requisite quality, what could it have been that this stout-hearted Slade lacked?—this bloody, desperate, kindly-mannered, urbane gentleman, who never hesitated to warn his most ruffianly enemies that he would kill them whenever or wherever he came across them next! I think it is a conundrum worth investigating.

CHAPTER XII

Just beyond the breakfast-station we overtook a Mormon emigrant train of thirty-three wagons; and tramping wearily along and driving their herd of loose cows, were dozens of coarse-clad and sad-looking men, women and children, who had walked as they were walking now, day after day for eight lingering weeks, and in that time had compassed the distance our stage had come in *eight days and three hours*—seven hundred and ninety-eight miles! They were dusty and uncombed, hatless, bonnetless and ragged, and they did look so tired!

After breakfast, we bathed in Horse Creek, a (previously) limpid, sparkling stream—an appreciated luxury, for it was very seldom that our furious coach halted long enough for an indulgence of that kind. We changed horses ten or twelve times in every twenty-four hours—changed mules, rather—six mules—and did it nearly every time in *four minutes*. It was lively work. As our coach rattled up to each station six harnessed mules stepped gayly from the stable; and in the twinkling of an eye, almost, the old team was out, and the new one in and we off and away again.

During the afternoon we passed Sweetwater Creek, Independence Rock, Devil's Gate and the Devil's Gap. The latter were wild specimens of rugged scenery, and full of interest—*we were in the heart of the Rocky Mountains, now*. And we also passed by "Alkali" or "Soda Lake," and we woke up to the fact that our journey had stretched a long way across the world when the driver said that the Mormons often came there from Great Salt Lake City to haul away saleratus. He said that a few days gone by they had shoveled up enough pure saleratus from the ground (it was a *dry* lake) to load two wagons, and that when they got these two wagon-loads of a drug that cost them nothing, to Salt Lake, they could sell it for twenty-five cents a pound.

In the night we sailed by a most notable curiosity, and one we had been hearing a good deal about for a day or two, and were suffering to see. This was what might be called a natural ice-house. It was August, now, and sweltering weather in the daytime, yet at one of the stations the men could scrape the soil on the hill-side under the lee of a range of boulders, and at a depth of six inches cut out pure blocks of ice—hard, compactly frozen, and clear as crystal!

Toward dawn we got under way again, and presently as we sat with raised curtains enjoying our early-morning smoke and contemplating the first splendor of the rising sun as it swept down the long array of mountain peaks, flushing and gilding crag after crag and summit after summit, as if the invisible Creator reviewed his gray veterans and they saluted with a smile, we hove in sight of South Pass City. The hotel-keeper, the postmaster, the blacksmith, the mayor, the constable, the city marshal and the principal citizen and property holder, all came out and greeted us cheerily, and we gave him good day. He gave us a little Indian news, and a little Rocky Mountain news, and we gave him some Plains information in return. He then retired to his lonely grandeur and we climbed on up among the bristling peaks and the ragged clouds. South Pass City consisted of four log cabins, one of which was unfinished, and the gentleman with all those offices and titles was the chiefest of the ten citizens of the place. Think of hotel-keeper, postmaster, blacksmith, mayor, constable, city marshal and principal citizen all condensed into one person and crammed into one skin. Bemis said he was "a perfect Allen's revolver of dignities." And he said that if he were to die as postmaster, or as blacksmith, or as postmaster and blacksmith both, the people might stand it; but if he were to die all over, it would be a frightful loss to the community.

Two miles beyond South Pass City we saw for the first time that mysterious marvel which all Western untraveled boys have heard of and fully believe in, but are sure to be astounded at when they see it with their own eyes, nevertheless—banks of snow in dead summer time. We were now far up toward the sky, and knew all the time that we must presently encounter lofty summits clad in the "eternal snow" which was so common-place a matter of mention in books, and yet when I did see it glittering in the sun on stately domes in the distance and knew the month was August and that my coat was hanging up because it was too warm to wear it, I was full as much amazed as if I never had heard of snow in August before. Truly, "seeing is believing"—and many a man lives a long life through, *thinking* he believes certain universally received and well established things, and yet never suspects that if he were confronted by those things once, he would discover that he did not *really* believe them before, but only thought he believed them.

In a little while quite a number of peaks swung into view with long claws of glittering snow clasping them; and with here and there, in the shade, down the mountain side, a little solitary patch of snow looking no larger than a lady's pocket-handkerchief, but being in reality as large as a "public square."

And now, at last, we were fairly in the renowned SOUTH PASS, and whirling gayly along high above the common world. We were perched upon the extreme summit of the great range of the Rocky Mountains, toward which we had been climbing, patiently climbing, ceaselessly climbing, for days and nights together— and about us was gathered a convention of Nature's kings that stood ten, twelve, and even thirteen thousand feet high—grand old fellows who would have to stoop to see Mount Washington, in the twilight. We were in such an airy elevation above the creeping populations of the earth, that now and then when the obstructing crags stood out of the way it seemed that we could look around and abroad and contemplate the whole great globe, with its dissolving views of mountains, seas and continents stretching away through the mystery of the summer haze.

As a general thing the Pass was more suggestive of a valley than a suspension bridge in the clouds—but it strongly suggested the latter at one spot. At that place the upper third of one or two majestic purple domes projected above our level on either hand and gave us a sense of a hidden great deep of mountains and plains and valleys down about their bases which we fancied we might see if we could step to the edge and look over. These Sultans of the fastnesses were turbaned with tumbled volumes of cloud, which shredded away from time to time and drifted off fringed and torn, trailing their continents of shadow after them; and catching presently on an intercepting peak, wrapped it about and brooded there—then shredded away again and left the purple peak, as they had left the purple domes, downy and white with new-laid snow. In passing, these monstrous rags of cloud hung low and swept along right over the spectator's head, swinging their tatters so nearly in his face that his impulse was to shrink when they came closest. In the one place I speak of, one could look below him upon a world of diminishing crags and canyons leading down, down, and away to a vague plain with a thread in it which was a road, and bunches of feathers in it which

were trees,—a pretty picture sleeping in the sunlight—but with
a darkness stealing over it and glooming its features deeper
and deeper under the frown of a coming storm; and then,
while no film or shadow marred the noon brightness of his
high perch, he could watch the tempest break forth down
there and see the lightning leap from crag to crag and the
sheeted rain drive along the canyon-sides, and here the
thunders peal and crash and roar. We had this spectacle; a
familiar one to many, but to us a novelty.

We bowled along cheerily, and presently, at the very summit
(though it had been all summit to us, and all equally level, for
half an hour or more), we came to a spring which spent its water
through two outlets and sent it in opposite directions. The conductor said that one of those streams which we were looking at,
was just starting on a journey westward to the Gulf of California
and the Pacific Ocean, through hundreds and even thousands of
miles of desert solitudes. He said that the other was just leaving
its home among the snow-peaks on a similar journey eastward—
and we knew that long after we should have forgotten the simple
rivulet it would still be plodding its patient way down the mountain sides, and canyon-beds, and between the banks of the
Yellowstone; and by and by would join the broad Missouri and
flow through unknown plains and deserts and unvisited wilder-
nesses; and add a long and troubled pilgrimage among snags and
wrecks and sandbars; and enter the Mississippi, touch the
wharves of St. Louis and still drift on, traversing shoals and
rocky channels, then endless chains of bottomless and ample
bends, walled with unbroken forests, then mysterious byways
and secret passages among woody islands, then the chained
bends again, bordered with wide levels of shining sugar-cane in
place of the sombre forests; then by New Orleans and still other
chains of bends—and finally, after two long months of daily and
nightly harassment, excitement, enjoyment, adventure, and
awful peril of parched throats, pumps and evaporation, pass the
Gulf and enter into its rest upon the bosom of the tropic sea,
never to look upon its snow-peaks again or regret them.

I freighted a leaf with a mental message for the friends at
home, and dropped it in the stream. But I put no stamp on it and
it was held for postage somewhere.

On the summit we overtook an emigrant train of many wagons, many tired men and women, and many a disgusted sheep
and cow. In the wofully dusty horseman in charge of the expedition I recognized John——. Of all persons in the world to meet
on top of the Rocky Mountains thousands of miles from home,
he was the last one I should have looked for. We were school-
boys together and warm friends for years. But a boyish prank of

mine had disruptured this friendship and it had never been renewed. The act of which I speak was this. I had been accustomed to visit occasionally an editor whose room was in the third story of a building and overlooked the street. One day this editor gave me a watermelon which I made preparations to devour on the spot, but chancing to look out of the window, I saw John standing directly under it and an irresistible desire came upon me to drop the melon on his head, which I immediately did. I was the loser, for it spoiled the melon, and John never forgave me and we dropped all intercourse and parted, but now met again under these circumstances.

We recognized each other simultaneously, and hands were grasped as warmly as if no coldness had ever existed between us, and no allusion was made to any. All animosities were buried and the simple fact of meeting a familiar face in that isolated spot so far from home, was sufficient to make us forget all things but pleasant ones, and we parted again with sincere "good-byes" and "God bless you" from both.

We had been climbing up the long shoulders of the Rocky Mountains for many tedious hours—we started *down* them, now. And we went spinning away at a round rate too.

We left the snowy Wind River Mountains and Uinta Mountains behind, and sped away, always through a splendid scenery but occasionally through long ranks of white skeletons of mules and oxen—monuments of the huge emigration of other days—and here and there were up-ended boards or small piles of stones which the driver said marked the resting-place of more precious remains. It was the loneliest land for a grave! A land given over to the cayote and the raven—which is but another name for desolation and utter solitude. On damp, murky nights, these scattered skeletons gave forth a soft, hideous glow, like very faint spots of moonlight starring the vague desert. It was because of the phosphorus in the bones. But no scientific explanation could keep a body from shivering when he drifted by one of those ghostly lights and knew that a skull held it.

At midnight it began to rain, and I never saw anything like it—indeed, I did not even see this, for it was too dark. We fastened down the curtains and even caulked them with clothing, but the rain streamed in in twenty places, notwithstanding. There was no escape. If one moved his feet out of a stream, he brought his body under one; and if he moved his body he caught one somewhere else. If he struggled out of the drenched blankets and sat up, he was bound to get one down the back of his neck. Meantime the stage was wandering about a plain with gaping gullies in it, for the driver could not see an inch before his face nor keep the road, and the storm pelted so pitilessly that there was no keeping the horses still. With the first abatement the conductor turned out with lanterns to look for the road, and the first dash he made was into a chasm about fourteen feet deep, his lantern following like a meteor. As soon as he touched bottom he sang out frantically:

"Don't come here!"

To which the driver, who was looking over the precipice where he had disappeared, replied, with an injured air: "Think I'm a dam fool?"

The conductor was more than an hour finding the road—a matter which showed us how far we had wandered and what chances we had been taking. He traced our wheel-tracks to the imminent verge of danger, in two places. I have always been glad that we were not killed that night. I do not know any particular reason, but I have always been glad.

In the morning, the tenth day out, we crossed Green River, a fine, large, limpid stream— stuck in it, with the water just up to the top of our mail-bed, and waited till extra teams were put on to haul us up the steep bank. But is was nice cool water, and besides it could not find any fresh place on us to wet.

At the Green River station we had breakfast—hot biscuits, fresh antelope steaks, and coffee—the only decent meal we tasted between the United States and Great Salt Lake City, and the only one we were ever really thankful for. Think of the monotonous execrableness of the thirty that went before it, to leave this one simple breakfast looming up in my memory like a shot-tower after all these years have gone by!

At five p.m. we reached Fort Bridger, one hundred and seventeen miles from the South Pass, and one thousand and twenty-five miles from St. Joseph. Fifty-two miles further on, near the head of Echo Canyon, we met sixty United States soldiers from Camp Floyd. The day before, they had fired upon three hundred or four hundred Indians, whom they supposed gathered together for no good purpose. In the fight that had ensued, four Indians were captured, and the main body chased four miles, but nobody killed. This looked like business. We had a notion to get out and join the sixty soldiers, but upon reflecting that there were four hundred of the Indians, we concluded to go on and join the Indians.

Echo Canyon is twenty miles long. It was like a long, smooth, narrow street, with a gradual descending grade, and shut in by enormous perpendicular walls of coarse conglomerate, four hundred feet high in many places, and turreted like medieval castles. This was the most faultless piece of road in the mountains, and the driver said he would "let his team out." He did, and if the Pacific express trains whiz through there now any faster than we did then in the stage-coach, I envy the passengers the exhilaration of it. We fairly seemed to pick up our wheels and fly—and the mail matter was lifted up free from everything and held in solution! I am not given to exaggeration, and when I say a thing I mean it.

However, time presses. At four in the afternoon we arrived on the summit of Big Mountain, fifteen miles from Salt Lake City, when all the world was glorified with the setting sun, and the most stupendous panorama of mountain peaks yet encountered burst on our sight. We looked out upon this sublime spectacle from under the arch of a brilliant rainbow! Even the overland stage-driver stopped his horses and gazed!

Half an hour or an hour later, we changed horses, and took supper with a Mormon "Destroying Angel." "Destroying Angels," as I understand it, are Latter-Day Saints who are set apart by the Church to conduct permanent disappearances of obnoxious citizens. I had heard a deal about these Mormon Destroying Angels and the dark and bloody deeds they had done, and when I entered this one's house I had my shudder all ready. But alas for all our romances, he was nothing but a loud, profane, offensive, old blackguard! He was murderous enough, possibly, to fill the bill of a Destroyer, but would you have *any* kind of an Angel devoid of dignity? Could you abide an Angel in an unclean shirt and no suspenders? Could you respect an Angel with a horse-laugh and a swagger like a buccaneer?

There were other blackguards present—comrades of this one. And there was one person that looked like a gentleman—Heber C. Kimball's son, tall and well made, and thirty years old, perhaps. A lot of slatternly women flitted hither and thither in a hurry, with coffee-pots, plates of bread, and other appurtenances to supper, and these were said to be the wives of the Angel—or some of them, at least. And of course they were; for if they had been hired "help" they would not have let an angel from above storm and swear at them as he did, let alone one from the place this one hailed from.

This was our first experience of the western "peculiar institution," and it was not very prepossessing. We did not tarry long to observe it, but hurried on to the home of the Latter-Day Saints, the stronghold of the prophets, the capital of the only absolute monarch in America—Great Salt Lake City. As the night closed in we took sanctuary in the Salt Lake House and unpacked our baggage.

CHAPTER XIII

We had a fine supper, of the freshest meats and fowls and vegetables—a great variety and as great abundance. We walked about the streets some, afterward, and glanced in at shops and stores; and there was fascination in surreptitiously staring at every creature we took to be a Mormon. This was fairy-land to us, to all intents and purposes—a land of enchantment, and goblins, and awful mystery. We felt a curiosity to ask every child how many mothers it had, and if it could tell them apart; and we experienced a thrill every time a dwelling-house door opened and shut as we passed, disclosing a glimpse of human heads and backs and shoulders—for we so longed to have a good satisfying look at a Mormon family in all its comprehensive ampleness, disposed in the customary concentric rings of its home circle.

By and by the Acting Governor of the Territory introduced us to other "Gentiles," and we spent a sociable hour with them. "Gentiles" are people who are not Mormons. Our fellow-passenger, Bemis, took care of himself, during this part of the evening, and did not make an overpowering success of it, either, for he came into our room in the hotel about eleven o'clock, full of cheerfulness, and talking loosely, disjointedly and indiscriminately, and every now and then tugging out a ragged word by the roots that had more hiccups than syllables in it. This, together with his hanging his coat on the floor on one side of a chair, and his vest on the floor on the other side, and piling his pants on the floor just in front of the same chair, and then contemplating the general result with superstitious awe, and finally pronouncing it "too many for *him*" and going to bed with his boots on, led us to fear that something he had eaten had not agreed with him.

But we knew afterward that it was something he had been drinking. It was the exclusively Mormon refresher, "valley tan." Valley tan (or, at least, one form of valley tan) is a kind of whisky, or first cousin to it; is of Mormon invention and manufactured only in Utah. Tradition says it is made of (imported) fire and brimstone. If I remember rightly no public drinking saloons were allowed in the kingdom by Brigham Young, and no private drinking permitted among the faithful, except they confined themselves to "valley tan."

Next day we strolled about everywhere through the broad, straight, level streets, and enjoyed the pleasant strangeness of a city of fifteen thousand inhabitants with no loafers perceptible in it; and no visible drunkards or noisy people; a limpid stream rippling and dancing through every street in place of a filthy gutter; block after block of trim dwellings, built of "frame" and sunburned brick—a great thriving orchard and garden behind every one of them, apparently—branches from the street stream winding and sparkling among the garden beds and fruit trees—and a grand general air of neatness, repair, thrift and comfort, around and about and over the whole. And everywhere were workshops, factories, and all manner of industries; and intent faces and busy hands were to be seen wherever one looked; and in one's ears was the ceaseless clink of hammers, the buzz of trade and the contented hum of drums and fly-wheels.

The armorial crest of my own State consisted of two dissolute bears holding up the head of a dead and gone cask between them and making the pertinent remark, "UNITED, WE STAND—(hic!)—DIVIDED WE FALL." It was always too figurative for the author of this book. But the Mormon crest was easy. And it was simple, unostentatious, and fitted like a glove. It was a representation of a GOLDEN BEEHIVE, with the bees all at work!

The city lies in the edge of a level plain as broad as the State of Connecticut, and crouches close down to the ground under a curving wall of mighty mountains whose heads are hidden in the clouds, and whose shoulders bear relics of the snows of winter all the summer long. Seen from one of these dizzy heights, twelve or fifteen miles off, Great Salt Lake City is toned down and diminished till it is suggestive of a child's toy-village reposing under the majestic protection of the Chinese wall.

On some of those mountains, to the southwest, it had been raining every day for two weeks, but not a drop had fallen in the city. And on hot days in late spring and early autumn the citizens could quit fanning and growling and go out and cool off by looking at the luxury of a glorious snow-storm going on in the mountains. They could enjoy it at a distance, at those seasons, every day, though no snow would fall in their streets, or anywhere near them.

Salt Lake City was healthy—an extremely healthy city. They declared there was only one physician in the place and he was arrested every week regularly and held to answer under the vagrant act for having "no visible means of support." [They always give you a good substantial article of truth in Salt Lake, and good measure and good weight, too. Very often, if you wished to weigh one of their airiest little commonplace statements you would want the hay scales.]

We desired to visit the famous inland sea, the American "Dead Sea," the great Salt Lake—seventeen miles, horseback, from the city—for we had dreamed about it, and thought about it, and talked about it, and yearned to see it, all the first part of our trip; but now when it was only arm's length away it had suddenly lost nearly every bit of its interest. And so we put if off, in a sort of general way, till next day—and that was the last we ever thought of it. We dined with some hospitable Gentiles; and visited the foundation of the prodigious temple; and talked long with that shrewd Connecticut Yankee, Heber C. Kimball (since deceased), a saint of high degree and a mighty man of commerce. We saw the "Tithing-House," and the "Lion House," and I do not know or remember how many more church and government buildings of various kinds and curious names. We flitted hither and thither and enjoyed every hour, and picked up a great deal of useful information and entertaining nonsense, and went to bed at night satisfied.

The second day, we made the acquaintance of Mr. Street (since deceased) and put on white shirts and went and paid a state visit to the king. He seemed a quiet, kindly, easy- mannered, dignified, self-possessed old gentleman of fifty-five or sixty, and had a gentle craft in his eye that probably belonged there. He was very simply dressed and was just taking off a straw hat as we entered. He talked about Utah, and the Indians, and Nevada, and general American matters and questions, with our secretary and certain government officials who came with us. But he never paid any attention to me, notwithstanding I made several attempts to "draw him out" on federal politics and his high handed attitude toward Congress. I thought some of the things I said were rather fine. But he merely looked around at me, at distant intervals, something as I have seen a benignant old cat look around to see which kitten was meddling with her tail. By and by I subsided into an indignant silence, and so sat until the end, hot and flushed, and execrating him in my heart for an ignorant savage. But he was calm. His conversation with those gentlemen flowed on as sweetly and peacefully and musically as any summer brook. When the audience was ended and we were retiring from the presence, he put his hand on my head, beamed down on me in an admiring way and said to my brother:

"Ah—your child, I presume? Boy, or girl?"

CHAPTER XIV

Mr. Street was very busy with his telegraphic matters—and considering that he had eight or nine hundred miles of rugged, snowy, uninhabited mountains, and waterless, treeless, melan-

choly deserts to traverse with his wire, it was natural and needful
that he should be as busy as possible. He could not go comfortably along and cut his poles by the roadside, either, but they
had to be hauled by ox teams across those exhausting deserts—
and it was two days' journey from water to water, in one or two
of them. Mr. Street's contract was a vast work, every way one
looked at it; and yet to comprehend what the vague words
"eight hundred miles of rugged mountains and dismal deserts"
mean, one must go over the ground in person—pen and ink
descriptions cannot convey the dreary reality to the reader. And
after all, Mr. S.'s mightiest difficulty turned out to be one which
he had never taken into the account at all. Unto Mormons he
had sub-let the hardest and heaviest half of his great undertaking, and all of a sudden they concluded that they were going to
make little or nothing, and so they tranquilly threw their poles
overboard in mountain or desert, just as it happened when they
took the notion, and drove home and went about their
customary business! They were under written contract to Mr.
Street, but they did not care anything for that. They said they
would "admire" to see a "Gentile" force a Mormon to fulfil a
losing contract in Utah! And they made themselves very merry
over the matter. Street said—for it was he that told us these
things:

"I was in dismay. I was under heavy bonds to complete my
contract in a given time, and this disaster looked very much like
ruin. It was an astounding thing; it was such a wholly unlooked-
for difficulty, that I was entirely nonplussed. I am a business
man—have always been a businessman—do not know anything
but business—and so you can imagine how like being struck by
lightning it was to find myself in a country where *written contracts were worthless!*—that main security, that sheet-anchor,
that absolute necessity, of business. My confidence left me.
There was no use in making new contracts—that was plain. I
talked with first one prominent citizen and then another. They
all sympathized with me, first rate, but they did not know how
to help me. But at last a Gentile said, 'Go to Brigham Young!—
these small fry cannot do you any good.' I did not think much of
the idea, for if the *law* could not help me, what could an individual do who had not even anything to do with either making
the laws or executing them? He might be a very good patriarch
of a church and preacher in its tabernacle, but something sterner
than religion and moral suasion was needed to handle a hundred
refractory, half-civilized sub-contractors. But what was a man
to do? I thought if Mr. Young could not do anything else, he

might probably be able to give me some advice and a valuable hint or two, and so I went straight to him and laid the whole case before him. He said very little, but he showed strong interest all the way through. He examined all the papers in detail, and whenever there seemed anything like a hitch, either in the papers or my statement, he would go back and take up the thread and follow it patiently out to an intelligent and satisfactory result. Then he made a list of the contractors' names. Finally he said:

" 'Mr. Street, this is all perfectly plain. These contracts are strictly and legally drawn, and are duly signed and certified. These men manifestly entered into them with their eyes open. I see no fault or flaw anywhere.'

"Then Mr. Young turned to a man waiting at the other end of the room and said: 'Take this list of names to So-and-so, and tell him to have these men here at such-and-such an hour.'

"They were there, to the minute. So was I. Mr. Young asked them a number of questions, and their answers made my statement good. Then he said to them:

" 'You signed these contracts and assumed these obligations of your own free will and accord?'

" 'Yes.'

" 'Then carry them out to the letter, if it makes paupers of you! Go!'

"And they *did* go, too! They are strung across the deserts now, working like bees. And I never hear a word out of them. There is a batch of governors, and judges, and other officials here, shipped from Washington, and they maintain the semblance of a republican form of government—but the petrified truth is that Utah is an absolute monarchy and Brigham Young is king!' "

Mr. Street was a fine man, and I believe his story. I knew him well during several years afterward in San Francisco.

Our stay in Salt Lake City amounted to only two days, and therefore we had no time to make the customary inquisition into the workings of polygamy and get up the usual statistics and deductions preparatory to calling the attention of the nation at large once more to the matter. I had the will to do it. With the gushing self-sufficiency of youth I was feverish to plunge in headlong and achieve a great reform here—until I saw the Mormon women. Then I was touched. My heart was wiser than my head. It warmed toward these poor, ungainly and pathetically "homely" creatures, and as I turned to hide the generous moisture in my eyes, I said, "No—the man that marries one of them has done an act of Christian charity which entitles him to

607

the kindly applause of mankind, not their harsh censure—and the man that marries sixty of them has done a deed of openhanded generosity so sublime that the nations should stand uncovered in his presence and worship in silence.''*

CHAPTER XV

It is a luscious country for thrilling evening stories about assassinations of intractable Gentiles. I cannot easily conceive of anything more cosy than the night in Salt Lake which we spent in a Gentile den, smoking pipes and listening to tales of how Burton galloped in among the pleading and defenceless "Morisites" and shot them down, men and women, like so many dogs. And how Bill Hickman, a Destroying Angel, shot Drown and Arnold dead for bringing suit against him for a debt. And how Porter Rockwell did this and that dreadful thing. And how heedless people often come to Utah and make remarks about Brigham, or polygamy, or some other sacred matter, and the very next morning at daylight such parties are sure to be found lying up some back alley, contentedly waiting for the hearse.

And the next most interesting thing is to sit and listen to these Gentiles talk about polygamy; and how some portly old frog of an elder, or a bishop, marries a girl—likes her, marries her sister—likes her, marries another sister—likes her, takes another—likes her, marries her mother—likes her, marries her father, grandfather, great grandfather, and then comes back hungry and asks for more. And how the pert young thing of eleven will chance to be the favorite wife and her own venerable grandmother have to rank away down toward D 4 in their mutual husband's esteem, and have to sleep in the kitchen, as like as not. And how this dreadful sort of thing, this hiving together in one foul nest of mother and daughters, and the making a young daughter superior to her own mother in rank and authority, are things which Mormon women submit to because their religion teaches them that the more wives a man has on earth, and the more children he rears, the higher the place they will all have in the world to come—and the warmer, maybe, though they do not seem to say anything about that.

According to these Gentile friends of ours, Brigham Young's harem contains twenty or thirty wives. They said that some of them had grown old and gone out of active service, but were comfortably housed and cared for in the henery—or the Lion

* For a brief sketch of Mormon history, and the noted Mountain Meadow massacre, see Appendices A and B.

House, as it is strangely named. Along with each wife were her children—fifty altogether. The house was perfectly quiet and orderly, when the children were still. They all took their meals in one room, and a happy and homelike sight it was pronounced to be. None of our party got an opportunity to take dinner with Mr. Young, but a Gentile by the name of Johnson professed to have enjoyed a sociable breakfast in the Lion House. He gave a preposterous account of the "calling of the roll," and other preliminaries, and the carnage that ensued when the buckwheat cakes came in. But he embellished rather too much. He said that Mr. Young told him several smart sayings of certain of his "two-year-olds," observing with some pride that for many years he had been the heaviest contributor in that line to one of the Eastern magazines; and then he wanted to show Mr. Johnson one of the pets that had said the last good thing, but he could not find the child. He searched the faces of the children in detail, but could not decide which one it was. Finally he gave it up with a sigh and said:

"I thought I would know the little cub again but I don't." Mr. Johnson said further, that Mr. Young observed that life was a sad, sad thing—"because the joy of every new marriage a man contracted was so apt to be blighted by the inopportune funeral of a less recent bride." And Mr. Johnson said that while he and Mr. Young were pleasantly conversing in private, one of the Mrs. Youngs came in and demanded a breast-pin, remarking that she had found out that he had been giving a breast-pin to No. 6, and *she*, for one, did not propose to let this partiality go on without making a satisfactory amount of trouble about it. Mr. Young reminded her that there was a stranger present. Mrs. Young said that if the state of things inside the house was not agreeable to the stranger, he could find room outside. Mr. Young promised the breast-pin, and she went away. But in a minute or two another Mrs. Young came in and demanded a breast-pin. Mr. Young began a remonstrance, but Mrs. Young cut him short. She said No. 6 had got one, and No. 11 was promised one, and it was "no use for him to try to impose on her—she hoped she knew her rights." He gave his promise, and she went. And presently three Mrs. Youngs entered in a body and opened on their husband a tempest of tears, abuse, and entreaty. They had heard all about No. 6, No. 11, and No. 14. Three more breast-pins were promised. They were hardly gone when nine more Mrs. Youngs filed into the presence, and a new tempest burst forth and raged round about the prophet and his guest. Nine breast-pins were promised, and the weird sisters filed out again. And in came eleven more, weeping and wailing and gnashing their teeth. Eleven promised breast-pins purchased peace once more.

"That is a specimen," said Mr. Young. "You see how it is. You see what a life I lead. A man *can't* be wise all the time. In a heedless moment I gave my darling No. 6—excuse my calling her thus, as her other name has escaped me for the moment—a breast-pin. It was only worth twenty-five dollars—that is, *apparently* that was its whole cost—but its ultimate cost was inevitably bound to be a good deal more. You yourself have seen it climb up to six hundred and fifty dollars—and alas, even that is not the end! For I have wives all over this Territory of Utah. I have dozen of wives whose *numbers*, even, I do not know without looking in the family Bible. They are scattered far and wide among the mountains and valleys of my realm. And mark you, every solitary one of them will hear of this wretched breast-pin, and every last one of them will have one or die. No. 6's breast-pin will cost me twenty-five hundred dollars before I see the end of it. And these creatures will compare these pins together, and if one is a shade finer than the rest, they will all be thrown on my hands, and I will have to order a new lot to keep peace in the family. Sir, you probably did not know it, but all the time you were present with my children your every movement was watched by vigilant servitors of mine. If you had offered to give a child a dime, or a stick of candy, or any trifle of the kind, you would have been snatched out of the house instantly, provided it could be done before your gift left your hand. Otherwise it would be absolutely necessary for you to make an exactly similar gift to all my children—and knowing by experience the importance of the thing, I would have stood by and seen to it myself that you did it, and did it thoroughly. Once a gentleman gave one of my children a tin whistle—a veritable invention of Satan, sir, and one which I have an unspeakable horror of, and so would you if you had eighty or ninety children in your house. But the deed was done—the man escaped. I knew what the result was going to be, and I thirsted for vengeance. I ordered out a flock of Destroying Angels, and they hunted the man far into the fastnesses of the Nevada mountains. But they never caught him. I am not cruel, sir—I am not vindictive except when sorely outraged—but if I had caught him, sir, so help me Joseph Smith, I would have locked him into the nursery till the brats whistled him to death! By the slaughtered body of St. Parley Pratt (whom God assoil!) there was never anything on this earth like it! *I* knew who gave the whistle to the child, but I could not make those jealous mothers believe me. They believed *I* did it, and the result was just what any man of reflection could have foreseen: I had to order a hundred and ten whistles—I think we had a hundred and ten children in the house then, but some of them are off at college now—I had to order a hundred and ten of those shrieking things, and I wish I may never speak another word if we didn't have to talk on our fingers entirely, from that time forth until the children got tired of the whistles. And if ever another man gives a whistle to a child of mine and I get my hands on him, I will hang him higher than Haman! That is the word with the bark on it! Shade of Nephi! *You* don't know anything about married life. I am rich, and everybody knows it. I am benevolent, and everybody takes advantage of it. I have a strong fatherly instinct and all the foundlings are foisted on me. Every time a woman wants to do well by her darling, she puzzles her brain to cipher out some scheme for getting it into my hands. Why, sir, a woman came here once with a child of a curious lifeless sort of complexion (and so had the woman), and swore that the child was mine and she my wife—that I had married her at such-and-such a time in such-and-such a place, but she had forgotten her number, and of course I could not remember her name. Well, sir, she called my attention to the fact that the child looked like me, and really it did seem to resemble me—a common thing in the Territory—and, to cut the story short, I put it in my nursery, and she left. And by the ghost of Orson Hyde, when they came to wash the paint off that child it was an Injun! Bless my soul, you don't know anything about married life. It is a perfect dog's life, sir—a perfect dog's life. You can't economize. It isn't possible. I have tried keeping one set of bridal attire for all occasions. But it is of no use. First you'll marry a combination of calico and consumption that's as thin as a rail, and next you'll get a creature that's nothing more than the dropsy in disguise, and then you've got to eke out that bridal dress with an old balloon. That is the way it goes. And think of the wash-bill—(excuse these tears)—nine hundred and eighty-four pieces a week! No, sir, there is no such a thing as economy in a family like mine. Why, just the one item of cradles—think of it! And vermifuge! Soothing syrup! Teething rings! And 'papa's watches' for the babies to play with! And things to scratch the furniture with! And lucifer matches for them to eat, and pieces of glass to cut themselves with! The item of glass alone would support *your* family, I venture to say, sir. Let me scrimp and squeeze all I can, I still can't get ahead as fast as I feel I ought to, with my opportunities. Bless you, sir, at a time when I had seventy-two wives in this house, I groaned under the pressure of keeping thousands of dollars tied up in seventy-two bedsteads when the money ought to have been out at interest;

and I just sold out the whole stock, sir, at a sacrifice, and built a bedstead seven feet long and ninety-six feet wide. But it was a failure, sir. I could *not* sleep. It appeared to me that the whole seventy-two women snored at once. The roar was deafening. And then the danger of it! That was what I was looking at. They would all draw in their breath at once, and you could actually see the walls of the house suck in—and then they would all exhale their breath at once, and you could see the walls swell out, and strain, and hear the rafters crack, and the shingles grind together. My friend, take an old man's advice, and *don't* encumber yourself with a large family—mind, I tell you, don't do it. In a small family, and in a small family only, you will find that comfort and that peace of mind which are the best at last of the blessings this world is able to afford us, and for the lack of which no accumulation of wealth, and no acquisition of fame, power, and greatness can ever compensate us. Take my word for it, ten or eleven wives is all you need—never go over it."

Some instinct or other made me set this Johnson down as being unreliable. And yet he was a very entertaining person, and I doubt if some of the information he gave us could have been acquired from any other source. He was a pleasant contrast to those reticent Mormons.

CHAPTER XVI

All men have heard of the Mormon Bible, but few except the "elect" have seen it, or, at least, taken the trouble to read it. I brought away a copy from Salt Lake. The book is a curiosity to me, it is such a pretentious affair, and yet so "slow," so sleepy; such an insipid mess of inspiration. It is chloroform in print. If Joseph Smith composed this book, the act was a miracle— keeping awake while he did it was, at any rate. If he, according to tradition, merely translated it from certain ancient and mysteriously-engraved plates of copper, which he declares he found under a stone, in an out-of-the-way locality, the work of translating was equally a miracle, for the same reason.

The book seems to be merely a prosy detail of imaginary history, with the Old Testament for a model; followed by a tedious plagiarism of the New Testament. The author labored to give his words and phrases the quaint, old-fashioned sound and structure of our King James's translation of the Scriptures; and the result is a mongrel—half modern glibness, and half ancient simplicity and gravity. The latter is awkward and constrained; the former natural, but grotesque by the contrast. Whenever he found his speech growing too modern—which was about every sentence or two—he ladled in a few such Scriptural phrases as "exceeding sore," "and it came to pass," etc., and made things satisfactory again. "And it came to pass" was his pet. If he had left that out, his Bible would have been only a pamphlet.

The title-page reads as follows:

THE BOOK OF MORMON: AN ACCOUNT WRITTEN BY THE HAND OF MORMON, UPON PLATES TAKEN FROM THE PLATES OF NEPHI.

Wherefore it is an abridgment of the record of the people of Nephi, and also of the Lamanites; written to the Lamanites, who are a remnant of the House of Israel; and also to Jew and Gentile; written by way of commandment, and also by the spirit of prophecy and of revelation. Written and sealed up, and hid up unto the Lord, that they might not be destroyed; to come forth by the gift and power of God unto the interpretation thereof; sealed by the hand of Moroni, and hid up unto the Lord, to come forth in due time by the way of Gentile; the interpretation thereof by the gift of God. An abridgment taken from the Book of Ether also; which is a record of the people of Jared; who were scattered at the time the Lord confounded the language of the people when they were building a tower to get to Heaven.

"Hid up" is good. And so is "wherefore"—though why "wherefore"? Any other word would have answered as well—though in truth it would not have sounded so Scriptural.

Next comes

THE TESTIMONY OF THREE WITNESSES

Be it known unto all nations, kindreds, tongues, and people unto whom this work shall come, that we, through the grace of God the Father, and our Lord Jesus Christ, have seen the plates which contain this record, which is a record of the people of Nephi, and also of the Lamanites, their brethren, and also of the people of Jared, who came from the tower of which hath been spoken; and we also know that they have been translated by the gift and power of God, for His voice hath declared it unto us; wherefore we know of a surety that the work is true. And we also testify that we have seen the engravings which are upon the plates; and they have been shown unto us by the power of God, and not of man. And we declare with words of soberness, that an angel of God came down from heaven, and he brought and laid before our eyes, that we beheld and saw the plates, and the engravings thereon; and we know that it is by the grace of God the Father, and our Lord Jesus Christ, that we beheld and bear record that these things are true; and it is marvellous in our eyes; nevertheless the voice of the Lord commanded us that we should bear record of it; wherefore, to be obedient unto the commandments of God, we bear testimony of these things. And we know that if we are faithful in Christ, we shall rid our garments of the blood of all men, and be found spotless before the judgment-seat of Christ, and shall dwell with Him eternally in the heavens. And the honor be to the Father, and to the Son, and to the Holy Ghost, which is one God. Amen.

OLIVER COWDERY,
DAVID WHITMER,
MARTIN HARRIS.

Some people have to have a world of evidence before they can come anywhere in the neighborhood of believing anything; but for me, when a man tells me that he has "seen the engravings which are upon the plates," and not only that, but an angel was there at the time, and saw him see them, and probably took his receipt for it, I am very far on the road to conviction, no matter whether I ever heard of that man before or not, and even if I do not know the name of the angel, or his nationality either.

Next is this:

AND ALSO THE TESTIMONY OF EIGHT WITNESSES

Be it known unto all nations, kindreds, tongues, and people unto whom this work shall come, that Joseph Smith, Jr., the translator of this work, has shown unto us the plates of which hath been spoken, which have the appearance of gold; and as many of the leaves as the said Smith has translated, we did handle with our hands; and we also saw the engravings thereon, all of which has the appearance of ancient work, and of curious workmanship. And this we bear record with words of soberness, that the said Smith has shown unto us, for we have seen and hefted, and know of a surety that the said Smith has got the plates of which we have spoken. And we give our names unto the world, to witness unto the world that which we have seen; and we lie not, God bearing witness of it.

CHRISTIAN WHITMER,	HIRAM PAGE,
JACOB WHITMER,	JOSEPH SMITH, SR.,
PETER WHITMER, JR.,	HYRUM SMITH,
JOHN WHITMER,	SAMUEL H. SMITH.

And when I am far on the road to conviction, and eight men, be they grammatical or otherwise, come forward and tell me that they have seen the plates too; and not only seen those plates but "hefted" them, I *am* convinced. I could not feel more satisfied and at rest if the entire Whitmer family had testified.

The Mormon Bible consists of fifteen "books"—being the books of Jacob, Enos, Jarom, Omni, Mosiah, Zeniff, Alma, Helaman, Ether, Moroni, two "books" of Mormon, and three of Nephi.

In the first book of Nephi is a plagiarism of the Old Testament, which gives an account of the exodus from Jerusalem of the "children of Lehi"; and it goes on to tell of their wanderings in the wilderness, during eight years, and their supernatural protection by one of their number, a party by the name of Nephi. They finally reached the land of "Bountiful," and camped by the sea. After they had remained there "for the space of many days"— which is more Scriptural than definite—Nephi was commanded from on high to build a ship wherein to "carry the people across the waters." He travestied Noah's ark—but he obeyed orders in the matter of the plan. He finished the ship *in a single day,* while his brethren stood by and made fun of it—and of him, too— "saying, our brother is a fool, for he thinketh that he can build a ship." They did not wait for the timbers to dry, but the whole tribe or nation sailed the next day. Then a bit of genuine nature cropped out, and is revealed by outspoken Nephi with Scriptural frankness—they all got on a spree! They, "and also their wives, began to make themselves merry, insomuch that they began to dance, and to sing, and to speak with much rudeness; yea, they were lifted up unto exceeding rudeness."

Nephi tried to stop these scandalous proceedings; but they tied him neck and heels, and went on with their lark. But observe how Nephi the prophet circumvented them by the aid of the invisible powers:

And it came to pass that after they had bound me, insomuch that I could not move, the compass, which had been prepared of the Lord, did cease to work; wherefore, they knew not whither they should steer the ship, insomuch that there arose a great storm, yea, a great and terrible tempest, and we were driven back upon the waters for the space of three days; and they began to be frightened exceedingly, lest they should be drowned in the sea; nevertheless they did not loose me. And on the fourth day, which we had been driven back, the tempest began to be exceeding sore.

And it came to pass that we were about to be swallowed up in the depths of the sea.

Then they untied him.

And it came to pass after they had loosed me, behold, I took the compass, and it did work whither I desired it. And it came to pass that I prayed unto the Lord; and after I had prayed, the winds did cease, and the storm did cease, and there was a great calm.

Equipped with their compass, these ancients appear to have had the advantage of Noah.

Their voyage was toward a "promised land"—the only name they give it. They reached it in safety.

Polygamy is a recent feature in the Mormon religion, and was added by Brigham Young after Joseph Smith's death. Before that, it was regarded as an "abomination." This verse from the Mormon Bible occurs in Chapter II. of the book of Jacob:

For behold, thus saith the Lord, this people begin to wax in iniquity; they understand not the Scriptures; for they seek to excuse themselves in committing whoredoms, because of the things which were written concerning David, and Solomon his son. Behold, David and Solomon truly had many wives and concubines, which thing was abominable before me, saith the Lord; wherefore, thus saith the Lord, I have led this people forth out of the land of Jerusalem, by the power of mine arm, that I might raise up unto me a righteous branch from the fruit of the loins of Joseph. Wherefore, I the Lord God, will not suffer that this people shall do like unto them of old.

However, the project failed—or at least the modern Mormon end of it—for Brigham "suffers" it. This verse is from the same chapter:

Behold, the Lamanites your brethren, whom ye hate, because of their filthiness and the cursings which hath come upon their skins, are more righteous than you; for they have not forgotten the commandment of the Lord, which was given unto our fathers, that they should have, save it were one wife; and concubines they should have none.

The following verse (from Chapter IX. of the Book of Nephi) appears to contain information not familiar to everybody:

And now it came to pass that when Jesus had ascended into heaven, the multitude did disperse, and every man did take his wife and his children, and did return to his own home.

And it came to pass that on the morrow, when the multitude was gathered together, behold, Nephi and his brother whom he had raised from the dead, whose name was Timothy, and also his son, whose name was Jonas, and also Mathoni, and Mathonihah, his brother, and Kumen, and Kumenonhi, and Jeremiah, and Shemnon, and Jonas, and Zedekiah, and Isaiah; now these were the names of the disciples whom Jesus had chosen.

In order that the reader may observe how much more grandeur and picturesqueness (as seen by these Mormon twelve) accompanied one of the tenderest episodes in the life of our Saviour than other eyes seem to have been aware of, I quote the following from the same "book"—Nephi:

And it came to pass that Jesus spake unto them, and bade them arise. And they arose from the earth, and He said unto them, Blessed are ye because of your faith. And now behold, My joy is full. And when He had said these words, He wept, and the multitude bear record of it, and He took their little children, one by one, and blessed them, and prayed unto the Father for them. And when He had done this He wept again, and He spake unto the multitude, and saith unto them, Behold your little ones. And as they looked to behold, they cast their eyes toward heaven, and they saw the heavens open, and they saw angels descending out of heaven as it were, in the midst of fire; and they came down and encircled those little ones about, and they were encircled about with fire; and the angels did minister unto them, and the multitude did see and hear and bear record; and they know that their record is true, for they all of them did see and hear, every man for himself; and they were in number about two thousand and five hundred souls; and they did consist of men, women, and children.

And what else would they be likely to consist of?

The Book of Ether is an incomprehensible medley of "history," much of it relating to battles and sieges among peoples whom the reader has possibly never heard of; and who inhabited a country which is not set down in the geography. There was a King with the remarkable name of Coriantumr, and he warred with Shared, and Lib, and Shiz, and others, in the "plains of Heshlon"; and the "valley of Gilgal"; and the "wilderness of Akish"; and the "land of Moran"; and the "plains of Agosh"; and "Ogath," and "Ramah," and the "land of Corihor," and the "hill Comnor," by "the waters of Ripliancum," etc., etc., etc. "And it came to pass," after a deal of fighting, that Coriantumr, upon making calculation of his losses, found that "there had been slain two millions of mighty men, and also their wives and their children"—say 5,000,000 or 6,000,000 in all—"and he began to sorrow in his heart." Unquestionably it was time. So he wrote to Shiz, asking a cessation of hostilities, and offering to give up his kingdom to save his people. Shiz declined, except upon condition that Coriantumr would come and let him cut his head off first—a thing which Coriantumr would not do. Then there was more fighting for a season; then *four years* were devoted to gathering the forces for a final struggle—after which ensued a battle, which, I take it, is the most remarkable set forth in history,—except, perhaps, that of the Kilkenny cats, which it resembles in some respects. This is the account of the gathering and the battle:

7. And it came to pass that they did gather together all the people, upon all the face of the land, who had not been slain, save it was Ether. And it came to pass that Ether did behold all the doings of the people; and he beheld that the people who were for Corianthumr, were gathered to the army of Coriantumr; and the people who were for Shiz, were gathered together to the army of Shiz; wherefore they were for the space of four years gathering together the people, that they might get all who were upon the face of the land, and that they might receive all the strength which it was possible that they could receive. And it came to pass that when they were all gathered together, every one to the army which he would, with their wives and their children; both men, women, and children being armed with weapons of war, having shields, and

breast-plates, and head-plates, and being clothed after the manner of war, they did march forth one against another, to battle; and they fought all that day, and conquered not. And it came to pass that when it was night they were weary, and retired to their camps; and after they had retired to their camps, they took up a howling and a lamentation for the loss of the slain of their people; and so great were their cries, their howlings and lamentations, that it did rend the air exceedingly. And it came to pass that on the morrow they did go again to battle, and great and terrible was that day; nevertheless they conquered not, and when the night came again, they did rend the air with their cries, and their howlings, and their mournings, for the loss of the slain of their people.

8. And it came to pass that Coriantumr wrote again an epistle unto Shiz, desiring that he would not come again to battle, but that he would take the kingdom, and spare the lives of the people. But behold, the Spirit of the Lord had ceased striving with them, and Satan had full power over the hearts of the people, for they were given up unto the hardness of their hearts, and the blindness of their minds that they might be destroyed; wherefore they went again to battle. And it came to pass that they fought all that day, and when the night came they slept upon their swords; and on the morrow they fought even until the night came; and when the night came they were drunken with anger, even as a man who is drunken with wine; and they slept again upon their swords; and on the morrow they fought again; and when the night came they had all fallen by the sword save it were fifty and two of the people of Coriantumr, and sixty and nine of the people of Shiz. And it came to pass that they slept upon their swords that night, and on the morrow they fought again, and they contended in their mights with their swords, and with their shields, all that day; and when the night came there were thirty and two of the people of Shiz, and twenty and seven of the people of Coriantumr.

9. And it came to pass that they ate and slept, and prepared for death on the morrow. And they were large and mighty men, as to the strength of men. And it came to pass that they fought for the space of three hours, and they fainted with the loss of blood. And it came to pass that when the men of Coriantumr had received sufficient strength, that they could walk, they were about to flee for their lives, but behold, Shiz arose, and also his men, and he swore in his wrath that he would slay Coriantumr, or he would perish by the sword: wherefore he did pursue them, and on the morrow he did overtake them; and they fought again with the sword. And it came to pass that when they had all fallen by the sword, save it were Coriantumr and Shiz, behold Shiz had fainted with loss of blood. And it came to pass that when Coriantumr had leaned upon his sword, that he rested a little, he smote off the head of Shiz. And it came to pass that after he had smote off the head of Shiz, that Shiz raised upon his hands and fell; and after that he had struggled for breath, he died. And it came to pass that Coriantumr fell to the earth, and became as if he had no life. And the Lord spake unto Ether, and said unto him, go forth. And he went forth, and beheld that the words

of the Lord had all been fulfilled; and he finished his record; and the hundredth part I have not written.

It seems a pity he did not finish, for after all his dreary former chapters of commonplace, he stopped just as he was in danger of becoming interesting.

The Mormon Bible is rather stupid and tiresome to read, but there is nothing vicious in its teachings. Its code of morals is unobjectionable—it is "smouched"* from the New Testament and no credit given.

CHAPTER XVII

At the end of our two days' sojourn, we left Great Salt Lake City hearty and well fed and happy—physically superb but not so very much wiser, as regards the "Mormon question," than we were when we arrived, perhaps. We had a deal more "information" than we had before, of course, but we did not know what portion of it was reliable and what was not—for it all came from acquaintances of a day—strangers, strictly speaking. We were told, for instance, that the dreadful "Mountain Meadows Massacre" was the work of the Indians entirely, and that the Gentiles had meanly tried to fasten it upon the Mormons; we were told, likewise, that the Indians were to blame, partly, and partly the Mormons; and we were told, likewise, and just as positively, that the Mormons were almost if not wholly and completely responsible for that most treacherous and pitiless butchery. We got the story in all these different shapes, but it was not till several years afterward that Mrs. Waite's book, "The Mormon Prophet," came out with Judge Cradlebaugh's trial of the accused parties in it and revealed the truth that the latter version was the correct one and that the Mormons *were* the assassins. All our "information" had three sides to it, and so I gave up the idea that I could settle the "Mormon question" in two days. Still I have seen newspaper correspondents do it in one.

I left Great Salt Lake a good deal confused as to what state of things existed there—and sometimes even questioning in my own mind whether a state of things existed there at all or not. But presently I remembered with a lightening sense of relief that we had learned two or three trivial things there which we could be certain of; and so the two days were not wholly lost. For in-

* Milton.

stance, we had learned that we were at last in a pioneer land, in absolute and tangible reality. The high prices charged for trifles were eloquent of high freights and bewildering distances of freightage. In the east, in those days, the smallest moneyed denomination was a penny and it represented the smallest purchasable quantity of any commodity. West of Cincinnati the smallest coin in use was the silver five-cent piece and no smaller quantity of an article could be bought than "five-cents' worth." In Overland City the lowest coin appeared to be the ten-cent piece; but in Salt Lake there did not seem to be any money in circulation smaller than a quarter, or any smaller quantity purchasable of any commodity than twenty-five cents' worth. We had always been used to half dimes and "five cents' worth" as the minimum of financial negotiations; but in Salt Lake if one wanted a cigar, it was a quarter; if he wanted a chalk pipe, it was a quarter; if he wanted a peach, or a candle, or a newspaper, or a shave, or a little Gentile whiskey to rub on his corns to arrest indigestion and keep him from having the toothache, twenty-five cents was the price, every time. When we looked at the shot-bag of silver, now and then, we seemed to be wasting our substance in riotous living, but if we referred to the expense account we could see that we had not been doing anything of the kind. But people easily get reconciled to big money and big prices, and fond and vain of both—it is a descent to little coins and cheap prices that is hardest to bear and slowest to take hold upon one's toleration. After a month's acquaintance with the twenty-five cent minimum, the average human being is ready to blush every time he thinks of his despicable five-cent days. How sunburnt with blushes I used to get in gandy Nevada, every time I thought of my first financial experience in Salt Lake. It was on this wise (which is a favorite expression of great authors, and a very neat one, too, but I never hear anybody *say* on this wise when they are talking). A young half-breed with a complexion like a yellow-jacket asked me if I would have my boots blacked. It was at the Salt Lake House the morning after we arrived. I said yes, and he blacked them. Then I handed him a silver five-cent piece, with the benevolent air of a person who is conferring wealth and blessedness upon poverty and suffering. The yellow-jacket took it with what I judged to be suppressed emotion, and laid it reverently down in the middle of his broad hand. Then he began to contemplate it, much as a philosopher contemplates a gnat's ear in the ample field of his microscope. Several mountaineers, teamsters, stage-drivers, etc., drew near and dropped into the tableau and fell to surveying the money with that attractive indifference to formality which is noticeable in the hardy pioneer.

Presently the yellow-jacket handed the half dime back to me and told me I ought to keep my money in my pocket-book instead of in my soul, and then I wouldn't get it cramped and shriveled up so!

What a roar of vulgar laughter there was! I destroyed the mongrel reptile on the spot, but I smiled and smiled all the time I was detaching his scalp, for the remark he made *was* good for an "Injun."

Yes, we had learned in Salt Lake to be charged great prices without letting the inward shudder appear on the surface—for even already we had overheard and noted the tenor of conversations among drivers, conductors, and hostlers, and finally among citizens of Salt Lake, until we were well aware that these superior beings despised "emigrants." We permitted no tell-tale shudders and winces in our countenances, for we wanted to seem pioneers, or Mormons, half-breeds, teamsters, stage-drivers, Mountain Meadow assassins—anything in the word that the plains and Utah respected and admired—but we were wretchedly ashamed of being "emigrants," and sorry enough that we had white shirts and could not swear in the presence of ladies without looking the other way.

And many a time in Nevada, afterwards, we had occasion to remember with humiliation that we were "emigrants," and consequently a low and inferior sort of creatures. Perhaps the reader has visited Utah, Nevada, or California, even in these latter days, and while communing with himself upon the sorrowful banishment of those countries from what he considers "the world," has had his wings clipped by finding that *he* is the one to be pitied, and that there are entire populations around him ready and willing to do it for him—yea, who are complacently doing it for him already, wherever he steps his foot. Poor thing, they are making fun of his hat; and the cut of his New York coat; and his conscientiousness about his grammar; and his feeble profanity; and his consumingly ludicrous ignorance of ores, shafts, tunnels, and other things which he never saw before, and never felt enough interest in to read about. And all the time that he is thinking what a sad fate it is to be exiled to that far country, that lonely land, the citizens around him are looking down on him with a blighting compassion because he is an "emigrant" instead of that proudest and blessedest creature that exists on all the earth, a "FORTY-NINER."

The accustomed coach life began again, now, and by midnight it almost seemed as if we never had been out of our snuggery among the mail sacks at all. We had made one alteration, however. We had provided enough bread, boiled ham and hard boiled eggs to last double the six hundred miles of staging we had still to do.

And it was comfort in those succeeding days to sit up and contemplate the majestic panorama of mountains and valleys spread out below us and eat ham and hard boiled eggs while our spiritual natures revelled alternately in rainbows, thunderstorms, and peerless sunsets. Nothing helps scenery like ham and eggs. Ham and eggs, and after these a pipe—an old, rank, delicious pipe—ham and eggs and scenery, a "down grade," a flying coach, a fragrant pipe and a contented heart—these make happiness. It is what all the ages have struggled for.

CHAPTER XVIII

At eight in the morning we reached the remnant and ruin of what had been the important military station of "Camp Floyd," some forty-five or fifty miles from Salt Lake City. At four P.M. we had doubled our distance and were ninety or a hundred miles from Salt Lake. And now we entered upon one of that species of deserts whose concentrated hideousness shames the diffused and diluted horrors of Sahara—an *"alkali"* desert. For sixty-eight miles there was but one break in it. I do not remember that this was really a break; indeed it seems to me that it was nothing but a watering depot *in the midst* of the stretch of sixty-eight miles. If my memory serves me, there was no well or spring at this place, but the water was hauled there by mule and ox teams from the further side of the desert. There was a stage station there. It was forty-five miles from the beginning of the desert, and twenty-three from the end of it.

We plowed and dragged and groped along, the whole livelong night, and at the end of this uncomfortable twelve hours we finished the forty-five-mile part of the desert and got to the stage station where the imported water was. The sun was just rising. It was easy enough to cross a desert in the night while we were asleep; and it was pleasant to reflect, in the morning, that we in actual person *had* encountered an absolute desert and could always speak knowingly of deserts in presence of the ignorant thenceforward. And it was pleasant also to reflect that this was not an obscure, back country desert, but a very celebrated one, the metropolis itself, as you may say. All this was very well and very comfortable and satisfactory—but now we were to cross a desert in *daylight*. This was fine—novel—romantic— dramatically adventurous—*this,* indeed, was worth living for, worth traveling for! We would write home all about it.

This enthusiasm, this stern thirst for adventure, wilted under the sultry August sun and did not last above one hour. One poor little hour—and then we were ashamed that we had "gushed" so. The poetry was all in the anticipation—there is none in the reality. Imagine a vast, waveless ocean stricken dead and turned to ashes; imagine this solemn waste tufted with ash-dusted sage-bushes; imagine the lifeless silence and solitude that belong to such a place; imagine a coach, creeping like a bug through the midst of this shoreless level, and sending up tumbled volumes of dust as if it were a bug that went by steam; imagine this aching monotony of toiling and plowing kept up hour after hour, and the shore still as far away as ever, apparently; imagine team, driver, coach and passengers so deeply coated with ashes that they are all one colorless color; imagine ash-drifts roosting above moustaches and eyebrows like snow accumulations on boughs and bushes. This is the reality of it.

The sun beats down with dead, blistering, relentless malignity; the perspiration is welling from every pore in man and beast, but scarcely a sign of it finds its way to the surface—it is absorbed before it gets there; there is not the faintest breath of air stirring; there is not a merciful shred of cloud in all the brilliant firmament; there is not a living creature visible in any direction whither one searches the blank level that stretches its monotonous miles on every hand; there is not a sound—not a sigh—not a whisper—not a buzz, or a whir of wings, or distant pipe of bird—not even a sob from the lost souls that doubtless people that dead air. And so the occasional sneezing of the resting mules, and the champing of the bits, grate harshly on the grim stillness, not dissipating the spell but accenting it and making one feel more lonesome and forsaken than before.

The mules, under violent swearing, coaxing and whipcracking, would make at stated intervals a "spurt," and drag the coach a hundred or may be two hundred yards, stirring up a billowy cloud of dust that rolled back, enveloping the vehicle to the wheel-tops or higher, and making it seem afloat in a fog. Then a rest followed, with the usual sneezing and bit-champing. Then another "spurt" of a hundred yards and another rest at the end of it. All day long we kept this up, without water for the mules and without ever changing the team. At least we kept it up ten hours, which, I take it, is a day, and a pretty honest one, in an alkali desert. It was from four in the morning till two in the afternoon. And it was so hot! and so close! and our water canteens went dry in the middle of the day and we got so thirsty! It was so stupid and tiresome and dull! and the tedious hours did lag and drag and limp along with such a cruel deliberation! It was so trying to give one's watch a good long undisturbed spell and then take it out and find that it had been fooling away the time and not trying to get ahead any! The alkali dust cut through our lips, it persecuted our eyes, it ate through the delicate membranes and made our noses bleed and *kept* them bleeding—and truly and seriously the romance all faded far away and disappeared, and left the desert trip nothing but a harsh reality—a thirsty, sweltering, longing, hateful reality!

Two miles and a quarter an hour for ten hours—that was what we accomplished. It was hard to bring the comprehension away down to such a snail-pace as that, when we had been used to making eight and ten miles an hour. When we reached the station on the farther verge of the desert, we were glad, for the first time, that the dictionary was along, because we never could have found language to tell how glad we were, in any sort of dictionary but an unabridged one with pictures in it. But there could not have been found in a whole library of dictionaries language sufficient to tell how tired those mules were after their twenty-three mile pull. To try to give the reader an idea of how *thirsty* they were, would be to "gild refined gold or paint the lily."

Somehow, now that it is there, the quotation does not seem to fit—but no matter, let it stay, anyhow. I think it is a graceful and attractive thing, and therefore have tried time and time again to work it in where it *would* fit, but could not succeed. These efforts have kept my mind distracted and ill at ease, and made my narrative seem broken and disjointed, in places. Under these circumstances it seems to me best to leave it in, as above, since this will afford at least a temporary respite from the wear and tear of trying to "lead up" to this really apt and beautiful quotation.

CHAPTER XIX

On the morning of the sixteenth day out from St. Joseph we arrived at the entrance of Rocky Canyon, two hundred and fifty miles from Salt Lake. It was along in this wild country somewhere, and far from any habitation of white men, except the stage stations, that we came across the wretchedest type of mankind I have ever seen, up to this writing. I refer to the Goshoot Indians. From what we could see and all we could learn, they are very considerably inferior to even the despised Digger Indians of California; inferior to all races of savages on our continent; inferior to even the Terra del Fuegans; inferior to the Hottentots, and actually inferior in some respects to the Kytches of Africa. Indeed, I have been obliged to look the bulky volumes of Wood's "Uncivilized Races of Men" clear through in order to find a savage tribe degraded enough to take rank with the Goshoots. I find but one people fairly open to that shameful verdict. It is the Bosjesmans (Bushmen) of South Africa. Such of the Goshoots as we saw, along the road and hanging about the stations, were small, lean, "scrawny" creatures; in complexion a dull black like the ordinary American negro; their faces and hands bearing dirt which they had been hoarding and accumulating for months, years, and even generations, according to the age of the proprietor; a silent, sneaking, treacherous looking race; taking note of everything, covertly, like all the other "Noble Red Men" that we (do not) read about, and betraying no sign in their countenances; indolent, everlastingly patient and tireless, like all other Indians; prideless beggars—for if the beggar instinct were left out of an Indian he would not "go," any more than a clock without a pendulum; hungry, always hungry, and yet never refusing anything that a hog would eat, though often eating what a hog would decline; hunters, but having no higher ambition than to kill and eat jackass rabbits, crickets and grasshoppers, and embezzle carrion from the buzzards and cayotes; savages who, when asked if they have the common Indian belief in a Great Spirit show a something which almost amounts to emotion, thinking whiskey is referred to; a thin, scattering race of almost naked black children, these Goshoots are, who produce nothing at all, and have no villages, and no gatherings together into strictly defined tribal communities—a people whose only shelter is a rag cast on a bush to keep off a portion of the snow, and yet who inhabit one of the most rocky, wintry, repulsive wastes that our country or any other can exhibit.

The Bushmen and our Goshoots are manifestly descended from the self-same gorilla, or kangaroo, or Norway rat, whichever animal-Adam the Darwinians trace them to.

One would as soon expect the rabbits to fight as the Goshoots, and yet they used to live off the offal and refuse of the stations a few months and then come some dark night when no mischief was expected, and burn down the buildings and kill the men from ambush as they rushed out. And once, in the night, they attacked the stage-coach when a District Judge, of Nevada Territory, was the only passenger, and with their first volley of arrows (and a bullet or two) they riddled the stage curtains, wounded ∴ horse or two and mortally wounded the driver. The latter was full of pluck, and so was his passenger. At the driver's call Judge Mott swung himself out, clambered to the box and seized the reins of the team, and away they plunged, through the racing mob of skeletons and under a hurtling storm of missiles. The stricken driver had sunk down on the boot as soon as he was wounded, but had held on to the reins and said he would manage to keep hold of them until relieved. And after they were taken from his relaxing grasp, he lay with his head between Judge Mott's feet, and tranquilly gave directions about the road; he said he believed he could live till the miscreants were outrun and left behind, and that if he managed that, the main difficulty would be at an end, and then if the Judge drove so and so (giving directions about bad places in the road, and general course) he would reach the next station without trouble. The Judge distanced the enemy and at last rattled up to the station and knew that the night's perils were done; but there was no comrade-in-arms for him rejoice with, for the soldierly driver was dead.

Let us forget that we have been saying harsh things about the Overland drivers, now. The disgust which the Goshoots gave me, a disciple of Cooper and a worshipper of the Red Man—even of the scholarly savages in the "Last of the Mohicans" who are fittingly associated with backwoodsmen who divide each sentence into two equal parts: one part critically grammatical, refined and choice of language, and the other part just such an attempt to talk like a hunter or a mountaineer, as a Broadway clerk might make after eating an edition of Emerson Bennett's works and studying frontier life at the Bowery Theatre a couple of weeks—I say that the nausea which the Goshoots gave me, an Indian worshipper, set me to examining authorities, to see if perchance I had been over-estimating the Red Man while viewing him through the mellow moonshine of romance. The revelations that came were disenchanting. It was curious to see how quickly the paint and tinsel fell away from him and left him treacherous, filthy and repulsive—and how quickly the evidences accumulated that wherever one finds an Indian tribe he has only found Goshoots more or less modified by circumstances and surroundings—but Goshoots, after all. They deserve pity, poor creatures; and they can have mine—at this distance. Nearer by, they never get anybody's.

There is an impression abroad that the Baltimore and Washington Railroad Company and many of its employes are Goshoots; but it is an error. There is only a plausible resemblance, which, while it is apt enough to mislead the ignorant, cannot deceive parties who have contemplated both tribes. But seriously, it was not only poor wit, but very wrong to start the report referred to above; for however innocent the motive may have been, the necessary effect was to injure the reputation of a class who have a hard enough time of it in the pitiless deserts of the Rocky Mountains, Heaven knows! If we cannot find it in our hearts to give those poor naked creatures our Christian sympathy and compassion, in God's name let us at least not throw mud at them.

CHAPTER XX

On the seventeenth day we passed the highest mountain peaks we had yet seen, and although the day was very warm the night that followed upon its heels was wintry cold and blankets were next to useless.

On the eighteenth day we encountered the eastward-bound telegraph-constructors at Reese River station and sent a message to his Excellency Gov. Nye at Carson City (distant one hundred and fifty-six miles).

On the nineteenth day we crossed the Great American Desert—forty memorable miles of bottomless sand, into which the coach wheels sunk from six inches to a foot. We worked our passage most of the way across. That is to say, we got out and walked. It was a dreary pull and a long and thirsty one, for we had no water. From one extremity of this desert to the other, the road was white with the bones of oxen and horses. It would hardly be an exaggeration to say that we could have walked the forty miles and set our feet on a bone at every step! The desert was one prodigious graveyard. And the log-chains, wagon tyres, and rotting wrecks of vehicles were almost as thick as the bones. I think we saw log-chains enough rusting there in the desert, to reach across any State in the Union. Do not these relics suggest something of an idea of the fearful suffering and privation the early emigrants to California endured?

At the border of the Desert lies Carson Lake, or The "Sink" of the Carson, a shallow, melancholy sheet of water some eighty or a hundred miles in circumference. Carson River empties into it and is lost—sinks mysteriously into the earth and never appears in the light of the sun again—for the lake has no outlet whatever.

There are several rivers in Nevada, and they all have this mysterious fate. They end in various lakes or "sinks," and that is the last of them. Carson Lake, Humboldt Lake, Walker Lake, Mono Lake, are all great sheets of water without any visible outlet. Water is always flowing into them; none is ever seen to flow out of them, and yet they remain always level full, neither receding nor overflowing. What they do with their surplus is only known to the Creator.

On the western verge of the Desert we halted a moment at Ragtown. It consisted of one loghouse and is not set down on the map.

This reminds me of a circumstance. Just after we left Julesburg, on the Platte, I was sitting with the driver, and he said:

"I can tell you a most laughable thing indeed, if you would like to listen to it. Horace Greeley went over this road once. When he was leaving Carson City he told the driver, Hank Monk, that he had an engagement to lecture at Placerville and was very anxious to go through quick. Hank Monk cracked his whip and started off at an awful pace. The coach bounced up and down in such a terrific way that it jolted the buttons all off of Horace's coat, and finally shot his head clean through the roof of the stage, and then he yelled at Hank Monk and begged him to go easier—said he warn't in as much of a hurry as he was awhile ago. But Hank Monk said, 'Keep your seat, Horace, and I'll get you there on time'—and you bet you he did, too, what was left of him!"

A day or two after that we picked up a Denver man at the cross roads, and he told us a good deal about the country and the Gregory Diggings. He seemed a very entertaining person and a man well posted in the affairs of Colorado. By and by he remarked:

"I can tell you a most laughable thing indeed, if you would like to listen to it. Horace Greeley went over this road once. When he was leaving Carson City he told the driver, Hank Monk, that he had an engagement to lecture at Placerville and was very anxious to go through quick. Hank Monk cracked his whip and started off at an awful pace. The coach bounced up and down in such a terrific way that it jolted the buttons all off of Horace's coat, and finally shot his head clean through the roof of the stage, and then he yelled at Hank Monk and begged him to go easier—said he warn't in as much of a hurry as he was awhile ago. But Hank Monk said, 'Keep your seat, Horace, and I'll get you there on time!'—and you bet you he did, too, what was left of him!"

At Fort Bridger, some days after this, we took on board a cavalry sergeant, a very proper and soldierly person indeed. From no other man during the whole journey, did we gather such a store of concise and well-arranged military information. It was surprising to find in the desolate wilds of our country a man so thoroughly acquainted with everything useful to know in his line of life, and yet of such inferior rank and unpretentious bearing. For as much as three hours we listened to him with unabated interest. Finally he got upon the subject of trans- continental travel, and presently said:

"I can tell you a very laughable thing indeed, if you would like to listen to it. Horace Greeley went over this road once. When he was leaving Carson City he told the driver, Hank Monk, that he had an engagement to lecture at Placerville and was very anxious to go through quick. Hank Monk cracked his whip and started off at an awful pace. The coach bounced up and down in such a terrific way that it jolted the buttons all off of Horace's coat, and finally shot his head clean through the roof of the stage, and then he yelled at Hank Monk and begged him to go easier—said he warn't in as much of a hurry as he was awhile ago. But Hank Monk said, 'Keep your seat, Horace, and I'll get you there on time!'—and you bet you he did, too, what was left of him!"

When we were eight hours out from Salt Lake City a Mormon preacher got in with us at a way station—a gentle, soft-spoken, kindly man, and one whom any stranger would warm to at first sight. I can never forget the pathos that was in his voice as he told, in simple language, the story of his people's wanderings and unpitied sufferings. No pulpit eloquence was ever so moving and so beautiful as this outcast's picture of the first Mormon pilgrimage across the plains, stuggling sorrowfully onward to the land of its banishment and marking its desolate way with graves and watering it with tears. His words so wrought upon us that it was a relief to us all when the conversation drifted into a more cheerful channel and the natural features of the curious country we were in came under treatment. One matter after another was pleasantly discussed, and at length the stranger said:

"I can tell you a most laughable thing indeed, if you would like to listen to it. Horace Greeley went over this road once. When he was leaving Carson City he told the driver, Hank Monk, that he had an engagement to lecture in Placerville, and was very anxious to go through quick. Hank Monk cracked his whip and started off at an awful pace. The coach bounced up and down in such a terrific way that it jolted the buttons all off of Horace's coat, and finally shot his head clean through the roof of the stage, and then he yelled at Hank Monk and begged him to go easier—said he warn't in as much of a hurry as he was awhile ago. But Hank Monk said, 'Keep your seat, Horace, and I'll get you there on time!'—and you bet you he did, too, what was left of him!"

Ten miles out of Ragtown we found a poor wanderer who had lain down to die. He had walked as long as he could, but his limbs had failed him at last. Hunger and fatigue had conquered him. It would have been inhuman to leave him there. We paid his fare to Carson and lifted him into the coach. It was some little time before he showed any very decided signs of life; but by dint of chafing him and pouring brandy between his lips we finally brought him to a languid consciousness. Then we fed him a little, and by and by he seemed to comprehend the situation and a grateful light softened his eye. We made his mail-sack bed as comfortable as possible, and constructed a pillow for him with our coats. He seemed very thankful. Then he looked up in our faces, and said in a feeble voice that had a tremble of honest emotion in it:

"Gentlemen, I know not who you are, but you have saved my life; and although I can never be able to repay you for it, I feel that I can at least make one hour of your long journey lighter. I take it you are strangers to this great thoroughfare, but I am entirely familiar with it. In this connection I can tell you a most laughable thing indeed, if you would like to listen to it. Horace Greeley—"

I said, impressively:

"Suffering stranger, proceed at your peril. You see in me the melancholy wreck of a once stalwart and magnificent manhood. What has brought me to this? That thing which you are about to tell. Gradually but surely, that tiresome old anecdote has sapped my strength, undermined my constitution, withered my life. Pity my helplessness. Spare me only just this once, and tell me about young George Washington and his little hatchet for a change."

We were saved. But not so the invalid. In trying to retain the anecdote in his system he strained himself and died in our arms.

I am aware, now, that I ought not to have asked of the sturdiest citizen of all that region, what I asked of that mere shadow of a man; for, after seven years' residence on the Pacific coast, I know that no passenger or driver on the Overland ever corked that anecdote in, when a stranger was by, and survived. Within a period of six years I crossed and recrossed the Sierras between Nevada and California thirteen times by stage and listened to that deathless incident four hundred and eighty-one or eighty-two times. I have the list somewhere. Drivers always told it, conductors told it, landlords told it, chance passengers told it, the very Chinamen and vagrant Indians recounted it. I have had the same driver tell it to me two or three times in the same afternoon. It has come to me in all the multitude of tongues that Babel bequeathed to earth, and flavored with whiskey, brandy, beer, cologne, sozodont, tobacco, garlic, onions, grasshoppers—everything that has a fragrance to it through all the long list of things that are gorged or guzzled by the sons of men.

I never have smelt any anecdote as often as I have smelt that one; never have smelt any anecdote that smelt so variegated as that one. And you never could learn to know it by its smell, because every time you thought you had learned the smell of it, it would turn up with a different smell. Bayard Taylor has written about this hoary anecdote, Richardson has published it; so have Jones, Smith, Johnson, Ross Browne, and every other correspondence-inditing being that ever set his foot upon the great overland road anywhere between Julesburg and San Francisco; and I have heard that it is in the Talmud. I have seen it in print in nine different foreign languages; I have been told that it is employed in the inquisition in Rome; and I now learn with regret that it is going to be set to music. I do not think that such things are right.

Stage-coaching on the Overland is no more, and stage drivers are a race defunct. I wonder if they bequeathed that bald-headed anecdote to their successors, the railroad brakemen and conductors, and if these latter still persecute the helpless passenger with it until he concludes, as did many a tourist of other days, that the real grandeurs of the Pacific coast are not Yo Semite and the Big Trees, but Hank Monk and his adventure with Horace Greeley.*

CHAPTER XXI

We were approaching the end of our long journey. It was the morning of the twentieth day. At noon we would reach Carson City, the capital of Nevada Territory. We were not glad, but sorry. It had been a fine pleasure trip; we had fed fat on wonders every day; we were now well accustomed to stage life, and very fond of it; so the idea of coming to a stand-still and settling down to a humdrum existence in a village was not agreeable, but on the contrary depressing.

Visibly our new home was a desert, walled in by barren, snow-clad mountains. There was not a tree in sight. There was no vegetation but the endless sage-brush and greasewood. All nature was gray with it. We were plowing through great deeps of powdery alkali dust that rose in thick clouds and floated across the plain like smoke from a burning house. We were coated with

---

* And what makes that worn anecdote the more aggravating, is, that the adventure it celebrates *never occurred*. If it were a good anecote, that seeming demerit would be its chiefest virtue, for creative power belongs to greatness; but what ought to be done to a man who would want only contrive so flat a one as this? If *I* were to suggest what ought to be done to him, I should be called extravagant—but what does the thirteenth chapter of Daniel say? Aha!

it like millers; so were the coach, the mules, the mail-bags, the driver—we and the sage-brush and the other scenery were all one monotonous color. Long trains of freight wagons in the distance enveloped in ascending masses of dust suggested pictures of prairies on fire. These teams and their masters were the only life we saw. Otherwise we moved in the midst of solitude, silence and desolation. Every twenty steps we passed the skeleton of some dead beast of burthen, with its dust-coated skin stretched tightly over its empty ribs. Frequently a solemn raven sat upon the skull or the hips and contemplated the passing coach with meditative serenity.

By and by Carson City was pointed out to us. It nestled in the edge of a great plain and was a sufficient number of miles away to look like an assemblage of mere white spots in the shadow of a grim range of mountains overlooking it, whose summits seemed lifted clear out of companionship and consciousness of earthly things.

We arrived, disembarked, and the stage went on. It was a "wooden" town; its population two thousand souls. The main street consisted of four or five blocks of little white frame stores which were too high to sit down on, but not too high for various other purposes; in fact, hardly high enough. They were packed close together, side by side, as if room were scarce in that mighty plain. The sidewalk was of boards that were more or less loose and inclined to rattle when walked upon. In the middle of the town, opposite the stores, was the "plaza" which is native to all towns beyond the Rocky Mountains—a large, unfenced, level vacancy, with a liberty pole in it, and very useful as a place for public auctions, horse trades, and mass meetings, and likewise for teamsters to camp in. Two other sides of the plaza were faced by stores, offices and stables. The rest of Carson City was pretty scattering.

We were introduced to several citizens, at the stage-office and on the way up to the Governor's from the hotel—among others, to a Mr. Harris, who was on horseback; he began to say something, but interrupted himself with the remark:

"I'll have to get you to excuse me a minute; yonder is the witness that swore I helped to rob the California coach—a piece of impertinent intermeddling, sir, for I am not even acquainted with the man."

Then he rode over and began to rebuke the stranger with a six-shooter, and the stranger began to explain with another. When the pistols were emptied, the stranger resumed his work (mending a whip-lash), and Mr. Harris rode by with a polite nod, homeward bound, with a bullet through one of his lungs, and several in his hips; and from them issued little rivulets of blood that coursed down the horse's sides and made the animal look quite picturesque. I never saw Harris shoot a man after that but it recalled to mind that first day in Carson.

This was all we saw that day, for it was two o'clock, now, and according to custom the daily "Washoe Zephyr" set in: a soaring dust-drift about the size of the United States set up edgewise came with it, and the capital of Nevada Territory disappeared from view. Still, there were sights to be seen which were not wholly uninteresting to new comers; for the vast dust cloud was thickly freckled with things strange to the upper air—things living and dead, that flitted hither and thither, going and coming, appearing and disappearing among the rolling billows of dust—hats, chickens and parasols sailing in the remote heavens; blankets, tin signs, sage-brush and shingles a shade lower; door-mats and buffalo robes lower still; shovels and coal scuttles on the next grade; glass doors, cats and little children on the next; disrupted lumber yards, light buggies and wheelbarrows on the next; and down only thirty or forty feet above ground was a scurrying storm of emigrating roofs and vacant lots.

It was something to see that much. I could have seen more, if I could have kept the dust out of my eyes.

But seriously a Washoe wind is by no means a trifling matter. It blows flimsy houses down, lifts shingle roofs occasionally, rolls up tin ones like sheet music, now and then blows a stage coach over and spills the passengers; and tradition says the reason there are so many bald people there, is, that the wind blows the hair off their heads while they are looking skyward after their hats. Carson streets seldom look inactive on Summer afternoons, because there are so many citizens skipping around their escaping hats, like chambermaids trying to head off a spider.

The "Washoe Zephyr" (Washoe is a pet nickname for Nevada) is a peculiarly Scriptural wind, in that no man knoweth "whence it cometh." That is to say, where it *originates*. It comes right over the mountains from the West, but when one crosses the ridge he does not find any of it on the other side! It probably is manufactured on the mountain-top for the occasion, and starts from there. It is a pretty regular wind, in the summer time. Its office hours are from two in the afternoon till two the next morning; and anybody venturing abroad during those twelve hours needs to allow for the wind or he will bring up a mile or two to leeward of the point he is aiming at. And yet the first complaint a Washoe visitor to San Francisco makes, is that the sea winds blow so, there! There is a good deal of human nature in that.

We found the state palace of the Governor of Nevada Territory to consist of a white frame one-story house with two small rooms in it and a stanchion supported shed in front—for grandeur—it compelled the respect of the citizen and inspired the Indians with awe. The newly arrived Chief and Associate Justices of the Territory, and other machinery of the government, were domiciled with less splendor. They were boarding around privately, and had their offices in their bedrooms.

The Secretary and I took quarters in the "ranch" of a worthy French lady by the name of Bridget O'Flannigan, a camp follower of his Excellency the Governor. She had known him in his prosperity as commander-in-chief of the Metropolitan Police of New York, and she would not desert him in his adversity as Governor of Nevada. Our room was on the lower floor, facing the plaza, and when we had got our bed, a small table, two chairs, the government fire-proof safe, and the Unabridged Dictionary into it, there was still room enough left for a visitor— may be two, but not without straining the walls. But the walls could stand it—at least the partitions could, for they consisted simply of one thickness of white "cotton domestic" stretched from corner to corner of the room. This was the rule in Carson—any other kind of partition was the rare exception. And if you stood in a dark room and your neighbors in the next had lights, the shadows on your canvas told queer secrets sometimes! Very often these partitions were made of old flour sacks basted together; and then the difference between the common herd and the aristocracy was, that the common herd had unornamented sacks, while the walls of the aristocrat were overpowering with rudimental fresco—*i.e.,* red and blue mill brands on the flour sacks. Occasionally, also, the better classes embellished their canvas by pasting pictures from *Harper's Weekly* on them. In many cases, too, the wealthy and the cultured rose to spittoons and other evidences of a sumptuous and luxurious taste.* We had a carpet and a genuine queen's-ware washbowl. Consequently we were hated without reserve by the other tenants of the O'Flannigan "ranch." When we added a painted oilcloth window curtain, we simply took our lives into our own hands. To prevent bloodshed I removed up stairs and took up quarters with the untitled plebeians in one of the four-

* Washoe people take a joke so hard that I must explain that the above description was only the rule; there were many honorable exceptions in Carson—plastered ceilings and houses that had considerable furniture in them.—M.T.

teen white pine cot-bedsteads that stood in two long ranks in the one sole room of which the second story consisted.

It was a jolly company, the fourteen. They were principally voluntary camp-followers of the Governor, who had joined his retinue by their own election at New York and San Francisco and came along, feeling that in the scuffle for little territorial crumbs and offices they could not make their condition more precarious than it was, and might reasonably expect to make it better. They were popularly known as the "Irish Brigade," though there were only four or five Irishmen among all the Governor's retainers. His good-natured Excellency was much annoyed at the gossip his henchmen created—especially when there arose a rumor that they were paid assassins of his, brought along to quietly reduce the democratic vote when desirable!

Mrs. O'Flannigan was boarding and lodging them at ten dollars a week apiece, and they were cheerfully giving their notes for it. They were perfectly satisfied, but Bridget presently found that notes that could not be discounted were but a feeble constitution for a Carson boarding-house. So she began to harry the Governor to find employment for the "Brigade." Her importunities and theirs together drove him to a gentle desperation at last, and he finally summoned the Brigade to the presence. Then, said he:

"Gentlemen, I have planned a lucrative and useful service for you—a service which will provide you with recreation amid noble landscapes, and afford you never ceasing opportunities for enriching your minds by observation and study. I want you to survey a railroad from Carson City westward to a certain point! When the legislature meets I will have the necessary bill passed and the remuneration arranged."

"What, a railroad over the Sierra Nevada Mountains?"

"Well, then, survey it eastward to a certain point!"

He converted them into surveyors, chain-bearers and so on, and turned them loose in the desert. It was "recreation" with a vengeance! Recreation on foot, lugging chains through sand and sage-brush, under a sultry sun and among cattle bones, cayotes and tarantulas. "Romantic adventure" could go no further. They surveyed very slowly, very deliberately, very carefully. They returned every night during the first week, dusty, footsore, tired, and hungry, but very jolly. They brought in great store of prodigious hairy spiders—tarantulas—and imprisoned them in covered tumblers up stairs in the "ranch." After the first week, they had to camp on the field, for they were getting well eastward. They made a good many inquiries as to the location of that indefinite "certain point," but got no information. At last, to a peculiarly urgent inquiry of "How far eastward?" Governor Nye telegraphed back:

"To the Atlantic Ocean, blast you!—and then bridge it and go on!"

This brought back the dusty toilers, who sent in a report and ceased from their labors. The Governor was always comfortable about it; he said Mrs. O'Flannigan would hold him for the Brigade's board anyhow, and he intended to get what entertainment he could out of the boys; he said, with his old-time pleasant twinkle, that he meant to survey them into Utah and then telegraph Brigham to hang them for trespass!

The surveyors brought back more tarantulas with them, and so we had quite a menagerie arranged along the shelves of the room. Some of these spiders could straddle over a common saucer with their hairy, muscular legs, and when their feelings were hurt, or their dignity offended, they were the wickedest-looking desperadoes the animal world can furnish. If their glass prison-houses were touched ever so lightly they were up and spoiling for a fight in a minute. Starchy?—proud? Indeed, they would take up a straw and pick their teeth like a member of Congress. There was as usual a furious "zephyr" blowing the first night of the brigade's return, and about midnight the roof of an adjoining stable blew off, and a corner of it came crashing through the side of our ranch. There was a simultaneous awakening, and a tumultuous muster of the brigade in the dark, and a general tumbling and sprawling over each other in the narrow aisle between the bed-rows. In the midst of the turmoil, Bob II—sprung up out of a sound sleep, and knocked down a shelf with his head. Instantly he shouted:

"Turn out, boys—the tarantulas is loose!"

No warning ever sounded so dreadful. Nobody tried, any longer, to leave the room, lest he might step on a tarantula. Every man groped for a trunk or a bed, and jumped on it. Then followed the strangest silence—a silence of grisly suspense it was, too—waiting, expectancy, fear. It was as dark as pitch, and one had to imagine the spectacle of those fourteen scant-clad men roosting gingerly on trunks and beds, for not a thing could be seen. Then came occasional little interruptions of the silence, and one could recognize a man and tell his locality by his voice, or locate any other sound a sufferer made by his gropings or changes of position. The occasional voices were not given to much speaking—you simply heard a gentle ejaculation of "Ow!" followed by a solid thump, and you knew the gentleman had felt a hairy blanket or something touch his bare skin and had skipped from a bed to the floor. Another silence. Presently you would hear a gasping voice say:

"Su-su-something's crawling up the back of my neck!"

Every now and then you could hear a little subdued scramble and a sorrowful "O Lord!" and then you knew that somebody was getting away from something he took for a tarantula, and not losing any time about it, either. Directly a voice in the corner rang out wild and clear:

"I've got him! I've got him!" [Pause, and probable change of circumstances.] "No, he's got me! Oh, ain't they *never* going to fetch a lantern!"

The lantern came at that moment, in the hands of Mrs. O'Flannigan, whose anxiety to know the amount of damage done by the assaulting roof had not prevented her waiting a judicious interval, after getting out of bed and lighting up, to see if the wind was done, now, up stairs, or had a larger contract.

The landscape presented when the lantern flashed into the room was picturesque, and might have been funny to some people, but was not to us. Although we were perched so strangely upon boxes, trunks and beds, and so strangely attired, too, we were too earnestly distressed and too genuinely miserable to see any fun about it, and there was not the semblance of a smile anywhere visible. I know I am not capable of suffering more than I did during those few minutes of suspense in the dark, surrounded by those creeping, bloody-minded tarantulas. I had skipped from bed to bed and from box to box in a cold agony, and every time I touched anything that was furzy I fancied I felt the fangs. I had rather go to war than live that episode over again. Nobody was hurt. The man who thought a tarantula had "got him" was mistaken—only a crack in a box had caught his finger. Not one of those escaped tarantulas was ever seen again. There were ten or twelve of them. We took candles and hunted the place high and low for them, but with no success. Did we go back to bed then? We did nothing of the kind. Money could not have persuaded us to do it. We sat up the rest of the night playing cribbage and keeping a sharp lookout for the enemy.

CHAPTER XXII

It was the end of August, and the skies were cloudless and the weather superb. In two or three weeks I had grown wonderfully fascinated with the curious new country, and concluded to put off my return to "the States" awhile. I had grown well accustomed to wearing a damaged slouch hat, blue woolen shirt, and pants crammed into boot-tops, and gloried in the absence of coat, vest and braces. I felt rowdyish and "bully," (as the historian Josephus phrases it, in his fine chapter upon the destruction of the Temple). It seemed to me that nothing could be so fine and so romantic. I had become an officer of the government, but that was for mere sublimity. The office was an unique sinecure. I had nothing to do and no salary. I was private Secretary to his majesty the Secretary and there was not yet writing enough for two of us. So Johnny K——and I devoted our time to amusement. He was the young son of an Ohio nabob and was out there for recreation. He got it. We had heard a world of talk about the marvellous beauty of Lake Tahoe, and finally curiosity drove us thither to see it. Three or four members of the Brigade had been there and located some timber lands on its shores and stored up a quantity of provisions in their camp. We strapped a couple of blankets on our shoulders and took an axe apiece and started—for we intended to take up a wood ranch or so ourselves and become wealthy. We were on foot. The reader will find it advantageous to go horseback. We were told that the distance was eleven miles. We tramped a long time on level ground, and then toiled laboriously up a mountain about a thousand miles high and looked over. No lake there. We descended on the other side, crossed the valley and toiled up another mountain three or four thousand miles high, apparently, and looked over again. No lake yet. We sat down tired and perspiring, and hired a couple of Chinamen to curse those people who had beguiled us. Thus refreshed, we presently resumed the march with renewed vigor and determination. We plodded on, two or three hours longer, and at last the Lake burst upon us—a noble sheet of blue water lifted six thousand three hundred feet above the level of the sea, and walled in by a rim of snow-clad mountain peaks that towered aloft full three thousand feet higher still! It was a vast oval, and one would have to use up eighty or a hundred good miles in traveling around it. As it lay there with the shadows of the mountains brilliantly photographed upon its still surface I thought it must surely be the fairest picture the whole earth affords.

We found the small skiff belonging to the Brigade boys, and without loss of time set out across a deep bend of the lake toward the landmarks that signified the locality of the camp. I got Johnny to row—not because I mind exertion myself, but because it makes me sick to ride backwards when I am at work. But I steered. A three-mile pull brought us to the camp just as the night fell, and we stepped ashore very tired and wolfishly hungry. In a "cache" among the rocks we found the provisions and the cooking utensils, and then, all fatigued as I was, I sat down on a boulder and superintended while Johnny gathered wood and cooked supper. Many a man who had gone through what I had, would have wanted to rest.

It was a delicious supper—hot bread, fried bacon, and black coffee. It was a delicious solitude we were in, too. Three miles away was a saw-mill and some workmen, but there were not fifteen other human beings throughout the wide circumference of the lake. As the darkness closed down and the stars came out and spangled the great mirror with jewels, we smoked meditatively in the solemn hush and forgot our troubles and our pains. In due time we spread our blankets in the warm sand between two large boulders and soon feel asleep, careless of the procession of ants that passed in through rents in our clothing and explored our persons. Nothing could disturb the sleep that fettered us, for it had been fairly earned, and if our consciences had any sins on them they had to adjourn court for that night, any way. The wind rose just as we were losing consciousness, and we were lulled to sleep by the beating of the surf upon the shore.

It is always very cold on that lake shore in the night, but we had plenty of blankets and were warm enough. We never moved a muscle all night, but waked at early dawn in the original positions, and got up at once, thoroughly refreshed, free from soreness, and brim full of friskiness. There is no end of wholesome medicine in such an experience. That morning we could have whipped ten such people as we were the day before—sick ones at any rate. But the world is slow, and people will go to "water cures" and "movement cures" and to foreign lands for health. Three months of camp life on Lake Tahoe would restore an Egyptian mummy to his pristine vigor, and give him an appetite like an alligator. I do not mean the oldest and driest mummies, of course, but the fresher ones. The air up there in the clouds is very pure and fine, bracing and delicious. And why shouldn't it be?—it is the same the angels breathe. I think that hardly any amount of fatigue can be gathered together that a man cannot sleep off in one night on the sand by its side. Not under a roof, but under the sky; it seldom or never rains there in the summer time. I know a man who went there to die. But he made a failure of it. He was a skeleton when he came, and could barely stand. He had no appetite, and did nothing but read tracts and reflect on the future. Three months later he was sleeping out of doors regularly, eating all he could hold, three times a day, and chasing game over mountains three thousand feet high for recreation. And he was a skeleton no longer, but weighed part of a ton. This is no fancy sketch, but the truth. His disease was consumption. I confidently commend his experience to other skeletons.

I superintended again, and as soon as we had eaten breakfast we got in the boat and skirted along the lake shore about three miles and disembarked. We liked the appearance of the place, and so we claimed some three hundred acres of it and stuck our "notices" on a tree. It was yellow pine timber land—a dense forest of trees a hundred feet high and from one to five feet through at the butt. It was necessary to fence our property or we could not hold it. That is to say, it was necessary to cut down trees here and there and make them fall in such a way as to form a sort of enclosure (with pretty wide gaps in it). We cut down three trees apiece, and found it such heart-breaking work that we decided to "rest our case" on those; if they held the property, well and good; if they didn't, let the property spill out through the gaps and go; it was no use to work ourselves to death merely to save a few acres of land. Next day we came back to build a house—for a house was also necessary, in order to hold the property. We decided to build a substantial log-house and excite the envy of the Brigade boys; but by the time we had cut and trimmed the first log it seemed unnecessary to be so elaborate, and so we concluded to build it of saplings. However, two saplings, duly cut and trimmed, compelled recognition of the fact that a still modester architecture would satisfy the law, and so we concluded to build a "brush" house. We devoted the next day to this work, but we did so much "sitting around" and discussing, that by the middle of the afternoon we had achieved only a half-way sort of affair which one of us had to watch while the other cut brush, lest if both turned our backs we might not be able to find it again, it had such a strong family resemblance to the surrounding vegetation. But we were satisfied with it.

We were land owners now, duly seized and possessed, and within the protection of the law. Therefore we decided to take up our residence on our own domain and enjoy that large sense of independence which only such an experience can bring. Late the next afternoon, after a good long rest, we sailed away from the Brigade camp with all the provisions and cooking utensils we could carry off—borrow is the more accurate word—and just as the night was falling we beached the boat at our own landing.

CHAPTER XXIII

If there is any life that is happier than the life we led on our timber ranch for the next two or three weeks, it must be a sort of life which I have not read of in books or experienced in person. We did not see a human being but ourselves during the time, or hear any sounds but those that were made by the wind and the waves, the sighing of the pines, and now and then the far-off thunder of an avalanche. The forest about us was dense and cool, the sky above us was cloudless and brilliant with sunshine, the broad lake before us was glassy and clear, or rippled and breezy, or black and storm-tossed, according to Nature's mood; and its circling border of mountain domes, clothed with forests, scarred with land-slides, cloven by canons and valleys, and helmeted with glittering snow, fitly framed and finished the noble picture. The view was always fascinating, bewitching, entrancing. The eye was never tired of gazing, night or day, in calm or storm; it suffered but one grief, and that was that it could not look always, but must close sometimes in sleep.

We slept in the sand close to the water's edge, between two protecting boulders, which took care of the stormy night-winds for us. We never took any paregoric to make us sleep. At the first break of dawn we were always up and running footraces to tone down excess of physical vigor and exuberance of spirits. That is, Johnny was—but I held his hat. While smoking the pipe of peace after breakfast we watched the sentinel peaks put on the glory of the sun, and followed the conquering light as it swept down among the shadows, and set the captive crags and forests free. We watched the tinted pictures grow and brighten upon the water till every little detail of forest, precipice and pinnacle was wrought in and finished, and the miracle of the enchanter complete. Then to "business."

That is, drifting around in the boat. We were on the north shore. There, the rocks on the bottom are sometimes gray, sometimes white. This gives the marvelous transparency of the water a fuller advantage than it has elsewhere on the lake. We usually pushed out a hundred yards or so from shore, and then lay down on the thwarts, in the sun, and let the boat drift by the hour whither it would. We seldom talked. It interrupted the Sabbath stillness, and marred the dreams the luxurious rest and indolence brought. The shore all along was indented with deep, curved bays and coves, bordered by narrow sand-beaches; and where the sand ended, the steep mountain-sides rose right up aloft into space—rose up like a vast wall a little out of the perpendicular, and thickly wooded with tall pines.

So singularly clear was the water, that where it was only twenty or thirty feet deep the bottom was so perfectly distinct that the boat seemed floating in the air! Yes, where it was even *eighty* feet deep. Every little pebble was distinct, every speckled trout, every hand's-breadth of sand. Often, as we lay on our faces, a granite boulder, as large as a village church, would start out of the bottom apparently, and seem climbing up rapidly to the surface, till presently it threatened to touch our faces, and we could not resist the impulse to seize an oar and avert the danger. But the boat would float on, and the boulder descend again, and then we could see that when we had been exactly above it, it must still have been twenty or thirty feet below the surface. Down through the transparency of these great depths, the water was not *merely* transparent, but dazzlingly, brilliantly so. All objects seen through it had a bright, strong vividness, not only of outline, but of every minute detail, which they would not have had when seen simply through the same depth of atmosphere. So empty and airy did all spaces seem below us, and so strong was the sense of floating high aloft in mid-nothingness, that we called these boat-excursions "balloon-voyages."

We fished a good deal, but we did not average one fish a week. We could see trout by the thousand winging about in the emptiness under us, or sleeping in shoals on the bottom, but they would not bite—they could see the line too plainly, perhaps. We frequently selected the trout we wanted, and rested the bait patiently and persistently on the end of his nose at a depth of eighty feet, but he would only shake it off with an annoyed manner, and shift his position.

We bathed occasionally, but the water was rather chilly, for all it looked so sunny. Sometimes we rowed out to the "blue water," a mile or two from shore. It was as dead blue as indigo there, because of the immense depth. By official measurement the lake in its centre is one thousand five hundred and twenty-five feet deep!

Sometimes, on lazy afternoons, we lolled on the sand in camp, and smoked pipes and read some old well-worn novels. At night, by the camp-fire, we played euchre and seven-up to strengthen the mind—and played them with cards so greasy and defaced that only a whole summer's acquaintance with them could enable the student to tell the ace of clubs from the jack of diamonds.

We never slept in our "house." It never occurred to us, for one thing; and besides, it was built to hold the ground, and that was enough. We did not wish to strain it.

By and by our provisions began to run short, and we went

back to the old camp and laid in a new supply. We were gone all day, and reached home again about night-fall, pretty tired and hungry. While Johnny was carrying the main bulk of the provisions up to our "house" for future use, I took the loaf of bread, some slices of bacon, and the coffee-pot, ashore, set them down by a tree, lit a fire, and went back to the boat to get the frying-pan. While I was at this, I heard a shout from Johnny, and looking up I saw that my fire was galloping all over the premises!

Johnny was on the other side of it. He had to run through the flames to get to the lake shore, and then we stood helpless and watched the devastation.

The ground was deeply carpeted with dry pine-needles, and the fire touched them off as if they were gunpowder. It was wonderful to see with what fierce speed the tall sheet of flame traveled! My coffee-pot was gone, and everything with it. In a minute and a half the fire seized upon a dense growth of dry manzanita chapparal six or eight feet high, and then the roaring and popping and crackling was something terrific. We were driven to the boat by the intense heat, and there we remained, spell-bound.

Within half an hour all before us was a tossing, blinding tempest of flame! It went surging up adjacent ridges—surmounted them and disappeared in the canons beyond—burst into view upon higher and farther ridges, presently—shed a grander illumination abroad, and dove again—flamed out again, directly, higher and still higher up the mountain-side— threw out skirmishing parties of fire here and there, and sent them trailing their crimson spirals away among remote ramparts and ribs and gorges, till as far as the eye could reach the lofty mountain-fronts were webbed as it were with a tangled network of red lava streams. Away across the water the crags and domes were lit with a ruddy glare, and the firmament above was a reflected hell!

Every feature of the spectacle was repeated in the glowing mirror of the lake! Both pictures were sublime, both were beautiful; but that in the lake had a bewildering richness about it that enchanted the eye and held it with the stronger fascination.

We sat absorbed and motionless through four long hours. We never thought of supper, and never felt fatigue. But at eleven o'clock the conflagration had traveled beyond our range of vision, and then darkness stole down upon the landscape again.

Hunger asserted itself now, but there was nothing to eat. The provisions were all cooked, no doubt, but we did not go to see. We were homeless wanderers again, without any property. Our fence was gone, our house burned down; no insurance. Our pine forest was well scorched, the dead trees all burned up, and our broad acres of manzanita swept away. Our blankets were on our usual sand-bed, however, and so we lay down and went to sleep. The next morning we started back to the old camp, but while out a long way from shore, so great a storm came up that we dared not try to land. So I baled out the seas we shipped, and Johnny pulled heavily through the billows till we had reached a point three or four miles beyond the camp. The storm was increasing, and it became evident that it was better to take the hazard of beaching the boat than go down in a hundred fathoms of water; so we ran in, with tall white-caps following, and I sat down in the stern-sheets and pointed her head-on to the shore. The instant the bow struck, a wave came over the stern that washed crew and cargo ashore, and saved a deal of trouble. We shivered in the lee of a boulder all the rest of the day, and froze all the night through. In the morning the tempest had gone down, and we paddled down to the camp without any unnecessary delay. We were so starved that we ate up the rest of the Brigade's provisions, and then set out to Carson to tell them about it and ask their forgiveness. It was accorded, upon payment of damages.

We made many trips to the lake after that, and had many a hair-breadth escape and blood-curdling adventure which will never be recorded in any history.

CHAPTER XXIV

I resolved to have a horse to ride. I had never seen such wild, free, magnificent horsemanship outside of a circus as these picturesquely-clad Mexicans, Californians and Mexicanized Americans displayed in Carson streets every day. How they rode! Leaning just gently forward out of the perpendicular, easy and nonchalant, with broad slouch-hat brim blown square up in front, and long *riata* swinging above the head, they swept through the town like the wind! The next minute they were only a sailing puff of dust on the far desert. If they trotted, they sat up gallantly and gracefully, and seemed part of the horse; did not go jiggering up and down after the silly Miss-Nancy fashion of the riding-schools. I had quickly learned to tell a horse from a cow, and was full of anxiety to learn more. I was resolved to buy a horse.

While the thought was rankling in my mind, the auctioneer came skurrying through the plaza on a black beast that had as many humps and corners on him as a dromedary, and was neces-

sarily uncomely; but he was "going, going, at twenty-two!—
horse, saddle and bridle at twenty-two dollars, gentlemen!" and
I could hardly resist.

A man whom I did not know (he turned out to be the auctioneer's brother) noticed the wistful look in my eye, and observed that that was a very remarkable horse to be going at such
a price; and added that the saddle alone was worth the money. It
was a Spanish saddle, with ponderous *tapidaros,* and furnished
with the ungainly sole-leather covering with the unspellable
name. I said I had half a notion to bid. Then this keen-eyed person appeared to me to be "taking my measure"; but I dismissed
the suspicion when he spoke, for his manner was full of guileless
candor and truthfulness. Said he:

"I know that horse—know him well. You are a stranger, I
take it, and so you might think he was an American horse, maybe, but I assure you he is not. He is nothing of the kind: but—
excuse my speaking in a low voice, other people being near—he
is, without the shadow of a doubt, a Genuine Mexican Plug!"

I did not know what a Genuine Mexican Plug was, but there
was something about this man's way of saying it, that made me
swear inwardly that I would own a Genuine Mexican Plug, or
die.

"Has he any other—er—advantages?" I inquired, suppress-
ing what eagerness I could.

He hooked his forefinger in the pocket of my army-shirt, led
me to one side, and breathed in my ear impressively these words:

"He can out-buck anything in America!"

"Going, going, going—at *twent—ty*-four dollars and a half,
gen—"

"Twenty-seven!" I shouted, in a frenzy.

"And sold!" said the auctioneer, and passed over the Genuine
Mexican Plug to me.

I could scarcely contain my exultation. I paid the money, and
put the animal in a neighboring livery-stable to dine and rest
himself.

In the afternoon I brought the creature into the plaza, and certain citizens held him by the head, and others by the tail, while I
mounted him. As soon as they let go, he placed all his feet in a
bunch together, lowered his back, and then suddenly arched it
upward, and shot me straight into the air a matter of three or
four feet! I came as straight down again, lit in the saddle, went
instantly up again, came down almost on the high pommel, shot
up again, and came down on the horse's neck—all in the space
of three or four seconds. Then he rose and stood almost straight
up on his hind feet, and I, clasping his lean neck desperately, slid

back into the saddle, and held on. He came down, and immediately hoisted his heels into the air, delivering a vicious kick at the sky, and stood on his forefeet. And then down he came once more, and began the original exercise of shooting me straight up again. The third time I went up I heard a stranger say:

"Oh, *don't* he buck, though!"

While I was up, somebody struck the horse a sounding thwack with a leathern strap, and when I arrived again the Genuine Mexican Plug was not there. A Californian youth chased him up and caught him, and asked if he might have a ride. I granted him that luxury. He mounted the Genuine, got lifted into the air once, but sent his spurs home as he descended, and the horse darted away like a telegram. He soared over three fences like a bird, and disappeared down the road toward the Washoe Valley.

I sat down on a stone, with a sigh, and by a natural impulse one of my hands sought my forehead, and the other the base of my stomach. I believe I never appreciated, till then, the poverty of the human machinery—for I still needed a hand or two to place elsewhere. Pen cannot describe how I was jolted up. Imagination cannot conceive how disjointed I was—how internally, externally and universally I was unsettled, mixed up and ruptured. There was a sympathetic crowd around me, though.

One elderly-looking comforter said:

"Stranger, you've been taken in. Everybody in this camp knows that horse. Any child, any Injun, could have told you that he'd buck; he is the very worst devil to buck on the continent of America. You hear *me*. I'm Curry. *Old* Curry. Old *Abe* Curry. And moreover, he is a simon-pure, out-and-out, genuine d—d Mexican plug, and an uncommon mean one at that, too. Why, you turnip, if you had laid low and kept dark, there's chances to buy an *American* horse for mighty little more than you paid for that bloody old foreign relic."

I gave no sign; but I made up my mind that if the auctioneer's brother's funeral took place while I was in the Territory I would postpone all other recreations and attend it.

After a gallop of sixteen miles the Californian youth and the Genuine Mexican Plug came tearing into town again, shedding foam-flakes like the spume-spray that drives before a typhoon, and, with one final skip over a wheelbarrow and a Chinaman, cast anchor in front of the "ranch."

Such panting and blowing! Such spreading and contracting of the red equine nostrils, and glaring of the wild equine eye! But was the imperial beast subjugated? Indeed he was not. His lordship the Speaker of the House thought he was, and mounted him to go down to the Capitol; but the first dash the creature made was over a pile of telegraph poles half as high as a church; and his time to the Capitol—one mile and three quarters—remains unbeaten to this day. But then he took an advantage—he left out the mile, and only did the three quarters. That is to say, he made a straight cut across lots, preferring fences and ditches to a crooked road; and when the Speaker got to the Capitol he said he had been in the air so much he felt as if he had made the trip on a comet.

In the evening the Speaker came home afoot for exercise, and got the Genuine towed back behind a quartz wagon. The next day I loaned the animal to the Clerk of the House to go down to the Dana silver mine, six miles, and *he* walked back for exercise, and got the horse towed. Everybody I loaned him to always walked back; they never could get enough exercise any other way. Still, I continued to loan him to anybody who was willing to borrow him, my idea being to get him crippled, and throw him on the borrower's hands, or killed, and make the borrower pay for him. But somehow nothing ever happened to him. He took chances that no other horse ever took and survived, but he always came out safe. It was his daily habit to try experiments that had always before been considered impossible, but he always got through. Sometimes he miscalculated a little, and did not get his rider through intact, but *he* always got through himself. Of course I had tried to sell him; but that was a stretch of simplicity which met with little sympathy. The auctioneer stormed up and down the streets on him for four days, dispersing the populace, interrupting business, and destroying children, and never got a bid—at least never any but the eighteen-dollar one he hired a notoriously substanceless bummer to make. The people only smiled pleasantly, and restrained their desire to buy, if they had any. Then the auctioneer brought in his bill, and I withdrew the horse from the market. We tried to trade him off at private vendue next, offering him at a sacrifice for second-hand tombstones, old iron, temperance tracts—any kind of property. But holders were stiff, and we retired from the market again. I never tried to ride the horse any more. Walking was good enough exercise for a man like me, that had nothing the matter with him except ruptures, internal injuries, and such things. Finally I tried to *give* him away. But it was a failure. Parties said earthquakes were handy enough on the Pacific coast—they did not wish to own one. As a last resort I offered him to the Governor for the use of the "Brigade." His face lit up eagerly at first, but toned down again, and he said the thing would be too palpable.

Just then the livery stable man brought in his bill for six weeks' keeping—stall-room for the horse, fifteen dollars; hay for the horse, two hundred and fifty! The Genuine Mexican Plug had eaten a ton of the article, and the man said he would have eaten a hundred if he had let him.

I will remark here, in all seriousness, that the regular price of hay during that year and a part of the next was really two hundred and fifty dollars a ton. During a part of the previous year it had sold at five hundred a ton, in gold, and during the winter before that there was such scarcity of the article that in several instances small quantities had brought eight hundred dollars a ton in coin! The consequence might be guessed without my telling it: peopled turned their stock loose to starve, and before the spring arrived Carson and Eagle valleys were almost literally carpeted with their carcases! Any old settler there will verify these statements.

I managed to pay the livery bill, and that same day I gave the Genuine Mexican Plug to a passing Arkansas emigrant whom fortune delivered into my hand. If this ever meets his eye, he will doubtless remember the donation.

Now whoever has had the luck to ride a real Mexican plug will recognize the animal depicted in this chapter, and hardly consider him exaggerated—but the uninitiated will feel justified in regarding his portrait as a fancy sketch, perhaps.

CHAPTER XXV

Originally, Nevada was a part of Utah and was called Carson county; and a pretty large county it was, too. Certain of its valleys produced no end of hay, and this attracted small colonies of Mormon stock-raisers and farmers to them. A few orthodox Americans straggled in from California, but no love was lost between the two classes of colonists. There was little or no friendly intercourse; each party staid to itself. The Mormons were largely in the majority, and had the additional advantage of being peculiarly under the protection of the Mormon government of the Territory. Therefore they could afford to be distant, and even peremptory toward their neighbors. One of the traditions of Carson Valley illustrates the condition of things that prevailed at the time I speak of. The hired girl of one of the American families was Irish, and a Catholic; yet it was noted with surprise that she was the only person outside of the Mormon ring who could get favors from the Mormons. She asked kindnesses of them often, and always got them. It was a mystery to everybody. But one day as she was passing out at the door, a large bowie knife dropped from under her apron, and when her mistress asked for an explanation she observed that she was going out to "borry a wash-tub from the Mormons!"

In 1858 silver lodes were discovered in "Carson County," and then the aspect of things changed. Californians began to flock in, and the American element was soon in the majority. Allegiance to Brigham Young and Utah was renounced, and a temporary territorial government for "Washoe" was instituted by the citizens. Governor Roop was the first and only chief magistrate of it. In due course of time Congress passed a bill to organize "Nevada Territory," and President Lincoln sent out Governor Nye to supplant Roop.

At this time the population of the Territory was about twelve or fifteen thousand, and rapidly increasing. Silver mines were being vigorously developed and silver mills erected. Business of all kinds was active and prosperous and growing more so day by day.

The people were glad to have a legitimately constituted government, but did not particularly enjoy having strangers from distant States put in authority over them—a sentiment that was natural enough. They thought the officials should have been chosen from among themselves—from among prominent citizens who had earned a right to such promotion, and who would be in sympathy with the populace and likewise thoroughly acquainted with the needs of the Territory. They were right in viewing the matter thus, without doubt. The new officers were "emigrants," and that was no title to anybody's affection or admiration either.

The new government was received with considerable coolness. It was not only a foreign intruder, but a poor one. It was not even worth plucking—except by the smallest of small fry office-seekers and such. Everybody knew that Congress had appropriated only twenty thousand dollars a year in greenbacks for its support—about money enough to run a quartz mill a month. And everybody knew, also, that the first year's money was still in Washington, and that the getting hold of it would be a tedious and difficult process. Carson City was too wary and too wise to open a credit account with the imported bantling with anything like indecent haste.

There is something solemnly funny about the struggles of a new-born Territorial government to get a start in this world. Ours had a trying time of it. The Organic Act and the "instructions" from the State Department commanded that a legislature should be elected at such-and-such a time, and its sittings inaugurated at such-and-such a date. It was easy to get legislators, even at three dollars a day, although board was four dollars and fifty cents, for distinction has its charm in Nevada as well as elsewhere, and there were plenty of patriotic souls out of employment; but to get a legislative hall for them to meet in was another matter altogether. Carson blandly declined to give a room rent-free, or let one to the government on credit.

But when Curry heard of the difficulty, he came forward, solitary and alone, and shouldered the Ship of State over the bar and got her afloat again. I refer to "Curry—*Old* Curry—Old *Abe* Curry." But for him the legislature would have been obliged to sit in the desert. He offered his large stone building just outside the capital limits, rent-free, and it was gladly accepted. Then he built a horse-railroad from town to the capitol, and carried the legislators gratis. He also furnished pine benches and chairs for the legislature, and covered the floors with clean saw-dust by way of carpet and spittoon combined. But for Curry the government would have died in its tender infancy. A canvas partition to separate the Senate from the House of Representatives was put up by the Secretary, at a cost of three dollars and forty cents, but the United States declined to pay for it. Upon being reminded that the "instructions" permitted the payment of a liberal rent for a legislative hall, and that that money was saved to the country by Mr. Curry's generosity, the United States said that did not alter the matter, and the three dollars and forty cents would be subtracted from the Secretary's eighteen hundred dollar salary—and it *was!*

The matter of printing was from the beginning an interesting feature of the new government's difficulties. The Secretary was sworn to obey his volume of written "instructions," and these commanded him to do two certain things without fail, viz. :

1. Get the House and Senate journals printed; and,

2. For this work, pay one dollar and fifty cents per "thousand" for composition, and one dollar and fifty cents per "token" for press-work, in greenbacks.

It was easy to swear to do these two things, but it was entirely impossible to do more than one of them. When greenbacks had gone down to forty cents on the dollar, the prices regularly charged everybody by printing establishments were one dollar and fifty cents per "thousand" and one dollar and fifty cents per "token," in *gold*. The "instructions" commanded that the Secretary regard a paper dollar issued by the government as equal to any other dollar issued by the government. Hence the printing of the journals was discontinued. Then the United States sternly rebuked the Secretary for disregarding the "instructions," and warned him to correct his ways. Wherefore he got some printing done, forwarded the bill to Washington with full exhibits of the high prices of things in the Territory, and called attention to a printed market report wherein it would be observed that even hay was two hundred and fifty dollars a ton. The United States responded by subtracting the printing-bill from the Secretary's suffering salary—and moreover remarked with dense gravity that he would find nothing in his "instructions" requiring him to purchase hay!

Nothing in this world is palled in such impenetrable obscurity as a U.S. Treasury Comptroller's understanding. The very fires of the hereafter could get up nothing more than a fitful glimmer in it. In the days I speak of he never could be made to comprehend why it was that twenty thousand dollars would not go as far in Nevada, where all commodities ranged at an enormous figure, as it would in the other Territories, where exceeding cheapness was the rule. He was an officer who looked out for the little expenses all the time. The Secretary of the Territory kept his office in his bedroom, as I before remarked; and he charged the United States no rent, although his "instructions" provided for that item and he could have justly taken advantage of it (a thing which I would have done with more than lightning promptness if I had been Secretary myself). But the United States never applauded this devotion. Indeed, I think my country was ashamed to have so improvident a person in its employ.

Those "instructions" (we used to read a chapter from them every morning, as intellectual gymnastics, and a couple of chapters in Sunday school every Sabbath, for they treated of all subjects under the sun and had much valuable religious matter in them along with the other statistics) those "instructions" commanded that pen-knives, envelopes, pens and writing-paper be furnished the members of the legislature. So the Secretary made the purchase and the distribution. The knives cost three dollars apiece. There was one too many, and the Secretary gave it to the Clerk of the House of Representatives. The United States said the Clerk of the House was not a "member" of the legislature, and took that three dollars out of the Secretary's salary, as usual.

White men charged three or four dollars a "load" for sawing up stove-wood. The Secretary was sagacious enough to know that the United States would never pay any such price as that; so he got an Indian to saw up a load of office wood at one dollar and a half. He made out the usual voucher, but signed no name to it—simply appended a note explaining that an Indian had done the work, and had done it in a very capable and satisfactory way, but could not sign the voucher owing to lack of ability in the necessary direction. The Secretary had to pay that dollar and a half. He thought the United States would admire both his economy and his honesty in getting the work done at half price and not putting a pretended Indian's signature to the voucher, but the United States did not see it in that light. The United States was too much accustomed to employing dollar-and-a-half thieves in all manner of official capacities to regard his explanation of the voucher as having any foundation in fact.

But the next time the Indian sawed wood for us I taught him to make a cross at the bottom of the voucher—it looked like a cross that had been drunk a year—and then I "witnessed" it and it went through all right. The United States never said a word. I was sorry I had not made the voucher for a thousand loads of wood instead of one. The government of my country snubs honest simplicity but fondles artistic villainy, and I think I might have developed into a very capable pickpocket if I had remained in the public service a year or two.

That was a fine collection of sovereigns, that first Nevada legislature. They levied taxes to the amount of thirty or forty thousand dollars and ordered expenditures to the extent of about a million. Yet they had their little periodical explosions of economy like all other bodies of the kind. A member proposed to save three dollars a day to the nation by dispensing with the Chaplain. And yet that short-sighted man needed the Chaplain more than any other member, perhaps, for he generally sat with his feet on his desk, eating raw turnips, during the morning prayer.

The legislature sat sixty days, and passed private toll-road franchises all the time. When they adjourned it was estimated that every citizen owned about three franchises, and it was believed that unless Congress gave the Territory another degree of longitude there would not be room enough to accomodate the toll-roads. The ends of them were hanging over the boundary line everywhere like a fringe.

The fact is, the freighting business had grown to such important proportions that there was nearly as much excitement over suddenly acquired toll-road fortunes as over the wonderful silver mines.

CHAPTER XXVI

By and by I was smitten with the silver fever. "Prospecting parties" were leaving for the mountains every day, and discovering and taking possession of rich silver-bearing lodes and ledges of quartz. Plainly this was the road to fortune. The great "Gould and Curry" mine was held at three or four hundred dollars a foot when we arrived; but in two months it had sprung up to eight hundred. The "Ophir" had been worth only a mere trifle, a year gone by, and now it was selling at nearly *four thousand dollars a foot!* Not a mine could be named that had not experienced an astonishing advance in value within a short time. Everybody was talking about these marvels. Go where you would, you heard nothing else, from morning till far into the night. Tom So-and-So had sold out of the "Amanda Smith" for $40,000—hadn't a cent when he "took up" the ledge six months ago. John Jones had sold half his interest in the "Bald Eagle and Mary Ann" for $65,000, gold coin, and gone to the States for his family. The widow Brewster had "struck it rich" in the "Golden Fleece" and sold ten feet for $18,000—hadn't money enough to buy a crape bonnet when Sing-Sing Tommy killed her husband at Baldy Johnson's wake last spring. The "Last Chance" had found a "clay casing" and knew they were "right on the ledge"—consequence, "feet" that went begging yesterday were worth a brick house apiece to-day, and seedy owners who could not get trusted for a drink at any bar in the country yesterday were roaring drunk on champagne to-day and had hosts of warm personal friends in a town where they had forgotten how to bow or shake hands from long-continued want of practice. Johnny Morgan, a common loafer, had gone to sleep in the gutter and waked up worth a hundred thousand dollars, in consequence of the decision in the "Lady Franklin and Rough and Ready" lawsuit. And so on—day in and day out the talk pelted our ears and the excitement waxed hotter and hotter around us.

I would have been more or less than human if I had not gone mad like the rest. Cart-loads of solid silver bricks, as large as pigs of lead, were arriving from the mills every day, and such sights as that gave substance to the wild talk about me. I succumbed and grew as frenzied as the craziest.

Every few days news would come of the discovery of a brannew mining region; immediately the papers would teem with accounts of its richness, and away the surplus population would scamper to take possession. By the time I was fairly inoculated with the disease, "Esmeralda" had just had a run and "Humboldt" was beginning to shriek for attention. "Humboldt! Humboldt!" was the new cry, and straightway Humboldt, the newest of the new, the richest of the rich, the most marvellous of the marvellous discoveries in silver-land, was occupying two columns of the public prints to "Esmeralda's" one. I was just on the point of starting to Esmeralda, but turned with the tide and got ready for Humboldt. That the reader may see what moved me, and what would as surely have moved him had he been there, I insert here one of the newspaper letters of the day. It and several other letters from the same calm hand were the main means of converting me. I shall not garble the extract, but put it in just as it appeared in the *Daily Territorial Enterprise*:

But what about our mines? I shall be candid with you. I shall express an honest opinion, based upon a thorough examination. Humboldt county is the richest mineral region upon God's footstool. Each mountain range is gorged with the precious ores. Humboldt is the true Golconda.

The other day an assay of mere *croppings* yielded exceeding *four thousand dollars to the ton*. A week or two ago an assay of just such surface developments made returns of *seven thousand* dollars to the ton. Our mountains are full of rambling prospectors. Each day and almost every hour reveals new and more startling evidences of the profuse and intensified wealth of our favored county. The metal is not silver alone. There are distinct ledges of auriferous ore. A late discovery plainly evinces cinnabar. The coarser metals are in gross abundance. Lately evidences of bituminous coal have been detected. My theory has ever been that coal is a ligneous formation. I told Col. Whitman, in times past, that the neighborhood of Dayton (Nevada) betrayed no present or previous manifestations of a ligneous foundation, and that hence I had no confidence in his lauded coal mines. I repeated the same doctrine to the exultant coal discoverers of Humboldt. I talked with my friend Captain Burch on the subject. My pyrhanism vanished upon his statement that in the very region referred to he had seen petrified trees of the length of two hundred feet. Then is the fact established that huge forests once cast their grim shadows over this remote section. I am firm in the coal faith. Have no fears of the mineral resources of Humboldt county. They are immense— incalculable.

Let me state one or two things which will help the reader to better comprehend certain items in the above. At this time, our near neighbor, Gold Hill, was the most successful silver mining locality in Nevada. It was from there that more than half the daily shipments of silver bricks came. "Very rich" (and scarce) Gold Hill ore yielded from $100 to $400 to the ton; but the usual yield was only $20 to $40 per ton—that is to say, each hundred pounds of ore yielded from one dollar to two dollars. But the reader will perceive by the above extract, that in Humboldt from one fourth to nearly half the mass was silver! That is to say, every one hundred pounds of the ore had from *two hundred* dollars up to about *three hundred and fifty* in it. Some days later this same correspondent wrote:

I have spoken of the vast and almost fabulous wealth of this region—it is incredible. The intestines of our mountains are gorged with precious ore to plethora. I have said that nature has so shaped our mountains as to furnish most excellent facilities for the working of our mines. I have also told you that the country about here is pregnant with the finest mill sites in the world. But what is the mining history of Humboldt? The Sheba mine is in the hands of energetic San Francisco capitalists. It would seem that the ore is combined with metals that render it difficult of reduction with our imperfect mountain machinery. The proprietors have combined the capital and labor hinted at in my exordium. They are toiling and probing. Their tunnel has reached the length of one hundred feet. From primal assays alone, coupled with the development of the mine and public confidence in the continuance of effort, the stock had reared itself to eight hundred dollars market value. I do not know that one ton of the ore has been converted into current metal. I do know that there are many lodes in this section that surpass the Sheba in primal assay value. Listen a moment to the calculations of the Sheba operators. They purpose transporting the ore concentrated to Europe. The conveyance from Star City (its locality) to Virginia City will cost seventy dollars per ton; from Virginia to San Francisco, forty dollars per ton; from thence to Liverpool, its destination, ten dollars per ton. Their idea is that its conglomerate metals will reimburse them their cost of original extraction, the price of transportation, and the expense of reduction, and that then a ton of the raw ore will net them twelve hundred dollars. The estimate may be extravagant. Cut it in twain, and the product is enormous, far transcending any previous developments of our racy Territory.

A very common calculation is that many of our mines will yield five hundred dollars to the ton. Such fecundity throws the Gould & Curry, the Ophir and the Mexican, of your neighborhood, in the darkest shadow. I have given you the estimate of the value of a single developed mine. Its richness is indexed by its market valuation. The people of Humboldt county are *feet* crazy. As I write, our towns are near deserted. They look as languid as a consumptive girl. What has become of our sinewy and athletic fellow-citizens? They are coursing through ravines and over mountain tops. Their tracks are visible in every direction. Occasionally a horseman will dash among us. His steed betrays hard usage. He alights before his adobe dwelling, hastily exchanges courtesies with his townsmen, hurries to an assay office and from thence to the District Recorder's. In the morning, having renewed his provisional supplies, he is off again on his wild and unbeaten route. Why, the fellow numbers already his feet by the thousands. He is the horse-leech. He has the craving stomach of the shark or anaconda. He would conquer metallic worlds.

This was enough. The instant we had finished reading the above article, four of us decided to go to Humboldt. We commenced getting ready at once. And we also commenced up-braiding ourselves for not deciding sooner—for we were in terror lest all the rich mines would be found and secured before we got there, and we might have to put up with ledges that would not yield more than two or three hundred dollars a ton, maybe. An hour before, I would have felt opulent if I had owned ten feet in a Gold Hill mine whose ore produced twenty-five dollars to the ton; now I was already annoyed at the prospect of having to put up with mines the poorest of which would be a marvel in Gold Hill.

CHAPTER XXVII

Hurry, was the word! We wasted no time. Our party consisted of four persons—a blacksmith sixty years of age, two young lawyers, and myself. We bought a wagon and two miserable old horses. We put eighteen hundred pounds of provisions and mining tools in the wagon and drove out of Carson on a chilly December afternoon. The horses were so weak and old that we soon found that it would be better if one or two of us got out and walked. It was an improvement. Next, we found that it would be better if a third man got out. That was an improvement also. It was at this time that I volunteered to drive, although I had never driven a harnessed horse before and many a man in such a position would have felt fairly excused from such a responsibility. But in a little while it was found that it would be a fine thing if the driver got out and walked also. It was at this time that I resigned the position of driver, and never resumed it again. Within the hour, we found that it would not only be better, but was absolutely necessary, that we four, taking turns, two at a time, should put our hands against the end of the wagon and push it through the sand, leaving the feeble horses little to do but keep out of the way and hold up the tongue. Perhaps it is well for one to know his fate at first, and get reconciled to it. We had learned ours in one afternoon. It was plain that we had to walk through the sand and shove that wagon and those horses two hundred miles. So we accepted the situation, and from that time forth we never rode. More than that, we stood regular and nearly constant watches pushing up behind.

We made seven miles, and camped in the desert. Young Clagett (now member of Congress from Montana) unharnessed and fed and watered the horses; Oliphant and I cut sage-brush, built the fire and brought water to cook with; and old Mr. Ballou the blacksmith did the cooking. This division of labor, and this appointment, was adhered to throughout the journey. We had no tent, and so we slept under our blankets in the open plain. We were so tired that we slept soundly.

We were fifteen days making the trip—two hundred miles; thirteen, rather, for we lay by a couple of days, in one place, to let the horses rest. We could really have accomplished the journey in ten days if we had towed the horses behind the wagon, but we did not think of that until it was too late, and so went on shoving the horses and the wagon too when we might have saved half the labor. Parties who met us, occasionally, advised us to put the horses *in* the wagon, but Mr. Ballou, through whose iron-clad earnestness no sarcasm could pierce, said that that would not do, because the provisions were exposed and would suffer, the horses being "bituminous from long deprivation." The reader will excuse me from translating. What Mr. Ballou customarily meant, when he used a long word, was a secret between himself and his Maker. He was one of the best and kindest hearted men that ever graced a humble sphere of life. He was gentleness and simplicity itself—and unselfishness, too. Although he was more than twice as old as the eldest of us, he never gave himself any airs, privileges, or exemptions on that account. He did a *young* man's share of the work; and did his share of conversing and entertaining from the general standpoint of *any* age—not from the arrogant, overawing summit-height of sixty years. His one striking peculiarity was his Partingtonian fashion of loving and using big words *for their own sakes*, and independent of any bearing they might have upon the thought he was purposing to convey. He always let his ponderous syllables fall with an easy unconsciousness that left them wholly without offensiveness. In truth his air was so natural and so simple that one was always catching himself accepting his stately sentences as meaning something, when they really meant nothing in the world. If a word was long and grand and resonant, that was sufficient to win the old man's love, and he would drop that word into the most out-of-the-way place in a sentence or a subject, and be as pleased with it as if it were perfectly luminous with meaning.

We four always spread our common stock of blankets together on the frozen ground, and slept side by side; and finding that our foolish, long-legged hound pup had a deal of animal heat in him, Oliphant got to admitting him to the bed, between himself and Mr. Ballou, hugging the dog's warm back to his breast and finding great comfort in it. But in the night the pup would get stretchy and brace his feet against the old man's back and shove, grunting complacently the while; and now and then, being warm and snug, grateful and happy, he would paw the old man's back simply in excess of comfort; and at yet other times he would dream of the chase and in his sleep tug at the old man's back hair and bark in his ear. The old gentleman complained mildly about these familiarities, at last, and when he got through with his statement he said that such a dog as that was not a proper animal to admit to bed with tired men, because he was "so meretricious in his movements and so organic in his emotions." We turned the dog out.

It was a hard, wearing, toilsome journey, but it had its bright side; for after each day was done and our wolfish hunger appeased with a hot supper of fried bacon, bread, molasses and black coffee, the pipe-smoking, song-singing and yarn-spinning around the evening camp-fire in the still solitudes of the desert was a happy, care-free sort of recreation that seemed the very summit and culmination of earthly luxury. It is a kind of life that has a potent charm for all men, whether city or country-bred. We are descended from desert-lounging Arabs, and countless ages of growth toward perfect civilization have failed to root out of us the nomadic instinct. We all confess to a gratified thrill at the thought of "camping out."

Once we made twenty-five miles in a day, and once we made forty miles (through the Great American Desert), and ten miles beyond—fifty in all—in twenty-three hours, without halting to eat, drink or rest. To stretch out and go to sleep, even on stony and frozen ground, after pushing a wagon and two horses fifty miles, is a delight so supreme that for the moment it almost seems cheap at the price.

We camped two days in the neighborhood of the "Sink of the Humboldt." We tried to use the strong alkaline water of the Sink, but it would not answer. It was like drinking lye, and not weak lye, either. It left a taste in the mouth, bitter and every way execrable, and a burning in the stomach that was very uncomfortable. We put molasses in it, but that helped it very little; we added a pickle, yet the alkali was the prominent taste, and so it was unfit for drinking. The coffee we made of this water was the meanest compound man has yet invented. It was really viler to the taste than the unameliorated water itself. Mr. Ballou, being the architect and builder of the beverage felt constrained to endorse and uphold it, and so drank half a cup, by little sips, making shift to praise it faintly the while, but finally threw out the remainder, and said frankly it was "too technical for *him*."

But presently we found a spring of fresh water, convenient, and then, with nothing to mar our enjoyment, and no stragglers to interrupt it, we entered into our rest.

CHAPTER XXVIII

After leaving the Sink, we traveled along the Humboldt river a little way. People accustomed to the monster mile-wide Mississippi, grow accustomed to associating the term "river" with a high degree of watery grandeur. Consequently, such people feel rather disappointed when they stand on the shores of the Humboldt or the Carson and find that a "river" in Nevada is a sickly rivulet which is just the counterpart of the Erie canal in all respects save that the canal is twice as long and four times as deep. One of the pleasantest and most invigorating exercises one can contrive is to run and jump across the Humboldt river till he is overheated, and then drink it dry.

On the fifteenth day we completed our march of two hundred miles and entered Unionville, Humboldt county, in the midst of a driving snow-storm. Unionville consisted of eleven cabins and a liberty-pole. Six of the cabins were strung along one side of a deep canyon, and the other five faced them. The rest of the landscape was made up of bleak mountain walls that rose so high into the sky from both sides of the canyon that the village was left, as it were, far down in the bottom of a crevice. It was always daylight on the mountain tops a long time before the darkness lifted and revealed Unionville.

We built a small, rude cabin in the side of the crevice and roofed it with canvas, leaving a corner open to serve as a chimney, through which the cattle used to tumble occasionally, at night, and mash our furniture and interrupt our sleep. It was very cold weather and fuel was scarce. Indians brought brush and bushes several miles on their backs; and when we could catch a laden Indian it was well—and when we could not (which was the rule, not the exception), we shivered and bore it.

I confess, without shame, that I expected to find masses of silver lying all about the ground. I expected to see it glittering in the sun on the mountain summits. I said nothing about this, for some instinct told me that I might possibly have an exaggerated idea about it, and so if I betrayed my thought I might bring derision upon myself. Yet I was as perfectly satisfied in my own mind as I could be of anything, that I was going to gather up, in a day or two, or at furthest a week or two, silver enough to make me satisfactorily wealthy—and so my fancy was already busy with plans for spending this money. The first opportunity that offered, I sauntered carelessly away from the cabin, keeping an eye on the other boys, and stopping and contemplating the sky when they seemed to be observing me; but as soon as the coast was manifestly clear, I fled away as guiltily as a thief might have done and never halted till I was far beyond sight and call. Then I began my search with a feverish excitement that was brimful of expectation—almost of certainty. I crawled about the ground, seizing and examining bits of stone, blowing the dust from them or rubbing them on my clothes, and then peering at them with anxious hope. Presently I found a bright fragment and my heart bounded! I hid behind a boulder and polished it and scrutinized it with a nervous eagerness and a delight that was more pronounced than absolute certainty itself could have afforded. The more I examined the fragment the more I was convinced that I had found the door to fortune. I marked the spot and carried away my specimen. Up and down the rugged mountain side I searched, with always increasing interest and always augmenting gratitude that I had come to Humboldt and come in time. Of all the experiences of my life, this secret search among the hidden treasures of silver-land was the nearest to unmarred ecstasy. It was a delirious revel. By and by, in the bed of a shallow rivulet, I found a deposit of shining yellow scales, and my breath almost forsook me! A gold mine, and in my simplicity I had been content with vulgar silver! I was so excited that I half believed my overwrought imagination was deceiving me. Then a fear came upon me that people might be observing me and would guess my secret. Moved by this thought, I made a circuit of the place, and ascended a knoll to reconnoiter. Solitude. No creature was near. Then I returned to my mine, fortifying myself against possible disappointment, but my fears were groundless—the shining scales were still there. I set about scooping them out, and for an hour I toiled down the windings of the stream and robbed its bed. But at last the descending sun warned me to give up the quest, and I turned homeward laden with wealth. As I walked along I could not help smiling at the thought of my being so excited over my fragment of silver when a nobler metal was almost under my nose. In this little time the former had so fallen in my estimation that once or twice I was on the point of throwing it away.

The boys were as hungry as usual, but I could eat nothing. Neither could I talk. I was full of dreams and far away. Their conversation interrupted the flow of my fancy somewhat, and annoyed me a little, too. I despised the sordid and commonplace things they talked about. But as they proceeded, it began to amuse me. It grew to be rare fun to hear them planning their poor little economies and sighing over possible privations and distresses when a gold mine, all our own, lay within sight of the cabin and I could point it out at any moment. Smothered hilarity began to oppress me, presently. It was hard to resist the impulse to burst out with exultation and reveal everything; but I did resist. I said within myself that I would filter the great news through my lips calmly and be serene as a summer morning while I watched its effect in their faces. I said:

"Where have you all been?"

"Prospecting."

"What did you find?"

"Nothing."

"Nothing? What do you think of the country?"

"Can't tell, yet," said Mr. Ballou, who was an old gold miner, and had likewise had considerable experience among the silver mines.

"Well, haven't you formed any sort of opinion?"

"Yes, a sort of a one. It's fair enough here, may be, but over-rated. Seven thousand dollar ledges are scarce, though. That Sheba may be rich enough, but we don't own it; and besides, the rock is so full of base metals that all the science in the world can't work it. We'll not starve, here, but we'll not get rich, I'm afraid."

"So you think the prospect is pretty poor?"

"No name for it!"

"Well, we'd better go back, hadn't we?"

"Oh, not yet—of course not. We'll try it a riffle, first."

"Suppose, now—this is merely a supposition, you know—suppose you could find a ledge that would yield, say, a hundred and fifty dollars a ton—would that satisfy you?"

"Try us once!" from the whole party.

"Or suppose—merely a supposition, of course—suppose you were to find a ledge that would yield two thousand dollars a ton—would *that* satisfy you?"

"Here—what do you mean? What are you coming at? Is there some mystery behind all this?"

"Never mind. I am not saying anything. You know perfectly well there are no rich mines here—of course you do. Because you have been around and examined for yourselves. Anybody would know that, that had been around. But just for the sake of argument, suppose—in a kind of general way—suppose some person were to tell you that two-thousand-dollar ledges were simply contemptible—contemptible, understand—and that right yonder in sight of this very cabin there were piles of pure gold and pure silver—oceans of it—enough to make you all rich in twenty-four hours! Come!"

"I should say he was as crazy as a loon!" said old Ballou, but wild with excitement, nevertheless.

"Gentlemen," said I, "I don't say anything—*I* haven't been around, you know, and of course don't know anything—but all I ask of you is to cast your eye on *that,* for instance, and tell me what you think of it!" and I tossed my treasure before them.

There was an eager scramble for it, and a closing of heads together over it under the candle-light. Then old Ballou said:

"Think of it? I think it is nothing but a lot of granite rubbish and nasty glittering mica that isn't worth ten cents an acre!"

So vanished my dream. So melted my wealth away. So toppled my airy castle to the earth and left me stricken and forlorn.

Moralizing, I observed, then, that "all that glitters is not gold."

Mr. Ballou said I could go further than that, and lay it up among my treasures of knowledge, that *nothing* that glitters is gold. So I learned then, once for all, that gold in its native state is but dull, unornamental stuff, and that only lowborn metals excite the admiration of the ignorant with an ostentatious glitter. However, like the rest of the world, I still go on underrating men of gold and glorifying men of mica. Commonplace human nature cannot rise above that.

CHAPTER XXIX

True knowledge of the nature of silver mining came fast enough. We went out "prospecting" with Mr. Ballou. We climbed the mountain sides, and clambered among sage-brush, rocks and snow till we were ready to drop with exhaustion, but found no silver—nor yet any gold. Day after day we did this. Now and then we came upon holes burrowed a few feet into the declivities and apparently abandoned; and now and then we found one or two listless men still burrowing. But there was no appearance of silver. These holes were the beginnings of tunnels, and the purpose was to drive them hundreds of feet into the mountain, and some day tap the hidden ledge where the silver was. Some day! It seemed far enough away, and very hopeless and dreary. Day after day we toiled, and climbed and searched, and we younger partners grew sicker and still sicker of the promiseless toil. At last we halted under a beetling rampart of rock which projected from the earth high upon the mountain. Mr. Ballou broke off some fragments with a hammer, and examined them long and attentively with a small eye-glass; threw them away and broke off more; said this rock was quartz, and quartz was the sort of rock that contained silver. *Contained* it! I had thought that at least it would be caked on the outside of it like a kind of veneering. He still broke off pieces and critically examined them, now and then wetting the piece with his tongue and applying the glass. At last he exclaimed:

"We've got it!"

We were full of anxiety in a moment. The rock was clean and white, where it was broken, and across it ran a ragged thread of blue. He said that that little thread had silver in it, mixed with base metals, such as lead and antimony, and other rubbish, and that there was a speck or two of gold visible. After a great deal of effort we managed to discern some little fine yellow specks, and judged that a couple of tons of them massed together might make a gold dollar, possibly. We were not jubilant, but Mr. Ballou said there were worse ledges in the world than that. He saved what he called the "richest" piece of the rock, in order to determine its value by the process called the "fire-assay." Then we named the mine "Monarch of the Mountains" (modesty of nomenclature is not a prominent feature in the mines), and Mr. Ballou wrote out and stuck up the following "notice," preserving a copy to be entered upon the books in the mining recorder's office in the town.

"NOTICE."

"We the undersigned claim three claims, of three hundred feet each (and one for discovery), on this silver-bearing quartz lead or lode, extending north and south from this notice, with all its dips, spurs, and angles, variations and sinuosities, together with fifty feet of ground on either side for working the same."

We put our names to it and tried to feel that our fortunes were made. But when we talked the matter all over with Mr. Ballou, we felt depressed and dubious. He said that this surface quartz was not all there was of our mine; but that the wall or ledge of rock called the "Monarch of the Mountains," extended down hundreds and hundreds of feet into the earth—he illustrated by saying it was like a curb-stone, and maintained a nearly uniform thickness—say twenty feet—away down into the bowels of the earth, and was perfectly distinct from the casing rock on each side of it; and that it kept to itself, and maintained its distinctive character always, no matter how deep it extended into the earth or how far it stretched itself through and across the hills and valleys. He said it might be a mile deep and ten miles long, for all we knew; and that wherever we bored into it above ground or below, we would find gold and silver in it, but no gold or silver in the meaner rock it was cased between. And he said that down in the great depths of the ledge was its richness, and the deeper it went the richer it grew. Therefore, instead of working here on the surface, we must either bore down into the rock with a shaft till we came to where it was rich—say a hundred feet or so—or else we must go down into the valley and bore a long tunnel into the mountain side and tap the ledge far under the earth. To do either was plainly the labor of months; for we could blast and bore only a few feet a day—some five or six. But this was not all. He said that after we got the ore out it must be hauled in wagons to a distant silver-mill, ground up, and the silver extracted by a tedious and costly process. Our fortune seemed a century away!

But we went to work. We decided to sink a shaft. So, for a week we climbed the mountain, laden with picks, drills, gads, crowbars, shovels, cans of blasting powder and coils of fuse and strove with might and main. At first the rock was broken and loose and we dug it up with picks and threw it out with shovels, and the hole progressed very well. But the rock became more compact, presently, and gads and crowbars came into play. But shortly nothing could make an impression but blasting powder. That was the weariest work! One of us held the iron drill in its place and another would strike with an eight-pound sledge—it was like driving nails on a large scale. In the course of an hour or two the drill would reach a depth of two or three feet, making a hole a couple of inches in diameter. We would put in a charge of powder, insert half a yard of fuse, pour in sand and gravel and ram it down, then light the fuse and run. When the explosion came and the rocks and smoke shot into the air, we would go back and find about a bushel of that hard, rebellious quartz jolted out. Nothing more. One week of this satisfied me. I resigned. Clagget and Oliphant followed. Our shaft was only twelve feet deep. We decided that a tunnel was the thing we wanted.

So we went down the mountain side and worked a week; at the end of which time we had blasted a tunnel about deep enough to hide a hogshead in, and judged that about nine hundred feet more of it would reach the ledge. I resigned again, and the other boys only held out one day longer. We decided that a tunnel was not what we wanted. We wanted a ledge that was already "developed." There were none in the camp.

We dropped the "Monarch" for the time being.

Meantime the camp was filling up with people, and there was a constantly growing excitement about our Humboldt mines. We fell victims to the epidemic and strained every nerve to acquire more "feet." We prospected and took up new claims, put "notices" on them and gave them grandiloquent names. We traded some of our "feet" for "feet" in other people's claims. In a little while we owned largely in the "Gray Eagle," the "Columbiana," the "Branch Mint," the "Maria Jane," the "Universe," the "Root-Hog-or-Die," the "Samson and Delilah," the "Treasure Trove," the "Golconda," the "Sultana," the "Boomerang," the "Great Republic," the "Grand Mogul," and fifty other "mines" that had never been molested by a shovel or scratched with a pick. We had not less than thirty thousand "feet" apiece in the "richest mines on earth" as the frenzied cant phrased it—and were in debt to the butcher. We were stark mad with excitement—drunk with happiness—smothered under mountains of prospective wealth—arrogantly compassionate toward the plodding millions who knew not our marvellous canyon—but our credit was not good at the grocer's.

It was the strangest phase of life one can imagine. It was a beggars' revel. There was nothing doing in the district—no mining—no milling—no productive effort—no income—and not enough money in the entire camp to buy a corner lot in an eastern village, hardly; and yet a stranger would have supposed he was walking among bloated millionaires. Prospecting parties swarmed out of town with the first flush of dawn, and swarmed in again at nightfall laden with spoil—rocks. Nothing but rocks. Every man's pockets were full of them; the floor of his cabin was littered with them; they were disposed in labeled rows on his shelves.

CHAPTER XXX

I met men at every turn who owned from one thousand to thirty thousand "feet" in undeveloped silver mines, every single foot of which they believed would shortly be worth from fifty to a thousand dollars—and as often as any other way they were men who had not twenty-five dollars in the world. Every man you met had his new mine to boast of, and his "specimens" ready; and if the opportunity offered, he would infallibly back you into a corner and offer as a favor to *you*, not to *him*, to part with just a few feet in the "Golden Age," or the "Sarah Jane," or some other unknown stack of croppings, for money enough to get a "square meal" with, as the phrase went. And you were never to reveal that he had made you the offer at such a ruinous price, for it was only out of friendship for you that he was willing to make the sacrifice. Then he would fish a piece of rock out of his pocket, and after looking mysteriously around as if he feared he might be waylaid and robbed if caught with such wealth in his possession, he would dab the rock against his tongue, clap an eyeglass to it, and exclaim:

"Look at that! Right there in that red dirt! See it? See the specks of gold? And the streak of silver? That's from the 'Uncle Abe.' There's a hundred thousand tons like that in sight! Right in sight, mind you! And when we get down on it and the ledge comes in solid, it will be the richest thing in the world! Look at the assay! I don't want you to believe *me*—look at the assay!"

Then he would get out a greasy sheet of paper which showed that the portion of rock assayed had given evidence of containing silver and gold in the proportion of so many hundreds or thousands of dollars to the ton. I little knew, then, that the custom was to hunt out the *richest* piece of rock and get it assayed! Very often, that piece, the size of a filbert, was the only fragment in a ton that had a particle of metal in it—and yet the assay made it pretend to represent the average value of the ton of rubbish it came from!

On such a system of assaying as that, the Humboldt world had gone crazy. On the authority of such assays its newspaper correspondents were frothing about rock worth four and seven thousand dollars a ton!

And does the reader remember, a few pages back, the calculations, of a quoted correspondent, whereby the ore is to be mined and shipped all the way to England, the metals extracted, and the gold and silver contents received back by the miners as clear profit, the copper, antimony and other things in the ore being sufficient to pay all the expenses incurred? Everybody's head was full of such "calculations" as those—such raving insanity, rather. Few people took *work* into their calculations—or outlay of money either; except the work and expeditures of other people.

We never touched our tunnel or our shaft again. Why? Because we judged that we had learned the *real* secret of success in silver mining—which was, *not* to mine the silver ourselves by the sweat of our brows and the labor of our hands, but to *sell* the ledges to the dull slaves of toil and let them do the mining!

Before leaving Carson, the Secretary and I had purchased "feet" from various Esmeralda stragglers. We had expected immediate returns of bullion, but were only afflicted with regular and constant "assessments" instead—demands for money wherewith to develop the said mines. These assessments had grown so oppressive that it seemed necessary to look into the matter personally. Therefore I projected a pilgrimage to Carson and thence to Esmeralda. I bought a horse and started, in company with Mr. Ballou and a gentleman named Ollendorff, a Prussian—not the party who has inflicted so much suffering on the world with his wretched foreign grammars, with their interminable repetitions of questions which never have occurred and are never likely to occur in any conversation among human beings. We rode through a snow-storm for two or three days, and arrived at "Honey Lake Smith's," a sort of isolated inn on the Carson river. It was a two-story log house situated in a small knoll in the midst of the vast basin or desert through which the sickly Carson winds its melancholy way. Close to the house were the Overland stage stables, built of sun-dried bricks. There was not another building within several leagues of the place. Towards sunset about twenty hay-wagons arrived and camped around the house and all the teamsters came in to supper—a very, very rough set. There were one or two Overland stage drivers there, also, and half a dozen vagabonds and stragglers; consequently the house was well crowded.

We walked out, after supper, and visited a small Indian camp in the vicinity. The Indian were in a great hurry about something, and were packing up and getting away as fast as they could. In their broken English they said, "By'm-by, heap water!" and by the help of signs made us understand that in their opinion a flood was coming. The weather was perfectly clear, and this was not the rainy season. There was about a foot of water in the insignificant river—or maybe two feet; the stream was not wider than a back alley in a village, and its banks were scarcely higher than a man's head. So, where was the flood to come from? We canvassed the subject awhile and then concluded it was a ruse, and that the Indians had some better reason for leaving in a hurry than fears of a flood in such an exceedingly dry time.

At seven in the evening we went to bed in the second story—with our clothes on, as usual, and all three in the same bed, for every available space on the floors, chairs, etc., was in request, and even then there was barely room for the housing of the inn's guests. An hour later we were awakened by a great turmoil, and springing out of bed we picked our way nimbly among the ranks of snoring teamsters on the floor and got to the front windows of the long room. A glance revealed a strange spectacle, under the moonlight. The crooked Carson was full to the brim, and its waters were raging and foaming in the wildest way—sweeping around the sharp bends at a furious speed, and bearing on their surface a chaos of logs, brush and all sorts of rubbish. A depression, where its bed had once been, in other times, was already filling, and in one or two places the water was beginning to wash over the main bank. Men were flying hither and thither, bringing cattle and wagons close up to the house, for the spot of high ground on which it stood extended only some thirty feet in front and about a hundred in the rear. Close to the old river bed just spoken of, stood a little log stable, and in this our horses were lodged. While we looked, the waters increased so fast in this place that in a few minutes a torrent was roaring by the little stable and its margin encroaching steadily on the logs. We suddenly realized that this flood was not a mere holiday spectacle, but meant damage—and not only to the small log stable but to the Overland buildings close to the main river, for the waves had now come ashore and were creeping about the foundations and invading the great hay-corral adjoining. We ran down and joined the crowd of excited men and frightened animals. We waded knee-deep into the log stable, unfastened the horses and waded out almost *waist*-deep, so fast the waters increased. Then the crowd rushed in a body to the hay-corral and began to tumble down the huge stacks of baled hay and roll the bales up on the high ground by the house. Meantime it was discovered that Owens, an overland driver, was missing, and a man ran to the large stable, and wading in, boot-top deep, discovered him asleep in his bed, awoke him, and waded out again. But Owens was drowsy and resumed his nap; but only for a minute or two, for presently he turned in his bed, his hand dropped over the side and came in contact with the cold water! It was up level with the mattrass! He waded out, breast-deep, almost, and the next moment the sun-burned bricks melted down like sugar and the big building crumbled to a ruin and was washed away in a twinkling.

At eleven o'clock only the roof of the little log stable was out of water, and our inn was on an island in mid-ocean. As far as the eye could reach, in the moonlight, there was no desert visible, but only a level waste of shining water. The Indians were true prophets, but how did they get their information? I am not able to answer the question.

We remained cooped up eight days and nights with that curious crew. Swearing, drinking and card playing were the order of the day, and occasionally a fight was thrown in for variety. Dirt and vermin—but let us forget those features; their profusion is simply inconceivable—it is better that they remain so.

There were two men—however, this chapter is long enough.

CHAPTER XXXI

There were two men in the company who caused me particular discomfort. One was a little Swede, about twenty-five years old, who knew only one song, and he was forever singing it. By day we were all crowded into one small, stifling bar-room, and so there was no escaping this person's music. Through all the profanity, whisky-guzzling, "old sledge" and quarreling, his monotonous song meandered with never a variation in its tiresome sameness, and it seemed to me, at last, that I would be content to die, in order to be rid of the torture. The other man was a stalwart ruffian called "Arkansas," who carried two revolvers in his belt and a bowie knife projecting from his boot, and who was always drunk and always suffering for a fight. But he was so feared, that nobody would accommodate him. He would try all manner of little wary ruses to entrap somebody into an offensive remark, and his face would light up now and then when he fancied he was fairly on the scent of a fight, but invariably his victim would elude his toils and then he would show a disappointment that was almost pathetic. The landlord, Johnson, was a meek, well-meaning fellow, and Arkansas fastened on him early, as a promising subject, and gave him no rest day or night, for awhile. On the fourth morning, Arkansas got drunk and sat himself down to wait for an opportunity. Presently Johnson came in, just comfortably sociable with whisky, and said:

"I reckon the Pennsylvania 'lection—"

Arkansas raised his finger impressively and Johnson stopped. Arkansas rose unsteadily and confronted him. Said he:

"Wha-what do you know a-about Pennsylvania? Answer me that. Wha-what do you know 'bout Pennsylvania?"

"I was only goin' to say—"

"You was only goin' to *say*. *You* was! You was only goin' to say—*what* was you goin' to say? That's it! That's what *I* want to know. *I* want to know wha-what you (*'ic*) what you know about Pennsylvania, since you're makin' yourself so d—d free. Answer me that!"

"Mr. Arkansas, if you'd only let me—"

"Who's a henderin' you? Don't you insinuate nothing agin me!—don't you do it. Don't you come in here bullyin' around, and cussin' and goin' on like a lunatic—don't you do it. 'Coz *I* won't *stand* it. If fight's what you want, out with it! I'm your man! Out with it!"

Said Johnson, backing into a corner, Arkansas following,

menacingly:

"Why, *I* never said nothing, Mr. Arkansas. You don't give a man no chance. I was only goin' to say that Pennsylvania was goin' to have an election next week—that was all—that was everything I was goin' to say—I wish I may never stir if it wasn't."

"Well then why d'n't you say it? What did you come swellin' around that way for, and tryin' to raise trouble?"

"Why *I* didn't come swelling' around, Mr. Arkansas—I just—"

"I'm a liar am I ! Ger-reat Caesar's ghost—"

"Oh, please, Mr. Arkansas, I never meant such a thing as that, I wish I may die if I did. All the boys will tell you that I've always spoke well of you, and respected you more'n any man in the house. Ask Smith. Ain't it so, Smith? Didn't I say, no longer ago than last night, that for a man that was a gentleman *all* the time and every way you took him, give me Arkansas? I'll leave it to any gentleman here if them warn't the very words I used. Come, now, Mr. Arkansas, le's take a drink—le's shake hands and take a drink. Come up—everybody! It's my treat. Come up, Bill, Tom, Bob, Scotty—come up. I want you all to take a drink with me and Arkansas—*old* Arkansas, I call him—bully old Arkansas. Gimme your hand agin. Look at him, boys—just take a *look* at him. Thar stands the whitest man in America!—and the man that denies it has got to fight *me*, that's all. Gimme that old flipper agin!"

They embraced, with drunken affection on the landlord's part and unresponsive toleration on the part of Arkansas, who, bribed by a drink, was disappointed of his prey once more. But the foolish landlord was so happy to have escaped butchery, that he went on talking when he ought to have marched himself out of danger. The consequence was that Arkansas shortly began to glower upon him dangerously, and presently said:

"Lan'lord, will you p-please make that remark over agin if you please?"

"I was a-sayin' to Scotty that my father was up'ards of eighty year old when he died."

"Was that *all* that you said?"

"Yes, that was all."

"Didn't say nothing but that?"

"No—nothing."

Then an uncomfortable silence.

Arkansas played with his glass a moment, lolling on his elbows on the counter. Then he meditatively scratched his left shin with his right boot, while the awkward silence continued. But presently he loafed away toward the stove, looking dissatisfied; roughly shouldered two or three men out of a comfortable position; occupied it himself, gave a sleeping dog a kick that sent him howling under a bench, then spread his long legs and his blanket-coat tails apart and proceeded to warm his back. In a little while he fell to grumbling to himself, and soon he slouched back to the bar and said:

"Lan'lord, what's your idea for rakin' up old personalities and blowin' about your father? Ain't this company agreeable to you? Ain't it? If this company ain't agreeable to you, p'r'aps we'd better leave. Is that your idea? Is that what you're coming at?"

"Why bless your soul, Arkansas, I warn't thinking of such a thing. My father and my mother—"

"Lan'lord, *don't* crowd a man! Don't do it. If nothing'll do you but a disturbance, out with it like a man ('*ic*)—but *don't* rake up old bygones and fling 'em in the teeth of a passel of people that wants to be peaceable if they could git a chance. What's the matter with you this mornin', anyway? I never see a man carry on so."

"Arkansas, I reely didn't mean no harm, and I won't go on with it if it's onpleasant to you. I reckon my licker's got into my head, and what with the flood, and havin' so many to feed and look out for—"

"So *that's* what's a-ranklin' in your heart, is it? You want us to leave do you? There's too many on us. You want us to pack up and swim. Is that it? Come!"

"Please be reasonable, Arkansas. Now *you* know that I ain't the man to—"

"Are you a threatenin' me? Are you? By George, the man don't live that can skeer me! Don't you try to come that game, my chicken—'cuz I can stand a good deal, but I won't stand that. Come out from behind that bar till I clean you! You want to drive us out, do you, you sneakin' underhanded hound! Come out from behind that bar! *I'll* learn you to bully and badger and browbeat a gentleman that's forever trying to befriend you and keep you out of trouble!"

"Please, Arkansas, please don't shoot! If there's got to be bloodshed—"

"Do you hear that, gentlemen? Do you hear him talk about bloodshed? So it's blood you want, is it, you ravin' desperado! You'd made up your mind to murder somebody this mornin'—I knowed it perfectly well. I'm the man, am I? It's me you're goin' to murder, is it? But you can't do it 'thout I get one chance first, you thievin' black-hearted, white-livered son of a nigger! Draw your weepon!"

With that, Arkansas began to shoot, and the landlord to

671

clamber over benches, men and every sort of obstacle in a frantic desire to escape. In the midst of the wild hubbub the landlord crashed through a glass door, and as Arkansas charged after him the landlord's wife suddenly appeared in the doorway and confronted the desperado with a pair of scissors! Her fury was magnificent. With head erect and flashing eye she stood a moment and then advanced, with her weapon raised. The astonished ruffian hesitated, and then fell back a step. She followed. She backed him step by step into the middle of the bar-room, and then, while the wondering crowd closed up and gazed, she gave him such another tongue-lashing as never a cowed and shamefaced braggart got before, perhaps! As she finished and retired victorious, a roar of applause shook the house, and every man ordered "drinks for the crowd" in one and the same breath.

The lesson was entirely sufficient. The reign of terror was over, and the Arkansas domination broken for good. During the rest of the season of island captivity, there was one man who sat apart in a state of permanent humiliation, never mixing in any quarrel or uttering a boast, and never resenting the insults the once cringing crew now constantly leveled at him, and that man was "Arkansas."

By the fifth or sixth morning the waters had subsided from the land, but the stream in the old river bed was still high and swift and there was no possibility of crossing it. On the eighth it was still too high for an entirely safe passage, but life in the inn had become next to insupportable by reason of the dirt, drunkenness, fighting, etc., and so we made an effort to get away. In the midst of a heavy snow-storm we embarked in a canoe, taking our saddles aboard and towing our horses after us by their halters. The Prussian, Ollendorff, was in the bow, with a paddle, Ballou paddled in the middle, and I sat in the stern holding the halters. When the horses lost their footing and began to swim, Ollendorff got frightened, for there was great danger that the horses would make our aim uncertain, and it was plain that if we failed to land at a certain spot the current would throw us off and almost surely cast us into the main Carson, which was a boiling torrent, now. Such a catastrophe would be death, in all probability, for we would be swept to sea in the "Sink" or overturned and drowned. We warned Ollendorff to keep his wits about him and handle himself carefully, but it was useless; the moment the bow touched the bank, he made a spring and the canoe whirled upside down in ten-foot water. Ollendorff seized some brush and dragged himself ashore, but Ballou and I had to swim for it, encumbered with our overcoats. But we held on to the canoe, and although we were washed down nearly to the Carson, we managed to push the boat ashore and make a safe landing. We were cold and water-soaked, but safe. The horses made a landing, too, but our saddles were gone, of course. We tied the animals in the sage-brush and there they had to stay for twenty-four hours. We baled out the canoe, and ferried over some food and blankets for them, but we slept one more night in the inn before making another venture on our journey.

The next morning it was still snowing furiously when we got away with our new stock of saddles and accoutrements. We mounted and started. The snow lay so deep on the ground that there was no sign of a road perceptible, and the snow-fall was so thick that we could not see more than a hundred yards ahead, else we could have guided our course by the mountain ranges. The case looked dubious, but Ollendorff said his instinct was as sensitive as any compass, and that he could "strike a bee-line" for Carson city and never diverge from it. He said that if he were to straggle a single point out of the true line his instinct would assail him like an outraged conscience. Consequently we dropped into his wake happy and content. For half an hour we poked along warily enough, but at the end of that time we came upon a fresh trail, and Ollendorff shouted proudly:

"I knew I was as dead certain as a compass, boys! Here we are, right in somebody's tracks that will hunt the way for us without any trouble. Let's hurry up and join company with the party."

So we put the horses into as much of a trot as the deep snow would allow, and before long it was evident that we were gaining on our predecessors, for the tracks grew more distinct. We hurried along, and at the end of an hour the tracks looked still newer and fresher—but what surprised us was, that the *number* of travelers in advance of us seemed to steadily increase. We wondered how so large a party came to be traveling at such a time and in such a solitude. Somebody suggested that it must be a company of soldiers from the fort, and so we accepted that solution and jogged along a little faster still, for they could not be far off now. But the tracks still multiplied, and we began to think the platoon of soldiers was miraculously expanding into a regiment—Ballou said they had already increased to five hundred! Presently he stopped his horse and said:

"Boys, these are our own tracks, and we've actually been circussing round and round in a circle for more than two hours, out here in this blind desert! By George this is perfectly hydraulic!"

Then the old man waxed wroth and abusive. He called Ollendorff all manner of hard names—said he never saw such a lurid fool as he was, and ended with the peculiarly venomous opinion that he "did not know as much as a logarythm!"

We certainly had been following our own tracks. Ollendorff and his "mental compass" were in disgrace from that moment. After all our hard travel, here we were on the bank of the stream again, with the inn beyond dimly outlined through the driving snow-fall. While we were considering what to do, the young Swede landed from the canoe and took his pedestrian way Carson-wards, singing his same tiresome song about his "sister and his brother" and "the child in the grave with its mother," and in a short minute faded and disappeared in the white oblivion. He was never heard of again. He no doubt got bewildered and lost, and Fatigue delivered him over to Sleep and Sleep betrayed him to Death. Possibly he followed our treacherous tracks till he became exhausted and dropped.

Presently the Overland stage forded the now fast receding stream and started toward Carson on its first trip since the flood came. We hesitated no longer, now, but took up our march in its wake, and trotted merrily along, for we had good confidence in the driver's bump of locality. But our horses were no match for the fresh stage team. We were soon left out of sight; but it was no matter, for we had the deep ruts the wheels made for a guide. By this time it was three in the afternoon, and consequently it was not very long before night came—and not with a lingering twilight, but with a sudden shutting down like a cellar door, as is its habit in that country. The snow-fall was still as thick as ever, and of course we could not see fifteen steps before us; but all about us the white glare of the snow-bed enabled us to discern the smooth sugar-loaf mounds made by the covered sage-bushes, and just in front of us the two faint grooves which we knew were the steadily filling and slowly disappearing wheel-tracks.

Now those sage-bushes were all about the same height—three or four feet; they stood just about seven feet apart, all over the vast desert; each of them was a mere snow-mound, now; in *any* direction that you proceeded (the same as in a well laid out orchard) you would find yourself moving down a distinctly defined avenue, with a row of these snow-mounds an either side of it—an avenue the customary width of a road, nice and level in its breadth, and rising at the sides in the most natural way, by reason of the mounds. But we had not thought of this. Then imagine the chilly thrill that shot through us when it finally occurred to us, far in the night, that since the last faint trace of the wheel-tracks had long ago been buried from sight, we might now be wandering down a mere sage-brush avenue, miles away from the road and diverging further and further away from it all the time. Having a cake of ice slipped down one's back is placid comfort compared to it. There was a sudden leap and stir of blood that had been asleep for an hour, and as sudden a rousing of all the drowsing activities in our minds and bodies. We were alive and awake at once—and shaking and quaking with consternation, too. There was an instant halting and dismounting, a bending low and an anxious scanning of the road-bed. Useless, of course; for if a faint depression could not be discerned from an altitude of four or five feet above it, it certainly could not with one's nose nearly against it.

CHAPTER XXXII

We seemed to be in a road, but that was no proof. We tested this by walking off in various directions—the regular snow-mounds and the regular avenues between them convinced each man that *he* had found the true road, and that the others had found only false ones. Plainly the situation was desperate. We were cold and stiff and the horses were tired. We decided to build a sage-brush fire and camp out till morning. This was wise, because if we were wandering from the right road and the snow-storm continued another day our case would be the next thing to hopeless if we kept on.

All agreed that a camp fire was what would come nearest to saving us, now, and so we set about building it. We could find no matches, and so we tried to make shift with the pistols. Not a man in the party had ever tried to do such a thing before, but not a man in the party doubted that it *could* be done, and without any trouble—because every man in the party had read about it in books many a time and had naturally come to believe it, with trusting simplicity, just as he had long ago accepted and believed *that other* common book-fraud about Indians and lost hunters making a fire by rubbing two dry sticks together.

We huddled together on our knees in the deep snow, and the horses put their noses together and bowed their patient heads over us; and while the feathery flakes eddied down and turned us into a group of white statuary, we proceeded with the momentous experiment. We broke twigs from a sage bush and piled them on a little cleared place in the shelter of our bodies. In the course of ten or fifteen minutes all was ready, and then, while conversation ceased and our pulses beat low with anxious suspense, Ollendorff applied his revolver, pulled the trigger and blew the pile clear out of the county! It was the flattest failure that ever was.

This was distressing, but it paled before a greater horror—the horses were gone! I had been appointed to hold the bridles, but in my absorbing anxiety over the pistol experiment I had unconsciously dropped them and the released animals had walked off in the storm. It was useless to try to follow them, for their footfalls could make no sound, and one could pass within two yards of the creatures and never see them. We gave them up without an effort at recovering them, and cursed the lying books that said horses would stay by their masters for protection and companionship in a distressful time like ours.

We were miserable enough, before; we felt still more forlorn, now. Patiently, but with blighted hope, we broke more sticks and piled them, and once more the Prussian shot them into annihilation. Plainly, to light a fire with a pistol was an art requiring practice and experience, and the middle of a desert at midnight in a snow-storm was not a good place or time for the acquiring of the accomplishment. We gave it up and tried the other. Each man took a couple of sticks and fell to chafing them together. At the end of half an hour we were thoroughly chilled, and so were the sticks. We bitterly execrated the Indians, the hunters and the books that had betrayed us with the silly device, and wondered dismally what was next to be done. At this critical moment Mr. Ballou fished out four matches from the rubbish of an overlooked pocket. To have found four gold bars would have seemed poor and cheap good luck compared to this. One cannot think how good a match looks under such circumstances—or how lovable and precious, and sacredly beautiful to the eye. This time we gathered sticks with high hopes; and when Mr. Ballou prepared to light the first match, there was an amount of interest centred upon him that pages of writing could not describe. The match burned hopefully a moment, and then went out. It could not have carried more regret with it if it had been a human life. The next match simply flashed and died. The wind puffed the third one out just as it was on the imminent verge of success. We gathered together closer than ever, and developed a solicitude that was rapt and painful, as Mr. Ballou scratched our last hope on his leg. It lit, burned blue and sickly, and then budded into a robust flame. Shading it with his hands, the old gentleman bent gradually down and every heart went with him—everybody, too, for that matter—and blood and breath stood still. The flame touched the sticks at last, took gradual hold upon them— hesitated—took a stronger hold—hesitated again—held its breath five heart-breaking seconds, then gave a sort of human gasp and went out.

Nobody said a word for several minutes. It was a solemn sort of silence; even the wind put on a stealthy, sinister quiet, and made no more noise than the falling flakes of snow. Finally a sad-voiced conversation began, and it was soon apparent that in each of our hearts lay the conviction that this was our last night with the living. I had so hoped that I was the only one who felt so. When the others calmly acknowledged their conviction, it sounded like the summons itself. Ollendorff said:

"Brothers, let us die together. And let us go without one hard feeling towards each other. Let us forget and forgive bygones. I know that you jave felt hard towards me for turning over the canoe, and for knowing too much and leading you round and round in the snow—but I meant well; forgive me. I acknowledge freely that I have had hard feelings against Mr. Ballou for abusing me and calling me a logarythm, which is a thing I do not know what, but no doubt a thing considered disgraceful and unbecoming in America, and it has scarcely been out of my mind and has hurt me a great deal—but let it go; I forgive Mr. Ballou with all my heart, and—"

Poor Ollendorff broke down and the tears came. He was not alone, for I was crying too, and so was Mr. Ballou. Ollendorff got his voice again and forgave me for things I had done and said. Then he got out his bottle of whisky and said that whether he lived or died he would never touch another drop. He said he had given up all hope of life, and although ill-prepared, was ready to submit humbly to his fate; that he wished he could be spared a little longer, not for any selfish reason, but to make a thorough reform in his character, and by devoting himself to helping the poor, nursing the sick, and pleading with the people to guard themselves against the evils of intemperance, make his life a beneficent example to the young, and lay it down at last with the precious reflection that it had not been lived in vain. He ended by saying that his reform should begin at this moment, even here in the presence of death, since no longer time was to be vouchsafed wherein to prosecute it to men's help and benefit— and with that he threw away the bottle of whisky.

Mr. Ballou made remarks of similar purport, and began the reform he could not live to continue, by throwing away the ancient pack of cards that had solaced our captivity during the flood and made it bearable. He said he never gambled, but still was satisfied that the meddling with cards in any way was immoral and injurious, and no man could be wholly pure and blemishless without eschewing them. "And therefore," continued he, "in doing this act I already feel more in sympathy with that spiritual saturnalia necessary to entire and obsolete reform." These rolling syllables touched him as no intelligible eloquence could have done, and the old man sobbed with a mournfulness not unmingled with satisfaction.

My own remarks were of the same tenor as those of my comrades, and I know that the feelings that prompted them were heartfelt and sincere. We were all sincere, and all deeply moved and earnest, for we were in the presence of death and without hope. I threw away my pipe, and in doing it felt that at last I was free of a hated vice and one that had ridden me like a tyrant all my days. While I yet talked, the thought of the good I might have done in the world and the still greater good I might *now* do, with these new incentives and higher and better aims to guide me if I could only be spared a few years longer, overcame me and the tears came again. We put our arms about each other's necks and awaited the warning drowsiness that precedes death by freezing.

It came stealing over us presently, and then we bade each other a last farewell. A delicious dreaminess wrought its web about my yielding senses, while the snow-flakes wove a winding sheet about my conquered body. Oblivion came. The battle of life was done.

CHAPTER XXXIII

I do not know how long I was in a state of forgetfulness, but it seemed an age. A vague consciousness grew upon me by degrees, and then came a gathering anguish of pain in my limbs and through all my body. I shuddered. The thought flitted through my brain, "this is death—this is the hereafter."

Then came a white upheaval at my side, and a voice said, with bitterness:

"Will some gentleman be so good as to kick me behind?"

It was Ballou—at least it was a towzled snow image in a sitting posture, with Ballou's voice.

I rose up, and there in the gray dawn, not fifteen steps from us, were the frame buildings of a stage station, and under a shed stood our still saddled and bridled horses!

An arched snow-drift broke up, now, and Ollendorff emerged from it, and the three of us sat and stared at the houses without speaking a word. We really had nothing to say. We were like the profane man who could not "do the subject justice," the whole situation was so painfully ridiculous and humiliating that words were tame and we did not know where to commence anyhow.

The joy in our hearts at our deliverance was poisoned; well-nigh dissipated, indeed. We presently began to grow pettish by degrees, and sullen; and then, angry at each other, angry at ourselves, angry at everything in general, we moodily dusted the snow from our clothing and in unsociable single file plowed our way to the horses, unsaddled them, and sought shelter in the station.

I have scarcely exaggerated a detail of this curious and absurd adventure. It occurred almost exactly as I have stated it. We actually went into camp in a snow-drift in a desert, at midnight in a storm, forlorn and hopeless, within fifteen steps of a comfortable inn.

For two hours we sat apart in the station and ruminated in disgust. The mystery was gone, now, and it was plain enough why the horses had deserted us. Without a doubt they were under that shed a quarter of a minute after they had left us, and they must have overheard and enjoyed all our confessions and lamentations.

After breakfast we felt better, and the zest of life soon came back. The world looked bright again, and existence was as dear to us as ever. Presently an uneasiness came over me—grew upon me—assailed me without ceasing. Alas, my regeneration was not complete—I wanted to smoke! I resisted with all my strength, but the flesh was weak. I wandered away alone and wrestled with myself an hour. I recalled my promises of reform and preached to myself persuasively, upbraidingly, exhaustively. But it was all vain, I shortly found myself sneaking among the snow-drifts hunting for my pipe. I discovered it after a considerable search, and crept away to hide myself and enjoy it. I remained behind the barn a good while, asking myself how I would feel if my braver, stronger, truer comrades should catch me in my degradation. At last I lit the pipe, and no human being can feel meaner and baser that I did then. I was ashamed of being in my own pitiful company. Still dreading discovery, I felt that perhaps the further side of the barn would be somewhat safer, and so I turned the corner. As I turned the one corner, smoking, Ollendorff turned the other with his bottle to his lips, and between us sat unconscious Ballou deep in a game of "solitaire" with the old greasy cards!

Absurdity could go no farther. We shook hands and agreed to say no more about "reform" and "examples to the rising generation."

The station we were at was at the verge of the Twenty-six-Mile Desert. If we had approached it half an hour earlier the night before, we must have heard men shouting there and firing pistols; for they were expecting some sheep drovers and their flocks and knew that they would infallibly get lost and wander out of reach of help unless guided by sounds. While we remained at the station, three of the drovers arrived, nearly exhausted with their wanderings, but two others of their party were never heard of afterward.

We reached Carson in due time, and took a rest. This rest, together with preparations for the journey to Esmeralda, kept us there a week, and the delay gave us the opportunity to be present at a trial of the great land-slide case of Hyde *vs.* Morgan—an episode which is famous in Nevada to this day. After a word or two of necessary explanation, I will set down the history of this singular affair just as it transpired.

CHAPTER XXXIV

The mountains are very high and steep about Carson, Eagle and Washoe Valleys—very high and very steep, and so when the snow gets to melting off fast in the Spring and the warm surface-earth begins to moisten and soften, the disastrous land-slides commence. The reader cannot know what a land-slide is, unless he has lived in that country and seen the whole side of a mountain taken off some fine morning and deposited down in the valley, leaving a vast, treeless, unsightly scar upon the mountain's front to keep the circumstance fresh in his memory all the years that he may go on living within seventy miles of that place.

General Buncombe was shipped out to Nevada in the invoice of Territorial officers, to be United States Attorney. He considered himself a lawyer of parts, and he very much wanted an opportunity to manifest it—partly for the pure gratification of it and partly because his salary was Territorially meagre (which is a strong expression). Now the older citizens of a new territory look down upon the rest of the world with a calm, benevolent compassion, as long as it keeps out of the way—when it gets in the way they snub it. Sometimes this latter takes the shape of a practical joke.

One morning Dick Hyde rode furiously up to General Buncombe's door in Carson city and rushed into his presence without stopping to tie his horse. He seemed much excited. He told the General that he wanted him to conduct a suit for him and would pay him five hundred dollars if he achieved a victory. And then, with violent gestures and a world of profanity, he poured out his griefs. He said it was pretty well known that for some years he had been farming (or ranching as the more customary term is) in Washoe District, and making a successful thing of it, and furthermore it was known that his ranch was situated just in the edge of the valley, and that Tom Morgan owned a ranch immediately above it on the mountain side. And now the trouble was, that one of those hated and dreaded land-slides had come and slid Morgan's ranch, fences, cabins, cattle, barns and everything down on top of *his* ranch and exactly covered up every single vestige of his property, to a depth of about thirty-eight feet. Morgan was in possession and refused to vacate the premises—said he was occupying his own cabin and not interfering with anybody else's—and said the cabin was standing on the same dirt and same ranch it had always stood on, and he would like to see anybody make him vacate.

"And when I reminded him," said Hyde, weeping, "that it was on top of my ranch and that he was trespassing, he had the infernal meanness to ask me why didn't I *stay* on my ranch and hold possession when I see him a-coming! Why didn't I *stay* on it, the blathering lunatic—by George, when I heard that racket and looked up that hill it was just like the whole world was a-ripping and a-tearing down that mountain side—splinters, and cord-wood, thunder and lightning, hail and snow, odds and ends of hay stacks, and awful clouds of dust!—trees going end over end in the air, rocks as big as a house jumping 'bout a thousand feet high and busting into ten million pieces, cattle turned inside out and a-coming head on with their tails hanging out between their teeth!—and in the midst of all that wrack and destruction sot that cussed Morgan on his gate-post, a-wondering why I didn't *stay and hold possession!* Laws bless me, I just took one glimpse, General, and lit out'n the county in three jumps exactly.

"But what grinds me is that that Morgan hangs on there and won't move off'n that ranch—says it's his'n and he's going to keep it—likes it better'n he did when it was higher up the hill. Mad! Well, I've been so mad for two days I couldn't find my way to town—been wandering around in the brush in a starving condition—got anything here to drink, General? But I'm here *now,* and I'm a-going to law. You hear *me!*"

Never in all the world, perhaps, were a man's feelings so out-raged as were the General's. He said he had never heard of such high-handed conduct in all his life as this Morgan's. And he said there was no use in going to law—Morgan had no shadow of right to remain where he was—nobody in the wide world would uphold him in it, and no lawyer would take his case and no judge listen to it. Hyde said that right there was where he was mistaken—everybody in town sustained Morgan; Hal Brayton, a very smart lawyer, had taken his case; the courts being in vacation, it was to be tried before a referee, and ex-Governor Roop had already been appointed to that office and would open his court in a large public hall near the hotel at two that afternoon.

The General was amazed. He said he had suspected before that the people of that Territory were fools, and now he knew it. But he said rest easy, rest easy and collect the witnesses, for the victory was just as certain as if the conflict were already over. Hyde wiped away his tears and left.

At two in the afternoon referee Roop's Court opened, and Roop appeared throned among his sheriffs, the witnesses, and spectators, and wearing upon his face a solemnity so awe- inspiring that some of his fellow-conspirators had misgivings that maybe he had not comprehended, after all, that this was merely a joke. An unearthly stillness prevailed, for at the slightest noise the judge uttered sternly the command:

"Order in the Court!"

And the sheriffs promptly echoed it. Presently the General elbowed his way through the crowd of spectators, with his arms full of law-books, and on his ears fell an order from the judge which was the first respectful recognition of his high official dignity that had ever saluted them, and it trickled pleasantly through his whole system:

"Way for the United States Attorney!"

The witnesses were called—legislators, high government officers, ranchmen, miners, Indians, Chinamen, negroes. Three fourths of them were called by the defendant Morgan, but no matter, their testimony invariably went in favor of the plaintiff Hyde. Each new witness only added new testimony to the absurdity of a man's claiming to own another man's property because his farm had slid down on top of it. Then the Morgan lawyers made their speeches, and seemed to make singularly weak ones—they did really nothing to help the Morgan cause. And now the General, with exultation in his face, got up and made an impassioned effort; he pounded the table, he banged the law-books, he shouted, and roared, and howled, he quoted from everything and everybody, poetry, sarcasm, statistics, history, pathos, bathos, blasphemy, and wound up with a grand war-whoop for free speech, freedom of the press, free schools, the Glorious Bird of America and the principles of eternal justice! [Applause.]

When the General sat down, he did it with the conviction that if there was anything in good strong testimony, a great speech and believing and admiring countenances all around, Mr.

Morgan's case was killed. Ex-Governor Roop leant his head upon his hand for some minutes, thinking, and the still audience waited for his decision. Then he got up and stood erect, with bended head, and thought again. Then he walked the floor with long, deliberate strides, his chin in his hand, and still the audience waited. At last he returned to his throne, seated himself, and began, impressively:

"Gentlemen, I feel the great responsibility that rests upon me this day. This is no ordinary case. On the contrary it is plain that it is the most solemn and awful that ever man was called upon to decide. Gentlemen, I have listened attentively to the evidence, and have perceived that the weight of it, the overwhelming weight of it, is in favor of the plaintiff Hyde. I have listened also to the remarks of counsel, with high interest—and especially will I commend the masterly and irrefutable logic of the distinguished gentleman who represents the plaintiff. But gentlemen, let us beware how we allow mere human testimony, human ingenuity in argument and human ideas of equity, to influence us at a moment so solemn as this. Gentlemen, it ill becomes us, worms as we are, to meddle with the decrees of Heaven. It is plain to me that Heaven, in its inscrutable wisdom, has seen fit to move this defendant's ranch for a purpose. We are but creatures, and we must submit. If Heaven has chosen to favor the defendant Morgan in this marked and wonderful manner; and if Heaven, dissatisfied with the position of the Morgan ranch upon the mountain side, has chosen to remove it to a position more eligible and more advantageous for its owner, it ill becomes us, insects as we are, to question the legality of the act or inquire into the reasons that prompted it. No—Heaven created the ranches and it is Heaven's prerogative to rearrange them, to experiment with them, to shift them around at its pleasure. It is for us to submit, without repining. I warn you that this thing which has happened is a thing with which the sacrilegious hands and brains and tongues of men must not meddle. Gentlemen, it is the verdict of this court that the plaintiff, Richard Hyde, has been deprived of his ranch by the visitation of God! And from this decision there is no appeal."

Buncombe seized his cargo of law-books and plunged out of the court-room frantic with indignation. He pronounced Roop to be a miraculous fool, an inspired idiot. In all good faith he returned at night and remonstrated with Roop upon his extravagant decision, and implored him to walk the floor and think for half an hour, and see if he could not figure out some sort of modification of the verdict. Roop yielded at last and got up to walk. He walked two hours and a half, and at last his face lit up happily and he told Buncombe it had occurred to him that the ranch underneath the new Morgan ranch still belonged to Hyde, that his title to the ground was just as good as it had ever been, and therefore he was of opinion that Hyde had a right to dig it out from under there and—

The General never waited to hear the end of it. He was always an impatient and irascible man, that way. At the end of two months the fact that he had been played upon with a joke had managed to bore itself, like another Hoosac Tunnel, through the solid adamant of his understanding.

CHAPTER XXXV

When we finally left for Esmeralda, horseback, we had an addition to the company in the person of Capt. John Nye, the Governor's brother. He had a good memory, and a tongue hung in the middle. This is a combination which gives immortality to conversation. Capt. John never suffered the talk to flag or falter once during the hundred and twenty miles of the journey. In addition to his conversational powers, he had one or two other endowments of a marked character. One was a singular "handiness" about doing anything and everything, from laying out a railroad or organizing a political party, down to sewing on buttons, shoeing a horse, or setting a broken leg, or a hen. Another was a spirit of accommodation that prompted him to take the needs, difficulties and perplexities of anybody and everybody upon his own shoulders at any and all times, and dispose of them with admirable facility and alacrity—hence he always managed to find vacant beds in crowded inns, and plenty to eat in the emptiest larders. And finally, wherever he met a man, woman or child, in camp, inn or desert, he either knew such parties personally or had been acquainted with a relative of the same. Such another traveling comrade was never seen before. I cannot forbear giving a specimen of the way in which he overcame difficulties. On the second day out, we arrived, very tired and hungry, at a poor little inn in the desert, and were told that the house was full, no provisions on hand, and neither hay nor barley to spare for the horses—we must move on. The rest of us wanted to hurry on while it was yet light, but Capt. John insisted on stopping awhile. We dismounted and entered. There was no welcome for us on any face. Capt. John began his blandishments, and within twenty minutes he had accomplished the following things, viz.: found old acquaintances in three teamsters; discovered that he used to go to school with the landlord's mother; recognized his wife as a lady whose life he had saved once in California, by stopping her runaway horse; mended a child's broken toy and won the favor of its mother, a guest of the inn; helped the hostler bleed a horse, and prescribed for another horse that had the "heaves"; treated the entire party three times at the landlord's bar; produced a later paper than anybody had seen for a week and sat himself down to read the news to a deeply interested audience. The result, summed up, was as follows: The hostler found plenty of feed for our horses; we had a trout supper, an exceedingly sociable time after it, good beds to sleep in, and a surprising breakfast in the morning—and when we left, we left lamented by all! Capt. John had some bad traits, but he had some uncommonly valuable ones to offset them with.

Esmeralda was in many respects another Humboldt, but in a little more forward state. The claims we had been paying assessments on were entirely worthless, and we threw them away. The principal one cropped out of the top of a knoll that was fourteen feet high, and the inspired Board of Directors were running a tunnel under that knoll to strike the ledge. The tunnel would have to be seventy feet long, and would then strike the ledge at the same depth that a *shaft* twelve feet deep would have reached! The Board were living on the "assessments." [N.B.—This hint comes too late for the enlightenment of New York silver miners; they have already learned all about this neat trick by experience.] The Board had no desire to strike the ledge, knowing that it was as barren of silver as a curbstone. This reminiscence calls to mind Jim Townsend's tunnel. He had paid assessments on a mine called the "Daley" till he was well-nigh penniless. Finally an assessment was levied to run a tunnel two hundred and fifty feet on the Daley, and Townsend went up on the hill to look into matters. He found the Daley cropping out of the apex of an exceedingly sharp-pointed peak, and a couple of men up there "facing" the proposed tunnel. Townsend made a calculation. Then he said to the men:

"So you have taken a contract to run a tunnel into this hill two hundred and fifty feet to strike this ledge?"

"Yes, sir."

"Well, do you know that you have got one of the most expensive and arduous undertakings before you that was ever conceived by man?"

"Why no—how is that?"

"Because this hill is only twenty-five feet through from side to side; and so you have got to build two hundred and twenty-five feet of your tunnel on trestle-work!"

The ways of silver mining Boards are exceedingly dark and sinuous.

We took up various claims, and *commenced* shafts and tunnels on them, but never finished any of them. We had to do a certain amount of work on each to "hold" it, else other parties could seize our property after the expiration of ten days. We were always hunting up new claims and doing a little work on them and then waiting for a buyer— who never came. We never found any ore that would yield more than fifty dollars a ton; and as the mills charged fifty dollars a ton for *working* ore and extracting the silver, our pocket-money melted steadily away and none returned to take its place. We lived in a little cabin and cooked for ourselves; and altogether it was a hard life, though a hopeful one—for we never ceased to expect fortune and a customer to burst upon us some day.

At last, when flour reached a dollar a pound, and money could not be borrowed on the best security at less than *eight per cent a month* (I being without the security, too), I abandoned mining and went to milling. That is to say, I went to work as a common laborer in a quartz mill, at ten dollars a week and board.

CHAPTER XXXVI

I had already learned how hard and long and dismal a task it is to burrow down into the bowels of the earth and get out the coveted ore; and now I learned that the burrowing was only half the work; and that to get the silver out of the ore was the dreary and laborious other half of it. We had to turn out at six in the morning and keep at it till dark. This mill was a six-stamp affair, driven by steam. Six tall, upright rods of iron, as large as a man's ankle, and heavily shod with a mass of iron and steel at their lower ends, were framed together like a gate, and these rose and fell, one after the other, in a ponderous dance, in an iron box called a "battery." Each of these rods or stamps weighed six hundred pounds. One of us stood by the battery all day long, breaking up masses of silver-bearing rock with a sledge and shoveling it into the battery. The ceaseless dance of the stamps pulverized the rock to powder, and a stream of water that trickled into the battery turned it to a creamy paste. The minutest particles were driven through a fine wire screen which fitted close around the battery, and were washed into great tubs warmed by super-heated steam—amalgamating pans, they are called. The mass of pulp in the pans was kept constantly stirred up by revolving "mullers." A quantity of quicksilver was kept always in the battery, and this seized some of the liberated gold and silver particles and held on to them; quicksilver was shaken in a fine shower into the pans, also, about every half hour, through a buckskin sack. Quantities of coarse salt and sulphate of copper were added, from time to time to assist the amalgamation by destroying base metals which coated the gold and silver and would not let it unite with the quicksilver. All these tiresome things we had to attend to constantly. Streams of dirty water flowed always from the pans and were carried off in broad wooden troughs to the ravine. One would not suppose that atoms of gold and silver would float on top of six inches of water, but they did; and in order to catch them, coarse blankets were laid in the troughs, and little obstructing "riffles" charged with quicksilver were placed here and there across the troughs also. These riffles had to be cleaned and the blankets washed out every evening, to get their precious accumulations—and after all this eternity of trouble one third of the silver and gold in a ton of rock would find its way to the end of the troughs in the ravine at last and have to be worked over again some day. There is nothing so aggravating as silver milling. There never was any idle time in that mill. There was always something to do. It is a pity that Adam could not have gone straight out of Eden into a quartz mill, in order to understand the full force of his doom to "earn his bread by the sweat of his brow." Every now and then, during the day, we had to scoop some pulp out of the pans, and tediously "wash" it in a horn spoon—wash it little by little over the edge till at last nothing was left but some little dull globules of quicksilver in the bottom. If they were soft and yielding, the pan needed some salt or some sulphate of copper or some other chemical rubbish to assist digestion; if they were crisp to the touch and would retain a dint, they were freighted with all the silver and gold they could seize and hold, and consequently the pans needed a fresh charge of quicksilver. When there was nothing else to do, one could always "screen tailings." That is to say, he could shovel up the dried sand that had washed down to the ravine through the troughs and dash it against an upright wire screen to free it from pebbles and prepare it for working over. The process of amalgamation differed in the various mills, and this included changes in style of pans and other machinery, and a great diversity of opinion existed as to the best in use, but none of the methods employed, involved the principle of milling ore without "screening the tailings." Of all recreations in the world, screening tailings on a hot day, with a long-handled shovel, is the most undesirable.

At the end of the week the machinery was stopped and we "cleaned up." That is to say, we got the pulp out of the pans and batteries, and washed the mud patiently away till nothing was left but the long accumulating mass of quicksilver, with its imprisoned treasures. This we made into heavy, compact snowballs, and piled them up in a bright, luxurious heap for inspection. Making these snow-balls cost me a fine gold ring—that and ignorance together; for the quicksilver invaded the ring with the same facility with which water saturates a sponge—separated its particles and the ring crumbled to pieces.

We put our pile of quicksilver into an iron retort that had a pipe leading from it to a pail of water, and then applied a roasting heat. The quicksilver turned to vapor, escaped through the pipe into the pail, and the water turned it into good wholesome quicksilver again. Quicksilver is very costly, and they never waste it. On opening the retort, there was our week's work—a lump of pure white, frosty looking silver, twice as large as a man's head. Perhaps a fifth of the mass was gold, but the color of it did not show—would not have shown if two thirds of it had been gold. We melted it up and made a solid brick of it by pouring it into an iron brick-mould.

By such a tedious and laborious process were silver bricks obtained. This mill was but one of many others in operation at the time. The first one in Nevada was built at Egan Canyon and was a small insignificant affair and compared most unfavorably with some of the immense establishments afterwards located at Virginia City and elsewhere.

From our bricks a little corner was chipped off for the "fire-assay"—a method used to determine the proportions of gold, silver and base metals in the mass. This is an interesting process. The chip is hammered out as thin as paper and weighed on scales so fine and sensitive that if you weigh a two-inch scrap of paper on them and then write your name on the paper with a coarse, soft pencil and weigh it again, the scales will take marked notice of the addition. Then a little lead (also weighed) is rolled up with the flake of silver and the two are melted at a great heat in a small vessel called a cupel, made by compressing bone ashes into a cup-shape in a steel mold. The base metals oxidize and are absorbed with the lead into the pores of the cupel. A button or globule of perfectly pure gold and silver is left behind, and by weighing it and noting the loss, the assayer knows the proportion of base metal the brick contains. He has to separate the gold from the silver now. The button is hammered out flat and thin, put in the furnace and kept some time at a red heat; after cooling it off it is rolled up like a quill and heated in a glass vessel containing nitric acid; the acid dissolves the silver and leaves the gold pure and ready to be weighed on its own merits. Then salt water is poured into the vessel containing the dissolved silver and the silver returns to palpable form again and sinks to the bottom. Nothing now remains but to weigh it; then the proportions of the several metals contained in the brick are known, and the assayer stamps the value of the brick upon its surface.

The sagacious reader will know now, without being told, that the speculative miner, in getting a "fire-assay" made of a piece of rock from his mine (to help him sell the same), was not in the habit of picking out the least valuable fragment of rock on his dump-pile, but quite the contrary. I have seen men hunt over a pile of nearly worthless quartz for an hour, and at last find a little piece as large as a filbert, which was rich in gold and silver—and this was reserved for a fire-assay! Of course the fire- assay would demonstrate that a ton of such rock would yield hundreds of dollars—and on such assays many an utterly worthless mine was sold.

Assaying was a good business, and so some men engaged in it, occasionally, who were not strictly scientific and capable. One assayer got such rich results out of all specimens brought to him that in time he acquired almost a monopoly of the business. But like all men who achieve success, he became an object of envy and suspicion. The other assayers entered into a conspiracy against him, and let some prominent citizens into the secret in order to show that they meant fairly. Then they broke a little fragment off a carpenter's grindstone and got a stranger to take it to the popular scientist and get it assayed. In the course of an hour the result came—whereby it appeared that a ton of that rock would yield $1,284.40 in silver and $366.36 in gold!

Due publication of the whole matter was made in the paper, and the popular assayer left town "between two days."

I will remark, in passing, that I only remained in the milling business one week. I told my employer I could not stay longer without an advance in my wages; that I liked quartz milling, indeed was infatuated with it; that I had never before grown so tenderly attached to an occupation in so short a time; that nothing, it seemed to me, gave such scope to intellectual activity as feeding a battery and screening tailings, and nothing so stimulated the moral attributes as retorting bullion and washing blankets—still, I felt constrained to ask an increase of salary.

He said he was paying me ten dollars a week, and thought it a good round sum. How much did I want?

I said about four hundred thousand dollars a month, and board, was about all I could reasonably ask, considering the hard times.

I was ordered off the premises! And yet, when I look back to those days and call to mind the exceeding hardness of the labor I performed in that mill, I only regret that I did not ask him seven hundred thousand.

Shortly after this I began to grow crazy, along with the rest of the population, about the mysterious and wonderful "cement mine," and to make preparations to take advantage of any opportunity that might offer to go and help hunt for it.

CHAPTER XXXVII

It was somewhere in the neighborhood of Mono Lake that the marvellous Whiteman cement mine was supposed to lie. Every now and then it would be reported that Mr. W. had passed stealthily through Esmeralda at dead of night, in disguise, and then we would have a wild excitement—because he must be steering for his secret mine, and now was the time to follow him. In less than three hours after daylight all the horses and mules and donkeys in the vicinity would be bought, hired or stolen, and half the community would be off for the mountains, following in the wake of Whiteman. But W. would drift about through the mountain gorges for days together, in a purposeless sort of way, until the provisions of the miners ran out, and they would have to go back home. I have known it reported at eleven at night, in a large mining camp, that Whiteman had just passed through, and in two hours the streets, so quiet before, would be swarming with men and animals. Every individual would be trying to be very secret, but yet venturing to whisper to just one neighbor that W. had passed through. And long before daylight—this in the dead of Winter—the stampede would be complete, the camp deserted, and the whole population gone chasing after W.

The tradition was that in the early immigration, more than twenty years ago, three young Germans, brothers, who had survived an Indian massacre on the Plains, wandered on foot through the deserts, avoiding all trails and roads, and simply holding a westerly direction and hoping to find California before they starved, or died of fatigue. And in a gorge in the mountains they sat down to rest one day, when one of them noticed a curious vein of cement running along the ground, shot full of lumps of dull yellow metal. They saw that it was gold, and that here was a fortune to be acquired in a single day. The vein was about as wide as a curbstone, and fully two thirds of it was pure gold. Every pound of the wonderful cement was worth well-nigh $200. Each of the brothers loaded himself with about twenty-five pounds of it, and then they covered up all traces of the vein, made a rude drawing of the locality and the principal landmarks in the vicinity, and started westward again. But troubles thickened about them. In their wanderings one brother fell and broke his leg, and the others were obliged to go on and leave him to die in the wilderness. Another, worn out and starving, gave up by and by, and laid down to die, but after two or three weeks of incredible hardships, the third reached the settlements of California exhausted, sick, and his mind deranged by his sufferings. He had thrown away all his cement but a few fragments, but these were sufficient to set everybody wild with excitement. However, he had had enough of the cement country, and nothing could induce him to lead a party thither. He was entirely content to work on a farm for wages. But he gave Whiteman his map, and described the cement region as well as he could, and thus transferred the curse to that gentleman—for when I had my one accidental glimpse of Mr. W. in Esmeralda he had been hunting for the lost mine, in hunger and thirst, poverty and sickness, for twelve or thirteen years. Some people believed he had found it, but most people believed he had not. I saw a piece of cement as large as my fist which was said to have been given to Whiteman by the young German, and it was of a seductive nature. Lumps of virgin gold were as thick in it as raisins in a slice of fruit cake. The privilege of working such a mine one week would be sufficient for a man of reasonable desires.

A new partner of ours, a Mr. Higbie, knew Whiteman well by sight, and a friend of ours, a Mr. Van Dorn, was well acquainted with him, and not only that, but had Whiteman's promise that he should have a private hint in time to enable him to join the next cement expedition. Van Dorn had promised to extend the hint to us. One evening Higbie came in greatly excited, and said he felt certain he had recognized Whiteman, up town, disguised and in a pretended state of intoxication. In a little while Van Dorn arrived and confirmed the news; and so we gathered in our cabin and with heads close together arranged our plans in impressive whispers.

We were to leave town quietly, after midnight, in two or three small parties, so as not to attract attention, and meet at dawn on the "divide" overlooking Mono Lake, eight or nine miles distant. We were to make no noise after starting, and not speak

above a whisper under any circumstances. It was believed that for once Whiteman's presence was unknown in the town and his expedition unsuspected. Our conclave broke up at nine o'clock, and we set about our preparations diligently and with profound secrecy. At eleven o'clock we saddled our horses, hitched them with their long *riatas* (or lassos), and then brought out a side of bacon, a sack of beans, a small sack of coffee, some sugar, a hundred pounds of flour in sacks, some tin cups and a coffee pot, frying pan and some few other necessary articles. All these things were "packed" on the back of a led horse—and whoever has not been taught, by a Spanish adept, to pack an animal, let him never hope to do the thing by natural smartness. That is impossible. Higbie had had some experience, but was not perfect. He put on the pack saddle (a thing like a saw-buck), piled the property on it and then wound a rope all over and about it and under it, "every which way," taking a hitch in it every now and then, and occasionally surging back on it till the horse's sides sunk in and he gasped for breath—but every time the lashings grew tight in one place they loosened in another. We never did get the load tight all over, but we got it so that it would do, after a fashion, and then we started, in single file, close order, and without a word. It was a dark night. We kept the middle of the road, and proceeded in a slow walk past the rows of cabins, and whenever a miner came to his door I trembled for fear the light would shine on us and excite curiosity. But nothing happened. We began the long winding ascent of the canyon, toward the "divide," and presently the cabins began to grow infrequent, and the intervals between them wider and wider, and then I began to breathe tolerably freely and feel less like a thief and a murderer. I was in the rear, leading the pack horse. As the ascent grew steeper he grew proportionately less satisfied with his cargo, and began to pull back on his *riata* occasionally and delay progress. My comrades were passing out of sight in the gloom. I was getting anxious. I coaxed and bullied the pack horse till I presently got him into a trot, and then the tin cups and pans strung about his person frightened him and he ran. His *riata* was wound around the pummel of my saddle, and so, as he went by he dragged me from my horse and the two animals traveled briskly on without me. But I was not alone—the loosened cargo tumbled overboard from the pack horse and fell close to me. It was abreast of almost the last cabin. A miner came out and said:
"Hello!"
I was thirty steps from him, and knew he could not see me, it was so very dark in the shadow of the mountain. So I lay still. Another head appeared in the light of the cabin door, and pres-

ently the two men walked toward me. They stopped within ten steps of me, and one said:

" 'St! Listen."

I could not have been in a more distressed state if I had been escaping justice with a price on my head. Then the miners appeared to sit down on a boulder, though I could not see them distinctly enough to be very sure what they did. One said:

"I heard a noise, as plain as I ever heard anything. It seemed to be about there—"

A stone whizzed by my head. I flattened myself out in the dust like a postage stamp, and thought to myself if he mended his aim ever so little he would probably hear another noise. In my heart, now, I execrated secret expeditions. I promised myself that this should be my last, though the Sierras were ribbed with cement veins. Then one of the men said:

"I'll tell you what! Welch knew what he was talking about when he said he saw Whiteman to-day. I heard horses—that was the noise. I am going down to Welch's, right away."

They left and I was glad. I did not care whither they went, so they went. I was willing they should visit Welch, and the sooner the better.

As soon as they closed their cabin door my comrades emerged from the gloom; they had caught the horses and were waiting for a clear coast again. We remounted the cargo on the pack horse and got under way, and as day broke we reached the "divide" and joined Van Dorn. Then we journeyed down into the valley of the Lake, and feeling secure, we halted to cook breakfast, for we were tired and sleepy and hungry. Three hours later the rest of the population filed over the "divide" in a long procession, and drifted off out of sight around the borders of the Lake!

Whether or not my accident had produced this result we never knew, but at least one thing was certain—the secret was out and Whiteman would not enter upon a search for the cement mine this time. We were filled with chagrin.

We held a council and decided to make the best of our misfortune and enjoy a week's holiday on the borders of the curious Lake. Mono, it is sometimes called, and sometimes the "Dead Sea of California." It is one of the strangest freaks of Nature to be found in any land, but it is hardly ever mentioned in print and very seldom visited, because it lies away off the usual routes of travel and besides is so difficult to get at that only men content to endure the roughest life will consent to take upon themselves the discomforts of such a trip. On the morning of our second day, we traveled around to a remote and particularly wild spot on the borders of the Lake, where a stream of fresh, ice-cold water entered it from the mountain side, and then we went regularly into camp. We hired a large boat and two shot-guns from a lonely ranchman who lived some ten miles further on, and made ready for comfort and recreation. We soon got thoroughly acquainted with the Lake and all its peculiarities.

CHAPTER XXXVIII

Mono Lake lies in a lifeless, treeless, hideous desert, eight thousand feet above the level of the sea, and is guarded by mountains two thousand feet higher, whose summits are always clothed in clouds. This solemn, silent, sailless sea—this lonely tenant of the loneliest spot on earth—is little graced with the picturesque. It is an unpretending expanse of grayish water, about a hundred miles in circumference, with two islands in its centre, mere upheavals of rent and scorched and blistered lava, snowed over with gray banks and drifts of pumice-stone and ashes, the winding sheet of the dead volcano, whose vast crater the lake has seized upon and occupied.

The lake is two hundred feet deep, and its sluggish waters are so strong with alkali that if you only dip the most hopelessly soiled garment into them once or twice, and wring it out, it will be found as clean as if it had been through the ablest of washer-women's hands. While we camped there our laundry work was easy. We tied the week's washing astern of our boat, and sailed a quarter of a mile, and the job was complete, all to the wringing out. If we threw the water on our heads and gave them a rub or so, the white lather would pile up three inches high. This water is not good for bruised places and abrasions of the skin. We had a valuable dog. He had raw places on him. He had more raw places on him than sound ones. He was the rawest dog I almost ever saw. He jumped overboard one day to get away from the flies. But it was bad judgment. In his condition, it would have been just as comfortable to jump into the fire. The alkali water nipped him in all the raw places simultaneously, and he struck out for the shore with considerable interest. He yelped and barked and howled as he went—and by the time he got to the shore there was no bark to him—for he had barked the bark all out of his inside, and the alkali water had cleaned the bark all off his outside, and he probably wished he had never embarked in any such enterprise. He ran round and round in a circle, and pawed the earth and clawed the air, and threw double somersaults, sometimes backward and sometimes forward, in the most extraordinary manner. He was not a demonstrative dog, as a general thing, but rather of a grave and serious turn of mind, and I never saw him take so much interest in anything before. He finally struck out over the mountains, at a gait which we estimated at about two hundred and fifty miles an hour, and he is going yet. This was about nine years ago. We look for what is left of him along here every day.

A white man cannot drink the water of Mono Lake, for it is nearly pure lye. It is said that the Indians in the vicinity drink it sometimes, though. It is not improbable, for they are among the purest liars I ever saw. [There will be no additional charge for this joke, except to parties requiring an explanation of it. This joke has received high commendation from some of the ablest minds of the age.]

There are no fish in Mono Lake—no frogs, no snakes, no polliwigs—nothing, in fact, that goes to make life desirable. Millions of wild ducks and sea-gulls swim about the surface, but no living thing exists *under* the surface, except a white feathery sort of worm, one half an inch long, which looks like a bit of white thread frayed out at the sides. If you dip up a gallon of water, you will get about fifteen thousand of these. They give to the water a sort of grayish-white appearance. Then there is a fly, which looks something like our house fly. These settle on the beach to eat the worms that wash ashore—and any time, you can see there a belt of flies an inch deep and six feet wide, and this belt extends clear around the lake—a belt of flies one hundred miles long. If you throw a stone among them, they swarm up so thick that they look dense, like a cloud. You can hold them under water as long as you please—they do not mind it—they are only proud of it. When you let them go, they pop up to the surface as dry as a patent office report, and walk off as unconcernedly as if they had been educated especially with a view to affording instructive entertainment to man in that particular way. Providence leaves nothing to go by chance. All things have their uses and their part and proper place in Nature's economy: the ducks eat the flies—the flies eat the worms—the Indians eat all three—the wild cats eat the Indians—the white folks eat the wild cats—and thus all things are lovely.

Mono Lake is a hundred miles in a straight line from the ocean—and between it and the ocean are one or two ranges of mountains—yet thousands of sea-gulls go there every season to lay their eggs and rear their young. One would as soon expect to find sea-gulls in Kansas. And in this connection let us observe another instance of Nature's wisdom. The islands in the lake being merely huge masses of lava, coated over with ashes and pumice-stone, and utterly innocent of vegetation or anything that would burn; and sea-gulls' eggs being entirely useless to anybody unless they be cooked, Nature has provided an unfailing spring of boiling water on the largest island, and you can put your eggs in there, and in four minutes you can boil them as hard as any statement I have made during the past fifteen years. Within ten feet of the boiling spring is a spring of pure cold water, sweet and wholesome. So, in that island you get your board and washing free of charge—and if nature had gone further and furnished a nice American hotel clerk who was crusty and disobliging, and didn't know anything about the time tables, or the railroad routes—or—anything—and was proud of it—I would not wish for a more desirable boarding-house.

Half a dozen little mountain brooks flow into Mono Lake, but *not a stream of any kind flows out of it.* It neither rises nor falls, apparently, and what it does with its surplus water is a dark and bloody mystery.

There are only two seasons in the region round about Mono Lake—and these are, the breaking up of one Winter and the beginning of the next. More than once (in Esmeralda) I have seen a perfectly blistering morning open up with the thermometer at ninety degrees at eight o'clock, and seen the snow fall fourteen inches deep and that same identical thermometer go down to forty-four degrees under shelter, before nine o'clock at night. Under favorable circumstances it snows at least once in every single month in the year, in the little town of Mono. So uncertain is the climate in Summer that a lady who goes out visiting cannot hope to be prepared for all emergencies unless she takes her fan under one arm and her snow shoes under the other. When they have a Fourth of July procession it generally snows on them, and they do say that as a general thing when a man calls for a brandy toddy there, the bar keeper chops it off with a hatchet and wraps it up in a paper, like maple sugar. And it is further reported that the old soakers haven't any teeth—wore them out eating gin cocktails and brandy punches. I do not endorse that statement—I simply give it for what it is worth—and it is worth—well, I should say, millions, to any man who can believe it without straining himself. But I do endorse the snow on the Fourth of July—because I know that to be true.

CHAPTER XXXIX

About seven o'clock one blistering hot morning—for it was now dead summer time—Higbie and I took the boat and started on a voyage of discovery to the two islands. We had often longed to do this, but had been deterred by the fear of storms; for they were frequent, and severe enough to capsize an ordinary row-boat like ours without great difficulty—and once capsized, death would ensue in spite of the bravest swimming, for that venomous water would eat a man's eyes out like fire, and burn him out inside, too, if he shipped a sea. It was called twelve miles, straight out to the islands—a long pull and a warm one—but the morning was so quiet and sunny, and the lake so smooth and glassy and dead, that we could not resist the temptation. So we filled two large tin canteens with water (since we were not acquainted with the locality of the spring said to exist on the large island), and started. Higbie's brawny muscles gave the boat good speed, but by the time we reached our destination we judged that we had pulled nearer fifteen miles than twelve.

We landed on the big island and went ashore. We tried the water in the canteens, now, and found that the sun had spoiled it; it was so brackish that we could not drink it; so we poured it out and began a search for the spring—for thirst augments fast as soon as it is apparent that one has no means at hand of quenching it. The island was a long, moderately high hill of ashes—nothing but gray ashes and pumice-stone, in which we sunk to our knees at every step—and all around the top was a forbidding wall of scorched and blasted rocks. When we reached the top and got within the wall, we found simply a shallow, far-reaching basin, carpeted with ashes, and here and there a patch of fine sand. In places, picturesque jets of steam shot up out of crevices, giving evidence that although this ancient crater had gone out of active business, there was still some fire left in its furnaces. Close to one of these jets of steam stood the only tree on the island—a small pine of most graceful shape and most faultless symmetry; its color was a brilliant green, for the steam drifted unceasingly through its branches and kept them always moist. It contrasted strangely enough, did this vigorous and beautiful outcast, with its dead and dismal surroundings. It was like a cheerful spirit in a mourning household.

We hunted for the spring everywhere, traversing the full length of the island (two or three miles), and crossing it twice—climbing ash-hills patiently, and then sliding down the other side in a sitting posture, plowing up smothering volumes of gray dust. But we found nothing but solitude, ashes and a heart-breaking silence. Finally we noticed that the wind had risen, and we forgot our thirst in a solicitude of greater importance; for, the lake being quiet, we had not taken pains about securing the boat. We hurried back to a point overlooking our landing place, and then—but mere words cannot describe our dismay—the boat was gone! The chances were that there was not another boat on the entire lake. The situation was not comfortable—in truth, to speak plainly, it was frightful. We were prisoners on a desolate island, in aggravating proximity to friends who were for the present helpless to aid us; and what was still more uncomfortable was the reflection that we had neither food nor water. But presently we sighted the boat. It was drifting along, leisurely, about fifty yards from shore, tossing in a foamy sea. It drifted, and continued to drift, but at the same safe distance from land, and we walked along abreast it and waited for fortune to favor us. At the end of an hour it approached a jutting cape, and Higbie ran ahead and posted himself on the utmost verge and prepared for the assault. If we failed there, there was no hope for us. It was driving gradually shoreward all the time, now; but whether it was driving fast enough to make the connection or not was the momentous question. When it got within thirty steps of Higbie I was so excited that I fancied I could hear my own heart beat. When, a little later, it dragged slowly along and seemed about to go by, only one little yard out of reach, it seemed as if my heart stood still; and when it was exactly abreast him and began to widen away, and he still standing like a watching statue, I knew my heart did stop. But when he gave a great spring, the next instant, and lit fairly in the stern, I discharged a war-whoop that woke the solitudes!

But it dulled my enthusiasm, presently, when he told me he had not been caring whether the boat came within jumping distance or not, so that it passed within eight or ten yards of him, for he had made up his mind to shut his eyes and mouth and swim that trifling distance. Imbecile that I was, I had not thought of that. It was only a long swim that could be fatal.

The sea was running high and the storm increasing. It was growing late, too—three or four in the afternoon. Whether to venture toward the mainland or not, was a question of some moment. But we were so distressed by thirst that we decided to try it, and so Higbie fell to work and I took the steering-oar. When we had pulled a mile, laboriously, we were evidently in serious peril, for the storm had greatly augmented; the billows ran very high and were capped with foaming crests, the heavens were hung with black, and the wind blew with great fury. We would have gone back, now, but we did not dare to turn the boat around, because as soon as she got in the trough of the sea she would upset, of course. Our only hope lay in keeping her head-on to the seas. It was hard work to do this, she plunged so, and so beat and belabored the billows with her rising and falling bows. Now and then one of Higbie's oars would trip on the top of a wave, and the other one would snatch the boat half around in spite of my cumbersome steering apparatus. We were drenched by the sprays constantly, and the boat occasionally shipped water. By and by, powerful as my comrade was, his great exertions began to tell on him, and he was anxious that I should change places with him till he could rest a little. But I told him this was impossible; for if the steering oar were dropped a moment while we changed, the boat would slue around into the trough of the sea, capsize, and in less than five minutes we would have a hundred gallons of soap-suds in us and be eaten up so quickly that we could not even be present at our own inquest.

But things cannot last always. Just as the darkness shut down we came booming into port, head on. Higbie dropped his oars to hurrah—I dropped mine to help—the sea gave the boat a twist, and over she went!

The agony that alkali water inflicts on bruises, chafes and blistered hands, is unspeakable, and nothing but greasing all over will modify it—but we ate, drank and slept well, that night, notwithstanding.

In speaking of the peculiarities of Mono Lake, I ought to have mentioned that at intervals all around its shores stand picturesque turret-looking masses and clusters of a whitish, coarse-grained rock that resembles inferior mortar dried hard; and if one breaks off fragments of this rock he will find perfectly shaped and thoroughly petrified gulls' eggs deeply imbedded in the mass. How did they get there? I simply state the fact—for it is a fact—and leave the geological reader to crack the nut at his leisure and solve the problem after his own fashion.

At the end of a week we adjourned to the Sierras on a fishing excursion, and spent several days in camp under snowy Castle Peak, and fished successfully for trout in a bright, miniature lake whose surface was between ten and eleven thousand feet about the level of the sea; cooling ourselves during the hot August noons by sitting on snow banks ten feet deep, under whose sheltering edges *fine grass and dainty flowers flourished luxuriously;* and at night entertaining ourselves by almost freezing to death. Then we returned to Mono Lake, and finding that the cement excitement was over for the present, packed up and went back to Esmeralda. Mr. Ballou reconnoitred awhile, and not liking the prospect, set out alone for Humboldt.

About this time occurred a little incident which has always had a sort of interest to me, from the fact that it came so near "instigating" my funeral. At a time when an Indian attack had been expected, the citizens hid their gunpowder where it would be safe and yet convenient to hand when wanted. A neighbor of ours hid six cans of rifle powder in the bake-oven of an old discarded cooking stove which stood on the open ground near a frame out-house or shed, and from and after that day never thought of it again. We hired a half-tamed Indian to do some washing for us, and he took up quarters under the shed with his tub. The ancient stove reposed within six feet of him, and before his face. Finally it occurred to him that hot water would be better than cold, and he went out and fired up under that forgotten powder magazine and set on a kettle of water. Then he returned to his tub. I entered the shed presently and threw down some more clothes, and was about to speak to him when the stove blew up with a prodigious crash, and disappeared, leaving not a splinter behind. Fragments of it fell in the streets full two hundred yards away. Nearly a third of the shed roof over our heads was destroyed, and one of the stove lids, after cutting a small stanchion half in two in front of the Indian, whizzed between us and drove partly through the weather-boarding beyond. I was as white as a sheet and as weak as a kitten and speechless. But the Indian betrayed no trepidation, no distress, not even discomfort. He simply stopped washing, leaned forward and surveyed the clean, blank ground a moment, and then remarked:

"Mph! Dam stove heap gone!"—and resumed his scrubbing as placidly as if it were an entirely customary thing for a stove to do. I will explain, that "heap" is "Injun-English" for "very much." The reader will perceive the exhaustive expressiveness of it in the present instance.

CHAPTER XL

I now come to a curious episode—the most curious, I think, that had yet accented my slothful, valueless, heedless career. Out of a hillside toward the upper end of the town, projected a wall of reddish looking quartz-croppings, the exposed comb of a silver-bearing ledge that extended deep down into the earth, of course. I was owned by a company entitled the "Wide West." There was a shaft sixty or seventy feet deep on the under side of the croppings, and everybody was acquainted with the rock that came from it—and tolerably rich rock it was, too, but nothing extraordinary. I will remark here, that although to the inexperienced stranger all the quartz of a peculiar "district" looks about alike, an old resident of the camp can take a glance at a mixed pile of rock, separate the fragments and tell you which mine each came from, as easily as a confectioner can separate and classify the various kinds and qualities of candy in a mixed heap of the article.

All at once the town was thrown into a state of extraordinary excitement. In mining parlance the Wide West had "struck it rich!" Everybody went to see the new developments, and for some days there was such a crowd of people about the Wide West shaft that a stranger would have supposed there was a mass meeting in session there. No other topic was discussed but the rich strike, and nobody thought or dreamed about anything else. Every man brought away a specimen, ground it up in a hand mortar, washed it out in his horn spoon, and glared speechless upon the marvelous result. It was not hard rock, but black, decomposed stuff which could be crumbled in the hand like a baked potato, and when spread out on a paper exhibited a thick sprinkling of gold and particles of "native" silver. Higbie brought a handful to the cabin, and when he had washed it out his amazement was beyond description. Wide West stock soared skywards. It was said that repeated offers had been made for it at a thousand dollars a foot, and promptly refused. We have all had the "blues"—the mere sky-blues—but mine were indigo, now—because I did not own in the Wide West. The world seemed hollow to me, and existence a grief. I lost my appetite, and ceased to take an interest in anything. Still I had to stay, and listen to other people's rejoicing, because I had no money to get out of the camp with.

The Wide West company put a stop to the carrying away of "specimens," and well they might, for every handful of the ore was worth a sum of some consequence. To show the exceeding value of the ore, I will remark that a sixteen-hundred-pounds parcel of it was sold, just as it lay, at the mouth of the shaft, at *one dollar a pound;* and the man who bought it "packed" it on mules a hundred and fifty or two hundred miles, over the mountains, to San Francisco, satisfied that it would yield at a rate that would richly compensate him for his trouble. The Wide West people also commanded their foreman to refuse any but their own operatives permission to enter the mine at any time or for any purpose. I kept up my "blue" meditations and Higbie kept up a deal of thinking, too, but of a different sort. He puzzled over the "rock," examined it with a glass, inspected it in different lights and from different points of view, and after each experiment delivered himself, in soliloquy, of one and the same unvarying opinion in the same unvarying formula:

"It is *not* Wide West rock!"

He said once or twice that he meant to have a look into the

Wide West Shaft if he got shot for it. I was wretched, and did not care whether he got a look into it or not. He failed that day, and tried again at night; failed again; got up at dawn and tried, and failed again. Then he lay in ambush in the sage brush hour after hour, waiting for the two or three hands to adjourn to the shade of a boulder for dinner; made a start once, but was premature—one of the men came back for something; tried it again, but when almost at the mouth of the shaft, another of the men rose up from behind the boulder as if to reconnoitre, and he dropped on the ground and lay quiet; presently he crawled on his hands and knees to the mouth of the shaft, gave a quick glance around, then seized the rope and slid down the shaft. He disappeared in the gloom of a "side drift" just as a head appeared in the mouth of the shaft and somebody shouted "Hello!"—which he did not answer. He was not disturbed any more. An hour later he entered the cabin, hot, red, and ready to burst with smothered excitement, and exclaimed in a stage whisper:

"I knew it! We are rich! IT'S A BLIND LEAD!"

I thought the very earth reeled under me. Doubt— conviction—doubt again—exultation—hope, amazement, belief, unbelief—every emotion imaginable swept in wild procession through my heart and brain, and I could not speak a word. After a moment or two of this mental fury, I shook myself to rights, and said:

"Say it again!"

"It's a blind lead!"

"Cal., let's—let's burn the house—or kill somebody! Let's get out where there's room to hurrah! But what is the use? It is a hundred times too good to be true."

"It's a blind lead, for a million!—hanging wall—foot wall—clay casings—everything complete!" He swung his hat and gave three cheers, and I cast doubt to the winds and chimed in with a will. For I was worth a million dollars, and did not care "whether school kept or not!"

But perhaps I ought to explain. A "blind lead" is a lead or ledge that does not "crop out" above the surface. A miner does not know where to look for such leads, but they are often stumbled upon by accident in the course of driving a tunnel or sinking a shaft. Higbie knew the Wide West rock perfectly well, and the more he had examined the new developments the more he was satisfied that the ore could not have come from the Wide West vein. And so had it occurred to him alone, of all the camp, that there was a blind lead down in the shaft, and that even the Wide West people themselves did not suspect it. He was right. When he went down the shaft, he found that the blind lead held its independent way through the Wide West vein, cutting it diagonally, and that it was enclosed in its own well-defined casing-rocks and clay. Hence it was public property. Both leads being perfectly well defined, it was easy for any miner to see which one belonged to the Wide West and which did not.

We thought it well to have a strong friend, and therefore we brought the foreman of the Wide West to our cabin that night and revealed the great surprise to him. Higbie said:

"We are going to take possession of this blind lead, record it and establish ownership, and then forbid the Wide West company to take out any more of the rock. You cannot help your company in this matter—nobody can help them. I will go into the shaft with you and prove to your entire satisfaction that it *is* a blind lead. Now we propose to take you in with us, and claim the blind lead in our three names. What do you say?"

What could a man say who had an opportunity to simply stretch forth his hand and take possession of a fortune without risk of any kind and without wronging any one or attaching the least taint of dishonor to his name? He could only say, "Agreed."

The notice was put up that night, and duly spread upon the recorder's books before ten o'clock. We claimed two hundred feet each—six hundred feet in all—the smallest and compactest organization in the district, and the easiest to manage.

No one can be so thoughtless as to suppose that we slept, that night. Higbie and I went to bed at midnight, but it was only to lie broad awake and think, dream, scheme. The floorless, tumbledown cabin was a palace, the ragged gray blankets silk, the furniture rosewood and mahogany. Each new splendor that burst out of my visions of the future whirled me bodily over in bed or jerked me to a sitting posture just as if an electric battery had been applied to me. We shot fragments of conversation back and forth at each other. Once Higbie said:

"When are you going home—to the States?"

"To-morrow!"—with an evolution or two, ending with a sitting position. "Well—no—but next month, at furthest."

"We'll go in the same steamer."

"Agreed."

A pause.

"Steamer of the 10th?"

"Yes. No, the 1st."

"All right."

Another pause.

"Where are you going to live?" said Higbie.

"San Francisco."

"That's me!"

Pause.

"Too high—too much climbing"—from Higbie.

"What is?"

"I was thinking of Russian Hill—building a house up there."

"Too much climbing? Shan't you keep a carriage?"

"Of course. I forgot that."

Pause.

"Cal., what kind of a house are you going to build?"

"I was thinking about that. Three-story and an attic."

"But what *kind?*"

"Well, I don't hardly know. Brick, I suppose."

"Brick—bosh."

"Why? What is your idea?"

"Brown stone front—French plate glass—billiard-room off the dining-room—statuary and paintings—shrubbery and two-acre grass plat—greenhouse—iron dog on the front stoop—gray horses—landau, and a coachman with a bug on his hat!"

"By George!"

A long pause.

"Cal., when are you going to Europe?"

"Well—I hadn't thought of that. When are you?"

"In the Spring."

"Going to be gone all summer?"

"All summer! I shall remain there three years."

"No—but are you in earnest?"

"Indeed I am."

"I will go along too."

"Why of course you will."

"What part of Europe shall you go to?"

"All parts. France, England, Germany—Spain, Italy, Switzerland, Syria, Greece, Palestine, Arabia, Persia, Egypt—all over—everywhere."

"I'm agreed."

"All right."

"Won't it be a swell trip!"

"We'll spend forty or fifty thousand dollars trying to make it one, anyway."

Another long pause.

"Higbie, we owe the butcher six dollars, and he has been threatening to stop our—"

"Hang the butcher!"

"Amen."

And so it went on. By three o'clock we found it was no use, and so we got up and played cribbage and smoked pipes till sunrise. It was my week to cook. I always hated cooking—now, I abhorred it.

The news was all over town. The former excitement was great—this one was greater still. I walked the streets serene and happy. Higbie said the foreman had been offered two hundred thousand dollars for his third of the mine. I said I would like to see myself selling for any such price. My ideas were lofty. My figure was a million. Still, I honestly believe that if I had been offered it, it would have had no other effect than to make me hold off for more.

I found abundant enjoyment in being rich. A man offered me a three-hundred-dollar horse, and wanted to take my simple, un-endorsed note for it. That brought the most realizing sense I had yet had that I was actually rich, beyond shadow of doubt. I was followed by numerous other evidences of a similar nature—among which I may mention the fact of the butcher leaving us a double supply of meat and saying nothing about money.

By the laws of the district, the "locators" or claimants of a ledge were obliged to do a fair and reasonable amount of work on their new property within ten days after the date of the loca-tion, or the property was forfeited, and anybody could go and seize it that chose. So we determined to go to work the next day. About the middle of the afternoon, as I was coming out of the post office, I met a Mr. Gardiner, who told me that Capt. John Nye was lying dangerously ill at his place (the "Nine-Mile Ranch"), and that he and his wife were not able to give him nearly as much care and attention as his case demanded. I said if he would wait for me a moment, I would go down and help in the sick room. I ran to the cabin to tell Higbie. He was not there, but I left a note on the table for him, a few minutes later I left town in Gardiner's wagon.

CHAPTER XLI

Captain Nye was very ill indeed, with spasmodic rheumatism. But the old gentleman was himself—which is to say, he was kind-hearted and agreeable when comfortable, but a singularly violent wild-cat when things did not go well. He would be smil-ing along pleasantly enough, when a sudden spasm of his disease would take him and he would go out of his smile into a perfect fury. He would groan and wail and howl with the anguish, and fill up the odd chinks with the most elaborate profanity that strong convictions and a fine fancy could contrive. With fair op-portunity he could swear very well and handle his adjectives with

705

considerable judgment; but when the spasm was on him it was painful to listen to him, he was so awkward. However, I had seen him nurse a sick man himself and put up patiently with the inconveniences of the situation, and consequently I was willing that he should have full license now that his own turn had come. He could not disturb me, with all his raving and ranting, for my mind had work on hand, and it labored on diligently, night and day, whether my hands were idle or employed. I was altering and amending the plans for my house, and thinking over the propriety of having the billiard-room in the attic, instead of on the same floor with the dining-room; also, I was trying to decide between green and blue for the upholstery of the drawing-room, for, although my preference was blue I feared it was a color that would be too easily damaged by dust and sunlight; likewise while I was content to put the coachman in a modest livery, I was uncertain about a footman—I needed one, and was even resolved to have one, but wished he could properly appear and perform his functions out of livery, for I somewhat dreaded so much show; and yet, inasmuch as my late grandfather had had a coachman and such things, but no liveries, I felt rather drawn to beat him;—or beat his ghost, at any rate; I was also systematizing the European trip, and managed to get it all laid out, as to route and length of time to be devoted to it—everything, with one exception—namely, whether to cross the desert from Cairo to Jerusalem per camel, or go by sea to Beirut, and thence down through the country per caravan. Meantime I was writing to the friends at home every day, instructing them concerning all my plans and intentions, and directing them to look up a handsome homestead for my mother and agree upon a price for it against my coming, and also directing them to sell my share of the Tennessee land and tender the proceeds to the widows' and orphans' fund of the typographical union of which I had long been a member in good standing. [This Tennessee land had been in the possession of the family many years, and promised to confer high fortune upon us some day; it still promises it, but in a less violent way.]

When I had been nursing the Captain nine days he was somewhat better, but very feeble. During the afternoon we lifted him into a chair and gave him an alcoholic vapor bath, and then set about putting him on the bed again. We had to be exceedingly careful, for the least jar produced pain. Gardiner had his shoulders and I his legs; in an unfortunate moment I stumbled and the patient fell heavily on the bed in an agony of torture. I never heard a man swear so in my life. He raved like a maniac, and tried to snatch a revolver from the table—but I got it. He ordered me out of the house, and swore a world of oaths that he would kill me wherever he caught me when he got on his feet again. It was simply a passing fury, and meant nothing. I knew he would forget it in an hour, and maybe be sorry for it, too; but it angered me a little, at the moment. So much so, indeed, that I determined to go back to Esmeralda. I thought he was able to get along alone, now, since he was on the war path. I took supper, and as soon as the moon rose, began my nine-mile journey, on foot. Ever millionaires needed no horses, in those days, for a mere nine-mile jaunt without baggage.

As I "raised the hill" overlooking the town, it lacked fifteen minutes of twelve. I glanced at the hill over beyond the canyon, and in the bright moonlight saw what appeared to be about half the population of the village massed on and around the Wide West croppings. My heart gave an exulting bound, and I said to myself, "They have made a new strike to-night—and struck it richer than ever, no doubt." I started over there, but gave it up. I said the "strike" would keep, and I had climbed hills enough for one night. I went on down through the town, and as I was passing a little German bakery, a woman ran out and begged me to come in and help her. She said her husband had a fit. I went in, and judged she was right—he appeared to have a hundred of them, compressed into one. Two Germans were there, trying to hold him, and not making much of a success of it. I ran up the street half a block or so and routed out a sleeping doctor, brought him down half dressed, and we four wrestled with the maniac, and doctored, drenched and bled him, for more than an hour, and the poor German woman did the crying. He grew quiet, now, and the doctor and I withdrew and left him to his friends.

It was a little after one o'clock. As I entered the cabin door, tired but jolly, the dingy light of a tallow candle revealed Higbie, sitting by the pine table gazing stupidly at my note, which he held in his fingers, and looking pale, old, and haggard. I halted, and looked at him. He looked at me, stolidly. I said:

"Higbie, what—what is it?"

"We're ruined—we didn't do the work—THE BLIND LEAD'S RELOCATED!"

It was enough. I sat down sick, grieved—broken-hearted, indeed. A minute before, I was rich and brimful of vanity; I was a pauper now, and very meek. We sat still an hour, busy with thought, busy with vain and useless self-upbraidings, busy with "Why *didn't* I do this, and why *didn't* I do that," but neither spoke a word. Then we dropped into mutual explanations, and the mystery was cleared away. It came out that Higbie had depended on me, as I had on him, and as both of us had on the foreman. The folly of it! It was the first time that ever staid and steadfast Higbie had left an important matter to chance or failed to be true to his full share of a responsibility.

But he had never seen my note till this moment, and this moment was the first time he had been in the cabin since the day he had seen me last. He, also, had left a note for me, on that same fatal afternoon—had ridden up on horseback, and looked through the window, and being in a hurry and not seeing me, had tossed the note into the cabin through a broken pane. Here it was, on the floor, where it had remained undisturbed for nine days:

"Don't fail to do the work before the ten days expire. W. has passed through and given me notice. I am to join him at Mono Lake, and we shall go on from there to-night. He says he will find it this time, sure. CAL."

"W." meant Whiteman, of course. That thrice accursed "cement!"

That was the way of it. An old miner, like Higbie, could no more withstand the fascination of a mysterious mining excitement like this "cement" foolishness, than he could refrain from eating when he was famishing. Higbie had been dreaming about the marvelous cement for months; and now, against his better judgment, he had gone off and "taken the chances" on my keeping secure a mine worth a million undiscovered cement veins. They had not been followed this time. His riding out of town in broad daylight was such a commonplace thing to do that it had not attracted any attention. He said they prosecuted their search in the fastnesses of the mountains during nine days, without success; they could not find the cement. Then a ghastly fear came over him that something might have happened to prevent the doing of the necessary work to hold the blind lead (though indeed he thought such a thing hardly possible), and forthwith he started home with all speed. He would have reached Esmeralda in time, but his horse broke down and he had to walk a great part of the distance. And so it happened that as he came into Esmeralda by one road, I entered it by another. His was the superior energy, however, for he went straight to the Wide West, instead of turning aside as I had done—and he arrived there about five or ten minutes too late! The "notice" was already up, the "relocation" of our mine completed beyond recall, and the crowd rapidly dispersing. He learned some facts before he left the ground. The foreman had not been seen about the streets since the night we had located the mine—a telegram had called him to California on a matter of life and death, it was said. At any rate he had done no work and the watchful eyes of the community were taking note of the fact. At midnight of this woful tenth day, the ledge would be "relocatable," and by eleven o'clock the hill was black with men prepared to do the relocating. That was the crowd I had seen when I fancied a new "strike" had been made—idiot that I was.]We three had the same right to relocate the lead that other people had, provided we were quick enough.] As midnight was announced, fourteen men, duly armed and ready to back their proceedings, put up their "notice" and proclaimed their ownership of the blind lead, under the new name of the "Johnson." But A. D. Allen our partner (the foreman) put in a sudden appearance about that time, with a cocked revolver in his hand, and said his name must be added to the list, or he would "thin out the Johnson company some." He was a manly, splendid, determined fellow, and known to be as good as his word, and therefore a compromise was effected. They put in his name for a hundred feet, reserving to themselves the customary two hundred feet each. Such was the history of the night's events, as Higbie gathered from a friend on the way home.

Higbie and I cleared out on a new mining excitement the next morning, glad to get away from the scene of our sufferings, and after a month or two of hardship and disappointment, returned to Esmeralda once more. Then we learned that the Wide West and the Johnson companies had consolidated; that the stock, thus united, comprised five thousand feet, or shares; that the foreman, apprehending tiresome litigation, and considering such a huge concern unwieldly, had sold his hundred feet for ninety thousand dollars in gold and gone home to the States to enjoy it. If the stock was worth such a gallant figure, with five thousand shares in the corporation, it makes me dizzy to think what it would have been worth with only our original six hundred in it. It was the difference between six hundred men owning a house and five thousand owning it. We would have been millionaires if we had only worked with pick and spade one little day on our property and so secured our ownership!

It reads like a wild fancy sketch, but the evidence of many witnesses, and likewise that of the official records of Esmeralda District, is easily obtainable in proof that it is a true history. I can always have it to say that I was absolutely and unquestionably worth a million dollars, once, for ten days.

A year ago my esteemed and in every way estimable old millionaire partner, Higbie, wrote me from an obscure little

mining camp in California that after nine or ten years of buffetings and hard striving, he was at last in a position where he
could command twenty-five hundred dollars, and said he meant
to go into the fruit business in a modest way. How such a
thought would have insulted him the night we lay in our cabin
planning European trips and brown stone houses on Russian
Hill!

CHAPTER XLII

What to do next?
It was a momentous question. I had gone out into the world to
shift for myself, at the age of thirteen (for my father had endorsed for friends; and although he left us a sumptuous legacy
of pride in his fine Virginian stock and its national distinction, I
presently found that I could not live on that alone without occasional bread to wash it down with). I had gained a livelihood in
various vocations, but had not dazzled anybody with my successes; still the list was before me, and the amplest liberty in the
matter of choosing, provided I wanted to work—which I did
not, after being so wealthy. I had once been a grocery clerk, for
one day, but had consumed so much sugar in that time that I was
relieved from further duty by the proprietor; said he wanted me
outside, so that he could have my custom. I had studied law an
entire week, and then given it up because it was so prosy and
tiresome. I had engaged briefly in the study of blacksmithing,
but wasted so much time trying to fix the bellows so that it
would blow itself, that the master turned me adrift in disgrace,
and told me I would come to no good. I had been a bookseller's
clerk for awhile, but the customers bothered me so much I could
not read with any comfort, and so the proprietor gave me a
furlough and forgot to put a limit to it. I had clerked in a drug
store part of a summer, but my prescriptions were unlucky, and
we appeared to sell more stomach pumps than soda water. So I
had to go. I had made of myself a tolerable printer, under the
impression that I would be another Franklin some day, but
somehow had missed the connection thus far. There was no
berth open in the Esmeralda *Union,* and besides I had always
been such a slow compositor that I looked with envy upon the
achievements of apprentices of two years' standing; and when I
took a "take," foremen were in the habit of suggesting that it
would be wanted "some time during the year." I was a good
average St. Louis and New Orleans pilot and by no means
ashamed of my abilities in that line; wages were two hundred

and fifty dollars a month and no board to pay, and I did long to stand behind a wheel again and never roam any more—but I had been making such an ass of myself lately in grandiloquent letters home about my blind lead and my European excursion that I did what many and many a poor disappointed miner had done before; said "It is all over with me now, and I will never go back home to be pitied—and snubbed." I had been a private secretary, a silver miner and a silver mill operative, and amounted to less than nothing in each, and now—

What to do next?

I yielded to Higbie's appeals and consented to try the mining once more. We climbed far up on the mountain side and went to work on a little rubbishy claim of ours that had a shaft on it eight feet deep. Higbie descended into it and worked bravely with his pick till he had loosened up a deal of rock and dirt and then I went down with a long-handled shovel (the most awkward invention yet contrived by man) to throw it out. You must brace the shovel forward with the side of your knee till it is full, and then, with a skilful toss, throw it backward over your left shoulder. I made the toss and landed the mess just on the edge of the shaft and it all came back on my head and down the back of my neck. I never said a word, but climbed out and walked home. I inwardly resolved that I would starve before I would make a target of myself and shoot rubbish at it with a long-handled shovel. I sat down, in the cabin, and gave myself up to solid misery—so to speak. Now in pleasanter days I had amused myself with writing letters to the chief paper of the Territory, the Virginia *Daily Territorial Enterprise,* and had always been surprised when they appeared in print. My good opinion of the editors had steadily declined; for it seemed to me that they might have found something better to fill up with than my literature. I had found a letter in the post office as I came home from the hill side, and finally I opened it. Eureka! [I never did know what Eureka meant, but it seems to be as proper a word to heave in as any when no other that sounds pretty offers.] It was a deliberate offer to me of Twenty-Five Dollars a week to come up to Virginia and be city editor of the *Enterprise.*

I would have challenged the publisher in the "blind lead" days—I wanted to fall down and worship him, now. Twenty-Five Dollars a week—it looked like bloated luxury—a fortune—a sinful and lavish waste of money. But my transports cooled when I thought of my inexperience and consequent unfitness for the position—and straightway, on top of this, my long array of failures rose up before me. Yet if I refused this place I must presently become dependent upon somebody for my bread, a thing necessarily distasteful to a man who had never experienced such a humiliation since he was thirteen years old. Not much to be proud of, since it is so common—but then it was all I had to *be* proud of. So I was scared into being a city editor. I would have declined, otherwise. Necessity is the mother of "taking chances." I do not doubt that if, at that time, I had been offered a salary to translate the Talmud from the original Hebrew, I would have accepted—albeit with diffidence and some misgivings—and thrown as much variety into it as I could for the money.

I went up to Virginia and entered upon my new vocation. I was a rusty looking city editor, I am free to confess—coatless, slouch hat, blue woolen shirt, pantaloons stuffed into boot-tops, whiskered half down to the waist, and the universal navy revolver slung to my belt. But I secured a more Christian costume and discarded the revolver. I had never had occasion to kill anybody, nor ever felt a desire to do so, but had worn the thing in deference to popular sentiment, and in order that I might not, by its absence, be offensively conspicuous, and a subject of remark. But the other editors, and all the printers, carried revolvers. I asked the chief editor and proprietor (Mr. Goodman, I will call him, since it describes him as well as any name could do) for some instructions with regard to my duties, and he told me to go all over town and ask all sorts of people all sorts of questions, make notes of the information gained, and write them out for publication. And he added:

"Never say 'We learn' so-and-so, or 'It is reported,' or 'It is rumored,' or 'We understand' so-and-so, but go to headquarters and get the absolute facts, and then speak out and say 'It *is* so-and-so.' Otherwise, people will not put confidence in your news. Unassailable certainty is the thing that gives a newspaper the firmest and most valuable reputation."

It was the whole thing in a nut-shell; and to this day when I find a reporter commencing his article with "We understand," I gather a suspicion that he has not taken as much pains to inform himself as he ought to have done. I moralize well, but I did not always practise well when I was a city editor; I let fancy get the upper hand of fact too often when there was a dearth of news. I can never forget my first day's experience as a reporter. I wandered about town questioning everybody, boring everybody, and finding out that nobody knew anything. At the end of five hours my notebook was still barren. I spoke to Mr. Goodman. He said:

"Dan used to make a good thing out of the hay wagons in a dry time when there were no fires or inquests. Are there no hay wagons in from the Truckee? If there are, you might speak of the renewed activity and all that sort of thing, in the hay business, you know. It isn't sensational or exciting, but it fills up and looks business like."

I canvassed the city again and found one wretched old hay truck dragging in from the country. But I made affluent use of it. I multiplied it by sixteen, brought it into town from sixteen different directions, made sixteen separate items out of it, and got up such another sweat about hay as Virginia City had never seen in the world before.

This was encouraging. Two nonpareil columns had to be filled, and I was getting along. Presently, when things began to look dismal again, a desperado killed a man in a saloon and joy returned once more. I never was so glad over any mere trifle before in my life. I said to the murderer:

"Sir, you are a stranger to me, but you have done me a kindness this day which I can never forget. If whole years of gratitude can be to you any slight compensation, they shall be yours. I was in trouble and you have relieved me nobly and at a time when all seemed dark and drear. Count me your friend from this time forth, for I am not a man to forget a favor."

If I did not really say that to him I at least felt a sort of itching desire to do it. I wrote up the murder with a hungry attention to details, and when it was finished experienced but one regret— namely, that they had not hanged my benefactor on the spot, so that I could work him up too.

Next I discovered some emigrant wagons going into camp on the plaza and found that they had lately come through the hostile Indian country and had fared rather roughly. I made the best of the item that the circumstances permitted, and felt that if I were not confined within rigid limits by the presence of the reporters of the other papers I could add particulars that would make the article much more interesting. However, I found one wagon that was going on to California, and made some judicious inquiries of the proprietor. When I learned, through his short and surly answers to my cross-questioning, that he was certainly going on and would not be in the city next day to make trouble, I got ahead of the other papers, for I took down his list of names and added his party to the killed and wounded. Having more scope here, I put this wagon through an Indian fight that to this day has no parallel in history.

My two columns were filled. When I read them over in the morning I felt that I had found my legitimate occupation at last. I reasoned within myself that news, and stirring news, too, was what a paper needed, and I felt that I was peculiarly endowed

713

with the ability to furnish it. Mr. Goodman said that I was as good a reporter as Dan. I desired no higher commendation. With encouragement like that, I felt that I could take my pen and murder all the immigrants on the plains if need be and the interests of the paper demanded it.

CHAPTER XLIII

However, as I grew better acquainted with the business and learned the run of the sources of information I ceased to require the aid of fancy to any large extent, and became able to fill my columns without diverging noticeably from the domain of fact.

I struck up friendships with the reporters of the other journals, and we swapped "regulars" with each other and thus economized work. "Regulars" are permanent sources of news, like courts, bullion returns, "clean-ups" at the quartz mills, and inquests. Inasmuch as everybody went armed, we had an inquest about every day, and so this department was naturally set down among the "regulars." We had lively papers in those days. My great competitor among the reporters was Boggs of the *Union*. He was an excellent reporter. Once in three or four months he would get a little intoxicated, but as a general thing he was a wary and cautious drinker although always ready to tamper a little with the enemy. He had the advantage of me in one thing; he could get the monthly public school report and I could not, because the principal hated the *Enterprise*. One snowy night when the report was due, I started out sadly wondering how I was going to get it. Presently, a few steps up the almost deserted street I stumbled on Boggs and asked him where he was going.

"After the school report."

"I'll go along with you."

"No, *sir*. I'll excuse you."

"Just as you say."

A saloon-keeper's boy passed by with a steaming pitcher of hot punch, and Boggs snuffed the fragrance gratefully. He gazed fondly after the boy and saw him start up the *Enterprise* stairs. I said:

"I wish you could help me get that school business, but since you can't, I must run up to the *Union* office and see if I can get them to let me have a proof of it after they have set it up, though I don't begin to suppose they will. Good night."

"Hold on a minute. I don't mind getting the report and sitting around with the boys a little, while you copy it, if you're willing to drop down to the principal's with me."

"Now you talk like a rational being. Come along."

We plowed a couple of blocks through the snow, got the report and returned to our office. It was a short document and soon copied. Meantime Boggs helped himself to the punch. I gave the manuscript back to him and we started out to get an inquest, for we heard pistol shots near by. We got the particulars with little loss of time, for it was only an inferior sort of barroom murder, and of little interest to the public, and then we separated. Away at three o'clock in the morning, when we had gone to press and were having a relaxing concert as usual—for some of the printers were good singers and others good performers on the guitar and on that atrocity the accordeon—the proprietor of the *Union* strode in and desired to know if anybody had heard anything of Boggs or the school report. We stated the case, and all turned out to help hunt for the delinquent. We found him standing on a table in a saloon, with an old tin lantern in one hand and the school report in the other, haranguing a gang of intoxicated Cornish miners on the iniquity of squandering the public moneys on education "when hundreds and hundreds of honest hard-working men are literally starving for whiskey." [Riotous applause.] He had been assisting in a regal spree with those parties for hours. We dragged him away and put him to bed.

Of course there was no school report in the *Union,* and Boggs held me accountable, though I was innocent of any intention or desire to compass its absence from that paper and was as sorry as any one that the misfortune had occurred.

But we were perfectly friendly. The day that the school report was next due, the proprietor of the "Genessee" mine furnished us a buggy and asked us to go down and write something about the property—a very common request and one always gladly acceded to when people furnished buggies, for we were as fond of pleasure excursions as other people. In due time we arrived at the "mine"—nothing but a hole in the ground ninety feet deep, and no way of getting down into it but by holding on to a rope and being lowered with a windlass. The workmen had just gone off somewhere to dinner. I was not strong enough to lower Boggs's bulk; so I took an unlighted candle in my teeth, made a loop for my foot in the end of the rope, implored Boggs not to go to sleep or let the windlass get the start of him, and then swung out over the shaft. I reached the bottom muddy and bruised about the elbows, but safe. I lit the candle, made an examination of the rock, selected some specimens and shouted to Boggs to hoist away. No answer. Presently a head appeared in the circle of daylight away aloft, and a voice came down:

"Are you all set?"

"All set—hoist away."

"Are you comfortable?"

"Perfectly."

"Could you wait a little?"

"Oh certainly—no particular hurry."

"Well—good by."

"Why? Where are you going?"

"After the school report!"

And he did. I staid down there an hour, and surprised the workmen when they hauled up and found a man on the rope instead of a bucket of rock. I walked home, too—five miles—up hill. We had no school report next morning; but the *Union* had.

Six months after my entry into journalism the grand "flush times" of Silverland began, and they continued with unabated splendor for three years. All difficulty about filling up the "local department" ceased, and the only trouble now was how to make the lengthened columns hold the world of incidents and happenings that came to our literary net every day. Virginia had grown to be the "livest" town, for its age and population, that America had ever produced. The sidewalks swarmed with people—to such an extent, indeed, that it was generally no easy matter to stem the human tide. The streets themselves were just as crowded with quartz wagons, freight teams and other vehicles. The procession was endless. So great was the pack, that buggies frequently had to wait half an hour for an opportunity to cross the principal street. Joy sat on every countenance, and there was a glad, almost fierce, intensity in every eye, that told of the money-getting schemes that were seething in every brain and the high hope that held sway in every heart. Money was as plenty as dust; every individual considered himself wealthy, and a melancholy countenance was nowhere to be seen. There were military companies, fire companies, brass bands, banks, hotels, theatres, "hurdy-gurdy houses," wide-open gambling palaces, political pow-wows, civic processions, street fights, murders, inquests, riots, a whiskey mill every fifteen steps, a Board of Aldermen, a Mayor, a City Surveyor, a City Engineer, a Chief of the Fire Department, with First, Second and Third Assistants, a Chief of Police, City Marshal and a large police force, two Boards of Mining Brokers, a dozen breweries and half a dozen jails and station-houses in full operation, and some talk of building a church. The "flush times" were in magnificent flower! Large fire-proof brick buildings were going up in the principal streets, and the wooden suburbs were spreading out in all directions. Town lots soared up to prices that were amazing.

The great "Comstock lode" stretched its opulent length straight through the town from north to south, and every mine on it was in diligent process of development. One of these mines alone employed six hundred and seventy-five men, and in the matter of elections the adage was, "as the 'Gould and Curry' goes, so goes the city." Laboring men's wages were four and six dollars a day, and they worked in three "shifts" or gangs, and the blasting and picking and shoveling went on without ceasing, night and day.

The "city" of Virginia roosted royally midway up the steep side of Mount Davidson, seven thousand two hundred feet above the level of the sea, and in the clear Nevada atmosphere was visible from a distance of fifty miles! It claimed a population of fifteen thousand to eighteen thousand, and all day long half of this little army swarmed the streets like bees and the other half swarmed among the drifts and tunnels of the "Comstock," hundreds of feet down in the earth directly under those same streets. Often we felt our chairs jar, and heard the faint boom of a blast down in the bowels of the earth under the office.

The mountain side was so steep that the entire town had a slant to it like a roof. Each street was a terrace, and from each to the next street below the descent was forty or fifty feet. The fronts of the houses were level with the street they faced, but their rear first floors were propped on lofty stilts; a man could stand at a rear first floor window of a C street house and look down the chimneys of the row of houses below him facing D street. It was a laborious climb, in that thin atmosphere, to ascend from D to A street, and you were panting and out of breath when you got there; but you could turn around and go down again like a house a-fire—so to speak. The atmosphere was so rarified, on account of the great altitude, that one's blood lay near the surface always, and the scratch of a pin was a disaster worth worrying about, for the chances were that a grievous erysipelas would ensue. But to offset this, the thin atmosphere seemed to carry healing to gunshot wounds, and therefore, to simply shoot your adversary through both lungs was a thing not likely to afford you any permanent satisfaction, for he would be nearly certain to be around looking for you within the month, and not with an opera glass, either.

From Virginia's airy situation one could look over a vast, far-reaching panorama of mountain ranges and deserts; and whether the day was bright or overcast, whether the sun was rising or setting, or flaming in the zenith, or whether night and the moon held sway, the spectacle was always impressive and beautiful. Over your head Mount Davidson lifted its gray dome,

717

and before and below you a rugged canyon clove the battlemented hills, making a sombre gateway through which a soft-tinted desert was glimpsed, with the silver thread of a river winding through it, bordered with trees which many miles of distance diminished to a delicate fringe; and still further away the snowy mountains rose up and stretched their long barrier to the filmy horizon—far enough beyond a lake that burned in the desert like a fallen sun, though that, itself, lay fifty miles removed. Look from your window where you would, there was fascination in the picture. At rare intervals—but very rare—there were clouds in our skies, and then the setting sun would gild and flush and glorify this mighty expanse of scenery with a bewildering pomp of color that held the eye like a spell and moved the spirit like music.

CHAPTER XLIV

My salary was increased to forty dollars a week. But I seldom drew it. I had plenty of other resources, and what were two broad twenty-dollar gold pieces to a man who had his pockets full of such and a cumbersome abundance of bright half dollars besides? [Paper money has never come into use on the Pacific coast.] Reporting was lucrative, and every man in the town was lavish with his money and his "feet." The city and all the great mountain side were riddled with mining shafts. There were more mines than miners. True, not ten of these mines were yielding rock worth hauling to a mill, but everybody said, "Wait till the shaft gets down where the ledge comes in solid, and then you will see!" So nobody was discouraged. These were nearly all "wild cat" mines, and wholly worthless, but nobody believed it then. The "Ophir," the "Gould & Curry," the "Mexican," and other great mines on the Comstock lead in Virginia and Gold Hill were turning out huge piles of rich rock every day, and every man believed that his little wild cat claim was as good as any on the "main lead" and would infallibly be worth a thousand dollars a foot when he "got down where it came in solid." Poor fellow, he was blessedly blind to the fact that he never would see that day. So the thousand wild cat shafts burrowed deeper and deeper into the earth day by day, and all men were beside themselves with hope and happiness. How they labored, prophesied, exulted! Surely nothing like it was ever seen before since the world began. Every one of these wild cat mines—not mines, but holes in the ground over imaginary mines—was incorporated and had handsomely engraved "stock" and the stock was salable, too. It was bought and sold with a feverish avidity in the boards every day. You could go up on the mountain side, scratch around and find a ledge (there was no lack of them), put up a "notice" with a grandiloquent name in it, start a shaft, get your stock printed, and with nothing whatever to prove that your mine was worth a straw, you could put your stock on the market and sell out for hundreds and even thousands of dollars. To make money, and make it fast, was as easy as it was to eat your dinner. Every man owned "feet" in fifty different wild cat mines and considered his fortune made. Think of a city with not one solitary poor man in it! One would suppose that when month after month went by and still not a wild cat mine [by wild cat I mean, in general terms, *any* claim not located on the mother vein, *i.e.,* the "Comstock") yielded a ton of rock worth crushing, the people would begin to wonder if they were not putting too much faith in their prospective riches; but there was not a thought of such a thing. They burrowed away, bought and sold, and were happy.

New claims were taken up daily, and it was the friendly custom to run straight to the newspaper offices, give the reporter forty or fifty "feet," and get them to go and examine the mine and publish a notice of it. They did not care a fig what you said about the property so you said something. Consequently we generally said a word or two to the effect that the "indications" were good, or that the ledge was "six feet wide," or that the rock "resembled the Comstock" (and so it did—but as a general thing the resemblance was not startling enough to knock you down). If the rock was moderately promising, we followed the custom of the country, used strong adjectives and frothed at the mouth as if a very marvel in silver discoveries had transpired. If the mine was a "developed" one, and had no pay ore to show (and of course it hadn't), we praised the tunnel; said it was one of the most infatuating tunnels in the land; driveled and driveled about the tunnel till we ran entirely out of ecstasies—but never said a word about the rock. We would squander half a column of adulation on a shaft, or a new wire rope, or a dressed pine windlass, or a fascinating force pump, and close with a burst of admiration of the "gentlemanly and efficient Superintendent" of the mine—but never utter a whisper about the rock. And those people were always pleased, always satisfied. Occasionally we patched up and varnished our reputation for discrimination and stern, undeviating accuracy, by giving some old abandoned claim a blast that ought to have made its dry bones rattle—and then somebody would seize it and sell it on the fleeting notoriety thus conferred upon it.

There was *nothing* in the shape of a mining claim that was not salable. We received presents of "feet" every day. If we needed a hundred dollars or so, we sold some; if not, we hoarded it away, satisfied that it would ultimately be worth a thousand dollars a foot. I had a trunk about half full of "stock." When a claim made a stir in the market and went up to a high figure, I searched through my pile to see if I had any of its stock—and generally found it.

The prices rose and fell constantly; but still a fall disturbed us little, because a thousand dollars a foot was our figure, and so we were content to let it fluctuate as much as it pleased till it reached it. My pile of stock was not all given to me by people who wished their claims "noticed." At least half of it was given me by persons who had no thought of such a thing, and looked for nothing more than a simple verbal "thank you"; and you were not even obliged by law to furnish that. If you are coming up the street with a couple of baskets of apples in your hands, and you meet a friend, you naturally invite him to take a few. That describes the condition of things in Virginia in the "flush times." Every man had his pockets full of stock, and it was the actual *custom* of the country to part with small quantities of it to friends without the asking. Very often it was a good idea to close the transaction instantly, when a man offered a stock present to a friend, for the offer was only good and binding at that moment, and if the price went to a high figure shortly afterward the procrastination was a thing to be regretted. Mr. Stewart (Senator, now, from Nevada) one day told me he would give me twenty feet of "Justis" stock if I would walk over to his office. It was worth five or ten dollars a foot. I asked him to make the offer good for next day, as I was just going to dinner. He said he would not be in town; so I risked it and took my dinner instead of the stock. Within the week the price went up to seventy dollars and afterward to a hundred and fifty, but nothing could make that man yield. I suppose he sold that stock of mine and placed the guilty proceeds in his own pocket. [My revenge will be found in the accompanying portrait.] I met three friends one afternoon, who said they had been buying "Overman" stock at auction at eight dollars a foot. One said if I would come up to his office he would give me fifteen feet; another said he would add fifteen; the third said he would do the same. But I was going after an inquest and could not stop. A few weeks afterward they sold all their "Overman" at six hundred dollars a foot and generously came around to tell me about it—and also to urge me to accept of the next forty-five feet of it that people tried to force on me. These are actual facts, and I could make the list a long one and still confine myself strictly to the truth. Many a time friends gave us as much as twenty-five feet of stock that was selling at twenty-five dollars a foot, and they thought no more of it than they would of offering a guest a cigar. These were "flush times" indeed! I thought they were going to last always, but somehow I never was much of a prophet.

To show what a wild spirit possessed the mining brain of the community, I will remark that "claims" were actually "located" in excavations for cellars, where the pick had exposed what seemed to be quartz veins—and not cellars in the suburbs, either, but in the very heart of the city; and forthwith stock would be issued and thrown on the market. It was small matter who the cellar belonged to—the "ledge" belonged to the finder, and unless the United States government interfered (inasmuch as the government holds the primary right to mines of the noble metals in Nevada—or at least did then), it was considered to be his privilege to work it. Imagine a stranger staking out a mining claim among the costly shrubbery in your front yard and calmly proceeding to lay waste the ground with pick and shovel and blasting powder! It has been often done in California. In the middle of one of the principal business streets of Virginia, a man "located" a mining claim and began a shaft on it. He gave me a hundred feet of the stock and I sold it for a fine suit of clothes because I was afraid somebody would fall down the shaft and sue for damages. I owned in another claim that was located in the middle of another street; and to show how absurd people can be, that "East India" stock (as it was called) sold briskly although there was an ancient tunnel running directly under the claim and any man could go into it and see that it did not cut a quartz ledge or anything that remotely resembled one.

One plan of acquiring sudden wealth was to "salt" a wild cat claim and sell out while the excitement was up. The process was simple. The schemer located a worthless ledge, sunk a shaft on it, bought a wagon load of rich "Comstock" ore, dumped a portion of it into the shaft and piled the rest by its side, above ground. Then he showed the property to a simpleton and sold it to him at a high figure. Of course the wagon load of rich ore was all that the victim ever got out of his purchase. A most remarkable case of "salting" was that of the "North Ophir." It was claimed that this vein was a remote "extension" of the original "Ophir," a valuable mine on the "Comstock." For a few days everybody was talking about the rich developments in the North Ophir. It was said that it yielded perfectly pure silver in small, solid lumps. I went to the place with the owners, and found a shaft six or eight feet deep, in the bottom of which was a badly shattered vein of dull, yellowish, unpromising rock. One would as soon expect to find silver in a grindstone. We got out a pan of the rubbish and washed it in a puddle, and sure enough, among the sediment we found half a dozen black, bullet-looking pellets of unimpeachable "native" silver. Nobody had ever heard of such a thing before; science could not account for such a queer novelty. The stock rose to sixty-five dollars a foot, and at this figure the world-renowned tragedian, McKean Buchanan, bought a commanding interest and prepared to quit the stage once more—he was always doing that. And then it transpired that the mine had been "salted"—and not in any hackneyed way, either, but in a singularly bold, barefaced and peculiarly original and outrageous fashion. On one of the lumps of "native" silver was discovered the minted legend, "TED STATES OF," and then it was plainly apparent that the mine had been "salted" with melted half-dollars! The lumps thus obtained had been blackened till they resembled native silver, and were then mixed with the shattered rock in the bottom of the shaft. It is literally true. Of course the price of the stock at once fell to nothing, and the tragedian was ruined. But for this calamity we might have lost McKean Buchanan from the stage.

CHAPTER XLV

The "flush times" held bravely on. Something over two years before, Mr. Goodman and another journeyman printer, had borrowed forty dollars and set out from San Francisco to try their fortunes in the new city of Virginia. They found the *Territorial Enterprise,* a poverty-stricken weekly journal, gasping for breath and likely to die. They bought it, type, fixtures, goodwill and all, for a thousand dollars, on long time. The editorial sanctum, news-room, pressroom, publication office, bedchamber, parlor, and kitchen were all compressed into one apartment and it was a small one, too. The editors and printers slept on the floor, a Chinaman did their cooking, and the "imposing-stone" was the general dinner table. But now things were changed. The paper was a great daily, printed by steam; there were five editors and twenty-three compositors; the subscription price was sixteen dollars a year; the advertising rates were exorbitant, and the columns crowded. The paper was clearing from six to ten thousand dollars a month, and the "Enterprise Building" was finished and ready for occupation—a stately fireproof brick. Every day from five all the way up to eleven columns of "live" advertisements were left out or crowded into spasmodic and irregular "supplements."

The "Gould & Curry" company were erecting a monster hundred-stamp mill at a cost that ultimately fell little short of a million dollars. Gould & Curry stock paid heavy dividends—a rare thing, and an experience confined to the dozen or fifteen claims located on the "main lead," the "Comstock." The Superintendent of the Gould & Curry lived, rent free, in a fine house built and furnished by the company. He drove a fine pair of horses which were a present from the company, and his salary was twelve thousand dollars a year. The superintendent of another of the great mines traveled in grand state, had a salary of twenty-eight thousand dollars a year, and in a law suit in after days claimed that he was to have had one per cent, on the gross yield of the bullion likewise.

Money was wonderfully plenty. The trouble was, not how to get it,—but how to spend it, how to lavish it, get rid of it, squander it. And so it was a happy thing that just at this juncture the news came over the wires that a great United States Sanitary Commission had been formed and money was wanted for the relief of the wounded sailors and soldiers of the Union languishing in the Eastern hospitals. Right on the heels of it came word that San Francisco had responded superbly before the telegram was half a day old. Virginia rose as one man! A Sanitary Committee was hurriedly organized, and its chairman mounted a vacant cart in C street and tried to make the clamorous multitude understand that the rest of the committee were flying hither and thither and working with all their might and main, and that if the town would only wait an hour, an office would be ready, books opened, and the Commission prepared to receive contributions. His voice was drowned and his information lost in a ceaseless roar of cheers, and demands that the money be received *now*—they swore they would not wait. The chairman pleaded and argued, but, deaf to all entreaty, men plowed their way through the throng and rained checks of gold coin into the cart and skurried away for more. Hands clutching money, were thrust aloft out of the jam by men who hoped this eloquent appeal would cleave a road their strugglings could not open. The very Chinamen and Indians caught the excitement and dashed their half dollars into the cart without knowing or caring what it was all about. Women plunged into the crowd, trimly attired, fought their way to the cart with their coin, and emerged again, by and by, with their apparel in a state of hopeless dilapidation. It was the wildest mob Virginia had ever seen and the most determined and ungovernable; and when at last it abated its fury and dispersed, it had not a penny in its pocket. To use its own phraseology, it came there "flush" and went away "busted."

After that, the Commission got itself into systematic working order, and for weeks the contributions flowed into its treasury in a generous stream. Individuals and all sorts of organizations levied upon themselves a regular weekly tax for the sanitary fund, graduated according to their means, and there was not another grand universal outburst till the famous "Sanitary Flour Sack" came our way. Its history is peculiar and interesting. A former schoolmate of mine, by the name of Reuel Gridley, was living at the little city of Austin, in the Reese river country, at this time, and was the Democratic candidate for mayor. He and the Republican candidate made an agreement that the defeated man should be publicly presented with a fifty-pound sack of flour by the successful one, and should carry it home on his shoulder. Gridley was defeated. The new mayor gave him the sack of flour, and he shouldered it and carried it a mile or two, from Lower Austin to his home in Upper Austin, attended by a band of music and the whole population. Arrived there, he said he did not need the flour, and asked what the people thought he had better do with it. A voice said:

"Sell it to the highest bidder, for the benefit of the Sanitary fund."

The suggestion was greeted with a round of applause, and Gridley mounted a dry-goods box and assumed the role of auctioneer. The bids went higher and higher, as the sympathies of the pioneers awoke and expanded, till at last the sack was knocked down to a mill man at two hundred and fifty dollars, and his check taken. He was asked where he would have the flour delivered, and he said:

"Nowhere—sell it again."

Now the cheers went up royally, and the multitude were fairly in the spirit of the thing. So Gridley stood there and shouted and perspired till the sun went down; and when the crowd dispersed he had sold the sack to three hundred different people, and had taken in eight thousand dollars in gold. And still the flour sack was in his possession.

The news came to Virginia, and a telegram went back:

"Fetch along your flour sack!"

Thirty-six hours afterward Gridley arrived, and an afternoon mass meeting was held in the Opera House, and the auction began. But the sack had come sooner than it was expected; the people were not thoroughly aroused, and the sale dragged. At nightfall only five thousand dollars had been secured, and there was a crestfallen feeling in the community. However, there was no disposition to let the matter rest here and acknowledge vanquishment at the hands of the village of Austin. Till late in the night the principal citizens were at work arranging the morrow's campaign, and when they went to bed they had no fears for the result. At eleven the next morning a procession of open carriages, attended by clamorous bands of music and adorned with a moving display of flags, filed along C street and was soon in danger of blockade by a huzzaing multitude of citizens. In the first carriage şat Gridley, with the flour sack in prominent view, the latter splendid with bright paint and gilt lettering; also in the same carriage sat the mayor and the recorder. The other carriages contained the Common Council, the editors and reporters, and other people of imposing consequence. The crowd pressed to the corner of C and Taylor streets, expecting the sale to begin there, but they were disappointed, and also unspeakably surprised; for the cavalcade moved on as if Virginia had ceased to be of importance, and took its way over the "divide," toward the small town of Gold Hill. Telegrams had gone ahead to Gold Hill, Silver City and Dayton, and those communities were at fever heat and rife for the conflict. It was a very hot day, and wonderfully dusty. At the end of a short half hour we descended into Gold Hill with drums beating and colors flying, and enveloped in imposing clouds of dust. The whole population—men, women and children, Chinamen and Indians, were massed in the main street, all the flags in town were at the mast head, and the blare of the bands was drowned in cheers. Gridley stood up and asked who would make the first bid for the National Sanitary Flour Sack. Gen. W. said:

"The Yellow Jacket silver mining company offers a thousand dollars, coin!"

A tempest of applause followed. A telegram carried the news to Virginia, and fifteen minutes afterward the city's population was massed in the streets devouring the tidings—for it was part of the programme that the bulletin boards should do a good work that day. Every few minutes a new dispatch was bulletined from Gold Hill, and still the excitement grew. Telegrams began to return to us from Virginia beseeching Gridley to bring back the flour sack; but such was not the plan of the campaign. At the end of an hour Gold Hill's small population had paid a figure for the flour sack that awoke all the enthusiasm of Virginia when the grand total was displayed upon the bulletin boards. Then the Gridley cavalcade moved on, a giant refreshed with new lager beer and plenty of it—for the people brought it to the carriages without waiting to measure it—and within three hours more the expedition had carried Silver City and Dayton by storm and was on its way back covered with glory. Every move had been telegraphed and bulletined, and as the procession entered Virginia and filed down C street at half past eight in the evening the town was abroad in the thoroughfares, torches were glaring, flags flying, bands playing, cheer on cheer cleaving the air, and the city ready to surrender at discretion. The auction began, every bid was greeted with bursts of applause, and at the end of two hours and a half a population of fifteen thousand souls had paid in coin for a fifty-pound sack of flour a sum equal to forty thousand dollars in greenbacks! It was at a rate in the neighborhood of three dollars for each man, woman and child of the population. The grand total would have been twice as large, but the streets were very narrow, and hundreds who wanted to bid could not get within a block of the stand, and could not make themselves heard. These grew tired of waiting and many of them went home long before the auction was over. This was the greatest day Virginia every saw, perhaps.

Gridley sold the sack in Carson city and several California towns; also in San Francisco. Then he took it east and sold it in one or two Atlantic cities, I think. I am not sure of that, but I know that he finally carried it to St. Louis, where a monster Sanitary Fair was being held, and after selling it there for a large sum and helping on the enthusiasm by displaying the portly silver bricks which Nevada's donation had produced, he had the flour baked up into small cakes and retailed them at high prices.

It was estimated that when the flour sack's mission was ended it had been sold for a grand total of a hundred and fifty thousand dollars in greenbacks! This is probably the only instance on record where common family flour brought three thousand dollars a pound in the public market.

It is due to Mr. Gridley's memory to mention that the expenses of his sanitary flour sack expedition of fifteen thousand miles, going and returning, were paid in large part, if not entirely, out of his own pocket. The time he gave to it was not less than three months. Mr. Gridley was a soldier in the Mexican war and a pioneer Californian. He died at Stockton, California, in December, 1870, greatly regretted.

CHAPTER XLVI

There were nabobs in those days—in the "flush times," I mean. Every rich strike in the mines created one or two. I call to mind several of these. They were careless, easy-going fellows, as a general thing, and the community at large was as much benefited by their riches as they were themselves—possibly more, in some cases.

Two cousins, teamsters, did some hauling for a man and had to take a small segregated portion of a silver mine in lieu of $300 cash. They gave an outsider a third to open the mine, and they went on teaming. But not long. Ten months afterward the mine was out of debt and paying each owner $8,000 to $10,000 a month—say $100,000 a year.

One of the earliest nabobs that Nevada was delivered of wore $6,000 worth of diamonds in his bosom, and swore he was unhappy because he could not spend his money as fast as he made it.

Another Nevada nabob boasted an income that often reached $16,000 a month; and he used to love to tell how he had worked in the very mine that yielded it, for five dollars a day, when he first came to the country.

The silver and sage-brush State has knowledge of another of these pets of fortune—lifted from actual poverty to affluence almost in a single night—who was able to offer $100,000 for a position of high official distinction, shortly afterward, and did offer it—but failed to get it, his politics not being as sound as his bank account.

Then there was John Smith. He was a good, honest, kind-hearted soul, born and reared in the lower ranks of life, and miraculously ignorant. He drove a team, and owned a small ranch—a ranch that paid him a comfortable living, for although it yielded but little hay, what little it did yield was worth from $250 to $300 in gold per ton in the market. Presently Smith traded a few acres of the ranch for a small undeveloped silver mine in Gold Hill. He opened the mine and built a little unpretending ten-stamp mill. Eighteen months afterward he retired from the hay business, for his mining income had reached a most comfortable figure. Some people said it was $30,000 a month, and others said it was $60,000. Smith was very rich at any rate.

And then he went to Europe and traveled. And when he came back he was never tired of telling about the fine hogs he had seen in England, and the gorgeous sheep he had seen in Spain, and the fine cattle he had noticed in the vicinity of Rome. He was full of the wonders of the old world, and advised everybody to travel. He said a man never imagined what surprising things there were in the world till he had traveled.

One day, on board ship, the passengers made up a pool of $500, which was to be the property of the man who should come nearest to guessing the run of the vessel for the next twenty-four hours. Next day, toward noon, the figures were all in the purser's hands in sealed envelopes. Smith was serene and happy, for he had been bribing the engineer. But another party won the prize! Smith said:

"Here, that won't do! He guessed two miles wider of the mark than I did."

The purser said, "Mr. Smith, you missed it further than any man on board. We traveled two hundred and eight miles yesterday."

"Well, sir," said Smith, "that's just where I've got you, for I guessed two hundred and nine. If you'll look at my figgers again you'll find a 2 and two 0's, which stands for 200, don't it?—and after 'em you'll find a 9 (2009), which stands for two hundred and nine. I reckon I'll take that money, if you please."

The Gould & Curry claim comprised twelve hundred feet, and it all belonged originally to the two men whose names it bears. Mr. Curry owned two third of it—and he said that he sold it out for twenty-five hundred dollars in cash, and an old plug horse that ate up his market value in hay and barley in seventeen days by the watch. And he said that Gould sold out for a pair of second-hand government blankets and a bottle of whiskey that killed nine men in three hours, and that an unoffending stranger that smelt the cork was disabled for life. Four years afterward the mine thus disposed of was worth in the San Francisco market seven millions six hundred thousand dollars in gold coin.

In the early days a poverty-stricken Mexican who lived in a canyon directly back of Virginia City, had a stream of water as large as a man's wrist trickling from the hill-side on his premises. The Ophir Company segregated a hundred feet of their mine and traded it to him for the stream of water. The hundred feet proved to be the richest part of the entire mine; four years after the swap, its market value (including its mill) was $1,500,000.

An individual who owned twenty feet in the Ophir mine before its great riches were revealed to men, traded it for a horse, and a very sorry looking brute he was, too. A year or so afterward, when Ophir stock went up to $3,000 a foot, this man, who had not a cent, used to say he was the most startling example of magnificence and misery the world had ever seen—because he was able to ride a sixty-thousand-dollar horse—yet could not scrape up cash enough to buy a saddle, and was obliged to borrow one or ride bareback. He said if fortune were to give him another sixty-thousand-dollar horse it would ruin him.

A youth of nineteen, who was a telegraph operator in Virginia on a salary of a hundred dollars a month, and who, when he could not make out German names in the list of San Francisco steamer arrivals, used to ingeniously select and supply substitutes for them out of an old Berlin city directory, made himself rich by watching the mining telegrams that passed through his hands and buying and selling stocks accordingly, through a friend in San Francisco. Once when a private dispatch was sent from Virginia announcing a rich strike in a prominent mine and advising that the matter be kept secret till a large amount of the stock could be secured, he bought forty "feet" of the stock at twenty dollars a foot, and afterward sold half of it at eight hundred dollars a foot and the rest at double that figure. Within three months he was worth $150,000, and had resigned his telegraphic position.

Another telegraph operator who had been discharged by the company for divulging the secrets of the office, agreed with a moneyed man in San Francisco to furnish him the result of a great Virginia mining lawsuit within an hour after its private reception by the parties to it in San Francisco. For this he was to have a large percentage of the profits on purchases and sales made on it by his fellow-conspirator. So he went, disguised as a teamster, to a little wayside telegraph office in the mountains, got acquainted with the operator, and sat in the office day after day, smoking his pipe, complaining that his team was fagged out and unable to travel—and meantime listening to the dispatches as they passed clicking through the machine from Virginia. Finally the private dispatch announcing the result of the lawsuit sped over the wires, and as soon as he heard it he telegraphed his friend in San Francisco:

"Am tired waiting. Shall sell the team and go home."

It was the signal agreed upon. The word "waiting" left out, would have signified that the suit had gone the other way. The mock teamster's friend picked up a deal of the mining stock, at low figures, before the news became public, and a fortune was the result.

For a long time after one of the great Virginia mines had been incorporated, about fifty feet of the original location were still in the hands of a man who had never signed the incorporation papers. The stock became very valuable, and every effort was made to find this man, but he had disappeared. Once it was heard that he was in New York, and one or two speculators went east but failed to find him. Once the news came that he was in the Bermudas, and straightway a speculator or two hurried east and sailed for Bermuda—but he was not there. Finally he was heard of in Mexico, and a friend of his, a bar-keeper on a salary, scraped together a little money and sought him out, bought his "feet" for a hundred dollars, returned and sold the property for $75,000.

But why go on? The traditions of Silverland are filled with instances like these, and I would never get through enumerating them were I to attempt to do it. I only desired to give the reader an idea of a peculiarity of the "flush times" which I could not present so strikingly in any other way, and which some mention of was necessary to a realizing comprehension of the time and the country.

I was personally acquainted with the majority of the nabobs I have referred to, and so, for old acquaintance sake, I have shifted their occupations and experiences around in such a way as to keep the Pacific public from recognizing these once notorious men. No longer notorious, for the majority of them have drifted back into poverty and obscurity again.

In Nevada there used to be current the story of an adventure of two of her nabobs, which may or may not have occurred. I give it for what it is worth:

Col. Jim had seen somewhat of the world, and knew more or less of its ways; but Col. Jack was from the back settlements of the States, had led a life of arduous toil, and had never seen a city. These two, blessed with sudden wealth, projected a visit to New York,—Col. Jack to see the sights, and Col. Jim to guard his unsophistication from misfortune. They reached San Francisco in the night, and sailed in the morning. Arrived in New York, Col. Jack said:

"I've heard tell of carriages all my life, and now I mean to have a ride in one; I don't care what it costs. Come along."

They stepped out on the sidewalk, and Col. Jim called a stylish barouche. But Col. Jack said:

"*No*, sir! None of your cheap-John turn-outs for me. I'm here to have a good time, and money ain't any object. I mean to have the nobbiest rig that's going. Now here comes the very trick. Stop that yaller one with the pictures on it—don't you fret—I'll stand all the expenses myself."

So Col. Jim stopped an empty omnibus, and they got in. Said Col. Jack:

"Ain't it gay, though? Oh, no, I reckon not! Cushions, and windows, and pictures, till you can't rest. What would the boys say if they could see us cutting a swell like this in New York? By George, I wish they *could* see us."

Then he put his head out of the window, and shouted to the driver:

"Say, Johnny, this suits *me!*—suits yours truly, you bet, you!

I want this shebang all day. I'm *on* it, old man! Let 'em out! Make 'em go! We'll make it all right with *you,* sonny!''

The driver passed his hand through the strap-hole, and tapped for his fare—it was before the gongs came into common use. Col. Jack took the hand, and shook it cordially. He said:

"You twig me, old pard! All right between gents. Smell of *that,* and see how you like it!''

And he put a twenty-dollar gold piece in the driver's hand. After a moment the driver said he could not make change.

"Bother the change! Ride it out. Put it in your pocket."

Then to Col. Jim, with a sounding slap on his thigh:

"*Ain't* it style, though? Hanged if I don't hire this thing every day for a week."

The omnibus stopped, and a young lady got in. Col. Jack stared a moment, then nudged Col. Jim with his elbow:

"Don't say a word," he whispered. "Let her ride, if she wants to. Gracious, there's room enough."

The young lady got out her porte-monnaie, and handed her fare to Col. Jack.

"What's this for?" said he.

"Give it to the driver, please."

"Take back your money, madam. We can't allow it. You're welcome to ride here as long as you please, but this shebang's chartered, and we can't let you pay a cent."

The girl shrunk into a corner, bewildered. An old lady with a basket climbed in, and proffered her fare.

"Excuse me," said Col. Jack. "You're perfectly welcome here, madam, but we can't allow you to pay. Set right down there, mum, and don't you be the least uneasy. Make yourself just as free as if you was in your own turn-out."

Within two minutes, three gentlemen, two fat women, and a couple of children, entered.

"Come right along, friends," said Col. Jack; "don't mind *us.* This is a free blow-out." Then he whispered to Col. Jim, "New York ain't no sociable place, I don't reckon—it ain't no *name* for it!"

He resisted every effort to pass fares to the driver, and made everybody cordially welcome. The situation dawned on the people, and they pocketed their money, and delivered themselves up to covert enjoyment of the episode. Half a dozen more passengers entered.

"Oh, there's *plenty* of room," said Col. Jack. "Walk right in, and make yourselves at home. A blow-out ain't worth anything *as* a blow-out, unless a body has company." Then in a whisper to Col. Jim: "But *ain,'t* these New Yorkers friendly? And ain't they cool about it, too? Icebergs ain't anywhere. I reckon they'd tackle a hearse, if it was going their way."

More passengers got in; more yet, and still more. Both seats were filled, and a file of men were standing up, holding on to the cleats overhead. Parties with baskets and bundles were climbing up on the roof. Half-suppressed laughter rippled up from all sides.

"Well, for clean, cool, out-and-out cheek, if this don't bang anything that ever I saw, I'm an Injun!" whispered Col. Jack.

A Chinaman crowded his way in.

"I weaken!" said Col. Jack. "Hold on, driver! Keep your seats, ladies and gents. Just make yourselves free—everything's paid for. Driver, rustle these folks around as long as they're a mind to go—friends of ours, you know. Take them everywheres—and if you want more money, come to the St. Nicholas, and we'll make it all right. Pleasant journey to you, ladies and gents—go it just as long as you please—it shan't cost you a cent!"

The two comrades got out, and Col. Jack said:

"Jimmy, it's the sociablest place *I* ever saw. The Chinaman waltzed in as comfortable as anybody. If we'd staid awhile, I reckon we'd had some niggers. B' George, we'll have to barricade our doors to-night, or some of these ducks will be trying to sleep with us."

CHAPTER XLVII

Somebody has said that in order to know a community, one must observe the style of its funerals and know what manner of men they bury with most ceremony. I cannot say which class we buried with most eclat in our "flush times," the distinguished public benefactor or the distinguished rough—possibly the two chief grades or grand divisions of society honored their illustrious dead about equally; and hence, no doubt the philosopher I have quoted from would have needed to see two representative funerals in Virginia before forming his estimate of the people.

There was a grand time over Buck Fanshaw when he died. He was a representative citizen. He had "killed his man"—not in his own quarrel, it is true, but in defence of a stranger unfairly beset by numbers. He had kept a sumptuous saloon. He had been the proprietor of a dashing helpmeet whom he could have discarded without the formality of a divorce. He had held a high position in the fire department and been a very Warwick in politics. When he died there was great lamentation throughout the town, but especially in the vast bottom-stratum of society.

On the inquest it was shown that Buck Fanshaw, in the delirium of a wasting typhoid fever, had taken arsenic, shot himself through the body, cut his throat, and jumped out of a four-story window and broken his neck—and after due deliberation, the jury, sad and tearful, but with intelligence unblinded by its sorrow, brought in a verdict of death "by the visitation of God." What could the world do without juries?

Prodigious preparations were made for the funeral. All the vehicles in town were hired, all the saloons put in mourning, all the municipal and fire-company flags hung at half-mast, and all the firemen ordered to muster in uniform and bring their machines duly draped in black. Now—let us remark in parenthesis—as all the peoples of the earth had representative adventurers in the Silverland, and as each adventurer had brought the slang of his nation or his locality with him, the combination made the slang of Nevada the richest and the most infinitely varied and copious that had ever existed anywhere in the world, perhaps, except in the mines of California in the "early days." Slang was the language of Nevada. It was hard to preach a sermon without it, and be understood. Such phrases as "You bet!" "Oh, no, I reckon not!" "No Irish need apply," and a hundred others, became so common as to fall from the lips of a speaker unconsciously—and very often when they did not touch the subject under discussion and consequently failed to mean anything.

After Buck Fanshaw's inquest, a meeting of the short-haired brotherhood was held, for nothing can be done on the Pacific coast without a public meeting and an expression of sentiment. Regretful resolutions were passed and various committees appointed; among others, a committee of one was deputed to call on the minister, a fragile, gentle, spirituel new fledgling from an Eastern theological seminary, and as yet unacquainted with the ways of the mines. The committeeman, "Scotty" Briggs, made his visit; and in after days it was worth something to hear the minister tell about it. Scotty was a stalwart rough, whose customary suit, when on weighty official business, like committee work, was a fire helmet, flaming red flannel shirt, patent leather belt with spanner and revolver attached, coat hung over arm, and pants stuffed into boot tops. He formed something of a contrast to the pale theological student. It is fair to say of Scotty, however, in passing, that he had a warm heart, and a strong love for his friends, and never entered into a quarrel when he could reasonably keep out of it. Indeed, it was commonly said that whenever one of Scotty's fights was investigated, it always turned out that it had originally been no affair of his, but that out of native goodheartedness he had dropped in of his own accord to help the man who was getting the worst of it. He and Buck Fanshaw were bosom friends, for years, and had often taken adventurous "pot-luck" together. On one occasion, they had thrown off their coats and taken the weaker side in a fight among strangers, and after gaining a hard-earned victory, turned and found that the men they were helping had deserted early, and not only that, but had stolen their coats and made off with them! But to return to Scotty's visit to the minister. He was on a sorrowful mission, now, and his face was the picture of woe. Being admitted to the presence he sat down before the clergyman, placed his fire-hat on an unfinished manuscript sermon under the minister's nose, took from it a red silk handkerchief, wiped his brow and heaved a sigh of dismal impressiveness, explanatory of his business. He choked, and even shed tears; but with an effort he mastered his voice and said in lugubrious tones:

"Are you the duck that runs the gospel-mill next door?"

"Am I the—pardon me, I believe I do not understand?"

With another sigh and a half-sob, Scotty rejoined:

"Why you see we are in a bit of trouble, and the boys thought maybe you would give us a lift, if we'd tackle you—that is, if I've got the rights of it and you are the head clerk of the doxology-works next door."

"I am the shepherd in charge of the flock whose fold is next door."

"The which?"

"The spiritual adviser of the little company of believers whose sanctuary adjoins these premises."

Scotty scratched his head, reflected a moment, and then said:

"You ruther hold over me, pard. I reckon I can't call that hand. Ante and pass the buck."

"How? I beg pardon. What did I understand you to say?"

"Well, you've ruther got the bulge on me. Or maybe we've both got the bulge, somehow. You don't smoke me and I don't smoke you. You see, one of the boys has passed in his checks and we want to give him a good send-off, and so the thing I'm on now is to roust out somebody to jerk a little chin-music for us and waltz him through handsome."

"My friend, I seem to grow more and more bewildered. Your observations are wholly incomprehensible to me. Cannot you simplify them in some way? At first I thought perhaps I understood you, but I grope now. Would it not expedite matters if you restricted yourself to categorical statements of fact unencumbered with obstructing accumulations of metaphor and allegory?"

Another pause, and more reflection. Then, said Scotty:

"I'll have to pass, I judge."

"How?"

"You've raised me out, pard."

"I still fail to catch your meaning."

"Why, that last lead of yourn is too many for me—that's the idea. I can't neither trump nor follow suit."

The clergyman sank back in his chair perplexed. Scotty leaned his head on his hand and gave himself up to thought. Presently his face came up, sorrowful but confident.

"I've got it now, so's you can savvy," he said. "What we want is a gospel-sharp. See?"

"A what?"

"Gospel-sharp. Parson."

"Oh! Why did you not say so before? I am a clergyman—a parson."

"Now you talk! You see my blind and straddle it like a man. Put it there!"—extending a brawny paw, which closed over the minister's small hand and gave it a shake indicative of fraternal sympathy and fervent gratification.

"Now we're all right, pard. Let's start fresh. Don't you mind my snuffling a little—becuz we're in a power of trouble. You see, one of the boys has gone up the flume—"

"Gone where?"

"Up the flume—throwed up the sponge, you understand."

"Thrown up the sponge?"

"Yes—kicked the bucket—"

"Ah—has departed to that mysterious country from whose bourne no traveler returns."

"Return! I reckon not. Why pard, he's *dead!*"

"Yes, I understand."

"Oh, you do? Well I thought maybe you might be getting tangled some more. Yes, you see he's dead again—"

"*Again?* Why, has he ever been dead before?"

"Dead before? No! Do you reckon a man has got as many lives as a cat? But you bet you he's awful dead now, poor old boy, and I wish I'd never seen this day. I don't want no better friend than Buck Fanshaw. I knowed him by the back; and when I know a man and like him, I freeze to him—you hear *me*. Take him all round, pard, there never was a bullier man in the mines.

No man ever knowed Buck Fanshaw to go back on a friend. But it's all up, you know, it's all up. It ain't no use. They've scooped him."

"Scooped him?"

"Yes—death has. Well, well, well, we've got to give him up. Yes indeed. It's a kind of a hard world, after all, *ain't* it? But pard, he was a rustler! You ought to seen him get started once. He was a bully boy with a glass eye! Just spit in his face and give him room according to his strength, and it was just beautiful to see him peel and go in. He was the worst son of a thief that ever drawed breath. Pard, he was *on* it! He was on it bigger than an Injun!"

"On it? On what?"

"On the shoot. On the shoulder. On the fight, you understand. *He* didn't give a continental for *any*body. *Beg* your pardon, friend, for coming so near saying a cuss-word—but you see I'm on an awful strain, in this palaver, on account of having to cramp down and draw everything so mild. But we've got to give him up. There ain't any getting around that, I don't reckon. Now if we can get you to help plant him—"

"Preach the funeral discourse? Assist at the obsequies?"

"Obs'quies is good. Yes. That's it—that's our little game. We are going to get the thing up regardless, you know. He was always nifty himself, and so you bet you his funeral ain't going to be no slouch—solid silver door-plate on his coffin, six plumes on the hearse, and a nigger on the box in a biled shirt and a plug hat—how's that for high? And we'll take care of *you,* pard. We'll fix you all right. There'll be a kerridge for you; and whatever you want, you just 'scape out and we'll 'tend to it. We've got a shebang fixed up for you to stand behind, in No. 1's house, and don't you be afraid. Just go in and toot your horn, if you don't sell a clam. Put Buck through as bully as you can, pard, for anybody that knowed him will tell you that he was one of the whitest men that was ever in the mines. You can't draw it too strong. He never could stand it to see things going wrong. He's done more to make this town quiet and peaceable than any man in it. I've seen him lick four Greasers in eleven minutes, myself. If a thing wanted regulating, *he* warn't a man to go browsing around after somebody to do it, but he would prance in and regulate it himself. He warn't a Catholic. Scasely. He was down on 'em. His word was, 'No Irish need apply!' But it didn't make no difference about that when it came down to what a man's rights was—and so, when some roughs jumped the Catholic bone-yard and started in to stake out town-lots in it he *went* for 'em! And he *cleaned* 'em, too! I was there, pard, and I seen it myself.''

"That was very well indeed—at least the impulse was—whether the act was strictly defensible or not. Had deceased any religious convictions? That is to say, did he feel a dependence upon, or acknowledge allegiance to a higher power?''

More reflection.

"I reckon you've stumped me again, pard. Could you say it over once more, and say it slow?''

"Well, to simplify it somewhat, was he, or rather had he ever been connected with any organization sequestered from secular concerns and devoted to self-sacrifice in the interests of morality?''

"All down but nine—set 'em up on the other alley, pard.''

"What did I understand you to say?''

"Why, you're most too many for me, you know. When you get in with your left I hunt grass every time. Every time you draw, you fill; but I don't seem to have any luck. Lets have a new deal.''

"How? Begin again?''

"That's it.''

"Very well. Was he a good man, and—''

"There—I see that; don't put up another chip till I look at my hand. A good man, says you? Pard, it ain't no name for it. He was the best man that ever—pard, you would have doted on that man. He could lam any galoot of his inches in America. It was him that put down the riot last election before it got a start; and everybody said he was the only man that could have done it. He waltzed in with a spanner in one hand and a trumpet in the other, and sent fourteen men home on a shutter in less than three minutes. He had that riot all broke up and prevented nice before anybody ever got a chance to strike a blow. He was always for peace, and he would *have* peace—he could not stand disturbances. Pard, he was a great loss to this town. It would please the boys if you could chip in something like that and do him justice. Here once when the Micks got to throwing stones through the Methodis' Sunday school windows, Buck Fanshaw, all of his own notion, shut up his saloon and took a couple of six-shooters and mounted guard over the Sunday school. Says he, 'No Irish need apply!' And they didn't. He was the bulliest man in the mountains, pard! He could run faster, jump higher, hit harder, and hold more tangle-foot whisky without spilling it than any man in seventeen counties. Put that in, pard—it'll please the boys more than anything you could say. And you can say, pard, that he never shook his mother.''

"Never shook his mother?"

"That's it—any of the boys will tell you so."

"Well, but why *should* he shake her?"

"That's what *I* say—but some people does."

"Not people of any repute?"

"Well, some that averages pretty so-so."

"In my opinion the man that would offer personal violence to his own mother, outght to—"

"Cheese it, pard; you've banked your ball clean outside the string. What I was a drivin' at, was, that he never *throwed off* on his mother—don't you see? No indeedy. He give her a house to live in, and town lots, and plenty of money; and he looked after her and took care of her all the time; and when she was down with the small-pox I'm d—d if he didn't set up nights and nuss her himself! *Beg* your pardon for saying it, but it hopped out too quick for yours truly. You've treated me like a gentleman, pard, and I ain't the man to hurt your feelings intentional. I think you're white. I think you're a square man, pard. I like you, and I'll lick any man that don't. I'll lick him till he can't tell himself from a last year's corpse! Put it *there!*" [Another fraternal handshake—and exit.]

The obsequies were all that "the boys" could desire. Such a marvel of funeral pomp had never been seen in Virginia. The plumed hearse, the dirge-breathing brass bands, the closed marts of business, the flags drooping at half mast, the long, plodding procession of uniformed secret societies, military battalions and fire companies, draped engines, carriages of officials, and citizens in vehicles and on foot, attracted multitudes of spectators to the sidewalks, roofs and windows; and for years afterward, the degree of grandeur attained by any civic display in Virginia was determined by comparison with Buck Fanshaw's funeral.

Scotty Briggs, as a pall-bearer and a mourner, occupied a prominent place at the funeral, and when the sermon was finished and the last sentence of the prayer for the dead man's soul ascended, he responded, in a low voice, but with feeling:

"Amen. No Irish need apply."

As the bulk of the response was without apparent relevancy, it was probably nothing more than a humble tribute to the memory of the friend that was gone; for, as Scotty had once said, it was "his word."

Scotty Briggs, in after days, achieved the distinction of becoming the only convert to religion that was ever gathered from the Virginia roughs; and it transpired that the man who had it in him to espouse the quarrel of the weak out of inborn nobility of spirit was no mean timber whereof to construct a Christian. The making him one did not warp his generosity or diminish his courage; on the contrary it gave intelligent direction to the one and a broader field to the other. If his Sunday-school class progressed faster than the other classes, was it matter for wonder? I think not. He talked to his pioneer small-fry in a language they understood! It was my large privilege, a month before he died, to hear him tell the beautiful story of Joseph and his brethren to his class "without looking at the book." I leave it to the reader to fancy what it was like, as it fell, riddled with slang, from the lips of that grave, earnest teacher, and was listened to by his little learners with a consuming interest that showed that they were as unconscious as he was that any violence was being done to the sacred proprieties!

CHAPTER XLVIII

The first twenty-six graves in the Virginia cemetery were occupied by *murdered* men. So everybody said, so everybody believed, and so they will always say and believe. The reason why there was so much slaughtering done, was, that in a new mining district the rough element predominates, and a person is not respected until he has "killed his man." That was the very expression used.

If an unknown individual arrived, they did not inquire if he was capable, honest, industrious, but—had he killed his man? If he had not, he gravitated to his natural and proper position, that of a man of small consequence; if he had, the cordiality of his reception was graduated according to the number of his dead. It was tedious work struggling up to a position of influence with bloodless hands; but when a man came with the blood of half a dozen men on his soul, his worth was recognized at once and his acquaintance sought.

In Nevada, for a time, the lawyer, the editor, the banker, the chief deperado, the chief gambler, and the saloon keeper, occupied the same level in society, and it was the highest. The cheapest and easiest way to become an influential man and be looked up to by the community at large, was to stand behind a bar, wear a cluster-diamond pin, and sell whisky. I am not sure but that the saloon-keeper held a shade higher rank than any other member of society. His opinion had weight. It was his privilege to say how the elections should go. No great movement could succeed without the countenance and direction of the saloon-keepers. It was a high favor when the chief saloon-keeper consented to serve in the legislature or the board of aldermen. Youthful ambition hardly aspired so much to the honors of the law, or the army and navy as to the dignity of proprietorship in a saloon.

To be a saloon-keeper and kill a man was to be illustrious. Hence the reader will not be surprised to learn that more than one man was killed in Nevada under hardly the pretext of provocation, so impatient was the slayer to achieve reputation and throw off the galling sense of being held in indifferent repute by his associates. I knew two youths who tried to "kill their men" for no other reason—and got killed themselves for their pains. "There goes the man that killed Bill Adams" was higher praise and a sweeter sound in the ears of this sort of people than any other speech that admiring lips could utter.

The men who murdered Virginia's original twenty-six cemetery-occupants were never punished. Why? Because Alfred the Great, when he invented trial by jury, and knew that he had admirably framed it to secure justice in his age of the world, was not aware that in the nineteenth century the condition of things would be so entirely changed that unless he rose from the grave and altered the jury plan to meet the emergency, it would prove the most ingenious and infallible agency for *defeating* justice that human wisdom could contrive. For how could he imagine that we simpletons would go on using his jury plan after circumstances had stripped it of its usefulness, any more than he could imagine that we would go on using his candle-clock after we had invented chronometers? In his day news could not travel fast, and hence he could easily find a jury of honest, intelligent men who had not heard of the case they were called to try—but in our day of telegraphs and newspapers his plan compels us to swear in juries composed of fools and rascals, because the system rigidly excludes honest men and men of brains.

I remember one of those sorrowful farces, in Virginia, which we call a jury trial. A noted desperado killed Mr. B., a good citizen, in the most wanton and cold-blooded way. Of course the papers were full of it, and all men capable of reading, read about it. And of course all men not deaf and dumb and idiotic, talked about it. A jury-list was made out, and Mr. B. L., a prominent banker and a valued citizen, was questioned precisely as he would have been questioned in any court in America:

"Have you heard of this homicide?"

"Yes."

"Have you held conversations upon the subject?"

"Yes."

"Have you formed or expressed opinions about it?"

"Yes."

"Have you read the newspaper accounts of it?"

"Yes."

"We do not want you."

A minister, intelligent, esteemed, and greatly respected; a merchant of high character and known probity; a mining superintendent of intelligence and unblemished reputation; a quartz mill owner of excellent standing, were all questioned in the same way, and all set aside. Each said the public talk and the newspaper reports had not so biased his mind but that sworn testimony would overthrow his previously formed opinions and enable him to render a verdict without prejudice and in accordance with the facts. But of course such men could not be trusted with the case. Ignoramuses alone could mete out unsullied justice.

When the peremptory challenges were all exhausted, a jury of twelve men was impaneled—a jury who swore they had neither heard, read, talked about nor expressed an opinion concerning a murder which the very cattle in the corrals, the Indians in the sage-brush and the stones in the streets were cognizant of! It was a jury composed of two desperadoes, two low beer-house politicians, three bar-keepers, two ranchmen who could not read, and three dull, stupid, human donkeys! It actually came out afterward, that one of these latter thought that incest and arson were the same thing.

The verdict rendered by this jury was, Not Guilty. What else could one expect?

The jury system puts a ban upon intelligence and honesty, and a premium upon ignorance, stupidity and perjury. It is a shame that we must continue to use a worthless system because it *was* good a thousand years ago. In this age, when a gentleman of high social standing, intelligence and probity, swears that testimony given under solemn oath will outweigh, with him, street talk and newspaper reports based upon mere hearsay, he is worth a hundred jurymen who will swear to their own ignorance and stupidity, and justice would be far safer in his hands than in theirs. Why could not the jury law be so altered as to give men of brains and honesty an *equal chance* with fools and miscreants? Is it right to show the present favoritism to one class of men and inflict a disability on another, in a land whose boast is that all its citizens are free and equal? I am a candidate for the legislature. I desire to tamper with the jury law. I wish to so alter it as to put a premium on intelligence and character, and close the jury box against idiots, blacklegs, and people who do not read news-papers. But no doubt I shall be defeated—every effort I make to save the country "misses fire."

My idea, when I began this chapter, was to say something about desperadoism in the "flush times" of Nevada. To attempt a portrayal of that era and that land, and leave out the blood and carnage, would be like portraying Mormondom and leaving out polygamy. The desperado stalked the streets with a swagger graded according to the number of his homicides, and a nod of recognition from him was sufficient to make a humble admirer happy for the rest of the day. The deference that was paid to a desperado of wide reputation, and who "kept his private graveyard," as the phrase went, was marked, and cheerfully ac-corded. When he moved along the sidewalk in his excessively long-tailed frock-coat, shiny stump-toed boots, and with dainty little slouch hat tipped over left eye, the small-fry roughs made room for his majesty; when he entered the restaurant, the waiters deserted bankers and merchants to overwhelm him with obsequious service; when he shouldered his way to a bar, the shouldered parties wheeled indignantly, recognized him, and —apologized. They got a look in return that froze their marrow, and by that time a curled and breast-pinned bar keeper was beaming over the counter, proud of the established acquaint-anceship that permitted such a familiar form of speech as:

"How're ye, Billy, old fel? Glad to see you. What'll you take—the old thing?"

The "old thing" meant his customary drink, of course.

The best known names in the Territory of Nevada were those belonging to these long-tailed heroes of the revolver. Orators, Governors, capitalists and leaders of the legislature enjoyed a degree of fame, but it seemed local and meagre when contrasted with the fame of such men as Sam Brown, Jack Williams, Billy Mulligan, Farmer Pease, Sugarfoot Mike, Pock Marked Jake, El Dorado Johnny, Jack McNabb, Joe McGee, Jack Harris, Six-fingered Pete, etc., etc. There was a long list of them. They were brave, reckless men, and traveled with their lives in their hands. To give them their due, they did their killing principally among themselves, and seldom molested peaceable citizens, for they considered it small credit to add to their trophies so cheap a bauble as the death of a man who was "not on the shoot," as they phrased it. They killed each other on slight provocation, and hoped and expected to be killed themselves—for they held it almost shame to die otherwise than "with their boots on," as they expressed it.

I remember an instance of a desperado's contempt for such

small game as a private citizen's life. I was taking a late supper in a restaurant one night, with two reporters and a little printer named—Brown, for instance—any name will do. Presently a stranger with a long-tailed coat on came in, and not noticing Brown's hat, which was lying in a chair, sat down on it. Little Brown sprang up and became abusive in a moment. The stranger smiled, smoothed out the hat, and offered it to Brown with profuse apologies couched in caustic sarcasm, and begged Brown not to destroy him. Brown threw off his coat and challenged the man to fight—abused him, threatened him, impeached his courage, and urged and even implored him to fight; and in the meantime the smiling stranger placed himself under our protection in mock distress. But presently he assumed a serious tone, and said:

"Very well, gentlemen, if we must fight, we must, I suppose. But don't rush into danger and then say I gave you no warning. I am more than a match for all of you when I get started. I will give you proofs, and then if my friend here still insists, I will try to accommodate him."

The table we were sitting at was about five feet long, and unusually cumbersome and heavy. He asked us to put our hands on the dishes and hold them in their places a moment—one of them was a large oval dish with a portly roast on it. Then he sat down, tilted up one end of the table, set two of the legs on his knees, took the end of the table between his teeth, took his hands away, and pulled down with his teeth till the table came up to a level position, dishes and all! He said he could lift a keg of nails with his teeth. He picked up a common glass tumbler and bit a semi-circle out of it. Then he opened his bosom and showed us a net-work of knife and bullet scars; showed us more on his arms and face, and said he believed he had bullets enough in his body to make a pig of lead. He was armed to the teeth. He closed with the remark that he was Mr.—— of Cariboo—a celebrated name whereat we shook in our shoes. I would publish the name, but for the suspicion that he might come and carve me. He finally inquired if Brown still thirsted for blood. Brown turned the thing over in his mind a moment, and then—asked him to supper.

With the permission of the reader, I will group together, in the next chapter, some samples of life in our small mountain village in the old days of desperadoism. I was there at the time. The reader will observe peculiarities in our *official* society; and he will observe also, an instance of how, in new countries, murders breed murders.

CHAPTER XLIX

An extract or two from the newspapers of the day will furnish a photograph that can need no embellishment:

FATAL SHOOTING AFFRAY.—An affray occurred, last evening, in a billiard saloon on C street, between *Deputy Marshal Jack Williams* and Wm. Brown, which resulted in the immediate death of the latter. There had been some difficulty between the parties for several months.

An inquest was immediately held, and the following testimony adduced:

Officer GEO. BIRDSALL, sworn, says:—I was told Wm. Brown was drunk and was looking for Jack Williams; so soon as I heard that I started for the parties to prevent a collision; went into the billiard saloon; saw Billy Brown running around, saying if anybody had anything against him to show cause; he was talking in a boisterous manner, and officer Perry took him to the other end of the room to talk to him; Brown came back to me; remarked to me that he thought he was as good as anybody, and knew how to take care of himself; he passed by me and went to the bar; don't know whether he drank or not; Williams was at the end of the billiard-table, next to the stairway; Brown, after going to the bar, came back and said he was as good as any man in the world; he had then walked out to the end of the first billiard-table from the bar; I moved closer to them, supposing there would be a fight; as Brown drew his pistol I caught hold of it; he had fired one shot at Williams; don't know the effect of it; caught hold of him with one hand, and took hold of the pistol and turned it up; think he fired once after I caught hold of the pistol; I wrenched the pistol from him; walked to the end of the billiard-table and told a party that I had Brown's pistol, and to stop shooting; I think four shots were fired in all; after walking out, Mr. Foster remarked that Brown was shot dead.

Oh, there was no excitement about it—he merely "remarked" the small circumstance!

Four months later the following item appeared in the same paper (the *Enterprise*). In this item the name of one of the city officers above referred to *(Deputy Marshal Jack Williams)* occurs again:

ROBBERY AND DESPERATE AFFRAY.—On Tuesday night, a German named Charles Hurtzal, engineer in a mill at Silver City, came to this place, and visited the hurdy-gurdy house on B street. The music, dancing and Teutonic maidens awakened memories of Faderland until our German friend was carried away with rapture. He evidently had money, and was spending it freely. Late in the evening Jack Williams and Andy Blessington invited him down stairs to take a cup of coffee. Williams proposed a game of cards and went up stairs to procure a deck, but not finding any returned. On the stairway he met the German, and drawing his pistol knocked him down and rifled his pockets of some seventy dollars. Hurtzal dared give no alarm, as he was told, with a pistol at this head, if he made any noise or exposed them, they would blow his brains out. So effectually was he frightened that he made no complaint, until his friends forced him. Yesterday a warrant was issued, but the culprits had disappeared.

This efficient city officer, Jack Williams, had the common reputation of being a burglar, a highwayman and a desperado. It was said that he had several times drawn his revolver and levied money contributions on citizens at dead of night in the public streets of Virginia.

Five months after the above item appeared, Williams was assassinated while sitting at a card table one night; a gun was thrust through the crack of the door and Williams dropped from his chair riddled with balls. It was said, at the time, that Williams had been for some time aware that a party of his own sort (desperadoes) had sworn away his life; and it was generally believed among the people that Williams's friends and enemies would make the assassination memorable—and useful, too—by a wholesale destruction of each other.*

It did not so happen, but still, times were not dull during the next twenty-four hours, for within that time a woman was killed by a pistol shot, a man was brained with a slung shot, and a man named Reeder was also disposed of permanently. Some matters in the *Enterprise* account of the killing of Reeder are worth noting—especially the accommodating complaisance of a Virginia justice of the peace. The italics in the following narrative are mine:

MORE CUTTING AND SHOOTING.—The devil seems to have again broken loose in our town. Pistols and guns explode and knives gleam in our streets as in early times. When there has been a long season of

---

*However, one prophecy was verified, at any rate. It was asserted by the desperadoes that one of their brethren (Joe McGee, *a special policeman*) was known to be the conspirator chosen by lot to assassinate Williams; and they also asserted that doom had been pronounced against McGee, and that he would be assassinated in exactly the same manner that had been adopted for the destruction of Williams—a prophecy which came true a year later. After twelve months of distress (for McGee saw a fancied assassin in every man that approached him), he made the last of many efforts to get out of the country unwatched. He went to Carson and sat down in a saloon to wait for the stage—it would leave at four in the morning. But as the night waned and the crowd thinned, he grew uneasy, and told the bar-keeper that assassins were on his track. The bar-keeper told him to stay in the middle of the room, then, and not go near the door, or the window by the stove. But a fatal fascination seduced him to the neighborhood of the stove every now and then, and repeatedly the bar-keeper brought him back to the middle of the room and warned him to remain there. But he could not. At three in the morning he again returned to the stove and sat down by a stranger. Before the bar-keeper could get to him with another warning whisper, some one outside fired through the window and riddled McGee's breast with slugs, killing him almost instantly. By the same discharge the stranger at McGee's side also received attentions which proved fatal in the course of two or three days.

quiet, people are slow to wet their hands in blood; but once blood is spilled, cutting and shooting come easy. Night before last Jack Williams was assassinated, and yesterday forenoon we had more bloody work, growing out of the killing of Williams, and on the same street in which he met his death. It appears that Tom Reeder, a friend of Williams, and George Gumbert were talking, at the meat market of the latter, about the killing of Williams the previous night, when Reeder said it was a most cowardly act to shoot a man in such a way, giving him "no show." Gumbert said that Williams had "as good a show as he gave Billy Brown," meaning the man killed by Williams last March. Reeder said it was a d—d lie, that Williams had no show at all. At this, Gumbert drew a knife and stabbed Reeder, cutting him in two places in the back. One stroke of the knife cut into the sleeve of Reeder's coat and passed downward in a slanting direction through his clothing, and entered his body at the small of the back; another blow struck more squarely, and made a much more dangerous wound. Gumbert gave himself up to the officers of justice, and was shortly after discharged by Justice Atwill, *on his own recognizance,* to appear for trial at six o'clock in the evening. In the meantime Reeder had been taken into the office of Dr. Owens, where his wounds were properly dressed. *One of his wounds was considered quite dangerous, and it was thought by many that it would prove fatal. But being considerably under the influence of liquor, Reeder did not feel his wounds as he otherwise would, and he got up and went into the street.* He went to the meat market and renewed his quarrel with Gumbert, threatening his life. Friends tried to interfere to put a stop to the quarrel and get the parties away from each other. In the Fashion Saloon Reeder made threats against the life of Gumbert, saying he would kill him, and it is said that *he requested the officers not to arrest Gumbert, as he intended to kill him.* After these threats Gumbert went off and procured a double-barreled shot gun, loaded with buck-shot or revolver balls, and went after Reeder. Two or three persons were assisting him along the street, trying to get him home, and had him just in front of the store of Klopstock & Harris, when Gumbert came across toward him from the opposite side of the street with his gun. He came up within about ten or fifteen feet of Reeder, and called out to those with him to "look out! get out of the way!" and they had only time to heed the warning, when he fired. Reeder was at the time attempting to screen himself behind a large cask, which stood against the awning post of Klopstock & Harris's store, but some of the balls took effect in the lower part of his breast, and he reeled around forward and fell in front of the cask. Gumbert then raised his gun and fired the second barrel, which missed Reeder and entered the ground. At the time that this occurred, there were a great many persons on the street in the vicinity, and a number of them called out to Gumbert, when they saw him raise his gun, to "hold on," and "don't shoot!" The cutting took place about ten o'clock and the shooting about twelve. After the shooting the street was instantly crowded with the inhabitants of that part of the town, some appearing much excited and laughing—declaring that it looked like the "good old times of '60.'' Marshal Perry and officer Birdsall were near when the shooting occurred, and Gumbert was immediately arrested and his gun taken from him, when he was marched off to jail. Many persons who were attracted to the spot where this bloody work had just taken place, looked bewildered and seemed to be asking themselves what was to happen next, appearing in doubt as to whether the killing mania had reached its climax, or whether we were to turn in and have a grand killing spell, shooting whoever might have given us offence. It was whispered around that it was not all over yet—five or six more were to be killed before night. Reeder was taken to the Virginia City Hotel, and doctors called in to examine his wounds. They found that two or three balls had entered his right side; one of them appeared to have passed through the substance of the lungs, while another passed into the liver. Two balls were also found to have struck one of his legs. As some of the balls struck the cask, the wounds in Reeder's leg were probably from these, glancing downwards, though they might have been caused by the second shot fired. After being shot, Reeder said when he got on his feet—smiling as he spoke—"It will take better shooting than that to kill me.'' The doctors consider it almost impossible for him to recover, but as he has an excellent constitution he may survive, notwithstanding the number and dangerous character of the wounds he has received. The town appears to be perfectly quiet at present, as though the late stormy times had cleared our moral atmosphere; but who can tell in what quarter clouds are lowering or plots ripening?

Reeder—or at least what was left of him—survived his wounds two days! Nothing was ever done with Gumbert.

Trial by jury is the palladium of our liberties. I do not know what a palladium is, having never seen a palladium, but it is a good thing no doubt at any rate. Not less than a hundred men have been murdered in Nevada—perhaps I would be within bounds if I said three hundred—and as far as I can learn, only two persons have suffered the death penalty there. However, four or five who had no money and no political influence have been punished by imprisonment—one languished in prison as much as eight months, I think. However, I do not desire to be extravagant—it may have been less.

CHAPTER L

These murder and jury statistics remind me of a certain very extraordinary trial and execution of twenty years ago; it is a scrap of history familiar to all old Californians, and worthy to be known by other peoples of the earth that love simple, straightforward justice unencumbered with nonsense. I would apologize for this digression but for the fact that the information I am about to offer is apology enough in itself. And since I digress constantly anyhow, perhaps it is as well to eschew apologies altogether and thus prevent their growing irksome.

Capt. Ned Blakely—that name will answer as well as any other fictitious one (for he was still with the living at last accounts, and may not desire to be famous)—sailed ships out of the harbor of San Francisco for many years. He was a stalwart, warm-hearted, eagle-eyed veteran, who had been a sailor nearly fifty years—a sailor from early boyhood. He was a rough, honest creature, full of pluck, and just as full of hard-headed simplicity, too. He hated trifling conventionalities—"business" was the word, with him. He had all a sailor's vindictiveness against the quips and quirks of the law, and steadfastly believed that the first and last aim and object of the law and lawyers was to defeat justice.

He sailed for the Chincha Islands in command of a guano ship. He had a fine crew, but his negro mate was his pet—on him he had for years lavished his admiration and esteem. It was Capt. Ned's first voyage to the Chinchas, but his fame had gone before him—the fame of being a man who would fight at the dropping of a handkerchief, when imposed upon, and would stand no nonsense. It was a fame well earned. Arrived in the islands, he found that the staple of conversation was the exploits of one Bill Noakes, a bully, the mate of a trading ship. This man had created a small reign of terror there. At nine o'clock at night, Capt. Ned, all alone, was pacing his deck in the starlight. A form ascended the side, and approached him. Capt. Ned said:

"Who goes there?"

"I'm Bill Noakes, the best man in the islands."

"What do you want aboard this ship?"

"I've heard of Capt. Ned Blakely, and one of us is a better man that 'tother—I'll know which, before I go ashore."

"You've come to the right shop—I'm your man. I'll learn you to come aboard this ship without an *in*vite."

He seized Noakes, backed him against the mainmast, pounded his face to a pulp, and then threw him overboard.

Noakes was not convinced. He returned the next night, got the pulp renewed, and went overboard head first, as before. He was satisfied.

A week after this, while Noakes was carousing with a sailor crowd on shore, at noonday, Capt. Ned's colored mate came along, and Noakes tried to pick a quarrel with him. The negro evaded the trap, and tried to get away. Noakes followed him up; the negro began to run; Noakes fired on him with a revolver and killed him. Half a dozen sea-captains witnessed the whole affair.

Noakes retreated to the small after-cabin of his ship, with two other bullies, and gave out that death would be the portion of any man that intruded there. There was no attempt made to follow the villains; there was no disposition to do it, and indeed very little thought of such an enterprise. There were no courts and no officers; there was no government; the islands belonged to Peru, and Peru was far away; she had no official representative on the ground; and neither had any other nation.

However, Capt. Ned was not perplexing his head about such things. They concerned him not. He was boiling with rage and furious for justice. At nine o'clock at night he loaded a double-barreled gun with slugs, fished out a pair of handcuffs, got a ship's lantern, summoned his quartermaster, and went ashore. He said:

"Do you see that ship there at the dock?"

"Ay-ay, sir."

"It's the Venus."

"Ay-ay, sir."

"You—you know *me*."

"Ay-ay, sir."

"Very well, then. Take the lantern. Carry it just under your chin. I'll walk behind you and rest this gun-barrel on your shoulder, p'inting forward—so. Keep your lantern well up, so's I can see things ahead of you good. I'm going to march in on Noakes—and take him—and jug the other chaps. If you flinch—well, you know *me*."

"Ay-ay, sir."

In this order they filed aboard softly, arrived at Noakes's den, the quartermaster pushed the door open, and the lantern revealed the three desperadoes sitting on the floor. Capt. Ned said:

"I'm Ned Blakely. I've got you under fire. Don't you move without orders—any of you. You two kneel down in the corner; faces to the wall—now. Bill Noakes, ptu these handcuffs on; now come up close. Quartermaster, fasten 'em. All right. Don't stir, sir. Quartermaster, put the key in the outside of the door. Now, men, I'm going to lock you two in; and if you try to burst through this door—well, you've heard of *me*. Bill Noakes, fall in ahead, and march. All set. Quartermaster, lock the door."

Noakes spent the night on board Blakely's ship, a prisoner under strict guard. Early in the morning Capt. Ned called in all the sea-captains in the harbor and invited them, with nautical ceremony, to be present on board his ship at nine o'clock to witness the hanging of Noakes at the yard-arm!

"What! The man has not been tried."

"Of course he hasn't. But didn't he kill the nigger?"

"Certainly he did; but you are not thinking of hanging him without a trial?"

"*Trial!* What do I want to try him for, if he killed the nigger?"

"Oh, Capt. Ned, this will *never* do. Think how it will sound."

"Sound be hanged! *Didn't he kill the nigger]*"

"Certainly, certainly, Capt. Ned,—nobody denies that,—but—"

"Then I'm going to *hang* him, that's all. Everybody I've talked to talks just the same way you do. Everybody says he killed the nigger, everybody knows he killed the nigger, and yet every lubber of you wants him *tried* for it. I don't understand such bloody foolishness as that. *Tried!* Mind you, I don't object to trying him, if it's got to be done to give satisfaction; and I'll be there, and chip in and help, too; but put it off till afternoon—put it off till afternoon, for I'll have my hands middling full till after the burying—"

"Why, what do you mean? Are you going to hang him *any how*—and try him afterward?"

"Didn't I *say* I was going to hang him? I never saw such people as you. What's the difference? You ask a favor, and then you ain't satisfied when you get it. Before or after's all one—*you* know how the trial will go. He killed the nigger. Say—I must be going. If your mate would like to come to the hanging, fetch him along. I like him."

There was a stir in the camp. The captains came in a body and pleaded with Capt. Ned not to do this rash thing. They promised that they would create a court composed of captains of the best character; they would empanel a jury; they would conduct everything in a way becoming the serious nature of the business in hand, and give the case an impartial hearing and the accused a fair trial. And they said it would be murder, and punishable by the American courts if he persisted and hung the accused on his ship. They pleaded hard. Capt. Ned said:

"Gentlemen, I'm not stubborn and I'm not unreasonable. I'm always willing to do just as near right as I can. How long will it take?"

"Probably only a little while."

"And can I take him up the shore and hang him as soon as you are done?"

"If he is proven guilty he shall be hanged without unnecessary delay."

"*If* he's proven guilty. Great Neptune, *ain't* he guilty? This beats my time. Why you all *know* he's guilty."

But at last they satisfied him that they were projecting nothing underhanded. Then he said:

"Well, all right. You go on and try him and I'll go down and overhaul his conscience and prepare him to go—like enough he needs it, and I don't want to send him off without a show for hereafter."

This was another obstacle. They finally convinced him that it was necessary to have the accused in court. Then they said they would send a guard to bring him.

"No, sir, I prefer to fetch him myself—he don't get out of *my* hands. Besides, I've got to go to the ship to get a rope, anyway."

The court assembled with due ceremony, empaneled a jury, and presently Capt. Ned entered, leading the prisoner with one hand and carrying a Bible and a rope in the other. He seated himself by the side of his captive and told the court to "up anchor and make sail." Then he turned a searching eye on the jury, and detected Noakes's friends, the two bullies. He strode over and said to them confidentially:

"You're here to interfere, you see. Now you vote right, do you hear?—or else there'll be a double-barreled inquest here when this trial's off, and your remainders will go home in a couple of baskets."

The caution was not without fruit. The jury was a unit—the verdict, "Guilty."

Capt. Ned sprung to his feet and said:

"Come along—you're my meat *now*, my lad, anyway. Gentlemen you've done yourselves proud. I invite you all to come and see that I do it all straight. Follow me to the canyon, a mile above here."

The court informed him that a sheriff had been appointed to do the hanging, and—

Capt. Ned's patience was at an end. His wrath was boundless. The subject of a sheriff was judiciously dropped.

When the crowd arrived at the canyon, Capt. Ned climbed a tree and arranged the halter, then came down and noosed his man. He opened his Bible, and laid aside his hat. Selecting a chapter at random, he read it through, in a deep bass voice and with sincere solemnity. Then he said:

"Lad, you are about to go aloft and give an account of yourself; and the lighter a man's manifest is, as far as sin's concerned, the better for him. Make a clean breast, man, and carry a log with you that'll bear inspection. You killed the nigger?"

No reply. A long pause.

The captain read another chapter, pausing, from time to time,

751

to impress the effect. Then he talked an earnest, persuasive sermon to him, and ended by repeating the question:

"Did you kill the nigger?"

No reply—other than a malignant scowl. The captain now read the first and second chapters of Genesis, with deep feeling— paused a moment, closed the book reverently, and said with a perceptible savor of satisfaction:

"There. Four chapters. There's few that would have took the pains with you that I have."

Then he swung up the condemned, and made the rope fast; stood by and timed him half an hour with his watch, and then delivered the body to the court. A little after, as he stood contemplating the motionless figure, a doubt came into his face; evidently he felt a twinge of conscience—a misgiving—and he said with a sigh:

"Well, p'raps I ought to burnt him, maybe. But I was trying to do for the best."

When the history of this affair reached California (it was in the "early days") it made a deal of talk, but did not diminish the captain's popularity in any degree. It increased it, indeed. California had a population then that "inflicted" justice after a fashion that was simplicity and primitiveness itself, and could therefore admire appreciatively when the same fashion was followed elsewhere.

CHAPTER LI

Vice flourished luxuriantly during the hey-day of our "flush times." The saloons were overburdened with custom; so were the police courts, the gambling dens, the brothels and the jails— unfailing signs of high prosperity in a mining region—in any region for that matter. Is it not so? A crowded police court docket is the surest of all signs that trade is brisk and money plenty. Still, there is one other sign; it comes last, but when it does come it establishes beyond cavil that the "flush times" are at the flood. This is the birth of the "literary" paper. The *Weekly Occidental*, "devoted to literature," made its appearance in Virginia. All the literary people were engaged to write for it. Mr. F. was to edit it. He was a felicitous skirmisher with a pen, and a man who could say happy things in a crisp, neat way. Once, while editor of the *Union*, he had disposed of a labored, incoherent, two-column attack made upon him by a cotemporary, with a single line, which, at first glance, seemed to contain a solemn and tremendous compliment—viz.: "THE LOGIC OF OUR

ADVERSARY RESEMBLES THE PEACE OF GOD,"—and left it to the reader's memory and after-thought to invest the remark with another and "more different" meaning by supplying for himself and at his own leisure the rest of the Scripture—*"in that it passeth understanding."* He once said of a little, half-starved, wayside community that had no subsistence except what they could get by preying upon chance passengers who stopped over with them a day when traveling by the overland stage, that in their Church service they had altered the Lord's Prayer to read: "Give us this day our daily stranger!"

We expected great things of the *Occidental.* Of course it could not get along without an original novel, and so we made arrangements to hurl into the work the full strength of the company. Mrs. F. was an able romancist of the ineffable school—I know no other name to apply to a school whose heroes are all dainty and all perfect. She wrote the opening chapter, and introduced a lovely blonde simpleton who talked nothing but pearls and poetry and who was virtuous to the verge of eccentricity. She also introduced a young French Duke of aggravated refinement, in love with the blonde. Mr. F. followed next week, with a brilliant lawyer who set about getting the Duke's estates into trouble, and a sparkling young lady of high society who fell to fascinating the Duke and impairing the appetite of the blonde. Mr. D., a dark and bloody editor of one of the dailies, followed Mr. F., the third week, introducing a mysterious Roscicrucian who transmuted metals, held consultations with the devil in a cave at dead of night, and cast the horoscope of the several heroes and heroines in such a way as to provide plenty of trouble for their future careers and breed a solemn and awful public interest in the novel. He also introduced a cloaked and masked melodramatic miscreant, put him on a salary and set him on the midnight tract of the Duke with a poisoned dagger. He also created an Irish coachman with a rich brogue and placed him in the service of the society-young-lady with an ulterior mission to carry billet-doux to the Duke.

About this time there arrived in Virginia a dissolute stranger with a literary turn of mind—rather seedy he was, but very quiet and unassuming; almost diffident, indeed. He was so gentle, and his manners were so pleasing and kindly, whether he was sober or intoxicated, that he made friends of all who came in contact with him. He applied for literary work, offered conclusive evidence that he wielded an easy and practiced pen, and so Mr. F. engaged him at once to help write the novel. His chapter was to follow Mr. D.'s, and mine was to come next. Now what does this fellow do but go off and get drunk and then proceed to his quarters and set to work with his imagination in a state of chaos, and that chaos in a condition of extravagant activity. The result may be guessed. He scanned the chapters of his predecessors, found plenty of heroes and heroines already created, and was satisfied with them; he decided to introduce no more; with all the confidence that whisky inspires and all the easy complacency it gives to its servant, he then launched himself lovingly into his work: he married the coachman to the society-young-lady for the sake of the scandal; married the Duke to the blonde's step-mother, for the sake of the sensation; stopped the desperado's salary; created a misunderstanding between the devil and the Roscicrucian; threw the Duke's property into the wicked lawyer's hands; made the lawyer's upbraiding conscience drive him to drink, thence to *delirium tremens,* thence to suicide; broke the coachman's neck; let his widow succumb to contumely, neglect, poverty and consumption; caused the blonde to drown herself, leaving her clothes on the bank with the customary note pinned to them forgiving the Duke and hoping he would be happy; revealed to the Duke, by means of the usual strawberry mark on left arm, that he had married his own long-lost mother and destroyed his long-lost sister; instituted the proper and necessary suicide of the Duke and the Duchess in order to compass poetical justice; opened the earth and let the Roscicrucian through, accompanied with the accustomed smoke and thunder and smell of brimstone, and finished with the promise that in the next chapter, after holding a general inquest, he would take up the surviving character of the novel and tell what became of the devil!

It read with singular smoothness, and with a "dead" earnestness that was funny enough to suffocate a body. But there was war when it came in. The other novelists were furious. The mild stranger, not yet more than half sober, stood there, under a scathing fire of vituperation, meek and bewildered, looking from one to another of his assailants, and wondering what he could have done to invoke such a storm. When a lull came at last, he said his say gently and appealingly—said he did not rightly remember what he had written, but was sure he had tried to do the best he could, and knew his object had been to make the novel not only pleasant and plausible but instructive and--

The bombardment began again. The novelists assailed his ill-chosen adjectives and demolished them with a storm of denunciation and ridicule. And so the siege went on. Every time the stranger tried to appease the enemy he only made matters worse. Finally he offered to rewrite the chapter. This arrested hostilities. The indignation gradually quieted down, peace reigned again and the sufferer retired in safety and got him to his own citadel.

But on the way thither the evil angel tempted him and he got drunk again. And again his imagination went mad. He led the heroes and heroines a wilder dance than ever; and yet all through it ran that same convincing air of honesty and earnestness that had marked his first work. He got the characters into the most extraordinary situations, put them through the most surprising performances, and made them talk the strangest talk! But the chapter cannot be described. It was symmetrically crazy; it was artistically absurd; and it had explanatory footnotes that were fully as curious as the text. I remember one of the "situations," and will offer it as an example of the whole. He altered the character of the brilliant lawyer, and made him a great-hearted, splendid fellow; gave him fame and riches, and set his age at thirty-three years. Then he made the blonde discover, through the help of the Roscicrucian and the melodramatic miscreant, that while the Duke loved her money ardently and wanted it, he secretly felt a sort of leaning toward the society-young-lady. Stung to the quick, she tore her affections from him and bestowed them with tenfold power upon the lawyer, who responded with consuming zeal. But the parents would none of it. What they wanted in the family was a Duke; and a Duke they were determined to have; though they confessed that next to the Duke the lawyer had their preference. Necessarily the blonde now went into a decline. The parents were alarmed. They pleaded with her to marry the Duke, but she steadfastly refused, and pined on. Then they laid a plan. They told her to wait a year and a day, and if at the end of that time she still felt that she could not marry the Duke, she might marry the lawyer with their full consent. The result was as they had foreseen: gladness came again, and the flush of returning health. Then the parents took the next step in their scheme. They had the family physician recommend a long sea voyage and much land travel for the thorough restoration of the blonde's strength; and they invited the Duke to be of the party. They judged that the Duke's constant presence and the lawyer's protracted absence would do the rest—for they did not invite the lawyer.

So they set sail in a steamer for America—and the third day out, when their sea-sickness called truce and permitted them to take their first meal at the public table, behold there sat the lawyer! The Duke and party made the best of an awkward situation; the voyage progressed, and the vessel neared America. But, by and by, two hundred miles off New Bedford, the ship took fire; she burned to the water's edge; of all her crew and passengers, only thirty were saved. They floated about the sea half an afternoon and all night long. Among them were our friends. The lawyer, by superhuman exertions, had saved the blonde and her parents, swimming back and forth two hundred yards and bringing one each time—(the girl first). The Duke had saved himself. In the morning two whale ships arrived on the scene and sent their boats. The weather was stormy and the embarkation was attended with much confusion and excitement. The lawyer did his duty like a man; helped his exhausted and insensible blonde, her parents and some others into a boat (the Duke helped himself in); then a child fell overboard at the other end of the raft and the lawyer rushed thither and helped half a dozen people fish it out, under the stimulus of its mother's screams. Then he ran back—a few seconds too late—the blonde's boat was under way. So he had to take the other boat, and go to the other ship. The storm increased and drove the vessels out of sight of each other—drove them whither it would. When it calmed, at the end of three days, the blonde's ship was seven hundred miles north of Boston and the other about seven hundred south of that port. The blonde's captain was bound on a whaling cruise in the North Atlantic and could not go back such a distance or make a port without orders; such being nautical law. The lawyer's captain was to cruise in the North Pacific, and *he* could not go back or make a port without orders. All the lawyer's money and baggage were in the blonde's boat and went to the blonde's ship—so his captain made him work his passage as a common sailor. When both ships had been cruising nearly a year, the one was off the coast of Greenland and the other in Behring's Strait. The blonde had long ago been well-nigh persuaded that her lawyer had been washed overboard and lost just before the whale ships reached the raft, and now, under the pleadings of her parents and the Duke she was at last beginning to nerve herself for the doom of the covenant, and prepare for the hated marriage. But she would not yield a day before the date set. The weeks dragged on, the time narrowed, orders were given to deck the ship for the wedding—a wedding at sea among icebergs and walruses. Five days more and all would be over. So the blonde reflected, with a sigh and a tear. Oh where was her true love—and why, why did he not come and save her? At that moment he was lifting his harpoon to strike a whale in Behring's Strait, five thousand miles away, by the way of the Arctic Ocean, or twenty thousand by the way of the Horn—that was the reason. He struck, but not with perfect aim—his foot slipped and he fell in the whale's mouth and went down his throat. He was insensible five days. Then he came to himself and heard voices; daylight was streaming through a hole cut in the whale's roof. He climbed out and astonished the sailors who were hoisting blubber up a ship's side. He recognized the vessel, flew aboard, surprised the wedding party at the altar and exclaimed:

"Stop the proceedings—I'm here! Come to my arms, my own!"

There were foot-notes to this extravagant piece of literature wherein the author endeavored to show that the whole thing was within the possibilities; he said he got the incident of the whale traveling from Behring's Strait to the coast of Greenland, five thousand miles in five days, through the Arctic Ocean, from Charles Reade's "Love Me Little Love Me Long," and considered that that established the fact that the thing could be done; and he instanced Jonah's adventure as proof that a man could live in a whale's belly, and added that if a preacher could stand it three days a lawyer could surely stand it five!

There was a fiercer storm than ever in the editorial sanctum now, and the stranger was peremptorily discharged, and his manuscript flung at his head. But he had already delayed things so much that there was not time for some one else to rewrite the chapter, and so the paper came out without any novel in it. It was but a feeble, struggling, stupid journal, and the absence of the novel probably shook public confidence; at any rate, before the first side of the next issue went to press, the *Weekly Occidental* died as peacefully as an infant.

An effort was made to resurrect it, with the proposed advantage of a telling new title, and Mr. F. said that *The Phenix* would be just the name for it, because it would give the idea of a resurrection from its dead ashes in a new and undreamed of condition of splendor; but some low-priced smarty on one of the dailies suggested that we call it the *Lazarus;* and inasmuch as the people were not profound in Scriptural matters but thought the resurrected Lazarus and the dilapidated mendicant that begged in the rich man's geteway were one and the same person, the name became the laughing stock of the town, and killed the paper for good and all.

I was sorry enough, for I was very proud of being connected with a literary paper—prouder than I have ever been of anything since, perhaps. I had written some rhymes for it—poetry I considered it—and it was a great grief to me that the production was on the "first side" of the issue that was not completed, and hence did not see the light. But time brings its revenges—I can put it in here; it will answer in place of a tear dropped to the memory of the lost *Occidental*. The idea (not the chief idea, but the vehicle that bears it) was probably suggested by the old song called "The Raging Canal," but I cannot remember now. I do remember, though, that at that time I thought my doggerel was one of the ablest poems of the age:

THE AGED PILOT MAN

On the Erie Canal, it was,
    All on a summer's day,
I sailed forth with my parents
    Far away to Albany.

From out the clouds at noon that day
    There came a dreadful storm,
That piled the billows high about,
    And filled us with alarm.

A man came rushing from a house,
    Saying, "Snub up * your boat I pray,
Snub up your boat, snub up, alas,
    Snub up while yet you may."

Our captain cast one glance astern,
    Then forward glanced he,
And said, "My wife and little ones
    I never more shall see."

Said Dollinger the pilot man,
    In noble words, but few,—
"Fear not, but lean on Dollinger,
    And he will fetch you through."

The boat drove on, the frightened mules
    Tore through the rain and wind,
And bravely still, in danger's post,
    The whip-boy strode behind.

"Come 'board, come 'board," the captain cried,
    "Nor tempt so wild a storm;"
But still the raging mules advanced,
    And still the boy strode on.

Then said the captain to us all,
    "Alas tis plain to me,
The greater danger is not there,
    But here upon the sea.

* The customary canal technicality for "tie up."

So let us strive, while life remains,
  To save all souls on board,
And then if die at last we must,
  Let . . . . I *cannot* speak the word!

Said Dollinger the pilot man,
  Tow'ring above the crew,
"Fear not, but trust in Dollinger,
  And he will fetch you through."

"Low bridge! low bridge!" all heads went down,
  The laboring bark sped on;
A mill we passed, we passed a church,
  Hamlets, and fields of corn;
And all the world came out to see,
  And chased along the shore

Crying, "Alas, alas, the sheeted rain,
  The wind, the tempest's roar!
Alas, the gallant ship and crew,
  Can *nothing* help them more?"

And from our deck sad eyes looked out
  Across the stormy scene:
The tossing wake of billows aft,
  The bending forests green,

The chickens sheltered under carts
  In lee of barn the cows,
The skurrying swine with straw in mouth,
  The wild spray from our bows!

    "She balances!
    She wavers!
Now let her go about!
If she misses stays and broaches to,
We're all"—[then with a shout,]
    "Huray! huray!
    Avast! belay!
    Take in more sail!
    Lord, what a gale!
Ho, boy, haul taut on the hind mule's tail!"

"Ho! lighten ship! ho! man the pump!
  Ho, hostler, heave the lead!
"A quarter-three!—'tis shoaling fast!
  Three feet large!—t-h-r-e-e feet!—
Three feet scant!" I cried in fright
  "Oh, is there *no* retreat?"

Said Dollinger, the pilot man,
　　As on the vessel flew,
"Fear not, but trust in Dollinger,
　　And he will fetch you through."

A panic struck the bravest hearts,
　　The boldest cheek turned pale;
For plain to all, this shoaling said
A leak had burst the ditch's bed!
And, straight as bolt from crossbow sped,
Our ship swept on, with shoaling lead,
　　Before the fearful gale!

"Sever the tow-line! Cripple the mules!"
　　Too late! . . . . . There comes a shock!
* 　 * 　 * 　 * 　 * 　 * 　 * 　 *
Another length, and the fated craft
　　Would have swum in the saving lock!

Then gathered together the shipwrecked crew
　　And took one last embrace,
While sorrowful tears from despairing eyes
　　Ran down each hopeless face;
And some did think of their little ones
　　Whom they never more might see,
And others of waiting wives at home,
　　And mothers that grieved would be.

But all the children of misery there
　　On that poor sinking frame,
But one spake words of hope and faith,
　　And I worshipped as they came:
Said Dollinger the pilot man,—
　　(O brave heart, strong and true!)—
"Fear not, but trust in Dollinger,
　　For he will fetch you through."

Lo! scarce the words have passed his lips
　　The dauntless prophet say'th,
When every soul about him seeth
　　A wonder crown his faith!

And count ye all, both great and small,
　　As numbered with the dead!
For mariner for forty year,
　　On Erie, boy and man,
I never yet saw such a storm,
　　Or one't with it began!"

So overboard a keg of nails
And anvils three we threw,
Likewise four bales of gunny-sacks,
Two hundred pounds of glue,
Two sacks of corn, four ditto wheat,
A box of books, a cow,
A violin, Lord Byron's works,
A rip-saw and a sow.

A curve! a curve! the dangers grow!
"Labbord!—stabbord!—s-t-e-a-d-y!— so!—
Hard-a-port, Dol!—hellum-a-lee!
Haw the head mule!—the aft one gee!
Luff!—bring her to the wind!"

For straight a farmer brought a plank,—
(Mysteriously inspired)—
And laying it unto the ship,
In silent awe retired.

Then every sufferer stood amazed
That pilot man before;
A moment stood. The wondering turned,
And speechless walked ashore.

CHAPTER LII

Since I desire, in this chapter, to say an instructive word or two about the silver mines, the reader may take this fair warning and skip, if he chooses. The year 1863 was perhaps the very top blossom and culmination of the "flush times." Virginia swarmed with men and vehicles to that degree that the place looked like a very hive—that is when one's vision could pierce through the thick fog of alkali dust that was generally blowing in summer. I will say, concerning this dust, that if you drove ten miles through it, you and your horses would be coated with it a sixteenth of an inch thick and present an outside appearance that was a uniform pale yellow color, and your buggy would have three inches of dust in it, thrown there by the wheels. The delicate scales used by the assayers were inclosed in glass cases intended to be air-tight, and yet some of this dust was so impalpable and so invisibly fine that it would get in, somehow, and impair the accuracy of those scales.

Speculation ran riot, and yet there was a world of substantial business going on, too. All freights were brought over the mountains from California (150 miles) by pack-train partly, and partly in huge wagons drawn by such long mule teams that each team amounted to a procession, and it did seem, sometimes, that the grand combined procession of animals stretched unbroken from Virginia to California. Its long route was traceable clear across the deserts of the Territory by the writhing serpent of dust it lifted up. By these wagons, freights over that hundred and fifty miles were $200 a ton for small lots (same price for all express matter brought by stage), and $100 a ton for full loads. One Virginia firm received one hundred tons of freight a month, and paid $10,000 a month freightage. In the winter the freights were much higher. All the bullion was shipped in bars by stage to San Francisco (a bar was usually about twice the size of a pig of lead and contained from $1,500 to $3,000 according to the amount of gold mixed with the silver), and the freight on it (when the shipment was large) was one and a quarter per cent. of its intrinsic value. So, the freight on these bars probably averaged something more than $25 each. Small shippers paid two per cent. There were three stages a day, each way, and I have seen the out-going stages carry away a third of a ton of bullion each, and more than once I saw them divide a two-ton lot and take it off. However, these were extraordinary events.* Two tons of silver bullion would be in the neighborhood of forty bars, and the freight on it over $1,000. Each coach always carried a deal of ordinary express matter beside, and also from fifteen to twenty passengers at from $25 to $30 a head. With six stages going all the time,

*Mr. Valentine, Wells Fargo's agent, has handled all the bullion shipped through the Virginia office for many a month. To his memory—which is excellent—we are indebted for the following exhibit of the company's business in the Virginia office since the first of January, 1862: From January 1st, to April 1st, about $270,000 worth of bullion passed through that office; during the next quarter, $570,000; next quarter, $800,000; next quarter, $956,000; next quarter, $1,275,000; and for the quarter ending on the 30th of last June, about $1,600,000. Thus in a year and a half, the Virginia office only shipped $5,330,000 in bullion. During the year 1862 they shipped $2,615,000, so we perceive the average shipments have more than doubled in the last six months. This gives us room to promise for the Virginia office $500,000 a month for the year 1863 (though perhaps, judging by the steady increase in the business, we are under estimating, somewhat). This gives us $6,000,000 for the year. Gold Hill and Silver City together can beat us—we will give them $10,000,000. To Dayton, Empire City, Ophir and Carson City, we will allow an aggregate of $8,000,000, which is not over the mark, perhaps, and may possibly be a little under it. To Emeralda we give $4,000,000. To Reese River and Humboldt $2,000,000, which is liberal now, but may not be before the year is out. So we prognosticate that the yield of bullion this year will be about $30,000,000. Placing the number of mills in the Territory at one hundred, this gives to each the labor of producing $300,000 in bullion during the twelve months. Allowing them to run three hundred days in the year (which none of them more than do), this makes their work average $1,000 a day. Say the mills average twenty tons of rock a day and this rock worth $50 as a general thing, and you have the actual work of our one hundred mills figured down "to a spot"—$1,000 a day each, and $30,000,000 a year in the aggregate.—*Enterprise.*
[A considerable over estimate.—M.T.]

Wells, Fargo and Co.'s Virginia City business was important and lucrative.

All along under the centre of Virginia and Gold Hill, for a couple of miles, ran the great Comstock silver lode—a vein of ore from fifty to eighty feet thick between its solid walls of rock—a vein as wide as some of New York's streets. I will remind the reader that in Pennsylvania a coal vein only eight feet wide is considered ample.

Virginia was a busy city of streets and houses above ground. Under it was another busy city, down in the bowels of the earth, where a great population of men thronged in and out among an intricate maze of tunnels and drifts, flitting hither and thither under a winking sparkle of lights, and over their heads towered a vast web of interlocking timbers that held the walls of the gutted Comstock apart. These timbers were as large as a man's body, and the framework stretched upward so far that no eye could pierce to its top through the closing gloom. It was like peering up through the clean-picked ribs and bones of some colossal skeleton. Imagine such a framework two miles long, sixty feet wide, and higher than any church spire in America. Imagine this stately lattice-work stretching down Broadway, from the St. Nicholas to Wall street, and a Fourth of July procession, reduced to pigmies, parading on top of it and flaunting their flags, high above the pinnacle of Trinity steeple. One can imagine that, but he cannot well imagine what that forest of timbers cost, from the time they were felled in the pineries beyond Washoe Lake, hauled up and around Mount Davidson at atrocious rates of freightage, then squared, let down into the deep maw of the mine and built up there. Twenty ample fortunes would not timber one of the greatest of those silver mines. The Spanish proverb says it requires a gold mine to "run" a silver one, and it is true. A beggar with a silver mine is a pitiable pauper indeed if he cannot sell.

I spoke of the underground Virginia as a city. The Gould and Curry is only one single mine under there, among a great many others; yet the Gould and Curry's streets of dismal drifts and tunnels were five miles in extent, altogether, and its population five hundred miners. Taken as a whole, the underground city had some thirty miles of streets and a population of five or six thousand. In this present day some of those populations are at work from twelve to sixteen hundred feet under Virginia and Gold Hill, and the signal-bells that tell them what the superintendent above ground desires them to do are struck by telegraph as we strike a fire alarm. Sometimes men fall down a shaft, there, a thousand feet deep. In such cases, the usual plan is to hold an inquest.

If you wish to visit one of those mines, you may walk through a tunnel about half a mile long if you prefer it, or you may take the quicker plan of shooting like a dart down a shaft, on a small platform. It is like tumbling down through an empty steeple, feet first. When you reach the bottom, you take a candle and tramp through drifts and tunnels where throngs of men are digging and blasting; you watch them send up tubs full of great lumps of stone—silver ore; you select choice specimens from the mass, as souvenirs; you admire the world of skeleton timbering; you reflect frequently that you are buried under a mountain, a thousand feet below daylight; being in the bottom of the mine you climb from "gallery" to "gallery," up endless ladders that stand straight up and down; when your legs fail you at last, you lie down in a small box-car in a cramped "incline" like a half-up-ended sewer and are dragged up to daylight feeling as if you are crawling through a coffin that has no end to it. Arrived at the top, you find a busy crowd of men receiving the ascending cars and tubs and dumping the ore from an elevation into long rows of bins capable of holding half a dozen tons each; under the bins are rows of wagons loading from chutes and trap-doors in the bins, and down the long street is a procession of these wagons wending toward the silver mills with their rich freight. It is all "done," now, and there you are. You need never go down again, for you have seen it all. If you have forgotten the process of reducing the ore in the mill and making the silver bars, you can go back and find it again in my Esmeralda chapters if so disposed.

Of course these mines cave in, in places, occasionally, and then it is worth one's while to take the risk of descending into them and observing the crushing power exerted by the pressing weight of a settling mountain. I published such an experience in the *Enterprise*, once, and from it I will take an extract:

AN HOUR IN THE CAVED MINES.—We journeyed down into the Ophir mine, yesterday, to see the earthquake. We could not go down the deep incline, because it still has a propensity to cave in places. Therefore we traveled through the long tunnel which enters the hill above the Ophir office, and then by means of a series of long ladders, climbed away down from the first to the fourth gallery. Traversing a drift, we came to the Spanish line, passed five sets of timbers still uninjured, and found the earthquake. Here was as complete a chaos as ever was seen—vast masses of earth and splintered and broken timbers piled confusedly together, with scarcely an aperture left large enough for a cat to creep through. Rubbish was still falling at intervals from above, and one timber which had braced others earlier in the day, was *now* crushed down out of its former position, showing that the caving and settling of the tremendous mass was still going on. We were in that portion of the Ophir known as the "north mines." Returning to the surface, we entered a tunnel leading into the Central, for the purpose of getting into the main Ophir. Descending a long incline in this tunnel, we traversed a drift or so, and then went down a deep shaft from whence we proceeded into the fifth gallery of the Ophir. From a side-drift we crawled through a small hole and got into the midst of the earthquake again— earth and broken timbers mingled together without regard to grace or symmetry. A large portion of the second, third and fourth galleries had caved in and gone to destruction—the two latter at seven o'clock on the previous evening.

At the turn-table, near the northern extremity of the fifth gallery, two big piles of rubbish had forced their way through from the fifth gallery, and from the looks of the timbers, more was about to come. These beams are solid—eighteen inches square; first, a great beam is laid on the floor, then upright ones, five feet high, stand on it, supporting another horizontal beam, and so on, square above square, like the framework of a window. The superincumbent weight was sufficient to mash the ends of those great upright beams fairly into the solid wood of the horizontal ones three inches, compressing and bending the upright beam till it curved like a bow. Before the Spanish caved in, some of their twelve-inch horizontal timbers were compressed in this way until they were only five inches thick! Imagine the power it must take to squeeze a solid log together in that way. Here, also, was a range of timbers, for a distance of twenty feet, tilted six inches out of the perpendicular by the weight resting upon them from the caved galleries above. You could hear things cracking and giving way, and it was not pleasant to know that the world overhead was slowly and silently sinking down upon you. The men down in the mine do not mind it, however.

Returning along the fifth gallery, we struck the safe part of the Ophir incline, and went down it to the sixth; but we found ten inches of water there, and had to come back. In repairing the damage done to the incline, the pump had to be stopped for two hours, and in the meantime the water gained about a foot. However, the pump was at work again, and the flood-water was decreasing. We climbed up to the fifth gallery again and sought a deep shaft, whereby we might descend to another part of the sixth, out of reach of the water, but suffered disappointment, as the men had gone to dinner, and there was no one to man the windlass. So, having seen the earthquake, we climbed out at the Union incline and tunnel, and adjourned, all dripping with candle grease and perspiration, to lunch at the Ophir office.

During the great flush year of 1863, Nevada [claims to have] produced $25,000,000 in bullion—almost, if not quite, a round million to each thousand inhabitants, which is very well, considering that she was without agriculture and manufactures.* Silver mining was her sole productive industry.

CHAPTER LIII

Every now and then, in these days, the boys used to tell me I ought to get one Jim Blaine to tell me the stirring story of his grandfather's old ram—but they always added that I must not mention the matter unless Jim was drunk at the time—just comfortably and sociably drunk. They kept this up until my curiosity was on the rack to hear the story. I got to haunting Blaine; but it was of no use, the boys always found fault with his condition; he was often moderately but never satisfactorily drunk. I never watched a man's condition with such absorbing interest, such anxious solicitude; I never so pined to see a man uncompromisingly drunk before. At last, one evening I hurried to his cabin, for I learned that this time his situation was such that even the most fastidious could find no fault with it—he was tranquilly, serenely, symmetrically drunk—not a hiccup to mar his voice, not a cloud upon his brain thick enough to obscure his memory. As I entered, he was sitting upon an empty powder-keg, with a clay pipe in one hand and the other raised to command silence. His face was round, red, and very serious; his throat was bare and his hair tumbled; in general appearance and costume he was a stalwart miner of the period. On the pine table stood a candle, and its dim light revealed "the boys" sitting here and there on bunks, candle-boxes, powder-kegs, etc. They said:

"Sh—! Don't speak—he's going to commence."

---

*Since the above was in type, I learn from an official source that the above figure is too high, and that the yield for 1863 did not exceed $20,000,000. However, the day for large figures is approaching; the Sutro Tunnel is to plow through the Comstock lode from end to end, at a depth of two thousand feet, and then mining will be easy and comparatively inexpensive; and the momentous matters of drainage, and hoisting and hauling of ore will cease to be burdensome. This vast work will absorb many years, and millions of dollars, in its completion; but it will early yield money, for that desirable epoch will begin as soon as it strikes the first end of the vein. The tunnel will be some eight miles long, and will develop astonishing riches. Cars will carry the ore through the tunnel and dump it in the mills and thus do away with the present costly system of double handling and transportation by mule teams. The water from the tunnel will furnish the motive power for the mills. Mr. Sutro, the originator of this prodigious enterprise, is one of the few men in the world who is gifted with the pluck and perseverance necessary to follow up and hound such an undertaking to its completion. He has converted several obstinate Congresses to a deserved friendliness toward his important work, and has gone up and down and to and fro in Europe until he has enlisted a great moneyed interest in it there.

THE STORY OF THE OLD RAM

I found a seat at once, and Blaine said:

"I don't reckon them times will ever come again. There never was a more bullier old ram than what he was. Grandfather fetched him from Illinois—got him of a man by the name of Yates—Bill Yates—maybe you might have heard of him; his father was a decon—Baptist—and he was a rustler, too; a man had to get up ruther early to get the start of old Thankful Yates; it was him that put the Greens up to jining teams with my grandfather when he moved west. Seth Green was prob'ly the pick of the flock; he married a Wilkerson—Sarah Wilkerson—good cretur, she was—one of the likeliest heifers that was ever raised in old Stoddard, everybody said that knowed her. She could heft a bar'l of flour as easy as I can flirt a flapjack. And spin? Don't mention it! Independent? Humph! When Sile Hawkins come a browsing around her, she let him know that for all his tin he couldn't trot in harness alongside of *her*. You see, Sile Hawkins was—no, it warn't Sile Hawkins, after all—it was a galoot by the name of Filkins—I disremember his first name; but he *was* a stump— come into pra'r meeting drunk, one night, hooraying for Nixon, becuz he thought it was a primary; and old deacon Ferguson up and scooted him through the window and he lit on old Miss Jefferson's head, poor old filly. She was a good soul—had a glass eye and used to lend it to old Miss Wagner, that hadn't any, to receive company in; it warn't big enough, and when Miss Wagner warn't noticing, it would get twisted around in the socket, and look up, maybe, or out to one side, and every which way, while t'other one was looking as straight ahead as a spy-glass. Grown people didn't mind it, but it most always made the children cry, it was so sort of scary. She tried packing it in raw cotton, but it wouldn't work, somehow—the cotton would get loose and stick out and look so kind of awful that the children couldn't stand it no way. She was always dropping it out, and turning up her old dead-light on the company empty, and making them oncomfortable, becuz *she* never could tell when it hopped out, being blind on that side, you see. So somebody would have to hunch her and say, "Your game eye has fetched loose, Miss Wagner dear"—and then all of them would have to sit and wait till she jammed it in again—wrong side before, as a general thing, and green as a bird's egg, being a bashful cretur and easy sot back before company. But being wrong side before warn't much difference, anyway, becuz her own eye was sky-blue and the glass one was yaller on the front

side, so whichever way she turned it it didn't match nohow. Old
Miss Wagner was considerable on the borrow, she was. When
she had a quilting, or Dorcas S'iety at her house she gen'ally
borrowed Miss Higgins's wooden leg to stump around on; it was
considerable shorter than her other pin, but much *she* minded
that. She said she couldn't abide crutches when she had company, becuz they were so slow; said when she had company and
things had to be done, she wanted to get up and hump herself.
She was as bald as a jug, and so she used to borrow Miss
Jacops's wig—Miss Jacops was the coffin-peddler's wife—a rat-
ty old buzzard, he was, that used to go roosting around where
people was sick, waiting for 'em; and there that old rip would sit
all day, in the shade, on a coffin that he judged would fit the
can'idate; and if it was a slow customer and kind of uncertain,
he'd fetch his rations and a blanket along and sleep in the coffin
nights. He was anchored out that way, in frosty weather, for
about three weeks, once, before old Robbins's place, waiting for
him; and after that, for as much as two years, Jacops was not on
speaking terms with the old man, on account of his disapp'inting
him. He got one of his feet froze, and lost money, too, becuz old
Robbins took a favorable turn and got well. The next time Robbins got sick, Jacops tried to makè up with him, and varnished
up the same old coffin and fetched it along; but old Robbins was
too many for him; he had him in, and 'peared to be powerful
weak; he bought the coffin for ten dollars and Jacops was to pay
it back and twenty-five more besides if Robbins didn't like the
coffin after he'd tried it. And then Robbins died, and at the
funeral he bursted off the lid and riz up in his shroud and told
the parson to let up on the performances, becuz he could *not*
stand such a coffin as that. You see he had been in a trance once
before, when he was young, and he took the chances on another,
cal'lating that if he made the trip it was money in his pocket, and
if he missed fire he couldn't lose a cent. And by George he sued
Jacops for the rhino and got jedgment; and he set up the coffin
in his back parlor and said he 'lowed to take his time, now. It
was always an aggravation to Jacops, the way that miserable old
thing acted. He moved back to Indiany pretty soon—went to
Wellsville—Wellsville was the place the Hogadorns was from.
Mighty fine family. Old Maryland stock. Old Squire Hogadorn
could carry around more mixed licker, and cuss better than most
any man I ever see. His second wife was the widder Billings—she
that was Becky Martin; her dam was deacon Dunlap's first wife.
Her oldest child, Maria, married a missionary and died in
grace—et up by the savages. They et *him*, too, poor feller—biled
him. It warn't the custom, so they say, but they explained to

friends of his'n that went down there to bring away his things, that they'd tried missionaries every other way and never could get any good out of 'em—and so it annoyed all his relations to find out that that man's life was fooled away just out of a dern'd experiment, so to speak. But mind you, there ain't anything ever reely lost; everything that people can't understand and don't see the reason of does good if you only hold on and give it a fair shake; Prov'dence don't fire no blank ca'tridges, boys. That there missionary's substance, unbeknowns to himself, actu'ly converted every last one of them heathens that took a chance at the barbacue. Nothing ever fetched them but that. Don't tell *me* it was an accident that he was biled. There ain't no such a thing as an accident. When my uncle Lem was leaning up agin a scaffolding once, sick, or drunk, or suthin, an Irishman with a hod full of bricks fell on him out of the third story and broke the old man's back in two places. People said it was an accident. Much accident there was about that. He didn't know what he was there for, but he was there for a good object. If he hadn't been there the Irishman would have been killed. Nobody can ever make me believe anything different from that. Uncle Lem's dog was there. Why didn't the Irishman fall on the dog? Becuz the dog would a seen him a-coming and stood from under. That's the reason the dog warn't appinted. A dog can't be depended on to carry out a special providence. Mark my words it was a put-up thing. Accidents don't happen, boys. Uncle Lem's dog—I wish you could a seen that dog. He was a reglar shepherd—or ruther he was part bull and part shepherd—splendid animal; belonged to parson Hagar before Uncle Lem got him. Parson Hagar belonged to the Western Reserve Hagars; prime family; his mother was a Watson; one of his sisters married a Wheeler; they settled in Morgan county, and he got nipped by the machinery in a carpet factory and went through in less than a quarter of a minute; his widder bought the piece of carpet that had his remains wove in, and people come a hundred mile to 'tend the funeral. There was fourteen years in the piece. She wouldn't let them roll him up, but planted him just so—full length. The church was middling small where they preached the funeral, and they had to let one end of the coffin stick out of the window. They didn't bury him—they planed one end, and let him stand up, same as a monument. And they nailed a sign on it and put— put on—put on it—sacred to—the m-e-m-o-r-y—of fourteen y-a-r-d-s—of three-ply—car - - - pet—containing all that was— m-o-r-t-a-l—of—of—W-i-l-l-i-a-m—W-h-e—''

Jim Blaine had been growing gradually drowsy and drowsier—his head nodded, once, twice, three times—dropped peacefully upon his breast, and he fell tranquilly asleep. The tears were running down the boys' cheeks—they were suffocating with suppressed laughter—and had been from the start, though I had never noticed it. I perceived that I was "sold." I learned then that Jim Blaine's peculiarity was that whenever he reached a certain stage of intoxication, no human power could keep him from setting out, with impressive unction, to tell about a wonderful adventure which he had once had with his grandfather's old ram—and the mention of the ram in the first sentence was as far as any man had ever heard him get, concerning it. He always maundered off, interminably, from one thing to another, till his whisky got the best of him and he fell asleep. What the thing was that happened to him and his grandfather's old ram is a dark mystery to this day, for nobody has ever yet found out.

CHAPTER LIV

Of course there was a large Chinese population in Virginia—it is the case with every town and city on the Pacific coast. They are a harmless race when white men either let them along or treat them no worse than dogs; in fact they are almost entirely harmless anyhow, for they seldom think of resenting the vilest insults or the cruelest injuries. They are quiet, peaceable, tractable, free from drunkenness, and they are as industrious as the day is long. A disorderly Chinaman is rare, and a lazy one does not exist. So long as a Chinaman has strength to use his hands he needs no support from anybody; white men often complain of want of work, but a Chinaman offers no such complaint; he always manages to find something to do. He is a great convenience to everybody—even to the worst class of white men, for he bears the most of their sins, suffering fines for their petty thefts, imprisonment for their robberies, and death for their murders. Any white man can swear a Chinaman's life away in the courts, but no Chinaman can testify against a white man. Ours is the "land of the free"—nobody denies that—nobody challenges it. [Maybe it is because we won't let other people testify.] As I write, news comes that in broad daylight in San Francisco, some boys have stoned an inoffensive Chinaman to death, and that although a large crowd witnessed the shameful deed, no one interfered.

There are seventy thousand (and possibly one hundred thousand) Chinamen on the Pacific coast. There were about a thousand in Virginia. They were penned into a "Chinese quarter"—a thing which they do not particularly object to, as they are fond of herding together. Their buildings were of wood; usually only one story high, and set thickly together along streets scarcely wide enough for a wagon to pass through. Their quarter was a little removed from the rest of the town. The chief employment of Chinamen in towns is to wash clothing. They always send a bill, pinned to the clothes. It is mere ceremony, for it does not enlighten the customer much. Their price for washing was $2.50 per dozen—rather cheaper than white people could afford to wash for at that time. A very common sign on the Chinese houses was: "See Yup, Washer and Ironer"; "Hong Wo, Washer"; "Sam Sing & Ah Hop, Washing." The house servants, cooks, etc., in California and Nevada, were chiefly Chinamen. There were few white servants and no Chinawomen so employed. Chinamen make good house servants, being quick, obedient, patient, quick to learn and tirelessly industrious. They do not need to be taught a thing twice, as a general thing. They are imitative. If a Chinaman were to see his master break up a centre table, in a passion, and kindle a fire with it, that Chinaman would be likely to resort to the furniture for fuel forever afterward.

All Chinamen can read, write and cipher with easy facility—pity but all our petted *voters* could. In California they rent little patches of ground and do a deal of gardening. They will raise surprising crops of vegetables on a sand pile. They waste nothing. What is rubbish to a Christian, a Chinaman carefully preserves and makes useful in one way or another. He gathers up all the old oyster and sardine cans that white people throw away, and procures marketable tin and solder from them by melting. He gathers up old bones and turns them into manure. In California he gets a living out of old mining claims that white men have abandoned as exhausted and worthless—and then the officers come down on him once a month with an exorbitant swindle to which the legislature has given the broad, general name of "foreign" mining tax, but it is usually inflicted on no foreigners but Chinamen. This swindle has in some cases been repeated once or twice on the same victim in the course of the same month—but the public treasury was not additionally enriched by it, probably.

Chinamen hold their dead in great reverence—they worship their departed ancestors, in fact. Hence, in China, a man's front yard, back yard, or any other part of his premises, is made his family burying ground, in order that he may visit the graves at any and all times. Therefore that huge empire is one mighty cemetery; it is ridged and wringled from its centre to its circumference with graves—and inasmuch as every foot of ground must be made to do its utmost, in China, lest the swarming population suffer for food, the very graves are cultivated and yield a harvest, custom holding this to be no dishonor to the dead. Since the departed are held in such worshipful reverence, a Chinaman cannot bear that any indignity be offered the places where they sleep. Mr. Burlingame said that herein lay China's bitter opposition to railroads; a road could not be built anywhere in the empire without disturbing the graves of their ancestors or friends.

A Chinaman hardly believes he could enjoy the hereafter except his body lay in his beloved China; also, he desires to receive, himself, after death, that worship with which he has honored his death that preceded him. Therefore, if he visits a foreign country, he makes arrangements to have his bones returned to China in case he dies; if he hires to go to a foreign country on a labor contract, there is always a stipulation that his body shall be taken back to China if he dies; if the government sells a gang of Coolies to a foreigner for the usual five-year term, it is specified in the contract that their bodies shall be restored to China in case of death. On the Pacific coast the Chinamen all belong to one or another of several great companies or organizations, and these companies keep track of their members, register their names, and ship their bodies home when they die. The See Yup Company is held to be the largest of these. The Ning Yeong Company is next, and numbers eighteen thousand members on the coast. Its headquarters are at San Francisco, where it has a costly temple, several great officers (one of whom keeps regal state in seclusion and cannot be approached by common humanity), and a numerous priesthood. In it I was shown a register of its members, with the dead and the date of their shipment to China duly marked. Every ship that sails from San Francisco carries away a heavy freight of Chinese corpses—or did, at least, until the legislature, with an ingenious refinement of Christian cruelty, forbade the shipments, as a neat underhanded way of deterring Chinese immigration. The bill was offered, whether it passed or not. It is my impression that it passed. There was another bill—it became a law—compelling every incoming Chinaman to be vaccinated on the wharf and pay a duly appointed quack (no decent doctor would defile himself with such legalized robbery) ten dollars for it. As few importers of Chinese would want to go to an expense like that, the lawmakers thought this would be another heavy blow to Chinese immigration.

What the Chinese quarter of Virginia was like—or, indeed, what the Chinese quarter of any Pacific coast town was and is like—may be gathered from this item which I printed in the *Enterprise* while reporting for that paper:

CHINATOWN.—Accompanied by a fellow reporter, we made a trip through our Chinese quarter the other night. The Chinese have built their portion of the city to suit themselves; and as they keep neither carriages nor wagons, their streets are not wide enough, as a general thing, to admit of the passage of vehicles. At ten o'clock at night the Chinaman may be seen in all his glory. In every little cooped-up, dingy cavern of a hut, faint with the odor of burning Josh-lights and with nothing to see the gloom by save the sickly, guttering tallow candle, were two or three yellow, long-tailed vagabonds, coiled up on a sort of short truckle-bed, smoking opium, motionless and with their lustreless eyes turned inward from excess of satisfaction—or rather the recent smoker looks thus, immediately after having passed the pipe to his neighbor—for opium-smoking is a comfortless operation, and requires constant attention. A lamp sits on the bed, the length of the long pipe-stem from the smoker's mouth; he puts a pellet of opium on the end of a wire, sets it on fire, and plasters it into the pipe much as a Christian would fill a hole with putty; then he applies the bowl to the lamp and proceeds to smoke—and the stewing and frying of the drug and the gurgling of the juices in the stem would wellnigh turn the stomach of statue. John likes it, though; it soothes him, he takes about two dozen whiffs, and then rolls over to dream, Heaven only knows what, for we could not imagine by looking at the soggy creature. Possibly in his visions he travels far away from the gross world and his regular washing, and feasts on succulent rats and birds'-nests in Paradise.

Mr. Ah Sing keeps a general grocery and provision store at No. 13 Wang street. He lavished his hospitality upon our party in the friendliest way. He had various kinds of colored and colorless wines and brandies, with unpronouncable names, imported from China in little crockery jugs, and which he offered to us in dainty little miniature wash-basins of porcelain. He offered us a mess of birds'-nests; also, small, neat sausages, of which we could have swallowed several yards if we had chosen to try, but we suspected that each link contained the corpse of a mouse, and therefore refrained. Mr. Sing had in his store a thousand articles of merchandise, curious to behold, impossible to imagine the uses of, and beyond our ability to describe.

His ducks, however, and his eggs, we could understand; the former were split open and flattened out like codfish, and came from China in that shape, and the latter were plastered over with some kind of paste which kept them fresh and palatable through the long voyage.

We found Mr. Hong Wo, No. 37 Chow-chow street, making up a lottery scheme—in fact we found a dozen others occupied in the same way in various parts of the quarter, for about every third Chinaman runs a lottery, and the balance of the tribe "buck" at it. "Tom," who speaks faultless English, and used to be chief and only cook to the *Territorial Enterprise,* when the establishment kept bachelor's hall two years ago, said that "Sometime Chinaman buy ticket one dollar hap, ketch um two tree hundred, sometime no ketch um anything; lottery like one man fight um seventy—may-be he whip, may-be he get whip herself, welly good." However, the percentage being sixty-nine against him, the chances are, as a general thing, that "he get whip heself." We could not see that these lotteries differed in any respect from our own, save that the figures being Chinese, no ignorant white man might ever hope to succeed in telling "t'other from which;" the manner of drawing is similar to ours.

Mr. See Yup keeps a fancy store on Live Fox street. He sold us fans of white feathers, gorgeously ornamented; perfumery that smelled like Limburger cheese, Chinese pens, and watch-charms made of a stone unscratchable with steel instruments, yet polished and tinted like the inner coat of a sea-shell.* As tokens of his esteem, See Yup presented the party with gaudy plumes made of gold tinsel and trimmed with peacocks' feathers.

We ate chow-chow with chop-sticks in the celestial restaurants; our comrade chided the moon-eyed damsels in front of the houses for their want of feminine reserve; we received protecting Josh-lights from our hosts and "dickered" for a pagan God or two. Finally, we were impressed with the genius of a Chinese book-keeper; he figured up his accounts on a machine like a gridiron with buttons strung on its bars; the different rows represented units, tens, hundreds and thousands. He fingered them with incredible rapidity—in fact, he pushed them from place to place as fast as a musical professor's fingers travel over the keys of a piano.

They are a kindly disposed, well-meaning race, and are respected and well treated by the upper classes, all over the Pacific coast. No Californian *gentleman or lady* ever abuses or oppresses a Chinaman, under any circumstances, an explanation that seems to be much needed in the East. Only the scum of the population do it—they and their children; they, and, naturally and consistently, the policemen and politicians, likewise, for these are the dust-licking pimps and slaves of the scum, there as well as elsewhere in America.

CHAPTER LV

I began to get tired of staying in one place so long. There was no longer satisfying variety in going down to Carson to report the proceedings of the legislature once a year, and horse-races and pumpkin-shows once in three months; (they had got to raising pumpkins and potatoes in Washoe Valley, and of course one of the first achievements of the legislature was to institute a ten-

*A peculiar species of the "jade-stone"—to a Chinaman peculiarly precious.

thousand-dollar Agricultural Fair to show off forty dollars' worth of those pumpkins in—however, the territorial legislature was usually spoken of as the "asylum"). I wanted to see San Francisco. I wanted to go somewhere. I wanted—I did not know *what* I wanted. I had the "spring fever" and wanted a change, principally, no doubt. Besides, a convention had framed a State Constitution; nine men out of every ten wanted an office; I believed that these gentlemen would "treat" the moneyless and the irresponsible among the population into adopting the constitution and thus wellnigh killing the country (it could not well carry such a load as a State government, since it had nothing to tax that could stand a tax, for undeveloped mines could not, and there were not fifty developed ones in the land, there was but little realty to tax, and it did seem as if nobody was ever going to think of the simple salvation of inflicting a money penalty on murder). I believed that a State government would destroy the "flush times," and I wanted to get away. I believed that the mining stocks I had on hand would soon be worth $100,000, and thought if they reached that before the Constitution was adopted, I would sell out and make myself secure from the crash the change of government was going to bring. I considered $100,000 sufficient to go home with decently, though it was but a small amount compared to what I had been expecting to return with. I felt rather downhearted about it, but I tried to comfort myself with the reflection that with such a sum I could not fall into want. About this time a schoolmate of mine whom I had not seen since boyhood, came tramping in on foot from Reese River, a very allegory of Poverty. The son of wealthy parents, here he was, in a strange land, hungry, bootless, mantled in an ancient horse-blanket, roofed with a brimless hat, and so generally and so extravagantly dilapidated that he could have "taken the shine out of the Prodigal Son himself," as he pleasantly remarked. He wanted to borrow forty-six dollars—twenty-six to take him to San Francisco, and twenty for something else; to buy some soap with, maybe, for he needed it. I found I had but little more than the amount wanted, in my pocket; so I stepped in and borrowed forty-six dollars of a banker (on twenty days' time, without the formality of a note), and gave it him, rather than walk half a block to the office, where I had some specie laid up. If anybody had told me that it would take me two years to pay back that forty-six dollars to the banker (for I did not expect it of the Prodigal, and was not disappointed), I would have felt injured. And so would the banker.

I wanted a change. I wanted variety of some kind. It came.

Mr. Goodman went away for a week and left me the post of chief editor. It destroyed me. The first day, I wrote my "leader" in the forenoon. The second day, I had no subject and put it off till the afternoon. The third day I put it off till evening, and then copied an elaborate editorial out of the "American Cyclopedia," that steadfast friend of the editor, all over this land. The fourth day I "fooled around" till midnight, and then fell back on the Cyclopedia again. The fifth day I cudgeled my brain till midnight, and then kept the press waiting while I penned some bitter personalities on six different people. The sixth day I labored in anguish till far into the night and brought forth—nothing. The paper went to press without an editorial. The seventh day I resigned. On the eighth, Mr. Goodman returned and found six duels on his hands—my personalities had borne fruit.

Nobody, except he has tried it, knows what it is to be an editor. It is easy to scribble local rubbish, with the facts all before you; it is easy to clip selections from other papers; it is easy to string out a correspondence from any locality; but it is unspeakable hardship to write editorials. *Subjects* are the trouble—the dreary lack of them, I mean. Every day, it is drag, drag, drag—think, and worry and suffer—all the world is a dull blank, and yet the editorial columns *must* be filled. Only give the editor a *subject,* and his work is done—it is no trouble to write it up; but fancy how you would feel if you had to pump your brains dry every day in the week, fifty-two weeks in the year. It makes one low spirited simply to think of it. The matter that each editor of a daily paper in America writes in the course of a year would fill from four to eight bulky volumes like this book! Fancy what a library an editor's work would make, after twenty or thirty years' service. Yet people often marvel that Dickens, Scott, Bulwer, Dumas, etc., have been able to produce so many books. If these authors had wrought as voluminously as newspaper editors do, the result would be something to marvel at, indeed. How editors can continue this tremendous labor, this exhausting consumption of brain fibre (for their work is creative, and not a mere mechanical laying-up of facts, like reporting), day after day and year after year, is incomprehensible. Preachers take two months' holiday in midsummer, for they find that to produce two sermons a week is wearing, in the long run. In truth it must be so, and is so; and therefore, how an editor can take from ten to twenty texts and build upon them from ten to twenty painstaking editorials a week and keep it up all the year round, is farther beyond comprehension than ever. Ever since I survived my week as editor, I have found at least one pleasure in any newspaper that comes to my hand; it is in admiring the long columns of editorial, and wondering to myself how in the mischief he did it!

Mr. Goodman's return relieved me of employment, unless I chose to become a reporter again. I could not do that; I could not serve in the ranks after being General of the army. So I thought I would depart and go abroad into the world somewhere. Just at this juncture, Dan, my associate in the reportorial department, told me, casually, that two citizens had been trying to persuade him to go with them to New York and aid in selling a rich silver mine which they had discovered and secured in a new mining district in our neighborhood. He said they offered to pay his expenses and give him one third of the proceeds of the sale. He had refused to go. It was the very opportunity I wanted. I abused him for keeping so quiet about it, and not mentioning it sooner. He said it had not occurred to him that I would like to go, and so he had recommended them to apply to Marshall, the reporter of the other paper. I asked Dan if it was a good, honest mine, and no swindle. He said the men had shown him nine tons of the rock, which they had got out to take to New York, and he could cheerfully say that he had seen but little rock in Nevada that was richer; and moreover, he said that they had secured a tract of valuable timber and a mill-site, near the mine. My first idea was to kill Dan. But I changed my mind, notwithstanding I was so angry, for I thought maybe the chance was not yet lost. Dan said it was by no means lost; that the men were absent at the mine again, and would not be in Virginia to leave for the East for some ten days; that they had requested him to do the talking to Marshall, and he had promised that he would either secure Marshall or somebody else for them by the time they got back; he would now say nothing to anybody till they returned, and then fulfil his promise by furnishing me to them.

It was splendid. I went to bed all on fire with excitement; for nobody had yet gone East to sell a Nevada silver mine, and the field was white for the sickle. I felt that such a mine as the one described by Dan would bring a princely sum in New York, and sell without delay or difficulty. I could not sleep, my fancy so rioted through its castles in the air. It was the "blind lead" come again.

Next day I got away, on the coach, with the usual eclat attending departures of old citizens,—for if you have only half a dozen friends out there they will make noise for a hundred rather than let you seem to go away neglected and unregretted— and Dan promised to keep strict watch for the men that had the mine to sell.

The trip was signalized but by one little incident, and that occurred just as we were about to start. A very seedy looking vagabond passenger got out of the stage a moment to wait till the usual ballast of silver bricks was thrown in. He was standing on the pavement, when an awkward express employé, carrying a brick weighing a hundred pounds, stumbled and let it fall on the bummer's foot. He instantly dropped on the ground and began to howl in the most heart-breaking way. A sympathizing crowd gathered around and were going to pull his boot off; but he screamed louder than ever and they desisted; then he fell to gasping, and between the gasps ejaculated "Brandy! for Heaven's sake, brandy!" They poured half a pint down him, and it wonderfully restored and comforted him. Then he begged the people to assist him to the stage, which was done. The express people urged him to have a doctor at their expense, but he declined, and said that if he only had a little brandy to take along with him, to soothe his paroxyms of pain when they came on, he would be grateful and content. He was quickly supplied with two bottles, and we drove off. He was so smiling and happy after that, that I could not refrain from asking him how he could possibly be so comfortable with a crushed foot.

"Well," said he, "I hadn't had a drink for twelve hours, and hadn't a cent to my name. I was most perishing—and so, when that duffer dropped that hundred-pounder on my foot, I see my chance. Got a cork leg, you know!" and he pulled up his pantaloons and proved it.

He was as drunk as a lord all day long, and full of chucklings over his timely ingenuity.

One drunken man necessarily reminds one of another. I once heard a gentleman tell about an incident which he witnessed in a Californian bar-room. He entitled it "Ye Modest Man Taketh a Drink." It was nothing but a bit of acting, but it seemed to me a perfect rendering, and worthy of Toodles himself. The modest man, tolerably far gone with beer and other matters, enters a saloon (twenty-five cents is the price for anything and everything, and specie the only money used) and lays down a half dollar; calls for whiskey and drinks it; the bar-keeper makes change and lays the quarter in a wet place on the counter; the modest man fumbles at it with nerveless fingers, but it slips and the water holds it; he contemplates it, and tries again; same result; observes that people are interested in what he is at, blushes; fumbles at the quarter again—blushes—puts his forefinger carefully, slowly down, to make sure of his aim—pushes the coin toward the bar-keeper, and says with a sigh:

"('ic!) Gimme a cigar!"

Naturally, another gentleman present told about another drunken man. He said he reeled toward home late at night; made a mistake and entered the wrong gate; thought he saw a dog on the stoop; and it was—an iron one. He stopped and considered; wondered if it was a dangerous dog; ventured to say "Be (hic) begone!" No effect. Then he approached warily, and adopted conciliation; pursed up his lips and tried to whistle, but failed; still approached, saying, "Poor dog!—doggy, doggy, doggy!— poor doggy-dog!" Got up on the stoop, still petting with fond names; till master of the advantages; then exclaimed, "Leave, you thief!"—planted a vindictive kick in his ribs, and went head-over-heels overboard, of course. A pause; a sigh or two of pain, and then a remark in a reflective voice:

"Awful solid dog. What could he ben eating? ('ic!) Rocks, p'raps. Such animals is dangerous. 'At's what *I* say—they're dangerous. If a man—('ic!)—if a man wants to feed a dog on rocks, let him *feed* him on rocks; 'at's all right; but let him keep him at *home*—not have him layin' round promiscuous, where ('ic!) where people's liable to stumble over him when they ain't noticin'!"

It was not without regret that I took a last look at the tiny flag (it was thirty-five feet long and ten feet wide) fluttering like a lady's handkerchief from the topmost peak of Mount Davidson, two thousand feet above Virginia's roofs, and felt that doubtless I was bidding a permanent farewell to a city which had afforded me the most vigorous enjoyment of life I had ever experienced. And this reminds me of an incident which the dullest memory Virginia could boast at the time it happened must vividly recall, at times, till its possessor dies. Late one summer afternoon we had a rain shower. That was astonishing enough, in itself, to set the whole town buzzing, for it only rains (during a week or two weeks) in the winter in Nevada, and even then not enough at a time to make it worth while for any merchant to keep umbrellas for sale. But the rain was not the chief wonder. It only lasted five or ten minutes; while the people were still talking about it all the heavens gathered to themselves a dense blackness as of midnight. All the vast eastern front of Mount Davidson, overlooking the city, put on such a funereal gloom that only the nearness and solidity of the mountain made its outlines even faintly distinguishable from the dead blackness of the heavens they rested against. This unaccustomed sight turned all eyes toward the mountain; and as they looked, a little tongue of rich golden flame was seen waving and quivering in the heart of the midnight, away up on the extreme summit! In a few minutes the streets were packed with people, gazing with hardly an uttered word, at the one brilliant mote in the brooding world of darkness. It flicked like a candle-flame, and looked no larger; but with such a background it was wonderfully bright, small as it was. It was the flag!—though no one suspected it at first, it seemed so like a supernatural visitor of some kind—a mysterious messenger of good tidings, some were fain to believe. It was the nation's emblem transfigured by the departing rays of a sun that was entirely palled from view; and on no other object did the glory fall, in all the broad panorama of mountain ranges and deserts. Not even upon the staff of the flag—for that, a needle in the distance at any time, was now untouched by the light and undistinguishable in the gloom. For a whole hour the weird visitor winked and burned in its lofty solitude, and still the thousands of uplifted eyes watched it with fascinated interest. How the people were wrought up! The superstition grew apace that this was a mystic courier come with great news from the war—the poetry of the idea excusing and commending it—and on it spread, from heart to heart, from lip to lip and from street to street, till there was a general impulse to have out the military and welcome the bright waif with a salvo of artillery!

And all that time one sorely tired man, the telegraph operator sworn to official secrecy, had to lock his lips and chain his tongue with a silence that was like to rend them; for he, and he only, of all the speculating multitude, knew the great things this sinking sun had seen that day in the east—Vicksburg fallen, and the Union arms victorious at Gettysburg!

But for the journalistic monopoly that forbade the slightest revealment of eastern news till a day after its publication in the California papers, the glorified flag on Mount Davidson would have been saluted and re-saluted, that memorable evening, as long as there was a charge of powder to thunder with; the city would have been illuminated, and every man that had any respect for himself would have got drunk,—as was the custom of the country on all occasions of public moment. Even at this distant day I cannot think of this needlessly marred supreme opportunity without regret. What a time we might have had!

CHAPTER LVI

We rumbled over the plains and valleys, climbed the Sierras to the clouds, and looked down upon summer-clad California. And I will remark here, in passing, that all scenery in California requires *distance* to give it its highest charm. The mountains are imposing in their sublimity and their majesty of form and altitude, from any point of view—but one must have distance to soften their ruggedness and enrich their tintings; a Californian forest is best at a little distance, for there is a sad poverty of variety in species, the trees being chiefly of one monotonous family—redwood, pine, spruce, fir—and so, at a near view there is a wearisome sameness of attitude in their rigid arms, stretched downward and outward in one continued and reiterated appeal to all men to "Sh!—don't say a word!—you might disturb somebody!" Close at hand, too, there is a reliefless and relentless smell of pitch and turpentine; there is a ceaseless melancholy in their sighing and complaining foliage; one walks over a soundless carpet of beaten yellow bark and dead spines of the foliage till he feels like a wandering spirit bereft of a footfall; he tires of the endless tufts of needles and yearns for substantial, shapely leaves; he looks for moss and grass to loll upon, and finds none, for where there is no bark there is naked clay and dirt, enemies to pensive musing and clean apparel. Often a grassy plain in California, is what it should be, but often, too, it is best contemplated at a distance, because although its grass blades are tall, they stand up vindictively straight and self-sufficient, and are unsociably wide apart, with uncomely spots of barrens and between.

One of the queerest things I know of, is to hear tourists from "the States" go into ecstasies over the loveliness of "everblooming California." And they always do go into that sort of ecstasies. But perhaps they would modify them if they knew how old Californians, with the memory full upon them of the dust-covered and questionable summer greens of Californian "verdure," stand astonished, and filled with worshipping admiration, in the presence of the lavish richness, the brilliant green, the infinite freshness, the spendthrift variety of form and species and foliage that make an Eastern landscape a vision of Paradise itself. The idea of a man falling into raptures over grave and sombre California, when that man has seen New England's meadow-expanses and her maples, oaks and cathedral-windowed elms decked in summer attire, or the opaline splendors of autumn descending upon her forests, comes very near being funny—would be, in fact, but that it is so pathetic. No land with an unvarying climate can be very beautiful. The tropics are not, for all the sentiment that is wasted on them. They seem beautiful at first, but sameness impairs the charm by and by. *Change* is the handmaiden Nature requires to do her miracles with. The land that has four well-defined seasons, cannot lack beauty, or pall with monotony. Each season brings a world of enjoyment and interest in the watching of its unfolding, its gradual, harmonious development, its culminating graces—and just as one begins to tire of it, it passes away and a radical change comes, with new witcheries and new glories in its train. And I think that to one in sympathy with nature, each season, in its turn, seems the loveliest.

San Francisco, a truly fascinating city to live in, is stately and handsome at a fair distance, but close at hand one notes that the architecture is mostly old-fashioned, many streets are made up of decaying, smoke-grimed, wooden houses, and the barren sand-hills toward the outskirts obtrude themselves too prominently. Even the kindly climate is sometimes pleasanter when read about than personally experienced, for a lovely, cloudless sky wears out its welcome by and by, and then when the longed for rain does come it *stays*. Even the playful earthquake is better contemplated at a dis— .

However there are varying opinions about that.

The climate of San Francisco is mild and singularly equable. The thermometer stands at about seventy degrees the year round. It hardly changes at all. You sleep under one or two light blankets Summer and Winter, and never use a mosquito bar. Nobody ever wears Summer clothing. You wear black broadcloth—if you have it—in August and January, just the same. It is no colder, and no warmer, in the one month than the other. You do not use overcoats and you do not use fans. It is as pleasant a climate as could well be contrived, take it all around, and is doubtless the most unvarying in the whole world. The wind blows there a good deal in the Summer months, but then you can go over to Oakland, if you choose—three or four miles away—it does not blow there. It has only snowed twice in San Francisco in nineteen years, and then it only remained on the ground long enough to astonish the children, and set them to wondering what the feathery stuff was.

During eight months of the year, straight along, the skies are bright and cloudless, and never a drop of rain falls. But when the other four months come along, you will need to go and steal an umbrella. Because you will require it. Not just one day, but one hundred and twenty days in hardly varying succession. When you want to go visiting, or attend church, or the theatre, you never look up at the clouds to see whether it is likely to rain or not—you look at the almanac. If it is Winter, it will *rain*—and if it is Summer, it *won't* rain, and you cannot help it. You never need a lightning-rod, because it never thunders and it never lightens. And after you have listened for six or eight weeks, every night, to the dismal monotony of those quiet rains, you will wish in your heart the thunder *would* leap and crash and

roar along those drowsy skies once, and make everything alive—
you will wish the prisoned lightnings *would* cleave the dull firmament asunder and light it with a blinding glare for *one* little
instant. You would give *anything* to hear the old familiar
thunder again and see the lightning strike somebody. And along
in the Summer, when you have suffered about four months of
lustrous, pitiless sunshine, you are ready to go down on your
knees and plead for rain—hail—snow—thunder and lightning—
anything to break the monotony—you will take an earthquake,
if you cannot do any better. And the chances are that you'll get
it, too.

San Francisco is built on sand hills, but they are prolific sand
hills. They yield a generous vegetation. All the rare flowers
which people in "the States" rear with such patient care in
parlor flower-pots and green-houses, flourish luxuriantly in the
open air there all the year round. Calla lilies, all sorts of
geraniums, passion flowers, moss roses—I do not know the
names of a tenth part of them. I only know that while New
Yorkers are burdened with banks and drifts of snow, Californians are burdened with banks and drifts of flowers, if they only
keep their hands off and let them grow. And I have heard that
they have also that rarest and most curious of all the flowers, the
beautiful *Espiritu Santo,* as the Spaniards call it—or flower of
the Holy Spirit—though I thought it grew only in Central
America—down on the Isthmus. In its cup is the daintiest little
fac-simile of a dove, as pure as snow. The Spaniards have a
superstitious reverence for it. The blossom has been conveyed to
the States, submerged in ether; and the bulb has been taken
thither also, but every attempt to make it bloom after it arrived,
has failed.

I have elsewhere spoken of the endless Winter of Mono,
California, and but this moment of the eternal Spring of San
Francisco. Now if we travel a hundred miles in a straight line, we
come to the eternal Summer of Sacramento. One never sees
Summer-clothing or mosquitoes in San Francisco—but they can
be found in Sacramento. Not always and unvaryingly, but about
one hundred and forty-three months out of twelve years, perhaps. Flowers bloom there, always, the reader can easily
believe—people suffer and sweat, and swear, morning, noon
and night, and wear out their stanchest energies fanning themselves. It gets hot there, but if you go down to Fort Yuma you
will find it hotter. Fort Yuma is probably the hottest place on
earth. The thermometer stays at one hundred and twenty in the
shade there all the time—except when it varies and goes higher.
It is a U.S. military post, and its occupants get so used to the ter-

rific heat that they suffer without it. There is a tradition (attributed to John Phenix*) that a very, very wicked soldier died there, once, and of course, went straight to the hottest corner of perdition,—and the next day he *telegraphed back for his blankets.* There is no doubt about the truth of this statement— there can be no doubt about it. I have seen the place where that soldier used to board. In Sacramento it is fiery Summer always, and you can gather roses, and eat strawberries and ice-cream, and wear white linen clothes, and pant and perspire, at eight or nine o'clock in the morning, and then take the cars, and at noon put on your furs and your skates, and go skimming over frozen Donner Lake, seven thousand feet above the valley, among snow banks fifteen feet deep, and in the shadow of grand mountain peaks that lift their frosty crags ten thousand feet above the level of the sea. There is a transition for you! Where will you find another like it in the Western hemisphere? And some of us have swept around snow-walled curves of the Pacific Railroad in that vicinity, six thousand feet above the sea, and looked down as the birds do, upon the deathless Summer of the Sacramento Valley, with its fruitful fields, its feathery foliage, its silver streams, all slumbering in the mellow haze of its enchanted atmosphere, and all infinitely softened and spiritualized by distance—a dreamy, exquisite glimpse of fairyland, made all the more charming and striking that it was caught through a forbidden gateway of ice and snow, and savage crags and precipices.

CHAPTER LVII

It was in this Sacramento Valley, just referred to, that a deal of the most lucrative of the early gold mining was done, and you may still see, in places, its grassy slopes and levels torn and guttered and disfigured by the avaricious spoilers of fifteen and twenty years ago. You may see such disfigurements far and wide over California—and in some such places, where only meadows and forests are visible—not a living creature, not a house, no stick or stone or remnant of a ruin, and not a sound, not even a whisper to disturb the Sabbath stillness—you will find it hard to believe that there stood at one time a fiercely-flourishing little city, of two thousand or three thousand souls, with its newspaper, fire company, brass band, volunteer militia, bank, hotels, noisy Fourth of July processions and speeches, gambling hells crammed with tobacco smoke, profanity, and rough-

*It has been purloined by fifty different scribblers who were too poor to invent a fancy but not ashamed to steal one.—M.T.

bearded men of all nations and colors, with tables heaped with gold dust sufficient for the revenues of a German principality—streets crowded and rife with business—town lots worth four hundred dollars a front foot—labor, laughter, music, dancing, swearing, fighting, shooting, stabbing—a bloody inquest and a man for breakfast every morning—*everything* that delights and adorns existence—all the appointments and appurtenances of a thriving and prosperous and promising young city,—and *now* nothing is left of it all but a lifeless, homeless solitude. The men are gone, the houses have vanished, even the *name* of the place is forgotten. In no other land, in modern times, have towns so absolutely died and disappeared, as in the old mining regions of California.

It was a driving, vigorous, restless population in those days. It was a *curious* population. It was the *only* population of the kind that the world has ever seen gathered together, and it is not likely that the world will ever see its like again. For, observe, it was an assemblage of two hundred thousand *young* men—not simpering, dainty, kid-gloved weaklings, but stalwart, muscular, dauntless young braves, brimful of push and energy, and royally endowed with every attribute that goes to make up a peerless and magnificent manhood—the very pick and choice of the world's glorious ones. No women, no children, no gray and stooping veterans,—none but erect, bright-eyed, quick-moving, strong-handed young giants—the strangest population, the finest population, the most gallant host that ever trooped down the startled solitudes of an unpeopled land. And where are they now? Scattered to the ends of the earth—or prematurely aged and decrepit—or shot or stabbed in street affrays—or dead of disappointed hopes and broken hearts—all gone, or nearly all—victims devoted upon the altar of the golden calf—the noblest holocaust that ever wafted its sacrificial incense heavenward. It is pitiful to think upon.

It was a splendid population—for all the slow, sleepy, sluggish-brained sloths staid at home—you never find that sort of people among pioneers—you cannot build pioneers out of that sort of material. It was that population that gave to California a name for getting up astounding enterprises and rushing them through with a magnificent dash and daring and a recklessness of cost or consequences, which she bears unto this day—and when she projects a new surprise, the grave world smiles as usual, and says "Well, that is California all over."

But they were rough in those times! They fairly reveled in gold, whisky, fights, and fandangoes, and were unspeakably happy. The honest miner raked from a hundred to a thousand dollars out of his claim a day, and what with the gambling dens and the other entertainments, he hadn't a cent the next morning, if he had any sort of luck. They cooked their own bacon and beans, sewed on their own buttons, washed their own shirts—blue woollen ones; and if a man wanted a fight on his hands without any annoying delay, all he had to do was to appear in public in a white shirt or a stove-pipe hat, and he would be accommodated. For those people hated aristocrats. They had a particular and malignant animosity toward what they called a "biled shirt."

It was a wild, free, disorderly, grotesque society! *Men*—only swarming hosts of stalwart *men*—nothing juvenile, nothing feminine, visible anywhere!

In those days miners would flock in crowds to catch a glimpse of that rare and blessed spectacle, a woman! Old inhabitants tell how, in a certain camp, the news went abroad early in the morning that a woman was come! They had seen a calico dress hanging out of a wagon down at the camping-ground—sign of emigrants from over the great plains. Everybody went down there, and a shout went up when an actual, bona fide dress was discovered fluttering in the wind! The man emigrant was visible. The miners said:

"Fetch her out!"

He said: "It is my wife, gentlemen—she is sick—we have been robbed of money, provisions, everything, by the Indians—we want to rest."

"Fetch her out! We've got to see her!"

"But, gentlemen, the poor thing, she—"

"FETCH HER OUT!"

He "fetched her out," and they swung their hats and sent up three rousing cheers and a tiger; and they crowded around and gazed at her, and touched her dress, and listened to her voice with the look of men who listened to a *memory* rather than a present reality—and then they collected twenty-five hundred dollars in gold and gave it to the man, and swung their hats again and gave three more cheers, and went home satisfied.

Once I dined in San Francisco with the family of a pioneer, and talked with his daughter, a young lady whose first experience in San Francisco was an adventure, though she herself did not remember it, as she was only two or three years old at the time. Her father said that, after landing from the ship, they were walking up the street, a servant leading the party with the little girl in her arms. And presently a huge miner, bearded, belted, spurred, and bristling with deadly weapons—just down from a long campaign in the mountains, evidently—barred the way, stopped the servant, and stood gazing, with a face all alive with gratification and astonishment. Then he said, reverently:

"Well, if it ain't a child!" And then he snatched a little leather sack out of his pocket and said to the servant:

"There's a hundred and fifty dollars in dust, there, and I'll give it to you to let me kiss the child!"

That anecdote is *true*.

But see how things change. Sitting at that dinner-table, listening to that anecdote, if I had offered double the money for the privilege of kissing the same child, I would have been refused. Seventeen added years have far more than doubled the price.

And while upon this subject I will remark that once in Star City, in the Humboldt Mountains, I took my place in a sort of long, post-office single file of miners, to patiently await my chance to peep through a crack in the cabin and get a sight of the splendid new sensation—a genuine, live Woman! And at the end of half of an hour my turn came, and I put my eye to the crack, and there she was, with one arm akimbo, and tossing flap-jacks in a frying-pan with the other. And she was one hundred and sixty-five* years old, and hadn't a tooth in her head.

CHAPTER LVIII

For a few months I enjoyed what to me was an entirely new phase of existence—a butterfly idleness; nothing to do, nobody to be responsible to, and untroubled with financial uneasiness. I fell in love with the most cordial and sociable city in the Union. After the sage-brush and alkali deserts of Washoe, San Francisco was Paradise to me. I lived at the best hotel, exhibited my clothes in the most conspicuous places, infested the opera, and learned to seem enraptured with music which oftener afflicted my ignorant ear than enchanted it, if I had had the vulgar honesty to confess it. However, I suppose I was not greatly worse than the most of my countrymen in that. I had longed to be a butterfly, and I was one at last. I attended private parties in sumptuous evening dress, simpered and aired my graces like a born beau, and polked and schottisched with a step peculiar to myself—and the kangaroo. In a word, I kept the due state of a man worth a hundred thousand dollars (prospectively,) and likely to reach absolute affluence when that silvermine sale should be ultimately achieved in the East. I spent money with a free hand, and meantime watched the stock sales with an interested eye and looked to see what might happen in Nevada.

*Being in calmer mood, now, I voluntarily knock off a hundred from that.—M.T.

Something very important happened. The property holders of Nevada voted against the State Constitution; but the folks who had nothing to lose were in the majority, and carried the measure over their heads. But after all it did not immediately look like a disaster, though unquestionably it was one. I hesitated, calculated the chances, and then concluded not to sell. Stocks went on rising; speculation went mad; bankers, merchants, lawyers, doctors, mechanics, laborers, even the very washerwomen and servant girls, were putting up their earnings on silver stocks, and every sun that rose in the morning went down on paupers enriched and rich men beggared. What a gambling carnival it was! Gould and Curry soared to six thousand three hundred dollars a foot! And then—all of a sudden, out went the bottom and everything and everybody went to ruin and destruction! The wreck was complete. The bubble scarcely left a microscopic moisture behind it. I was an early beggar and a thorough one. My hoarded stocks were not worth the paper they were printed on. I threw them all away. I, the cheerful idiot that had been squandering money like water, and thought myself beyond the reach of misfortune, had not now as much as fifty dollars when I gathered together my various debts and paid them. I removed from the hotel to a very private boarding house. I took a reporter's berth and went to work. I was not entirely broken in spirit, for I was building confidently on the sale of the silver mine in the east. But I could not hear from Dan. My letters miscarried or were not answered.

One day I did not feel vigorous and remained away from the office. The next day I went down toward noon as usual, and found a note on my desk which had been there twenty-four hours. It was signed "Marshall"—the Virginia reporter—and contained a request that I should call at the hotel and see him and a friend or two that night, as they would sail for the east in the morning. A postscript added that their errand was a big mining speculation! I was hardly ever so sick in my life. I abused myself for leaving Virginia and entrusting to another man a matter I ought to have attended to myself; I abused myself for remaining away from the office on the one day of all the year that I should have been there. And thus berating myself I trotted a mile to the steamer wharf and arrived just in time to be too late. The ship was in the stream and under way.

I comforted myself with the thought that may be the speculation would amount to nothing—poor comfort at best—and then went back to my slavery, resolved to put up with my thirty-five dollars a week and forget all about it.

A month afterward I enjoyed my first earthquake. It was one

which was long called the "great" earthquake, and is doubtless so distinguished till this day. It was just after noon, on a bright October day. I was coming down Third street. The only objects in motion anywhere in sight in that thickly built and populous quarter, were a man in a buggy behind me, and a street car wending slowly up the cross street. Otherwise, all was solitude and a Sabbath stillness. As I turned the corner, around a frame house, there was a great rattle and jar, and it occurred to me that here was an item!—no doubt a fight in that house. Before I could turn and seek the door, there came a really terrific shock; the ground seemed to roll under me in waves, interrupted by a violent joggling up and down, and there was a heavy grinding noise as of brick houses rubbing together. I fell up against the frame house and hurt my elbow. I knew what it was, now, and from mere reportorial instinct, nothing else, took out my watch and noted the time of day; at that moment a third and still severer shock came, and as I reeled about on the pavement trying to keep my footing, I saw a sight! The entire front of a tall four-story brick building in Third street sprung outward like a door and fell sprawling across the street, raising a dust like a great volume of smoke! And here came the buggy—overboard went the man, and in less time than I can tell it the vehicle was distributed in small fragments along three hundred yards of street. One could have fancied that somebody had fired a charge of chair-rounds and rags down the thoroughfare. The street car had stopped, the horses were rearing and plunging, the passengers were pouring out at both ends, and one fat man had crashed half way through a glass window on one side of the car, got wedged fast and was squirming and screaming like an impaled madman. Every door, of every house, as far as the eye could reach, was vomiting a stream of human beings; and almost before one could execute a wink and begin another, there was a massed multitude of people stretching in endless procession down every street my position commanded. Never was solemn solitude turned into teeming life quicker.

Of the wonders wrought by "the great earthquake," these were all that came under my eye; but the tricks it did, elsewhere, and far and wide over the town, made toothsome gossip for nine days. The destruction of property was trifling—the injury to it was wide-spread and somewhat serious.

The "curiosities" of the earthquake were simply endless. Gentlemen and ladies who were sick, or were taking a siesta, or had dissipated till a late hour and were making up lost sleep, thronged into the public streets in all sorts of queer apparel, and some without any at all. One woman who had been washing a naked child, ran down the street holding it by the ankles as if it were a dressed turkey. Prominent citizens who were supposed to keep the Sabbath strictly, rushed out of saloons in their shirt-sleeves, with billiard cues in their hands. Dozens of men with necks swathed in napkins, rushed from barber-shops, lathered to the eyes or with one cheek clean shaved and the other still bearing a hairy stubble. Horses broke from stables, and a frightened dog rushed up a short attic ladder and out on to a roof, and when his scare was over had not the nerve to go down again the same way he had gone up. A prominent editor flew down stairs, in the principal hotel, with nothing on but one brief undergarment—met a chambermaid, and exclaimed:

"Oh, what *shall* I do! Where shall I go!"

She responded with naive serenity:

"If you have no choice, you might try a clothing-store!"

A certain foreign consul's lady was the acknowledged leader of fashion, and every time she appeared in anything new or extraordinary, the ladies in the vicinity made a raid on their husbands' purses and arrayed themselves similarly. One man who had suffered considerably and growled accordingly, was standing at the window when the shocks came, and the next instant the consul's wife, just out of the bath, fled by with no other apology for clothing than—a bath-towel! The sufferer rose superior to the terrors of the earthquake, and said to his wife:

"Now *that* is something *like!* Get out your towel my dear!"

The plastering that fell from ceilings in San Francisco that day, would have covered several acres of ground. For some days afterward, groups of eyeing and pointing men stood about many a building, looking at long zig-zag cracks that extended from the eaves to the ground. Four feet of the tops of three chimneys on one house were broken square off and turned around in such a way as to completely stop the draft. A crack a hundred feet long gaped open six inches wide in the middle of one street and then shut together again with such force, as to ridge up the meeting earth like a slender grave. A lady sitting in her rocking and quaking parlor, saw the wall part at the ceiling, open and shut twice, like a mouth, and then-drop the end of a brick on the floor like a tooth. She was a woman easily disgusted with foolishness, and she arose and went out of there. One lady who was coming down stairs was astonished to see a bronze Hercules lean forward on its pedestal as if to strike her with its club. They both reached the bottom of the flight at the same time,—the woman insensible from the fright. Her child, born some little time afterward, was club-footed. However—on second thought,—if the reader sees any coincidence in this, he must do it at his own risk.

The first shock brought down two or three huge organ-pipes in one of the churches. The minister, with uplifted hands, was just closing the services. He glanced up, hesitated, and said:

"However, we will omit the benediction!"—and the next instant there was a vacancy in the atmosphere where he had stood.

After the first shock, an Oakland minister said:

"Keep your seats! There is no better place to die than this"—

And added, after the third:

"But outside is good enough!" He then skipped out at the back door.

Such another destruction of mantel ornaments and toilet bottles as the earthquake created, San Francisco never saw before. There was hardly a girl or a matron in the city but suffered losses of this kind. Suspended pictures were thrown down, but oftener still, by a curious freak of the earthquake's humor, they were whirled completely around with their faces to the wall! There was great difference of opinion, at first, as to the course or direction the earthquake traveled, but water that splashed out of various tanks and buckets settled that. Thousands of people were made so sea-sick by the rolling and pitching of floors and streets that they were weak and bed-ridden for hours, and some few for even days afterward.—Hardly an individual escaped nausea entirely.

The queer earthquake—episodes that formed the staple of San Francisco gossip for the next week would fill a much larger book than this, and so I will diverge from the subject.

By and by, in the due course of things, I picked up a copy of the *Enterprise* one day, and fell under this cruel blow:

NEVADA MINES IN NEW YORK.—G.M. Marshall, Sheba Hurs and Amos H. Rose, who left San Francisco last July for New York City, with ores from mines in Pine Wood District, Humboldt County, and on the Reese River range, have disposed of a mine containing six thousand feet and called the Pine Mountains Consolidated, for the sum of $3,000,000. The stamps on the deed, which is now on its way to Humboldt County, from New York, for record, amounted to $3,000, which is said to be the largest amount of stamps ever placed on one document. A working capital of $1,000,000 has been paid into the treasury, and machinery has already been purchased for a large quartz mill, which will be put up as soon as possible. The stock in this company is all full paid and entirely unassessable. The ores of the mines in this district somewhat resemble those of the Sheba mine in Humboldt. Sheba Hurst, the discoverer of the mines, with his friends corralled all the best leads and all the land and timber they desired before making public their whereabouts. Ores from there, assayed in this city, showed them to be exceedingly rich in silver and gold—silver predominating. There is an abundance of wood and water in the District. We are glad to know that New York capital has been enlisted in the development of the mines of this region. Having seen the ores and assays, we are satisfied that the mines of the District are very valuable—anything but wild-cat.

Once more native imbecility had carried the day, and I had lost a million! It was the "blind lead" over again.

Let us not dwell on this miserable matter. If I were inventing these things, I could be wonderfully humorous over them; but they are too true to be talked of with hearty levity, even at this distant day.* Suffice it that I so lost heart, and so yielded myself up to repinings and sighings and foolish regrets, that I neglected my duties and became about worthless, as a reporter for a brisk newspaper. And at last one of the proprietors took me aside, with a charity I still remember with considerable respect, and gave me an opportunity to resign my berth and so save myself the disgrace of a dismissal.

CHAPTER LIX

For a time I wrote literary screeds for the *Golden Era.* C. H. Webb had established a very excellent literary weekly called the *Californian,* but high merit was no guaranty of success; it languished, and he sold out to three printers, and Bret Harte became editor at $20 a week, and I was employed to contribute an article a week at $12. But the journal still languished, and the printers sold out to Captain Ogden, a rich man and a pleasant gentleman who chose to amuse himself with such an expensive luxury without much caring about the cost of it. When he grew tired of the novelty, he re-sold to the printers, the paper presently died a peaceful death, and I was out of work again. I would not mention these things but for the fact that they so aptly illustrate the ups and downs that characterize life on the Pacific coast. A man could hardly stumble into such a variety of queer vicissitudes in any other country.

---

*True, and yet not exactly as given in the above figures, possibly. I saw Marshall, months afterward, and although he had plenty of money he did not claim to have captured an entire *million.* In fact I gathered that he had not then received $50,000. Beyond that figure his fortune appeared to consist of uncertain vast expectations rather than prodigious certainties. However, when the above item appeared in print I put full faith in it, and incontinently wilted and went to seed under it.

For two months my sole occupation was avoiding acquaintances; for during that time I did not earn a penny, or buy an article of any kind, or pay my board. I became a very adept at
"slinking." I slunk from back street to back street, I slunk away
from approaching faces that looked familiar, I slunk to my
meals, ate them humbly and with a mute apology for every
mouthful I robbed my generous landlady of, and at midnight,
after wanderings that were but slinkings away from cheerfulness
and light, I slunk to my bed. I felt meaner, and lowlier and more
despicable than the worms. During all this time I had but one
piece of money—a silver ten cent piece—and I held to it and
would not spend it on any account, lest the consciousness
coming strong upon me that I was *entirely* penniless, might suggest suicide. I had pawned every thing but the clothes I had on;
so I clung to my dime desperately, till it was smooth with handling.

However, I am forgetting. I did have one other occupation
beside that of "slinking." It was the entertaining of a collector
(and being entertained by him,) who had in his hands the
Virginia banker's bill for the forty-six dollars which I had loaned
my schoolmate, the "Prodigal." This man used to call regularly
once a week and dun me, and sometimes oftener. He did it from
sheer force of habit, for he knew he could get nothing. He would
get out his bill, calculate the interest for me, at five per cent a
month, and show me clearly that there was no attempt at fraud
in it and no mistakes; and then plead, and argue and dun with all
his might for any sum—any little trifle—even a dollar—even
half a dollar, on account. Then his duty was accomplished and
his conscience free. He immediately dropped the subject there
always; got out a couple of cigars and divided, put his feet in the
window, and then we would have a long, luxurious talk about
everything and everybody, and he would furnish me a world of
curious dunning adventures out of the ample store in his
memory. By and by he would clap his hat on his head, shake
hands and say briskly:

"Well, business is business—can't stay with you always!"—
and was off in a second.

The idea of pining for a dun! And yet I used to long for him to
come, and would get as uneasy as any mother if the day went by
without his visit, when I was expecting him. But he never collected that bill, at last nor any part of it. I lived to pay it to the
banker myself.

Misery loves company. Now and then at night, in out-of-the-
way, dimly lighted places, I found myself happening on another
child of misfortune. He looked so seedy and forlorn, so home-

less and friendless and forsaken, that I yearned toward him as a brother. I wanted to claim kinship with him and go about and enjoy our wretchedness together. The drawing toward each other must have been mutual; at any rate we got to falling together oftener, though still seemingly by accident; and although we did not speak or evince any recognition, I think the dull anxiety passed out of both of us when we saw each other, and then for several hours we would idle along contentedly, wide apart, and glancing furtively in at home lights and fireside gatherings, out of the night shadows, and very much enjoying our dumb companionship.

Finally we spoke, and were inseparable after that. For our woes were identical, almost. He had been a reporter too, and lost his berth, and this was his experience, as nearly as I can recollect it. After losing his berth, he had gone down, down, down, with never a halt: from a boarding house on Russian Hill to a boarding house in Kearney street; from thence to Dupont; from thence to a low sailor den; and from thence to lodgings in goods boxes and empty hogsheads near the wharves. Then, for a while, he had gained a meagre living by sewing up bursted sacks of grain on the piers; when that failed he had found food here and there as chance threw it in his way. He had ceased to show his face in daylight, now, for a reporter knows everybody, rich and poor, high and low, and cannot well avoid familiar faces in the broad light of day.

This mendicant Blucher—I call him that for convenience— was a splendid creature. He was full of hope, pluck and philosophy; he was well read and a man of cultivated taste; he had a bright wit and was a master of satire; his kindliness and his generous spirit made him royal in my eyes and changed his curbstone seat to a throne and his damaged hat to a crown.

He had an adventure, once, which sticks fast in my memory as the most pleasantly grotesque that ever touched my sympathies. He had been without a penny for two months. He had shirked about obscure streets, among friendly dim lights, till the thing had become second nature to him. But at last he was driven abroad in daylight. The cause was sufficient; *he had not tasted food for forty-eight hours,* and he could not endure the misery of his hunger in idle hiding. He came along a back street, glowering at the loaves in bake-shop windows, and feeling that he could trade his life away for a morsel to eat. The sight of the bread doubled his hunger; but it was good to look at it, any how, and imagine what one might do if one only had it. Presently, in the middle of the street he saw a shining spot—looked again— did not, and could not, believe his eyes—turned away, to try them, then looked again. It was a verity—no vain, hunger-inspired delusion—it was a silver dime! He snatched it—gloated over it; doubted it—bit it—found it genuine—choked his heart down, and smothered a halleluiah. Then he looked around—saw that nobody was looking at him—threw the dime down where it was before—walked away a few steps, and approached again, pretending he did not know it was there, so that he could re-enjoy the luxury of finding it. He walked around it, viewing it from different points; then sauntered about with his hands in his pockets, looking up at the signs and now and then glancing at it and feeling the old thrill again. Finally he took it up, and went away, fondling it in his pocket. He idled through unfrequented streets, stopping in doorways and corners to take it out and look at it. By and by he went home to his lodgings—an empty queensware hogshead,—and employed himself till night trying to make up his mind what to buy with it. But it was hard to do. To get the most for it was the idea. He knew that at the Miner's Restaurant he could get a plate of beans and a piece of bread for ten cents; or a fish-ball and some few trifles, but they gave "no bread with one fish-ball" there. At French Pete's he could get a veal cutlet, plain, and some radishes and bread, for ten cents; or a cup of coffee—a pint at least—and a slice of bread; but the slice was not thick enough by the eighth of an inch, and sometimes they were still more criminal than that in the cutting of it. At seven o'clock his hunger was wolfish; and still his mind was not made up. He turned out and went up Merchant street, still ciphering; and chewing a bit of stick, as is the way of starving men. He passed before the lights of Martin's restaurant, the most aristocratic in the city, and stopped. It was a place where he had often dined, in better days, and Martin knew him well. Standing aside, just out of the range of the light, he worshiped the quails and steaks in the show window, and imagined that may be the fairy times were not gone yet and some prince in disguise would come along presently and tell him to go in there and take whatever he wanted. He chewed his stick with a hungry interest as he warmed to his subject. Just at this juncture he was conscious of some one at his side, sure enough; and then a finger touched his arm. He looked up, over his shoulder, and saw an apparition—a very allegory of Hunger! It was a man six feet high, gaunt, unshaven, hung with rags; with a haggard face and sunken cheeks, and eyes that pleaded piteously. This phantom said:

"Come with me—please."

He locked his arm in Blucher's and walked up the street to where the passengers were few and the light not strong, and then facing about, put out his hands in a beseeching way, and said:

"Friend—stranger—look at me! Life is easy to you— you go about, placid and content, as I did once, in my day—you have been in there, and eaten your sumptuous supper, and picked your teeth, and hummed your tune, and thought your pleasant thoughts, and said to yourself it is a good world—but you've never *suffered!* You don't know what trouble is—you don't know what misery is— nor hunger! Look at me! Stranger have pity on a poor friendless, homeless dog! As God is my judge, I have not tasted food for eight and forty hours!—look in my eyes and see if I lie! Give me the least trifle in the world to keep me from starving—anything—twenty-five cents! Do it, stranger— do it, *please.* It will be nothing to you, but life to me. Do it, and I will go down on my knees and lick the dust before you! I will kiss your footprints—I will worship the very ground you walk on! Only twenty-five cents! I am famishing—perishing— starving by inches! For God's sake don't desert me!"

Blucher was bewildered—and touched, too—stirred to the depths. He reflected. Thought again. Then an idea struck him, and he said:

"Come with me."

He took the outcast's arm, walked him down to Martin's restaurant, seated him at a marble table, placed the bill of fare before him, and said:

"Order what you want, friend. Charge it to me, Mr. Martin."

"All right, Mr. Blucher," said Martin.

Then Blucher stepped back and leaned against the counter and watched the man stow away cargo after cargo of buckwheat cakes at seventy-five cents a plate; cup after cup of coffee, and porter house steaks worth two dollars apiece; and when six dollars and a half's worth of destruction had been accomplished, and the stranger's hunger appeased, Blucher went down to French Pete's, bought a veal cutlet plain, a slice of bread, and three radishes, with his dime, and set to and feasted like a king!

Take the episode all around, it was as odd as any that can be culled from the myriad curiosities of Californian life, perhaps.

CHAPTER LX

By and by, an old friend of mine, a miner, came down from one of the decayed mining camps of Tuolumne, California, and I went back with him. We lived in a small cabin on a verdant hillside, and there were not five other cabins in view over the wide expanse of hill and forest. Yet a flourishing city of two or three thousand population had occupied this grassy dead solitude during the flush times of twelve or fifteen years before, and where our cabin stood had once been the heart of the teeming hive, the centre of the city. When the mines gave out the town fell into decay, and in a few years wholly disappeared— streets, dwellings, shops, everything—and left no sign. The grassy slopes were as green and smooth and desolate of life as if they had never been disturbed. The mere handful of miners still remaining, had seen the town spring up, spread, grow and flourish in its pride; and they had seen it sicken and die, and pass away like a dream. With it their hopes had died, and their zest of life. They had long ago resigned themselves to their exile, and ceased to correspond with their distant friends or turn longing eyes toward their early homes. They had accepted banishment, forgotten the world and been forgotten of the world. They were far from telegraphs and railroads, and they stood, as it were, in a living grave, dead to the events that stirred the globe's great populations, dead to the common interests of men, isolated and outcast from brotherhood with their kind. It was the most singular, and almost the most touching and melancholy exile that fancy can imagine.—One of my associates in this locality, for two or three months, was a man who had had a university education; but now for eighteen years he had decayed there by inches, a bearded, rough-clad, clay-stained miner, and at times, among his sighings and soliloquizings, he unconsciously interjected vaguely remembered Latin and Greek sentences—dead and musty tongues, meet vehicles for the thoughts of one whose dreams were all of the past, whose life was a failure; a tired man, burdened with the present, and indifferent to the future; a man without ties, hopes, interests, waiting for rest and the end.

In that one little corner of California is found a species of mining which is seldom or never mentioned in print. It is called "pocket mining" and I am not aware that any of it is done outside of that little corner. The gold is not evenly distributed through the surface dirt, as in ordinary placer mines, but is collected in little spots, and they are very wide apart and exceedingly hard to find, but when you do find one you reap a rich and sudden harvest. There are not now more than twenty pocket miners in that entire little region. I think I know every one of them personally. I have known one of them to hunt patiently about the hill-sides every day for eight months without finding gold enough to make a snuff-box—his grocery bill running up relentlessly all the time—and then find a pocket and take out of it two thousand dollars in two dips of his shovel. I have known him to take out three thousand dollars in two hours, and go and pay up every cent of his indebtedness, then enter on a dazzling spree that finished the last of his treasure before the night was gone. And the next day he bought his groceries on credit as usual, and shouldered his pan and shovel and went off to the hills hunting pockets again happy and content. This is the most fascinating of all the different kinds of mining, and furnishes a very handsome percentage of victims to the lunatic asylum.

Pocket hunting is an ingenious process. You take a spadeful of earth from the hill-side and put it in a large tin pan and dissolve and wash it gradually away till nothing is left but a teaspoonful of fine sediment. Whatever gold was in that earth has remained, because, being the heaviest, it has sought the bottom. Among the sediment you will find half a dozen yellow particles no larger than pin-heads. You are delighted. You move off to one side and wash another pan. If you find gold again, you move to one side further, and wash a third pan. If you find *no* gold this time, you are delighted again, because you know you are on the right scent. You lay an imaginary plan, shaped like a fan, with its handle up the hill—for just where the end of the handle is, you argue that the rich deposit lies hidden, whose vagrant grains of gold have escaped and been washed down the hill, spreading farther and farther apart as they wandered. And so you proceed up the hill, washing the earth and narrowing your lines every time the absence of gold in the pan shows that you are outside the spread of the fan; and at last, twenty yards up the hill your lines have converged to a point—a single foot from that point you cannot find any gold. Your breath comes short and quick, you are feverish with excitement; the dinner-bell may ring its clapper off, you pay no attention; friends may die, weddings transpire, houses burn down, they are nothing to you; you sweat and dig and delve with a frantic interest—and all at once you strike it! Up comes a spadeful of earth and quartz that is all lovely with soiled lumps and leaves and sprays of gold. Sometimes that one spadeful is all—$500. Sometimes the nest contains $10,000, and it takes you three or four days to get it all out. The pocket-miners tell of one nest that yielded $60,000 and two men exhausted it in two weeks, and then sold the ground for $10,000 to a party who never got $300 out of it afterward.

The hogs are good pocket hunters. All the summer they root around the bushes, and turn up a thousand little piles of dirt, and then the miners long for the rains; for the rains beat upon these little piles and wash them down and expose the gold, possibly right over a pocket. Two pockets were found in this way by the same man in one day. One had $5,000 in it and the other

$8,000. That man could appreciate it, for he hadn't had a cent for about a year.

In Tuolumne lived two miners who used to go to the neighboring village in the afternoon and return every night with household supplies. Part of the distance they traversed a trail, and nearly always sat down to rest on a great boulder that lay beside the path. In the course of thirteen years they had worn that boulder tolerably smooth, sitting on it. By and by two vagrant Mexicans came along and occupied the seat. They began to amuse themselves by chipping off flakes from the boulder with a sledge-hammer. They examined one of these flakes and found it rich with gold. That boulder paid them $800 afterward. But the aggravating circumstance was that these "Greasers" knew that there must be more gold where that boulder came from, and so they went panning up the hill and found what was probably the richest pocket that region has yet produced. It took three months to exhaust it, and it yielded $120,000. The two American miners who used to sit on the boulder are poor yet, and they take turn about in getting up early in the morning to curse those Mexicans—and when it comes down to pure ornamental cursing, the native American is gifted above the sons of men.

I have dwelt at some length upon this matter of pocket mining because it is a subject that is seldom referred to in print, and therefore I judged that it would have for the reader that interest which naturally attaches to novelty.

CHAPTER LXI

One of my comrades there—another of those victims of eighteen years of unrequited toil and blighted hopes—was one of the gentlest spirits that ever bore its patient cross in a weary exile: grave and simple Dick Baker, pocket-miner of Dead-House Gulch.—He was forty-six, gray as a rat, earnest, thoughtful, slenderly educated, slouchily dressed and clay-soiled, but his heart was finer metal than any gold his shovel ever brought to light—than any, indeed, that ever was mined or minted.

Whenever he was out of luck and a little down-hearted, he would fall to mourning over the loss of a wonderful cat he used to own (for where women and children are not, men of kindly impulses take up with pets, for they must love something). And he always spoke of the strange sagacity of that cat with the air of a man who believed in his secret heart that there was something human about it—may be even supernatural.

I heard him talking about this animal once. He said:

"Gentlemen, I used to have a cat here, by the name of Tom Quartz, which you'd a took an interest in I reckon—most any body would. I had him here eight year—and he was the remarkablest cat *I* ever see. He was a large gray one of the Tom specie, an' he had more hard, natchral sense than any man in this camp—'n' a *power* of dignity—he wouldn't let the Gov'ner of Californy be familiar with him. He never ketched a rat in his life—'peared to be above it. He never cared for nothing but mining. He knowed more about mining, that cat did, than any man *I* ever, ever see. You couldn't tell *him* noth'n' 'bout placer diggin's—'n' as for pocket mining, why he was just born for it. He would dig out after me an' Jim when we went over the hills prospect'n', and he would trot along behind us for as much as five mile, if we went so fur. An' he had the best judgment about mining ground—why you never see anything like it. When we went to work, he'd scatter a glance around, 'n' if he didn't think much of the indications, he would give a look as much as to say, 'Well, I'll have to get you to excuse *me*,' 'n' without another word he'd hyste his nose into the air 'n' shove for home. But if the ground suited him, he would lay low 'n' keep dark till the first pan was washed, 'n' then he would sidle up 'n' take a look, an' if there was about six or seven grains of gold *he* was satisfied—he didn't want no better prospect 'n' that—'n' then he would lay down on our coats and snore like a steamboat till we'd struck the pocket, an' then get up 'n' superintend. He was nearly lightnin' on superintending.

"Well, bye an' bye, up comes this yer quartz excitement. Every body was into it—every body was pick'n' 'n' blast'n' instead of shovelin' dirt on the hill side—every body was put'n' down a shaft instead of scrapin' the surface. Noth'n' would do Jim, but *we* must tackle the ledges, too, 'n' so we did. We commenced put'n' down a shaft, 'n' Tom Quartz he begin to wonder what in the Dickens it was all about. *He* hadn't ever seen any mining like that before, 'n' he was all upset, as you may say—he couldn't come to a right understanding of it no way—it was too many for *him*. He was down on it, too, you bet you—he was down on it powerful—'n' always appeared to consider it the cussedest foolishness out. But that cat, you know, was *always* agin new fangled arrangements—somehow he never could abide 'em. *You* know how it is with old habits. But by an' by Tom Quartz begin to git sort of reconciled a little, though he never *could* altogether understand that eternal sinkin' of a shaft an' never pannin' out any thing. At last he got to comin' down in the shaft, hisself, to try to cipher it out. An' when he'd git the blues, 'n' feel kind o' scruffy, 'n' aggravated 'n' disgusted—knowin' as he did, that the bills was runnin' up all the time an' we warn't makin' a cent—he would curl up on a gunny sack in the corner an' go to sleep. Well, one day when the shaft was down about eight foot, the rock got so hard that we had to put in a blast—the first blast'n' we'd ever done since Tom Quartz was born. An' then we lit the fuse 'n' clumb out 'n' got off 'bout fifty yards— 'n' forgot 'n' left Tom Quartz sound asleep on the gunny sack. In 'bout a minute we seen a puff of smoke bust up out of the hole, 'n' then everything let go with an awful crash, 'n' about four million ton of rocks 'n' dirt 'n' smoke 'n' splinters shot up 'bout a mile an' a half into the air, an' by George, right in the dead centre of it was old Tom Quartz a goin' end over end, an' a snortin' an' a sneez'n', an' a clawin' an' a reachin' for things like all possessed. But it warn't no use, you know, it warn't no use. An' that was the last we see of *him* for about two minutes 'n' a half, an' then all of a sudden it begin to rain rocks and rubbage, an' directly he come down ker-whop about ten foot off f'm where we stood. Well, I reckon he was p'raps the orneriest lookin' beast you ever see. One ear was sot back on his neck, 'n' his tail was stove up, 'n' his eye-winkers was swinged off, 'n' he was all blacked up with powder an' smoke, an' all sloppy with mud 'n' slush f'm one end to the other. Well sir, it warn't no use to try to apologize—we couldn't say a word. He took a sort of a disgusted look at hisself, 'n' then he looked at us—an' it was just exactly the same as if he had said—'Gents, may be *you* think it's smart to take advantage of a cat that ain't had no experience of quartz minin', but *I* think *different'*—an' then he turned on his heel 'n' marched off home without ever saying another word.

"That was jest his style. An' may be you won't believe it, but after that you never see a cat so prejudiced agin quartz mining as what he was. An' by an' bye when he *did* get to goin' down in the shaft agin, you'd 'a been astonished at his sagacity. The minute we'd tetch off a blast 'n' the fuse'd begin to sizzle, he'd give a look as much as to say: 'Well, I'll have to git you to excuse *me*,' an' it was surpris'n' the way he'd shin out of that hole 'n' go f'r a tree. Sagacity? It ain't no name for it. 'Twas *inspiration!*"

I said, "Well, Mr. Baker, his prejudice against quartz-mining *was* remarkable, considering how he came by it. Couldn't you ever cure him of it?"

"*Cure him!* No! When Tom Quartz was sot once, he was *always* sot—and you might a blowed him up as much as three million times 'n' you'd never a broken him of his cussed prejudice agin quartz mining."

The affection and the pride that lit up Baker's face when he delivered this tribute to the firmness of his humble friend of other days, will always be a vivid memory with me.

At the end of two months we had never "struck" a pocket. We had panned up and down the hillsides till they looked plowed like a field; we could have put in a crop of grain, then, but there would have been no way to get it to market. We got many good "prospects," but when the gold gave out in the pan and we dug down, hoping and longing, we found only emptiness—the pocket that should have been there was as barren as our own.— At last we shouldered our pans and shovels and struck out over the hills to try new localities. We prospected around Angel's Camp, in Calaveras county, during three weeks, but had no success. Then we wandered on foot among the mountains, sleeping under the trees at night, for the weather was mild, but still we remained as centless as the last rose of summer. That is a poor joke, but it is in pathetic harmony with the circumstances, since we were so poor ourselves. In accordance with the custom of the country, our door had always stood open and our board welcome to tramping miners—they drifted along nearly every day, dumped their paust shovels by the threshold and took "pot luck" with us—and now on our own tramp we never found cold hospitality.

Our wanderings were wide and in many directions; and now I could give the reader a vivid description of the Big Trees and the marvels of the Yo Semite—but what has this reader done to me that I should persecute him? I will deliver him into the hands of less conscientious tourists and take his blessing. Let me be charitable, though I fail in all virtues else.

Some of the phrases in the above are mining technicalities, purely, and may be a little obscure to the general reader. In *"placer diggings"* the gold is scattered all through the surface dirt; in *"pocket"* diggings it is concentrated in one little spot; in *"quartz"* the gold is in a solid, continuous vein of rock, enclosed between distinct walls of some other kind of stone—and this is the most laborious and expensive of all the different kinds of mining. *"Prospecting"* is hunting for a *"placer"*; *"indications"* are signs of its presence; *"panning out"* refers to the washing process by which the grains of gold are separated from the dirt; a *"prospect"* is what one finds in the first panful of dirt—and its value determines whether it is a good or a bad prospect, and whether it is worth while to tarry there or seek further.

CHAPTER LXII

After a three months' absence, I found myself in San Francisco again, without a cent. When my credit was about exhausted, (for I had become too mean and lazy, now, to work on a morning paper, and there were no vacancies on the evening journals,) I was created San Francisco correspondent of the *Enterprise*, and at the end of five months I was out of debt, but my interest in my work was gone; for my correspondence being a daily one, without rest or respite, I got unspeakably tired of it. I wanted another change. The vagabond interest was strong upon me. Fortune favored and I got a new berth and a delightful one. It was to go down to the Sandwich Islands and write some letters for the Sacramento *Union*, an excellent journal and liberal with employés.

We sailed in the propeller *Ajax*, in the middle of winter. The almanac called it winter, distinctly enough, but the weather was a compromise between spring and summer. Six days out of port, it became summer altogether. We had some thirty passengers; among them a cheerful soul by the name of Williams, and three sea-worn old whaleship captains going down to join their vessels. These latter played euchre in the smoking room day and night, drank astonishing quantities of raw whisky without being in the least affected by it, and were the happiest people I think I ever saw. And then there was "the old Admiral—" a retired whaleman. He was a roaring, terrific combination of wind and lightning and thunder, and earnest, whole-souled profanity. But nevertheless he was tender-hearted as a girl. He was a raving, deafening, devastating typhoon, laying waste the cowering seas but with an unvexed refuge in the centre where all comers were safe and at rest. Nobody could know the "Admiral" without liking him; and in a sudden and dire emergency I think no friend of his would know which to choose—to be cursed by him or prayed for by a less efficient person.

His title of "Admiral" was more strictly "official" than any ever worn by a naval officer before or since, perhaps—for it was the voluntary offering of a whole nation, and came direct from the *people* themselves without any intermediate red tape—the people of the Sandwich Islands. It was a title that came to him freighted with affection, and honor, and appreciation of his unpretending merit. And in testimony of the genuineness of the title it was publicly ordained that an exclusive flag should be devised for him and used solely to welcome his coming and wave him God-speed in his going. From that time forth, whenever his ship was signaled in the offing, or he catted his anchor and stood out to sea, that ensign streamed from the royal halliards on the parliament house and the nation lifted their hats to it with spontaneous accord.

Yet he had never fired a gun or fought a battle in his life. When I knew him on board the *Ajax*, he was seventy-two years old and had plowed the salt water sixty-one of them. For sixteen years he had gone in and out of the harbor of Honolulu in command of a whaleship, and for sixteen more had been captain of a San Francisco and Sandwich Island passenger packet and had never had an accident or lost a vessel. The simple natives knew him for a friend who never failed them, and regarded him as children regard a father. It was a dangerous thing to oppress them when the roaring Admiral was around.

Two years before I knew the Admiral, he had retired from the sea on a competence, and had sworn a colossal nine-jointed oath that he would "never go within *smelling* distance of the salt water again as long as he lived." And he had conscientiously kept it. That is to say, *he* considered he had kept it, and it would have been more than dangerous to suggest to him, even in the gentlest way, that making eleven long sea voyages, as a passenger, during the two years that had transpired since he "retired," was only keeping the general spirit of it and not the strict letter.

The Admiral knew only one narrow line of conduct to pursue in any and all cases where there was a fight, and that was to shoulder his way straight in without an inquiry as to the rights or the merits of it, and take the part of the weaker side.—And this was the reason why he was always sure to be present at the trial of any universally execrated criminal to oppress and intimidate the jury with a vindictive pantomime of what he would do to them if he ever caught them out of the box. And this was why harried cats and outlawed dogs that knew him confidently took sanctuary under his chair in time of trouble. In the beginning he was the most frantic and bloodthirsty Union man that drew breath in the shadow of the Flag; but the instant the Southerners began to go down before the sweep of the Northern armies, he ran up the Confederate colors and from that time till the end was a rampant and inexorable secessionist.

He hated intemperance with a more uncompromising animosity than any individual I have ever met, of either sex; and he was never tired of storming against it and beseeching friends and strangers alike to be wary and drink with moderation. And yet if any creature had been guileless enough to intimate that his absorbing nine gallons of "straight" whisky during our voyage was any fraction short of rigid or inflexible abstemiousness, in that self-same moment the old man would have spun him to the uttermost parts of the earth in the whirlwind of his wrath. Mind, I am not saying his whisky ever affected his head or his legs, for it did not, in even the slightest degree. He was a capacious container, but he did not hold enough for that. He took a level tumblerful of whisky every morning before he put his clothes on—"to sweeten his bilgewater," he said.—He took another after he got the most of his clothes on, "to settle his mind and give him clean bearings." He then shaved, and put on a clean shirt; after which he recited the Lord's Prayer in a fervent, thundering bass that shook the ship to her kelson and suspended all conversation in the main cabin. Then, at this stage, being invariably "by the head," or "by the stern," or "listed to port or starboard," he took one more to "put him on an even keel so that he would mind his hellum and not miss stays and go about, every time he came up in the wind."—And now, his state-room door swung open and the sun of his benignant face beamed redly out upon men and women and children, and he roared his "Shipmets a'hoy!" in a way that was calculated to wake the dead and precipitate the final resurrection; and forth he strode, a picture to look at and a presence to enforce attention. Stalwart and portly; not a gray hair; broad-brimmed slouch hat; semisailor toggery of blue navy flannel—roomy and ample; a stately expanse of shirt-front and a liberal amount of black silk neckcloth tied with a sailor knot; large chain and imposing seals impending from his fob; awe-inspiring feet, and "a hand like the hand of Providence," as his whaling brethren expressed it; wrist-bands and sleeves pushed back half way to the elbow, out of respect for the warm weather, and exposing hairy arms, gaudy with red and blue anchors, ships, and goddesses of liberty tattooed in India ink. But these details were only secondary matters—his face was the lodestone that chained the eye. It was a sultry disk, glowing determinedly out through a weather beaten mask of mahogany, and studded with warts, seamed with scars, "blazed" all over with unfailing fresh slips of the razor; and with cheery eyes, under shaggy brows, contemplating the world from over the back of a gnarled crag of a nose that loomed vast and lonely out of the undulating immensity that spread away from its foundations. At his heels frisked the darling of his bachelor estate, his terrier "Fan," a creature no larger than a squirrel. The main part of his daily life was occupied in looking after "Fan," in a motherly way, and doctoring her for a hundred ailments which existed only in his imagination.

The Admiral seldom read newspapers; and when he did he never believed anything they said. He read nothing, and believed in nothing, but "The Old Guard," a secession periodical published in New York. He carried a dozen copies of it with him, always, and referred to them for all required information. If it was not there, he supplied it himself, out of a bountiful fancy, inventing history, names, dates, and every thing else necessary to make his point good in an argument. Consequently he was a formidable antagonist in a dispute. Whenever he swung clear of the record and began to create history, the enemy was helpless and had to surrender. Indeed, the enemy could not keep from betraying some little spark of indignation at his manufactured history—and when it came to indignation, that was the Admiral's very "best hold." He was always ready for a political argument, and if nobody started one he would do it himself. With his third retort his temper would begin to rise, and within five minutes he would be blowing a gale, and within fifteen his smoking-room audience would be utterly stormed away and the old man left solitary and alone, banging the table with his fist, kicking the chairs, and roaring a hurricane of profanity. It got so, after a while, that whenever the Admiral approached, with politics in his eye, the passengers would drop out with quiet accord, afraid to meet him; and he would camp on a deserted field.

But he found his match at last, and before a full company. At one time or another, everybody had entered the lists against him and been routed, except the quiet passenger Williams. He had never been able to get an expression of opinion out of him on politics. But now, just as the Admiral drew near the door and the company were about to slip out, Williams said:

"Admiral, are you *certain* about that circumstance concerning the clergymen you mentioned the other day?"—referring to a piece of the Admiral's manufactured history.

Every one was amazed at the man's rashness. The idea of deliberately inviting annihilation was a thing incomprehensible. The retreat came to a halt; then everybody sat down again wondering, to await the upshot of it. The Admiral himself was as surprised as any one. He paused in the door, with his red handkerchief half raised to his sweating face, and contemplated the daring reptile in the corner.

"*Certain* of it? Am I *certain* of it? Do you think I've been lying about it? What do you take me for? Anybody that don't know that circumstance, don't know anything; a child ought to know it. Read up your history! Read it up —— —— —— ——, and don't come asking a man if he's *certain* about a bit of A B C stuff that the very southern niggers know all about."

Here the Admiral's fires began to wax hot, the atmosphere thickened, the coming earthquake rumbled, he began to thunder and lighten. Within three minutes his volcano was in full irruption and he was discharging flames and ashes of indignation, belching black volumes of foul history aloft, and vomiting redhot torrents of profanity from his crater. Meantime Williams sat silent, and apparently deeply and earnestly interested in what the old man was saying. By and by, when the lull came, he said in the most deferential way, and with the gratified air of a man who has had a mystery cleared up which had been puzzling him uncomfortably:

"*Now* I understand it. I always thought I knew that piece of history well enough, but was still afraid to trust it, because there was not that convincing particularity about it that one likes to have in history; but when you mentioned every name, the other day, and every date, and every little circumstance, in their just order and sequence, I said to myself, *this* sounds something like—*this* is history—*this* is putting it in a shape that gives a man confidence; and I said to myself afterward, I will just ask the Admiral if he is perfectly certain about the details, and if he is I will come out and thank him for clearing this matter up for me. And that is what I want to do now—for until you set that matter right it was nothing but just a confusion in my mind, without head or tail to it."

Nobody ever saw the Admiral look so mollified before, and so pleased. Nobody had ever received his bogus history as gospel before; its genuineness had always been called in question either by words or looks; but here was a man that not only swallowed it all down, but was grateful for the dose. He was taken a back; he hardly knew what to say; even his profanity failed him. Now, Williams continued, modestly and earnestly:

"But Admiral, in saying that this was the first stone thrown, and that this precipitated the war, you have overlooked a circumstance which you are perfectly familiar with, but which has escaped your memory. Now I grant you that what you have stated is correct in every detail—to wit: that on the 16th of October, 1860, two Massachusetts clergymen, named Waite and Granger, went in disguise to the house of John Moody, in Rockport, at dead of night, and dragged forth two southern women and their two little children, and after tarring and feathering them conveyed them to Boston and burned them alive in the State House square; and I also grant your proposition that this deed is what led to the secession of South Carolina on the 20th of December following. Very well." [Here the company were pleasantly surprised to hear Williams proceed to come back at the Admiral with his own invincible weapon—clean, pure, *manufactured history*, without a word of truth in it.] "Very well, I say. But Admiral, why overlook the Willis and Morgan case in South Carolina? You are too well informed a man not to know all about that circumstance. Your arguments and your conversations have shown you to be intimately conversant with every detail of this national quarrel. You develop matters of history every day that show plainly that you are no smatterer in it, content to nibble about the surface, but a man who has searched the depths and possessed yourself of everything that has a bearing upon the great question. Therefore, let me just recall to your mind that Willis and Morgan case—though I see by your face that the whole thing is already passing through your memory at this moment. On the 12th of August, 1860, *two months* before the Waite and Granger affair, two South Carolina clergymen, named John H. Morgan and Winthrop L. Willis, one a Methodist and the other an Old School Baptist, disguised themselves, and went at midnight to the house of a planter named Thompson—Archibald F. Thompson, Vice President under Thomas Jefferson,—and took thence, at midnight, his widowed aunt, (a Northern woman,) and her adopted child, an orphan named Mortimer Hughie, afflicted with epilepsy and suffering at the time from white swelling on one of his legs, and compelled to walk on crutches in consequence; and the two ministers, in spite of the pleadings of the victims, dragged them to the bush, tarred and feathered them, and afterward burned them at the stake in the city of Charleston. You remember perfectly well what a stir it made; you remember perfectly well that even the Charleston *Courier* stigmatized the act as being unpleasant, of questionable propriety, and scarcely justifiable, and likewise that it would not be a matter of surprise if retaliation ensued. And you remember also, that this thing was the *cause* of the Massachusetts outrage. Who, indeed, were the two Massachusetts ministers? and who were the two Southern women they burned? I do not need to remind *you*, Admiral, with your intimate knowledge of history; that Waite was the nephew of the woman burned in Charleston; the Granger was her cousin in the second degree, and that the woman they burned in Boston was the wife of John H. Morgan, and the still loved but divorced wife of Winthrop L. Willis. Now, Admiral, it is only fair that you should acknowledge that the first provocation came from the Southern preachers and that the Northern ones were justified in retaliating. In your arguments you never yet have shown the least disposition to withhold a just verdict or be in anywise unfair, when authoritative history condemned your position, and therefore I have no hesitation in asking you to take the original blame from the Massachusetts ministers, in this matter, and transfer it to the South Carolina clergymen where it justly belongs."

The Admiral was conquered. This sweet spoken creature who swallowed his fraudulent history as if it were the bread of life; basked in his furious blasphemy as if it were generous sunshine; found only calm, even-handed justice in his rampart partisanship; and flooded him with invented history so sugar-coated with flattery and deference that there was no rejecting it, was "too many" for him. He stammered some awkward, profane sentences about the —— —— —— —— Willis and Morgan business having escaped his memory, but that he "remembered it now," and then, under pretence of giving Fan some medicine for an imaginary cough, drew out of the battle and went away, a vanquished man. Then cheers and laughter went up, and Williams, the ship's benefactor was a hero. The news went about the vessel, champagne was ordered, an enthusiastic reception instituted in the smoking room, and everybody flocked thither to shake hands with the conqueror. The wheelsman said afterward, that the Admiral stood up behind the pilot house and "ripped and cursed all to himself" till he loosened the smokestack guys and becalmed the mainsail.

The Admiral's power was broken. After that, if he began an argument, somebody would bring Williams, and the old man would grow weak and begin to quiet down at once. And as soon as he was done, Williams in his dulcet, insinuating way, would invent some history (referring for proof, to the old man's own excellent memory and to copies of "The Old Guard" known not to be in his possession) that would turn the tables completely and leave the Admiral all abroad and helpless. By and by he came to so dread Williams and his gilded tongue that he would stop talking when he saw him approach, and finally ceased to mention politics altogether, and from that time forward there was entire peace and serenity in the ship.

CHAPTER LXIII

On a certain bright morning the Islands hove in sight, lying low on the lonely sea, and everybody climbed to the upper deck to look. After two thousand miles of watery solitude the vision was a welcome one. As we approached, the imposing promontory of Diamond Head rose up out of the ocean its rugged front softened by the hazy distance, and presently the details of the land began to make themselves manifest: first the line of beach; then the plumed coacoanut trees of the tropics; then cabins of the natives; then the white town of Honolulu, said to contain between twelve and fifteen thousand inhabitants spread over a dead level; with streets from twenty to thirty feet wide, solid and level as a floor, most of them straight as a line and few as crooked as a corkscrew.

The further I traveled through the town the better I liked it. Every step revealed a new contrast—disclosed something I was unaccustomed to. In place of the grand mud-colored brown fronts of San Francisco, I saw dwellings built of straw, adobies, and cream-colored pebble-and-shell-conglomerated coral, cut into oblong blocks and laid in cement; also a great number of neat white cottages, with green window-shutters; in place of front yards like billiard-tables with iron fences around them, I saw these homes surrounded by ample yards, thickly clad with green grass, and shaded by tall trees, through whose dense foliage the sun could scarcely penetrate; in place of the customary geranium, calla lily, etc., languishing in dust and general debility, I saw luxurious banks and thickets of flowers, fresh as a meadow after a rain, and glowing with the richest dyes; in place of the dingy horrors of San Francisco's pleasure grove, the "Willows," I saw huge-bodied, wide-spreading forest trees, with strange names and stranger appearance—trees that cast a shadow like a thundercloud, and were able to stand alone without being tied to green poles; in place of gold fish, wiggling around in glass globes, assuming countless shades and degrees of distortion through the magnifying and diminishing qualities of their transparent prison houses, I saw cats—Tom-cats, Mary Ann cats, long-tailed cats, bob-tailed cats, blind cats, one-eyed cats, wall-eyed cats, cross-eyed cats, gray cats, black cats, white cats, yellow cats, striped cats, spotted cats, tame cats, wild cats, singed cats, individual cats, groups of cats, platoons of cats, companies of cats, regiments of cats, armies of cats, multitudes of cats, millions of cats, and all of them sleek, fat, lazy and sound asleep.

I looked on a multitude of people, some white, in white coats, vests, pantaloons, even white cloth shoes, made snowy with chalk duly laid on every morning; but the majority of the people were almost as dark as negroes—women with comely features, fine black eyes, rounded forms, inclining to the voluptuous, clad in a single bright red or white garment that fell free and unconfined from shoulder to heel, long black hair falling loose, gypsy hats, encircled with wreaths of natural flowers of a brilliant carmine tint; plenty of dark men in various costumes, and some with nothing on but a battered stove-pipe hat tilted on the nose, and a very scant breech-clout;—certain smoke-dried children were clothed in nothing but sunshine—a very neat fitting and picturesque apparel indeed.

In place of roughs and rowdies staring and blackguarding on the corners, I saw long-haired, saddle-colored Sandwich Island maidens sitting on the ground in the shade of corner houses, gazing indolently at whatever or whoever happened along; instead of wretched cobble-stone pavements, I walked on a firm foundation of coral, built up from the bottom of the sea by the absurd but persevering insect of that name, with a light layer of lava and cinders overlying the coral, belched up out of fathomless perdition long ago through the seared and blackened crater that stands dead and harmless in the distance now; instead of cramped and crowded street-cars, I met dusky native women sweeping by, free as the wind, on fleet horses and astride, with gaudy riding-sashes, streaming like banners behind them; instead of the combined stenches of Chinadom and Brannan street slaughter-houses, I breathed the balmy fragrance of jesamine, oleander, and the Pride of India; in place of the hurry and bustle and noisy confusion of San Francisco, I moved in the midst of a Summer calm as tranquil as dawn in the Garden of Eden; in place of the Golden City's skirting sand hills and the placid bay, I saw on the one side a frame-work of tall, precipitous mountains close at hand, clad in refreshing green, and cleft by deep, cool, chasm-like valleys—and in front the grand sweep of the ocean: a brilliant, transparent green near the shore, bound and bordered by a long white line of foamy spray dashing against the reef, and further out the dead blue water of the deep sea, flecked with "white caps," and in the far horizon a single, lonely sail—a mere accent-mark to emphasize a slumberous calm and a solitude that were without sound or limit. When the sun sunk down—the one intruder from other realms and persistent in suggestions of them—it was tranced luxury to sit in the perfumed air and forget that there was any world but these enchanted islands.

It was such ecstacy to dream, and dream—till you got a bite. A scorpion bite. Then the first duty was to get up out of the grass and kill the scorpion; and the next to bathe the bitten place with alcohol or brandy; and the next to resolve to keep out of the grass in future. Then came an adjournment to the bed-chamber and the pastime of writing up the day's journal with one hand and the destruction of mosquitoes with the other—a whole community of them at a slap. Then, observing an enemy approaching—a hairy tarantula on stilts—why not set the spitoon on him? It is done, and the projecting ends of his paws give a luminous idea of the magnitude of his reach. Then to bed and become a promenade for a centipede with forty-two legs and every foot hot enough to burn a hole through a raw-hide. More soaking with alcohol, and a resolution to examine the bed before entering it, in future. Then wait, and suffer, till all the mosquitoes in the neighborhood have crawled in under the bar, then slip out quickly, shut them in and sleep peacefully on the floor till morning. Meantime it is comforting to curse the tropics in occasional wakeful intervals.

We had an abundance of fruit in Honolulu, of course. Oranges, pine-apples, bananas, strawberries, lemons, limes, mangoes, guavas, melons, and a rare and curious luxury called the chirimoya, which is deliciousness itself. Then there is the tamarind. I thought tamarinds were made to eat, but that was probably not the idea. I ate several, and it seemed to me that they were rather sour that year. They pursed up my lips, till they resembled the stem-end of a tomato, and I had to take my sustenance through a quill for twenty-four hours. They sharpened my teeth till I could have shaved with them, and gave them a "wire edge" that I was afraid would stay; but a citizen said "no, it will come off when the enamel does"—which was comforting, at any rate. I found, afterward, that only strangers eat tamarinds—but they only eat them once.

CHAPTER LXIV

In my diary of our third day in Honolulu, I find this:

I am probably the most sensitive man in Hawaii to-night—especially about sitting down in the presence of my betters. I have ridden fifteen or twenty miles on horseback since 5 P.M. and to tell the honest truth, I have a delicacy about sitting down at all.

An excursion to Diamond Head and the King's Coacoanut Grove was planned to-day—time, 4:30 P.M.—the party to consist of half a dozen gentlemen and three ladies. They all started at the appointed hour except myself. I was at the Government prison, (with Captain Fish and another whaleship-skipper, Captain Phillips,) and got so interested in its examination that I did not notice how quickly the time was passing. Somebody remarked that it was twenty minutes past five o'clock, and that woke me up. It was a fortunate circumstance that Captain Phillips was along with his "turn out," as he calls a top-buggy that Captain Cook brought here in 1778, and a horse that was here when Captain Cook came. Captain Phillips takes a just pride in his driving and in the speed of his horse, and to his passion for displaying them I owe it that we were only sixteen minutes coming from the prison to the American Hotel—a distance which has been estimated to be over half a mile. But it took some fearful driving. The Captain's whip came down fast, and the blows started so much dust out of the horse's hide that during the last half of the journey we rode through an impenetrable fog, and ran by a pocket compass in the hands of Captain Fish, a whaler of twenty-six years experience, who sat there through the perilous voyage as self-possessed as if he had been on the euchre-deck of his own ship, and calmly said, "Port your helm—port," from time to time, and "Hold her a little free—steady—so-o," and "Luff—hard down to starboard!" and never once lost his presence of mind or betrayed the least anxiety by voice or manner. When we came to anchor at last, and Captain Phillips looked at his watch and said, "Sixteen minutes—I told you it was in her! that's over three miles an hour!" I could see he felt entitled to a compliment, and so I said I had never seen lightning go like that horse. And I never had.

The landlord of the American said the party had been gone nearly an hour, but that he could give me my choice of several horses that could overtake them. I said, never mind—I preferred a safe horse to a fast one—I would like to have an excessively gentle horse—a horse with no spirit whatever—a lame one, if he had such a thing. Inside of five minutes I was mounted, and perfectly satisfied with my outfit. I had no time to label him "This is a horse," and so if the public took him for a sheep I cannot help it. I was satisfied, and that was the main thing. I could see that he had as many fine points as any man's horse, and so I hung my hat on one of them, behind the saddle, and swabbed the perspiration from my face and started. I named him after this island, "Oahu" (pronounced O-waw-hee). The first gate he came to he started in; I had neither whip nor spur, and so I simply argued the case with him. He resisted argument, but ultimately yielded to insult and abuse. He backed out of that gate and steered for another one on the other side of the street. I triumphed by my former process. Within the next six hundred yards he crossed the street fourteen times and attempted thirteen gates, and in the meantime the tropical sun was beating down and threatening to cave the top of my head in, and I was literally dripping with perspiration. He abandoned the gate business after that and went along peaceably enough, but absorbed in meditation. I noticed this latter circumstance, and it soon began to fill me with apprehension. I said to myself, this creature is planning some new outrage, some fresh deviltry or other—no horse ever thought over a subject so profoundly as this one is doing just for nothing. The more this thing preyed upon my mind the more uneasy I became, until the suspense became almost unbearable and I dismounted to see if there was anything wild in his eye—for I had heard that the eye of this noblest of our domestic animals is very expressive. I cannot describe what a load of anxiety was lifted from my mind when I found that he was only asleep. I woke him up and started him into a faster walk, and then the villainy of his nature came out again. He tried to climb over a stone wall, five or six feet high. I saw that I must apply force to this horse, and that I might as well begin first as last. I plucked a stout switch from a tamarind tree, and the moment he saw it, he surrendered. He broke into a convulsive sort of a canter, which had three short steps in it and one long one, and reminded me alternately of the clattering shake of the great earthquake, and the sweeping plunging of the Ajax in a storm.

And now there can be no fitter occasion than the present to pronounce a left-handed blessing upon the man who invented the American saddle. There is no seat to speak of about it— one might as well sit in a shovel—and the stirrups are nothing but an ornamental nuisance. If I were to write down here all the abuse I expended on those stirrups, it would make a large book, even without pictures. Sometimes I got one foot so far through, that he stirrup partook of the nature of an anklet; sometimes both feet were through, and I was handcuffed by the legs; and sometimes my feet got clear out and left the stirrups wildly dangling about my shins. Even when I was in proper position and carefully balanced upon the balls of my feet, there was no comfort in it, on account of my nervous dread that they were going to slip one way or the other in a moment. But the subject is too exasperating to write about.

A mile and a half from town, I came to a grove of tall cocoanut trees, with clean, branchless stems reaching straight up sixty or seventy feet and topped with a spray of green foliage sheltering clusters of cocoa-nuts—not more picturesque than a forest of collossal ragged parasols, with bunches of magnified grapes under them, would be. I once heard a grouty northern invalid say that a cocoanut tree might be poetical, possibly it was; but it looked like a feather-duster struck by lightning. I think that describes it better than a picture—and yet, without any question, there is something fascinating about a cocoa-nut tree—and graceful, too.

About a dozen cottages, some frame and the others of native grass, nestled sleepily in the shade here and there. The grass cabins are of a grayish color, are shaped much like our own cottages, only with higher and steeper roofs usually, and are made of some kind of weed strongly bound together in bundles. The roofs are very thick, and so are the walls; the latter have square holes in them for windows. At a little distance these cabins have a furry appearance, as if they might be made of bear skins. They are very cool and pleasant inside. The King's flag was flying from the roof of one of the cottages, and His Majesty was probably within. He owns the whole concern thereabouts, and passes his time there frequently, on sultry days "laying off." The spot is called "The King's Grove."

Near by is an interesting ruin—the meagre remains of an ancient heathen temple—a place where human sacrifices were offered up in those old bygone days when the simple child of nature, yielding momentarily to sin when sorely tempted, acknowledged his error when calm reflection had shown it him, and came forward with noble frankness and offered up his grandmother as an atoning sacrifice—in those old days when the luckless sinner could keep on cleansing his conscience and achieving periodical happiness as long as his relations held out; long, long before the missionaries braved a thousand privations to come and make them permanently miserable by telling them how beautiful and how blissful a place heaven is, and how nearly impossible it is to get there; and showed the poor native how dreary a place perdition is and what unnecessarily liberal facilities there are for going to it; showed him how, in his ignorance he had gone and fooled away all his kinfolks to no purpose; showed him what rapture it is to work all day long for fifty cents to buy food for next day with, as compared with fishing for pastime and lolling in the shade through eternal Summer, and eating of the bounty that nobody labored to provide but Nature. How sad it is to think of the multitudes who have gone to their graves in this beautiful island and never knew there was a hell!

This ancient temple was built of rough blocks of lava, and was simply a roofless inclosure a hundred and thirty feet long and seventy feet wide—nothing but naked walls, very thick, but not much higher than a man's head. They will last for ages no doubt, if left unmolested. Its three altars and other sacred appurtenances have crumbled and passed away years ago. It is said that in the old times thousands of human beings were slaughtered here, in the presence of naked and howling savages. If these mute stones could speak, what tales they could tell, what pictures they could describe, of fettered victims writhing under the knife; of massed forms straining forward out of the gloom, with ferocious faces lit up by the sacrificial fires; of the background of ghostly trees; of the dark pyramid of Diamond Head standing sentinel over the uncanny scene, and the peaceful moon looking down upon it through rifts in the cloud-rack!

When Kamehameha (pronounced Ka-may-ha-may-ah) the Great—who was a sort of a Napoleon in military genius and uniform success—invaded this island of Oahu three quarters of a century ago, and exterminated the army sent to oppose him, and took full and final possession of the country, he searched out the dead body of the King of Oahu, and those of the principal chiefs, and impaled their heads on the walls of this temple.

Those were savage times when this old slaughter-house was in its prime. The King and the chiefs ruled the common herd with a rod of iron; made them gather all the provisions the masters needed; build all the houses and temples; stand all the expenses of whatever kind; take kicks and cuffs for thanks; drag out lives well flavored with misery, and then suffer deatfences or yield up their lives on the sacrificial altars to purchase favors from the gods for their hard rulers. The missionaries have clothed them, educated them, broken up the tyrannous authority of their chiefs, and given them freedom and the right to enjoy whatever their hands and brains produce with equal laws for all, and punishment for all alike who transgress them. The contrast is so strong—the benefit conferred upon this people by the missionaries is so prominent, so palpable and so unquestionable, that the frankest compliment I can pay them, and the best, is simply to point to the condition of the Sandwich Islanders of Captain Cook's time, and their condition to-day. Their work speaks for itself.

CHAPTER LXV

By and by, after a rugged climb, we halted on the summit of a hill which commanded a far-reaching view. The moon rose and flooded mountain and valley and ocean with a mellow radiance, and out of the shadows of the foliage the distant lights of Honolulu glinted like an encampment of fireflies. The air was heavy with the fragrance of flowers. The halt was brief.—Gayly laughing and talking, the party galloped on, and I clung to the pommel and cantered after. Presently we came to a place where no grass grew—a wide expanse of deep sand. They said it was an old battle ground. All around everywhere, not three feet apart, the bleached bones of men gleamed white in the moonlight. We picked up a lot of them for mementoes. I got quite a number of arm bones and leg bones—of great chiefs, may be, who had fought savagely in that fearful battle in the old days, when blood flowed like wine where we now stood.—and wore the choicest of them out on Oahu afterward, trying to make him go. All sorts of bones could be found except skulls; but a citizen said, irreverently, that there had been an unusual number of "skull-hunters" there lately—a species of sportsmen I had never heard of before.

Nothing whatever is known about this place—its story is a secret that will never be revealed. The oldest natives make no pretense of being possessed of its history. They say these bones were here when they were children. They were here when their grandfathers were children—but how they came here, they can only conjecture. Many people believe this spot to be an ancient battle-ground, and it is usual to call it so; and they believe that these skeletons have lain for ages just where their proprietors fell in the great fight. Other people believe that Kamehameha I. fought his first battle here. On this point, I have heard a story, which may have been taken from one of the numerous books which have been written concerning these islands—I do not know where the narrator got it. He said that when Kamehameha (who was at first merely a subordinate chief on the island of Hawaii), landed here, he brought a large army with him, and encamped at Waikiki. The Oahuans marched against him, and so confident were they of success that they readily acceded to a demand of their priests that they should draw a line where these bones now lie, and take an oath that, if forced to retreat at all, they would never retreat beyond this boundary. The priests told them that death and everlasting punishment would overtake any who violated the oath, and the march was resumed. Kamehameha drove them back step by step; the priests fought in the front rank and exhorted them both by voice and inspiriting example to remember their oath—to die, if need be, but never cross the fatal line. The struggle was manfully maintained, but at last the chief priest fell, pierced to the heart with a spear, and the unlucky omen fell like a blight upon the brave souls at his back; with a triumphant shout the invaders pressed forward— the line was crossed—the offended gods deserted the despairing army, and, accepting the doom their perjury had brought upon them, they broke and fled over the plain where Honolulu stands now—up the beautiful Nuuanu Valley—paused a moment, hemmed in by precipitous mountains on either hand and the frightful precipice of the Pari in front, and then were driven over—a sheer plunge of six hundred feet!

The story is pretty enough, but Mr. Jarves' excellent history says the Oahuans were intrenched in Nuuanu Valley; that Kamehameha ousted them, routed them, pursued them up the valley and drove them over the precipice. He makes no mention of our bone-yard at all in his book.

Impressed by the profound silence and repose that rested over the beautiful landscape, and being, as usual, in the rear, I gave voice to my thoughts. I said:

"What a picture is here slumbering in the solemn glory of the moon! How strong the rugged outlines of the dead volcano stand out against the clear sky! What a snowy fringe marks the bursting of the surf over the long, curved reef! How calmly the dim city sleeps yonder in the plain! How soft the shadows lie upon the stately mountains that border the dream-haunted Mauoa Valley! What a grand pyramid of billowy clouds towers above the storied Pari! How the grim warriors of the past seem flocking in ghostly squadrons to their ancient battlefield again— how the wails of the dying well up from the—"

At this point the horse called Oahu sat down in the sand. Sat down to listen, I suppose. Never mind what he heard, I stopped apostrophising and convinced him that I was not a man to allow contempt of Court on the part of a horse. I broke the back-bone of a Chief over his rump and set out to join the cavalcade again.

Very considerably fagged out we arrived in town at 9 o'clock at night, myself in the lead—for when my horse finally came to understand that he was homeward bound and hadn't far to go, he turned his attention strictly to business.

This is a good time to drop in a paragraph of information. There is no regular livery stable in Honolulu, or, indeed, in any part of the kingdom of Hawaii; therefore unless you are acquainted with wealthy residents (who all have good horses), you must hire animals of the wretchedest description from the Kanakas. (i.e. natives.) Any horse you hire, even though it be from a white man, is not often of much account, because it will be brought in for you from some ranch, and has necessarily been leading a hard life. If the Kanakas who have been caring for him (inveterate riders they are) have not ridden him half to death every day themselves, you can depend upon it they have been doing the same thing by proxy, by clandestinely hiring him out. At least, so I am informed. The result is, that no horse has a chance to eat, drink, rest, recuperate, or look well or feel well, and so strangers go about the Islands mounted as I was to-day.

In hiring a horse from a Kanaka, you must have all your eyes about you, because you can rest satisfied that you are dealing with a shrewd unprincipled rascal. You may leave your door open and your trunk unlocked as long as you please, and he will not meddle with your property; he has no important vices and no inclination to commit robbery on a large scale; but if he can get ahead of you in the horse business, he will take a genuine delight in doing it. This trait is characteristic of horse jockeys, the world over, is it not? He will overcharge you if he can; he will hire you a fine-looking horse at night (anybody's—may be the King's, if the royal steed be in convenient view), and bring you the mate to my Oahu in the morning, and contend that it is the same animal. If you make trouble, he will get out by saying it was not himself who made the bargain with you, but his brother, "who went out in the country this morning." They have always got a "brother" to shift the responsibility upon. A victim said to one of these fellows one day:

"But I know I hired the horse of you, because I noticed that scar on your cheek."

The reply was not bad: "Oh, yes—yes—my brother all same—we twins!"

A friend of mine, J. Smith, hired a horse yesterday, the Kanaka warranting him to be in excellent condition. Smith had a saddle and blanket of his own, and he ordered the Kanaka to put these on the horse. The Kanaka protested that he was perfectly willing to trust the gentleman with the saddle that was already on the animal, but Smith refused to use it. The change was made; then Smith noticed that the Kanaka had only changed the saddles, and had left the original blanket on the horse; he said he forgot to change the blankets, and so, to cut the bother short, Smith mounted and rode away. The horse went lame a mile from town, and afterward got to cutting up some extraordinary capers. Smith got down and took off the saddle, but the blanket stuck fast to the horse—glued to a procession of raw places. The Kanaka's mysterious conduct stood explained.

Another friend of mine bought a pretty good horse from a native, a day or two ago, after a tolerably thorough examination. He discovered today that the horse was as blind as a bat, in one eye. He meant to have examined that eye, and came home with a general notion that he had done it; but he remembers now that every time he made the attempt his attention was called to something else by his victimizer.

One more instance, and then I will pass to something else. I am informed that when a certain Mr. L., a visiting stranger, was here, he bought a pair of very respectable-looking match horses from a native. They were in a little stable with a partition through the middle of it—one horse in each apartment. Mr. L. examined one of them critically through a window (the Kanaka's "brother" having gone to the country with the key), and then went around the house and examined the other through a window on the other side. He said it was the neatest match he had ever seen, and paid for the horses on the spot. Whereupon the Kanaka departed to join his brother in the country. The fellow had shamefully swindled L. There was only one "match" horse, and he had examined his starboard side through one window and his port side through another! I decline to believe this story, but I give it because it is worth something as a fanciful illustration of a fixed fact— namely, that the Kanaka horse-jockey is fertile in invention and elastic in conscience.

You can buy a pretty good horse for forty or fifty dollars, and a good enough horse for all practical purposes for two dollars and a half. I estimate "Oahu" to be worth somewhere in the neighborhood of thirty-five cents. A good deal better animal than he is was sold here day before yesterday for a dollar and seventy-five cents, and sold again to-day for two dollars and twenty-five cents; Williams bought a handsome and lively little pony yesterday for ten dollars; and about the best common horse on the island (and he is a really good one) sold yesterday, with Mexican saddle and bridle, for seventy dollars—a horse which is well and widely known, and greatly respected for his speed, good disposition and everlasting bottom. You give your horse a little grain once a day; it comes from San Francisco, and is worth about two cents a pound; and you give him as much hay as he wants; it is cut and brought to the market by natives, and is not very good it is baled into long, round bundles, about the size of a large man; one of them is stuck by the middle on each end of a six-foot pole, and the Kanaka shoulders the pole and walks about the streets between the upright bales in search of customers. These hay bales, thus carried, have a general resemblance to a colossal capital H.

The hay-bundles cost twenty-five cents apiece, and one will last a horse about a day. You can get a horse for a song, a week's hay for another song, and you can turn your animal loose among the luxuriant grass in your neighbor's broad front yard without a song at all—you do it at midnight, and stable the beast again before morning. You have been at no expense thus far, but when you buy a saddle and bridle they will cost you from twenty to thirty-five dollars. You can hire a horse, saddle and bridle at from seven to ten dollars a week, and the owner will take care of them at his own expense.

It is time to close this day's record—bed time. As I prepare for sleep, a rich voice rises out of the still night, and, far as this ocean rock is toward the ends of the earth, I recognize a familiar home air. But the words seem somewhat out of joint:

"Waikiki lantoni œ Kaa hooly hooly wawhoo."

Translated, that means, "When we were marching through Georgia."

CHAPTER LXVI

Passing through the market place we saw that feature of Honolulu under its most favorable auspices—that is, in the full glory of Saturday afternoon, which is a festive day with the natives. The native girls by twos and threes and parties of a dozen, and sometimes in whole platoons and companies, went cantering up and down the neighboring streets astride of fleet but homely horses, and with their gaudy riding habits streaming like banners behind them. Such a troop of free and easy riders, in their natural home, the saddle, makes a gay and graceful spectacle. The riding habit I speak of is simply a long, broad scarf, like a tavern table cloth brilliantly colored, wrapped around the loins once, then apparently passed between the limbs and each end thrown backward over the same, and floating and flapping behind on both sides beyond the horse's tail like a couple of fancy flags; then, slipping the stirrup-irons between her toes, the girl throws her chest forward, sits up like a Major General and goes sweeping by like the wind.

The girls put on all the finery they can on Saturday afternoon—fine black silk robes; flowing red ones that nearly put your eyes out; others as white as snow; still others that discount the rainbow; and they wear their hair in nets, and trim their jaunty hats with fresh flowers, and encircle their dusky throats with home-made necklaces of the brilliant vermillion-tinted blossom of the *ohia*; and they fill the markets and the adjacent streets with their bright presences, and smell like a rag factory on fire with their offensive cocoanut oil.

Occasionally you see a heathen from the sunny isles away down in the South Seas, with his face and neck tattooed till he looks like the customary mendicant from Washoe who has been blown up in a mine. Some are tattooed a dead blue color down to the upper lip—masked, as it were—leaving the natural light yellow skin of Micronesia unstained from thence down; some with broad marks drawn down from hair to neck, on both sides of the face, and a strip of the original yellow skin, two inches wide, down the center—a gridiron with a spoke broken out; and some with the entire face discolored with the popular mortification tint, relieved only by one or two thin, wavy threads of natural yellow running across the face from ear to ear, and eyes twinkling out of this darkness, from under shadowing hat-brims, like stars in the dark of the moon.

Moving among the stirring crowds, you come to the poi merchants, squatting in the shade on their hams, in true native fashion, and surrounded by purchasers. (The Sandwich Islanders always squat on their hams, and who knows but they may be the old original "ham sandwiches?" The thought is pregnant with interest.) The poi looks like common flour paste, and is kept in large bowls formed of a species of gourd, and capable of holding from one to three or four gallons. Poi is the chief article of food among the natives, and is prepared from the *taro* plant. The taro root looks like a thick, or, if you please, a corpulent sweet potato, in shape, but is of light purple color when boiled. When boiled it answers as a passable substitute for bread. The buck Kanakas bake it under ground, then mash it up well with a heavy lava pestle, mix water with it until it becomes a paste, set it aside and let it ferment, and then it is poi—and an unseductive mixture it is, almost tasteless before it ferments and too sour for a luxury afterward. But nothing is more nutritious. When solely used, however,it produces acrid humors, a fact which sufficiently accounts for the humorous character of the Kanakas. I think there must be as much of a knack in handling poi as there is in eating with chopsticks. The forefinger is thrust into the mess and stirred quickly round several times and drawn as quickly out, thickly coated, just as if it were poulticed; the head is thrown back, the finger inserted in the mouth and the delicacy stripped off and swallowed—the eye closing gently, meanwhile, in a languid sort of ecstasy. Many a different finger goes into the same bowl and many a different kind of dirt and shade and quality of flavor is added to the virtues of its contents.

Around a small shanty was collected a crowd of natives buying the *awa* root. It is said that but for the use of this root the destruction of the people in former times by certain imported diseases would have been far greater than it was, and by others it is said that this is merely a fancy. All agree that poi will rejuvenate a man who is used up and his vitality almost annihilated by hard drinking, and that in some kinds of diseases it will restore health after all medicines have failed; but all are not willing to allow to the *awa* the virtues claimed for it. The natives manufacture an intoxicating drink from it which is fearful in its effects when persistently indulged in. It covers the body with dry, white scales, inflames the eyes, and causes premature decrepitude. Although the man before whose establishment we stopped has to pay a Government license of eight hundred dollars a year for the exclusive right to sell *awa* root, it is said that he makes a small fortune every twelve-month; while saloon keepers, who pay a thousand dollars a year for the privilege of retailing whiskey, etc., only make a bare living.

We found the fish market crowded; for the native is very fond of fish, and *eats the article raw and alive!* Let us change the subject.

In old times here Saturday was a grand gala day indeed. All the native population of the town forsook their labors, and those of the surrounding country journeyed to the city. Then the white folks had to stay indoors, for every street was so packed with charging cavaliers and cavalieresses that it was next to impossible to thread one's way through the cavalcades without getting crippled.

At night they feasted and the girls danced the lascivious *hula hula*—a dance that is said to exhibit the very perfection of educated motion of limb and arm, hand, head and body, and the exactest uniformity of movement and accuracy of "time." It was performed by a circle of girls with no raiment on them to speak of, who went through an infinite variety of motions and figures without prompting, and yet so true was their "time," and in such perfect concert did they move that when they were placed in a straight line, hands, arms, bodies, limbs and heads waved, swayed, gesticulated, bowed, stooped, whirled, squirmed, twisted and undulated as if they were part and parcel of a single individual; and it was difficult to believe they were not moved in a body by some exquisite piece of mechanism.

Of late years, however, Saturday has lost most of its quondam gala features. This weekly stampede of the natives interfered too much with labor and the interest of the white folks, and by sticking in a law here, and preaching a sermon there, and by various other means, they gradually broke it up. The demoralizing *hula hula* was forbidden to be performed, save at night, with closed doors, in presence of few spectators, and only by permission duly procured from the authorities and the payment of ten dollars for the same. There are few girls now-a-days able to dance this ancient national dance in the highest perfection of the art.

The missionaries have christianized and educated all the natives. They all belong to the Church, and there is not one of them, above the age of eight years, but can read and write with facility in the native tongue. It is the most universally educated race of people outside of China. They have any quantity of books, printed in the Kanaka language, and all the natives are fond of reading. They are inveterate church-goers—nothing can keep them away. All this ameliorating cultivation has at last built up in the native women a profound respect for chastity—in other people. Perhaps that is enough to say on that head. The national sin will die out when the race does, but perhaps not earlier.—But doubtless this purifying is not far off, when we reflect that contact with civilization and the whites has reduced the native population from *four hundred thousand* (Captain Cook's estimate,) to *fifty-five thousand* in something over eighty years!

Society is a queer medley in this notable missionary, whaling and governmental centre. If you get into conversation with a stranger and experience that natural desire to know what sort of ground you are treading on by finding out what manner of man your stranger is, strike out boldly and address him as "Captain." Watch him narrowly, and if you see by his countenance that you are on the wrong tack, ask him where he preaches. It is a safe bet that he is either a missionary or captain of a whaler. I am now personally acquainted with seventy-two captains and ninety-six missionaries. The captains and ministers form one-half of the population; the third fourth is composed of common Kanakas and mercantile foreigners and their families, and the final fourth is made up of high officers of the Hawaiian Government. And there are just about cats enough for three apiece all around.

A solemn stranger met me in the suburbs the other day, and said:

"Good morning, your reverence. Preach in the stone church yonder, no doubt?"

"No, I don't. I'm not a preacher."

"Really, I beg your pardon, Captain. I trust you had a good season. How much oil"—

"Oil? What do you take me for? I'm not a whaler."

"Oh, I beg a thousand pardons, your Excellency. Major General in the household troops, no doubt? Minister of the Interior, likely? Secretary of war? First Gentleman of the Bedchamber? Commissioner of the Royal"—

"Stuff! I'm no official. I'm not connected in any way with the Government."

"Bless my life! Then, who the mischief are you? what the mischief are you? and how the mischief did you get here, and where in thunder did you come from?"

"I'm only a private personage—an unassuming stranger—lately arrived from America."

"No? Not a missionary! Not a whaler! not a member of his Majesty's Government! not even Secretary of the Navy! Ah, Heaven! it is too blissful to be true; alas, I do but dream. And yet that noble, honest countenance—those oblique, ingenuous eyes—that massive head, incapable of—of—anything; your hand; give me your hand, bright waif. Excuse these tears. For sixteen weary years I have yearned for a moment like this, and"—

Here his feelings were too much for him, and he swooned away. I pitied this poor creature from the bottom of my heart. I was deeply moved. I shed a few tears on him and kissed him for his mother. I then took what small change he had and "shoved."

CHAPTER LXVII

I still quote from my journal:

I found the national Legislature to consist of half a dozen white men and some thirty or forty natives. It was a dark assemblage. The nobles and Ministers (about a dozen of them altogether) occupied the extreme left of the hall, with David Kalakaua (the King's Chamberlain) and Prince William at the head. The President of the Assembly, His Royal Highness M. Kekuanaoa,* and the Vice President (the latter a white man,) sat in the pulpit, if I may so term it.

The President is the King's father. He is an erect, strongly built, massive featured, white-haired, tawny old gentleman of eighty years of age or thereabouts. He was simply but well dressed, in a blue cloth coat and white vest, and white pantaloons, without spot, dust or blemish upon them. He bears himself with a calm, stately dignity, and is a man of noble presence. He was a young man and a distinguished warrior under that terrific fighter, Kamehameha I., more than half a century ago. A knowledge of his career suggested some such thought as this: "This man, naked as the day he was born, and war-club and spear in hand, has charged at the head of a horde of savages against other hordes of savages more than a generation and a half ago, and reveled in slaughter and carnage; has worshipped wooden images on his devout knees; has seen hundreds of his race offered up in heathen temples as sacrifices to wooden idols, at a time when no missionary's foot had ever pressed this soil, and he had never heard of the white man's God; has believed his enemy could secretly pray him to death; has seen the day, in his childhood, when it was a crime punishable by death for a man to eat with his wife, or for a plebeian to let his shadow fall upon the King—and now look at

*Since dead.

825

him; an educated Christian; neatly and handsomely dressed; a high-minded, elegant gentleman; a traveler, in some degree, and one who has been the honored guest of royalty in Europe; a man practiced in holding the reins of an enlightened government, and well versed in the politics of his country and in general, practical information. Look at him, sitting there presiding over the deliberations of a legislative body, among whom are white men—a grave, dignified, statesmanlike personage, and as seemingly natural and fitted to the place as if he had been born in it and had never been out of it in his life time. How the experiences of this old man's eventful life shame the cheap inventions of romance!"

Kekuanaoa is not of the blood royal. He derives his princely rank from his wife, who was a daughter of Kamehameha the Great. Under other monarchies the male line takes precedence of the female in tracing genealogies, but here the opposite is the case—the female line takes precedence. Their reason for this is exceedingly sensible, and I recommend it to the aristocracy of Europe: They say it is easy to know who a man's mother was, but, etc, etc.

The christianizing of the natives has hardly even weakened some of their barbarian superstitions, much less destroyed them. I have just referred to one of these. It is still a popular belief that if your enemy can get hold of any article belonging to you he can get down on his knees over it and *pray you to death*. Therefore many a native gives up and dies merely because he *imagines* that some enemy is putting him through a course of damaging prayer. This praying an individual to death seems absurb enough at a first glance, but then when we call to mind some of the pulpit efforts of certain of our own ministers the thing looks plausible.

In former times, among the Islanders, not only a plurality of wives was customary, but a *plurality of husbands* likewise. Some native women of noble rank had as many as six husbands. A woman thus supplied did not reside with all her husbands at once, but lived several months with each in turn. An understood sign hung at her door during these months. When the sign was taken down, it meant "NEXT."

In those days woman was rigidly taught to "know her place." Her place was to do all the work, take all the cuffs, provide all the food, and content herself with what was left after her lord had finished his dinner. She was not only forbidden, by ancient law, and under penalty of death, to eat with her husband or enter a canoe, but was debarred, under the same penalty, from eating bananas, pine-apples, oranges and other choice fruits at any time or in any place. She had to confine herself pretty strictly to "poi" and hard work. These poor ignorant heathen seem to have had a sort of groping idea of what came of woman eating fruit in the garden of Eden, and they did not choose to take any more chances. But the missionaries broke up this satisfactory arrangement of things. They liberated woman and made her the equal of man.

The natives had a romantic fashion of burying some of their children alive when the family became larger than necessary. The missionaries interfered in this matter too, and stopped it.

To this day the natives are able to *lie down and die whenever they want to,* whether there is anything the matter with them or not. If a Kanaka takes a notion to die, that is the end of him; nobody can persuade him to hold on; all the doctors in the world could not save him.

A luxury which they enjoy more than anything else, is a large funeral. If a person wants to get rid of a troublesome native, it is only necessary to promise him a fine funeral and name the hour and he will be on hand to the minute—at least his remains will.

All the natives are Christians, now, but many of them still desert to the Great Shark God for temporary succor in time of trouble. An irruption of the great volcano of Kilauea, or an earthquake, always brings a deal of latent loyalty to the Great Shark God to the surface. It is common report that the King, educated, cultivated and refined Christian gentleman as he undoubtedly is, still turns to the idols of his fathers for help when disaster threatens. A planter caught a shark, and one of his christianized natives testified his emancipation from the thrall of ancient superstition by assisting to dissect the shark after a fashion forbidden by his abandoned creed. But remorse shortly began to torture him. He grew moody and sought solitude; brooded over his sin, refused food, and finally said he must die and ought to die, for he had sinned against the Great Shark God and could never know peace any more. He was proof against persuasion and ridicule, and in the course of a day or two took to his bed and died, although he showed no symptom of disease. His young daughter followed his lead and suffered a like fate within the week. Superstition is ingrained in the native blood and bone and it is only natural that it should crop out in time of distress. Wherever one goes in the Islands, he will find small piles of stones by the wayside, covered with leafy offerings, placed there by the natives to appease evil spirits or honor local deities belonging to the mythology of former days.

In the rural districts of any of the Islands, the traveler hourly comes upon parties of dusky maidens bathing in the streams or in the sea without any clothing on and exhibiting no very intemperate zeal in the matter of hiding their nakedness. When the missionaries first took up their residence in Honolulu, the native women would pay their families frequent friendly visits, day by day, not even clothed with a blush. It was found a hard matter to convince them that this was rather indelicate. Finally the missionaries provided them with long, loose calico robes, and that ended the difficulty—for the women would troop through the town, stark naked, with their robes folded under their arms, march to the missionary houses and then proceed to dress!—The natives soon manifested a strong proclivity for clothing, but it was shortly apparent that they only wanted it for grandeur. The missionaries imported a quantity of hats, bonnets, and other male and female wearing apparel, instituted a general distribution, and begged the people not to come to church naked, next Sunday, as usual. And they did not; but the national spirit of unselfishness led them to divide up with neighbors who were not at the distribution, and next Sabbath the poor preachers could hardly keep countenance before their vast congregations. In the midst of the reading of a hymn a brown, stately dame would sweep up the aisle with a world of airs, with nothing in the world on but a "stovepipe" hat and a pair of cheap gloves; another dame would follow, tricked out in a man's shirt, and nothing else; another one would enter with a flourish, with simply the sleeves of a bright calico dress tied around her waist and the rest of the garment dragging behind like a peacock's tail off duty; a stately "buck" Kanaka would stalk in with a woman's bonnet on, wrong side before—only this, and nothing more; after him would stride his fellow, with the legs of a pair of pantaloons tied around his neck, the rest of his person untrammeled; in his rear would come another gentleman simply gotten up in a fiery neck-tie and a striped vest. The poor creatures were beaming with complacency and wholly unconscious of any absurdity in their appearance. They gazed at each other with happy admiration, and it was plain to see that the young girls were taking note of what each other had on, as naturally as if they had always lived in a land of Bibles and knew what churches were made for; here was the evidence of a dawning civilization. The spectacle which the congregation presented was so extraordinary and withal so moving, that the missionaries found it difficult to keep to the text and go on with the services; and by and by when the simple children of the sun began a general swapping of garments in open meeting and produced some irresistibly grotesque effects in the course of re-dressing, there was nothing for it but to cut the thing short with the benediction and dismiss the fantastic assemblage.

In our country, children play "keep house;" and in the same high-sounding but miniature way the grown folk here, with the poor little material of slender territory and meagre population, play "empire." There is his royal Majesty the King, with a New York detective's income of thirty or thirty-five thousand dollars a year from the "royal civil list" and the "royal domain." He lives in a two-story frame "palace."

And there is the "royal family"—the customary hive of royal brothers, sisters, cousins and other noble drones and vagrants usual to monarchy,—all with a spoon in the national pap-dish, and all bearing such titles as his or her Royal Highness the Prince or Princess So-and-so. Few of them can carry their royal splendors far enough to ride in carriages, however; they sport the economical Kanaka horse or "hoof it"* with the plebeians.

Then there is his Excellency the "royal Chamberlain"—a sinecure, for his majesty dresses himself with his own hands, except when he is ruralizing at Waikiki and then he requires no dressing.

Next we have his Excellency the Commander-in-chief of the Household Troops, whose forces consist of about the number of soldiers usually placed under a corporal in other lands.

Next comes the royal Steward and the Grand Equerry in Waiting—high dignitaries with modest salaries and little to do.

Then we have his Excellency the First Gentleman of the Bedchamber—an office as easy as it is magnificent.

Next we come to his Excellency the Prime Minister, a renegade American from New Hampshire, all jaw, vanity, bombast and ignorance, a lawyer of "shyster" calibre, a fraud by nature, a humble worshiper of the sceptre above him, a reptile never tired of sneering at the land of his birth or glorifying the ten-acre kingdom that has adopted him—salary, $4,000 a year, vast consequence, and no perquisites.

Then we have his Excellency the Imperial Minister of Finance, who handles a million dollars of public money a year, sends in his annual "budget" with great ceremony, talks prodigiously of "finance," suggests imposing schemes for paying off the "national debt" (of $150,000,) and does it all for $4,000 a year and unimaginable glory.

Next we have his Excellency the Minister of War, who holds sway over the royal armies—they consist of two hundred and

*Missionary phrase.

thirty uniformed Kanakas, mostly Brigadier Generals, and if the country ever gets into trouble with a foreign power we shall probably hear from them. I knew an American whose copperplate visiting card bore this impressive legend: "Lieutenant-Colonel in the Royal Infantry." To say that he was proud of this distinction is stating it but tamely. The Minister of War has also in his charge some venerable swivels on Punch-Bowl Hill wherewith royal salutes are fired when foreign vessels of war enter the port.

Next comes his Excellency the Minister of the Navy—a nabob who rules the "royal fleet," (a steam-tug and a sixty-ton schooner.)

And next comes his Grace the Lord Bishop of Honolulu, the chief dignitary of the "Established Church"—for when the American Presbyterian missionaries had completed the reduction of the nation to a compact condition of Christianity, native royalty stepped in and erected the grand dignity of an "Established (Episcopal) Church" over it, and imported a cheap ready-made Bishop from England to take charge. The chagrin of the missionaries has never been comprehensively expressed, to this day, profanity not being admissible.

Next comes his Excellency the Minister of Public Instruction.

Next , their Excellencies the Governors of Oahu, Hawaii, etc., and after them a string of High Sheriffs and other small fry too numerous for computation.

Then there are their Excellencies the Envoy Extraordinary and Minister Plenipotentiary of his Imperial Majesty the Emperor of the French; her British Majesty's Minister; the Minister Resident, of the United States; and some six or eight representatives of other foreign nations, all with sounding titles, imposing dignity and prodigious but economical state.

Imagine all this grandeur in a play-house "kingdom" whose population falls absolutely short of sixty thousand souls!

The people are so accustomed to nine-jointed titles and colossal magnates that a foreign prince makes very little more stir in Honolulu than a Western Congressman does in New York.

And let it be borne in mind that there is a strictly defined "court costume" of so "stunning" a nature that it would make the clown in a circus look tame and commonplace by comparison; and each Hawaiian official dignitary has a gorgeous vari-colored, gold-laced uniform peculiar to his office—no two of them are alike, and it is hard to tell which one is the "loudest." The King had a "drawing-room" at stated intervals, like other monarchs, and when these varied uniforms congregate there weak-eyed people have to contemplate the spectacle through smoked glass. Is there not a gratifying contrast between this latter-day exhibition and the one the ancestors of some of these magnates afforded the missionaries the Sunday after the old-time distribution of clothing? Behold what religion and civilization have wrought!

CHAPTER LXVIII

While I was in Honolulu I witnessed the ceremonious funeral of the King's sister, her Royal Highness the Princess Victoria. According to the royal custom, the remains had lain in state at the palace *thirty days*, watched day and night by a guard of honor. And during all that time a great multitude of natives from the several islands had kept the palace grounds well crowded and had made the place a pandemonium every night with their howlings and wailings, beating of tom-toms and dancing of the (at other times) forbidden "hula-hula" by half-clad maidens to the music of songs of questionable decency chanted in honor of the deceased. The printed programme of the funeral procession interested me at the time; and after what I have just said of Hawaiian grandiloquence in the matter of "playing empire," I am persuaded that a perusal of it may interest the reader:

After reading the long list of dignitaries, etc., and remembering the sparseness of the population, one is almost inclined to wonder where the material for that portion of the procession devoted to "Hawaiian Population Generally" is going to be procured:

Undertaker.
Royal School.   Kawaiahao School.
Roman Catholic School.   Miæmæ School.
Honolulu Fire Department.
Mechanics' Benefit Union.
Attending Physicians.
Knonohikis (Superintendents) of the Crown Lands, Konohikis of the
Private Lands of His Majesty Konohikis of Private Lands of
Her late Royal Highness.
Governor of Oahu and Staff.
Hulumanu (Military Company).
Household Troops.
The Prince of Hawaii's Own (Military Company).
The King's household servants.
Servants of Her late Royal Highness.
Protestant Clergy.   The Clergy of the Roman Catholic Church.
His Lordship Louis Maigret, The Right Rev. Bishop of Arathea,
Vicar-Apostolic of the Hawaiian Islands.

The Clergy of the Hawaiian Reformed Catholic Church.
His Lordship the Right Rev. Bishop of Honolulu.

Escort Hawaiian Cavalry.*
Large Kahilis.
Small Kahilis.
Pall Bearers.

[HEARSE.]

Escort Hawaiian Cavalry.
Large Kahilis.
Small Kahalis.
Pall Bearers.

Her Majesty Queen Emma's Carriage.
His Majesty's Staff.
Carriage of Her late Royal Highness.
Carriage of Her Majesty the Queen Dowager.
The King's Chancellor.
Cabinet Ministers.
His Excellency the Minister Resident of the United States.
H. I. M's Commissioner.
H. B. M's Acting Commissioner.
Judges of Supreme Court.
Privy Councillors.
Members of Legislative Assembly.
Consular Corps.
Circuit Judges.
Clerks of Government Departments.
Members of the Bar.
Collector General, Custom-house Officers and
Officers of the Customs.
Marshal and Sheriffs of the different Islands.
King's Yeomanry.
Foreign Residents.
Ahahui Kaahumanu.
Hawaiian Population Generally.
Hawaiian Cavalry.
Police Force.

I resume my journal at the point where the procession arrived at the royal mausoleum:

As the procession filed through the gate, the military deployed handsomely to the right and left and formed an avenue through which the long column of mourners passed to the tomb. The coffin was borne through the door of the mausoleum, followed by the King and his chiefs, the great officers of the kingdom, foreign Consuls, Embassadors and distinguished guests (Burlingame and General Van Valkenburgh). Several of the kahilis were then fastened to a frame-

*Ranks of long-handled mops made of gaudy feathers—sacred to royalty. They are stuck in the ground around the tomb and left there.

work in front of the tomb, there to remain until they decay and fall to pieces, or, forestalling this, until another scion of royalty dies. At this point of the proceedings the multitude set up such a heart-broken wailing as I hope never to hear again. The soldiers fired three volleys of musketry—the wailing being previously silenced to permit of the guns being heard. His Highness Prince William, in a showy military uniform (the "true prince," this—scion of the house over-thrown by the present dynasty—he was formerly betrothed to the Princess but was not allowed to marry her), stood guard and paced back and forth within the door. The privileged few who followed the coffin into the mausoleum remained sometime, but the King soon came out and stood in the door and near one side of it. A stranger could have guessed his rank (although he was so simply and unpretentiously dressed) by the profound deference paid him by all persons in his vicinity; by seeing his high officers receive his quiet orders and suggestions with bowed and uncovered heads; and by observing how careful those persons who came out of the mausoleum were to avoid "crowding" him (although there was room enough in the doorway for a wagon to pass, for that matter); how respectfully they edged out sideways, scraping their backs against the wall and always presenting a front view of their persons to his Majesty, and never putting their hats on until they were well out of the royal presence.

He was dressed entirely in black—dress-coat and silk hat—and looked rather democratic in the midst of the showy uniforms about him. On his breast he wore a large gold star, which was half hidden by the lapel of his coat. He remained at the door a half hour, and occasionally gave an order to the men who were erecting the *kahilis* before the tomb. He had the good taste to make one of them substitute black crape for the ordinary hempen rope he was about to tie one of them to the frame-work with. Finally he entered his carriage and drove away, and the populace shortly began to drop into his wake. While he was in view there was but one man who attracted more attention than himself, and that was Harris (the Yankee Prime Minister). This feeble personage had crape enough around his hat to express the grief of an entire nation, and as usual he neglected no opportunity of making himself conspicuous and exciting the admiration of the simple Kanakas. Oh! noble ambition of this modern Richelieu!

It is interesting to contrast the funeral ceremonies of the Princess Victoria with those of her noted ancestor Kamehameha the Conqueror, who died fifty years ago—in 1819, the year before the first missionaries came.

"On the 8th of May, 1819, at the age of sixty-six, he died, as he had lived, in the faith of his country. It was his misfortune not to have come in contact with men who could have rightly influenced his religious aspirations. Judged by his advantages and compared with the most eminent of his countrymen he may be justly styled not only great, but good. To this day his memory warms the heart and elevates the national feelings of Hawaiians. They are proud of their old warrior King; they love his name; his deeds form their historical age; and an enthusiasm everywhere prevails, shared even by foreigners who knew his worth, that constitutes the firmest pillar of the throne of his dynasty.

"In lieu of human victims (the custom of that age), a sacrifice of three hundred dogs attended his obsequies—no mean holocaust when their national value and the estimation in which they were held are considered. The bones of Kamehameha, after being kept for a while, were so carefully concealed that all knowledge of their final resting place is now lost. There was a proverb current among the common people that the bones of a cruel King could not be hid; they made fishhooks and arrows of them, upon which, in using them, they vented their abhorrence of his memory in bitter execrations."

The account of the circumstances of his death, as written by the native historians, is full of minute detail, but there is scarcely a line of it which does not mention or illustrate some by-gone custom of the country. In this respect it is the most comprehensive document I have yet met with. I will quote it entire:

"When Kamehameha was dangerously sick, and the priests were unable to cure him, they said: 'Be of good courage and build a house for the god' (his own private god or idol), that thou mayest recover.' The chiefs corroborated this advice of the priests, and a place or worship was prepared for Kukailimoku, and consecrated in the evening. They proposed also to the King, with a view to prolong his life, that human victims should be sacrificed to his deity; upon which the greater part of the people absconded through fear of death, and concealed themselves in hiding places till the *tabu** in which destruction impended, was past. It is doubtful whether Kamehameha approved of the plan of the chiefs and priests to sacrifice men, as he was known to say, 'The men are sacred for the King;' meaning that they were for the service of his successor. This information was derived from Liholiho, his son.

"After this, his sickness increased to such a degree that he had not strength to turn himself in his bed. When another season, consecrated for worship at the new temple (*heiau*) arrived, he said to his son, Liholiho, 'Go thou and make supplication to thy god; I am not able to go, and will offer my prayers at home.' When his devotions to his feathered god, Kukuailimoku, were concluded, a certain religiously disposed individual, who had a bird god, suggested to the King that through its influence his sickness might be removed. The name of this god was Pua; its body was made of a bird, now eaten by the Hawaiians, and called in their language *alae*. Kamehameha was willing that a trial should be made, and two houses were constructed to facilitate the ex-

---

*Tabu (pronounced tah-boo,) means prohibition (we have borrowed it,) or sacred. The tabu was sometimes permanent, sometimes temporary; and the person or thing placed under tabu was for the time being sacred to the purpose for which it was set apart. In the above case the victims selected under the tabu would be sacred to the sacrifice.

periment; but while dwelling in them he became so very weak as not to receive food. After lying there three days, his wives, children and chiefs, perceiving that he was very low, returned him to his own house. In the evening he was carried to the eating house,* where he took a little food in his mouth which he did not swallow; also a cup of water. The chiefs requested him to give them his counsel; but he made no reply, and was carried back to the dwelling house; but when near midnight— ten o'clock, perhaps—he was carried again to the place to eat; but, as before, he merely tasted of what was presented to him. Then Kaikioewa addressed him thus: 'Here we all are, your younger brethren, your son Liholiho and your foreigner; impart to us your dying charge, that Liholiho and Kaahumanu may hear.' Then Kamehameha inquired, 'What do you say?' Kaikioewa repeated, 'Your counsels for us.' He then said, 'Move on in my good way and—.' He could proceed no further. The foreigner, Mr. Young, embraced and kissed him. Hoapili also embraced him, whispering something in his ear, after which he was taken back to the house. About twelve he was carried once more to the house for eating, into which his head entered, while his body was in the dwelling house immediately adjoining. It should be remarked that this frequent carrying of a sick chief from one house to another resulted from the *tabu* system, then in force. There were at that time six houses (huts) connected with an establishment—one was for worship, one for the men to eat in, an eating house for the women, a house to sleep in, a house in which to manufacture kapa (native cloth) and one where, at certain intervals, the women might dwell in seclusion.

"The sick was once more taken to his house, when he expired; this was at two o'clock, a circumstance from which Leleiohoku derived his name. As he breathed his last, Kalaimoku came to the eating house to order those in it to go out. There were two aged persons thus directed to depart; one went, the other remained on account of love to the King, by whom he had formerly been kindly sustained. The children also were sent away. Then Kalaimoku came to the house, and the chiefs had a consultation. One of them spoke thus: 'This is my thought—we will eat him raw.'† Kaahumanu (one of the dead King's widows) replied, 'Perhaps his body is not at our disposal; that is more properly with his successor. Our part in him—his breath—has departed; his remains will be disposed of by Liholiho.'

"After this conversation the body was taken into the consecrated house for the performance of the proper rites by the priest and the new King. The name of this ceremony is *uko;* and when the sacred hog was baked the priest offered it to the dead body, and it became a god, the King at the same time repeating the customary prayers.

"Then the priest, addressing himself to the King and chiefs, said: 'I will now make known to you the rules to be observed respecting per-

*It was deemed pollution to eat in the same hut a person slept in—the fact that the patient was dying could not modify the rigid etiquette.

†This sounds suspicious, in view of the fact that all Sandwich Island historians, white and black, protest cannibalism never existed in the islands. However, since they only proposed to "eat him raw" we "won't count that". But it would certainly have been cannibalism if they had cooked him.—[M. T.]

sons to be sacrificed on the burial of this body. If you obtain one man before the corpse is removed, one will be sufficient; but after it leaves this house four will be required. If delayed until we carry the corpse to the grave there must be ten; but after it is deposited in the grave there must be fifteen. To-morrow morning there will be a *tabu*, and, if the sacrifice be delayed until that time, forty men must die.'

"Then the high priest, Hewahewa, inquired of the chiefs, 'Where shall be the residence of King Liholiho?' They replied, 'Where, indeed? You, of all men, ought to know.' Then the priest observed, 'There are two suitable places; one is Kau, the other is Kohala.' The chiefs preferred the latter, as it was more thickly inhabited. The priest added, 'These are proper places for the King's residence; but he must not remain in Kona, for it is polluted.' This was agreed to. It was now break of day. As he was being carried to the place of burial the people perceived that their King was dead, and they wailed. When the corpse was removed from the house to the tomb, a distance of one chain, the procession was met by a certain man who was ardently attached to the deceased. He leaped upon the chiefs who were carrying the King's body; he desired to die with him on account of his love. The chiefs drove him away. He persisted in making numerous attempts, which were unavailing. Kalaimoka also had it in his heart to die with him, but was prevented by Hookio.

"The morning following Kamehameha's death, Liholiho and his train departed for Kohala, according to the suggestions of the priest, to avoid the defilement occasioned by the dead. At this time if a chief died the land was polluted, and the heirs sought a residence in another part of the country until the corpse was dissected and the bones tied in a bundle, which being done, the season of defilement terminated. If the deceased were not a chief, the house only was defiled which became pure again on the burial of the body. Such were the laws on this subject.

"On the morning on which Liholiho sailed in his canoe for Kohala, the chiefs and people mourned after their manner on occasion of a chief's death, conducting themselves like madmen and like beasts. Their conduct was such as to forbid description; The priests, also, put into action the sorcery apparatus, that the person who had prayed the King to death might die; for it was not believed that Kamehameha's departure was the effect either of sickness or old age. When the sorcerers set up by their fire-places stick with a strip of kapa flying at the top, the chief Keeaumoku, Kaahumanu's brother, came in a state of intoxication and broke the flag-staff of the sorcerers, from which it was inferred that Kaahumanu and her friends had been instrumental in the King's death. On this account they were subjected to abuse."

You have the contrast, now, and a strange one it is. This great Queen, Kaahumanu, who was "subjected to abuse" during the frightful orgies that followed the King's death, in accordance with ancient custom, afterward became a devout Christian and a steadfast and powerful friend of the missionaries.

Dogs were, and still are, reared and fattened for food, by the natives—hence the reference to their value in one of the above paragraphs.

Forty years ago it was the custom in the Islands to suspend all law for a certain number of days after the death of a royal personage; and then a saturnalia ensued which one may picture to himself after a fashion, but not in the full horror of the reality. The people shaved their heads, knocked out a tooth or two, plucked out an eye sometimes, cut, bruised, mutilated or burned their flesh, got drunk, burned each other's huts, maimed or murdered one another according to the caprice of the moment, and both sexes gave themselves up to brutal and unbridled licentiousness. And after it all, came a torpor from which the nation slowly emerged bewildered and dazed, as if from a hideous half-remembered nightmare. They were not the salt of the earth, those "gentle children of the sun."

The natives still keep up an old custom of theirs which cannot be comforting to an invalid. When they think a sick friend is going to die, a couple of dozen neighbors surround his hut and keep up a deafening wailing night and day till he either dies or gets well. No doubt this arrangement has helped many a subject to a shroud before his appointed time.

They surround a hut and wail in the same heart-broken way when its occupant returns from a journey. This is their dismal idea of a welcome. A very little of it would go a great way with most of us.

CHAPTER LXIX

Bound for Hawaii (a hundred and fifty miles distant,) to visit the great volcano and behold the other notable things which distinguish that island above the remainder of the group, we sailed from Honolulu on a certain Saturday afternoon, in the good schooner Boomerang.

The Boomerang was about as long as two street cars, and about as wide as one. She was so small (though she was larger than the majority of the inter-island coasters) that when I stood on her deck I felt but little smaller than the Colossus of Rhodes must have felt when he had a man-of-war under him. I could reach the water when she lay over under a strong breeze. When the Captain and my comrade (a Mr. Billings), myself and four other persons were all assembled on the little after portion of the deck which is sacred to the cabin passengers, it was full—there was not room for any more quality folks. Another section of the deck, twice as large as ours, was full of natives of both sexes, with their customary dogs, mats, blankets, pipes, calabashes of poi, fleas, and other luxuries and baggage of minor importance. As soon as we set sail the natives all lay down on the deck as thick as negroes in a slave-pen, and smoked, conversed, and spit on each other, and were truly sociable.

The little low-ceiled cabin below was rather larger than a hearse, and as dark as a vault. It had two coffins on each side—I mean two bunks. A small table, capable of accommodating three persons at dinner, stood against the forward bulkhead, and over it hung the dingiest whale oil lantern that ever peopled the obscurity of a dungeon with ghostly shapes. The floor room unoccupied was not extensive. One might swing a cat in it, perhaps, but not a long cat. The hold forward of the bulkhead had but little freight in it, and from morning till night a portly old rooster, with a voice like Baalam's ass, and the same disposition to use it, strutted up and down in that part of the vessel and crowed. He usually took dinner at six o'clock, and then, after an hour devoted to meditation, he mounted a barrel and crowed a good part of the night. He got hoarser and hoarser all the time, but he scorned to allow any personal consideration to interfere with his duty, and kept up his labors in defiance of threatened diphtheria.

Sleeping was out of the question when he was on watch. He was a source of genuine aggravation and annoyance. It was worse than useless to shout at him or apply offensive epithets to him—he only took these things for applause, and strained himself to make more noise. Occasionally, during the day, I threw potatoes at him through an aperture in the bulkhead, but he only dodged and went on crowing.

The first night, as I lay in my coffin, idly watching the dim lamp swinging to the rolling of the ship, and snuffing the nauseous odors of bilge water, I felt something gallop over me. I turned out promptly. However, I turned in again when I found it was only a rat. Presently something galloped over me once more. I knew it was not a rat this time, and I thought it might be a centipede, because the Captain had killed one on deck in the afternoon. I turned out. The first glance at the pillow showed me a repulsive sentinel perched upon each end of it—cockroaches as large as peach leaves—fellows with long, quivering antennae and fiery, malignant eyes. They were grating their teeth like tobacco worms, and appeared to be dissatisfied about something. I had often heard that these reptiles were in the habit of eating off sleeping sailors' toe nails down to the quick, and I would not get in the bunk any more. I lay down on the floor. But a rat came and bothered me, and shortly afterward a procession of cockroaches arrived and camped in my hair. In a few moments the rooster was crowing with uncommon spirit and a party of fleas were throwing double somersaults about my person in the wildest disorder, and taking a bite every time they struck. I was beginning to feel really annoyed. I got up and put my clothes on and went on deck.

The above is not overdrawn; it is a truthful sketch of interisland schooner life. There is no such thing as keeping a vessel in elegant condition, when she carries molasses and Kanakas.

It was compensation for my sufferings to come unexpectedly upon so beautiful a scene as met my eye—to step suddenly out of the sepulchral gloom of the cabin and stand under the strong light of the moon—in the centre, as it were, of a glittering sea of liquid silver—to see the broad sails straining in the gale, the ship keeled over on her side, the angry foam hissing past her lee bulwarks, and sparkling sheets of spray dashing high over her bows and raining upon her decks; to brace myself and hang fast to the first object that presented itself, with hat jammed down and coat tails whipping in the breeze, and feel that exhilaration that thrills in one's hair and quivers down his back bone when he knows that every inch of canvas is drawing and the vessel cleaving through the waves at her utmost speed. There was no darkness, no dimness, no obscurity there. All was brightness, every object was vividly defined. Every prostrate Kanaka; every coil of rope; every calabash of poi; every puppy; every seam in the flooring; every bolthead; every object, however minute, showed sharp and distinct in its every outline; and the shadow of the broad mainsail lay black as a pall upon the deck, leaving Billing's white upturned face glorified and his body in a total eclipse.

Monday morning we were close to the island of Hawaii. Two of its high mountains were in view—Mauna Loa and Hualaiai. The latter is an imposing peak, but being only ten thousand feet high is seldom mentioned or heard of. Mauna Loa is said to be sixteen thousand feet high. The rays of glittering snow and ice, that clasped its summit like a claw, looked refreshing when viewed from the blistering climate we were in. One could stand on that mountain (wrapped up in blankets and furs to keep warm), and while he nibbled a snowball or an icicle to quench his thirst he could look down the long sweep of its sides and see spots where plants are growing that grow only where the bitter cold of Winter prevails; lower down he could see sections devoted to productions that thrive in the temperate zone alone; and at the bottom of the mountain he could see the home of the tufted cocoa-palms and other species of vegetation that grow only in the sultry atmosphere of eternal Summer. He could see all the climes of the world at a single glance of the eye, and that glance would only pass over a distance of four or five miles as the bird flies!

By and by we took boat and went ashore at Kailua, designing to ride horseback through the pleasant orange and coffee region of Kona, and rejoin the vessel at a point some leagues distant. This journey is well worth taking. The trail passes along on high ground—say a thousand feet above sea level—and usually about a mile distant from the ocean, which is always in sight, save that occasionally you find yourself buried in the forest in the midst of a rank tropical vegetation and a dense growth of trees, whose great bows overarch the road and shut out sun and sea and everything, and leave you in a dim, shady tunnel, haunted with invisible singing birds and fragrant with the odor of flowers. It was pleasant to ride occasionally in the warm sun, and feast the eye upon the ever-changing panorama of the forest (beyond and below us), with its many tints, its softened lights and shadows, its billowy undulations sweeping gently down from the mountain to the sea. It was pleasant also, at intervals, to leave the sultry sun and pass into the cool, green depths of this forest and indulge in sentimental reflections under the inspiration of its brooding twilight and its whispering foliage.

We rode through one orange grove that had ten thousand trees in it! They were all laden with fruit.

At one farmhouse we got some large peaches of excellent flavor. This fruit, as a general thing, does not do well in the Sandwich Islands. It takes a sort of almond shape, and is small and bitter. It needs frost, they say, and perhaps it does; if this be so, it will have a good opportunity to go on needing it, as it will not be likely to get it. The trees from which the fine fruit I have spoken of, came, had been planted and replanted *sixteen times*, and to this treatment the proprietor of the orchard attributed his success.

We passed several sugar plantations—new ones and not very extensive. The crops were, in most cases, third rattoons. [Note.—The first crop is called "plant cane;" subsequent crops which spring from the original roots, without replanting, are called "rattoons."] Almost everywhere on the island of Hawaii sugar-cane matures in twelve months, both rattoons and plant, and although it ought to be taken off as soon as it tassels, no doubt, it is not absolutely necessary to do it until about four months afterward. In Kona, the average yield of an acre of ground is *two tons* of sugar, they say. This is only a moderate yield for these islands, but would be astounding for Louisiana and most other sugar growing countries. The plantations in Kona being on pretty high ground—up among the light and frequent rains—no irrigation whatever is required.

CHAPTER LXX

We stopped some time at one of the plantations, to rest ourselves and refresh the horses. We had a chatty conversation with several gentlemen present; but there was one person, a middle aged man, with an absent look in his face, who simply glanced up, gave us good-day and lapsed again into the meditations which our coming had interrupted. The planters whispered us not to mind him—crazy. They said he was in the Islands for his health; was a preacher; his home, Michigan. They said that if he woke up presently and fell to talking about a correspondence which he had some time held with Mr. Greeley about a trifle of some kind, we must humor him and listen with interest; and we must humor his fancy that this correspondence was the talk of the world.

It was easy to see that he was a gentle creature and that his madness had nothing vicious in it. He looked pale, and a little worn, as if with perplexing thought and anxiety of mind. He sat a long time, looking at the floor, and at intervals muttering to himself and nodding his head acquiescingly or shaking it in mild protest. He was lost in his thought, or in his memories. We continued our talk with the planters, branching from subject to subject. But at last the word "circumstance," casually dropped, in the course of conversation, attracted his attention and brought an eager look into his countenance. He faced about in his chair and said:

"Circumstance? What circumstance? Ah, I know—I know too well. So you have heard of it too." [With a sigh.] "Well, no matter—all the world has heard of it. All the world. The whole world. It is a large world, too, for a thing to travel so far in—now isn't it? Yes, yes—the Greeley correspondence with Erickson has created the saddest and bitterest controversy on both sides of the ocean—and still they keep it up! It makes us famous, but at what a sorrowful sacrifice! I was so sorry when I heard that it had caused that bloody and distressful war over there in Italy. It was little comfort to me, after so much bloodshed, to know that the victors sided with me, and the vanquished with Greeley.—It is little comfort to know that Horace Greeley is responsible for the battle of Sadowa, and not me. Queen Victoria wrote me that she felt just as I did about it—she said that as much as she was opposed to Greeley and the spirit he showed in the correspondence with me, she would not have had Sadowa happen for hundreds of dollars. I can show you her letter, if you would like to see it. But gentlemen, much as you may think you know about that unhappy correspondence, you cannot know the *straight* of it till you hear it from my lips. It has always been garbled in the journals, and even in history. Yes, even in history—think of it! Let me—*please* let me, give you the matter, exactly as it occurred. I truly will not abuse your confidence.''

Then he leaned forward, all interest, all earnestness, and told his story—and told it appealingly, too, and yet in the simplest and most unpretentious way; indeed, in such a way as to suggest to one, all the time, that this was a faithful, honorable witness, giving evidence in the sacred interest of justice, and under oath. He said:

"Mrs. Beazeley—Mrs. Jackson Beazeley, widow, of the village of Campbellton, Kansas,—wrote me about a matter which was near her heart—a matter which many might think trivial, but to her it was a thing of deep concern. I was living in Michigan, then—serving in the ministry. She was, and is, an estimable woman—a woman to whom poverty and hardship have proven incentives to industry, in place of discouragements. Her only treasure was her son William, a youth just verging upon manhood; religious, amiable, and sincerely attached to agriculture. He was the widow's comfort and her pride. And so, moved by her love for him, she wrote me about a matter, as I have said before, which lay near her' heart—because it lay near her boy's. She desired me to confer with Mr. Greeley about turnips. Turnips were the dream of her child's young ambition. While other youths were frittering away in frivolous amusements the precious years of budding vigor which God had given them for useful preparation, this boy was patiently enriching his mind with information concerning turnips. The sentiment which he felt toward the turnip was akin to adoration. He could not think of the turnip without emotion; he could not speak of it calmly; he could not contemplate it without exaltation. He could not eat it without shedding tears. All the poetry in his sensitive nature was in sympathy with the gracious vegetable. With the earliest pipe of dawn he sought his patch, and when the curtaining night drove him from it he shut himself up with his books and garnered statistics till sleep overcame him. On rainy days he sat and talked hours together with his mother about turnips. When company came, he made it his loving duty to put aside everything else and converse with them all the day long of his great joy in the turnip. And yet, was this joy rounded and complete? Was there no secret alloy of unhappiness in it? Alas, there was. There was a canker gnawing at his heart; the noblest inspiration of his soul eluded his endeavor—viz: he could not make of the turnip a climbing vine. Months went by; the bloom forsook his cheek, the fire faded out of his eye; sighings and abstraction usurped the place of smiles and cheerful converse. But a watchful eye noted these things and in time a motherly sympathy unsealed the secret. Hence the letter to me. She pleaded for attention—she said her boy was dying by inches.

"I was a stranger to Mr. Greeley, but what of that? The matter was urgent. I wrote and begged him to solve the difficult problem if possible and save the student's life. My interest grew, until it partook of the anxiety of the mother. I waited in much suspense.—At last the answer came.

"I found that I could not read it readily, the handwriting being unfamiliar and my emotions somewhat wrought up. It seemed to refer in part to the boy's case, but chiefly to other and irrelevant matters—such as paving-stones, electricity, oysters, and something which I took to be 'absolution' or 'agrarianism,' I could not be certain which; still, these appeared to be simply casual mentions, nothing more; friendly in spirit, without doubt, but lacking the connection or coherence necessary to make them useful.—I judged that my understanding was affected by my feelings, and so laid the letter away till morning.

"In the morning I read it again, but with difficulty and uncertainty still, for I had lost some little rest and my mental vision seemed clouded. The note was more connected, now, but did not meet the emergency it was expected to meet. It was too discursive. It appeared to read as follows, though I was not certain of some of the words:

'Polygamy dissembles majesty; extracts redeem polarity; causes hitherto exist. Ovations pursue wisdom, or warts inherit and condemn. Boston, botany, cakes, folony undertakes, but who shall allay? We fear not. Yrxwly,

HEVACE EVEELOJ.'

"But there did not seem to be a word about turnips. There seemed to be no suggestion as to how they might be made to grow like vines. There was not even a reference to the Beazeleys. I slept upon the matter; I ate no supper, neither any breakfast next morning. So I resumed my work with a brain refreshed, and was very hopeful. *Now* the letter took a different aspect—all save the signature, which latter I judged to be only a harmless affectation of Hebrew. The epistle was necessarily from Mr.

New-York Tribune.

New York 18 18

[handwritten letter, largely illegible, signed] Horace Greeley

Greeley, for it bore the printed heading of *The Tribune,* and I had written to no one else there. The letter, I say, had taken a different aspect, but still its language was eccentric and avoided the issue. It now appeared to say:

'Bolivia extemporizes mackerel; borax esteems polygamy; sausages wither in the east. Creation perdu, is done; for woes inherent one can damn. Buttons, buttons, corks, geology underrates but we shall allay. My beer's out. Yrxwly,

HEVACE EVEELOJ.'

"I was evidently overworked. My comprehension was impaired. Therefore I gave two days to recreation, and then returned to my task greatly refreshed. The letter now took this form:

'Poultices do sometimes choke swine; tulips reduce posterity; causes leather to resist. Our notions empower wisdom, her let's afford while we can. Butter but any cakes, fill any undertaker, we'll wean him from his filly. We feel hot.
Yrxwly,   HEVACE EVEELOJ.'

"I was still not satisfied. These generalities did not meet the question. They were crisp, and vigorous, and delivered with a confidence that almost compelled conviction; but at such a time as this, with a human life at stake, they seemed inappropriate, worldly, and in bad taste. At any other time I would have been not only glad, but proud, to receive from a man like Mr. Greeley a letter of this kind, and would have studied it earnestly and tried to improve myself all I could; but now, with that poor boy in his far home languishing for relief, I had no heart for learning.

"Three days passed by, and I read the note again. Again its tenor had changed. It now appeared to say:

'Potations do sometimes wake wines; turnips restrain passion; causes necessary to state. Infest the poor widow; her lord's effects will be void. But dirt, bathing, etc., etc., followed unfairly, will worm him from his folly—so swear not.
Yrxwly,   HEVACE EVEELOJ.'

"This was more like it. But I was unable to proceed. I was too much worn. The word 'turnips' brought temporary joy and encouragement, but my strength was so much impaired, and the delay might be so perilous for the boy, that I relinquished the idea of pursuing the translation further, and resolved to do what I ought to have done at first. I sat down and wrote Mr. Greeley as follows:

"DEAR SIR: I fear I do not entirely comprehend your kind note. It cannot be possible, Sir, that 'turnips restrain passion'—at least the study or contemplation of turnips cannot—for it is this very employment that has scorched our poor friend's mind and sapped his bodily strength.—But if they *do* restrain it, will you bear with us a little further and explain how they should be prepared? I observe that you say 'causes necessary to state,' but you have omitted to state them.

"Under a misapprehension, you seem to attribute to me interested motives in this matter—to call it by no harsher term. But I assure you, dear sir, that if I seem to be 'infesting the widow,' it is all *seeming*, and void of reality. It is from no seeking of mine that I am in this position. She asked me, herself, to write you. I never have infested her—indeed I scarcely know her. I do not infest anybody. I try to go along, in my humble way, doing as near right as I can, never harming anybody, and never *throwing out insinuations*. As for 'her lord and his effects,' they are of no interest to me. I trust I have effects enough of my own—shall endeavor to get along with them, at any rate, and not go mousing around to get hold of somebody's that are 'void.' But do you not see?—this woman is a *widow*—she has no 'lord.' He is dead—or pretended to be, when they buried him. Therefore, no amount of 'dirt, bathing,' etc., etc., howsoever 'unfairly followed' will be likely to 'worm him from his folly'—if being dead and a ghost is 'folly.' Your closing remark is as unkind as it was uncalled for; and if report says true you might have applied it to yourself, sir, with more point and less impropriety.   Very Truly Yours,   SIMON ERICKSON.

"In the course of a few days, Mr. Greeley did what would have saved a world of trouble, and much mental and bodily suffering and misunderstanding, if he had done it sooner. To wit, he sent an intelligible rescript or translation of his original note, made in a plain hand by his clerk. Then the mystery cleared, and I saw that his heart had been right, all the time. I will recite the note in its clarified form:

[Translation.]

'Potatoes do sometimes make vines; turnips remain passive: cause unnecessary to state. Inform the poor widow her lad's efforts will be vain. But diet, bathing, etc., etc., followed uniformly, will wean him from his folly—so fear not.
     Yours,   HORACE GREELEY.'

"But alas, it was too late, gentlemen—too late. The criminal delay had done its work—young Beazely was no more. His spirit had taken its flight to a land where all anxieties shall be charmed away, all desires gratified, all ambitions realized. Poor lad, they laid him to his rest with a turnip in each hand."

So ended Erickson, and lapsed again into nodding, mumbling, and abstraction. The company broke up, and left him so . . . . But they did not say what drove him crazy. In the momentary confusion, I forgot to ask.

CHAPTER LXXI

At four o'clock in the afternoon we were winding down a mountain of dreary and desolate lava to the sea, and closing our pleasant land journey. This lava is the accumulation of ages; one torrent of fire after another has rolled down here in old times, and built up the island structure higher and higher. Underneath, it is honey-combed with caves; it would be of no use to dig wells in such a place; they would not hold water—you would not find any for them to hold, for that matter. Consequently, the planters depend upon cisterns.

The last lava flow occurred here so long ago that there are none now living who witnessed it. In one place it enclosed and burned down a grove of cocoa-nut trees, and the holes in the lava where the trunks stood are still visible; their sides retain the impression of the bark; the trees fell upon the burning river, and becoming partly submerged, left in it the perfect counterpart of every knot and branch and leaf, and even nut, for curiosity seekers of a long distant day to gaze upon and wonder at.

There were doubtless plenty of Kanaka sentinels on guard hereabouts at that time, but they did not leave casts of their figures in the lava as the Roman sentinels at Herculaneum and Pompeii did. It is a pity it is so, because such things are so interesting; but so it is. They probably went away. They went away early, perhaps. However, they had their merits; the Romans exhibited the higher pluck, but the Kanakas showed the sounder judgment.

Shortly we came in sight of that spot whose history is so familiar to every school-boy in the wide world—Kealakekua Bay—the place where Captain Cook, the great circumnavigator, was killed by the natives, nearly a hundred years ago. The setting sun was flaming upon it, a Summer shower was falling, and it was spanned by two magnificent rainbows. Two men who were in advance of us rode through one of these and for a moment their garments shone with a more than regal splendor. Why did not Captain Cook have taste enough to call his great discovery the Rainbow Islands? These charming spectacles are present to you at every turn; they are common in all the islands; they are visible every day, and frequently at night also—not the silvery bow we see once in an age in the States, by moonlight, but barred with all bright and beautiful colors, like the children of the sun and rain. I saw one of them a few nights ago. What the sailors call "rain dogs"—little patches of rainbow—are often seen drifting about the heavens in these latitudes, like stained cathedral windows.

Kealakekua Bay is a little curve like the last kink of a snail-shell, winding deep into the land, seemingly not more than a mile wide from shore to shore. It is bounded on one side—where the murder was done—by a little flat plain, on which stands a cocoanut grove and some ruined houses; a steep wall of lava, a thousand feet high at the upper end and three or four hundred at the lower, comes down from the mountain and bounds the inner extremity of it. From this wall the place takes its name, *Kealakekua,* which in the native tongue signifies "The Pathway of the Gods." They say, (and still believe, in spite of their liberal education in Christianity), that the great god *Lono,* who used to live upon the hillside, always traveled that causeway when urgent business connected with heavenly affairs called him down to the seashore in a hurry.

As the red sun looked across the placid ocean through the tall, clean stems of the cocoanut trees, like a blooming whiskey bloat through the bars of a city prison, I went and stood in the edge of the water on the flat rock pressed by Captain Cook's feet when the blow was dealt which took away his life, and tried to picture in my mind the doomed man struggling in the midst of the multitude of exasperated savages—the men in the ship crowding to the vessel's side and gazing in anxious dismay toward the shore—the—but I discovered that I could not do it.

It was growing dark, the rain began to fall, we could see that the distant Boomerang was helplessly becalmed at sea, and so I adjourned to the cheerless little box of a warehouse and sat down to smoke and think, and wish the ship would make the land—for we had not eaten for ten hours and were viciously hungry.

Plain unvarnished history takes the romance out of Captain Cook's assassination, and renders a deliberate verdict of justifiable homicide. Wherever he went among the islands, he was cordially received and welcomed by the inhabitants, and his ships lavishly supplied with all manner of food. He returned these kindnesses with insult and ill-treatment. Perceiving that the people took him for the long vanished and lamented god Lono, he encouraged them in the delusion for the sake of the limitless power it gave him; but during the famous disturbance at this spot, and while he and his comrades were surrounded by fifteen thousand maddened savages, he received a hurt and betrayed his earthly origin with a groan. It was his death warrant. Instantly a shout went up: "He groans!—he is not a god!" So they closed in upon him and dispatched him.

His flesh was stripped from the bones and burned (except nine pounds of it which were sent on board the ships). The heart was hung up in a native hut, where it was found and eaten by three children, who mistook it for the heart of a dog. One of these children grew to be a very old man, and died in Honolulu a few years ago. Some of Cook's bones were recovered and consigned to the deep by the officers of the ships.

Small blame should attach to the natives for the killing of Cook. They treated him well. In return, he abused them. He and his men inflicted bodily injury upon many of them at different times, and killed at least three of them before they offered any proportionate retaliation.

Near the shore we found "Cook's Monument"—only a cocoanut stump, four feet high and about a foot in diameter at the butt. It had lava boulders piled around its base to hold it up and keep it in its place, and it was entirely sheathed over, from top to bottom, with rough, discolored sheets of copper, such as ships' bottoms are coppered with. Each sheet had a rude inscription scratched upon it—with a nail, apparently—and in every case the execution was wretched. Most of these merely recorded the visits of British naval commanders to the spot, but one of them bore this legend:

"Near this spot fell
CAPTAIN JAMES COOK,
The Distinguished Circumnavigator, who Discovered these
Islands A.D. 1778.

After Cook's murder, his second in command, on board the ship, opened fire upon the swarms of natives on the beach, and one of his cannon balls cut this cocoanut tree short off and left this monumental stump standing. It looked sad and lonely enough to us, out there in the rainy twilight. But there is no other monument to Captain Cook. True, up on the mountain side we had passed by a large inclosure like an ample hog-pen, built of lava blocks, which marks the spot where Cook's flesh was stripped from his bones and burned; but this is not properly a monument, since it was erected by the natives themselves, and less to do honor to the circumnavigator than for the sake of convenience in roasting him. A thing like a guide-board was elevated above this pen on a tall pole, and formerly there was an inscription upon it describing the memorable occurrence that had there taken place; but the sun and the wind have long ago so defaced it as to render it illegible.

Toward midnight a fine breeze sprang up and the schooner soon worked herself into the bay and cast anchor. The boat came ashore for us, and in a little while the clouds and the rain were all gone. The moon was beaming tranquilly down on land and sea, and we two were stretched upon the deck sleeping the refreshing sleep and dreaming the happy dreams that are only vouchsafed to the weary and the innocent.

CHAPTER LXXII

In the breezy morning we went ashore and visited the ruined temple of the last god Lono. The high chief cook of this temple—the priest who presided over it and roasted the human sacrifices—was uncle to Obookia, and at one time that youth was an apprentice-priest under him. Obookia was a young native of fine mind, who, together with three other native boys, was taken to New England by the captain of a whaleship during the reign of Kamehameha I, and they were the means of attracting the attention of the religious world to their country. This resulted in the sending of missionaries there. And this Obookia was the very same sensitive savage who sat down on the church steps and wept because his people did not have the Bible. That incident has been very elaborately painted in many a charming Sunday School book—aye, and told so plaintively and so tenderly that I have cried over it in Sunday School myself, on general principles, although at a time when I did not know much and could not understand why the people of the Sandwich Islands needed to worry so much about it as long as they did not know there was a Bible at all.

Obookia was converted and educated, and was to have returned to his native land with the first missionaries, had he lived. The other native youths made the voyage, and two of them did good service, but the third, William Kanui, fell from grace afterward, for a time, and when the gold excitement broke out in California he journeyed thither and went to mining, although he was fifty years old. He succeeded pretty well, but the failure of Page, Bacon & Co. relieved him of six thousand dollars, and then, to all intents and purposes, he was a bankrupt in his old age and he resumed service in the pulpit again. He died in Honolulu in 1864.

Quite a broad tract of land near the temple, extending from the sea to the mountain top, was sacred to the god Lono in olden times—so sacred that if a common native set his sacrilegious foot upon it it was judicious for him to make his will, because his time had come. He might go around it by water, but he could not cross it. It was well sprinkled with pagan temples and stocked with awkward, homely idols carved out of logs of wood. There was a temple devoted to prayers for rain—and with fine sagacity it was placed at a point so well up on the mountain side that if you prayed there twenty-four times a day for rain you would be likely to get it every time. You would seldom get to your Amen before you would have to hoist your umbrella.

And there was a large temple near at hand which was built in a single night, in the midst of storm and thunder and rain, by the ghastly hands of dead men! Tradition says that the weird glare of the lightning a noiseless multitude of phantoms were seen at their strange labor far up the mountain side at dead of night—flitting hither and thither and bearing great lava-blocks clasped in their nerveless fingers—appearing and disappearing as the pallid lustre fell upon their forms and faded away again. Even to this day, it is said, the natives hold this dread structure in awe and reverence, and will not pass by it in the night.

At noon I observed a bevy of nude native young ladies bathing in the sea, and went and sat down on their clothes to keep them from being stolen. I begged them to come out, for the sea was rising and I was satisfied that they were running some risk. But they were not afraid, and presently went on with their sport. They were finished swimmers and divers, and enjoyed themselves to the last degree. The swam races, splashed and ducked and tumbled each other about, and filled the air with their laughter. It is said that the first thing an Islander learns is how to swim; learning how to walk being a matter of smaller consequence, comes afterward. One hears tales of native men and women swimming ashore from vessels many miles at sea—more miles, indeed, than I dare vouch for or even mention. And they tell of a native diver who went down in thirty or forty-foot waters and brought up an anvil! I think he swallowed the anvil afterward, if my memory serves me. However I will not urge this point.

I have spoken, several times, of the god Lono—I may as well furnish two or three sentences concerning him.

The idol the natives worshiped for him was a slender, unornamented staff twelve feet long. Tradition says he was a favorite god on the Island of Hawaii—a great king who had been deified for meritorious services—just our own fashion of rewarding heroes, with the difference that we would have made him a Postmaster instead of a god, no doubt. In an angry moment he slew his wife, a goddess named Kaikilani Aiii. Remorse of conscience drove him mad, and tradition presents us the singular spectacle of a god traveling "on the shoulder;" for in his gnawing grief he wandered about from place to place boxing and wrestling with all whom he met. Of course this pastime soon lost its novelty, inasmuch as it must necessarily have been the case when so powerful a deity sent a frail human opponent "to grass" he never came back any more. Therefore, he instituted games called makahiki, and ordered that they should be held in his honor, and then sailed for foreign lands on a three-cornered raft, stating that he would return some day—and that was the last of Lono. He was never seen any more; his raft got swamped, perhaps. But the people always expected his return, and thus they were easily led to accept Captain Cook as the restored god.

Some of the old natives believed Cook was Lono to the day of their death; but many did not, for they could not understand how he could die if he was a god.

Only a mile or so from Kealakekua Bay is a spot of historic interest—the place where the last battle was fought for idolatry. Of course we visited it, and came away as wise as most people do who go and gaze upon such mementoes of the past when in an unreflective mood.

While the first missionaries were on their way around the Horn, the idolatrous customs which had obtained in the island, as far back as tradition reached were suddenly broken up. Old Kamehameha I. was dead, and his son, Liholiho, the new King was a free liver, a roystering, dissolute fellow, and hated the restraints of the ancient *tabu*. His assistant in the Government, Kaahumanu, the Queen dowager, was proud and high-spirited, and hated the *tabu* because it restricted the privileges of her sex and degraded all women very nearly to the level of brutes. So the case stood. Liholiho had half a mind to put his foot down, Kaahumanu had a whole mind to badger him into doing it, and whiskey did the rest. It was probably the rest. It was probably the first time whiskey ever prominently figured as an aid to civilization. Liholiho came up to Kailua as drunk as a piper, and attended a great feast; the determined Queen spurred his drunken courage up to a reckless pitch, and then, while all the multitude stared in blank dismay, he moved deliberately forward and sat down with the women! They saw him eat from the same vessel with them, and were appalled! Terrible moments drifted slowly by, and still the King ate, still he lived, still the lightnings of the insulted gods were withheld! Then conviction came like a revelation—the superstitions of a hundred generations passed from before the people like a cloud, and a shout went up, "the *tabu* is broken! the *tabu* is broken!"

Thus did King Liholiho and his dreadful whiskey preach the first sermon and prepare the way for the new gospel that was speeding southward over the waves of the Atlantic.

The *tabu* broken and destruction failing to follow the awful sacrilege, the people, with that childlike precipitancy which has always characterized them, jumped to the conclusion that their gods were a weak and wretched swindle, just as they formerly jumped to the conclusion that Captain Cook was no god, merely because he groaned, and promptly killed him without stopping to inquire whether a god might not groan as well as a man if it suited his convenience to do it; and satisfied that the idols were powerless to protect themselves they went to work at once and pulled them down—hacked them to pieces—applied the torch—annihilated them!

The pagan priests were furious. And well they might be; they had held the fattest offices in the land, and now they were beggared; they had been great—they had stood above the chiefs—and now they were vagabonds. They raised a revolt; they scared a number of people into joining their standard, and Bekuokalani, an ambitious offshoot of royalty, was easily persuaded to become their leader.

In the first skirmish the idolaters triumphed over the royal army sent against them, and full of confidence they resolved to march upon Kailua. The King sent an envoy to try and conciliate them, and came very near being an envoy short by the operation; the savages not only refused to listen to him, but wanted to kill him. So the King sent his men forth under Major General Kalaimoku and the two hosts met at Kuamoo. The battle was long and fierce—men and women fighting side by side, as was the custom—and when the day was done the rebels were flying in every direction in hopeless panic, and idolatry and the *tabu* were dead in the land!

The royalists marched gayly home to Kailua glorifying the new dispensation. "There is no power in the gods," said they; "they are a vanity and a lie. The army with idols was weak; the army without idols was strong and victorious!"

The nation was without a religion.

The missionary ship arrived in safety shortly afterward, timed by providential exactness to meet the emergency, and the Gospel was planted as in a virgin soil.

CHAPTER LXXIII

At noon, we hired a Kanaka to take us down to the ancient ruins at Honaunau in his canoe—price two dollars—reasonable enough, for a sea voyage of eight miles, counting both ways.

The native canoe is an irresponsible looking contrivance. I cannot think of anything to liken it to but a boy's sled runner hollowed out, and that does not quite convey the correct idea. It is about fifteen feet long, high and pointed at both ends, is a foot and a half or two feet deep, and so narrow that if you wedged a fat man into it you might not get him out again. It sits on top of the water like a duck, but it has an outrigger and does not upset easily, if you keep still. This outrigger is formed of two long bent sticks like plow handles, which project from one side, and to their outer ends is bound a curved beam composed of an extremely light wood, which skims along the surface of the water and thus saves you from an upset on that side, while the outrigger's weight is not so easily lifted as to make an upset on the other side a thing to be greatly feared. Still, until one gets used to sitting perched upon this knife-blade, he is apt to reason within himself that it would be more comfortable if there were just an outrigger or so on the other side also.

I had the bow seat, and Billings sat amidships and faced the Kanaka, who occupied the stern of the craft and did the paddling. With the first stroke the trim shell of a thing shot out from the shore like an arrow. There was not much to see. While we were on the shallow water of the reef, it was pastime to look down into the limpid depths at the large bunches of branching coral—the unique shrubbery of the sea. We lost that, though, when we got out into the dead blue water of the deep. But we had the picture of the surf, then, dashing angrily against the crag-bound shore and sending a foaming spray high into the air. There was interest in this beetling border, too, for it was honeycombed with quaint caves and arches and tunnels, and had a rude resemblance of the dilapidated architecture of ruined keeps and castles rising out of the restless sea. When this novelty ceased to be a novelty, we turned our eyes shoreward and gazed at the long mountain with its rich green forests stretching up into the curtaining clouds, and at the specks of houses in the rearward distance and the diminished schooner riding sleepily at anchor. And when these grew tiresome we dashed boldly into the midst of a school of huge, beastly porpoises engaged at their eternal game of arching over a wave and disappearing, and then doing it over again and keeping it up—always circling over, in that way, like so many well-submerged wheels. But the porpoises wheeled themselves away, and then we were thrown upon our own resources. It did not take many minutes to discover that the sun was blazing like a bonfire, and that the weather was of a melting temperature. It had a drowsing effect, too.

In one place we came upon a large company of naked natives, of both sexes and all ages, amusing themselves with the national pastime of surf-bathing. Each heathen would paddle three or four hundred yards out to sea, (taking a short board with him), then face the shore and wait for a particularly prodigious billow to come along; at the right moment he would fling his board upon its foamy crest and himself upon the board, and here he would come whizzing by like a bombshell! It did not seem that a lightning express train could shoot along at a more hair-lifting speed. I tried surf-bathing once, subsequently, but made a failure of it. I got the board placed right, and at the right moment, too; but missed connection myself.—The board struck the shore in three quarters of a second, without any cargo, and I struck the bottom about the same time, with a couple of barrels of water in me. None but natives ever master the art of surf-bathing thoroughly.

At the end of an hour, we had made the four miles, and landed on a level point of land, upon which was a wide extent of old ruins, with many a tall cocoanut tree growing among them. Here was the ancient City of Refuge—a vast inclosure, whose stone walls were twenty feet thick at the base, and fifteen feet high; an oblong square, a thousand and forty feet one way and a fraction under seven hundred the other. Within this inclosure, in early times, has been three rude temples; each two hundred and ten feet long by one hundred wide, and thirteen high.

In those days, if a man killed another anywhere on the island the relatives were privileged to take the murderer's life; and then a chase for life and liberty began—the outlawed criminal flying through pathless forests and over mountain and plain, with his hopes fixed upon the protecting walls of the City of Refuge, and the avenger of blood following hotly after him! Sometimes the race was kept up to the very gates of the temple, and the panting pair sped through long files of excited natives, who watched the contest with flashing eye and dilated nostril, encouraging the hunted refugee with sharp, inspiriting ejaculations, and sending up a ringing shout of exultation when the saving gates closed upon him and the cheated pursuer sank exhausted at the threshold. But sometimes the flying criminal fell under the hand of the avenger at the very door, when one more brave stride, one more brief second of time would have brought his feet upon the sacred ground and barred him against all harm. Where did these isolated pagans get this idea of a City of Refuge—this ancient Oriental custom?

This old sanctuary was sacred to all—even to rebels in arms and invading armies. Once within its walls, and confession made to the priest and absolution obtained, the wretch with a price upon his head could go forth without fear and without danger—he was *tabu,* and to harm him was death. The routed rebels in the lost battle for idolatry fled to this place to claim sanctuary, and many were thus saved.

Close to the corner of the great inclosure is a round structure of stone, some six or eight feet high, with a level top about ten or twelve in diameter. This was the place of execution. A high palisade of cocoanut piles shut out the cruel scenes from the vulgar multitude. Here criminals were killed, the flesh stripped from the bones and burned, and the bones secreted in holes in the body of the structure. If the man had been guilty of a high crime, the entire corpse was burned.

The walls of the temple are a study. The same food for speculation that is offered the visitor to the Pyramids of Egypt he will find here—the mystery of how they were constructed by a people unacquainted with science and mechanics. The natives have no invention of their own for hoisting heavy weights, they had no beasts of burden, and they have never even shown any knowledge of the properties of the lever. Yet some of the lava blocks quarried out, brought over rough, broken ground, and built into this wall, six or seven feet from the ground, are of prodigious size and would weigh tons. How did they transport and raise them?

Both the inner and the outer surfaces of the walls present a smooth front and are very creditable specimens of masonry. The blocks are of all manner of shapes and sizes, but yet are fitted together with the neatest exactness. The gradual narrowing of the wall from the base upward is accurately preserved.

No cement was used, but the edifice is firm and compact and is capable of resisting storm and decay for centuries. Who built this temple, and how was it built, and when, are mysteries that may never be unraveled.

Outside of these ancient walls lies a sort of coffin-shaped stone eleven feet four inches long and three feet square at the small end (it would weigh a few thousand pounds), which the high chief who held sway over this district many centuries ago brought thither on his shoulder one day to use as a lounge! This circumstance is established by the most reliable traditions. He used to lie down on it, in his indolent way, and keep an eye on his subjects at work for him and see that there were no "soldiering" done. And no doubt there was not any done to speak of, because he was a man of that sort of build that incites to attention to business on the part of an employee. He was fourteen or fifteen feet high. When he stretched himself at full length on his lounge, his legs hung down over the end, and when he snored he woke the dead. These facts are all attested by irrefragable tradition.

On the other side of the temple is a monstrous seven-ton rock, eleven feet long, seven feet wide and three feet thick. It is raised a foot or a foot and a half above the ground, and rests upon half a dozen little stony pedestals. The same old fourteen-footer brought it down from the mountain, merely for fun (he had his own notions about fun), and propped it up as we find it now and as others may find it a century hence, for it would take a score of horses to budge it from its position. They say that fifty or sixty years ago the proud Queen Kaahumanu used to fly to this rock for safety, whenever she had been making trouble with her fierce husband, and hide under it until his wrath was appeased. But these Kanakas will lie, and this statement is one of their ablest efforts—for Kaahumanu was six feet high—she was bulky—she was built like an ox—and she could no more have squeezed herself under that rock than she could have passed between the cylinders of a sugar mill. What could she gain by it, even if she succeeded? To be chased and abused by a savage husband could not be otherwise than humiliating to her high spirit, yet it could never make her feel so flat as an hour's repose under that rock would.

We walked a mile over a raised macadamized road of uniform width; a road paved with flat stones and exhibiting in its every detail a considerable degree of engineering skill. Some say that that wise old pagan, Kamehameha I., planned and built it, but others say it was built so long before his time that the knowledge of who constructed it has passed out of the traditions. In either case, however, as the handiwork of an untaught and degraded race it is a thing of pleasing interest. The stones are worn and smooth, and pushed apart in places, so that the road has the exact appearance of those ancient paved highways leading out of Rome which one sees in pictures.

The object of our tramp was to visit a great natural curiosity at the base of the foothills—a congealed cascade of lava. Some old forgotten volcanic eruption sent its broad river of fire down the mountain side here, and it poured down in a great torrent from an overhanging bluff some fifty feet high to the ground below. The flaming torrent cooled in the winds from the sea, and remains there to-day, all seamed, and frothed and rippled a petrified Niagara. It is very picturesque, and withal so natural that one might almost imagine it still flowed. A smaller stream trickled over the cliff and built up an isolated pyramid about thirty feet high, which has the semblance of a mass of large gnarled and knotted vines and roots and stems intricately twisted and woven together.

We passed in behind the cascade and the pyramid, and found the bluff pierced by several cavernous tunnels, whose crooked courses we followed a long distance.

Two of these winding tunnels stand as proof of Nature's mining abilities. Their floors are level, they are seven feet wide, and their roofs are gently arched. Their height is not uniform, however. We passed through one a hundred feet long, which leads through a spur of the hill and opens out well up in the sheer wall of a precipice whose foot rests in the waves of the sea. It is a commodious tunnel, except that there are occasional places in it where one must stoop to pass under. The roof is lava, of course, and is thickly studded with little lava-pointed icicles an inch long, which hardened as they dripped. They project as closely together as the iron teeth of a corn-sheller, and if one will stand up straight and walk any distance there, he can get his hair combed free of charge.

CHAPTER LXXIV

We got back to the schooner in good time, and then sailed down to Kau, where we disembarked and took final leave of the vessel. Next day we bought horses and bent our way over the summer-clad mountain-terraces, toward the great volcano of Kilauea (Ke-low-way-ah). We made nearly a two days' journey of it, but that was on account of laziness. Toward sunset on the second day, we reached an elevation of some four thousand feet above sea level, and as we picked our careful way through billowy wastes of lava long generations ago stricken dead and cold in the climax of its tossing fury, we began to come upon signs of the near presence of the volcano—signs in the nature of ragged fissures that discharged jets of sulphurous vapor into the air, hot from the molten ocean down in the bowels of the mountain.

Shortly the crater came into view. I have seen Vesuvius since, but it was a mere toy, a child's volcano, a soup-kettle, compared to this. Mount Vesuvius is a shapely cone thirty-six hundred feet high; its crater an inverted cone only three hundred feet deep, and not more than a thousand feet in diameter, if as much as that; its fires meagre, modest, and docile.—But here was a vast, perpendicular, walled cellar, nine hundred feet deep in some places, thirteen hundred in others, level-floored, and *ten miles in circumference!* Here was a yawning pit upon whose floor the armies of Russia could camp, and have room to spare.

Perched upon the edge of the crater, at the opposite end from where we stood, was a small look-out house—say three miles away. It assisted us, by comparison, to comprehend and appreciate the great depth of the basin—it looked like a tiny martin-box clinging at the eaves of a cathedral. After some little time spent in resting and looking and ciphering, we hurried on to the hotel.

By the path it is half a mile from the Volcano House to the lookout-house. After a hearty supper we waited until it was thoroughly dark and then started to the crater. The first glance in that direction revealed a scene of wild beauty. There was a heavy fog over the crater and it was splendidly illuminated by the glare from the fires below. The illumination was two miles wide and a mile high, perhaps; and if you ever, on a dark night and at a distance beheld the light from thirty or forty blocks of distant buildings all on fire at once, reflected strongly against overhanging clouds, you can form a fair idea of what this looked like.

A colossal column of cloud towered to a great height in the air immediately above the crater, and the outer swell of every one of its vast folds was dyed with a rich crimson luster, which was subdued to a pale rose tint in the depressions between. It glowed like a muffled torch and stretched upward to a dizzy height toward the zenith. I thought it just possible that its like had not been seen since the children of Israel wandered on their long march through the desert so many centuries ago over a path illuminated by the mysterious "pillar of fire." And I was sure that I now had a vivid conception of what the majestic "pillar of fire" was like, which almost amounted to a revelation.

Arrived at the little thatched lookout house, we rested our elbows on the railing in front and looked abroad over the wide crater and down over the sheer precipice at the seething fires beneath us. The view was a startling improvement on my daylight experience. I turned to see the effect on the balance of the company and found the reddest-faced set of men I almost ever saw. In the strong light every countenance glowed like red-hot iron, every shoulder was suffused with crimson and shaded rearward into dingy, shapeless obscurity! The place below looked like the infernal regions and these men like half-cooled devils just come up on a furlough.

I turned my eyes upon the volcano again. The "cellar" was tolerably well lighted up. For a mile and a half in front of us and half a mile on either side, the floor of the abyss was magnificently illuminated; beyond these limits the mists hung down their gauzy curtains and cast a deceptive gloom over all that made the twinkling fires in the remote corners of the crater seem countless leagues removed—made them seem like the camp-fires of a great army far away. Here was room for the imagination to work! You could imagine those lights the width of a continent away—

and that hidden under the intervening darkness were hills, and winding rivers, and weary wastes of plain and desert—and even then the tremendous vista stretched on, and on, and on!—to the fires and far beyond! You could not compass it—it was the idea of eternity made tangible—and the longest end of it made visible to the naked eye!

The greater part of the vast floor of the desert under us was as black as ink, and apparently smooth and level; but over a mile square of it was ringed and streaked and striped with a thousand branching streams of liquid and gorgeously brilliant fire! It looked like a colossal railroad map of the State of Massachusetts done in chain lightning on a midnight sky. Imagine it— imagine a coal-black sky shivered into a tangled net-work of angry fire!

Here and there were gleaming holes a hundred feet in diameter, broken in the dark crust, and in them the melted lava—the color a dazzling white just tinged with yellow—was boiling and surging furiously; and from these holes branched numberless bright torrents in many directions, like the spokes of a wheel, and kept a tolerably straight course for a while and then swept round in huge rainbow curves, or made a long succession of sharp worm-fence angles, which looked precisely like the fiercest jagged lightning. These streams met other streams, and they mingled with and crossed and recrossed each other in every conceivable direction, like skate tracks on a popular skating ground. Sometimes streams twenty or thirty feet wide flowed from the holes to some distance without dividing—and through the opera-glasses we could see that they ran down small, steep hills and were genuine cataracts of fire, white at their source, but soon cooling and turning to the richest red, grained with alternate lines of black and gold. Every now and then masses of the dark crust broke away and floated slowly down these streams like rafts down a river. Occasionally the molten lava flowing under the superincumbent crust broke through—split a dazzling streak, from five hundred to a thousand feet long, like a sudden flash of lightning, and then acre after acre of the cold lava parted into fragments, turned up edgewise like cakes of ice when a great river breaks up, plunged downward and were swallowed in the crimson cauldron. Then the wide expanse of the "thaw" maintained a ruddy glow for a while, but shortly cooled and became black and level again. During a "thaw," every dismembered cake was marked by a glittering white border which was superbly shaded inward by aurora borealis rays, which were a flaming yellow where they joined the white border, and from thence toward their points tapered into glowing crimson, then into a rich, pale carmine, and finally into a faint blush that held its own a moment and then dimmed and turned black. Some of the streams preferred to mingle together in a tangle of fantastic circles, and then they looked something like the confusion of ropes one sees on a ship's deck when she has just taken in sail and dropped anchor—provided one can imagine those ropes on fire.

Through the glasses, the little fountains scattered about looked very beautiful. They boiled, and coughed, and spluttered, and discharged sprays of stringy red fire—of about the consistency of mush, for instance—from ten to fifteen feet into the air, along with a shower of brilliant white sparks—a quaint and unnatural mingling of gouts of blood and snow-flakes!

We had circles and serpents and streaks of lightning all twined and wreathed and tied together, without a break throughout an area more than a mile square (that amount of ground was covered, though it was not strictly "square"), and it was with a feeling of placid exultation that we reflected that many years had elapsed since any visitor had seen such a splendid display—since any visitor had seen anything more than the now snubbed and insignificant "North" and "South" lakes in action. We had been reading old files of Hawaiian newspapers and the "Record Book" at the Volcano House, and were posted.

I could see the North Lake lying out on the black floor away off in the outer edge of our panorama, and knitted to it by a web-work of lava streams. In its individual capacity it looked very little more respectable than a schoolhouse on fire. True, it was about nine hundred feet long and two or three hundred wide, but then, under the present circumstances, it necessarily appeared rather insignificant, and besides it was so distant from us.

I forgot to say that the noise made by the bubbling lava is not great, heard as we heard it from our lofty perch. It makes three distinct sounds—a rushing, a hissing, and a coughing or puffing sound; and if you stand on the brink and close your eyes it is no trick at all to imagine that you are sweeping down a river on a large low-pressure steamer, and that you hear the hissing of the steam about her boilers, the puffing from her escape-pipes and the churning rush of the water abaft her wheels. The smell of sulphur is strong, but not unpleasant to a sinner.

We left the lookout house at ten o'clock in a half cooked condition, because of the heat from Pele's furnaces, and wrapping up in blankets, for the night was cold, we returned to our Hotel.

CHAPTER LXXV

The next night was appointed for a visit to the bottom of the crater, for we desired to traverse its floor and see the "North Lake" (of fire) which lay two miles away, toward the further wall. After dark half a dozen of us set out, with lanterns and native guides, and climbed down a crazy, thousand-foot pathway in a crevice fractured in the crater wall, and reached the bottom in safety.

The irruption of the previous evening had spent its force and the floor looked black and cold; but when we ran out upon it we found it hot yet, to the feet, and it was likewise riven with crevices which revealed the underlying fires gleaming vindictively. A neighboring cauldron was threatening to overflow, and this added to the dubiousness of the situation. So the native guides refused to continue the venture, and then every body deserted except a stranger named Marlette. He said he had been in the crater a dozen times in daylight and believed he could find his way through it at night. He thought that a run of three hundred yards would carry us over the hottest part of the floor and leave us our shoe-soles. His pluck gave me back-bone. We took one lantern and instructed the guides to hang the other to the roof of the look-out house to serve as a beacon for us in case we got lost, and then the party started back up the precipice and Marlette and I made our run. We skipped over the hot floor and over the red crevices with brisk dispatch and reached the cold lava safe but with pretty warm feet. Then we took things leisurely and comfortably, jumping tolerably wide and probably bottomless chasms, and threading our way through picturesque lava upheavals with considerable confidence. When we got fairly away from the cauldrons of boiling fire, we seemed to be in a gloomy desert, and a suffocating dark one, surrounded by dim walls that seemed to tower to the sky. The only cheerful objects were the glinting stars high overhead.

By and by Marlette shouted "Stop!" I never stopped quicker in my life. I asked what the matter was. He said we were out of the path. He said we must not try to go on till we found it again, for we were surrounded with beds of rotten lava through which we could easily break and plunge down a thousand feet. I thought eight hundred would answer for me, and was about to say so when Marlette partly proved his statement by accidentally crushing through and disappearing to his arm-pits. He got out and we hunted for the path with the lantern. He said there was only one path and that it was but vaguely defined. We could not find it. The lava surface was all alike in the lantern light. But he was an ingenious man. He said it was not the lantern that had informed him that we were out of the path, but his *feet*. He had noticed a crisp grinding of fine lava-needles under his feet, and some instinct reminded him that in the path these were all worn away. So he put the lantern behind him, and began to search with his boots instead of his eyes. It was good sagacity. The first time his foot touched a surface that did not grind under it he announced that the trail was found again; and after that we kept up a sharp listening for the rasping sound and it always warned us in time.

It was a long tramp, but an exciting one. We reached the North Lake between ten and eleven o'clock, and sat down on a huge overhanging lava-shelf, tired but satisfied. The spectacle presented was worth coming double the distance to see. Under us, and stretching away before us, was a heaving sea of molten fire of seemingly limitless extent. The glare from it was so blinding that it was some time before we could bear to look upon it steadily. It was like gazing at the sun at noonday, except that the glare was not quite so white. At unequal distances all around the shores of the lake were nearly white-hot chimneys or hollow drums of lava, four or five feet high, and up through them were bursting gorgeous sprays of lava-gouts and gem spangles, some white, some red and some golden—a ceaseless bombardment, and one that fascinated the eye with its unapproachable splendor. The more distant jets, sparkling up through an intervening gossamer veil of vapor, seemed miles away; and the further the curving ranks of fiery fountains receded, the more fairy-like and beautiful they appeared.

Now and then the surging bosom of the lake under our noses would calm down ominously and seem to be gathering strength for an enterprise; and then all of a sudden a red dome of lava of the bulk of an ordinary dwelling would heave itself aloft like an escaping balloon, then burst asunder, and out if its heart would flit a pale-green film of vapor, and float upward and vanish in the darkness—a released soul soaring homeward from captivity with the damned, no doubt. The crashing plunge of the ruined dome into the lake again would send a world of seething billows lashing against the shores and shaking the foundations of our perch. By and by, a loosened mass of the hanging shelf we sat on tumbled into the lake, jarring the surroundings like an earthquake and delivering a suggestion that may have been intended for a hint, and may not. We did not wait to see.

We got lost again on our way back, and were more than an hour hunting for the path. We were where we could see the beacon lantern at the look-out house at the time, but thought it was a star and paid no attention to it. We reached the hotel at two o'clock in the morning pretty well fagged out.

Kilauea never overflows its vast crater, but bursts a passage for its lava through the mountain side when relief is necessary, and then the destruction is fearful. About 1840 it rent its over-burdened stomach and sent a broad river of fire careering down to the sea, which swept away forests, huts, plantations and every thing else that lay in its path. The stream was *five miles broad,* in places, and *two hundred feet deep,* and the distance it traveled was forty miles. It tore up and bore away acre-patches of land on its bosom like rafts—rocks, trees and all intact. At night the red glare was visible a hundred miles at sea; and at a distance of forty miles fine print could be read at midnight. The atmosphere was poisoned with sulphurous vapors and choked with falling ashes, pumice stones and cinders; countless columns of smoke rose up and blended together in a tumbled canopy that hid the heavens and glowed with a ruddy flush reflected from the fires below; here and there jets of lava sprung hundreds of feet into the air and burst into rocket-sprays that returned to earth in a crimson rain; and all the while the laboring mountain shook with Nature's great palsy, and voiced its distress in moanings and the muffled booming and subterranean thunders.

Fishes were killed for twenty miles along the shore, where the lava entered the sea. The earthquakes caused some loss of human life, and a prodigious tidal wave swept inland, carrying every thing before it and drowning a number of natives. The devastation consummated along the route traversed by the river of lava was complete and incalculable. Only a Pompeii and a Herculaneum were needed at the foot of Kilauea to make the story of the irruption immortal.

CHAPTER LXXVI

We rode horseback all around the island of Hawaii (the crooked road making the distance two hundred miles), and en-joyed the journey very much. We were more than a week making the trip, because our Kanaka horses would not go by a house or a hut without stopping—whip and spur could not alter their minds about it, and so we finally found that it economized time to let them have their way. Upon inquiry the mystery was ex-plained: the natives are such thorough-going gossips that they never pass a house without stopping to swap news, and conse-quently their horses learn to regard that sort of thing as an essential part of the whole duty of man, and his salvation not to be compassed without it. However, at a former crisis of my life I had once taken an aristocratic young lady out driving, behind a horse that had just retired from a long and honorable career as the moving impulse of a milk wagon, and so this present experience awoke a reminiscent sadness in me in place of the exasperation more natural to the occasion. I remembered how helpless I was that day, and how humiliated; how ashamed I was of having intimated to the girl that I had always owned the horse and was accustomed to grandeur; how hard I tried to appear easy, and even vivacious, under suffering that was consuming my vitals; how placidly and maliciously the girl smiled, and kept on smiling, while my hot blushes baked themselves into a permanent blood-pudding in my face; how the horse ambled from one side of the street to the other and waited complacently before every third house two minutes and a quarter while I belabored his back and reviled him in my heart; how I tried to keep him from turning corners, and failed; how I moved heaven and earth to get him out of town, and did not succeed; how he traversed the entire settlement and delivered imaginary milk at a hundred and sixty-two different domiciles, and how he finally brought up at a dairy depot and refused to budge further, thus rounding and completing the revealment of what the plebeian service of his life had been; how, in eloquent silence, I walked the girl home, and how, when I took leave of her, her parting remark scorched my soul and appeared to blister me all over: she said that my horse was a fine, capable animal, and I must have taken great comfort in him in my time—but that if I would take along some milk tickets next time, and appear to deliver them at the various halting places, it might expedite his movements a little. There was a coolness between us after that.

In one place in the island of Hawaii, we saw a laced and ruffled cataract of limpid water leaping from a sheer precipice fifteen hundred feet high; but that sort of scenery finds its stanchest ally in the arithmetic rather than in spectacular effect. If one desires to be so stirred by a poem of Nature wrought in the happily commingled graces of picturesque rocks, glimpsed distances, foliage, color, shifting lights and shadows, and falling water, that the tears almost come into his eyes so potent is the charm exerted, he need not go away from America to enjoy such an experience. The Rainbow Fall, in Watkins Glen (N. Y.), on the Erie railway, is an example. It would recede into pitiable insignificance if the callous tourist drew an arithmetic on it; but left to compete for the honors simply on scenic grace and beauty—the grand, the august and the sublime being barred the contest—it could challenge the old world and the new to produce its peer.

In one locality, on our journey, we saw some horses that had been born and reared on top of the mountains, above the range of running water, and consequently they had never drank that fluid in their lives, but had been always accustomed to quenching their thirst by eating dew-laden or shower-wetted leaves. And now it was destructively funny to see them sniff suspiciously at a pail of water, and then put in their noses and try to take a *bite* out of the fluid, as if it were a solid. Finding it liquid, they would snatch away their heads and fall to trembling, snorting and showing other evidences of fright. When they became convinced at last that the water was friendly and harmless, they thrust in their noses up to their eyes, brought out a mouthful of the water, and proceeded to *chew* it complacently. We saw a man coax, kick and spur one of them five or ten minutes before he could make it cross a running stream. It spread its nostrils, distended its eyes and trembled all over, just as horses customarily do in the presence of a serpent—and for aught I know it thought the crawling stream *was* a serpent.

In due course of time our journey came to an end at Kawaehae (usually pronounced To-a-*hi*—and before we find fault with this elaborate orthographical method of arriving at such an unostentatious result, let us lop off the *ugh* from our word "though"). I made this horseback trip on a mule. I paid ten dollars for him at Kau (Kah-oo), added four to get him shod, rode him two hundred miles, and then sold him for fifteen dollars. I mark the circumstance with a white stone (in the absence of chalk—for I never saw a white stone that a body could mark anything with, though out of respect for the ancients I have tried it often enough); for up to that day and date it was the first strictly commercial transaction I have ever entered into, and come out winner. We returned to Honolulu, and from thence sailed to the island of Maui, and spent several weeks there very pleasantly. I still remember, with a sense of indolent luxury, a picnicing excursion up a romantic gorge there, called the Iao Valley. The trail lay along the edge of a brawling stream in the bottom of the gorge—a shady route, for it was well roofed with the verdant domes of forest trees. Through openings in the foliage we glimpsed picturesque scenery that revealed ceaseless changes and new charms with every step of our progress. Perpendicular walls from one to three thousand feet high guarded the way, and were sumptuously plumed with varied foliage, in places, and in places swathed in waving ferns. Passing shreds of cloud trailed their shadows across these shining fronts, mottling them with blots; billowy masses of white vapor hid the turreted summits, and far above the vapor swelled a background of gleaming green crags and cones that came and went, through the veiling mists, like islands drifting in a fog; sometimes the cloudy curtain descended till half the canon wall was hidden, then shredded gradually away till only airy glimpses of the ferny front appeared through it—then swept aloft and left it glorified in the sun again. Now and then, as our position changed, rocky bastions swung out from the wall, a mimic ruin of castellated ramparts and crumbling towers clothed with mosses and hung with garlands of swaying vines, and as we moved on they swung back again and hid themselves once more in the foliage. Presently a verdure-clad needle of stone, a thousand feet high, stepped out from behind a corner, and mounted guard over the mysteries of the valley. It seemed to me that if Captain Cook needed a monument, here was one ready made—therefore, why not put up his sign here, and sell out the venerable cocoanut stump?

But the chief pride of Maui is her dead volcano of Haleakala—which means, translated, "the house of the sun." We climbed a thousand feet up the side of this isolated colossus one afternoon; then camped, and next day climbed the remaining nine thousand feet, and anchored on the summit, where we built a fire and froze and roasted by turns, all night. With the first pallor of dawn we got up and saw things that were new to us. Mounted on a commanding pinnacle, we watched Nature work her silent wonders. The sea was spread abroad on every hand, its tumbled surface seeming only wrinkled and dimpled in the distance. A broad valley below appeared like an ample checker-board, its velvety green sugar plantations alternating with dun squares of barrenness and groves of trees diminished to mossy tufts. Beyond the valley were mountains picturesquely grouped together; but bear in mind, we fancied that we were looking *up* at these things—not down. We seemed to sit in the bottom of a symmetrical bowl ten thousand feet deep, with the valley and the skirting sea lifted away into the sky above us! It was curious; and not only curious, but aggravating; for it was having our trouble all for nothing, to climb ten thousand feet toward heaven and then have to look *up* at our scenery. However, we had to be content with it and make the best of it; for, all we could do we could not coax our landscape down out of the clouds. Formerly, when I had read an article in which Poe treated of this singular fraud perpetrated upon the eye by isolated great altitudes, I had looked upon the matter as an invention of his own fancy.

I have spoken of the outside view—but we had an inside one, too. That was the yawning dead crater, into which we now and then tumbled rocks, half as large as a barrel, from our perch, and saw them go careering down the almost perpendicular sides, bounding three hundred feet at a jump; kicking up dust-clouds wherever they struck; diminishing to our view as they sped farther into distance; growing invisible, finally, and only betraying their course by faint little puffs of dust; and coming to a halt at last in the bottom of the abyss, two thousand five hundred feet down from where they started! It was magnificent sport. We wore ourselves out at it.

The crater of Vesuvius, as I have before remarked, is a modest pit about a thousand feet deep and three thousand in circumference; that of Kilauea is somewhat deeper, and *ten miles* in circumference. But what are either of them compared to the vacant stomach of Haleakala? I will not offer any figures of my own, but give official ones—those of Commander Wilkes, U. S. N., who surveyed it and testifies that it is *twenty-seven miles in circumference!* If it had a level bottom it would make a fine site for a city like London. It must have afforded a spectacle worth contemplating in the old days when its furnaces gave full rein to their anger.

Presently vagrant white clouds came drifting along, high over the sea and the valley; then they came in couples and groups; then in imposing squadrons; gradually joining their forces, they banked themselves solidly together, a thousand feet under us, and *totally shut out land and ocean*—not a vestige of *anything* was left in view but just a little of the rim of the crater, circling away from the pinnacle whereon we sat (for a ghostly procession of wanderers from the filmy hosts without had drifted through a chasm in the crater wall and filed round and round, and gathered and sunk and blended together till the abyss was stored to the brim with a fleecy fog). Thus banked, motion ceased, and silence reigned. Clear to the horizon, league on league, the snowy floor stretched without a break—not level, but in rounded folds, with shallow creases between, and with here and there stately piles of vapory architecture lifting themselves aloft out of the common plain—some near at hand, some in the middle distances, and others relieving the monotony of the remote solitudes. There was little conversation, for the impressive scene overawed speech. I felt like the Last Man, neglected of the judgment, and left pinnacled in mid-heaven, a forgotten relic of a vanished world.

While the hush yet brooded, the messengers of the coming resurrection appeared in the East. A growing warmth suffused the horizon, and soon the sun emerged and looked out over the cloud-waste, flinging bars of ruddy light across it, staining its folds and billow-caps with blushes, purpling the shaded troughs between, and glorifying the massy vapor-palaces and cathedrals with a wasteful splendor of all blendings and combinations of rich coloring.

It was the sublimest spectacle I ever witnessed, and I think the memory of it will remain with me always.

CHAPTER LXXVII

I stumbled upon one curious character in the Island of Maui. He became a sore annoyance to me in the course of time. My first glimpse of him was in a sort of public room in the town of Lahaina. He occupied a chair at the opposite side of the apartment, and sat eyeing our party with interest for some minutes, and listening as critically to what we were saying as if he fancied we were talking to him and expecting him to reply. I thought it very sociable in a stranger. Presently, in the course of conversation, I made a statement bearing upon the subject under discussion—and I made it with due modesty, for there was nothing extraordinary about it, and it was only put forth in illustration of a point at issue. I had barely finished when this person spoke out with rapid utterance and feverish anxiety:

"Oh, that was certainly remarkable, after a fashion, but you ought to have seen *my* chimney—you ought to have seen *my* chimney, sir! Smoke! I wish I may hang if—Mr. Jones, *you* remember that chimney—you *must* remember that chimney! No, no—I recollect, now, you warn't living on this side of the island then. But I am telling you nothing but the truth, and I wish I may never draw another breath if that chimney didn't smoke so that the smoke actually got *caked* in it and I had to dig it out with a pickaxe! You may smile, gentlemen, but the High Sheriff's got a hunk of it which I dug out before his eyes, and so it's perfectly easy for you to go and examine for yourselves."

The interruption broke up the conversation, which had already begun to lag, and we presently hired some natives and an out-rigger canoe or two, and went out to overlook a grand surf-bathing contest.

Two weeks after this, while talking in a company, I looked up and detected this same man boring through and through me with his intense eye, and noted again his twitching muscles and his feverish anxiety to speak. The moment I paused, he said:

"*Beg* your pardon, sir, beg your pardon, but it can only be considered remarkable when brought into strong outline by isolation. Sir, contrasted with a circumstance which occurred in my own experience, it instantly becomes commonplace. No, not that—for I will not speak so discourteously of any experience in the career of a stranger and a gentleman—but I am *obliged* to say that you could not, and you *would* not ever again refer to this tree as a *large* one, if you could behold, as I have, the great Yakmatack tree, in the island of Ounaska, sea of Kamtchatka— a tree, sir, not one inch less than four hundred and fifteen feet in solid diameter!—and I wish I may die in a minute if it isn't so! Oh, you needn't look so questioning, gentlemen; here's old Cap Saltmarsh can say whether I know what I'm talking about or not. I showed him the tree."

Captain Saltmarsh.—"Come, now, cat your anchor, lad— you're heaving too taut. You *promised* to show me that stunner, and I walked more than eleven mile with you through the cussedest jungle *I* ever see, a hunting for it; but the tree you showed me finally warn't as big around as a beer cask, and *you* know that your own self, Markiss."

"Hear the man talk! Of *course* the tree was reduced that way, but didn't I *explain* it? Answer me, didn't I? Didn't I say I wished you could have seen it when *I* first saw it? When you got up on your ear and called me names, and said I had brought you eleven miles to look at a sapling, didn't I *explain* to you that all the whale-ships in the North Seas had been wooding off of it for more than twenty-seven years? And did you s'pose the tree could last for-*ever*, con-*found* it? I don't see why you want to keep back things that way, and try to injure a person that's never done *you* any harm."

Somehow this man's presence made me uncomfortable, and I was glad when a native arrived at that moment to say that Muckawow, the most companionable and luxurious among the rude war-chiefs of the Islands, desired us to come over and help him enjoy a missionary whom he had found trespassing on his grounds.

I think it was about ten days afterward that, as I finished a statement I was making for the instruction of a group of friends and acquaintances, and which made no pretence of being extraordinary, a familiar voice chimed instantly in on the heels of my last word, and said:

"But, my dear sir, there was *nothing* remarkable about that horse, or the circumstance either—nothing in the world! I mean no sort of offence when I say it, sir, but you really do not know anything whatever about speed. Bless your heart, if you could only have seen my mare Margaretta; *there* was a beast!—*there* was lightning for you! Trot! Trot is no name for it—she flew! How she *could* whirl a buggy along! I started her out once, sir—Colonel Bilgewater, *you* recollect that animal perfectly well—I started her out about thirty or thirty-five yards ahead of the awfullest storm I ever saw in my life, and it chased us upwards of eighteen miles! It did, by the everlasting hills! And I'm telling you nothing but the unvarnished truth when I say that not one single drop of rain fell on me—not a single *drop,* sir! And I swear to it! But my dog was a-swimming behind the wagon all they way!''

For a week or two I stayed mostly within doors, for I seemed to meet this person everywhere, and he had become utterly hateful to me. But one evening I dropped in on Captain Perkins and his friends, and we had a sociable time. About ten o'clock I chanced to be talking about a merchant friend of mine, and without really intending it, the remark slipped out that he was a little mean and parsimonious about paying his workmen. Instantly, through the steam of a hot whiskey punch on the opposite side of the room, a remembered voice shot—and for a moment I trembled on the imminent verge of profanity:

''Oh, my dear sir, really you expose yourself when you parade *that* as a surprising circumstance. Bless your heart and hide, you are ignorant of the very A B C of meanness! ignorant as the unborn babe! ignorant as unborn *twins!* You don't know *any thing* about it! It is pitiable to see you, sir, a well-spoken and prepossessing stranger, making such an enormous pow-wow here about a subject concerning which your ignorance is perfectly humiliating! Look me in the eye, if you please; look me in the eye. John James Godfrey was the son of poor but honest parents in the State of Mississippi—boyhood friend of mine—bosom comrade in later years. Heaven rest his noble spirit, he is gone from us now. John James Godfrey was hired by the Hayblossom Mining Company in California to do some blasting for them—the ''Incorporated Company of Mean Men,'' the boys used to call it. Well, one day he drilled a hole about four feet deep and put in an awful blast of powder, and was standing over it ramming it down with an iron crowbar about nine foot long, when the cussed thing struck a spark and fired the powder, and scat! away John Godfrey whizzed like a skyrocket, him and his crowbar! Well, sir, he kept on going up in the air higher and higher, till he didn't look any bigger than a boy—and he kept going on up higher and higher, till he didn't look any bigger than a doll—and he kept on going up higher and higher, till he didn't look any bigger than a little small bee—and then he went out of sight! Presently he came in sight again, looking like a little small bee—and he came along down further and further, till he looked as big as a doll again—and down further and further, till he was a full-sized man once more; and then him and his crowbar came a wh-izzing down and lit right exactly in the same old tracks and went to r-ramming down, and r-ramming down, and r-ramming down again, just the same as if nothing had happened! Now do you know, that poor cuss warn't gone only sixteen minutes, and yet that Incorporated Company of Mean Men DOCKED HIM FOR THE LOST TIME!''

I said I had the headache, and so excused myself and went home. And on my diary I entered "another night spoiled" by this offensive loafer. And a fervent curse was set down with it to keep the item company. And the very next day I packed up, out of all patience, and left the Island.

Almost from the very beginning, I regarded that man as a liar.

. . . . . .

The line of points represents an interval of years. At the end of which time the opinion hazarded in that last sentence came to be gratifyingly and remarkably endorsed, and by wholly disinterested persons. The man Markiss was found one morning hanging to a beam of his own bedroom (the doors and windows securely fastened on the inside), dead; and on his breast was pinned a paper in his own handwriting begging his friends to suspect no innocent person of having any thing to do with his death, for that it was the work of his own hands entirely. Yet the jury brought in the astounding verdict that deceased came to his death "by the hands of some person or persons unknown!" They explained that the perfectly undeviating consistency of Markiss's character for thirty years towered aloft as colossal and indestructible testimony, that whatever statement he chose to make was entitled to instant and unquestioning acceptance as a *lie*. And they furthermore stated their belief that he was not dead, and instanced the strong circumstantial evidence of his own word that he *was* dead—and beseeched the coroner to delay the funeral as long as possible, which was done. And so in the tropical climate of Lahaina the coffin stood open for seven days, and then even the loyal jury gave him up. But they sat on him again, and changed their verdict to "suicide, induced by mental aberration"—because, said they, with penetration, "he said he was dead, and he *was* dead; and would he have told the truth if he had been in his right mind? *No,* sir."

CHAPTER LXXVIII

After half a year's luxurious vagrancy in the islands, I took shipping in a sailing vessel, and regretfully returned to San Francisco—a voyage in every way delightful, but without an incident: unless lying two long weeks in a dead calm, eighteen hundred miles from the nearest land, may rank as an incident. Schools of whales grew so tame that day after day they played about the ship among the porpoises and the sharks without the least apparent fear of us, and we pelted them with empty bottles for lack of better sport. Twenty-four hours afterward these bottles would be still lying on the glassy water under our noses, showing that the ship had not moved out of her place in all that time. The calm was absolutely breathless, and the surface of the sea absolutely without a wrinkle. For a whole day and part of a night we lay so close to another ship that had drifted to our vicinity, that we carried on conversations with her passengers, introduced each other by name, and became pretty intimately acquainted with people we had never heard of before, and have never heard of since. This was the only vessel we saw during the whole lonely voyage. We had fifteen passengers, and to show how hard pressed they were at last for occupation and amusement, I will mention that the gentlemen gave a good part of their time every day, during the calm, to trying to sit on an empty champagne bottle (lying on its side), and thread a needle without touching their heels to the deck, or falling over; and the ladies sat in the shade of the mainsail, and watched the enterprise with absorbing interest. We were at sea five Sundays; and yet, but for the almanac, we never would have known but that all the other days were Sundays too.

I was home again, in San Francisco, without means and without employment. I tortured my brain for a saving scheme of some kind, and at last a public lecture occurred to me! I sat down and wrote one, in a fever of hopeful anticipation. I showed it to several friends, but they all shook their heads. They said nobody would come to hear me, and I would make a humiliating failure of it. They said that as I had never spoken in public, I would break down in the delivery, anyhow. I was disconsolate now. But at last an editor slapped me on the back and told me to "go ahead." He said, "Take the largest house in town, and charge a dollar a ticket." The audacity of the proposition was charming; it seemed fraught with practical worldly wisdom, however. The proprietor of the several theatres endorsed the advice, and said I might have his handsome new opera-house at half price—fifty dollars. In sheer desperation I took it—on credit, for sufficient reasons. In three days I did a hundred and fifty dollars' worth of printing and advertising, and was the most distressed and frightened creature on the Pacific coast. I could not sleep—who could, under such circumstances? For other people there was facetiousness in the last line of my posters, but to me it was plaintive with a pang when I wrote it:

"Doors open at 7½. The trouble will begin at 8."

That line has done good service since. Showmen have borrowed it frequently. I have even seen it appended to a newspaper advertisement reminding school pupils in vacation what time next term would begin. As those three days of suspense dragged by, I grew more and more unhappy. I had sold two hundred tickets among my personal friends, but I feared they might not come. My lecture, which had seemed "humorous" to me, at first, grew steadily more and more dreary, till not a vestige of fun seemed left, and I grieved that I could not bring a coffin on the stage and turn the thing into a funeral. I was so panic-stricken, at last, that I went to three old friends, giants in stature, cordial by nature, and stormy-voiced, and said:

"This thing is going to be a failure; the jokes in it are so dim that nobody will ever see them; I would like to have you sit in the parquette, and help me through."

They said they would. Then I went to the wife of a popular citizen, and said that if she was willing to do me a very great kindness, I would be glad if she and her husband would sit prominently in the left-hand stage-box, where the whole house could see them. I explained that I should need help, and would turn toward her and smile, as a signal, when I had been delivered of an obscure joke—"and then," I added, "don't wait to investigate, but *respond!*"

She promised. Down the street I met a man I never had seen before. He had been drinking, and was beaming with smiles and good nature. He said:

"My name's Sawyer. You don't know me, but that don't matter. I haven't got a cent, but if you knew how bad I wanted to laugh, you'd give me a ticket. Come, now, what do you say?"

"Is your laugh hung on a hair-trigger?—that is, is it critical, or can you get it off *easy?*"

My drawling infirmity of speech so affected him that he laughed a specimen or two that struck me as being about the article I wanted, and I gave him a ticket, and appointed him to sit in the second circle, in the centre, and be responsible for that division of the house. I gave him minute instructions about how to detect indistinct jokes, and then went away, and left him chuckling placidly over the novelty of the idea.

I ate nothing on the last of the three eventful days—I only suffered. I had advertised that on this third day the box-office would be opened for the sale of reserved seats. I crept down to the theatre at four in the afternoon to see if any sales had been made. The ticket seller was gone, the box-office was locked up. I had to swallow suddenly, or my heart would have got out. "No sales," I said to myself; "I might have known it." I thought of suicide, pretended illness, flight. I thought of these things in earnest, for I was very miserable and scared. But of course I had to drive them away, and prepare to meet my fate. I could not wait for half-past seven—I wanted to face the horror, and end it—the feeling of many a man doomed to hang, no doubt. I went down back street at six o'clock, and entered the theatre by the back door. I stumbled my way in the dark among the ranks of canvas scenery, and stood on the stage. The house was gloomy and silent, and its emptiness depressing. I went into the dark among the scenes again, and for an hour and a half gave myself up to the horrors, wholly unconscious of everything else. Then I heard a murmur; it rose higher and higher, and ended in a crash, mingled with cheers. It made my hair raise, it was so close to me, and so loud. There was a pause, and then another; presently came a third, and before I well knew what I was about, I was in the middle of the stage, staring at a sea of faces, bewildered by the fierce glare of the lights, and quaking in every limb with a terror that seemed like to take my life away. The house was full, aisles and all!

The tumult in my heart and brain and legs continued a full minute before I could gain any command over myself. Then I recognized the charity and the friendliness in the faces before me, and little by little my fright melted away, and I began to talk. Within three or four minutes I was comfortable, and even content. My three chief allies, with three auxiliaries, were on hand, in the parquette, all sitting together, all armed with bludgeons, and all ready to make an onslaught upon the feeblest joke that might show its head. And whenever a joke did fall, their bludgeons came down and their faces seemed to split from ear to ear; Sawyer, whose hearty countenance was seen looming redly in the centre of the second circle, took it up, and the house was carried handsomely. Inferior jokes never fared so royally before. Presently I delivered a bit of serious matter with impressive unction (it was my pet), and the audience listened with an absorbed hush that gratified me more than any applause; and as I dropped the last word of the clause, I happened to turn and catch Mrs. ——'s intent and waiting eye; my conversation with her flashed upon me, and in spite of all I could do I smiled. She took it for the signal, and promptly delivered a mellow laugh that touched off the whole audience; and the explosion that followed was the triumph of the evening. I thought that that honest man Sawyer would choke himself; and as for the bludgeons, they performed like pile-drivers. But my poor little morsel of pathos was ruined. It was taken in good faith as an intentional joke, and the prize one of the entertainment, and I wisely let it go at that.

All the papers were kind in the morning; my appetite returned; I had abundance of money. All's well that ends well.

CHAPTER LXXIX

I launched out as a lecturer, now, with great boldness. I had the field all to myself, for public lectures were almost an unknown commodity in the Pacific market. They are not so rare, now, I suppose. I took an old personal friend along to play agent for me, and for two or three weeks we roamed through Nevada and California and had a very cheerful time of it. Two days before I lectured in Virginia City, two stagecoaches were robbed within two miles of the town. The daring act was committed just at dawn, by six masked men, who sprang up alongside the coaches, presented revolvers at the heads of the drivers and passengers, and commanded a general dismount. Everybody climbed down, and the robbers took their watches and every cent they had. Then they took gunpowder and blew up the express specie boxes and got their contents. The leader of the robbers was a small, quick-spoken man, and the fame of his vigorous manner and his intrepidity was in everybody's mouth when we arrived.

The night after instructing Virginia, I walked over the desolate "divide" and down to Gold Hill, and lectured there. The lecture done, I stopped to talk with a friend, and did not start back till eleven. The "divide" was high, unoccupied ground, between the towns, the scene of twenty midnight murders and a hundred robberies. As we climbed up and stepped out on this eminence, the Gold Hill lights dropped out of sight at our backs, and the night closed down gloomy and dismal. A sharp wind swept the place, too, and chilled our perspiring bodies through.

"I tell you I don't like this place at night," said Mike the agent.

"Well, don't speak so loud," I said. "You needn't remind anybody that we are here."

Just then a dim figure approached me from the direction of Virginia—a man, evidently. He came straight at me, and I stepped aside to let him pass; he stepped in the way and confronted me again. Then I saw that he had a mask on and was holding something in my face—I heard a click-click and recognized a revolver in dim outline. I pushed the barrel aside with my hand and said:

"Don't!"

He ejaculated sharply:

"Your watch! Your money!"

I said:

"You can have them with pleasure—but take the pistol away from my face, please. It makes me shiver."

"No remarks! Hand out your money!"

"Certainly—I—"

"Put up your hands! Don't you go for a weapon! Put 'em up! Higher!"

I held them above my head.

A pause. Then:

"Are you going to hand out your money or not?"

I dropped my hands to my pockets and said:

"Certainly! I—"

"Put up your *hands!* Do you want your head blown off? Higher!"

I put them above my head again.

Another pause.

"*Are* you going to hand out your money or *not?* Ah-ah—again? Put up your hands! By George, you want the head shot off you awful bad!"

"Well, friend, I'm trying my best to please you. You tell me to give up my money, and when I reach for it you tell me to put up my hands. If you would only—. Oh, now—don't! All six of you at me! That other man will get away while.—Now please take some of those revolvers out of my face—*do,* if you *please!* Every time one of them clicks, my liver comes up into my throat! If you have a mother—any of you—or if any of you have ever *had* a mother—or a—grandmother—or a—"

"Cheese it! *Will* you give up your money, or have we got to—. There-there—none of that! Put up your *hands!*"

"Gentlemen—I know you are gentlemen by your—"

"Silence! If you want to be facetious, young man, there are times and places more fitting. *This* is a serious business."

"You prick the marrow of my opinion. The funerals I have attended in my time were comedies compared to it. Now *I* think—"

"Curse your palaver! Your money!—your money!—your money! Hold!—put up your hands!"

"Gentlemen, listen to reason. You *see* how I am situated—now *don't* put those pistols so close—I smell the powder. You see how I am situated. If I had four hands—so that I could hold up two and—"

"Throttle him! Gag him! Kill him!"

"Gentlemen, *don't!* Nobody's watching the other fellow. Why don't some of you—. Ouch! Take it away, please! Gentlemen, you see that I've got to hold up my hands; and so I can't take out my money—but if you'll be so kind as to take it out for me, I will do as much for you some—"

"Search him Beauregard—and stop his jaw with a bullet, quick, if he wags it again. Help Beauregard, Stonewall."

Then three of them, with the small, spry leader, adjourned to Mike and fell to searching him. I was so excited that my lawless fancy tortured me to ask my two men all manner of facetious questions about their rebel brother-generals of the South, but, considering the order they had received, it was but common prudence to keep still. When everything had been taken from me,—watch, money, and a multitude of trifles of small value,—I supposed I was free, and forthwith put my cold hands into my empty pockets and began an inoffensive jig to warm my feet and stir up some latent courage—but instantly all pistols were at my head, and the order came again:

"Be still! Put up your hands! And *keep* them up!"

They stood Mike up alongside of me, with strict orders to keep his hands above his head, too, and then the chief highwayman said:

"Beauregard, hide behind that boulder; Phil Sheridan, you hide behind that other one; Stonewall Jackson, put yourself behind that sage-bush there. Keep you pistols bearing on these fellows, and if they take down their hands within ten minutes, or move a single peg, let them have it!"

Then three disappeared in the gloom toward the several ambushes, and the other three disappeared down the road toward Virginia. .

It was depressingly still, and miserably cold. Now this whole thing was a practical joke, and the robbers were personal friends of ours in disguise, and twenty more lay hidden within ten feet of us during the whole operation, listening. Mike knew all this, and was in the joke, but I suspected nothing of it. To me it was most uncomfortably genuine.

When we had stood there in the middle of the road five minutes, like a couple of idiots, with our hands aloft, freezing to death by inches, Mike's interest in the joke began to wane. He said:

"The time's up, now, aint it?"

"No, you keep still. Do you want to take any chances with those bloody savages?"

Presently Mike said:

"*Now* the time's up, anyway. I'm freezing."

"Well freeze. Better freeze than carry your brains home in a basket. Maybe the time *is* up, but how do *we* know?—got no watch to tell by. I mean to give them good measure. I calculate to stand here fifteen minutes or die. Don't you move."

So, without knowing it, I was making one joker very sick of his contract. When we took our arms down at last, they were aching with cold and fatigue, and when we went sneaking off, the dread I was in that the time might not yet be up and that we would feel bullets in a moment, was not sufficient to draw all my attention from the misery that racked my stiffened body.

The joke of these highwayman friends of ours was mainly a joke upon themselves; for they had waited for me on the cold hill-top two full hours before I came, and there was very little fun in that; they were so chilled that it took them a couple of weeks to get warm again. Moreover, I never had a thought that they would kill me to get money which it was so perfectly easy to get without any such folly, and so they did not really frighten me bad enough to make their enjoyment worth the trouble they had taken. I was only afraid that their weapons would go off accidently. Their very numbers inspired me with confidence that no blood would be intentionally spilled. They were not smart; they ought to have sent only *one* highwayman, with a double-barrelled shot gun, if they desired to see the author of this volume climb a tree.

However, I suppose that in the long run I got the largest share of the joke at last; and in a shape not foreseen by the highwaymen; for the chilly exposure on the "divide" while I was in a perspiration gave me a cold which developed itself into a troublesome disease and kept my hands idle some three months, besides costing me quite a sum in doctor's bills. Since then I play no practical jokes on people and generally lose my temper when one is played upon me.

When I returned to San Francisco I projected a pleasure journey to Japan and thence westward around the world; but a desire to see home again changed my mind, and I took a berth in the steamship, bade good-bye to the friendliest land and livest, heartiest community on our continent, and came by the way of the Isthmus to New York—a trip that was not much of a pic-nic excursion, for the cholera broke out among us on the passage and we buried two or three bodies at sea every day. I found home a dreary place after my long absence; for half the children I had known were now wearing whiskers or waterfalls, and few of the grown people I had been acquainted with remained at their hearthstones prosperous and happy—some of them had wandered to other scenes, some were in jail, and the rest had been hanged. These changes touched me deeply, and I went away and joined the famous Quaker City European Excursion and carried my tears to foreign lands.

Thus, after seven years of vicissitudes, ended a "pleasure trip" to the silver mines of Nevada which had originally been intended to occupy only three months. However, I usually miss my calculations further than that.

MORAL

If the reader thinks he is done, now, and that this book has no moral to it, he is in error. The moral of it is this: If you are of any account, stay at home and make your way by faithful diligence; but if you are "no account," go away from home, and then you will *have* to work, whether you want to or not. Thus you become a blessing to your friends by ceasing to be a nuisance to them—if the people you go among suffer by the operation.

APPENDIX

A

BRIEF SKETCH OF MORMON HISTORY

Mormonism is only about forty years old, but its career has been full of stir and adventure from the beginning, and is likely to remain so to the end. Its adherents have been hunted and hounded from one end of the country to the other, and the result is that for years they have hated all "Gentiles" indiscriminately and with all their might. Joseph Smith, the finder of the Book of Mormon and founder of the religion, was driven from State to State with his mysterious copperplates and the miraculous stones he read their inscriptions with. Finally he instituted his "church" in Ohio and Brigham Young joined it. The neighbors began to persecute, and apostasy commenced. Brigham held to the faith and worked hard. He arrested desertion. He did more—he added converts in the midst of the trouble. He rose in favor and importance with the brethren. He was made one of the Twelve Apostles of the Church. He shortly fought his way to a higher post and a more powerful—President of the Twelve. The neighbors rose up and drove the Mormons out of Ohio, and they settled in Missouri. Brigham went with them. The Missourians drove them out and they retreated to Nauvoo, Illinois. They prospered there, and built a temple which made some pretensions to architectural grace and achieved some celebrity in a section of country where a brick court-house with a tin dome and a cupola on it was contemplated with reverential awe. But the Mormons were badgered and harried again by their neighbors. All the proclamations Joseph Smith could issue denouncing polygamy and repudiating it as utterly anti-Mormon were of no avail; the people of the neighborhood, on both sides of the Mississippi, claimed that polygamy was practised by the Mormons, and not only polygamy but a little of everything that was bad. Brigham returned from a mission to England, where he had established a Mormon newspaper, and he brought back with him several hundred converts to his preaching. His influence among the brethren augmented with every move he made. Finally Nauvoo was invaded by the Missouri and Illinois Gentiles, and Joseph Smith killed. A Mormon named Rigdon assumed the Presidency of the Mormon church and government, in Smith's place, and even tried his hand at a prophecy or two. But a greater than he was at hand. Brigham seized the advantage of the hour and without other authority than superior brain and nerve and will, hurled Rigdon from his high place and occupied it himself. He did more. He launched an elaborate curse at Rigdon and his disciples; and he pronounced Rigdon's "prophecies" emanations from the devil, and ended by "handing the false prophet over to the buffetings of Satan for a thousand years"—probably the longest term ever inflicted in Illinois. The people recognized their master. They straightway elected Brigham Young President, by a prodigious majority, and have never faltered in their devotion to him from that day to this. Brigham had forecast—a quality which no other prominent Mormon has probably ever possessed. He recognized that it was better to move to the wilderness than *be* moved. By his command the people gathered together their meagre effects, turned their backs upon their homes, and their faces toward the wilderness, and on a bitter night in February filed in sorrowful procession across the frozen Mississippi, lighted on their way by the glare from their burning temple, whose sacred furniture their own hands had fired! They camped, several days afterward, on the western verge of Iowa, and poverty, want, hunger, cold, sickness, grief and persecution did their work, and many succumbed and died—martyrs, fair and true, whatever else they might have been. Two years the remnant remained there, while Brigham and a small party crossed the country and founded Great Salt Lake City, purposely choosing a land which was *outside the ownership and jurisdiction of the hated American nation.* Note that. This was in 1847. Brigham moved his people there and got them settled just in time to see disaster fall again. For the war closed and Mexico ceded Brigham's refuge to the enemy—the United States! In 1849 the Mormons organized a "free and independent" government and erected the "State of Deseret," with Brigham Young as its head. But the very next year Congress deliberately snubbed it and created the "Territory of Utah" out of the same accumulation of mountains, sage-brush, alkali and general desolation,—but made Brigham Governor of it. Then for years the enormous migration across the plains to California poured through the land of the Mormons and yet the church remained staunch and true to its lord and master. Neither hunger, thirst, poverty, grief, hatred, contempt, nor persecution could drive the Mormons from their faith or their allegiance; and even the thirst for gold, which gleaned the flower of the youth and strength of many nations was not able to entice them! That was the final test. An experiment that could survive that was an experiment with some substance to it somewhere.

Great Salt Lake City throve finely, and so did Utah. One of the last things which Brigham Young had done before leaving Iowa, was to appear in the pulpit dressed to personate the worshipped and lamented prophet Smith and confer the prophetic succession, with all its dignities, emoluments and authorities, upon "President Brigham Young!" The people accepted the pious fraud with the maddest enthusiasm, and Brigham's power was sealed and secured for all time. Within five years afterward he openly added polygamy to the tenets of the church by authority of a "revelation" which he pretended had been received nine years before by Joseph Smith, albeit Joseph is amply on record as denouncing polygamy to the day of his death.

Now was Brigham become a second Andrew Johnson in the small beginning and steady progress in his official grandeur. He had served successively as a disciple in the ranks; home missionary; foreign missionary; editor and publisher; Apostle; President of the Board of Apostles; President of all Mormondom, civil and ecclesiastical; successor to the great Joseph by the will of heaven; "prophet," "seer," "revelator." There was but one dignity higher which he *could* aspire to, and he reached out modestly and took that—he proclaimed himself a God!

He claims that he is to have a heaven of his own hereafter, and that he will be its God, and his wives and children its goddesses, princes and princesses. Into it all faithful Mormons will be admitted, with their families, and will take rank and consequence according to the number of their wives and children. If a disciple dies before he has had time to accumulate enough wives and children to enable him to be respectable in the next world any friend can marry a few wives and raise a few children for him *after he is dead,* and they are duly credited to his account and his heavenly status advanced accordingly.

Let it be borne in mind that the majority of the Mormons have always been ignorant, simple, of an inferior order of intellect, unacquainted with the world and its ways; and let it be borne in mind that the wives of these Mormons are necessarily after the same pattern and their children likely to be fit representatives of such a conjunction; and then let it be remembered that *for forty years* these creatures have been driven, driven, driven, relentlessly! and mobbed, beaten, and shot down; cursed, despised, expatriated; banished to a remote desert, whither they journeyed gaunt with famine and disease, disturbing the ancient solitudes with their lamentations and marking the long way with graves of their dead—and all because they were simply trying to live and worship God in the way which *they* believed with all their hearts and souls to be the true one. Let all these things be borne in mind, and then it will not be hard to account for the deathless hatred which the Mormons bear our people and our government.

That hatred has "fed fat its ancient grudge" ever since Mormon Utah developed into a self-supporting realm and the church waxed rich and strong. Brigham as Territorial Governor made it plain that Mormondom was for the Mormons. The United States tried to rectify all that by appointing territorial officers from New England and other anti-Mormon localities, but Brigham prepared to make their entrance into his dominions difficult. Three thousand United States troops had to go across the plains and put these gentlemen in office. And after they were in office they were as helpless as so many stone images. They made laws which nobody minded and which could not be executed. The federal judges opened court in a land filled with crime and violence and sat as holiday spectacles for insolent crowds to gape at—for there was nothing to try, nothing to do, nothing on the dockets! And if a Gentile brought a suit, the Mormon jury would do just as it pleased about bringing in a verdict, and when the judgment of the court was rendered no Mormon cared for it and no officer could execute it. Our Presidents shipped one cargo of officials after another to Utah, but the result was always the same—they sat in a blight for awhile, they fairly feasted on scowls and insults day by day, they saw every attempt to do their official duties find its reward in darker and darker looks, and in secret threats and warnings of a more and more dismal nature—and at last they either succumbed and became despised tools and toys of the Mormons, or got scared and discomforted beyond all endurance and left the Territory. If a brave officer kept on courageously till his pluck was proven, some pliant Buchanan or Pierce would remove him and appoint a stick in his place. In 1857 General Harney came very near being appointed Governor of Utah. And so it came very near being Harney governor and Cradlebaugh judge!—two men who never had any idea of fear further than the sort of murky comprehension of it which they were enabled to gather from the dictionary. Simply (if for nothing else) for the variety they would have made in a rather monotonous history of Federal servility and helplessness, it is a pity they were not fated to hold office together in Utah.

Up to the date of our visit to Utah, such had been the Territorial record. The Territorial government established there had been a hopeless failure, and Brigham Young was the only real power in the land. He was an absolute monarch—a monarch who defied our President—a monarch who laughed at our armies when they camped about his capital—a monarch who received without emotion the news that the august Congress of the United States had enacted a solemn law against polygamy, and then went forth calmly and married twenty-five or thirty more wives.

B

THE MOUNTAIN MEADOWS MASSACRE

The persecutions which the Mormons suffered so long—and which they consider they still suffer in not being allowed to govern themselves—they have endeavored and are still endeavoring to repay. The now almost forgotten "Mountain Meadows massacre" was their work. It was very famous in its day. The whole United States rang with its horrors. A few items will refresh the reader's memory. A great emigrant train from Missouri and Arkansas passed through Salt Lake City and a few disaffected Mormons joined it for the sake of the strong protection it afforded for their escape. In that matter lay sufficient cause for hot retaliation by the Mormon chiefs. Besides, these one hundred and forty-five or one hundred and fifty unsuspecting emigrants being in part from Arkansas, where a noted Mormon missionary had lately been killed, and in part from Missouri, a State remembered with execrations as a bitter persecutor of the saints when they were few and poor and friendless, here were substantial additional grounds for lack of love for these wayfarers. And finally, this train was rich, very rich in cattle, horses, mules and other property—and how could the Mormons consistently keep up their coveted resemblance to the Israelitish tribes and not seize the "spoil" of an enemy when the Lord had so manifestly "delivered it into their hand?"

Wherefore, according to Mrs. C.V. Waite's entertaining book, "The Mormon Prophet," it transpired that—

"A 'revelation' from Brigham Young, as Great Grand Archee or God, was dispatched to President J.C. Haight, Bishop Higbee and J.D. Lee (adopted son of Brigham), commanding them to raise all the forces they could muster and trust, follow those cursed Gentiles (so read the revelation), attack them disguised as Indians, and with the arrows of the Almighty make a clean sweep of them, and leave none to tell the tale; and if they needed any assistance they were commanded to hire the Indians as their allies, promising them a share of the booty. They were to be neither slothful nor negligent in their duty, and to be punctual in sending the teams back to him before winter set in, for this was the mandate of Almighty God."

The command of the "revelation" was faithfully obeyed. A large party of Mormons, painted and tricked out as Indians, overtook the train of emigrant wagons some three hundred miles south of Salt Lake City, and made an attack. But the emigrants threw up earthworks, made fortresses of their wagons and defended themselves gallantly and successfully for five days! Your Missouri or Arkansas gentleman is not much afraid of the sort of scurvy apologies for "Indians" which the southern part of Utah affords. He would stand up and fight five hundred of them.

At the end of the five days the Mormons tried military strategy. They retired to the upper end of the "Meadows," resumed civilized apparel, washed off their paint, and then, heavily armed, drove down in wagons to the beleaguered emigrants, bearing a flag of truce! When the emigrants saw white men coming they threw down their guns and welcomed them with cheer after cheer! And, all unconscious of the poetry of it, no doubt, they lifted a little child aloft, dressed in white, in answer to the flag of truce!

The leaders of the timely white "deliverers" were President Haight and Bishop John D. Lee, of the Mormon Church. Mr. Cradlebaugh, who served a term as a Federal Judge in Utah and afterward was sent to Congress from Nevada, tells in a speech delivered in Congress how these leaders next proceeded:

"They professed to be on good terms with the Indians, and represented them as being very mad. They also proposed to intercede and settle the matter with the Indians. After several hours parley they, having (apparently) visited the Indians, gave the *ultimatum* of the savages; which was, that the emigrants should march out of their camp, leaving everything behind them, even their guns. It was promised by the Mormon bishops that they would bring a force and guard the emigrants back to the settlements. The terms were agreed to, the emigrants being desirous of saving the lives of their families. The Mormons retired, and subsequently appeared with thirty or forty armed men. The emigrants were marched out, the women and children in front and the men behind, the Mormon guard being in the rear. When they had marched in this way about a mile, at a given signal the slaughter commenced. The men were almost all shot down at the first fire from the guard. Two only escaped, who fled to the desert, and were followed one hundred and fifty miles before they were overtaken and slaughtered. The women and children ran on, two or three hundred yards further, when they were overtaken and with the aid of the Indians they were slaughtered. Seventeen individuals only, of all the emigrant party, were spared, and they were little children, the eldest of them being only seven years old. Thus, on the 10th day of September, 1857, was consummated one of the most cruel, cowardly and bloody murders known in our history."

The number of persons butchered by the Mormons on this occasion was *one hundred and twenty.*

With unheard-of temerity Judge Cradlebaugh opened his court and proceeded to make Mormondom answer for the massacre. And what a spectacle it must have been to see this grim veteran, solitary and alone in his pride and his pluck, glowering down on his Mormon jury and Mormon auditory, deriding them by turns, and by turns "breathing threatenings and slaughter!"

An editorial in the *Territorial Enterprise* of that day says of him and of the occasion:

"He spoke and acted with the fearlessness and resolution of a Jackson; but the jury failed to indict, or even report on the charges, while threats of violence were heard in every quarter, and an attack on the U.S. troops intimated, if he persisted in his course.

"Finding that nothing could be done with the juries, they were discharged, with a scathing rebuke from the judge. And then, sitting as a committing magistrate, *he commenced his task alone.* He examined witnesses, made arrests in every quarter, and created a consternation in the camps of the saints greater than any they had ever witnessed before, since Mormondom was born. At last accounts terrified elders and bishops were decamping to save their necks; and developments of the most startling character were being made, implicating the highest Church dignitaries in the many murders and robberies committed upon the Gentiles during the past eight years."

Had Harney been Governor, Cradlebaugh would have been supported in his work, and the absolute proofs adduced by him of Mormon guilt in this massacre and in a number of previous murders, would have conferred gratuitous coffins upon certain citizens, together with occasion to use them. But Cumming was the Federal Governor, and he, under a curious pretense of impartiality, sought to screen the Mormons from the demands of justice. On one occasion he even went so far as to publish his protest against the use of the U.S. troops in aid of Cradlebaugh's proceedings.

Mrs. C.V. Waite closes her interesting detail of the great massacre with the following remark and accompanying summary of the testimony—and the summary is concise, accurate and reliable:

"For the benefit of those who may still be disposed to doubt the guilt of Young and his Mormons in this transaction, the testimony is here collated and circumstances given which go not merely to implicate but to fasten conviction upon them by 'confirmations strong as proofs of Holy Writ:'

"1. The evidence of Mormons themselves, engaged in the affair, as shown by the statements of Judge Cradlebaugh and Deputy U.S. Marshal Rodgers.

"2. The failure of Brigham Young to embody any account of it in his Report as Superintendent of Indian Affairs. Also his failure to make any allusion to it whatever from the pulpit, until several years after the occurrence.

"3. The flight to the mountains of men high in authority in the Mormon Church and State, when this affair was brought to the ordeal of a judicial investigation.

"4. The failure of the *Deseret News,* the Church organ, and the only paper then published in the Territory, to notice the massacre until several months afterward, and then only to deny that Mormons were engaged in it.

"5. The testimony of the children saved from the massacre.

"6. The children and the property of the emigrants found in possession of the Mormons, and that possession traced back to the very day after the massacre.

"7. The statements of Indians in the neighborhood of the scene of the massacre: these statements are shown, not only by Cradlebaugh and Rodgers, but by a number of military officers, and by J. Forney, who was, in 1859, Superintendent of Indian Affairs for the Territory. To all these were such statements freely and frequently made by the Indians.

"8. The testimony of R.P. Campbell, Capt. 2d Dragoons, who was sent in the Spring of 1859 to Santa Clara, to protect travelers on the road to California and to inquire into Indian depredations."

C

CONCERNING A FRIGHTFUL ASSASSINATION THAT WAS NEVER CONSUMMATED

[If ever there was a harmless man, it is Conrad Wiegand, of Gold Hill, Nevada. If ever there was a gentle spirit that thought itself unfired gunpowder and latent ruin, it is Conrad Wiegand. If ever there was an oyster that fancied itself a whale; or a jack-o'lantern, confined to a swamp, that fancied itself a planet with a billion-mile orbit; or a summer zephyr that deemed itself a hurricane, it is Conrad Wiegand. Therefore, what wonder is it that when he says a thing, he thinks the world listens; that when he does a thing the world stands to look; and that when he suffers, there is a convulsion of nature? When I met Conrad, he was "Superintendent of the Gold Hill Assay Office"—and he was not only its Superintendent, but its entire force. And he was a street preacher, too, with a mongrel religion of his own invention, whereby he expected to regenerate the universe. This was years ago. Here latterly he has entered journalism; and his journalism is what it might be expected to be: colossal to ear, but pigmy to the eye. It is extravagant grandiloquence confined to a newspaper about the size of a double letter sheet. He doubtless edits, sets the type, and prints his paper, all alone; but he delights to speak of the concern as if it occupies a block and employs a thousand men.

[Something less than two years ago, Conrad assailed several people mercilessly in his little "People's Tribune," and got himself into trouble. Straightway he airs the affair in the "Territorial Enterprise," in a communication over his own signature, and I propose to reproduce it here, in all its native simplicity and more than human candor. Long as it is, it is well worth reading, for it is the richest specimen of journalistic literature the history of America can furnish, perhaps:]

THE UNABRIDGED MARK TWAIN II

From the Territorial Enterprise, Jan. 20, 1870.

A SEEMING PLOT FOR ASSASSINATION MISCARRIED

TO THE EDITOR OF THE ENTERPRISE: Months ago, when Mr. Sutro incidentally exposed mining management on the Comstock, and among others roused me to protest against its continuance, in great kindness you warned me that any attempt by publications, by public meetings and by legislative action, aimed at the correction of chronic mining evils in Storey County, must entail upon me (*a*) business ruin, (*b*) the burden of all its costs, (*c*) personal violence, and if my purpose were persisted in, then (*d*) assassination, and after all nothing would be effected.

YOUR PROPHECY FULFILLING

In large part at least your prophecies have been fulfilled, for (*a*) assaying, which was well attended to in the Gold Hill Assay Office (of which I am superintendent), in consequence of my publications, has been taken elsewhere, so the President of one of the companies assures me. With no reason *assigned,* other work has been taken away. With but one or two important exceptions, our assay business now consists simply of the *gleanings* of the vicinity. (*b*) Though my own personal donations to the People's Tribune Association have already exceeded $1,500, outside of our own numbers we have received (in money) less than $300 as contributions and subscriptions for the journal. (*c*) On Thursday last, on the main street in Gold Hill, near noon, with neither warning nor cause assigned, by a powerful blow I was felled to the ground, and while down I was kicked by a man who it would seem had been led to *believe* that I had spoken derogatorily of him. By whom he was so induced to believe I am as yet unable to say. On Saturday last I was again assailed and beaten by a man who first informed me why he did so, and who persisted in making his assault even after the erroneous impression under which he *also* was at first laboring had been clearly and repeatedly pointed out. This same man, after failing through intimidation to elicit from me the names of our editorial contributors, against giving which he knew me to be pledged, beat himself weary upon me with a raw hide, I not resisting, and then pantingly threatened me with permanent disfiguring mayhem, if ever again I should introduce his name into print, and who but a few minutes before his attack upon me assured me that the only reason I was "permitted" to reach home alive on Wednesday evening last (at which time the People's Tribune was issued) was, that he deems me only half-witted, and be it remembered the very next morning I *was* knocked down and kicked by a man who seemed to be *prepared* for flight.

[*He sees doom impending:*]

WHEN WILL THE CIRCLE JOIN?

How long before the whole of your prophecy will be fulfilled I cannot say, but under the shadow of so much fulfillment in so short a time, and with such threats from a man who is one of the most prominent exponents of the San Francisco mining-ring staring me and this whole community defiantly in the face and *pointing* to a completion of your augury, do you blame me for feeling that this communication is the last I shall ever write for the Press, especially when a sense alike of personal self-respect, of duty to this money-oppressed and fear-ridden community, and of American fealty to the spirit of true Liberty all command me, and each more loudly than love of life itself, to declare the name of that prominent man to be JOHN B. WINTERS, President of the Yellow Jacket Company, a political aspirant and a military General? The name of his partially duped accomplice and abettor in this last marvelous assault, is none other than PHILIP LYNCH, Editor and Proprietor of the Gold Hill *News*.

Despite the insult and wrong heaped upon me by John B. Winters, on Saturday afternoon, only a glimpse of which I shall be able to afford your readers, so much do I deplore clinching (by publicity) a serious mistake of any one, man or woman, committed under natural and not self-wrought passion, in view of his great apparent excitement at the time and in view of the almost perfect privacy of the assault, I am far from sure that I should not have given him space for repentance before exposing him, were it not that he himself has so far exposed the matter as to make it the common talk of the town that he has horsewhipped me. That fact having been made public, all the facts in connection need to be also, or silence on my part would seem *more* than singular, and with many would be proof either that I was conscious of some unworthy aim in publishing the article, or else that my "non-combatant" principles are but a convenient cloak alike of physical and moral cowardice. I therefore shall try to present a graphic but truthful picture of this whole affair, but shall forbear all comments, presuming that the editors of our own journal, if others do not, will speak freely and fittingly upon this subject in our next number, whether I shall then be dead or living, for my death will not stop, though it may suspend, the publication of the PEOPLE'S TRIBUNE.

[*The "non-combatant" sticks to principle, but takes along a friend or two of a conveniently different stripe:*]

THE TRAP SET

On Saturday morning John B. Winters sent verbal word to the Gold Hill Assay Office that he desired to see me at the Yellow Jacket office. Though such a request struck me as decidedly cool in view of his own recent discourtesies to me there alike as a publisher and as a stockholder in the Yellow Jacket mine, and though it seemed to me more like a summons than the courteous request by one gentleman to another for a favor, hoping that some conference with Sharon looking to the betterment of mining matters in Nevada might arise from it, I felt strongly inclined to overlook what *possibly* was simply an oversight in courtesy. But as then it had only been two days since I had been bruised and beaten under a hasty and false apprehension of facts, my caution was somewhat aroused. Moreover I remembered sensitively his contemptuousness of manner to me at my last interview in his office. I therefore felt it needful, if I went at all, to go accompanied by a friend whom he would not dare to treat with incivility, and whose presence with me might secure exemption from insult. Accordingly I asked a neighbor to accompany me.

THE TRAP ALMOST DETECTED

Although I was not then aware of this fact, it would seem that previous to my request this same neighbor had heard Dr. Zabriskie state publicly in a saloon, that Mr. Winters had told him he had decided either to kill or to horsewhip me, but had not finally decided on which. My neighbor, therefore, felt unwilling to go down with me until he had *first* called on Mr. Winters alone. He therefore paid him a visit. From that interview he assured me that he gathered the impression that he did not believe I would have any difficulty with Mr. Winters, and that he (Winters) would call on me at four o'clock in my own office.

MY OWN PRECAUTIONS

As Sheriff Cummings was in Gold Hill that afternoon, and as I desired to converse with him about the previous assault, I invited him to my office, and he came. Although a half hour had passed beyond four o'clock, Mr. Winters had not called, and we both of us began preparing to go home. Just then, Philip Lynch, Publisher of the Gold Hill *News*, came in and said, blandly and cheerily, as if bringing good news:

"Hello, John B. Winters wants to see you."

I replied, "Indeed! Why he sent me word that he would call on me *here* this afternoon at four o'clock!"

"O, well, it don't do to be too ceremonious just now, he's in my office, and that will do as well—come on in. Winters wants to consult with you alone. He's got something to say to you."

Though slightly uneasy at this change of programme, yet believing that in an *editor's* house I ought to be safe, and anyhow that I would be within hail of the street, I hurriedly, and but partially whispered my dim apprehension to Mr. Cummings, and asked him if he would not keep near enough to hear my voice in case I should call. He consented to do so while waiting for some other parties, and to come in if he heard my voice or thought I had need of protection.

On reaching the editorial part of the *News* office, which viewed from the street is dark, I did not see Mr. Winters, and again my misgivings arose. Had I paused long enough to consider the case, I should have invited Sheriff Cummings in, but as Lynch went down stairs, he said: "*This* way, Wiegand—it's best to be private," or some such remark.

[I do not desire to strain the reader's fancy, hurtfully, and yet it would be a favor to me if he would try to fancy this lamb in battle, or the duelling ground or at the head of a vigilance committee—M.T.:]

I followed, and *without* Mr. Cummings, and without arms, which I never do or will carry, unless as a soldier in war, or unless I should yet come to feel I must fight a duel, or to join and aid in the ranks of a *necessary* Vigilance Committee. But by following I made a fatal mistake. Following was entering a trap, and whatever animal suffers itself to be *caught* should expect the common fate of a caged rat, as I fear events to come will prove.

Traps commonly are not set for *benevolence.*

[*His body-guard is shut out:*]

THE TRAP INSIDE

I followed Lynch down stairs. At their foot a door to the left opened into a small room. From *that* room another door opened into yet *another* room, and once entered I found myself inveigled into what many will ever henceforth regard as a private subterranean Gold Hill den, admirably adapted in proper hands to the purposes of murder, raw or disguised, for from it, with both or even one door closed, when too late, I saw that I *could* not be heard by Sheriff Cummings, and from it, BY VIOLENCE AND BY FORCE, I was prevented from making a peaceable exit, when I thought I saw the studious object of this "consultation" was no other than to compass my killing, *in the presence of Philip Lynch as a witness,* as soon as by insult a proverbially excitable man should be exasperated to the point of assailing Mr. Winters, so that Mr. Lynch, by his conscience and by his well known tenderness of heart toward the rich and potent would be *compelled* to testify that he saw Gen. John B. Winters kill Conrad Wiegand in "self-defence." But I am going too fast.

OUR HOST

Mr. Lynch was present during the most of the time (say a little short of an hour) but three times he left the room. His testimony, therefore, would be available only as to the bulk of what transpired. On entering this carpeted den I was invited to a seat near one corner of the room. Mr. Lynch took a seat near the window. J. B. Winters sat (at first) near the door, and began his remarks essentially as follows:

"I have come here to exact of you a retraction, in black and white, of those damnably false charges which you have preferred against me in that —— —— infamous lying sheet of yours, and you must declare yourself their author, that you published them knowing them to be false, and that your motives were malicious."

"Hold, Mr. Winters. Your language is insulting and your demand an enormity. I trust I was not invited here to be insulted or coerced. I supposed myself here by invitation of Mr. Lynch, at your request."

"Nor did I come here to insult you. I have already told you that I am here for a very different purpose."

"Yet your language *has* been offensive, and even now shows strong excitement. If insult is repeated I shall either leave the room or call in

Sheriff Cummings, whom I just left standing and waiting for me outside the door."

"No, you won't, sir. You may just as well understand it at once as not. *Here* you are my man, and I'll tell you why! Months ago you put your property out of your hands, boasting that you did so to escape losing it on prosecution for libel."

"It is true that I did convert all my immovable property into personal property, such as I could trust safely to others, and chiefly to escape ruin through possible libel suits."

"Very good, sir. Having placed yourself beyond the pale of the law, *may God help your soul if you* DON'T make precisely such a retraction as I have demanded. I've got you now, and by —— before you can get out of this room you've *got* to both write and sign precisely the retraction I have demanded, and before you go, anyhow—you —— —— low-lived——lying —— ——, I'll teach you what *personal* responsibility is *outside* of the law; and, by ——, Sheriff Cummings and all the friends you've got in the world besides, can't save you, you —— ——, etc.! *No*, sir. I'm *alone* now, and I'm *prepared* to be shot down just here and now rather than be villified by you as I have been, and suffer you to escape me after publishing those charges, not only here where I am known and universally respected, but where I am *not* personally known and may be injured."

I confess this speech, with its terrible and but too plainly *implied* threat of killing me if I did not sign the paper he demanded, terrified me, especially as I saw he was working himself up to the highest possible pitch of passion, and instinct told me that any reply other than one of seeming concession to his demands would only be fuel to a raging fire, so I replied:

"Well, if I've *got* to sign——," and then I paused some time. Resuming, I said, "But, Mr. Winters, you are greatly excited. Besides, I see you are laboring under a total misapprehension. It is your duty not to inflame but to calm yourself. I am prepared to show you, if you will only point out the article that you allude to, that *you* regard as 'charges' what no calm and logical mind has any *right* to regard as such. *Show* me the charges, and I will try, at all events; and if it becomes plain that no charges *have* been preferred, then plainly there can be nothing to retract, and no one could rightly *urge* you to demand a retraction. You should beware of making so serious a mistake, for however *honest* a man may be, every one is liable to misapprehend. Besides you *assume* that *I* am the author of some certain article which you have not pointed out. It is *hasty* to do so."

He then pointed to some numbered paragraphs in a TRIBUNE article, headed "What's the Matter with Yellow Jacket?" saying "*That's* what I refer to."

To gain time for general reflection and resolution, I took up the paper and looked it over for awhile, he remaining silent, and as I hoped, cooling. I then resumed, saying, "As I supposed. I do not *admit* having written that article, nor have you any right to *assume* so important a point, and then base important action upon your assumption.

You might deeply regret it afterwards. In my published Address to the People, I notified the world that no information as to the authorship of any article would be given without the consent of the writer. I therefore cannot honorably tell you *who* wrote that article, nor can you exact it."

"If you are *not* the author, then I *do* demand to know who is?"

"I must decline to say."

"Then, by ——, I brand *you* as its author, and shall treat you accordingly."

"Passing that point, the most important misapprehension which I notice is, that you regard them as 'charges' at all, when their context, both at their beginning and end, show they are not. These words introduce them: '*Such an investigation* [just before indicated], *we think MIGHT result in showing some of the following points.*' Then follow eleven specifications, and the succeeding paragraph shows that the suggested investigation 'might EXONERATE those who are generally believed guilty.' You see, therefore, the context *proves* they are not preferred *as* charges, and this you seem to have overlooked."

While making those comments, Mr. Winters frequently interrupted me in such a way as to convince me that he was *resolved* not to consider candidly the thoughts contained in my words. He insisted upon it that they *were* charges, and "By ——," he would make me take them back *as* charges, and he referred the question to Philip Lynch, to whom I then appealed as a literary man, as a logician, and as an editor, calling his attention especially to the introductory paragraph just before quoted.

He replied, "If they are *not* charges, they are certainly *insinuations*," whereupon Mr. Winters renewed his demands for retraction precisely such as he had before named, except that he would allow me to state who *did* write the article if I did not myself, and this time shaking his fist in my face with more cursings and epithets.

When he threatened me with his clenched fist, instinctively I tried to rise from my chair, but Winters then forcibly thrust me down, as he did every other time (at least seven or eight) when under similar imminent danger of bruising by his fist (or for aught I could know worse than that after the first stunning blow) which he could easily and safely to himself have dealt me so long as he kept me down and stood over me.

This fact it was, which more than anything else, convinced me that by plan and plot I was purposely made powerless in Mr. Winters' hands, and that he did not mean to allow me that advantage of being afoot, which he possessed. Moreover, I then became convinced, that Philip Lynch (and for what *reason* I wondered) would do absolutely nothing to protect me in his own house. I realized then the situation thoroughly. I had found it equally vain to protest or argue, and I would make no unmanly appeal for pity, still less apologize. Yet my life had been by the plainest possible implication threatened. I was a weak man. I was unarmed. I was helplessly down, and Winters was afoot and probably armed. Lynch was the only "witness." The statements demanded, if given and not explained, would utterly sink me in my own self-respect, in my family's eyes, and in the eyes of the community. On the other hand, should I give the author's name how could I ever expect that confidence of the People which I should no longer deserve, and how much dearer to me and to my family was *my* life than the life of the real author to *his* friends. Yet life seemed dear and each minute that remained seemed precious if not solemn. I sincerely trust that neither you nor any of your readers, and especially none with families, may ever be placed in such seeming *direct* proximity to death while obliged to decide the one question I was compelled to, viz.: What should I do—I, a man of family, and *not* as Mr. Winters is, "alone."

[*The reader is requested not to skip the following—M. T.:*]

STRATEGY AND MANNERISM

To gain time for further reflection, and hoping that by a *seeming* acquiescence I might regain my personal liberty, at least till I could give an alarm, or take advantage of some momentary inadvertence of Winters, and then without a *cowardly* flight escape, I resolved to write a certain kind of retraction, but previously had inwardly decided

First.—That I would studiously avoid every action which might be *construed* into the drawing of a weapon, even by a self-infuriated man, no matter what amount of insult might be heaped upon me, for it seemed to me that this great excess of compound profanity, foulness and epithet must be more than a mere indulgence, and therefore must have some object. "Surely in vain the net is spread in the sight of any bird." Therefore, as before without thought, I thereafter by intent kept my hands away from my pockets, and generally in sight upon my knees.

Second.—I resolved to make no motion with my arms or hands which could possibly be construed into aggression.

Third.—I resolved completely to govern my outward manner and suppress indignation. To do this, I must govern my spirit. To do that, by force of imagination I was obliged like actors on the boards to resolve myself into an unnatural mental state and see all things through the eyes of an assumed *character*.

Fourth.—I resolved to try on Winters, silently, and unconsciously to himself a mesmeric power which I possess over certain kinds of people, and which at times I have found to work even in the dark over the lower animals.

Does any one smile at these last counts? God save you from ever being *obliged* to beat in a game of chess, whose stake is your life, you having but four poor pawns and pieces and your adversary with his full force unshorn. But if you are, provided you have any strength with breadth of will, do not despair. Though mesmeric power may not *save* you, it may help you; *try* it at all events. In this instance I was conscious of power coming into me, and by a law of nature, I know Winters was correspondingly weakened. If I could have gained more time I am sure he would not even have struck me.

It takes time to both form such resolutions and to recite them. That time, however, I gained while thinking of my retraction, which I first wrote in pencil, altering it from time to time till I got it to suit me, my aim being to make it look like a concession to demands, while in fact it should tersely speak the truth into Mr. Winters' mind. When it was finished, I copied it in ink, and if correctly copied from my first draft it should read as follows. In copying I do not think I made any material change.

COPY

To Philip Lynch, Editor of the Gold Hill News: I learn that Gen. John B. Winters believes the following (pasted on) clipping from the PEOPLE'S TRIBUNE of January to contain distinct charges of mine against him personally and that as such he desires me to retract them unqualifiedly.

In compliance with his request, permit me to say that, although Mr. Winters and I see this matter differently, in view of his strong feelings in the premises, I hereby declare that I do not know those "charges" (if such they are) to be true, and I hope that a critical examination would altogether disprove them. CONRAD WIEGAND.
Gold Hill, January 15, 1870.

I then read what I had written and handed it to Mr. Lynch, whereupon Mr. Winters said:

"That's not satisfactory, and it won't do;" and then addressing himself to Mr. Lynch, he further said: "How does it strike *you?*"

"Well, I confess I don't see that it *retracts* anything."

"Nor do I," said Winters; "in fact, I regard it as adding insult to injury. Mr. Wiegand you've got to do better than that. *You* are not the man who can pull wool over *my* eyes."

"That, sir, is the only retraction I can write."

"No, it isn't, sir, and if you so much as *say* so again you do it at your peril, for I'll thrash you to within an inch of your life, and, by ——, sir, I don't pledge myself to spare you even that inch either. I want you to understand I have asked you for a very different paper, and that paper you've got to sign."

"Mr. Winters, I assure you that I *do* not wish to irritate you, but, at the same time, it is utterly *impossible* for me to write any other paper than that which I have written. If you are resolved to *compel* me to *sign* something, Philip Lynch's hand must write at your dictation, and if, when written, I *can* sign it I will do so, but such a document as you say you *must* have from me, I never can sign. I mean what I say."

"Well, sir, what's to be done must be done quickly, for I've been here long enough already. I'll put the thing in another shape (and then pointing to the paper); don't you know those charges to be false?"

"I do not."

"Do you know them to be true?"

"Of my own personal knowledge I do not."

"Why then did you print them?"

"Because rightly considered in their connection they are *not* charges, but pertinent and useful *suggestions* in answer to the queries of a correspondent who stated facts which are inexplicable."

"Don't you know that *I* know they are false?"

"If you *do*, the proper course is simply to deny them and court an investigation."

"And do YOU claim the right to make ME come out and deny anything you may choose to write and print?"

To that question I think I made no reply, and then he further said: "Come, now, we've talked about the matter long enough. I want your final answer—did you write that article or not?"

"I cannot in honor tell you *who* wrote it."

"Did you not see it before it was printed?"

"Most certainly, sir."

"And did you deem it a fit thing to publish?"

"Most assuredly, sir, or I would never have consented to its appearance. Of its *authorship* I can say nothing whatever, but for its *publication* I assume full, sole and personal responsibility."

"And do you then retract it or not?"

"Mr. Winters, if my refusal to sign such a paper as you have demanded *must* entail me all that your language in this room fairly implies, then I ask a few minutes for prayer."

"Prayer! —— —— you, this is not your *hour* for praˑˑer—your time to pray was when you were writing those —— lying charges. Will you sign or not?"

"You already have my answer."

"What! do you still refuse?"

"I do, sir."

"Take *that,* then," and to my amazement and inexpressible relief he drew only a rawhide instead of what I expected—a bludgeon or pistol. With it, as he spoke, he struck at my left ear downwards, as if to tear it off, and afterwards on the side of the head. As he moved away to get a better chance for a more effective shot, for the first time I gained a chance under peril to rise, and I did so pitying him from the very bottom of my soul. to think that one so naturally capable of true dignity, power and nobility could, by the temptations of this State, and by unfortunate associations and aspirations, be so deeply debased as to find in such brutality anything which he could call satisfaction—but the great hope for us all is in progress and growth, and John B. Winters, I trust, will yet be able to comprehend my feelings.

He continued to beat me with all his great force, until absolutely weary, exhausted and panting for breath. I still adhered to my purpose of non-aggressive defence, and made no other use of my arms than to defend my head and face from further disfigurement. The mere pain arising from the blows he inflicted upon my person was of course transient, and my clothing to some extent deadened its severity, as it now hides all remaining traces.

When I supposed he was through, taking the butt end of his weapon and shaking it in my face, he warned me, if I correctly understood him, of more yet to come, and furthermore said, if ever I again dared to introduce his name to print, in either my own or any other public journal, he would cut off my left ear (and I do not *think* he was jesting) and send me home to my family a visibly mutilated man, to be a standing warning to all low-lived puppies who seek to blackmail gentlemen and to injure their good names. And when he *did* so operate, he informed me that his implement would not be a whip but a knife.

When he had said this, unaccompanied by Mr. Lynch, as I remember it, he left the room, for I sat down by Mr. Lynch, exclaiming: "The man is mad—he is *utterly* mad—this step is his ruin—it is a mistake—it would be ungenerous in me, despite of all the ill usage I have here received, to expose him, at least until he has had an opportunity to reflect upon the matter. I shall be in no haste."

"Winters *is* very mad just now," replied Mr. Lynch, "but when he is himself he is one of the finest men I ever met. In fact, he told me the reason he did not meet you upstairs was to spare you the humiliation of a beating in the sight of others."

I submit that that unguarded remark of Philip Lynch convicts him of having been privy in advance to Mr. Winters' intentions whatever they may have been, or at least to his meaning to make an assault upon me, but I leave to others to determine how much censure an *editor* deserves for inveigling a weak, non-combatant man, also a publisher, to a pen of his own to be horsewhipped, if no worse, for the simple printing of what is verbally in the mouth of nine out of ten men, and women too, upon the street.

While writing this account two theories have occurred to me as *possibly* true respecting this most remarkable assault:

First.—The aim *may* have been simply to extort from me such admissions as in the hands of money and influence would have sent me to the Penitentiary for libel. This, however, seems unlikely, because any statements elicited by fear or force could not be evidence in law or could be so explained as to have no force. The statements wanted so badly must have been desired for some other purpose.

Second.—The other theory has so dark and wilfully murderous a look that I shrink from writing it, yet as in all probability my death at the earliest practicable moment has already been decreed, I feel I should do all I can before my hour arrives, at least to show others how to break up that aristocratic rule and combination which has robbed all Nevada of true freedom, if not of manhood itself. Although I do not prefer this hypothesis as a *"charge,"* I feel that as an American citizen I still have a right both to think and to speak my thoughts even in the land of Sharon and Winters, and as much so respecting the theory of a brutal assault (especially when I have been its subject) as respecting any other apparent enormity. I give the matter simply as a suggestion which may explain to the proper authorities and to the people whom they should represent, a well ascertained but notwithstanding a darkly mysterious fact. The scheme of the assault *may* have been

First—To terrify me by making me conscious of my own helplessness after making actual though not legal threats against my life.

Second—To imply that I could save my life only by writing or signing certain specific statements which if not subsequently explained would eternally have branded me as infamous and would have consigned my family to shame and want, and to the deadful compassion and patronage of the rich.

Third—To blow my brains out *the moment I had signed,* thereby preventing me from making any subsequent explanation such as *could* remove the infamy.

Fourth—Philip Lynch to be compelled to testify that I was killed by John B. Winters in self-defence, for the conviction of Winters would bring *him* in as an accomplice. If that *was* the programme in John B. Winters' mind nothing saved my life but my persistent *refusal* to sign, when that refusal seemed clearly to me to be the choice of death.

The remarkable assertion made to me by Mr. Winters, that pity only spared my life on Wednesday evening last, almost compels me to believe that at first he *could* not have intended me to leave that room alive; and why I was allowed to, unless through mesmeric *or some other invisible influence,* I cannot divine. The more I reflect upon this matter, the more probable as true does this horrible interpretation become.

The narration of these things I might have spared both to Mr. Winters and to the public had he himself observed silence, but as he has both verbally spoken and suffered a thoroughly garbled statement of facts to appear in the Gold Hill *News* I feel it due to myself no less than to this community, and to the entire independent press of America and Great Britain, to give a true account of what even the Gold Hill *News* has pronounced a disgraceful affair, and which it deeply regrets because of some alleged telegraphic mistake in the account of it. [Who received the erroneous telegrams?]

Though he may not deem it prudent to take my life just now, the publication of this article I feel sure must compel Gen. Winters (with his peculiar views about *his* right to exemption from criticism by *me*) to resolve on my violent death, though it may take years to compass it. Notwithstanding *I* bear *him* no ill will; and if W. C. Ralston and William Sharon, and other members of the San Francisco mining and milling Ring feel that he above all other men in this State and California is the most fitting man to supervise and control Yellow Jacket matters, until I am able to vote more than half their stock I presume he will be retained to grace his present post.

Meantime, I cordially invite all who know of any sort of important villainy which only *can* be cured by exposure (and who would expose it if they felt sure they would not be betrayed under bullying threats), to communicate with the People's Tribune; for until I *am* murdered, so long as I can raise the means to publish, I propose to continue my *efforts* at least to revive the liberties of the State, to curb oppression, and to benefit man's world and God's earth.　　CONRAD WIEGAND.

[It does seem a pity that the Sheriff was shut out, since the good sense of a general of militia and of a prominent editor failed to teach them that the merited castigation of this weak, half-witted child was a thing that ought to have been done in the street, where the poor thing could have a chance to run. When a journalist maligns a citizen, or attacks his good name on hearsay evidence, he deserves to be thrashed for it, even if he *is* a "non-combatant" weakling; but a generous adversary would at least allow such a lamb the use of his legs at such a time.—M.T.]

"How To Tell a Story" *was written for the October 3, 1895 issue of* Youth's Companion, *and was first collected in* How To Tell a Story and Other Essays, *published by Harper & Brothers in 1897. It contains a hairraising ghost story, "The Golden Arm," that Twain first heard as a boy on his uncle's farm. He used the tale on many of his lecture tours, and it was one of the most effective parts of the program. The story always terrified his daughter Susy, and she disliked it intensely.*

How To Tell a Story

THE HUMOROUS STORY AN AMERICAN DEVELOPMENT.—ITS DIFFERENCE FROM COMIC AND WITTY STORIES.

I do not claim that I can tell a story as it ought to be told. I only claim to know how a story ought to be told, for I have been almost daily in the company of the most expert story-tellers for many years.

There are several kinds of stories, but only one difficult kind—the humorous. I will talk mainly about that one. The humorous story is American, the comic story is English, the witty story is French. The humorous story depends for its effect upon the *manner* of the telling; the comic story and the witty story upon the *matter*.

The humorous story may be spun out to great length, and may wander around as much as it pleases, and arrive nowhere in particular; but the comic and witty stories must be brief and end with a point. The humorous story bubbles gently along, the others burst.

The humorous story is strictly a work of art—high and delicate art—and only an artist can tell it; but no art is necessary in telling the comic and the witty story; anybody can do it. The art of telling a humorous story—understand, I mean by word of mouth, not print—was created in America, and has remained at home.

The humorous story is told gravely; the teller does his best to conceal the fact that he even dimly suspects that there is anything funny about it; but the teller of the comic story tells you beforehand that it is one of the funniest things he has ever heard, then tells it with eager delight, and is the first person to laugh when he gets through. And sometimes, if he has had good success, he is so glad and happy that he will repeat the "nub" of it and glance around from face to face, collecting applause, and then repeat it again. It is a pathetic thing to see.

Very often, of course, the rambling and disjointed humorous story finishes with a nub, point, snapper, or whatever you like to call it. Then the listener must be alert, for in many cases the teller will divert attention from that nub by dropping it in a carefully casual and indifferent way, with the pretence that he does not know it is a nub.

Artemus Ward used that trick a good deal; then when the belated audience presently caught the joke he would look up with innocent surprise, as if wondering what they had found to laugh at. Dan Setchell used it before him, Nye and Riley and others use it to-day.

But the teller of the comic story does not slur the nub; he shouts it at you—every time. And when he prints it, in England, France, Germany, and Italy, he italicizes it, puts some whooping exclamation-points after it, and sometimes explains it in a parenthesis. All of which is very depressing, and makes one want to renounce joking and lead a better life.

Let me set down an instance of the comic method, using an anecdote which has been popular all over the world for twelve or fifteen hundred years. The teller tells it in this way:

THE WOUNDED SOLDIER

In the course of a certain battle a soldier whose leg had been shot off appealed to another soldier who was hurrying by to carry him to the rear, informing him at the same time of the loss which he had sustained; whereupon the generous son of Mars, shouldering the unfortunate, proceeded to carry out his desire. The bullets and cannon-balls were flying in all directions, and presently one of the latter took the wounded man's head off— without, however, his deliverer being aware of it. In no long time he was hailed by an officer, who said:

"Where are you going with that carcass?"

"To the rear, sir—he's lost his leg!"

"His leg, forsooth?" responded the astonished officer: "you mean his head, you booby."

Whereupon the soldier dispossessed himself of his burden, and stood looking down upon it in great perplexity. At length he said:

"It is true, sir, just as you have said." Then after a pause he added, *"But he* TOLD *me* IT WAS HIS LEG!!!!!"

Here the narrator bursts into explosion after explosion of thunderous horse-laughter, repeating that nub from time to time through his gaspings and shriekings and suffocatings.

It takes only a minute and a half to tell that in its comic-story form; and isn't worth the telling, after all. Put into the humorous-story form it takes ten minutes, and is about the funniest thing I have ever listened to—as James Whitcomb Riley tells it.

He tells it in the character of a dull-witted old farmer who has just heard it for the first time, thinks it is unspeakably funny, and is trying to repeat it to a neighbor. But he can't remember it; so he gets all mixed up and wanders helplessly round and round, putting in tedious details that don't belong in the tale and only retard it; taking them out conscientiously and putting in others that are just as useless; making minor mistakes now and then and stopping to correct them and explain how he came to make them; remembering things which he forgot to put in in their proper place and going back to put them in there; stopping his narrative a good while in order to try to recall the name of the soldier that was hurt, and finally remembering that the soldier's name was not mentioned, and remarking placidly that the name is of no real importance, anyway—better, of course, if one knew it, but not essential, after all—and so on, and so on, and so on.

The teller is innocent and happy and pleased with himself, and has to stop every little while to hold himself in and keep from laughing outright; and does hold in, but his body quakes in a jelly-like way with interior chuckles; and at the end of the ten minutes the audience have laughed until they are exhausted, and the tears are running down their faces.

The simplicity and innocence and sincerity and unconsciousness of the old farmer are perfectly simulated, and the result is a performance which is thoroughly charming and delicious. This is art—and fine and beautiful, and only a master can compass it; but a machine could tell the other story.

To string incongruities and absurdities together in a wandering and sometimes purposeless way, and seem innocently unaware that they are absurdities, is the basis of the American art, if my position is correct. Another feature is the slurring of the point. A third is the dropping of a studied remark apparently without knowing it, as if one were thinking aloud. The fourth and last is the pause.

Artemus Ward dealt in numbers three and four a good deal. He would begin to tell with great animation something which he seemed to think was wonderful; then lose confidence, and after an apparently absent-minded pause add an incongruous remark in a soliloquizing way; and that was the remark intended to explode the mine—and it did.

For instance, he would say eagerly, excitedly, "I once knew a man in New Zealand who hadn't a tooth in his head"—here his animation would die out; a silent, reflective pause would follow, then he would say dreamily, and as if to himself, "and yet that man could beat a drum better than any man I ever saw." The pause is an exceedingly important feature in any kind of story, and a frequently recurring feature, too. It is a dainty thing, and delicate, and also uncertain and treacherous; for it must be exactly the right length—no more and no less—or it fails of its purpose and makes trouble. If the pause is too short the impressive point is passed, and the audience have had time to divine that a surprise is intended—and then you can't surprise them, of course.

One the platform I used to tell a negro ghost story that had a pause in front of the snapper on the end, and that pause was the most important thing in the whole story. If I got it the right length precisely, I could spring the finishing ejaculation with effect enough to make some impressive girl deliver a startled little yelp and jump out of her seat—and that was what I was after. This story was called "The Golden Arm," and was told in this fashion. You can practise with it yourself—and mind you look out for the pause and get it right.

THE GOLDEN ARM

Once 'pon a time dey wuz a monsus mean man, en he live 'way out in de prairie all 'lone by hisself, 'cept'n he had a wife. En bimeby she died, en he tuck en toted her way out dah in de prairie en buried her. Well, she had a golden arm—all solid gold, fum de shoulder down. He wuz pow'ful mean—pow'ful; en dat night he couldn't sleep, caze he want dat golden arm so bad.

When it come midnight he couldn't stan' it no mo'; so he git up, he did, en tuck his lantern en shoved out thoo de storm en dug her up en got de golden arm; en he bent his head down 'gin de win', en plowed en plowed en plowed thoo de snow. Den all on a sudden he stop (make a considerable pause here, and look startled, and take a listening attitude) en say: "My *lan'*, what's dat!"

En he listen—en listen—en de win' say (set your teeth together and imitate the wailing and wheezing singsong of the wind), "Bzzz-z-zzz"—en den, way back yonder whah de grave is, he hear a *voice!*—he hear a voice all mix' up in de win'—can't hardly tell 'em 'part—"Bzzz-zzz—W-h-o—g-o-t—m-y—g-o-l-d-

904

e-n *arm?*—zzz—zzz—W-h-o g-o-t m-y g-o-l-d-e-n *arm?* (You must begin to shiver violently now.)

En he begin to shiver en shake, en say, "Oh, my! *Oh,* my lan'!" en de win' blow de lantern out, en de snow en sleet blow in his face en mos' choke him, en he start a-plowin' knee-deep towards home mos' dead, he so sk'yerd—en pooty soon he hear de voice agin, en (pause) it'us comin' *after* him! "Buzz—zzz—zzz—W-h-o—g-o-t—m-y—g-o-l-d-e-n—*arm?*"

When he git to de pasture he hear it agin—closter now, en a-*comin'!*—a-comin' back dah in de dark en de storm—(repeat the wind and the voice). When he git to de house he rush upstairs en jump in de bed en kiver up, head and years, en lay dah shiverin' en shakin'—en den way out dah he hear it *agin!*—en a *comin'!* En bimeby he hear (pause—awed, listening attitude)—pat—pat—pat—*hit's a-comin' up-stairs!* Den he hear de latch, en he *know* it's in de room!

Den pooty soon he know it's a-*stannin' by de bed!* (Pause.) Den—he know it's a-*bendin' down over him*—he cain't skasely git his breath! Den—den—he seem to feel someth'n *c-o-l-d,* right down 'most agin his head! (Pause.)

Den de voice say, *right at his year*—"W-h-o—g-o-t—m-y—g-o-l-d-e-n *arm?*" (You must wail it out very plaintively and accusingly; then you stare steadily and impressively into the face of the farthest-gone auditor—a girl, preferably—and let that awe-inspiring pause begin to build itself in the deep hush. When it has reached exactly the right length, jump suddenly at that girl and yell, *"You've* got it!"

If you've got the *pause* right, she'll fetch a dear little yelp and spring right out of her shoes. But you *must* get the pause right; and you will find it the most troublesome and aggravating and uncertain thing you ever undertook.)

In August of 1869, Twain used a loan from his future father-in-law to buy a share in the Buffalo Express. Following his marriage to Olivia Langdon, he tried to settle down to the life of a newspaper proprietor, and he spent the next few years running the paper, contributing a series of sketches and commentaries, usually for its Saturday edition. "A Curious Dream" appeared in the Express on April 30 and May 7, 1870. In 1872, it was included in a collection published by George Routledge & Sons in London called A Curious Dream and Other Stories, and also appeared in an unauthorized collection called A Book for an Hour which was brought out in New York in 1873 by B.J. Such. In 1875, Twain reprinted the tale in Mark Twain's Sketches New and Old.

A Curious Dream
CONTAINING A MORAL

Night before last I had a singular dream. I seemed to be sitting on a doorstep (in no particular city perhaps), ruminating, and the time of night appeared to be about twelve or one o'clock. The weather was balmy and delicious. There was no human sound in the air, not even a footstep. There was no sound of any kind to emphasize the dead stillness, except the occasional hollow barking of a dog in the distance and the fainter answer of a further dog. Presently up the street I heard a bony clack-clacking, and guessed it was the castanets of a serenading party. In a minute more a tall skeleton, hooded, and half-clad in a tat-tered and mouldy shroud, whose shreds were flapping about the ribby lattice-work of its person swung by me with a stately stride, and disappeared in the grey gloom of the starlight. It had a broken and worm-eaten coffin on its shoulder and a bundle of something in its hand. I knew what the clack-clacking was then; it was this party's joints working together, and his elbows knocking against his sides as he walked. I may say I was sur-prised. Before I could collect my thoughts and enter upon any speculations as to what this apparition might portend, I heard another one coming—for I recognized his clack-clack. He had two-thirds of a coffin on his shoulder, and some foot- and head-boards under his arm. I mightily wanted to peer under his hood and speak to him, but when he turned and smiled upon me with his cavernous sockets and his projecting grin as he went by, I thought I would not detain him. He was hardly gone when I heard the clacking again, and another one issued from the shadowy half-light. This one was bending under a heavy gravestone, and dragging a shabby coffin after him by a string. When he got to me he gave me a steady look for a moment or two, and then rounded to and backed up to me, saying:

"Ease this down for a fellow, will you?"

I eased the gravestone down till it rested on the ground, and in doing so noticed that it bore the name of "John Baxter Copmanhurst," with "May 1839," as the date of his death. Deceased sat wearily down by me, and wiped his os frontis with his major maxillary—chiefly from former habit I judged, for I could not see that he brought away any perspiration.

"It is too bad, too bad," said he, drawing the remnant of the shroud about him and leaning his jaw pensively on his hand. Then he put his left foot up on his knee and fell to scratching his ankle bone absently with a rusty nail which he got out of his coffin.

"What is too bad, friend?"

"Oh, everything, everything. I almost wish I never had died."

"You surprise me. Why do you say this? Has anything gone wrong? What is the matter?"

"Matter! Look at this shroud—rags. Look at this gravestone, all battered up. Look at that disgraceful old coffin. All a man's property going to ruin and destruction before his eyes, and ask him if anything is wrong? Fire and brimstone!"

"Calm yourself, calm yourself," I said. "It *is* too bad—it is certainly too bad, but then I had not supposed that you would much mind such matters, situated as you are."

"Well, my dear sir, I *do* mind them. My pride is hurt, and my comfort is impaired—destroyed, I might say. I will state my case—I will put it to you in such a way that you can comprehend it, if you will let me," said the poor skeleton, tilting the hood of his shroud back, as if he were clearing for action, and thus unconsciously giving himself a jaunty and festive air very much at variance with the grave character of his position in life—so to speak—and in prominent contrast with his distressful mood.

"Proceed," said I.

"I reside in the shameful old graveyard a block or two above you here, in this street—there, now, I just expected that cartilage would let go!—third rib from the bottom, friend, hitch the end of it to my spine with a string, if you have got such a thing about you, though a bit of silver wire is a deal pleasanter, and more durable and becoming, if one keeps it polished—to think of shredding out and going to pieces in this way, just on account of the indifference and neglect of one's posterity!"—and the poor ghost grated his teeth in a way that gave me a wrench and a shiver—for the effect is mightily increased by the absence of muffling flesh and cuticle. "I reside in that old graveyard, and have for these thirty years; and I tell you things are changed since I first laid this old tired frame there, and turned over, and stretched out for a long sleep, with a delicious sense upon me of being *done* with bother, and grief, and anxiety, and doubt, and fear, for ever and ever, and listening with comfortable and increasing satisfaction to the sexton's work, from the startling clatter of his first spadeful on my coffin till it dulled away to the faint patting that shaped the roof of my new home—delicious! My! I wish you could try it to-night!" and out of my reverie deceased fetched me with a rattling slap with a bony hand.

"Yes, sir, thirty years ago I laid me down there, and was happy. For it was out in the country, then—out in the breezy, flowery, grand old woods, and the lazy winds gossiped with the leaves, and the squirrels capered over us and around us, and the creeping things visited us, and the birds filled the tranquil solitude with music. Ah, it was worth ten years of a man's life to be dead then! Everything was pleasant. I was in a good neighborhood, for all the dead people that lived near me belonged to the best families in the city. Our posterity appeared to think the world of us. They kept our graves in the very best condition; the fences were always in faultless repair, head-boards were kept painted or whitewashed, and were replaced with new ones as soon as they began to look rusty or decayed; monuments were kept upright, railings intact and bright, the rosebushes and shrubbery trimmed, trained, and free from blemish, the walks clean and smooth and gravelled. But that day is gone by. Our descendants have forgotten us. My grandson lives in a stately house built with money made by these old hands of mine, and I sleep in a neglected grave with invading vermin that gnaw my shroud to build them nests withal! I and friends that lie with me founded and secured the prosperity of this fine city, and the stately bantling of our loves leaves us to rot in a dilapidated cemetery which neighbors curse and strangers scoff at. See the difference between the old time and this—for instance: Our graves are all caved in, now; our headboards have rotted away and tumbled down; our railings reel this way and that with one foot in the air, after a fashion of unseemly levity; our monuments lean wearily, and our gravestones bow their heads discouraged; there be no adornments any more—no roses, nor shrubs, nor gravelled walks, nor anything that is a comfort to the eye; and even the paintless old board fence that did make a show of holding us sacred from companionship with beasts and the defilement of heedless feet, has tottered till it overhangs the

909

street, and only advertises the presence of our dismal resting-place and invites yet more derision to it. And now we cannot hide our poverty and tatters in the friendly woods, for the city has stretched its withering arms abroad and taken us in, and all that remains of the cheer of our old home is the cluster of lugubrious forest trees that stand, bored and weary of a city life, with their feet in our coffins, looking into the hazy distance and wishing they were there. I tell you it is disgraceful!

"You begin to comprehend—you begin to see how it is. While our descendants are living sumptuously on our money, right around us in the city, we have to fight hard to keep skull and bones together. Bless you, there isn't a grave in our cemetery that doesn't leak—not one. Every time it rains in the night we have to climb out and roost in the trees—and sometimes we are wakened suddenly by the chilly water trickling down the back of our necks. Then I tell you there is a general heaving up of old graves and kicking over of old monuments, and scampering of old skeletons for the trees! Bless me, if you had gone along there some such nights after twelve you might have seen as many as fifteen of us roosting on one limb, with our joints rattling drearily and the wind wheezing through our ribs! Many a time we have perched there for three or four dreary hours, and then come down, stiff and chilled through and drowsy, and borrowed each other's skulls to bale out our graves with—if you will glance up in my mouth, now as I tilt my head back, you can see that my head-piece is half full of old dry sediment—how top-heavy and stupid it makes me sometimes! Yes, sir, many a time if you had happened to come along just before the dawn you'd have caught us baling out the graves and hanging our shrouds on the fence to dry. Why, I had an elegant shroud stolen from there one morning—think a party by the name of Smith took it, that resides in a plebeian graveyard over yonder—I think so because the first time I ever saw him he hadn't anything on but a check-shirt, and the last time I saw him, which was at a social gathering in the new cemetery, he was the best dressed corpse in the company—and it is a significant fact that he left when he saw me; and presently an old woman from here missed her coffin— she generally took it with her when she went anywhere, because she was liable to take cold and bring on the spasmodic rheumatism that originally killed her if she exposed herself to the night air much. She was named Hotchkiss—Anna Matilda Hotchkiss—you might know her? She has two upper front teeth, is tall, but a good deal inclined to stoop, one rib on the left side gone, has one shred of rusty hair hanging from the left side of her head, and one little tuft just above and a little forward of her right ear, has her under jaw wired on one side where it had worked loose, small bone of left forearm gone—lost in a fight— has a kind of swagger in her gait and a 'gallus' way of going with her arms akimbo and her nostrils in the air—has been pretty free and easy, and is all damaged and battered up till she looks like a queensware crate in ruins—maybe you have met her?''

"God forbid!" I involuntarily ejaculated, for somehow I was not looking for that form of question, and it caught me a little off my guard. But I hastened to make amends for my rudeness, and say, "I simply meant I had not had the honor—for I would not deliberately speak discourteously of a friend of yours. You were saying that you were robbed—and it was a shame, too— but it appears by what is left of the shroud you have on that it was a costly one in its day. How did—"

A most ghastly expression began to develop among the decayed features and shrivelled integuments of my guest's face, and I was beginning to grow uneasy and distressed, when he told me he was only working up a deep, sly smile, with a wink in it, to suggest that about the time he acquired his present garment a ghost in a neighboring cemetery missed one. This reassured me, but I begged him to confine himself to speech thenceforth, because his facial expression was uncertain. Even with the most elaborate care it was liable to miss fire. Smiling should especially be avoided. What *he* might honestly consider a shining success was likely to strike me in a very different light. I said I liked to see a skeleton cheerful, even decorously playful, but I did not think smiling was a skeleton's best hold.

"Yes, friend," said the poor skeleton, "the facts are just as I have given them to you. Two of these old graveyards—the one that I resided in and one further along—have been deliberately neglected by our descendants of to-day until there is no occupying them any longer. Aside from the osteological discomfort of it—and that is no light matter this rainy weather—the present state of things is ruinous to property. We have got to move or be content to see our effects wasted away and utterly destroyed. Now, you will hardly believe it, but it is true, nevertheless, that there isn't a single coffin in good repair among all my acquaintance—now that is an absolute fact. I do not refer to low people who come in a pine box mounted on an express wagon, but I am talking about your high-toned, silver mounted burial-case, your monumental sort, that travel under black plumes at the head of a procession and have choice of cemetery lots—I mean folks like the Jarvises, and the Bledsoes and Burlings, and such. They are all about ruined. The most substantial people in our set, they were. And now look at them—utterly used up and poverty-stricken. One of the Bledsoes actually traded his monument to a late bar-keeper for some fresh shavings to put under his head. I tell you it speaks volumes, for there is nothing a corpse takes so much pride in as his monument. He loves to read the inscription. He comes after awhile to believe what it says himself, and then you may see him sitting on the fence night after night enjoying it. Epitaphs are cheap, and they do a poor chap a world of good after he is dead, especially if he had hard luck while he was alive. I wish they were used more. Now, I don't complain, but confidentially I *do* think it was a little shabby in my descendants to give me nothing but this old slab of a gravestone—and all the more that there isn't a compliment on it. It used to have

'GONE TO HIS JUST REWARD'

on it, and I was proud when I first saw it, but by-and-by I noticed that whenever an old friend of mine came along he would hook his chin on the railing and pull a long face and read along down till he came to that, and then he would chuckle to himself and walk off, looking satisfied and comfortable. So I scratched it off to get rid of those fools. But a dead man always takes a deal of pride in his monument. Yonder goes half-a-dozen of the Jarvises, now, with the family monument along. And Smithers and some hired spectres went by with his a while ago. Hello, Higgins, good-bye, old friend! That's Meredith Higgins—died in '44—belongs to our set in the cemetery—fine old family—great-grandmother was an Injun—I am on the most familiar terms with him—he didn't hear me was the reason he didn't answer me. And I am sorry, too, because I would have liked to introduce you. You would admire him. He is the most disjointed, sway-backed, and generally distorted old skeleton you ever saw, but he is full of fun. When he laughs it sounds like rasping two stones together, and he always starts it off with a cheery screech like raking a nail across a window-pane. Hey, Jones! That is old Columbus Jones—shroud cost four hundred dollars—entire trousseau, including monument, twenty-seven hundred. This was in the spring of '26. It was enormous style for those days. Dead people came all the way from the Alleghanies to see his things—the party that occupied the grave next to mine remembers it well. Now do you see that individual going along with a piece of a head-board under his arm, one leg-bone below his knee gone, and not a thing in the world on? That is Barstow Dalhousie, and next to Columbus Jones he was the most sumptuously outfitted person that ever entered our cemetery. We are all leaving. We cannot tolerate the treatment we are receiving at the hands of our descendants. They open new cemeteries, but they leave us to our ignominy. They mend the streets, but they never mend anything that is about us or belongs to us. Look at that coffin of mine—yet I tell you in its day it was a piece of furniture that would have attracted attention in any drawing-room in this city. You may have it if you want it—I can't afford to repair it. Put a new bottom in her, and part of a new top, and a bit of fresh lining along the left side, and you'll find her about as comfortable as any receptacle of her species you ever tried. No thanks—no, don't mention it—you have been civil to me, and I would give you all the property I have got before I would seem ungrateful. Now this winding-sheet is a kind of a sweet thing in its way, if you would like to—No? Well, just as you say, but I wished to be fair and liberal—there's nothing mean about *me*. Good-by, friend, I must be going. I may have a good way to go to-night—don't know. I only know one thing for certain, and that is, that I am on the emigrant trail, now, and I'll never sleep in that crazy old cemetery again. I will travel till I find respectable quarters, if I have to hoof it to New Jersey. All the boys are going. It was decided in public conclave, last night, to emigrate, and by the time the sun rises there won't be a bone left in our old habitations. Such cemeteries may suit my surviving friends, but they do not suit the remains that have the honor to make these remarks. My opinion is the general opinion. If you doubt it, go and see how the departing ghosts upset things before they started. They were almost riotous in their demonstrations of distaste. Hello, here are some of the Bledsoes, and if you will give me a lift with this tombstone I guess I will join company and jog along with them—mighty respectable old family, the Bledsoes, and used to always come out in six-horse hearses, and all that sort of thing fifty years ago when I walked these streets in daylight. Good-by, friend."

And with his gravestone on his shoulder he joined the grisly procession, dragging his damaged coffin after him, for notwithstanding he pressed it upon me so earnestly, I utterly refused his hospitality. I suppose that for as much as two hours these sad outcasts went clacking by, laden with their dismal effects, and all that time I sat pitying them. One or two of the youngest and least dilapidated among them inquired about midnight trains on the railways, but the rest seemed unacquainted with that mode of travel, and merely asked about common public roads to various towns and cities, some of which are not on the map now, and vanished from it and from the earth as much as thirty years ago, and some few of them never *had* existed anywhere but on maps, and private ones in real estate agencies at that. And they asked about the condition of the cemeteries in these towns and cities, and about the reputation the citizens bore as to reverence for the dead.

This whole matter interested me deeply, and likewise compelled my sympathy for these homeless ones. And it all seeming real, and I not knowing it was a dream, I mentioned to one shrouded wanderer an idea that had entered my head to publish an account of this curious and very sorrowful exodus, but said also that I could not describe it truthfully, and just as it occurred, without seeming to trifle with a grave subject and exhibit an irreverence for the dead that would shock and distress their surviving friends. But this bland and stately remnant of a former citizen leaned him far over my gate and whispered in my ear, and said:—

"Do not let that disturb you. The community that can stand such graveyards as those we are emigrating from can stand anything a body can say about the neglected and forsaken dead that lie in them."

At that very moment a cock crowed, and the weird procession vanished and left not a shred or a bone behind. I awoke, and found myself lying with my head out of the bed and "sagging" downwards considerably—a position favorable to dreaming dreams with morals in them, maybe, but not poetry.

Note.—The reader is assured that if the cemeteries in his town are kept in good order, this Dream is not levelled at his town at all, but is levelled particularly and venomously at the *next* town.

The first appearance of "My Late Senatorial Secretaryship" in book form in this country was in Mark Twain's Sketches New and Old, published in 1875 by the American Publishing Company. It had been written for a New York monthly called Galaxy, where it appeared in the May 1868 issue under the title "Facts Concerning the Late Senatorial Secretaryship." The essay is a burlesque of Twain's experiences in Washington as private secretary to Senator William M. Stewart of Nevada, an arrangement which suited neither of the parties involved and was terminated after two months.

My Late Senatorial Secretaryship

I am not a private secretary to a senator any more, now. I held the berth two months in security and in great cheerfulness of spirit, but my bread began to return from over the waters, then—that is to say, my works came back and revealed themselves. I judged it best to resign. The way of it was this. My employer sent for me one morning tolerably early, and, as soon as I had finished inserting some conundrums clandestinely into his last great speech upon finance, I entered the presence. There was something portentous in his appearance. His cravat was untied, his hair was in a state of disorder, and his countenance bore about it the signs of a suppressed storm. He held a package of letters in his tense grasp, and I knew that the dreaded Pacific mail was in. He said—

"I thought you were worthy of confidence."

I said, "Yes, sir."

He said, "I gave you a letter from certain of my constituents in the State of Nevada, asking the establishment of a post-office at Baldwin's Ranch, and told you to answer it, as ingeniously as you could, with arguments which should persuade them that there was no real necessity for an office at that place."

I felt easier. "Oh, if that is all, sir, I *did* do that."

"Yes, you *did*. I will read your answer, for your own humiliation:

"WASHINGTON, Nov. 24.

" 'Messrs. Smith, Jones, and others.

" 'GENTLEMEN: What the mischief do you suppose you want with a post-office at Baldwin's Ranche? It would not do you any good. If any letters came there, you couldn't read them, you know; and, besides, such letters as ought to pass through, with money in them, for other localities, would not be likely to *get* through, you must perceive at once; and that would make trouble for us all. No, don't bother about a post-office in your camp. I have your best interests at heart, and feel that it would only be an ornamental folly. What you want is a nice jail, you know—a nice, substantial jail and a free school. These will be a lasting benefit to you. These will make you really contented and happy. I will move in the matter at once.

" 'Very truly, etc.,
" 'MARK TWAIN,
" 'For James W.N**, U.S. Senator.'

"That is the way you answered that letter. Those people say they will hang me, if I ever enter that district again; and I am perfectly satisfied they *will*, too."

"Well, sir, I did not know I was doing any harm. I only wanted to convince them."

"Ah. Well you *did* convince them, I make no manner of doubt. Now, here is another specimen. I gave you a petition from certain gentlemen of Nevada, praying that I would get a bill through Congress incorporating the Methodist Episcopal Church of the State of Nevada. I told you to say, in reply, that the creation of such a law came more properly within the province of the State Legislature; and to endeavor to show them that, in the present of feebleness of the religious element in that new commonwealth, the expediency of incorporating the church was questionable. What did you write?

" 'WASHINGTON, Nov. 24.

" 'Rev. John Halifax and others.

" 'GENTLEMEN: You will have to go to the State Legislature about that speculation of yours—Congress don't know anything about religion. But don't you hurry to go there, either; because this thing you propose to do out in that new country isn't expedient—in fact, it is ridiculous. Your religious people there are too feeble, in intellect, in morality, in piety—in everything, pretty much. You had better drop this—you can't make it work. You can't issue stock on an incorporation like that—or if you could, it would only keep you in trouble all the time. The other denominations would abuse it, and "bear" it, and "sell it short," and break it down. They would do with it just as they would with one of your silver mines out there—they would try to make all the world believe it was "wildcat." You ought not to do anything that is calculated to bring a sacred thing into disrepute. You ought to be ashamed of yourselves—that is what *I* think about it. You close your petition with the words: "And we will ever pray." I think you had better—you need to do it.

" 'Very truly, etc.,
" 'MARK TWAIN,
" 'For James W.N**, U.S. Senator.'

"That luminous epistle finishes me with the religious element among my constituents. But that my political murder might be made sure, some evil instinct prompted me to hand you this memorial from the grave company of elders composing the Board of Aldermen of the city of San Francisco, to try your hand upon—a memorial praying that the city's right to the water-lots upon the city front might be established by law of Congress. I told you this was a dangerous matter to move in. I told you to write a non-committal letter to the Aldermen—an ambiguous letter—a letter that should avoid, as far as possible, all real consideration and discussion of the water-lot question. If there is any feeling left in you—any shame—surely this letter you wrote, in obedience to that order, ought to evoke it, when its words fall upon your ears:

" 'WASHINGTON, NOV.17.
" 'The Hon. Board of Aldermen, etc.
" 'GENTLEMEN: George Washington, the revered Father of his Country is dead. His long and brilliant career is closed, alas! forever. He was greatly respected in this section of the country, and his untimely decease cast a gloom over the whole community. He died on the 14th day of December, 1799. He passed peacefully away from the scene of his honors and his great achievements, the most lamented hero and the best beloved that ever earth hath yielded unto Death. At such a time as this, *you* speak of water-lots!—what a lot was his!
" 'What is fame! Fame is an accident. Sir Isaac Newton discovered an apple falling to the ground—a trivial discovery, truly, and one which a million men had made before him—but his parents were influential, and so they tortured that small circumstance into something wonderful, and, lo! the simple world took up the shout and, in almost the twinkling of an eye, that man was famous. Treasure these thoughts.
" 'Poesy, sweet poesy, who shall estimate what the world owes to thee!

"Mary had a little lamb, its fleece was white as snow—
And everywhere that Mary went, the lamb was sure to go."

"Jack and Gill went up the hill
To draw a pail of water.
Jack fell down and broke his crown,
And Gill came tumbling after."

For simplicity, elegance of diction, and freedom from immoral tendencies, I regard those two poems in the light of gems. They are suited to all grades of intelligence, to every sphere of life— to the field, to the nursery, to the guild. Especially should no Board of Aldermen be without them.

" 'Venerable fossils! write again. Nothing improves one so much as friendly correspondence. Write again—and if there is anything in this memorial of yours that refers to anything in particular, do not be backward about explaining it. We shall always be happy to hear you chirp.

" 'Very Truly, etc.

" 'MARK TWAIN.

" 'For James W.N**, U.S. Senator.

"That is an atrocious, a ruinous epistle! Distraction!"

"Well, sir, I am really sorry if there is anything wrong about it—but—but it appears to me to dodge the water-lot question."

"Dodge the mischief! Oh—but never mind. As long as destruction must come now, let it be complete. Let it be complete—let this last of your performances, which I am about to read, make a finality of it. I am a ruined man. I *had* my misgivings when I gave you the the letter from Humboldt, asking that the post route from Indian Gulch to Shakespeare Gap and intermediate points, be changed partly to the old Mormon trail. But I told you it was a delicate question, and warned you to deal with it deftly—to answer it dubiously5 and leave them a little in the dark. And your fatal imbecility impelled you to make *this* disastrous reply. I should think you would stop your ears, if you are not dead to all shame:

" 'WASHINGTON, Nov. 30.

" '*Messrs. Perkins, Wagner, et al.*

" 'GENTLEMEN: It is a delicate question about this Indian trail, but, handled with proper deftness and dubiousness, I doubt not we shall succeed in some measure or otherwise, because the place where the route leaves the Lassen Meadows, over beyond where those two Shawnee chiefs, Dilapidated-Vengeance and Biter-of-the-Clouds, were scalped last winter, this being the favorite direction to some, but others preferring something else in consequence of things, the Mormon trail leaving Mosby's at three in the morning, and passing through Jawbone Flat to Blucher, and then down by a Jug-Handle, the road passing to the right of it, and naturally leaving it on the right, too, and Dawson's on the left of the trail where it passes to the left of said Dawson's and onward thence to Tomahawk, thus making the route cheaper, easier of access to all who can get at it, and compassing all the desirable objects so considered by others, and, therefore, conferring the most good upon the greatest number, and, consequently, I am encouraged to hope we shall. However, I shall be ready, and happy, to afford you still further information upon the subject, from time to time, as you may desire it and the Post-office Department be enabled to furnish it to me. .

" 'Very truly, etc.
" 'MARK TWAIN,
" 'For, James W.N**, U.S. Senator.'

"There—now *what* do you think of that?"

"Well, I don't know, sir. It—well, it appears to me—to be dubious enough."

"Du—leave the house! I am a ruined man. Those Humboldt savages never will forgive me for tangling their brains up with this inhuman letter. I have lost the respect of the Methodist Church, the Board of Aldermen——"

"Well, I haven't anything to say about that, because I may have missed it a little in their cases, but I *was* too many for the Baldwin's Ranch people, General!"

"Leave the house! Leave it for ever and for ever, too!"

I regarded that as a sort of covert intimation that my service could be dispensed with, and so I resigned. I never will be a private secretary to a senator again. You can't please that kind of people. They don't know anything. They can't appreciate a party's efforts.

"A Mysterious Visit" appeared in *the* Buffalo Express *on March 19, 1870, and was later collected in* Mark Twain's Sketches New and Old *in 1875. Written while Twain was a proprietor of and regular contributor to the newspaper, it describes the sudden interest taken in him—a man who had recently married a wealthy woman and published an enormously successful book—by the Internal Revenue Department.*

A Mysterious Visit

The first notice that was taken of me when I "settled down" recently, was by a gentleman who said he was an assessor, and connected with the U.S. Internal Revenue Department. I said I had never heard of his branch of business before, but I was very glad to see him all the same—would he sit down? He sat down. I did not know anything particular to say, and yet I felt that people who have arrived at the dignity of keeping house must be conversational, must be easy and sociable in company. So, in default of anything else to say, I asked him if he was opening his shop in our neighborhood?

He said he was. [I did not wish to appear ignorant, but I *had* hoped he would mention what he had for sale.]

I ventured to ask him "How was trade?" And he said "So- so."

I then said we would drop in, and if we liked his house as well as any other, we would give him our custom.

He said he thought we would like his establishment well enough to confine ourselves to it—said he never saw anybody who would go off and hunt up another man in his line after trading with him once.

That sounded pretty complacent, but barring that natural expression of villainy which we all have, the man looked honest enough.

I do not know how it came about exactly, but gradually we appeared to melt down and run together, conversationally speaking, and then everything went along as comfortably as clockwork.

We talked, and talked, and talked—at least I did; and we laughed, and laughed, and laughed—at least he did. But all the time I had my presence of mind about me—I had my native shrewdness turned on "full head," as the engineers say. I was determined to find out all about his business in spite of his obscure answers—and I was determined I would have it out of him without his suspecting what I was at. I meant to trap him with a deep, deep ruse. I would tell him all about my own business, and he would naturally so warm to me during this seductive burst of confidence that he would forget himself, and tell me all about *his* affairs before he suspected what I was about. I thought to myself, My son, you little know what an old fox you are dealing with. I said—

"Now you never would guess what I made lecturing this winter and last spring?"

"No—don't believe I could, to save me. Let me see—let me see. About two thousand dollars, maybe? But no; no sir, I know you couldn't have made that much. Say seventeen hundred, maybe?"

"Ha! ha! I knew you couldn't. My lecturing receipts for last spring and this winter were fourteen thousand seven hundred and fifty dollars. What do you think of that?"

"Why, it is amazing—perfectly amazing. I will make a note of it. And you say even this wasn't all?"

"All! Why bless you, there was my income from the *Daily Warwhoop* for four months—about—about—well, what should you say to about eight thousand dollars, for instance?"

"Say! Why, I should say I should like to see myself rolling in just such another ocean of affluence. Eight thousand! I'll make a note of it. Why man!—and on top of all this I am to understand that you had still more income?"

"Ha! ha! ha! Why, you're only in the suburbs of it, so to speak. There's my book, 'The Innocents Abroad'—price $3.50 to $5.00, according to the binding. Listen to me. Look me in the eye. During the last four months and a half, saying nothing of sales before that, but just simply during the four months and a half, we've sold ninety-five thousand copies of that book. Ninety-five thousand! Think of it. Average four dollars a copy, say. It's nearly four hundred thousand dollars, my son. I get half."

"The suffering Moses! I'll set *that* down. Fourteen-seven-fifty—eight—two hundred. Total, say—well, upon my word, the grand total is about two hundred and thirteen or fourteen thousand dollars! *Is* that possible?"

"Possible! If there's any mistake it's the other way. Two hundred and fourteen thousand, cash, is my income for this year if *I* know how to cipher."

Then the gentleman got up to go. It came over me most uncomfortably that maybe I had made my revelations for nothing, besides being flattered into stretching them considerably by the stranger's astonished exclamations. But no; at the last moment the gentleman handed me a large envelope, and said it contained his advertisement; and that I would find out all about his business in it; and that he would be happy to have my custom—would in fact, be *proud* to have the custom of a man of such prodigious income; and that he used to think there were several wealthy men in the city, but when they came to trade with him, he discovered that they barely had enough to live on; and that, in truth it had been such a weary, weary age since he had seen a rich man face to face, and talked to him, and touched him with his hands, that he could hardly refrain from embracing me—in fact, would esteem it a great favor if I would *let* him embrace me.

This so pleased me that I did not try to resist, but allowed this simple-hearted stranger to throw his arms about me and weep a few tranquilizing tears down the back of my neck. Then he went his way.

As soon as he was gone I opened his advertisement. I studied it attentively for four minutes. I then called up the cook, and said—

"Hold me while I faint! Let Marie turn the griddle-cakes."

By and by, when I came to, I sent down to the rum mill on the corner and hired an artist by the week to sit up nights and curse that stranger, and give me a lift occasionally in the daytime when I came to a hard place.

Ah, what a miscreant he was! His "advertisement" was nothing in the world but a wicked tax-return—a string of impertinent questions about my private affairs, occupying the best part of four foolscap pages of fine print—questions, I may remark, gotten up with such marvelous ingenuity, that the oldest man in the world couldn't understand what the most of them were driving at—questions, too, that were calculated to make a man report about four times his actual income to keep from swearing to a falsehood. I looked for a loophole, but there did not appear to be any. Inquiry No. I covered my case as generously and as amply as an umbrella could cover an ant hill—

"What were your profits, during the past year, from any trade, business, or vocation, wherever carried on?"

And that inquiry was backed up by thirteen others of an

equally searching nature, the most modest of which required information as to whether I had committed any burglary or highway robbery, or by any arson or other secret source of emolument, had acquired property which was not enumerated in my statement of income as set opposite to inquiry No. I.

It was plain that that stranger had enabled me to make a goose of myself. It was very, very plain; and so I went out and hired another artist. By working on my vanity, the stranger had seduced me into declaring an income of $214,000. By law, $1000 of this was exempt from income-tax—the only relief I could see, and it was only a drop in the ocean. At the legal five per cent, I must pay to the Government the sum of ten thousand six hundred and fifty dollars, income-tax!

[I may remark, in this place, that I did not do it.]

I am acquainted with a very opulent man, whose house is a palace, whose table is regal, whose outlays are enormous, yet a man who has no income, as I have often noticed by the revenue returns; and to him I went for advice, in my distress. He took my dreadful exhibition of receipts, he put on his glasses, he took his pen, and presto!—I was a pauper! It was the neatest thing that ever was. He did it simply by deftly manipulating the bill of "DEDUCTIONS." He set down my "State, national, and municipal taxes" at so much; my "losses by shipwreck, fire, etc.," at so much; my "losses on sales of real estate"—on "live stock sold"—on "payments for rent of homestead"—on "repairs, improvements, interest"—on "previously taxed salary as an officer of the United States' army, navy, revenue service," and other things. He got astonishing "deductions" out of each and every one of these matters—each and every one of them. And when he was done he handed me the paper, and I saw at a glance that during the year my income, in the way of profits, had been *one thousand two hundred and fifty dollars and forty cents.*

"Now," said he, "the thousand dollars is exempt by law. What you want to do is to go and swear this document in and pay tax on the two hundred and fifty dollars."

[While he was making this speech his little boy Willie lifted a two dollar greenback out of his vest pocket and vanished with it, and I would wager anything that if my stranger were to call on that little boy to-morrow he would make a false return of his income.]

"Do you," said I, "do you always work up the 'deductions' after this fashion in your own case, sir?"

"Well, I should say so! If it weren't for those eleven saving clauses under the head of 'Deduction' I should be beggared every year to support this hateful and wicked, this extortionate and tyrannical government.''

This gentleman stands away up among the very best of the solid men of the city—the men of moral weight, of commercial integrity, of unimpeachable social spotlessness—and so I bowed to his example. I went down to the revenue office, and under the accusing eyes of my old visitor I stood up and swore to lie after lie, fraud after fraud, villainy after villainy, till my soul was coated inches and inches thick with perjury, and my self-respect gone for ever and ever.

But what of it? It is nothing more than thousands of the richest and proudest, and most respected, honored, and courted men in America do every year. And so I don't care. I am not ashamed. I shall simply, for the present, talk little, and eschew fire-proof gloves, lest I fall into certain dreadful habits irrevocably.

"Journalism in Tennessee" was written for Twain's column in the Buffalo Express, *where it appeared on September 4, 1869. In 1871, the story was part of a volume of pirated material called* Eye Openers *that was published in London by John Camden Hotten, an enterprising man who had assembled several cheap editions of Twain's work for the British market. This infuriated Twain, not only because he did not collect royalties on any of the books, but also because Hotten was in the habit of filling out collections like* Eye Openers *with sketches that he had written himself. In a blast at Hotten in the London* Spectator *of September 20, 1872, Twain directed loyal readers to patronize his official English publishers, George Routledge & Sons. At home, Twain continued to be a client of the American Publishing Company, which issued* Mark Twain's Sketches New and Old *(including "Journalism in Tennessee") in 1875. The story was reissued as a pamphlet with several other selections in Girard, Kansas, around 1923.*

Journalism in Tennessee

The editor of the Memphis *Avalanche* swoops thus mildly down upon a correspondent who posted him as a Radical:—"While he was writing the first word, the middle, dotting his i's, crossing his t's, and punching his period, he knew he was concocting a sentence that was saturated with infamy and reeking with falsehood."—*Exchange*

I was told by the physician that a Southern climate would improve my health, and so I went down to Tennessee, and got a berth on the *Morning Glory and Johnson County War-Whoop* as associate editor. When I went on duty I found the chief editor sitting tilted back in a three-legged chair with his feet on a pine table. There was another pine table in the room and another afflicted chair, and both were half buried under newspapers and scraps and sheets of manuscript. There was a wooden box of sand, sprinkled with cigar stubs and "old soldiers," and a stove with a door hanging by its upper hinge. The chief editor had a long-tailed black cloth frock coat on, and white linen pants. His boots were small and neatly blacked. He wore a ruffled shirt, a large seal ring, a standing collar of obsolete pattern, and a checkered neckerchief with the ends hanging down. Date of costume about 1848. He was smoking a cigar, and trying to think of a word, and in pawing his hair he had rumpled his locks a good deal. He was scowling fearfully, and I judged that he was concocting a particularly knotty editorial. He told me to take the exchanges and skim through them and write up the "Spirit of the Tennessee Press," condensing into the article all of their contents that seemed of interest.

929

I wrote as follows:—

"SPIRIT OF THE TENNESSEE PRESS

"The editors of the *Semi-Weekly Earthquake* evidently labor under a misapprehension with regard to the Ballyhack railroad. It is not the object of the company to leave Buzzardville off to one side. On the contrary, they consider it one of the most important points along the line, and consequently can have no desire to slight it. The gentlemen of the *Earthquake* will, of course, take pleasure in making the correction.

"John W. Blossom, Esq., the able editor of the Higginsville *Thunderbolt and Battle Cry of Freedom,* arrived in the city yesterday. He is stopping at the Van Buren House.

"We observe that our contemporary of the Mud Springs *Morning Howl* has fallen into the error of supposing that the election of Van Werter is not an established fact, but he will have discovered his mistake before this reminder reaches him, no doubt. He was doubtless misled by incomplete election returns.

"It is pleasant to note that the city of Blathersville is endeavoring to contract with some New York gentlemen to pave its well-nigh impassable streets with the Nicholson pavement. The *Daily Hurrah* urges the measure with ability, and seems confident of ultimate success."

I passed my manuscript over to the chief editor for acceptance, alteration, or destruction. He glanced at it and his face clouded. He ran his eye down the pages, and his countenance grew portentous. It was easy to see that something was wrong. Presently he sprang up and said—

"Thunder and lightning! Do you suppose I am going to speak of those cattle that way? Do you suppose my subscribers are going to stand such gruel as that? Give me the pen!"

I never saw a pen scrape and scratch its way so viciously, or plough through another man's verbs and adjectives so relentlessly. While he was in the midst of his work, somebody shot at him through the open window, and marred the symmetry of my ear.

"Ah," said he, "that is that scoundrel Smith, of the *Moral Volcano*—he was due yesterday." And he snatched a navy revolver from his belt and fired. Smith dropped, shot in the thigh. The shot spoiled Smith's aim, who was just taking a second chance, and he crippled a stranger. It was me. Merely a finger shot off.

Then the chief editor went on with his erasures and interlineations. Just as he finished them a hand-grenade came down the stove pipe, and the explosion shivered the stove into a thousand fragments. However, it did no further damage, except that a vagrant piece knocked a couple of my teeth out.

"That stove is utterly ruined," said the chief editor.

I said I believed it was.

"Well, no matter—don't want it this kind of weather. I know the man that did it. I'll get him. Now, *here* is the way this stuff ought to be written."

I took the manuscript. It was scarred with erasures and interlineations till its mother wouldn't have known it if it had had one. It now read as follows:—

"SPIRIT OF THE TENNESSEE PRESS

"The inveterate liars of the *Semi-Weekly Earthquake* are evidently endeavoring to palm off upon a noble and chivalrous people another of their vile and brutal falsehoods with regard to that most glorious conception of the nineteenth century, the Ballyhack railroad. The idea that Buzzardville was to be left off at one side originated in their own fulsome brains—or rather in the settlings which *they* regard as brains. They had better swallow this lie if they want to save their abandoned reptile carcasses the cowhiding they so richly deserve.

"That ass, Blossom, of the Higginsville *Thunderbolt and Battle Cry of Freedom,* is down here again sponging at the Van Buren.

"We observe that the besotted blackguard of the Mud Springs *Morning Howl* is giving out, with his usual propensity for lying, that Van Werter is not elected. The heaven-born mission of journalism is to disseminate truth; to eradicate error; to educate, refine, and elevate the tone of public morals and manners, and make all men more gentle, more virtuous, more charitable, and in all ways better, and holier, and happier; and yet this black-hearted scoundrel degrades his great office persistently to the dissemination of falsehood, calumny, vituperation, and vulgarity.

"Blathersville wants a Nicholson pavement—it wants a jail and a poorhouse more. The idea of a pavement in a one horse town composed of two gin mills, a blacksmith's shop, and that mustard-plaster of a newspaper, the *Daily Hurrah!* The crawling insect, Buckner, who edits the *Hurrah,* is braying about this business with his customary imbecility, and imagining that he is talking sense."

"Now *that* is the way to write—peppery and to the point. Mush-and-milk journalism gives me the fan-tods."

About this time a brick came through the window with a splintering crash, and gave me a considerable of a jolt in the back. I moved out of range—I began to feel in the way.

The chief said, "That was the Colonel, likely. I've been expecting him for two days. He will be up, now, right away."

He was correct. The Colonel appeared in the door a moment afterward with a dragoon revolver in his hand.

He said, "Sir, have I the honor of addressing the poltroon who edits this mangy sheet?"

"You have. Be seated, sir. Be careful of the chair, one of its legs is gone. I believe I have the honor of addressing the putrid liar, Col. Blatherskite Tecumseh?"

"Right, sir. I have a little account to settle with you. If you are at leisure we will begin."

"I have an article on the 'Encouraging Progress of Moral and Intellectual Development in America' to finish, but there is no hurry. Begin."

Both pistols rang out their fierce clamor at the same instant. The chief lost a lock of his hair, and the Colonel's bullet ended its career in the fleshy part of my thigh. The Colonel's left shoulder was clipped a little. They fired again. Both missed their men this time, but I got my share, a shot in the arm. At the third fire both gentlemen were wounded slightly, and I had a knuckle chipped. I then said, I believed I would go out and take a walk, as this was a private matter, and I had a delicacy about participating in it further. But both gentlemen begged me to keep my seat, and assured me that I was not in the way.

They then talked about the elections and the crops while they reloaded, and I fell to tying up my wounds. But presently they opened fire again with animation, and every shot took effect— but it is proper to remark that five out of the six fell to my share. The sixth one mortally wounded the colonel, who remarked, with fine humor, that he would have to say good morning now, as he had business up town. He then inquired the way to the undertaker's and left.

The chief turned to me and said, "I am expecting company to dinner, and shall have to get ready. It will be a favor to me if you will read proof and attend to the customers."

I winced a little at the idea of attending to the customers, but I was too bewildered by the fusilade that was still ringing in my ears to think of anything to say.

He continued, "Jones will be here at 3—cowhide him. Gillespie will call earlier, perhaps—throw him out of the window. Ferguson will be along about 4—kill him. That is all for to-day, I believe. If you have any odd time, you may write a blistering article on the police—give the Chief Inspector rats. The cowhides are under the table; weapons in the drawer— ammunition there in the corner—lint and bandages up there in the pigeon-holes. In case of accident, go to Lancet, the surgeon, down-stairs. He advertises—we take it out in trade."

He was gone. I shuddered. At the end of the next three hours I had been through perils so awful that all peace of mind and all cheerfulness were gone from me. Gillespie had called and thrown *me* out of the window. Jones arrived promptly, and when I got ready to do the cowhiding he took the job off my hands. In an encounter with a stranger, not in the bill of fare, I had lost my scalp. Another stranger, by the name of Thompson, left me a mere wreck and ruin of chaotic rags. And at last, at bay in the corner, and beset by an infuriated mob of editors, blacklegs, politicians, and desperadoes, who raved and swore and flourished their weapons about my head till the air shimmered with glancing flashes of steel, I was in the act of resigning my berth on the paper when the chief arrived, and with him a rabble of charmed and enthusiastic friends. Then ensued a scene of riot and carnage such as no human pen, or steel one either, could describe. People were shot, probed, dismembered, blown up, thrown out of the window. There was a brief tornado of murky blasphemy, with a confused and frantic war-dance glimmering through it, and then all was over. In five minutes there was silence, and the gory chief and I sat alone and surveyed the sanguinary ruin that strewed the floor around us.

He said, "You'll like this place when you get used to it".

I said, "I'll have to get you to excuse me; I think maybe I might write to suit you after a while; as soon as I had had some practice and learned the language I am confident I could. But, to speak the plain truth, that sort of energy of expression has its inconveniences, and a man is liable to interruption. You see that yourself. Vigorous writing is calculated to elevate the public, no doubt, but, then I do not like to attract so much attention as it calls forth. I can't write with comfort when I am interrupted so much as I have been to-day. I like this berth well enough, but I don't like to be left here to wait on the customers. The experiences are novel, I grant you, and entertaining too, after a fashion, but they are not judiciously distributed. A gentleman shoots at you through the window and cripples *me;* a bomb-shell comes down the stove-pipe for your gratification and sends the stove-door down *my* throat; a friend drops in to swap compliments with you, and freckles *me* with bullet-holes till my skin won't hold my principles; you go to dinner, and Jones comes with his cowhide, Gillespie throws me out of the window, Thompson tears all my clothes off, and an entire stranger takes my scalp with the easy freedom of an old acquaintance; and in less than five minutes all the blackguards in the country arrive in their war-paint, and proceed to scare the rest of me to death with their tomahawks. Take it altogether, I never had such a spirited time in all my life as I have had to-day. No; I like you, and I like your calm unruffled way of explaining things to the customers, but you see I am not used to it. The Southern heart is too impulsive; Southern hospitality is too lavish with the stranger. The

933

paragraphs which I have written to-day, and into whose cold sentences your masterly hand has infused the fervent spirit of Tennessean journalism, will wake up another nest of hornets. All that mob of editors will come—and they will come hungry, too, and want somebody for breakfast. I shall have to bid you adieu. I decline to be present at these festivities. I came South for my health, I will go back on the same errand, and suddenly. Tennesseean journalism is too stirring for me."

After which we parted with mutual regret, and I took apartments at the hospital.

This travelogue was originally called "A Day at Niagara" when it appeared in the Buffalo Express *on August 21, 1869. In 1872, it surfaced in London in one of John Camden Hotten's pirated volumes,* Practical Jokes. *The next year, Twain contributed the tale to a collection issued in Philadelphia called* One Hundred Choice Selections. *Retitled "A Visit to Niagara," it was also included in the American Publishing Company's* Mark Twain's Sketches New and Old *in 1875.*

A Visit to Niagara

Niagara Falls is a most enjoyable place of resort. The hotels are excellent, and the prices not at all exorbitant. The opportunities for fishing are not even equalled elsewhere. Because, in other localities, certain places in the streams are much better than others; but at Niagara one place is just as good as another, for the reason that the fish do not bite anywhere, and so there is no use in your walking five miles to fish, when you can depend on being just as unsuccessful nearer home. The advantages of this state of things have never heretofore been properly placed before the public.

The weather is cool in summer, and the walks and drives are all pleasant and none of them fatiguing. When you start out to "do" the Falls you first drive down about a mile, and pay a small sum for the privilege of looking down from a precipice into the narrowest part of the Niagara river. A railway "cut" through a hill would be as comely if it had the angry river tumbling and foaming through its bottom. You can descend a staircase here a hundred and fifty feet down, and stand at the edge of the water. After you have done it, you will wonder why you did it; but you will then be too late.

The guide will explain to you, in his blood-curdling way, how he saw the little steamer, *Maid of the Mist,* descend the fearful rapids—how first one paddle-box was out of sight behind the raging billows, and then the other, and at what point it was that her smokestack toppled overboard, and where her planking began to break and part asunder—and how she did finally live through the trip, after accomplishing the incredible feat of travelling seventeen miles in six minutes, or six miles in seventeen minutes, I have really forgotten which. But it was very extraordinary, anyhow. It is worth the price of admission to hear the guide tell the story nine times in succession to different parties, and never miss a word or alter a sentence or a gesture.

Then you drive over the Suspension Bridge, and divide your misery between the chances of smashing down two hundred feet into the river below, and the chances of having the railway train overhead smashing down on to you. Either possibility is discomforting taken by itself, but mixed together, they amount in the aggregate to positive unhappiness.

On the Canada side you drive along the chasm between long ranks of photographers standing guard behind their cameras, ready to make an ostentatious frontispiece of you and your decaying ambulance, and your solemn crate with a hide on it, which you are expected to regard in the light of a horse, and a diminished and unimportant background of sublime Niagara; and a great many people have the incredible effrontery or the native depravity to aid and abet this sort of crime.

Any day, in the hands of these photographers, you may see stately pictures of papa and mamma, Johnny and Bub and Sis, or a couple of country cousins, all smiling vacantly, and all disposed in studied and uncomfortable attitudes in their carriage, and all looming up in their awe-inspiring imbecility before the snubbed and diminished presentment of that majestic presence whose ministering spirits are the rainbows, whose voice is the thunder, whose awful front is veiled in clouds, who was monarch here dead and forgotten ages before this hackful of small reptiles was deemed temporarily necessary to fill a crack in the world's unnoted myriads, and will still be monarch here ages and decades of ages after they shall have gathered themselves to their blood relations, the other worms, and been mingled with the unremembering dust.

There is no actual harm in making Niagara a background whereon to display one's marvelous insignificance in a good strong light, but it requires a sort of superhuman self-complacency to enable one to do it.

When you have examined the stupendous Horseshoe Fall till you are satisfied you cannot improve on it, you return to America by the new Suspension Bridge, and follow up the bank to where they exhibit the Cave of the Winds.

Here I followed instructions, and divested myself of all my clothing, and put on a waterproof jacket and overalls. This costume is picturesque, but not beautiful. A guide, similarly dressed, led the way down a flight of winding stairs, which wound and wound, and still kept on winding long after the thing ceased to be a novelty, and then terminated long before it had begun to be a pleasure. We were then well down under the precipice, but still considerably above the level of the river.

We now began to creep along flimsy bridges of a single plank, our persons shielded from destruction by a crazy wooden railing, to which I clung with both hands—not because I was afraid, but because I wanted to. Presently the descent became steeper, and the bridge flimsier, and sprays from the American Fall began to rain down on us in fast-increasing sheets that soon became blinding, and after that our progress was mostly in the nature of groping. Now a furious wind began to rush out from behind the waterfall, which seemed determined to sweep us from the bridge, and scatter us on the rocks and among the torrents below. I remarked that I wanted to go home; but it was too late. We were almost under the monstrous wall of water thundering down from above, and speech was in vain in the midst of such a pitiless crash of sound.

In another moment the guide disappeared behind the deluge, and bewildered by the thunder, driven helplessly by the wind, and smitten by the arrowy tempest of rain, I followed. All was darkness. Such a mad storming, roaring, and bellowing of warring wind and water never crazed my ears before. I bent my head, and seemed to receive the Atlantic on my back. The world seemed going to destruction. I could not see anything, the flood poured down so savagely. I raised my head, with open mouth, and the most of the American cataract went down my throat. If I had sprung a leak now, I had been lost. And at this moment I discovered that the bridge had ceased, and we must trust for a foothold to the slippery and precipitous rocks. I never was so scared before and survived it. But we got through at last, and emerged into the open day, where we could stand in front of the laced and frothy and seething world of descending water, and look at it. When I saw how much of it there was, and how fearfully in earnest it was, I was sorry I had gone behind it.

The noble Red Man has always been a friend and darling of mine. I love to read about him in tales and legends and romances. I love to read of his inspired sagacity, and his love of the wild free life of mountain and forest, and his general nobility of character, and his stately metaphorical manner of speech, and his chivalrous love for the dusky maiden, and the picturesque pomp of his dress and accoutrements. Especially the picturesque pomp of his dress and accoutrements. When I found the shops at Niagara Falls full of dainty Indian bead-work, and stunning moccasins, and equally stunning toy figures representing human beings who carried their weapons in holes bored through their arms and bodies, and had feet shaped like a pie, I was filled with emotion. I knew that now, at last, I was going to come face to face with the noble Red Man.

A lady clerk in a shop told me, indeed, that all her grand array of curiosities were made by the Indians, and that they were plenty about the Falls, and that they were friendly, and it would not be dangerous to speak to them. And sure enough, as I approached the bridge leading over to Luna Island, I came upon a noble Son of the Forest sitting under a tree, diligently at work on a bead reticule. He wore a slouch hat and brogans, and had a short black pipe in his mouth. Thus does the baneful contact with our effeminate civilization dilute the picturesque pomp which is so natural to the Indian when far removed from us in his native haunts. I addressed the relic as follows:—

"Is the Wawhoo-Wang-Wang of the Whack-a-Whack happy? Does the great Speckled Thunder sigh for the warpath, or is his heart contented with dreaming of the dusky maiden, the Pride of the Forest? Does the mighty Sachem yearn to drink the blood of his enemies, or is he satisfied to make bead reticules for the pappooses of the paleface? Speak, sublime relic of bygone grandeur—venerable ruin, speak!"

The relic said—

"An' is it mesilf, Dennis Hooligan, that ye'd be takin' for a dirty Injin, ye drawlin', lantern-jawed, spider-legged divil! By the piper that played before Moses, I'll ate ye!"

I went away from there.

By and by, in the neighborhood of the Terrapin Tower, I came upon a gentle daughter of the aborigines in fringed and beaded buckskin moccasins and leggins, seated on a bench, with her pretty wares about her. She had just carved out a wooden chief that had a strong family resemblance to a clothes-pin, and was now boring a hole through his abdomen to put his bow through. I hesitated a moment, and then addressed her:

"Is the heart of the forest maiden heavy? Is the Laughing Tadpole lonely? Does she mourn over the extinguished council-fires of her race, and the vanished glory of her ancestors? Or does her sad spirit wander afar toward the hunting grounds whither her brave Gobbler-of-the-Lightning is gone? Why is my daughter silent? Has she aught against the paleface stranger?"

The maiden said—

"Faix, an' is it Biddy Malone ye dare to be callin' names? Lave this, or I'll shy your lean carcass over the cataract, ye sniveling blaggard!"

I adjourned from there also.

"Confound these Indians!" I said. "They told me they were tame; but, if appearances go for anything, I should say they were all on the warpath."

I made one more attempt to fraternize with them, and only one. I came upon a camp of them gathered in the shade of a great tree, making wampum and moccasins, and addressed them in the language of friendship:

"Noble Red Men, Braves, Grand Sachems, War Chiefs, Squaws, and High Muck-a-Mucks, the paleface from the land of the setting sun greets you! You, Beneficent Polecat—you, Devourer of Mountains—you, Roaring Thundergust—you, Bully Boy with a Glass eye—the paleface from beyond the great waters greets you all! War and pestilence have thinned your ranks, and destroyed your once proud nation. Poker and seven-up, and a vain modern expense for soap, unknown to your glorious ancestors, have depleted your purses. Appropriating, in your simplicity, the property of others, has gotten you into trouble. Misrepresenting facts, in your simple innocence, has damaged your reputation with the soulless usurper. Trading for forty-rod whisky, to enable you to get drunk and happy and tomahawk your families, has played the everlasting mischief with the picturesque pomp of your dress, and here you are, in the broad light of the nineteenth century, gotten up like the ragtag and bobtail of the purlieus of New York. For shame! Remember your ancestors! Recall their mighty deeds! Remember Uncas!—and Red Jacket!—and Hole in the Day!—and Whoopdedoodledo! Emulate their achievements! Unfurl yourselves under my banner, noble savages, illustrious gutter-snipes"—

"Down wid him!" "Scoop the blaggard!" "Burn him!" "Hang him!" "Dhround him!"

It was the quickest operation that ever was. I simply saw a sudden flash in the air of clubs, brickbats, fists, bead-baskets, and moccasins—a single flash, and they all appeared to hit me at once, and no two of them in the same place. In the next instant the entire tribe was upon me. They tore half the clothes off me; they broke my arms and legs; they gave me a thump that dented the top of my head till it would hold coffee like a saucer; and, to crown their disgraceful proceedings and add insult to injury, they threw me over the Niagara Falls, and I got wet.

About ninety or a hundred feet from the top, the remains of my vest caught on a projecting rock, and I was almost drowned before I could get loose. I finally fell, and brought up in a world of white foam at the foot of the Fall, whose celled and bubbly

941

masses towered up several inches above my head. Of course I got into the eddy. I sailed round and round in it forty-four times—chasing a chip and gaining on it—each round trip a half mile—reaching for the same bush on the bank forty-four times, and just exactly missing it by a hair's-breadth every time.

At last a man walked down and sat down close to that bush, and put a pipe in his mouth, and lit a match, and followed me with one eye and kept the other on the match, while he sheltered it in his hands from the wind. Presently a puff of wind blew it out. The next time I swept around he said—

"Got a match?"

"Yes; in my other vest. Help me out, please."

"Not for Joe."

When I came round again, I said—

"Excuse the seemingly impertinent curiosity of a drowning man, but will you explain this singular conduct of yours?"

"With pleasure. I am the coroner. Don't hurry on my account. I can wait for you. But I wish I had a match."

I said—"Take my place, and I'll go and get you one."

He declined. This lack of confidence on his part created a coldness between us, and from that time forward I avoided him. It was my idea, in case anything happened, to so time the occurrence as to throw my custom into the hands of the opposition coroner over on the American side.

At last a policeman came along, and arrested me for disturbing the peace by yelling at people on shore for help. The judge fined me, but I had the advantage of him. My money was with my pantaloons, and my pantaloons were with the Indians.

Thus I escaped. I am now lying in a very critical condition. At least I am lying anyway—critical or not critical. I am hurt all over, but I cannot tell the full extent yet, because the doctor is not done taking inventory. He will make out my manifest this evening. However, thus far he thinks only sixteen of my wounds are fatal. I don't mind the others.

Upon regaining my right mind, I said—

"It is an awful savage tribe of Indians that do the bead work and moccasins for Niagara Falls, doctor. Where are they from?"

"Limerick, my son."

"The Experiences of the McWilliamses With the Membranous Croup" made its first appearance *in* Mark Twain's Sketches New and Old *in 1875. The narrator of the tale, Mortimer McWilliams, was the classic hen-pecked husband; he was also one of Twain's favorite characters.*

The Experiences of the McWilliamses with Membranous Croup

[As related to the author of this book by Mr. McWilliams, a pleasant New York gentleman whom the said author met by chance on a journey.]

Well, to go back to where I was before I digressed to explain to you how that frightful and incurable disease, membranous croup, was ravaging the town and driving all mothers mad with terror, I called Mrs. McWilliams's attention to little Penelope and said:

"Darling, I wouldn't let that child be chewing that pine stick if I were you."

"Precious, where is the harm in it?" said she, but at the same time preparing to take away the stick—for some women cannot receive even the most palpably judicious suggestion without arguing it; that is, married women.

I replied:

"Love, it is notorious that pine is the least nutritious wood that a child can eat."

My wife's hand paused, in the act of taking the stick, and returned itself to her lap. She bridled perceptibly, and said:

"Hubby, you know better than that. You know you do. Doctors *all* say that the turpentine in pine wood is good for weak back and the kidneys."

"Ah—I was under a misapprehension. I did not know that the child's kidneys and spine were affected, and that the family physician had recommended—"

"Who said the child's spine and kidneys were affected?"

"My love, you intimated it."

"The idea! I never intimated anything of the kind."

"Why my dear, it hasn't been two minutes since you said—"

"Bother what I said! I don't care what I did say. There isn't any harm in the child's chewing a bit of pine stick if she wants to, and you know it perfectly well. And she *shall* chew it, too. So there, now!"

"Say no more, my dear. I now see the force of your reasoning, and I will go and order two or three cords of the best pine wood to-day. No child of mine shall want while I—"

"O *please* go along to your office and let me have some peace. A body can never make the simplest remark but you must take it up and go to arguing and arguing and arguing till you don't know what you are talking about, and you *never* do."

"Very well, it shall be as you say. But there is a want of logic in your last remark which—"

However, she was gone with a flourish before I could finish, and had taken the child with her. That night at dinner she confronted me with a face as white as a sheet:

"O, Mortimer, there's another! Little Georgie Gordon is taken."

"Membranous croup?"

"Membranous croup."

"Is there any hope for him?"

"None in the wide world. O, what is to become of us!"

By and by a nurse brought in our Penelope to say good-night and offer the customary prayer at the mother's knee. In the midst of "Now I lay me down to sleep," she gave a slight cough! My wife fell back like one stricken with death. But the next moment she was up and brimming with the activities which terror inspires.

She commanded that the child's crib be removed from the nursery to our bed-room; and she went along to see the order executed. She took me with her, of course. We got matters arranged with speed. A cot bed was put up in my wife's dressing room for the nurse. But now Mrs. McWilliams said we were too far away from the other baby, and what if *he* were to have the symptoms in the night—and she blanched again, poor thing.

We then restored the crib and the nurse to the nursery and put up a bed for ourselves in a room adjoining.

Presently, however, Mrs. McWilliams said suppose the baby should catch it from Penelope? This thought struck a new panic to her heart, and the tribe of us could not get the crib out of the nursery again fast enough to satisfy my wife, though she assisted in her own person and well nigh pulled the crib to pieces in her frantic hurry.

We moved down stairs; but there was no place there to stow

the nurse, and Mrs. McWilliams said the nurse's experience would be an inestimable help. So we returned, bag and baggage, to our own bed-room once more, and felt a great gladness, like storm-buffeted birds that have found their nest again.

Mrs. McWilliams sped to the nursery to see how things were going on there. She was back in a moment with a new dread. She said:

"What *can* make Baby sleep so?"

I said:

"Why, my darling, Baby *always* sleeps like a graven image."

"I know. I know; but there's something peculiar about his sleep, now. He seems to—to—he seems to breathe so *regularly*. O, this is dreadful."

"But my dear he always breathes regularly."

"Oh, I know it, but there's something frightful about it now. His nurse is too young and inexperienced. Maria shall stay there with her, and be on hand if anything happens."

"That is a good idea, but who will help *you*?"

"You can help me all I want. I wouldn't allow anybody to do anything but myself, any how, at such a time as this."

I said I would feel mean to lie abed and sleep, and leave her to watch and toil over our little patient all the weary night.—But she reconciled me to it. So old Maria departed and took up her ancient quarters in the nursery.

Penelope coughed twice in her sleep.

"Oh, why *don't* that doctor come! Mortimer, this room is too warm. This room is certainly too warm. Turn off the register—quick!"

I shut it off, glancing at the thermometer at the same time, and wondering to myself if 70 *was* too warm for a sick child.

The coachman arrived from down town, now, with the news that our physician was ill and confined to his bed.—Mrs. McWilliams turned a dead eye upon me, and said in a dead voice:

"There is a Providence in it. It is foreordained. He never was sick before.—Never. We have not been living as we ought to live, Mortimer. Time and time again I have told you so. Now you see the result. Our child will never get well. Be thankful if you can forgive yourself; I never can forgive *my*self."

I said, without intent to hurt, but with heedless choice of words, that I could not see that we had been living such an abandoned life.

"*Mortimer!* Do you want to bring the judgment upon Baby, too!"

Then she began to cry, but suddenly exclaimed:

"The doctor must have sent medicines!"

I said:

"Certainly. They are here. I was only waiting for you to give me a chance."

"Well, do give them to me! Don't you know that every moment is precious now? But what was the use in sending medicines, when he *knows* that the disease is incurable?"

I said that while there was life there was hope.

"Hope! Mortimer, you know no more what you are talking about than the child unborn. If you would—. As I live, the directions say give one teaspoonful once an hour! Once an hour!—as if we had a whole year before us to save the child in! Mortimer, please hurry. Give the poor perishing thing a table-spoonful, and *try* to be quick!"

"Why, my dear, a table-spoonful might—"

"*Don't* drive me frantic!. . . . .There, there, there, my precious, my own; it's nasty bitter stuff, but it's good for Nelly—good for Mother's precious darling; and it will make her well. There, there, there, put the little head on Mamma's breast and go to sleep, and pretty soon—Oh, I know she can't live till morning! Mortimer, a table-spoonful every half hour will—. Oh, the child needs belladonna too; I know she does—and aconite. Get them, Mortimer. Now do let me have my way. You know nothing about these things."

We now went to bed, placing the crib close to my wife's pillow. All this turmoil had worn upon me, and within two minutes I was something more than half asleep. Mrs. McWilliams roused me:

"Darling, is that register turned on?"

"No."

"I thought as much. Please turn it on at once. This room is cold."

I turned it on, and presently fell asleep again. I was aroused once more:

"Dearie, would you mind moving the crib to your side of the bed? It is nearer the register."

I moved it, but had a collision with the rug and woke up the child. I dozed off once more, while my wife quieted the sufferer. But in a little while these words came murmuring remotely through the fog of my drowsiness:

"Mortimer, if we only had some goose-grease—will you ring?"

I climbed dreamily out, and stepped on a cat, which responded with a protest and would have got a convincing kick for it if a chair had not got it instead.

"Now, Mortimer, why do you want to turn up the gas and wake up the child again?"

"Because I want to see how much I am hurt, Caroline."

"Well look at the chair, too—I have no doubt it is ruined. Poor cat, suppose you had—"

"Now I am not going to suppose anything about the cat. It never would have occurred if Maria had been allowed to remain here and attend to these duties, which are in her line and are not in mine."

"Now Mortimer, I should think you would be ashamed to make a remark like that. It is a pity if you cannot do the few little things I ask of you at such an awful time as this when our child—"

"There, there, I will do anything you want. But I can't raise anybody with this bell. They're all gone to bed. Where is the goose-grease?"

"On the mantel-piece in the nursery. If you'll step there and speak to Maria—"

I fetched the goose-grease and went to sleep again. Once more I was called:

"Mortimer, I so hate to disturb you, but the room is still too cold for me to try to apply this stuff. Would you mind lighting the fire? It is all ready to touch a match to."

I dragged myself out and lit the fire, and then sat down disconsolate.

"Mortimer, don't sit there and catch your death of cold. Come to bed."

As I was stepping in, she said:

"But wait a moment. Please give the child some more of the medicine."

Which I did. It was a medicine which made a child more or less lively; so my wife made use of its waking interval to strip it and grease it all over with the goose-oil. I was soon asleep once more, but once more I had to get up.

"Mortimer, I feel a draft. I feel it distinctly. There is nothing so bad for this disease as a draft. Please move the crib in front of the fire."

I did it; and collided with the rug again, which I threw in the fire. Mrs. McWilliams sprang out of bed and rescued it and we had some words. I had another trifling interval of sleep, and then got up, by request, and constructed a flax-seed poultice.

This was placed upon the child's breast and left there to do its healing work.

A wood fire is not a permanent thing. I got up every twenty minutes and renewed ours, and this gave Mrs. McWilliams the opportunity to shorten the times of giving the medicines by ten minutes, which was a great satisfaction to her. Now and then, between times, I reorganized the flax-seed poultices, and applied sinapisms and other sorts of blisters where unoccupied places could be found upon the child. Well, toward morning the wood gave out and my wife wanted me to go down cellar and get some more. I said:

"My dear, it is a laborious job, and the child must be nearly warm enough, with her extra clothing. Now mightn't we put on another layer of poultices and—"

I did not finish, because I was interrupted. I lugged wood up from below for some little time, and then turned in and fell to snoring as only a man can whose strength is all gone and whose soul is worn out. Just at broad daylight I felt a grip on my shoulder that brought me to my senses suddenly.—My wife was glaring down upon me and gasping. As soon as she could command her tongue she said:

"It is all over! All over! The child's perspiring! What *shall* we do?"

"Mercy, how you terrify me! *I* don't know what we ought to do. Maybe if we scraped her and put her in the draft again—"

"O, idiot! There is not a moment to lose! Go for the doctor. Go yourself. Tell him he *must* come, dead or alive."

I dragged that poor sick man from his bed and brought him. He looked at the child and said she was not dying. This was joy unspeakable to me, but it made my wife as mad as if he had offered her a personal affront. Then he said the child's cough was only caused by some trifling irritation or other in the throat. At this I thought my wife had a mind to show him the door.—Now the doctor said he would make the child cough harder and dislodge the trouble. So he gave her something that sent her into a spasm of coughing, and presently up came a little wood splinter or so.

"This child has no membranous croup," said he. "She has been chewing a bit of pine shingle or something of the kind, and got some little slivers in her throat. They won't do her any hurt."

"No," said I, "I can well believe that. Indeed the turpentine that is in them is very good for certain sorts of diseases that are peculiar to children. My wife will tell you so."

But she did not. She turned away in disdain and left the room; and since that time there is one episode in our life which we never refer to. Hence the tide of our days flows by in deep and untroubled serenity.

[Very few married men have such an experience as McWilliams's, and so the author of this book thought that maybe the novelty of it would give it a passing interest to the reader.]

"Mrs. McWilliams and the Lightning" is one of several tales Twain wrote about the domestic problems of the McWilliams family. The story made its debut in the September 1880 issue of the Atlantic *and appeared the next year in an anthology called* Choice Selections No. 19. *In 1882, it was included in a collection of Twain's sketches called* The Stolen White Elephant, *published by James R. Osgood and Company.*

Mrs. McWilliams and the Lightning

Well, sir,—continued Mr. McWilliams, for this was not the beginning of his talk,—the fear of lightning is one of the most distressing infirmities a human being can be afflicted with. It is mostly confined to women; but now and then you find it in a little dog, and sometimes in a man. It is a particularly distressing infirmity, for the reason that it takes the sand out of a person to an extent which no other fear can, and it can't be *reasoned* with, and neither can it be shamed out of a person. A woman who could face the very devil himself—or a mouse— loses her grip and goes all to pieces in front of a flash of lightning. Her fright is something pitiful to see.

Well, as I was telling you, I woke up, with that smothered and unlocatable cry of "Mortimer! Mortimer!" wailing in my ears; and as soon as I could scrape my faculties together I reached over in the dark and then said,—

"Evangeline, is that you calling? What is the matter? Where are you?"

"Shut up in the boot-closet. You ought to be ashamed to lie there and sleep so, and such an awful storm going on."

"Why, how *can* one be ashamed when he is asleep? It is unreasonable; a man *can't* be ashamed when he is asleep, Evangeline."

"You never try, Mortimer,—you know very well you never try."

I caught the sound of muffled sobs.

953

That sound smote dead the sharp speech that was on my lips,
and I changed it to—

"I'm sorry, dear,—I'm truly sorry. I never meant to act so.
Come back and—"

"MORTIMER!"

"Heavens! what is the matter, my love?"

"Do you mean to say you are in that bed yet?"

"Why, of course."

"Come out of it instantly. I should think you would take
some *little* care of your life, for *my* sake and the children's, if
you will not for your own."

"But my love—"

"Don't talk to me, Mortimer. You *know* there is no place so
dangerous as a bed, in such a thunder-storm as this,—all the
books say that; yet there you would lie, and deliberately throw
away your life,—for goodness knows what, unless for the sake
of arguing and arguing, and—"

"But, confound it, Evangeline, I'm *not* in the bed, *now*.
I'm—"

[Sentence interrupted by a sudden glare of lightning, followed
by a terrified little scream from Mrs. McWilliams and a tremendous blast of thunder.]

"There! You see the result. Oh, Mortimer, how *can* you be so
profligate as to swear at such a time as this?"

"I *didn't* swear. And that *wasn't* a result of it, any way. It
would have come, just the same, if I hadn't said a word; and you
know very well, Evangeline,—at least you ought to know,—that
when the atmosphere is charged with electricity—"

"Oh, yes, now argue it, and argue it, and argue it!—I don't
see how you can act so, when you *know* there is not a lightning-
rod on the place, and your poor wife and children are absolutely
at the mercy of Providence. What *are* you doing?—lighting a
match at such a time as this! Are you stark mad?"

"Hang it, woman, where's the harm? The place is as dark as
the inside of an infidel, and—"

"Put it out! put it out instantly! Are you determined to
sacrifice us all? You *know* there is nothing attracts lightning like
a light. [*Fzt!—crash! boom—boloom-boom-boom!*] Oh, just
hear it! Now you see what you've done!"

"No, I *don't* see what I've done. A match may attract lightning, for all I know, but it don't *cause* lightning,—I'll go odds
on that. And it didn't attract it worth a cent this time; for if that
shot was levelled at my match, it was blessed poor marksmanship,—about an average of none out of a possible million, I

should say. Why, at Dollymount, such marksmanship as that—"

"For shame, Mortimer! Here we are standing right in the very presence of death, and yet in so solemn a moment you are capable of using such language as that. If you have no desire to—Mortimer!"

"Well?"

"Did you say your prayers to-night?"

"I— I— meant to, but I got to trying to cipher out how much twelve times thirteen is, and—"

[*Fzt!—boom-beroom-boom! bumble-umble bang-*SMASH!]

"Oh, we are lost, beyond all help! How *could* you neglect such a thing at such a time as this?"

"But it *wasn't* 'such a time as this.' There wasn't a cloud in the sky. How could *I* know there was going to be all this rumpus and pow-wow about a little slip like that? And I don't think it's just fair for you to make so much out of it, any way, seeing it happens so seldom; I haven't missed before since I brought on that earthquake, four years ago."

"MORTIMER! How you talk! Have you forgotten the yellow fever?"

"My dear, you are always throwing up the yellow fever to me, and I think it is perfectly unreasonable. You can't even send a telegraphic message as far as Memphis without relays, so how is a little devotional slip of mine going to carry so far? I'll *stand* the earthquake, because it was in the neighborhood; but I'll be hanged if I'm going to be responsible for every blamed—"

[*Fzt!—*BOOM *beroom-*boom! boom!—BANG!]

"Oh, dear, dear, dear! I *know* it struck something, Mortimer. We never shall see the light of another day; and if it will do you any good to remember, when we are gone, that your dreadful language—*Mortimer!*"

"WELL! What now?"

"Your voice sounds as if—Mortimer, are you actually standing in front of that open fireplace?"

"That is the very crime I am committing."

"Get away from it, this moment. You do seem determined to bring destruction on us all. Don't you *know* that there is no better conductor for lightning than an open chimney? *Now* where have you got to?"

"I'm here by the window."

"Oh, for pity's sake, have you lost your mind? Clear out from there, this moment. The very children in arms know it is fatal to stand near a window in a thunder-storm. Dear, dear, I know I shall never see the light of another day. Mortimer?"

"Yes?"

"What is that rustling?"

"It's me."

"What are you doing?"

"Trying to find the upper end of my pantaloons."

"Quick! throw those things away! I do believe you would deliberately put on those clothes at such a time as this; yet you know perfectly well that *all* authorities agree that woollen stuffs attract lightning. Oh, dear, dear, it isn't sufficient that one's life must be in peril from natural causes, but you must do everything you can possibly think of to augment the danger. Oh, *don't* sing! What *can* you be thinking of?"

"Now where's the harm in it?"

"Mortimer, if I have told you once, I have told you a hundred times, that singing causes vibrations in the atmosphere which interrupt the flow of the electric fluid, and—What on *earth* are you opening that door for?"

"Goodness gracious, woman, is there any harm in *that?*"

"*Harm?* There's *death* in it. Anybody that has given this subject any attention knows that to create a draught is to invite the lightning. You haven't half shut it; shut it *tight,*—and do hurry, or we are all destroyed. Oh, it is an awful thing to be shut up with a lunatic at such a time as this. Mortimer, what *are* you doing?"

"Nothing. Just turning on the water. This room is smothering hot and close. I want to bathe my face and hands."

"You have certainly parted with the remnant of your mind! Where lightning strikes any other substance once, it strikes water fifty times. Do turn it off. Oh, dear, I am sure that nothing in this world can save us. I does seem to me that—Mortimer, what was that?"

"It was a da— it was a picture. Knocked it down."

"Then you are close to the wall! I never heard of such imprudence! Don't you *know* that there's no better conductor for lightning than a wall? Come away from there! And you came as near as anything to swearing, too. Oh, how can you be so desperately wicked, and your family in such peril? Mortimer, did you order a feather bed, as I asked you to do?"

"No. Forgot it."

"Forgot it! It may cost you your life. If you had a feather bed, now, and could spread it in the middle of the room and lie on it, you would be perfectly safe. Come in here,—come quick, before you have a chance to commit any more frantic indiscretions."

I tried, but the little closet would not hold us both with the door shut, unless we could be content to smother. I gasped awhile, then forced my way out. My wife called out,—

"Mortimer, something *must* be done for your preservation. Give me that German book that is on the end of the mantel-piece, and a candle; but don't light it; give me a match; I will light it in here. That book has some directions in it."

I got the book,—at cost of a vase and some other brittle things; and the madam shut herself up with her candle. I had a moment's peace; then she called out,—

"Mortimer, what was that?"

"Nothing but the cat."

"The cat! Oh, destruction! Catch her, and shut her up in the wash-stand. Do be quick, love; cats are *full* of electricity. I just know my hair will turn white with this night's awful perils."

I heard the muffled sobbings again. But for that, I should not have moved hand or foot in such a wild enterprise in the dark.

However, I went at my task,—over chairs, and against all sorts of obstructions, all of them hard ones, too, and most of them with sharp edges,—and at last I got kitty cooped up in the commode, at an expense of over four hundred dollars in broken furniture and shins. Then these muffled words came from the closet:—

"It says the safest thing is to stand on a chair in the middle of the room, Mortimer; and the legs of the chair must be insulated, with non-conductors. That is, you must set the legs of the chair in glass tumblers. [*Fzt!—boom—bang!—smash!*] Oh, hear that! Do hurry, Mortimer, before you are struck."

I managed to find and secure the tumblers. I got the last four,—broke all the rest. I insulated the chair legs, and called for further instructions.

"Mortimer, it says, 'Während eines Gewitters entferne man Metalle, wie z. B., Ringe, Uhren, Schlüssel, etc., von sich und halte sich auch nicht an solchen Stellen auf, wo viele Metalle bei einander liegen, oder mit andern Körpern verbunden sind, wie an Herden, Oefen, Eisengittern u. dgl.' What does that mean, Mortimer? Does it mean that you must keep metals *about* you, or keep them *away* from you?"

"Well, I hardly know. It appears to be a little mixed. All German advice is more or less mixed. However, I think that that sentence is mostly in the dative case, with a little genitive and ac-cusative sifted in, here and there, for luck; so I reckon it means that you must keep some metals *about* you."

"Yes, that must be it. It stands to reason that it is. They are in the nature of lightning-rods, you know. Put on your fireman's helmet, Mortimer; that is mostly metal."

I got it and put it on,—a very heavy and clumsy and uncomfortable thing on a hot night in a close room. Even my night-dress seemed to be more clothing that I strictly needed.

"Mortimer, I think your middle ought to be protected. Won't you buckle on your militia sabre, please?"

I complied.

"Now, Mortimer, you ought to have some way to protect your feet. Do please put on your spurs."

I did it,—in silence,—and kept my temper as well as I could.

"Mortimer, it says, 'Das Gewitter läuten ist sehr gefährlich, weil die Glocke selbst, sowie der durch das Läuten veranlasste Luftzug und die Höhe des Thurmes den Blitz anziehen könnten.' Mortimer, does that mean that it is dangerous not to ring the church bells during a thunder-storm?"

"Yes, it seems to mean that,—if that is the past participle of the nominative case singular, and I reckon it is. Yes, I think it means that on account of the height of the church tower and the absence of *Luftzug* it would be very dangerous (*sehr gefährlich*) not to ring the bells in time of a storm; and moreover, don't you see, the very wording—"

"Never mind that, Mortimer; don't waste the precious time in talk. Get the large dinner-bell; it is right there in the hall. Quick, Mortimer dear; we are almost safe. Oh, dear, I do believe we are going to be saved at last!"

Our little summer establishment stands on top of a high range of hills, overlooking a valley. Several farm-houses are in our neighborhood,—the nearest some three or four hundred yards away.

When I, mounted on the chair, had been clanging that dreadful bell a matter of seven or eight minutes, our shutters were suddenly torn open from without, and a brilliant bull's-eye lantern was thrust in at the window, followed by a hoarse inquiry:—

"What in the nation is the matter here?"

The window was full of men's heads, and the heads were full of eyes that stared wildly at my night-dress and my warlike accoutrements.

I dropped the bell, skipped down from the chair in confusion, and said,—

"There is nothing the matter, friends,—only a little discomfort on account of the thunder-storm. I was trying to keep off the lightning."

"Thunder-storm? Lightning? Why, Mr. McWilliams, have you lost your mind? It is a beautiful starlight night; there has been no storm."

I looked out, and I was so astonished I could hardly speak for a while. Then I said,—

"I do not understand this. We distinctly saw the glow of the flashes through the curtains and shutters, and heard the thunder."

One after another of those people lay down on the ground to laugh,—and two of them died. One of the survivors remarked,—

"Pity you didn't think to open your blinds and look over to the top of the high hill yonder. What you heard was cannon; what you saw was the flash. You see, the telegraph brought some news, just at midnight: Garfield's nominated,—and that's what's the matter!"

Yes, Mr. Twain, as I was saying in the beginning (said Mr. McWilliams), the rules for preserving people against lightning are so excellent and so innumerable that the most incomprehensible thing in the world to me is how anybody ever manages to get struck.

So saying, he gathered up his satchel and umbrella, and departed; for the train had reached his town.

"The Stolen White Elephant" first appeared in a volume of the same name published by James R. Osgood and Company in 1882. This outrageous farce lampoons detectives, the heroes of the popular fiction of the period.

The Stolen White Elephant*

I

The following curious history was related to me by a chance railway acquaintance. He was a gentleman more than seventy years of age, and his thoroughly good and gentle face and earnest and sincere manner imprinted the unmistakable stamp of truth upon every statement which fell from his lips. He said:—

You know in what reverence the royal white elephant of Siam is held by the people of that country. You know it is sacred to kings, only kings may possess it, and that it is indeed in a measure even superior to kings, since it receives not merely honor but worship. Very well; five years ago, when the troubles concerning the frontier line arose between Great Britain and Siam, it was presently manifest that Siam had been in the wrong. Therefore every reparation was quickly made, and the British representative stated that he was satisfied and the past should be forgotten. This greatly relieved the King of Siam, and partly as a token of gratitude, but partly also, perhaps, to wipe out any little remaining vestige of unpleasantness which England might feel toward him, he wished to send the Queen a present,—the sole sure way of propitiating an enemy, according to Oriental ideas. This present ought not only to be a royal one, but transcendently royal. Wherefore, what offering could be so meet as

---

*Left out of "A Tramp Abroad," because it was feared that some of the particulars had been exaggerated, and that others were not true. Before these suspicions had been proven groundless, the book had gone to press.—M.T.

that of a white elephant? My position in the Indian civil service was such that I was deemed peculiarly worthy of the honor of conveying the present to her Majesty. A ship was fitted out for me and my servants and the officers and attendants of the elephant, and in due time I arrived in New York harbor and placed my royal charge in admirable quarters in Jersey City. It was necessary to remain awhile in order to recruit the animal's health before resuming the voyage.

All went well during a fortnight,—then my calamities began. The white elephant was stolen! I was called up at dead of night and informed of this fearful misfortune. For some moments I was beside myself with terror and anxiety; I was helpless. Then I grew calmer and collected my faculties. I soon saw my course,— for indeed there was but the one course for an intelligent man to pursue. Late as it was, I flew to New York and got a policeman to conduct me to the headquarters of the detective force. Fortunately I arrived in time, though the chief of the force, the celebrated Inspector Blunt, was just on the point of leaving for his home. He was a man of middle size and compact frame, and when he was thinking deeply he had a way of knitting his brows and tapping his forehead reflectively with his finger, which impressed you at once with the conviction that you stood in the presence of a person of no common order. The very sight of him gave me confidence and made me hopeful. I stated my errand. It did not flurry him in the least; it had no more visible effect upon his iron self-possession than if I had told him somebody had stolen my dog. He motioned me to a seat, and said calmly,—

"Allow me to think a moment, please."

So saying, he sat down at his office table and leaned his head upon his hand. Several clerks were at work at the other end of the room; the scratching of their pens was all the sound I heard during the next six or seven minutes. Meantime the inspector sat there, buried in thought. Finally he raised his head, and there was that in the firm lines of his face which showed me that his brain had done its work and his plan was made. Said he,—and his voice was low and impressive,—

"This is no ordinary case. Every step must be warily taken; each step must be made sure before the next is ventured. And secrecy must be observed,—secrecy profound and absolute. Speak to no one about the matter, not even the reporters. I will take care of *them;* I will see that they get only what it may suit my ends to let them know." He touched a bell; a youth appeared. "Alaric, tell the reporters to remain for the present." The boy retired. "Now let us proceed to business,—and systematically. Nothing can be accomplished in this trade of mine without strict and minute method.''

He took a pen and some paper. "Now—name of the elephant?''

"Hassan Ben Ali Ben Selim Abdallah Mohammed Moisé Alhammal Jamsetjejeebhoy Dhuleep Sultan Ebu Bhudpoor.''

"Very well. Given name?''

"Jumbo.''

"Very well. Place of birth?''

"The capital city of Siam.''

"Parents living?''

"No,—dead.''

"Had they any other issue besides this one?''

"None. He was an only child.''

"Very well. These matters are sufficient under that head. Now please describe the elephant, and leave out no particular, however insignificant,—that is, insignificant from *your* point of view. To men in my profession there *are* no insignificant particulars; they do not exist.''

I described,—he wrote. When I was done, he said,—

"Now listen. If I have made any mistakes, correct me.''

He read as follows:—

"Height, 19 feet; length from apex of forehead to insertion of tail, 26 feet; length of trunk, 16 feet; length of tail, 6 feet; total length, including trunk and tail, 48 feet; length of tusks, 9½ feet; ears in keeping with these dimensions; footprint resembles the mark left when one up-ends a barrel in the snow; color of the elephant, a dull white; has a hole the size of a plate in each ear for the insertion of jewelry, and possesses the habit in a remarkable degree of squirting water upon spectators and of maltreating with his trunk not only such persons as he is acquainted with, but even entire strangers; limps slightly with his right hind leg, and has a small scar in his left armpit caused by a former boil; had on, when stolen, a castle containing seats for fifteen persons, and a gold-cloth saddle-blanket the size of an ordinary carpet.''

There were no mistakes. The inspector touched the bell, handed the description to Alaric, and said,—

"Have fifty thousand copies of this printed at once and mailed to every detective office and pawnbroker's shop on the continent.'' Alaric retired. "There,—so far, so good. Next, I must have a photograph of the property.''

I gave him one. He examined it critically, and said,—

"It must do, since we can do no better; but he has his trunk curled up and tucked into his mouth. That is unfortunate, and is calculated to mislead, for of course he does not usually have it in that position." He touched his bell.

"Alaric, have fifty thousand copies of this photograph made, the first thing in the morning, and mail them with the descriptive circulars."

Alaric retired to execute his orders. The inspector said,—

"It will be necessary to offer a reward, of course. Now as to the amount?"

"What sum would you suggest?"

"To *begin* with, I should say,—well, twenty-five thousand dollars. It is an intricate and difficult business; there are a thousand avenues of escape and opportunities of concealment. These thieves have friends and pals everywhere—"

"Bless me, do you know who they are?"

The wary face, practised in concealing the thoughts and feelings within, gave me no token, nor yet the replying words, so quietly uttered:—

"Never mind about that. I may, and I may not. We generally gather a pretty shrewd inkling of who our man is by the manner of his work and the size of the game he goes after. We are not dealing with a pickpocket or a hall thief, now, make up your mind to that. This property was not 'lifted' by a novice. But, as I was saying, considering the amount of travel which will have to be done, and the diligence with which the thieves will cover up their traces as they move along, twenty-five thousand may be too small a sum to offer, yet I think it worth while to start with that."

So we determined upon that figure, as a beginning. Then this man, whom nothing escaped which could by any possibility be made to serve as a clew, said:—

"There are cases in detective history to show that criminals have been detected through peculiarities in their appetites. Now, what does this elephant eat, and how much?"

"Well, as to *what* he eats,—he will eat *anything*. He will eat a man, he will eat a Bible,—he will eat anything *between* a man and a Bible."

"Good,—very good indeed, but too general. Details are necessary,—details are the only valuable things in our trade. Very well,—as to men. At one meal,—or, if you prefer, during one day,—how many men will he eat, if fresh?"

"He would not care whether they were fresh or not; at a single meal he would eat five ordinary men."

"Very good; five men; we will put that down. What nationalities would he prefer?"

"He is indifferent about nationalities. He prefers acquaintances, but is not prejudiced against strangers."

"Very good. Now, as to Bibles. How many Bibles would he eat at a meal?"

"He would eat an entire edition."

"It is hardly succinct enough. Do you mean the ordinary octavo, or the family illustrated?"

"I think he would be indifferent to illustrations; that is, I think he would not value illustrations above simple letter-press."

"No, you do not get my idea. I refer to bulk. The ordinary octavo Bible weighs about two pounds and a half, while the great quarto with the illustrations weighs ten or twelve. How many Doré Bibles would he eat at a meal?"

"If you knew this elephant, you could not ask. He would take what they had."

"Well, put it in dollars and cents, then. We must get at it somehow. The Doré costs a hundred dollars a copy, Russia leather, bevelled."

"He would require about fifty thousand dollars' worth,—say an edition of five hundred copies."

"Now that is more exact. I will put that down. Very well; he likes men and Bibles; so far, so good. What else will he eat? I want particulars."

"He will leave Bibles to eat bricks, he will leave bricks to eat bottles, he will leave bottles to eat clothing, he will leave clothing to eat cats, he will leave cats to eat oysters, he will leave oysters to eat ham, he will leave ham to eat sugar, he will leave sugar to eat pie, he will leave pie to eat potatoes, he will leave potatoes to eat bran, he will leave bran to eat hay, he will leave hay to eat oats, he will leave oats to eat rice, for he was mainly raised on it. There is nothing whatever that he will not eat but European butter, and he would eat that if he could taste it."

"Very good. General quantity at a meal,—say about—"

"Well, anywhere from a quarter to half a ton."

"And he drinks—"

"Everything that is fluid. Milk, water, whiskey, molasses, castor oil, camphene, carbolic acid,—it is no use to go into particulars; whatever fluid occurs to you set it down. He will drink anything that is fluid, except European coffee."

"Very good. As to quantity?"

"Put it down five to fifteen barrels,—his thirst varies; his other appetites do not."

"These things are unusual. They ought to furnish quite good clews toward tracing him."

965

He touched the bell.

"Alaric, summon Captain Burns."

Burns appeared. Inspector Blunt unfolded the whole matter to him, detail by detail. Then he said in the clear, decisive tones of a man whose plans are clearly defined in his head, and who is accustomed to command,—

"Captain Burns, detail Detectives Jones, Davis, Halsey, Bates, and Hackett to shadow the elephant."

"Yes, sir."

"Detail Detectives Moses, Dakin, Murphy, Rogers, Tupper, Higgins, and Bartholomew to shadow the thieves."

"Yes, sir."

"Place a strong guard—a guard of thirty picked men, with a relief of thirty—over the place from whence the elephant was stolen, to keep strict watch there night and day, and allow none to approach—except reporters—without written authority from me."

"Yes, sir."

"Place detectives in plain clothes in the railway, steamship, and ferry depots, and upon all roadways leading out of Jersey City, with orders to search all suspicious persons."

"Yes, sir."

"Furnish all these men with photograph and accompanying description of the elephant, and instruct them to search all trains and outgoing ferry-boats and other vessels."

"Yes, sir."

"If the elephant should be found, let him be seized, and the information forwarded to me by telegraph."

"Yes, sir."

"Let me be informed at once if any clews should be found,—footprints of the animal, or anything of that kind."

"Yes, sir."

"Get an order commanding the harbor police to patrol the frontages vigilantly."

"Yes, sir."

"Despatch detectives in plain clothes over all the railways, north as far as Canada, west as far as Ohio, south as far as Washington."

"Yes, sir."

"Place experts in all the telegraph offices to listen to all messages; and let them require that all cipher despatches be interpreted to them."

"Yes, sir."

"Let all these things be done with the utmost secrecy,—mind, the most impenetrable secrecy."

"Yes, sir."

"Report to me promptly at the usual hour."

"Yes, sir."

"Go!"

"Yes, sir."

He was gone.

Inspector Blunt was silent and thoughtful a moment, while the fire in his eye cooled down and faded out. Then he turned to me and said in a placid voice,—

"I am not given to boasting, it is not my habit; but—we shall find the elephant."

I shook him warmly by the hand and thanked him; and I *felt* my thanks, too. The more I had seen of the man the more I liked him, and the more I admired him and marvelled over the mysterious wonders of his profession. Then we parted for the night, and I went home with a far happier heart than I had carried with me to his office.

II

Next morning it was all in the newspapers, in the minutest detail. It even had additions,—consisting of Detective This, Detective That, and Detective The Other's "Theory" as to how the robbery was done, who the robbers were, and whither they had flown with their booty. There were eleven of these theories, and they covered all the possibilities; and this single fact shows what independent thinkers detectives are. No two theories were alike, or even much resembled each other, save in one striking particular, and in that one all the eleven theories were absolutely agreed. That was, that although the rear of my building was torn out and the only door remained locked, the elephant had not been removed through the rent, but by some other (undiscovered) outlet. All agreed that the robbers had made that rent only to mislead the detectives. That never would have occurred to me or to any other layman, perhaps, but it had not deceived the detectives for a moment. Thus, what I had supposed was the only thing that had no mystery about it was in fact the very thing I had gone furthest astray in. The eleven theories all named the supposed robbers, but no two named the same robbers; the total number of suspected persons was thirty-seven. The various newspaper accounts all closed with the most important opinion of all,—that of Chief Inspector Blunt. A portion of this statement read as follows:—

"The chief knows who the principals are, namely, 'Brick' Duffy and 'Red' McFadden. Ten days before the robbery was achieved he was already aware that it was to be attempted, and had quietly proceeded to shadow these two noted villains; but unfortunately on the night in question their track was lost, and before it could be found again the bird was flown,—that is, the elephant.

"Duffy and McFadden are the boldest scoundrels in the profession; the chief has reasons for believing that they are the men who stole the stove out of the detective headquarters on a bitter night last winter,—in consequence of which the chief and every detective present were in the hands of the physicians before morning, some with frozen feet, others with frozen fingers, ears, and other members."

When I read the first half of that I was more astonished than ever at the wonderful sagacity of this strange man. He not only saw everything in the present with a clear eye, but even the future could not be hidden from him. I was soon at his office, and said I could not help wishing he had had those men arrested, and so prevented the trouble and loss; but his reply was simple and unanswerable:—

"It is not our province to prevent crime, but to punish it. We cannot punish it until it is committed."

I remarked that the secrecy with which we had begun had been marred by the newspapers; not only all our facts but all our plans and purposes had been revealed; even all the suspected persons had been named; these would doubtless disguise themselves now, or go into hiding.

"Let them. They will find that when I am ready for them my hand will descend upon them, in their secret places, as unerringly as the hand of fate. As to the newspapers, we *must* keep in with them. Fame, reputation, constant public mention,— these are the detective's bread and butter. He must publish his facts, else he will be supposed to have none; he must publish his theory, for nothing is so strange or striking as a detective's theory, or brings him so much wondering respect; we must publish our plans, for these the journals insist upon having, and we could not deny them without offending. We must constantly show the public what we are doing, or they will believe we are doing nothing. It is much pleasanter to have a newspaper say, 'Inspector Blunt's ingenious and extraordinary theory is as follows,' than to have it say some harsh thing, or, worse still, some sarcastic one."

"I see the force of what you say. But I noticed that in one part of your remarks in the papers this morning you refused to reveal your opinion upon a certain minor point."

"Yes, we always do that; it has a good effect. Besides, I had not formed any opinion on that point, any way."

I deposited a considerable sum of money with the inspector, to meet current expenses, and sat down to wait for news. We were expecting the telegrams to begin to arrive at any moment now. Meantime I reread the newspapers and also our descriptive circular, and observed that our $25,000 reward seemed to be offered only to detectives. I said I thought it ought to be offered to anybody who would catch the elephant. The inspector said:—

"It is the detectives who will find the elephant, hence the reward will go to the right place. If other people found the animal, it would only be by watching the detectives and taking advantage of clews and indications stolen from them, and that would entitle the detectives to the reward, after all. The proper office of a reward is to stimulate the men who deliver up their time and their trained sagacities to this sort of work, and not to confer benefits upon chance citizens who stumble upon a capture without having earned the benefits by their own merits and labors."

This was reasonable enough, certainly. Now the telegraphic machine in the corner began to click, and the following despatch was the result:—

FLOWER STATION, N.Y., 7:30 A.M.

Have got a clew. Found a succession of deep tracks across a farm near here. Followed them two miles east without result; think elephant went west. Shall now shadow him in that direction.

DARLEY, *Detective.*

"Darley's one of the best men on the force," said the inspector. "We shall hear from him again before long."

Telegram No. 2 came:—

BARKER'S, N.J., 7.40 A.M.

Just arrived. Glass factory broken open here during night, and eight hundred bottles taken. Only water in large quantity near here is five miles distant. Shall strike for there. Elephant will be thirsty. Bottles were empty.

BAKER, *Detective.*

"That promises well, too," said the inspector. "I told you the creature's appetites would not be bad clews."

Telegram No. 3:—

TAYLORVILLE, L.I., 8.15 A.M.

A haystack near here disappeared during night. Probably eaten. Have got a clew, and am off.

HUBBARD, *Detective.*

969

"How he does move around!" said the inspector. "I knew we had a difficult job on hand, but we shall catch him yet."

FLOWER STATION, N.Y., 9 A.M.

Shadowed the tracks three miles westward. Large, deep and ragged. Have just met a farmer who says they are not elephant tracks. Says they are holes where he dug up saplings for shade-trees when ground was frozen last winter. Give me orders how to proceed.

DARLEY, *Detective.*

"Aha! a confederate of the thieves! The thing grows warm," said the inspector.

He dictated the following telegram to Darley:—

Arrest the man and force him to name his pals. Continue to follow the tracks,—to the Pacific, if necessary.

Chief BLUNT.

Next telegram:—

CONEY POINT, PA., 8.45 A.M.

Gas office broken open here during night and three months' unpaid gas bills taken. Have got a clew and am away.

MURPHY, *Detective.*

"Heavens!" said the inspector; "would he eat gas bills?"

"Through ignorance,—yes; but they cannot support life. At least, unassisted."

Now came this exciting telegram:—

IRONVILLE, N.Y., 9.30 A.M.

Just arrived. This village in consternation. Elephant passed through here at five this morning. Some say he went east, some say west, some north, some south,—but all say they did not wait to notice particularly. He killed a horse; have secured a piece of it for a clew. Killed it with his trunk; from style of blow, think he struck it left-handed. From position in which horse lies, think elephant travelled northward along line of Berkley railway. Has four and a half hours' start, but I move on his track at once.

HAWES, *Detective.*

I uttered exclamations of joy. The inspector was as self-contained as a graven image. He calmly touched his bell.

"Alaric, send Captain Burns here."

Burns appeared.

"How many men are ready for instant orders?"

"Ninety-six, sir."

"Send them north at once. Let them concentrate along the line of the Berkley road north of Ironville."

"Yes, sir."

"Let them conduct their movements with the utmost secrecy. As fast as others are at liberty, hold them for orders."

"Yes, sir."

"Go!"

"Yes, sir."

Presently came another telegram:—

SAGE CORNERS, N.Y., 10.30.

Just arrived. Elephant passed through here at 8.15. All escaped from the town but a policeman. Apparently elephant did not strike at policeman, but at the lamp-post. Got both. I have secured a portion of the policeman as clew.

STUMM, *Detective.*

"So the elephant has turned westward," said the inspector. "However, he will not escape, for my men are scattered all over that region."

The next telegram said:—

GLOVER'S, 11.15.

Just arrived. Village deserted, except sick and aged. Elephant passed through three quarters of an hour ago. The anti-temperance mass meeting was in session; he put his trunk in at a window and washed it out with water from cistern. Some swallowed it—since dead; several drowned. Detectives Cross and O'Shaughnessy were passing through town, but going south,—so missed elephant. Whole region for many miles around in terror,—people flying from their homes. Wherever they turn they meet elephant, and many are killed.

BRANT, *Detective.*

I could have shed tears, this havoc so distressed me. But the inspector only said,—

"You see,—we are closing in on him. He feels our presence; he has turned eastward again."

Yet further troublous news was in store for us. The telegraph brought this:—

HOGANPORT, 12.19.

Just arrived. Elephant passed through half an hour ago, creating wildest fright and excitement. Elephant raged around streets; two plumbers going by, killed one—other escaped. Regret general.

O'FLAHERTY, *Detective.*

"Now he is right in the midst of my men," said the inspector. "Nothing can save him."

A succession of telegrams came from detectives who were scattered through New Jersey and Pennsylvania, and who were following clews consisting of ravaged barns, factories, and Sunday school libraries, with high hopes,—hopes amounting to certainties, indeed. The inspector said,—

"I wish I could communicate with them and order them north, but that is impossible. A detective only visits a telegraph office to send his report; then he is off again, and you don't know where to put your hand on him."

Now came this despatch:—

> BRIDGEPORT, CT., 12.15.
> Barnum offers rate of $4,000 a year for exclusive privilege of using elephant as travelling advertising medium from now till detectives find him. Wants to paste circus-posters on him. Desires immediate answer.
>> BOGGS, *Detective*.

"That is perfectly absurd!" I exclaimed.

"Of course it is," said the inspector. "Evidently Mr. Barnum, who thinks he is so sharp, does not know me,—but I know him."

Then he dictated this answer to the despatch:—

> Mr. Barnum's offer declined. Make it $7,000 or nothing.
>> *Chief* BLUNT.

"There. We shall not have to wait long for an answer. Mr. Barnum is not at home; he is in the telegraph office,—it is his way when he has business on hand. Inside of three—"

> DONE.—P.T. BARNUM.

So interrupted the clicking telegraphic instrument. Before I could make a comment upon this extraordinary episode, the following despatch carried my thoughts into another and very distressing channel:—

> BOLIVIA, N.Y., 12.50.
> Elephant arrived here from the south and passed through toward the forest at 11.50, dispersing a funeral on the way, and diminishing the mourners by two. Citizens fired some small cannon-balls into him, and then fled. Detective Burke and I arrived ten minutes later, from the north, but mistook some excavations for footprints, and so lost a good deal of time; but at last we struck the right trail and followed it to the woods. We then got down on our hands and knees and continued to keep a sharp eye on the track, and so shadowed it into the brush. Burke was in advance. Unfortunately the animal had stopped to rest; there-

fore, Burke having his head down, intent upon the track, butted up against the elephant's hind legs before he was aware of his vicinity. Burke instantly rose to his feet, seized the tail, and exclaimed joyfully, "I claim the re——" but got no further, for a single blow of the huge trunk laid the brave fellow's fragments low in death. I fled rearward, and the elephant turned and shadowed me to the edge of the wood, making tremendous speed, and I should inevitably have been lost, but that the remains of the funeral providentially intervened again and diverted his attention. I have just learned that nothing of that funeral is now left; but this is no loss, for there is an abundance of material for another. Meantime, the elephant has disappeared again.

MULROONEY, *Detective.*

We heard no news except from the diligent and confident detectives scattered about New Jersey, Pennsylvania, Delaware, and Virginia,—who were all following fresh and encouraging clews,—until shortly after 2 P.M., when this telegram came:—

BAXTER CENTRE, 2.15.

Elephant been here, plastered over with circus-bills, and broke up a revival, striking down and damaging many who were on the point of entering upon a better life. Citizens penned him up, and established a guard. When Detective Brown and I arrived, some time after, we entered enclosure and proceeded to identify elephant by photograph and description. All marks tallied exactly except one, which we could not see,—the boil-scar under armpit. To make sure, Brown crept under to look, and was immediately brained,—that is, head crushed and destroyed, though nothing issued from debris. All fled; so did elephant, striking right and left with much effect. Has escaped, but left bold blood-track from cannon-wounds. Rediscovery certain. He broke southward, through a dense forest.

BRENT, *Detective.*

That was the last telegram. At nightfall a fog shut down which was so dense that objects but three feet away could not be discerned. This lasted all night. The ferry-boats and even the omnibuses had to stop running.

III

Next morning the papers were as full of detective theories as before; they had all our tragic facts in detail also, and a great many more which they had received from their telegraphic correspondents. Column after column was occupied, a third of its way down, with glaring head-lines, which it made my heart sick to read. Their general tone was like this:—

THE WHITE ELEPHANT AT LARGE! HE MOVES UPON HIS FATAL MARCH! WHOLE VILLAGES DESERTED BY THEIR FRIGHT-STRICKEN OCCUPANTS! PALE TERROR GOES BEFORE HIM. DEATH AND DEVASTATION FOLLOW AFTER! AFTER THESE, THE DETECTIVES. BARNS DESTROYED, FACTORIES GUTTED, HARVESTS DEVOURED, PUBLIC ASSEMBLAGES DISPERSED, ACCOMPANIED BY SCENES OF CARNAGE IMPOSSIBLE TO DESCRIBE! THEORIES OF THIRTY-FOUR OF THE MOST DISTINGUISHED DETECTIVES ON THE FORCE! THEORY OF CHIEF BLUNT!"

"There!" said Inspector Blunt, almost betrayed into excitement, "this is magnificent! This is the greatest windfall that any detective organization ever had. The fame of it will travel to the ends of the earth, and endure to the end of time, and my name with it."

But there was no joy for me. I felt as if I had committed all those red crimes, and that the elephant was only my irresponsible agent. And how the list had grown! In one place he had "interfered with an election and killed five repeaters." He had followed this act with the destruction of two poor fellows, named O'Donahue and McFlannigan, who had "found a refuge in the home of the oppressed of all lands only the day before, and were in the act of exercising for the first time the noble right of American citizens at the polls, when stricken down by the relentless hand of the Scourge of Siam." In another, he had "found a crazy sensation-preacher preparing his next season's heroic attacks on the dance, the theatre, and other things which can't strike back, and had stepped on him." And in still another place he had "killed a lightning-rod agent." And so the list went on, growing redder and redder, and more and more heartbreaking. Sixty persons had been killed, and two hundred and forty wounded. All the accounts bore just testimony to the activity and devotion of the detectives, and all closed with the remark that "three hundred thousand citizens and four detectives saw the dread creature, and two of the latter he destroyed."

I dreaded to hear the telegraphic instrument begin to click again. By and by the messages began to pour in, but I was happily disappointed in their nature. It was soon apparent that all trace of the elephant was lost. The fog had enabled him to search out a good hiding-place unobserved. Telegrams from the most absurdly distant points reported that a dim vast mass had been glimpsed there through the fog at such and such an hour, and was "undoubtedly the elephant." This dim vast mass had been glimpsed in New Haven, in New Jersey, in Pennsylvania, in interior New York, in Brooklyn, and even in the city of New York itself! But in all cases the dim vast mass had vanished quickly and left no trace. Every detective of the large force scattered over this huge extent of country sent his hourly report, and each and every one of them had a clew, and was shadowing something, and was hot upon the heels of it.

But the day passed without other result.

The next day the same.

The next just the same.

The newspaper reports began to grow monotonous with facts that amounted to nothing, clews which led to nothing, and theories which had nearly exhausted the elements which surprise and delight and dazzle.

By advice of the inspector I doubled the reward.

Four more dull days followed. Then came a bitter blow to the poor, hard-working detectives,—the journalists declined to print their theories, and coldly said, "Give us a rest."

Two weeks after the elephant's disappearance I raised the reward to $75,000 by the inspector's advice. It was a great sum, but I felt that I would rather sacrifice my whole private fortune than lose my credit with my government. Now that the detectives were in adversity, the newspapers turned upon them, and began to fling the most stinging sarcasms at them. This gave the minstrels an idea, and they dressed themselves as detectives and hunted the elephant on the stage in the most extravagant way. The caricaturists made pictures of detectives scanning the country with spy-glasses, while the elephant, at their backs, stole apples out of their pockets. And they made all sorts of ridiculous pictures of the detective badge,—you have seen that badge printed in gold on the back of detective novels, no doubt,—it is a wide-staring eye, with the legend, "WE NEVER SLEEP." When detectives called for a drink, the would-be facetious bar-keeper resurrected an obsolete form of expression and said, "Will you have an eye-opener?" All the air was thick with sarcasms.

But there was one man who moved calm, untouched, unaffected, through it all. It was that heart of oak, the Chief Inspector. His brave eye never drooped, his serene confidence never wavered. He always said,—

"Let them rail on; he laughs best who laughs last."

My admiration for the man grew into a species of worship. I was at his side always. His office had become an unpleasant place to me, and now became daily more and more so. Yet if he could endure it I meant to do so also; at least, as long as I could. So I came regularly, and stayed,—the only outsider who seemed to be capable of it. Everybody wondered how I could; and often it seemed to me that I must desert, but at such times I looked into that calm and apparently unconscious face, and held my ground.

About three weeks after the elephant's disappearance I was about to say, one morning, that I should *have* to strike my colors and retire, when the great detective arrested the thought by proposing one more superb and masterly move.

This was to compromise with the robbers. The fertility of this man's invention exceeded anything I have ever seen, and I have had a wide intercourse with the world's finest minds. He said he was confident he could compromise for $100,000 and recover the elephant. I said I believed I could scrape the amount together, but what would become of the poor detectives who had worked so faithfully? He said,—

"In compromises they always get half."

This removed my only objection. So the inspector wrote two notes, in this form:—

DEAR MADAM,—Your husband can make a large sum of money (and be entirely protected from the law) by making an immediate appointment with me.

Chief BLUNT.

He sent one of these by his confidential messenger to the "reputed wife" of Brick Duffy, and the other to the reputed wife of Red McFadden.

Within the hour these offensive answers came:—

YE OWLD FOOL: brick McDuffys bin ded 2 yere.

BRIDGET MAHONEY.

CHIEF BAT,—Red McFadden is hung and in heving 18 month. Any Ass but a detective knose that.

MARY O'HOOLIGAN.

"I had long suspected these facts," said the inspector; "this testimony proves the unerring accuracy of my instinct."

The moment one resource failed him he was ready with another. He immediately wrote an advertisement for the morning papers, and I kept a copy of it:—

A.—xwblv.242 N. Tjnd—fz328wmlg. Ozpo,—; 2m!ogw. Mum.

He said that if the thief was alive this would bring him to the usual rendezvous. He further explained that the usual rendezvous was a place where all business affairs between detectives and criminals were conducted. This meeting would take place at twelve the next night.

We could do nothing till then, and I lost no time in getting out of the office, and was grateful indeed for the privilege.

At 11 the next night I brought $100,000 in bank-notes and put them into the chief's hands, and shortly afterward he took his leave, with the brave old undimmed confidence in his eye. An almost intolerable hour dragged to a close; then I heard his welcome tread, and rose gasping and tottered to meet him. How his fine eyes flamed with triumph! He said,—

"We've compromised! The jokers will sing a different tune to-morrow! Follow me!"

He took a lighted candle and strode down into the vast vaulted basement where sixty detectives always slept, and where a score were now playing cards to while the time. I followed close after him. He walked swiftly down to the dim remote end of the place, and just as I succumbed to the pangs of suffocation and was swooning away he stumbled and fell over the outlying members of a mighty object, and I heard him exclaim as he went down,—

"Our noble profession is vindicated. Here is your elephant!"

I was carried to the office above and restored with carbolic acid. The whole detective force swarmed in, and such another season of triumphant rejoicing ensued as I had never witnessed before. The reporters were called, baskets of champagne were opened, toasts were drunk, the handshakings and congratulations were continuous and enthusiastic. Naturally the chief was the hero of the hour, and his happiness was so complete and had been so patiently and worthily and bravely won that it made me happy to see it, though I stood there a homeless beggar, my priceless charge dead, and my position in my country's service lost to me through what would always seem my fatally careless execution of a great trust. Many an eloquent eye testified its deep admiration for the chief, and many a detective's voice murmured, "Look at him,—just the king of the profession,—only give him a clew, it's all he wants, and there ain't anything hid that he can't find." The dividing of the $50,000 made great pleasure; when it was finished the chief made a little speech while he put his share in his pocket, in which he said, "Enjoy it, boys, for you've earned it; and more than that you've earned for the detective profession undying fame."

A telegram arrived, which read:—

MONROE, MICH., 10 P.M.

First time I've struck a telegraph office in over three weeks. Have followed those footprints, horseback, through the woods, a thousand miles to here, and they get stronger and bigger and fresher every day.

Don't worry—inside of another week I'll have the elephant. This is dead sure.

DARLEY, *Detective.*

The chief ordered three cheers for "Darley, one of the finest minds on the force," and then commanded that he be telegraphed to come home and receive his share of the reward.

So ended that marvelous episode of the stolen elephant. The newspapers were pleasant with praises once more, the next day, with one contemptible exception. This sheet said, "Great is the detective! He may be a little slow in finding a little thing like a mislaid elephant,—he may hunt him all day and sleep with his rotting carcass all night for three weeks, but he will find him at last—if he can get the man who mislaid him to show him the place!"

Poor Hassan was lost to me forever. The cannon-shots had wounded him fatally, he had crept to that unfriendly place in the fog, and there, surrounded by his enemies and in constant danger of detection, he had wasted away with hunger and suffering till death gave him peace.

The compromise cost me $100,000; my detective expenses were $42,000 more; I never applied for a place again under my government; I am a ruined man and a wanderer in the earth,—but my admiration for that man, whom I believe to be the greatest detective the world has ever produced, remains undimmed to this day, and will so remain unto the end.

Twain claimed that he had written the "Legend of Sagenfeld, in Germany" for A Tramp Abroad, *but the tale was cut from the final version of the travelogue that was published in 1880. Instead, the story made its first appearance two years later· in* The Stolen White Elephant, *a collection of sketches issued by James R. Osgood and Company.*

Legend of Sagenfeld, in Germany*

I

More than a thousand years ago this small district was a kingdom,—a little bit of a kingdom, a sort of dainty little toy kingdom, as one might say. It was far removed from the jealousies, strifes, and turmoils of that old warlike day, and so its life was a simple life, its people a gentle and guileless race; it lay always in a deep dream of peace, a soft Sabbath tranquility; there was no malice, there was no envy, there was no ambition, consequently there were no heart-burnings, there was no unhappiness in the land.

In the course of time the old king died and his little son Hubert came to the throne. The people's love for him grew daily; he was so good and so pure and so noble, that by and by this love became a passion, almost a worship. Now at his birth the soothsayers had diligently studied the stars and found something written in that shining book to this effect:—

In Hubert's fourteenth year a pregnant event will happen; the animal whose singing shall sound sweetest in Hubert's ear shall save Hubert's life. So long as the king and the nation shall honor this animal's race for this good deed, the ancient dynasty shall not fail of an heir, nor the nation know war or pestilence or poverty. But beware an erring choice!

* Left out of "A Tramp Abroad" because its authenticity seemed doubtful, and could not at that time be proved.—M.T.

981

All through the king's thirteenth year but one thing was talked of by the soothsayers, the statesmen, the little parliament, and the general people. That one thing was this: How is the last sentence of the prophecy to be understood? What goes before seems to mean that the saving animal will choose *itself*, at the proper time; but the closing sentence seems to mean that the *king* must choose beforehand, and say what singer among the animals pleases him best, and that if he choose wisely the chosen animal will save his life, his dynasty, his people, but that if he should make "an erring choice"—beware!

By the end of the year there were as many opinions about this matter as there had been in the beginning; but a majority of the wise and the simple were agreed that the safest plan would be for the little king to make choice beforehand, and the earlier the better. So an edict was sent forth commanding all persons who owned singing creatures to bring them to the great hall of the palace in the morning of the first day of the new year. This command was obeyed. When everything was in readiness for the trial, the king made his solemn entry with the great officers of the crown, all clothed in their robes of state. The king mounted his golden throne and prepared to give judgment. But he presently said,—

"These creatures all sing at once; the noise is unendurable; no one can choose in such a turmoil. Take them all away, and bring back one at a time."

This was done. One sweet warbler after another charmed the young king's ear and was removed to make way for another candidate. The precious minutes slipped by; among so many bewildering songsters he found it hard to choose, and all the harder because that promised penalty for an error was so terrible that it unsettled his judgment and made him afraid to trust his own ears. He grew nervous and his face showed distress. His ministers saw this, for they never took their eyes from him a moment. Now they began to say in their hearts,—

"He has lost courage—the cool head is gone—he will err—he and his dynasty and his people are doomed!"

At the end of an hour the king sat silent awhile, and then said,—

"Bring back the linnet."

The linnet trilled forth her jubilant music. In the midst of it the king was about to uplift his sceptre in sign of choice, but checked himself and said,—

"But let us be sure. Bring back the thrush; let them sing together."

The thrush was brought, and the two birds poured out their

marvels of song together. The king wavered, then his inclination began to settle and strengthen—one could see it in his countenance. Hope budded in the hearts of the old ministers, their pulses began to beat quicker, the sceptre began to rise slowly, when—

There was a hideous interruption! It was a sound like this—just at the door:—

"Waw . . . . . . *he!*—waw . . . . . . *he!*—waw-he! waw-he!—waw he!"

Everybody was sorely startled—and enraged at himself for showing it.

The next instant the dearest, sweetest, prettiest little peasant maid of nine years came tripping in, her brown eyes glowing with childish eagerness; but when she saw that august company and those angry faces she stopped and hung her head and put her poor coarse apron to her eyes. Nobody gave her welcome, none pitied her. Presently, she looked up timidly through her tears, and said,—

"My lord the king, I pray you pardon me, for I meant no wrong. I have no father and no mother, but I have a goat and a donkey, and they are all in all to me. My goat gives me the sweetest milk, and when my good dear donkey brays it seems to me there is no music like it. So when my lord the king's jester said the sweetest singer among all the animals should save the crown and nation, and moved me to bring him here—"

All the court burst into a rude laugh, and the child fled away crying, without trying to finish her speech. The chief minister gave a private order that she and her disastrous donkey be flogged beyond the precincts of the palace and commanded to come within them no more.

Then the trial of the birds was resumed. The two birds sang their best, but the sceptre lay motionless in the king's hand. Hope died slowly out in the breasts of all. An hour went by; two hours; still no decision. The day waned to its close, and the waiting multitudes outside the palace grew crazed with anxiety and apprehension. The twilight came on, the shadows fell deeper and deeper. The king and his court could no longer see each other's faces. No one spoke—none called for lights. The great trial had been made; it had failed; each and all wished to hide their faces from the light and cover up their deep trouble in their own hearts.

Finally—hark! A rich, full strain of the divinest melody streamed forth from a remote part of the hall,—the nightingale's voice!

"Up!" shouted the king, "let all the bells make proclamation to the people, for the choice is made and we have not erred. King, dynasty, and nation are saved. From henceforth let the nightingale be honored throughout the land forever. And publish it among all the people that whosoever shall insult a nightingale, or injure it, shall suffer death. The king hath spoken."

All that little world was drunk with joy. The castle and the city blazed with bonfires all night long, the people danced and drank and sang, and the triumphant clamor of the bells never ceased.

From that day the nightingale was a sacred bird. Its song was heard in every house; the poets wrote its praises; the painters painted it; its sculptured image adorned every arch and turret and fountain and public building. It was even taken into the king's councils; and no grave matter of state was decided until the soothsayers had laid the thing before the state nightingale and translated to the ministry what it was that the bird had sung about it.

II

The young king was very fond of the chase. When the summer was come he rose forth with hawk and hound, one day, in a brilliant company of his nobles. He got separated from them, by and by, in a great forest, and took what he imagined a near cut, to find them again; but it was a mistake. He rode on and on, hopefully at first, but with sinking courage finally. Twilight came on, and still he was plunging through a lonely and unknown land. Then came a catastrophe. In the dim light he forced his horse through a tangled thicket overhanging a steep and rocky declivity. When horse and rider reached the bottom, the former had a broken neck and the latter a broken leg. The poor little king lay there suffering agonies of pain, and each hour seemed a long month to him. He kept his ear strained to hear any sound that might promise hope of rescue; but he heard no voice, no sound of horn or bay of hound. So at last he gave up all hope, and said, "Let death come, for come it must."

Just then the deep, sweet song of a nightingale swept across the still wastes of the night.

"Saved!" the king said. "Saved! It is the sacred bird, and the prophecy is come true. The gods themselves protected me from error in the choice."

He could hardly contain his joy; he could not word his gratitude. Every few moments, now, he thought he caught the sound of approaching succor. But each time it was a disappointment; no succor came. The dull hours drifted on. Still no help came,—but still the sacred bird sang on. He began to have misgivings about his choice, but he stifled them. Toward dawn the bird ceased. The morning came, and with it thirst and hunger; but no succor. The day waxed and waned. At last the king cursed the nightingale.

Immediately the song of the thrush came out from the wood. The king said in his heart, "This was the true bird—my choice was false—succor will come now."

But it did not come. Then he lay many hours insensible. When he came to himself, a linnet was singing. He listened—with apathy. His faith was gone. "These birds," he said, "can bring no help; I and my house and my people are doomed." He turned him about to die; for he was grown very feeble from hunger and thirst and suffering, and felt that his end was near. In truth, he wanted to die, and be released from pain. For long hours he lay without thought or feeling or motion. Then his senses returned. The dawn of the third morning was breaking. Ah, the world seemed very beautiful to those worn eyes. Suddenly a great longing to live rose up in the lad's heart, and from his soul welled a deep and fervent prayer that Heaven would have mercy upon him and let him see his home and his friends once more. In that instant a soft, a faint, a far-off sound, but oh, how inexpressibly sweet to his waiting ear, came floating out of the distance,—

"Waw . . . . . *he!*—waw . . . . . . *he!*—waw-he!—waw-he!—waw-he!"

"*That*, oh, *that* song is sweeter, a thousand times sweeter, than the voice of nightingale, thrush, or linnet, for it brings not mere hope, but *certainty* of succor; and now indeed am I saved! The sacred singer has chosen itself, as the oracle intended; the prophecy is fulfilled, and my life, my house, and my people are redeemed. The ass shall be sacred from this day!"

The divine music grew nearer and nearer, stronger and stronger,—and ever sweeter and sweeter to the perishing sufferer's ear. Down the declivity the docile little donkey wandered, cropping herbage and singing as he went; and when at last he saw the dead horse and the wounded king, he came and snuffed at them with simple and marvelling curiosity. The king petted him, and he knelt down as had been his wont when his little mistress desired to mount. With great labor and pain the lad drew himself upon the creature's back, and held himself there by aid of the generous ears. The ass went singing forth from the place and carried the king to the little peasant maid's hut. She gave him her pallet for a bed, refreshed him with goat's milk, and then flew to tell the great news to the first scouting party of searchers she might meet.

The king got well. His first act was to proclaim the sacredness and inviolability of the ass; his second was to add this particular ass to his cabinet and make him chief minister of the crown; his third was to have all the statues and effigies of nightingales throughout his kingdom destroyed, and replaced by statues and effigies of the sacred donkey; and his fourth was to announce that when the little peasant maid should reach her fifteenth year he would make her his queen,—and he kept his word.

Such is the legend. This explains why the mouldering image of the ass adorns all these old crumbling walls and arches; and it explains why, during many centuries, an ass was always the chief minister in that royal cabinet, just as is still the case in most cabinets to this day; and it also explains why, in that little kingdom, during many centuries, all great poems, all great speeches, all great books, all public solemnities, and all royal proclamations, always began with these stirring words,—

"Waw . . . . . . *he!*—waw . . . . . . *he!*—waw-he!—waw-he!—waw-he!"

"Some Rambling Notes of an Idle Excursion," which describes Twain's visit to the island of Bermuda, was written for the Atlantic, *where it appeared in monthly installments from October 1877 to January 1878. The piece appeared in a small collection called* Punch, Brothers, Punch!, *published by Slote, Woodman & Company of New York in 1878. It was also published in another of Twain's collections,* The Stolen White Elephant, *issued by James R. Osgood and Company in 1882.*

Some Rambling Notes
of an Idle Excursion

I

All the journeyings I had ever done had been purely in the way
of business. The pleasant May weather suggested a novelty,
namely, a trip for pure recreation, the bread-and-butter element
left out. The Reverend said he would go, too: a good man, one
of the best of men, although a clergyman. By eleven at night we
were in New Haven and on board the New York boat. We
bought our tickets, and then went wandering around, here and
there, in the solid comfort of being free and idle, and of putting
distance between ourselves and the mails and telegraphs.

After a while I went to my state-room and undressed, but the
night was too enticing for bed. We were moving down the bay
now, and it was pleasant to stand at the window and take the
cool night-breeze and watch the gliding lights on shore. Presently, two elderly men sat down under that window and began a
conversation. Their talk was properly no business of mine, yet I
was feeling friendly toward the world and willing to be entertained. I soon gathered that they were brothers, that they were
from a small Connecticut village, and that the matter in hand
concerned the cemetery. Said one,—

"Now, John, we talked it all over amongst ourselves, and this
is what we've done. You see, every body was a-movin' from the
old buryin' ground, and our folks was most about left to their-
selves, as you may say. They was crowded, too, as you know; lot
wa'n't big enough in the first place; and last year, when Seth's

wife died, we couldn't hardly tuck her in. She sort o' overlaid Deacon Shorb's lot, and he soured on her, so to speak, and on the rest of us, too. So we talked it over, and I was for a lay-out in the new simitery on the hill. They wa'n't unwilling, if it was cheap. Well the two best and biggest plots was No. 8 and No. 9—both of a size; nice comfortable room for twenty-six— twenty-six full-growns, that is; but you reckon in children and other shorts, and strike an everage, and I should say you might lay in thirty, or maybe thirty-two or three, pretty genteel—no crowdin' to signify.''

"That's a plenty, William. Which one did you buy?''

"Well, I'm a-coming to that, John. You see, No. 8 was thirteen dollars, No. 9 fourteen—''

"I see. So 's 't you took No. 8.''

"You wait. I took No. 9. And I'll tell you for why. In the first place, Deacon Shorb wanted it. Well, after the way he'd gone on about Seth's wife overlappin' his prem'ses, I'd 'a' beat him out of that No. 9 if I'd 'a' had to stand two dollars extra, let alone one. That's the way I felt about it. Says I, what's a dollar any way? Life's on'y a pilgrimage, says I; we ain't here for good, and we can't take it with us, says I. So I just dumped it down, knowin' the Lord don't suffer a good deed to go for nothin', and cal'latin' to take it out o' somebody in the course o' trade. Then there was another reason, John. No. 9's a long way the handiest lot in the simitery, and the likeliest for situation. It lays right on top of a knoll, in the dead centre of the buryin' ground; and you can see Millport from there, and Tracy's, and Hopper Mount, and a raft o' farms, and so on. There ain't no better outlook from a buryin' plot in the State. Si Higgins says so, and I reckon he ought to know. Well, and that ain't all. 'Course Shorb had to take No. 8; wa'n't no help for 't. Now, No. 8 jines on to No. 9, but it's on the slope of the hill, and every time it rains, it 'll soak right down on to the Shorbs. Si Higgins says 't when the deacon's time comes, he better take out fire and marine insurance both on his remains.''

Here there was the sound of a low, placid, duplicate chuckle of appreciation and satisfaction.

"Now, John, here's a little rough draft of the ground, that I've made on a piece of paper. Up here in the left-hand corner we've bunched the departed; took them from the old grave-yard and stowed them one along side o' t' other, on a first-come-first-served plan, no partialities, with gran'ther Jones for a starter, on'y because it happened so, and windin' up indiscriminate with Seth's twins. A little crowded towards the end of the lay-out, maybe, but we reckoned 't wa'n't best to scatter the twins. Well, next comes the livin'. Here, where it's marked A, we're goin' to put Mariar and her family, when they're called; B, that's for brother Hosea and his'n; C, Calvin and tribe. What's left is these two lots here,—just the gem of the whole patch for general style and outlook; they're for me and my folks, and you and yourn. Which of them would you ruther be buried in?''

''I swan you've took me mighty onexpected, William! It sort of started the shivers. Fact is, I was thinkin' so busy about makin' things comfortable for the others, I hadn't thought about being buried myself.''

''Life's on'y a fleetin' show, John, as the sayin' is. We've all got to go, sooner or later. To go with a clean record's the main thing. Fact is, it's the on'y thing worth strivin' for, John.''

''Yes, that's so, William, that's so; there ain't no getting around it. Which of these lots would you recommend?''

''Well, it depends, John. Are you particular about outlook?''

''I don't say I am, William; I don't say I ain't. Reely I don't know. But mainly, I reckon, I'd set store by a south exposure.''

''That's easy fixed, John. They're both south exposure. They take the sun and the Shorbs get the shade.''

''How about sile, William?''

''D's a sandy sile, E's mostly loom.''

''You may gimme E, then, William; a sandy sile caves in, more or less, and costs for repairs.''

''All right; set your name down here, John, under E. Now, if you don't mind payin' me your share of the fourteen dollars, John, while we're on the business, every thing's fixed.''

After some higgling and sharp bargaining, the money was paid, and John bade his brother good-night and took his leave. There was silence for some moments; then a soft chuckle welled up from the lonely William, and he muttered: ''I declare for't, if I haven't made a mistake! It's D that's mostly loom, not E. And John's booked for a sandy sile after all.''

There was another soft chuckle, and William departed to his rest, also.

The next day, in New York, was a hot one. Still we managed to get more or less entertainment out of it. Toward the middle of the afternoon we arrived on board the stanch steamship Bermuda, with bag and baggage, and hunted for a shady place. It was blazing summer weather, until we were half way down the harbor. Then I buttoned my coat closely; half an hour later I put on a spring overcoat and buttoned that. As we passed the light-ship I added an ulster and tied a handkerchief around the collar to hold it snug to my neck. So rapidly had the summer gone and winter come again!

By nightfall we were far out at sea, with no land in sight. No telegrams could come here, no letters, no news. This was an uplifting thought. It was still more uplifting to reflect that the millions of harassed people on shore behind us were suffering just as usual.

The next day brought us into the midst of the Atlantic solitudes—out of smoke-colored soundings into fathomless deep blue; no ships visible anywhere over the wide ocean; no company but Mother Cary's chickens wheeling, darting, skimming the waves in the sun. There were some seafaring men among the passengers, and conversation drifted into matters concerning ships and sailors. One said that "true as the needle to the pole" was a bad figure, since the needle seldom pointed to the pole. He said a ship's compass was not faithful to any particular point, but was the most fickle and treacherous of the servants of man. It was forever changing. It changed every day in the year; consequently the amount of the daily variation had to be ciphered out and allowance made for it, else the mariner would go utterly astray. Another said there was a vast fortune waiting for the genius who should invent a compass that would not be affected by the local influences of an iron ship. He said there was only one creature more fickle than a wooden ship's compass, and that was the compass of an iron ship. Then came reference to the well-known fact that an experienced mariner can look at the compass of a new iron vessel, thousands of miles from her birthplace, and tell which way her head was pointing when she was in process of building.

Now an ancient whale-ship master fell to talking about the sort of crew they used to have in his early days. Said he—

"Sometimes we'd have a batch of college students. Queer lot. Ignorant? Why, they didn't know the cat-heads from the main brace. But if you took them for fools you'd get bit, sure. They'd learn more in a month than another man would in a year. We had one, once, in the Mary Ann, that came aboard with gold spectacles on. And besides, he was rigged out from main truck to keelson in the nobbiest clothes that ever saw a fo'castle. He had a chest full, too: cloaks, and broadcloth coats, and velvet vests; every thing swell, you know; and didn't the salt water fix them out for him? I guess not! Well, going to sea, the mate told him to go aloft and help shake out the fore-to'-gallants'l. Up he shins to the foretop, with his spectacles on, and in a minute down he comes again, looking insulted. Says the mate, 'What did you come for?' Says the chap, 'P'raps you didn't notice that there ain't any ladders above there.' You see we hadn't any shrouds above the foretop. The men bursted out in a laugh such

as I guess you never heard the like of. Next night, which was
dark and rainy, the mate ordered this chap to go aloft about
something, and I'm dummed if he didn't start up with an umbrella and a lantern! But no matter; he made a mighty good
sailor before the voyage was done, and we had to hunt up
something else to laugh at. Years afterwards, when I had forgot
all about him, I comes into Boston, mate of a ship, and was loafing around town with the second mate, and it so happened that
we stepped into the Revere House, thinking maybe we would
chance the salt-horse in that big dining-room for a flyer, as the
boys say. Some fellows were talking just at our elbow, and one
says, 'Yonder's the new governor of Massachusetts—at that
table over there, with the ladies.' We took a good look, my mate
and I, for we hadn't either of us ever seen a governor before. I
looked and looked at that face, and then all of a sudden it
popped on me! But I didn't give any sign. Says I, 'Mate, I've a
notion to go over and shake hands with him.' Says he, 'I think I
see you doing it, Tom.' Says I, 'Mate, I'm a-going to do it.' Says
he, 'Oh, yes, I guess so! Maybe you don't want to bet you will,
Tom?' Says I, 'I don't mind going a V on it, mate.' Says he, 'Put
it up.' 'Up she goes,' says I, planking the cash. This surprised
him. But he covered it, and says, pretty sarcastic, 'Hadn't you
better take your grub with the governor and the ladies, Tom?'
Says I, 'Upon second thoughts, I will.' Says he, 'Well, Tom, you
are a dum fool.' Says I, 'Maybe I am, maybe I ain't; but the
main question is, Do you want to risk two and a half that I won't
do it?' 'Make it a V,' says he. 'Done,' says I. I started, him a-
giggling and slapping his hand on his thigh, he felt so good. I
went over there and leaned my knuckles on the table a minute,
and looked the governor in the face, and says I, 'Mister Gard-
ner, don't you know me?' He stared, and I stared, and he stared.
Then all of a sudden he sings out, 'Tom Bowling, by the holy
poker! Ladies, it's old Tom Bowling, that you've heard me talk
about—shipmate of mine in the Mary Ann.' He rose up and
shook hands with me ever so hearty—I sort of glanced around
and took a realizing sense of my mate's saucer eyes—and then,
says the governor, 'Plant yourself, Tom; plant yourself; you
can't cat your anchor again till you've had a feed with me and
the ladies!' I planted myself alongside the governor, and canted
my eye around towards my mate. Well, sir, his dead-lights were
bugged out like tompions; and his mouth stood that wide open
that you could have laid a ham in it without him noticing it.''

There was great applause at the conclusion of the old captain's story; then, after a moment's silence, a grave, pale young
man said:

"Had you ever met the governor before?"

The old captain looked steadily at this inquirer a while, and then got up and walked aft without making any reply. One passenger after another stole a furtive glance at the inquirer, but failed to make him out, and so gave him up. It took some little work to get the talk-machinery to running smoothly again after this derangement; but at length a conversation sprang up about that important and jealously guarded instrument, a ship's time-keeper; its exceeding delicate accuracy, and the wreck and destruction that have sometimes resulted from its varying a few seemingly trifling moments from the true time; then, in due course, my comrade, the Reverend, got off on a yarn, with a fair wind and every thing drawing. It was a true story, too—about Captain Rounceville's shipwreck—true in every detail. It was to this effect:

Captain Rounceville's vessel was lost in mid-Atlantic, and likewise his wife and his two little children. Captain Rounceville and seven seamen escaped with life, but with little else. A small, rudely constructed raft was to be their home for eight days. They had neither provisions nor water. They had scarcely any clothing; no one had a coat but the captain. This coat was changing hands all the time, for the weather was very cold. Whenever a man became exhausted with the cold, they put the coat on him and laid him down between two shipmates until the garment and their bodies had warmed life into him again. Among the sailors was a Portuguese who knew no English. He seemed to have no thought of his own calamity, but was concerned only about the captain's bitter loss of wife and children. By day, he would look his dumb compassion in the captain's face; and by night, in the darkness and the driving spray and rain, he would seek out the captain, and try to comfort him with caressing pats on the shoulder. One day, when hunger and thirst were making their sure inroads upon the men's strength and spirits, a floating barrel was seen at a distance. It seemed a great find, for doubtless it contained food of some sort. A brave fellow swam to it, and, after long and exhausting effort, got it to the raft. It was eagerly opened. It was a barrel of magnesia! On the fifth day an onion was spied. A sailor swam off and got it. Although perishing with hunger, he brought it in its integrity and put it into the captain's hand. The history of the sea teaches that among starving, ship-wrecked men selfishness is rare, and a wonder-compelling magnanimity the rule. The onion was equally divided into eight parts, and eaten with deep thanksgivings. On the eighth day a distant ship was sighted. Attempts were made to hoist an oar, with Captain Rounceville's coat on it for a signal. There were many failures, for the men were but skeletons now, and strengthless. At last success was achieved, but the signal brought no help. The ship faded out of sight and left despair behind her. By and by another ship appeared, and passed so near that the castaways, every eye eloquent with gratitude, made ready to welcome the boat that would be sent to save them. But this ship also drove on, and left these men staring their unutterable surprise and dismay into each other's ashen faces. Late in the day, still another ship came up out of the distance, but the men noted with a pang that her course was one which would not bring her nearer. Their remnant of life was nearly spent; their lips and tongues were swollen, parched, cracked with eight days' thirst; their bodies starved; and here was their last chance gliding relentlessly from them; they would not be alive when the next sun rose. For a day or two past the men had lost their voices, but now Captain Rounceville whispered, "Let us pray." The Portuguese patted him on the shoulder in sign of deep approval. All knelt at the base of the oar that was waving the signal-coat aloft, and bowed their heads. The sea was tossing; the sun rested, a red, rayless disk, on the sea-line in the west. When the men presently raised their heads they would have roared a hallelujah if they had had a voice—the ship's sails lay wrinkled and flapping against her masts; she was going about! Here was rescue at last, and in the very last instant of time that was left for it. No, not rescued yet—only the imminent prospect of it. The red disk sank under the sea and darkness blotted out the ship. By and by came a pleasant sound—oars moving in a boat's rowlocks. Nearer it came and nearer—within thirty steps—but nothing visible. Then a deep voice: "Hol-*lo!*" The castaways could not answer; their swollen tongues refused voice. The boat skirted round and round the raft, started away—the agony of it!—returned, rested the oars, close at hand, listening, no doubt. The deep voice again: "Hol-*lo!* Where are ye, shipmates?" Captain Rounceville whispered to his men, saying: "Whisper your best, boys; now—all at once!" So they sent out an eight-fold whisper in hoarse concert: "Here!" There was life in it if it succeeded; death if it failed; after that supreme moment Captain Rounceville was conscious of nothing until he came to himself on board the saving ship. Said the Reverend, concluding:

"There was one little moment of time in which that raft could be visible from that ship, and only one. If that one little fleeting moment had passed unfruitful, those men's doom was sealed. As close as that does God shave events foreordained from the beginning of the world. When the sun reached the water's edge that day, the captain of that ship was sitting on deck reading his prayer-book. The book fell; he stooped to pick it up, and happened to glance at the sun. In that instant that far-off raft appeared for a second against the red disk, its needle-like oar and diminutive signal cut sharp and black against the bright surface, and in the next instant was thrust away into the dusk again. But that ship, that captain, and that pregnant instant had their work appointed for them in the dawn of time, and could not fail of the performance. The chronometer of God never errs!''

There was deep, thoughtful silence for some moments; then the grave, pale young man said:

''What is the chronometer of God?''

II

At dinner, six o'clock, the same people assembled whom we had talked with on deck and seen at luncheon and breakfast this second day out, and at dinner the evening before. That is to say, three journeying ship-masters, a Boston merchant, and a returning Bermudian who had been absent from his Bermuda thirteen years; these sat on the starboard side. On the port side sat the Reverend in the seat of honor; the pale young man next to him; I next; next to me an aged Bermudian, returning to his sunny islands after an absence of twenty-seven years. Of course our captain was at the head of the table, the purser at the foot of it. A small company, but small companies are pleasantest.

No racks upon the table; the sky cloudless, the sun brilliant, the blue sea scarcely ruffled. Then what had become of the four married couples, the three bachelors, and the active and obliging doctor from the rural districts of Pennsylvania? for all these were on deck when we sailed down New York harbor. This is the explanation. I quote from my note-book:

Thursday, 3.30 P.M. Under way, passing the Battery. The large party, of four married couples, three bachelors, and a cheery, exhilarating doctor from the wilds of Pennsylvania, are evidently travelling together. All but the doctor grouped in camp-chairs on deck.

Passing principal fort. The doctor is one of those people who has an infallible preventive of sea-sickness; is flitting from friend to friend administering it, and saying, ''Don't you be afraid; I *know* this medicine; absolutely infallible; prepared under my own supervision.'' Takes a dose himself, intrepidly.

4.15 P.M. Two of those ladies have struck their colors, notwithstanding the ''infallible.'' They have gone below. The other two begin to show distress.

5 P.M. Exit one husband and one bachelor. These still had their infallible in cargo when they started, but arrived at the companion-way without it.

5.10. Lady No. 3, two bachelors, and one married man have gone below with their own opinion of the infallible.

5.20. Passing Quarantine Hulk. The infallible has done the business for all the party except the Scotchman's wife and the author of that formidable remedy.

Nearing the Light-Ship. Exit the Scotchman's wife, head drooped on stewardess's shoulder.

Entering the open sea. Exit doctor!

The rout seems permanent; hence the smallness of the company at table since the voyage began. Our captain is a grave, handsome Hercules of thirty-five, with a brown hand of such majestic size that one cannot eat for admiring it, and wondering if a single kid or calf could furnish material for gloving it.

Conversation not general; drones along between couples. One catches a sentence here and there. Like this, from Bermudian of thirteen years' absence: "It is the nature of women to ask trivial, irrelevant, and pursuing questions,—questions that pursue you from a beginning in nothing to a run-to-cover in nowhere." Reply of Bermudian of twenty-seven years' absence: "Yes; and to think they have logical, analytical minds and argumentative ability. You see 'em begin to whet up whenever they smell argument in the air." Plainly these be philosophers.

Twice since we left port our engines have stopped for a couple of minutes at a time. Now they stop again. Says the pale young man, meditatively, "There! that engineer is sitting down to rest again."

Grave stare from the captain, whose mighty jaws cease to work, and whose harpooned potato stops in mid-air on its way to his open, paralyzed mouth. Presently says he, in measured tones, "Is it your idea that the engineer of this ship propels her by a crank turned by his own hands?"

The pale young man studies over this a moment, then lifts up his guileless eyes, and says, "Don't he?"

Thus gently falls the death-blow to further conversation, and the dinner drags to its close in a reflective silence, disturbed by no sounds but the murmurous wash of the sea and the subdued clash of teeth.

After a smoke and a promenade on deck, where is no motion to discompose our steps, we think of a game of whist. We ask the brisk and capable stewardess from Ireland if there are any cards in the ship.

"Bless your soul, dear, indeed there is. Not a whole pack, true for ye, but not enough missing to signify."

However, I happened by accident to bethink me of a new pack in a morocco case, in my trunk, which I had placed there by mistake, thinking it to be a flask of something. So a party of us conquered the tedium of the evening with a few games, and were ready for bed at six bells, mariner's time, the signal for putting out the lights.

There was much chat in the smoking-cabin on the upper deck after luncheon to-day, mostly whaler yarns from those old sea-captains. Captain Tom Bowling was garrulous. He had that garrulous attention to minor detail which is born of secluded farm life or life at sea on long voyages, where there is little to do and time no object. He would sail along till he was right in the most exciting part of a yarn, and then say, "Well, as I was saying, the rudder was fouled, ship driving before the gale, head on, straight for the iceberg, all hands holding their breath, turned to stone, top-hamper giving way, sails blown to ribbons, first one stick going, then another, boom! smash! crash! duck your head and stand from under! when up comes Johnny Rogers, capstan bar in hand, eyes a-blazing, hair a-flying—no, 't wa'n't Johnny Rogers—lemme see—seems to me Johnny Rogers wa'n't along that voyage; he was along *one* voyage, I know that mighty well, but somehow it seems to me that he signed the articles for this voyage, but—but—whether he come along or not, or got left, or something happened—"

And so on and so on, till the excitement all cooled down and nobody cared whether the ship struck the iceberg or not.

In the course of his talk he rambled into a criticism upon New England degrees of merit in ship-building. Said he, "You get a vessel built away down Maine-way; Bath, for instance; what's the result? First thing you do, you want to heave her down for repairs,—*that's* the result! Well, sir, she hain't been hove down a week till you can heave a dog through her seams. You send that vessel to sea, and what's the result? She wets her oakum the first trip! Leave it to any man if 't a'n't so. Well, you let *our* folks build you a vessel—down New Bedford-way. What's the result? Well, sir, you might take that ship and heave her down, and keep her hove down six months, and she'll never shed a tear!"

Every body, landsmen and all, recognized the descriptive neatness of that figure, and applauded, which greatly pleased the old man. A moment later, the meek eyes of the pale young fellow heretofore mentioned came up slowly, rested upon the old man's face a moment, and the meek mouth began to open.

"Shet your head!" shouted the old mariner.

It was a rather startling surprise to every body, but it was effective in the matter of its purpose. So the conversation flowed on instead of perishing.

There was some talk about the perils of the sea, and a landsman delivered himself of the customary nonsense about the poor mariner wandering in far oceans, tempest-tossed, pursued by dangers, every storm blast and thunderbolt in the home skies moving the friends by snug firesides to compassion for that poor mariner, and prayers for his succor. Captain Bowling put up with this for a while, and then burst out with a new view of the matter.

"Come, belay there! I have read this kind of rot all my life in poetry and tales and such like rubbage. Pity for the poor mariner! sympathy for the poor mariner! All right enough, but not in the way the poetry puts it. Pity for the mariner's wife! all right again, but not in the way the poetry puts it. Look-a-here! whose life's the safest in the whole world? The poor mariner's. You look at the statistics, you'll see. So don't you fool away any sympathy on the poor mariner's dangers and privations and sufferings. Leave that to the poetry muffs. Now you look at the other side a minute. Here is Captain Brace, forty years old, been at sea thirty. On his way now to take command of his ship and sail south from Bermuda. Next week he'll be under way: easy times; comfortable quarters; passengers, sociable company; just enough to do to keep his mind healthy and not tire him; king over his ship, boss of every thing and every body; thirty years' safety to learn him that his profession a'n't a dangerous one. Now you look back at his home. His wife's a feeble woman; she's a stranger in New York; shut up in blazing hot or freezing cold lodgings, according to the season; don't know any body hardly; no company but her lonesomeness and her thoughts; husband gone six months at a time. She has borne eight children; five of them she has buried without her husband ever setting eyes on them. She watched them all the long nights till they died—he comfortable on the sea; she followed them to the grave, she heard the clods fall that broke her heart—he comfortable on the sea; she mourned at home, weeks and weeks, missing them every day and every hour—he cheerful at sea, knowing nothing about it. Now look at it a minute—turn it over in your mind and size it: five children born, she among strangers, and him not by to hearten her; buried, and him not by to comfort her; think of that! Sympathy for the poor mariner's perils is rot; give it to his wife's hard lines, where it belongs! Poetry makes out that all the wife worries about is the dangers her husband's running. She's got substantialer things to worry over, I tell you. Poetry's always pitying the poor mariner on account of his perils at sea; better a blamed sight pity him for the nights he can't sleep for thinking of how he had to leave his wife in her very birth pains, lonesome and friendless, in the thick of disease and trouble and death. If there's one thing that can make me madder than another, it's this sappy, damned maritime poetry!''

Captain Brace was a patient, gentle, seldom-speaking man, with a pathetic something in his bronzed face that had been a mystery up to this time, but stood interpreted now, since we had heard his story. He had voyaged eighteen times to the Mediterranean, seven times to India, once to the arctic pole in a discovery-ship, and "between times" had visited all the remote seas and ocean corners of the globe. But he said that twelve years ago, on account of his family, he "settled down," and ever since then had ceased to roam. And what do you suppose was this simple-hearted, life-long wanderer's idea of settling down and ceasing to roam? Why, the making of two five-month voyages a year between Surinam and Boston for sugar and molasses!

Among other talk, to-day, it came out that whaleships carry no doctor. The captain adds the doctorship to his own duties. He not only gives medicines, but sets broken limbs after notions of his own, or saws them off and sears the stump when amputation seems best. The captain is provided with a medicine-chest, with the medicines numbered instead of named. A book of directions goes with this. It describes diseases and symptoms, and says, "Give a tea-spoonful of No. 9 once an hour," or "Give ten grains of No. 12 every half hour," etc. One of our sea-captains came across a skipper in the North Pacific who was in a state of great surprise and perplexity. Said he:

"There's something rotten about this medicine-chest business. One of my men was sick—nothing much the matter. I looked in the book: it said, 'Give him a tea-spoonful of No. 15.' I went to the medicine-chest, and I see I was out of No. 15. I judged I'd got to get up a combination somehow that would fill the bill; so I hove into the fellow half a tea-spoonful of No. 8 and half a tea-spoonful of No. 7, and I'll be hanged if it didn't kill him in fifteen minutes! There's something about this medicine-chest system that's too many for me!''

There was a good deal of pleasant gossip about old Captain "Hurricane" Jones, of the Pacific Ocean—peace to his ashes! Two or three of us present had known him; I, particularly well, for I had made four sea-voyages with him. He was a very remarkable man. He was born in a ship; he picked up what little education he had among his shipmates; he began life in the forecastle, and climbed grade by grade to the captaincy. More than fifty years of his sixty-five were spent at sea. He had sailed all oceans, seen all lands, and borrowed a tint from all climates. When a man has been fifty years at sea; he necessarily knows nothing of men, nothing of the world but its surface, nothing of the world's thought, nothing of the world's learning but its A B C, and that blurred and distorted by the unfocused lenses of an untrained mind. Such a man is only a gray and bearded child. That is what old Hurricane Jones was—simply an innocent, lovable old infant. When his spirit was in repose, he was as sweet and gentle as a girl; when his wrath was up, he was a hurricane that made his nickname seem tamely descriptive. He was formidable in a fight, for he was of powerful build and dauntless courage. He was frescoed from head to heel with pictures and mottoes tattooed in red and blue India ink. I was with him one voyage when he got his last vacant space tattooed; this vacant space was around his left ankle. During three days he stumped about the ship with his ankle bare and swollen, and this legend gleaming red and angry out from a clouding of India ink: "Virtue is its own R'd." (There was a lack of room.) He was deeply and sincerely pious, and swore like a fishwoman. He considered swearing blameless; because sailors would not understand an order unillumined by it. He was a profound Biblical scholar— that is, he thought he was. He believed every thing in the Bible, but he had his own methods of arriving at his beliefs. He was of the "advanced" school of thinkers, and applied natural laws to the interpretation of all miracles, somewhat on the plan of the people who make the six days of creation six geological epochs, and so forth. Without being aware of it, he was a rather severe satire on modern scientific religionists. Such a man as I have been describing is rabidly fond of disquisition and argument; one knows that without being told it.

One trip the captain had a clergyman on board, but did not know he was a clergyman, since the passenger list did not betray the fact. He took a great liking to this Rev. Mr. Peters, and talked with him a great deal; told him yarns, gave him toothsome scraps of personal history, and wove a glittering streak of profanity through his garrulous fabric that was refreshing to a spirit weary of the dull neutralities of undecorated speech. One day the captain said, "Peters, do you ever read the Bible?"

"Well—yes."

"I judge it a'n't often, by the way you say it. Now, you tackle it in dead earnest once, and you'll find it'll pay. Don't you get discouraged, but hang right on. First you won't understand it; but by and by things will begin to clear up, and then you wouldn't lay it down to eat."

"Yes, I have heard that said."

"And it's so, too. There a'n't a book that begins with it; it lays over 'em all, Peters. There's some pretty tough things in it— there a'n't any getting around that—but you stick to them and think them out, and when once you get on the inside every thing's plain as day."

"The miracles, too, captain?"

"Yes, sir! the miracles, too. Every one of them. Now, there's that business with the prophets of Baal; like enough that stumped you?"

"Well, I don't know but—"

"Own up, now; it stumped you. Well, I don't wonder. You hadn't had any experience in ravelling such things out, and naturally it was too many for you. Would you like to have me explain that thing to you, and show you how to get at the meat of these matters?"

"Indeed I would, captain, if you don't mind."

Then the captain proceeded as follows:

"I'll do it with pleasure. First, you see, I read and read, and thought and thought, till I got to understand what sort of people they were in the old Bible times, and then after that it was all clear and easy. Now, this was the way I put it up concerning Isaac* and the prophets of Baal. There was some mighty sharp men amongst the public characters of that old ancient day, and Isaac was one of them. Isaac had his failings—plenty of them, too. It a'n't for me to apologize for Isaac; he played it on the prophets of Baal, and like enough he was justifiable, considering the odds that was against him. No, all I say is, 'twa'n't any miracle, and that I'll show you so's't you can see it yourself.

"Well, times had been getting rougher and rougher for prophets—that is, prophets of Isaac's denomination. There was four hundred and fifty prophets of Baal in the community, and only one Presbyterian; that is, if Isaac *was* a Presbyterian, which I reckon he was, but it don't say. Naturally, the prophets of Baal took all the trade. Isaac was pretty low-spirited, I reckon, but he was a good deal of a man, and no doubt he went a-prophesying around, letting on to be doing a land-office business, but 'twa'n't any use; he couldn't run any opposition to amount to any thing. By and by things got desperate with him; he sets his head to work and thinks it all out, and then what does he do?

*This is the captain's own mistake.

1002

Why, he begins to throw out hints that the other parties are this and that and 't other—nothing very definite, may be, but just kind of undermining their reputation in a quiet way. This made talk, of course, and finally got to the king. The king asked Isaac what he meant by his talk. Says Isaac, 'Oh! nothing particular; only, can they pray down fire from heaven on an altar? It a'n't much, may be, your majesty, only, can they *do* it? that's the idea.' So the king was a good deal disturbed, and he went to the prophets of Baal, and they said, pretty airy, that if he had an altar ready, *they* were ready; and they intimated he better get it insured, too.

"So next morning all the children of Israel and their parents and the other people gathered themselves together. Well, here was that great crowd of prophets of Baal packed together on one side, and Isaac walking up and down all alone on the other, putting up his job. When time was called, Isaac let on to be comfortable and indifferent; told the other team to take the first innings. So they went at it, the whole four hundred and fifty, praying around the altar, very hopeful, and doing their level best. They prayed an hour—two hours—three hours—and so on, plumb till noon. It wa'n't any use; they hadn' took a trick. Of course they felt kind of ashamed before all those people, and well they might. Now, what would a magnanimous man do? Keep still, wouldn't he? Of course. What did Isaac do? He gravelled the prophets of Baal every way he could think of. Says he, 'You don't speak up loud enough; your God's asleep, like enough, or may be he's taking a walk; you want to holler, you know'—or words to that effect; I don't recollect the exact language. Mind, I don't apologize for Isaac; he had his faults.

"Well, the prophets of Baal prayed along the best they knew how all the afternoon, and never raised a spark. At last, about sundown, they were all tuckered out, and they owned up and quit.

"What does Isaac do now? He steps up and says to some friends of his there, 'Pour four barrels of water on the altar!' Every body was astonished; for the other side had prayed at it dry, you know, and got whitewashed. They poured it on. Says he, 'Heave on four more barrels.' Then he says, 'Heave on four more.' Twelve barrels, you see, altogether. The water ran all over the altar, and all down the sides, and filled up a trench around it that would hold a couple of hogsheads—'measures,' it says; I reckon it means about a hogshead. Some of the people were going to put on their things and go, for they allowed he was crazy. They didn't know Isaac. Isaac knelt down and began to pray: he strung along, and strung along, about the heathen in distant lands, and about the sister churches, and about the state and the country at large, and about those that's in authority in the government, and all the usual programme, you know, till every body had got tired and gone to thinking about something else, and then, all of a sudden, when nobody was noticing, he outs with a match and rakes it on the under side of his leg, and pff! up the whole thing blazes like a house afire! Twelve barrels of *water? Petroleum,* sir, PETROLEUM! that's what it was."

"Petroleum, captain?"

"Yes, sir; the country was full of it. Isaac knew all about that. You read the Bible. Don't you worry about the tough places. They a'n't tough when you come to think them out and throw light on them. There a'n't a thing in the Bible but what is true; all you want is to go prayerfully to work and cipher out how 't was done."

At eight o'clock on the third morning out from New York, land was sighted. Away across the sunny waves one saw a faint dark stripe stretched along under the horizon—or pretended to see it, for the credit of his eyesight. Even the Reverend said he saw it, a thing which was manifestly not so. But I never have seen any one who was morally strong enough to confess that he could not see land when others claimed that they could.

By and by the Bermuda Islands were easily visible. The principal one lay upon the water in the distance, a long, dull-colored body, scalloped with slight hills and valleys. We could not go straight at it, but had to travel all the way around it, sixteen miles from shore, because it is fenced with an invisible coral reef. At last we sighted buoys, bobbing here and there, and then we glided into a narrow channel among them, "raised the reef," and came upon shoaling blue water that soon further shoaled into pale green, with a surface scarcely rippled. Now came the resurrection hour; the berths gave up their dead. Who are these pale spectres in plug hats and silken flounces that file up the companion-way in melancholy procession and step upon the deck? These are they which took the infallible preventive of sea-sickness in New York harbor, and then disappeared and were forgotten. Also there came two or three faces not seen before until this moment. One's impulse is to ask, "Where did you come aboard?"

We followed the narrow channel a long time, with land on both sides—low hills that might have been green and grassy, but had a faded look instead. However, the land-locked water was lovely at any rate, with its glittering belts of blue and green where moderate soundings were, and its broad splotches of rich brown where the rocks lay near the surface. Every body was feeling so well that even the grave, pale young man (who, by a sort of kindly common consent, had come latterly to be referred to as "the Ass") received frequent and friendly notice—which was right enough, for there was no harm in him.

At last we steamed between two island points whose rocky jaws allowed only just enough room for the vessel's body, and now before us loomed Hamilton on her clustered hill-sides and summits, the whitest mass of terraced architecture that exists in the world, perhaps.

It was Sunday afternoon, and on the pier were gathered one or two hundred Bermudians, half of them black, half of them white, and all of them nobbily dressed, as the poet says.

Several boats came off to the ship, bringing citizens. One of these citizens was a faded, diminutive old gentleman, who approached our most ancient passenger with a childlike joy in his twinkling eyes, halted before him, folded his arms, and said, smiling with all his might and with all the simple delight that was in him, "You don't know me, John! Come, out with it, now; you know you don't!"

The ancient passenger scanned him perplexedly, scanned the napless, threadbare costume of venerable fashion that had done Sunday service no man knows how many years, contemplated the marvellous stovepipe hat of still more ancient and venerable pattern, with its poor pathetic old stiff brim canted up "gallusly" in the wrong places, and said, with a hesitation that indicated strong internal effort to "place" the gentle old apparition, 'Why—let me see—plague on it—there's *something* about you that—er—er—but I've been gone from Bermuda for twenty-seven years, and—hum, hum—I don't seem to get at it, somehow, but there's something about you that is just as familiar to me as—"

"Likely it might be his hat," murmured the Ass, with innocent, sympathetic interest.

III

So the Reverend and I had at last arrived at Hamilton, the principal town in the Bermuda Islands. A wonderfully white town; white as snow itself. White as marble; white as flour. Yet looking like none of these, exactly. Never mind, we said; we shall hit upon a figure by and by that will describe this peculiar white.

It was a town that was compacted together upon the sides and tops of a cluster of small hills. Its outlying borders fringed off and thinned away among the cedar forests, and there was no woody distance of curving coast, or leafy islet sleeping upon the dimpled, painted sea, but was flecked with shining white points—half-concealed houses peeping out of the foliage. The architecture of the town was mainly Spanish, inherited from the colonists of two hundred and fifty years ago. Some ragged-topped cocoapalms, glimpsed here and there, gave the land a tropical aspect.

There was an ample pier of heavy masonry; upon this, under shelter, were some thousands of barrels containing that product which has carried the fame of Bermuda to many lands, the potato. With here and there an onion. That last sentence is facetious; for they grow at least two onions in Bermuda to one potato. The onion is the pride and joy of Bermuda. It is her jewel, her gem of gems. In her conversation, her pulpit, her literature, it is her most frequent and eloquent figure. In Bermudian metaphor it stands for perfection—perfection absolute.

The Bermudian weeping over the departed, exhausts praise when he says, "He was an onion!" The Bermudian extolling the living hero, bankrupts applause when he says, "He is an onion!" The Bermudian, setting his son upon the stage of life to dare and do for himself, climaxes all counsel, supplication, admonition, comprehends all ambition, when he says, "Be an onion!"

When parallel with the pier, and ten or fifteen steps outside it, we anchored. It was Sunday, bright and sunny. The groups upon the pier—men, youths, and boys—were whites and blacks in about equal proportion. All were well and neatly dressed, many of them nattily, a few of them very stylishly. One would have to travel far before he would find another town of twelve thousand inhabitants that could represent itself so respectably, in the matter of clothes, on a freight-pier, without premeditation or effort. The women and young girls, black and white, who occasionally passed by, were nicely clad, and many were elegantly and fashionably so. The men did not affect summer clothing much, but the girls and women did, and their white garments were good to look at, after so many months of familiarity with sombre colors.

Around one isolated potato-barrel stood four young gentlemen, two black, two white, becomingly dressed, each with the head of a slender cane pressed against his teeth, and each with a foot propped up on the barrel. Another young gentleman came up, looked longingly at the barrel, but saw no rest for his foot there, and turned pensively away to seek another barrel. He wandered here and there, but without result. Nobody sat upon a barrel, as is the custom of the idle in other lands, yet all the isolated barrels were humanly occupied. Whosoever had a foot to spare, put it on a barrel, if all the places on it were not already taken. The habits of all peoples are determined by their circumstances. The Bermudians lean upon barrels because of the scarcity of lampposts.

Many citizens came on board and spoke eagerly to the officers—inquiring about the Turco-Russian war news, I supposed. However, by listening judiciously I found that this was not so. They said, "What is the price of onions?" or, "How's onions?" Naturally enough, this was their first interest; but they dropped into the war the moment it was satisfied.

We went ashore and found a novelty of a pleasant nature; there were no hackmen, hacks, or omnibuses on the pier or about it anywhere, and nobody offered his services to us, or molested us in any way. I said it was like being in heaven. The Reverend rebukingly and rather pointedly advised me to make the most of it, then. We knew of a boarding-house, and what we needed now was somebody to pilot us to it. Presently a little barefooted colored boy came along, whose raggedness was conspicuously un-Bermudian. His rear was so marvellously bepatched with colored squares and triangles that one was half persuaded he had got it out of an atlas. When the sun struck him right, he was as good to follow as a lightning-bug. We hired him and dropped into his wake. He piloted us through one picturesque street after another, and in due course deposited us where we belonged. He charged nothing for his map, and but a trifle for his services; so the Reverend doubled it. The little chap received the money with a beaming applause in his eye which plainly said, "This man's an onion!"

We had brought no letters of introduction; our names had been misspelt in the passenger list; nobody knew whether we were honest folk or otherwise. So we were expecting to have a good private time in case there was nothing in our general aspect to close boarding-house doors against us. We had no trouble. Bermuda has had but little experience of rascals, and is not suspicious. We got large, cool, well-lighted rooms on a second floor, overlooking a bloomy display of flowers and flowering shrubs—calla and annunciation lilies, lantanas, heliotrope, jessamine, roses, pinks, double geraniums, oleanders, pomegranates, blue morning-glories of a great size, and many plants that were unknown to me.

We took a long afternoon walk, and soon found out that that exceedingly white town was built of blocks of white coral. Bermuda is a coral island, with a six-inch crust of soil on top of it, and every man has a quarry on his own premises. Everywhere you go you see square recesses cut into the hill-sides, with perpendicular walls unmarred by crack or crevice, and perhaps you fancy that a house grew out of the ground there, and has been removed in a single piece from the mould. If you do, you err. But the material for a house has been quarried there. They cut right down through the coral, to any depth that is convenient—ten to twenty feet—and take it out in great square blocks. This cutting is done with a chisel that has a handle twelve or fifteen feet long, and is used as one uses a crowbar when he is drilling a hole, or a dasher when he is churning. Thus soft is this stone. Then with a common handsaw they saw the great blocks into handsome, huge bricks, that are two feet long, a foot wide, and about six inches thick. These stand loosely piled during a month to harden; then the work of building begins. The house is built of these blocks; it is roofed with broad coral slabs an inch thick, whose edges lap upon each other, so that the roof looks like a succession of shallow steps or terraces; the chimneys are built of the coral blocks and sawed into graceful and picturesque patterns; the ground-floor verandah is paved with coral blocks; also the walk to the gate; the fence is built of coral blocks—built in massive panels, with broad cap-stones and heavy gate-posts, and the whole trimmed into easy lines and comely shape with the saw. Then they put a hard coat of whitewash, as thick as your thumb nail, on the fence and all over the house, roof, chimneys, and all; the sun comes out and shines on this spectacle, and it is time for you to shut your unaccustomed eyes, lest they be put out. Is is the whitest white you can conceive of, and the blindingest. A Bermuda house does not look like marble; it is a much intenser white than that; and besides, there is a dainty, indefinable something else about its look that is not marble-like. We put in a great deal of solid talk and reflection over this matter of trying to find a figure that would describe the unique white of a Bermuda house, and we contrived to hit upon it at last. It is exactly the white of the icing of a cake, and has the same unemphasized and scarcely perceptible polish. The white of marble is modest and retiring compared with it.

After the house is cased in its hard scale of whitewash, not a crack, or sign of a seam, or joining of the blocks, is detectable, from base-stone to chimney-top; the building looks as if it had been carved from a single block of stone, and the doors and windows sawed out afterwards. A white marble house has a cold, tomb-like, unsociable look, and takes the conversation out of a body and depresses him. Not so with a Bermuda house. There is something exhilarating, even hilarious, about its vivid whiteness when the sun plays upon it. If it be of picturesque shape and graceful contour—and many of the Bermudian dwellings are—it will so fascinate you that you will keep your eyes on it until they ache. One of those clean-cut, fanciful chimneys—too pure and white for this world—with one side glowing in the sun and the other touched with a soft shadow, is an object that will charm one's gaze by the hour. I know of no other country that has chimneys worthy to be gazed at and gloated over. One of those snowy houses half-concealed and half-glimpsed through green foliage is a pretty thing to see; and if it takes one by surprise and suddenly, as he turns a sharp corner of a country road, it will wring an exclamation from him, sure.

Wherever you go, in town or country, you find those snowy houses, and always with masses of bright-colored flowers about them, but with no vines climbing their walls; vines cannot take hold of the smooth, hard whitewash. Wherever you go, in the town or along the country roads, among little potato farms and patches or expensive country-seats, these stainless white dwellings, gleaming out from flowers and foliage, meet you at every turn. The least little bit of a cottage is as white and blemishless as the stateliest mansion. Nowhere is there dirt or stench, puddle or hog-wallow, neglect, disorder, or lack of trimness and neatness. The roads, the streets, the dwellings, the people, the clothes—this neatness extends to every thing that falls under the eye. It is the tidiest country in the world. And very much the tidiest, too.

Considering these things, the question came up, Where do the poor live? No answer was arrived at. Therefore, we agreed to leave this conundrum for future statesmen to wrangle over.

What a bright and startling spectacle one of those blazing white country palaces, with its brown-tinted window caps and ledges, and green shutters, and its wealth of caressing flowers and foliage, would be in black London! And what a gleaming surprise it would be in nearly any American city one could mention, too!

Bermuda roads are made by cutting down a few inches into the solid white coral—or a good many feet, where a hill intrudes itself—and smoothing off the surface of the road-bed. It is a simple and easy process. The grain of the coral is coarse and porous; the road-bed has the look of being made of coarse white sugar. Its excessive cleanness and whiteness are a trouble in one way: the sun is reflected into your eyes with such energy as you walk along that you want to sneeze all the time. Old Captain Tom Bowling found another difficulty. He joined us in our walk, but kept wandering unrestfully to the roadside. Finally he explained. Said he, "Well, I chew, you know, and the road's so plaguy clean."

We walked several miles that afternoon in the bewildering glare of the sun, the white roads, and the white buildings. Our eyes got to paining us a good deal. By and by a soothing, blessed twilight spread its cool balm around. We looked up in pleased surprise, and saw that it proceeded from an intensely black negro who was going by. We answered his military salute in the grateful gloom of his near presence, and then passed on into the pitiless white glare again.

The colored women whom we met usually bowed and spoke; so did the children. The colored men commonly gave the military salute. They borrow this fashion from the soldiers no doubt; England has kept a garrison here for generations. The younger men's custom of carrying small canes is also borrowed from the soldiers, I suppose, who always carry a cane, in Bermuda as everywhere else in Britain's broad dominions.

The country roads curve and wind hither and thither, in the delightfulest way, unfolding pretty surprises at every turn: billowy masses of oleander that seem to float out from behind distant projections like the pink cloud-banks of sunset; sudden plunges among cottages and gardens, life and activity, followed by as sudden plunges into the sombre twilight and stillness of the woods; flitting visions of white fortresses and beacon towers pictured against the sky on remote hill-tops; glimpses of shining green sea caught for a moment through opening headlands, then lost again; more woods and solitude; and by and by another turn lays bare, without warning, the full sweep of the inland ocean, enriched with its bars of soft color, and graced with its wandering sails.

Take any road you please, you may depend upon it you will not stay in it half a mile. Your road is every thing that a road ought to be: it is bordered with trees, and with strange plants and flowers; it is shady and pleasant, or sunny and still pleasant; it carries you by the prettiest and peacefulest and most homelike of homes, and through stretches of forest that lie in a deep hush sometimes, and sometimes are alive with the music of birds; it curves always, which is a continual promise, whereas straight roads reveal every thing at a glance and kill interest. Your road is all this, and yet you will not stay in it half a mile, for the reason that little, seductive, mysterious roads are always branching out from it on either hand, and as these curve sharply also and hide what is beyond, you cannot resist the temptation to desert your own chosen road and explore them. You are usually paid for your trouble; consequently, your walk inland always turns out to be one of the most crooked, involved, purposeless, and interesting experiences a body can imagine. There is enough of variety. Sometimes you are in the level open, with marshes thick grown with flag-lances that are ten feet high on the one hand, and potato and onion orchards on the other; next you are on a hill-top, with the ocean and the Islands spread around you; presently the road winds through a deep cut, shut in by perpendicular walls thirty or forty feet high, marked with the oddest and abruptest stratum lines, suggestive of sudden and eccentric old upheavals, and garnished with here and there a clinging adventurous flower, and here and there a dangling vine; and by and by your way is along the sea edge, and you may look down a fathom or two through the transparent water and watch the diamond-like flash and play of the light upon the rocks and sands on the bottom until you are tired of it—if you are so constituted as to be able to get tired of it.

You may march the country roads in maiden meditation, fancy free, by field and farm, for no dog will plunge out at you from unsuspected gate, with breath-taking surprise of ferocious bark, notwithstanding it is a Christian land and a civilized. We saw upwards of a million cats in Bermuda, but the people are very abstemious in the matter of dogs. Two or three nights we prowled the country far and wide, and never once were accosted by a dog. It is a great privilege to visit such a land. The cats were no offence when properly distributed, but when piled they obstructed travel.

As we entered the edge of the town that Sunday afternoon, we stopped at a cottage to get a drink of water. The proprietor, a middle-aged man with a good face, asked us to sit down and rest. His dame brought chairs, and we grouped ourselves in the shade of the trees by the door. Mr. Smith—that was not his name, but it will answer—questioned us about ourselves and our country, and we answered him truthfully, as a general thing, and questioned him in return. It was all very simple and pleasant and sociable. Rural, too; for there was a pig and a small donkey and a hen anchored out, close at hand, by cords to their legs, on a spot that purported to be grassy. Presently, a woman passed along, and although she coldly said nothing she changed the drift of our talk. Said Smith:

"She didn't look this way, you noticed? Well, she is our next neighbor on one side, and there's another family that's our next neighbors on the other side; but there's a general coolness all around now, and we don't speak. Yet these three families, one generation and another, have lived here side by side and been as friendly as weavers for a hundred and fifty years, till about a year ago."

"Why, what calamity could have been powerful enough to break up so old a friendship?"

"Well, it was too bad, but it couldn't be helped. It happened like this: About a year or more ago, the rats got to pestering my place a good deal, and I set up a steel-trap in the back-yard. Both of these neighbors run considerable to cats, and so I warned them about the trap, because their cats were pretty sociable around here nights, and they might get into trouble without my intending it. Well, they shut up their cats for a while, but you know how it is with people; they got careless, and sure enough one night the trap took Mrs. Jones's principal tomcat into camp, and finished him up. In the morning Mrs. Jones comes here with the corpse in her arms, and cries and takes on the same as if it was a child. It was a cat by the name of Yelverton—Hector G. Yelverton—a troublesome old rip, with no more principle than an Injun, though you couldn't make *her* believe it. I said all a man could to comfort her, but no, nothing would do but I must pay for him. Finally, I said I warn't investing in cats now as much as I was, and with that she walked off in a huff, carrying the remains with her. That closed our intercourse with the Joneses. Mrs. Jones joined another church and took her tribe with her. She said she would not hold fellowship with assassins. Well, by and by comes Mrs. Brown's turn—she that went by here a minute ago. She had a disgraceful old yellow cat that she thought as much of as if he was twins, and one night he tried that trap on his neck, and it fitted him so, and was so sort of satisfactory, that he laid down and curled up and stayed with it. Such was the end of Sir John Baldwin."

"Was that the name of the cat?"

"The same. There's cats around here with names that would surprise you. Maria" (to his wife), "what was that cat's name that eat a keg of ratsbane by mistake over at Hooper's, and started home and got struck by lightning and took the blind staggers and fell in the well and was most drowned before they could fish him out?"

"That was that colored Deacon Jackson's cat. I only remember the last end of its name, which was To-Be-Or-Not-To-Be- That-Is-The-Question Jackson."

"Sho! that ain't the one. That's the one that eat up an entire box of Seidlitz powders, and then hadn't any more judgment than to go and take a drink. He was considered to be a great loss, but I never could see it. Well, no matter about the names. Mrs. Brown wanted to be reasonable, but Mrs. Jones wouldn't let her. She put her up to going to law for damages. So to law she went, and had the face to claim seven shillings and sixpence. It made a great stir. All the neighbors went to court. Every body took sides. It got hotter and hotter, and broke up all the friendships for three hundred yards around—friendships that had lasted for generations and generations.

"Well, I proved by eleven witnesses that the cat was of a low character and very ornery, and warn't worth a cancelled postage-stamp, any way, taking the average of cats here; but I lost the case. What could I expect? The system is all wrong here, and is bound to make revolution and bloodshed some day. You see, they give the magistrate a poor little starvation salary, and then turn him loose on the public to gouge for fees and costs to live on. What is the natural result? Why he never looks into the justice of a case—never once. All he looks at is which client has got the money. So this one piled the fees and costs and every thing on to me. I could pay specie, don't you see? and he knew mighty well that if he put the verdict on to Mrs. Brown, where it belonged, he'd have to take his swag in currency."

"Currency? Why, has Bermuda a currency?" ·

"Yes—onions. And they were forty per cent discount, too, then, because the season had been over as much as three months. So I lost my case. I had to pay for that cat. But the general trouble the case made was the worse thing about it. Broke up so much good feeling. The neighbors don't speak to each other now. Mrs. Brown had named a child after me. But she changed its name right away. She is a Baptist. Well, in the course of baptizing it over again, it got drowned. I was hoping we might get to be friendly again some time or other, but of course this drowning the child knocked that all out of the question. It would have saved a world of heart-break and ill blood if she had named it dry."

I knew by the sigh that this was honest. All this trouble and all this destruction of confidence in the purity of the bench on account of a seven-shilling lawsuit about a cat! Somehow, it seemed to "size" the country.

At this point we observed that an English flag had just been placed at half-mast on a building a hundred yards away. I and my friends were busy in an instant trying to imagine whose death, among the island dignitaries, could command such a mark of respect as this. Then a shudder shook them and me at the same moment, and I knew that we had jumped to one and the same conclusion: "The governor has gone to England; it is for the British admiral!"

At this moment Mr. Smith noticed the flag. He said with emotion:

"That's on a boarding-house. I judge there's a boarder dead."

A dozen other flags within view went to half-mast.

"It's a boarder, sure," said Smith.

"But would they half-mast the flags here for a boarder, Mr. Smith?"

"Why, certainly they would, if he was *dead*."

That seemed to size the country again.

IV

The early twilight of a Sunday evening in Hamilton, Bermuda, is an alluring time. There is just enough of whispering breeze, fragrance of flowers, and sense of repose, to raise one's thoughts heavenward; and just enough amateur piano music to keep him reminded of the other place. There are many venerable pianos in Hamilton, and they all play at twilight. Age enlarges and enriches the powers of some musical instruments—notably those of the violin—but it seems to set a piano's teeth on edge. Most of the music in vogue there is the same that those pianos prattled in their innocent infancy; and there is something very pathetic about it when they go over it now, in their asthmatic second childhood, dropping a note here and there, where a tooth is gone.

We attended evening service at the stately Episcopal church on the hill, where were five or six hundred people, half of them white and the other half black, according to the usual Bermudian proportions; and all well dressed—a thing which is also usual in Bermuda, and to be confidently expected. There was good music, which we heard, and doubtless a good sermon, but there was a wonderful deal of coughing, and so only the high parts of the argument carried over it. As we came out, after service, I overheard one young girl say to another,

"Why, you don't mean to say you pay duty on gloves and laces! I only pay postage; have them done up and sent in the Boston *Advertiser*."

There are those who believe that the most difficult thing to create is a woman who can comprehend that it is wrong to smuggle; and that an impossible thing to create is a woman who will not smuggle, whether or no, when she gets a chance. But these may be errors.

We went wandering off toward the country, and were soon far down in the lonely black depths of a road that was roofed over with the dense foliage of a double rank of great cedars. There was no sound of any kind, there; it was perfectly still. And it was so dark that one could detect nothing but sombre outlines. We strode farther and farther down this tunnel, cheering the way with chat.

Presently, the chat took this shape: "How insensibly the character of a people and of a government makes its impress upon a stranger, and gives him a sense of security or of insecurity without his taking deliberate thought upon the matter or asking any body a question! We have been in this land half a day; we have seen none but honest faces; we have noted the British flag flying, which means efficient government and good order; so without inquiry we plunge unarmed and with perfect confidence into this dismal place, which in almost any other country would swarm with thugs and garroters—"

'Sh! What was that? Stealthy footsteps! Low voices! We gasp, we close up together, and wait. A vague shape glides out of the dusk and confronts us. A voice speaks—demands money!

"A shilling, gentlemen, if you please, to help build the new Methodist church."

Blessed sound! Holy sound! We contribute with thankful avidity to the new Methodist church, and are happy to think how lucky it was that those little colored Sunday-school scholars did not seize upon every thing we had with violence, before we recovered from our momentary helpless condition. By the light of cigars we write down the names of weightier philanthropists than ourselves on the contribution-cards, and then pass on into the farther darkness, saying, What sort of government do they call this, where they allow little black pious children, with contribution-cards, to plunge out upon peaceable strangers in the dark and scare them to death?

We prowled on several hours, sometimes by the seaside, sometimes inland, and finally managed to get lost, which is a feat that requires talent in Bermuda. I had on new shoes. They were No. 7's when I started, but were not more than 5's now, and still diminishing. I walked two hours in those shoes after that, before we reached home. Doubtless I could have the reader's sympathy for the asking. Many people have never had the headache or the toothache, and I am one of those myself; but every body has worn tight shoes for two or three hours, and known the luxury of taking them off in a retired place and seeing his feet swell up and obscure the firmament. Few of us will ever forget the exquisite hour we were married. Once when I was a callow, bashful cub, I took a plain, unsentimental country girl to a comedy one night. I had known her a day; she seemed divine; I wore my new boots. At the end of the first half hour she said, "Why do you fidget so with your feet?" I said, "Did I?" Then I put my attention there and kept still. At the end of another half hour she said, "Why do you say, 'Yes, oh! yes!' and 'Ha, ha! oh! certainly! very true!' to every thing I say, when half the time those are entirely irrelevant answers?" I blushed, and explained that I had been a little absent-minded. At the end of another half hour she said, "Please, why do you grin so steadfastly at vacancy, and yet look so sad?" I explained that I always did that when I was reflecting. An hour passed, and then she turned and contemplated me with her earnest eyes and said, "Why do you cry all the time?" I explained that very funny comedies always made me cry. At last human nature surrendered, and I secretly slipped my boots off. This was a mistake. I was not able to get them on any more. It was a rainy night; there were no omnibuses going our way; and as I walked home, burning up with shame, with the girl on one arm and my boots under the other, I was an object worthy of some compassion—especially in those moments of martyrdom when I had to pass through the glare that fell upon the pavement from street lamps. Finally, this child of the forest said, "Where are your boots?" and being taken unprepared, I put a fitting finish to the follies of the evening with the stupid remark, "The higher classes do not wear them to the theatre."

The Reverend had been an army chaplain during the war, and while we were hunting for a road that would lead to Hamilton, he told me a story about two dying soldiers which interested me in spite of my feet. He said that in the Potomac hospitals rough pine coffins were furnished by government, but that it was not always possible to keep up with the demand; so when a man died, if there was no coffin at hand he was buried without one. One night late, two soldiers lay dying in a ward. A man came in with a coffin on his shoulder, and stood trying to make up his mind which of these two poor fellows would be likely to need it first. Both of them begged for it with their fading eyes—they were past talking. Then one of them protruded a wasted hand from his blankets and made a feeble beckoning sign with the fingers, to signify, "Be a good fellow; put it under my bed, please." The man did it, and left. The lucky soldier painfully turned himself in his bed until he faced the other warrior, raised himself partly on his elbow, and began to work up a mysterious expression of some kind in his face. Gradually, irksomely, but surely and steadily, it developed, and at last it took definite form as a pretty successful wink. The sufferer fell back exhausted with his labor, but bathed in glory. Now entered a personal friend of

No. 2, the despoiled soldier. No. 2 pleaded with him with eloquent eyes, till presently he understood, and removed the coffin
from under No. 1's bed and put it under No. 2's. No. 2 indicated
his joy, and made some more signs; the friend understood again,
and put his arm under No. 2's shoulders and lifted him partly
up. Then the dying hero turned the dim exultation of his eye
upon No. 1, and began a slow and labored work with his hands;
gradually he lifted one hand up toward his face; it grew weak
and dropped back again; once more he made the effort, but
failed again. He took a rest; he gathered all the remnant of his
strength, and this time he slowly but surely carried his thumb to
the side of his nose, spread the gaunt fingers wide in triumph,
and dropped back dead. That picture sticks by me yet. Thl
"situation" is unique.

The next morning, at what seemed a very early hour, the little
white table-waiter appeared suddenly in my room and shot a
single word out of himself: "Breakfast!"

This was a remarkable boy in many ways. He was about
eleven years old; he had alert, intent black eyes; he was quick of
movement; there was no hesitation, no uncertainty about him
anywhere; there was a military decision in his lip, his manner,
his speech, that was an astonishing thing to see in a little chap
like him; he wasted no words; his answers always came so quick
and brief that they seemed to be part of the question that had
been asked, instead of a reply to it. When he stood at table with
his fly-brush, rigid, erect, his face set in a cast-iron gravity, he
was a statue till he detected a dawning want in somebody's eye;
then he pounced down, supplied it, and was instantly a statue
again. When he was sent to the kitchen for any thing, he
marched upright till he got to the door; he turned hand-springs
the rest of the way.

"Breakfast!"

I thought I would make one more effort to get some conversation out of this being.

"Have you called the Reverend, or are—"

"Yes, s'r!"

"Is it early, or is—"

"Eight-five!"

"Do you have to do all the 'chores,' or is there somebody to
give you a l—"

"Colored girl!"

"Is there only one parish in this island, or are there—"

"Eight!"

"Is the big church on the hill a parish church, or is it—"

"Chapel-of-ease!"

"Is taxation here classified into poll, parish, town, and—"
"Don't know!"

Before I could cudgel another question out of my head, he was below, hand-springing across the back yard. He had slid down the balusters, head first. I gave up trying to provoke a discussion with him. The essential element of discussion had been left out of him; his answers were so final and exact that they did not leave a doubt to hang conversation on. I suspect that there is the making of a mighty man or a mighty rascal in this boy,—according to circumstances,—but they are going to apprentice him to a carpenter. It is the way the world uses its opportunities.

During this day and the next we took carriage drives about the island and over to the town of St. George's, fifteen or twenty miles away. Such hard, excellent roads to drive over are not to be found elsewhere out of Europe. An intelligent young colored man drove us, and acted as guide-book. In the edge of town we saw five or six mountain-cabbage palms (atrocious name!) standing in a straight row, and equidistant from each other. These were not the largest or the tallest trees I have ever seen, but they were the stateliest, the most majestic. That row of them must be the nearest that nature has ever come to counterfeiting a colonnade. These trees are all the same height, say sixty feet; the trunks as gray as granite, with a very gradual and perfect taper; without a sign of branch or knot or flaw; the surface not looking like bark, but like granite that has been dressed and not polished. Thus all the way up the diminishing shaft for fifty feet; then it begins to take the appearance of being closely wrapped, spool-fashion, with gray cord, or of having been turned in a lathe. Above this point there is an outward swell, and thence upwards, for six feet or more, the cylinder is a bright, fresh green, and is formed of wrappings like those of an ear of green Indian corn. Then comes the great spraying palm plume, also green. Other palm-trees always lean out of the perpendicular, or have a curve in them. But the plumb-line could not detect a deflection in any individual of this stately row; they stand as straight as the colonnade of Baalbec; they have its great height, they have its gracefulness, they have its dignity; in moonlight or twilight, and shorn of their plumes, they would duplicate it.

The birds we came across in the country were singularly tame; even that wild creature, the quail, would pick around in the grass at ease while we inspected it and talked about it at leisure. A small bird of the canary species had to be stirred up with the butt end of the whip before it would move, and then it moved only a couple of feet. It is said that even the suspicious flea is tame and sociable in Bermuda, and will allow himself to be caught and caressed without misgivings. This should be taken with allowance, for doubtless there is more or less brag about it. In San Francisco they used to claim that their native flea could kick a child over, as if it were a merit in a flea to be able to do that; as if the knowledge of it, trumpeted abroad, ought to entice immigration. Such a thing in nine cases out of ten would be almost sure to deter a thinking man from coming.

We saw no bugs or reptiles to speak of, and so I was thinking of saying in print, in a general way, that there were none at all; but one night after I had gone to bed, the Reverend came into my room carrying something, and asked, "Is this your boot?" I said it was, and he said he had met a spider going off with it. Next morning he stated that just at dawn the same spider raised his window and was coming in to get a shirt, but saw him and fled.

I inquired, "Did he get the shirt?"

"No."

"How did you know it was a shirt he was after?"

"I could see it in his eye."

We inquired around, but could hear of no Bermudian spider capable of doing these things. Citizens said that their largest spiders could not more than spread their legs over an ordinary saucer, and that they had always been considered honest. Here was testimony of a clergyman against the testimony of mere worldlings—interested ones, too. On the whole, I judged it best to lock up my things.

Here and there on the country roads we found lemon, papaia, orange, lime, and fig trees; also several sorts of palms, among them the cocoa, the date, and the palmetto. We saw some bamboos forty feet high, with stems as thick as a man's arm. Jungles of the mangrove-tree stood up out of swamps, propped on their interlacing roots as upon a tangle of stilts. In drier places the noble tamarind sent down its grateful cloud of shade. Here and there the blossomy tamarisk adorned the roadside. There was a curious gnarled and twisted black tree, without a single leaf on it. It might have passed itself off for a dead apple-tree but for the fact that it had a star-like, red-hot flower sprinkled sparsely over its person. It had the scattery red glow that a constellation might have when glimpsed through smoked glass. It is possible that our constellations have been so constructed as to be invisible through smoked glass; if this is so, it is a great mistake.

We saw a tree that bears grapes, and just as calmly and unostentatiously as a vine would do it. We saw an India-rubber tree, but out of season, possibly, so there were no shoes on it, nor suspenders, nor any thing that a person would properly expect to find there. This gave it an impressively fraudulent look. There was exactly one mahogany tree on the island. I know this to be reliable, because I saw a man who said he had counted it many a time and could not be mistaken. He was a man with a hare lip and a pure heart, and every body said he was as true as steel. Such men are all too few.

One's eye caught near and far the pink cloud of the oleander and the red blaze of the pomegranate blossom. In one piece of wild-wood the morning-glory vines had wrapped the trees to their very tops, and decorated them all over with couples and clusters of great blue bells—a fine and striking spectacle, at a little distance. But the dull cedar is everywhere, and it is the prevailing foliage. One does not appreciate how dull it is until the varnished, bright green attire of the infrequent lemon-tree pleasantly intrudes its contrast. In one thing Bermuda is eminently tropical—was in May, at least—the unbrilliant, slightly faded, unrejoicing look of the landscape. For forests arrayed in a blemishless magnificence of glowing green foliage that seems to exult in its own existence, and can move the beholder to an enthusiasm that will make him either shout or cry, one must go to countries that have malignant winters.

We saw scores of colored farmers digging their crops of potatoes and onions, their wives and children helping—entirely contented and comfortable, if looks go for any thing. We never met a man, or woman, or child anywhere in this sunny island who seemed to be unprosperous, or discontented, or sorry about any thing. This sort of monotony became very tiresome presently, and even something worse. The spectacle of an entire nation grovelling in contentment is an infuriating thing. We felt the lack of something in this community—a vague, an undefinable, an elusive something, and yet a lack. But after considerable thought we made out what it was—tramps. Let them go there, right now, in a body. It is utterly virgin soil. Passage is cheap. Every true patriot in America will help buy tickets. Whole armies of these excellent beings can be spared from our midst and our polls; they will find a delicious climate and a green, kind-hearted people. There are potatoes and onions for all, and a generous welcome for the first batch that arrives, and elegant graves for the second.

It was the Early Rose potato the people were digging. Later in the year they have another crop, which they call the Garnet. We buy their potatoes (retail) at fifteen dollars a barrel; and those colored farmers buy ours for a song, and live on them. Havana might exchange cigars with Connecticut in the same advantageous way, if she thought of it.

We passed a roadside grocery with a sign up, "Potatoes Wanted." An ignorant stranger, doubtless. He could not have gone thirty steps from his place without finding plenty of them.

In several fields the arrow-root crop was already sprouting. Bermuda used to make a vast annual profit out of this staple before fire-arms came into such general use.

The island is not large. Somewhere in the interior a man ahead of us had a very slow horse. I suggested that we had better go by him; but the driver said the man had but a little way to go. I waited to see, wondering how he could know. Presently the man did turn down another road. I asked, "How did you know he would?"

"Because I knew the man, and where he lived."

I asked him, satirically, if he knew every body in the island; he answered, very simply, that he did. This gives a body's mind a good substantial grip on the dimensions of the place.

At the principal hotel in St. George's, a young girl, with a sweet, serious face, said we could not be furnished with dinner, because we had not been expected, and no preparation had been made. Yet it was still an hour before dinner time. We argued, she yielded not ; we supplicated, she was serene. The hotel had not been expecting an inundation of two people, and so it seemed that we should have to go home dinnerless. I said we were not very hungry; a fish would do. My little maid answered, it was not the market-day for fish. Things began to look serious; but presently the boarder who sustained the hotel came in, and when the case was laid before him, he was cheerfully willing to divide. So we had much pleasant chat at table about St. George's chief industry, the repairing of damaged ships; and in between we had a soup that had something in that seemed to taste like the hereafter, but it proved to be only pepper of a particularly vivacious kind. And we had an iron-clad chicken that was deliciously cooked, but not in the right way. Baking was not the thing to convince his sort. He ought to have been put through a quartz mill until the "tuck" was taken out of him, and then boiled till we came again. We got a good deal of sport out of him, but not enough sustenance to leave the victory on our side. No matter; we had potatoes and a pie and a sociable good time. Then a ramble through the town, which is a quaint one, with interesting, crooked streets, and narrow, crooked lanes, with here and there a grain of dust. Here, as in Hamilton, the dwellings had Venetian blinds of a very sensible pattern. They were not double shutters, hinged at the sides, but a single broad shutter, hinged at the top; you push it outward, from the bottom, and fasten it at any angle required by the sun or desired by yourself.

All about the island one sees great white scars on the hill-slopes. These are dished spaces where the soil has been scraped off and the coral exposed and glazed with hard whitewash. Some of these are a quarter-acre in size. They catch and carry the rain-fall to reservoirs; for the wells are few and poor, and there are no natural springs and no brooks.

They say that the Bermuda climate is mild and equable, with never any snow or ice, and that one may be very comfortable in spring clothing the year round, there. We had delightful and decided summer weather in May, with a flaming sun that permit-ted the thinnest of raiment, and yet there was a constant breeze; consequently we were never discomforted by heat. At four or five in the afternoon the mercury began to go down, and then it became necessary to change to thick garments. I went to St. George's in the morning clothed in the thinnest of linen, and reached home at five in the afternoon with two overcoats on. The nights are said to be always cool and bracing. We had mos-quito nets, and the Reverend said the mosquitoes persecuted him a good deal. I often heard him slapping and banging at these imaginary creatures with as much zeal as if they had been real. There are no mosquitoes in the Bermudas in May.

The poet Thomas Moore spent several months in Bermuda more than seventy years ago. He was sent out to be registrar of the admiralty. I am not quite clear as to the function of a registrar of the admiralty of Bermuda, but I think it is his duty to keep a record of all the admirals born there. I will inquire into this. There was not much doing in admirals, and Moore got tired and went away. A reverently preserved souvenir of him is still one of the treasures of the islands. I gathered the idea, vaguely, that it was a jug, but was persistently thwarted in the twenty-two efforts I made to visit it. However, it was no matter, for I found afterwards that it was only a chair.

There are several "sights" in the Bermudas, of course, but they are easily avoided. This is a great advantage—one cannot have it in Europe. Bermuda is the right country for a jaded man to "loaf" in. There are no harassments; the deep peace and quiet of the country sink into one's body and bones and give his conscience a rest, and chloroform the legion of invisible small devils that are always trying to whitewash his hair. A good many Americans go there about the first of March and remain until the early spring weeks have finished their villainies at home.

The Bermudians are hoping soon to have telegraphic communication with the world. But even after they shall have acquired this curse, it will still be a good country to go to for a vacation; for there are charming little islets scattered about the inclosed sea where one could live secure from interruption. The telegraph boy would have to come in a boat, and one could easily kill him while he was making his landing.

We had spent four days in Bermuda—three bright ones out of doors and one rainy one in the house, we being disappointed about getting a yacht for a sail; and now our furlough was ended.

We made the run home to New York quarantine in three days and five hours, and could have gone right along up to the city if we had had a health permit. But health permits are not granted after seven in the evening, partly because a ship cannot be inspected and overhauled with exhaustive thoroughness except in daylight, and partly because health officers are liable to catch cold if they expose themselves to the night air. Still, you can *buy* a permit after hours for five dollars extra, and the officer will do the inspecting next week. Our ship and passengers lay under expense and in humiliating captivity all night, under the very nose of the little official reptile who is supposed to protect New York from pestilence by his vigilant "inspections." This imposing rigor gave every body a solemn and awful idea of the beneficent watchfulness of our government, and there were some who wondered if any thing finer could be found in other countries.

In the morning we were all a-tiptoe to witness the intricate ceremony of inspecting the ship. But it was a disappointing thing. The health officer's tug ranged alongside for a moment, our purser handed the lawful three-dollar permit fee to the health officer's boot-black, who passed us a folded paper in a forked stick, and away we went. The entire "inspection" did not occupy thirteen seconds.

The health officer's place is worth a hundred thousand dollars a year to him. His system of inspection is perfect, and therefore cannot be improved on; but it seems to me that his system of collecting his fees might be amended. For a great ship to lie idle all night is a most costly loss of time; for her passengers to have to do the same thing works to them the same damage, with the addition of an amount of exasperation and bitterness of soul that the spectacle of that health officer's funeral could hardly sweeten. Now why would it not be better and simpler to let the ships pass in unmolested, and the fees and permits be exchanged once a year by post?

"Travelling With a Reformer" was written for the December 1893 edition of Cosmopolitan. *Twain included it in a collection entitled* How To Tell a Story and Other Essays, *published by Harper & Brothers in 1897.*

Travelling with a Reformer

Last spring I went out to Chicago to see the Fair, and although I did not see it my trip was not wholly lost—there were compensations. In New York I was introduced to a major in the regular army who said he was going to the Fair, and we agreed to go together. I had to go to Boston first, but that did not interfere; he said he would go along, and put in the time. He was a handsome man, and built like a gladiator. But his ways were gentle, and his speech was soft and persuasive. He was companionable, but exceedingly reposeful. Yes, and wholly destitute of the sense of humor. He was full of interest in everything that went on around him, but his serenity was indestructible; nothing disturbed him, nothing excited him.

But before the day was done I found that deep down in him somewhere he had a passion, quiet as he was—a passion for reforming petty public abuses. He stood for citizenship—it was his hobby. His idea was that every citizen of the republic ought to consider himself an unofficial policeman, and keep unsalaried watch and ward over the laws and their execution. He thought that the only effective way of preserving and protecting public rights was for each citizen to do his share in preventing or punishing such infringements of them as came under his personal notice.

It was a good scheme, but I thought it would keep a body in trouble all the time; it seemed to me that one would be always trying to get offending little officials discharged, and perhaps getting laughed at for all reward. But he said no, I had the wrong idea; that there was no occasion to get anybody discharged; that in fact you *musn't* get anybody discharged; that that would itself be a failure; no, one must reform the man—reform him and make him useful where he was.

"Must one report the offender and then beg his superior not to discharge him, but reprimand him and keep him?"

"No, that is not the idea; you don't report him at all, for then you risk his bread and butter. You can act as if you are *going* to report him—when nothing else will answer. But that's an extreme case. That is a sort of *force*, and force is bad. Diplomacy is the effective thing. Now if a man has tact—if a man will exercise diplomacy—"

For two minutes we had been standing at a telegraph wicket, and during all this time the Major had been trying to get the attention of one of the young operators, but they were all busy skylarking. The Major spoke now, and asked one of them to take his telegram. He got for reply:

"I reckon you can wait a minute, can't you?" and the skylarking went on.

The Major said yes, he was not in a hurry. Then he wrote another telegram:

"President Western Union Tel. Co.:
"Come and dine with me this evening. I can tell you how business is conducted in one of your branches."

Presently the young fellow who had spoken so pertly a little before reached out and took the telegram, and when he read it he lost color and began to apologize and explain. He said he would lose his place if this deadly telegram was sent, and he might never get another. If he could be let off this time he would give no cause for complaint again. The compromise was accepted.

As we walked away, the Major said:

"Now, you see, that was diplomacy—and you see how it worked. It wouldn't do any good to bluster, the way people are always doing—that boy can always give you as good as you send, and you'll come out defeated and ashamed of yourself pretty nearly always. But you see he stands no chance against diplomacy. Gentle words and diplomacy—those are the tools to work with."

"Yes, I see; but everybody wouldn't have had your opportunity. It isn't everybody that is on those familiar terms with the president of the Western Union."

"Oh, you misunderstand. I don't know the president—I only

use him diplomatically. It is for his good and for the public good. There's no harm in it."

I said, with hesitation and diffidence:

"But is it ever right or noble to tell a lie?"

He took no note of the delicate self-righteousness of the question, but answered, with undisturbed gravity and simplicity:

"Yes, sometimes. Lies told to injure a person, and lies told to profit yourself are not justifiable, but lies told to help another person, and lies told in the public interest—oh, well, that is quite another matter. Anybody knows that. But never mind about the methods: you see the result. That youth is going to be useful now, and well-behaved. He had a good face. He was worth saving. Why, he was worth saving on his mother's account if not his own. Of course, he has a mother—sisters, too. Damn these people who are always forgetting that! Do you know, I've never fought a duel in my life—never once—and yet have been challenged, like other people. I could always see the other man's unoffending women folks or his little children standing between him and me. *They* hadn't done anything—I couldn't break *their* hearts, you know."

He corrected a good many little abuses in the course of the day, and always without friction—always with a fine and dainty "diplomacy" which left no sting behind; and he got such happiness and such contentment out of these performances that I was obliged to envy him his trade—and perhaps would have adopted it if I could have managed the necessary deflections from fact as confidently with my mouth as I believe I could with a pen, behind the shelter of print, after a little practice.

Away late that night we were coming uptown in a horse-car when three boisterous roughs got aboard, and began to fling hilarious obscenities and profanities right and left among the timid passengers, some of whom were women and children. Nobody resisted or retorted; the conductor tried soothing words and moral suasion, but the roughs only called him names and laughed at him. Very soon I saw that the Major realized that this was a matter which was in his line; evidently he was turning over his stock of diplomacy in his mind and getting ready. I felt that the first diplomatic remark he made in this place would bring down a land-slide of ridicule upon him and maybe something worse; but before I could whisper to him and check him, he had begun, and it was too late. He said, in a level and dispassionate tone:

"Conductor, you must put these swine out. I will help you."

I was not looking for that. In a flash the three roughs plunged at him. But none of them arrived. He delivered three such blows as one could not expect to encounter outside the prize-ring, and neither of the men had life enough left in him to get up from where he fell. The Major dragged them out and threw them off the car, and we got under way again.

I was astonished; astonished to see a lamb act so; astonished at the strength displayed, and the clean and comprehensive result; astonished at the brisk and business-like style of the whole thing. The situation had a humorous side to it, considering how much I had been hearing about mild persuasion and gentle diplomacy all day from this pile-driver, and I would have liked to call his attention to that feature and do some sarcasms about it; but when I looked at him I saw that it would be of no use—his placid and contented face had no ray of humor in it; he would not have understood. When we left the car, I said:

"That was a good stroke of diplomacy—three good strokes of diplomacy, in fact."

"*That?* That wasn't diplomacy. You are quite in the wrong. Diplomacy is a wholly different thing. One cannot apply it to that sort, they would not understand it. No, that was not diplomacy; it was force."

"Now that you mention it, I—yes, I think perhaps you are right."

"Right? Of course I am right. It was just force."

"I think, myself, it had an outside aspect of it. Do you often have to reform people in that way?"

"Far from it. It hardly ever happens. Not oftener than once in half a year, at the outside."

"Those men will get well?"

"Get well? Why, certainly they will. They are not in any danger. I know how to hit and where to hit. You noticed that I did not hit them under the jaw. That would have killed them."

I believed that. I remarked—rather wittily, as I thought—that he had been a lamb all day, but now had all of a sudden developed into a ram—battering-ram; but with dulcet frankness and simplicity he said no, a battering-ram was quite a different thing and not in use now. This was maddening, and I came near bursting out and saying he had no more appreciation of wit than a jackass—in fact, I had it right on my tongue, but did not say it, knowing there was no hurry and I could say it just as well some other time over the telephone.

We started to Boston the next afternoon. The smoking-compartment in the parlor-car was full, and we went into the regular smoker. Across the aisle in the front seat sat a meek, farmer-looking old man with a sickly pallor in his face, and he was holding the door open with his foot to get the air. Presently a big brakeman came rushing through, and when he got to the door he stopped, gave the farmer an ugly scowl, then wrenched the door to with such energy as to almost snatch the old man's boot off. Then on he plunged about his business. Several passengers laughed, and the old gentleman looked pathetically shamed and grieved.

After a little the conductor passed along, and the Major stopped him and asked him a question in his habitually courteous way:

"Conductor, where does one report the misconduct of a brakeman? Does one report to you?"

"You can report him at New Haven if you want to. What has he been doing?"

The Major told the story. The conductor seemed amused. He said, with just a touch of sarcasm in his bland tones:

"As I understand you, the brakeman didn't *say* anything."

"No, he didn't say anything."

"But he scowled, you say."

"Yes."

"And snatched the door loose in a rough way."

"Yes."

"That's the whole business, is it?"

"Yes, that is the whole of it."

The conductor smiled pleasantly, and said:

"Well, if you want to report him, all right, but I don't quite make out what it's going to amount to. You'll say—as I understand you—that the brakeman insulted this old gentleman. They'll ask you what he *said*. You'll say he didn't say anything at all. I reckon they'll say, how are you going to make out an insult when you acknowledge yourself that he didn't say a word."

There was a murmur of applause at the conductor's compact reasoning, and it gave him pleasure—you could see it in his face. But the Major was not disturbed. He said:

"There—now you have touched upon a crying defect in the complaint-system. The railway officials—as the public think and as you also seem to think—are not aware that there are any kind of insults except *spoken* ones. So nobody goes to headquarters and reports insults of manners, insults of gestures, look, and so forth; and yet these are sometimes harder to bear than any words. They are bitter hard to bear because there is nothing tangible to take hold of; and the insulter can always say, if called before the railway officials, that he never dreamed of intending any offence. It seems to me that the officials ought to specially and urgently request the public to report *unworded* affronts and incivilities."

The conductor laughed, and said:

"Well, that *would* be trimming it pretty fine, sure!"

"But not too fine, I think. I will report this matter at New Haven, and I have an idea that I'll be thanked for it."

The conductor's face lost something of its complacency; in fact, it settled to a quite sober cast as the owner of it moved away. I said:

"You are not really going to bother with that trifle, are you?"

"It isn't a trifle. Such things ought always to be reported. It is a public duty, and no citizen has a right to shirk it. But I sha'n't have to report this case."

"Why?"

"It won't be necessary. Diplomacy will do the business. You'll see."

Presently the conductor came on his rounds again, and when he reached the Major he leaned over and said:

"That's all right. You needn't report him. He's responsible to me, and if he does it again I'll give him a talking to."

The Major's response was cordial:

"Now that is what I like! You mustn't think that I was moved by any vengeful spirit, for that wasn't the case. It was duty—just a sense of duty, that was all. My brother-in-law is one of the directors of the road, and when he learns that you are going to reason with your brakeman the very next time he brutally insults an unoffending old man it will please him, you may be sure of that."

The conductor did not look as joyous as one might have thought he would, but on the contrary looked sickly and uncomfortable. He stood around a little; then said:

"*I* think something ought to be done to him *now*. I'll discharge him."

"Discharge him? What good would that do? Don't you think it would be better wisdom to teach him better ways and keep him?"

"Well, there's something in that. What would you suggest?"

"He insulted the old gentleman in presence of all these people. How would it do to have him come and apologize in their presence?"

"I'll have him here right off. And I want to say this: If people would do as you've done, and report such things to me instead of keeping mum and going off and blackguarding the road, you'd see a different state of things pretty soon. I'm much obliged to you."

The brakeman came and apologized. After he was gone the Major said:

"Now, you see how simple and easy that was. The ordinary citizen would have accomplished nothing—the brother-in-law of a director can accomplish anything he wants to."

"But are you really the brother-in-law of a director?"

"Always. Always when the public interests require it. I have a brother-in-law on all the boards—everywhere. It saves me a world of trouble."

"It is a good wide relationship."

"Yes. I have over three hundred of them."

"Is the relationship never doubted by a conductor?"

"I have never met with a case. It is the honest truth—I never have."

"Why didn't you let him go ahead and discharge the brakeman, in spite of your favorite policy? You know he deserved it."

The Major answered with something which really had a sort of distant resemblance to impatience:

"If you would stop and think a moment you wouldn't ask such a question as that. Is a brakeman a dog, that nothing but dog's methods will do for him? He is a man, and has a man's fight for life. And he always has a sister, or a mother, or wife and children to support. Always—there are no exceptions. When you take his living away from him you take theirs away too—and what have they done to you? Nothing. And where is the profit in discharging an uncourteous brakeman and hiring another just like him? It's unwisdom. Don't you see that the rational thing to do is to *reform* the brakeman and keep him? Of course it is."

Then he quoted with admiration the conduct of a certain division superintendent of the Consolidated road, in a case where a switchman of two years' experience was negligent once and threw a train off the track and killed several people. Citizens came in a passion to urge the man's dismissal, but the superintendent said:

"No, you are wrong. He has learned his lesson, he will throw no more trains off the track. He is twice as valuable as he was before. I shall keep him."

We had only one more adventure on the trip. Between Hartford and Springfield the train-boy came shouting in with an armful of literature and dropped a sample into a slumbering gentleman's lap, and the man woke up with a start. He was very angry, and he and a couple of friends discussed the outrage with much heat. They sent for the parlor-car conductor and described the matter, and were determined to have the boy expelled from his situation. The three complainants were wealthy Holyoke merchants, and it was evident that the conductor stood in some awe of them. He tried to pacify them, and explained that the boy was not under his authority, but under that of one of the news companies; but he accomplished nothing.

Then the Major volunteered some testimony for the defence. He said:

"I saw it all. You gentlemen have not meant to exaggerate the circumstances, but still that is what you have done. The boy has done nothing more than all train-boys do. If you want to get his ways softened down and his manners reformed, I am with you and ready to help, but it isn't fair to get him discharged without giving him a chance."

But they were angry, and would hear no compromise. They were well acquainted with the president of the Boston & Albany, they said, and would put everything aside next day and go up to Boston and fix that boy.

The Major said he would be on hand too, and would do what he could to save the boy. One of the gentlemen looked him over, and said:

"Apparently it is going to be a matter of who can wield the most influence with the president. Do you know Mr. Bliss personally?"

The Major said, with composure:

"Yes; he is my uncle."

The effect was satisfactory. There was an awkward silence for a minute or more; then the hedging and the half-confessions of overhaste and exaggerated resentment began, and soon everything was smooth and friendly and sociable, and it was resolved to drop the matter and leave the boy's bread-and-butter unmolested.

It turned out as I had expected: the president of the road was not the Major's uncle at all—except by adoption, and for this day and train only.

We got into no episodes on the return journey. Probably it was because we took a night train and slept all the way.

We left New York Saturday night by the Pennsylvania road. After breakfast the next morning we went into the parlor-car, but found it a dull place and dreary. There were but few people in it and nothing going on. Then we went into the little smoking-compartment of the same car and found three gentlemen in there. Two of them were grumbling over one of the rules of the road—a rule which forbade card-playing on the trains on Sunday. They had started an innocent game of high-low-jack and been stopped. The Major was interested. He said to the third gentleman:

"Did you object to the game?"

"Not at all. I am a Yale professor and a religious man, but my prejudices are not extensive."

Then the Major said to the others:

"You are at perfect liberty to resume your game, gentlemen; no one here objects."

One of them declined the risk, but the other one said he would like to begin again if the Major would join him. So they spread an overcoat over their knees and the game proceeded. Pretty soon the parlor-car conductor arrived, and said, brusquely:

"There, there, gentlemen, that won't do. Put up the cards— it's not allowed."

The Major was shuffling. He continued to shuffle, and said:

"By whose order is it forbidden?"

"It's my order. I forbid it."

The dealing began. The Major asked:

"Did you invent the idea?"

"What idea?"

"The idea of forbidding card-playing on Sunday."

"No—of course not."

"Who did?"

"The company."

"Then it isn't your order, after all, but the company's. Is that it?"

"Yes. But you don't stop playing; I have to require you to stop playing immediately."

"Nothing is gained by hurry, and often much is lost. Who authorized the company to issue such an order?"

"My dear sir, that is a matter of no consequence to me, and—"

"But you forget that you are not the only person concerned. It may be a matter of consequence to me. It is indeed a matter of very great importance to me. I cannot violate a legal requirement of my country without dishonoring myself; I cannot allow any man or corporation to hamper my liberties with illegal rules—a thing which railway companies are always trying to do—without dishonoring my citizenship. So I come back to that question: By whose authority has the company issued this order?"

"I don't *know*. That's *their* affair."

"Mine, too. I doubt if the company has any right to issue such a rule. This road runs through several States. Do you know what State we are in now, and what its laws are in matters of this kind?"

"Its laws do not concern me, but the company's orders do. It is my duty to stop this game, gentlemen, and it *must* be stopped."

1033

"Possibly; but still there is no hurry. In hotels they post certain rules in the rooms, but they always quote passages from the State law as authority for these requirements. I see nothing posted here of this sort. Please produce your authority and let us arrive at a decision, for you see yourself that you are marring the game."

"I have nothing of the kind, but I have my orders, and that is sufficient. They must be obeyed."

"Let us not jump to conclusions. It will be better all around to examine into the matter without heat or haste, and see just where we stand before either of us makes a mistake—for the curtailing of the liberties of a citizen of the United States is a much more serious matter than you and the railroads seem to think, and it cannot be done in my person until the curtailer proves his right to do so. Now—"

"My dear sir, *will* you put down those cards?"

"All in good time, perhaps. It depends. You say this order must be obeyed. *Must.* It is a strong word. You see yourself how strong it is. A wise company would not arm you with so drastic an order as this, of *course*, without appointing a penalty for its infringement. Otherwise it runs the risk of being a dead letter and a thing to laugh at. What is the appointed penalty for an infringement of this law?"

"Penalty? I never heard of any."

"Unquestionably you must be mistaken. Your company orders you to come here and rudely break up an innocent amusement, and furnishes you no way to enforce the order? Don't you see that that is nonsense. What do you *do* when people refuse to obey this order? Do you take the cards away from them?"

"No."

"Do you put the offender off at the next station?"

"Well, no—of course we couldn't if he had a ticket."

"Do you have him up before a court?"

The conductor was silent and apparently troubled. The Major started a new deal, and said:

"You see that you are helpless, and that the company has placed you in a foolish position. You are furnished with an arrogant order, and you deliver it in a blustering way, and when you come to look into the matter you find you haven't any way of enforcing obedience."

The conductor said, with chill dignity:

"Gentlemen, you have heard the order, and my duty is ended. As to obeying it or not, you will do as you think fit." And he turned to leave.

"But wait. The matter is not yet finished. I think you are

mistaken about your duty being ended; but if it really is, I myself have a duty to perform yet."

"How do you mean?"

"Are you going to report my disobedience at headquarters in Pittsburg?"

"No. What good would that do?"

"You must report me, or I will report you."

"Report me for what?"

"For disobeying the company's orders in not stopping this game. As a citizen it is my duty to help the railway companies keep their servants to their work."

"Are you in earnest?"

"Yes, I am in earnest. I have nothing against you as a man, but I have this against you as an officer—that you have not carried out that order, and if you do not report me I must report you. And I will."

The conductor looked puzzled, and was thoughtful for a moment; then he burst out with:

"I seem to be getting *myself* into a scrape! It's all a muddle; I can't make head or tail of it; it's never happened before; they always knocked under and never said a word, and so *I* never saw how ridiculous that stupid order with no penalty is. *I* don't want to report anybody, and I don't want to *be* reported—why, it might do me no end of harm! Now *do* go on with the game— play the whole day if you want—and don't let's have any more trouble about it!"

"No, I only sat down here to establish this gentleman's rights—he can have his place now. But before you go won't you tell me what you think the company made this rule for? Can you imagine an excuse for it? I mean a rational one—an excuse that is not on its face silly, and the invention of an idiot?"

"Why, surely I can. The reason it was made is plain enough. It is to save the feelings of the other passengers—the religious ones among them, I mean. They would not like it, to have the Sabbath desecrated by card-playing on the train."

"I just thought as much. They are willing to desecrate it themselves by travelling on Sunday, but they are not willing that other people—"

"By gracious, you've hit it! I never thought of that before. The fact is, it *is* a silly rule when you come to look into it."

At this point the train-conductor arrived, and was going to shut down the game in a very high-handed fashion, but the parlor-car conductor stopped him and took him aside to explain. Nothing more was heard of the matter.

I was ill in bed eleven days in Chicago and got no glimpse of the Fair, for I was obliged to return east as soon as I was able to travel. The Major secured and paid for a state-room in a sleeper the day before we left, so that I could have plenty of room and be comfortable; but when we arrived at the station a mistake had been made and our car had not been put on. The conductor had reserved a section for us—it was the best he could do, he said. But the Major said we were not in a hurry, and would wait for the car to be put on. The conductor responded, with pleasant irony:

"It may be that *you* are not in a hurry, just as you say, but we *are:* Come, get aboard, gentlemen, get aboard—don't keep us waiting."

But the Major would not get aboard himself nor allow me to do it. He wanted his car, and said he must have it. This made the hurried and perspiring conductor impatient, and he said:

"It's the best we can *do*—we can't do impossibilities. You will take the section or go without. A mistake has been made and can't be rectified at this late hour. It's a thing that happens now and then, and there is nothing for it but to put up with it and make the best of it. Other people do."

"Ah, that is just it, you see. If they had stuck to their rights and enforced them you wouldn't be trying to trample mine underfoot in this bland way now. I haven't any disposition to give you unnecessary trouble, but it is my duty to protect the next man from this kind of imposition. So I must have my car. Otherwise I will wait in Chicago and sue the company for violating its contract."

"Sue the company?—for a thing like that!"

"Certainly."

"Do you really mean that?"

"Indeed, I do."

The conductor looked the Major over wonderingly, and then said:

"It beats me—it's bran-new—I've never struck the mate to it before. But I swear I think you'd do it. Look here, I'll send for the station-master."

When the station-master came he was a good deal annoyed—at the Major, not at the person who had made the mistake. He was rather brusque, and took the same position which the conductor had taken in the beginning; but he failed to move the soft-spoken artilleryman, who still insisted that he must have his car. However, it was plain that there was only one strong side in this case, and that that side was the Major's. The station-master banished his annoyed manner, and became pleasant and even half-apologetic. This made a good opening for a compromise, and the Major made a concession. He said he would give up the engaged state-room, but he must have *a* state-room. After a deal of ransacking, one was found whose owner was persuadable; he exchanged it for our section, and we got away at last. The conductor called on us in the evening, and was kind and courteous and obliging, and we had a long talk and got to be good friends. He said he wished the public would make trouble oftener—it would have a good effect. He said that the railroads could not be expected to do their whole duty by the traveller unless the traveller would take some interest in the matter himself.

I hoped that we were done reforming for the trip now, but it was not so. In the hotel-car, in the morning, the Major called for broiled chicken. The waiter said:

"It's not in the bill of fare, sir; we do not serve anything but what is in the bill."

"That gentleman yonder is eating a broiled chicken."

"Yes, but that is different. He is one of the superintendents of the road."

"Then all the more must I have broiled chicken. I do not like these discriminations. Please hurry—bring me a broiled chicken."

The waiter brought the steward, who explained in a low and polite voice that the thing was impossible—it was against the rule, and the rule was rigid.

"Very well, then, you must either apply it impartially or break it impartially. You must take that gentleman's chicken away from him or bring me one."

The steward was puzzled, and did not quite know what to do. He began an incoherent argument, but the conductor came along just then, and asked what the difficulty was. The steward explained that here was a gentleman who was insisting on having a chicken when it was dead against the rule and not in the bill. The conductor said:

"Stick by your rules—you haven't any option. Wait a minute—is this the gentleman?" Then he laughed and said: "Never mind your rules—it's my advice, and sound; give him anything he wants—don't get him started on his rights. Give him whatever he asks for; and if you haven't got it, stop the train and get it."

The Major ate the chicken, but said he did it from a sense of duty and to establish a principle, for he did not like chicken.

I missed the Fair it is true, but I picked up some diplomatic tricks which I and the reader may find handy and useful as we go along.

"The Loves of Alonzo Fitz Clarence and Rosannah Ethelton" appeared in March, 1878, in the Atlantic *magazine and almost simultaneously in a collection of sketches called* Punch, Brothers, Punch! *That same year it was also published separately in pamphlet form in The Chimney Corner Series.*

The Loves of Alonzo Fitz Clarence and Rosannah Ethelton

I

It was well along in the forenoon of a bitter winter's day. The town of Eastport, in the State of Maine, lay buried under a deep snow that was newly fallen. The customary bustle in the streets was wanting. One could look long distances down them and see nothing but a dead-white emptiness, with silence to match. Of course I do not mean that you could *see* the silence,—no, you could only hear it. The sidewalks were merely long, deep ditches, with steep snow walls on either side. Here and there you might hear the faint, far scrape of a wooden shovel, and if you were quick enough you might catch a glimpse of a distant black figure stooping and disappearing in one of those ditches, and reappearing the next moment with a motion which you would know meant the heaving out of a shovelful of snow. But you needed to be quick, for that black figure would not linger, but would soon drop that shovel and scud for the house, thrashing itself with its arms to warm them. Yes, it was too venomously cold for snow shovelers or any body else to stay out long.

Presently the sky darkened; then the wind rose and began to blow in fitful, vigorous gusts, which sent clouds of powdery snow aloft, and straight ahead, and everywhere. Under the impulse of one of these gusts, great white drifts banked themselves like graves across the streets; a moment later, another gust shifted them around the other way, driving a fine spray of snow from their sharp crests, as the gale drives the spume-flakes from wave-crests at sea; a third gust swept that place as clean as your hand, if it saw fit. This was fooling, this was play; but each and all of the gusts dumped some snow into the sidewalk ditches, for that was business.

Alonzo Fitz Clarence was sitting in his snug and elegant little parlor, in a lovely blue silk dressing-gown, with cuffs and facings of crimson satin, elaborately quilted. The remains of his breakfast were before him, and the dainty and costly little table service added a harmonious charm to the grace, beauty, and richness of the fixed appointments of the room. A cheery fire was blazing on the hearth.

A furious gust of wind shook the windows, and a great wave of snow washed against them with a drenching sound, so to speak. The handsome young bachelor murmured—

"That means, no going out to-day. Well, I am content. But what to do for company? Mother is well enough, aunt Susan is well enough; but these, like the poor, I have with me always. On so grim a day as this, one needs a new interest, a fresh element, to whet the dull edge of captivity. That was very neatly said, but it doesn't mean any thing. One doesn't *want* the edge of captivity sharpened up, you know, but just the reverse."

He glanced at his pretty French mantel clock.

"That clock's wrong again. That clock hardly ever knows what time it is; and when it does know, it lies about it—which amounts to the same thing. Alfred!"

There was no answer.

"Alfred!—Good servant, but as uncertain as the clock."

Alonzo touched an electrical bell-button in the wall. He waited a moment, then touched it again; waited a few moments more, and said—

"Battery out of order, no doubt. But now that I have started, I *will* find out what time it is." He stepped to a speaking-tube in the wall, blew its whistle, and called, "Mother!" and repeated it twice.

"Well, *that's* no use. Mother's battery is out of order, too. Can't raise any body down-stairs—that is plain."

He sat down at a rose-wood desk, leaned his chin on the left-hand edge of it, and spoke, as if to the floor: "Aunt Susan!"

A low, pleasant voice answered, "Is that you, Alonzo?"

"Yes. I'm too lazy and comfortable to go downstairs; I am in extremity, and I can't seem to scare up any help."

"Dear me, what is the matter?"

"Matter enough, I can tell you!"

"Oh, don't keep me in suspense, dear! What *is* it?"

"I want to know what time it is."

"You abominable boy, what a turn you did give me! Is that all?"

"All—on my honor. Calm yourself. Tell me the time, and receive my blessing."

"Just five minutes after nine. No charge—keep your blessing."

"Thanks. It wouldn't have impoverished me, aunty, nor so enriched you that you could live without other means." He got up, murmuring, "Just five minutes after nine," and faced his clock. "Ah," said he, "you are doing better than usual. You are only thirty-four minutes wrong. Let me see—let me see—Thirty-three and twenty-one are fifty-four; four times fifty-four are two hundred and thirty-six. One off, leaves two hundred and thirty-five. That's right."

He turned the hands of the clock forward till they marked twenty-five minutes to one, and said, "Now see if you can't keep right for a while—else I'll raffle you!"

He sat down at the desk again, and said, "Aunt Susan!"

"Yes, dear."

"Had breakfast?"

"Yes indeed, an hour ago."

"Busy?"

"No—except sewing. Why?"

"Got any company?"

"No, but I expect some at half past nine."

"I wish *I* did. I'm lonesome. I want to talk to somebody."

"Very well, talk to me."

"But this is very private."

"Don't be afraid—talk right along; there's nobody here but me."

"I hardly know whether to venture or not, but—"

"But what? Oh, don't stop there! You *know* you can trust me, Alonzo—you know you can."

"I feel it, aunt, but this is very serious. It affects me deeply—me, and all the family—even the whole community."

"Oh, Alonzo, tell me! I will never breathe a word of it. What is it?"

"Aunt, if I might dare—"

"Oh, please go on! I love you, and can feel for you. Tell me all. Confide in me. What *is* it?"

"The weather!"

"Plague take the weather! I don't see how you can have the heart to serve me so, Lon."

"There, there, aunty dear, I'm sorry; I am, on my honor. I won't do it again. Do you forgive me?"

"Yes, since you seem so sincere about it, though I know I oughtn't to. You will fool me again as soon as I have forgotten this time."

"No, I won't, honor bright. But such weather, oh, such weather! You've *got* to keep your spirits up artificially. It is snowy, and blowy, and gusty, and bitter cold! How is the weather with you?"

"Warm and rainy and melancholy. The mourners go about the streets with their umbrellas running streams from the end of every whalebone. There's an elevated double pavement of umbrellas stretching down the sides of the streets as far as I can see. I've got a fire for cheerfulness, and the windows open to keep cool. But it is vain, it is useless: nothing comes in but the balmy breath of December, with its burden of mocking odors from the flowers that possess the realm outside, and rejoice in their lawless profusion whilst the spirit of man is low, and flaunt their gaudy splendors in his face whilst his soul is clothed in sackcloth and ashes and his heart breaketh."

Alonzo opened his lips to say, "You ought to print that, and get it framed," but checked himself, for he heard his aunt speaking to some one else. He went and stood at the window and looked out upon the wintry prospect. The storm was driving the snow before it more furiously than ever; window shutters were slamming and banging; a forlorn dog, with bowed head and tail withdrawn from service, was pressing his quaking body against a windward wall for shelter and protection; a young girl was plowing knee-deep through the drifts, with her face turned from the blast, and the cape of her water-proof blowing straight rearward over her head. Alonzo shuddered, and said with a sigh, "Better the slop, and the sultry rain, and even the insolent flowers, than this!"

He turned from the window, moved a step, and stopped in a listening attitude. The faint, sweet notes of a familiar song caught his ear. He remained there, with his head unconsciously bent forward, drinking in the melody, stirring neither hand nor foot, hardly breathing. There was a blemish in the execution of the song, but to Alonzo it seemed an added charm instead of a defect. This blemish consisted of a marked flatting of the third, fourth, fifth, sixth, and seventh notes of the refrain or chorus of the piece. When the music ended, Alonzo drew a deep breath, and said, "Ah, I never heard 'In the Sweet By and By' sung like that before!"

He stepped quickly to the desk, listened a moment, and said in a guarded, confidential voice, "Aunty, who is this divine singer?"

"She is the company I was expecting. Stays with me a month or two. I will introduce you. Miss—"

"For goodness' sake, wait a moment, Aunt Susan! You never stop to think what you are about!"

He flew to his bed-chamber, and returned in a moment perceptibly changed in his outward appearance, and remarking, snappishly—

"Hang it, she would have introduced me to this angel in that sky-blue dressing-gown with red-hot lapels! Women never think, when they get a-going."

He hastened and stood by the desk, and said eagerly, "Now, aunty, I am ready," and fell to smiling and bowing with all the persuasiveness and elegance that were in him.

"Very well. Miss Rosannah Ethelton, let me introduce to you my favorite nephew, Mr. Alonzo Fitz Clarence. There! You are both good people, and I like you; so I am going to trust you together while I attend to a few household affairs. Sit down, Rosannah; sit down, Alonzo. Good-by; I shan't be gone long."

Alonzo had been bowing and smiling all the while, and motioning imaginary young ladies to sit down in imaginary chairs, but now he took a seat himself, mentally saying, "Oh, this is luck! Let the winds blow now, and the snow drive, and the heavens frown! Little I care!"

While these young people chat themselves into an acquaintanceship, let us take the liberty of inspecting the sweeter and fairer of the two. She sat alone, at her graceful ease, in a richly furnished apartment which was manifestly the private parlor of a refined and sensible lady, if signs and symbols may go for anything. For instance, by a low, comfortable chair stood a dainty, top-heavy work-stand, whose summit was a fancifully embroidered shallow basket, with vari-colored crewels, and other strings and odds and ends, protruding from under the gaping lid and hanging down in negligent profusion. On the floor lay bright shreds of Turkey red, Prussian blue, and kindred fabrics, bits of ribbon, a spool or two, a pair of scissors, and a roll or so of tinted silken stuffs. On a luxurious sofa upholstered with some sort of soft Indian goods wrought in black and gold threads interwebbed with other threads not so pronounced in color, lay a great square of coarse white stuff, upon whose surface a rich bouquet of flowers was growing, under the deft cultivation of the crochet needle. The household cat was asleep on this work of art. In a bay-window stood an easel with an unfinished picture on it, and a palette and brushes on a chair beside it. There were books everywhere: Robertson's Sermons, Tennyson, Moody and Sankey, Hawthorne, Rab and his Friends, cook-books, prayer-books, pattern-books, and books about all kinds of odious and exasperating pottery, of course. There was a piano, with a deck-load of music, and more in a tender. There was a great plenty of pictures on the walls, on the shelves of the mantel-piece, and around generally; where coigns of vantage offered were statuettes, and quaint and pretty gimcracks, and rare and costly specimens of peculiarly devilish china. The bay-window gave upon a garden that was ablaze with foreign and domestic flowers and flowering shrubs.

But the sweet young girl was the daintiest thing those premises, within or without, could offer for contemplation: delicately chiseled features, of Grecian cast; her complexion the pure snow of a japonica that is receiving a faint reflected enrichment from some scarlet neighbor of the garden; great, soft, blue eyes fringed with long, curving lashes; an expression made up of the trustfulness of a child and the gentleness of a fawn; a beautiful head crowned with its own prodigal gold; a lithe and rounded figure, whose every attitude and movement were instinct with native grace.

Her dress and adornment were marked by that exquisite harmony that can come only of a fine natural taste perfected by culture. Her gown was of a simple magenta tulle, cut bias, traversed by three rows of light blue flounces, with the selvage edges turned up with ashes-of-roses chenille; overdress of dark bay tarleton, with scarlet satin lambrequins; corn-colored polonaise, *en panier*, looped with mother-of-pearl buttons and silver cord, and hauled aft and made fast by buff-velvet lashings; basque of lavender reps, picked out with valenciennes; low neck, short sleeves; maroon-velvet necktie edged with delicate pink silk; inside handkerchief of some simple three-ply ingrain fabric of a soft saffron tint; coral bracelets and locket-chain; coiffure of forget-me-nots and lilies of the valley massed around a noble calla.

This was all; yet even in this subdued attire she was divinely beautiful. Then what must she have been when adorned for the festival or the ball?

All this time she has been busily chatting with Alonzo, unconscious of our inspection. The minutes still sped, and still she talked. But by and by she happened to look up, and saw the clock. A crimson blush sent its rich flood through her cheeks, and she exclaimed—

"There, good-by, Mr. Fitz Clarence; I must go now!"

She sprang from her chair with such haste that she hardly heard the young man's answering good-by. She stood radiant, graceful, beautiful, and gazed, wondering, upon the accusing clock. Presently her pouting lips parted, and she said—

"Five minutes after eleven! Nearly two hours, and it did not seem twenty minutes! Oh, dear, what will he think of me!"

At the self-same moment Alonzo was staring at *his* clock. And presently he said—

"Twenty-five minutes to three! Nearly two hours, and I didn't believe it was two minutes! Is it possible that this clock is humbugging again? Miss Ethelton! Just one moment, please. Are you there yet?"

"Yes, but be quick; I'm going right away."

"Would you be so kind as to tell me what time it is?"

The girl blushed again, murmured to herself, "It's right down cruel of him to ask me!" and then spoke up and answered with admirably counterfeited unconcern, "Five minutes after eleven."

"Oh, thank you! You have to go now, have you?"

"Yes."

"I'm sorry."

No reply.

"Miss Ethelton!"

"Well?"

"You—you're there yet, *ain't* you?"

"Yes, but please hurry. What did you want to say?"

"Well, I—well, nothing in particular. It's very lonesome here. It's asking a great deal, I know, but would you mind talking with me again by and by—that is, if it will not trouble you too much?"

"I don't know—but I'll think about it. I'll try."

"O thanks! Miss Ethelton?—Ah me, she's gone, and here are the black clouds and the whirling snow and the raging winds come again! But she said *good-by!* She didn't say good morning, she said good-by!—The clock was right, after all. What a lightning-winged two hours it was!"

He sat down, and gazed dreamily into his fire for a while, then heaved a sigh and said—

"How wonderful it is! Two little hours ago I was a free man, and now my heart's in San Francisco!"

About that time Rosannah Ethelton, propped in the window-seat of her bed-chamber, book in hand, was gazing vacantly out over the rainy seas that washed the Golden Gate, and whispering to herself, "How different he is from poor Burley, with his empty head and his single little antic talent of mimicry!"

II

Six weeks later Mr. Sydney Algernon Burley was entertaining a gay luncheon company, in a sumptuous drawing-room on Telegraph Hill, with some capital imitations of the voices and gestures of certain popular actors and San Franciscan literary people and Bonanza grandees. He was elegantly upholstered, and was a handsome fellow, barring a trifling cast in his eye. He seemed very jovial, but nevertheless he kept his eye on the door with an expectant and uneasy watchfulness. By and by a nobby lackey appeared, and delivered a message to the mistress, who nodded her head understandingly. That seemed to settle the thing for Mr. Burley; his vivacity decreased little by little, and a dejected look began to creep into one of his eyes and a sinister one into the other.

The rest of the company departed in due time, leaving him with the mistress, to whom he said—

"There is no longer any question about it. She avoids me. She continually excuses herself. If I could see her, if I could speak to her only a moment,—but this suspense—"

"Perhaps her seeming avoidance is mere accident, Mr. Burley. Go to the small drawing-room up-stairs and amuse yourself a moment. I will dispatch a household order that is on my mind, and then I will go to her room. Without doubt she will be persuaded to see you."

Mr. Burley went up-stairs, intending to go to the small drawing-room, but as he was passing "aunt Susan's" private parlor, the door of which stood slightly ajar, he heard a joyous laugh which he recognized; so without knock or announcement he stepped confidently in. But before he could make his presence known he heard words that harrowed up his soul and chilled his young blood. He heard a voice say—

"Darling, it has come!"

Then he heard Rosannah Ethelton, whose back was toward him, say—

"So has yours, dearest!"

He saw her bowed form bend lower; he heard her kiss something—not merely once, but again and again! His soul raged within him. The heart-breaking conversation went on:

"Rosannah, I knew you must be beautiful, but this is dazzling, this is blinding, this is intoxicating!"

"Alonzo, it is such happiness to hear you say it. I know it is not true, but I am *so* grateful to have you think it is, nevertheless! I knew you must have a noble face, but the grace and majesty of the reality beggar the poor creation of my fancy."

Burley heard the rattling shower of kisses again.

"Thank you, my Rosannah! The photograph flatters me, but you must not allow yourself to think of that. Sweetheart?"

"Yes, Alonzo."

"I am so happy, Rosannah."

"Oh, Alonzo, none that have gone before me knew what love was, none that come after me will ever know what happiness is. I float in a gorgeous cloudland, a boundless firmament of enchanted and bewildering ecstasy!"

"Oh, my Rosannah!—for you are mine, are you not?"

"Wholly, oh, wholly yours, Alonzo, now and forever! All the day long, and all through my nightly dreams, one song sings itself, and its sweet burden is, 'Alonzo Fitz Clarence, Alonzo Fitz Clarence, Eastport, State of Maine!' "

"Curse him, I've got his address, any way!" roared Burley inwardly, and rushed from the place.

Just behind the unconscious Alonzo stood his mother, a picture of astonishment. She was so muffled from head to heel in furs that nothing of herself was visible but her eyes and nose. She was a good allegory of winter, for she was powdered all over with snow.

Behind the unconscious Rosannah stood "aunt Susan," another picture of astonishment. She was a good allegory of summer, for she was lightly clad, and was vigorously cooling the perspiration on her face with a fan.

Both of these women had tears of joy in their eyes.

"So ho!" exclaimed Mrs. Fitz Clarence, "this explains why nobody has been able to drag you out of your room for six weeks, Alonzo!"

"So ho!" exclaimed Aunt Susan, "this explains why you have been a hermit for the past six weeks, Rosannah!"

The young people were on their feet in an instant, abashed, and standing like detected dealers in stolen goods awaiting Judge Lynch's doom.

"Bless you, my son! I am happy in your happiness. Come to your mother's arms, Alonzo!"

"Bless you, Rosannah, for my dear nephew's sake! Come to my arms!"

Then was there a mingling of hearts and tears of rejoicing on Telegraph Hill and in Eastport Square.

Servants were called by the elders, in both places. Unto one was given the order, "Pile this fire high with hickory wood, and bring me a roasting-hot lemonade."

Unto the other was given the order, "Put out this fire, and bring me two palm-leaf fans and a pitcher of ice-water."

Then the young people were dismissed, and the elders sat down to talk the sweet surprise over and make the wedding plans.

Some minutes before this Mr. Burley rushed from the mansion on Telegraph Hill without meeting or taking formal leave of anybody. He hissed through his teeth in unconscious imitation of a popular favorite in melodrama, "Him shall she never wed! I have sworn it! Ere great Nature shall have doffed her winter's ermine to don the emerald gauds of spring, she shall be mine!"

III

Two weeks later. Every few hours, during some three or four days, a very prim and devout looking Episcopal clergyman, with a cast in his eye, had visited Alonzo. According to his card, he was the Rev. Melton Hargrave, of Cincinnati. He said he had retired from the ministry on account of his health. If he had said on account of ill health, he would probably have erred, to judge by his wholesome looks and firm build. He was the inventor of an improvement in telephones, and hoped to make his bread by selling the privilege of using it. "At present," he continued, "a man may go and tap a telegraph wire which is conveying a song or a concert from one State to another, and he can attach his private telephone and steal a hearing of that music as it passes along. My invention will stop all that."

"Well," answered Alonzo, "if the owner of the music could not miss what was stolen, why should he care?"

"He shouldn't care," said the Reverend.

"Well?" said Alonzo, inquiringly.

"Suppose," replied the Reverend, "suppose that instead of music that was passing along and being stolen, the burden of the wire was loving endearments of the most private and sacred nature?"

Alonzo shuddered from head to heel. "Sir, it is a priceless invention," said he; "I must have it at any cost."

But the invention was delayed somewhere on the road from Cincinnati, most unaccountably. The impatient Alonzo could hardly wait. The thought of Rosannah's sweet words being shared with him by some ribald thief was galling to him. The Reverend came frequently and lamented the delay, and told of measures he had taken to hurry things up. This was some little comfort to Alonzo.

One forenoon the Reverend ascended the stairs, and knocked

at Alonzo's door. There was no response. He entered, glanced eagerly around, closed the door softly, then ran to the telephone. The exquisitely soft remote strains of the "Sweet By and By" came floating through the instrument. The singer was flatting, as usual, the five notes that follow the first two in the chorus, when the Reverend interrupted her with this word, in a voice which was an exact imitation of Alonzo's, with just the faintest flavor of impatience added—

"Sweetheart?"

"Yes, Alonzo?"

"Please don't sing that any more this week—try something modern."

The agile step that goes with a happy heart was heard on the stairs, and the Reverend, smiling diabolically, sought sudden refuge behind the heavy folds of the velvet window curtains. Alonzo entered and flew to the telephone. Said he—

"Rosannah, dear, shall we sing something together?"

"Something *modern?*" asked she, with sarcastic bitterness.

"Yes, if you prefer."

"Sing it yourself, if you like!"

This snappishness amazed and wounded the young man. He said—

Rosannah, that was not like you."

"I suppose it becomes me as much as your very polite speech became you, Mr. Fitz Clarence."

"*Mister* Fitz Clarence! Rosannah, there was nothing impolite about my speech."

"Oh, indeed! Of course, then, I misunderstood you, and I most humbly beg your pardon, ha-ha-ha! No doubt you said, 'Don't sing it any more *to-day.*'"

"Sing *what* any more to-day?"

"The song you mentioned, of course. How very obtuse we are, all of a sudden!"

"I never mentioned any song."

"Oh, you *didn't!*"

"No, I *didn't!*"

"I am compelled to remark that you *did.*"

"And I am obliged to reiterate that I *didn't.*"

"A second rudeness! That is sufficient, sir. I will never forgive you. All is over between us."

Then came a muffled sound of crying. Alonzo hastened to say—

"Oh, Rosannah, unsay those words! There is some dreadful mystery here, some hideous mistake. I am utterly earnest and sincere when I say I never said any thing about any song. I would not hurt you for the whole world . . . Rosannah, dear? . . . Oh, speak to me, won't you?''

There was a pause; then Alonzo heard the girl's sobbings retreating, and knew she had gone from the telephone. He rose with a heavy sigh, and hastened from the room, saying to himself, "I will ransack the charity missions and the haunts of the poor for my mother. She will persuade her that I never meant to wound her."

A minute later, the Reverend was crouching over the telephone like a cat that knoweth the ways of the prey. He had not very many minutes to wait. A soft repentant voice, tremulous with tears, said—

"Alonzo, dear, I have been wrong. You *could* not have said so cruel a thing. It must have been some one who imitated your voice in malice or in jest."

The Reverend coldly answered, in Alonzo's tones—

"You have said all was over between us. So let it be. I spurn your proffered repentance, and despise it!"

Then he departed, radiant with fiendish triumph, to return no more with his imaginary telephonic invention forever.

Four hours afterward, Alonzo arrived with his mother from her favorite haunts of poverty and vice. They summoned the San Francisco household; but there was no reply. They waited, and continued to wait, upon the voiceless telephone.

At length, when it was sunset in San Francisco, and three hours and a half after dark in Eastport, an answer came to the oft-repeated cry of "Rosannah!"

But, alas, it was aunt Susan's voice that spake. She said—

"I have been out all day; just got in. I will go and find her."

The watchers waited two minutes—five minutes—ten minutes. Then came these fatal words, in a frightened tone—

"She is gone, and her baggage with her. To visit another friend, she told the servants. But I found this note on the table in her room. Listen: 'I am gone; seek not to trace me out; my heart is broken; you will never see me more. Tell him I shall always think of him when I sing my poor 'Sweet By and By,' but never of the unkind words he said about it.' That is her note. Alonzo, Alonzo, what does it mean? What has happened?"

But Alonzo sat white and cold as the dead. His mother threw back the velvet curtains and opened a window. The cold air refreshed the sufferer, and he told his aunt his dismal story. Meantime his mother was inspecting a card which had disclosed itself upon the floor when she cast the curtains back. It read, "Mr. Sidney Algernon Burley, San Francisco."

"The miscreant!" shouted Alonzo, and rushed forth to seek

the false Reverend and destroy him; for the card explained every thing, since in the course of the lovers' mutual confessions they had told each other all about all the sweethearts they had ever had, and thrown no end of mud at their failings and foibles—for lovers always do that. It has a fascination that ranks next after billing and cooing.

IV

During the next two months, many things happened. It had early transpired that Rosannah, poor suffering orphan, had neither returned to her grandmother in Portland, Oregon, nor sent any word to her save a duplicate of the woful note she had left in the mansion on Telegraph Hill. Whosoever was sheltering her—if she was still alive—had been persuaded not to betray her whereabouts, without doubt; for all efforts to find trace of her had failed.

Did Alonzo give her up? Not he. He said to himself, "She will sing that sweet song when she is sad; I shall find her." So he took his carpet sack and a portable telephone, and shook the snow of his native city from his arctics, and went forth into the world. He wandered far and wide and in many States. Time and again, strangers were astounded to see a wasted, pale, and woe-worn man laboriously climb a telegraph pole in wintry and lonely places, perch sadly there an hour, with his ear at a little box, then come sighing down, and wander wearily away. Sometimes they shot at him, as peasants do at aeronauts, thinking him mad and dangerous. Thus his clothes were much shredded by bullets and his person grievously lacerated. But he bore it all patiently.

In the beginning of his pilgrimage he used often to say, "Ah, if I could but hear the 'Sweet By and By!' But toward the end of it he used to shed tears of anguish and say, "Ah, if I could but hear something else!"

Thus a month and three weeks drifted by, and at last some humane people seized him and confined him in a private mad-house in New York. He made no moan, for his strength was all gone, and with it all heart and all hope. The superintendent, in pity, gave up his own comfortable parlor and bed-chamber to him and nursed him with affectionate devotion.

At the end of a week the patient was able to leave his bed for the first time. He was lying, comfortably pillowed, on a sofa, listening to the plaintive Miserere of the bleak March winds, and the muffled sound of tramping feet in the street below—for it was about six in the evening, and New York was going home from work. He had a bright fire and the added cheer of a couple of student lamps. So it was warm and snug within, though bleak and raw without; it was light and bright within, though outside it was as dark and dreary as if the world had been lit with Hartford gas. Alonzo smiled feebly to think how his loving vagaries had made him a maniac in the eyes of the world, and was proceeding to pursue his line of thought further, when a faint, sweet strain, the very ghost of sound, so remote and attenuated it seemed, struck upon his ear. His pulses stood still; he listened with parted lips and bated breath. The song flowed on—he waiting, listening, rising slowly and unconsciously from his recumbent position. At last he exclaimed—

"It is! it is she! Oh, the divine flatted notes!"

He dragged himself eagerly to the corner whence the sounds proceeded, tore aside a curtain, and discovered a telephone. He bent over, and as the last note died away he burst forth with the exclamation—

"Oh, thank Heaven, found at last! Speak to me, Rosannah, dearest! The cruel mystery has been unravelled; it was the villain Burley who mimicked my voice and wounded you with insolent speech!"

There was a breathless pause, a waiting age to Alonzo; then a faint sound came, framing itself into language—

"Oh, say those precious words again, Alonzo!"

"They are the truth, the veritable truth, my Rosannah, and you shall have the proof, ample and abundant proof!"

"Oh, Alonzo, stay by me! Leave me not for a moment! Let me feel that you are near me! Tell me we shall never be parted more! Oh, this happy hour, this blessed hour, this memorable hour!"

"We will make record of it, my Rosannah; every year, as this dear hour chimes from the clock, we will celebrate it with thanksgivings, all the years of our life."

"We will, we will, Alonzo!"

"Four minutes after six, in the evening, my Rosannah, shall henceforth—"

"Twenty-three minutes after twelve, afternoon, shall—"

"Why, Rosannah, darling, where are you?"

"In Honolulu, Sandwich Islands. And where are you? Stay by me; do not leave me for a moment. I cannot bear it. Are you at home?"

"No, dear, I am in New York—a patient in the doctor's hands."

An agonizing shriek came buzzing to Alonzo's ear, like the

sharp buzzing of a hurt gnat; it lost power in travelling five thousand miles. Alonzo hastened to say—

"Calm yourself, my child. It is nothing. Already I am getting well under the sweet healing of your presence. Rosannah?"

"Yes, Alonzo? Oh, how you terrified me! Say on."

"Name the happy day, Rosannah!"

There was a little pause. Then a diffident small voice replied, "I blush—but it is with pleasure, it is with happiness. Would—would you like to have it soon?"

"This very night, Rosannah! Oh, let us risk no more delays. Let it be now!—this very night, this very moment!"

"Oh, you impatient creature! I have nobody here but my good old uncle, a missionary for a generation, and now retired from service—nobody but him and his wife. I would so dearly like it if your mother and your aunt Susan—"

"*Our* mother and *our* aunt Susan, my Rosannah."

"Yes, *our* mother and *our* aunt Susan—I am content to word it so if it pleases you; I would so like to have them present."

"So would I. Suppose you telegraph aunt Susan. How long would it take her to come?"

"The steamer leaves San Francisco day after tomorrow. The passage is eight days. She would be here the 31st of March."

"Then name the 1st of April; do, Rosannah, dear."

"Mercy, it would make us April fools, Alonzo!"

"So we be the happiest ones that that day's sun looks down upon in the whole broad expanse of the globe, why need we care? Call it the 1st of April, dear."

"Then the 1st of April it shall be, with all my heart!"

"Oh, happiness! Name the hour too, Rosannah."

"I like the morning, it is so blithe. Will eight in the morning do, Alonzo?"

"The loveliest hour in the day, since it will make you mine."

There was a feeble but frantic sound for some little time, as if wool-lipped, disembodied spirits were exchanging kisses; then Rosannah said, "Excuse me just a moment, dear; I have an appointment, and am called to meet it."

The young girl sought a large parlor and took her place at a window which looked out upon a beautiful scene. To the left one could view the charming Nuuana Valley, fringed with its ruddy flush of tropical flowers and its plumed and graceful cocoa palms; its rising foothills, clothed in the shining green of lemon, citron, and orange groves; its storied precipice beyond, where the first Kamehameha drove his defeated foes over to their destruction, a spot that had forgotten its grim history, no doubt, for now it was smiling, as almost always at noonday, under the glowing arches of a succession of rainbows. In front of the window one could see the quaint town, and here and there a picturesque group of dusky natives, enjoying the blistering weather; and far to the right lay the restless ocean, tossing its white mane in the sunshine.

Rosannah stood there, in her filmy white raiment, fanning her flushed and heated face, waiting. A Kanaka boy, clothed in a damaged blue neck-tie and part of a silk hat, thrust his head in at the door, and announced, " 'Frisco *haole!*"

"Show him in," said the girl, straightening herself up and assuming a meaning dignity. Mr. Sidney Algernon Burley entered, clad from head to heel in dazzling snow—that is to say, in the lightest and whitest of Irish linen. He moved eagerly forward, but the girl made a gesture and gave him a look which checked him suddenly. She said, coldly, "I am here as I promised. I believed your assertions. I yielded to your importunities, and said I would name the day. I name the 1st of April—eight in the morning. Now go!"

"Oh, my dearest, if the gratitude of a lifetime—"

"Not a word. Spare me all sight of you, all communication with you, until that hour. No, no supplications; I will have it so."

When he was gone, she sank exhausted in a chair, for the long siege of troubles she had undergone had wasted her strength. Presently she said, "What a narrow escape! If the hour appointed had been an hour earlier—Oh, horror, what an escape I have made! And to think I had come to imagine I was loving this beguiling, this truthless, this treacherous monster! Oh! he shall repent his villainy!"

Let us now draw this history to a close, for little more needs to be told. On the 2d of the ensuing April, the Honolulu Advertiser contained this notice:

MARRIED.—In this city, by telephone, yesterday morning, at eight o'clock, by Rev. Nathan Hays, assisted by Rev. Nathaniel Davis, of New York, Mr. Alonzo Fitz Clarence, of Eastport, Maine, U. S., and Miss Rosannah Ethelton, of Portland, Oregon, U. S. Mrs. Susan Howland, of San Francisco, a friend of the bride, was present, she being the guest of the Rev. Mr. Hays and wife, uncle and aunt of the bride. Mr. Sidney Algernon Burley, of San Francisco, was also present, but did not remain till the conclusion of the marriage service. Captain Hawthorne's beautiful yacht, tastefully decorated, was in waiting, and the happy bride and her friends immediately departed on a bridal trip to Lahaina and Haleakala.

The New York papers of the same date contained this notice:

MARRIED.—In this city, yesterday, by telephone, at half past two in the morning, by Rev. Nathaniel Davis, assisted by Rev. Nathan Hays, of Honolulu, Mr. Alonzo Fitz Clarence, of Eastport, Maine, and Miss Rosannah Ethelton, of Portland, Oregon. The parents and several friends of the bridegroom were present, and enjoyed a sumptuous breakfast and much festivity until nearly sunrise, and then departed on a bridal trip to the Aquarium, the bridegroom's state of health not admitting of a more extended journey.

Toward the close of that memorable day, Mr. and Mrs. Alonzo Fitz Clarence were buried in sweet converse concerning the pleasures of their several bridal tours, when suddenly the young wife exclaimed: "O Lonny, I forgot! I did what I said I would."

"Did you, dear?"

"Indeed I did. I made *him* the April fool! And I told him so too! Ah, it was a charming surprise! There he stood, sweltering in a black dress suit, with the mercury leaking out of the top of the thermometer, waiting to be married. You should have seen the look he gave when I whispered it in his ear! Ah, his wickedness cost me many of heartache and many a tear, but the score was all squared up, then. So the vengeful feeling went right out of my heart, and I begged him to stay, and said I forgave him every thing. But he wouldn't. He said he would live to be avenged; said he would make our lives a curse to us. But he can't, *can* he dear?"

"Never in this world, my Rosannah!" .

Aunt Susan, the Oregonian grandmother, and the young couple and their Eastport parents are all happy at this writing, and likely to remain so. Aunt Susan brought the bride from the Islands, accompanied her across our continent, and had the happiness of witnessing the rapturous meeting between an adoring husband and wife who had never seen each other until that moment.

A word about the wretched Burley, whose wicked machinations came so near wrecking the hearts and lives of our poor young friends, will be sufficient. In a murderous attempt to seize a crippled and helpless artisan who he fancied had done him some small offence, he fell into a caldron of boiling oil and expired before he could be extinguished.

"The $30,000 Bequest" *was completed in a villa outside* *Florence where Twain had taken his wife Livy in a vain* *attempt to restore her failing health. The Twains had* *been troubled by financial difficulties for some time,* *and this tale perhaps reflects some of the wisdom gained* *from their close escape from bankruptcy. The story* *made its first appearance in the December 10, 1904 issue* *of* Harper's Weekly, *and was collected in* The $30,000 Bequest and Other Stories, *published by Harper &* Brothers in 1906.

The $30,000 Bequest

I

Lakeside was a pleasant little town of five or six thousand inhabitants, and a rather pretty one, too, as towns go in the Far West. It had church accommodations for 35,000, which is the way of the Far West and the South, where everybody is religious, and where each of the Protestant sects is represented and has a plant of its own. Rank was unknown in Lakeside—unconfessed, anyway; everybody knew everybody and his dog, and a sociable friendliness was the prevailing atmosphere.

Saladin Foster was book-keeper in the principal store, and the only high-salaried man of his profession in Lakeside. He was thirty-five years old, now; he had served that store for fourteen years; he had begun in his marriage-week at four hundred dollars a year, and had climbed steadily up, a hundred dollars a year, for four years; from that time forth his wage had remained eight hundred—a handsome figure indeed, and everybody conceded that he was worth it.

His wife, Electra, was a capable helpmeet, although—like himself—a dreamer of dreams and a private dabbler in romance. The first thing she did, after her marriage—child as she was, aged only nineteen—was to buy an acre of ground on the edge of the town, and pay down the cash for it—twenty-five dollars, all her fortune. Saladin had less, by fifteen. She instituted a vegetable garden there, got it farmed on shares by the nearest neighbor, and made it pay her a hundred per cent. a year. Out of

1057

Saladin's first year's wage she put thirty dollars in the savings-bank, sixty out of his second, a hundred out of his third, a hundred and fifty out of his fourth. His wage went to eight hundred a year, then, and meantime two children had arrived and increased the expenses, but she banked two hundred a year from the salary, nevertheless, thenceforth. When she had been married seven years she built and furnished a pretty and comfortable two-thousand-dollar house in the midst of her garden-acre, paid half of the money down and moved her family in. Seven years later she was out of debt and had several hundred dollars out earning its living.

Earning it by the rise in landed estate; for she had long ago bought another acre or two and sold the most of it at a profit to pleasant people who were willing to build, and would be good neighbors and furnish a general comradeship for herself and her growing family. She had an independent income from safe investments of about a hundred dollars a year; her children were growing in years and grace; and she was a pleased and happy woman. Happy in her husband, happy in her children, and the husband and the children were happy in her. It is at this point that this history begins.

The youngest girl, Clytemnestra—called Clytie for short—was eleven; her sister, Gwendolen—called Gwen for short—was thirteen; nice girls, and comely. The names betray the latent romance-tinge in the parental blood, the parents' names indicate that the tinge was an inheritance. It was an affectionate family, hence all four of its members had pet names. Saladin's was a curious and unsexing one—Sally; and so was Electra's— Aleck. All day long Sally was a good and diligent book-keeper and salesman; all day long Aleck was a good and faithful mother and housewife, and thoughtful and calculating business-woman; but in the cosey living-room at night they put the plodding world away, and lived in another and a fairer, reading romances to each other, dreaming dreams, comrading with kings and princes and stately lords and ladies in the flash and stir and splendor of noble palaces and grim and ancient castles.

II

Now came great news! Stunning news—joyous news, in fact. It came from a neighboring State, where the family's only surviving relative lived. It was Sally's relative—a sort of vague and indefinite uncle or second or third cousin by the name of Tilbury Foster, seventy and a bachelor, reputed well-off and correspondingly sour and crusty. Sally had tried to make up to him once, by letter, in a by-gone time, and had not made that mistake again. Tilbury now wrote to Sally, saying he should shortly die, and should leave him thirty thousand dollars, cash; not for love, but because money had given him most of his troubles and exasperations, and he wished to place it where there was good hope that it would continue its malignant work. The bequest would be found in his will, and would be paid over. *Provided, that Sally should be able to prove to the executors that he had taken no notice of the gift by spoken word or by letter, had made no inquiries concerning the moribund's progress towards the everlasting tropics, and had not attended the funeral.*

As soon as Aleck had partially recovered from the tremendous emotions created by the letter, she sent to the relative's habitat and subscribed for the local paper.

Man and wife entered into a solemn compact, now, to never mention the great news to any one while the relative lived, lest some ignorant person carry the fact to the death-bed and distort it and make it appear that they were disobediently thankful for the bequest, and just the same as confessing it and publishing it, right in the face of the prohibition.

For the rest of the day Sally made havoc and confusion with his books, and Aleck could not keep her mind on her affairs, nor even take up a flower-pot or book or a stick of wood without forgetting what she had intended to do with it. For both were dreaming.

"Thir-ty thousand dollars!"

All day long the music of those inspiring words sang through those people's heads.

From his marriage-day forth, Aleck's grip had been upon the purse, and Sally had seldom known what it was to be privileged to squander a dime on non-necessities.

"Thir-ty thousand dollars!" the song went on and on. A vast sum, an unthinkable sum!

All day long Aleck was absorbed in planning how to invest it, Sally in planning how to spend it.

There was no romance-reading that night. The children took themselves away early, for the parents were silent, distraught, and strangely unentertaining. The good-night kisses might as well have been impressed upon vacancy, for all the response they got; the parents were not aware of the kisses, and the children had been gone an hour before their absence was noticed. Two pencils had been busy during that hour—note-making; in the way of plans. It was Sally who broke the stillness at last. He said, with exultation—

"Ah, it'll be grand, Aleck! Out of the first thousand we'll have a horse and a buggy for summer, and a cutter and a skin lap-robe for winter."

Aleck responded with decision and composure—

"Out of the *capital?* Nothing of the kind. Not if it was a million!"

Sally was deeply disappointed; the glow went out of his face. "Oh, Aleck!" he said, reproachfully. "We've always worked so hard and been so scrimped; and now that we are rich, it does seem—"

He did not finish, for he saw her eye soften; his supplication had touched her. She said, with gentle persuasiveness—

"We must not spend the capital, dear, it would not be wise. Out of the income from it—"

"That will answer, that will answer, Aleck! How dear and good you are! There will be a noble income, and if we can spend that—"

"Not *all* of it, dear, not all of it, but you can spend a part of it. That is, a reasonable part. But the whole of the capital—every penny of it—must be put right to work, and kept at it. You see the reasonableness of that, don't you?"

"Why, ye-s. Yes, of course. But we'll have to wait so long. Six months before the first interest falls due."

"Yes—maybe longer."

"Longer, Aleck? Why? Don't they pay half-yearly?"

"*That* kind of an investment—yes; but I sha'n't invest in that way."

"What way then?"

"For big returns."

"Big. That's good. Go on, Aleck. What is it?"

"Coal. The new mines. Cannel. I mean to put in ten thousand. Ground floor. When we organize, we'll get three shares for one."

"By George, but it sounds good, Aleck! Then the shares will be worth—how much? And when?"

"About a year. They'll pay ten per cent. half-yearly, and be worth thirty thousand. I know all about it; the advertisement is in the Cincinnati paper here."

"Land, thirty thousand for ten—in a year! Let's jam in the whole capital and pull out ninety! I'll write and subscribe right now—to-morrow it may be too late."

He was flying to the writing-desk, but Aleck stopped him and put him back in his chair. She said:

"Don't lose your head so. We mustn't subscribe till we've got the money; don't you know that?"

Sally's excitement went down a degree or two, but he was not wholly appeased.

"Why, Aleck, we'll *have* it, you know—and so soon, too. He's probably out of his troubles before this, it's a hundred to nothing he's selecting his brimstone-shovel this very minute. Now, I think—"

Aleck shuddered, and said:

"How *can* you, Sally! Don't talk in that way, it is perfectly scandalous."

"Oh well, make it a halo, if you like, *I* don't care for his outfit, I was only just talking. Can't you let a person talk?"

"But why should you *want* to talk in that dreadful way? How would you like to have people talk so about *you,* and you not cold yet?"

"Not likely to be, for *one* while, I reckon, if my last act was giving away money for the sake of doing somebody a harm with it. But never mind about Tilbury, Aleck, let's talk about something worldly. It does seem to me that that mine is the place for the whole thirty. What's the objection?"

"All the eggs in one basket—that's the objection."

"All right, if you say so. What about the other twenty? What do you mean to do with that?"

"There is no hurry; I am going to look around before I do anything with it."

"All right, if your mind's made up," sighed Sally. He was deep in thought awhile, then he said:

"There'll be twenty thousand profit coming from the ten a year from now. We can spend that, can't we, Aleck?"

Aleck shook her head.

"No, dear," she said, "it won't sell high till we've had the first semi-annual dividend. You can spend part of that."

"Shucks, only *that*—and a whole year to wait! Confound it, I—"

"Oh, do be patient! It might even be declared in three months—it's quite within the possibilities."

"Oh, jolly! oh, thanks!" and Sally jumped up and kissed his wife in gratitude. "It'll be three thousand—three whole thousand! how much of it can we spend, Aleck? Make it liberal—do, dear, that's a good fellow."

Aleck was pleased; so pleased that she yielded to the pressure and conceded a sum which her judgment told her was a foolish extravagance—a thousand dollars. Sally kissed her half a dozen times and even in that way could not express all his joy and thankfulness. This new access of gratitude and affection carried Aleck quite beyond the bounds of prudence, and before she could restrain herself she had made her darling another grant—a couple of thousand out of the fifty or sixty which she meant to clear within a year out of the twenty which still remained of the bequest. The happy tears sprang to Sally's eyes, and he said:

"Oh, I want to hug you!" And he did it. Then he got his notes and sat down and began to check off, for first purchase, the luxuries which he should earliest wish to secure. "Horse—buggy—cutter—lap-robe—patent-leathers—dog—plug hat—church-pew—stem-winder—new teeth—*say,* Aleck!"

"Well?"

"Ciphering away, aren't you? That's right. Have you got the twenty thousand invested yet?"

"No, there's no hurry about that; I must look around first, and think."

"But you are ciphering; what's it about?"

"Why, I have to find work for the thirty thousand that comes out of the coal, haven't I?"

"Scott, what a head! I never thought of that. How are you getting along? Where have you arrived?"

"Not very far—two years or three. I've turned it over twice; once in oil and once in wheat."

"Why, Aleck, it's splendid! How does it aggregate?"

"I think—well, to be on the safe side, about a hundred and eighty thousand clear, though it will probably be more."

"My! isn't it wonderful! By gracious! luck has come our way at last, after all the hard sledding. Aleck!"

"Well?"

"I'm going to cash-in a whole three hundred on the missionaries—what real right have we to care for expenses!"

"You couldn't do a nobler thing, dear; and it's just like your generous nature, you unselfish boy."

The praise made Sally poignantly happy, but he was fair and just enough to say it was rightfully due to Aleck rather than to himself, since but for her he should never have had the money.

Then they went up to bed, and in their delirium of bliss they forgot and left the candle burning in the parlor. They did not remember until they were undressed; then Sally was for letting it burn; he said they could afford it, if it was a thousand. But Aleck went down and put it out.

A good job, too; for on her way back she hit on a scheme that would turn the hundred and eighty thousand into half a million before it had had time to get cold.

III

The little newspaper which Aleck had subscribed for was a Thursday sheet; it would make the trip of five hundred miles from Tilbury's village and arrive on Saturday. Tilbury's letter had started on Friday, more than a day too late for the benefactor to die and get into that week's issue, but in plenty of time to make connection for the next output. Thus the Fosters had to wait almost a complete week to find out whether anything of a satisfactory nature had happened to him or not. It was a long, long week, and the strain was a heavy one. The pair could hardly have borne it if their minds had not had the relief of wholesome diversion. We have seen that they had that. The woman was piling up fortunes right along; the man was spending them—spending all his wife would give him a chance at, at any rate.

At last the Saturday came, and the *Weekly Sagamore* arrived. Mrs. Eversly Bennett was present. She was the Presbyterian parson's wife, and was working the Fosters for a charity. Talk now died a sudden death—on the Foster side. Mrs. Bennett presently discovered that her hosts were not hearing a word she was saying; so she got up, wondering and indignant, and went away. The moment she was out of the house, Aleck eagerly tore the wrapper from the paper, and her eyes and Sally's swept the columns for the death notices. Disappointment! Tilbury was not anywhere mentioned. Aleck was a Christian from the cradle, and duty and the force of habit required her to go through the motions. She pulled herself together and said, with a pious two-per-cent. trade joyousness:

"Let us be humbly thankful that he has been spared; and—"

"Damn his treacherous hide, I wish—"

"Sally! For shame!"

"I don't care!" retorted the angry man. "It's the way *you* feel, and if you weren't so immorally pious you'd be honest and say so."

Aleck said, with wounded dignity:

"I do not see how you can say such unkind and unjust things. There is no such thing as immoral piety."

Sally felt a pang, but tried to conceal it under a shuffling attempt to save his case by changing the form of it—as if changing the form while retaining the juice could deceive the expert he was trying to placate. He said:

"I didn't mean so bad as that, Aleck; I didn't really mean immoral piety, I only meant—meant—well, conventional piety, you know; er—shop piety; the—the—why, *you* know what I mean, Aleck—the—well, where you put up the plated article and play it for solid, you know, without intending anything improper but just out of trade habit, ancient policy, petrified custom, loyalty to—to—hang it, I can't find the right words, but *you* know what I mean, Aleck, and that there isn't any harm in it. I'll try again. You see, it's this way. If a person—"

"You have said quite enough," said Aleck, coldly; let the subject be dropped."

"*I'm* willing," fervently responded Sally, wiping the sweat from his forehead and looking the thankfulness he had no words for. Then, musingly, he apologized to himself. "I certainly held threes—I *know* it—but I drew and didn't fill. That's where I'm so often weak in the game. If I had stood pat—but I didn't. I never do. I don't know enough."

Confessedly defeated, he was properly tame now and subdued. Aleck forgave him with her eyes.

The grand interest, the supreme interest, came instantly to the front again; nothing could keep it in the background many minutes on a stretch. The couple took up the puzzle of the absence of Tilbury's death notice. They discussed it every way, more or less hopefully, but they had to finish where they began, and concede that the only really sane explanation of the absence of the notice must be—and without doubt was—that Tilbury was not dead. There was something sad about it, something even a little unfair, maybe, but there it was, and had to be put up with. They were agreed as to that. To Sally it seemed a strangely inscrutable dispensation; more inscrutable than usual, he thought; one of the most unnecessarily inscrutable he could call to mind, in fact—and said so, with some feeling; but if he was hoping to draw Aleck he failed; she reserved her opinion, if she one; she had not the habit of taking injudicious risks in any market, worldy or other.

The pair must wait for next week's paper—Tilbury had evidently postponed. That was their thought and their decision. So they put the subject away, and went about their affairs again with as good heart as they could.

Now, if they had but known it, they had been wronging Tilbury all the time. Tilbury had kept faith, kept it to the letter; he was dead, he had died to schedule. He was dead more than four days now and used to it; entirely dead, perfectly dead, as dead as any other new person in the cemetery; dead in abundant time to get into that week's *Sagamore,* too, and only shut out by an accident; an accident which could not happen to a metropolitan journal, but which happens easily to a poor little village rag like the *Sagamore*. On this occasion, just as the editorial page was being locked up, a gratis quart of strawberry water-ice arrived from Hostetter's Ladies' and Gents' Ice-Cream Parlors, and the stickful of rather chilly regret over Tilbury's translation got crowded out to make room for the editor's frantic gratitude.

On its way to the standing-galley Tilbury's notice got pied. Otherwise it would have gone into some future edition, for *Weekly Sagamores* do not waste "live" matter, and in their galleys "live" matter is immortal, unless a pi accident intervenes. But a thing that gets pied is dead, and for such there is no resurrection; its chance of seeing print is gone, forever and ever. And so, let Tilbury like it or not, let him rave in his grave to his fill, no matter—no mention of his death would ever see the light in the *Weekly Sagamore*.

IV

Five weeks drifted tediously along. The *Sagamore* arrived regularly on the Saturdays, but never once contained a mention of Tilbury Foster. Sally's patience broke down at this point, and he said, resentfully:

"Damn his livers, he's immortal!"

Aleck gave him a very severe rebuke, and added, with icy solemnity:

"How would you feel if you were suddenly cut off just after such an awful remark had escaped out of you?"

Without sufficient reflection Sally responded:

"I'd feel I was lucky I hadn't got caught with it *in* me."

Pride had forced him to say something, and as he could not think of any rational thing to say he flung that out. Then he stole a base—as he called it—that is, slipped from the presence, to keep from getting brayed in his wife's discussion-mortar.

Six months came and went. The *Sagamore* was still silent about Tilbury. Meantime, Sally had several times thrown out a feeler—that is, a hint that he would like to know. Aleck had ignored the hints. Sally now resolved to brace up and risk a frontal attack. So he squarely proposed to disguise himself and go to Tilbury's village and surreptitiously find out as to the prospects. Aleck put her foot on the dangerous project with energy and decision. She said:

"What can you be thinking of? You do keep my hands full! You have to be watched all the time, like a little child, to keep you from walking into the fire. You'll stay right where you are!''

"Why, Aleck, I could do it and not be found out—I'm certain of it.''

"Sally Foster, don't you know you would have to inquire around?''

"Of course, but what of it? Nobody would suspect who I was.''

"Oh, listen to the man! Some day you've got to prove to the executors that you never inquired. What then?''

He had forgotten that detail. He didn't reply; there wasn't anything to say. Aleck added:

"Now then, drop that notion out of your mind, and don't ever meddle with it again. Tilbury set that trap for you. Don't you know it's a trap? He is on the watch, and fully expecting you to blunder into it. Well, he is going to be disappointed—at least while I am on deck. Sally!''

"Well?''

"As long as you live, if it's a hundred years, don't you ever make an inquiry. Promise!''

"All right,'' with a sigh and reluctantly.

Then Aleck softened and said:

"Don't be impatient. We are prospering; we can wait; there is no hurry. Our small dead-certain income increases all the time; and as to futures, I have not made a mistake yet—they are piling up by the thousands and the tens of thousands. There is not another family in the State with such prospects as ours. Already we are beginning to roll in eventual wealth. You know that, don't you?''

"Yes, Aleck, it's certainly so.''

"Then be grateful for what God is doing for us, and stop worrying. You do not believe we could have achieved these prodigious results without His special help and guidance, do you?''

Hesitatingly, "No-no, I suppose not.'' Then, with feeling and admiration, "And yet, when it comes to judiciousness in watering a stock or putting up a hand to skin Wall Street I don't give in that *you* need any outside amateur help, if I do I wish I—''

"Oh, *do* shut up! I know you do not mean any harm or any irreverence, poor boy, but you can't seem to open your mouth without letting out things to make a person shudder. You keep me in constant dread. For you and for all of us. Once I had no fear of the thunder, but now when I hear it I—''

Her voice broke, and she began to cry, and could not finish. The sight of this smote Sally to the heart and he took her in his arms and petted her and comforted her and promised better conduct, and upbraided himself and remorsefully pleaded for forgiveness. And he was in earnest, and sorry for what he had done and ready for any sacrifice that could make up for it.

And so, in privacy, he thought long and deeply over the matter, resolving to do what should seem best. It was easy to *promise* reform; indeed he had already promised it. But would that do any real good, any permanent good? No, it would be but temporary—he knew his weakness, and confessed it to himself with sorrow—he could not keep the promise. Something surer and better must be devised; and he devised it. At cost of precious money which he had long been saving up, shilling by shilling, he put a lightning-rod on the house.

At a subsequent time he relapsed.

What miracles habit can do! and how quickly and how easily habits are acquired—both trifling habits and habits which profoundly change us. If by accident we wake at two in the morning a couple of nights in succession, we have need to be uneasy, for another repetition can turn the accident into a habit; and a month's dallying with whiskey—but we all know these commonplace facts.

The castle-building habit, the day-dreaming habit—how it grows! what a luxury it becomes; how we fly to its enchantments at every idle moment, how we revel in them, steep our souls in them, intoxicate ourselves with their beguiling fantasies—oh yes, and how soon and how easily our dream-life and our material life become so intermingled and so fused together that we can't quite tell which is which, any more.

By-and-by Aleck subscribed for a Chicago daily and for the *Wall Street Pointer*. With an eye single to finance she studied these as diligently all the week as she studied her Bible Sundays. Sally was lost in admiration, to note with what swift and sure strides her genius and judgment developed and expanded in the forecasting and handling of the securities of both the material and spiritual markets. He was proud of her nerve and daring in exploiting worldly stocks, and just as proud of her conservative caution in working her spiritual deals. He noted that she never lost her head in either case; that with a splendid courage she often went short on worldly futures, but heedfully drew the line there—she was always long on the others. Her policy was quite sane and simple, as she explained it to him: what she put into earthly futures was for speculation, what she put into spiritual futures was for investment; she was willing to go into the one on a margin, and take chances, but in the case of the other, "margin her no margins"—she wanted to cash-in a hundred cents per dollar's-worth, and have the stock transferred on the books.

It took but a very few months to educate Aleck's imagination and Sally's. Each day's training added something to the spread and effectiveness of the two machines. As a consequence, Aleck made imaginary money much faster than at first she had dreamed of making it, and Sally's competency in spending the overflow of it kept pace with the strain put upon it, right along. In the beginning, Aleck had given the coal speculation a twelvemonth in which to materialize, and had been loath to grant that this term might possibly be shortened by nine months. But that was the feeble work, the nursery work, of a financial fancy that had had no teaching, no experience, no practice. These aids soon came, then that nine months vanished, and the imaginary ten-thousand-dollar investment came marching home with three hundred per cent. profit on its back!

It was a great day for the pair of Fosters. They were speechless for joy. Also speechless for another reason: after much watching of the market, Aleck had lately, with fear and trembling, made her first flyer on a "margin," using the remaining twenty thousand of the bequest in this risk. In her mind's eye she had seen it climb, point by point—always with a chance that the market would break—until at last her anxieties were too great for further endurance—she being new to the margin-business and unhardened as yet—and she gave her imaginary broker an imaginary order by imaginary telegraph to sell. She said forty thousand dollars profit was enough. The sale was made on the very day that the coal-venture had returned with its rich freight. As I have said, the couple were speechless. They sat dazed and blissful that night, trying to realize the immense fact, the overwhelming fact, that they were actually worth a hundred thousand dollars in clean, imaginary cash. Yet so it was.

It was the last time that ever Aleck was afraid of a margin; at least afraid enough to let it break her sleep and pale her cheek to the extent that this first experience in that line had done.

Indeed it was a memorable night. Gradually the realization that they were rich sank securely home into the souls of the pair, then they began to place the money. If we could have looked out through the eyes of these dreamers, we should have seen their tidy little wooden house disappear, and a two-story brick with a cast-iron fence in front of it take its place; we should have seen a three-globed gas-chandelier grow down from the parlor ceiling; we should have seen the homely rag carpet turn to noble Brussels, a dollar and a half a yard; we should have seen the plebeian fireplace vanish away and a recherché, big base-burner with isinglass windows take position and spread awe around.

And we should have seen other things, too; among them the buggy, the lap-robe, the stove-pipe hat, and so on.

From that time forth, although the daughters and the neighbors saw only the same old wooden house there, it was a two-story brick to Aleck and Sally; and not a night went by that Aleck did not worry about the imaginary gas-bills, and get for all comfort Sally's reckless retort, "What of it? we can afford it."

Before the couple went to bed, that first night that they were rich, they had decided that they must celebrate. They must give a party—that was the idea. But how to explain it—to the daughters and the neighbors? They could not expose the fact that they were rich. Sally was willing, even anxious, to do it; but Aleck kept her head and would not allow it. She said that although the money was as good as in, it would be as well to wait until it was actually in. On that policy she took her stand, and would not budge. The great secret must be kept, she said—kept from the daughters and everybody else.

The pair were puzzled. They must celebrate, they were determined to celebrate, but since the secret must be kept, what could they celebrate? No birthdays were due for three months. Tilbury wasn't available, evidently he was going to live forever; what the nation *could* they celebrate? That was Sally's way of putting it; and he was getting impatient, too, and harassed. But at last he hit it—just by sheer inspiration, as it seemed to him—and all their troubles were gone in a moment; they would celebrate the Discovery of America. A splendid idea!

Aleck was almost too proud of Sally for words—she said *she* never would have thought of it. But Sally, although he was bursting with delight in the compliment and with wonder at himself, tried not to let on, and said it wasn't really anything, anybody could have done it. Whereat Aleck, with a prideful toss of her happy head, said:

"Oh, certainly! Anybody could—oh, anybody! Hosannah Dilkins, for instance! Or maybe Adelbert Peanut—oh, *dear*—yes! Well, I'd like to see them try it, that's all. Dear-me-suz, if they could think of the discovery of a forty-acre island it's more than *I* believe they could; and as for a whole continent, why, Sally Foster, you know perfectly well it would strain the livers and lights out of them and *then* they couldn't!"

The dear woman, she knew he had talent; and if affection made her over-estimate the size of it a little, surely it was a sweet and gentle crime, and forgiveable for its source's sake.

V

The celebration went off well. The friends were all present, both the young and the old. Among the young were Flossie and Gracie Peanut and their brother Adelbert, who was a rising young journeyman tinner, also Hosannah Dilkins, Jr., journeyman plasterer, just out of his apprenticeship. For many months Adelbert and Hosannah had been showing interest in Gwendolen and Clytemnestra Foster, and the parents of the girls had noticed this with private satisfaction. But they suddenly realized now that that feeling had passed. They recognized that the changed financial conditions had raised up a social bar between their daughters and the young mechanics. The daughters could now look higher—and must. Yes, must. They need marry nothing below the grade of lawyer or merchant; poppa and momma would take care of this; there must be no mésalliances.

However, these thinkings and projects of theirs were private, and did not show on the surface, and therefore threw no shadow upon the celebration. What showed upon the surface was a serene and lofty contentment and a dignity of carriage and gravity of deportment which compelled the admiration and likewise the wonder of the company. All noticed it, all commented upon it, but none was able to divine the secret of it. It was a marvel and a mystery. Three several persons remarked, without suspecting what clever shots they were making:

"It's as if they'd come into property."

That was just it, indeed.

Most mothers would have taken hold of the matrimonial matter in the old regulation way; they would have given the girls a talking to, of a solemn sort and untactful—a lecture calculated to defeat its own purpose, by producing tears and secret rebellion; and the said mothers would have further damaged the business by requesting the young mechanics to discontinue their attentions. But this mother was different. She was practical. She said nothing to any of the young people concerned, nor to any one else except Sally. He listened to her and understood; understood and admired. He said:

"I get the idea. Instead of finding fault with the samples on view, thus hurting feelings and obstructing trade without occasion, you merely offer a higher class of goods for the money, and leave nature to take her course. It's wisdom, Aleck, solid wisdom, and sound as a nut. Who's your fish? Have you nominated him yet?"

No, she hadn't. They must look the market over—which they did. To start with, they considered and discussed Bradish, rising young lawyer, and Fulton, rising young dentist. Sally must invite them to dinner. But not right away; there was no hurry, Aleck said. Keep an eye on the pair, and wait; nothing would be lost by going slowly in so important a matter.

It turned out that this was wisdom, too; for inside of three weeks Aleck made a wonderful strike which swelled her imaginary hundred thousand to four hundred thousand of the same quality. She and Sally were in the clouds that evening. For the first time they introduced champagne at dinner. Not real champagne, but plenty real enough for the amount of imagination expended on it. It was Sally that did it, and Aleck weakly submitted. At bottom both were troubled and ashamed, for he was a high-up Son of Temperance, and at funerals wore an apron which no dog could look upon and retain his reason and his opinion; and she was a W.C.T.U., with all that that implies of boiler-iron virtue and unendurable holiness. But there it was; the pride of riches was beginning its disintegrating work. They had lived to prove, once more, a sad truth which had been proven many times before in the world: that whereas principle is a great and noble protection against showy and degrading vanities and vices, poverty is worth six of it. More than four hundred thousand dollars to the good! They took up the matrimonial matter again. Neither the dentist nor the lawyer was mentioned; there was no occasion, they were out of the running. Disqualified. They discussed the son of the pork-packer and the son of the village banker. But finally, as in the previous case, they concluded to wait and think, and go cautiously and sure.

Luck came their way again. Aleck, ever watchful, saw a great and risky chance, and took a daring flyer. A time of trembling, of doubt, of awful uneasiness followed, for non-success meant absolute ruin and nothing short of it. Then came the result, and Aleck, faint with joy, could hardly control her voice when she said:

"The suspense is over, Sally—and we are worth a cold million!"

Sally wept for gratitude, and said:

"Oh, Electra, jewel of women, darling of my heart, we are free at last, we roll in wealth, we need never scrimp again. It's a case for Veuve Cliquot!" and he got out a pint of spruce-beer and made sacrifice, he saying "Damn the expense," and she rebuking him gently with reproachful but humid and happy eyes.

They shelved the pork-packer's son and the banker's son, and sat down to consider the Governor's son and the son of the Congressman.

VI

It were a weariness to follow in detail the leaps and bounds the Foster fictitious finances took from this time forth. It was marvellous, it was dizzying, it was dazzling. Everything Aleck touched turned to fairy gold, and heaped itself glittering towards the firmament. Millions upon millions poured in, and still the mighty stream flowed thundering along, still its vast volume increased. Five millions—ten millions—twenty—thirty—was there never to be an end?

Two years swept by in a splendid delirium, the intoxicated Fosters scarcely noticing the flight of time. They were now worth three hundred million dollars; they were in every board of directors of every prodigious combine in the country; and still, as time drifted along, the millions went on piling up, five at a time, ten at a time, as fast as they could tally them off, almost. The three hundred doubled itself—then doubled again—and yet again—and yet once more.

Twenty-four hundred millions!

The business was getting a little confused. It was necessary to take an account of stock, and straighten it out. The Fosters knew it, they felt it, they realized that it was imperative; but they also knew that to do it properly and perfectly the task must be carried to a finish without a break when once it was begun. A ten-hours' job; and where could *they* find ten leisure hours in a bunch? Sally was selling pins and sugar and calico all day and every day; Aleck was cooking and washing dishes and sweeping and making beds all day and every day, with none to help, for the daughters were being saved up for high society. The Fosters knew there was one way to get the ten hours, and only one. Both were ashamed to name it; each waited for the other to do it. Finally Sally said:

"Somebody's got to give in. It's up to me. Consider that I've named it—never mind pronouncing it out loud."

Aleck colored, but was grateful. Without further remark, they fell. Fell, and—broke the Sabbath. For that was their only free ten-hour stretch. It was but another step in the downward path. Others would follow. Vast wealth has temptations which fatally and surely undermine the moral structure of persons not habituated to its possession.

They pulled down the shades and broke the Sabbath. With hard and patient labor they overhauled their holdings and listed them. And a long-drawn procession of formidable names it was! Starting with the Railway Systems, Steamer Lines, Standard Oil, Ocean Cables, Diluted Telegraph, and all the rest, and winding up with Klondike, De Beers, Tammany Graft, and Shady Privileges in the Post-office Department.

Twenty-four hundred millions, and all safely planted in Good Things, gilt-edged and interest-bearing. Income, $120,000,000 a year. Aleck fetched a long purr of soft delight, and said:

"Is it enough?"

"It is, Aleck."

"What shall we do?"

"Stand pat."

"Retire from business?"

"That's it."

"I am agreed. The good work is finished; we will take a long rest and enjoy the money."

"Good! Aleck!"

"Yes, dear?"

"How much of the income can we spend?"

"The whole of it."

It seemed to her husband that a ton of chains fell from his limbs. He did not say a word; he was happy beyond the power of speech.

After that, they broke the Sabbaths right along, as fast as they turned up. It is the first wrong steps that count. Every Sunday they put in the whole day, after morning service, on inventions—inventions of ways to spend the money. They got to continuing this delicious dissipation until past midnight; and at every séance Aleck lavished millions upon great charities and religious enterprises, and Sally lavished like sums upon matters to which (at first) he gave definite names. Only at first. Later the names gradually lost sharpness of outline, and eventually faded into "sundries," thus becoming entirely—but safely— undescriptive. For Sally was crumbling. The placing of these millions added seriously and most uncomfortably to the family expenses—in tallow candles. For a while Aleck was worried. Then, after a little, she ceased to worry, for the occasion of it was gone. She was pained, she was grieved, she was ashamed; but she said nothing, and so became an accessory. Sally was taking candles; he was robbing the store. It is ever thus. Vast wealth, to the person unaccustomed to it, is a bane; it eats into the flesh and bone of his morals. When the Fosters were poor, they could have been trusted with untold candles. But now they—but let us not dwell upon it. From candles to apples is but a step: Sally got to taking apples; then soap; then maple-sugar; then canned-goods; then crockery. How easy it is to go from bad to worse, when once we have started upon a downward course!

Meantime, other effects had been milestoning the course of

the Fosters' splendid financial march. The fictitious brick-dwelling had given place to an imaginary granite one with a checker-board mansard roof; in time this one disappeared and gave place to a still grander home—and so on and so on. Mansion after mansion, made of air, rose, higher, broader, finer, and each in its turn vanished away; until now, in these latter great days, our dreamers were in fancy housed, in a distant region, in a sumptuous vast palace which looked out from a leafy summit upon a noble prospect of vale and river and receding hills steeped in tinted mists—and all private, all the property of the dreamers; a palace swarming with liveried servants, and populous with guests of fame and power, hailing from all the world's capitals, foreign and domestic.

This palace was far, far away towards the rising sun, immeasurably remote, astronomically remote, in Newport, Rhode Island, Holy Land of High Society, ineffable Domain of the American Aristocracy. As a rule, they spent a part of every Sabbath—after morning service—in this sumptuous home, the rest of it they spent in Europe, or in dawdling around in their private yacht. Six days of sordid and plodding Fact-life at home on the ragged edge of Lakeside and straitened means, the seventh in Fairyland—such had become their programme and their habit.

In their sternly restricted Fact-life they remained as of old—plodding, diligent, careful, practical, economical. They stuck loyally to the little Presbyterian Church, and labored faithfully in its interests and stood by its high and tough doctrines with all their mental and spiritual energies. But in their Dream-life they obeyed the invitations of their fancies, whatever they might be, and howsoever the fancies might change. Aleck's fancies were not very capricious, and not frequent, but Sally's scattered a good deal. Aleck, in her dream-life, went over to the Episcopal camp, on account of its large official titles; next she became High-church on account of the candles and shows; and next she naturally changed to Rome, where there were cardinals and more candles. But these excursions were as nothing to Sally's. His Dream-life was a glowing and continuous and persistent excitement, and he kept every part of it fresh and sparkling by frequent changes, the religious part along with the rest. He worked his religions hard, and changed them with his shirt.

The liberal spendings of the Fosters upon their fancies began early in their prosperities, and grew in prodigality step by step with their advancing fortunes. In time they became truly enormous. Aleck built a university or two per Sunday; also a hospital or two; also a Rowton hotel or so; also a batch of churches; now and then a cathedral; and once, with untimely and ill-chosen playfulness, Sally said, "It was a cold day when she didn't ship a cargo of missionaries to persuade unreflecting Chinamen to trade off twenty-four carat Confucianism for counterfeit Christianity."

This rude and unfeeling language hurt Aleck to the heart, and she went from the presence crying. That spectacle went to his own heart, and in his pain and shame he would have given worlds to have those unkind words back. She had uttered no syllable of reproach—and that cut him. Not one suggestion that he look at his own record—and she could have made, oh, so many, and such blistering ones! Her generous silence brought a swift revenge, for it turned his thoughts upon himself, it summoned before him a spectral procession, a moving vision of his life as he had been leading it these past few years of limitless prosperity, and as he sat there reviewing it his cheeks burned and his soul was steeped in humiliation. Look at her life—how fair it was, and tending upward; and look at his own—how frivolous, how charged with mean vanities, how selfish, how empty, how ignoble! And its trend—never upward, but downward, ever downward!

He instituted comparisons between her record and his own. He had found fault with her—so he mused—*he!* And what could he say for himself? When she built her first church what was he doing? Gathering other blasé multimillionaires into a Poker Club; defiling his own palace with it; losing hundreds of thousands to it at every sitting, and sillily vain of the admiring notoriety it made for him. When she was building her first university, what was he doing? Polluting himself with a gay and dissipated secret life in the company of other fast bloods, multimillionaires in money and paupers in character. When she was building her first foundling asylum, what was he doing? Alas! When she was projecting her noble Society for the Purifying of the Sex, what was he doing? Ah, what, indeed! When she and the W.C.T.U. and the Woman with the Hatchet, moving with resistless march, were sweeping the fatal bottle from the land, what was he doing? Getting drunk three times a day. When she, builder of a hundred cathedrals, was being gratefully welcomed and blest in papal Rome and decorated with the Golden Rose which she had so honorably earned, what was he doing? Breaking the bank at Monte Carlo.

He stopped. He could go no farther; he could not bear the rest. He rose up, with a great resolution upon his lips: this secret life should be revealed, and confessed; no longer would he live it clandestinely; he would go and tell her All.

And that is what he did. He told her All; and wept upon her bosom; wept, and moaned, and begged for her forgiveness. It was a profound shock, and she staggered under the blow, but he was her own, the core of her heart, the blessing of her eyes, her all in all, she could deny him nothing, and she forgave him. She felt that he could never again be quite to her what he had been before; she knew that he could only repent, and not reform; yet all morally defaced and decayed as he was, was he not her own, her very own, the idol of her deathless worship? She said she was his serf, his slave, and she opened her yearning heart and took him in.

VII

One Sunday afternoon some time after this they were sailing the summer seas in their dream-yacht, and reclining in lazy luxury under the awning of the after-deck. There was silence, for each was busy with his own thoughts. These seasons of silence had insensibly been growing more and more frequent of late; the old nearness and cordiality were waning. Sally's terrible revelation had done its work; Aleck had tried hard to drive the memory of it out of her mind, but it would not go, and the shame and bitterness of it were poisoning her gracious dream-life. She could see now (on Sundays) that her husband was becoming a bloated and repulsive Thing. She could not close her eyes to this, and in these days she no longer looked at him, Sundays, when she could help it.

But she—was she herself without blemish? Alas, she knew she was not. She was keeping a secret from him, she was acting dishonorably towards him, and many a pang it was costing her. *She was breaking the compact, and concealing it from him.* Under strong temptation she had gone into business again; she had risked their whole fortune in a purchase of all the railway systems and coal and steel companies in the country on a margin, and she was now trembling, every Sabbath hour, lest through some chance word of hers he find it out. In her misery and remorse for this treachery she could not keep her heart from going out to him in pity; she was filled with compunctions to see him lying there, drunk and content, and never suspecting. Never suspecting—trusting her with a perfect and pathetic trust, and she holding over him by a thread a possible calamity of so devastating a—

"*Say*—Aleck?"

The interrupting words brought her suddenly to herself. She

was grateful to have that persecuting subject from her thoughts, and she answered, with much of the old-time tenderness in her tone:

"Yes, dear."

"Do you know, Aleck, I think we are making a mistake—that is, you are. I mean about the marriage business." He sat up, fat and froggy and benevolent, like a bronze Buddha, and grew earnest. "Consider—it's more than five years. You've continued the same policy from the start: with every rise, always holding on for five points higher. Always when I think we are going to have some weddings, you see a bigger thing ahead, and I undergo another disappointment. *I* think you are too hard to please. Some day we'll get left. First, we turned down the dentist and the lawyer. That was all right—it was sound. Next, we turned down the banker's son and the pork-butcher's heir— right again, and sound. Next, we turned down the Congress-man's son and the Governor's—right as a trivet, I confess it. Next, the Senator's son and the son of the Vice-President of the United States—perfectly right, there's no permanency about those little distinctions. Then you went for the aristocracy; and I thought we had struck oil at last—yes. We would make a plunge at the Four Hundred, and pull in some ancient lineage, venerable, holy, ineffable, mellow with the antiquity of a hun-dred and fifty years, disinfected of the ancestral odors of salt cod and pelts all of a century ago, and unsmirched by a day's work since; and then! why, then the marriages, of course. But no, along comes a pair of real aristocrats from Europe, and straightway you throw over the half-breeds. It was awfully discouraging, Aleck! Since then, what a procession! You turned down the baronets for a pair of barons; you turned down the barons for a pair of viscounts; the viscounts for a pair of earls; the earls for a pair of marquises; the marquises for a brace of dukes. *Now,* Aleck, cash-in!—you've played the limit. You've got a job lot of four dukes under the hammer; of four na-tionalities; all sound in wind and limb and pedigree, all bankrupt and in debt up to the ears. They come high, but we can afford it. Come, Aleck, don't delay any longer, don't keep up the suspense: take the whole lay-out, and leave the girls to choose!"

Aleck had been smiling blandly and contentedly all through this arraignment of her marriage-policy; a pleasant light, as a triumph with perhaps a nice surprise peeping out through it, rose in her eyes, and she said, as calmly as she could:

"Sally, what would you say to—*royalty?*"

Prodigious! Poor man, it knocked him silly, and he fell over the garboard-strake and barked his shin on the cat-heads. He was dizzy for a moment, then he gathered himself up and limped over and sat down by his wife and beamed his old-time admiration and affection upon her in floods, out of his bleary eyes.

"By George!" he said, fervently, "Aleck, you *are* great—the greatest woman in the whole earth! I can't ever learn the whole size of you. I can't ever learn the immeasurable deeps of you. Here I've been considering myself qualified to criticise your game. *I!* Why, if I had stopped to think, I'd have known you had a lone hand up your sleeve. Now, dear heart, I'm all red-hot impatience—tell me about it!"

The flattered and happy woman put her lips to his ear and whispered a princely name. It made him catch his breath, it lit his face with exultation.

"Land!" he said, "it's a stunning catch! He's got a gambling-hell, and a graveyard, and a bishop, and a cathedral—all his very own. And all gilt-edged five-hundred-per-cent. stock, every detail of it; the tidiest little property in Europe. And that graveyard—it's the selectest in the world: none but suicides admitted; *yes,* sir, and the free-list suspended, too, *all* the time. There isn't much land in the principality, but there's enough: eight hundred acres in the graveyard and forty-two outside. It's a *sovereignty*—that's the main thing; *land's* nothing. There's plenty land, Sahara's drugged with it."

Aleck glowed; she was profoundly happy. She said:

"Think of it, Sally—it is a family that has never married outside the Royal and Imperial Houses of Europe: our grandchildren will sit upon thrones!"

"True as you live, Aleck—and bear sceptres, too; and handle them as naturally and nonchalantly as I handle a yardstick. It's a grand catch, Aleck. He's corralled, is he? Can't get away? You didn't take him on a margin?"

"No. Trust me for that. He's not a liability, he's an asset. So is the other one."

"Who is it, Aleck?"

"His Royal Highness Sigismund-Siegfried-Lauenfeld- Dinkel-spiel-Schwartzenberg Blutwurst, Hereditary Grand Duke of Katzenyammer."

"No! You can't mean it!"

"It's as true as I'm sitting here, I give you my word," she answered.

His cup was full, and he hugged her to his heart with rapture, saying:

"How wonderful it all seems, and how beautiful! It's one of the oldest and noblest of the three hundred and sixty-four ancient German principalities, and one of the few that was allowed to retain its royal estate when Bismarck got done trimming them. I know that farm, I've been there. It's got a ropewalk and a candle-factory and an army. Standing army. Infantry and cavalry. Three soldiers and a horse. Aleck, it's been a long wait, and full of heartbreak and hope deferred, but God knows I am happy now. Happy, and grateful to yof, my own, who have done it all. When is it to be?''

"Next Sunday.''

"Good. And we'll want to do these weddings up in the very regalest style that's going. It's properly due to the royal quality of the parties of the first part. Now as I understand it, there is only one kind of marriage that is sacred to royalty, exclusive to royalty: it's the morganatic.''

"What do they call it that for, Sally?''

"I don't know; but anyway it's royal, and royal only.''

"Then we will insist upon it. More—I will compel it. It is morganatic marriage or none.''

"That settles it!'' said Sally, rubbing his hands with delight. "And it will be the very first in America. Aleck, it will make Newport sick.''

Then they fell silent, and drifted away upon their dream-wings to the far regions of the earth to invite all the crowned heads and their families and provide gratis transportation for them.

VIII

During three days the couple walked upon air, with their heads in the clouds. They were but vaguely conscious of their surroundings; they saw all things dimly, as through a veil; they were steeped in dreams, often they did not hear when they were spoken to; they often did not understand when they heard; they answered confusedly or at random; Sally sold molasses by weight, sugar by the yard, and furnished soap when asked for candles, and Aleck put the cat in the wash and fed milk to the soiled linen. Everybody was stunned and amazed, and went about muttering, "What *can* be the matter with the Fosters?''

Three days. Then came events! Things had taken a happy turn, and for forty-eight hours Aleck's imaginary corner had been booming. Up—up—still up! Cost-point was passed. Still up—and up—and up! Five points above cost—then ten—fifteen—twenty! Twenty points cold profit on the vast venture, now, and Aleck's imaginary brokers were shouting frantically by imaginary long-distance, "Sell! sell! for Heaven's sake *sell!*''

She broke the splendid news to Sally, and he, too, said, "Sell!

sell—oh, don't make a blunder, now, you own the earth!—sell, sell!'' But she set her iron will and lashed it amidships, and said she would hold on for five points more if she died for it.

It was a fatal resolve. The very next day came the historic crash, the record crash, the devastating crash, when the bottom fell out of Wall Street, and the whole body of gilt-edged stocks dropped ninety-five points in five hours, and the multimillionaire was seen begging his bread in the Bowery. Aleck sternly held her grip and "put up" as long as she could, but at last there came a call which she was powerless to meet, and her imaginary brokers sold her out. Then, and not till then, the man in her was vanquished, and the woman in her resumed sway. She put her arms about her husband's neck and wept, saying:

"I am to blame, do not forgive me, I cannot bear it. We are paupers! Paupers, and I am so miserable. The weddings will never come off; all that is past; we could not even buy the dentist, now.''

A bitter reproach was on Sally's tongue: "I *begged* you to sell, but you—'' He did not say it; he had not the heart to add a hurt to that broken and repentant spirit. A nobler thought came to him and he said:

"Bear up, my Aleck, all is not lost! You really never invested a penny of my uncle's bequest, but only its unmaterialized future; what we have lost was only the increment harvested from that future by your incomparable financial judgement and sagacity. Cheer up, banish these griefs; we still have the thirty thousand untouched; and with the experience which you have acquired, think what you will be able to do with it in a couple of years! The marriages are not off, they are only postponed.''

These were blessed words. Aleck saw how true they were, and the influence was electric; her tears ceased to flow, and her great spirit rose to its full stature again. With flashing eye and grateful heart, and with hand uplifted in pledge and prophecy, she said:

"Now and here I proclaim—''

But she was interrupted by a visitor. It was the editor and proprietor of the *Sagamore*. He had happened into Lakeside to pay a duty-call upon an obscure grandmother of his who was nearing the end of her pilgrimage, and with the idea of combining business with grief he had looked up the Fosters, who had been so absorbed in other things for the past four years that they had neglected to pay up their subscription. Six dollars due. No visitor could have been more welcome. He would know all about Uncle Tilbury and what his chances might be getting to be, cemeterywards. They could, of course, ask no questions, for that would squelch the bequest, but they could nibble around on the edge of the subject and hope for results. The scheme did not work. The obtuse editor did not know he was being nibbled at; but at last, chance accomplished what art had failed in. In illustration of something under discussion which required the help of metaphor, the editor said:

"Land, it's as tough as Tilbury Foster!—as *we* say."

It was sudden, and it made the Fosters jump. The editor noticed it, and said, apologetically:

"No harm intended, I assure you. It's just a saying; just a joke, you know—nothing in it. Relation of yours?"

Sally crowded his burning eagerness down, and answered with all the indifference he could assume:

"I—well, not that I know of, but we've heard of him." The editor was thankful, and resumed his composure. Sally added: "Is he—is he—well?"

"Is he *well?* Why, bless you he's in Sheol these five years!"

The Fosters were trembling with grief, though it felt like joy. Sally said, non-commitally—and tentatively:

"Ah, well, such is life, and none can escape—not even the rich are spared."

The editor laughed.

"If you are including Tilbury," said he, "it don't apply. *He* hadn't a cent; the town had to bury him."

The Fosters sat petrified for two minutes; petrified and cold. Then, white-faced and weak-voiced, Sally asked:

"Is it true? Do you *know* it to be true?"

"Well, I should say! I was one of the executors. He hadn't anything to leave but a wheelbarrow, and he left that to me. It hadn't any wheel, and wasn't any good. Still, it was something, and so, to square up, I scribbled off a sort of a little obituarial send-off for him, but it got crowded out."

The Fosters were not listening—their cup was full, it could contain no more. They sat with bowed heads, dead to all things but the ache at their hearts.

An hour later. Still they sat there, bowed, motionless, silent, the visitor long ago gone, they unaware.

Then they stirred, and lifted their heads wearily, and gazed at each other wistfully, dreamily, dazed; then presently began to twaddle to each other in a wandering and childish way. At intervals they lapsed into silences, leaving a sentence unfinished, seemingly either unaware of it or losing their way. Sometimes, when they woke out of these silences they had a dim and transient consciousness that something had happened to their minds; then with a dumb and yearning solicitude they would softly caress each other's hands in mutual compassion and support, as if they would say: "I am near you, I will not forsake you, we will bear it together; somewhere there is release and forgetfulness, somewhere there is a grave and peace; be patient, it will not be long."

They lived yet two years, in mental night, always brooding, steeped in vague regrets and melancholy dreams, never speaking; then release came to both on the same day.

Towards the end the darkness lifted from Sally's ruined mind for a moment, and he said:

"Vast wealth, acquired by sudden and unwholesome means, is a snare. It did us no good, transient were its feverish pleasures; yet for its sake we threw away our sweet and simple and happy life—let others take warning by us."

He lay silent awhile, with closed eyes; then as the chill of death crept upward towards his heart, and consciousness was fading from his brain, he muttered:

"Money had brought him misery, and he took his revenge upon us, who had done him no harm. He had his desire: with base and cunning calculation he left us but thirty thousand, knowing we would try to increase it, and ruin our life and break our hearts. Without added expense he could have left us far above desire of increase, far above the temptation to speculate, and a kinder soul would have done it; but in him was no generous spirit, no pity, no—"

This burlesque was written when Twain was a newspaperman in San Francisco; it appeared as a feature in the Golden Era *on September 20, 1863, and was reprinted in the January 1864 issue of the monthly* Yankee Notions. *The tale was first collected in* The Celebrated Jumping Frog of Calaveras County and Other Sketches, *published by C.H. Webb in 1867, and was later included in the American Publishing Company's edition of* Mark Twain's Sketches New and Old *in 1875.*

Curing a Cold

It is a good thing, perhaps, to write for the amusement of the public, but it is a far higher and nobler thing to write for their instruction, their profit, their actual and tangible benefit. The latter is the sole object of this article. If it prove the means of restoring to health one solitary sufferer among my race, of lighting up once more the fire of hope and joy in his faded eyes, of bringing back to his dead heart again the quick, generous impulses of other days, I shall be amply rewarded for my labor; my soul will be permeated with the sacred delight a Christian feels when he has done a good, unselfish deed.

Having led a pure and blameless life, I am justified in believing that no man who knows me will reject the suggestions I am about to make, out of fear that I am trying to deceive him. Let the public do itself the honor to read my experience in doctoring a cold, as herein set forth, and then follow in my footsteps.

When the White House was burned in Virginia City, I lost my home, my happiness, my constitution, and my trunk. The loss of the two first-named articles was a matter of no great consequence, since a home without a mother or a sister, or a distant young female relative in it, to remind you, by putting your soiled linen out of sight and taking your boots down off the mantelpiece, that there are those who think about you and care for you, is easily obtained. And I cared nothing for the loss of my happiness, because not being a poet, it could not be possible that melancholy would abide with me long. But to lose a good constitution and a better trunk were serious misfortunes. On the day of the fire my constitution succumbed to a severe cold, caused by undue exertion in getting ready to do something. I suffered to no purpose, too, because the plan I was figuring at for the extinguishing of the fire was so elaborate that I never got it completed until the middle of the following week.

The first time I began to sneeze, a friend told me to go and bathe my feet in hot water and go to bed. I did so. Shortly afterwards, another friend advised me to get up and take a cold shower-bath. I did that also. Within the hour, another friend assured me that it was policy to "feed a cold and starve a fever." I had both. So I thought it best to fill myself up for the cold, and then keep dark and let the fever starve awhile.

In a case of this kind, I seldom do things by halves; I ate pretty heartily; I conferred my custom upon a stranger who had just opened his restaurant that morning: he waited near me in respectful silence until I had finished feeding my cold, when he inquired if the people about Virginia City were much afflicted with colds? I told him I thought they were. He then went out and took in his sign.

I started down toward the office, and on the way encountered another bosom friend, who told me that a quart of salt water, taken warm, would come as near curing a cold as anything in the world. I hardly thought I had room for it, but I tried it anyhow. The result was surprising. I believed I had thrown up my immortal soul.

Now, as I am giving my experience only for the benefit of those who are troubled with the distemper I am writing about, I feel that they will see the propriety of my cautioning them against following such portions of it as proved inefficient with me, and acting upon this conviction, I warn them against warm salt water. It may be a good enough remedy, but I think it is too severe. If I had another cold in the head, and there were no course left me but to take either an earthquake or a quart of warm salt water, I would take my chances on the earthquake.

After the storm which had been raging in my stomach had subsided, and no more good Samaritans happening along, I went on borrowing handkerchiefs again and blowing them to atoms, as had been my custom in the early stages of my cold, until I came across a lady who had just arrived from over the plains, and who said she had lived in a part of the country where doctors were scarce, and had from necessity acquired considerable skill in the treatment of simple "family complaints." I knew she must have had much experience, for she appeared to be a hundred and fifty years old.

She mixed a decoction composed of molasses, aquafortis,

turpentine, and various other drugs, and instructed me to take a wine-glass full of it every fifteen minutes. I never took but one dose; that was enough; it robbed me of all moral principle, and awoke every unworthy impulse of my nature. Under its malign influence my brain conceived miracles of meanness, but my hands were too feeble to execute them; at that time, had it not been that my strength had surrendered to a succession of assaults from infallible remedies for my cold, I am satisfied that I would have tried to rob the graveyard. Like most other people, I often feel mean, and act accordingly; but until I took that medicine I had never revelled in such supernatural depravity, and felt proud of it. At the end of two days I was ready to go to doctoring again. I took a few more unfailing remedies, and finally drove my cold from my head to my lungs.

I got to coughing incessantly, and my voice fell below zero; I conversed in a thundering base, two octaves below my natural tone; I could only compass my regular nightly repose by coughing myself down to a state of utter exhaustion, and then the moment I began to talk in my sleep, my discordant voice woke me up again.

My case grew more and more serious every day. Plain gin was recommended; I took it. Then gin and molasses; I took that also. Then gin and onions; I added the onions, and took all three. I detected no particular result, however, except that I had acquired a breath like a buzzard's.

I found I had to travel for my health. I went to Lake Bigler with my reportorial comrade, Wilson. It is gratifying to me to reflect that we traveled in considerable style; we went in the Pioneer coach, and my friend took all his baggage with him, consisting of two excellent silk handkerchiefs and a daguerreotype of his grandmother. We sailed and hunted and fished and danced all day, and I doctored my cough all night. By managing in this way, I made out to improve every hour in the twenty-four. But my disease continued to grow worse.

A sheet-bath was recommended. I had never refused a remedy yet, and it seemed poor policy to commence then; therefore I determined to take a sheet-bath, notwithstanding I had no idea what sort of arrangement it was. It was administered at midnight, and the weather was very frosty. My breast and back were bared, and a sheet (there appeared to be a thousand yards of it) soaked in ice-water, and wound around me until I resembled a swab for a Columbiad.

It is a cruel expedient. When the chilly rag touches one's warm flesh, it makes him start with sudden violence, and gasp for breath just as men do in the death agony. It froze the marrow in my bones, and stopped the beating of my heart. I thought my time had come.

Young Wilson said the circumstance reminded him of an anecdote about a negro who was being baptized, and who slipped from the parson's grasp, and came near being drowned. He floundered around, though, and finally rose up out of the water considerably strangled, and furiously angry, and started ashore at once, spouting water like a whale, and remarking, with great asperity, that "one o' dese days some gent'l'man's nigger gwyne to get killed wid jis' such dam foolishness as dis!"

Never take a sheet-bath—never. Next to meeting a lady acquaintance, who, for reasons best known to herself, don't see you when she looks at you, and don't know you when she does see you, it is the most uncomfortable thing in the world.

But, as I was saying, when the sheet-bath failed to cure my cough, a lady friend recommended the application of a mustard plaster to my breast. I believe that would have cured me effectually, if it had not been for young Wilson. When I went to bed, I put my mustard plaster—which was a very gorgeous one, eighteen inches square—where I could reach it when I was ready for it. But young Wilson got hungry in the night and—here is food for the imagination.

After sojourning a week at Lake Bigler, I went to Steamboat Springs, and beside the steam baths, I took a lot of the vilest medicines that were ever concocted. They would have cured me, but I had to go back to Virginia City, where, notwithstanding the variety of new remedies I absorbed every day, I managed to aggravate my disease by carelessness and undue exposure.

I finally concluded to visit San Francisco, and the first day I got there, a lady at the hotel told me to drink a quart of whisky every twenty-four hours, and a friend up town recommended precisely the same course. Each advised me to take a quart; that made half a gallon. I did it, and still live.

Now, with the kindest motives in the world, I offer for the consideration of consumptive patients the variegated course of treatment I have lately gone through. Let them try it: if it don't cure, it can't more than kill them.

This scathing satire appeared in the May 1870 issue of Galaxy. At the time, Twain had an arrangement with the magazine to contribute a monthly column called "Memoranda," and he often used his allotted space to comment on various injustices, particularly to the Chinese, about which he had not been able to write freely while he was a newspaperman in San Francisco. In 1871, the essay appeared in an unauthorized publication in Toronto called Mark Twain's Memoranda from the Galaxy. *He included it in his own collection,* Mark Twain's Sketches New and Old, *in 1875.*

Disgraceful Persecution of a Boy

In San Francisco, the other day, "A well-dressed boy, on his way to Sunday-school, was arrested and thrown into the city prison for stoning Chinamen."

What a commentary is this upon human justice! What sad prominence it gives to our human disposition to tyrannize over the weak! San Francisco has little right to take credit to herself for her treatment of this poor boy. What had the child's education been? How should he suppose it was wrong to stone a Chinaman? Before we side against him, along with outraged San Francisco, let us give him a chance—let us hear the testimony for the defense.

He was a "well-dressed" boy, and a Sunday-school scholar, and therefore, the chances are that his parents were intelligent, well-to-do people, with just enough natural villainy in their composition to make them yearn after the daily papers, and enjoy them; and so this boy had opportunities to learn all through the week how to do right, as well as on Sunday.

It was in this way that he found out that the great commonwealth of California imposes an unlawful mining-tax upon John the foreigner, and allows Patrick the foreigner to dig gold for nothing—probably because the degraded Mongol is at no expense for whisky, and the refined Celt cannot exist without it.

It was in this way that he found out that a respectable number of the tax-gatherers—it would be unkind to say all of them—collect the tax twice, instead of once; and that, inasmuch as they do it solely to discourage Chinese immigration into the mines, it is a thing that is much applauded, and likewise regarded as being singularly facetious.

It was in this way that he found out that when a white man robs a sluice-box (by the term white man is meant Spaniards, Mexicans, Portuguese, Irish, Hondurans, Peruvians, Chileans, &c., &c.), they make him leave the camp; and when a Chinaman does that thing, they hang him.

It was in this way that he found out that in many districts of the vast Pacific coast, so strong is the wild, free love of justice in the hearts of the people, that whenever any secret and mysterious crime is committed, they say, "Let justice be done, though the heavens fall," and go straightNay and swing a Chinaman.

It was in this way that he found out that by studying one half of each day's "local items," it would appear that the police of San Francisco were either asleep or dead, and by studying the other half it would seem that the reporters were gone mad with admiration of the energy, the virtue, the high effectiveness, and the dare-devil intrepidity of that very police—making exultant mention of how "the Argus-eyed officer So-and-so," captured a wretched knave of a Chinaman who was stealing chickens, and brought him gloriously to the city prison and how "the gallant officer Such-and-such-a-one," quietly kept an eye on the movements of an "unsuspecting, almond-eyed son of Confucius" (your reporter is nothing if not facetious), following him around with that far-off look of vacancy and unconsciousness always so finely affected by that inscrutable being, the forty-dollar policeman, during a waking interval, and captured him at last in the very act of placing his hands in a suspicious manner upon a paper of tacks, left by the owner in an exposed situation; and how one officer performed this prodigious thing, and another officer that, and another the other—and pretty much every one of these performances having for a dazzling central incident a Chinaman guilty of a shilling's worth of crime, an unfortunate, whose misdemeanor must be hurrahed into something enormous in order to keep the public from noticing how many really important rascals went uncaptured in the meantime, and how overrated those glorified policemen actually are.

It was in this way that the boy found out that the Legislature, being aware that the Constitution has made America an asylum for the poor and the oppressed of all nations, and that, therefore, the poor and oppressed who fly to our shelter must not be charged a disabling admission fee, made a law that every

Chinaman, upon landing, must be *vaccinated* upon the wharf, and pay to the State's appointed officer *ten dollars* for the service, when there are plenty of doctors in San Francisco who would be glad enough to do it for him for fifty cents.

It was in this way that the boy found out that a Chinaman had no rights that any man was bound to respect; that he had no sorrows that any man was bound to pity; that neither his life nor his liberty was worth the purchase of a penny when a white man needed a scapegoat; that nobody loved Chinamen, nobody befriended them, nobody spared them suffering when it was convenient to inflict it; everybody, individuals, communities, the majesty of the State itself, joined in hating, abusing, and persecuting these humble strangers.

And, therefore, what *could* have been more natural than for this sunny-hearted boy, tripping along to Sunday-school, with his mind teeming with freshly-learned incentives to high and virtuous action, to say to himself—

"Ah, there goes a Chinaman! God will not love me if I do not stone him."

And for this he was arrested and put in the city jail.

Everything conspired to teach him that it was a high and holy thing to stone a Chinaman, and yet he no sooner attempts to do his duty that he is punished for it—he, poor chap, who has been aware all his life that one of the principal recreations of the police, out toward the Gold Refinery, is to look on with tranquil enjoyment while the butchers of Brannan Street set their dogs on unoffending Chinamen, and make them flee for their lives.*

Keeping in mind the tuition in the humanities which the entire "Pacific coast" gives its youth, there is a very sublimity of incongruity in the virtuous flourish with which the good city fathers of San Francisco proclaim (as they have lately done) that "The police are positively ordered to arrest all boys, of every description and wherever found, who engage in assaulting Chinamen."

Still, let us be truly glad they have made the order, notwithstanding its inconsistency; and let us rest perfectly confident the police are glad, too. Because there is no personal peril in ar-

*I have many such memories in my mind, but am thinking just at present of one particular one, where the Brannan Street butchers set their dogs on a Chinaman who was quietly passing with a basket of clothes on his head; and while the dogs mutilated his flesh, a butcher increased the hilarity of the occasion by knocking some of the Chinaman's teeth down his throat with half a brick. This incident sticks in my memory with a more malevolent tenacity, perhaps, on account of the fact that I was in the employ of a San Francisco journal at the time, and was not allowed to publish it because it might offend some of the peculiar element that subscribed for the paper.

resting boys, provided they be of the small kind, and the reporters will have to laud their performances just as loyally as ever, or go without items.

The new form for local items in San Francisco will now be:— "The ever vigilant and efficient officer So-and-so succeeded, yesterday afternoon, in arresting Master Tommy Jones, after a determined resistance," etc., etc, followed by the customary statistics and final hurrah, with its unconscious sarcasm: "We are happy in being able to state that this is the forty-seventh boy arrested by this gallant officer since the new ordinance went into effect. The most extraordinary activity prevails in the police department. Nothing like it has been seen since we can remember."

This burlesque on the mania of the collector was written for the December 1876 issue of the Atlantic. *The following year, it appeared as "The Echo That Did Not Answer" in the London publication* Beeton's Christmas Annual. *Its first appearance in book form in America was in* Punch, Brothers, Punch!, *a collection of sketches issued by Slote, Woodman & Company in 1878.*

The Canvasser's Tale

Poor, sad-eyed stranger! There was that about his humble mien, his tired look, his decayed-gentility clothes, that almost reached the mustard-seed of charity that still remained, remote and lonely, in the empty vastness of my heart, notwithstanding I observed a portfolio under his arm, and said to myself, Behold, Providence hath delivered his servant into the hands of another canvasser.

Well, these people always get one interested. Before I well knew how it came about, this one was telling me his history, and I was all attention and sympathy. He told it something like this:

My parents died, alas! when I was a little, sinless child. My uncle Ithuriel took me to his heart and reared me as his own. He was my only relative in the wide world; but he was good and rich and generous. He reared me in the lap of luxury. I knew no want that money could satisfy.

In the fulness of time I was graduated, and went with two of my servants—my chamberlain and my valet—to travel in foreign countries. During four years I flitted upon careless wing amid the beauteous gardens of the distant strand, if you will permit this form of speech in one whose tongue was ever attuned to poesy; and indeed I so speak with confidence, as one unto his kind, for I perceive by your eyes that you too, sir, are gifted with the divine inflation. In those far lands I reveled in the ambrosial food that fructifies the soul, the mind, the heart. But of all things, that which most appealed to my inborn aesthetic taste was the prevailing custom there, among the rich, of making collections of elegant and costly rarities, dainty *objets de vertu*, and in an evil hour I tried to uplift my uncle Ithuriel to a plane of sympathy with this exquisite employment.

I wrote and told him of one gentleman's vast collection of shells; another's noble collection of meerschaum pipes; another's elevating and refining collection of undecipherable autographs; another's priceless collection of old china; another's enchanting collection of postage-stamps—and so forth and so on. Soon my letters yielded fruit. My uncle began to look about for something to make a collection of. You may know, perhaps, how fleetly a taste like this dilates. His soon became a raging fever, though I knew it not. He began to neglect his great pork business; presently he wholly retired and turned an elegant leisure into a rabid search for curious things. His wealth was vast, and he spared it not. First he tried cow-bells. He made a collection which filled five large *salons*, and comprehended all the different sorts of cow-bells that ever had been contrived, save one. That one—an antique, and the only specimen extant—was possessed by another collector. My uncle offered enormous sums for it, but the gentleman would not sell. Doubtless you know what necessarily resulted. A true collector attaches no value to a collection that is not complete. His great heart breaks, he sells his hoard, he turns his mind to some field that seems unoccupied.

Thus did my uncle. He next tried brickbats. After piling up a vast and intensely interesting collection, the former difficulty supervened; his great heart broke again; he sold out his soul's idol to the retired brewer who possessed the missing brick. Then he tried flint hatchets and other implements of Primeval Man, but by and by discovered that the factory where they were made was supplying other collectors as well as himself. He tried Aztec inscriptions and stuffed whales—another failure, after incredible labor and expense. When his collection seemed at last perfect, a stuffed whale arrived from Greenland and an Aztec inscription from the Cundurango regions of Central America that made all former specimens insignificant. My uncle hastened to secure these noble gems. He got the stuffed whale, but another collector got the inscription. A real Cundurango, as possibly you know, is a possession of such supreme value that, when once a collector gets it, he will rather part with his family than with it. So my uncle sold out, and saw his darlings go forth, never more to return; and his coal-black hair turned white as snow in a single night.

Now he waited, and thought. He knew another disappointment might kill him. He was resolved that he would choose things next time that no other man was collecting. He carefully made up his mind, and once more entered the field—this time to make a collection of echoes.

"Of what?" said I.

Echoes, sir. His first purchase was an echo in Georgia that repeated four times; his next was a six-repeater in Maryland; his next was a thirteen-repeater in Maine; his next was a nine-repeater in Kansas; his next was a twelve-repeater in Tennessee, which he got cheap, so to speak, because it was out of repair, a portion of the crag which reflected it having tumbled down. He believed he could repair it at a cost of a few thousand dollars, and, by increasing the elevation with masonry, treble the repeating capacity; but the architect who undertook the job had never built an echo before, and so he utterly spoiled this one. Before he meddled with it, it used to talk back like a mother-in-law, but now it was only fit for the deaf and dumb asylum. Well, next he bought a lot of cheap little double-barreled echoes, scattered around over various States and Territories; he got them at twenty per cent off by taking the lot. Next he bought a perfect Gatling gun of an echo in Oregon, and it cost a fortune, I can tell you. You may know, sir, that in the echo market the scale of prices is cumulative, like the carat-scale in diamonds; in fact, the same phraseology is used. A single-carat echo is worth but ten dollars over and above the value of the land it is on; a two-carat or double-barreled echo is worth thirty dollars; a five-carat is worth nine hundred and fifty; a ten-carat is worth thirteen thousand. My uncle's Oregon echo, which he called the Great Pitt Echo, was a twenty-two carat gem, and cost two hundred and sixteen thousand dollars—they threw the land in, for it was four hundred miles from a settlement.

Well, in the mean time my path was a path of roses. I was the accepted suitor of the only and lovely daughter of an English earl, and was beloved to distraction. In that dear presence I swam in seas of bliss. The family were content, for it was known that I was sole heir to an uncle held to be worth five millions of dollars. However, none of us knew that my uncle had become a collector, at least in any thing more than a small way, for aesthetic amusement.

Now gathered the clouds above my unconscious head. That divine echo, since known throughout the world as the Great Koh-i-noor, or Mountain of Repetitions, was discovered. It was a sixty-five-carat gem. You could utter a word and it would talk back at you for fifteen minutes, when the day was otherwise quiet. But behold, another discovery was made at the same time: another echo-collector was in the field. The two rushed to make the purchase. The property consisted of a couple of small hills with a shallow swale between, out yonder among the back settlements of New York State. Both men arrived on the ground at the same time, and neither knew the other was there. The echo was not all owned by one man; a person by the name of Williamson Bolivar Jarvis owned the east hill, and a person by the name of Harbison J. Bledso owned the west hill; the swale between was the dividing line. So, while my uncle was buying Jarvis's hill for three million two hundred and eighty-five thousand dollars, the other party was buying Bledso's hill for a shade over three million.

Now, do you perceive the natural result? Why, the noblest collection of echoes on earth was forever and ever incomplete, since it possessed but the one half of the king echo of the universe. Neither man was content with this divided ownership, yet neither would sell to the other. There were jawings, bickerings, heart-burnings. And at last, that other collector, with a malignity which only a collector can feel toward a man and a brother, proceeded to cut down his hill.

You see, as long as he could not have the echo, he was resolved that nobody should have it. He would remove his hill, and then there would be nothing to reflect my uncle's echo. My uncle remonstrated with him, but the man said, "I own one end of this echo; I choose to kill my end; you must take care of your own end yourself."

Well, my uncle got an injunction put on him. The other man appealed and fought it in a higher court. They carried it on up, clear to the Supreme Court of the United States. It made no end of trouble there. Two of the judges believed that an echo was personal property, because it was impalpable to sight and touch, and yet was purchasable, salable, and consequently taxable; two others believed that an echo was real estate, because it was manifestly attached to the land, and was not removable from place to place; other of the judges contended that an echo was not property at all.

It was finally decided that the echo was property; that the hills were property; that the two men were separate and independent owners of the two hills, but tenants in common in the echo; therefore, defendant was at full liberty to cut down his hill, since it belonged solely to him, but must give bonds in three million dollars as indemnity for damages which might result to my uncle's half of the echo. This decision also debarred my uncle from using defendant's hill to reflect his part of the echo, without defendant's consent; he must use only his own hill; if his part of the echo would not go, under these circumstances, it was sad, of course, but the court could find no remedy. The court also debarred defendant from using my uncle's hill to reflect *his* end of the echo, without consent. You see the grand result! Neither man would give consent, and so that astonishing and most noble echo had to cease from its great powers; and since that day that magnificent property is tied up and unsalable.

A week before my wedding day, while I was still swimming in bliss and the nobility were gathering from far and near to honor our espousals, came news of my uncle's death, and also a copy of his will, making me his sole heir. He was gone; alas, my dear benefactor was no more. The thought surcharges my heart even at this remote day. I handed the will to the earl; I could not read it for the blinding tears. The earl read it; then he sternly said, "Sir, do you call this wealth? But doubtless you do in your inflated country. Sir, you are left sole heir to a vast collection of echoes—if a thing can be called a collection that is scattered far and wide over the huge length and breadth of the American continent. Sir, this is not all; you are head and ears in debt; there is not an echo in the lot but has a mortgage on it. Sir, I am not a hard man, but I must look to my child's interest; if you had but one echo which you could honestly call your own; if you had but one echo which was free from encumbrances, so that you could retire to it with my child, and by humble, painstaking industry cultivate and improve it, and thus wrest from it a maintenance, I would not say you nay; but I cannot marry my child to a beggar. Leave his side, my darling; go, sir, take your mortgage-ridden echoes and quit my sight forever."

My noble Celestine clung to me in tears, with loving arms, and swore she would willingly, nay, gladly marry me, though I had not an echo in the world. But it could not be. We were torn asunder; she to pine and die within the twelvemonth, I to toil life's long journey sad and lone, praying daily, hourly, for that release which shall join us together again in that dear realm where the wicked cease from troubling and the weary are at rest. Now, sir, if you will be so kind as to look at these maps and plans in my portfolio, I am sure that I can sell you an echo for less money than any man in the trade. Now this one, which cost my uncle ten dollars thirty years ago, and is one of the sweetest things in Texas, I will let you have for—

"Let me interrupt you," I said. "My friend, I have not had a moment's respite from canvassers this day. I have bought a sewing machine which I did not want; I have bought a map which is mistaken in all its details, I have bought a clock which will not go; I have bought a moth poison which the moths prefer to any other beverage; I have bought no end of useless inventions, and now I have had enough of this foolishness. I would not have one of your echoes if you were even to give it to me. I would not let it stay on the place. I always hate a man that tries to sell me echoes. You see this gun? Now take your collection and move on; let us not have bloodshed.''

But he only smiled a sad, sweet smile, and got out some more diagrams. You know the result perfectly well, because you know that when you have once opened the door to a canvasser, the trouble is done, and you have got to suffer defeat.

I compromised with this man at the end of an intolerable hour. I bought two double-barreled echoes in good condition, and he threw in another, which he said was not salable because it only spoke German. He said, "She was a perfect polyglot once, but somehow her palate got down.''

"At the Appetite-Cure," a story that *Twain says was originally intended for inclusion in* A Tramp Abroad, *first appeared in* Cosmopolitan *in August 1898. It was collected in* How To Tell a Story and Other Essays *in 1900.*

At the Appetite-Cure

I

This establishment's name is Hochberghaus. It is in Bohemia, a short day's journey from Vienna, and being in the Austrian empire is of course a health resort. The empire is made up of health resorts; it distributes health to the whole world. Its waters are all medicinal. They are bottled and sent throughout the earth; the natives themselves drink beer. This is self-sacrifice, apparently—but outlanders who have drunk Vienna beer have another idea about it. Particularly the Pilsner which one gets in a small cellar up an obscure back lane in the First Bezirk—the name has escaped me, but the place is easily found: You inquire for the Greek church; and when you get to it, go right along by—the next house is that little beer-mill. It is remote from all traffic and all noise; it is always Sunday there. There are two small rooms, with low ceilings supported by massive arches; the arches and ceilings are whitewashed, otherwise the rooms would pass for cells in the dungeons of a bastile. The furniture is plain and cheap, there is no ornamentation anywhere; yet it is a heaven for the self-sacrificers, for the beer there is incomparable; there is nothing like it elsewhere in the world. In the first room you will find twelve or fifteen ladies and gentlemen of civilian quality; in the other one a dozen generals and ambassadors. One may live in Vienna many months and not hear of this place; but having once heard of it and sampled it, the sampler will afterward infest it.

However, this is all incidental—a mere passing note of gratitude for blessings received—it has nothing to do with my subject. My subject is health resorts. All unhealthy people ought to domicile themselves in Vienna, and use that as a base, making flights from time to time to the outlying resorts, according to need. A flight to Marienbad to get rid of fat; a flight to Carlsbad to get rid of rheumatism; a flight to Kaltenleutgeben to take the water cure and get rid of the rest of the diseases. It is all so handy. You can stand in Vienna and toss a biscuit into Kaltenleutgeben, with a twelve-inch gun. You can run out thither at any time of the day; you go by the phenomenally slow trains, and yet inside of an hour you have exchanged the glare and swelter of the city for wooded hills, and shady forest paths, and soft cool airs, and the music of birds, and the repose and peace of paradise.

And there are plenty of other health resorts at your service and convenient to get at from Vienna; charming places, all of them; Vienna sits in the centre of a beautiful world of mountains with now and then a lake and forests; in fact, no other city is so fortunately situated.

There are an abundance of health resorts, as I have said. Among them this place—Hochberghaus. It stands solitary on the top of a densely wooded mountain, and is a building of great size. It is called the Appetite Anstallt, and people who have lost their appetites come here to get them restored. When I arrived I was taken by Professor Haimberger to his consulting-room and questioned:

"It is six o'clock. When did you eat last?"

"At noon."

"What did you eat?"

"Next to nothing."

"What was on the table?"

"The usual things."

"Chops, chickens, vegetables, and so on?"

"Yes; but don't mention them—I can't bear it."

"Are you tired of them?"

"Oh, utterly. I wish I might never hear of them again."

"The mere sight of food offends you, does it?"

"More, it revolts me."

The doctor considered awhile, then got out a long menu and ran his eye slowly down it.

"I think," said he, "that what you need to eat is—but here, choose for yourself."

I glanced at the list, and my stomach threw a handspring. Of all the barbarous layouts that were ever contrived, this was the most atrocious. At the top stood "tough, underdone, overdue tripe, garnished with garlic"; half-way down the bill stood "young cat; old cat; scrambled cat"; at the bottom stood "sailor-boots, softened with tallow—served raw." The wide intervals of the bill were packed with dishes calculated to insult a cannibal. I said:

"Doctor, it is not fair to joke over so serious a case as mine. I came here to get an appetite, not to throw away the remnant that's left."

He said gravely: "I am not joking; why should I joke?"

"But I can't eat these horrors."

"Why not?"

He said it with a naiveté that was admirable, whether it was real or assumed.

"Why not? Because—why, doctor, for months I have seldom been able to endure anything more substantial than omelettes and custards. These unspeakable dishes of yours—"

"Oh, you will come to like them. They are very good. And you *must* eat them. It is the rule of the place, and is strict. I cannot permit any departure from it."

I said, smiling: "Well, then, doctor, you will have to permit the departure of the patient. I am going."

He looked hurt, and said in a way which changed the aspect of things:

"I am sure you would not do me that injustice. I accepted you in good faith—you will not shame that confidence. This appetite-cure is my whole living. If you should go forth from it with the sort of appetite which you now have, it could become known, and you can see, yourself, that people would say my cure failed in your case and hence can fail in other cases. You will not go; you will not do me this hurt."

I apologized and said I would stay.

"That is right. I was sure you would not go; it would take the food from my family's mouths."

"Would they mind that? Do they eat these fiendish things?"

"They? My family?" His eyes were full of gentle wonder. "Of course not."

"Oh, they don't! Do you?"

"Certainly not."

"I see. It's another case of a physician who doesn't take his own medicine."

"I don't need it. It is six hours since you lunched. Will you have supper now—or later?"

"I am not hungry, but now is as good a time as any, and I would like to be done with it and have it off my mind. It is about my usual time, and regularity is commanded by all the authorities. Yes, I will try to nibble a little now—I wish a light horsewhipping would answer instead."

The professor handed me that odious menu.

"Choose—or will you have it later?"

"Oh, dear me, show me to my room; I forgot your hard rule."

"Wait just a moment before you finally decide. There is another rule. If you choose now, the order will be filled at once; but if you wait, you will have to await my pleasure. You cannot get a dish from that entire bill until I consent."

"All right. Show me to my room, and send the cook to bed; there is not going to be any hurry."

The professor took me up one flight of stairs and showed me into a most inviting and comfortable apartment consisting of parlor, bedchamber, and bathroom.

The front windows looked out over a far-reaching spread of green glades and valleys, and tumbled hills clothed with forests—a noble solitude unvexed by the fussy world. In the parlor were many shelves filled with books. The professor said he would now leave me to myself; and added:

"Smoke and read as much as you please, drink all the water you like. When you get hungry, ring and give your order, and I will decide whether it shall be filled or not. Yours is a stubborn, bad case, and I think the first fourteen dishes in the bill are each and all too delicate for its needs. I ask you as a favor to restrain yourself and not call for them."

"Restrain myself, is it? Give yourself no uneasiness. You are going to save money by me. The idea of coaxing a sick man's appetite back with this buzzard-fare is clear insanity."

I said it with bitterness, for I felt outraged by this calm, cold talk over these heartless new engines of assassination. The doctor looked grieved, but not offended. He laid the bill of fare on the commode at my bed's head, "so that it would be handy," and said:

"Yours is not the worst case I have encountered, by any means; still it is a bad one and requires robust treatment; therefore I shall be gratified if you will restrain yourself and skip down to No. 15 and begin with that."

Then he left me and I began to undress, for I was dog-tired and very sleepy. I slept fifteen hours and woke up finely refreshed at ten the next morning. Vienna coffee! It was the first thing I thought of—that unapproachable luxury—that sumptuous coffee-house coffee, compared with which all other European coffee and all American hotel coffee is mere fluid poverty.

I rang, and ordered it; also Vienna bread, that delicious invention. The servant spoke through the wicket in the door and said—but you know what he said. He referred me to the bill of fare. I allowed him to go—I had no further use for him.

After the bath I dressed and started for a walk, and got as far as the door. It was locked on the outside. I rang and the servant came and explained that it was another rule. The seclusion of the patient was required until after the first meal. I had not been particularly anxious to get out before; but it was different now. Being locked in makes a person wishful to get out. I soon began to find it difficult to put in the time. At two o'clock I had been twenty-six hours without food. I had been growing hungry for some time; I recognized that I was not only hungry now, but hungry with a strong adjective in front of it. Yet I was not hungry enough to face the bill of fare.

I must put in the time somehow. I would read and smoke. I did it; hour by hour. The books were all of one breed—shipwrecks; people lost in deserts; people shut up in caved-in mines; people starving in besieged cities. I read about all the revolting dishes that ever famishing men had stayed their hunger with. During the first hours these things nauseated me: hours followed in which they did not so affect me; still other hours followed in which I found myself smacking my lips over some tolerably infernal messes. When I had been without food forty-five hours I ran eagerly to the bell and ordered the second dish in the bill, which was a sort of dumplings containing a compost made of caviar and tar.

It was refused me. During the next fifteen hours I visited the bell every now and then and ordered a dish that was further down the list. Always a refusal. But I was conquering prejudice after prejudice, right along; I was making sure progress; I was creeping up on No. 15 with deadly certainty, and my heart beat faster and faster, my hopes rose higher and higher.

At last when food had not passed my lips for sixty hours, victory was mine, and I ordered No. 15:

"Soft-boiled spring chicken—in the egg; six dozen, hot and fragrant!"

In fifteen minutes it was there; and the doctor along with it, rubbing his hands with joy. He said with great excitement:

"It's a cure, it's a cure! I knew I could do it. Dear sir, my grand system never fails—never. You've got your appetite back—you know you have; say it and make me happy."

"Bring on your carrion—I can eat anything in the bill!"

"Oh, this is noble, this is splendid—but I knew I could do it, the system never fails. How are the birds?"

"Never was anything so delicious in the world; and yet as a rule I don't care for game. But don't interrupt me, don't—I can't spare my mouth, I really can't."

Then the doctor said:

"The cure is perfect. There is no more doubt nor danger. Let the poultry alone; I can trust you with a beefsteak, now."

The beefsteak came—as much as a basketful of it—with potatoes, and Vienna bread and coffee; and I ate a meal then that was worth all the costly preparation I had made for it. And dripped tears of gratitude into the gravy all the time—gratitude to the doctor for putting a little plain common-sense into me when I had been empty of it so many, many years.

II

Thirty years ago Haimberger went off on a long voyage in a sailing-ship. There were fifteen passengers on board. The table-fare was of the regulation pattern of the day: At 7 in the morning, a cup of bad coffee in bed; at 9, breakfast: bad coffee, with condensed milk; soggy rolls, crackers, salt fish; at 1 P.M., luncheon: cold tongue, cold ham, cold corned beef, soggy cold rolls, crackers; 5 P.M., dinner: thick pea soup, salt fish, hot corned beef and sour kraut, boiled pork and beans, pudding; 9 till 11 P.M., supper: tea, with condensed milk, cold tongue, cold ham, pickles, sea-biscuit, pickled oysters, pickled pig's feet, grilled bones, golden buck.

At the end of the first week eating had ceased, nibbling had taken its place. The passengers came to the table, but it was partly to put in the time, and partly because the wisdom of the ages commanded them to be regular in their meals. They were tired of the coarse and monotonous fare, and took no interest in it, had no appetite for it. All day and every day they roamed the ship half hungry, plagued by their gnawing stomachs, moody, untalkative, miserable. Among them were three confirmed dyspeptics. These became shadows in the course of three weeks. There was also a bedridden invalid; he lived on boiled rice; he could not look at the regular dishes.

Now came shipwreck and life in open boats, with the usual paucity of food. Provisions ran lower and lower. The appetites improved, then. When nothing was left but raw ham and the ration of that was down to two ounces a day per person, the appetites were perfect. At the end of fifteen days the dyspeptics, the invalid, and the most delicate ladies in the party were chewing sailor-boots in ecstasy, and only complaining because the supply of them was limited. Yet these were the same people who couldn't endure the ship's tedious corned beef and sour kraut and other crudities. They were rescued by an English vessel. Within ten days the whole fifteen were in as good condition as they had been when the shipwreck occurred.

"They had suffered no damage by their adventure," said the professor. "Do you note that?"

"Yes."

"Do you note it well?"

"Yes—I think I do."

"But you don't. You hesitate. You don't rise to the importance of it. I will say it again—with emphasis—*not one of them suffered any damage.*"

"Now I begin to see. Yes, it was indeed remarkable."

"Nothing of the kind. It was perfectly natural. There was no reason why they should suffer damage. They were undergoing Nature's Appetite Cure, the best and wisest in the world."

"Is that where you got your idea?"

"That is where I got it."

"It taught those people a valuable lesson."

"What makes you think that?"

"Why shouldn't I? You seem to think it taught you one."

"That is nothing to the point. I am not a fool."

"I see. Were they fools?"

"They were human beings."

"Is it the same thing?"

"Why do you ask? You know it yourself. As regards his health—and the rest of the things—the average man is what his environment and his superstitions have made him; and their function is to make him an ass. He can't add up three or four new circumstances together and perceive what they mean; it is beyond him. He is not capable of observing for himself; he has to get everything at second-hand. If what are miscalled the lower animals were as silly as man is, they would all perish from the earth in a year."

"Those passengers learned no lesson, then?"

"Not a sign of it. They went to their regular meals in the English ship, and pretty soon they were nibbling again—nibbling, appetiteless, disgusted with the food, moody, miserable, half hungry, their outraged stomachs cursing and swearing and whining and supplicating all day long. And in vain, for they were the stomachs of fools."

"Then, as I understand it, your scheme is—"

"Quite simple. Don't eat till you are hungry. If the food fails to taste good, fails to satisfy you, rejoice you, comfort you, don't eat again until you are *very* hungry. Then it will rejoice you— and do you good, too.''

"And I observe no regularity, as to hours?''

"When you are conquering a bad appetite—no. After it is conquered, regularity is no harm, so long as the appetite remains good. As soon as the appetite wavers, apply the corrective again—which is starvation, long or short according to the needs of the case.''

"The best diet, I suppose—I mean the wholesomest—''

"All diets are wholesome. Some are wholesomer than others, but all the ordinary diets are wholesome enough for the people who use them. Whether the food be fine or coarse it will taste good and it will nourish if a watch be kept upon the appetite and a little starvation introduced every time it weakens. Nansen was used to fine fare, but when his meals were restricted to bear-meat months at a time he suffered no damage and no discomfort, because his appetite was kept at par through the difficulty of getting his bear-meat regularly.''

"But doctors arrange carefully considered and delicate diets for invalids.''

"They can't help it. The invalid is full of inherited superstitions and won't starve himself. He believes it would certainly kill him.''

"It would weaken him, wouldn't it?''

"Nothing to hurt. Look at the invalids in our shipwreck. They lived fifteen days on pinches of raw ham, a suck at sailor-boots, and general starvation. It weakened them, but it didn't hurt them. It put them in fine shape to eat heartily of hearty food and build themselves up to a condition of robust health. But they do not perceive that; they lost their opportunity; they remained invalids; it served them right. Do you know the tricks that the health-resort doctors play?''

"What is it?''

"My system disguised—covert starvation. Grape-cure, bath-cure, mud-cure—it is all the same. The grape and the bath and the mud make a show and do a trifle of the work—the real work is done by the surreptitious starvation. The patient accustomed to four meals and late hours—at both ends of the day—now consider what he has to do at a health resort. He gets up at 6 in the morning. Eats one egg. Tramps up and down a promenade two hours with the other fools. Eats a butterfly. Slowly drinks a glass of filtered sewage that smells like a buzzard's breath. Promenades another two hours, but alone; if you speak to him he says anxiously, 'My water!—I am walking off my water!— please don't interrupt,' and goes stumping along again. Eats a candied rose-leaf. Lies at rest in the silence and solitude of his room for hours; mustn't read, mustn't smoke. The doctor comes and feels of his heart, now, and his pulse, and thumps his breast and his back and his stomach, and listens for results through a penny flageolet; then orders the man's bath—half a degree, Reamur, cooler than yesterday. After the bath another egg. A glass of sewage at 3 or 4 in the afternoon, and promenade solemnly with the other freaks. Dinner at 6—half a doughnut and a cup of tea. Walk again. Half-past 8, supper—more butterfly; at 9, to bed. Six weeks of this régime—think of it. It starves a man out and puts him in splendid condition. It would have the same effect in London, New York, Jericho—anywhere."

"How long does it take to put a person in condition here?"

"It ought to take but a day or two; but in fact it takes from one to six weeks, according to the character and mentality of the patient."

"How is that?"

"Do you see that crowd of women playing football, and boxing, and jumping fences yonder? They have been here six or seven weeks. They were spectral poor weaklings when they came. They were accustomed to nibbling at dainties and delicacies at set hours four times a day, and they had no appetite for anything. I questioned them, and then locked them into their rooms—the frailest ones to starve nine or ten hours, the others twelve or fifteen. Before long they began to beg; and indeed they suffered a good deal. They complained of nausea, headache, and so on. It was good to see them eat when the time was up. They could not remember when the devouring of a meal had afforded them such rapture—that was their word. Now, then, that ought to have ended their cure, but it didn't. They were free to go to any meals in the house, and they chose their accustomed four. Within a day or two I had to interfere. Their appetites were weakening. I made them knock out a meal. That set them up again. Then they resumed the four. I begged them to learn to knock out a meal themselves, without waiting for me. Up to a fortnight ago they couldn't; they really hadn't manhood enough; but they were gaining it, and now I think they are safe. They drop out a meal every now and then of their own accord. They are in fine condition now, and they might safely go home, I think, but their confidence is not quite perfect yet, so they are waiting awhile."

"Other cases are different?"

"Oh yes. Sometimes a man learns the whole trick in a week. Learns to regulate his appetite and keep it in perfect order.

Learns to drop out a meal with frequency and not mind it."

"But why drop the entire meal out? Why not a part of it?"

"It's a poor device, and inadequate. If the stomach doesn't call vigorously—with a shout, as you may say—it is better not to pester it but just give it a real rest. Some people can eat more meals than others, and still thrive. There are all sorts of people, and all sorts of appetites. I will show you a man presently who was accustomed to nibble at eight meals a day. It was beyond the proper gait of his appetite by two. I have got him down to six a day, now, and he is all right, and enjoys life. How many meals do you affect per day?"

"Formerly—for twenty-two years—a meal and a half; during the past two years, two and a half: coffee and a roll at 9, luncheon at 1, dinner at 7:30 or 8."

"Formerly a meal and a half—that is, coffee and a roll at 9, dinner in the evening, nothing between—is that it?"

"Yes."

"Why did you add a meal?"

"It was the family's idea. They were uneasy. They thought I was killing myself."

"You found a meal and a half per day enough, all through the twenty-two years?"

"Plenty."

"Your present poor condition is due to the extra meal. Drop it out. You are trying to eat oftener than your stomach demands. You don't gain, you lose. You eat less food now, in a day, on two and a half meals, than you formerly ate on one and half."

"True—a good deal less; for in those old days my dinner was a very sizable thing."

"Put yourself on a single meal a day, now—dinner—for a few days, till you secure a good, sound, regular, trustworthy appetite, then take to your one and a half permanently, and don't listen to the family any more. When you have any ordinary ailment, particularly of a feverish sort, eat nothing at all during twenty-four hours. That will cure it. It will cure the stubbornest cold in the head, too. No cold in the head can survive twenty-four hours' unmodified starvation."

"I know it. I have proved it many a time."

This petition to Congress concerning copyright was published in Mark Twain's Sketches New and Old in 1875, and describes inequities against which Twain lobbied throughout his life. His most famous appearance on its behalf took place on December 7, 1906, when he testified before a joint congressional committee on copyright at the Library of Congress. It was one of the first times that Twain was seen in a white serge suit, a costume that was soon to become his trademark.

Petition to Congress

TO THE HONORABLE THE SENATE AND HOUSE OF REPRESENTATIVES IN CONGRESS ASSEMBLED:

Whereas, The Constitution guarantees equal rights to all, backed by the Declaration of Independence; and

Whereas, Under our laws, the right of property in real estate is perpetual; and

Whereas, Under our laws, the right of property in the literary result of a citizen's intellectual labor is restricted to forty-two years; and

Whereas, Forty-two years seems an exceedingly just and righteous term, and a sufficiently long one for the retention of property:

Therefore, Your petitioner, having the good of his country solely at heart, humbly prays that "equal rights" and fair and equal treatment may be meted out to all citizens, by the restriction of rights in *all* property, real estate included, to the beneficent term of forty-two years. Then shall all men bless your honorable body and be happy. And for this will your petitioner ever pray.

MARK TWAIN

A PARAGRAPH NOT ADDED TO THE PETITION

The charming absurdity of restricting property-rights in books to forty-two years sticks prominently out in the fact that hardly any man's books ever *live* forty-two years, or even half of it; and so, for the sake of getting a shabby advantage of the heirs of about one Scott or Burns or Milton in a hundred years, the law makers of the "Great" Republic are content to leave that poor little pilfering edict upon the statute books. It is like an emperor lying in wait to rob a phenix's nest, and waiting the necessary century to get the chance.